SIR ARTHUR CONAN DOYLE

THE HISTORICAL NOVELS

VOLUME ONE

SIR ARTHUR CONAN DOYLE

THE HISTORICAL NOVELS

VOLUME ONE

The White Company
Sir Nigel
The Exploits of Brigadier Gerard
Adventures of Gerard

by
Sir Arthur Conan Doyle

New Orchard Editions
Poole · New York · Sydney

Copyright © 1986 New Orchard Editions Ltd

This edition first published 1986 by
New Orchard Editions Ltd
Robert Rogers House
New Orchard
Poole, Dorset, BH15 1LU

ISBN: 1 85079 041 8 Vol. One
1 85079 042 6 Vol. Two
1 85079 045 0 Two Volume Set

Printed in Great Britain by
The Bath Press, Avon

CONTENTS

PREFACE

MY husband was intensely thorough in all his literary work. He took enormous pains to have everything right. For instance before writing *The White Company* he soaked his brain with a knowledge of the period he intended to portray. He read over sixty books dealing with heraldry—armour—falconry—the medieval habits of the peasants of that time—the social customs of the higher folk of the land, etc. Only when he knew those days as though he had lived in them—when he had got the very atmosphere steeped into his brain— did he put pen to paper and let loose the creations of his mind. That perfect knight—Sir Nigel—so human and attractive and so lovable, is an example of all that a gentleman—a true knight in life—should be, and in portraying Sir Nigel's adventurous life my husband has given a wonderful and living description of that romantic and chivalrous period of English history.

His literary versatility was truly remarkable. When one considers the wide range of subjects and characters created by that one mind: His historical romances covering several different eras—his sporting novels— his poems—the detective stories—his brilliantly imaginative works, such as *The Lost World*, *The Maracot Deep*, his pirate and adventure yarns—his simple human study as embodied in *The Duet*—his plays—his marvellously accurate and humanly described Histories of the Boer

PREFACE

War and the Great War, as well as all his psychic books, etc.—how many finely cut facets to be parts of one brain !

Apart from all my husband's literary inspiration and genius there was in his work—as in his life—such sincerity and thoroughness, honesty and fearlessness. His big heart and human understanding was the keynote —the undercurrent of his great brain and personality.

Jean Conan Doyle

WINDLESHAM,
    CROWBOROUGH,
      1931.

NOTE

White Company is given first in this volume, as it was published before *Sir Nigel*. It should, however, be read as a sequel to *Sir Nigel*.

THE WHITE COMPANY

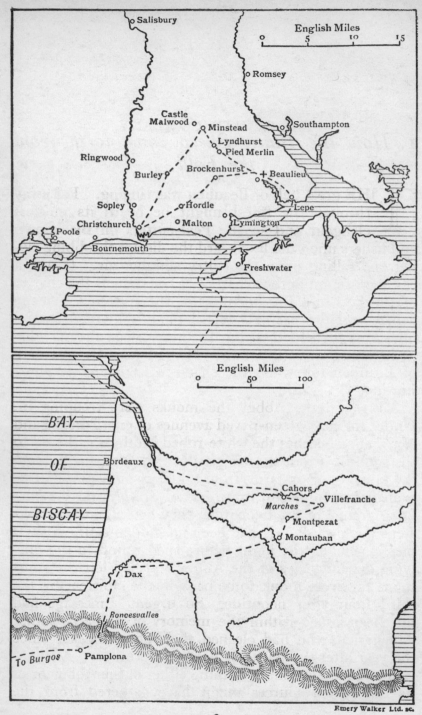

1. *How the Black Sheep came forth from the Fold*

THE great bell of Beaulieu was ringing. Far away through the forest might be heard its musical clangour and swell. Peat-cutters on Blackdown and fishers upon the Exe heard the distant throbbing rising and falling upon the sultry summer air. It was a common sound in those parts—as common as the chatter of the jays and the booming of the bittern. Yet the fishers and the peasants raised their heads and looked questions at each other, for the Angelus had already gone and Vespers was still far off. Why should the great bell of Beaulieu toll when the shadows were neither short nor long?

All round the Abbey the monks were trooping in. Under the long green-paved avenues of gnarled oaks and of lichened beeches the white-robed brothers gathered to the sound. From the vineyard and the vinepress, from the bouvary or ox-farm, from the marl-pits and salterns, even from the distant ironworks of Sowley and the outlying grange of St. Leonard's, they had all turned their steps homewards. It had been no sudden call. A swift messenger had the night before sped round to the outlying dependencies of the Abbey and had left the summons for every monk to be back in the cloisters by the third hour after noontide. So urgent a message had not been issued within the memory of old lay-brother Athanasius, who had cleaned the Abbey knocker since the year after the Battle of Bannockburn.

A stranger who knew nothing either of the Abbey or of its immense resources might have gathered from the appearance of the brothers some conception of the varied duties which they were called upon to perform, and of the busy widespread life which centred in the old monastery. As they swept gravely in by twos and by threes, with bended heads and muttering lips, there were few who did not bear upon them some signs of their daily toil. Here were two with wrists and sleeves all spotted with the ruddy grape juice. There again was a bearded brother with a broad-headed axe and a bundle of faggots upon his shoulders, while beside him walked another with the shears under his arm and the white wool still clinging to his whiter gown. A long straggling troop bore spades and mattocks, while the two rearmost of all staggered along under a huge basket of fresh-caught carp—for the morrow was Friday, and there were fifty platters to be filled and as many sturdy trenchermen behind them. Of all the throng there was scarce one who was not labour-stained and weary, for Abbot Berghersh was a hard man to himself and to others.

Meanwhile, in the broad and lofty chamber set apart for occasions of import, the Abbot himself was pacing impatiently backwards and forwards, with his long white nervous hands clasped in front of him. His thin thought-worn features and sunken haggard cheeks bespoke one who had indeed beaten down that inner foe whom every man must face, but had none the less suffered sorely in the contest. In crushing his passions he had well-nigh crushed himself. Yet, frail as was his person, there gleamed out ever and anon from under his drooping brows a flash of fierce energy, which recalled to men's minds that he came of a fighting stock, and that even now his twin brother, Sir Bartholomew Berghersh, was one of the most famous of those stern warriors who had planted the Cross of St. George before the gates of Paris. With lips compressed and clouded brow, he strode up and down the oaken floor, the very genius and impersonation of asceticism, while the great bell still thundered and clanged above his head. At last the uproar died away in three last, measured throbs, and ere their echo had ceased the Abbot struck a small gong which summoned a lay-brother to his presence.

" Have the brethren come ? " he asked, in the Anglo-French dialect used in religious houses.

" They are here," the other answered, with his eyes cast down, and his hands crossed upon his chest.

" All ? "

" Two-and-thirty of the seniors and fifteen of the novices, most holy father. Brother Mark of the Spicarium is sore smitten with a fever and could not come. He said that——"

" It boots not what he said. Fever or no, he should have come at my call. His spirit must be chastened, as must that of many more in this Abbey. You yourself, brother Francis, have twice raised your voice, so that it hath come to my ears, when the reader in the refectory hath been dealing with the lives of God's most blessed saints. What hast thou to say ? "

The lay-brother stood meek and silent, with his arms still crossed in front of him.

" One thousand Aves and as many Credos, said standing with arms outstretched before the shrine of the Virgin, may help thee to remember that the Creator hath given us two ears and but one mouth, as a token that there is twice the work for the one as for the other. Where is the master of the novices ? "

" He is without, most holy father."

" Send him hither."

The sandalled feet clattered over the wooden floor, and the iron-bound door creaked upon its hinges. In a few moments it opened again to admit a short square monk with a heavy composed face and authoritative manner.

" You have sent for me, holy father ? "

" Yes, brother Jerome, I wish that this matter be disposed of with as little scandal as may be ; and yet it is needful that the example should be a public one." The Abbot spoke in Latin now, as a language which was more

5

fitted by its age and solemnity to convey the thoughts of two high dignitaries of the order.

" It would perchance be best that the novices be not admitted," suggested the master. " This mention of a woman may turn their minds from their pious meditations to worldly and evil thoughts."

" Woman ! woman ! " groaned the Abbot. " Well has the holy Chrysostom termed them *radix malorum*. From Eve downwards, what good hath come from any of them ? Who brings the plaint ? "

" It is brother Ambrose."

" A holy and devout young man."

" A light and a pattern to every novice."

" Let the matter be brought to an issue, then, according to our old-time monastic habit. Bid the chancellor and the sub-chancellor lead in the brothers according to age, together with brother John the accused and brother Ambrose the accuser."

" And the novices ? "

" Let them bide in the north alley of the cloisters. Stay ! Bid the sub-chancellor send out to them Thomas the lector to read unto them from the ' Gesta beati Benedicti.' It may save them from foolish and pernicious babbling."

The Abbot was left to himself once more, and bent his thin grey face over his illuminated breviary. So he remained while the senior monks filed slowly and sedately into the chamber, seating themselves upon the long oaken benches which lined the wall on either side. At the farther end, in two high chairs as large as that of the Abbot, though hardly as elaborately carved, sat the master of the novices and the chancellor, the latter a broad and portly priest, with dark mirthful eyes and a thick outgrowth of crisp black hair all round his tonsured head. Between them stood a lean white-faced brother who appeared to be ill at ease, shifting his feet from side to side and tapping his chin nervously with the long parchment roll which he held in his hand. The Abbot, from his point of vantage, looked down on the two lines of faces, placid and sun-browned for the most part, with the large bovine eyes and unlined features which told of their easy, unchanging existence. Then he turned his eager, fiery gaze upon the pale-faced monk who faced him.

" This plaint is thine, as I learn, brother Ambrose," said he. " May the holy Benedict, patron of our house, be present this day and aid us in our findings. How many counts are there ? "

" Three, most holy father," the brother answered in a low and quavering voice.

" Have you set them forth according to rule ? "

" They are here set down, most holy father, upon a cantle of sheepskin."

" Let the sheepskin be handed to the chancellor. Bring in brother John, and let him hear the plaints which have been urged against him."

At this order a lay-brother swung open the door, and two other lay-brothers entered, leading between them a young novice of the order. He was a man of huge stature, dark-eyed and red-headed, with a peculiar half humorous, half defiant expression upon his bold, well-marked features. His cowl was thrown back upon his shoulders, and his gown, unfastened at the top, disclosed a round sinewy neck, ruddy and corded like the bark of the fir. Thick muscular arms, covered with a reddish down, protruded from the wide sleeves of his habit, while his white skirt, looped up upon one side, gave a glimpse of a huge leg, scarred and torn with the scratches of brambles. With a bow to the Abbot, which had in it perhaps more pleasantry than reverence, the novice strode across to the carved prie-dieu which had been set apart for him, and stood silent and erect with his hand upon the gold bell which was used in the private orisons of the Abbot's own household. His dark eyes glanced rapidly over the assembly, and finally settled with a grim and menacing twinkle upon the face of his accuser.

The chancellor rose, and having slowly unrolled the

parchment scroll, proceeded to read it out in a thick and pompous voice, while a subdued rustle and movement among the brothers bespoke the interest with which they followed the proceedings.

" Charges brought upon the second Thursday after the feast of the Assumption, in the year of our Lord thirteen hundred and sixty-six, against brother John, formerly known as Hordle John, or John of Hordle, but now a novice in the holy monastic order of the Cistercians. Read upon the same day at the Abbey of Beaulieu in the presence of the most reverend Abbot Berghersh and of the assembled order.

" The charges against the said brother John are the following, namely, to wit :

" First, that on the above-mentioned feast of the Assumption, small beer having been served to the novices in the proportion of one quart to each four, the said brother John did drain the pot at one draught to the detriment of brother Paul, brother Porphyry, and brother Ambrose, who could scarce eat their none-meat of salted stock-fish, on account of their exceeding dryness."

At this solemn indictment the novice raised his hand and twitched his lip, while even the placid senior brothers glanced across at each other and coughed to cover their amusement. The Abbot alone sat grey and immutable, with a drawn face and a brooding eye.

" Item, that having been told by the master of the novices that he should restrict his food for two days to a single three-pound loaf of bran and beans, for the greater honouring and glorifying of St. Monica, mother of the holy Augustine, he was heard by brother Ambrose and others to say that he wished twenty thousand devils would fly away with the said Monica, mother of the holy Augustine, or any other saint who came between a man and his meat. Item, that upon brother Ambrose reproving him for this blasphemous wish, he did hold the said brother face downwards over the piscatorium or fishpond for a space during which the said brother was able to repeat a

8

Pater and four Aves for the better fortifying of his soul against impending death."

There was a buzz and murmur among the white-frocked brethren at this grave charge ; but the Abbot held up his long quivering hand. " What then ? " said he.

" Item, that between Nones and Vespers on the feast of James the Less the said brother John was observed upon the Brockenhurst road, near the spot which is known as Hatchett's Pond, in converse with a person of the other sex, being a maiden of the name of Mary Sowley, the daughter of the King's verderer. Item, that after sundry japes and jokes the said brother John did lift up the said Mary Sowley and did take, carry, and convey her across a stream, to the infinite relish of the devil and the exceeding detriment of his own soul, which scandalous and wilful falling away was witnessed by three members of our order."

A dead silence throughout the room, with a rolling of heads and upturning of eyes, bespoke the pious horror of the community. The Abbot drew his grey brows low over his fiercely questioning eyes.

" Who can vouch for this thing ? " he asked.

" That can I," answered the accuser. " So too can brother Porphyry, who was with me, and brother Mark of the Spicarium, who hath been so much stirred and inwardly troubled by the sight that he now lies in a fever through it."

" And the woman ? " asked the Abbot. " Did she not break into lamentation and woe that a brother should so demean himself ? "

" Nay, she smiled sweetly upon him and thanked him. I can vouch it, and so can brother Porphyry."

" Canst thou ? " cried the Abbot, in a high, tempestuous tone. " Canst thou so ? Hast forgotten that the five-and-thirtieth rule of the order is that in the presence of a woman the face should be ever averted and the eyes cast down ? Hast forgot it, I say ? If your eyes were upon your sandals, how came ye to see this smile of which ye prate ? A week in your cells, false brethren, a week of rye-bread and lentils, with double Lauds and double Matins, may help ye to a remembrance of the laws under which ye live."

At this sudden outflame of wrath the two witnesses sank their faces on to their chests, and sat as men crushed. The Abbot turned his angry eyes away from them and bent them upon the accused, who met his searching gaze with a firm and composed face.

" What hast thou to say, brother John, upon these weighty things which are urged against thee ? "

" Little enough, good father, little enough," said the novice, speaking English with a broad West Saxon drawl. The brothers, who were English to a man, pricked up their ears at the sound of the homely and yet unfamiliar speech : but the Abbot flushed red with anger, and struck his hand upon the oaken arm of his chair.

" What talk is this ? " he cried. " Is this a tongue to be used within the walls of an old and well-famed monastery ? But grace and learning have ever gone hand in hand, and when one is lost it is needless to look for the other."

" I know not about that," said brother John ; " I know only that the words come kindly to my mouth, for it was the speech of my fathers before me. Under your favour I shall either use it now or hold my peace."

The Abbot patted his foot and nodded his head, as one who passes a point but does not forget it.

" For the matter of the ale," continued brother John, " I had come in hot from the fields and had scarce got the taste of the thing before mine eye lit upon the bottom of the pot. It may be, too, that I spoke somewhat shortly concerning the bran and the beans, the same being poor provender and unfitted for a man of my inches. It is true also that I did lay my hands upon this jack-fool of a brother Ambrose, though, as you can see, I did him little scathe. As regards the maid, too, it is true that I did heft her over the stream, she having on her hosen and shoon, whilst I had but my wooden sandals, which could take no hurt from the water. I should have thought shame upon my manhood, as well as my monkhood, if I had held back my hand from her." He glanced around as he spoke, with the half-amused look which he had worn during the whole proceedings.

" There is no need to go further," said the Abbot. " He has confessed to all. It only remains for me to portion out the punishment which is due to his evil conduct."

He rose, and the two long lines of brothers followed his example, looking sideways with scared faces at the angry prelate.

" John of Hordle," he thundered, " you have shown yourself during the two months of your novitiate to be a recreant monk, and one who is unworthy to wear the white garb which is the outer symbol of the spotless spirit. That dress shall therefore be stripped from thee, and thou shalt be cast into the outer world without benefit of clerkship, and without lot or part in the graces and blessings of those who dwell under the care of the blessed Benedict. Thou shalt come back neither to Beaulieu nor to any of the granges of Beaulieu, and thy name shall be struck off the scrolls of the order."

The sentence appeared a terrible one to the older monks, who had become so used to the safe and regular life of the Abbey that they would have been as helpless as children in the outer world. From their pious oasis they looked dreamily out at the desert of life—a place full of stormings and strivings, comfortless, restless, and overshadowed by evil. The young novice, however, appeared to have other thoughts, for his eyes sparkled and his smile broadened. It needed but that to add fresh fuel to the fiery mood of the prelate.

" So much for thy spiritual punishment," he cried. " But it is to the grosser feelings that we must turn in such natures as thine, and as thou art no longer under the shield of holy Church there is the less difficulty. Ho there ! lay-brothers—Francis, Naomi, Joseph—seize him and bind his arms ! Drag him forth, and let the foresters and the porters scourge him from the precincts ! "

As these three brothers advanced towards him to carry out the Abbot's direction the smile faded from the novice's face, and he glanced right and left with his fierce brown eyes ; like a bull at a baiting. Then, with a sudden deep-chested shout, he tore up the heavy oaken prie-dieu, and poised it to strike, taking two steps backward the while, that none might take him at a vantage.

" By the black rood of Waltham ! " he roared, " if any knave among you lays a finger-end upon the edge of my gown, I will crush his skull like a filbert ! " With his thick knotted arms, his thundering voice, and his bristle of red hair, there was something so repellent in the man that the three brothers flew back at the very glare of him ; and the two rows of white monks strained away from him like poplars in a tempest. The Abbot only sprang forward with shining eyes ; but the chancellor and the master hung upon either arm and wrested him back out of danger's way.

" He is possessed of a devil ! " they shouted. " Run, brother Ambrose, brother Joachim ! Call Hugh of the Mill, and Woodman Wat, and Raoul with his arbalest and bolts. Tell them that we are in fear of our lives ! Run, run ! for the love of the Virgin ! "

But the novice was a strategist as well as a man of action. Springing forward, he hurled his unwieldy weapon at brother Ambrose, and, as desk and monk clattered on to the floor together, he sprang through the open door and down the winding stair. Sleepy old brother Athanasius, at the porter's cell, had a fleeting vision of twinkling feet and flying skirts ; but before he had time to rub his eyes the recreant had passed the lodge, and was speeding as fast as his sandals could patter along the Lyndhurst road.

2. *How Alleyne Edricson came out into the World*

NEVER had the peaceful atmosphere of the old Cistercian house been so rudely ruffled. Never had there been insurrection so sudden, so short, and so successful. Yet the Abbot Berghersh was a man of too firm a grain to allow one bold outbreak to imperil the settled order of his great household. In a few hot and bitter words, he compared their false brother's exit to the expulsion of our first parents from the garden, and more than hinted that unless a reformation occurred some others of the community might find themselves in the same evil and perilous case. Having thus pointed the moral and reduced his flock to a fitting state of docility, he dismissed them once more to their labours and withdrew himself to his own private chamber, there to seek spiritual aid in the discharge of the duties of his high office.

The Abbot was still on his knees, when a gentle tapping at the door of his cell broke in upon his orisons. Rising in no very good humour at the interruption, he gave the word to enter ; but his look of impatience softened down into a pleasant and paternal smile as his eyes fell upon his visitor.

He was a thin-faced, yellow-haired youth, rather above the middle size, comely and well shapen, with straight lithe figure and eager boyish features. His clear, pensive grey eyes, and quick delicate expression, spoke of a nature which had unfolded far from the boisterous joys and sorrows of the world. Yet there was a set of the mouth and a prominence of the chin which relieved him of any trace of effeminacy. Impulsive he might be, enthusiastic, sensitive, with something sympathetic and adaptive in his disposition ; but an observer of nature's tokens would have confidently pledged himself that there was native firmness and strength underlying his gentle, monk-bred ways.

The youth was not clad in monastic garb, but in lay attire, though his jerkin, cloak, and hose were all of a sombre hue, as befitted one who dwelt in sacred precincts. A broad leather strap hanging from his shoulder supported a scrip or satchel such as travellers were wont to carry. In one hand he grasped a thick staff pointed and shod with metal, while in the other he held his coif or bonnet, which bore in its front a broad pewter medal stamped with the image of Our Lady of Rocamadour.

"Art ready, then, fair son?" said the Abbot. "This is indeed a day of comings and of goings. It is strange that in one twelve hours the Abbey should have cast off its foulest weed, and should now lose what we are fain to look upon as our choicest blossom."

"You speak too kindly, father," the youth answered. "If I had my will I should never go forth, but should end my days here in Beaulieu. It hath been my home as far back as my mind can carry me, and it is a sore thing for me to have to leave it."

"Life brings many a cross," said the Abbot gently. "Who is without them? Your going forth is a grief to us as well as to yourself. But there is no help. I had given my foreword and sacred promise to your father, Edric the Franklin, that at the age of twenty you should be sent out into the world to see for yourself how you liked the savour of it. Seat thee upon the settle, Alleyne, for you may need rest ere long."

The youth sat down as directed, but reluctantly and with diffidence. The Abbot stood by the narrow window, and his long black shadow fell slantwise across the rush-strewn floor.

"Twenty years ago," he said, "your father, the Franklin of Minstead, died, leaving to the Abbey three hides of rich land in the hundred of Malwood, and leaving to us also his infant son on condition that we should rear him until he came to man's estate. This he did partly because your mother was dead, and partly because your elder brother, now Socman of Minstead, had already

14

given sign of that fierce and rude nature which would make him no fit companion for you. It was his desire and request, however, that you should not remain in the cloisters, but should at a ripe age return into the world."

" But, father," interrupted the young man, " it is surely true that I am already advanced several degrees in clerkship ? "

" Yes, fair son, but not so far as to bar you from the garb you now wear or the life which you must now lead. You have been porter ? "

" Yes, father."

" Exorcist ? "

" Yes, father."

" Reader ? "

" Yes, father."

" Acolyte ? "

" Yes, father."

" But have sworn no vow of constancy or chastity ? "

" No, father."

" Then you are free to follow a worldly life. But let me hear, ere you start, what gifts you take away with you from Beaulieu. Some I already know. There is the playing of the citole and the rebec. Our choir will be dumb without you. You carve, too ? "

The youth's pale face flushed with the pride of the skilled workman. " Yes, holy father," he answered. " Thanks to good brother Bartholomew, I carve in wood and in ivory, and can do something also in silver and in bronze. From brother Francis I have learned to paint on vellum, on glass, and on metal, with a knowledge of those pigments and essences which can preserve the colour against damp or a biting air. Brother Luke hath given me some skill in damask work, and in the enamelling of shrines, tabernacles, diptychs and triptychs. For the rest, I know a little of the making of covers, the cutting of precious stones, and the fashioning of instruments."

" A goodly list, truly," cried the superior with a smile. " What clerk of Cambrig or of Oxenford could say as much? But of thy reading—hast not so much to show there, I fear?"

"No, father, it hath been slight enough. Yet, thanks to our good chancellor, I am not wholly unlettered. I have read Ockham, Bradwardine, and other of the schoolmen, together with the learned Duns Scotus and the book of the holy Aquinas."

"But of the things of this world, what have you gathered from your reading? From this high window you may catch a glimpse over the wooded point and the smoke of Bucklershard, of the mouth of the Exe, and the shining sea. Now, I pray you, Alleyne, if a man were to take a ship and spread sail across yonder waters, where might he hope to arrive?"

The youth pondered, and drew a plan amongst the rushes with the point of his staff. "Holy father," said he, "he would come upon those parts of France which are held by the King's Majesty. But if he trended to the south he might reach Spain and the Barbary States. To his north would be Flanders and the country of the Eastlanders and of the Muscovites."

"True. And how if, after reaching the King's possessions, he still journeyed on to the eastward?"

"He would then come upon that part of France which is still in dispute, and he might hope to reach the famous city of Avignon, where dwells our blessed father, the prop of Christendom."

"And then?"

"Then he would pass through the land of the Almains and the great Roman Empire, and so to the country of the Huns and of the Lithuanian pagans, beyond which lie the great city of Constantine and the kingdom of the unclean followers of Mahmoud."

"And beyond that, fair son?"

"Beyond that is Jerusalem and the Holy Land, and the great river which hath its source in the Garden of Eden."

"And then?"

" Nay, good father, I cannot tell. Methinks the end of the world is not far from there."

" Then we can still find something to teach thee, Alleyne," said the Abbot complaisantly. " Know that many strange nations lie betwixt there and the end of the world. There is the country of the Amazons, and the country of the dwarfs, and the country of the fair but evil women who slay with beholding, like the basilisk. Beyond that again is the kingdom of Prester John and of the Great Cham. These things I know for very sooth, for I had them from that pious Christian and valiant knight, Sir John de Mandeville, who stopped twice at Beaulieu on his way to and from Southampton, and discoursed to us concerning what he had seen from the reader's desk in the refectory, until there was many a good brother who got neither bit nor sup, so stricken were they by his strange tales."

" I would fain know, father," asked the young man, " what there may be at the end of the world ? "

" There are some things," replied the Abbot gravely, " into which it was never intended that we should inquire. But you have a long road before you. Whither will you first turn ? "

" To my brother's at Minstead. If he be indeed an ungodly and violent man, there is the more need that I should seek him out and see whether I cannot turn him to better ways."

The Abbot shook his head. " The Socman of Minstead hath earned an evil name over the countryside," he said. " If you must go to him, see at least that he doth not turn you from the narrow path upon which you have learned to tread. But you are in God's keeping, and Godward should you ever look in danger and in trouble. Above all, shun the snares of women, for they are ever set for the foolish feet of the young. Kneel down, my child, and take an old man's blessing."

Alleyne Edricson bent his head while the Abbot poured out his heartfelt supplication that Heaven would watch

17

over this young soul, now going forth into the darkness and danger of the world. It was no mere form for either of them. To them the outside life of mankind did indeed seem to be one of violence and of sin, beset with physical and still more with spiritual danger. Heaven, too, was very near to them in those days. God's direct agency was to be seen in the thunder and the rainbow, the whirlwind and the lightning. To the believer, clouds of angels and confessors, and martyrs, armies of the sainted and the saved, were ever stooping over their struggling brethren upon earth, raising, encouraging, and supporting them. It was then with a lighter heart and a stouter courage that the young man turned from the Abbot's room, while the latter, following him to the stair-head, finally commended him to the protection of the holy Julian, patron of travellers.

Underneath, in the porch of the Abbey, the monks had gathered to give him a last God-speed. Many had brought some parting token by which he should remember them. There was brother Bartholomew with a crucifix of rare carved ivory, and brother Luke with a white-backed psalter adorned with golden bees, and brother Francis with the " Slaying of the Innocents" most daintily set forth upon vellum. All these were duly packed away deep in the traveller's scrip, and above them old pippin-faced brother Athanasius had placed a parcel of simnel bread and rammel cheese, with a small flask of the famous blue-sealed Abbey wine. So, amid hand-shakings and laughings and blessings, Alleyne Edricson turned his back upon Beaulieu.

At the turn of the road he stopped and gazed back. There was the widespread building which he knew so well, the Abbot's house, the long church, the cloisters with their line of arches, all bathed and mellowed in the evening sun. There too was the broad sweep of the river Exe, the old stone well, the canopied niche of the Virgin, and, in the centre of all, the cluster of white-robed figures who waved their hands to him. A sudden mist swam up before the young man's eyes, and he turned away upon his journey with a heavy heart and a choking throat.

3. *How Hordle John cozened the Fuller of Lymington*

IT is not, however, in the nature of things that a lad of twenty, with young life glowing in his veins and all the wide world before him, should spend his first hours of freedom in mourning for what he had left. Long ere Alleyne was out of sound of the Beaulieu bells he was striding sturdily along, swinging his staff and whistling as merrily as the birds in the thicket. It was an evening to raise a man's heart. The sun shining slantwise through the trees threw delicate traceries across the road, with bars of golden light between. Away in the distance, before and behind, the green boughs, now turning in places to a coppery redness, shot their broad arches across the track. The still summer air was heavy with the resinous smell of the great forest. Here and there a tawny brook prattled out from among the underwood and lost itself again in the ferns and brambles upon the farther side. Save the dull piping of insects and the sough of the leaves, there was silence everywhere—the sweet restful silence of nature.

And yet there was no want of life—the whole wide wood was full of it. Now it was a lithe, furtive stoat which shot across the path upon some fell errand of its own ; then it was a wild cat which squatted upon the out-lying branch of an oak and peeped at the traveller with a yellow and dubious eye. Once it was a wild sow which scuttled out of the bracken, with two young sounders at her heels ; and once a lordly red staggard walked daintily out from among the tree-trunks and looked around him with the fearless gaze of one who lived under the king's own high protection. Alleyne gave his staff a merry flourish, however, and the red deer bethought him that the king was far off, so bounded away whence he came.

The youth had now journeyed considerably beyond the farthest domains of the Abbey. He was the more surprised therefore when, on coming round a turn in the path, he perceived a man clad in the familiar garb of the order, and seated in a clump of heather by the roadside. Alleyne had known every brother well, but this was a face which was new to him—a face which was very red and puffed, working this way and that, as though the man were sore perplexed in his mind. Once he shook both hands furiously in the air, and twice he sprang from his seat and hurried down the road. When he rose, however, Alleyne observed that his robe was much too long and loose for him in every direction, trailing upon the ground and bagging about his ankles, so that even with trussed-up skirts he could make little progress. He ran once, but the long gown clogged him so that he slowed down into a shambling walk, and finally plumped into the heather once more.

" Young friend," said he, when Alleyne was abreast of him, " I fear from thy garb that thou canst know little of the Abbey of Beaulieu."

" Then you are in error, friend," the clerk answered, " for I have spent all my days within its walls."

" Hast so indeed ? " cried he. " Then perhaps canst tell me the name of a great loathly lump of a brother wi' freckled face an' a hand like a spade. His eyes were black an' his hair was red an' his voice like the parish bull. I trow that there cannot be two alike in the same cloisters."

" That surely can be no other than brother John," said Alleyne. " I trust he has done you no wrong, that you should be so hot against him."

" Wrong, quotha ? " cried the other, jumping out of the heather. " Wrong ! why, he hath stolen every plack of clothing off my back, if that be a wrong, and hath left me here in this sorry frock of white falding, so that I have shame to go back to my wife, lest she think that I have donned her old kirtle. Harrow and alas that ever I should have met him ! "

" But how came this ? " asked the young clerk, who could scarce keep from laughter at the sight of the hot little man so swathed in the great white cloak.

" It came in this way," he said, sitting down once more : " I was passing this way, hoping to reach Lymington ere nightfall, when I came on this red-headed knave seated even where we are sitting now. I uncovered and louted as I passed, thinking that he might be a holy man at his orisons, but he called to me and asked me if I had heard speak of the new indulgence in favour of the Cistercians. " Not I," I answered. " Then the worse for thy soul," said he ; and with that he broke into a long tale how that on account of the virtues of the Abbot Berghersh it had been decreed by the Pope that whoever should wear the habit of a monk of Beaulieu for as long as he might say the seven psalms of David should be assured of the kingdom of Heaven. When I heard this I prayed him on my knees that he would give me the use of his gown, which after many contentions he at last agreed to do, on my paying him three marks towards the regilding of the image of Laurence the martyr. Having stripped his robe, I had no choice but to let him have the wearing of my good leathern jerkin and hose, for, as he said, it was chilling to the blood and unseemly to the eye to stand frockless whilst I made my orisons. He had scarce got them on, and it was a sore labour, seeing that my inches will scarce match my girth—he had scarce got them on, I say, and I not yet at the end of the second psalm, when he bade me do honour to my new dress, and with that set off down the road as fast as feet would carry him. For myself, I could no more run that if I had been sewn in a sack ; so here I sit, and here I am like to sit, before I set eyes upon my clothes again."

" Nay, friend, take it not so sadly," said Alleyne, clapping the disconsolate one upon the shoulder. " Canst change thy robe for a jerkin once more at the Abbey, unless perchance you have a friend near at hand."

"That have I," he answered, "and close; but I care not to go nigh him in this plight, for his wife hath a gibing tongue, and would spread the tale until I could not show my face in any market from Fordingbridge to Southampton. But if you, fair sir, out of your kind charity, would be pleased to go a matter of two bow-shots out of your way, you would do me such a service as I could scarce repay."

"With all my heart," said Alleyne readily.

"Then take this pathway on the left, I pray thee, and then the deer-track which passes on the right. You will then see under a great beech-tree the hut of a charcoal-burner. Give him my name, good sir, the name of Peter the Fuller, of Lymington, and ask him for a change of raiment, that I may pursue my journey without delay. There are reasons why he would be loth to refuse me."

Alleyne started off along the path indicated, and soon found the log-hut where the burner dwelt. He was away faggot-cutting in the forest; but his wife, a ruddy, bustling dame, found the needful garments and tied them into a bundle. While she busied herself in finding and folding them Alleyne Edricson stood by the open door looking in at her with much interest and some distrust, for he had never been so nigh to a woman before. She had red arms, a dress of some sober woollen stuff, and a brass brooch the size of a cheese-cake stuck in the front of it.

"Peter the Fuller!" she kept repeating. "Marry come up! if I were Peter the Fuller's wife, I would teach him better than to give his clothes to the first knave who asks for them. But he was always a poor, fond, silly creature, was Peter, though we are beholden to him for helping to bury our second son, Wat, who was a 'prentice to him at Lymington in the year of the Black Death. But who are you, young sir?"

"I am a clerk on my road from Beaulieu to Minstead."

" Aye, indeed ! Hast been brought up at the Abbey then. I could read it from thy reddened cheek and down-cast eye. Hast learned from the monks, I trow, to fear a woman as thou wouldst a lazar-house. Out upon them that they should dishonour their own mothers by such teaching ! A pretty world it would be with all the women out of it."

" Heaven forefend that such a thing should come to pass ! " said Alleyne.

" Amen and amen ! But thou art a pretty lad, and the prettier for thy modest ways. It is easy to see from thy cheek that thou hast not spent thy days in the rain and the heat and the wind, as my poor Wat hath been forced to do."

" I have indeed seen little of life, good dame."

" Wilt find nothing in it to pay thee for the loss of thy own freshness. Here are the clothes, and Peter can leave them when next he comes this way. Holy Virgin ! see the dust upon thy doublet. It were easy to see that there is no woman to tend to thee. So !—that is better. Now buss me, boy."

Alleyne stooped and kissed her, for the kiss was the common salutation of the age, and, as Erasmus long after-wards remarked, more used in England than in any other country. Yet it sent the blood to his temples again, and he wondered, as he turned away, what the Abbot Berg-hersh would have answered to so frank an invitation. He was still tingling from this new experience when he came out upon the high road and saw a sight which drove all other thoughts from his mind.

Some way down from where he had left him the un-fortunate Peter was stamping and raving tenfold worse than before. Now, however, instead of the great white cloak, he had no clothes on at all, save a short woollen shirt and a pair of leather shoes. Far down the road a long-legged figure was running, with a bundle under one arm and the other hand to his side, like a man who laughs until he is sore.

" See him ! " yelled Peter. " Look to him ! You shall be my witness. He shall see Winchester gaol for this. See where he goes with my cloak under his arm ! "

" Who then ! " cried Alleyne.

" Who but that cursed brother John ! He hath not left me clothes enough to make a galleybagger. The double thief hath cozened me out of my gown."

" Stay though, my friend, it was his gown," objected Alleyne.

" It boots not. He hath them all—gown, jerkin, hosen, and all. Gramercy to him that he left me the shirt and the shoon ! I doubt not that he will be back for them anon."

" But how came this ? " asked Alleyne, open-eyed with astonishment.

" Are those the clothes ? For dear charity's sake, give them to me. Not the Pope himself shall have these from me though he sent the whole college of cardinals to ask it. How came it ? Why, you had scarce gone ere this loathly John came running back again, and when I oped mouth to reproach him, he asked me whether it was indeed likely that a man of prayer would leave his own godly raiment in order to take a layman's jerkin. He had, he said, but gone for a while that I might be the freer for my devotions. On this I plucked off the gown, and he with much show of haste did begin to undo his points ; but when I threw his frock down he clipped it up and ran off all untrussed, leaving me in this sorry plight. He laughed so the while, like a great croaking frog, that I might have caught him, had my breath not been as short as his legs were long."

The young man listened to this tale of wrong with all the seriousness that he could maintain ; but at the sight of the pursy red-faced man and the dignity with which he bore him, the laughter came so thick upon him that he had to lean up against a tree-trunk. The fuller looked sadly and gravely at him ; but finding that he still laughed, he bowed with much mock politeness and stalked onwards in his borrowed clothes. Alleyne watched him until he was small in the distance, and then, wiping the tears from his eyes, he set off briskly once more upon his journey.

4. *How the Bailiff of Southampton slew the Two Masterless Men*

THE road along which he travelled was scarce as populous as most other roads in the kingdom, and far less so than those which lie between the larger towns. Yet from time to time Alleyne met other wayfarers, and more than once was overtaken by strings of pack-mules and horsemen journeying in the same direction as himself. Once a begging friar came limping along in a brown habit, imploring him in a most dolorous voice to give him a single groat to buy bread wherewith to save himself from impending death. Alleyne passed him swiftly by, for he had learned from the monks to have no love for the wandering friars, and, besides, there was a great half-gnawed mutton-bone sticking out of his pouch to prove him a liar. Swiftly as he went, however, he could not escape the curse of the four blessed Evangelists which the mendicant howled behind him. So dreadful were his execrations that the frightened lad thrust his fingers into his ear-holes, and ran until the fellow was but a brown smirch upon the yellow road.

Farther on, at the edge of the woodland, he came upon a chapman and his wife, who sat upon a fallen tree. He had put his pack down as a table, and the two of them were devouring a great pasty, and washing it down with some drink from a stone jar. The chapman broke a rough jest as he passed, and the woman called shrilly to Alleyne to come and join them, on which the man, turning suddenly from mirth to wrath, began to belabour her with his cudgel. Alleyne hastened on, lest he make more mischief, and his heart was heavy as lead within him. Look where he would, he seemed to see nothing but injustice and violence, and the hardness of man to man.

But even as he brooded sadly over it, and pined for the sweet peace of the Abbey, he came on an open space dotted with holly-bushes, where was the strangest sight that he had yet chanced upon. Near to the pathway lay a long clump of greenery, and from behind this there stuck straight up into the air four human legs clad in parti-coloured hosen, yellow and black. Strangest of all was it when a brisk tune struck suddenly up and the four legs began to kick and twitter in time to the music. Walking on tiptoe round the bushes, he stood in amazement to see two men bounding about on their heads while they played, the one a viol and the other a pipe, as merrily and as truly as though they were seated in choir. Alleyne crossed himself as he gazed at this unnatural sight, and could scarce hold his ground with a steady face, when the two dancers, catching sight of him, came bouncing in his direction. A spear's length from him they each threw a somersault into the air, and came down upon their feet with smirking faces and their hands over their hearts.

"A guerdon—a guerdon, my knight of the staring eyes!" cried one.

"A gift, my prince!" shouted the other. "Any trifle will serve—a purse of gold, or even a jewelled goblet."

Alleyne thought of what he had read of demoniac possession—the jumpings, the twitchings, the wild talk. It was in his mind to repeat over the exorcism proper to such attacks; but the two burst out a-laughing at his scared face, and, turning on to their heads once more, clapped their heels in derision.

"Hast never seen tumblers before?" asked the elder, a black-browed swarthy man, as brown and supple as a hazel-twig. "Why shrink from us, then, as though we were the spawn of the Evil One?"

"Why shrink, my honey-bird? Why so afeard, my sweet cinnamon?" exclaimed the other, a loose-jointed lanky youth with a dancing roguish eye.

" Truly, sirs, it is a new sight to me," the clerk answered. " When I saw your four legs above the bush I could scarce credit my own eyes. Why is it that you do this thing ? "

" A dry question to answer," cried the younger, coming back on to his feet. " A most husky question, my fair bird ! But how ? A flask, a flask !—by all that is wonderful ! " He shot out his hand as he spoke, and plucking Alleyne's bottle out of his scrip, he deftly knocked the neck off, and poured the half of it down his throat. The rest he handed to his comrade, who drank the wine, and then, to the clerk's increasing amazement, made a show of swallowing the bottle, with such skill that Alleyne seemed to see it vanish down his throat. A moment later, however, he flung it over his head, and caught it bottom downwards upon the calf of his left leg.

" We thank you for the wine, kind sir," said he, " and for the ready courtesy wherewith you offered it. Touching your question, we may tell you that we are strollers and jugglers, who, having performed with much applause at Winchester fair, are now on our way to the great Michaelmas market at Ringwood. As our art is a very fine and delicate one, however, we cannot let a day go by without exercising ourselves in it, to which end we choose some quiet and sheltered spot, where we may break our journey. Here you find us ; and we cannot wonder that you, who are new to tumbling, should be astounded, since many great barons, earls, marshals, and knights, who have wandered as far as the Holy Land, are of one mind in saying that they have never seen a more noble or gracious performance. If you will be pleased to sit upon that stump, we will now continue our exercise."

Alleyne sat down willingly as directed, with two great bundles on either side of him which contained the strollers' dresses—doublets of flame-coloured silk and girdles of leather, spangled with brass and tin. The jugglers were on their heads once more, bounding about with rigid necks, playing the while in perfect time and tune. It chanced that out of one of the bundles there stuck the end of what the clerk saw to be a cittern, so, drawing it forth, he tuned it up and twanged a harmony to the merry lilt which the dancers played. On that they dropped their own instruments, and putting their hands to the ground they hopped about faster and faster, ever shouting to him to play more briskly, until at last for very weariness all three had to stop.

" Well played, sweet poppet ! " cried the younger. " Hast a rare touch on the strings."

" How knew you the tune ? " asked the other.

" I knew it not. I did but follow the notes I heard."

Both opened their eyes at this, and stared at Alleyne with as much amazement as he had shown at them.

" You have a fine trick of ear, then," said one. " We have long wished to meet such a man. Wilt join us and jog on to Ringwood ? Thy duties shall be light, and thou shalt have twopence a day and meat for supper every night.'

" With as much beer as you can put away," said the other, " and a flask of Gascon wine on Sabbaths."

" Nay, it may not be. I have other work to do. I have tarried with you over long," quoth Alleyne, and resolutely set forth upon his journey once more. They ran behind him some little way, offering him first four-pence and then sixpence a day ; but he only smiled and shook his head, until at last they fell away from him. Looking back, he saw that the smaller had mounted on the younger's shoulders, and that they stood so, some ten feet high, waving their adieus to him. He waved back to them, and then hastened on, the lighter of heart for having fallen in with these strange men of pleasure.

Alleyne had gone no great distance for all the many small passages that had befallen him. Yet to him, used as he was to a life of such quiet that the failure of a brew-ing, or the altering of an anthem, had seemed to be of the deepest import, the quick changing play of the lights and shadows of life was strangely startling and interesting. A gulf seemed to divide this brisk, uncertain existence from the old steady round of work and of prayer which he had left behind him. The few hours that had passed since he saw the Abbey tower stretched out in his memory until they outgrew whole months of the stagnant life of the cloister. As he walked and munched the soft bread from his scrip, it seemed strange to him to feel that it was still warm from the ovens of Beaulieu.

When he passed Penerley, where were three cottages and a barn, he reached the edge of the tree country, and found the great barren heath of Blackdown stretching in front of him, all pink with heather and bronzed with the fading ferns. On the left the woods were still thick, but the road edged away from them and wound over the open. The sun lay low in the west upon a purple cloud, whence it threw a mild chastening light over the wild moorland and glittered on the fringe of forest, turning the withered leaves into flakes of dead gold, the brighter for the black depths behind them. To the seeing eye decay is as fair as growth, and death as life. The thought stole into Alleyne's heart as he looked upon the autumnal country-side and marvelled at its beauty. He had little time to dwell upon it, however, for there were still six good miles between him and the nearest inn. He sat down by the roadside to partake of his bread and cheese, and then with a lighter scrip he hastened upon his way.

There appeared to be more wayfarers on the down than in the forest. First he passed two Dominicans in their long black dresses, who swept by him with downcast looks and pattering lips, without so much as a glance at him. Then there came a grey friar, or minorite, with a good paunch upon him, walking slowly and looking about him with the air of a man who was at peace with himself and with all men. He stopped Alleyne to ask him whether it were not true that there was a hostel some-where in those parts which was especially famous for the stewing of eels. The clerk having made answer that he had heard the eels of Sowley well spoken of, the friar sucked in his lips and hurried forward. Close at his heels came three labourers walking abreast, with spade and mattock over their shoulders. They sang some rude chorus right tunefully as they walked, but their English was so coarse and rough that to the ears of a cloister-bred man it sounded like a foreign and barbarous tongue. One of them carried a young bittern which they had caught upon the moor, and they offered it to Alleyne for a silver groat. Very glad he was to get safely past them, for, with their bristling red beards and their fierce blue eyes, they were uneasy men to bargain with upon a lonely moor.

Yet it is not always the burliest and the wildest who are the most to be dreaded. The workers looked hungrily at him, and then jogged onwards upon their way in slow lumbering Saxon style. A worse man to deal with was a wooden-legged cripple who came hobbling down the path, so weak and so old to all appearance that a child need not stand in fear of him. Yet when Alleyne had passed him, of a sudden, out of pure devilment, he screamed out a curse at him, and sent a jagged flint-stone hurtling past his ear. So horrid was the causeless rage of the crooked creature, that the clerk came over a cold thrill, and took to his heels until he was out of shot from stone or word. It seemed to him that in this country of England there was no protection for a man save that which lay in the strength of his own arm and the speed of his own foot. In the cloisters he had heard vague talk of the law—the mighty law which was higher than prelate or baron, yet no sign could he see of it. What was the benefit of a law written fair upon parchment, he wondered, if there were no officers to enforce it ? As it fell out, however, he had that very evening, ere the sun had set, a chance of seeing how stern was the grip of the English law when it did happen to seize the offender.

A mile or so out upon the moor the road takes a very sudden dip into a hollow, with a peat-coloured stream running swiftly down the centre of it. To the right of this stood, and stands to this day, an ancient barrow, or burying mound, covered deeply in a bristle of heather and bracken. Alleyne was plodding down the slope upon one side, when he saw an old dame coming towards him upon the other, limping with weariness and leaning heavily upon a stick. When she reached the edge of the stream she stood helpless, looking to right and to left for some ford. Where the path ran down a great stone had been fixed in the centre of the brook, but it was too far from the bank for her aged and uncertain feet. Twice she thrust forward at it, and twice she drew back, until at last, giving it up in despair, she sat herself down by the brink and wrung her hands wearily. There she still sat when Alleyne reached the crossing.

"Come, mother," quoth he, "it is not so very perilous a passage."

"Alas! good youth," she answered, "I have a humour in the eyes, and though I can see that there is a stone there, I can by no means be sure as to where it lies."

"That is easily amended," said he cheerily, and picking her lightly up, for she was much worn with time, he passed across with her. He could not but observe, however, that as he placed her down her knees seemed to fail her, and she could scarcely prop herself up with her staff.

"You are weak, mother," said he. "Hast journeyed far, I wot."

"From Wiltshire, friend," said she, in a quavering voice; "three days have I been on the road. I go to my son, who is one of the king's regarders at Brockenhurst. He has ever said that he would care for me in mine old age."

"And rightly, too, mother, since you cared for him in his youth. But when have you broken fast?"

"At Lyndenhurst; but, alas! my money is at an end, and I could but get a dish of bran-porridge from the nunnery. Yet I trust that I may be able to reach Brockenhurst to-night, where I may have all that heart can desire; for, oh, sir! but my son is a fine man, with a kindly heart of his own, and it is as good as food to me to think that he should have a doublet of Lincoln-green to his back and be the king's own paid man."

" It is a long road yet to Brockenhurst," said Alleyne ; " but here is such bread and cheese as I have left, and here, too, is a penny which may help you to supper. May God be with you ! "

" May God be with you, young man ! " she cried. " May He make your heart as glad as you have made mine ! " She turned away, still mumbling blessings, and Alleyne saw her short figure and her long shadow stumbling slowly up the slope.

He was moving away himself, when his eyes lit upon a strange sight, and one which sent a tingling through his skin. Out of the tangled scrub on the old overgrown barrow two human faces were looking at him ; the sinking sun glimmered full upon them, showing up every line and feature. The one was an oldish man with a thin beard, a crooked nose, and a broad red smudge from a birth-mark over his temple ; the other was a negro, a thing rarely met in England at that day, and rarer still in the quiet south-land parts. Alleyne had read of such folk, but had never seen one before, and could scarce take his eyes from the fellow's broad pouting lip and shining teeth. Even as he gazed, however, the two came writhing out from among the heather, and came down towards him with such a guilty, slinking carriage, that the clerk felt that there was no good in them, and hastened onwards upon his way.

He had not gained the crown of the slope, when he heard a sudden scuffle behind him, and a feeble voice bleating for help. Looking round, there was the old dame down upon the roadway, with her red wimple fly-ing on the breeze, while the two rogues, black and white, stooped over her, wresting away from her the penny and such other poor trifles as were worth the taking. At the sight of her thin limbs struggling in weak resistance, such a glow of fierce anger passed over Alleyne as set his head in a whirl. Dropping his scrip, he bounded over the stream once more, and made for the two villains, with his staff whirled over his shoulder, and his grey eyes blazing with fury.

The robbers, however, were not disposed to leave their victim until they had worked their wicked will upon her. The black man, with the woman's crimson scarf tied round his swarthy head, stood forward in the centre of the path, with a long dull-coloured knife in his hand, while the other, waving a ragged cudgel, cursed at Alleyne and dared him to come on. His blood was fairly aflame, however, and he needed no such challenge. Dashing at the black man, he smote at him with such good will that he let his knife tinkle into the roadway, and hopped howling to a safer distance. The second rogue, however, made of sterner stuff, rushed in upon the clerk, and clipped him round the waist with a grip like a bear, shouting the while to his comrade to come round and stab him in the back. At this the negro took heart of grace, and, picking up his dagger again, he came stealing with prowling step and murderous eye, while the two swayed backwards and forwards, staggering this way and that. In the very midst of the scuffle, however, whilst Alleyne braced himself to feel the cold blade between his shoulders, there came a sudden scurry of hoofs, and the black man yelled with terror, and ran for his life through the heather. The man with the birth-mark, too, struggled to break away, and Alleyne heard his teeth chatter and felt his limbs grow limp to his hand. At this sign of coming aid the clerk held on the tighter, and at last was able to pin his man down and glance behind him to see whence all the noise was coming.

Down the slanting road there was riding a big burly man, clad in a tunic of purple velvet and driving a great black horse as hard as it could gallop. He leaned well over its neck as he rode, and made a heaving with his shoulders at every bound as though he were lifting the steed instead of it carrying him. In the rapid glance Alleyne saw that he had white doeskin gloves, a curling white feather in his flat velvet cap, and a broad gold

embroidered baldric across his bosom. Behind him rode
six others, two and two, clad in sober brown jerkins, with
the long yellow staves of their bows thrusting out from
behind their right shoulders. Down the hill they thundered, over the brook, and up to the scene of the contest.

" Here is one ! " said the leader, springing down from
his reeking horse, and seizing the white rogue by the edge
of his jerkin. " This is one of them. I know him by
that devil's touch upon his brow. Where are your cords,
Peterkin ? So ! Bind him hand and foot. His last
hour has come. And you, young man, who may you be ? "

" I am a clerk, sir, travelling from Beaulieu."

" A clerk ! " cried the other. " Art from Oxenford
or from Cambridge ? Hast thou a letter from the chancellor of thy college, giving thee a permit to beg ? Let me
see thy letter." He had a stern square face, with bushy
side whiskers, and a very questioning eye.

" I am from Beaulieu Abbey, and I have no need to
beg," said Alleyne, who was all of a tremble now that the
ruffle was over.

" The better for thee," the other answered. " Dost
know who I am ? "

" No, sir, I do not."

" I am the law ! "—nodding his head solemnly. " I
am the law of England and the mouthpiece of his most
gracious and royal majesty, Edward the Third."

Alleyne louted low to the king's representative.

" Truly you came in good time, honoured sir," said he.
" A moment later and they would have slain me."

" But there should be another one," cried the man in
the purple coat. " There should be a black man. A
shipman with St. Anthony's fire, and a black man who had
served him as cook—those are the pair that we are in chase
of."

" The black man fled over to that side," said Alleyne,
pointing towards the barrow.

" He could not have gone far, sir bailiff," cried one of
the archers, unslinging his bow. " He is in hiding some-

where, for he knew well, black paynim as he is, that our horses' four legs could outstrip his two."

" Then we shall have him," said the other. " It shall never be said whilst I am Bailiff of Southampton, that any waster, riever, drawlatch or murtherer came scathless away from me and my posse. Leave that rogue lying. Now stretch out in line, my merry ones, with arrow on string, and I shall show you such sport as only the king can give. You on the left, Howett, and Thomas of Redbridge upon the right. So ! Beat high and low among the heather, and a pot of wine to the lucky marksman."

As it chanced, however, the searchers had not far to seek. The negro had burrowed down into his hiding-place upon the barrow, where he might have lain snug enough, had it not been for the red gear upon his head. As he raised himself to look over the bracken at his enemies, the staring colour caught the eye of the bailiff, who broke into a long screeching whoop and spurred forward sword in hand. Seeing himself discovered, the man rushed out from his hiding-place, and bounded at the top of his speed down the line of archers, keeping a good hundred paces to the front of them. The two who were on either side of Alleyne bent their bows as calmly as though they were shooting at the popinjay at a village fair.

" Seven yards windage, Hal," said one, whose hair was streaked with grey.

" Five," replied the other, letting loose his string. Alleyne gave a gulp in his throat, for the yellow streak seemed to pass through the man ; but he still ran forward.

" Seven, you jack-fool," growled the first speaker, and his bow twanged like a harpstring. The black man sprang high up into the air, and shot out both his arms and his legs, coming down all asprawl among the heather. " Right under the blade bone ! " quoth the archer, sauntering forward for his arrow.

" The old hound is the best when all is said," quoth the Bailiff of Southampton, as they made back for the roadway. " That means a quart of the best malmsey in

Southampton this very night, Matthew Atwood. Art sure that he is dead ? "

" Dead as Pontius Pilate, worshipful sir."

" It is well. Now, as to the other knave. There are trees and to spare over yonder, but we have scarce leisure to make for them. Draw thy sword, Thomas of Redbridge, and hew me his head from his shoulders."

" A boon, gracious sir, a boon ! " cried the condemned man.

" What then ? " asked the bailiff.

" I will confess to my crime. It was indeed I and the black cook, both from the ship *La Rose de Gloire*, of Southampton, who did set upon the Flanders merchant and rob him of his spicery and his mercery, for which, as we well know, you hold a warrant against us."

" There is little merit in this confession," quoth the bailiff sternly. "Thou hast done evil within my baili- wick, and must die."

" But, sir," urged Alleyne, who was white to the lips at these bloody doings, " he hath not yet come to trial."

" Young clerk," said the bailiff, " you speak of that of which you know nothing. It is true that he hath not come to trial, but the trial hath come to him. He hath fled the law and is beyond its pale. Touch not that which is no concern of thine. But what is this boon, rogue, which you would crave ? "

" I have in my shoe, most worshipful sir, a strip of wood which belonged once to the bark wherein the blessed Paul was dashed up against the island of Melita. I bought it for two rose nobles from a shipman who came from the Levant. The boon I crave is that you will place it in my hands and let me die still grasping it. In this manner, not only shall my own eternal salvation be secured, but thine also, for I shall never cease to intercede for thee."

At the command of the bailiff they plucked off the fellow's shoe, and there sure enough at the side of the instep, wrapped in a piece of fine sendal, lay a long dark splinter of wood. The archers doffed their caps at the sight of it, and the bailiff crossed himself devoutly as he handed it to the robber.

" If it should chance," he said, " that through the surpassing merits of the blessed Paul your sin-stained soul should gain way into paradise, I trust that you will not forget that intercession which you have promised. Bear in mind, too, that it is Herward the Bailiff for whom you pray, and not Herward the Sheriff, who is my uncle's son. Now, Thomas, I pray you despatch, for we have a long ride before us and sun has already set."

Alleyne gazed upon the scene—the portly velvet-clad official, the knot of hard-faced archers with their hands to the bridles of their horses, the thief with his arms trussed back and his doublet turned down upon his shoulders. By the side of the track the old dame was standing, fastening her red wimple once more round her head. Even as he looked one of the archers drew his sword with a sharp whirr of steel and stepped up to the lost man. The clerk hurried away in horror ; but, ere he had gone many paces, he heard a sudden, sullen thump, with a choking, whistling sound at the end of it. A minute later the bailiff and four of his men rode past him on their journey back to Southampton, the other two having been chosen as grave-diggers. As they passed, Alleyne saw that one of the men was wiping his sword-blade upon the mane of his horse. A deadly sickness came over him at the sight, and sitting down by the wayside he burst out a-weeping, with his nerves all in a jangle. It was a terrible world, thought he, and it was hard to know which were the more to be dreaded, the knaves or the men of the law.

5. *How a Strange Company gathered at the "Pied Merlin"*

THE night had already fallen, and the moon was shining between the rifts of ragged drifting clouds, before Alleyne Edricson, footsore and weary from the unwonted exercise, found himself in front of the forest inn which stood upon the outskirts of Lyndhurst. The building was long and low, standing back a little from the road, with two flambeaux blazing on either side of the door as a welcome to the traveller. From one window there thrust forth a long pole with a bunch of greenery tied to the end of it—a sign that liquor was to be sold within. As Alleyne walked up to it he perceived that it was rudely fashioned out of beams of wood, with twinkling lights all over where the glow from within shone through the chinks. The roof was poor and thatched; but in strange contrast to it there ran all along under the eaves a line of wooden shields, most gorgeously painted with chevron, bend, saltire, and every heraldic device. By the door a horse stood tethered, the ruddy glow beating strongly upon his brown head and patient eyes, while his body stood back in the shadow.

Alleyne stood still in the roadway for a few minutes reflecting upon what he should do. It was, he knew, only a few miles farther to Minstead, where his brother dwelt. On the other hand, he had never seen his brother since childhood, and the reports which had come to his ears concerning him were seldom to his advantage. By all accounts he was a hard and a bitter man. It might be an evil start to come to his door so late and claim the shelter of his roof. Better to sleep here at this inn and then travel on to Minstead in the morning. If his brother would take him in, well and good. He would bide with him for a time and do what he might to serve him. If, on the other hand, he should have hardened his heart against him, he could only go on his way and do the best he might by his skill as a craftsman and a scrivener. At the end of a year he would be free to return to the cloisters, for such had been his father's bequest. A monkish upbringing, one year in the world after the age of twenty, and then free selection one way or the other—it was a strange course which had been marked out for him. Such as it was, however, he had no choice but to follow it, and if he were to begin by making a friend of his brother he had best wait until morning before he knocked at his dwelling.

The rude plank door was ajar, but as Alleyne approached it there came from within such a gust of rough laughter and clatter of tongues that he stood irresolute upon the threshold. Summoning courage, however, and reflecting that it was a public dwelling, in which he had as much right as any other man, he pushed it open and stepped into the common room.

Though it was an autumn evening and somewhat warm, a huge fire of heaped billets of wood crackled and sparkled in a broad, open grate, some of the smoke escaping up a rude chimney, but the greater part rolling out into the room, so that the air was thick with it, and a man coming from without could scarce catch his breath. On this fire a great caldron bubbled and simmered, giving forth a rich and promising smell. Seated round it were a dozen or so folk, of all ages and conditions, who set up such a shout as Alleyne entered that he stood peering at them through the smoke uncertain what this riotous greeting might portend.

" A rouse ! A rouse ! " cried one rough-looking fellow in a tattered jerkin. " One more round of mead or ale and the score to the last comer."

" 'Tis the law of the ' Pied Merlin,' " shouted another. " Ho, there, Dame Eliza ! Here is fresh custom come to the house, and not a drain for the company."

" I will take your orders, gentles ; I will assuredly take your orders," the landlady answered, bustling in with her hands full of leathern drinking-cups. " What is that you drink then ? Beer for the lads of the forest, mead for the gleeman, strong waters for the tinker, and wine for the rest. It is an old custom of the house, young sir. It has been the use at the ' Pied Merlin ' this many a year back that the company should drink to the health of the last comer. Is it your pleasure to humour it ? "

" Why, good dame," said Alleyne, " I would not offend the customs of your house, but it is only sooth when I say that my purse is a thin one. As far as two pence will go, however, I shall be right glad to do my part."

"Plainly said and bravely spoken, my sucking friar," roared a deep voice, and a heavy hand fell upon Alleyne's shoulder. Looking up, he saw beside him his former cloister companion, the renegade monk, Hordle John.

"By the thorn of Glastonbury! ill days are coming upon Beaulieu," said he. "Here they have got rid in one day of the only two men within their walls—for I have had mine eyes upon thee, youngster, and I know that for all thy baby-face there is the making of a man in thee. Then there is the Abbot, too. I am no friend of his, nor he of mine; but he has warm blood in his veins. He is the only man left among them. The others, what are they?"

"They are holy men," Alleyne answered gravely.

"Holy men? Holy cabbages! Holy bean-pods! What do they do but live and suck in sustenance and grow fat? If that be holiness, I could show you hogs in this forest who are fit to head the Calendar. Think you it was for such a life that this good arm was fixed upon my shoulder, or that head placed upon your neck? There is work in the world, man, and it is not by hiding behind stone walls that we shall do it."

"Why, then, did you join the brothers?" asked Alleyne.

"A fair enough question; but it is as fairly answered. I joined them because Margery Alspaye, of Bolder, married Crooked Thomas of Ringwood, and left a certain John of Hordle in the cold, for that he was a ranting, roving blade who was not to be trusted in wedlock. That was why, being fond and hot-headed, I left the world; and that is why, having had time to take thought, I am right glad to find myself back in it once more. Ill betide the day that ever I took off my yeoman's jerkin to put on the white gown!"

Whilst he was speaking the landlady came in again, bearing a broad platter, upon which stood all the beakers and flagons charged to the brim with the brown ale or the ruby wine. Behind her came a maid with a high pile of wooden plates, and a great sheaf of spoons, one of which she handed round to each of the travellers. Two of the company, who were dressed in the weather-stained green doublet of foresters, lifted the big pot off the fire, and a third with a huge pewter ladle, served out a portion of steaming collops to each guest. Alleyne bore his share and his ale-mug away with him to a retired trestle in the corner, where he could sup in peace and watch the strange scene, which was so different to those silent and well-ordered meals to which he was accustomed.

The room was not unlike a stable. The low ceiling, smoke-blackened and dingy, was pierced by several square trap-doors with rough-hewn ladders leading up to them. The walls of bare unpainted planks were studded here and there with great wooden pins, placed at irregular intervals and heights, from which hung overtunics, wallets, whips, bridles, and saddles. Over the fireplace were suspended six or seven shields of wood, with coats-of-arms rudely daubed upon them, which showed by their varying degrees of smokiness and dirt that they had been placed there at different periods. There was no furniture, save a single long dresser covered with coarse crockery, and a number of wooden benches and trestles, the legs of which sank deeply into the soft clay floor, while the only light, save that of the fire, was furnished by three torches stuck in sockets on the wall, which flickered and crackled, giving forth a strong resinous odour. All this was novel and strange to the cloister-bred youth ; but most interesting of all was the motley circle of guests who sat eating their collops round the blaze. They were a humble group of wayfarers, such as might have been found that night in any inn through the length and breadth of England ; but to him they represented that vague world against which he had been so frequeutly and so earnestly warned. It did not seem to him from what he could see of it to be such a very wicked place after all.

Three or four of the men round the fire were evidently under-keepers and verderers from the forest, sunburned and bearded, with the quick restless eye and lithe movements of the deer among which they lived. Close to the corner of the chimney sat a middle-aged gleeman, clad in a faded garb of Norwich cloth, the tunic of which was so outgrown that it did but fasten at the neck and at the waist. His face was swollen and coarse, and its watery protruding eyes spoke of a life which never wandered very far from the wine-pot. A gilt harp, blotched with many stains and with two of its strings missing, was tacked under one of his arms, while with the other he scooped greedily at his platter. Next to him sat two other men of about the same age, one with a trimming of fur to his coat, which gave him a dignity which was evidently dearer to him than his comfort, for he still drew it around him in spite of the hot glare of the faggots. The other, clad in a dirty russet suit with a long sweeping doublet, had a cunning foxy face with keen twinkling eyes and a peaky beard. Next to him sat Hordle John, and beside him three other rough unkempt fellows with tangled beards and matted hair—free labourers from the adjoining farms, where small patches of freehold property had been suffered to remain scattered about in the heart of the royal demesne. The company was completed by a peasant in a rude dress of undyed sheepskin, with the old-fashioned galligaskins about his legs, and a gaily dressed young man with striped cloak jagged at the edges and parti-coloured hosen, who looked about him with a high disdain upon his face, and held a blue smelling flask to his nose with one hand, while he brandished a busy spoon with the other. In the corner a very fat man was lying all asprawl upon a truss, snoring stertorously, and evidently in the last stage of drunkenness.

" That is Wat the Limner," quoth the landlady, sitting down beside Alleyne, and pointing with the ladle to the sleeping man. " That is he who paints the signs and the tokens. Alack and alas that ever I should have been fool enough to trust him ! Now, young man, what manner of a bird would you suppose a pied merlin to be—that being the proper sign of my hostel ? "

" Why," said Alleyne, " a merlin is a bird of the same form as an eagle or a falcon. I can well remember that learned brother Bartholomew, who is deep in all the secrets of Nature, pointed one out to me as we walked together near Vinney Ridge."

" A falcon, or an eagle, quotha ? And pied, that is of two several colours. So any man would say except this barrel of lies. He came to me, look you, saying that if I would furnish him with a gallon of ale, wherewith to strengthen himself as he worked, and also the pigments and a board, he would paint for me a noble pied merlin which I might hang along with the blazonry over my door. I, poor simple fool, gave him the ale and all that he cared, leaving him alone too, because he said that a man's mind must be left untroubled when he had great work to do. When I came back the gallon jar was empty, and he lay as you see him, with the board in front of him with this sorry device." She raised up a panel which was leaning against the wall, and showed a rude painting of a scraggy and angular fowl, with very long legs and a spotted body. " Was that," she asked, " like the bird which thou hast seen ? "

Alleyne shook his head, smiling.

" No, nor any other bird that ever wagged a feather. It is most like a plucked pullet which has died of the spotted fever. And scarlet, too ! What would the gentles, Sir Nicholas Borhunte, or Sir Bernard Brocas, of Roche Court, say if they saw such a thing—or, perhaps, even the king's own majesty himself, who often has ridden past this way, and who loves his falcons, as he loves his sons ? It would be the downfall of my house."

" The matter is not past mending," said Alleyne. " I pray you, good dame, to give me those three pigment-pots and the brush, and I shall try whether I cannot better this painting."

Dame Eliza looked doubtfully at him, as though fearing some other stratagem, but, as he made no demand for ale, she finally brought the paints, and watched him as he

43

smeared on his background, talking the while about the folk round the fire.

" The four forest lads must be jogging soon," she said. " They bide at Emery Down, a mile or more from here. Yeomen-prickets they are, who tend to the king's hunt. The gleeman is called Floyting Will. He comes from the north country, but for many years he hath gone the round of the forest from Southampton to Christchurch. He drinks much and pays little ; but it would make your ribs crackle to hear him sing the ' Jest of Hendy Tobias.' Mayhap he will sing it when the ale has warmed him."

" Who are those next to him ? " asked Alleyne, much interested. " He of the fur mantle has a wise and reverent face."

" He is a seller of pills and salves, very learned in humours, and rheums, and fluxes, and all manner of ailments. He wears, as you perceive, the vernicle of Sainted Luke, the first physician, upon his sleeve. May good St. Thomas of Kent grant that it may be long before either I or mine need his help ! He is here to-night for herbergage, as are the others, except the foresters. His neighbour is a tooth-drawer. That bag at his girdle is full of the teeth that he drew at Winchester fair. I warrant that there are more sound ones than sorry, for he is quick at his work, and a trifle dim in the eye. The lusty man next to him with the red head I have not seen before. The four on this side are all workers, three of them in the service of the bailiff of Sir Baldwin Redvers, and the other, he with the skeepskin, is, as I hear, a villein from the midlands who hath run from his master. His year and day are well-nigh up, when he will be a free man."

" And the other ? " asked Alleyne in a whisper. " He is surely some very great man, for he looks as though he scorned those who were about him."

The landlady looked at him in a motherly way and shook her head. " You have had no great truck with the world," she said, " or you would have learned that it is the small men and not the great who hold their noses in the air. Look at those shields upon my wall and under my eaves. Each of them is the device of some noble lord or gallant knight who hath slept under my roof at one time or another. Yet milder men or easier to please I have never seen : eating my bacon and drinking my wine with a merry face, and paying my score with some courteous word or jest which was dearer to me than my profit. Those are the true gentles. But your chapman or your bearward will swear that there is a lime in the wine, and water in the ale, and fling off at the last with a curse instead of a blessing. This youth is a scholar from Cambrig, where men are wont to be blown out by a little knowledge, and lose the use of their hands in learning the laws of the Romans. But I must away to lay down the beds. So may the saints keep you and prosper you in your undertaking ! "

Thus left to himself, Alleyne drew his panel of wood where the light of one of the torches would strike full upon it, and worked away with all the pleasure of the trained craftsman, listening the while to the talk which went on round the fire. The peasant in the sheepskins, who had sat glum and silent all evening, had been so heated by his flagon of ale that he was talking loudly and angrily with clenched hands and flashing eyes.

" Sir Humphrey Tennant of Ashby may till his own fields for me," he cried. " The castle has thrown its shadow upon the cottage over long. For three hundred years my folk have swinked and sweated, day in and day out, to keep the wine on the lord's table and the harness on the lord's back. Let him take off his plates and delve himself, if delving must be done."

" A proper spirit, my fair son ! " said one of the free labourers. " I would that all men were of thy way of thinking."

" He would have sold me with his acres," the other cried, in a voice which was hoarse with passion. " ' The man, the woman, and their litter '—so ran the words of the dotard bailiff. Never a bullock on the farm was sold

45

more lightly. Ha ! he may wake some black night to find the flames licking about his ears—for fire is a good friend to the poor man, and I have seen a smoking heap of ashes where overnight there stood just such another castlewick as Ashby."

" This is a lad of metal ! " shouted another of the labourers. " He dares to give tongue to what all men think. Are we not all from Adam's loins, all with flesh and blood, and with the same mouth that must needs have food and drink ? Where all this difference, then, between the ermine cloak and the leathern tunic, if what they cover is the same ? "

" Aye, Jenkin," said another, " our foeman is under the stole and the vestment as much as under the helmet and plate of proof. We have as much to fear from the tonsure as from the hauberk. Strike at the noble and the priest shrieks, strike at the priest and the noble lays his hand upon glaive. They are twin thieves who live upon our labour."

" It would take a clever man to live upon thy labour, Hugh," remarked one of the foresters, " seeing that the half of thy time is spent in swilling mead at the ' Pied Merlin.' "

" Better that than stealing the deer that thou art placed to guard, like some folk I know."

" If you dare open that swine's mouth against me," shouted the woodman, " I'll crop your ears for you before the hangman has the doing of it, thou long-jawed lackbrain."

" Nay, gentles, gentles ! " cried Dame Eliza, in a singsong, heedless voice, which showed that such bickerings were nightly things among her guests. " No brawling or brabbling, gentles ! Take heed to the good name of the house."

" Besides, if it comes to the cropping of ears, there are other folk who may say their say," quoth the third labourer. " We are all freemen, and I trow that a yeoman's cudgel is as good as a forester's knife. By St.

Anslem ! it would be an evil day if we had to bend to our masters' servants as well to our masters."

" No man is my master save the king," the woodman answered. " Who is there, save a false traitor, who would refuse to serve the English king ? "

" I know not about the English king," said the man Jenkin. " What sort of English king is it who cannot lay his tongue to a word of English ? You mind last year when he came down to Malwood, with his inner marshal and his outer marshal, his justiciar, his seneschal, and his four-and-twenty guardsmen. One noontide I was by Franklin Swinton's gate, when up he rides with a yeoman-pricker at his heels. ' Ouvre,' he cried, ' ouvre,' or some such word, making sign for me to open the gate ; and then ' Merci,' as though he were adrad of me. And you talk of an English king ! "

" I do not marvel at it," cried the Cambrig scholar, speaking in the high drawling voice which was common among his class. " It is not a tongue for men of sweet birth and delicate upbringing. It is a foul, snorting, snarling manner of speech. For myself, I swear by the learned Polycarp that I have most ease with Hebrew, and after that perchance with Arabian."

" I will not hear a word against old King Ned," cried Hordle John in a voice like a bull. " What if he is fond of a bright eye and a saucy face ? I know one of his subjects who could match him at that. If he cannot speak like an Englishman, I trow that he can fight like an Englishman ; and he was hammering at the gates of Paris while alehouse topers were grutching and grumbling at home."

This loud speech, coming from a man of so formidable an appearance, somewhat daunted the disloyal party, and they fell into a sudden silence, which enabled Alleyne to hear something of the talk which was going on in the farther corner between the physician, the tooth-drawer, and the gleeman.

" A raw rat," the man of drugs was saying, " that is

what it is ever my use to order for the plague—a raw rat with its paunch cut open."

" Might it not be broiled, most learned sir ? " asked the tooth-drawer. " A raw rat sounds a most sorry and cheerless dish."

" Not to be eaten," cried the physician, in high disdain. " Why should any man eat such a thing ? "

" Why, indeed ? " asked the gleeman, taking a long drain at his tankard.

" It is to be placed on the sore or swelling. For the rat, mark you, being a foul-living creature, hath a natural drawing or affinity for all foul things, so that the noxious humours pass from the man into the unclean beast."

" Would that cure the black death, master ? " asked Jenkin.

" Aye, truly would it, my fair son."

" Then I am right glad that there were none who knew of it. The black death is the best friend that ever the common folk had in England."

" How that then ? " asked Hordle John.

" Why, friend, it is easy to see that you have not worked with your hands, or you would not need to ask. When half the folk in the country were dead it was then that the other half could pick and choose who they would work for, and for what wage. That is why I say that the murrain was the best friend that the borel folk ever had."

" True, Jenkin," said another workman ; " but it is not all good that is brought by it either. We well know that through it corn land has been turned into pasture, so that flocks of sheep with perchance a single shepherd wander now where once a hundred men had work and wage."

" There is no great harm in that," remarked the tooth-drawer, " for the sheep give many folk their living. There is not only the herd, but the shearer and brander, and then the dresser, the curer, the dyer, the fuller, the webster, the merchant, and a score of others."

" If it come to that," said one of the foresters, " the
48

tough meat of them will wear folks' teeth out, and there is a trade for the man who can draw them."

A general laugh followed this sally at the dentist's expense, in the midst of which the gleeman placed his battered harp upon his knee, and began to pick out a melody upon the frayed strings.

" Elbow room for Floyting Will ! " cried the woodmen. " Twang us a merry lilt."

" Aye, aye, the ' Lasses of Lancaster,' " one suggested.

" Or ' St. Simeon and the Devil.' "

" Or the ' Jest of Hendy Tobias.' "

To all these suggestions the jongleur made no response, but sat with his eye fixed abstractedly upon the ceiling, as one who calls words to his mind. Then, with a sudden sweep across the strings, he broke out into a song so gross and so foul that ere he had finished a verse the pure-minded lad sprang to his feet with the blood tingling in his face.

" How can you sing such things ? " he cried. " You, too, an old man who should be an example to others."

The wayfarers all gazed in the utmost astonishment at the interruption.

" By the holy Dicon of Hampole ! our silent clerk has found his tongue," said one of the woodmen. " What is amiss with the song then ? How has it offended your baby-ship ? "

" A milder and better mannered song hath never been heard within these walls," cried another. " What sort of talk is this for a public inn ? "

" Shall it be a litany, my good clerk ? " shouted the third ; " or would a hymn be good enough to serve ? "

The jongleur had put down his harp in high dudgeon. " Am I to be preached to by a child ? " he cried, staring across at Alleyne with an inflamed and angry countenance. " Is a hairless infant to raise his tongue against me, when I have sung in every fair from Tweed to Trent, and have twice been named aloud by the High Court of the Minstrels at Beverley ? I shall sing no more to-night."

" Nay, but you will so," said one of the labourers.
" Hi ! Dame Eliza, bring a stoup of your best to Will to
clear his throat. Go forward with thy song, and if our
girl-faced clerk does not love it he can take to the road and
go whence he came."

" Nay, but not too fast," broke in Hordle John.
" There are two words in this matter. It may be that my
little comrade has been over quick in reproof, he having
gone early into the cloisters and seen little of the rough
ways and words of the world. Yet there is truth in what
he says, for, as you know well, the song was not of the
cleanest. I shall stand by him, therefore, and he shall
neither be put out on the road, nor shall his ears be
offended indoors."

" Indeed, your high and mighty grace," sneered one
of the yeomen, " have you in sooth so ordained ? "

" By the Virgin ! " said a second, " I think that you may
both chance to find yourselves upon the road before long."

" And so belaboured as to be scarce able to crawl along
it," cried a third.

" Nay, I shall go ! I shall go ! " said Alleyne hurriedly,
as Hordle John began to slowly roll up his sleeve, and bare
an arm like a leg of mutton. " I would not have you
brawl about me."

" Hush, lad ! " he whispered, " I count them not a fly.
They may find they have more tow on their distaff than
they know how to spin. Stand thou clear and give me
space."

Both the foresters and the labourers had risen from
their bench, and Dame Eliza and the travelling doctor had
flung themselves between the two parties with soft words
and soothing gestures, when the door of the ' Pied Merlin '
was flung violently open, and the attention of the company
was drawn from their own quarrel to the new-comer who
had burst so unceremoniously upon them.

6. *How Samkin Aylward wagered His Feather-bed*

HE was a middle-sized man, of most massive and robust build, with an arching chest and extra-ordinary breadth of shoulder. His shaven face was as brown as a hazel-nut, tanned and dried by the weather, with harsh well-marked features, which were not improved by a long white scar which stretched from the corner of his left nostril to the angle of the jaw. His eyes were bright and searching, with something of menace and of authority in their quick glitter, and his mouth was firm set and hard, as befitted one who was wont to set his face against danger. A straight sword by his side and a painted long-bow jutting over his shoulder proclaimed his profession, while his scarred brigandine of chain-mail and his dinted steel cap showed that he was no holiday soldier, but one who was even now fresh from the wars. A white surcoat with the lion of St. George in red upon the centre covered his broad breast, while a sprig of new-plucked broom at the side of his headgear gave a touch of gaiety and grace to his grim war-worn equipment.

" Ha ! " he cried, blinking like an owl in the sudden glare. " Good even to you, camarades ! Hola ! a woman, by my soul ! " and in an instant he had clipped Dame Eliza round the waist and was kissing her violently. His eye happening to wander upon the maid, however, he instantly abandoned the mistress and danced off after the other, who scurried in confusion up one of the ladders, and dropped the heavy trap-door upon her pursuer. He then turned back and saluted the landlady once more with the utmost relish and satisfaction.

" La petite is frightened," said he. " Ah, c'est l'amour, l'amour ! Curse this trick of French, which will stick to my throat. I must wash it out with some good English ale. By my hilt ! camarades, there is no drop of French blood in my body, and I am a true English bowman,

Samkin Aylward by name, once of Crooksbury ; and I
tell you, mes amis, that it warms my very heartroots to
set my feet on the dear old land once more.   When I came
off the galley at Hythe, this very day, I down on my bones,
and I kissed the good brown earth, as I kiss thee now, ma
belle, for it was eight long years since I had seen it.   The
very smell of it seemed life to me.   But where are my six
rascals ?   Hola, there !   En avant ! "

At the order, six men, dressed as common drudges,
marched solemnly into the room, each bearing a huge
bundle upon his head.   They formed in military line,
while the soldier stood in front of them with stern eyes,
checking off their several packages.

" Number one—a French feather-bed with the two
counterpanes of white sendal," said he.

" Here, worthy sir," answered the first of the bearers,
laying a great package down in the corner.

" Number two—seven ells of red Turkey cloth and nine
ells of cloth of gold.   Put it down by the other.   Good
dame, I prythee give each of these men a bottrine of wine
or a jack of ale.   Three—a full piece of white Genoan
velvet with twelve ells of purple silk.   Thou rascal,
there is dirt on the hem !   Thou hast brushed it against
some wall, coquin ! "

" Not I, most worthy sir," cried the carrier, shrinking
away from the fierce eyes of the bowman.

" I say yes, dog !   By the three kings !   I have seen a
man gasp out his last breath for less.   Had you gone
through the pain and unease that I have done to earn these
things you would be at more care.   I swear by my ten
finger-bones that there is not one of them that hath not cost
its weight in French blood !   Four—an incense boat, an
ewer of silver, a gold buckle and a cope worked in pearls.   I
found them, camarades, at the Church of St. Denis in the
harrying of Narbonne, and I took them away with me lest
they fall into the hands of the wicked.   Five—a cloak
of fur turned up with minever, a gold goblet with stand
and cover, and a box of rose-coloured sugar.   See that

you lay them together. Six—a box of monies, three pounds of Limousine gold-work, a pair of boots, silver tagged, and, lastly, a store of naping linen. So, the tally is complete! Here is a groat apiece and you may go."

"Go whither, worthy sir?" asked one of the carriers.

"Whither? To the devil if ye will. What is it to me? Now, ma belle, to supper. A pair of cold capons, a mortress of brawn, or what you will, with a flask or two of the right Gascony. I have crowns in my pouch, my sweet, and I mean to spend them. Bring in wine while the food is dressing. Buvons, my brave lads! you shall each empty a stoup with me."

Here was an offer which the company in an English inn at that or any other date are slow to refuse. The flagons were regathered, and came back with the white foam dripping over their edges. Two of the woodmen and three of the labourers drank their portions off hurriedly and trooped off together, for their homes were distant and the hour late. The others, however, drew closer, leaving the place of honour to the right of the gleeman to the free-handed new-comer. He had thrown off his steel cap and his brigandine, and had placed them with his sword, his quiver and his painted long-bow, on the top of his varied heap of plunder in the corner. Now, with his thick and somewhat bowed legs stretched in front of the blaze, his green jerkin thrown open, and a great quart pot held in his corded fist, he looked the picture of comfort and of good fellowship. His hard-set face had softened, and the thick crop of crisp brown curls which had been hidden by his helmet grew low upon his massive neck. He might have been forty years of age, though hard toil and harder pleasure had left their grim marks upon his features. Alleyne had ceased painting his pied merlin, and sat, brush in hand, staring with open eyes at a type of man so strange and so unlike any whom he had met. Men had been good or had been bad in his catalogue, but here was a man who was fierce one instant and gentle the next, with a curse on his lips and a smile in his eye. What was to be made of such a man as that ?

It chanced that the soldier looked up and saw the questioning glance which the young clerk threw upon him. He raised his flagon and drank to him, with a merry flash of his white teeth.

" À toi, mon garçon ! " he cried. " Hast surely never seen a man-at-arms, that thou shouldst stare so ? "

" I never have," said Alleyne frankly, " though I have oft heard talk of their deeds."

" By my hilt ! " cried the other, " if you were to cross the narrow sea you would find them as thick as bees at a tee-hole. Couldst not shoot a bolt down any street of Bordeaux, I warrant, but you would pink archer, squire or knight. There are more breastplates than gaberdines to be seen, I promise you."

" And where got you all those pretty things ? " asked Hordle John, pointing at the heap in the corner.

" Where there is as much more waiting for any brave lad to pick it up. Where a good man can always earn a good wage, and where he need look upon no man as his paymaster, but just reach his hand out and help himself. Aye, it is a goodly and a proper life. And here I drink to mine old comrades, and the saints be with them ! A rouse all together, mes enfants, under pain of my displeasure ! To Sir Claude Latour and the White Company ! "

" Sir Claude Latour and the White Company ! " shouted the travellers, draining off their goblets.

" Well quaffed, mes braves ! It is for me to fill your cups again, since you have drained them to my dear lads of the white jerkin. Hola ! mon ange, bring wine and ale. How runs the old stave ?

> We'll drink all together
> To the grey goose feather
> And the land where the grey goose flew.

He roared out the catch in a harsh unmusical voice, and

ended with a shout of laughter. " I trust that I am a better bowman than a minstrel," said he.

" Methinks I have some remembrance of the lilt," remarked the gleeman, running his finger over the strings. " Hoping that it will give thee no offence, most holy sir " —with a vicious snap at Alleyne—" and with the kind permit of the company, I will even venture upon it."

Many a time in the after days Alleyne Edricson seemed to see that scene, for all that so many which were stranger and more stirring were soon to crowd upon him. The fat, red-faced gleeman, the listening group, the archer with upraised finger beating in time to the music, and the huge sprawling figure of Hordle John, all thrown into red light and black shadow by the flickering fire in the centre—memory was to come often lovingly back to it.

At the time he was lost in admiration at the deft way in which the jongleur disguised the loss of his two missing strings, and the lusty, hearty fashion in which he trolled out his little ballad of the outland bowmen, which ran in some such fashion as this :

> What of the bow ?
> The bow was made in England :
> Of true wood, of yew-wood,
> The wood of English bows ;
> So men who are free
> Love the old yew-tree
> And the land where the yew-tree grows.

> What of the cord ?
> The cord was made in England :
> A rough cord, a tough cord,
> A cord that bowmen love ;
> So we'll drain our jacks
> To the English flax
> And the land where the hemp was wove.

> What of the shaft ?
> The shaft was cut in England :
> A long shaft, a strong shaft,
> Barbed and trim and true ;
> So we'll drink all together
> To the grey goose feather
> And the land where the grey goose flew.

What of the men ?
　The men were bred in England :
　The bowmen—the yeomen—
　The lads of dale and fell.
　　Here's to you—and to you !
　　To the hearts that are true
And the land where the true hearts dwell.

" Well sung, by my hilt ! " shouted the archer in high delight. " Many a night have I heard that song, both in the old war-time and after, in the days of the White Company, when Black Simon of Norwich would lead the stave and four hundred of the best bowmen that ever drew string would come roaring in upon the chorus. I have seen old John Hawkwood, the same who has led half the Company into Italy, stand laughing in his beard as he heard it, until his plates rattled again. But to get the full smack of it ye must yourselves be English bowmen, and be far off upon an outland soil."

Whilst the song had been singing Dame Eliza and the maid had placed a board across two trestles, and had laid upon it the knife, the spoon, the salt, the tranchoir of bread, and finally the smoking dish which held the savoury supper. The archer settled himself to it like one who had known what it was to find good food scarce ; but his tongue still went as merrily as his teeth.

" It passes me," he cried, " how all you lusty fellows can bide scratching your backs at home when there are such doings over the seas. Look at me—what have I to do ? It is but the eye to the cord, the cord to the shaft, and the shaft to the mark. There is the whole song of it. It is but what you do yourselves for pleasure upon a Sunday evening at the parish village butts."

" And the wage ? " asked a labourer.

" You see what the wage brings," he answered. " I eat of the best, and I drink deep. I treat my friend, and I ask no friend to treat me. I clap a silk gown on my girl's back. Never a knight's lady shall be better betrimmed and betrinketed. How of all that, mon garçon ? And how of the heap of trifles that you can see for yourselves in yonder corner ? They are from the South French, every one, upon whom I have been making war. By my hilt ! camarades, I think that I may let my plunder speak for itself."

" It seems indeed to be a goodly service," said the tooth-drawer.

" Tête bleue ! yes, indeed. Then there is the chance of a ransom. Why, look you, in the affair at Brignais, some four years back, when the companies slew James of Bourbon, and put his army to the sword, there was scarce a man of ours who had not count, baron, or knight. Peter Karsdale, who was but a common country lout newly brought over, with the English fleas still hopping under his doublet, laid his great hands upon the Sieur Amaury de Chatonville, who owns half Picardy, and had five thousand crowns out of him, with horse and harness. 'Tis true that a French wench took it all off Peter as quick as the Frenchman paid it ; but what then ? By the twang of string ! it would be a bad thing if money was not made to be spent ; and how better than on woman—eh, ma belle ? "

" It would indeed be a bad thing if we had not our brave archers to bring wealth and kindly customs into the country," quoth Dame Eliza, on whom the soldier's free and open ways had made a deep impression.

" À toi, ma chérie ! " said he, with his hand over his heart. " Hola ! there is la petite peeping from behind the door. À toi, aussi, ma petite ! Mon Dieu ! but the lass has a good colour ! "

" There is one thing, fair sir," said the Cambridge student in his piping voice, " which I would fain that you would make more clear. As I understand it, there was a peace made at the town of Brétigny some six years back between our most gracious monarch and the King of the French. This being so, it seems most passing strange that you should talk so loudly of war and of companies when there is no quarrel between the French and us."

" Meaning that I lie," said the archer, laying down his knife.

" May heaven forefend ! " cried the student hastily.
" *Magna est veritas sed rara*, which means in the Latin
tongue that archers are all honourable men. I come to
you seeking knowledge, for it is my trade to learn."

" I fear that you are yet a 'prentice to that trade," quoth
the soldier ; " for there is no child over the water but
could answer what you ask. Know, then, that though
there may be peace between our own provinces and the
French, yet within the marches of France there is always
war, for the country is much divided against itself, and
is furthermore harried by bands of flayers, skinners,
Brabaçons, tardvenus, and the rest of them. When
every man's grip is on his neighbour's throat, and every
five-sous-piece of a baron is marching with tuck of drum
to fight whom he will, it would be a strange thing if five
hundred brave English boys could not pick up a living.
Now that Sir John Hawkwood hath gone with the East
Anglian lads and the Nottingham woodmen into the
service of the Marquis of Montferrat to fight against the
Lord of Milan, there are but ten-score of us left ; yet I
trust that I may be able to bring some back with me to fill
the ranks of the White Company. By the tooth of Peter !
it would be a bad thing if I could not muster many a
Hamptonshire man who would be ready to strike in under
the red flag of St. George, and the more so if my old
master Sir Nigel Loring, of Christchurch, should don
hauberk once more and take the lead of us."

" Ah ! you would indeed be in luck then," quoth a
woodman ; " for it is said that, setting aside the prince,
and mayhap good old Sir John Chandos, there was not
in the whole army a man of such tried courage."

" It is sooth, every word of it," the archer answered.
" I have seen him with these two eyes on stricken fields
and never did man carry himself better. Mon Dieu ! yes,
ye would not credit to look at him, or to hearken to his
soft voice, but for clear twenty years, there was not
skirmish, onfall, sally, bushment, escalado, or battle, but
Sir Nigel was in the heart of it. I go now to Christchurch

with a letter to him from Sir Claude Latour, to ask him if he will take the place of Sir John Hawkwood ; and there is the more chance that he will if I bring one or two likely men at my heels. What say you, woodman : wilt leave the bucks to loose a shaft at a nobler mark ? "

The forester shook his head. " I have wife and child at Emery Down," quoth he ; " I would not leave them for such a venture."

"You then, young sir ? " asked the archer.

" Nay, I am a man of peace," said Alleyne Edricson. " Besides, I have other work to do."

" Peste ! " growled the soldier, striking his flagon on the board until the dishes danced again. " What, in the name of the devil, hath come over the folk ? Why sit ye all moping by the fireside, like crows round a dead horse, when there is man's work to be done within a few short leagues of ye ? Out upon you all, as a set of laggards and hang-backs ! By my hilt ! I believe that the men of England are all in France already, and that what is left behind are in sooth the women dressed up in their paltocks and hosen."

" Archer," quoth Hordle John, " you have lied more than once and more than twice ; for which, and also because I see much in you to mislike, I am sorely tempted to lay you upon your back."

" By my hilt ! then, I have found a man at last ! " shouted the bowman. " And, 'fore God, you are a better man than I take you for if you can lay me on my back, mon garçon. I have won the ram more times than there are toes to my feet, and for seven long years I have found no man in the Company who could make my jerkin dusty."

" We have had enough bobance and boasting," said Hordle John, rising and throwing off his doublet. " I will show you that there are better men left in England than ever went thieving to France."

" Pasques Dieu ! " cried the archer, loosening his jerkin, and eyeing his foeman over with the keen glance of one who is a judge of manhood. " I have only once before seen such a body of a man. By your leave, my red-headed friend, I should be right sorry to exchange buffets with you ; and I will allow that there is no man in the Company who would pull against you on a rope ; so let that be a salve to your pride. On the other hand, I should judge that you have led a life of ease for some months back, and that my muscle is harder than your own. I am ready to wager upon myself against you, if you are not afeard."

" Afeard, thou lurden ! " growled big John. " I never saw the face yet of the man that I was afeard of. Come out, and we shall see who is the better man."

" But the wager ? "

" I have nought to wager. Come out for the love and the lust of the thing."

" Nought to wager ! " cried the soldier. " Why, you have that which I covet above all things. It is that big body of thine that I am after. See, now, mon garçon. I have a French feather-bed there, which I have been at pains to keep these years back. I had it at the sacking of Issodun, and the king himself hath not such a bed. If you throw me, it is thine ; but, if I throw you, then you are under a vow to take bow and bill and hie with me to France, there to serve in the White Company as long as we be enrolled."

" A fair wager ! " cried all the travellers, moving back their benches and trestles, so as to give fair field for the wrestlers.

" Then you may bid farewell to your bed, soldier," said Hordle John.

" Nay ; I shall keep the bed, and I shall have you to France in spite of your teeth, and you shall live to thank me for it. How shall it be, then, mon enfant ? Collar and elbow, or close-lock, or catch how you can ? "

" To the devil with your tricks," said John, opening and shutting his great red hands. " Stand forth, and let me clip thee."

" Shalt clip me as best you can, then," quoth the archer, moving out into the open space, and keeping a most wary eye upon his opponent. He had thrown off his green jerkin, and his chest was covered only by a pink silk jupon, or undershirt, cut low in the neck and sleeveless. Hordle John was stripped from his waist upwards, and his huge body, with his great muscles swelling out like the gnarled roots of an oak, towered high above the soldier. The other, however, though near a foot shorter, was a man of great strength ; and there was a gloss upon his white skin which was wanting in the heavier limbs of the renegade monk. He was quick on his feet, too, and skilled at the game ; so that it was clear, from the poise of head and shine of eye, that he counted the chances to be in his favour. It would have been hard that night, through the whole length of England, to set up a finer pair in face of each other.

Big John stood waiting in the centre with a sullen, menacing eye, and his red hair in a bristle, while the archer paced lightly and swiftly to the right and the left with crooked knee and hands advanced. Then, with a sudden dash, so swift and fierce that the eye could scarce follow it, he flew in upon his man and locked his leg round him. It was a grip that, between men of equal strength, would mean a fall ; but Hordle John tore him off from him as he might a rat, and hurled him across the room, so that his head cracked up against the wooden wall.

" Ma foi ! " cried the bowman, passing his fingers through his curls, " you were not far from the feather-bed then, mon gar. A little more, and this good hostel would have a new window."

Nothing daunted, he approached his man once more ; but this time with more caution than before. With a quick feint he threw the other off his guard, and then, bounding upon him, threw his legs round his waist and his arms round his bull-neck, in the hope of bearing him to the ground with the sudden shock. With a bellow of rage, Hordle John squeezed him limp in his huge arms ;

and then, picking him up, cast him down upon the floor
with a force which might well have splintered a bone or
two, had not the archer with the most perfect coolness
clung to the other's forearms to break his fall. As it was,
he dropped upon his feet and kept his balance, though it
sent a jar through his frame which set every joint a-
creaking. He bounded back from his perilous foeman ;
but the other, heated by the bout, rushed madly after
him, and so gave the practised wrestler the very vantage
for which he had planned. As big John flung himself
upon him, the archer ducked under the great red hands
that clutched for him, and, catching his man round the
thighs, hurled him over his shoulder—helped as much by
his own mad rush as by the trained strength of the heave.
To Alleyne's eye, it was as if John had taken unto himself
wings and flown. As he hurtled through the air, with
giant limbs revolving, the lad's heart was in his mouth ;
for surely no man ever yet had such a fall and came scathless out of it. In truth, hardy as the man was, his neck
had been assuredly broken had he not pitched head first
on the very midriff of the drunken artist, who was slumbering so peacefully in the corner, all unaware of these
stirring doings. The luckless limner, thus suddenly
brought out from his dreams, sat up with a piercing yell,
while Hordle John bounded back into the circle almost
as rapidly as he had left it.

" One more fall, by all the saints ! " he cried, throwing
out his arms.

" Not I," quoth the archer, pulling on his clothes. " I
have come well out of the business. I would sooner
wrestle with the great bear of Navarre."

" It was a trick," cried John.

" Aye was it. By my ten finger-bones ! it is a trick
that will add a proper man to the ranks of the Company."

" Oh, for that," said the other, " I count it not a fly ;
for I had promised myself a good hour ago that I should go
with thee, since the life seems to be a goodly and proper
one. Yet I would fain have had the feather-bed."

" I doubt it not, mon ami," quoth the archer, going back to his tankard. " Here is to thee, lad, and may we be good comrades to each other ! But hola ! what is it that ails our friend of the wrathful face ? "

The unfortunate limner had been sitting up, rubbing himself ruefully and staring about with a vacant gaze, which showed that he knew neither where he was nor what had occurred to him. Suddenly, however, a flash of intelligence had come over his sodden features, and he rose and staggered for the door. " 'Ware the ale ! " he said in a hoarse whisper, shaking a warning finger at the company. " Oh, holy Virgin, 'ware the ale ! " and clapping his hands to his injury, he flitted off into the darkness, amid a shout of laughter, in which the vanquished joined as merrily as the victor. The remaining forester and the two labourers were also ready for the road, and the rest of the company turned to the blankets which Dame Eliza and the maid had laid out for them upon the floor. Alleyne, weary with the unwonted excitements of the day, was soon in a deep slumber, broken only by fleeting visions of twittering legs, cursing beggars, black robbers, and the many strange folk whom he had met at the " Pied Merlin."

7. *How the Three Comrades journeyed through the Woodlands*

AT early dawn the country inn was all alive, for it was rare indeed that an hour of daylight would be wasted at a time when lighting was so scarce and dear. Indeed, early as it was when Dame Eliza began to stir, it seemed that others could be earlier still, for the door was ajar and the learned student of Cambridge had taken himself off, with a mind which was too intent upon the high things of antiquity to stoop to consider the fourpence which he owed for bed and board. It was the shrill outcry of the landlady when she found her loss, and the clucking of the hens, which had streamed in through the open door, that first broke in upon the slumbers of the tired wayfarers.

Once afoot, it was not long before the company began to disperse. A sleek mule with red trappings was brought round from some neighbouring shed for the physician, and he ambled away with much dignity upon his road to Southampton. The tooth-drawer and the gleeman called for a cup of small ale apiece, and started off together for Ringwood Fair, the old jongleur looking very yellow in the eye and swollen in the face after his overnight potations. The archer, however, who had drunk more than any man in the room, was as merry as a grig, and having kissed the matron and chased the maid up the ladder once more, he went out to the brook, and came back with the water dripping from his face and hair.

" Hola ! my man of peace," he cried to Alleyne, " whither are you bent this morning ? "

" To Minstead," quoth he. " My brother Simon Edricson is socman there, and I go to bide with him for a while. I prythee, let me have my score, good dame."

" Score, indeed ! " cried she, standing with upraised hands in front of the panel on which Alleyne had worked the night before. " Say, rather, what it is that I owe to thee, good youth. Aye, this is indeed a pied merlin, and with a leveret under its claws, as I am a living woman. By the rood of Waltham ! but thy touch is deft and dainty."

" And see the red eye of it ! " cried the maid.

" Aye, and the open beak."

" And the ruffled wing," added Hordle John.

" By my hilt ! " cried the archer, " it is the very bird itself."

The young clerk flushed with pleasure at this chorus of praise, rude and indiscriminate indeed, and yet so much heartier and less grudging than any which he had ever heard from the critical brother Jerome or the short-spoken Abbot. There was, it would seem, great kindness as well as great wickedness in this world, of which he had heard so little that was good. His hostess would hear nothing of his paying either for bed or for board, while the archer and Hordle John placed a hand upon either shoulder and led him off to the board, where some smoking fish, a dish of spinach, and a jug of milk were laid out for their breakfast.

"I should not be surprised to learn, mon camarade," said the soldier, as he heaped a slice of the fish upon Alleyne's tranchoir of bread, " that you could read written things, since you are so ready with your brushes and pigments."

" It would be shame to the good brothers of Beaulieu if I could not," he answered, " seeing that I have been their clerk this ten years back."

The bowman looked at him with great respect. " Think of that ! " said he. " And you with not a hair to your face, and a skin like a girl. I can shoot three hundred and fifty paces with my little popper there, and four hundred and twenty with the great war-bow ; yet I can make nothing of this, nor read my own name if you were to set ' Sam Aylward ' up against me. In the whole Company there was only one man who could read, and he fell down a well at the taking of Ventadour, which proves that the thing is not suited to a soldier, though most needful to a clerk."

" I can make some show at it," said big John ; " though I was scarce long enough among the monks to catch the whole trick of it."

" Here, then, is something to try upon," quoth the archer, pulling a square of parchment from the inside of his tunic. It was tied securely with a broad band of purple silk, and firmly sealed at either end with a large red seal. John pored long and earnestly over the inscription upon the back, with his bows bent as one who bears up against great mental strain.

" Not having read much of late," he said, " I am loth to say too much about what this may be. Some might say one thing and some another, just as one bowman loves the yew, and a second will not shoot save with the ash. To me, by the length and look of it, I should judge this to be a verse from one of the Psalms."

The bowman shook his head. " It is scarce likely," he said, " that Sir Claude Latour should send me all the way across seas with nought more weighty than a psalm-verse. You have clean overshot the butts this time, mon camarade. Give it to the little one. I will wager my feather-bed that he makes more sense of it."

" Why, it is written in the French tongue," said Alleyne, " and in a right clerkly hand. This is how it runs : ' À le moult puissant et moult honorable chevalier, Sir Nigel Loring de Christchurch, de sont très fidèle amis Sir Claude Latour, capitaine de la Compagnie blanche, châtelain de Biscar, grand seigneur de Montchâteau, vavaseur de le renommé Gaston, Comte de Foix, tenant les droits de la haute justice, de la milieu, et de la basse.' Which signifies in our speech : ' To the very powerful and very honourable knight, Sir Nigel Loring of Christchurch, from his very faithful friend Sir Claude Latour, captain of the White Company, chatelain of Biscar, grand lord of Montchâteau, and vassal to the renowned Gaston, Count of Foix, who holds the rights of the high justice, the middle and the low.' "

" Look at that now ! " cried the bowman in triumph. " That is just what he would have said."

" I can see now that it is even so," said John, examining the parchment again. " Though I scarce understand this high, middle, and low."

" By my hilt ! you would understand it if you were Jacques Bonhomme. The low justice means that you fleece him, and the middle that you may torture him, and the high that you may slay him. That is about the truth of it. But this is the letter which I am to take ; and since the platter is clean it is time that we trussed up and were afoot. You come with me, mon gros Jean ; and as to you, little one, where did you say that you journeyed ? "

" To Minstead."

" Ah yes, I know this forest-country well, though I was born myself in the Hundred of Easebourne, in the Rape of Chichester, hard by the village of Midhurst. Yet I have not a word to say against the Hampton men, for there are no better comrades or truer archers in the whole Company than some who learned to loose the string in these very parts. We shall travel round with you to Minstead, lad, seeing that it is little out of our way."

" I am ready," said Alleyne, right pleased at the thought of such company upon the road.

" So am not I. I must store my plunder at this inn, since the hostess is an honest woman. Hola, my chérie, I wish to leave with you my gold-work, my velvet, my silk, my feather-bed, my incense-boat, my ewer, my naping linen, and all the rest of it. I take only the money in a linen bag, and the box of rose-coloured sugar, which is a gift from my Captain to the Lady Loring. Wilt guard my treasure for me ? "

" It shall be put in the safest loft, good archer. Come when you may, you shall find it ready for you."

" Now there is a true friend ! " cried the bowman, taking her hand. " There is a bonne amie ! English land and English women, say I, and French wine and French plunder. I shall be back anon, mon ange. I am a lonely man, my sweeting, and I must settle some day when the wars are over and done. Mayhap you and I—— Ah, méchante, méchante ! There is la petite peeping from behind the door. Now, John, the sun is over the trees ; you must be brisker than this when the bugleman blows ' Bows and Bills.' "

" I have been waiting this time back," said Hordle John gruffly.

" Then we must be off. Adieu, ma vie ! The two livres shall settle the score and buy some ribbons against the next kermesse. Do not forget Sam Aylward, for his heart shall ever be thine alone—and thine, ma petite ! So, marchons, and may St. Julian grant us as good quarters elsewhere ! "

The sun had risen over Ashurst and Denny woods, and was shining brightly, though the eastern wind had a sharp flavour to it, and the leaves were flickering thickly from the trees. In the High Street of Lyndhurst the way-farers had to pick their way, for the little town was crowded with the guardsmen, grooms, and yeomen-prickers who were attached to the king's hunt. The king himself was staying at Castle Malwood, but several of his suite had been compelled to seek such quarters as they might find in the wooden or wattle-and-daub cottages of the village. Here and there a small escutcheon, peeping from a glassless window, marked the night's lodging of knight or baron. These coats-of-arms could be read, where a scroll would be meaningless, and the bowman, like most men of his age, was well versed in the common symbols of heraldry.

" There is the Saracen's head of Sir Bernard Brocas," quoth he. " I saw him last at the ruffle at Poictiers some ten years back, when he bore himself like a man. He is the master of the king's horse, and can sing a right jovial stave, though in that he cannot come nigh to Sir John Chandos, who is the first at the board or in the saddle. Three martlets on a field azure. That must be one of the Luttrells. By the crescent upon it, it should be the second son of old Sir Hugh, who had a bolt through his ankle at the intaking of Romorantin, he having rushed into the fray ere his squire had time to clasp his solleret to his greave. There too is the hackle which is the old device of the De Brays. I have served under Sir Thomas de Bray, who was as jolly as a pie, and a lusty swordsman until he got too fat for his harness."

So the archer gossiped as the three wayfarers threaded their way among the stamping horses, the busy grooms, and the knots of pages and squires who disputed over the merits of their master's horses and deerhounds. As they passed the old church, which stood upon a mound at the left-hand side of the village street, the door was flung open, and a stream of worshippers wound down the sloping path, coming from the morning mass, all chattering like a cloud of jays. Alleyne bent knee and doffed hat at the sight of the open door ; but ere he had finished an ave, his comrades were out of sight round the curve of the path, and he had to run to overtake them.

"What !" he said, "not one word of prayer before God's own open house ? How can ye hope for His blessing upon the day ? "

"My friend," said Hordle John, "I have prayed so much during the last two months, not only during the day, but at matins, lauds, and the like, when I could scarce keep my head upon my shoulders for nodding, that I feel that I have somewhat overprayed myself."

"How can a man have too much religion ? " cried Alleyne earnestly. "It is the one thing that availeth. A man is but a beast as he lives from day to day, eating and drinking, breathing and sleeping. It is only when he raises himself, and concerns himself with the immortal spirit within him, that he becomes in very truth a man. Bethink ye how sad a thing it would be that the blood of the Redeemer should be spilled to no purpose."

"Bless the lad, if he doth not blush like any girl, and yet preach like the whole College of Cardinals," cried the archer.

"In truth I blush that anyone so weak and so unworthy as I should try to teach another that which he finds it so passing hard to follow himself."

"Prettily said, mon garçon. Touching that same slaying of the Redeemer, it was a bad business. A good padre in France read to us from a scroll the whole truth of the matter. The soldiers came upon Him in the garden. In truth, these Apostles of His may have been holy men, but they were of no great account as men-at-arms. There was one, indeed, Sir Peter, who smote out like a true man ; but, unless he is belied, he did but clip a varlet's ear, which was no very knightly deed. By these ten finger-bones ! had I been there, with Black Simon of Norwich, and but one score picked men of the Company, we had held them in play. Could we do no more, we had at least filled the false knight, Sir Judas, so full of English arrows that he would curse the day that ever he came on such an errand."

The young clerk smiled at his companion's earnestness. " Had He wished help," he said, " He could have summoned legions of archangels from heaven, so what need had He of your poor bow and arrow ? Besides, bethink you of His own words—that those who live by the sword shall perish by the sword."

"And how could man die better ? " asked the archer. " If I had my wish, it would be to fall so—not, mark you, in any mere skirmish of the Company, but in a stricken field, with the great lion banner waving over us and the red oriflamme in front, amid the shouting of my fellows and the twanging of the strings. But let it be sword, lance or bolt that strikes me down : for I should think it shame to die from an iron ball from fire-crake or bombard or any such unsoldierly weapon, which is only fitted to scare babes with its foolish noise and smoke."

" I have heard much even in the quiet cloisters of these new and dreadful engines," quoth Alleyne. " It is said, though I can scarce bring myself to believe it, that they will send a ball twice as far as a bowman can shoot his shaft, and with such force as to break through armour of proof."

" True enough, my lad. But while the armourer is thrusting in his devil's lust, and dropping his ball, and lighting his flambeau, I can very easily loose six shafts, or, eight maybe, so he hath no great vantage after all. Yet I will not deny that at the intaking of a town it is well to have good store of bombards. I am told that at Calais they made dints in the wall that a man might put his head into. But surely, comrades, someone who is grievously hurt hath passed along this road before us."

All along the woodland track there did indeed run a scattered straggling trail of blood-marks, sometimes in single drops, and in other places in broad ruddy gouts, smudged over the dead leaves or crimsoning the white flint stones.

" It must a stricken deer," said John.

" Nay, I am woodman enough to see that no deer hath passed this way this morning ; and yet the blood is fresh. But hark to the sound ! "

They stood listening all three with sidelong heads. Through the silence of the great forest there came a swishing, whistling sound, mingled with the most dolorous groans, and the voice of a man raised in a high quavering kind of song. The comrades hurried onwards eagerly, and topping the brow of a small rising they saw upon the other side the source from which these strange noises arose.

A tall man, much stooped in the shoulders, was walking slowly with bended head and clasped hands in the centre of the path. He was dressed from head to foot in a long white linen cloth, and a high white cap with a red cross printed upon it. His gown was turned back from his shoulders, and the flesh there was a sight to make a man wince, for it was all beaten to a pulp, and the blood was soaking into his gown and trickling down upon the ground. Behind him walked a smaller man, with his hair touched with grey, who was clad in the same white garb. He intoned a long whining rhyme in the French tongue, and at the end of every line he raised a thick cord, all jagged with pellets of lead, and smote his companion across the shoulders until the blood spurted again. Even as the three wayfarers stared, however, there was a sudden change, for the smaller man, having finished his song, loosened his own gown and handed the scourge to the other, who took up the stave once more and lashed his companion with all the strength of his bare and sinewy arm. So, alternately beating and beaten, they made their dolorous way through the beautiful woods and under the amber arches of the fading beech-trees, where the calm strength and majesty of Nature might serve to rebuke the foolish energies and misspent strivings of mankind.

Such a spectacle was new to Hordle John and to Alleyne Edricson ; but the archer treated it lightly, as a common matter enough.

" These are the Beating Friars, otherwise called the Flagellants," quoth he. " I marvel that ye should have come upon none of them before, for across the water they are as common as gallybaggers. I have heard that there are no English among them, but that they are from France, Italy and Bohemia. En avant, camarades ! that we may have speech with them."

As they came up to them, Alleyne could hear the doleful dirge which the beater was chanting, bringing down his heavy whip at the end of each line, while the groans of the sufferer formed a sort of dismal chorus. It was in old French, and ran somewhat in this way :

> Or avant, entre nous tous frères
> Battons nos charognes bien fort
> En remembrant la grant misère
> De Dieu et sa piteuse mort,
> Qui fut pris en la gent amère
> Et vendus et trais à tort
> Et bastu sa chair, vierge et dère
> Au nom de ce battons plus fort.

Then at the end of the verse the scourge changed hands and the chanting began anew.

" Truly, holy fathers," said the archer in French as they came abreast of them, " you have beaten enough for to-day. The road is all spotted like a shambles at Martinmas. Why should ye mishandle yourselves thus ? "

" C'est pour vos péchés—pour vos péchés," they droned, looking at the travellers with sad lack-lustre eyes and then bent to their bloody work once more without heed to the prayers and persuasions which were addressed to them. Finding all remonstrance useless, the three comrades hastened on their way, leaving these strange travellers to their dreary task.

" Mort Dieu ! " cried the bowman. " There is a bucketful or more of my blood over in France, but it was all spilled in hot fight, and I should think twice before I drew it drop by drop as these friars are doing. By my hilt! our young one here is as white as a Picardy cheese. What is amiss then, mon cher?"

"It is nothing," Alleyne answered. "My life has been too quiet. I am not used to such sights."

"Ma foi!" the other cried. "I have never yet seen a man who was so stout of speech and yet so weak of heart."

"Not so, friend," quoth big John; "it is not weakness of heart, for I know the lad well. His heart is as good as thine or mine, but he hath more in his pate than ever you will carry under that tin pot of thine, and as a consequence he can see farther into things, so that they weigh upon him more."

"Surely to any man it is a sad sight," said Alleyne, "to see these holy men, who have done no sin themselves, suffering so for the sin of others. Saints are they, if in this age any may merit so high a name."

"I count them not a fly," cried Hordle John; "for who is the better for all their whipping and yowling? They are like other friars, I trow, when all is done. Let them leave their backs alone, and beat the pride out of their hearts."

"By the three kings! there is sooth in what you say," remarked the archer. "Besides, methinks if I were le bon Dieu, it would bring me little joy to see a poor devil cutting the flesh off his bones; and I should think that he had but a small opinion of me, that he should hope to please me by such provost-marshal work. No, by my hilt! I should look with a more loving eye upon a jolly archer who never harmed a fallen foe and never feared a hale one."

"Doubtless you mean no sin," said Alleyne. "If your words are wild, it is not for me to judge them. Can you not see that there are other foes in this world besides Frenchmen, and as much glory to be gained in conquering them? Would it not be a proud day for knight or squire if he could overthrow seven adversaries in the lists?

Yet here are we in the lists of life, and there come the
seven black champions against us : Sir Pride, Sir Covet-
ousness, Sir Lust, Sir Anger, Sir Gluttony, Sir Envy,
and Sir Sloth. Let a man lay those seven low, and he
shall have the prize of the day, from the hands of the
fairest queen of beauty, even from the Virgin-Mother
herself. It is for this that these men mortify their flesh,
and to set us an example, who would pamper ourselves
overmuch. I say again that they are God's own saints
and I bow my head to them."

"And so you shall, mon petit," replied the archer.
"I have not heard a man speak better since old Dom
Bertrand died, who was at one time chaplain to the White
Company. He was a very valiant man, but at the battle
of Brignais he was spitted through the body by a Hainault
man-at-arms. For this we had an excommunication
read against the man, when next we saw our holy father
at Avignon ; but as we had not his name, and knew
nothing of him, save that he rode a dapple-grey roussin,
I have feared sometimes that the blight may have settled
upon the wrong man."

"Your Company has been, then, to bow knee before
our holy father, the Pope Urban, the prop and centre of
Christendom ? " asked Alleyne, much interested. " Perchance you have yourself set eyes upon his august face ? "

"Twice I saw him," said the archer. " He was a lean
little rat of a man, with a scab on his chin. The first
time we had five thousand crowns out of him, though he
made much ado about it. The second time we asked
ten thousand, but it was three days before we could come
to terms, and I am of opinion myself that we might have
done better by plundering the palace. His chamberlain
and cardinals came forth, as I remember, to ask whether
we would take seven thousand crowns with his blessing
and a plenary absolution, or the ten thousand with his
solemn ban by bell, book and candle. We were all of
one mind that it was best to have the ten thousand with
the curse ; but in some way they prevailed upon Sir

John, so that we were blessed and shriven against our will. Perchance it is as well, for the Company were in need of it about that time."

The pious Alleyne was deeply shocked by this reminiscence. Involuntarily he glanced up and around to see if there were any trace of those opportune levin-flashes and thunderbolts which, in the "Acta Sanctorum," were wont so often to cut short the loose talk of the scoffer. The autumn sun streamed down as brightly as ever, and the peaceful red path still wound in front of them through the rustling yellow-tinted forest. Nature seemed to be too busy with her own concerns to heed the dignity of an outraged pontiff. Yet he felt a sense of weight and reproach within his breast, as though he had sinned himself in giving ear to such words. The teachings of twenty years cried out against such licence. It was not until he had thrown himself down before one of the many wayside crosses, and had prayed from his heart both for the archer and for himself that the dark cloud rolled back again from his spirit.

8. *The Three Friends*

ALLEYNE'S companions had passed on whilst he was at his orisons ; but his young blood and the fresh morning air both invited him to a scamper. His staff in one hand and his scrip in the other, with springy step and floating locks, he raced along the forest path, as active and as graceful as a young deer. He had not far to go, however, for, on turning a corner, he came on a roadside cottage with a wooden fence-work around it, where stood big John and Aylward the bowman, staring at something within. As he came up with them he saw that two little lads, the one about nine years of age and the other somewhat older, were standing on the plot in front of the cottage, each holding out a round stick in their left hands, with their arms stiff and straight from the shoulder, as silent and still as two small statues. They were pretty blue-eyed yellow-haired lads, well made and sturdy, with bronzed skins, which spoke of a woodland life.

" Here are young chips from an old bow-stave ! " cried the soldier in great delight. " This is the proper way to raise children. By my hilt! I could not have trained them better had I the ordering of it myself."

" What is it, then ? " asked Hordle John. " They stand very stiff, and I trust that they have not been struck so."

" Nay, they are training their left arms, that they may have a steady grasp of the bow. So my own father trained me, and six days a week I held out his walking-staff till my arm was heavy as lead. Hola, mes enfants ! how long will you hold out ? "

" Until the sun is over the great lime-tree, good master, the elder answered.

"What would ye be, then? Woodmen? Verderers?"

" Nay, soldiers," they cried both together.

" By the beard of my father ! but ye are whelps of the true breed. Why so keen, then, to be soldiers ? "

" That we may fight the Scots," they answered. " Daddy will send us to fight the Scots."

" And why the Scots, my pretty lads ? We have seen French and Spanish galleys no farther away than Southampton, but I doubt that it will be some time before the Scots find their way to these parts."

" Our business is with the Scots," quoth the elder ; " for it was the Scots who cut off daddy's string fingers and his thumbs."

" Aye, lads, it was that," said a deep voice from behind Alleyne's shoulder. Looking round, the wayfarers saw a gaunt big-boned man, with sunken cheeks and a sallow face, who had come up behind them. He held up his two hands as he spoke, and showed that the thumbs and two first fingers had been torn away from each of them.

" Ma foi, camarade ! " cried Aylward. " Who hath served thee in so shameful a fashion ? "

" It is easy to see, friend, that you were born far from the marches of Scotland," quoth the stranger, with a bitter smile. " North of Humber there is no man who would not know the handiwork of Devil Douglas, the black Lord James."

" And how fell you into his hands ? " asked John.

" I am a man from the north country, from the town of Beverley and the wapentake of Holderness," he answered. " There was a day when, from Trent to Tweed, there was no better marksman than Robin Heathcot. Yet, as you see, he hath left me, as he hath left many another poor border archer, with no grip for bill or bow. Yet the king hath given me a living here in the southlands, and please God these two lads of mine will pay off a debt that hath been owing over long. What is the price of daddy's thumbs, boys ? "

" Twenty Scottish lives," they answered together.

" And for the fingers ? "

" Half a score."

" When they can bend my war-bow, and bring down a squirrel at a hundred paces, I send them to take service under Johnny Copeland, the Lord of the Marches and Governor of Carlisle. By my soul, I would give the rest of my fingers to see the Douglas within arrow-flight of them."

" May you live to see it," quoth the bowman. " And hark ye, mes enfants, take an old soldier's rede and lay your bodies to the bow, drawing from hip and thigh as much as from arm. Learn also, I pray you, to shoot with a dropping shaft ; for though a bowman may at times be called upon to shoot straight and fast, yet it is more often that he has to do with a town-guard behind a wall, or an arbalestier with his mantlet raised, when you cannot hope to do him scathe unless your shaft fall straight upon him from the clouds. I have not drawn string for two weeks, but I may be able to show ye how such shots should be made." He loosened his long bow, slung his quiver round to the front, and then glanced keenly round for a fitting mark. There was a yellow and withered stump some way off, seen under the drooping branches of a lofty oak. The archer measured the distance with his eye ; and then, drawing three shafts, he shot them off with such speed that the first had not reached the mark ere the last was on the string. Each arrow passed high over the oak ; and, of the three, two stuck fair into the stump ; while the third, caught in some wandering puff of wind, was driven a foot or two to one side.

" Good ! " cried the north countryman. " Hearken to him, lads ! He is a master bowman. Your dad says amen to every word he says."

" By my hilt ! " said Aylward, " if I am to preach on bowmanship, the whole long day would scarce give me time for my sermon. We have marksmen in the Company who will notch with a shaft every crevice and joint of a man-at-arm's harness, from the clasp of his bassinet to the hinge of his greave. But, with your favour, friend, I must gather my arrows again, for while a shaft costs a penny, a poor man can scarce leave them sticking in wayside stumps. We must, then, on our road again, and I hope from my heart that you may train these two young goshawks here until they are ready for a cast even at such a quarry as you speak of."

Leaving the thumbless archer and his brood, the way-farers struck through the scattered huts of Emery Down, and out on to the broad rolling heath covered deep in ferns and in heather, where droves of the half-wild black forest pigs were rooting about amongst the hillocks. The woods about this point fall away to the left and the right, while the road curves upwards and the wind sweeps keenly over the swelling uplands. The broad strips of bracken glowed red and yellow against the black peaty soil, and a queenly doe who grazed among them turned her white front and her great questioning eyes towards the wayfarers. Alleyne gazed in admiration at the supple beauty of the creature, but the archer's fingers played with his quiver, and his eyes glistened with the fell instinct which urges a man to slaughter.

" Tête Dieu ! " he growled, " were this France, or even Guienne, we should have a fresh haunch for our none-meat. Law or no law, I have a mind to loose a bolt at her."

" I would break your stave across my knee first," cried John, laying his great hand upon the bow. " What ! man, I am forest born, and I know what comes of it. In our own township of Hordle two have lost their eyes and one his skin for this very thing. On my troth, I felt no great love when I first saw you, but since then I have conceived over much regard for you to wish to see the verderer's flayer at work upon you."

" It is my trade to risk my skin," growled the archer ; but none the less he thrust his quiver over his hip again and turned his face for the west.

As they advanced, the path still trended upwards, running from heath into copses of holly and yew, and so back into heath again. It was joyful to hear the merry whistle of blackbirds as they darted from one clump of greenery to the other. Now and again a peaty amber-coloured stream rippled across their way, with ferny overgrown banks, where the blue kingfisher flitted busily from side to side, or the grey and pensive heron, swollen with trout and dignity, stood ankle-deep among the sedges. Chattering jays and loud wood-pigeons flapped thickly overhead, while ever and anon the measured tapping of Nature's carpenter, the great green woodpecker, sounded from each wayside grove. On either side, as the path mounted, the long sweep of country broadened and expanded, sloping down on the one side through yellow forest and brown moor to the distant smoke of Lymington and the blue misty channel which lay alongside of the sky-line, while to the north the woods rolled away, grove topping grove, to where in the farthest distance the white spire of Salisbury stood out hard and clear against the cloudless sky. To Alleyne, whose days had been spent in the low-lying coastland, the eager upland air and the wide free country-side gave a sense of life and of the joy of living which made his young blood tingle in his veins. Even the heavy John was not unmoved by the beauty of their road, while the bowman whistled lustily or sang snatches of French love songs in a voice which might have scared the most stout-hearted maiden that ever hearkened to serenade.

"I have a liking for that north countryman," he remarked presently. "He hath good power of hatred. Couldst see by his cheek and eye that he is as bitter as verjuice. I warm to a man who hath some gall in his liver."

"Ah me !" sighed Alleyne. "Would it not be better if he hath some love in his heart ?"

"I would not say nay to that. By my hilt ! I shall never be said to be a traitor to the little king. Let a man love the sex. Pasques Dieu ! they are made to be loved, les petites, from wimple down to shoe-string ! I am right glad, mon garçon, to see that the good monks have trained thee so wisely and so well."

"Nay, I meant not worldly love, but rather that his heart should soften towards those who have wronged him."

The archer shook his head. "A man should love those of his own breed," said he. "But it is not in nature that an English-born man should love a Scot or a Frenchman. Ma foi ! you have not seen a drove of Nithsdale raiders on their Galloway nags, or you would not speak of loving them. I would as soon take Beelzebub himself to my arms. I fear, mon gar, that they have taught thee but badly at Beaulieu, for surely a bishop knows more of what is right and what is ill than an abbot can do, and I myself with these very eyes saw the Bishop of Lincoln hew into a Scottish hobeler with a battle-axe, which was a passing strange way of showing him that he loved him."

Alleyne scarce saw his way to argue in the face of so decided an opinion on the part of a high dignity of the Church. "You have borne arms against the Scots, then ?" he asked.

" Yes, I have many times taken the field against them. Ma foi! it is rough soldiering, and a good school for one who would learn to be hardy and war-wise."

" I have heard that the Scots are good men of war," said Hordle John.

" For axemen and for spearmen I have not seen their match," the archer answered. " They can travel, too, with bag of meal and gridiron slung to their sword-belt, so that it is ill to follow them. There are scant crops, and few beeves in the borderland, where a man must reap his grain with sickle in one fist and brown bill in the other. On the other hand, they are the sorriest archers that I have ever seen, and cannot so much as aim with the arbalest, to say nought of the long-bow. Again, they are mostly poor folk, even the nobles among them, so that there are few who can buy as good a brigandine of chain mail as that which I am wearing, and it is ill for them to stand up against our own knights, who carry the price of five Scotch farms upon their chest and shoulders. Man for man, with equal weapons, they are as worthy and valiant men as could be found in the whole of Christendom."

" And the French?" asked Alleyne, to whom the archer's light gossip had all the relish that the words of the man of action have for the recluse.

" The French are also very worthy men. We have had great good fortune in France, and it hath led to much bobance and camp-fire talk, but I have ever noticed that those who know the most have the least to say about it. I have seen Frenchmen fight both in open field, in the intaking and defending of towns or castlewicks, in escalados, camisades, night forays, bushments, sallies, outfalls, and knightly spear-runnings. Their knights and squires, lad, are every whit as good as ours, and I could pick out a score of those who ride behind De Guesclin who would hold the lists with sharpened lances against the best men in the army of England. On the other hand, their common folk are so crushed down with gabelle, and poll-tax, and every manner of cursed tallage, that the spirit has passed right out of them. It is a fool's plan to teach a man to be a cur in peace, and think that he will be a lion in war. Fleece them like sheep, and sheep they will remain. If the nobles had not conquered the poor folk it is like enough that we should not have conquered the nobles."

" But they must be sorry folk to bow down to the rich in such a fashion," said big John. " I am but a poor commoner of England myself, and yet I know something of charters, liberties, franchises, usuages, privileges, customs and the like. If these be broken, then all men know that it is time to buy arrow-heads."

" Aye, but the men of the law are strong in France as well as the men of war. By my hilt ! I hold that a man has more to fear there from the ink-pot of the one than from the iron of the other. There is ever some cursed sheepskin in their strong boxes to prove that the rich man should be richer and the poor man poorer. It would scarce pass in England, but they are quiet folk over the water."

" And what other nations have you seen in your travels, good sir ? " asked Alleyne Edricson. His young mind hungered for plain facts of life, after the long course of speculation and of mysticism on which he had been trained.

" I have seen the Low-countryman in arms, and I have nought to say against him. Heavy and slow is he by nature, and is not to be brought into battle for the sake of a lady's eye-lash or the twang of a minstrel's string, like the hotter blood of the south. But, ma foi ! lay hand on his wool-bales, or trifle with his velvet of Bruges, and out buzzes every stout burgher, like bees from the tee-hole, ready to lay on as though it were his one business in life. By Our Lady ! they have shown the French at Courtrai and elsewhere that they are as deft in wielding steel as in welding it."

" And the men of Spain ? "

" They too are very hardy soldiers, the more so as for many hundred years they have had to fight hard against the cursed followers of the black Mahound, who have pressed upon them from the south, and still, as I understand, hold the fairer half of the country. I had a turn with them upon the sea when they came over to Winchelsea, and the good queen with her ladies sat upon the cliffs looking down at us, as if it had been joust or tourney. By my hilt ! it was a sight that was worth the seeing, for all that was best in England was out on the water that day. We went forth in little ships and came back in great galleys— for, of fifty tall ships of Spain over two score flew the Cross of St. George ere the sun had set. But now, youngster, I have answered you freely, and I trow it is time that you answered me. Let things be plat and plain between us. I am a man who shoots straight at his mark. You saw the things I had with me at yonder hostel ; name which you will, save only the box of rose-coloured sugar which I take to the Lady Loring, and you shall have it if you will but come with me to France."

" Nay, said Alleyne, " I would gladly come with ye to France or where else ye will, just to list to your talk, and because ye are the only two friends that I have in the whole wide world outside of the cloisters ; but indeed it may not be, for my duty is towards my brother, seeing that father and mother are dead, and he my elder. Besides, when ye talk of taking me to France, ye do not conceive how useless I should be to you, seeing that neither by training nor by nature am I fitted for the wars, and there seems to be nought but strife in those parts."

" That comes from my fool's talk," cried the archer ; " for being a man of no learning myself, my tongue turns to blades and targets even as my hand does. Know then that for every parchment in England there are twenty in France. For every statue, cut gem, shrine, carven screen, or what else might please the eye of a learned clerk, there are a good hundred to our one. At the spoiling of Carcassonne I have seen chambers stored

with writings, though not one man in our Company
could read them. Again, in Arles and Nîmes, and other
towns that I could name, there are the great arches and
fortalices still standing which were built of old by giant
men who came from the south. Can I not see by your
brightened eye how you would love to look upon these
things ? Come then with me, and by these ten finger-
bones ! there is not one of them which you shall not
see."

" I should indeed love to look upon them," Alleyne
answered ; " but I have come from Beaulieu for a purpose
and I must be true to my service, even as thou art true to
thine."

" Bethink you again, mon ami," quoth Aylward, " that
you might do much good yonder, since there are three
hundred men in the Company, and none who has ever
a word of grace for them, and yet the Virgin knows that
there was never a set of men who were in more need of it.
Sickerly the one duty may balance the other. Your
brother hath done without you this many a year, and, as
I gather, he hath never walked as far as Beaulieu to see
you during all that time, so he cannot be in any great need
of you."

" Besides," said John, " the Socman of Minstead is a
bye-word through the forest, from Bramshaw Hill to
Holmesley Walk. He is a drunken, brawling, perilous
churl, as you may find to your cost."

" The more reason that I should strive to mend him,"
quoth Alleyne. " There is no need to urge me, friends,
for my own wishes would draw me to France, and it
would be a joy to me if I could go with you. But indeed
and indeed it cannot be, so here I take my leave of you,
for yonder square tower amongst the trees upon the right
must surely be the church of Minstead, and I may reach
it by this path through the woods."

" Well, God be with thee, lad ! " cried the archer,
pressing Alleyne to his heart. " I am quick to love, and
quick to hate, and 'fore God I am loth to part."

" Would it not be well," said John, " that we should wait here, and see what manner of greeting you have from your brother ? You may prove to be as welcome as the king's purveyor to the village dame."

" Nay, nay," he answered ; " ye must not bide for me, for where I go I stay."

" Yet it may be as well that you should know whither we go," said the archer. " We shall now journey south through the woods until we come out upon the Christ-church road, and so onwards, hoping to-night to reach the castle of Sir William Montacute, Earl of Salisbury, of which Sir Nigel Loring is constable. There we shall bide and it is like enough that for a month or more you may find us there, ere we are ready for our viage back to France."

It was hard indeed for Alleyne to break away from these two new but hearty friends, and so strong was the combat between his conscience and his inclinations that he dared not look round, lest his resolution should slip away from him. It was not until he was deep among the tree trunks that he cast a glance backwards, when he found that he could still see them through the branches on the road above him. The archer was standing with folded arms, his bow jutting from over his shoulder, and the sun gleaming brightly upon his head-piece and the links of his chain-mail. Beside him stood his giant recruit, still clad in the home-spun and ill-fitting garments of the fuller of Lymington, with arms and legs shooting out of his scanty garb. Even as Alleyne watched them they turned upon their heels and plodded off together upon their way.

9. How Strange Things befell in Minstead Wood

THE path which the young clerk had now to follow lay through a magnificent forest of the very heaviest timber, where the giant boles of oak and of beech formed long aisles in every direction, shooting up their huge branches to build the majestic arches of Nature's own cathedral. Beneath lay a broad carpet of the softest and greenest moss, flecked over with fallen leaves, but yielding pleasantly to the foot of the traveller. The track which guided him was one so seldom used that in places it lost itself entirely among the grass, to reappear as a reddish rut between the distant tree trunks. It was very still here in the heart of the woodlands. The gentle rustle of the branches and the distant cooing of pigeons were the only sounds which broke in upon the silence, save that once Alleyne heard afar off a merry call upon a hunting bugle and the shrill yapping of the hounds.

It was not without some emotion that he looked upon the scene around him, for, in spite of his secluded life, he knew enough of the ancient greatness of his own family to be aware that the time had been when they had held undisputed and paramount sway over all that tract of country. His father could trace his pure Saxon lineage back to that Godfrey Malf who had held the manors of Bisterne and of Minstead at the time when the Norman first set mailed foot upon English soil. The afforestation of the district, however, and its conversion into a royal demesne had clipped off a large section of his estate, while other parts had been confiscated as a punishment for his supposed complicity in an abortive Saxon rising. The fate of the ancestor had been typical of that of his descendants. During three hundred years their domains had gradually contracted, sometimes through royal or feudal encroachment, and sometimes through such gifts to the Church as that with which Alleyne's father had opened the doors of Beaulieu Abbey to his younger son. The importance of the family had thus dwindled, but they still retained the old Saxon manor-house, with a couple of farms and a grove large enough to afford pannage to a hundred pigs—" sylva de centum porcis," as the old family parchments describe it. Above all, the owner of the soil could still hold his head high as the veritable Socman of Minstead—that is, as holding the land in free socage, with no feudal superior, and answerable to no man lower than the king. Knowing this, Alleyne felt some little glow of worldly pride as he looked for the first time upon the land with which so many generations of his ancestors had been associated. He pushed on the quicker, twirling his staff merrily, and looking out at every turn of the path for some sign of the old Saxon residence. He was suddenly arrested, however, by the appearance of a wild-looking fellow armed with a club, who sprang out from behind a tree and barred his passage. He was a rough, powerful peasant, with cap and tunic of untanned sheepskin, leather breeches, and galligaskins round legs and feet.

" Stand ! " he shouted, raising his heavy cudgel to enforce the order. " Who are you who walk so freely through the wood ? Whither would you go, and what is your errand ? "

" Why should I answer your questions, my friend ? " said Alleyne, standing on his guard.

" Because your tongue may save your pate. But where have I looked upon your face before ? "

" No longer ago than last night at the ' Pied Merlin,' " the clerk answered, recognising the escaped serf who had been so outspoken as to his wrongs.

" By the Virgin ! yes. You were the little clerk who sat so mum in the corner, and then cried fy on the gleeman. What hast in the scrip ? "

" Nought of any price."

" How can I tell that, clerk ? Let me see."

" Not I."

" Fool ! I could pull you limb from limb like a pullet. What would you have ? Hast forgot that we are alone, far from all men ? How can your clerkship help you ? Wouldst lose scrip and life too ? "

" I will part with neither without a fight."

" A fight, quotha ? A fight betwixt spurred cock and new-hatched chicken ! Thy fighting days may soon be over."

" Hadst asked me in the name of charity I would have given freely," cried Alleyne. " As it stands, not one farthing shall you have with my free will, and when I see my brother, the Socman of Minstead, he will raise hue and cry from vill to vill, from hundred to hundred, until you are taken as a common robber and a scourge to the country."

The outlaw sank his club. " The Socman's brother ! " he gasped. " Now, by the keys of Peter ! I had rather that hand withered and tongue was palsied ere I had struck or miscalled you. If you are the Socman's brother you are one of the right side, I warrant, for all your clerkly dress."

" His brother I am," replied Alleyne. " But even if I were not, is that reason why you should molest me on the king's ground ? "

" I give not the pip of an apple for king or for noble," cried the serf passionately. " Ill have I had from them, and ill I shall repay them. I am a good friend to my friends, and, by the Virgin ! an evil foeman to my foes."

" And therefore the worst of foemen to thyself," said Alleyne. " But I pray you since you seem to know him, to point out to me the shortest path to my brother's house."

The serf was about to reply, when the clear ringing call of a bugle burst from the wood close behind them, and Alleyne caught sight for an instant of the dun side and white breast of a lordly stag glancing swiftly betwixt the distant tree trunks. A minute later came the shaggy deerhounds, a dozen or fourteen of them, running on a hot scent, with nose to earth and tail in air. As they streamed past the silent forest around broke suddenly into loud life, with galloping of hoofs, crackling of brushwood, and the short sharp cries of the hunters. Close behind the pack rode a fourrier and a yeoman-pricker, whooping on the laggards and encouraging the leaders, in the shrill half-French jargon which was the language of venery and woodcraft. Alleyne was still gazing after them, listening to the loud " Hyke-a-Bayard ! Hyke-a-Pomers ! Hyke-a-Lebryt ! " with which they called upon their favourite hounds, when a group of horsemen crashed out through the underwood at the very spot where the serf and he were standing.

The one who led was a man between fifty and sixty years of age, war-worn and weather-beaten, with a broad thoughtful forehead and eyes which shone brightly from under his fierce and overhung brows. His beard, streaked thickly with grey, bristled forward from his chin, and spoke of a passionate nature, while the long finely-cut face and firm mouth marked the leader of men. His figure was erect and soldierly, and he rode his horse with the careless grace of a man whose life had been spent in the saddle. In common garb, his masterful face and flashing eye would have marked him as one who was born to rule ; but now, with his silken tunic powdered with golden fleurs-de-lis, his velvet mantle lined with the royal mine-ver, and the lions of England stamped in silver upon his harness, none could fail to recognise the noble Edward, most warlike and powerful of all the long line of fighting monarchs who had ruled the Anglo-Norman race. Alleyne doffed hat and bowed head at the sight of him, but the serf folded his hands and leaned them upon his cudgel, looking with little love at the knot of nobles and knights-in-waiting who rode behind the king.

" Ha ! " cried Edward, reining up for an instant his powerful black steed, " Le cerf est passé ? Non ? Ici, Brocas ; tu parles Anglais."

" The deer, clowns ? " said a hard-visaged, swarthy-faced man, who rode at the king's elbow. " If ye have headed it back, it is as much as your ears are worth."

" It passed by the blighted beech there," said Alleyne, pointing, " and the hounds were hard at his heels."

" It is well," cried Edward, still speaking in French ; for, though he could understand English, he had never learned to express himself in so barbarous and unpolished a tongue. " By my faith, sirs," he continued, half turning in his saddle to address his escort, " unless my woodcraft is sadly at fault, it is a stag of six tines and the finest that we have roused this journey. A golden St. Hubert to the man who is the first to sound the mort." He shook his bridle as he spoke, and thundered away, his knights lying low upon their horses and galloping as hard as whip and spur would drive them, in the hope of winning the king's prize. Away they drove down the long green glade—bay horses, black and grey, riders clad in every shade of velvet, fur, or silk, with glint of brazen horn and flash of knife and spear. One only lingered, the black-browed Baron Brocas, who, making a gambade which brought him within arms' sweep of the serf, slashed him across the face with his riding whip. " Doff, dog, doff," he hissed, " when a monarch deigns to lower his eyes to such as you ! "—then spurred through the underwood and was gone, with a gleam of steel shoes and flutter of dead leaves.

The villein took the cruel blow without wince or cry, as one to whom stripes are a birthright and an inheritance. His eyes flashed, however, and he shook his bony hand with a fierce wild gesture after the retreating figure.

" Black hound of Gascony," he muttered, " evil the day that you and those like you set foot in free England ! I know thy kennel of Rochecourt. The night will come when I may do to thee and thine what you and yours have wrought upon mine and me. May God smite me if I fail to smite thee, thou French robber, with thy wife and thy child, and all that is under thy castle roof ! "

" Forbear ! " cried Alleyne. " Mix not God's name with these unhallowed threats ! And yet it was a cow-ard's blow, and one to stir the blood and loose the tongue of the most peaceful. Let me find some soothing simples and lay them on the weal to draw the sting."

" Nay, there is but one thing that can draw the sting, and that the future may bring to me. But, clerk, if you would see your brother you must on, for there is a meeting to-day, and his merry men will await him ere the shadows turn from west to east. I pray you not to hold him back, for it would be an evil thing if all the stout lads were there and the leader a-missing. I would come with you, but sooth to say I am stationed here and may not move. The path over yonder, betwixt the oak and the thorn, should bring you out into his netherfield."

Alleyne lost no time in following the directions of the wild, masterless man, whom he left among the trees where he had found him. His heart was the heavier for the encounter, not only because all bitterness and wrath were abhorrent to his gentle nature, but also because it disturbed him to hear his brother spoken of as though he were a chief of outlaws or the leader of a party against the State. Indeed, of all the things which he had seen yet in the world to surprise him, there was none more strange than the hate which class appeared to bear to class. The talk of the labourer, woodman and villein in the inn had all pointed to the widespread mutiny, and now his brother's name was spoken as though he were the very centre of the universal discontent. In good truth, the commons throughout the length and breadth of the land were heart-weary of this fine game of chivalry which had been played so long at their expense. So long as knight and baron were a strength and a guard to the kingdom they might be endured ; but now, when all men knew that the great battles in France had been won by English yeomen and Welsh stabbers, warlike fame, the only fame to which his class had ever aspired, appeared to have deserted the plate-clad horseman. The sports of the lists had done much in days gone by to impress the minds of the people, but the plumed and unwieldy champion was no longer an object either of fear or of reverence to men whose fathers and brothers had shot into the press at Crécy, or Poictiers, and seen the proudest chivalry in the world unable to make head against the weapons of disciplined peasants. Power had changed hands. The protector had become the protected, and the whole fabric of the feudal system was tottering to a fall. Hence the fierce mutterings of the lower classes and the constant discontent breaking out into local tumult and outrage and culminating some years later in the great rising of Tyler. What Alleyne saw and wondered at in Hampshire would have appealed equally to the traveller in any other English county from the Channel to the marches of Scotland.

He was following the track, his misgivings increasing with every step which took him nearer to that home which he had never seen, when of a sudden the trees began to thin and the sward to spread out into a broad green lawn, where five cows lay in the sunshine and droves of black swine wandered unchecked. A brown forest stream swirled down the centre of this clearing, with a rude bridge flung across it, and on the other side was a second field sloping up to a long, low-lying wooden house, with thatched roof and open squares for windows. Alleyne gazed across at it with flushed cheeks and sparkling eyes—for this, he knew, must be the home of his fathers. A wreath of blue smoke floated up through a hole in the thatch, and was the only sign of life in the place, save a great black hound which lay sleeping chained to the doorpost. In the yellow shimmer of the autumn sunshine it lay as peacefully and as still as he had oft pictured it to himself in his dreams.

He was roused, however, from his pleasant reverie by the sound of voices, and two people emerged from the forest some little way to his right and moved across the field in the direction of the bridge. The one was a man with yellow flowing beard and very long hair of the same tint drooping over his shoulders ; his dress of good Norwich cloth and his assured bearing marked him as a man of position, while the sombre hue of his clothes and the absence of all ornament contrasted with the flash and glitter which had marked the king's retinue. By his side walked a woman, tall and slight and dark, with lithe graceful figure and clear-cut composed features. Her jet-black hair was gathered back under a light pink coif, her head poised proudly upon her neck, and her step long and springy, like that of some wild tireless woodland creature. She held her left hand in front of her, covered with a red velvet glove, and on the wrist a little brown falcon, very fluffy and bedraggled, which she smoothed and fondled as she walked. As she came out into the sunshine, Alleyne noticed that her light gown, slashed with pink, was all stained with earth and with moss upon one side from shoulder to hem. He stood in the shadow of an oak staring at her with parted lips, for this woman seemed to him to be the most beautiful and graceful creature that mind could conceive of. Such had he imagined the angels, and such he had tried to paint them in the Beaulieu missals ; but here there was something human, were it only in the battered hawk and discoloured dress, which sent a tingle and thrill through his nerves such as no dream of radiant and stainless spirit had ever been able to conjure up. Good, quiet, uncomplaining mother Nature, long slighted and miscalled, still bides her time and draws to her bosom the most errant of her children.

The two walked swiftly across the meadow to the narrow bridge, he in front and she a pace or two behind. There they paused, and stood for a few minutes face to face talking earnestly. Alleyne had read and had heard of love and of lovers. Such were these, doubtless—this golden-bearded man and the fair damsel with the cold proud face. Why else should they wander together in the woods or be so lost in talk by the rustic streams ? And yet as he watched, uncertain whether to advance from the cover or to choose some other path to the house, he soon came to doubt the truth of this first conjecture. The man stood, tall and square, blocking the entrance to the bridge, and throwing out his hands as he spoke in a wild eager fashion, while the deep tones of his stormy voice rose at times into accents of menace and of anger. She stood fearlessly in front of him, still stroking her bird ; but twice she threw a swift questioning glance over her shoulder, as one who is in search of aid. So moved was the young clerk by these mute appeals, that he came forth from the trees and crossed the meadow, uncertain what to do, and yet loth to hold back from one who might need his aid. So intent were they upon each other that neither took note of his approach ; until, when he was close upon them, the man threw his arm roughly round the damsel's waist and drew her towards him, she straining her lithe supple figure away and striking fiercely at him, while the hooded hawk screamed with ruffled wings and pecked blindly in its mistress's defence. Bird and maid, however, had but little chance against their assailant, who, laughing loudly, caught her wrist in one hand while he drew her towards him with the other.

" The best rose has ever the longest thorns," said he. " Quiet, little one, or you may do yourself a hurt. Must pay Saxon toll on Saxon land, my proud Maude, for all your airs and graces."

" You boor ! " she hissed. " You base underbred clod ! Is this your care and your hospitality ? I would rather wed a branded serf from my father's fields. Leave go, I say—— Ah ! good youth, Heaven has sent you. Make him loose me ! By the honour of your mother, I pray you to stand by me and to make this knave loose me."

" Stand by you I will, and that blithely," said Alleyne. " Surely, sir, you should take shame to hold the damsel againt her will."

The man turned a face upon him which was lion-like in its strength and in its wrath. With his tangle of golden hair, his fierce blue eyes, and his large, well-marked features, he was the most comely man whom Alleyne had ever seen ; and yet there was something so sinister and so fell in his expression that child or beast might well have shrunk from him. His brows were drawn, his cheek flushed, and there was a mad sparkle in his eyes which spoke of a wild untamable nature.

" Young fool ! " he cried, holding the woman still to

his side, though every line of her shrinking figure spoke her abhorrence. " Do you keep your spoon in your own broth. I rede you to go on your way, lest worse befall you. This little wench has come with me, and with me she shall bide."

" Liar ! " cried the woman ; and, stooping her head, she suddenly bit fiercely into the broad brown hand which held her. He whipped it back with an oath, while she tore herself free and slipped behind Alleyne, cowering up against him like the trembling leveret who sees the falcon poising for the swoop above him.

" Stand off my land ! " the man said fiercely, heedless of the blood which trickled freely from his fingers. " What have you to do here ? By your dress you should be one of those cursed clerks who overrun the land like vile rats, poking and prying into other men's concerns, too caitiff to fight and too lazy to work. By the rood ! if I had my will upon ye, I should nail you upon the abbey doors, as they hang vermin before their holes. Art neither man nor woman, young shaveling. Get thee back to thy fellows ere I lay hands upon you : for your foot is on my land, and I may slay you as a common draw-latch."

" Is this your land, then ? " gasped Alleyne.

" Would you dispute it, dog ? Would you wish by trick or quibble to juggle me out of these last acres ? Know, base-born knave, that you have dared this day to stand in the path of one whose race have been the advisers of kings and the leaders of hosts, ere ever this vile crew of Norman robbers came into the land, or such half-blood hounds as you were let loose to preach that the thief should have his booty and the honest man should sin if he strove to win back his own."

" You are the Socman of Minstead ! "

" That am I ; and the son of Edric the Socman, of the pure blood of Godfrey the thane, by the only daughter of the house of Aluric, whose forefathers held the white-horse banner at the fatal fight where our shield was broken and our sword shivered. I tell you, clerk, that my folk held this land from Bramshaw Wood to the Ringwood road ; and by the soul of my father ! it will be a strange thing if I am to be bearded upon the little that is left of it. Begone, I say, and meddle not with my affair."

" If you leave me now," whispered the woman, " then shame for ever upon your manhood."

" Surely, sir," said Alleyne, speaking in as persuasive and soothing a way as he could, " if your birth is gentle, there is more reason that your manners should be gentle too. I am well persuaded that you did but jest with this lady, and that you will now permit her to leave your land either alone or with me as a guide, if she should need one, through the wood. As to birth, it does not become me to boast, and there is sooth in what you say as to the unworthiness of clerks, but it is none the less true that I am as well born as you ! "

" Dog ! " cried the furious Socman, " there is no man in the south who can say as much."

" Yet can I," said Alleyne, smiling ; " for indeed I also am the son of Edric the Socman, of the pure blood of Godfrey the thane, by the only daughter of Aluric of Brockenhurst. Surely, dear brother," he continued, holding out his hand, " you have a warmer greeting than this for me. There are but two boughs left upon this old Saxon trunk."

His elder brother dashed his hand aside with an oath, while an expression of malignant hatred passed over his passion-drawn features. " You are the young cub of Beaulieu, then ? " said he. " I might have known it by the sleek face and the slavish manner, too monk-ridden and craven in spirit to answer back a rough word. Thy father, shaveling, with all his faults, had a man's heart ; and there were few who could look him in the eyes on the day of his anger. But you ! Look there, rat, on yonder field where the cows graze, and on that other beyond, and on the orchard hard by the church. Do you know that all these were squeezed out of your dying father by greedy priests, to pay for your upbringing in the cloisters ! I, the Socman, am shorn of my lands that you may snivel Latin and eat bread for which you never yet did hand's turn. You rob me first, and now you would come preaching and whining, in search mayhap of another field or two for your priestly friends. Knave ! my dogs shall be set upon you ; but, meanwhile, stand out of my path, and stop me at your peril ! " As he spoke he rushed forward, and throwing the lad to one side, caught the woman's wrist ; Alleyne however, as active as a young deer-hound, sprang to her aid and seized her by the other arm, raising his iron-shod staff as he did so.

" You may say what you will to me," he said between his clenched teeth—" it may be no better than I deserve ; but, brother or no, I swear by my hopes of salvation that I will break your arm if you do not leave hold of the maid."

There was a ring in his voice and a flash in his eyes which promised that the blow would follow quick at the heels of the word. For a moment the blood of the long line of hot-headed thanes was too strong for the soft whisperings of the doctrine of meekness and mercy. He was conscious of a fierce wild thrill through his nerves and a throb of mad gladness at his heart, as his real human self burst for an instant the bonds of custom and of teaching which had held it so long. The Socman sprang back, looking to left and to right for some stick or stone which might serve him for weapon ; but, finding none, he turned and ran at the top of his speed for the house, blowing the while upon a shrill whistle.

" Come ! " gasped the woman. " Fly, friend, ere he come back."

" Nay, let him come ! " cried Alleyne. " I shall not budge a foot for him or his dogs."

" Come, come ! " she cried, tugging at his arm. " I know the man : he will kill you. Come, for the Virgin's sake, or for my sake, for I cannot go and leave you here."

" Come, then," said he ; and they ran together to the

cover of the woods. As they gained the edge of the brushwood, Alleyne, looking back, saw his brother come running out of the house again, with the sun gleaming upon his hair and his beard. He held something which flashed in his right hand, and he stooped at the threshold to unloose the black hound.

" This way ! " the woman whispered, in a low eager voice. " Through the bushes to that forked ash. Do not heed me : I can run as fast as you, I trow. Now into the stream—right in, over ankles, to throw the dog off, though I think it is but a common cur, like its master." As she spoke, she sprang herself into the shallow stream and ran swiftly up the centre of it, with the brown water bubbling over her feet, and her hand outstretched to ward off the clinging branches of bramble or sapling. Alleyne followed close at her heels with his mind in a whirl at this black welcome and sudden shifting of all his plans and hopes. Yet, grave as were his thoughts, they would still turn to wonder as he looked at the twinkling feet of his guide and saw her lithe figure bend this way and that, dipping under boughs, springing over stones, with a lightness and ease which made it no small task for him to keep up with her. At last, when he was almost out of breath, she suddenly threw herself down upon a mossy bank, between two holly bushes, and looked ruefully at her own dripping feet and bedraggled skirt.

" Holy Mary ! " said she, " what shall I do ? Mother will keep me to my chamber for a month, and make me work at the tapestry of the nine bold knights. She promised as much last week, when I fell into Wilverley bog, and yet she knows that I cannot abide needlework."

Alleyne, still standing in the stream, glanced down at the graceful pink-and-white figure, the curve of raven-black hair, and the proud, sensitive face, which looked up frankly and confidingly at his own.

" We had best on," he said. " He may yet overtake us."

" Not so. We are well off his land now, nor can he

tell in this great wood which way we have taken. But you—you had him at your mercy. Why did you not kill him ? "

" Kill him ! My brother ! "

" And why not ? "—with a quick gleam of her white teeth. " He would have killed you. I know him, and I read it in his eyes. Had I had your staff I would have tried—aye, and done it, too." She shook her clenched white hand as she spoke, and her lips tightened ominously.

" I am already sad in heart for what I have done," said he, sitting down on the bank, and sinking his face into his hands, " God help me !—all that is worst in me seemed to come uppermost. Another instant, and I had smitten him ; the son of my own mother, the man whom I have longed to take to my heart. Alas ! that I should still be so weak ! "

" Weak ! " she exclaimed, raising her black eyebrows. " I do not think that even my father himself, who is a hard judge of manhood, would call you that. But it is, as you may think, sir, a very pleasant thing for me to hear that you are grieved at what you have done, and I can but rede that we should go back together, and you should make your peace with the Socman by handing back your prisoner. It is a sad thing that so small a thing as a woman should come between two who are of one blood."

Simple Alleyne opened his eyes at this little spurt of feminine bitterness. " Nay, lady," said he, " that were worst of all. What man would be so caitiff and thrall as to fail you at your need ? I have turned my brother against me, and now, alas ! I appear to have given you offence also with my clumsy tongue. But, indeed, lady, I am torn both ways, and can scarce grasp in my mind what it is that has befallen."

" Nor can I marvel at that," said she, with a little tinkling laugh. " You came in as the knight does in the jongleur's romances, between dragon and damsel, with small time for the asking of questions. Come," she went on, springing to her feet, and smoothing down her rumpled frock, " let us walk through the shaw together, and we may come upon Bertrand with the horses. If poor Troubadour had not cast a shoe, we should not have had this trouble. Nay, I must have your arm : for, though I speak lightly, now that all is happily over I am as frightened as my brave Roland. See how his chest heaves, and his dear feathers all awry—the little knight who would not have his lady mishandled." So she prattled on to her hawk, while Alleyne walked by her side, stealing a glance from time to time at this queenly and wayward woman. In silence they wandered together over the velvet turf and on through the broad Minstead woods, where the old lichen-draped beeches threw their circles of black shadow upon the sunlit sward.

" You have no wish, then, to hear my story ? " said she, at last.

" If it pleases you to tell it me," he answered.

" Oh ! " she cried, tossing her head, " if it is of so little interest to you, we had best let it bide."

" Nay," said he eagerly, " I would fain hear it."

" You have a right to know it, if you have lost a brother's favour through it. And yet—— Ah, well, you are, as I understand, a clerk, so I must think of you as one step further in orders, and make you my father-confessor. Know then that this man has been a suitor for my hand, less as I think for my own sweet sake than because he hath ambition, and had it on his mind that he might improve his fortunes by dipping into my father's strong-box— though the Virgin knows that he would have found little enough therein. My father, however, is a proud man, a gallant knight and tried soldier of the oldest blood, to whom this man's churlish birth and low descent—— Oh, lackaday ! I had forgot that he was of the same strain as yourself."

" Nay, trouble not for that," said Alleyne, " we are all from good mother Eve."

" Streams may spring from one source, and yet some be clear and some be foul," quoth she quickly. " But, to be brief over the matter, my father would have none of his wooing, or in sooth would I. On that he swore a vow against us, and as he is known to be a perilous man, with many outlaws and others at his back, my father forbade that I should hawk or hunt in any part of the wood to the north of Christchurch road. As it chanced, however, this morning my little Roland here was loosed at a strong-winged heron, and page Bertrand and I rode on, with no thoughts but for the sport, until we found ourselves in Minstead Woods. Small harm then, but that my horse Troubadour trod with a tender foot upon a sharp stick, rearing and throwing me to the ground. See to my gown, the third that I have befouled within the week. Woe worth me when Agatha the tirewoman sets eyes upon it."

" And what then, lady ? " asked Alleyne.

" Why, then away ran Troubadour, for belike I spurred him in falling, and Bertrand rode after him as hard as hoofs could bear him. When I rose there was the Socman himself by my side, with the news that I was on his land, but with so many courteous words besides, and such gallant bearing, that he prevailed upon me to come to his house for shelter, there to wait until the page return. By the grace of the Virgin and the help of my patron St. Magdalen, I stopped short ere I reached his door, though, as you saw, he strove to hale me up to it. And then— ah-h-h-h ! "—she shivered and chattered like one in an ague fit.

" What is it ? " cried Alleyne, looking about in alarm.

" Nothing, friend, nothing ! I was but thinking how I bit into his hand. Sooner would I bite living toad or poisoned snake. Oh, I shall loathe my lips for ever ! But you—how brave you were, and how quick ! How meek for yourself, and how bold for a stranger ! If I were a man, I should wish to do what you have done."

" It is a small thing," he answered, with a tingle of pleasure at these sweet words of praise. " But you— what will you do ? "

" There is a great oak near here, and I think that Bertrand will bring the horses there, for it is an old hunting-tryst of ours. Then hey for home, and no more hawking to-day ! A twelve-mile gallop will dry feet and skirt."

" But your father ? "

" Not one word shall I tell him. You do not know him ; but I can tell you he is not a man to disobey as I have disobeyed him. He would avenge me, it is true, but it is not to him that I shall look for vengeance. Some day, perchance in joust or in tourney, knight may wish to wear my colours, and then I shall tell him that if he does indeed crave my favour there is wrong unredressed, and the wronger the Socman of Minstead. So my knight shall find a venture such as bold knights love, and my debt shall be paid, and my father none the wiser, and one rogue the less in the world. Say, is not that a brave plan ? "

" Nay, lady, it is a thought which is unworthy of you. How can such as you speak of violence and of vengeance ? Are none to be gentle and kind, none to be piteous and forgiving ? Alas ! it is a hard, cruel world, and I would that I had never left my abbey cell. To hear such words from your lips is as though I heard an angel of grace preaching the devil's own creed."

She started from him as a young colt who first feels the bit. " Gramercy for your rede, young sir ! " she said, with a little curtsey. " As I understand your words, you are grieved that you ever met me, and look upon me as a preaching devil. Why, my father is a bitter man when he is wroth, but hath never called me such a name as that. It may be his right and duty, but certes it is none of thine. So it would be best, since you think so lowly of me, that you should take this path to the left while I keep on upon this one ; for it is clear that I can be no fit companion for you." So saying, with downcast lids and a dignity which was somewhat marred by her bedraggled skirt, she swept off down the ruddy track, leaving Alleyne standing staring ruefully after her. He waited in vain for some backward glance or sign of relenting, but she walked on with a rigid neck until her dress was only a white flutter among the leaves. Then, with a sunken head and a heavy heart, he plodded wearily down the other path, wroth with himself for the rude and uncouth tongue which had given offence where so little was intended.

He had gone some way, lost in doubt and in self-reproach, his mind all tremulous with a thousand new-found thoughts and fears and wonderments, when of a sudden there was a light rustle of the leaves behind him, and glancing round, there was this graceful, swift-footed creature, treading in his very shadow, with her proud head bowed, even as his was—the picture of humility and repentance.

" I shall not vex you, nor even speak," she said ; " but I would fain keep with you while we are in the wood."

" Nay, you cannot vex me," he answered, all warm again at the very sight of her. " It was my rough words which vexed you ; but I have been thrown among men all my life, and indeed, with all the will, I scarce know how to temper my speech to a lady's ear."

" Then unsay it," cried she quickly ; " say that I was right to wish to have vengeance on the Socman."

" Nay, I cannot do that," he answered gravely.

" Then who is ungentle and unkind now ? " she cried in triumph. " How stern and cold you are for one so young ! Art surely no mere clerk, but bishop or cardinal at the least. Shouldst have crozier for staff and mitre for cap. Well, well, for your sake I will forgive the Socman and take vengeance on none but on my own wilful self who must needs run into danger's path. So will that please you, sir ? "

" There spoke your true self," said he ; " and you will find more pleasure in such forgiveness than in any vengeance."

She shook her head, as if by no means assured of it, and then with a sudden little cry, which had more of surprise than of joy in it, " Here is Bertrand with the horses ! "

Down the glade there came a little green-clad page with laughing eyes, and long curls floating behind him. He sat perched on a high bay horse, and held on to the bridle of a spirited black palfrey, the hides of both glistening from a long run.

" I have sought you everywhere, dear Lady Maude," said he in a piping voice, springing down from his horse and holding the stirrup. " Troubadour galloped as far as Holmhill ere I could catch him. I trust that you had no hurt or scath ? " He shot a questioning glance at Alleyne as he spoke.

" No, Bertrand," said she, " thanks to this courteous stranger. And now, sir," she continued, springing into her saddle, " it is not fit that I leave you without a word more. Clerk or no, you have acted this day as becomes a true knight. King Arthur and all his table could not have done more. It may be that, as some small return, my father or his kin may have power to advance your interest. He is not rich, but he is honoured and hath great friends. Tell me what is your purpose, and see if he may not aid it."

" Alas ! lady, I have now no purpose. I have but two friends in the world, and they have gone to Christchurch, where it is likely I shall join them."

" And where in Christchurch ? "

" At the castle which is held by the brave knight, Sir Nigel Loring, constable to the Earl of Salisbury."

To his surprise she burst out a-laughing, and, spurring her palfrey, dashed off down the glade, with her page riding behind her. Not one word did she say, but as she vanished amid the trees she half turned in her saddle and waved a last greeting. Long time he stood, half hoping that she might again come back to him ; but the thud of the hoofs had died away, and there was no sound in all the woods but the gentle rustle and dropping of the leaves. At last he turned away and made his way back to the high road—another person from the light-hearted boy who had left it a short three hours before.

10. *How Hordle John found a Man whom he might Follow*

IF he might not return to Beaulieu within the year, and if his brother's dogs were to be set upon him if he showed face upon Minstead land, then indeed he was adrift upon the earth. North, south, east and west—he might turn where he would, but all was equally chill and cheerless. The Abbot had rolled ten silver crowns in a lettuce-leaf and hid them away in the bottom of his scrip, but that would be a sorry support for twelve long months. In all the darkness there was but the one bright spot of the sturdy comrades whom he had left that morning ; if he could find them again all would be well. The afternoon was not very advanced, for all that had befallen him. When a man is afoot at cock-crow much may be done in the day. If he walked fast he might yet overtake his friends ere they reached their destination. He pushed on, therefore, now walking and now running. As he journeyed he bit into a crust which remained from his Beaulieu bread, and he washed it down with a draught from a woodland stream.

It was no easy or light thing to journey through this great forest, which was some twenty miles from east to west and a good sixteen from Bramshaw Woods in the north to Lymington in the south. Alleyne, however, had the good fortune to fall in with a woodman, axe upon shoulder, trudging along in the very direction that he wished to go. With his guidance he passed the fringe of Bolderwood Walk, famous for old ash and yew, through Mark Ash, with its giant beech trees, and on through the Knightwood groves, where the giant oak was already a great tree, but only one of many comely brothers. They plodded along together, the woodman and Alleyne, with little talk on either side for, their thoughts were as far asunder as the poles. The peasant's gossip had been of the hunt, of the bracken, of the grey-headed kites that had nested in Wood Fidley, and of the great catch of herring brought back by the boats of Pitt's Deep. The clerk's mind was on his brother, on his future—above all on this strange, fierce, melting, beautiful woman who had broken so suddenly into his life, and as suddenly had passed out of it again. So *distrait* was he, and so random his answers, that the woodman took to whistling, and soon branched off upon the track to Burley, leaving Alleyne upon the main Christchurch road.

Down this he pushed as fast as he might, hoping at every turn and rise to catch sight of his companions of the morning. From Vinney Ridge to Rhinefield Walk the woods grow thick and dense up to the very edges of the track, but beyond the country opens up into broad dun-coloured moors, flecked with clumps of trees, and topping each other in long low curves up to the dark lines of forest in the farthest distance. Clouds of insects danced and buzzed in the golden autumn light, and the air was full of the piping of the song-birds. Long glinting dragon-flies shot across the path, or hung tremulous with gauzy wings and gleaming bodies. Once a white-necked sea eagle soared screaming high over the traveller's head, and again a flock of brown bustards popped up from among the bracken, and blundered away in their clumsy fashion, half running, half flying, with strident cry and whirr of wings.

There were folk, too, to be met upon the road—beggars and couriers, chapmen and tinkers—cheery fellows for the most part, with a rough jest and homely greeting for each other and for Alleyne. Near Shotwood he came upon five seamen, on their way from Poole to Southampton—rude red-faced men, who shouted at him in a jargon which he could scarce understand, and held out to him a great pot from which they had been drinking—nor would they let him pass until he had dipped pannikin in and taken a mouthful which set him coughing and choking, with the tears running down his cheeks. Farther on he met a sturdy black-bearded man, mounted on a brown horse, with a rosary in his right hand and a long two-handed sword jangling against his stirrup-iron. By his black robe and the eight-pointed cross upon his sleeve, Alleyne recognised him as one of the Knights Hospitallers of St. John of Jerusalem, whose presbytery was at Baddesley. He held up two fingers as he passed, with a " *Benedic, fili mi !* " whereat Alleyne doffed hat and bent knee, looking with much reverence at one who had devoted his life to the overthrow of the infidel. Poor simple lad ! he had not learned yet that what men are and what men profess to be are very wide asunder, and that the Knights of St. John, having come into large part of the riches of the ill-fated Templars, were very much too comfortable to think of exchanging their palace for a tent, or the cellars of England for the thirsty deserts of Syria. Yet ignorance may be more precious than wisdom, for Alleyne as he walked on braced himself to a higher life by the thought of this other's sacrifice, and strengthened himself by his example, which he could scarce have done had he known that the Hospitaller's mind ran more upon malmsey than on Mamelukes, and on venison rather than victories.

As he pressed on the plain turned to woods once more in the region of Wilverley Walk, and a cloud swept up from the south with the sun shining through the chinks of it. A few great drops came pattering loudly down, and then in a moment the steady swish of a brisk shower, with the dripping and dropping of the leaves. Alleyne, glancing round for shelter, saw a thick and lofty hollybush, so hollowed out beneath that no house could have been drier. Under this canopy of green two men were already squatted, who waved their hands to Alleyne that he should join them. As he approached he saw that they had five dried herrings laid out in front of them, with a great hunch of wheaten bread and a leathern flask full of milk, but instead of setting to at their food they appeared to have forgotten all about it, and were disputing together with flushed faces and angry gestures. It was easy to see by their dress and manner that they were two of those wandering students who formed about this time so enormous a multitude in every country in Europe. The one was long and thin, with melancholy features, while the other was fat and sleek, with a loud voice and the air of a man who is not to be gainsaid.

" Come hither, good youth," he cried, " come hither ! *Vultus ingenui puer.* Heed not the face of my good coz here. *Foenum habet in cornu*, as Dan Horace has it ; but I warrant him harmless for all that."

" Stint your bull's bellowing ! " exclaimed the other. " If it come to Horace, I have a line in my mind : *Loquaces si sapiat——* How doth it run ? The English o't being that a man of sense should ever avoid a great talker. That being so, if all were men of sense, then thou wouldst be a lonesome man, coz."

" Alas ! Dicon, I fear that your logic is as bad as your philosophy or your divinity—and God wot it would be hard to say a worse word than that for it. For, hark ye : granting, *propter argumentum*, that I am a talker, then the true reasoning runs that since all men of sense should avoid me, and thou hast not avoided me, but art at the present moment eating herrings with me under a holly-bush, ergo you are no man of sense, which is exactly what I have been dinning into your long ears ever since I first clapped eyes on your sunken chops."

" Tut, tut ! " cried the other. " Your tongue goes like the clapper of a mill-wheel. Sit down here, friend, and partake of this herring. Understand, first, however, that there are certain conditions attached to it."

" I had hoped," said Alleyne, falling into the humour of the twain, " that a tranchoir of bread and a draught of milk might be attached to it."

" Hark to him, hark to him ! " cried the little fat man. " It is ever thus, Dicon ! Wit, lad, is a catching thing, like the itch or the sweating sickness. I exude it around me ; it is an aura. I tell you, coz, that no man can come within seventeen feet of me without catching a spark. Look at your own case. A duller man never stepped, and yet within the week you have said three things which might pass, and one thing the day we left Fordingbridge which I should not have been ashamed of myself."

" Enough, rattlepate, enough ! " said the other. " The milk you shall have and the bread also, friend, together with the herring, but you must hold the scales between us."

" If he hold the herring he holds the scales, my sapient brother," cried the fat man. " But I pray you, good youth, to tell us whether you are a learned clerk, and, if so, whether you have studied at Oxenford or at Paris."

" I have some small stock of learning," Alleyne answered, picking at his herring, " but I have been at neither of these places. I was bred amongst the Cistercian monks at Beaulieu Abbey."

" Pooh, pooh ! " they cried both together. " What sort of an upbringing is that ? "

" *Non cuivis contingit adire Corinthum,*" quoth Alleyne.

" Come, brother Stephen, he hath some tincture of letters," said the melancholy man more hopefully. " He may be the better judge, since he hath no call to side with either of us. Now, attention, friend, and let your ears work as well as your nether jaw. *Judex damnatur*—you know the old saw. Here am I upholding the good fame of the learned Duns Scotus against the foolish quibblings and poor silly reasonings of Willie Ockham."

" While I," quoth the other loudly, " do maintain the good sense and extraordinary wisdom of that most learned William against the crack-brained fantasies of the muddy Scotchman, who hath hid such little wit as he has under so vast a pile of words, that it is like one drop of Gascony in a firkin of ditch-water. Solomon his wisdom would not suffice to say what the rogue means."

" Certes, Stephen Hapgood, his wisdom doth not suffice," cried the other. " It is as though a mole cried out against the morning star, because he could not see it. But our dispute, friend, is concerning the nature of that subtle essence which we call thought. For I hold with the learned Scotus that thought is in very truth a thing, even as vapour or fumes, or many other substances which our gross bodily eyes are blind to. For, look you, that which produces a thing must be itself a thing, and if a man's thought may produce a written book, then must thought itself be a material thing, even as the book is. Have I expressed it ? Do I make it plain ? "

" Whereas I hold," shouted the other, " with my revered preceptor, *doctor præclarus et excellentissimus*, that all things are but thought ; for when thought is gone I prythee where are the things then ? Here are trees about us, and I see them because I think I see them ; but if I have swooned, or sleep, or am in wine, then my thought having gone forth from me, lo the trees go forth also. How now, coz, have I touched thee on the raw ? "

Alleyne sat between them munching his bread while the twain disputed across his knees, leaning forward with flushed faces and darting hands, in all the heat of argument. Never had he heard such jargon of scholastic philosophy, such fine-drawn distinctions, such cross-fire of major and minor proposition, syllogism, attack and refutation. Question clattered upon answer like a sword on a buckler. The ancients, the fathers of the Church, the moderns, the Scriptures, the Arabians, were each sent hurtling against the other, while the rain still dripped and the dark holly-leaves glistened with the moisture. At last the fat man seemed to weary of it, for he set to work quietly upon his meal, while his opponent, as proud as a rooster who is left unchallenged upon the midden, crowed away in a last long burst of quotation and deduction. Suddenly, however, his eyes dropped upon his food, and he gave a howl of dismay.

" You double thief ! " he cried, " you have eaten my herrings, and I without bite or sup since morning."

" That," quoth the other complacently, " was my final argument, my crowning effort, or *peroratio*, as the orators have it. For, coz, since all thoughts are things, you have but to think a pair of herrings, and then conjure up a pottle of milk wherewith to wash them down."

" A brave piece of reasoning," cried the other, " and I know of but one reply to it." On which, leaning forward, he caught his comrade a rousing smack across his rosy cheek. " Nay, take it not amiss," he said ; " since all things are but thoughts, then that also is but a thought, and may be disregarded."

This last argument, however, by no means commended itself to the pupil of Ockham, who plucked a great stick from the ground and signified his dissent by smiting the realist over the pate with it. By good fortune, the wood was so light and rotten that it went to a thousand splinters ; but Alleyne thought it best to leave the twain to settle the matter at their leisure, the more so as the sun was shining brightly once more. Looking back down the pool-strewn road, he saw the two excited philosophers waving their hands and shouting at each other, but their babble soon became a mere drone in the distance, and a turn in the road hid them from his sight.

And now, after passing Holmesley Walk and the Wooton Heath, the forest began to shred out into scattered belts of trees, with gleam of cornfield and stretch of pasture-land between. Here and there by the wayside stood little knots of wattle-and-daub huts, with shock-haired labourers lounging by the doors and red-cheeked children sprawling in the roadway. Back among the groves he could see the high gable ends and thatched roofs of the franklins' houses, on whose fields these men found employment, or more often a thick dark column of smoke marked their position and hinted at the coarse plenty within. By these signs Alleyne knew that he was on the very fringe of the forest, and therefore no great way from Christchurch. The sun was lying low in the west and shooting its level rays across the long sweep of rich green country, glinting on the white-fleeced sheep, and throwing long shadows from the red kine who waded knee-deep in the juicy clover. Right glad was the traveller to see the high tower of Christchurch Priory gleaming in the mellow evening light, and gladder still

when, on rounding a corner, he came upon his comrades
of the morning seated astraddle upon a fallen tree. They
had a flat space before them, on which they alternately
threw little square pieces of bone, and were so intent
upon their occupation that they never raised eye as he
approached them. He observed with astonishment, as
he drew near, that the archer's bow was on John's back,
the archer's sword by John's side, and the steel cap laid
upon the tree-trunk between them.

" Mort de ma vie ! " Aylward shouted, looking down at
the dice. " Never had I such cursed luck. A murrain
on the bones ! I have not thrown a good main since I
left Navarre. A one and a three ! En avant, camarade ! "

" Four and three," cried Hordle John, counting on his
great fingers, " that makes seven. Ho, archer, I have thy
cap ! Now have at thee for thy jerkin ! "

" Mon Dieu ! " he growled, " I am like to reach Christchurch in my shirt." Then suddenly glancing up,
" Hola, by the splendour of heaven, here is our cher
petit ! Now, by my ten finger-bones ! this is a rare sight
to mine eyes." He sprang up and threw his arms round
Alleyne's neck, while John, no less pleased, but more
backward and Saxon in his habits, stood grinning and
bobbing by the wayside, with his newly won steel cap
stuck wrong side foremost upon his tangle of red hair.

" Hast come to stop ? " cried the bowman, patting
Alleyne all over in his delight. " Shall not get away from
us again ! "

" I wish no better," said he, with a pringling in the
eyes at this hearty greeting.

" Well said, lad ! " cried big John. " We three shall
to the wars together, and the devil may fly away with the
Abbot of Beaulieu ! But your feet and hosen are all
besmudged. Hast been in the water, or I am the more
mistaken."

" I have in good sooth," Alleyne answered, and then as
they journeyed on their way he told them the many things
that had befallen him, his meeting with the villein, his

sight of the king, his coming upon his brother, with all the tale of the black welcome and of the fair damsel. They strode on either side, each with an ear slanting towards him, but ere he had come to the end of his story the bowman had spun round upon his heel, and was hastening back the way they had come, breathing loudly through his nose.

" What then ? " asked Alleyne, trotting after him and gripping at his jerkin.

" I am back for Minstead, lad."

" And why, in the name of sense ? "

" To thrust a handful of steel into the Socman. What ! hale a demoiselle against her will, and then loose dogs at his own brother ! Let me go ! "

" Nenny, nenny ! " cried Alleyne, laughing. " There was no scath done. Come back, friend "—and so, by mingled pushing and entreaties, they got his head round for Christchurch once more. Yet he walked with his chin upon his shoulder, until, catching sight of a maiden by a wayside well, the smiles came back to his face and peace to his heart.

" But you," said Alleyne, " there have been changes with you also. Why should not the workman carry his tools ? Where are bow, and sword, and cap—and why so warlike, John ? "

" It is a game which friend Aylward hath been a-teaching of me."

" And I found him an over-apt pupil," grumbled the bowman. " He hath stripped me as though I had fallen into the hands of the tardvenus. But, by my hilt ! you must render them back to me, camarade, lest you bring discredit upon my mission, and I will pay you for them at armourers' prices."

" Take them back, man, and never heed the pay," said John. " I did but wish to learn the feel of them, since I am like to have such trinkets hung to my own girdle for some years to come."

" Ma foi, he was born for a free companion ! " cried

Aylward. " He hath the very trick of speech and turn of thought. I take them back then, and indeed it gives me unease not to feel my yew-stave tapping against my leg-bone. But see, mes garçons, on this side of the church rises the square and darkling tower of Earl Salisbury's castle, and even from here I seem to see on yonder banner the red roebuck of the Montacutes."

" Red upon white," said Alleyne, shading his eyes ; " but whether roebuck or no is more than I could vouch. How black is the great tower, and how bright the gleam of arms upon the wall ! See below the flag, how it twinkles like a star ! "

" Aye, it is the steel head-piece of the watchman," re-marked the archer. " But we must on, if we are to be there before the drawbridge rises at the vespers bugle ; for it is likely that Sir Nigel, being so renowned a soldier, may keep hard discipline within the walls, and let no man enter after sundown." So saying, he quickened his pace, and the three comrades were soon close to the straggling and broadspread town which centred round the noble church and the frowning castle.

It chanced on that very evening that Sir Nigel Loring, having supped before sunset, as was his custom, and having himself seen that Pommers and Cadsand, his two war-horses, with the thirteen hacks, the five jennets, my lady's three palfreys, and the great dapple-grey roussin, had all their needs supplied, had taken his dogs for an evening breather. Sixty or seventy of them, large and small, smooth and shaggy—deer-hound, boar-hound, blood-hound, wolf-hound, mastiff, alaun, talbot, lurcher, terrier, spaniel—snapping, yelling and whining, with score of lolling tongues and waving tails, came surging down the narrow lane which leads from the Twynham kennels to the bank of Avon. Two russet-clad varlets, with loud halloo and cracking whips, walked thigh-deep amid the swarm, guiding, controlling, and urging. Be-hind came Sir Nigel himself, with Lady Loring upon his arm, the pair walking slowly and sedately, as befitted both their age and their condition, while they watched with a smile in their eyes the scrambling crowd in front of them. They paused, however, at the bridge, and, leaning their elbows upon the stonework, they stood looking down at their own faces in the glassy stream, and at the swift flash of speckled trout against the tawny gravel.

Sir Nigel was a slight man of poor stature, with soft lisping voice and gentle ways. So short was he that his wife, who was no very tall woman, had the better of him by the breadth of three fingers. His sight having been injured in his early wars by a basketful of lime which had been emptied over him when he led the Earl of Derby's stormers up the breach at Bergerac, he had contracted something of a stoop, with a blinking, peering expression of face. His age was six-and-forty, but the constant practice of arms, together with a cleanly life, had preserved his activity and endurance unimpaired, so that from a distance he seemed to have the slight limbs and swift grace of a boy. His face, however, was tanned of a dull yellow tint, with a leathery poreless look, which spoke of rough outdoor doings, and the little pointed beard which he wore, in deference to the prevailing fashion, was streaked and shot with grey. His features were small, delicate, and regular, with clear-cut curving nose, and eyes which jutted forward from the lids. His dress was simple and yet spruce. A Flandrish hat of beevor, bearing in the band the token of Our Lady of Embrun, was drawn low upon the left side to hide that ear which had been partly shorn from his head by a Flemish man-at-arms in a camp broil before Tournay. His cote-hardie, or tunic, and trunk-hosen were of a purple plum colour, with long weepers which hung from either sleeve to below his knees. His shoes were of red leather, daintily pointed at the toes, but not yet prolonged to the extravagant lengths which the succeeding reign was to bring into fashion. A gold-embroidered belt of knighthood encircled his loins, with his arms, five roses gules on a field argent, cunningly worked upon the clasp. So stood Sir

Nigel Loring upon the bridge of Avon, and talked lightly with his lady.

And, certes, had the two visages alone been seen, and the stranger been asked which were the more likely to belong to the bold warrior whose name was loved by the roughest soldiery of Europe, he had assuredly selected the lady's. Her face was square and strong, with thick brows, and the eyes of one who was accustomed to rule. Taller and broader than her husband, her flowing gown of sendal, and fur-lined tippet, could not conceal the full outlines of her figure. It was the age of martial women. The deeds of Black Agnes of Dunbar, of Lady Salisbury and of the Countess of Montfort, were still fresh in the public mind. With such examples before them, the wives of the English captains had become as warlike as their mates, and ordered their castles in their absence with the prudence and discipline of veteran seneschals. Right easy were the Montacutes of their Castle of Twynham, and little had they to dread from roving galley or French squadron while Lady Mary Loring had the ordering of it. There were men who said that of all the stern passages and daring deeds by which Sir Nigel Loring had proved the true temper of his courage, not the least was his wooing and winning of so high-mettled a dame.

" I tell you, my fair lord," she was saying, " that it is no fit training for a demoiselle : hawks and hounds, rotes and citoles, singing a French rondel, or reading the Gestes de Doon de Mayence, as I found her yesternight, pretending sleep, the artful, with the corner of the scroll thrusting forth from under her pillow. Lent her by Father Christopher of the Priory, forsooth—that is ever her answer. How shall all this help her when she has castle of her own to keep, with a hundred mouths all agape for beef and beer ? "

" True, my sweet bird, true," answered the knight, picking a comfit from his gold drageoir. " The maid is like the young filly, which kicks heels and plunges for very lust of life. Give her time, dame, give her time."

" Well I know that my father would have given me, not time, but a good hazel-stick across my shoulders. Ma foi ! I know not what the world is coming to, when young maids may flout their elders. I wonder that you do not correct her, my fair lord."

" Nay, my heart's comfort, I never raised hand to woman yet, and it would be a passing strange thing if I began upon my own flesh and blood. It was a woman's hand which cast this lime into mine eyes, and though I saw her stoop, and might well have stopped her ere she threw, I deemed it unworthy of my knighthood to hinder or balk one of her sex."

" The hussy ! " cried Lady Loring, clenching her broad right hand. " I would I had been at the side of her ! "

" And so would I, since you would have been the nearer me, my own. But I doubt not that you are right, and that Maude's wings need clipping, which I may leave in your hands when I am gone, for, in sooth, this peaceful life is not for me, and were it not for your gracious kindness and loving care I could not abide it a week. I hear that there is talk of warlike muster at Bordeaux once more, and by St. Paul ! it would be a new thing if the lions of England and the red pile of Chandos were to be seen in the field, and the roses of Loring were not waving by their side."

" Now woe worth me but I feared it ! " cried she, with the colour all struck from her face. " I have noted your absent mind, your kindling eye, your trying and riveting of old harness. Consider, my sweet lord, that you have already won much honour, that we have seen but little of each other, that you bear upon your body the scars of over twenty wounds received in I know not how many bloody encounters. Have you not done enough for honour and the public cause ? "

" My lady, when our liege lord the king at nigh threescore, and my Lord Chandos at threescore and ten, are blithe and ready to lay lance in rest for England's cause, it would ill beseem me to prate of service done. It is sooth that I have received seven-and-twenty wounds. There is the more reason that I should be thankful that I am still long of breath and sound in limb. I have also seen some bickering and scuffling. Six great land battles I count, with four upon the sea, and seven-and-fifty onfalls, skirmishes and bushments. I have held two-and-twenty towns, and I have been at the intaking of thirty-one. Surely then it would be bitter shame to me, and also to you, since my fame is yours, that I should now hold back if a man's work is to be done. Besides, bethink you how low is our purse, with bailiff and reeve ever croaking of empty farms and wasting lands. Were it not for this constableship which the Earl of Salisbury hath bestowed upon us we could scarce uphold the state which is fitting to our degree. Therefore, my sweeting, there is the more need that I should turn to where there is good pay to be earned and brave ransoms to be won."

" Ah, my dear lord," quoth she, with sad, weary eyes. " I thought that at last I had you to mine own self, even though your youth had been spent afar from my side. Yet my voice, as I know well, should speed you on to glory and renown, not hold you back when fame is to be won. Yet what can I say ?—for all men know that your valour needs the curb and not the spur. It goes to my heart that you should ride forth now a mere knight bachelor, when there is no noble in the land who has so good a claim to the square pennon, save only that you have not the money to uphold it."

" And whose fault that, my sweet bird ? " said he.

" No fault, my fair lord, but a virtue ; for how many rich ransoms have you won, and yet have scattered the crowns among page and archer and varlet, until in a week you had not as much as would buy food and forage. It is a most knightly largesse, and yet withouten money how can man rise ? "

" Dirt and dross ! " cried he. " What matter rise or fall, so that duty be done and honour gained ! Banneret or bachelor, square pennon or forked, I would not give a denier for the difference, and the less since Sir John Chandos, chosen flower of English chivalry, is himself but a humble knight. But meanwhile fret not thyself, my heart's dove, for it is like that there may be no war waged, and we must await the news. But here are three strangers, and one, as I take it, a soldier fresh from service. It is likely that he may give us word of what is stirring over the water."

Lady Loring glancing up, saw in the fading light three companions walking abreast down the road, all grey with dust, and stained with travel, yet chattering merrily between themselves. He in the midst was young and comely, with boyish open face and bright grey eyes, which glanced from right to left as though he found the world around him both new and pleasing. To his right walked a huge red-headed man with broad smile and merry twinkle, whose clothes seemed to be bursting and splitting at every seam, as though he were some lusty chick who was breaking bravely from his shell. On the other side, with his knotted hand upon the young man's shoulder, came a stout and burly archer, brown and fierce-eyed, with sword at belt and long yellow yew-stave peeping over his shoulder. Hard face, battered headpiece, dinted brigandine, with faded red lion of St. George ramping on a discoloured ground, all proclaimed as plainly as words that he was indeed from the land of war. He looked keenly at Sir Nigel as he approached, and then, plunging his hand under his breast-plate, he stepped up to him with a rough uncouth bow to the lady.

" Your pardon, fair sir," said he, " but I fear you forget one who was once your humble friend and comrade."

" Nay, it is Samkin Aylward," cried the knight. " Often have I wondered what cheer you made, for it is indeed many years since I last set eyes upon your face."

" Aye, my master ; it is other days since we set forth together from Tilford with our faces towards the wars," said the archer.

" It is great joy to see you once again. Rest awhile, and you shall come to the hall anon and tell us what is passing in France, for I have heard that it is likely that our pennons may flutter to the south of the great Spanish mountains ere another year be passed."

" There was talk of it in Bordeaux," answered the archer, " and I saw myself that the armourers and smiths were as busy as rats in a wheat-rick. But I bring you this letter from the valiant Gascon knight, Sir Claude Latour. And to you, lady," he added after a pause, " I bring from him this box of red sugar of Narbonne, with every cour-teous and knightly greeting which a gallant cavalier may make to a fair and noble dame."

This little speech had cost the blunt bowman much pains and planning ; but he might have spared his breath, for the lady was quite as much absorbed as her lord in the letter, which they held between them, a hand on either corner, spelling it out very slowly, with drawn brows and muttering lips. As they read it, Alleyne, who stood with Hordle John a few paces back from their comrade, saw the lady catch her breath, while the knight laughed softly to himself.

" You see, dear heart," said he, " that they will not leave the old dog in his kennel when the game is afoot. And what of this White Company, Aylward ? "

" Ah, sir, you speak of dogs," cried Aylward ; " but there are a pack of lusty hounds who are ready for any quarry, if they have but a good huntsman to halloo them on. Sir, we have been in the wars together, and I have seen many a brave following, but never such a set of woodland boys as this. They do but want you at their head, and who will bar the way to them ? "

" Pardieu ! " said Sir Nigel, " if they are all like their messengers they are indeed men of whom a leader may be proud. What is the name of this giant behind you ? "

" He is big John, of Hordle, a forest man, who hath now taken service in the Company."

" A proper figure of a man-at-arms," said the little knight. " Why, man, you are no chicken, yet I warrant him the stronger man. See to that great stone from the coping which hath fallen upon the bridge. Four of my lazy varlets strove this day to carry it hence. I would that you two could put them to shame by budging it, though I fear that I overtask you, for it is of a grievous weight."

He pointed as he spoke to a huge rough-hewn block which lay by the roadside, deep sunken from its own weight in the reddish earth. The archer approached it, rolling back the sleeves of his jerkin, but with no very hopeful countenance, for indeed it was a mighty rock. John, however, put him aside with his left hand, and, stooping over the stone, he plucked it single-handed from its soft bed and swung it far into the stream. There it fell with mighty splash, one jagged end peaking out above the surface, while the waters bubbled and foamed with far-circling eddy.

" Good lack ! " cried Sir Nigel, and " Good lack ! " cried his lady, while John stood laughing and wiping the caked dirt from his fingers.

" I have felt his arms round my ribs," said the bowman, " and they crackle yet at the thought of it. This other comrade of mine is a right learned clerk, for all that he is so young, hight Alleyne, the son of Edric, brother to the Socman of Minstead."

" Young man," quoth Sir Nigel sternly, " if you are of the same way of thought as your brother, you may not pass under portcullis of mine."

" Nay, fair sir," cried Aylward hastily, " I will be pledge for it that they have no thought in common ; for this very day his brother hath set his dogs upon him, and driven him from his lands."

" And are you, too, of the White Company ? " asked Sir Nigel. " Hast had small experience of war, if I may judge by your looks and bearing."

" I would fain to France with my friends here,"

Alleyne answered ; " but I am a man of peace—a reader, exorcist, acolyte, and clerk."

" That need not hinder," quoth Sir Nigel.

" No, fair sir," cried the bowman joyously. " Why, I myself have served two terms with Arnold de Cervolles, he whom they called the archpriest. By my hilt ! I have seen him ere now, with monk's gown trussed to his knees, over his sandals in blood in the forefront of the battle. Yet, ere the last string had twanged, he would be down on his four bones among the stricken, and have them all houseled and shriven, as quick as shelling peas. Ma foi ! there were those who wished that he would have less care for their souls and a little more for their bodies ! "

" It is well to have a learned clerk in every troop," said Sir Nigel. " By St. Paul ! there are men so caitiff that they think more of a scrivener's pen than of their lady's smile, and do their devoir in hopes that they may fill a line in a chronicle or make a tag to a jongleur's romance. I remember well that, at the siege of Retters, there was a little, sleek, fat clerk of the name of Chaucer, who was so apt at rondel, sirvente, or tonson, that no man dare give back a foot from the walls, lest he find it all set down in his rhymes and sung by every underling and varlet in the camp. But, my soul's bird, you hear me prate as though all were decided, when I have not yet taken counsel either with you or with my lady mother. Let us to the chamber, while these strangers find such fare as pantry and cellar may furnish."

" The night air strikes chill," said the lady, and turned down the road with her hand upon her lord's arm. The three comrades dropped behind and followed : Aylward much the lighter for having accomplished his mission, Alleyne full of wonderment at the humble bearing of so renowned a captain, and John loud with snorts and sneers, which spoke his disappointment and contempt.

" What ails the man ? " asked Aylward in surprise.

" I have been cozened and bejaped," quoth he gruffly.

" By whom, Sir Samson the strong ? "

" By thee, Sir Balaam the false prophet."

" By my hilt ! " cried the archer, " though I be not
Balaam, yet I hold converse with the very creature that
spake to him. What is amiss, then, and how have I
played you false ? "

" Why, marry, did you not say, and Alleyne here will
be my witness, that, if I would hie to the wars with you,
you would place me under a leader who was second to
none in all England for valour ? Yet here you bring me
to a shred of a man, peaky and ill-nourished, with eyes
like a moulting owl, who must needs, forsooth, take
counsel with his mother ere he buckle sword to girdle."

" Is that where the shoe galls ? " cried the bowman, and
laughed aloud. " I will ask you what you think of him
three months hence, if we be all alive ; for sure I am
that——"

Aylward's words were interrupted by an extraordinary
hubbub which broke out that instant some little way down
the street in the direction of the Priory. There was deep-
mouthed shouting of men, frightened shrieks of women,
howling and barking of curs, and over all a sullen thunderous rumble, indescribably menacing and terrible. Round
the corner of the narrow street there came rushing a brace
of whining dogs with tails tucked under their legs, and
after them a white-faced burgher, with outstretched
hands and widespread fingers, his hair all abristle and his
eyes glinting back from one shoulder to the other, as
though some great terror were at his very heels. " Fly,
my lady, fly ! " he screeched, and whizzed past them like
a bolt from bow ; while close behind came lumbering a
huge black bear, with red tongue lolling from his mouth,
and a broken chain jangling behind him. To right and
left the folk flew for arch and doorway. Hordle John
caught up the Lady Loring as though she had been a
feather, and sprang with her into an open porch ; while
Aylward, with a whirl of French oaths, plucked at his
quiver and tried to unsling his bow. Alleyne, all unnerved at so strange and unwonted a sight, shrank up

against a wall with his eyes fixed upon the frenzied creature, which came bounding along with ungainly speed, looking the larger in the uncertain light, its huge jaws agape, with blood and slaver trickling to the ground. Sir Nigel alone, unconscious to all appearance of the universal panic, walked with unfaltering step up the centre of the road, a silken handkerchief in one hand and his gold comfit-box in the other. It sent the blood cold through Alleyne's veins to see that as they came together —the man and the beast—the creature reared up, with eyes ablaze with fear and hate, and whirled its great paws above the knight to smite him to the earth. He, however, blinking with puckered eyes, reached up his kerchief, and flicked the beast twice across the snout with it. " Ah, saucy ! saucy ! " quoth he, with gentle chiding ; on which the bear, uncertain and puzzled, dropped its fore legs to earth again, and waddling back, was soon swathed in ropes by the bear-ward and a crowd of peasants who had been in close pursuit.

A scared man was the keeper ; for, having chained the brute to a stake while he drank a stoup of ale at the inn, it had been baited by stray curs until, in wrath and madness, it had plucked loose the chain, and smitten or bitten all who came in its path. Most scared of all was he to find that the creature had come nigh to harm the Lord and Lady of the castle, who had power to place him in the stretch-neck or to have the skin scourged from his shoulders. Yet, when he came with bowed head and humble entreaty for forgiveness, he was met with a handful of small silver from Sir Nigel, whose dame, however, was less charitably disposed, being much ruffled in her dignity by the manner in which she had been hustled from her lord's side. As they passed through the castle gate, John plucked at Aylward's sleeve, and the two fell behind.

" I must crave your pardon, comrade," said he, bluntly. " I was a fool not to know that a little rooster may be the gamest. I believe that this man is indeed a leader whom we may follow."

11. *How a Young Shepherd had a Perilous Flock*

BLACK was the mouth of Twynham Castle, though a pair of torches burning at the farther end of the gateway cast a red glare over the outer bailey, and sent a dim ruddy flicker through the rough-hewn arch, rising and falling with fitful brightness. Over the door the travellers could discern the escutcheon of the Montacutes, a roebuck gules on a field argent, flanked on either side by smaller shields which bore the red roses of the veteran constable. As they passed over the drawbridge Alleyne marked the gleam of arms in the embrasures to right and left, and they had scarce set foot upon the causeway ere a hoarse blare burst from a bugle, and with screech of hinge and clank of chain, the ponderous bridge swung up into the air, drawn by unseen hands. At the same instant the huge portcullis came rattling down from above, and shut off the last fading light of day. Sir Nigel and his lady walked on in deep talk, while a fat understeward took charge of the three comrades, and led them to the buttery, where beef, bread, and beer were kept ever in readiness for the wayfarer. After a hearty meal and a dip in the trough to wash the dust from them, they strolled forth into the bailey, where the bowman peered about through the darkness at wall and at keep, with the carping eyes of one who has seen something of sieges, and is not lightly to be satisfied. To Alleyne and to John, however, it appeared to be as great and as stout a fortress as could be built by the hands of man.

Erected by Sir Baldwin de Redvers in the old fighting days of the twelfth century, when men thought much of war and little of comfort, Castle Twynham had been designed as a stronghold pure and simple, unlike those later and more magnificent structures where warlike strength had been combined with the magnificence of a palace. From the time of the Edwards such buildings as

125

Conway and Caernarvon Castles, to say nothing of Royal
Windsor, had shown that it was possible to secure luxury
in peace as well as security in times of trouble. Sir
Nigel's trust, however, still frowned above the smooth-
flowing waters of the Avon, very much as the stern race
of early Anglo-Normans had designed it. There were
the broad outer and inner bailies, not paved, but sown
with grass to nourish the sheep and cattle which might
be driven in on sign of danger. All round were high
and turreted walls, with at the corner a bare square-faced
keep, gaunt and windowless, rearing up from a lofty
mound, which made it almost inaccessible to an assailant.
Against the bailey-walls were rows of frail wooden houses
and leaning sheds, which gave shelter to the archers and
men-at-arms who formed the garrison. The doors of
these humble dwellings were mostly open, and against
the yellow glare from within Alleyne could see the
bearded fellows cleaning their harness, while their wives
would come out for a gossip, with their needlework in
their hands, and their long black shadows streaming across
the yard. The air was full of the clack of their voices and
the merry prattling of children, in strange contrast to the
flash of arms and constant warlike challenge from the
walls above.

" Methinks a company of school lads could hold this
place against an army," quoth John.

" And so say I," said Alleyne.

" Nay, there you are wide of the clout," the bowman
said gravely. " By my hilt ! I have seen a stronger
fortalice carried in a summer evening. I remember such
a one in Picardy, with a name as long as a Gascon's
pedigree. It was when I served under Sir Robert
Knolles, before the days of the Company ; and we came
by good plunder at the sacking of it. I had myself a great
silver bowl, with two goblets, and a plastron of Spanish
steel. Pasques Dieu ! there are some fine women over
yonder ! Mort de ma vie ! see to that one in the doorway ;
I will go speak to her. But whom have we here ? "

126

" Is there an archer here hight Sam Aylward ? " asked a gaunt man-at-arms, clanking up to them across the courtyard.

" My name, friend," quoth the bowman.

" Then sure I have no need to tell thee mine," saith the other.

" By the rood ! if it is not Black Simon of Norwich ! " cried Aylward. " À mon cœur, camarade, à mon cœur ! Ah, but I am blithe to see thee ! " The two fell upon each other and hugged like bears.

" And where from, old blood and bones ? " asked the bowman.

" I am in service here. Tell me, comrade, is it sooth that we shall have another fling at these Frenchmen ? It is so rumoured in the guard-room, and that Sir Nigel will take the field once more."

" It is like enough, mon gar, as things go."

" Now may the Lord be praised ! " cried the other. " This very night will I set apart a golden ouche to be offered on the shrine of my name-saint. I have pined for this, Aylward, as a young maid pines for her lover."

" Art so set on plunder then ? Is the purse so light that there is not enough for a rouse ? I have a bag at my belt, camarade, and you have but to put your fist into it for what you want. It was ever share and share between us."

" Nay, friend, it is not the Frenchman's gold, but the Frenchman's blood that I would have. I should not rest quiet in the grave, coz, if I had not another turn at them. For with us in France it has ever been fair and honest war —a shut fist for the man, but a bended knee for the woman. But how was it at Winchelsea when their galleys came down upon it some few years back ? I had an old mother there, lad, who had come down thither from the Midlands to be nearer her son. They found her after-wards by her own hearthstone, thrust through by a Frenchman's bill. My second sister, my brother's wife, and her two children, they were but ash-heaps in the smoking ruins of their house. I will not say that we have not wrought great scath upon France, but women and children have been safe from us. And so, old friend, my heart is hot within me, and I long to hear the old battle-cry again, and, by God's truth, if Sir Nigel unfurls his pennon, here is one who will be right glad to feel the saddle-flaps under his knees."

"We have seen good work together, old war-dog," quoth Aylward ; "and, by my hilt ! we may hope to see more ere we die. But we are more like to hawk at the Spanish woodcock than at the French heron, though certes it is rumoured that Du Guesclin, with all the best lances of France, have taken service under the lions and towers of Castile. But, comrade, it is in my mind that there is some small matter of dispute still open between us."

"'Fore God, it is sooth," cried the other. "I had forgot it. The provost-marshal and his men tore us apart when last we met."

"On which, friend, we vowed that we should settle the point when next we come together. Hast thy sword, I see, and the moon throws glimmer enough for such old nightbirds as we. On guard, mon gar ! I have not heard clink of steel this month or more."

"Out from the shadow, then," said the other, drawing his sword. "A vow is a vow, and not lightly to be broken."

"A vow to the saints," cried Alleyne, "is indeed not to be set aside ; but this is a devil's vow, and, simple clerk as I am, I am yet the mouthpiece of the true Church when I say that it were mortal sin to fight on such a quarrel. What ! shall two grown men carry malice for years, and fly like snarling curs at each other's throats ? "

"No malice, my young clerk, no malice," quoth Black Simon. "I have not a bitter drop in my heart for mine old comrade ; but the quarrel, as he hath told you, is still open and unsettled. Fall on, Aylward ! "

"Not whilst I can stand between you," cried Alleyne, springing before the bowman. "It is shame and sin to see two Christian Englishmen turn swords against each other like the frenzied bloodthirsty paynim."

" And, what is more," said Hordle John, suddenly appearing out of the buttery with the huge board upon which the pastry was rolled, " if either raise sword I shall flatten him like Shrove-tide pancake. By the black rood ! I shall drive him into the earth like a nail into a door, rather than see you do scath to each other."

" 'Fore God, this is a strange way of preaching peace," cried Black Simon. " You may find the scath yourself, my lusty friend, if you raise your great cudgel to me. I had as lief have the castle drawbridge drop upon my pate."

" Tell me, Aylward," said Alleyne earnestly, with hands outstretched to keep the pair asunder, " what is the cause of quarrel, that we may see whether honourable settlement may not be arrived at ? "

The bowman looked down at his feet and then up at the moon. " Parbleu ! " he cried, " the cause of quarrel ? Why, mon petit, it was years ago in Limousin, and how can I bear in mind what was the cause of it ? Simon there hath it at the end of his tongue."

" Not I, in troth," replied the other ; " I have had other things to think of. There was some sort of bickering over dice, or wine, or was it a woman, coz ? "

" Pasques Dieu ! but you have nicked it," cried Aylward, " it was indeed about a woman ; and the quarrel must go forward, for I am still of the same mind as before."

" What of the woman, then ? " asked Simon. " May the murrain strike me if I can call to mind aught about her."

" It was La Blanche Rose, maid at the sign of the ' Trois Corbeaux ' at Limoges. Bless her pretty heart ! Why, mon gar, I loved her."

" So did a many," quoth Simon. " I call her to mind now. On the very day that we fought over the little hussy, she went off with Evan ap Price, a long-legged Welsh dagsman. They have a hostel of their own now, somewhere on the banks of Garonne, where the landlord drinks so much of the liquor that there is little left for the customers."

" So ends our quarrel, then," said Aylward, sheathing his sword. " A Welsh dagsman, i' faith ! C'était mauvais goût, camarade, and the more so when she had a jolly archer and a lusty man-at-arms to choose from."

" True, old lad. And it is as well that we can compose our differences honourably, for Sir Nigel had been out at the first clash of steel ; and he hath sworn that if there be quarrelling in the garrison he would smite the right hand from the broilers. You know him of old, and that he is like to be as good as his word."

" Mort Dieu ! yes. But there are ale, mead, and wine in the buttery, and the steward a merry rogue, who will not haggle over a quart or two. Buvons, mon gar, for it is not every day that two old friends come together."

The old soldiers and Hordle John strode off together in all good-fellowship. Alleyne had turned to follow them, when he felt a touch upon his shoulder, and found a young page by his side.

" The Lord Loring commands," said the boy, " that you will follow me to the great chamber, and await him there."

" But my comrades ? "

" His commands were for you alone."

Alleyne followed the messenger to the east end of the courtyard, where a broad flight of steps led up to the door-way of the main hall, the outer wall of which is washed by the waters of the Avon. As designed at first, no dwelling had been allotted to the lord of the castle and his family but the dark and dismal basement story of the keep. A more civilised or more effeminate generation, however, had refused to be pent up in such a cellar, and the hall with its neighbouring chambers had been added for their accommodation. Up the broad steps Alleyne went, still following his boyish guide, until at the folding oak doors the latter paused, and ushered him into the main hall of the castle.

On entering the room the clerk looked round ; but, seeing no one, he continued to stand, his cap in his hand, examining with the greatest interest a chamber which was so different to any to which he was accustomed. The days had gone by when a nobleman's hall was but a barn-like rush-strewn enclosure, the common lounge and eating room of every inmate of the castle. The Crusaders had brought back with them experiences of domestic luxuries, of Damascus carpets and rugs of Aleppo, which made them impatient of the hideous bareness and want of privacy which they found in their ancestral strongholds. Still stronger, however, had been the influence of the great French war ; for, however well matched the nations might be in martial exercises, there could be no question but that our neighbours were infinitely superior to us in the arts of peace. A stream of returning knights, of wounded soldiers, and of unransomed French noblemen, had been for a quarter of a century continually pouring into England, every one of whom exerted an influence in the direction of greater domestic refinement ; while ship-loads of French furniture from Calais, Rouen and other plundered towns, had supplied our own artisans with models on which to shape their work. Hence, in most English castles, and in Castle Twynham among the rest, chambers were to be found which would seem to be not wanting either in beauty or in comfort.

In the great stone fireplace a log fire was spurting and crackling, throwing out a ruddy glare which, with the four bracket-lamps which stood at each corner of the room, gave a bright and lightsome air to the whole apartment. Above was a wreath-work of blazonry, extending up to the carved and corniced oaken roof ; while on either side stood the high canopied chairs placed for the master of the house and for his most honoured guest. The walls were hung all round with most elaborate and brightly coloured tapestry representing the achievements of Sir Bevis of Hampton, and behind this convenient screen were stored the tables dormant and benches which would be needed for banquet or high festivity. The floor was of polished tiles, with a square of red and black diapered Flemish carpet in the centre ; and many settees, cushions, folding chairs and carved bancals littered all over it. At the further end was a long black buffet or dresser, thickly covered with gold cups, silver salvers and other such valuables. All this Alleyne examined with curious eyes ; but most interesting of all to him was a small ebony table at his very side, on which, by the side of a chess-board and the scattered chessmen, there lay an open manuscript written in a right clerkly hand, and set forth with brave flourishes and devices along the margins. In vain Alleyne bethought him of where he was, and of those laws of good breeding and decorum which should restrain him : those coloured capitals and black even lines drew his hand down to them as the loadstone draws the needle, until, almost before he knew it, he was standing with the romance of Garin de Montglane before his eyes, so absorbed in its contents as to be completely oblivious both of where he was and why he had come there.

He was brought back to himself, however, by a sudden little ripple of quick feminine laughter. Aghast, he dropped the manuscript among the chessmen and stared in bewilderment round the room. It was as empty and as still as ever. Again he stretched his hand out to the romance, and again came that roguish burst of merriment. He looked up at the ceiling, back at the closed door, and round at the stiff folds of motionless tapestry. Of a sudden, however, he caught a quick shimmer from the corner of a high-backed bancal in front of him, and, shifting a pace or two to the side, saw a white slender hand, which held a mirror of polished silver in such a way that the concealed observer could see without being seen. He stood irresolute, uncertain whether to advance or to take no notice ; but, even as he hesitated, the mirror was whipped in, and a tall and stately young lady swept out from behind the oaken screen, with a dancing light of mischief in her eyes. Alleyne started with astonishment as he recognised the very maiden who had suffered from his brother's violence in the forest. She no longer wore her gay riding-dress, however, but was attired in a long sweeping robe of black velvet of Bruges, with delicate tracery of white lace at neck and at wrist, scarce to be seen against her ivory skin. Beautiful as she had seemed to him before, the lithe charm of her figure and the proud, free grace of her bearing were enhanced now by the rich simplicity of her attire.

"Ah, you start," said she, with the same sidelong look of mischief, "and I cannot marvel at it. Didst not look to see the distressed damozel again. Oh that I were a minstrel, that I might put it into rhyme, with the whole romance—the luckless maid, the wicked socman and the virtuous clerk! So might our fame have gone down together for all time, and you be numbered with Sir Percival or Sir Galahad, or all the other rescuers of oppressed ladies."

"What I did," said Alleyne, "was too small a thing for thanks; and yet, if I may say it without offence, it was too grave and near a matter for mirth and raillery. I had counted on my brother's love, but God has willed that it should be otherwise. It is a joy to me to see you again, lady, and to know that you have reached home in safety, if this be indeed your home."

"Yes, in sooth, Castle Twynham is my home, and Sir Nigel Loring my father. I should have told you so this morning, but you said that you were coming hither, so I bethought me that I might hold it back as a surprise to you. Oh dear, but it was brave to see you!" she cried, bursting out a-laughing once more, standing with her hand pressed to her side, and her half-closed eyes twinkling with amusement. "You drew back and came forward with your eyes upon my book there, like the mouse who sniffs the cheese and yet dreads the trap."

"I take shame," said Allyene, "that I should have touched it."

"Nay, it warmed my very heart to see it. So glad was

I that I laughed for very pleasure. My fine preacher can himself be tempted then, thought I ; he is not made of another clay to the rest of us."

"God help me! I am the weakest of the weak," groaned Alleyne. "I pray that I may have more strength."

"And to what end ?" she asked sharply. "If you are, as I understand, to shut yourself for ever in your cell within the four walls of an abbey, then of what use would it be were your prayer to be answered ?"

"The use of my own salvation."

She turned from him with a pretty shrug and wave. "Is that all ?" she said. "Then you are no better than Father Christopher and the rest of them. Your own, your own, ever your own ! My father is the king's man, and when he rides into the press of fight he is not thinking ever of the saving of his own poor body ; he recks little enough if he leave it on the field. Why then should you, who are soldier of the spirit, be ever moping and hiding in cell or in cave, with minds full of your own concerns, while the world, which you should be mending, is going on its way, and neither sees nor hears you ? Were ye all as thoughtless of your own souls as the soldier is of his body, ye would be of more avail to the souls of others."

"There is sooth in what you say, lady," Alleyne answered ; "and yet I scarce can see what you would have the clergy and the church to do."

"I would have them live as others, and do men's work in the world, preaching by their lives rather than their words. I would have them come forth from their lonely places, mix with the borel folks, feel the pains and the pleasures, the cares and the rewards, the temptings and the stirrings of the common people. Let them toil, and swinken, and labour, and plough the land, and take wives to themselves——"

"Alas ! alas !" cried Alleyne, aghast, "you have surely sucked this poison from the man Wicliffe, of whom I have heard such evil things."

" Nay, I know him not. I have learned it by looking from mine own chamber window and marking these poor monks of the priory, their weary life, their profitless round. I have asked myself if the best which can be done with virtue is to shut it within high walls as though it were some savage creature. If the good will lock themselves up, and if the wicked will still wander free, then alas for the world ! "

Alleyne looked at her in astonishment for her cheek was flushed, her eyes gleaming, and her whole pose full of eloquence and conviction. Yet in an instant she had changed again to her old expression of merriment leavened with mischief.

" Wilt do what I ask ? " said she.

" What is it, lady ? "

" Oh, most ungallant clerk ! A true knight would never have asked, but would have vowed upon the instant. 'Tis but to bear me out in what I say to my father."

" In what ? "

" In saying, if he ask, that it was south of the Christchurch road that I met you. I shall be shut up with the tirewomen else, and have a week of spindle and bodkin, when I would fain be galloping Troubadour up Wilverley Walk, or loosing little Roland at the Vinney Ridge herons."

" I shall not answer him if he ask."

" Not answer ! But he will have an answer. Nay, but you must not fail me, or it will go ill with me."

" But, lady," cried poor Alleyne in great distress, " how can I say that it was to the south of the road when I know well that it was four miles to the north ? "

" You will not say it ? "

" Surely, you will not, too, when you know that it is not so ?"

" Oh, I weary of your preaching ! " she cried, and swept away with a toss of her beautiful head, leaving Alleyne as cast down and ashamed as though he had himself proposed some infamous thing. She was back again in an instant, however, in another of her varying moods.

" Look at that, my friend ! " said she. " If you had been shut up in an abbey or in cell this day you could not have taught a wayward maiden to abide by the truth. Is it not so ? What avail is the shepherd if he leave his sheep ? "

" A sorry shepherd ! " said Alleyne humbly. " But here is your noble father."

" And you shall see how worthy a pupil I am. Father, I am much beholden to this young clerk, who was of service to me and helped me this very morning in Minstead Woods, four miles to the north of the Christchurch road, where I had no call to be, you having ordered it otherwise." All this she reeled off in a loud voice, and then glanced with sidelong questioning eyes at Alleyne for his approval.

Sir Nigel, who had entered the room with a silvery-haired old lady upon his arm, stared aghast at this sudden burst of candour.

" Maude, Maude ! " said he, shaking his head, " it is more hard for me to gain obedience from you than from the ten score drunken archers who followed me to Guienne. Yet, hush ! little one, for your fair lady-mother will be here anon, and there is no need that she should know it. We will keep you from the provost-marshal this journey. Away to your chamber, sweeting, and keep a blithe face, for she who confesses is shriven. And now, fair mother," he continued when his daughter had gone, " sit you here by the fire, for your blood runs colder than it did. Alleyne Edricson, I would have a word with you, for I would fain that you should take service under me. And here in good time comes my lady, without whose counsel it is not my wont to decide aught of import ; but, indeed, it was her own thought that you should come."

" For I have formed a good opinion of you, and can see that you are one who may be trusted," said the Lady

Loring. " And in good sooth my dear lord hath need of such a one by his side, for he recks so little of himself that there should be one there to look to his needs and meet his wants. You have seen the cloisters : it were well that you should see the world too, ere you make choice for life between them."

" It was for that very reason that my father willed that I should come forth into the world at my twentieth year," said Alleyne.

" Then your father was a man of good counsel," said she, " and you cannot carry out his will better than by going on this path, where all that is noble and gallant in England will be your companions."

" You can ride ? " asked Sir Nigel, looking at the youth with puckered eyes.

" Yes, I have ridden much at the abbey."

" Yet there is a difference betwixt a friar's hack and a warrior's destrier. You can sing and play ? "

" On citole, flute and rebeck."

" Good ! You can read blazonry ? "

" Indifferent well."

" Then read this," quoth Sir Nigel, pointing upwards to one of the many quarterings which adorned the wall over the fireplace.

" Argent," Alleyne answered, " a fess azure charged with three lozenges dividing three mullets sable. Over all, on an escutcheon of the first, a jambe gules."

" A jambe gules erased," said Sir Nigel, shaking his head solemnly. " Yet it is not amiss for a monk-bred man. I trust that you are lowly and serviceable ? "

" I have served all my life, my lord."

" Canst carve too ? "

" I have carved two days a week for the brethren."

" A model truly ! Wilt make a squire of squires. But tell me, I pray, canst curl hair ? "

" No, my lord, but I could learn."

" It is of import," said he, " for I love to keep my hair well ordered, seeing that the weight of my helmet for

thirty years hath in some degree frayed it upon the top."
He pulled off his velvet cap of maintenance as he spoke,
and displayed a pate which was as bald as an egg, and
shone bravely in the firelight. " You see," said he,
whisking round, and showing one little strip where a line
of scattered hairs, like the last survivors in some fatal
field, still barely held their own against the fate which had
fallen upon their comrades ; " these locks need some
little oiling and curling, for I doubt not that if you look
slantwise at my head, when the light is good, you will
yourself perceive that there are places where the hair is
sparse."

" It is for you also to bear the purse," said the lady ;
" for my sweet lord is of so free and gracious a temper
that he would give it gaily to the first who asked alms of
him. All these things, with some knowledge of venerie,
and of the management of horse, hawk and hound, with
the grace and hardihood and courtesy which are proper
to your age, will make you a fit squire for Sir Nigel
Loring."

" Alas ! lady," Alleyne answered, " I know well the
great honour that you have done me in deeming me
worthy to wait upon so renowned a knight, yet I am so
conscious of my own weakness that I scarce dare incur
duties which I might be so ill-fitted to fulfil."

" Modesty and a humble mind," said she, " are the
very first and rarest gifts in page or squire. Your words
prove that you have these, and all the rest is but the work
of use and of time. But there is no call for haste. Rest
upon it for the night, and let your orisons ask for guidance
in the matter. We knew your father well, and would fain
help his son, though we have small cause to love your
brother the socman, who is for ever stirring up strife in
the county."

" We can scarce hope," said Nigel, " to have all ready
for our start before the feast of St. Luke, for there is much
to be done in the time. You will have leisure therefore,
if it please you to take service under me, in which to learn

your devoir. Bertrand, my daughter's page, is hot to go ; but in sooth he is over young for such rough work as may be before us."

" And I have one favour to crave from you," added the lady of the castle, as Alleyne turned to leave their presence. " You have, as I understand, much learning which you have acquired at Beaulieu."

" Little enough, lady, compared with those who were my teachers."

" Yet enough for my purpose, I doubt not. For I would have you give an hour or two a day whilst you are with us in discoursing with my daughter, the Lady Maude ; for she is somewhat backward, I fear, and hath no love for letters, save for these poor fond romances, which do but fill her empty head with dreams of enchanted maidens and of errant cavaliers. Father Christopher comes over after nones from the priory, but he is stricken with years and slow of speech, so that she gets small profit from his teaching. I would have you do what you can with her, and with Agatha my young tire-woman, and with Dorothy Pierpoint."

And so Alleyne found himself not only chosen as squire to a knight, but also as squire to three damozels, which was even farther from the part which he had thought to play in the world. Yet he could but agree to do what he might, and so went forth from the castle hall with his face flushed and his head in a whirl at the thought of the strange and perilous paths which his feet were destined to tread.

12. *How Alleyne Learned more than he could Teach*

AND now there came a time of stir and bustle, of furbishing of arms and clang of hammer from all the southland counties. Fast spread the tidings from thorpe to thorpe and from castle to castle, that the old game was afoot once more, and the lions and lilies to be in the field with the early spring. Great news this for that fierce old country, whose trade for a generation had been war, her exports archers and her imports prisoners. For six years her sons had chafed under an unwonted peace. Now they flew to their arms as to their birthright. The old soldiers of Crécy, of Nogent and of Poictiers were glad to think that they might hear the war-trumpet once more, and gladder still were the hot youth who had chafed for years under the martial tales of their sires. To pierce the great mountains of the south, to fight the tamers of the fiery Moors, to follow the greatest captain of the age, to find sunny cornfields and vineyards, when the marches of Picardy and Normandy were as bare and bleak as the Jedburgh forests—here was a golden prospect for a race of warriors. From sea to sea there was stringing of bows in the cottage and clang of steel in the castle.

Nor did it take long for every stronghold to pour forth its cavalry, and every hamlet its footmen. Through the late autumn and the early winter every road and country lane resounded with nakir and trumpet, with the neigh of the war horse and the clatter of marching men. From the Wrekin in the Welsh marches to the Cotswolds in the west, or Butser in the south, there was no hill-top from which the peasant might not have seen the bright shimmer of arms, the toss and flutter of plume and of pensil. From bye-path, from woodland clearing or from winding moor-side track these little rivulets of steel united in the larger roads to form a broader stream, growing ever fuller and larger as it approached the nearest or most commodious seaport. And there all day, and day after day, there was bustle and crowding and labour, while the great ships loaded up, and one after the other spread their white pinions and darted off to the open sea, amid the clash of cymbals and rolling of drums and lusty shouts of those who went and of those who waited. From Orwell to the Dart there was no port which did not send forth its little fleet, gay with streamer and bunting, as for a joyous festival. Thus in the season of the waning days the might of England put forth on to the waters.

In the ancient and populous county of Hampshire there was no lack of leaders or of soldiers for a service which promised either honour or profit. In the north the Saracen's head of the Brocas and the scarlet fish of the De Roches were waving over a strong body of archers from Holt, Woolmer and Harewood forests. De Borhunte was up in the east, and Sir John de Montague in the west. Sir Luke de Ponynges, Sir Thomas West, Sir Maurice de Bruin, Sir Arthur Lipscombe, Sir Walter Ramsey and stout Sir Oliver Buttesthorn were all marching south with levies from Andover, Alresford, Odiham and Winchester, while from Sussex came Sir John Clinton, Sir Thomas Cheyne and Sir John Fallislee, with a troop of picked men-at-arms, making for their port at Southampton. Greatest of all the musters, however, was that at Twynham Castle, for the name and the fame of Sir Nigel Loring drew towards him the keenest and boldest spirits, all eager to serve under so valiant a leader. Archers from the New Forest and the Forest of Bere, billmen from the pleasant country which is watered by the Stour, the Avon and the Itchen, young cavaliers from the ancient Hampshire houses, all were pushing for Christchurch to take service under the banner of the five scarlet roses.

And now, could Sir Nigel have shown the bachelles of land which the laws of rank required, he might well have cut his forked pennon into a square banner, and taken such a following into the field as would have supported the dignity of a banneret. But poverty was heavy upon him, his land was scant, his coffers empty, and the very castle which covered him the holding of another. Sore was his heart when he saw rare bowmen and war-hardened spearmen turned away from his gates, for the lack of the money which might equip and pay them. Yet the letter which Aylward had brought him gave him powers which he was not slow to use. In it Sir Claude Latour, the Gascon lieutenant of the White Company, assured him that there remained in his keeping enough to fit out a hundred archers and twenty men-at-arms, which, joined to the three hundred veteran companions already in France, would make a force which any leader might be proud to command. Carefully and sagaciously the veteran knight chose out his men from the swarm of volunteers. Many an anxious consultation he held with Black Simon, Sam Aylward and other of his more experienced followers, as to who should come and who should stay. By All Saints' Day, however, ere the last leaves had fluttered to earth in the Wilverley and Holmesley glades, he had filled up his full numbers, and mustered under his banner as stout a following of Hampshire foresters as ever twanged their war-bows. Twenty men-at-arms, too, well mounted and equipped, formed the cavalry of the party, while young Peter Terlake of Fareham, and Walter Ford of Botley, the martial sons of martial sires, came at their own cost to wait upon Sir Nigel and to share with Alleyne Edricson the duties of his squireship.

Yet, even after the enrolment, there was much to be done ere the party could proceed upon its way. For armour, swords and lances there was no need to take much forethought, for they were to be had both better and cheaper in Bordeaux than in England. With the long-bow, however, it was different. Yew staves indeed might be got in Spain, but it was well to take enough and to spare with them. Then three spare cords should be carried for each bow, with a great store of arrow-heads, besides the brigandines of chain mail, the wadded steel caps, and the brassarts or arm-guards, which were the proper equipment of the archer. Above all, the women for miles round were hard at work cutting the white surcoats which were the badge of the Company, and adorning them with the red lion of St. George upon the centre of the breast. When all was completed and the muster called in the castle yard, the oldest soldier of the French wars was fain to confess that he had never looked upon a better equipped or more warlike body of men, from the old knight with

his silk jupon, sitting his great black war-horse in the front
of them, to Hordle John, the giant recruit, who leaned
carelessly upon a huge black bow-stave in the rear. Of
the six score, fully half had seen service before, while a
fair sprinkling were men who had followed the wars all
their lives, and had a hand in those battles which had made
the whole world ring with the fame and the wonder of the
island infantry.

Six long weeks were taken in these preparations, and it
was close on Martinmas ere all was ready for a start.
Nigh two months had Alleyne Edricson been in Castle
Twynham—months which were fated to turn the whole
current of his life, to divert it from that dark and lonely
bourne towards which it tended, and to guide it into freer
and more sunlit channels. Already he had learned to bless
his father for that wise provision which had made him
seek to know the world ere he had ventured to renounce it.

For it was a very different place from that which he had
pictured—very different from that which he had heard
described when the master of the novices held forth to
his charges upon the ravening wolves who lurked for
them beyond the peaceful folds of Beaulieu. There was
cruelty in it, doubtless, and lust and sin and sorrow ; but
were there not virtues to atone, robust positive virtues,
which did not shrink from temptation, which held their
own in all the rough blasts of the work-a-day world ?
How colourless by contrast appeared the sinlessness which
came from inability to sin, the conquest which was
attained by flying from the enemy ! Monk-bred as he
was, Alleyne had native shrewdness and a mind which was
young enough to form new conclusions and to outgrow old
ones. He could not fail to see that the men with whom
he was thrown in contact, rough-tongued, fierce and
quarrelsome as they were, were yet of deeper nature and
of more service in the world than the ox-eyed brethren
who rose and ate and slept from year's end to year's end
in their own narrow stagnant circle of existence. Abbot
Berghersh was a good man, but how was he better than

this kindly knight, who lived as simple a life, held as lofty and inflexible an ideal of duty, and did with all his fearless heart whatever came to his hand to do ?   In turning from the service of the one to that of the other, Alleyne could not feel that he was lowering his aims in life.   True that his gentle and thoughtful nature recoiled from the grim work of war, yet in those days of martial orders and militant brotherhoods there was no gulf fixed betwixt the priest and the soldier.   The man of God and the man of the sword might without scandal be united in the same individual.   Why then should he, a mere clerk, have scruples when so fair a chance lay in his way of carrying out the spirit as well as the letter of his father's provision ? Much struggle it cost him, anxious spirit-questionings and midnight prayings, with many a doubt and a misgiving ; but the issue was that ere he had been three days in Castle Twynham he had taken service under Sir Nigel, and had accepted horse and harness, the same to be paid for out of his share of the profits of the expedition.   Henceforth for seven hours a day he strove in the tiltyard to qualify himself to be a worthy squire to so worthy a knight.   Young, supple and active, with all the pent energies from years of pure and healthy living, it was not long before he could manage his horse and his weapon well enough to earn an approving nod from critical men-at-arms, or to hold his own against Terlake and Ford, his fellow-servitors.

But were there no other considerations which swayed him from the cloisters towards the world ?   So complex is the human spirit that it can itself scarce discern the deep springs which impel it to action.   Yet to Alleyne had been opened now a side of life of which he had been as innocent as a child, but one which was of such deep import that it could not fail to influence him in choosing his path.   A woman, in monkish precepts, had been the embodiment and concentration of what was dangerous and evil—a focus whence spread all that was to be dreaded and avoided.   So defiling was her presence that a true

Cistercian might not raise his eyes to her face or touch her finger-tips under ban of church and fear of deadly sin. Yet here, day after day, for an hour after nones, and for an hour before vespers, he found himself in close communion with three maidens, all young, all fair, and all therefore doubly dangerous from the monkish standpoint. Yet he found that in their presence he was conscious of a quick sympathy, a pleasant ease, a ready response to all that was most gentle and best in himself, which filled his soul with a vague and new-found joy.

And yet the Lady Maude Loring was no easy pupil to handle. An older and more world-wise man might have been puzzled by her varying moods, her sudden prejudices, her quick resentment at all constraint and authority. Did a subject interest her, was there space in it for either romance or imagination, she would fly through it with her subtle active mind, leaving her two fellow-students and even her teacher toiling behind her. On the other hand, were there dull patience needed with steady toil and strain of memory, no single fact could by any driving be fixed in her mind. Alleyne might talk to her of the stories of old gods and heroes, of gallant deeds and lofty aims, or he might hold forth upon moon and stars, and let his fancy wander over the hidden secrets of the universe, and he would have a rapt listener with flushed cheeks and eloquent eyes, who could repeat after him the very words which had fallen from his lips. But when it came to almagest and astrolabe, the counting of figures and reckoning of epicycles, away would go her thoughts to horse and hound, and a vacant eye and listless face would warn the teacher that he had lost his hold upon his scholar. Then he had but to bring out the old romance book from the priory, with befingered cover of sheepskin and gold letters upon a purple ground, to entice her wayward mind back to the paths of learning.

At times, too, when the wild fit was upon her, she would break into pertness and rebel openly against Alleyne's gentle firmness. Yet he would jog quietly on with his teachings, taking no heed to her mutiny, until suddenly she would be conquered by his patience, and break into self-revilings a hundred times stronger than her fault demanded. It chanced however that, on one of these mornings when the evil mood was upon her, Agatha, the young tirewoman, thinking to please her mistress, began also to toss her head and make tart rejoinder to the teacher's questions. In an instant the Lady Maude had turned upon her two blazing eyes and a face which was blanched with anger.

"You would dare!" said she. "You would dare!"

The frightened tirewoman tried to excuse herself. "But, my fair lady," she stammered, "what have I done? I have said no more than I heard."

"You would dare!" repeated the lady in a choking voice. "You, a graceless baggage, a foolish lack-brain, with no thought above the hemming of shifts! And he so kindly, and hendy and long-suffering! You would—ha, you may well flee the room!"

She had spoken with a rising voice, and a clasping and opening of her long white fingers, so that it was no marvel that ere the speech was over the skirts of Agatha were whisking round the door and the click of her sobs to be heard dying swiftly away down the corridor.

Alleyne stared open-eyed at this tigress who had sprung so suddenly to his rescue. "There is no need for such anger," he said mildly. "The maid's words have done me no scath. It is yourself who have erred."

"I know it," she cried; "I am a most wicked woman. But it is bad enough that one should misuse you. Ma foi! I will see that there is not a second one."

"Nay, nay, no one has misused me," he answered. "But the fault lies in your hot and bitter words. You have called her a baggage and a lack-brain, and I know not what."

"And you are he who taught me to speak the truth," she cried. "Now I have spoken it, and yet I cannot please you. Lack-brain she is, and lack-brain I shall call her."

Such was the sample of the sudden janglings which marred the peace of that little class. As the weeks passed, however, they became fewer and less violent, as Alleyne's firm and constant nature gained sway and influence over the Lady Maude. And yet, sooth to say, there were times when he had to ask himself whether it was not the Lady Maude who was gaining sway and influence over him. If she were changing, so was he. In drawing her up from the world, he was day by day being himself dragged down towards it. In vain he strove and reasoned with himself as to the madness of letting his mind rest upon Sir Nigel's daughter. What was he—a younger son, a penniless clerk, a squire unable to pay for his own harness—that he should dare to raise his eyes to the fairest maid in Hampshire ? So spake reason ; but, in spite of all, her voice was ever in his ears and her image in his heart. Stronger than reason, stronger than cloister teachings, stronger than all that might hold him back, was that old, old tyrant who will brook no rival in the kingdom of youth.

And yet it was a surprise and a shock to himself to find how deeply she had entered into his life ; how completely those vague ambitions and yearnings which had filled his spiritual nature centred themselves now upon this thing of earth. He had scarce dared to face the change which had come upon him, when a few sudden chance words showed it all up hard and clear, like a lightning flash in the darkness.

He had ridden over to Poole, one November day, with his fellow-squire, Peter Terlake, in quest of certain yew-staves from Wat Swathling, the Dorsetshire armourer. The day for their departure had almost come, and the two youths spurred it over the lonely downs at the top of their speed on their homeward course, for evening had fallen and there was much to be done. Peter was a hard, wiry, brown-faced country-bred lad, who looked on the coming war as the schoolboy looks on his holidays. This day, however, he had been sombre and mute, with scarce a word a mile to bestow upon his comrade.

" Tell me, Alleyne Edricson," he broke out, suddenly, as they clattered along the winding track which leads over the Bournemouth hills, " has it not seemed to you that of late the Lady Maude is paler and more silent than is her wont ? "

" It may be so," the other answered shortly.

" And would rather sit distrait by her oriel than ride gaily to the chase as of old. Methinks, Alleyne, it is this learning which you have taught her that has taken all the life and sap from her. It is more than she can master, like a heavy spear to a light rider."

" Her lady-mother has so ordered it," said Alleyne.

" By our Lady ! and withouten disrespect," quoth Terlake, " it is in my mind that her lady-mother is more fitted to lead a company to a storming than to have the up-bringing of this tender and milk-white maid. Hark ye, lad Alleyne, to what I never told man or woman yet. I love the fair Lady Maude, and would give the last drop of my heart's blood to serve her." He spoke with a gasping voice, and his face flushed crimson in the moon-light.

Alleyne said nothing, but his heart seemed to turn to a lump of ice in his bosom.

" My father has broad acres," the other continued, " from Fareham Creek to the slope of the Portsdown Hill. There is filling of granges, hewing of wood, malting of grain and herding of sheep as much as heart could wish, and I the only son. Sure am I that Sir Nigel would be blithe at such a match."

" But how of the lady ? " asked Alleyne, with dry lips.

" Ah, lad, there lies my trouble. It is a toss of the head and a droop of the eyes if I say one word of what is in my mind. 'Twere as easy to woo the snow-dame that we shaped last winter in our castle yard. I did but ask her yesternight for her green veil, that I might bear it as a token or lambrequin upon my helm ; but she flashed out at me that she kept it for a better man, and then all in a breath asked pardon for that she had spoke so rudely.

148

Yet she would not take back the words either, nor would she grant the veil. Has it seemed to thee, Alleyne, that she loves anyone ? ''

" Nay, I cannot say," said Alleyne, with a wild throb of sudden hope in his heart.

" I have thought so, and yet I cannot name the man. Indeed, save myself, and Walter Ford, and you, who are half a clerk, and Father Christopher of the Priory, and Bertrand the page, who is there whom she sees ? ''

" I cannot tell," quoth Alleyne shortly : and the two squires rode on again, each intent upon his own thoughts.

Next day at morning lesson the teacher observed that his pupil was indeed looking pale and jaded, with listless eyes and a weary manner. He was heavy-hearted to note the grievous change in her.

" Your mistress, I fear, is ill, Agatha," he said to the tire-woman, when the Lady Maude had sought her chamber.

The maid looked aslant at him with laughing eyes. " It is not an illness that kills," quoth she.

" Pray God not ! " he cried. " But tell me, Agatha, what it is that ails her."

" Methinks that I could lay my hand upon another who is smitten with the same trouble," said she, with the same sidelong look. " Canst not give a name to it, and thou so skilled in leechcraft ? ''

" Nay, save that she seems aweary."

" Well, bethink you that it is but three days ere you will all be gone, and Castle Twynham be as dull as the Priory. Is there not enough there to cloud a lady's brow ? ''

" In sooth, yes," he answered ; " I had forgot that she is about to lose her father."

" Her father ! " cried the tirewoman, with a little trill of laughter. " Oh, simple, simple ! " And she was off down the passage like arrow from bow, while Alleyne stood gazing after her, betwixt hope and doubt, scarce daring to put faith in the meaning which seemed to underlie her words.

13. *How the White Company set forth to the Wars*

ST. LUKE'S day had come and had gone, and it was in the season of Martinmas, when the oxen are driven in to the slaughter, that the White Company was ready for its journey. Loud shrieked the brazen bugles from keep and from gateway, and merry was the rattle of the war-drum, as the men gathered in the outer bailey, with torches to light them, for the morn had not yet broken. Alleyne, from the window of the armoury, looked down upon the strange scene—the circles of yellow flickering light, the lines of stern and bearded faces, the quick shimmer of arms and the lean heads of the horses. In front stood the bowmen, ten deep, with a fringe of under-officers, who paced hither and thither marshalling the ranks with curt precept or short rebuke. Behind were the little clump of steel-clad horsemen, their lances raised, with long pensils drooping down the oaken shafts. So silent and still were they, that they might have been metal-sheathed statues, were it not for the occasional quick impatient stamp of their chargers, or the rattle of chamfron against neck plates as they tossed and strained. A spear's length in front of them sat the spare and long-limbed figure of Black Simon, the Norwich fighting man, his fierce, deep-lined face framed in steel, and the silk guidon marked with the five scarlet roses slanting over his right shoulder. All round, in the edge of the circle of the light, stood the castle servants, the soldiers who were to form the garrison, and little knots of women, who sobbed in their aprons and called shrilly to their name-saints to watch over the Wat, or Will, or Peterkin who had turned his hand to the work of war.

The young squire was leaning forward, gazing at the stirring and martial scene, when he heard a short quick gasp at his shoulder, and there was the Lady Maude, with her hand to her heart, leaning up against the wall, slender and fair like a half-plucked lily. Her face was turned away from him, but he could see, by the sharp intake of her breath, that she was weeping bitterly.

" Alas ! alas ! " he cried, all unnerved at the sight, " why is it that you are so sad, lady ? "

" It is the sight of these brave men," she answered ; " and to think how many of them go and how few are like to find their way back. I have seen it before, when I was a little maid, in the year of the Prince's great battle. I remember then how they mustered in the bailey, even as they do now, and my lady-mother holding me in her arms at this very window that I might see the show."

" Please God, you will see them all back ere another year be out," said he.

She shook her head, looking round at him with flushed cheeks and eyes which sparkled in the lamp-light. " Oh, but I hate myself for being a woman ! " she cried, with a stamp of her little foot. " What can I do that is good ? Here I must bide, and talk and sew and spin, and spin and sew and talk. Ever the same dull round, with nothing at the end of it. And now you are going too, who could carry my thoughts out of these grey walls, and raise my mind above tapestry and distaffs. What can I do ? I am of no more use or value than that broken bow-stave."

" You are of such value to me," he cried, in a whirl of hot passionate words, " that all else has become nought. You are my heart, my life, my one and only thought. Oh, Maude, I cannot live without you, I cannot leave you without a word of love. All is changed to me since I have known you. I am poor and lowly and all unworthy of you ; but if great love may weigh down such defects, then mine may do it. Give me but one word of hope to take to the wars with me—but one. Ah, you shrink, you shudder ! My wild words have frightened you."

Twice she opened her lips, and twice no sound came from them. At last she spoke in a hard and measured voice, as one who dare not trust herself to speak too freely.

" This is over-sudden," she said ; " it is not so long

since the world was nothing to you. You have changed once ; perchance you may change again."

" Cruel ! " he cried, " who hath changed me ? "

" And then your brother," she continued with a little laugh, disregarding his question. " Methinks this hath become a family custom amongst the Edricsons. Nay, I am sorry ; I did not mean a jibe. But indeed, Alleyne, this hath come suddenly upon me, and I scarce know what to say."

" Say some word of hope, however distant—some kind word that I may cherish in my heart."

" Nay, Alleyne, it were a cruel kindness, and you have been too good and true a friend to me that I should use you despitefully. There cannot be a closer link between us. It is madness to think of it. Were there no other reasons, it is enough that my father and your brother would both cry out against it."

" My brother, what has he to do with it ? And your father——"

" Come, Alleyne, was it not you who would have me act fairly to all men, and, certes, to my father amongst them ? "

" You say truly," he cried, " you say truly. But you do not reject me, Maude ? You give me some ray of hope ? I do not ask pledge or promise. Say only that I am not hateful to you—that on some happier day I may hear kinder words from you."

Her eyes softened upon him, and a kind answer was on her lips, when a hoarse shout, with the clatter of arms and stamping of steeds, rose up from the bailey below. At the sound her face set, her eyes sparkled, and she stood with flushed cheek and head thrown back—a woman's body but a soul of fire.

" My father hath gone down," she cried. " Your place is by his side. Nay, look not at me, Alleyne. It is no time for dallying. Win my father's love, and all may follow. It is when the brave soldier hath done his devoir that he hopes for his reward. Farewell, and may God be with you ! " She held out her white, slim hand to him, but as he bent his lips over it she whisked away and was gone, leaving in his outstretched hand the very green veil for which poor Peter Terlake had craved in vain. Again the hoarse cheering burst out from below, and he heard the clang of the rising portcullis. Pressing the veil to his lips, he thrust it into the bosom of his tunic, and rushed as fast as feet could bear him to arm himself and join the muster.

The raw morning had broken ere the hot spiced ale was served round and the last farewell spoken. A cold wind blew up from the sea and ragged clouds drifted swiftly across the sky. The Christchurch townsfolk stood huddled about the Bridge of Avon, the women pulling tight their shawls and the men swathing themselves in their gaberdines, while down the winding path from the castle came the van of the little army, their feet clanging on the hard frozen road. First came Black Simon with his banner, bestriding a lean and powerful dapple-grey charger, as hard and wiry and warwise as himself. After him, riding three abreast, were nine men-at-arms, all picked soldiers, who had followed the French wars before, and knew the marches of Picardy as they knew the downs of their native Hampshire. They were armed to the teeth with lance, sword and mace, with square shields notched at the upper right-hand corner to serve as a spear-rest. For defence each man wore a coat of inter-laced leathern thongs strengthened at the shoulder, elbow and upper arm with slips of steel. Greaves and knee-pieces were also of leather backed by steel, and their gauntlets and shoes were of iron plates, craftily jointed. So, with jingle of arms and clatter of hoofs, they rode across the Bridge of Avon, while the burghers shouted lustily for the flag of the five roses and its gallant guard.

Close at the heels of the horses came two score archers, bearded and burly, their round targets on their backs and their long yellow bows, the most deadly weapon that the wit of man had yet devised, thrusting forth from behind their shoulders. From each man's girdle hung sword or axe, according to his humour, and over the right hip there jutted out the leathern quiver, with its bristle of goose, pigeon and peacock feathers. Behind the bowmen strode two drummers beating their nakirs, and two trumpeters in parti-coloured clothes. After them came twenty-seven sumpter-horses carrying tent-poles, cloth, spare arms, spurs, wedges, cooking kettles, horse-shoes, bags of nails, and the hundred other things which experience had shown to be needful in a harried and hostile country. A white mule with red trappings, led by a varlet, carried Sir Nigel's own napery and table comforts. Then came two score more archers, ten more men-at-arms, and finally a rearguard of twenty bowmen, with big John towering in the front rank and the veteran Aylward marching by his side, his battered harness and faded surcoat in strange contrast with the snow-white jupons and shining brigandines of his companions. A quick cross-fire of greetings and questions and rough West Saxon jests flew from rank to rank, or were bandied about betwixt the marching archers and the gazing crowd.

" Hola, Gaffer Higginson ! " cried Aylward, as he spied the portly figure of the village innkeeper. " No more of thy nut-brown, mon gar. We leave it behind us."

" By St. Paul, no ! " cried the other. " You take it with you. Devil a drop have you left in the great kilderkin. It was time for you to go."

" If your cask is leer, I warrant your purse is full, gaffer," shouted Hordle John. " See that you lay in good store of the best for our home-coming."

" See that you keep your throat whole for the drinking of it, archer," cried a voice, and the crowd laughed at the rough pleasantry.

" If you will warrant the beer, I will warrant the throat," said John composedly.

" Close up the ranks ! " cried Aylward. " En avant, mes enfants ! Ah, by my finger-bones, there is my sweet Mary from the Priory Mill ! Ma foi, but she is beautiful !

Adieu, Mary, ma chérie ! Mon cœur est toujours à toi. Brace your belt, Watkin, man, and swing your shoulders as a free companion should. By my hilt ! your jerkins will be as dirty as mine ere you clap eyes on Hengistbury Head again."

The Company had marched to the turn of the road ere Sir Nigel Loring rode out from the gateway, mounted on Pommers, his great black war-horse, whose ponderous foot-fall on the wooden drawbridge echoed loudly from the gloomy arch which spanned it. Sir Nigel was still in his velvet dress of peace, with flat velvet cap of maintenance, and curling ostrich feather clasped in a golden brooch. To his three squires riding behind him it looked as though he bore the bird's egg as well as its feather, for the back of his bald pate shone like a globe of ivory. He bore no arms save the long and heavy sword which hung at his saddle-bow ; but Terlake carried in front of him the high wivern-crested bassinet, Ford the heavy ash spear with swallow-tail pennon, while Alleyne was entrusted with the emblazoned shield. The Lady Loring rode her palfrey at her lord's bridle-arm, for she would see him as far as the edge of the forest, and ever and anon she turned her hard-lined face up wistfully to him and ran a questioning eye over his apparel and appointments.

" I trust that there is nothing forgot," she said, beckoning to Alleyne to ride on her farther side. " I trust him to you, Edricson. Hosen, shirts, cyclas and under-jupons are in the brown basket on the left side of the mule. His wine he takes hot when the nights are cold, malvoisie or vernage, with as much spice as would cover the thumb-nail. See that he hath a change if he come back hot from the tilting. There is goose-grease in a box, if the old scars ache at the turn of the weather. Let his blankets be dry and——"

" Nay, my heart's life," the little knight interrupted, " trouble not now about such matters. Why so pale and wan, Edricson ? Is it not enow to make a man's heart dance to see this noble company, such valiant men-at-arms, such lusty archers ? By St. Paul ! I should be ill to please if I were not blithe to see the red roses flying at the head of so noble a following ! "

" The purse I have already given you, Edricson," continued the lady. " There are in it twenty-three marks, one noble, three shillings and fourpence, which is a great treasure for one man to carry. And I pray you to bear in mind, Edricson, that he hath two pair of shoes, those of red leather for common use, and the others with golden toe-chains, which he may wear should he chance to drink wine with the Prince or with Chandos."

" My sweet bird," said Sir Nigel, " I am right loth to part from you, but we are now at the fringe of the forest, and it is not right that I should take the chatelaine too far from her trust."

" But oh, my dear lord," she cried with a trembling lip, " let me bide with you for one furlong further—or one and a half, perhaps. You may spare me this out of the weary miles that you will journey alone."

" Come then, my heart's comfort," he answered. " But I must crave a gage from thee. It is my custom, dearling, and hath been since I have first known thee, to proclaim by herald in such camps, townships or fortalices as I may chance to visit, that my ladylove being beyond compare the fairest and sweetest in Christendom, I should deem it great honour and kindly condescension if any cavalier would run three courses against me with sharpened lances, should he chance to have a lady whose claim he was willing to advance. I pray you then, my fair dove, that you will vouchsafe to me one of those doe-skin gloves, that I may wear it as the badge of her whose servant I shall ever be."

" Alack and alas for the fairest and sweetest ! " she cried. " Fair and sweet I would fain be for your dear sake, my lord, but old I am and ugly, and the knights would laugh should you lay lance in rest in such a cause."

" Edricson," quoth Sir Nigel, " you have young eyes,

and mine are somewhat bedimmed. Should you chance to see a knight laugh, or smile, or even, look you, arch his brows, or purse his mouth, or in any way show surprise that I should uphold the Lady Mary, you will take particular note of his name, his coat-armour and his lodging. Your glove, my life's desire!"

The Lady Mary Loring slipped her hand from her yellow leather gauntlet, and he, lifting it with dainty reverence, bound it to the front of his velvet cap.

"It is with mine other guardian angels," quoth he, pointing at the saints' medals which hung beside it. "And now, my dearest, you have come far enow. May the Virgin guard and prosper thee! One kiss!" He bent down from his saddle, and then striking spurs into his horse's sides, he galloped at top speed after his men, with his three squires at his heels. Half a mile farther, where the road topped a hill, they looked back, and the Lady Mary on her white palfrey was still where they had left her. A moment later they were on the downward slope, and she had vanished from their view.

14. *How Sir Nigel sought for a Wayside Venture*

FOR a time Sir Nigel was very moody and downcast, with bent brows and eyes upon the pommel of his saddle. Edricson and Terlake rode behind him in little better case, while Ford, a careless and light-hearted youth, grinned at the melancholy of his companions, and flourished his lord's heavy spear, making a point to right and a point to left, as though he were a paladin contending against a host of assailants. Sir Nigel happening, however, to turn himself in his saddle, Ford instantly became as stiff and as rigid as though he had been struck with a palsy. The four rode alone, for the archers had passed a curve in the road, though Alleyne could still hear the heavy clump, clump of their marching,

or catch a glimpse of the sparkle of steel through the tangle
of leafless branches.

"Ride by my side, friends, I entreat of you," said the
knight, reigning in his steed that they might come abreast
of him. "For since it hath pleased you to follow me to
the wars, it were well that you should know how you may
best serve me. I doubt not, Terlake, that you will show
yourself a worthy son of a valiant father, and you, Ford, of
yours; and you, Edricson, that you are mindful of the
old-time house from which all men know that you are
sprung. And first I would have you bear very steadfastly in
mind that our setting forth is by no means for the purpose
of gaining spoil or exacting ransom, though it may well
happen that such may come to us also. We go to France,
and from thence, I trust, to Spain, in humble search of a
field in which we may win advancement and perchance
some small share of glory. For this purpose I would
have you know that it is not my wont to let any occasion
pass where it is in any way possible that honour may be
gained. I would have you bear this in mind, and give
great heed to it that you may bring me word of all cartels,
challenges, wrongs, tyrannies, infamies and wronging of
damsels. Nor is any occasion too small to take note of,
for I have known such trifles as the dropping of a gauntlet,
or the flicking of a breadcrumb, when well and properly
followed up, lead to a most noble spear-running. But,
Edricson, do I not see a cavalier who rides down yonder
road amongst the nether shaw? It would be well, perchance, that you should give him greeting from me, and,
should he be of gentle blood, it may be that he would care
to exchange thrusts with me."

"Why, my lord," quoth Ford, standing in his stirrups
and shading his eyes, "it is old Hob Davidson, the fat
miller of Milton!"

"Ah, so it is, indeed," said Sir Nigel, puckering his
cheeks; "but wayside ventures are not to be scorned, for
I have seen no finer passages than are to be had from
such chance meetings, when cavaliers are willing to ad-

vance themselves. I can well remember that two leagues
from the town of Rheims I met a very valiant and courteous cavalier of France, with whom I had gentle and most
honourable contention for upwards of an hour. It hath
ever grieved me that I had not his name, for he smote
upon me with a mace and went upon his way ere I was in
condition to have much speech with him ; but his arms
were an allurion in chief above a fess azure. I was also
on such an occasion thrust through the shoulder by Lyon
de Montcourt, whom I met on the high road betwixt
Libourne and Bordeaux. I met him but the once, but I
have never seen a man for whom I bear a greater love and
esteem. And so also with the squire Le Bourg Capillet,
who would have been a very valiant captain had he
lived."

" He is dead then ? " asked Alleyne Edricson.

" Alas ! it was my ill fate to slay him in a bickering
which broke out in a field near the township of Tarbes. I
cannot call to mind how the thing came about, for it was
in the year of the Prince's ride through Languedoc, when
there was much fine skirmishing to be had at barriers.
By St. Paul ! I do not think that any honourable cavalier
could ask for better chance of advancement than might
be had by spurring forth before the army and riding to the
gateways of Narbonne, or Bergerac, or Mont Giscar,
where some courteous gentleman would ever be at wait
to do what he might to meet your wish to ease you of your
vow. Such a one at Ventadour ran three courses with
me betwixt daybreak and sunrise, to the great exaltation
of his lady."

" And did you slay him also, my lord ? " asked Ford
with reverence.

" I could never learn, for he was carried within the
barrier, and as I had chanced to break the bone of my leg
it was a great unease to me to ride or even to stand. Yet
by the goodness of heaven and the pious intercession of
the valiant St. George, I was able to sit my charger in the
great battle, which was no very long time afterwards.

But what have we here ?   A very fair and courtly maiden, or I mistake."

It was indeed a tall and buxom country lass, with a basket of spinach leaves upon her head, and a great slab of bacon tucked under one arm.   She bobbed a frightened curtsy as Sir Nigel swept his velvet hat from his head and reined up his great charger.

" God be with thee, fair maiden ! " said he.

" God guard thee, my lord ! " she answered, speaking in the broadest West Saxon speech and balancing herself first on one foot and then on the other in her bashfulness.

" Fear not, my fair damsel," said Sir Nigel, " but tell me if perchance a poor and most unworthy knight can in any wise be of service to you.   Should it chance that you have been used despitefully, it may be that I may obtain justice for you."

" Lawk no, kind sir," she answered, clutching her bacon the tighter, as though some design upon it might be hid under this knightly offer.   " I be the milking wench o' fairmer Arnold, and he be as kind a maister as heart could wish."

" It is well," said he, and with a shake of the bridle rode on down the woodland path.   " I would have you bear in mind," he continued to his squires, " that gentle courtesy is not, as is the base use of so many false knights, to be shown only to maidens of high degree, for there is no woman so humble that a true knight may not listen to her tale of wrong.   But here comes a cavalier who is indeed in haste.   Perchance it would be well that we should ask him whither he rides, for it may be that he is one who desires to advance himself in chivalry."

The bleak, hard, wind-swept road dipped down in front of them into a little valley, and then, writhing up the heathy slope upon the other side, lost itself among the gaunt pine-trees.   Far away between the black lines of trunks the quick glitter of steel marked where the Company pursued its way.   To the north stretched the tree country, but to the south, between two swelling downs, a glimpse might be caught of the cold grey shimmer of the sea, with the white fleck of a galley sail upon the distant sky-line. Just in front of the travellers a horseman was urging his steed up the slope, driving it on with whip and spur as one who rides for a set purpose. As he clattered up, Alleyne could see that the roan horse was grey with dust and flecked with foam, as though it had left many a mile behind it. The rider was a stern-faced man, hard of mouth and dry of eye, with a heavy sword clanking at his side, and a stiff white bundle swathed in linen balanced across the pommel of his saddle.

" The king's messenger ! " he bawled as he came up to them. " The messenger of the king ! Clear the causeway for the king's own man."

" Not so loudly, friend," quoth the little knight, reining his horse half round to bar the path. " I have myself been the king's man for thirty years and more, but I have not been wont to halloo about it on a peaceful highway."

" I ride in his service," cried the other, " and I carry that which belongs to him. You bar my path at your peril."

" Yet I have known the king's enemies claim to ride in his name," said Sir Nigel. " The foul fiend may lurk beneath a garment of light. We must have some sign or warrant of your mission."

" Then must I hew a passage," cried the stranger, with his shoulder braced round and his hand upon his hilt. " I am not to be stopped on the king's service by every gadabout."

" Should you be a gentleman of quarterings and coat-armour," lisped Sir Nigel, " I shall be very blithe to go further into the matter with you. If not, I have three very worthy squires, any one of whom would take the thing upon himself, and debate it with you in a very honourable way."

The man scowled from one to the other, and his hand stole away from his sword.

" You ask me for a sign," he said. " Here is a sign for

you, since you must have one." As he spoke he whirled
the covering from the object in front of him and showed
to their horror that it was a newly severed human leg.
" By God's tooth ! " he continued, with a brutal laugh,
" you ask me if I am a man of quarterings, and it is even
so, for I am officer to the verderer's court at Lyndhurst.
This thievish leg is to hang at Milton, and the other is
already at Brockenhurst, as a sign to all men of what comes
of being over fond of venison pasty."

" Faugh ! " cried Sir Nigel. " Pass on the other side
of the road, fellow, and let us have the wind of you. We
shall trot our horses, my friends, across this pleasant
valley, for, by Our Lady, a breath of God's fresh air is
right welcome after such a sight."

" We hoped to snare a falcon," said he presently, " but
we netted a carrion-crow. Ma foi ! but there are men
whose hearts are tougher than a boar's hide. For me, I
have played the old game of war since ever I had hair on
my chin, and I have seen ten thousand brave men in one
day with their faces to the sky, but I swear by Him who
made me that I cannot abide the work of the butcher."

" And yet, my fair lord," said Edricson, " there has,
from what I hear, been much of such devil's work in
France."

" Too much, too much," he answered. " But I have
ever observed that the foremost in the field are they who
would scorn to mishandle a prisoner ! By St. Paul ! it is
not they who carry the breach who are wont to sack the
town, but the laggard knaves who come crowding in when
a way has been cleared for them. But what is this among
the trees ? "

" It is a shrine of Our Lady," said Terlake, " and a
blind beggar who lives by the alms of those who worship
there."

" A shrine ! " cried the knight. " Then let us put up
an orison." Pulling off his cap, and clasping his hands, he
chaunted in a shrill voice : " Benedictus dominus Deus
meus, qui docet manus meas ad prœlium, et digitos meos

ad bellum." A strange figure he seemed to his three squires, perched on his huge horse, with his eyes upturned and the wintry sun shimmering upon his bald head. " It is a noble prayer," he remarked, putting on his hat again, " and it was taught to me by the noble Chandos himself. But how fares it with you, father ? Methinks that I should have ruth upon you, seeing that I am myself like one who looks through a horn window while his neighbours have the clear crystal. Yet, by St. Paul ! there is a long stride between the man who hath a horn casement and him who is walled in on every hand."

" Alas ! fair sir," cried the blind old man, " I have not seen the blessed blue of heaven this two score years, since a levin flash burned the sight out of my head."

" You have been blind to much that is goodly and fair," quoth Sir Nigel, " but you have also been spared much that is sorry and foul. This very hour our eyes have been shocked with that which would have left you unmoved. But, by St. Paul ! we must on, or our Company will think that they have lost their captain somewhat early in the venture. Throw the man my purse, Edricson, and let us go."

Alleyne, lingering behind, bethought him of the Lady Loring's counsel, and reduced the noble gift which the knight had so freely bestowed to a single penny, which the beggar with many mumbled blessings thrust away into his wallet. Then, spurring his steed, the young squire rode at the top of his speed after his companions, and overtook them just at the spot where the trees fringe off into the moor and the straggling hamlet of Hordle lies scattered on either side of the winding and deeply rutted track. The Company was already well-nigh through the village ; but as the knight and his squires closed up upon them, they heard the clamour of a strident voice, followed by a roar of deep-chested laughter from the ranks of the archers. Another minute brought them up with the rear-guard, where every man marched with his beard on his shoulder and a face which was agrin with merriment. By the side of the column walked a huge red-headed bowman, with his hands thrown out in argument and expostulation, while close at his heels followed a little wrinkled woman, who poured forth a shrill volley of abuse, varied by an occasional thwack from her stick, given with all the force of her body, though she might have been beating one of the forest trees for all the effect that she seemed likely to produce.

" I trust, Aylward," said Sir Nigel gravely, as he rode up, " that this doth not mean that any violence hath been offered to women. If such a thing happened, I tell you that the man shall hang, though he were the best archer that ever wore brassart."

" Nay, my fair lord," Aylward answered with a grin, " it is violence which is offered to a man. He comes from Hordle, and this is his mother who hath come forth to welcome him."

" You rammucky lurden," she was howling, with a blow between each catch of her breath, " you shammocking yaping over-long good-for-nought. I will teach thee ! I will baste thee ! Aye, by my faith ! "

" Whist, mother," said John, looking back at her from the tail of his eye. " I go to France as an archer to give blows and to take them."

" To France, quotha ? " cried the old dame. " Bide here with me, and I shall warrant you more blows than you are like to get in France. If blows be what you seek, you need not go further than Hordle."

" By my hilt ! the good dame speaks truth," said Aylward. " It seems to be the very home of them."

" What have you to say, you clean-shaved galley-bagger ? " cried the fiery dame, turning upon the archer. " Can I not speak with my own son but you must let your tongue clack ? A soldier, quotha, and never a hair on his face. I have seen a better soldier with pap for food and swaddling clothes for harness."

" Stand to it, Aylward," cried the archers, amid a fresh burst of laughter.

" Do not thwart her, comrade," said big John. " She hath a proper spirit for her years and cannot abide to be thwarted. It is kindly and homely to me to hear her voice and to feel that she is behind me. But I must leave you now, mother, for the way is over-rough for your feet ; but I will bring you back a silken gown, if there be one in France, or Spain, and I will bring Jinny a silver penny ; so good-bye to you, and God have you in his keeping ! " Whipping up the little woman, he lifted her lightly to his lips, and then, taking his place in the ranks again, marched on with the laughing Company.

" That was ever his way," she cried, appealing to Sir Nigel, who reined up his horse and listened with the gravest courtesy. " He would jog on his own road for all that I could do to change him. First he must be a monk forsooth, and all because a wench was wise enough to turn her back on him. Then he joins a rascally crew and must needs trapse off to the wars, and me with no one to bait the fire if I be out, or tend the cow if I be home. Yet I have been a good mother to him. Three hazel switches a day have I broke across his shoulders, and he takes no more notice than you have seen him to-day."

" Doubt not that he will come back to you both safe and prosperous, my fair dame," quoth Sir Nigel. " Meanwhile it grieves me that, as I have already given my purse to a beggar up the road, I——"

" Nay, my lord," said Alleyne, " I still have some monies remaining."

" Then I pray you to give them to this very worthy woman." He cantered on as he spoke, while Alleyne, having dispensed two more pence, left the old dame standing by the farthest cottage of Hordle with her shrill voice raised in blessings instead of revilings.

There were two cross-roads before they reached the Lymington Ford, and at each of them Sir Nigel pulled up his horse, and waited with many a curvet and gambade, craning his neck this way and that to see if fortune would send him a venture. Cross-roads had, as he explained, been rare places for knightly spear-runnings, and in his youth it was no uncommon thing for a cavalier to abide for weeks at such a point, holding gentle debate with all comers, to his own advancement and the great honour of his lady. The times were changed, however, and the forest tracks wound away from them deserted and silent, with no trample of war-horse or clang of armour which might herald the approach of an adversary—so that Sir Nigel rode on his way disconsolate. At the Lymington river they splashed through the ford, and lay in the meadows on the farther side to eat the bread and salt meat which they carried upon the sumpter horses. Then, ere the sun was up the slope of the heavens, they had deftly trussed up again, and were swinging merrily upon their way, two hundred feet moving like two.

There is a third cross-road where the track from Boldre runs down to the old fishing village of Pitt's Deep. Down this, as they came abreast of it, there walked two men, the one a pace or two behind the other. The cavaliers could not but pull up their horses to look at them, for a stranger pair were never seen journeying together. The first was a misshapen squalid man with cruel cunning eyes and a shock of tangled red hair, bearing in his hands a small unpainted cross, which he held high so that all men might see it. He seemed to be in the last extremity of fright, with a face the colour of clay and his limbs all ashake as one who hath an ague. Behind him, with his toe ever rasping upon the other's heels, there walked a very stern black-bearded man with a hard eye and a set mouth. He bore over his shoulder a great knotted stick with three jagged nails stuck in the head of it, and from time to time he whirled it up in the air with a quivering arm, as though he could scarce hold back from dashing his companion's brains out. So in silence they walked under the spread of the branches on the grass-grown path from Boldre.

" By St. Paul ! " quoth the knight, " but this is a passing strange sight, and perchance some very perilous and honourable venture may arise from it. I pray you,

Edricson, to ride up to them and to ask them the cause of it."

There was no need, however, for him to move, for the twain came swiftly towards them until they were within a spear's length, when the man with the cross sat himself down sullenly upon a tussock of grass by the wayside, while the other stood beside him with his great cudgel still hanging over his head. So intent was he that he raised his eyes neither to knight nor squires, but kept them ever fixed with a savage glare upon his comrade.

" I pray you, friend," said Sir Nigel, " to tell us truthfully who you are, and why you follow this man with such bitter enmity."

" So long as I am within the pale of the king's law," the stranger answered, " I cannot see why I should render account to every passing wayfarer."

" You are no very shrewd reasoner, fellow," quoth the knight ; " for if it be within the law for you to threaten him with your club, then it is also lawful for me to threaten you with my sword."

The man with the cross was down in an instant on his knees upon the ground, with hands clasped above him and his face shining with hope. " For dear Christ's sake, my fair lord," he cried in a crackling voice, " I have at my belt a bag with a hundred rose nobles, and I will give it to you freely if you will but pass your sword through this man's body."

" How, you foul knave ? " exclaimed Sir Nigel hotly. " Do you think that a cavalier's arm is to be bought like a packman's ware ? By St. Paul ! I have little doubt that this fellow hath some very good cause to hold you in hatred."

" Indeed, my fair sir, you speak sooth," quoth he with the club, while the other seated himself once more by the wayside. " For this man is Peter Peterson, a very noted rieve, drawlatch and murtherer, who has wrought much evil for many years in the parts about Winchester. It was but the other day, upon the feast of the blessed Simon and Jude, that he slew my younger brother William in Bere

Forest—for which, by the black thorn of Glastonbury ! I shall have his heart's blood, though I walked behind him to the further end of the earth."

" But if this be indeed so," asked Sir Nigel, " why is it that you have come with him so far through the forest ? "

" Because I am an honest Englishman, and will take no more than the law allows. For when the deed was done this foul and base wretch fled to sanctuary at St. Cross, and I, as you may think, after him with all the posse. The Prior, however, hath so ordered that while he holds this cross no man may lay hand upon him without the ban of church, which heaven forefend from me or mine. Yet, if for an instant he lay the cross aside, or if he fail to journey to Pitt's Deep, where it is ordered that he shall take ship to outland parts, or if he take not the first ship, or if until the ship be ready he walk not every day into the sea as far as his loins, then he becomes outlaw, and I shall forthwith dash out his brains."

At this the man on the ground snarled up at him like a rat, while the other clenched his teeth, and shook his club, and looked down at him with murder in his eyes. Knight and squires gazed from rogue to avenger, but as it was a matter which none could mend they tarried no longer, but rode upon their way. Alleyne, looking back, saw that the murderer had drawn bread and cheese from his scrip, and was silently munching it, with the protecting cross still hugged to his breast, while the other, black and grim, stood in the sunlit road and threw his dark shadow athwart him.

15. *How the Yellow Cog sailed forth from Lepe*

THAT night the Company slept at St. Leonard's, in the great monastic barns and spicarium—ground well known both to Alleyne and to John, for they were almost within sight of the Abbey of Beaulieu. A strange thrill it gave to the young squire to see the well-remembered white dress once more, and to hear the measured tolling of the deep vespers bell. At early dawn they passed across the broad, sluggish, reed-girt stream—men, horses and baggage in the flat ferry barges—and so journeyed on through the fresh morning air past Exbury to Lepe. Topping the heathy down, they came of a sudden full in sight of the old seaport—a cluster of houses, a trail of blue smoke and a bristle of masts. To right and left the long blue curve of the Solent lapped in a fringe of foam upon the yellow beach. Some way out from the town a line of pessoners, creyers and other small craft were rolling lazily on the gentle swell. Farther out still lay a great merchant-ship, high ended, deep waisted, painted of a canary yellow, and towering above the fishing boats like a swan among ducklings.

" By St. Paul ! " said the knight, " our good merchant of Southampton hath not played us false, for methinks I can see our ship down yonder. He said that she would be of great size and of a yellow shade."

" By my hilt, yes ! " muttered Aylward ; " she is yellow as a kite's claw, and would carry as many men as there are pips in a pomegranate."

" It is as well," remarked Terlake ; " for methinks, my fair lord, that we are not the only ones who are waiting a passage to Gascony. Mine eyes catches at times a flash and sparkle from among yonder houses which assuredly never came from shipman's jacket or the gaberdine of a burgher."

" I can also see it," said Alleyne, shading his eyes with his hand. " And I can see men-at-arms in yonder boats which ply betwixt the vessel and the shore. But me-thinks that we are very welcome here, for already they come forth to meet us."

A tumultuous crowd of fishermen, citizens and women had indeed swarmed out from the northern gate, ap-proached them up the side of the moor, waving their hands and dancing with joy, as though a great fear had been rolled back from their minds. At their head rode a very large and solemn man with a long chin and a drooping lip. He wore a fur tippet round his neck and a heavy gold chain over it, with a medallion which dangled in front of him.

"Welcome, most puissant and noble lord," he cried, doffing his bonnet to Black Simon. "I have heard of your lordship's valiant deeds, and in sooth they might be expected from your lordship's face and bearing. Is there any small matter in which I may oblige you?"

"Since you ask me," said the man-at-arms, "I would take it kindly if you could spare a link or two of the chain which hangs round your neck."

"What, the corporation chain!" cried the other in horror. "The ancient chain of the township of Lepe! This is but a sorry jest, Sir Nigel."

"What the plague did you ask me for, then?" said Simon. "But if it is Sir Nigel Loring with whom you would speak, that is he upon the black horse."

The Mayor of Lepe gazed with amazement on the mild face and slender frame of the famous warrior.

"Your pardon, my very gracious lord," he cried. "You see in me the mayor and chief magistrate of the ancient and powerful town of Lepe. I bid you very heartily welcome, and the more so as you are come at a moment when we are sore put to it for means of defence."

"Ha!" cried Sir Nigel, pricking up his ears.

"Yes, my lord, for the town being very ancient, and the walls as old as the town, it follows that they are very ancient too. But there is a certain villainous and blood-thirsty Norman pirate hight Tête-noire, who, with a Genoan called Tito Caracci, commonly known as Spade-beard, hath been a mighty scourge upon these coasts. Indeed, my lord, they are very cruel and black-hearted men, graceless and ruthless, and if they should come to the ancient and powerful town of Lepe, then——"

"Then good-bye to the ancient and powerful town of Lepe," quoth Ford, whose lightness of tongue could at times rise above his awe of Sir Nigel.

The knight, however, was too much intent upon the matter in hand to give heed to the flippancy of his squire. " Have you then cause," he asked, " to think that these men are about to venture an attempt upon you ? "

" They have come in two great galleys," answered the mayor, " with two bank of oars on either side, and great store of engines of war and of men-at-arms. At Weymouth and at Portland they have murdered and ravished. Yesterday morning they were at Cowes, and we saw the smoke from the burning crofts. To-day they lie at their ease near Freshwater, and we fear much lest they come upon us and do us a mischief."

" We cannot tarry," said Sir Nigel, riding towards the town, with the mayor upon his left side ; " the Prince awaits us at Bordeaux, and we may not be behind the general muster. Yet I will promise you that on our way we shall find time to pass Freshwater and to prevail upon these rovers to leave you in peace."

" We are much beholden to you ! " cried the mayor. " But I cannot see, my lord, how, without a war-ship you may venture against these men. With your archers, however, you might well hold the town and do them great scath if they attempt to land."

" There is a very proper cog out yonder," said Sir Nigel ; " it would be a very strange thing if any ship were not a war-ship when it had such men as these upon her decks. Certes, we shall do as I say, and that no later than this very day."

" My lord," said a rough-haired, dark-faced man, who walked by the knight's other stirrup, with his head sloped to catch all that he was saying. " By your leave, I have no doubt that you are skilled in land fighting and the marshalling of lances, but, by my soul ! you will find it another thing upon the sea. I am the master-shipman of this yellow cog, and my name is Goodwin Hawtayne. I have sailed since I was as high as this staff, and I have fought against these Normans and against the Genoese, as well as the Scotch, the Bretons, the Spanish and the Moors.

I tell you, sir, that my ship is over light and over frail for such work, and it will but end in our having our throats cut, or being sold as slaves to the Barbary heathen."

"I also have experienced one or two gentle and honourable ventures upon the sea," quoth Sir Nigel, "and I am right blithe to have so fair a task before us. I think, good master-shipman, that you and I may win great honour in this matter, and I can see very readily that you are a brave and stout man."

"I like it not," said the other sturdily. "In God's name, I like it not. And yet Goodwin Hawtayne is not the man to stand back when his fellows are for pressing forward. By my soul! be it sink or swim, I shall turn her beak into Freshwater Bay, and if good Master Witherton, of Southampton, like not my handling of his ship, then he may find another master-shipman."

They were close by the old north gate of the little town, and Alleyne, half turning in his saddle, looked back at the motley crowd who followed. The bowmen and men-at-arms had broken their ranks and were intermingled with the fishermen and citizens, whose laughing faces and hearty gestures bespoke the weight of care from which this welcome arrival had relieved them. Here and there among the moving throng of dark jerkins and of white surcoats were scattered dashes of scarlet or blue, the wimples or shawls of the women. Aylward, with a fishing lass on either arm, was vowing constancy alternately to her on the right and her on the left, while big John towered in the rear with a little chubby maiden enthroned upon his great shoulder, her soft white arm curled round his shining headpiece. So the throng moved on, until at the very gate it was brought to a stand by a wondrously fat man, who came darting forth from the town with rage in every feature of his rubicund face.

"How now, Sir Mayor?" he roared, in a voice like a bull. "How now, Sir Mayor? How of the clams and the scallops?"

"By our Lady, my sweet Sir Oliver," cried the mayor,

" I have had so much to think of, with these wicked villains so close upon us, that it had quite gone out of my head."

" Words, words ! " shouted the other furiously. " Am I to be put off with words ? I say to you again, how of the clams and scallops ? "

" My fair sir, you flutter me," cried the mayor. " I am a peaceful trader, and I am not wont to be so shouted at upon so small a matter."

" Small ! " shrieked the other. " Small ! Clams and scallops ! Ask me to your table to partake of the dainty of the town, and when I come a barren welcome and a bare board ! Where is my spear-bearer ? "

" Nay, Sir Oliver, Sir Oliver ! " cried Sir Nigel, laughing. " Let your anger be appeased, since instead of this dish you come upon an old friend and comrade."

" By St. Martin of Tours ! " shouted the fat knight, his wrath all changed in an instant to joy, " if it is not my dear little game rooster of the Garonne. Ah, my sweet coz, I am right glad to see you. What days we have seen together ! "

" Aye, by my faith," cried Sir Nigel, with sparkling eyes, " we have seen some valiant men, and we have shown our pennons in some noble skirmishes. By St. Paul ! we have had great joys in France."

" And sorrows also," quoth the other. " I have some sad memories of the land. Can you recall that which befell us at Libourne ? "

" Nay, I cannot call to mind that we ever so much as drew sword at the place."

" Man, man," cried Sir Oliver, " your mind still runs on nought but blades and bassinets. Hast no space in thy frame for the softer joys ? Ah, even now I can scarce speak of it unmoved. So noble a pie, such tender pigeons, and sugar in the gravy instead of salt ! You were by my side that day, as were Sir Claude Latour and the Lord of Pommers."

" I remember it," said Sir Nigel, laughing, " and how

you harried the cook down the street, and spoke of setting fire to the inn. By St. Paul ! most worthy mayor, my old friend is a perilous man, and I rede you that you compose your difference with him on such terms as you may."

"The clams and scallops shall be ready within the hour," the mayor answered. "I had asked Sir Oliver Buttesthorn to do my humble board the honour to partake at it of the dainty upon which we take some little pride, but in sooth this alarm of pirates hath cast such a shadow on my wits that I am like one distrait. But I trust, Sir Nigel, that you will also partake of none-meat with me ?"

"I have overmuch to do," Sir Nigel answered, "for we must be aboard, horse and man, as early as we may. How many do you muster, Sir Oliver ?"

"Three-and-forty. The forty are drunk, and three are but indifferent sober. I have them all safe upon the ship."

"They had best find their wits again, for I shall have work for every man of them ere the sun set. It is my intention, if it seems good to you, to try to venture against these Norman and Genoese rovers."

"They carry caviare, and certain very noble spices from the Levant aboard of ships from Genoa," quoth Sir Oliver. "We may come to great profit through the business. I pray you, master-shipman, that when you go on board you pour a helmetful of sea-water over any of my rogues who you may see there."

Leaving the lusty knight and the Mayor of Lepe, Sir Nigel led the Company straight down to the water's edge, where long lines of flat lighters swiftly bore them to their vessel. Horse after horse was slung by main force up from the barges, and after kicking and plunging in empty air was dropped into the deep waist of the yellow cog, where rows of stalls stood ready for their safe-keeping. Englishmen in those days were skilled and prompt in such matters, for it was not so long before that Edward had embarked as many as fifty thousand men in the port of Orwell, with their horses and their baggage, all in the space of four-and-twenty hours. So urgent was Sir Nigel on the shore, and so prompt was Goodwin Hawtayne on the cog, that Sir Oliver Buttesthorn had scarce swallowed his last scallop ere the peal of trumpet and clang of nakir announced that all was ready and the anchor drawn. In the last boat which left the shore the two commanders sat together in the sheets, a strange contrast to one another, while under the feet of the rowers was a litter of huge stones which Sir Nigel had ordered to be carried to the cog. These once aboard, the ship set her broad mainsail, purple in colour, with a golden St. Christopher bearing Christ upon his shoulder in the centre of it. The breeze blew, the sail bellied, over heeled the portly vessel, and away she plunged through the smooth blue rollers, amid the clang of the minstrels on her poop and the shouting of the crowd who fringed the yellow beach. To the left lay the green Island of Wight, with its long low curving hills peeping over each other's shoulders to the sky-line ; to the right the wooded Hampshire coast as far as eye could reach ; above a steel-blue heaven, with a wintry sun shimmering down upon them, and enough of frost to set the breath a-smoking.

" By St. Paul ! " said Sir Nigel gaily, as he stood upon the poop and looked on either side of him, " it is a land which is very well worth fighting for, but it were pity to go to France for what may be had at home. Did you not spy a crooked man upon the beach ? "

" Nay, I spied nothing," grumbled Sir Oliver, " for I was hurried down with a clam stuck in my gizzard and an untasted goblet of Cyprus on the board behind me."

" I saw him, my fair lord," said Terlake, " an old man with one shoulder higher than the other."

" 'Tis a sign of good fortune," quoth Sir Nigel. " Our path was also crossed by a woman and by a priest, so all should be well with us. What say you, Edricson ? "

" I cannot tell, my fair lord. The Romans of old were a very wise people, yet, certes, they placed their faith in such matters. So, too, did the Greeks, and divers other ancient peoples who were famed for their learning. Yet of the moderns there are many who scoff at all omens."

"There can be no manner of doubt about it," said Sir Oliver Buttesthorn. "I can well remember that in Navarre one day it thundered on the left out of a cloudless sky. We knew that ill would come of it, nor had we long to wait. Only thirteen days after, a haunch of prime venison was carried from my very tent door by the wolves, and on the same day two flasks of old vernage turned sour and muddy."

"You may bring my harness from below," said Sir Nigel to his squires, " and also, I pray you, bring up Sir Oliver's, and we shall don it here. Ye may then see to your own gear ; for this day you will, I hope, make a very honourable entrance into the field of chivalry, and prove yourselves to be very worthy and valiant squires. And now, Sir Oliver, as to our dispositions : would it please you that I should order them or will you ? "

"You, my cockerel, you. By our Lady ! I am no chicken, but I cannot claim to know as much of war as the squire of Sir Walter Manny. Settle the matter to your own liking."

"You shall fly your pennon upon the fore part, then, and I upon the poop. For foreguard I shall give you your own forty men, with two score archers. Two score men, with my own men-at-arms and squires, may serve as a poop guard. Ten archers, with thirty shipmen, under the master may hold the waist while ten lie aloft with stones and arbalests. How like you that ? "

"Good, by my faith, good ! But here comes my harness, and I must to work, for I cannot slip into it as I was wont when first I set my face to the wars."

Meanwhile there had been bustle and preparation in all parts of the great vessel. The archers stood in groups about the decks, new-stringing their bows, and testing that they were firm at the nocks. Among them moved

Aylward and other of the older soldiers, with a few whispered words of precept here and of warning there.

"Stand to it, my hearts of gold," said the old bowman as he passed from knot to knot. "By my hilt! we are in luck this journey. Bear in mind the old saying of the Company."

"What is that, Aylward?" cried several, leaning on their bows and laughing at him.

"'Tis the master-bowman's rede : 'Every bow well bent. Every shaft well sent. Every stave well nocked. Every string well locked.' There, with that jingle in his head, a bracer on his left hand, a shooting glove on his right, and a farthing's-worth of wax in his girdle, what more doth a bowman need?"

"It would not be amiss," said Hordle John, "if under his girdle he had four farthings'-worth of wine!"

"Work first, wine afterwards, mon camarade. But it is time that we took our order, for methinks that between the Needle rocks and the Alum cliffs yonder I can catch a glimpse of the topmasts of the galleys. Hewett, Cook, Johnson, Cunningham, your men are of the poop-guard. Thornbury, Walters, Hackett, Baddlesmere, you are with Sir Oliver to the forecastle. Simon, you bide with your lord's banner ; but ten men must go forward."

Quietly and promptly the men took their places, lying flat upon their faces on the deck, for such was Sir Nigel's order. Near the prow was planted Sir Oliver's spear, with his arms—a boar's head gules upon a field of gold. Close by the stern stood Black Simon with the pennon of the house of Loring. In the waist gathered the South-ampton mariners, hairy and burly men, with their jerkins thrown off, their waists braced tight, swords, mallets, and pole-axes in their hands. Their leader, Goodwin Hawtayne, stood upon the poop and talked with Sir Nigel, casting his eye up sometimes at the swelling sail, and then glancing back at the two seamen who held the tiller.

"Pass the word," said Sir Nigel, "that no man shall

stand to arms or draw his bowstring until my trumpeter shall sound. It would be well that we should seem to be a merchant-ship from Southampton and appear to flee from them."

"We shall see them anon," said the master-shipman. "Ha! said I not so? There they lie, the water-snakes in Freshwater Bay; and mark the reek of smoke from yonder point, where they have been at their devil's work. See how their shallops pull from the land! They have seen us and called their men aboard. Now they draw upon the anchor. See them like ants upon the forecastle! They stoop and heave like handy shipmen. But, my fair lord, these are no niefs. I doubt but we have taken in hand more than we can do. Each of these ships is a galeasse, and of the largest and swiftest make."

"I would I had your eyes," said Sir Nigel, blinking at the pirate galleys. "They seem very gallant ships, and I trust that we shall have much pleasance from our meeting with them. It would be well to pass the word that we should neither give nor take quarter this day. Have you perchance a priest or friar aboard this ship, Master Hawtayne?"

"No, my fair lord."

"Well, well, it is no great matter for my Company, for they were all houseled and shriven ere we left Twynham Castle; and Father Christopher of the Priory gave me his word that they were as fit to march to heaven as to Gascony. But my mind misdoubts me as to these Winchester men who have come with Sir Oliver, for they appear to be a very ungodly crew. Pass the word that the men kneel, and that the under-officers repeat to them the pater, the ave, and the credo."

With a clank of arms, the rough archers and seamen took to their knees, with bent heads and crossed hands, listening to the hoarse mutter from the file-leaders. It was strange to mark the hush; so that the lapping of the water, the straining of the sail, and the creaking of the timbers grew louder of a sudden upon the ear. Many of the bowmen had drawn amulets and relics from their bosoms, while he who possessed some more than usually sanctified treasure passed it down the line of his comrades that all might kiss and reap the virtue.

The yellow cog had now shot out from the narrow waters of the Solent, and was plunging and rolling on the long heave of the open channel. The wind blew freshly from the east, with a very keen edge to it ; and the great sail bellied roundly out, laying the vessel over until the water hissed beneath her lee bulwarks. Broad and ungainly she floundered from wave to wave, dipping her round bows deeply into the blue rollers, and sending the white flakes of foam in a spatter over her decks. On her larboard quarter lay the two dark galleys, which had already hoisted sail, and were shooting out from Freshwater Bay in swift pursuit, their double line of oars giving them a vantage which could not fail to bring them up with any vessel which trusted to sails alone. High and bluff the English cog ; long, black and swift the pirate galleys, like two fierce lean wolves which have seen a lordly and unsuspecting stag walk past their forest lair.

" Shall we turn, my fair lord, or shall we carry on ? " asked the master-shipman, looking behind him with anxious eyes.

" Nay, we must carry on, and play the part of the helpless merchant."

" But your pennons ? They will see that we have two knights with us."

" Yet it would not be to a knight's honour or good name to lower his pennon. Let them be, and they will think that we are a wine-ship for Gascony, or that we bear the wool-bales of some mercer of the Staple. Ma foi ! but they are very swift ! They swoop upon us like two goshawks on a heron. Is there not some symbol or device upon their sails ? "

" That on the right," said Edricson, " appears to have the head of an Ethiop upon it."

" 'Tis the badge of Tête-noire, the Norman," cried

the seaman-mariner. " I have seen it before when he
harried us at Winchelsea. He is a wondrous large and
strong man, with no ruth for man, woman, or beast.
They say that he hath the strength of six ; and, certes,
he hath the crimes of six upon his soul. See, now, to
the poor souls who swing at either end of his yard-arm ! "

At each end of the yard there did indeed hang the dark
figure of a man, jolting and lurching with hideous jerkings
of its limbs at every plunge and swoop of the galley.

" By St. Paul ! " said Sir Nigel, " and by the help of
St. George and Our Lady, it will be a very strange thing
if our black-headed friend does not himself swing thence
ere he be many hours older. But what is that upon the
other galley ? "

" It is the red cross of Genoa. This Spade-beard is a
very noted captain, and it is his boast there there are no
seamen and no archers in the world who can compare
with those who serve the Doge Boccanegra."

" That we shall prove," said Goodwin Hawtayne ;
" but it would be well, ere they close with us, to raise up
the mantlets and pavises as a screen against their bolts."
He shouted a hoarse order, and his seamen worked swiftly
and silently, heightening the bulwarks and strengthening
them. The three ship's anchors were at Sir Nigel's
command carried into the waist, and tied to the mast,
with twenty feet of cable between, each under the care
of four seamen. Eight others were stationed with leather
water-bags to quench any fire-arrows which might come
aboard, while others were sent up the mast, to lie along
the yard and drop stones or shoot arrows as the occasion
served.

" Let them be supplied with all that is heavy and
weighty in the ship," said Sir Nigel.

" Then we must send them up Sir Oliver Buttesthorn,"
quoth Ford.

The knight looked at him with a face which struck the
smile from his lips. " No squire of mine," he said,
" shall ever make jest of a belted knight. And yet," he

added, his eyes softening, " I know that it is but a boy's mirth, with no sting in it. Yet I should do ill my part towards your father if I did not teach you to curb your tongue-play."

" They will lay us aboard on either quarter, my lord," cried the master. " See how they stretch out from each other ! The Norman hath a mangonel or a trabuch upon the forecastle. See, they bend to the levers ! They are about to loose it."

" Aylward," cried the knight, " pick your three trustiest archers, and see if you cannot do something to hinder their aim. Methinks they are within long arrow flight."

" Seventeen score paces," said the archer, running his eye backwards and forwards. " By my ten finger-bones ! it would be a strange thing if we could not notch a mark at that distance. Here, Watkin of Sowley, Arnold, Long Williams, let us show the rogues that they have English bowmen to deal with."

The three archers named stood at the farther end of the poop, balancing themselves with feet widely spread and bows drawn, until the heads of the cloth-yard arrows were level with the centre of the stave. " You are the surer, Watkin," said Aylward, standing by them with shaft upon string. " Do you take the rogue with the red coif. You two bring down the man with the head-piece and I will hold myself ready if you miss. Ma foi ! they are about to loose her. Shoot, mes garçons, or you will be too late."

The throng of pirates had cleared away from the great wooden catapult, leaving two of their number to discharge it. One in a scarlet cap bent over it, steadying the jagged rock which was balanced on the spoon-shaped end of the long wooden lever. The other held the loop of the rope which would release the catch and send the unwieldy missile hurtling through the air. So for an instant they stood, showing hard and clear against the white sail behind them. The next, redcap had fallen across the stone with an arrow between his ribs ; and the other, struck in the leg and in the throat, was writhing and spluttering upon the ground. As he toppled backwards he had loosed the spring and the huge beam of wood, swinging round with tremendous force, cast the corpse of his comrade so close to the English ship that its mangled and distorted limbs grazed their very stern. As to the stone, it glanced off obliquely and fell midway between the vessels. A roar of cheering and of laughter broke from the rough archers and seamen at the sight, answered by a yell of rage from their pursuers.

"Lie low, mes infants," cried Aylward, motioning with his left hand. "They will learn wisdom. They are bringing forward shield and mantlet. We shall have some pebbles about our ears ere long."

16. *How the Yellow Cog fought the Two Rover Galleys*

THE three vessels had been sweeping swiftly westwards, the cog still well to the front, although the galleys were slowly drawing in upon either quarter. To the left was a hard sky-line unbroken by a sail. The island already lay like a cloud behind them, while right in front was St. Alban's Head, with Portland looming mistily in the farthest distance. Alleyne stood by the tiller, looking backwards, the fresh wind full in his teeth, the crisp winter air tingling on his face and blowing his yellow curls from under his bassinet. His cheeks were flushed and his eyes shining, for the blood of a hundred fighting Saxon ancestors was beginning to stir in his veins.

"What was that?" he asked, as a hissing, sharp-drawn voice seemed to whisper in his ear. The steersman smiled, and pointed with his foot to where a short heavy cross-bow quarrel stuck quivering in the boards. At the same instant the man stumbled forward upon his knee, and lay lifeless upon the deck, a blood-stained feather jutting out from his back. As Alleyne stooped to raise him, the air seemed to be alive with the sharp zip-zip of the bolts, and he could hear them pattering on the deck like apples at a tree-shaking.

" Raise two more mantlets by the poop-lanthorn," said Sir Nigel quietly.

" And another man to the tiller," cried the master shipman.

" Keep them in play, Aylward, with ten of your men," the knight continued. " And let ten of Sir Oliver's bow-men do as much for the Genoese. I have no mind as yet to show them how much they have to fear from us."

Ten picked shots under Aylward stood in line across the broad deck, and it was a lesson to the young squires who had seen nothing of war to note how orderly and how cool were these old soldiers, how quick the command, and how prompt the carrying out, ten moving like one. Their comrades crouched beneath the bulwarks, with many a rough jest and many a scrap of criticism or advice. " Higher, Wat, higher ! " " Put thy body into it, Will ! " " Forget not the wind, Hal ! " So ran the muttered chorus, while high above it rose the sharp twanging of the strings, the hiss of the shafts, and the short " Draw your arrow ! Nick your arrow ! Shoot wholly together ! " from the master-bowman.

And now both mangonels were at work from the galleys but so covered and protected that, save at the moment of discharge, no glimpse could be caught of them. A huge brown rock from the Genoese sang over their heads and plunged sullenly into the slope of a wave. Another from the Norman whizzed into the waist, broke the back of a horse, and crashed its way through the side of the vessel. Two others, flying together, tore a great gap in the St. Christopher upon the sail, and brushed three of Sir Oliver's men-at-arms from the forecastle. The master-shipman looked at the knight with a troubled face.

" They keep their distance from us," said he. " Our archery is over good, and they will not close. What defence can we make against the stones ? "

" I think I may trick them," the knight answered cheerfully, and passed his order to the archers. Instantly five of them threw up their hands and fell prostrate upon the deck. One had already been slain by a bolt, so that there were but four upon their feet.

" That should give them heart," said Sir Nigel, eyeing the galleys, which crept along on either side with a slow measured swing of their great oars, the water swirling and foaming under their sharp stems.

" They still hold aloof," cried Hawtayne.

" Then down with two more," shouted their leader. " That will do. Ma foi ! but they come to our lure like chicks to the fowler. To your arms, men ! The pennon behind me, and the squires round the pennon. Stand fast with the anchors in the waist, and be ready for a cast. Now blow out the trumpets, and may God's benison be with the honest men ! "

As he spoke the roar of voices and a roll of drums came from either galley, and the water was lashed into spray by the hurried beat of a hundred oars. Down they swooped, one on the right, one on the left, the sides and shrouds black with men and bristling with weapons. In heavy clusters they hung upon the forecastle all ready for a spring—faces white, faces brown, faces yellow, and faces black, fair Norsemen, swarthy Italians, fierce rovers from the Levant, and fiery Moors from the Barbary States, of all hues and countries, and marked solely by the common stamp of a wild-beast ferocity. Rasping up on either side, with oars trailing to save them from snapping, they poured in a living torrent with horrid yell and shrill whoop upon the defenceless merchantman.

But wilder yet was the cry, and shriller still the scream, when there rose up from the shadow of those silent bulwarks the long lines of the English bowmen, and the arrows whizzed in a deadly sleet among the unprepared masses upon the pirate decks. From the higher sides of the cog the bowmen could shoot straight down, at a range which was so short as to enable a cloth-yard shaft to pierce through mailcoats or to transfix a shield, though it were an inch thick of toughened wood. One moment Alleyne saw the galley's poop crowded with rushing figures, waving arms, exultant faces ; the next it was a blood-smeared shambles, with bodies piled three deep upon each other, the living cowering behind the dead to shelter themselves from that sudden storm-blast of death. On either side the seamen whom Sir Nigel had chosen for the purpose had cast their anchors over the side of the galleys, so that the three vessels, locked in an iron grip, lurched heavily forward upon the swell.

And now set in a fell and fierce fight, one of a thousand of which no chronicler has spoken and no poet sung. Through all the centuries, and over all those southern waters, nameless men have fought in nameless places, their sole monument a protected coast and an unravaged country-side.

Fore and aft the archers had cleared the galleys' decks, but from either side the rovers had poured down into the waist, where the seamen and bowmen were pushed back and so mingled with their foes that it was impossible for their comrades above to draw string to help them. It was a wild chaos where axe and sword rose and fell, while Englishmen, Norman, and Italian staggered and reeled on a deck which was cumbered with bodies and slippery with blood. The clang of blows, the cries of the stricken, the short deep shout of the islanders, and the fierce whoops of the rovers, rose together in a deafening tumult, while the breath of the panting men went up in the wintry air like the smoke from a furnace. The giant Tête-noir, towering above his fellows and clad from head to foot in plate of proof, led on his boarders, waving a huge mace in the air, with which he struck to the deck every man who opposed him. On the other side, Spade-beard, a dwarf in height, but of great breadth of shoulder and length of arm, had cut a road almost to the mast, with threescore Genoese men-at-arms close at his heels. Between these two formidable assailants the seamen were being slowly wedged more closely together, until they stood back to back under the mast with the rovers raging upon every side of them.

But help was close at hand. Sir Oliver Buttesthorn with his men-at-arms had swarmed down from the forecastle, while Sir Nigel, with his three squires, Black Simon, Aylward, Hordle John, and a score more, threw themselves from the poop and hurled themselves into the thickest of the fight. Alleyne, as in duty bound, kept his eyes fixed ever on his lord and pressed forward close at his heels. Often had he heard of Sir Nigel's prowess and skill with all knightly weapons, but all the tales that had reached his ears fell far short of the real quickness and coolness of the man. It was as if the devil was in him, for he sprang here and sprang there, now thrusting and now cutting, catching blows on his shield, turning them with his blade, stooping under the swing of an axe, springing over the sweep of a sword, so swift and so erratic that the man who braced himself for a blow at him might find him six paces off ere he could bring it down. Three pirates had fallen before him, and he had wounded Spade-beard in the neck when the Norman giant sprang at him from the side with a slashing blow from his deadly mace. Sir Nigel stooped to avoid it, and at the same instant turned a thrust from the Genoese swordsman; but, his foot slipping in a pool of blood, he fell heavily to the boards. Alleyne sprang in front of the Norman, but his sword was shattered and he himself beaten to the boards by a second blow from the ponderous weapon. Ere the pirate chief could repeat it, however, John's iron grip fell upon his wrist, and he found that for once he was in the hands of a stronger man than himself. Fiercely he strove to disengage his weapon, but Hordle John bent his arm slowly back until, with a sharp crack, like a breaking stave, it turned limp in his grasp, and the mace dropped from the nerveless fingers. In vain he tried to pluck it up with the other hand. Back and back still his foeman bent him, until, with a roar of pain and of fury the giant clanged his full length upon the boards, while the glimmer of a knife before the bars of his helmet warned him that short would be his shrift if he moved.

Cowed and disheartened by the loss of their leader, the Normans had given back and were now streaming over the bulwarks on to their own galley, dropping a dozen at a time on to her deck. But the anchor still held them in its crooked claw, and Sir Oliver with fifty men was hard upon their heels. Now, too, the archers had room to draw their bows once more, and great stones from the yard of the cog came thundering and crashing among the flying rovers. Here and there they rushed with wild screams and curses, diving under the sail, crouching behind booms, huddling into corners like rabbits when the ferrets are upon them, as helpless and as hopeless. They were stern days, and if the honest soldier, too poor for a ransom, had no prospect of mercy upon the battle-field, what ruth was there for sea-robbers, the enemies of human kind, taken in the very deed, with proofs of their crimes still swinging upon their yard-arm ?

But the fight had taken a new and a strange turn upon the other side. Spade-beard and his men had given slowly back, hard pressed by Sir Nigel, Aylward, Black Simon, and the poop-guard. Foot by foot the Italian had retreated, his armour running blood at every joint, his shield split, his crest shorn, his voice fallen away to a mere gasping and croaking. Yet he faced his foemen with dauntless courage, dashing in, springing back, sure-footed, steady-handed, with a point which seemed to menace three at once. Beaten back on to the deck of his own vessel, and closely followed by a dozen Englishmen, he disengaged himself from them, ran swiftly down the deck, sprang back into the cog once more, cut the rope which held the anchor, and was back in an instant among his crossbowmen. At the same time the Genoese sailors thrust with their oars against the side of the cog, and a rapidly widening rift appeared between the two vessels.

" By St. George ! " cried Ford, " we are cut off from Sir Nigel."

" He is lost," gasped Terlake. " Come, let us spring for it." The two youths jumped with all their strength to reach the departing galley. Ford's feet reached the edge of the bulwarks, and his hand clutching a rope he swung himself on board. Terlake fell short, crashed in among the oars, and bounded off into the sea. Alleyne, staggering to the side, was about to hurl himself after him, but Hordle John dragged him back by the girdle.

" You can scarce stand, lad, far less jump," said he. " See how the blood drips from your bassinet."

" My place is by the flag," cried Alleyne, vainly struggling to break from the other's hold.

" Bide here, man. You would need wings ere you could reach Sir Nigel's side."

The vessels were indeed so far apart now that the Genoese could use the full sweep of their oars, and draw rapidly away from the cog.

" My God, but it is a noble fight ! " shouted big John, clapping his hands. " They have cleared the poop, and they spring into the waist. Well struck, my lord ! Well struck, Aylward ! See to Black Simon, how he storms among the shipmen ! But this Spade-beard is a gallant warrior. He rallies his men upon the forecastle. He hath slain an archer. Ha ! my lord is upon him. Look to it, Alleyne ! See to the whirl and glitter of it ! "

" By heaven, Sir Nigel is down ! " cried the squire.

" Up ! " roared John. " It was but a feint. He bears him back. He drives him to the side. Ah, by Our Lady, his sword is through him ! They cry for mercy. Down goes the red cross, and up springs Simon with the scarlet roses ! "

The death of the Genoese leader did indeed bring the resistance to an end. Amid a thunder of cheering from cog and from galleys the forked pennon fluttered upon the forecastle, and the galley, sweeping round, came slowly back, as the slaves who rowed it learned the wishes of their new masters.

The two knights had come aboard the cog, and the grapplings having been thrown off, the three vessels now moved abreast. Through all the storm and rush of the fight Alleyne had been aware of the voice of Goodwin Hawtayne, the master-shipman, with his constant " Hale the bowline ! Veer the sheet ! " and strange it was to him to see how swiftly the blood-stained sailors turned from the strife to the ropes and back. Now the cog's head was turned Francewards, and the shipman walked the deck, a peaceful master-mariner once more.

" There is sad scath done to the cog, Sir Nigel," said he. " Here is a hole in the side two ells across, the sail split through the centre, and the wood as bare as a friar's poll. In good sooth, I know not what I shall say to Master Witherton when I see the Itchen once more."

" By St. Paul ! it would be a very sorry thing if we suffered you to be the worse for this day's work," said Sir Nigel. " You shall take these galleys back with you, and Master Witherton may sell them. Then from the monies he shall take as much as may make good the damage, and the rest he shall keep until our home-coming, when every man shall have his share. An image of silver fifteen inches high I have vowed to the Virgin, to be placed in her chapel within the Priory, for that she was pleased to allow me to come upon this Spade-beard, who seemed to me from what I have seen of him to be a very sprightly and valiant gentleman. But how fares it with you, Edricson ? "

" It is nothing, my fair lord," said Alleyne, who had now loosened his bassinet, which was cracked across by the Norman's blow. Even as he spoke, however, his head swirled round, and he fell to the deck with the blood gushing from his nose and mouth.

" He will come to anon," said the knight, stooping over him and passing his fingers through his hair. " I have lost one very valiant and gentle squire this day. I can ill afford to lose another. How many men have fallen ? ''

" I have pricked off the tally," said Aylward, who had come aboard with his lord. " There are seven of the Winchester men, eleven seamen, your squire, young Master Terlake, and nine archers ! ''

" And of the others ? ''

" They are all dead—save only the Norman knight who stands behind you. What would you that we should do with him ? ''

" He must hang on his own yard," said Sir Nigel. " It was my vow and must be done."

The pirate leader had stood by the bulwarks, a cord round his arms, and two stout archers on either side. At Sir Nigel's words he started violently, and his swarthy features blanched to a livid grey.

" How, Sir Knight ? '' he cried in broken English. " Que dites-vous ? To hang, la mort du chien ! To hang ! ''

" It is my vow," said Sir Nigel shortly. " From what I hear, you thought little enough of hanging others."

" Peasants, base roturiers," cried the other. " It is their fitting death. Mais Le Seigneur d'Andelys, avec le sang des rois dans ses veines ! C'est incroyable ! ''

Sir Nigel turned upon his heel, while the seamen cast a noose over the pirate's neck. At the touch of the cord he snapped the bonds which bound him, dashed one of the archers to the deck, and seizing the other round the waist sprang with him into the sea.

" By my hilt, he is gone ! '' cried Aylward, rushing to the side. " They have sunk together like a stone."

" I am right glad of it," answered Sir Nigel ; " for though it was against my vow to loose him, I deem that he has carried himself like a very gentle and débonnaire cavalier."

17. *How the Yellow Cog crossed the Bar of Gironde*

FOR two days the yellow cog ran swiftly before a north-easterly wind, and on the dawn of the third the highland of Ushant lay like a mist upon the shimmering sky-line. There came a plump of rain towards midday and the breeze died down, but it freshened again before nightfall, and Goodwin Hawtayne veered his sheet and held her head for the south. Next morning they had passed Belle Isle, and ran through the midst of a fleet of transports returning from Guienne. Sir Nigel Loring and Sir Oliver Buttesthorn at once hung their shields over the side, and displayed their pennons as was the custom, noting with the keenest interest the answering symbols which told the names of the cavaliers who had been constrained by ill health or wounds to leave the prince at so critical a time.

That evening a great dun-coloured cloud banked up in the west, and an anxious man was Goodwin Hawtayne, for a third part of his crew had been slain and half of the remainder were aboard the galleys, so that, with an injured ship, he was little fit to meet such a storm as sweeps over those waters. All night it blew in short fitful puffs, heeling the great cog over until the water curled over her lee bulwarks. As the wind still freshened the yard was lowered halfway down the mast in the morning. Alleyne, wretchedly ill and weak, with his head still ringing from the blow which he had received, crawled up upon deck. Water-swept and aslant, it was preferable to the noisome rat-haunted dungeons which served as cabins. There, clinging to the stout halliards of the sheet, he gazed with amazement at the long lines of black waves, each with its curling ridge of foam, racing in endless succession from out the inexhaustible west. A huge sombre cloud, flecked with livid blotches, stretched

191

over the whole seaward sky-line, with long ragged
streamers whirled out in front of it. Far behind them
the two galleys laboured heavily, now sinking between
the rollers until their yards were level with the waves, and
again shooting up with a reeling scooping motion until
every spar and rope stood out hard against the sky. On
the left the low-lying land stretched in a dim haze, rising
here and there into a darker blur which marked the higher
capes and headlands. The land of France ! Alleyne's
eyes shone as he gazed upon it. The land of France !—
the very words sounded as the call of a bugle in the ears
of the youth of England. The land where their fathers
had bled, the home of chivalry and of knightly deeds, the
country of gallant men, of courtly women, of princely
buildings, of the wise, the polished and the sainted.
There it lay, so still and grey beneath the drifting wrack—
the home of things noble and of things shameful—the
theatre where a new name might be made or an old one
marred. From his bosom to his lips came the crumpled
veil, and he breathed a vow that if valour and goodwill
could raise him to his lady's side, then death alone should
hold him back from her. His thoughts were still in the
woods of Minstead and the old armoury of Twynham
Castle, when the hoarse voice of the master-shipman
brought them back once more to the Bay of Biscay.

" By my troth, young sir," he said, " you are as long
in the face as the devil at a christening, and I cannot
marvel at it, for I have sailed these waters since I was as
high as this whinyard, and yet I never saw more sure
promise of an evil night."

" Nay, I had other things upon my mind," the squire
answered.

" And so has every man," cried Hawtayne, in an
injured voice. " Let the shipman see to it. It is the
master-shipman's affair. Put it all upon good Master
Hawtayne ! Never had I so much care since first I blew
trumpet and showed cartel at the west gate of Southampton."

" What is amiss then ? " asked Alleyne, for the man's words were as gusty as the weather.

" Amiss, quotha ? Here am I with but half my mariners, and a hole in the ship, where that twenty-devil stone struck us, big enough to fit the fat widow of Northam through. It is well enough on this tack, but I would have you tell me what I am to do on the other. We are like to have salt water upon us until we be found pickled like the herrings in an Easterling's barrels."

" What says Sir Nigel to it ? "

" He is below pricking out the coat-armour of his mother's uncle. ' Pester me not with such small matters,' was all that I could get from him. Then there is Sir Oliver. ' Fry them in oil with a dressing of Gascony,' quoth he, and then swore at me because I had not been the cook. ' Walawa,' thought I, ' mad master, sober man '—so away forward to the archers. Harrow and alas ! but they were worse than the others."

" Would they not help you then ? "

" Nay, they sat tway and tway at a board, him that they call Aylward and the great red-headed man who snapped the Norman's arm-bone, and the black man from Norwich, and a score of others, rattling their dice in an archer's gauntlet for want of a box. ' The ship can scarce last much longer, my masters,' quoth I. ' That is your business, old swine's head,' cried the black galliard. ' Le Diable t'emporte ! ' says Aylward. ' A five, a four, and the main,' shouted the big man, with a voice like the flap of a sail. Hark to them now, young sir, and say if I speak not sooth."

As he spoke, there sounded high above the shriek of the gale and the straining of the timbers a gust of oaths with a roar of deep-chested mirth from the gamblers in the forecastle.

" Can I be of avail ? " asked Alleyne. " Say the word and the thing is done, if two hands may do it."

" Nay, nay, your head I can see is still totty, and i' faith little head would you have, had your bassinet not stood your friend. All that may be done is already carried out, for we have stuffed the gape with sails and corded it without and within. Yet when we hale our bowline and veer the sheet our lives will hang upon the breach remaining blocked. See how yonder headland looms upon us through the mist! We must tack within three arrow flights, or we may find a rock through our timbers. Now, St. Christopher be praised! here is Sir Nigel, with whom I may confer."

" I prythee that you will pardon me," said the knight, clutching his way along the bulwark. " I would not show lack of courtesy toward a worthy man, but I was deep in a matter of some weight, concerning which, Alleyne, I should be glad of your rede. It touches the question of dimidiation or impalement in the coat of mine uncle, Sir John Leighton of Shropshire, who took unto wife the widow of Sir Henry Oglander of Nunwell. The case has been much debated by pursuivants and kings-of-arms. But how is it with you, master-shipman?"

" Ill enough, my fair lord. The cog must go about anon, and I know not how we may keep the water out of her."

" Go call Sir Oliver!" said Sir Nigel, and presently the portly knight made his way all astraddle down the slippery deck.

" By my soul, master-shipman, this passes all patience!" he cried wrathfully. " If this ship of yours must needs dance and skip like a clown at a kermesse, then I pray you that you will put me into one of these galeasses. I had but sat down to a flask of malvoisie and a mortress of brawn, as is my use about this hour, when there comes a cherking, and I find my wine over my legs and the flask in my lap, and then as I stoop to clip it there comes another cursed cherk, and there is a mortress of brawn stuck fast to the nape of my neck. At this moment I have two pages coursing after it from side to side, like hounds behind a leveret. Never did living pig gambol more lightly. But you have sent for me, Sir Nigel?"

" I would fain have your rede, Sir Oliver, for Master Hawtayne hath fears that when we veer there may come danger from the hole in our side."

" Then do not veer," quoth Sir Oliver hastily. " And now, fair sir, I must hasten back to see how my rogues have fared with the brawn."

" Nay, but this will scarce suffice," cried the shipman. " If we do not veer we shall be upon the rocks within the hour."

" Then veer," said Sir Oliver. " There is my rede ; and now, Sir Nigel, I must crave——"

At this instant, however, a startled shout rang out from two seamen upon the forecastle. " Rocks ! " they yelled, stabbing into the air with their forefingers, " rocks beneath our very bows ! " Through the belly of a great great black wave, not one hundred paces to the front of them, there thrust forth a huge jagged mass of brown stone, which spouted spray as though it were some crouching monster, while a dull menacing boom and roar filled the air.

" Yare ! yare ! " screamed Goodwin Hawtayne, flinging himself upon the long pole which served as a tiller. " Cut the halliard ! Haul her over ! Lay her two courses to the wind ! "

Over swung the great boom, and the cog trembled and quivered within five spear lengths of the breakers.

" She can scarce draw clear," cried Hawtayne, with his eyes from the sail to the seething line of foam. " May the holy Julian stand by us and the thrice-sainted Christopher ! "

" If there be such peril, Sir Oliver," quoth Sir Nigel, " it would be very knightly and fitting that we should show our pennons. I pray you, Edricson, that you will command my guidon-bearer to put forward my banner."

" And sound the trumpets ! " cried Sir Oliver. " In manus tuas, Domine ! I am in the keeping of James of Compostella, to whose shrine I shall make pilgrimage, and in whose honour I vow that I will eat a carp each year upon his feast-day. Mon Dieu, but the waves roar! How is it with us now, master-shipman?"

" We draw! We draw!" cried Hawtayne, with his eyes still fixed upon the foam which hissed under the very bulge of the side. " Ah, Holy Mother, be with us now!"

As he spoke the cog rasped along the edge of the reef and a long white curling sheet of wood was planed off from her side from waist to poop by a jutting horn of the rock. At the same instant she lay suddenly over, the sail drew full, and she plunged seawards amid the shoutings of the seamen and the archers.

" The Virgin be praised!" cried the shipman, wiping his brow. " For this shall bell swing and candle burn when I see Southampton Water once more. Cheerily, my hearts! Pull yarely on the bowline!"

" By my soul! I would rather have a dry death," quoth Sir Oliver. " Though, Mort Dieu! I have eaten so many fish that it were but justice that the fish should eat me. Now I must back to the cabin, for I have matters there which crave my attention."

" Nay, Sir Oliver, you had best bide with us, and still show your ensign," Sir Nigel answered; " for, if I understand the matter aright, we have but turned from one danger to the other."

" Good Master Hawtayne," cried the boatswain, rushing aft, " the water comes in upon us apace. The waves have driven in the sail wherewith we strove to stop the hole." As he spoke the seamen came swarming on to the poop and the forecastle to avoid the torrent which poured through the huge leak into the waist. High above the roar of the wind and the clash of the sea rose the shrill half-human cries of the horses, as they found the water rising rapidly around them.

" Stop it from without!" cried Hawtayne, seizing the end of the wet sail with which the gap had been plugged. " Speedily, my hearts, or we are gone!" Swiftly they rove ropes to the corners, and then, rushing forward to the bows they lowered them under the keel, and drew them tight in such a way that the sail should cover the outer face of the gap. The force of the rush of water was checked by this obstacle, but it still squirted plentifully from every side of it. At the sides the horses were above the belly, and in the centre a man from the poop could scarce touch the deck with a seven-foot spear. The cog lay lower in the water and the waves splashed freely over the weather bulwark.

" I fear that we can scarce bide upon this tack," cried Hawtayne ; " and yet the other will drive us on the rocks."

" Might we not haul down sail and wait for better times ? " suggested Sir Nigel.

" Nay, we should drift upon the rocks. Thirty years have I been on the sea, and never yet in greater straits. Yet we are in the hands of the Saints."

" Of whom," cried Sir Oliver, " I look more particularly to Saint James of Compostella, who hath already befriended us this day, and on whose feast I hereby vow that I shall eat a second carp, if he will but interpose a second time."

The wrack had thickened to seaward, and the coast was but a blurred line. Two vague shadows in the offing showed where the galeasses rolled and tossed upon the great Atlantic rollers. Hawtayne looked wistfully in their direction. " If they would but lie closer we might find safety, even should the cog founder. You will bear me out with good Master Witherton of Southampton that I have done all that a shipman might. It would be well that you should doff camail and greaves, Sir Nigel, for, by the black rood, it is like enough that we shall have to swim for it."

" Nay," said the little knight, " it would be scarce fitting that a cavalier should throw off his harness for the fear of every puff of wind and puddle of water. I would rather that my Company should gather round me here on the poop, where we might abide together whatever God may be pleased to send. But, certes, Master

Hawtayne, for all that my sight is none of the best, it is not the first time that I have seen that headland upon the left."

The seaman shaded his eyes with his hand, and gazed earnestly through the haze and spray. Suddenly he threw up his arms, and shouted aloud in his joy.

" 'Tis the Point of La Tremblade ! " he cried. " I had not thought that we were as far as Oléron. The Gironde lies before us, and once over the bar, and under shelter of the Tour de Cordouan, all will be well with us. Veer again, my hearts, and bring her to try with the main course."

The sail swung round once more, and the cog, battered and torn and well-nigh water-logged, staggered in for this haven of refuge. A bluff cape to the north and a long spit to the south marked the mouth of the noble river, with a low-lying island of silted sand in the centre, all shrouded and curtained by the spume of the breakers. A line of broken water traced the dangerous bar, which in clear day and balmy weather has cracked the back of many a tall ship.

" There is a channel," said Hawtayne, " which was shown to me by the prince's own pilot. Mark yonder tree upon the bank, and see the tower which rises behind it. If these two be held in a line, even as we hold them now, it may be done, though our ship draws two good ells more than when she put forth."

" God speed you, Master Hawtayne ! " cried Sir Oliver. " Twice have we come scathless out of peril, and now for the third time I commend me to the blessed James of Compostella, to whom I vow——"

" Nay, nay, old friend," whispered Sir Nigel. " You are like to bring a judgment upon us with these vows, which no living man could accomplish. Have I not already heard you vow to eat two carp in one day, and now you would venture upon a third ? "

" I pray you that you will order the Company to lie down," cried Hawtayne, who had taken the tiller and was gazing ahead with a fixed eye. " In three minutes we shall either be lost or in safety."

Archers and seamen lay flat upon the deck, waiting in stolid silence for whatever fate might come. Hawtayne bent his weight upon the tiller, and crouched to see under the bellying sail. Sir Oliver and Sir Nigel stood erect with hands crossed in front of the poop. Down swooped the great cog into the narrow channel which was the portal to safety. On either bow roared the shallow bar. Right ahead one small lane of black swirling water marked the pilot's course. But true was the eye and firm the hand which guided. A dull scraping came from beneath, the vessel quivered and shook, at the waist, at the quarter, and behind sounded that grim roaring of the waters, and with a plunge the yellow cog was over the bar and speeding swiftly up the broad and tranquil estuary of the Gironde.

18. *How Sir Nigel Loring put a Patch upon His Eye*

IT was on the morning of Friday, the eight-and-twentieth day of November, two days before the feast of St. Andrew, that the cog and her two prisoners, after a weary tacking up the Gironde and the Garonne, dropped anchor at last in front of the noble city of Bordeaux. With wonder and admiration, Alleyne, leaning over the bulwarks, gazed at the forest of masts, the swarm of boats darting hither and thither on the bosom of the broad curving stream, and the grey crescent-shaped city which stretched with many a tower and minaret along the western shore. Never had he in his quiet life seen so great a town, nor was there in the whole of England, save London alone, one which might match it in size or in wealth. Here came the merchandise of all the fair countries which are watered by the Garonne and the Dordogne—the cloths of the south, the skins of Guienne, the wines of the Médoc

—to be borne away to Hull, Exeter, Dartmouth, Bristol or Chester, in exchange for the wools and woolfels of England. Here too dwelt those famous smelters and welders who had made the Bordeaux steel the most trusty upon earth, and could give a temper to lance or to sword which might mean dear life to its owner. Alleyne could see the smoke of their forges reeking up in the clear morning air. The storm had died down now to a gentle breeze, which wafted to his ears the long-drawn stirring bugle-calls which sounded from the ancient ramparts.

" Holà, mon petit ! " said Aylward, coming up where to he stood. " Thou art a squire now, and like enough to win the golden spurs, while I am still the master-bowman, and master-bowman I shall abide. I dare scarce wag my tongue so freely with you as when we tramped together past Wilverley Chase, else I might be your guide now, for indeed I know every house in Bordeaux as a friar knows the beads on his rosary."

" Nay, Aylward," said Alleyne, laying his hand upon the sleeve of his companion's frayed jerkin, " you cannot think me so thrall as to throw aside an old friend because I have had some small share of good fortune. I take it unkind that you should have thought such evil of me."

" Nay, mon gar. 'Twas but a flight shot to see if the wind blew steady, though I were a rogue to doubt it."

" Why, had I not met you, Aylward, at the Lyndhurst inn, who can say where I had now been ? Certes, I had not gone to Twynham Castle, nor become squire to Sir Nigel, nor met——" He paused abruptly and flushed to his hair, but the bowman was too busy with his own thoughts to notice his young companion's embarrassment.

" It was a good hostel, that of the ' Pied Merlin,' " remarked Aylward. " By my ten finger-bones ! when I hang bow on nail and change my brigandine for a tunic, I might do worse than take over the dame and her business."

" I thought," said Alleyne, " that you were betrothed to someone at Christchurch."

" To three," Aylward answered moodily, " to three. I fear I may not go back to Christchurch. I might chance to see hotter service in Hampshire than I have ever done in Gascony. But mark you now yonder lofty turret in the centre, which stands back from the river and hath a broad banner upon the summit. See the rising sun flashes full upon it and sparkles on the golden lions. 'Tis the royal banner of England, crossed by the prince's label. There he dwells in the Abbey of St. Andrew, where he hath kept his court these years back. Beside it is the minster of the same saint, who hath the town under his very special care."

" And how of yon grey turret on the left ? "

" 'Tis the fane of St. Michael, as that upon the right is of St. Remi. There, too, above the poop of yonder nief, you see the towers of St. Croix and of Pey Berland. Mark also the mighty ramparts which are pierced by the three watergates, and sixteen others to the landward side."

" And how is it, good Aylward, that there comes so much music from the town ? I seem to hear a hundred trumpets, all calling in chorus."

" It would be strange else, seeing that all the great lords of England and of Gascony are within the walls, and each would have his trumpeter blow as loud as his neighbour, lest it might be thought that his dignity had been abated. Ma foi ! they make as much louster as a Scotch army, where every man fills himself with girdle-cakes, and sits up all night to blow upon the toodle-pipe. See all along the banks how the pages water the horses, and there beyond the town how they gallop them over the plain ! For every horse you see a belted knight hath herbergage in the town, for, as I learn, the men-at-arms and archers have already gone forward to Dax."

" I trust, Aylward," said Sir Nigel, coming upon deck, " that the men are ready for the land. Go tell them that the boats will be for them within the hour."

The archer raised his hand in salute, and hastened forward. In the meantime Sir Oliver had followed his brother knight, and the two paced the poop together, Sir Nigel in his plum-coloured velvet suit with flat cap of the same, adorned in front with the Lady Loring's glove and girt round with a curling ostrich feather. The lusty knight, on the other hand, was clad in the very latest mode, with côte-hardie, doublet, pourpoint, court-pie, and paltock of olive-green, picked out with pink and jagged at the edges. A red chaperon or cap, with long hanging cornette, sat daintily on the back of his black-curled head, while his gold-hued shoes were twisted up *à la poulaine*, as though the toes were shooting forth a tendril which might hope in time to entwine itself around his massive leg.

" Once more, Sir Oliver," said Sir Nigel, looking shorewards with sparkling eyes, " do we find ourselves at the gate of honour, the door which hath so often led us to all that is knightly and worthy. There flies the prince's banner, and it would be well that we haste ashore and pay our obeisance to him. The boats already swarm from the bank."

" There is a goodly hostel near the west gate, which is famed for the stewing of spiced pullets," remarked Sir Oliver. " We might take the edge of our hunger off ere we seek the prince, for though his tables are gay with damask and silver, he is no trencherman himself, and hath no sympathy for those who are his betters."

" His betters ! "

" His betters before the tranchoir, lad. Sniff not treason where none is meant. I have seen him smile in his quiet way because I had looked for the fourth time towards the carving squire. And indeed to watch him dallying with a little gobbet of bread, or sipping his cup of thrice-watered wine, is enough to make a man feel shame at his own hunger. Yet war and glory, my good friend, though well enough in their way, will not serve to tighten such a belt as clasps my waist."

" How read you that coat which hangs over yonder galley, Alleyne ? " asked Sir Nigel.

" Argent, a bend vert between cotises dancetté gules."

" It is a northern coat. I have seen it in the train of the Percies. From the shields, there is not one of these vessels which hath not knight or baron aboard. I would mine eyes were better. How read you this upon the left ? "

" Argent and azure, a barry wavy of six."

" Ha, it is the sign of the Wiltshire Stourtons ! And there beyond I see the red and silver of the Worsleys of Apuldercombe, who like myself are of Hampshire lineage. Close behind us is the moline cross of the gallant William Molyneux, and beside it the bloody chevrons of the Norfolk Woodhouses, with the annulets of the Musgraves of Westmoreland. By Saint Paul ! it would be a very strange thing if so noble a company were to gather without some notable deed of arms arising from it. And here is our boat, Sir Oliver, so it seems best to me that we should go to the abbey with our squires, leaving Master Hawtayne to have his own way in the unloading."

The horses both of knights and squires were speedily lowered into a broad lighter, and reached the shore almost as soon as their masters. Sir Nigel bent his knee devoutly as he put foot on land, and taking a small black patch from his bosom he bound it tightly over his left eye.

" May the blessed George and the memory of my sweet lady-love raise high in my heart ! " quoth he. " And as a token I vow that I will not take this patch from mine eye until I have seen something of this country of Spain, and done such a small deed as it lies in me to do. And this I swear upon the cross of my sword and upon the glove of my lady."

" In truth, you take me back twenty years, Nigel," quoth Sir Oliver, as they mounted and rode slowly through the water-gate. " After Cadsand, I deem that the French thought that we were an army of the blind, for there was scarce a man who had not closed an eye for the greater love and honour of his lady. Yet it goes hard with you that you should darken one side, when with both open you can scarce tell a horse from a mule. In truth, friend, I think that you step over the line of reason in this matter."

" Sir Oliver Buttesthorn," said the little knight shortly, " I would have you to understand that, blind as I am, I can yet see the path of honour very clearly, and that that is a road upon which I do not crave another man's guidance."

" By my soul," said Sir Oliver, " you are as tart as verjuice this morning ! If you are bent upon a quarrel with me I must leave you to your humour and drop into the ' Tête d'Or ' here, for I marked a varlet pass the door who bare a smoking dish, which had, methought, a most excellent smell."

" Nenny, nenny," cried his comrade, laying his hand upon his knee ; " we have known each other over long to fall out, Oliver, like two raw pages at their first épreuves. You must come with me first to the prince, and then back to the hostel ; though sure I am that it would grieve his heart that any gentle cavalier should turn from his board to a common tavern. But is not that my Lord Delewar who waves to us ? Ha ! my fair lord, God and Our Lady be with you ! And there is Sir Robert Cheney. Good morrow, Robert ! I am right glad to see you."

The two knights walked their horses abreast, while Alleyne and Ford, with John Norbury, who was squire to Sir Oliver, kept some paces behind them, a spear's length in front of Black Simon and of the Winchester guidon-bearer. Norbury, a lean silent man, had been to those parts before, and sat his horse with a rigid neck ; but the two young squires gazed eagerly to right or left, and plucked each other's sleeves to call attention to the many strange things on every side of them.

" See to the brave stalls ! " cried Alleyne. " See to the noble armour set forth, and the costly taffeta—and oh, Ford, see to where the scrivener sits with the pigments and the ink-horns, and the rolls of sheepskin as white as the Beaulieu napery ! Saw man ever the like before ? "

" Nay, man, there are finer stalls in Cheapside," answered Ford, whose father had taken him to London on occasion of one of the Smithfield joustings. " I have seen a silversmith's booth there which would serve to buy either side of this street. But mark these houses, Alleyne, how they thrust forth upon the top. And see to the coats-of-arms at every window, and banner or pensil on the roof."

" And the churches ! " cried Alleyne. " The Priory at Christchurch was a noble pile, but it was cold and bare, methinks, by one of these, with their frettings, and their carvings and their traceries, as though some great ivy-plant of stone had curled and wantoned over the walls."

" And hark to the speech of the folk ! " said Ford. " Was ever such a hissing and clacking ? I wonder that they have not wit to learn English now that they have come under the English crown. By Richard of Hampole ! there are fair faces amongst them. See the wench with the brown wimple ! Out on you, Alleyne, that you would rather gaze upon dead stone than on living flesh ! "

It was little wonder that the richness and ornament, not only of church and of stall, but of every private house as well, should have impressed itself upon the young squires. The town was now at the height of its fortunes. Besides its trade and its armourers, other causes had combined to pour wealth into it. War, which had wrought evil upon so many fair cities around, had brought nought but good to this one. As her French sisters decayed she increased, for here, from north, and from east, and from south, came the plunder to be sold and the ransom money to be spent. Through all her sixteen landward gates there had set for many years a double tide of empty-handed soldiers hurrying Francewards, and of enriched and laden bands who brought their spoils home. The prince's court, too, with its swarms of noble barons and wealthy knights, many of whom, in imitation of their master, had brought their ladies and their children from England, all hoped to swell the coffers of the burghers.

Now with this fresh influx of noblemen and cavaliers, food and lodgings were scarce to be had, and the prince was hurrying his forces to Dax in Gascony to relieve the overcrowding of his capital.

In front of the minster and abbey of St. Andrew's was a large square crowded with priests, soldiers, women, friars, and burghers, who made it their common centre for sight-seeing and gossip. Amid the knots of noisy and gesticulating townsfolk many small parties of mounted knights and squires threaded their way towards the prince's quarters, where the huge iron-clamped doors were thrown back to show that he held audience within. Two score archers stood about the gateway, and beat back from time to time with their bow-staves the inquisitive and chattering crowd who swarmed round the portal. Two knights in full armour, with lances raised and closed vizors, sat their horses on either side, while in the centre, with two pages to tend upon him, there stood a noble-faced man in flowing purple gown, who pricked off upon a sheet of parchment the style and title of each applicant, marshalling them in their due order, and giving to each the place and facility which his rank demanded. His long white beard and searching eyes imparted to him an air of masterful dignity, which was increased by his tabard-like vesture and the heraldic barret cap with triple plume which bespoke his office.

" It is Sir William de Pakington, the prince's own herald and scrivener," whispered Sir Nigel, as they pulled up amid the line of knights who awaited admission. " Ill fares it with the man who should venture to deceive him. He hath by rote the name of every knight of France or of England, and all the tree of his family, with his kinships, coat-armour, marriages, augmentations, abatements, and I know not what beside. We may leave our horses here with the varlets, and push forward with our squires."

Following Sir Nigel's counsel, they pressed on upon foot until they were close to the prince's secretary, who was in high debate with a young and foppish knight, who was bent upon making his way past him.

" Mackworth ! " said the king-at-arms. " It is in my mind, young sir, that you have not been presented before."

" Nay, it is but a day since I set foot in Bordeaux, but I feared lest the prince should think it strange that I had not waited upon him."

" The prince hath other things to think upon," quoth Sir William de Pakington ; " but if you be a Mackworth you must be a Mackworth of Normanton, and indeed I see now that your coat is sable and ermine."

" I am a Mackworth of Normanton," the other answered, with some uneasiness of manner.

" Then you must be Sir Stephen Mackworth, for I learn that when old Sir Guy died he came in for the arms and the name, the war-cry and the profit."

" Sir Stephen is my elder brother, and I am Arthur, the second son," said the youth.

" In sooth and in sooth ! " cried the king-at-arms with scornful eyes. " And pray, sir second son, where is the cadency mark which should mark your rank ? Dare you to wear your brother's coat without the crescent which should stamp you as his cadet ? Away to your lodgings, and come not nigh the prince until the armourer hath placed the true charge upon your shield." As the youth withdrew in confusion, Sir William's keen eye singled out the five red roses from amid the overlapping shields and clouds of pennons which faced him.

" Ha ! " he cried, " there are charges here which are above counterfeit. The roses of Loring and the boar's head of Buttesthorn may stand back in peace, but, by my faith ! they are not to be held back in war. Welcome, Sir Oliver, Sir Nigel ! Chandos will be glad to his very heart-roots when he sees you. This way, my fair sirs. Your squires are doubtless worthy the fame of their masters. Down this passage, Sir Oliver ! Edricson ! Ha ! one of the old strain of Hampshire Edricsons, I doubt not.

And Ford, they are of a south Saxon stock, and of good repute. There are Norburys in Cheshire and in Wilt-shire, and also, as I have heard, upon the borders. So, my fair sirs, and I shall see that you are shortly admitted."

He had finished his professional commentary by flinging open a folding-door, and ushering the party into a broad hall, which was filled with a great number of people who were waiting, like themselves, for an audience. The room was very spacious, lighted on one side by three arched and mullioned windows, while opposite was a huge fireplace in which a pile of faggots was blazing merrily. Many of the company had crowded round the flames, for the weather was bitterly cold ; but the two knights seated themselves upon a bancal, with their squires standing behind them. Looking down the room, Alleyne marked that both floor and ceiling were of the richest oak, the latter spanned by twelve arching beams which were adorned at either end by the lilies and the lions of the royal arms. On the farther side was a small door, on each side of which stood men-at-arms. From time to time an elderly man in black with rounded shoulders and a long white wand in his hand came softly from this inner room and beckoned to one or other of the company, who doffed cap and followed him.

The two knights were deep in talk, when Alleyne became aware of a remarkable individual who was walk-ing round the room in their direction. As he passed each knot of cavaliers every head turned to look after him, and it was evident, from the bows and respectful salutations on all sides, that the interest which he excited was not due merely to his strange personal appearance. He was tall and as straight as a lance, though of a great age, for his hair, which curled from under his black velvet cap of maintenance, was as white as the new-fallen snow. Yet, from the swing of his stride and spring of his step, it was clear that he had not yet lost the fire and activity of his youth. His fierce hawk-like face was clean shaven like that of a priest, save for a long thin wisp of white moustache which dropped down halfway to his shoulder. That he had been handsome might be easily judged from his high aquiline nose and clear-cut chin ; but his features had been so distorted by the seams and scars of old wounds, and by the loss of one eye which had been torn from the socket, that there was little to remind one of the dashing young knight who had been fifty years ago the fairest as well as the boldest of the English chivalry. Yet what knight was there in that hall of St. Andrew's who would not have gladly laid down youth, beauty, and all that he possessed to win the fame of this man ? For who could be named with Chandos, the stainless knight, the wise councillor, the valiant warrior, the hero of Crécy, of Winchelsea, of Poictiers, of Auray, and of as many other battles as there were years to his life ?

" Ha, my little heart of gold ! " he cried, darting forward suddenly and throwing his arms round Sir Nigel. " I heard that you were here, and have been seeking you."

" My fair and dear lord," said the knight, returning the warrior's embrace, " I have indeed come back to you, for where else shall I go that I may learn to be a gentle and a hardy knight ? "

" By my troth," said Chandos with a smile, " it is very fitting that we should be companions, Nigel, for since you have tied up one of your eyes, and I have had the mischance to lose one of mine, we have but a pair between us. Ah, Sir Oliver ! you were on the blind side of me and I saw you not. A wise woman hath made prophecy that this blind side will one day be the death of me. We shall go in to the prince anon ; but in truth he hath much upon his hands, for what with Pedro, and the King of Majorca, and the King of Navarre, who is no two days of the same mind, and the Gascon barons, who are all chaffering for terms like so many hucksters, he hath an uneasy part to play. But how left you the Lady Loring ? "

" She was well, my fair lord, and sent her service and greetings to you."

" I am ever her knight and slave. And your journey,
I trust that it was pleasant ? "

" As heart could wish. We had sight of two rover
galleys, and even came to have some slight bickering with
them."

" Ever in luck's way, Nigel ! " quoth Sir John. " We
must hear the tale anon. But I deem it best that ye
should leave your squires and come with me, for, how-
soe'er pressed the prince may be, I am very sure that he
would be loth to keep two old comrades in arms upon
the farther side of the door. Follow close behind me,
and I will forestall old Sir William, though I can scarce
promise to roll forth your style and rank as is his wont."
So saying, he led the way to the inner chamber, the two
companions treading close at his heels, and nodding to
right and left as they caught sight of familiar faces among
the crowd.

19. *How there was Stir at the Abbey of St. Andrew's*

THE prince's reception room, although of no great
size, was fitted up with all the state and luxury which
the fame and power of its owner demanded. A high
dais at the further end was roofed in by a broad canopy
of scarlet velvet spangled with silver fleurs-de-lis, and
supported at either corner by silver rods. This was
approached by four steps carpeted with the same material,
while all round were scattered rich cushions, Oriental
mats, and costly rugs of fur. The choicest tapestries
which the looms of Arras could furnish draped the walls,
whereon the battles of Judas Maccabæus were set forth,
with the Jewish warriors in plate of proof, with crest and
lance and banderole, as the naïve artists of the day were
wont to depict them. A few rich settles and bancals,
choicely carved and decorated with glazed leather
hangings of the sort termed *or basané*, completed the

furniture of the apartment, save that at one side of the dais there stood a lofty perch, upon which a cast of three solemn Prussian gerfalcons sat, hooded and jesseled, as silent and motionless as the royal fowler who stood beside them.

In the centre of the dais were two very high chairs with dorserets, which arched forwards over the heads of the occupants, the whole covered with light blue silk thickly powdered with golden stars. On that to the right sat a very tall and well-formed man with red hair, a livid face, and a cold blue eye, which had in it something peculiarly sinister and menacing. He lounged back in a careless position, and yawned repeatedly as though heartily weary of the proceedings, stooping from time to time to fondle a shaggy Spanish greyhound which lay stretched at his feet. On the other throne there was perched bolt up-right, with prim demeanour, as though he felt himself to be upon his good behaviour, a little round, pippin-faced person, who smiled and bobbed to every one whose eye he chanced to meet. Between, and a little in front of them, on a humber charette or stool, sat a slim, dark young man, whose quiet attire and modest manner would scarce proclaim him to be the most noted prince in Europe. A jupon of dark blue cloth, tagged with buckles and pendants of gold, seemed but a sombre and plain attire amidst the wealth of silk and ermine and gilt tissue of fustian with which he was surrounded. He sat with his two hands clasped round his knee, his head slightly bent, and an expression of impatience and of trouble upon his clear well-chiselled features. Behind the thrones there stood two men in purple gowns, with ascetic, clean-shaven faces, and half a dozen other high dignitaries and office-holders of Aquitaine. Below on either side of the steps were forty or fifty barons, knights, and courtiers, ranged in a triple row to the right and the left, with a clear passage in the centre.

" There sits the prince," whispered Sir John Chandos as they entered. " He on the right is Pedro, whom we are about to put upon the Spanish throne. The other is Don James, whom we purpose with the aid of God to help to his throne in Majorca. Now follow me, and take it not to heart, if he be a little short in his speech, for indeed his mind is full of many very weighty concerns."

The prince, however, had already observed their entrance, and, springing to his feet, he had advanced with a winning smile and the light of welcome in his eyes.

" We do not need your good offices as herald here, Sir John," said he in a low but clear voice ; " these valiant knights are very well known to me. Welcome to Aquitaine, Sir Nigel Loring and Sir Oliver Buttesthorn. Nay, keep your knee for my sweet father at Windsor. I would have your hands, my friends. We are like to give you some work to do ere you see the downs of Hampshire once more. Know you ought of Spain, Sir Oliver ? "

" Nought, my sire, save that I have heard men say that there is a dish named an olla which is prepared there, though I have never been clear in my mind as to whether it was but a ragout such as is to be found in the south, or whether there is some seasoning such as fennel or garlic which is peculiar to Spain."

" Your doubts, Sir Oliver, shall soon be resolved," answered the prince, laughing heartily, as did many of the barons who surrounded them. " His Majesty here will doubtless order that you have this dish hotly seasoned when we are all safely in Castile."

" I will have a hotly seasoned dish for some folk I know of," answered Don Pedro with a cold smile.

" But my friend Sir Oliver can fight right hardily without either bite or sup," remarked the prince. " Did I not see him at Poictiers, when for two days we had not more than a crust of bread and a cup of foul water, yet carrying himself most valiantly ? With my own eyes I saw him in the rout sweep the head from a knight of Picardy with one blow of his sword."

" The rogue got between me and the nearest French victualwain," muttered Sir Oliver, amid a fresh titter from those who were near enough to catch his words.

" How many have you in your train ? " asked the prince, assuming a graver mien.

" I have forty men-at-arms, sire," said Sir Oliver.

" And I have one hundred archers and a score of lances, but there are two hundred men who wait for me on this side of the water upon the borders of Navarre."

" And who are they, Sir Nigel ? "

" They are a free company, sire, and they are called the White Company."

To the astonishment of the knight, his words provoked a burst of merriment from the barons round, in which the two kings and the prince were fain to join. Sir Nigel blinked mildly from one to the other, until at last, perceiving a stout black-bearded knight at his elbow, whose laugh rang somewhat louder than the others, he touched him lightly upon the sleeve.

" Perchance, my fair sir," he whispered, " there is some small vow of which I may relieve you. Might we not have some honourable debate upon the matter ? Your gentle courtesy may perhaps grant me an exchange of thrusts."

" Nay, nay, Sir Nigel," cried the prince, " fasten not the offence upon Sir Robert Briquet, for we are one and all bogged in the same mire. Truth to say, our ears have just been vexed by the doings of the same Company, and I have even now made vow to hang the man who held the rank of captain over it. I little thought to find him among the bravest of my own chosen chieftains. But the vow is now nought, for, as you have never seen your Company, it would be a fool's act to blame you for their doings."

" My liege," said Sir Nigel, " it is a very small matter that I should be hanged, albeit the manner of death is somewhat more ignoble than I had hoped for. On the other hand, it would be a very grievous thing that you, the Prince of England, and the flower of knighthood, should make a vow, whether in ignorance or no, and fail to bring it to fulfilment."

" Vex not your mind on that," the prince answered,

smiling. " We have had a citizen from Montauban here this very day, who told us such a tale of sack and murder and pillage that it moved our blood ; but our wrath was turned upon the man who was in authority over them, and not on him who had never set eyes upon them."

" My dear and honoured master," cried Nigel, in great anxiety, " I fear me much that in your gentleness of heart you are straining this vow which you have taken. If there be so much as a shadow of a doubt as to the form of it, it were a thousand times best——"

" Peace ! peace ! " cried the prince impatiently. " I am very well able to look to my own vows and their performance. We hope to see you both in the banquet-hall anon. Meanwhile you will attend upon us with our train." He bowed, and Chandos, plucking Sir Oliver by the sleeve, led them both away to the back of the press of courtiers.

" Why, little coz," he whispered, " you are very eager to have your neck in a noose. By my soul ! had you asked as much from our new ally, Don Pedro, he had not baulked you. Between friends, there is overmuch of the hangman in him, and too little of the prince. But indeed this White Company is a rough band, and may take some handling ere you find yourself safe in your captaincy."

" I doubt not, with the help of St. Paul, that I shall bring them to some order," Sir Nigel answered. " But there are many faces here which are new to me, though others have been before me since first I waited upon my dear master, Sir Walter. I pray you to tell me, Sir John, who are these priests upon the dais ? "

" The one is the Archbishop of Bordeaux, Nigel, and the other the Bishop of Agen."

" And the dark knight with grey-streaked beard ? By my troth, he seems to be a man of much wisdom and valour."

" He is Sir William Felton, who, with my unworthy self, is the chief counsellor of the prince, he being high steward and I the seneschal of Aquitaine."

" And the knights upon the right, beside Don Pedro ? "

" They are cavaliers of Spain who have followed him in his exile.   The one at his elbow is Fernando de Castro, who is as brave and true a man as heart could wish.   In front to the right are the Gascon lords.   You may well tell them by their clouded brows, for there hath been some ill-will of late betwixt the prince and them.   The tall and burly man is the Captal de Buch, whom I doubt not that you know, for a braver knight never laid lance in rest. That heavy-faced cavalier who plucks his skirts and whispers in his ear is Lord Oliver de Clisson, known also as the Butcher.   He it is who stirs up strife, and for ever blows the dying embers into flame.   The man with the mole upon his cheek is the Lord Pommers, and his two brothers stand behind him, with the Lord Lesparre, Lord de Rosem, Lord de Mucident, Sir Perducas d' Albret, the Souldich de la Trane, and others.   Further back are knights from Quercy, Limousin, Saintonge, Poitou, and Aquitaine, with the valiant Sir Guiscard d'Angle.   That is he in the rose-coloured doublet with the ermine."

" And the knights upon this side ? "

" They are all Englishmen, some of the household and others who, like yourself, are captains of companies. There is Lord Neville, Sir Stephen Cossington, and Sir Matthew Gourney, with Sir Walter Huet, Sir Thomas Banaster, and Sir Thomas Felton, who is the brother of the high steward.   Mark well the man with the high nose and flaxen beard who hath placed his hand upon the shoulder of the dark hard-faced cavalier in the rust-stained jupon."

" Aye, by St. Paul ! " observed Sir Nigel, " they both bear the print of their armour upon their côtes-hardies. Methinks they are men who breathe freer in a camp than a court."

" There are many of us who do that, Nigel," said Chandos, " and the head of the court is, I dare warrant, among them.   But of these two men the one is Sir Hugh Calverley, and the other is Sir Robert Knolles."

Sir Nigel and Sir Oliver craned their necks to have the clearer view of these famous warriors, the one a chosen leader of free companies, the other a man who by his fierce valour and energy had raised himself from the lowest ranks until he was second only to Chandos himself in the esteem of the army.

" He hath no light hand in war, hath Sir Robert," said Chandos. " If he passes through a country you may tell it for some years to come. I have heard that in the north it is still the use to call a house which hath but the two gable-ends left, without walls and roof, a Knolles' mitre."

" I have served under him," said Sir Nigel, " and I have hoped to be so far honoured as to run a course with him. But hark, Sir John, what is amiss with the prince ? "

Whilst Chandos had been conversing with the two knights a continuous stream of suitors had been ushered in, adventurers seeking to sell their swords, and merchants clamouring over some grievance, a ship detained for the carriage of troops, or a tun of sweet wine which had the bottom knocked out by a troop of thirsty archers. A few words from the prince disposed of each case, and if the applicant liked not the judgment, a quick glance from the prince's dark eyes sent him to the door with the grievance all gone out of him. The young ruler had sat listlessly upon his stool with the two puppet monarchs enthroned behind him, but of a sudden a dark shadow passed over his face, and he sprang to his feet in one of those gusts of passion which were the single blot upon his noble and generous character.

"How now, Don Martin de la Carra ? " he cried. " How now, sirrah ? What message do you bring to us from our brother of Navarre ? "

The new-comer to whom this abrupt query had been addressed was a tall and exceedingly handsome cavalier who had just been ushered into the apartment. His swarthy cheek and raven black hair spoke of the fiery south, and he wore his long black coat swathed across his chest and over his shoulders in a graceful sweeping fashion, which was neither English nor French. With stately steps and many profound bows he advanced to the foot of the dais before replying to the prince's question.

" My powerful and illustrious master," he began, " Charles, King of Navarre, Earl of Evreux, Count of Champagne, who also writeth himself Overlord of Bearn, hereby sends his love and greetings to his dear cousin Edward, the Prince of Wales, Governor of Aquitaine, Grand Commander of——"

" Tush ! tush ! Don Martin ! " interrupted the prince, who had been beating the ground with his foot impatiently during this stately preamble. " We already know our cousin's titles and style, and, certes, we know our own. To the point, man, and at once. Are the passes open to us, or does your master go back from his word pledged to me at Libourne no later than last Michaelmas ? "

" It would ill become my gracious master, sire, to go back from promise given. He does but ask some delay and certain conditions and hostages——"

" Conditions ! Hostages ! Is he speaking to the Prince of England, or is it to the bourgeois provost of some half-captured town ? Conditions, quotha ? He may find much to mend in his own condition ere long. The passes are, then, closed to us ? "

" Nay, sire——"

" They are open, then ? "

" Nay, sire, if you would but——"

" Enough, enough, Don Martin," cried the prince. " It is a sorry sight to see so true a knight pleading in so false a cause. We know the doings of our Cousin Charles. We know that while with the right hand he takes our fifty thousand crowns for the holding of the passes open, he hath his left outstretched to Henry of Trastamare, or to the King of France, all ready to take as many more for the keeping them closed. I know our good Charles, and, by my blessed name-saint the Confessor, he shall learn that

I know him. He sets his kingdom up to the best bidder, like some scullion farrier selling a glandered horse. He is——"

" My lord," cried Don Martin. " I cannot stand here to hear such words of my master. Did they come from other lips I should know better how to answer them."

Don Pedro frowned and curled his lip, but the prince smiled and nodded his approbation.

" Your bearing and your words, Don Martin, are such as I should have looked for in you," he remarked. " You will tell the king, your master, that he hath been paid his price, and that if he holds to his promise he hath my word for it that no scath shall come to his people, nor to their houses or gear. If, however, we have not his leave, I shall come close at the heels of this message without his leave, and bearing a key with me which shall open all that he may close." He stooped and whispered to Sir Robert Knolles and Sir Hugh Calverley, who smiled as men well pleased, and hastened from the room.

" Our Cousin Charles has had experience of our friendship," the prince continued, " and now, by the Saints ! he shall feel a touch of our displeasure. I send now a message to our Cousin Charles which his whole kingdom may read. Let him take heed lest worse befall him. Where is my Lord Chandos ? Ha, Sir John, I commend this worthy knight to your care. You will see that he hath refection, and such a purse of gold as may defray his charges, for indeed it is great honour to any court to have within it so noble and gentle a cavalier. How say you, sire ? " he asked turning to the Spanish refugee, while the herald of Navarre was conducted from the chamber by the old warrior.

" It is not our custom in Spain to reward pertness in a messenger," Don Pedro answered, patting the head of his greyhound. " Yet we have all heard the lengths to which your royal generosity runs."

" In sooth, yes," cried the King of Majorca.

" Who should know it better than we," said Don Pedro

bitterly, " since we have had to fly to you in our trouble as to the natural protector of all who are weak ? "

" Nay, nay, as brothers to a brother," cried the prince, with sparkling eyes. " We doubt not, with the help of God, to see you very soon restored to those thrones from which you have been so traitorously thrust."

" When that happy day comes," said Pedro, " then Spain shall be to you as Aquitaine, and, be your project what it may, you may ever count on every troop and every ship over which flies the banner of Castile."

" And," added the other, " upon every aid which the wealth and power of Majorca can bestow."

" Touching the hundred thousand crowns in which I stand your debtor," continued Pedro carelessly, " it can no doubt——"

" Not a word, sire, not a word ! " cried the prince. " It is not now when you are in grief that I would vex your mind with such base and sordid matters. I have said once and for ever that I am yours with every bow-string of my army and every florin in my coffers."

" Ah ! here is indeed a mirror of chivalry," said Don Pedro. " I think, Sir Fernando, since the prince's bounty is stretched so far, that we may make further use of his gracious goodness to the extent of fifty thousand crowns. Good Sir William Felton, here, will doubtless settle the matter with you."

The stout old English councillor looked somewhat blank at this prompt acceptance of his master's bounty.

" If it please you, sire," he said, " the public funds are at their lowest, seeing that I have paid twelve thousand men of the companies, and the new taxes—the hearth tax and the wine tax—not yet come in. If you could wait until the promised help from England comes——"

" Nay, nay, my sweet cousin," cried Don Pedro. " Had we known that your own coffers were so low, or that this sorry sum could have weighed one way or the other, we had been loth indeed——"

" Enough, sire, enough ! " said the prince, flushing with

vexation. " If the public funds be, indeed, so backward, Sir William, there is still, I trust, my own private credit, which hath never been drawn upon for my own uses, but is now ready in the cause of a friend in adversity. Go, raise this money upon our own jewels, if nought else may serve, and see that it be paid over to Don Fernando."

" In security I offer——" cried Don Pedro.

" Tush ! tush ! " said the prince. " I am not a Lombard, sire. Your kingly pledge is my security, without bond or seal. But I have tidings for you, my lords and lieges, that our brother of Lancaster is on his way for our capital with four hundred lances and as many archers to aid us in our venture. When he hath come, and when our fair consort is recovered in her health, which I trust by the grace of God may be ere many weeks be past, we shall then join the army at Dax, and set our banners to the breeze once more."

A buzz of joy at the prospect of immediate action arose up from the group of warriors. The prince smiled at the martial ardour which shone upon every face around him.

" It will hearten you to know," he continued, " that I have sure advices that this Henry is a very valiant leader, and that he has it in his power to make such a stand against us as promises to give us much honour and pleasure. Of his own people he hath brought together, as I learn, some fifty thousand, with twelve thousand of the French free companies, who are, as you know, very valiant and expert men-at-arms. It is certain, also, that the brave and worthy Bertrand du Guesclin hath ridden into France to the Duke of Anjou, and purposes to take back with him great levies from Picardy and Brittany. We hold Bertrand in high esteem, for he has oft before been at great pains to furnish us with an honourable encounter. What think you of it, my worthy Captal ? He took you at Cocherel, and, by my soul ! you will have the chance now to pay that score."

The Gascon warrior winced a little at the allusion, nor were his countrymen around him better pleased, for on the only occasion when they had encountered the arms of France without English aid they had met with a heavy defeat.

"There are some who say, sire," said the burly De Clisson, "that the score is already overpaid, for that without Gascon help Bertrand had not been taken at Auray, nor had King John been overborne at Poictiers."

"By heaven, but this is too much!" cried an English nobleman. "Methinks that Gascony is too small a cock to crow so lustily."

"The smaller cock, my Lord Audley, may have the longer spur," remarked the Captal de Buch.

"May have its comb clipped if it make overmuch noise," broke in an Englishman.

"By Our Lady of Rocamadour!" cried the Lord of Mucident, "this is more than I can abide. Sir John Charnell, you shall answer to me for those words!"

"Freely, my lord, and when you will," returned the Englishman carelessly.

"My Lord de Clisson," cried Lord Audley, "you look somewhat fixedly in my direction. By God's soul! I should be right glad to go further into the matter with you."

"And you, my Lord of Pommers," said Sir Nigel, pushing his way to the front, "it is in my mind that we might break a lance in gentle and honourable debate over the question."

For a moment a dozen challenges flashed backwards and forwards at this sudden bursting of the cloud which had lowered so long between the knights of the two nations. Furious and gesticulating the Gascons, white and cold and sneering the English, while the prince with a half-smile glanced from one party to the other, like a man who loved to dwell upon a fiery scene, and yet dreaded lest the mischief go so far that he might find it beyond his control.

"Friends, friends!" he cried at last, "this quarrel must go no further. The man shall answer to me, be he Gascon or English, who carries it beyond this room. I have overmuch need for your swords that you should turn them upon each other. Sir John Charnell, Lord Audley, you do not doubt the courage of our friends of Gascony ? "

" Not I, sire," Lord Audley answered. " I have seen them fight too often not to know that they are very hardy and valiant gentlemen."

" And so say I," quoth the other Englishman ; " but, certes, there is no fear of our forgetting it while they have a tongue in their heads."

" Nay, Sir John," said the prince, reprovingly, " all peoples have their own use and customs. There are some who might call us cold and dull and silent. But you hear, my lords of Gascony, that these gentlemen had no thought to throw a slur upon your honour or your valour, so let all anger fade from your mind. Clisson, Captal, De Pommers, I have your word ? "

" We are your subjects, sire," said the Gascon barons, though with no very good grace. "Your words are our law."

" Then shall we bury all cause of unkindness in a flagon of malvoisie," said the prince, cheerily. " Ho, there ! the doors of the banquet-hall ! I have been overlong from my sweet spouse, but I shall be back with you anon. Let the sewers serve and the minstrels play, while we drain a cup to the brave days that are before us in the south ! " He turned away, accompanied by the two monarchs, while the rest of the company, with many a compressed lip and menacing eye, filed slowly through the side-door to the great chamber in which the royal tables were set forth.

20. *How Alleyne won his Place in an Honourable Guild*

WHILST the prince's council was sitting, Alleyne and Ford had remained in the outer hall, where they were soon surrounded by a noisy group of young Englishmen of their own rank, all eager to hear the latest news from England.

" How is it with the old man at Windsor ? " asked one.

" And how with the good Queen Philippa ? "

" And how with Dame Alice Perrers ? " cried a third.

" The devil take your tongue, Wat ! " shouted a tall young man, seizing the last speaker by the collar and giving him an admonitory shake. " The prince would take your head off for those words."

" By God's coif ! Wat would miss it but little," said another. " It is as empty as a beggar's wallet."

" As empty as an English squire, coz," cried the first speaker. " What a devil has become of the maître-des-tables and his sewers ? They have not put forth the trestles yet."

" Mon Dieu ! if a man could eat himself into knight-hood, Humphrey, you had been a banneret at the least," observed another, amid a burst of laughter.

" And if you could drink yourself in, old leather-head, you had been first baron of the realm," cried the aggrieved Humphrey. " But how of England, my lads of Loring ? "

" I take it," said Ford, " that it is much as it was when you were there last, save that perchance there is a little less noise there."

" And why less noise, young Solomon ? "

" Ah, that is for your wit to discover."

" Pardieu ! here is a paladin come over, with the Hampshire mud still sticking to his shoes. He means that the noise is less for our being out of the country."

" They are very quick in these parts," said Ford, turning to Alleyne.

" How are we to take this, sir ? " asked the ruffling squire.

" You may take it as it comes," said Ford carelessly.

" Here is pertness ! " cried the other.

" Sir, I honour your truthfulness," said Ford.

" Stint it, Humphrey," said the tall squire, with a burst of laughter. " You will have little credit from this gentle-man, I perceive. Tongues are sharp in Hampshire, sir."

" And swords ? "

223

" Hum ! we may prove that. In two days' time is the vêpres du tournoi, when we may see if your lance is as quick as your wit."

" All very well, Roger Harcomb," cried a burly bull-necked young man, whose square shoulders and massive limbs told of exceptional personal strength. " You pass too lightly over the matter. We are not to be so easily overcrowed. The Lord Loring hath given his proofs : but we know nothing of his squires, save that one of them hath a railing tongue. And how of you, young sir ? " bringing his heavy hand down on Alleyne's shoulder.

" And what of me, young sir ? "

" Ma foi ! this is my lady's page come over. Your cheek will be browner and your hand harder ere you see your mother again."

" If my hand is not hard, it is ready."

" Ready ? Ready for what ? For the hem of my lady's train ? "

" Ready to chastise insolence, sir ! " cried Alleyne with flashing eyes.

" Sweet little coz ! " answered the burly squire. " Such a dainty colour ! Such a mellow voice ! Eyes of a bash-ful maid, and hair like a three years' babe ! Voilà ! " He passed his thick fingers roughly through the youth's crisp golden curls.

" You seek to force a quarrel, sir," said the young man white with anger.

" And what then ? "

" Why, you do it like a country boor, and not like a gentle squire. Hast been ill bred and as ill taught ? I serve a master who could show you how such things should be done."

" And how would he do it, oh pink of squires ? "

" He would neither be loud nor would he be un-mannerly, but rather more gentle than is his wont. He would say, ' Sir, I should take it as an honour to do some small deed of arms against you, not for mine own glory or advancement, but rather for the fame of my lady and for the upholding of chivalry.' Then he would draw his glove, thus, and throw it on the ground : or, if he had cause to think that he had to deal with a churl, he might throw it in his face—as I do now ! "

A buzz of excitement went up from the knot of squires as Alleyne, his gentle nature turned by this causeless attack into fiery resolution, dashed his glove with all his strength into the sneering face of his antagonist. From all parts of the hall squires and pages came running, until a dense swaying crowd surrounded the disputants.

" Your life for this ! " said the bully, with a face which was distorted with rage.

" If you can take it," returned Alleyne.

" Good lad," whispered Ford. " Stick to it close as wax."

" I shall see justice," cried Norbury, Sir Oliver's silent attendant.

" You brought it upon yourself, John Tranter," said the tall squire, who had been addressed as Roger Harcomb. " You must ever plague the new-comers. But it were shame if this went further. The lad hath shown a proper spirit."

" But a blow ! a blow ! " cried several of the older squires. " There must be a finish to this."

" Nay ; Tranter first laid hand upon his head," said Harcomb. " How say you, Tranter ? The matter may rest where it stands ? "

" My name is known in these parts," said Tranter, proudly, " I can let pass what might leave a stain upon another. Let him pick up his glove and say that he has done amiss."

" I would see him in the claws of the devil first," whispered Ford.

" You hear, young sir ? " said the peacemaker. " Our friend will overlook the matter if you do but say that you have acted in heat and haste."

" I cannot say that," answered Alleyne.

" It is our custom, young sir, when new squires come

amongst us from England, to test them in some such way. Bethink you that if a man have a destrier or a new lance he will ever try it in time of peace, lest in days of need it may fail him. How much more then is it proper to test those who are our comrades in arms ? "

" I should draw out if it may honourably be done," murmured Norbury in Alleyne's ear. " The man is a noted swordsman and far above your strength."

Edricson came, however, of that sturdy Saxon blood which is very slowly heated, but once up not easily to be cooled. The hint of danger which Norbury threw out was the thing needed to harden his resolution.

" I came here at the back of my master," he said, " and I looked on every man here as an Englishman and a friend. This gentleman hath shown me a rough welcome, and if I have answered him in the same spirit he has but himself to thank. I will pick the glove up ; but, certes, I shall abide by what I have done unless he first crave my pardon for what he hath said and done."

Tranter shrugged his shoulders. " You have done what you could to save him, Harcomb," said he. " We had best settle at once."

" So say I," cried Alleyne.

" The council will not break up until the banquet," remarked a grey-haired squire. " You have a clear two hours."

" And the place ? "

" The tilting-yard is empty at this hour."

" Nay ; it must not be within the grounds of the court, or it may go hard with all concerned if it come to the ears of the prince."

" But there is a quiet spot near the river," said one youth. " We have but to pass through the abbey grounds along the armoury wall, past the church of St. Remi, and so down the Rue des Apôtres."

" En avant, then ! " cried Tranter shortly, and the whole assembly flocked out into the open air, save only those whom the special orders of their masters held to their posts. These unfortunates crowded to the small casements, and craned their necks after the throng as far as they could catch a glimpse of them.

Close to the bank of the Garonne there lay a little tract of green sward, with the high wall of a prior's garden upon one side and an orchard with a thick bristle of leafless apple-trees upon the other. The river ran deep and swift up to the steep bank ; but there were few boats upon it, and the ships were moored far out in the centre of the stream. Here the two combatants drew their swords and threw off their doublets, for neither had any defensive armour. The duello with its stately etiquette had not yet come into vogue, but rough and sudden encounters were as common as they must ever be when hot-headed youth goes abroad with a weapon strapped to its waist. In such combats, as well as in the more formal sports of the tilting-yard, Tranter had won a name for strength and dexterity which had caused Norbury to utter his well-meant warning. On the other hand, Alleyne had used his weapons in constant exercise and practice for every day for many months, and being by nature quick of eye and prompt of hand, he might pass now as no mean swordsman. A strangely opposed pair they appeared as they approached each other : Tranter dark and stout and stiff, with hairy chest and corded arms ; Alleyne a model of comeliness and grace, with his golden hair and his skin as fair as a woman's. An unequal fight it seemed to most ; but there were a few and they the most experienced who saw something in the youth's steady grey eye and wary step which left the issue open to doubt.

" Hold, sirs, hold ! " cried Norbury, ere blow had been struck. " This gentleman hath a two-handed sword, a good foot longer than that of our friend."

" Take mine, Alleyne ! " said Ford.

" Nay, friends," he answered, " I understand the weight and balance of mine own. To work, sir, for our lord may need us at the abbey ! "

Tranter's great sword was indeed a mighty vantage in

his favour. He stood with his feet close together, his knees bent outwards, ready for a dash inwards or a spring out. The weapon he held straight up in front of him with blade erect, so that he might either bring it down with a swinging blow, or by a turn of the heavy blade he might guard his own head and body. A further protection lay in the broad and powerful guard which crossed the hilt, and which was furnished with a deep and narrow notch, in which an expert swordsman might catch his foeman's blade, and by a quick turn of his wrist might snap it across. Alleyne, on the other hand, must trust for his defence to his quick eye and active foot—for his sword, though keen as a whetstone could make it, was of a light and graceful build, with a narrow sloping pommel and a tapering steel.

Tranter well knew his advantage and lost little time in putting it to use. As his opponent walked towards him he suddenly bounded forward and sent in a whistling cut which would have severed the other in twain had he not sprung lightly back from it. So close was it that the point ripped a gash in the jutting edge of his linen cyclas. Quick, as a panther, Alleyne sprang in with a thrust, but Tranter, who was as active as he was strong, had already recovered himself and turned it aside with a movement of his heavy blade. Again he whizzed in a blow which made the spectators hold their breath, and again Alleyne very quickly and swiftly slipped from under it, and sent back two lightning thrusts which the other could scarce parry. So close were they to each other that Alleyne had no time to spring back from the next cut, which beat down his sword and grazed his forehead, sending the blood streaming into his eyes and down his cheeks. He sprang out beyond sword sweep, and the pair stood breathing heavily, while the crowd of young squires buzzed their applause.

"Bravely struck on both sides!" called Roger Harcomb. "You have both won honour from this meeting, and it would be sin and shame to let it go further."

"You have done enough, Edricson," said Norbury.

" You have carried yourself well," cried several of the older squires.

" For my part, I have no wish to slay this young man," said Tranter, wiping his heated brow.

" Does this gentleman crave my pardon for having used me despitefully ? " asked Alleyne.

" Nay, not I."

" Then stand on your guard, sir ! " With a clatter and clash the two blades met once more, Alleyne pressing in so as to keep within the full sweep of the heavy blade, while Tranter as continually sprang back to have space for one of his fatal cuts. A three-parts parried blow drew blood from Alleyne's left shoulder, but at the same moment he wounded Tranter slightly upon the thigh. Next instant, however, his blade had slipped into the fatal notch, there was a sharp cracking sound with a tinkling upon the ground, and he found a splintered piece of steel fifteen inches long was all that remained to him of his weapon.

" Your life is in my hands ! " cried Tranter, with a bitter smile.

" Nay, nay, he makes submission ! " broke in several squires.

" Another sword ! " cried Ford.

" Nay, sir," said Harcomb, " that is not the custom."

" Throw down your hilt, Edricson," cried Norbury.

" Never ! " said Alleyne. " Do you crave my pardon, sir ? "

" You are mad to ask it."

" Then on guard again ! " cried the young squire, and sprang in with a fire and a fury which more than made up for the shortness of his weapon. It had not escaped him that his opponent was breathing in short hoarse gasps, like a man who is dizzy with fatigue. Now was the time for the purer living and the more agile limb to show their value. Back and back gave Tranter, ever seeking time for a last cut. On and on came Alleyne, his jagged point now at his foeman's face, now at his throat,

now at his chest, still stabbing and thrusting to pass the
line of steel which covered him. Yet his experienced
foeman knew well that such efforts could not be long
sustained. Let him relax for one instant and his death-
blow had come. Relax he must! Flesh and blood could
not stand the strain. Already the thrusts were less fierce,
the foot less ready, although there was no abatement of
the spirit in the steady grey eyes. Tranter, cunning and
wary from years of fighting, knew that his chance had
come. He brushed aside the frail weapon which was
opposed to him, whirled up his great blade, sprang back
to get the fairer sweep—and vanished into the waters of
the Garonne.

So intent had the squires, both combatants and spectators, been on the matter in hand, that all thought of the
steep bank and swift still stream had gone from their
minds. It was not until Tranter, giving back before the
other's fiery rush, was upon the very brink, that a general
cry warned him of his danger. That last spring, which
he hoped would have brought the fight to a bloody end,
carried him clear of the edge, and he found himself in an
instant eight feet deep in the ice-cold stream. Once and
twice his gasping face and clutching fingers broke up
through the still green water, sweeping outwards in the
swirl of the current. In vain were sword-sheaths, apple
branches, and belts linked together, thrown out to him
by his companions. Alleyne had dropped his shattered
sword and was standing, trembling in every limb, with
his rage all changed in an instant to pity. For the third
time the drowning man came to the surface, his hands full
of green slimy water-plants, his eyes turned in despair to
the shore. Their glance fell upon Alleyne, and he could
not withstand the mute appeal which he read in them.
In an instant he, too, was in the Garonne, striking out with
powerful strokes for his late foeman.

Yet the current was swift and strong, and, good swim-
mer as he was, it was no easy task which Alleyne had set
himself. To clutch at Tranter and to seize him by the

hair was the work of a few seconds, but to hold his head above water and to make their way out of the current was another matter. For a hundred strokes he did not seem to gain an inch. Then at last, amid a shout of joy and praise from the bank, they slowly drew clear into more stagnant water, at the instant that a rope, made of a dozen sword-belts linked together by the buckles, was thrown by Ford into their very hands. Three pulls from eager arms, and the two combatants, dripping and pale, were dragged up the bank and lay panting upon the grass.

John Tranter was the first to come to himself, for, although he had been longer in the water, he had done nothing during that fierce battle with the current. He staggered to his feet and looked down upon his rescuer, who had raised himself upon his elbow, and was smiling faintly at the buzz of congratulation and of praise which broke from the squires around him.

" I am much beholden to you, sir," said Tranter, though in no very friendly voice. " Certes, I should have been in the river now but for you, for I was born in Warwickshire, which is but a dry county, and there are few who swim in those parts."

" I ask no thanks," Alleyne answered shortly. " Give me your hand to rise."

" The river has been my enemy," said Tranter, " but it hath been a good friend to you, for it hath saved your life this day."

" That is as it may be," returned Alleyne.

" But all is now well over," quoth Harcomb, " and no scath come of it, which is more than I had at one time hoped for. Our young friend here hath very fairly and honestly earned his right to be craftsman of the Honourable Guild of the Squires of Bordeaux. Here is your doublet, Tranter."

" Alas, for my poor sword which lies at the bottom of the Garonne ! " said the squire.

" Here is your pourpoint, Edricson," cried Norbury.

" Throw it over your shoulders, that you may have at least one dry garment."

" And now away back to the abbey," said several.

" One moment, sirs," cried Alleyne, who was leaning on Ford's shoulder, with the broken sword, which he had picked up, still clutched in his right hand. " My ears may be somewhat dulled by the water, and perchance what has been said has escaped me, but I have not yet heard this gentleman crave pardon for the insult which he put upon me in the hall."

" What ! do you still pursue the quarrel ? " asked Tranter.

" And why not, sir ? I am slow to take up such things, but once afoot I shall follow it while I have life or breath."

" Ma foi ! you have not too much of either, for you are as white as marble," said Harcomb bluntly. " Take my rede, sir, and let it drop, for you have come very well out from it."

" Nay," said Alleyne, " this quarrel is none of my making, but, now that I am here, I swear to you that I shall never leave this spot until I have that which I have come for : so ask my pardon, sir, or choose another glaive and to it again."

The young squire was deadly white from his exertions, both on the land and in the water. Soaking and stained, with a smear of blood on his white shoulder, and another on his brow, there was still in his whole pose and set of face the trace of an inflexible resolution. His opponent's duller and more material mind quailed before the fire and intensity of a higher spiritual nature.

" I had not thought that you had taken it so amiss," said he awkwardly. " It was but such a jest as we play upon each other, and, if you must have it so, I am sorry for it."

" Then I am sorry too," quoth Alleyne warmly, " and here is my hand upon it."

" And the none-meat horn has blown three times," quoth Harcomb, as they all streamed in chattering groups from the ground. " I know not what the prince's maîtrede-cuisine will say or think.   By my troth ! master Ford, your friend here is in need of a cup of wine, for he hath drunk deeply of Garonne water.   I had not thought from his fair face that he had stood to this matter so shrewdly."

" Faith," said Ford, " this air of Bordeaux hath turned our turtle-dove into a game-cock.   A milder or more courteous youth never came out of Hampshire."

" His master also, as I understand, is a very mild and courteous gentleman," remarked Harcomb ; " yet I do not think that they are either of them men with whom it is very safe to trifle."

21. *How Agostino Pisano risked his Head*

EVEN the squires' table at the Abbey of St. Andrew's at Bordeaux was on a very sumptuous scale while the prince held his court there.   Here first, after the meagre fare of Beaulieu and the stinted board of the Lady Loring, Alleyne learned the lengths to which luxury and refinement might be pushed.   Roasted peacocks, with the feathers all carefully replaced so that the bird lay upon the dish even as it had strutted in life, boars' heads with the tusks gilded and the mouth lined with silver foil, jellies in the shape of the Twelve Apostles, and a great pasty which formed an exact model of the king's new castle at Windsor—these were a few of the strange dishes which faced him.   An archer had brought him a change of clothes from the cog, and he had already, with the elasticity of youth, shaken off the troubles and fatigues of the morning.   A page from the inner banqueting-hall had come with word that their master intended to drink wine at the lodgings of the Lord Chandos that night, and that he desired his squires to sleep at the hotel of the " Half Moon," on the Rue des Apôtres. Thither, then, they both set out in the twilight after the long course of juggling tricks and glee-singing with which the principal meal was concluded.

A thin rain was falling as the two youths, with their cloaks over their heads, made their way on foot through the streets of the old town, leaving their horses in the royal stables. An occasional oil-lamp at the corner of a street, or in the portico of some wealthy burgher, threw a faint glimmer over the shining cobble-stones and the varied motley crowd who, in spite of the weather, ebbed and flowed along every highway. In those escattered circles of dim radiance might be seen the whole busy panorama of life in a wealthy and martial city. Here passed the round-faced burgher, swollen with prosperity, his sweeping dark-clothed gaberdine, flat velvet cap, broad leather belt and dangling pouch all speaking of comfort and of wealth. Behind him his serving-wench, her blue wimple over her head, and one hand thrust forward to bear the lanthorn which threw a golden bar of light along her master's path. Behind them a group of swaggering half-drunken Yorkshire dalesmen, speaking a dialect which their own southland countrymen could scarce comprehend, their jerkins marked with the rampant lion, which showed that they had come over in the train of the north-country Stapletons. The burgher glanced back at their fierce faces and quickened his step, while the girl pulled her wimple closer round her ; for there was a meaning in their wild eyes as they stared at the purse and the maiden, which men of all tongues could understand. Then came archers of the guard, shrill-voiced women of the camp, English pages with their fair skins and blue wondering eyes, dark-robed friars, lounging men-at-arms, swarthy loud-tongued Gascon serving-men, seamen from the river, rude peasants of the Médoc, and becloaked and befeathered squires of the court, all jostling and pushing in an ever-changing many-coloured stream ; while English, French, Welsh, Basque, and the varied dialects of Gascony and Guienne filled the air with their babel. From time to time the throng would be burst asunder and a lady's horse-litter would trot past towards the abbey, or there would come a knot of torch-bearing archers walking in front of Gascon baron or English knight, as he sought his lodgings after the palace revels. Clatter of hoofs, clinking of weapons, shouts from the drunken brawlers, and high laughter of women, they all rose up, like the mist from a marsh, out of the crowded streets of the dim-lit city.

One couple out of the moving throng especially engaged the attention of the two young squires, the more so as they were going in their own direction and immediately in front of them. They consisted of a man and a girl, the former very tall with rounded shoulders, a limp of one foot, and a large flat object covered with dark cloth under his arm. His companion was young and straight, with a quick elastic step and graceful bearing, though so swathed in a black mantle that little could be seen of her face save a flash of dark eyes and a curve of raven hair. The tall man leaned heavily upon her to take the weight off his tender foot, while he held his burden betwixt himself and the wall, cuddling it jealously to his side, and thrusting forward his young companion to act as a buttress whenever the pressure of the crowd threatened to bear him away. The evident anxiety of the man, the appearance of his attendant, and the joint care with which they defended their concealed possession, excited the interest of the two young Englishmen who walked within hand-touch of them.

" Courage, child ! " they heard the tall man exclaim in strange hybrid French. " If we can win another sixty paces we are safe."

" Hold it safe, father," the other answered, in the same soft, mincing dialect. " We have no cause for fear."

" Verily, they are heathens and barbarians," cried the man ; " mad, howling, drunken barbarians ! Forty more paces, Tita mia, and I swear to the holy Eloi, patron of all learned craftsmen, that I will never set foot over my docr again until the whole swarm are safely hived in their camp of Dax, or wherever else they curse with their presence. Twenty more paces, my treasure ! Ah, my God ! how they push and brawl ! Get in their way, Tita mia ! Put your little elbow bravely out ! Set your shoulders squarely against them, girl ! Why should you give way to these mad islanders ? Ah, cospetto ! we are ruined and destroyed ! "

The crowd had thickened in front, so that the lame man and the girl had come to a stand. Several half-drunken English archers, attracted, as the squires had been, by their singular appearance, were facing towards them, and peering at them through the dim light.

" By the three kings ! " cried one, " here is an old dotard shrew to have so goodly a crutch ! Use the leg that God hath given you, man, and do not bear so heavily upon the wench."

" Twenty devils fly away with him ! " shouted another. " What, how, man ! are brave archers to go maidless while an old man uses one as a walking-staff ? "

" Come with me, my honey-bird ! " cried a third, plucking at the girl's mantle.

" Nay, with me, my heart's desire ! " said the first. " By St. George ! our life is short, and we should be merry while we may. May I never see Chester Bridge again, if she is not a right winsome lass ! "

" What hath the old toad under his arm ? " cried one of the others. " He hugs it to him as the devil hugged the pardoner."

" Let us see, old bag of bones ; let us see what it is that you have under your arm ! " They crowded in upon him, while he, ignorant of their language, could but clutch the girl with one hand and the parcel with the other, looking wildly about in search of help.

" Nay, lads, nay ! " cried Ford, pushing back the nearest archer. " This is but scurvy conduct. Keep your hands off, or it will be the worse for you."

" Keep your tongue still, or it will be the worse for you," shouted the most drunken of the archers. " Who are you to spoil sport ? "

" A raw squire, new landed," said another. " By St.

Thomas of Kent ! we are at the beck of our master, but we are not to be ordered by every babe whose mother hath sent him as far as Aquitaine."

" Oh, gentlemen," cried the girl in broken French, " for dear Christ's sake stand by us, and do not let these terrible men do us an injury."

" Have no fears, lady," Alleyne answered. " We shall see that all is well with you. Take your hand from the girl's wrist, you north-country rogue ! "

" Hold to her, Wat ! " said a great black-bearded man-at-arms, whose steel breast-plate glimmered in the dusk. " Keep your hands from your bodkins, you two, for that was my trade before you were born, and, by God's soul ! I will drive a handful of steel through you if you move a finger."

" Thank God ! " said Alleyne suddenly, as he spied in the lamp-light a shock of blazing red hair which fringed a steel cap high above the heads of the crowd. " Here is John, and Aylward, too ! Help us, comrades, for there is wrong being done to this maid and to the old man."

" Holà, mon petit," said the old bowman, pushing his way through the crowd, with the huge forester at his heels. " What is all this, then ? By the twang of string ! I think that you will have some work upon your hands if you are to right all the wrongs that you may see upon this side of the water. It is not to be thought that a troop of bowmen, with the wine buzzing in their ears, will be as soft-spoken as so many young clerks in an orchard. When you have been a year with the Company you will think less of such matters. But what is amiss here ? The provost-marshal with his archers is coming this way, and some of you may find yourselves in the stretch-neck, if you take not heed."

" Why, it is old Sam Aylward of the White Company ! " shouted the man-at-arms. " Why, Samkin, what hath come upon thee ? I can call to mind the day when you were as roaring a blade as ever called himself a free com-

panion. By my soul ! from Limoges to Navarre, who
was there who would kiss a wench or cut a throat as readily
as bowman Aylward of Hawkwood's Company ? "

" Like enough, Peter," said Aylward, " and, by my
hilt ! I may not have changed so much. But it was ever
a fair loose and a clear mark with me. The wench must
be willing, or the man must be standing up against me,
else, by these ten finger-bones ! either were safe enough
for me."

A glance at Aylward's resolute face, and at the huge
shoulders of Hordle John, had convinced the archers that
there was little to be got by violence. The girl and the
old man began to shuffle on in the crowd without their
tormentors venturing to stop them. Ford and Alleyne
followed slowly behind them, but Aylward caught the
latter by the shoulder.

" By my hilt ! camarade," said he, " I hear that you
have done great things at the Abbey to-day, but I pray
you to have a care, for it was I who brought you into the
Company, and it would be a black day for me if aught
were to befall you."

" Nay, Aylward, I will have a care."

" Thrust not forward into danger too much, mon petit.
In a little time your wrist will be stronger and your cut
more shrewd. There will be some of us at the ' Rose de
Guienne ' to-night, which is two doors from the hotel of
the ' Half Moon,' so if you would drain a cup with a few
simple archers you will be right welcome."

Alleyne promised to be there if his duties would allow,
and then, slipping through the crowd, he rejoined Ford,
who was standing in talk with the two strangers, who had
now reached their own doorstep.

" Brave young signor," cried the tall man, throwing his
arms round Alleyne, " how can we thank you enough for
taking our parts against those horrible drunken barbarians ? What should we have done without you ? My
Tita would have been dragged away, and my head would
have been shivered into a thousand fragments."

" Nay, I scarce think that they would have mishandled you so," said Alleyne in surprise.

" Ho, ho ! " cried he with a high crowing laugh, " it is not the head upon my shoulders that I think of. Cospetto ! no. It is the head under my arm which you have preserved."

" Perhaps the signori would deign to come under our roof, father," said the maiden. " If we bide here, who knows that some fresh tumult may not break out ? "

" Well said, Tita ! Well said, my girl ! I pray you, sirs, to honour my unworthy roof so far. A light, Giacomo ! There are five steps up. Now, two more. So ! Here we are at last in safety. Corpo di Baccho ! I would not have given ten maravedi for my head when those children of the devil were pushing us against the wall. Tita mia, you have been a brave girl, and it was better that you should be pulled and pushed than that my head should be broken."

" Yes, indeed, father," said she earnestly.

" But those English ! Ach ! Take a Goth, a Hun, and a Vandal ; mix them together and add a Barbary rover ; then take this creature and make him drunk— and you have an Englishman. My God ! were ever such people upon earth ? What place is free from them ? I hear that they swarm in Italy even as they swarm here. Everywhere you will find them, except in heaven."

" Dear father," cried Tita, still supporting the angry old man, as he limped up the curved oaken stair. " You must not forget that these good signori who have pre- served us are also English."

" Ah yes. My pardon, sirs ! Come into my room here. There are some who might find some pleasure in these paintings, but I learn that the art of war is the only art which is held in honour in your island."

The low-roofed, oak-panelled room into which he con- ducted them was brilliantly lighted by four scented oil- lamps. Against the walls, upon the table, on the floor, and in every part of the chamber, were great sheets of glass painted in the most brilliant colours. Ford and Edricson gazed around them in amazement, for never had they seen such magnificent works of art.

" You like them, then," the lame artist cried, in answer to the look of pleasure and of surprise in their faces. " There are, then, some of you who have a taste for such trifling."

" I could not have believed it," exclaimed Alleyne. " What colour ! What outlines ! See to this martyrdom of the holy Stephen, Ford. Could you not yourself pick up one of these stones which lie to the hand of the wicked murtherers ? "

" And see this stag, Alleyne, with the cross betwixt its horns. By my faith ! I have never seen a better one at the Forest of Bere."

" And the green of this grass—how bright and clear ! Why, all the painting that I have seen is but child's play beside this. This worthy gentleman must be one of those great painters of whom I have oft heard brother Bartholomew speak in the old days at Beaulieu."

The dark mobile face of the artist shone with pleasure at the unaffected delight of the two young Englishmen. His daughter had thrown off her mantle and disclosed a face of the finest and most delicate Italian beauty, which soon drew Ford's eyes from the pictures in front of him. Alleyne, however, continued with little cries of admiration and of wonderment to turn from the walls to the table and yet again to the walls.

" What think you of this, young sir ? " asked the painter, tearing off the cloth which concealed the flat object which he had borne beneath his arm. It was a leaf-shaped sheet of glass, bearing upon it a face with a halo round it, so delicately outlined, and of so perfect a tint, that it might have been indeed a human face which gazed with sad and thoughtful eyes upon the young squire. He clapped his hands, with that thrill of joy which true art will ever give to a true artist.

" It is great ! " he cried. " It is wonderful ! But I

marvel, sir, that you should have risked a work of such beauty and value by bearing it at night through so unruly a crowd."

" I have indeed been rash," said the artist. " Some wine, Tita, from the Florence flask ! Had it not been for you, I tremble to think of what might have come of it. See to the skin tint : it is not to be replaced ; for, paint as you will, it is not once in a hundred times that it is not either burned too brown in the furnace or else the colour will not hold, and you get but a sickly white. There you can see the very veins and the throb of the blood. Yes, diavolo ! if it had broken my heart would have broken too. It is for the choir window in the church of St. Remi, and we had gone, my little helper and I, to see if it was indeed of the size for the stonework. Night had fallen ere we finished, and what could we do save carry it home as best we might ? But you, young sir, you speak as if you too knew something of the art."

" So little that I scarce dare speak of it in your presence," Alleyne answered. " I have been cloister bred, and it was no very great matter to handle the brush better than my brother novices."

" There are pigments, brush, and paper," said the old artist. " I do not give you glass, for that is another matter, and takes much skill in the mixing of colours. Now I pray you to show me a touch of your art. I thank you, Tita ! The Venetian glasses, cara mia, and fill them to the brim. A seat, signor ! "

While Ford, in his English-French, was conversing with Tita in her Italian-French, the old man was carefully examining his precious head to see that no scratch had been left upon its surface. When he glanced up again, Alleyne had, with a few bold strokes of the brush, tinted in a woman's face and neck upon the white sheet in front of him.

" Diavolo ! " exclaimed the old artist, standing with his head on one side, " you have power ; yes, cospetto ! you have power. It is the face of an angel ! "

241

" It is the face of the Lady Maude Loring ! " cried
Ford, even more astonished.

" Why, on my faith, it is not unlike her ! " said Alleyne,
in some confusion.

" Ah ! a portrait ! So much the better. Young man,
I am Agostino Pisano, the son of Andrea Pisano, and I say
again that you have power. Further, I say that, if you
will stay with me I will teach you all the secrets of the
glass-stainers' mystery : the pigments and their thickening,
which will fuse into the glass and which will not, the furnace
and the glazing—every trick and method you shall know."

" I would be right glad to study under such a master,"
said Alleyne ; " but I am sworn to follow my lord while
this war lasts."

" War ! war ! " cried the old Italian. " Ever this talk
of war. And the men that you hold to be great—what are
they ? Have I not heard their names ? Soldiers,
butchers, destroyers ! Ah, per Baccho ! we have men in
Italy who are in very truth great. You pull down, you
despoil ; but they build up, they restore. Ah, if you
could but see my own dear Pisa, the duomo, the cloisters
of Campo Santo, the high campanile, with the mellow
throb of her bells upon the warm Italian air ! Those are
the works of great men. And I have seen them with my
own eyes, these very eyes which look upon you. I have
seen Andrea Orcagna, Taddeo Gaddi, Giottino, Stefano,
Simone Memmi—men whose very colours I am not
worthy to mix. And I have seen the aged Giotto, and
he in turn was pupil to Cimabue, before whom there was
no art in Italy, for the Greeks were brought to paint the
chapel of the Gondi at Florence. Ah, signori, these are
the real great men whose names will be held in honour
when your soldiers are shown to have been the enemies
of human kind."

" Faith, sir," said Ford, " there is something to say for
the soldiers, also ; for, unless they be defended, how are
all these gentlemen whom you have mentioned to preserve
the pictures which they have painted ? "

" And all these ? " said Alleyne. " Have you indeed done them all ?—and where are they to go ? "

" Yes, signor, they are all from my hand. Some are, as you see, upon one sheet, and some are in many pieces which may fasten together. There are some who do but paint upon the glass, and then, by placing another sheet of glass upon the top and fastening it, they keep the air from their painting. Yet I hold that the true art of my craft lies as much in the furnace as in the brush. See this rose window, which is from the model of the Church of the Holy Trinity at Vendôme, and this other of the ' Finding of the Grail,' which is for the apse of the Abbey church. Time was when none but my country-men could do these things ; but there is Clement of Chartres and others in France who are very worthy work-men. But, ah ! there is that ever-shrieking brazen tongue which will not let us forget for one short hour that it is the arm of the savage, and not the hand of the master, which rules over the world."

A stern clear bugle call had sounded close at hand to summon some following together for the night.

" It is a sign to us as well," said Ford. " I would fain stay here for ever amid all these beautiful things "— staring hard at the blushing Tita as he spoke—" but we must be back at our lord's hostel ere he reach it."

Amid renewed thanks and with promises to come again, the two squires bade their leave of the old Italian glass-stainer and his daughter. The streets were clearer now, and the rain had stopped, so they made their way quickly from the Rue du Roi, in which their new friends dwelt, to the Rue des Apôtres, where the hostel of the " Half Moon " was situated.

22. *How the Bowmen held Wassail at the "Rose de Guienne"*

" MON DIEU ! Alleyne, saw you ever so lovely a face ? " cried Ford as they hurried along together. " So pure, so peaceful, and so beautiful ! "

" In sooth, yes. And the hue of the skin the most perfect that ever I saw. Marked you also how the hair curled round the brow ? It was wonder-fine."

" Those eyes too ! " cried Ford. " How clear and how tender—simple, and yet so full of thought ! "

" If there was a weakness, it was in the chin," said Alleyne.

" Nay, I saw none."

" It was well curved, it is true."

" Most daintily so."

" And yet——"

" What then, Alleyne ? Wouldst find flaw in the sun ? "

" Well, bethink you, Ford, would not more power and expression have been put into the face by a long and noble beard ? "

" Holy Virgin ! " cried Ford, " the man is mad. A beard on the face of little Tita ! "

" Tita ! Who spoke of Tita ? "

" Who spoke of aught else ? "

" It was the picture of St. Remi, man, of which I have been discoursing."

" You are, indeed," cried Ford, laughing, " a Goth, Hun, and Vandal, with all the other hard names which the old man called us. How could you think so much of a smear of pigments, when there was such a picture painted by the good God Himself in the very room with you ? But who is this ? "

" If it please you, sirs," said an archer, running across to them, " Aylward and others would be right glad to see you. They are within here. He bade me say to you that the Lord Loring will not need your service to-night, as he sleeps with the Lord Chandos."

"By my faith!" said Ford, "we do not need a guide to lead us to their presence." As he spoke there came a roar of singing from the tavern upon the right, with shouts of laughter and stamping of feet. Passing under a low door, and down a stone-flagged passage, they found themselves in a long narrow hall lighted up by a pair of blazing torches, one at either end. Trusses of straw had been thrown down along the walls, and reclining on them were some twenty or thirty archers, all of the Company, their steel caps and jacks thrown off, their tunics open, and their great limbs sprawling upon the clay floor. At every man's elbow stood his leather black-jack of beer, while at the farther end a hogshead with its end knocked in promised an abundant supply for the future. Behind the hogshead, on a half-circle of kegs, boxes, and rude settles, sat Aylward, John, Black Simon and three or four other leading men of the archers, together with Goodwin Hawtayne, the master-shipman, who had left his yellow cog in the river to have a last rouse with his friends of the Company. Ford and Alleyne took their seats between Aylward and Black Simon, without their entrance checking in any degree the hubbub which was going on.

"Ale, mes camarades?" cried the bowman, "or shall it be wine? Nay, but ye must have the one or the other. Here, Jacques, thou limb of the devil, bring a bottrine of the oldest vernage, and see that you do not shake it. Hast heard the news?"

"Nay," cried both the squires.

"That we are to have a brave tourney."

"A tourney?"

"Aye, lads. For the Captal de Buch hath sworn that he will find five knights from this side of the water who will ride over any five Englishmen who ever threw leg over saddle; and Chandos hath taken up the challenge, and the prince hath promised a golden vase for the man who carries himself best, and all the court is in a buzz over it."

" Why should the knights have all the sport ? " growled Hordle John. " Could they not set up five archers for the honour of Aquitaine and of Gascony ? "

" Or five men-at-arms," said Black Simon.

" But who are the English knights ? " asked Haw-tayne.

" There are three hundred and forty-one in the town," said Aylward, " and I hear that three hundred and forty cartels and defiances have already been sent in, the only one missing being Sir John Ravensholme, who is in his bed with the sweating sickness, and cannot set foot to ground."

" I have heard of it from one of the archers of the guard," cried a bowman from among the straw ; " I hear that the prince wished to break a lance, but that Chandos would not hear of it, for the game is likely to be a rough one."

" Then there is Chandos."

" Nay, the prince would not permit it. He is to be marshal of the lists, with Sir William Felton and the Duc d'Armagnac. The English will be the Lord Audley, Sir Thomas Percy, Sir Thomas Wake, Sir William Beau-champ, and our own very good lord and leader."

" Hurrah for him, and God be with him ! " cried several. " It is honour to draw string in his service."

" So you may well say," said Aylward. " By my ten finger-bones ! if you march behind the pennon of the five roses you are like to see all that a good bowman would wish to see. Ha ! yes, mes garçons, you laugh, but, by my hilt ! you may not laugh when you find yourselves where he will take you, for you can never tell what strange vow he may not have sworn to. I see that he has a patch over his eye. There will come bloodshed of that patch, or I am the more mistaken."

" How chanced it at Poictiers, good Master Aylward ? " asked one of the younger archers, leaning upon his elbows, with his eyes fixed respectfully upon the old bow-man's rugged face.

" Aye, Aylward, tell us of it," cried Hordle John.

" Here is to old Samkin Aylward ! " shouted several at the farther end of the room, waving their black-jacks in the air.

" Ask him ! " said Aylward, modestly, nodding towards Black Simon.   " He saw more than I did.   And yet, by the holy nails ! there was not very much that I did not see either."

" Ah, yes," said Simon, shaking his head, " it was a great day.   I never hope to see such another.   There were some fine archers who drew their last shaft that day. We shall never see better men, Aylward."

" By my hilt ! no.   There was little Robby Withstaff, and Andrew Salblaster, and Wat Alspaye, who broke the neck of the German.   Mon Dieu ! what men they were ! Take them how you would, at long butts or short, hoyles, rounds, or rovers, better bowmen never twirled a shaft over their thumbnails."

" But the fight, Aylward, the fight ! " cried several, impatiently.

" Let me fill my jack first, boys, for it is a thirsty tale. It was at the first fall of the leaf that the prince set forth, and he passed through Auvergne, and Berry, and Anjou, and Touraine.   In Auvergne the maids are kind, but the wines are sour.   In Berry it is the women that are sour, but the wines are rich.   Anjou, however, is a very good land for bowmen, for wine and women are all that heart could wish.   In Touraine I got nothing save a broken pate, but at Vierzon I had a great good fortune, for I had a golden pyx from the minster, for which I afterwards got nine Genoan janes from the goldsmith in the Rue Mont Olive.   From thence we went to Bourges, where I had a tunic of flame-coloured silk and a very fine pair of shoes, with tassels of silk, and drops of silver."

" From a stall, Aylward ? " asked one of the young archers.

" Nay, from a man's feet, lad. I had reason to think that he might not need them again, seeing that a thirty-inch shaft had feathered in his back."

" And what then, Aylward ? "

" On we went, coz, some six thousand of us, until we came to Issodun, and there again a very great thing befell."

" A battle, Aylward ? "

" Nay, nay ; a greater thing than that. There is little to be gained out of a battle, unless one have the fortune to win a ransom. At Issodun I and three Welshmen came upon a house which all others had passed, and we had the profit of it to ourselves. For myself, I had a fine feather-bed—a thing which you will not see in a long day's journey in England. You have seen it, Alleyne, and you, John. You will bear me out that it is a noble bed. We put it on a sutler's mule, and bore it after the army. It was in my mind that I would lay it by until I came to start house of mine own, and I have it now in a very safe place near Lyndhurst."

" And what then, master-bowman ? " asked Hawtayne. " By St. Christopher ! it is indeed a fair and goodly life which you have chosen, for you gather up the spoil as a Warsash man gathers lobsters, without grace or favour from any man."

" You are right, master-shipman," said another of the older archers. " It is an old bowyer's rede that the second feather of a fenny goose is better than the pinion of a tame one. Draw on, old lad, for I have come between you and the clout."

" On we went then," said Aylward, after a long pull at his black-jack. " There were some six thousand of us, with the prince and his knights, and the feather-bed upon a sutler's mule in the centre. We made great havoc in Touraine, until we came into Romorantin, where I chanced upon a gold chain and two bracelets of jasper, which were stolen from me the same day by a black-eyed wench from the Ardennes. Mon Dieu ! there are some folk who have no fear of Domesday in them, and no sign of grace in their souls, for ever clutching and clawing at another man's chattels."

" But the battle, Aylward, the battle ! " cried several, amid a burst of laughter.

" I come to it, my young war-pups. Well, then, the King of France had followed us with fifty thousand men, and he made great haste to catch us ; but when he had us he scarce knew what to do with us, for we were so drawn up among hedges and vineyards that they could not come nigh us, save by one lane. On both sides were archers, men-at-arms and knights behind, and in the centre the baggage, with my feather-bed upon a sutler's mule. Three hundred chosen knights came straight for it, and, indeed, they were very brave men, but such a drift of arrows met them that few came back. Then came the Germans, and they also fought very bravely, so that one or two broke through the archers and came as far as the feather-bed, but all to no purpose. Then out rides our own little hothead and my lord Audley with his four Cheshire squires, and a few others of like kidney, and after them went the prince and Chandos, and then the whole throng of us, with axe and sword, for we had shot away our arrows. Ma foi ! it was a foolish thing, for we came forth from the hedges, and there was nought to guard the baggage had they ridden round behind us. But all went well with us, and the king was taken, and little Robby Withstaff and I fell in with a wain with twelve firkins of wine for the king's own table, and, by my hilt ! if you asked me what happened after that, I cannot answer you, nor can little Robby Withstaff either."

" And next day ? "

" By my faith ! we did not tarry long, but we hied back to Bordeaux, where we came in safety with the King of France and also the feather-bed. I sold my spoil, mes garçons, for as many gold pieces as I could hold in my hufken, and for seven days I lit twelve wax candles upon the altar of Saint Andrew : for if you forget the blessed when things are well with you, they are very likely to forget you when you have need of them. I have a score of one hundred and nineteen pounds of wax against the holy Andrew, and, as he was a very just man, I doubt not that I shall have full weight and measure when I have most need of it."

" Tell me, Master Aylward," cried a young, fresh-faced archer at the farther end of the room, " what was this great battle about ? "

" Why, you jack-fool, what would it be about save who should wear the crown of France ? "

" I thought that mayhap it might be as to who should have this feather-bed of thine."

" If I come down to you, Silas, I may lay my belt across your shoulders," Aylward answered, amid a general shout of laughter. " But it is time young chickens went to roost when they dare cackle against their elders. It is late, Simon."

" Nay, let us have another song."

" Here is Arnold of Sowley will troll as good a stave as any man in the Company."

" Nay, we have one here who is second to none," said Hawtayne, laying his hand upon big John's shoulder. " I have heard him on the cog with a voice like the wave upon the shore. I pray you, friend, to give us ' The Bells of Milton,' or, if you will, ' The Franklin's Maid.' "

Hordle John drew the back of his hand across his mouth, fixed his eyes upon the corner of the ceiling, and bellowed forth, in a voice which made the torches flicker, the southland ballad for which he had been asked :

> The franklin he hath gone to roam,
> The franklin's maid she bides at home.
> But she is cold and coy and staid,
> And who may win the franklin's maid ?

> There came a knight of high renown
> In bassinet and ciclatoun ;
> On bended knee full long he prayed :
> He might not win the franklin's maid.

There came a squire so debonair,
His dress was rich, his words were fair,
He sweetly sang, he deftly played :
He could not win the franklin's maid.

There came a mercer wonder-fine
With velvet cap and gaberdine :
For all his ships, for all his trade,
He could not buy the franklin's maid.

There came an archer bold and true,
With bracer guard and stave of yew ;
His purse was light, his jerkin frayed :
Haro, alas ! the franklin's maid !

Oh, some have laughed and some have cried,
And some have scoured the country-side ;
But off they ride through wood and glade,
The bowman and the franklin's maid.

A roar of delight from his audience, with stamping of feet and beating of black-jacks against the ground, showed how thoroughly the song was to their taste, while John modestly retired into a quart pot, which he drained in four giant gulps, " I sang that ditty in Hordle ale-house ere I ever thought to be an archer myself," quoth he.

" Fill up your stoups ! " cried Black Simon, thrusting his own goblet into the open hogshead in front of him. " Here is a last cup to the White Company, and every brave boy who walks behind the rose of Loring ! "

" To the wood, the flax, and the gander's wing ! " said an old grey-headed archer on the right.

" To a gentle loose, and the King of Spain for a mark at fourteen score ! " cried another.

" To a bloody war ! " shouted a fourth. " Many to go and few to come ! "

" With the most gold to the best steel ! " added a fifth.

" And a last cup to the maids of our heart ! " cried Aylward. " A steady hand and a true eye, boys ; so let two quarts be a bowman's portion." With shout and jest and snatch of song they streamed from the room, and all was peaceful once more in the " Rose de Guienne."

23. *How England held the Lists at Bordeaux*

SO used were the good burghers of Bordeaux to martial display and knightly sport, that an ordinary joust or tournament was an everyday matter with them. The fame and brilliancy of the prince's court had drawn the knights-errant and pursuivants-of-arms from every part of Europe. In the long lists by the Garonne on the landward side of the northern gate there had been many a strange combat, when the Teutonic knight, fresh from the conquest of the Prussian heathen, ran a course against the knight of Calatrava, hardened by continual struggle against the Moors, or cavaliers from Portugal broke a lance with Scandinavian warriors from the farther shore of the great Northern Ocean. Here fluttered many an outland pennon, bearing symbol and blazonry from the banks of the Danube, the wilds of Lithuania, and the mountain strongholds of Hungary : for chivalry was of no clime and of no race, nor was any land so wild that the fame and name of the prince had not sounded through it from border to border.

Great, however, was the excitement through town and district when it was learned that on the third Wednesday in Advent there would be held a passage-at-arms in which five knights of England would hold the lists against all comers. The great concourse of noblemen and famous soldiers, the national character of the contest, and the fact that this was a last trial of arms, before what promised to be an arduous and bloody war, all united to make the event one of the most notable and brilliant that Bordeaux had ever seen. On the eve of the contest the peasants flocked in from the whole district of the Médoc, and the fields beyond the walls were whitened with the tents of those who could find no warmer lodging. From the distant camp of Dax, too, and from Blaye, Bourg, Libourne, St. Emilion, Castillon, St. Macaire, Cardillac, Ryons, and all the cluster of flourishing towns which looked upon Bordeaux as their mother, there thronged an unceasing stream of horsemen and of footmen, all converging upon the great city. By the morning of the day on which the courses were to be run, not less than eighty thousand people had assembled round the lists and along the low grassy ridge which looks down upon the scene of the encounter.

It was, as may well be imagined, no easy matter among so many noted cavaliers to choose out five on either side who should have precedence over their fellows. A score of secondary combats had nearly arisen from the rivalries and bad blood created by the selection, and it was only the influence of the prince and the efforts of the older barons which kept the peace among so many eager and fiery soldiers. Not till the day before the courses were the shields finally hung out for the inspection of the ladies and the heralds, so that all men might know the names of the champions and have the opportunity to prefer any charge against them should there be stain upon them which should disqualify them from taking part in so noble and honourable a ceremony.

Sir Hugh Calverley and Sir Robert Knolles had not yet returned from their raid into the marches of Navarre, so that the English party were deprived of two of their most famous lances. Yet there remained so many good names that Chandos and Felton, to whom the selection had been referred, had many an earnest consultation, in which every feat of arms and failure or success of each candidate was weighed and balanced against the rival claims of his companions. Lord Audley of Cheshire, the hero of Poictiers, and Loring of Hampshire, who was held to be the second lance in the army, were easily fixed upon. Then, of the younger men, Sir Thomas Percy of Northumberland, Sir Thomas Wake of Yorkshire, and Sir William Beauchamp of Gloucestershire, were finally selected to uphold the honour of England. On the other side were the veteran Captal de Buch and the brawny Olivier de Clisson, with the free companion Sir Perducas d'Albret, the valiant

Lord of Mucident and Sigismond von Altenstat, of the Teutonic order. The older soldiers among the English shook their heads as they looked upon the escutcheons of these famous warriors, for they were all men who had spent their lives upon the saddle, and bravery and strength can avail little against experience and wisdom of war.

" By my faith ! Sir John," said the prince, as he rode through the winding streets on his way to the lists, " I should have been glad to have splintered a lance to-day. You have seen me hold a spear since I had strength to lift one, and should know best whether I do not merit a place among this honourable company."

" There is no better seat and no truer lance, sire," said Chandos ; " but, if I may say so without fear of offence, it were not fitting that you should join in this debate."

" And why, Sir John ? "

" Because, sire, it is not for you to take part with Gascons against English, or with English against Gascons, seeing that you are lord of both. We are not too well loved by the Gascons now, and it is but the golden link of your princely coronet which holds us together. If that be snapped I know not what would follow."

" Snapped, Sir John ! " cried the prince, with an angry sparkle in his dark eyes. " What manner of talk is this ? You speak as though the allegiance of our people were a thing which might be thrown off or on like a falcon's jessel.

" With a sorry hack one uses whip and spur, sire," said Chandos ; " but with a horse of blood and spirit a good cavalier is gentle and soothing, coaxing rather than forcing. These folk are strange people, and you must hold their love, even as you have it now, for you will get from their kindness what all the pennons in your army could not wring from them."

" You are over-grave to-day, John," the prince answered. " We may keep such questions for our council chamber. But how now, my brothers of Spain and of Majorca, what think you of this challenge ? "

" I look to see some handsome jousting," said Don

Pedro, who rode with the King of Majorca upon the right of the prince, while Chandos was on the left. " By St. James of Compostella ! but these burghers would bear some taxing. See to the broadcloth and velvet that the rogues bear upon their backs. By my troth ! if they were my subjects they would be glad enough to wear falding and leather ere I had done with them. But mayhap it is best to let the wool grow long ere you clip it."

" It is our pride," the prince answered coldly, " that we rule over freemen and not slaves."

" Every man to his own humour," said Pedro carelessly. " Carajo ! there is a sweet face at yonder window ! Don Fernando, I pray you to mark the house, and to have the maid brought to us at the abbey."

" Nay, brother, nay ! " cried the prince impatiently. " I have had occasion to tell you more than once that things are not ordered in this way in Aquitaine."

" A thousand pardons, dear friend," the Spaniard answered quickly, for a flush of anger had sprung to the dark cheek of the English prince. " You make my exile so like a home that I forget at times that I am not in very truth back in Castile. Every land hath indeed its own ways and manners ; but I promise you, Edward, that when you are my guest in Toledo or Madrid you shall not yearn in vain for any commoner's daughter on whom you may design to cast your eye."

" Your talk, sire," said the prince still more coldly, " is not such as I love to hear from your lips. I have no taste for such amours as you speak of, and I have sworn that my name shall be coupled with that of no woman save my ever dear wife."

" Ever the mirror of true chivalry ! " exclaimed Pedro, while James of Majorca, frightened at the stern countenance of their all-powerful protector, plucked hard at the mantle of his brother-exile.

" Have a care, cousin," he whispered, " for the sake of the Virgin have a care, for you have angered him."

" Pshaw ! fear not," the other answered, in the same

low tone. " If I miss one stoop I will strike him on the next. Mark me else. Fair cousin," he continued, turning to the prince, " these be rare men-at-arms, and lusty bowmen. It would be hard indeed to match them."

" They have journeyed far, sire, but they have never yet found their match."

" Nor ever will, I doubt not. I feel myself to be back upon my throne when I look at them. But tell me, dear coz, what shall we do next, when we have driven this bastard Henry from the kingdom which he hath filched ? "

" We shall then compel the King of Aragon to place our good friend and brother James of Majorca upon the throne."

" Noble and generous prince ! " cried the little monarch.

" That done," said King Pedro, glancing out of the corners of his eyes at the young conqueror, " we shall unite the forces of England, of Aquitaine, of Spain, and of Majorca. It would be shame to us if we did not do some great deed with such forces ready to our hand."

" You say truly, brother," cried the prince, his eyes kindling at the thought. " Methinks that we could not do anything more pleasing to Our Lady than to drive the heathen Moors out of the country."

" I am with you, Edward, as true as hilt to blade. But, by St. James ! we shall not let these Moors make mock at us from over the sea. We must take ship and thrust them from Africa."

" By heaven, yes ! " cried the prince. " And it is the dream of my heart that our English pennons shall wave upon the Mount of Olives, and the lions and lilies float over the holy city."

" And why not, dear coz ? Your bowmen have cleared a path to Paris, and why not to Jerusalem ? Once there, your arms might rest."

" Nay, there is more to be done," cried the prince, carried away by the ambitious dream. " There is still the city of Constantine to be taken, and war to be waged against the Soldan of Damascus. And beyond him again there is tribute to be levied from the Cham of Tartary, and from the kingdom of Cathay. Ha! John, what say you? Can we not go as far eastward as Richard of the Lion Heart?"

"Old John will bide at home, sire," said the rugged soldier. "By my soul! as long as I am seneschal of Aquitaine I will find enough to do in guarding the marches which you have entrusted to me. It would be a blithe day for the king of France when he heard that the sea lay between him and us."

"By my soul! John," said the prince, "I have never known you turn laggard before."

"The babbling hound, sire, is not always the first at the mort," the old knight answered.

"Nay, my true-heart! I have tried you too often not to know. But, by my soul! I have not seen so dense a throng since the day that we brought King John down Cheapside."

It was, indeed, an enormous crowd which covered the whole vast plain from the line of vineyards to the river bank. From the northern gate the prince and his companions looked down at a dark sea of heads, brightened here and there by the coloured hoods of the women or by the sparkling head-pieces of archers and men-at-arms. In the centre of this vast assemblage the lists seemed but a narrow strip of green marked out with banners and streamers, while a gleam of white with a flutter of pennons at either end showed where the marquees were pitched, which served as the dressing-rooms of the combatants. A path had been staked off from the city gate to the stands, which had been erected for the court and the nobility. Down this, amid the shouts of the enormous multitude, the prince cantered with his two attendant kings, his high officers of state, and his long train of lords and ladies, courtiers, counsellors, and soldiers, with toss of plume and flash of jewel, sheen of silk and glint of gold—as rich and gallant a show as heart could wish. The head of the cavalcade had reached the lists ere the rear had come clear of the city gate, for the fairest and the bravest had assembled from all the broad lands which are watered by the Dordogne and the Garonne. Here rode dark-browed cavaliers from the sunny south, fiery soldiers from Gascony, graceful courtiers of Limousin or Saintonge, and gallant young Englishmen from beyond the seas. Here, too, were the beautiful brunettes of the Gironde, with eyes which out-flashed their jewels, while beside them rode their blonde sisters of England clear cut and aquiline, swathed in swans'-down and in ermine, for the air was biting, though the sun was bright. Slowly the long and glittering train wound into the lists, until every horse had been tethered by the varlets in waiting, and every lord and lady seated in the long stands which stretched, rich in tapestry and velvet and blazoned arms, on either side of the centre of the arena.

The holders of the lists occupied the end which was nearest to the city gate. There, in front of their respective pavilions, flew the martlets of Audley, the roses of Loring, the scarlet bars of Wake, the lion of the Percys, and the silver wings of the Beauchamps, each supported by a squire clad in hanging green stuff to represent so many Tritons, and bearing a huge conch-shell in their left hands. Behind the tents the great war-horses, armed at all points, champed and reared, while their masters sat at the doors of their pavilions, with their helmets upon their knees, chatting as to the order of the day's doings. The English archers and men-at-arms had mustered at that end of the lists, but the vast majority of the spectators were in favour of the attacking party, for the English had declined in popularity ever since the bitter dispute as to the disposal of the royal captive after the battle of Poictiers. Hence the applause was by no means general when the herald-at-arms proclaimed, after a flourish of trumpets, the names and styles of the knights who were prepared, for the honour of their country and for the love of their ladies, to hold the field against all who might do them the favour to run a course with them. On the other hand, a deafening burst of cheering greeted the rival herald, who, advancing from the other end of the lists, rolled forth the well-known titles of the five famous warriors who had accepted the defiance.

" Faith, John," said the prince, " it sounds as though you were right. Ha ! my grace D'Armagnac, it seems that our friends on this side will not grieve if our English champions lose the day."

" It may be so, sire," the Gascon nobleman answered. " I have little doubt that in Smithfield or at Windsor an English crowd would favour their own countrymen."

" By my faith ! that's easily seen," said the prince, laughing, " for a few score English archers at yonder end are bellowing as though they would outshout the mighty multitude. I fear that they will have little to shout over this tourney, for my gold vase has small prospect of crossing the water. What are the conditions, John ? "

" They are to tilt singly not less than three courses, sire and the victory to rest with that party which shall have won the greater number of courses, each pair continuing till one or other have the vantage. He who carries himself best of the victors hath the prize, and he who is judged best of the other party hath a jewelled clasp. Shall I order that the nakirs sound, sire ? "

The prince nodded, and the trumpets rang out, while the champions rode forth one after the other, each meeting his opponent in the centre of the lists. Sir William Beauchamp went down before the practised lance of the Captal de Buch, Sir Thomas Percy won the vantage over the Lord of Mucident, and the Lord Audley struck Sir Perducas d'Albret from the saddle. The burly De Clisson, however, restored the hopes of the attackers by beating to the ground Sir Thomas Wake of Yorkshire. So far, there was little to choose betwixt challengers and challenged.

" By Saint James of Santiago ! " cried Don Pedro, with a tinge of colour upon his pale cheeks, " win who will, this has been a most noble contest."

" Who comes next for England, John ? " asked the prince, in a voice which quivered with excitement.

" Sir Nigel Loring of Hampshire, sire."

" Ha ! he is a man of good courage, and skilled in the use of all weapons."

" He is indeed, sire. But his eyes, like my own, are the worse for the wars. Yet he can tilt or play his part at handstrokes as merrily as ever. It was he, sire, who won the golden crown which Queen Philippa, your royal mother, gave to be jousted for by all the knights of England after the harrying of Calais. I have heard that at Twynham Castle there is a buffet which groans beneath the weight of his prizes."

" I pray that my vase may join them," said the prince. " But here is the cavalier of Germany, and, by my soul ! he looks like a man of great valour and hardiness. Let them run their full three courses, for the issue is over-great to hang upon one."

As the prince spoke, amid a loud flourish of trumpets and the shouting of the Gascon party, the last of the assailants rode gallantly into the lists. He was a man of great size, clad in black armour without blazonry or ornament of any kind, for all worldly display was forbidden by the rules of the military brotherhood to which he belonged. No plume or nobloy fluttered from his plain tilting salade, and even his lance was devoid of the customary banderole. A white mantle fluttered behind him, upon the left side of which was marked the broad black cross picked out with silver which was the well-known badge of the Teutonic order. Mounted upon a horse as black and as forbidding as himself, he cantered slowly forward, with none of those prancings and gambades with which a cavalier was accustomed to show his command over his charger. Gravely and sternly he inclined his head to the prince, and took his place at the farther end of the arena.

He had scarce done so before Sir Nigel rode out from the holders' enclosure, and galloping at full speed down

the lists, drew his charger up before the prince's stand
with a jerk which threw it back upon its haunches. With
white armour, blazoned shield, and plume of ostrich-
feathers from his helmet, he carried himself in so jaunty
and joyous a fashion, with tossing pennon and curveting
charger, that a shout of applause ran the full circle of the
arena. With the air of a man who hastes to a joyous
festival, he waved his lance in salute, and reining the
pawing horse round without permitting its fore-feet to
touch the ground, he hastened back to his station.

A great hush fell over the huge multitude as the last two
champions faced each other. A double issue seemed to
rest upon their contest, for their personal fame was at
stake as well as their party's honour. Both were famous
warriors, but as their exploits had been performed in
widely sundered countries, they had never before been
able to cross lances. A course between such men would
have been enough in itself to cause the keenest interest,
apart from its being the crisis which would decide who
should be the victors of the day. For a moment they
waited—the German sombre and collected, Sir Nigel
quivering in every fibre with eagerness and fiery resolution. Then, amid a long-drawn breath from the spectators, the glove fell from the marshal's hand, and the two
steel-clad horsemen met like a thunder-clap in front of the
royal stand. The German, though he reeled for an
instant before the thrust of the Englishman, struck his
opponent so fairly upon the vizor that the laces burst, the
plumed helmet flew to pieces, and Sir Nigel galloped on
down the list with his bald head shimmering in the sunshine. A thousand waving scarves and tossing caps
announced that the first bout had fallen to the popular
party.

The Hampshire knight was not a man to be disheartened
by a reverse. He spurred back to his pavilion, and was
out in a few instants with another helmet. The second
course was so equal that the keenest judges could not
discern any vantage. Each struck fire from the other's

shield, and each endured the jarring shock as though welded to the horse beneath him. In the final bout, however, Sir Nigel struck his opponent with so true an aim that the point of the lance caught between the bars of his vizor and tore the front of his helmet out, while the German, aiming somewhat low, and half stunned by the shock, had the misfortune to strike his adversary upon the thigh, a breach of the rules of the tilting-yard, by which he not only sacrificed his chances of success, but would also have forfeited his horse and his armour, had the English knight chosen to claim them. A roar of applause from the English soldiers, with an ominous silence from the vast crowd who pressed round the barriers, announced that the balance of victory lay with the holders. Already the ten champions had assembled in front of the prince to receive his award, when a harsh bugle call from the farther end of the lists drew all eyes to a new and un-expected arrival.

24. *How a Champion came forth from the East*

THE Bordeaux lists were, as has already been ex-plained, situated upon the plain near the river upon those great occasions when the tilting-ground in front of the Abbey of St. Andrew's was deemed to be too small to contain the crowd. On the eastern side of this plain the country-side sloped upwards, thick with vines in summer, but now ridged with the brown bare enclosures. Over the gently rising plain curved the white road which leads inland, usually flecked with travellers, but now with scarce a living form upon it, so completely had the lists drained all the district of its inhabitants. Strange it was to see so vast a concourse of people, and then to look upon that broad, white, empty highway which wound away, bleak and deserted, until it narrowed itself to a bare streak against the distant uplands.

Shortly after the contest had begun, anyone looking from the lists along this road might have remarked, far away in the extreme distance, two brilliant and sparkling points which glittered and twinkled in the bright shimmer of the winter sun. Within an hour these points had become clearer and nearer, until they might be seen to come from the reflection from the head-pieces of two horsemen who were riding at the top of their speed in the direction of Bordeaux. Another half-hour had brought them so close that every point of their bearing and equipment could be discerned. The first was a knight in full armour, mounted upon a brown horse with a white blaze upon breast and forehead. He was a short man of great breadth of shoulder, with vizor closed, and no blazonry upon his simple white surcoat or plain black shield. The other, who was evidently his squire and attendant, was unarmed save for the helmet upon his head, but bore in his right hand a very long and heavy oaken spear which belonged to his master. In his left hand the squire held not only the reins of his own horse but those of a great black war-horse fully harnessed, which trotted along at his side. Thus the three horses and their two riders rode swiftly to the lists, and it was the blare of the trumpet sounded by the squire as his lord rode into the arena which had broken in upon the prize-giving and drawn away the attention and interest of the spectators.

" Ha, John ! " cried the prince, craning his neck, " who is this cavalier, and what is it that he desires ? "

" On my word, sire," replied Chandos, with the utmost surprise upon his face, " it is my opinion that he is a Frenchman."

" A Frenchman ! " repeated Don Pedro. " And how can you tell that, my Lord Chandos, when he has neither coat-armour, crest, nor blazonry ? "

" By his armour, sire, which is rounder at elbow and at shoulder than any of Bordeaux or of England. Italian he might be were his bassinet more sloped, but I will swear that those plates were welded betwixt this and Rhine.

Here comes his squire, however, and we shall hear what strange fortune hath brought him over the marches."

As he spoke the attendant cantered up the grassy enclosure, and pulling up his steed in front of the royal stand, blew a second fanfare upon his bugle. He was a raw-boned, swarthy-cheeked man, with black bristling beard and a swaggering bearing. Having sounded his call, he thrust the bugle into his belt, and pushing his way betwixt the groups of English and of Gascon knights, he reined up within a spear's length of the royal party.

" I come," he shouted in a hoarse thick voice, with a strong Breton accent, " as squire and herald from my master, who is a very valiant pursuivant-of-arms, and a liegeman to the great and powerful monarch, Charles, king of the French. My master has heard that there is jousting here, and prospect of honourable advancement, so he has come to ask that some English cavalier will vouchsafe for the love of his lady to run a course with sharpened lances with him, or to meet him with sword, mace, battle-axe, or dagger. He bade me say, however, that he would fight only with a true Englishman, and not with any mongrel who is neither English nor French, but speaks with the tongue of the one, and fights under the banner of the other."

" Sir ! " cried De Clisson, with a voice of thunder, while his countrymen clapped their hands to their swords. The squire, however, took no notice of their angry faces, but continued with his master's message.

" He is now ready, sire," he said, " albeit his destrier has travelled many miles this day, and fast, for we were in fear lest we come too late for the jousting.

" Ye have indeed come too late," said the prince, " seeing that the prize is about to be awarded ; yet I doubt not that one of these gentlemen will run a course for the sake of honour with this cavalier of France."

" And as to the prize, sire," quoth Sir Nigel, " I am sure that I speak for all when I say this French knight hath our leave to bear it away with him if he can fairly win it."

" Bear word of this to your master," said the prince, " and ask him which of these five Englishmen he would desire to meet. But stay ; your master bears no coat-armour, and we have not yet heard his name."

" My master, sire, is under vow to the Virgin neither to reveal his name nor to open his vizor until he is back upon French ground once more."

" Yet what assurance have we," said the prince, " that this is not some varlet masquerading in his master's harness, or some caitiff knight, the very touch of whose lance might bring infamy upon an honourable gentle-man ? "

" It is not so, sire," cried the squire earnestly. " There is no man upon earth who would demean himself by breaking a lance with my master."

" You speak out boldly, squire," the prince answered ; " but unless I have some further assurance of your master's noble birth and gentle name I cannot match the choicest lances of my court against him."

" You refuse, sire ? "

" I do refuse."

" Then, sire, I was bidden to ask you from my master whether you would consent if Sir John Chandos, upon hearing my master's name, should assure you that he was indeed a man with whom you might yourself cross swords without indignity."

" I ask no better," said the prince.

" Then I must ask, Lord Chandos, that you will step forth. I have your pledge that the name shall remain ever a secret, and that you will neither say nor write one word which might betray it ? The name is——" He stooped down from his horse and whispered something into the old knight's ear which made him start with surprise, and stare with much curiosity at the distant knight, who was sitting his charger at the farther end of the arena.

" Is this indeed sooth ? " he exclaimed.

" It is, my lord, and I swear it by St. Ives of Brittany."

" I might have known it," said Chandos, twisting his moustache, and still looking thoughtfully at the cavalier.

" What then, Sir John ? " asked the prince.

" Sire, this is a knight whom it is indeed great honour to meet, and I would that your grace would grant me leave to send my squire for my harness, for I would dearly love to run a course with him."

" Nay, nay, Sir John, you have gained as much honour as one man can bear, and it were hard if you could not rest now. But I pray you, squire, to tell your master that he is very welcome to our court, and that wines and spices will be served him if he would refresh himself before jousting."

" My master will not drink," said the squire.

" Let him then name the gentleman with whom he would break a spear."

" He would contend with these five knights, each to choose such weapons as suit him best."

" I perceive," said the prince, " that your master is a man of great heart and high of enterprise. But the sun already is low in the west, and there will scarce be light for these courses. I pray you, gentlemen, to take your places, that we may see whether this stranger's deeds are as bold as his words."

The unknown knight had sat like a statue of steel looking neither to the right nor to the left during these preliminaries. He had changed from the horse upon which he had ridden, and bestrode the black charger which his squire had led beside him. His immense breadth, his stern composed appearance, and the mode in which he handled his shield and his lance, were enough in themselves to convince the thousands of critical spectators that he was a dangerous opponent. Aylward, who stood in the front row of the archers with Simon, big John, and others of the Company, had been criticising the proceedings from the commencement with the ease and freedom of a man who had spent his life under arms and had learned in a hard school to know at a glance the points of a horse and his rider. He stared now at the stranger with a wrinkled brow and the air of a man who is striving to stir his memory.

" By my hilt ! I have seen the thick body of him before to-day. Yet I cannot call to mind where it could have been. At Nogent belike, or was it at Auray ? Mark me, lads, this man will prove to be one of the best lances of France, and there are no better in the world."

" It is but child's play, this poking game," said John. " I would fain try my hand at it, for, by the black rood ! I think that it might be amended."

" What, then, would you do, John ? " asked several.

" There are many things which might be done," said the forester thoughtfully. " Methinks that I would begin by breaking my spear."

" So they all strive to do."

" Nay, but not upon another man's shield. I would break it over my own knee."

" And what the better for that, old beef and bones ? " asked Black Simon.

" So I would turn what is but a lady's bodkin of a weapon into a very handsome club."

" And then, John ? "

" Then I would take the other's spear into my arm or my leg, or where it pleased him best to put it, and I would dash out his brains with my club."

" By my ten finger-bones ! old John," said Aylward. " I would give my feather-bed to see you at a spear-running. This is a most courtly and gentle sport which you have devised."

" So it seems to me," said John seriously. " Or, again, one might seize the other round the middle, pluck him off his horse and bear him to the pavilion, there to hold him to ransom."

" Good ! " cried Simon, amid a roar of laughter from all the archers round. " By Thomas of Kent ! we shall make a camp-marshal of thee, and thou shalt draw up rules for our jousting. But, John, who is it that you would uphold in this knightly and pleasing fashion ? "

" What mean you ? "

" Why, John, so strong and strange a tilter must fight for the brightness of his lady's eyes or the curl of her eyelash, even as Sir Nigel does for the Lady Loring."

" I know not about that," said the big archer, scratching his head in perplexity. " Since Mary hath played me false, I can scarce fight for her."

" Yet any woman will serve."

" There is my mother, then," said John. " She was at much pains at my upbringing, and, by my soul ! I will uphold the curve of her eye-lashes, for it tickleth my very heartroot to think of her. But who is here ? "

" It is Sir William Beauchamp. He is a valiant man, but I fear that he is scarce firm enough upon the saddle to bear the thrust of such a tilter as this stranger promises to be."

Aylward's words were speedily justified, for even as he spoke the two knights met in the centre of the lists. Beauchamp struck his opponent a shrewd blow upon the helmet, but was met with so frightful a thrust that he whirled out of his saddle and rolled over and over upon the ground. Sir Thomas Percy met with little better success, for his shield was split, his vambrace torn, and he himself wounded slightly in the side. Lord Audley and the unknown knight struck each other fairly upon the helmet ; but while the stranger sat as firm and rigid as ever upon his charger the Englishman was bent back to his horse's crupper by the weight of the blow and had galloped half-way down the lists ere he could recover himself. Sir Thomas Wake was beaten to the ground with a battle-axe—that being the weapon which he had selected—and had to be carried to his pavilion. These rapid successes, gained one after the other over four celebrated warriors, worked the crowd up to a pitch of wonder and admiration. Thunders of applause from the English soldiers, as well as from the citizens and peasants, showed how far the love of brave and knightly deeds could rise above the rivalries of race.

" By my soul ! John," cried the prince, with his cheek flushed and his eyes shining, " this is a man of good courage and great hardiness. I could not have thought that there was any single arm upon earth which could have overthrown these four champions."

" He is indeed, as I have said, sire, a knight from whom much honour is to be gained. But the lower edge of the sun is wet, and it will be beneath the sea ere long."

" Here is Sir Nigel Loring, on foot and with his sword," said the prince. " I have heard that he is a fine swordsman."

" The finest in your army, sire," Chandos answered. " Yet I doubt not that he will need all his skill this day."

As he spoke, the two combatants advanced from either end in full armour with their two-handed swords sloping over their shoulders. The stranger walked heavily and with a measured stride, while the English knight advanced as briskly as though there was no iron shell to weigh down the freedom of his limbs. At four paces distance they stopped, eyed each other for a moment, and then in an instant fell to work with a clatter and clang as though two sturdy smiths were busy upon their anvils. Up and down went the long shining blades, round and round they circled in curves of glimmering light, crossing, meeting, disengaging, with flash of sparks at every parry. Here and there bounded Sir Nigel, his head erect, his jaunty plume fluttering in the air, while his dark opponent sent in crashing blow upon blow, following fiercely up with cut and with thrust, but never once getting past the practised blade of the skilled swordsman. The crowd roared with delight as Sir Nigel would stoop his head to avoid a blow, or by some slight movement of his body allow some terrible thrust to glance harmlessly past him. Suddenly, however, his time came. The Frenchman, whirling up his sword, showed for an instant a chink betwixt his shoulder-piece and the rerebrace which guarded his upper arm. In dashed Sir Nigel, and out again so swiftly that the eye could not follow the quick play of his blade, but a trickle of blood from the stranger's shoulder, and a rapidly widening red smudge upon his white surcoat, showed where the thrust had taken effect. The wound was, however, but a slight one, and the Frenchman was about to renew his onset, when, at a sign from the prince, Chandos threw down his bâton, and the marshals of the lists struck up the weapons and brought the contest to an end.

" It were time to check it," said the prince, smiling, " for Sir Nigel is too good a man for me to lose, and, by the five holy wounds ! if one of those cuts came home I should have fears for our champion. What think you, Pedro ? "

" I think, Edward, that the little man was very well able to take care of himself. For my part, I should wish to see so well matched a pair fight on while a drop of blood remained in their veins."

" We must have speech with him. Such a man must not go from my court without rest or sup. Bring him hither, Chandos, and, certes, if the Lord Loring hath resigned his claim upon this goblet, it is right and proper that this cavalier should carry it to France with him as a sign of the prowess that he has shown this day."

As he spoke, the knight-errant, who had remounted his war-horse, galloped forward to the royal stand, with a silken kerchief bound round his wounded arm. The setting sun cast a ruddy glare upon his burnished armour, and sent his long black shadow streaming behind him up the level clearing. Pulling up his steed, he slightly inclined his head, and sat in the stern and composed fashion with which he had borne himself throughout, heedless of the applauding shouts and the flutter of kerchiefs from the long lines of brave men and of fair women who were looking down upon him.

" Sir knight," said the prince, " we have all marvelled this day at the great skill and valour with which God has been pleased to endow you. I would fain that you should tarry at our court, for a time at least, until your hurt is healed and your horses rested."

" My hurt is nothing, sire, nor are my horses weary," returned the stranger in a deep stern voice.

" Will you not at least hie back to Bordeaux with us, that you may drain a cup of muscadine and sup at our table ? "

" I will neither drink your wine nor sit at your table," returned the other. " I bear no love for you or for your race, and there is nought that I wish at your hands until the day when I see the last sail which bears you back to your island vanishing away against the western sky."

" These are bitter words, sir knight," said Prince Edward, with an angry frown.

" And they come from a bitter heart," answered the unknown knight. " How long is it since there has been peace in my hapless country ? Where are the steadings and orchards and vineyards which made France fair ? Where are the cities which made her great ? From Provence to Burgundy we are beset by all the prowling hirelings in Christendom, who rend and tear the country which you have left too weak to guard her own marches. Is it not a byword that a man may ride all day in that unhappy land without seeing thatch upon roof or hearing the crow of cock ? Does not one fair kingdom content you, that you should strive so for this other one which has no love for you ? Pardieu ! a true Frenchman's words may well be bitter, for bitter is his lot, and bitter his thoughts as he rides through his thrice unhappy country."

" Sir knight," said the prince, " you speak like a brave man, and our cousin of France is happy in having a cavalier who is so fit to uphold his cause either with tongue or with sword. But if you think such evil of us, how comes it that you have trusted yourself to us without warranty of safe-conduct ? "

" Because I knew that you would be here, sire. Had the man who sits upon your right been ruler of this land,

I had indeed thought twice before I looked to him for aught that was knightly or generous." With a soldierly salute, he wheeled round his horse, and, galloping down the lists, disappeared amid the dense crowd of footmen and of horsemen who were streaming away from the scene of the tournament.

" The insolent villain ! " cried Pedro, glaring furiously after him. " I have seen a man's tongue torn from his jaws for less. Would it not be well, even now, Edward, to send horsemen to hale him back ? Bethink you that it may be one of the royal house of France, or at least some knight whose loss would be a heavy blow to his master. Sir William Felton, you are well mounted, gallop after the caitiff, I pray you."

" Do so, Sir William," said the prince, " and give him this purse of a hundred nobles as a sign of the respect which I bear for him ; for, by St. George ! he has served his master this day even as I would wish liegemen of mine to serve me." So saying, the prince turned his back upon the king of Spain, and, springing upon his horse, rode slowly homewards to the Abbey of St. Andrew's.

25. *How Sir Nigel wrote to Twynham Castle*

ON the morning after the jousting, when Alleyne Edricson went, as was his custom, into his master's chamber to wait upon him in his dressing, and to curl his hair, he found him already up and very busily at work. He sat at a table by the window, a deer-hound on one side of him and a lurcher on the other, his feet tucked away under the trestle on which he sat, and his tongue in his cheek, with the air of a man who is much perplexed. A sheet of vellum lay upon the board in front of him, and he held a pen in his hand, with which he had been scribbling in a rude schoolboy hand. So many were the blots, however, and so numerous the scratches and erasures, that he had at last given it up in despair, and sat with his single uncovered eye cocked upwards at the ceiling, as one who waits upon inspiration.

" By Saint Paul ! " he cried, as Alleyne entered, " you are the man who will stand by me in this matter. I have been in sore need of you, Alleyne."

" God be with you, my fair lord ! " the squire answered. " I trust that you have taken no hurt from all that you have gone through yesterday."

" Nay ; I feel the fresher for it, Alleyne. It has eased my joints, which were somewhat stiff from these years of peace. I trust, Alleyne, that thou didst very carefully note and mark the bearing and carriage of this knight of France : for it is time, now when you are young, that you should see all that is best, and mould your own actions in accordance. This was a man from whom much honour might be gained, and I have seldom met anyone for whom I have conceived so much love and esteem. Could I but learn his name, I should send you to him with my cartel, that we might have further occasion to watch his goodly feats of arms."

" It is said, my fair lord, that none know his name, save only the Lord Chandos, and that he is under vow not to speak it. So ran the gossip at the squires' table."

" Be he who he might, he was a very hardy gentleman. But I have a task here, Alleyne, which is harder to me than aught that was set before me yesterday."

" Can I help you, my lord ? "

" That indeed you can. I have been writing my greetings to my sweet wife ; for I hear that a messenger goes from the prince to Southampton within the week, and he would gladly take a packet for me. I pray you, Alleyne, to cast your eyes upon what I have written, and see if they are such words as my lady will understand. My fingers, as you can see, are more used to iron and leather than to the drawing of strokes and turning of letters. What then ? Is there aught amiss, that you should stare so ? "

" It is this first word, my lord. In what tongue were you pleased to write ? "

" In English ; for my lady talks it more than she doth French."

" Yet this is no English word, my sweet lord. Here are four t's and never a letter betwixt them."

" By Saint Paul ! it seemed strange to my eye when I wrote it," said Sir Nigel. " They bristle up together like a clump of lances. We must break their ranks and set them farther apart. The word is ' that.' Now I will read it to you, Alleyne, and you shall write it out fair ; for we leave Bordeaux this day, and it would be great joy to me to think that the Lady Loring had word from me."

Alleyne sat down as ordered, with a pen in his hand and a fresh sheet of parchment before him, while Sir Nigel slowly spelled out his letter, running his forefinger on from word to word.

" That my heart is with thee, my dear sweeting, is what thine own heart will assure thee of. All is well with us here, save that Pepin hath the mange on his back, and Pommers hath scarce yet got clear of his stiffness from being four days on ship-board ; and the more so because the sea was very high, and we were like to founder on account of a hole in her side, which was made by a stone cast at us by certain sea-rovers, who may the saints have in their keeping, for they have gone from amongst us, as has young Terlake and two score mariners and archers who would be the more welcome here, as there is like to be a very fine war, with much honour and all hopes of advancement ; for which I go to gather my Company together, who are now at Montaubon, where they pillage and destroy ; yet I hope that, by God's help, I may be able to show that I am their master, even as, my sweet lady, I am thy servant." " How of that, Alleyne ? " continued Sir Nigel, blinking at his squire, with an expression of some pride upon his face. " Have I not told her all that hath befallen us ? "

" You have said much, my fair lord ; and yet, if I may

say so, it is somewhat crowded together, so that my Lady Loring can, mayhap, scarce follow it. Were it in shorter periods——"

"Nay, it boots not how you marshal them, as long as they are all there at the muster. Let my lady have the words, and she will place them in such order as pleases her best. But I would have you add what it would please her to know."

"That will I," said Alleyne, blithely, and bent to the task.

"My fair lady and mistress," he wrote, "God hath had us in His keeping, and my lord is well and in good cheer. He hath won much honour at the jousting before the prince, when he alone was able to make it good against a very valiant man from France. Touching the monies, there is enough and to spare until we reach Montaubon. Herewith, my fair lady, I send my humble regards, entreating you that you will give the same to your daughter, the Lady Maude. May the holy saints have you both in their keeping is ever the prayer of thy servant,

"ALLEYNE EDRICSON."

"That is very fairly set forth," said Sir Nigel, nodding his bald head as each sentence was read to him. "And for thyself, Alleyne, if there be any dear friend to whom you would fain give greeting, I can send it for thee within this packet."

"There is none," said Alleyne, sadly.

"Have you no kinsfolk, then?"

"None, save my brother."

"Ha! I had forgot that there was ill-blood betwixt you. But are there none in all England who love thee?"

"None that I dare say so."

"And none whom you love?"

"Nay, I will not say that," said Alleyne.

Sir Nigel shook his head and laughed softly to himself. "I see how it is with you," he said. "Have I not noted your frequent sighs, and vacant eye? Is she fair?"

" She is indeed," cried Alleyne from his heart, all tingling at this sudden turn of the talk.

" And good ? "

" As an angel."

" And yet she loves you not ? "

" Nay, I cannot say that she loves another."

" Then you have hopes ? "

" I could not live else."

" Then must you strive to be worthy of her love. Be brave and pure, fearless to the strong and humble to the weak ; and so, whether this love prosper or no, you will have fitted yourself to be honoured by a maiden's love, which is, in sooth, the highest guerdon which a true knight can hope for."

" Indeed, my lord, I do so strive," said Alleyne ; " but she is so sweet, so dainty, and of so noble a spirit, that I fear me that I shall never be worthy of her."

" By thinking so you become worthy. Is she then of noble birth ? "

" She is, my lord," faltered Alleyne.

" Of a knightly house ? "

" Yes."

" Have a care, Alleyne, have a care ! " said Sir Nigel kindly. " The higher the steed the greater the fall. Hawk not at that which may be beyond thy flight."

" My lord, I know little of the ways and usages of the world," cried Alleyne, " but I would fain ask your rede upon the matter. You have known my father and my kin : is not my family one of good standing and repute ? "

" Beyond all question."

" And yet you warn me that I must not place my love too high."

" Were Minstead yours, Alleyne, then, by Saint Paul ! I cannot think that any family in the land would not be proud to take you among them, seeing that you come of so old a strain. But while the Socman lives—— Ha, by my soul ! if this is not Sir Oliver's step I am the more mistaken."

As he spoke, a heavy footfall was heard without, and the portly knight flung open the door and strode into the room.

" Why, my little coz," said he, " I have come across to tell you that I live above the barber's in the Rue de la Tour, and that there is a venison pasty in the oven and two flasks of the right vintage on the table. By St. James ! a blind man might find the place, for one has but to get in the wind from it, and follow the savoury smell. Put on your cloak, then, and come, for Sir Walter Hewett and Sir Robert Briquet, with one or two others, are awaiting us."

" Nay, Oliver, I cannot be with you, for I must to Montaubon this day."

" To Montaubon ? But I have heard that your Company is to come with my forty Winchester rascals to Dax."

" If you will take charge of them, Oliver. For I will go to Montaubon with none save my two squires and two archers. Then, when I have found the rest of my Company, I shall lead them to Dax. We set forth this morning."

" Then I must back to my pasty," said Sir Oliver. " You will find us at Dax, I doubt not, unless the prince throw me into prison, for he is very wroth against me."

" And why, Oliver ? "

" Pardieu ! because I have sent my cartel, gauntlet and defiance to Sir John Chandos and to Sir William Felton."

" To Chandos ? In God's name, Oliver, why have you done this ? "

" Because he and the other have used me despitefully."

" And how ? "

" Because they have passed me over in choosing those who should joust for England. Yourself and Audley I could pass, coz, for you are mature men ; but who are Wake, and Percy, and Beauchamp ? By my soul ! I was prodding for my food into a camp-kettle when they were howling for their pap. Is a man of my weight and substance to be thrown aside for the first three half-grown lads who have learned the trick of the tilt-yard ? But hark ye, coz, I think of sending my cartel also to the prince."

" Oliver ! Oliver ! You are mad ! "

" Not I, i' faith ! I care not a denier whether he be prince or no. By Saint James ! I see that your squire's eyes are starting from his head like a trussed crab. Well, friend, we are all three men of Hampshire, and not lightly to be jeered at."

" Has he jeered at you then ? "

" Pardieu ! yes. ' Old Sir Oliver's heart is still stout,' said one of his court. ' Else had it been out of keeping with the rest of him,' quoth the prince. ' And his arm is strong,' said another. ' So is the backbone of his horse,' quoth the prince. This very day I will send him my cartel and defiance."

" Nay, nay, my dear Oliver," said Sir Nigel, laying his hand upon his angry friend's arm. " There is nought in this, for it was but saying that you were a strong and robust man, who had need of a good destrier. And as to Chandos and Felton, bethink you that if when you your-self were young the older lances had ever been preferred, how would you then have had the chance to earn the good name and fame which you now bear ? You do not ride as light as you did, Oliver, and I ride lighter by the weight of my hair, but it would be an ill thing if in the evening of our lives we showed that our hearts were less true and loyal than of old. If such a knight as Sir Oliver Buttes-thorn may turn against his own prince for the sake of a light word, then where are we to look for steadfast faith and constancy ? "

" Ah ! my dear little coz, it is easy to sit in the sunshine and preach to the man in the shadow. Yet you could ever win me over to your side with that soft voice of yours. Let us think no more of it then. But, Holy Mother ! I had forgot the pasty, and it will be as scorched as Judas Iscariot ! Come, Nigel, lest the foul fiend get the better of me again."

" For one hour, then ; for we march at mid-day. Tell Aylward, Alleyne, that he is to come with me to Montaubon, and to choose one archer for his comrade. The rest will to Dax when the prince starts, which will be before the feast of the Epiphany. Have Pommers ready at midday with my sycamore lance, and place my harness on the sumpter mule."

With these brief directions, the two old soldiers strode off together, while Alleyne hastened to get all in order for their journey.

26. *How the Three Comrades gained a Mighty Treasure*

IT was a bright crisp winter's day when the little party set off from Bordeaux on their journey to Montaubon, where the missing half of their Company had last been heard of. Sir Nigel and Ford had ridden on in advance, the knight upon his hackney, while his great war-horse trotted beside his squire. Two hours later Alleyne Edricson followed ; for he had the tavern reckoning to settle, and many other duties which fell to him as squire of the body. With him came Aylward and Hordle John, armed as of old, but mounted for their journey upon a pair of clumsy Landes horses, heavy-headed and shambling, but of great endurance, and capable of jogging along all day even when between the knees of the huge archer, who turned the scale at two hundred and seventy pounds. They took with them the sumpter mules which carried in panniers the wardrobe and table furniture of Sir Nigel ; for the knight, though neither fop nor epicure, was very dainty in small matters and loved, however bare the board or hard the life, that his napery should still be white and his spoon of silver.

There had been frost during the night, and the white hard road rang loud under their horses' irons as they spurred through the east gate of the town, along the same broad highway which the unknown French champion had traversed on the day of the jousts. The three rode abreast, Alleyne Edricson with his eyes cast down and his mind distrait, for his thoughts were busy with the conversation which he had had with Sir Nigel in the morning. Had he done well to say so much, or had he not done better to have said more ? What would the knight have said had he confessed to his love for the Lady Maude ? Would he cast him off in disgrace, or might he chide him as having abused the shelter of his roof ? It had been ready upon his tongue to tell him all when Sir Oliver had broken in upon them. Perchance Sir Nigel, with his love of all the dying usages of chivalry, might have contrived some strange ordeal or feat of arms, by which his love should be put to the test. Alleyne smiled as he wondered what fantastic and wondrous deed would be exacted from him. Whatever it was, he was ready for it, whether it were to hold the lists in the court of the King of Tartary, to carry a cartel to the Sultan of Baghdad, or to serve a term against the wild heathen of Prussia. Sir Nigel had said that his birth was high enough for any lady, if his fortune could but be amended. Often had Alleyne curled his lip at the beggarly craving for land or for gold which blinded man to the higher and more lasting issues of life. Now it seemed as though it were only by this same land and gold that he might hope to reach his heart's desire. But then, again, the Socman of Minstead was no friend to the constable of Twynham Castle. It might happen that, should he amass riches by some happy fortune of war, this feud might hold the two families aloof. Even if Maude loved him, he knew her too well to think that she would wed him without the blessing of her father. Dark and murky was it all, but hope mounts high in youth, and it ever fluttered over all the turmoil of his thoughts like a white plume amid the shock of horsemen.

If Alleyne Edricson had enough to ponder over as he rode through the bare plains of Guienne, his two com-

panions were more busy with the present and less thoughtful of the future. Aylward rode for half a mile with his
chin upon his shoulder, looking back at a white kerchief
which fluttered out of the gable window of a high house
which peeped over the corner of the battlements. When
at last a dip of the road hid it from his view, he cocked his
steel cap, shrugged his broad shoulders, and rode on with
laughter in his eyes, and his weather-beaten face all ashine
with pleasant memories. John also rode in silence, but
his eyes wandered slowly from one side of the road to the
other, and he stared and pondered and nodded his head
like a traveller who makes his notes and saves them up for
the re-telling.

" By the rood ! " he broke out suddenly, slapping his
thigh with his great red hand, " I knew that there was
something a-missing, but I could not bring to my mind
what it was."

" What was it then ? " asked Alleyne, coming with a
start out of his reverie.

" Why, it is the hedgerows," roared John, with a shout
of laughter. " The country is all scraped as clear as a
friar's poll. But indeed I cannot think much of the folk
in these parts. Why do they not get to work and dig up
these long rows of black and crooked stumps which I see
on every hand ? A franklin of Hampshire would think
shame to have such litter upon his soil."

" Thou foolish old John ! " quoth Aylward. " You
should know better, since I have heard that the monks of
Beaulieu could squeeze a good cup of wine from their
own grapes. Know then that if these rows were dug up
the wealth of the country would be gone, and mayhap
there would be dry throats and gaping mouths in England,
for in three months' time these black roots will blossom
and shoot and burgeon, and from them will come many
a good ship-load of Médoc and Gascony which will cross
the narrow seas. But see the little church in the hollow,
and the folk who cluster in the churchyard ! By my hilt !
it is a burial, and there is a passing bell ! " He pulled off

his steel cap as he spoke and crossed himself, with a muttered prayer for the repose of the dead.

" There too," remarked Alleyne, as they rode on again, " that which seems to the eye to be dead is still full of the sap of life, even as the vines were. Thus God hath written Himself and His laws very broadly on all that is around us, if our poor dull eyes and duller souls could but read what He hath set before us."

" Ha ! mon petit," cried the bowman, " you take me back to the days when you were new-fledged, as sweet a little chick as ever pecked his way out of a monkish egg. I had feared that in gaining our debonair young man-at-arms we had lost our soft-spoken clerk. In truth, I have noted much change in you since we came from Twynham Castle."

" Surely it would be strange else, seeing that I have lived in a world so new to me. Yet I trust that there are many things in which I have not changed. If I have turned to serve an earthly master, and to carry arms for an earthly king, it would be an ill thing if I were to lose all thought of the great high King and Master of all, whose humble and unworthy servant I was ere ever I left Beaulieu. You, John, are also from the cloisters, but I trow that you do not feel that you have deserted the old service in taking on the new."

" I am a slow-witted man," said John, " and, in sooth, when I try to think about such matters it casts a gloom upon me. Yet I do not look upon myself as a worse man in an archer's jerkin than I was in a white cowl, if that be what you mean."

" You have but changed from one white company to the other," quoth Aylward. " But, by these ten finger-bones ! it is a passing strange thing to me to think that it was but in the last fall of the leaf that we walked from Lyndhurst together, he so gentle and maidenly, and you, John, like a great red-limbed over-grown mooncalf ; and now here you are as sprack a squire and as lusty an archer as ever passed down the highway from Bordeaux, while

I am still the same old Samkin Aylward, with never a change, save that I have a few more sins on my soul, and a few less crowns in my pouch. But I never heard yet, John, what the reason was why you should come out of Beaulieu."

" There were seven reasons," said John, thoughtfully. " The first of them was that they threw me out."

" Ma foi ! camarade, to the devil with the other six ! That is enough for me and for thee also. I can see that they are very wise and discreet folk at Beaulieu. Ah ! mon ange, what have you in the pipkin ? "

" It is milk, worthy sir," answered the peasant-maid, who stood by the door of a cottage with a jug in her hand. " Would it please you, gentles, that I should bring you out three horns of it ? "

" Nay, ma petite, but here is a two-sous piece for thy kindly tongue and for the sight of thy pretty face. Ma foi ! but she has a bonne mine. I have a mind to bide and speak with her."

" Nay, nay, Aylward," cried Alleyne. " Sir Nigel will await us, and he in haste."

" True, true, camarade ! Adieu, ma chérie ! mon cœur est toujours à toi. Her mother is a well-grown woman also. See where she digs by the wayside. Ma foi ! the riper fruit is ever the sweeter. Bon jour, ma belle dame ! God have you in His keeping ! Said Sir Nigel where he would await us ? "

" At Marmande or Aiguillon. He said that we could not pass him, seeing that there is but the one road."

" Aye, and it is a road that I know as I know the Midhurst parish butts," quoth the bowman. " Thirty times have I journeyed it, forward and backward, and by the twang of string ! I am wont to come back this way more laden than I went. I have carried all that I had into France in a wallet, and it hath taken four sumpter mules to carry it back again. God's benison on the man who first turned his hand to the making of war ! But there, down in the dingle, is the church of Cardillac, and you may see the inn where three poplars grow beyond the village. Let us on, for a stoup of wine would hearten us upon our way."

The highway had lain through the swelling vineyard country, which stretched away to the north and east in gentle curves, with many a peeping spire and feudal tower, and cluster of village houses, all clear cut and hard in the bright wintry air. To their right stretched the blue Garonne running swiftly seawards, with boats and barges dotted over its broad bosom. On the other side lay a strip of vineyard, and beyond it the desolate and sandy region of the Landes, all tangled with faded gorse and heath and broom, stretching away in unbroken gloom to the blue hills which lay low upon the farthest sky-line. Behind them might still be seen the broad estuary of the Gironde, with the high towers of Saint André and Saint Remi shooting up from the plain. In front, amid radiating lines of poplars, lay the riverside townlet of Cardillac —grey walls, white houses and a feather of blue smoke. " This is the ' Mouton d'Or,' " said Aylward, as they pulled up their horses at a whitewashed straggling hostel. " What ho there ! " he continued, beating upon the door with the hilt of his sword. " Tapster, ostler, varlet, hark hither, and a wannion on your lazy limbs ! Ha ! Michel, as red in the nose as ever ! Three jacks of the wine of the country, Michel—for the air bites shrewdly. I pray you, Alleyne, to take note of this door, for I have a tale concerning it."

" Tell me, friend," said Alleyne to the portly, red-faced innkeeper, " have a knight and a squire passed this way within the hour ? "

" Nay, sir, it would be two hours back. Was he a small man, weak in the eyes, with a want of hair, and speaks very quiet when he is most to be feared ? "

" The same," the squire answered. " But I marvel how you should know how he speaks when he is in wrath, for he is very gentle-minded with those who are beneath him."

" Praise to the saints ! it was not I who angered him,"
said the fat Michel.

" Who, then ? "

" It was young Sieur de Brissac of Saintonge, who
chanced to be here, and made game of the Englishman,
seeing that he was but a small man and hath a face which
is full of peace. But indeed this good knight was a very
quiet and patient man, for he saw that the Sieur de
Brissac was still young and spoke from an empty head,
so he sat his horse and quaffed his wine, even as you are
doing now, all heedless of his clacking tongue."

" And what then, Michel ? "

" Well, messieurs, it chanced that the Sieur de Brissac,
having said this and that, for the laughter of the varlets,
cried out at last about the glove that the knight wore in his
coif, asking if it was the custom in England for a man to
wear a great archer's glove in his cap. Pardieu ! I have
never seen a man get off his horse as quick as did that
stranger Englishman. Ere the words were past the other's
lips he was beside him, his face nigh touching, and his
breath hot upon his cheeks. ' I think, young sir,' quoth
he softly, looking into the other's eyes, ' that now that I
am nearer, you will very clearly see that the glove is not
an archer's glove.' ' Perchance not,' said the Sieur de
Brissac, with a twitching lip. ' Nor is it large, but very
small,' quoth the Englishman. ' Less large than I had
thought,' said the other, looking down, for the knight's
gaze was heavy upon his eyelids. ' And in every way such
a glove as might be warn by the fairest and sweetest lady
in England,' quoth the Englishman. ' It may be so,'
said the Sieur de Brissac, turning his face from him.
' I am myself weak in the eyes, and have often taken one
thing for another,' quoth the knight, as he sprang back
into his saddle and rode off, leaving the Sieur de Brissac
biting his nails before my door. Ha ! by the five wounds,
many men of war have drunk my wine, but never one
who was more to my fancy than this little Englishman."

" By my hilt ! he is our master, Michel," quoth

285

Aylward, " and such men as we do not serve under a laggart. But here are four deniers, Michel, and God be with you ! En avant, camarades ! for we have a long road before us."

At a brisk trot the three friends left Cardillac and its wine-house behind them, riding without a halt, past St. Macaire, and on by ferry over the river Dorpt. At the farther side the road winds through La Réolle, Bazaille and Marmande, with the sunlit river still gleaming upon the right, and the bare poplars bristling up upon either side. John and Alleyne rode silent on either side, but every inn, farm-steading, or castle brought back to Aylward some remembrance of love, foray, or plunder, with which to beguile the way.

" There is the smoke from Bazas, on the further side of Garonne," quoth he. " There were three sisters yonder, the daughters of a farrier, and, by these ten finger-bones ! a man might ride for a long June day and never set eyes upon such maidens. There was Marie, tall and grave, and Blanche, petite and gay, and the dark Agnes, with eyes that went through you like a waxed arrow. I lingered there as long as four days, and was betrothed to them all : for it seemed shame to set one above her sisters, and might cause ill blood in the family. Yet, for all my care, things were not merry in the house, and I thought it well to come away. There, too, is the mill of Le Souris. Old Le Pierre Carron, who owned it, was a right good comrade, and had ever a seat and a crust for a weary archer. He was a man who wrought hard at all that he turned his hand to ; but he heated himself in grinding bones to mix with his flour, and so through over-diligence he brought a fever upon himself and died."

" Tell me, Aylward," said Alleyne, " what was amiss with the door of yonder inn that you should ask me to observe it."

" Pardieu ! yes, I had well-nigh forgot. What saw you on yonder door ? "

" I saw a square hole, through which doubtless the

host may peep when he is not too sure of those who knock."

" And you saw nought else ? "

" I marked that beneath this hole there was a deep cut in the door, as though a great nail had been driven in."

" And nought else ? "

" No."

" Had you looked more closely you might have seen that there was a stain upon the wood. The first time that I ever heard my comrade Black Simon laugh was in front of that door. I heard him once again when he slew a French squire with his teeth, he being unarmed and the Frenchman having a dagger."

" And why did Simon laugh in front of the inn-door ? " asked John.

" Simon is a hard and perilous man when he hath the bitter drop in him ; and, by my hilt ! he was born for war, for there is little sweetness or rest in him. This inn, the ' Mouton d'Or,' was kept in the old days by one François Gourval, who had a hard fist and a harder heart. It was said that many and many an archer coming from the wars had been served with wine with simples in it, until he slept, and had then been stripped of all by this Gourval. Then on the morrow, if he made complaint this wicked Gourval would throw him out upon the road or beat him, for he was a very lusty man, and had many stout varlets in his service. This chanced to come to Simon's ears when we were at Bordeaux together, and he would have it that we should ride to Cardillac with a good hempen cord and give this Gourval such a scourging as he merited. Forth we rode then, but when we came to the ' Mouton d'Or,' Gourval had had word of our coming and its purpose, so that the door was barred, nor was there any way into the house. ' Let us in, good Master Gourval ! ' cried Simon, and ' Let us in, good Master Gourval ! ' cried I, but no word could we get through the hole in the door, save that he would draw an arrow upon us unless we went on our way. ' Well,

Master Gourval,' quoth Simon at last, ' this is but a sorry welcome, seeing that we have ridden so far just to shake you by the hand.' ' Canst shake me by the hand without coming in,' said Gourval. ' And how that ? ' asked Simon. ' By passing in your hand through the hole,' said he. ' Nay, my hand is wounded,' quoth Simon, ' and of such a size that I cannot pass it in.' ' That need not hinder,' said Gourval, who was hot to be rid of us ; ' pass in your left hand.' ' But I have something for thee, Gourval,' said Simon. ' What then ? ' he asked. ' There was an English archer who slept here last week of the name of Hugh of Nutbourne.' ' We have had many rogues here,' said Gourval. ' His conscience hath been heavy within him because he owes you a debt of fourteen deniers, having drunk wine for which he hath never paid. For the easing of his soul he asked me to pay the money to you as I passed.' Now this Gourval was very greedy for money, so he thrust forth his hand for the fourteen deniers, but Simon had his dagger ready and he pinned his hand to the door. ' I have paid the Englishman's debt, Gourval ! ' quoth he, and so rode away, laughing so that he could scarce sit his horse, leaving mine host still nailed to his door. Such is the story of the hole which you have marked, and of the smudge upon the wood. I have heard that from that time English archers have been better treated in the auberge of Cardillac. But what have we here by the wayside ? "

" It appears to be a very holy man," said Alleyne.

" And, by the rood ! he hath some strange wares," cried John. " What are these bits of stone, and of wood, and rusted nails, which are set out in front of him ? "

The man whom they had remarked sat with his back against a cherry-tree, and his legs shooting out in front of him, like one who is greatly at his ease. Across his thighs was a wooden board, and scattered over it all manner of slips of wood and knobs of brick and stone, each laid separate from the other as a huckster places his wares. He was dressed in a long grey gown, and wore a broad hat of the same colour, much weather-stained, with three scallop-shells dangling from the brim. As they approached, the travellers observed that he was advanced in years, and that his eyes were upturned and yellow.

" Dear knights and gentlemen," he cried in a high crackling voice, " worthy Christian cavaliers, will ye ride past and leave an aged pilgrim to die of hunger ? The sight hath been burned from mine eyes by the sands of the Holy Land, and I have had neither crust of bread nor cup of wine these two days past."

" By my hilt ! father," said Aylward, looking keenly at him, " it is a marvel to me that thy girdle should have so goodly a span and clip thee so closely, if you have in sooth had so little to place within it."

" Kind stranger," answered the pilgrim, " you have unwittingly spoken words which are very grievous to me to listen to. Yet I should be loth to blame you, for I doubt not that what you said was not meant to sadden me, nor to bring my sore affliction back to my mind. It ill becomes me to prate too much of what I have endured for the faith, and yet, since you have observed it, I must tell you that this sickness and roundness of the waist is caused by a dropsy brought on by over-haste in journeying from the house of Pilate to the Mount of Olives."

" There, Aylward," said Alleyne, with a reddened cheek, " let that curb your blunt tongue. How could you bring a fresh pang to this holy man, who hath endured so much and hath journeyed as far as Christ's own blessed tomb ? "

" May the foul fiend strike me dumb ! " cried the bowman in hot repentance ; but both the palmer and Alleyne threw up their hands to stop him.

" I forgive thee from my heart, dear brother," piped the blind man. " But, oh, these wild words of thine are worse to mine ears than aught which you could say of me."

" Not another word shall I speak," said Aylward ; " but here is a florin for thee and I crave thy blessing."

" And here is another," said Alleyne.

"And another," cried Hordle John.

But the blind palmer would have none of their alms. "Foolish, foolish pride!" he cried beating upon his chest with his large brown hand. "Foolish, foolish pride! How long then will it be ere I can scourge it forth? Am I then never to conquer it? Oh, strong, strong are the ties of flesh, and hard it is to subdue the spirit! I come, friends, of a noble house, and I cannot bring myself to touch this money, even though it be to save me from the grave."

"Alas! father," said Alleyne, "how then can we be of help to thee?"

"I had sat down here to die," quoth the palmer, "but for many years I have carried in my wallet these precious things which you see set forth now before me. It were sin, thought I, that my secret should perish with me. I shall therefore sell these things to the first worthy passers-by, and from them I shall have enough money to take me to the shrine of Our Lady at Rocamadour, where I hope to lay these old bones."

"What are the treasures, then, father?" asked Hordle John. "I can but see an old rusty nail, with bits of stone and slips of wood."

"My friend," answered the palmer, "not all the money that is in this country could pay a just price for these wares of mine. This nail," he continued, pulling off his hat and turning up his sightless orbs, "is one of those wherewith man's salvation was secured. I had it, together with this piece of the true rood, from the five-and-twentieth descendant of Joseph of Arimathea, who still lives in Jerusalem alive and well, though latterly much afflicted by boils. Aye, you may well cross yourselves, and I beg that you will not breathe upon it or touch it with your fingers."

"And the wood and stone, holy father?" asked Alleyne, with bated breath, as he stared awe-struck at his precious relics.

"This cantle of wood is from the true cross, this

other from Noah his ark, and the third is from the door-post of the temple of the wise King Solomon. This stone was thrown at the sainted Stephen, and the other two are from the Tower of Babel. Here, too, is part of Aaron's rod and a lock of hair from Elisha the prophet."

" But father," quoth Alleyne, " the holy Elisha was bald, which brought down upon him the revilements of the wicked children."

" It is very true that he had not much hair," said the palmer quickly, " and it is this which makes this relic so exceedingly precious. Take now your choice of these, my worthy gentlemen, and pay such a price as your consciences will suffer you to offer ; for I am not a chapman nor a huckster, and I would never part with them, did I not know that I am very near to my reward."

" Aylward," said Alleyne excitedly, " this is such a chance as few folk have twice in one life. The nail I must have, and I will give it to the Abbey of Beaulieu, so that all the folk in England may go thither to wonder and to pray."

" And I will have the stone from the temple," cried Hordle John. " What would not my old mother give to have it hung over her bed ? "

" And I will have Aaron's rod," quoth Aylward. " I have but five florins in the world, and here are four of them."

" Here are three more," said John.

" And here five more," added Alleyne. " Holy father, I hand you twelve florins, which is all that we can give, though we well know how poor a pay it is for the wondrous things which you sell us."

" Down, pride, down ! " cried the pilgrim, still beating upon his chest. " Can I not bend myself then to take this sorry sum which is offered me for that which has cost me the labours of a life ? Give me the dross ! Here are the precious relics, and, oh, I pray you that you will handle them softly and with reverence, else had I rather left my unworthy bones here by the wayside."

With doffed caps and eager hands, the comrades took their new and precious possessions, and pressed onwards upon their journey, leaving the aged palmer still seated under the cherry-tree. They rode in silence, each with his treasure in his hand, glancing at it from time to time, and scarcely able to believe that chance had made them sole owners of relics of such holiness and worth that every abbey and church in Christendom would have bid eagerly for their possession. So they journeyed, full of this good fortune, until opposite the town of Le Mas, where John's horse cast a shoe, and they were glad to find a wayside smith who might set the matter to rights. To him Aylward narrated the good hap which had befallen them ; but the smith, when his eyes lit upon the relics, leaned up against his anvil and laughed, with his hand to his side, until the tears hopped down his sooty cheeks.

" Why, masters," quoth he, " this man is a coquillart, or seller of false relics, and was here in this smithy not two hours ago. This nail that he hath sold you was taken from my nail box, and as to the wood and the stonet, you will see a heap of both outside from which he hath filled his scrip."

" Nay, nay," cried Alleyne, " this was a holy man who had journeyed to Jerusalem, and acquired a dropsy by running from the house of Pilate to the Mount of Olives."

" I know not about that," said the smith, " but I know that a man with a grey palmer's hat and gown was here no very long time ago, and that he sat on yonder stump and ate a cold pullet and drank a flask of wine. Then he begged from me one of my nails, and filling his scrip with stones, he went upon his way. Look at these nails, and see if they are not the same as that which he has sold you."

" Now may God save us ! " cried Alleyne, all aghast. " Is there then no end to the wickedness of human kind ? He so humble, so aged, so loth to take our money—and yet a villain and a cheat ! Whom can we trust or believe in ? "

" I will after him," said Aylward, flinging himself into
the saddle. " Come, Alleyne, we may catch him ere
John's horse be shod."

Away they galloped together, and ere long they saw the
old grey palmer walking slowly along in front of them.
He turned, however, at the sound of their hoofs, and it
was clear that his blindness was a cheat like all the rest of
him, for he ran swiftly through a field and so into a wood,
where none could follow him. They hurled their relics
after him, and so rode back to the blacksmith's the poorer
both in pocket and in faith.

27. *How Roger Club-foot was passed into Paradise*

IT was evening before the three comrades came into
Aiguillon. There they found Sir Nigel Loring and
Ford safely lodged at the sign of the " Bâton Rouge,"
where they supped on good fare and slept between laven-
der-scented sheets. It chanced, however, that a knight of
Poitou, Sir Gaston d'Estelle, was staying there on his way
back from Lithuania, where he had served a term with the
Teutonic knights under the land-master of the presbytery
of Marienberg. He and Sir Nigel sat late in high converse as to bushments, outfalls, and the intaking of cities,
with many tales of warlike men and valiant deeds. Then
their talk turned to minstrelsy, and the stranger knight
drew forth a cittern, upon which he played the minne-
lieder of the north, singing the while in a high cracked
voice of Hildebrand and Brunhild and Siegfried, and all
the strength and beauty of the land of Almain. To this
Sir Nigel answered with the romances of Sir Eglamour and
of Sir Isumbras, and so through the long winter night they
sat by the crackling wood-fire answering each other's songs
until the crowing cocks joined in their concert. Yet, with
scarce an hour of rest, Sir Nigel was as blithe and bright
as ever as they set forth after breakfast upon their way.

" This Sir Gaston is a very worthy man," said he to his squires as they rode from the " Bâton Rouge." " He hath a very strong desire to advance himself, and would have entered upon some small knightly debate with me, had he not chanced to have his arm-bone broken by the kick of a horse. I have conceived a great love for him, and I have promised him that when his bone is mended I will exchange thrusts with him. But we must keep to this road upon the left."

" Nay, my fair lord," quoth Aylward. " The road to Montabon is over the river, and so through Quercy and the Agenois."

" True, my good Aylward ; but I have learned from this worthy knight, who hath come over the French marches, that there is a company of Englishmen who are burning and plundering in the country round Ville-franche. I have little doubt, from what he says, that they are those whom we seek."

" By my hilt ! it is like enough," said Aylward. " By all accounts they had been so long at Montaubon, that there would be little there worth the taking. Then, as they have already been in the south, they would come north to the country of the Aveyron."

" We shall follow the Lot until we come to Cahors, and then cross the marches into Villefranche," said Sir Nigel. " By Saint Paul ! as we are but a small band, it is very likely that we may have some very honourable and pleasing adventure, for I hear that there is little peace upon the French border."

All morning they rode down a broad and winding road barred with the shadows of poplars. Sir Nigel rode in front with his squires, while the two archers followed behind with the sumpter mule between them. They had left Aiguillon and the Garonne far to the south, and rode now by the tranquil Lot, which curves blue and placid through a gently rolling country. Alleyne could not but mark that, whereas in Guienne there had been many townlets and few castles, there were now many castles and few houses. On either hand grey walls and square grim keeps peeped out at every few miles from amid the forests, while the few villages which they passed were all ringed round with rude walls, which spoke of the constant fear and sudden foray of a wild frontier land. Twice during the morning there came bands of horsemen swooping down upon them from the black gateways of wayside strongholds, with short stern questions as to whence they came and what their errand. Bands of armed men clanked along the highway and the few lines of laden mules which carried the merchandise of the trader were guarded by armed varlets, or by archers hired for the service.

" The peace of Bretigny hath not made much change in these parts," quoth Sir Nigel, " for the country is overrun with free companies and masterless men. Yonder towers, between the wood and the hill, mark the town of Cahors and beyond it is the land of France. But here is a man by the wayside, and as he hath two horses and a squire I make little doubt that he is a knight. I pray you, Alleyne, to give him greeting from me, and to ask him for his titles and coat-armour. It may be that I can relieve him of some vow, or perchance he hath a lady whom he would wish to advance."

" Nay, my fair lord," said Alleyne, " these are not horses and a squire, but mules and a varlet. The man is a mercer, for he hath a great bundle beside him."

" Now, God's blessing on your honest English voice ! " cried the stranger, pricking up his ears at the sound of Alleyne's words. " Never have I heard music that was so sweet to mine ear. Come, Watkin lad, throw the bales over Laura's back ! My heart was nigh broke, for it seemed that I had left all that was English behind me, and that I would never set eyes upon Norwich market square again." He was a tall, lusty, middle-aged man with a ruddy face, a brown forked beard shot with grey, and a broad Flanders hat set at the back of his head. His servant, as tall as himself, but gaunt and raw-boned, had swung the bales on the back of one mule, while the merchant mounted upon the other and rode to join the party. It was easy to see, as he approached, from the quality of his dress and the richness of his trappings, that he was a man of some wealth and position.

" Sir knight," said he, " my name is David Micheldene, and I am a burgher and alderman of the good town of Norwich, where I live five doors from the church of Our Lady, as all men know on the banks of Yare. I have here my bales of cloth which I carry to Cahors—woe worth the day that ever I started on such an errand ! I crave your gracious protection upon the way for me, my servant, and my mercery ; for I have already had many perilous passages, and have learned now that Roger Club-foot, the robber-knight of Quercy, is out upon the road in front of me. I hereby agree to give you one rose-noble if you bring me safe to the inn of the ' Angel ' in Cahors, the same to be repaid to me or my heirs if any harm come to me or my goods."

" By Saint Paul ! " answered Sir Nigel, " I should be a sorry knight if I asked pay for standing by a countryman in a strange land. You may ride with me and welcome, Master Micheldene, and your varlet may follow with my archers."

" God's benison upon thy bounty ! " cried the stranger. " Should you come to Norwich you may have cause to remember that you have been of service to Alderman Micheldene. It is not very far to Cahors, for surely I see the cathedral towers against the sky-line ; but I have heard much of this Roger Club-foot, and the more I hear the less do I wish to look upon his face. Oh, but I am sick and weary of it all, and I would give half that I am worth to see my good dame sitting in peace beside me, and to hear the bells of Norwich town."

" Your words are strange to me," quoth Sir Nigel, " for you have the appearance of a stout man, and I see that you wear a sword by your side."

" Yet it is not my trade," answered the merchant. " I

doubt not that if I set you down in my shop at Norwich you might scarce tell fustian from falding, and know little difference between the velvet of Genoa and the three-piled cloth of Bruges. There you might well turn to me for help. But here on a lone roadside, with thick woods and robber-knights, I turn to you, for it is the business to which you have been reared."

" There is sooth in what you say, Master Micheldene," said Sir Nigel, " and I trust that we may come upon this Roger Club-foot, for I have heard that he is a very stout and skilful soldier, and a man from whom much honour is to be gained."

" He is a bloody robber," said the trader, curtly, " and I wish I saw him kicking at the end of a halter."

" It is such men as he," Sir Nigel remarked, " who give the true knight honourable deeds to do, whereby he may advance himself."

" It is such men as he," retorted Micheldene, " who are like rats in a wheat-rick or moth in a woolfels, a harm and a hindrance to all peaceful and honest men."

" Yet if the dangers of the road weigh so heavily upon you, master alderman, it is a great marvel to me that you should venture so far from home."

" And, sometimes, sir knight, it is a marvel to myself. But I am a man who may grutch and grumble, but when I have set my face to do a thing I will not turn my back upon it until it be done. There is one François Villet, at Cahors, who will send me wine-casks for my cloth-bales, so to Cahors I will go, though all the robber-knights of Christendom were to line the roads like yonder poplars."

" Stoutly spoken, master alderman ! But how have you fared hitherto ? "

" As a lamb fares in a land of wolves. Five times we have had to beg and pray ere we could pass. Twice I have paid toll to the wardens of the road. Three times we have had to draw, and once at La Réolle we stood over our wool-bales, Watkin and I, and we laid about us for as long as a man might chant a litany, slaying one rogue and wounding two others. By God's coif ! we are men of peace, but we are free English burghers, not to be mishandled either in our country or abroad. Neither lord, baron, knight, nor commoner shall have as much as a strike of flax of mine whilst I have strength to wag this sword."

" And a passing strange sword it is," quoth Sir Nigel. " What make you, Alleyne, of these black lines which are drawn across the sheath ? "

" I cannot tell what they are, my fair lord."

" Nor can I," said Ford.

The merchant chuckled to himself. " It was a thought of mine own," said he ; " for the sword was made by Thomas Wilson, the armourer, who is betrothed to my second daughter Margery. Know then that the sheath is one cloth-yard in length, marked off according to feet and inches to serve me as a measuring wand. It is also of the exact weight of two pounds, so that I may use it in the balance."

" By Saint Paul ! " quoth Sir Nigel, " it is very clear to me that the sword is like thyself, good alderman, apt either for war or for peace. But I doubt not that even in England you have had much to suffer from the hands of robbers and outlaws."

" It was only last Lammastide, sir knight, that I was left for dead near Reading as I journeyed to Winchester fair. Yet I had the rogues up at the court of pie-powder, and they will harm no more peaceful traders."

" You travel much, then ? "

" To Winchester, Linn mart, Bristol fair, Stourbridge, and Bartholomew's in London Town. The rest of the year you may ever find me five doors from the church of Our Lady, where I would from my heart that I was at this moment, for there is no air like Norwich air, and no water like the Yare, nor can all the wines of France compare with the beer of old Sam Yelverton who keeps the ' Dun Cow.' But, out and alack, here is an evil fruit which hangs upon this chestnut-tree."

As he spoke they had ridden round a curve of the road

and come upon a great tree which shot one strong brown branch across their path. From the centre of this branch there hung a man, with his head at a horrid slant to his body and his toes just touching the ground. He was naked save for a linen under-shirt and pair of woollen drawers. Beside him on a green bank there sat a small man with a solemn face, and a great bundle of papers of all colours thrusting forth from the scrip which lay beside him. He was very richly dressed, with furred robes, a scarlet hood, and wide hanging sleeves lined with flame-coloured silk. A great gold chain hung round his neck, and rings glittered from every finger of his hands. On his lap he had a little pile of gold and of silver, which he was dropping, coin by coin, into a plump pouch which hung from his girdle.

" May the saints be with you, good travellers ! " he shouted, as the party rode up. " May the four Evange-lists watch over you ! May the twelve Apostles bear you up ! May the blessed army of martyrs direct your feet and lead you to eternal bliss ! "

" Gramercy for these good wishes ! " said Sir Nigel. " But I perceive, master alderman, that this man who hangs here is, by mark of foot, the very robber-knight of whom we have spoken. But there is a cartel pinned upon his breast, and I pray you, Alleyne, to read it to me."

The dead robber swung slowly to and fro in the wintry wind, a fixed smile upon his swarthy face, and his bulging eyes still glaring down the highway of which he had so long been the terror ; on a sheet of parchment upon his breast was printed in rude characters :

ROGER PIED-BOT.

Par l'ordre du Sénéchal de
Castelnau, et de l'Échevin de
Cahors, servantes fidèles du
très vaillant et très puissant
Édouard, Prince de Galles et
d'Aquitaine.
Ne touchez pas,
Ne coupez pas,
Ne dépêchez pas.

" He took a sorry time in dying," said the man who sat
beside him. " He could stretch one toe to the ground and
bear himself up, so that I thought he would never have
done. Now at last, however, he is safely in paradise, and
so I may jog on upon my earthly way." He mounted, as
he spoke, a white mule which had been grazing by the
wayside, all gay with fustian of gold and silver bells, and
rode onward with Sir Nigel's party.

" How know you then that he is in paradise ? " asked
Sir Nigel. " All things are possible to God, but, certes,
without a miracle, I should scarce expect to find the soul
of Roger Club-foot amongst the just."

" I know that he is there because I have just passed him
in there," answered the stranger, rubbing his bejewelled
hands together in placid satisfaction. " It is my holy
mission to be a sompnour or pardoner. I am the unworthy servant and delegate of him who holds the keys.
A contrite heart and ten nobles to holy Mother Church
may stave off perdition ; but he hath a pardon of the first
degree, with a twenty-five livre benison, so that I doubt
if he will so much as feel a twinge of purgatory. I came
up even as the seneschal's archers were tying him up, and
I gave him my foreword that I would bide with him until
he had passed. There were two leaden crowns among the
silver, but I would not for that stand in the way of his
salvation."

" By Saint Paul ! " said Sir Nigel, " if you have indeed
this power to open and to shut the gates of hope, then
indeed you stand high above mankind. But if you do but
claim to have it, and yet have it not, then it seems to me,
master clerk, that you may yourself find the gate barred
when you shall ask admittance."

" Small of faith ! Small of faith ! " cried the sompnour. " Ah, Sir Didymus yet walks upon earth ! And
yet no words of doubt can bring anger to mine heart, or
a bitter word to my lip, for am I not a poor unworthy
worker in the cause of gentleness and peace ? Of all
these pardons which I bear every one is stamped and

signed by our holy father, the prop and centre of Christendom."

" Which of them ? " asked Sir Nigel.

" Ha, ha ! " cried the pardoner, shaking a jewelled
forefinger. " Thou wouldst be deep in the secrets of
Mother Church ? Know then that I have both in my
scrip. Those who hold with Urban shall have Urban's
pardon, while I have Clement's for the Clementist—or
he who is in doubt may have both, so that come what may
he shall be secure. I pray you that you will buy one, for
war is bloody work, and the end is sudden, with little
time for thought or shrift. Or you, sir, for you seem to
me a man who would do ill to trust to your own merits."
This to the alderman of Norwich, who had listened to
him with a frowning brow and a sneering lip.

" When I sell my cloth," quoth he, " he who buys may
weigh and feel and handle. These goods which you sell
are not to be seen, nor is there any proof that you hold
them. Certes, if mortal man might control God's mercy,
it would be one of a lofty and God-like life, and not one
who is decked out with rings and chains and silks, like a
pleasure-wench at a kermesse."

" Thou wicked and shameless man ! " cried the clerk.
" Dost thou dare to raise thy voice against the unworthy
servant of Mother Church ? "

" Unworthy enough ! " quoth David Micheldene. " I
would have you to know, clerk, that I am a free English
burgher, and that I dare say my mind to our father the
Pope himself, let alone such a lacquey's lacquey as you ! "

" Base-born and foul-mouthed knave ! " cried the
sompnour. " You prate of holy things to which your
hog's mind can never rise. Keep silence, lest I call a
curse upon you ! "

" Silence yourself ! " roared the other. " Foul bird !
we found thee by the gallows like a carrion-crow. A fine
life thou hast of it with thy silks and thy baubles, cozening
the last few shillings from the pouches of dying men. A
fig for thy curse ! Bide here, if you will take my rede, for

we will make England too hot for such as you when
Master Wicliff has the ordering of it. Thou vile thief!
it is you, and such as you, who bring an evil name upon
the many churchmen who lead a pure and a holy life.
Thou outside the door of heaven! Art more like to be
inside the door of hell."

At this crowning insult the sompnour, with a face
ashen with rage, raised up a quivering hand and began
pouring Latin imprecations upon the angry alderman.
The latter, however, was not a man to be quelled by words,
for he caught up his ell-measure sword-sheath and belaboured the cursing clerk with it. The latter, unable to
escape from the shower of blows, set spurs to his mule and
rode for his life, with his enemy thundering behind him.
At sight of his master's sudden departure, the varlet
Watkin set off after him, with the pack-mule beside him,
so that the four clattered away down the road together,
until they swept round a curve, and their babble was but
a drone in the distance. Sir Nigel and Alleyne gazed
in astonishment at one another, while Ford burst out
a-laughing.

" Pardieu ! " said the knight, " this David Micheldene
must be one of those Lollards about whom Father
Christopher of the priory had so much to say. Yet he
seemed to be no bad man from what I have seen of him."

" I have heard that Wicliff hath many followers in
Norwich," answered Alleyne.

" By Saint Paul ! I have no great love for them,"
quoth Sir Nigel. " I am a man who am slow to change ;
and, if you take away from me the faith that I have been
taught, it would be long ere I could learn one to set in its
place. It is but a chip here and a chip there, yet it may
bring the tree down in time. Yet, on the other hand, I
cannot but think it shame that a man should turn God's
mercy on and off, as a cellarman doth wine with a spigot."

" Nor is it," said Alleyne, " part of the teachings of that
Mother Church of which he had so much to say. There
was sooth in what the alderman said of it."

" Then, by Saint Paul ! they may settle it betwixt them," quoth Sir Nigel. " For me, I serve God, the king and my lady ; and so long as I can keep the path of honour I am well content. My creed shall ever be that of Chandos :

> ' Fais ce que dois—adviegne que peut.
> C'est commandé au chevalier.' "

28. *How the Comrades came over the Marches of France*

AFTER passing Cahors, the party branched away from the main road, and leaving the river to the north of them, followed a smaller track which wound over a vast and desolate plain. This path led them amid marshes and woods, until it brought them out into a glade with a broad stream swirling swiftly down the centre of it. Through this the horses splashed their way, and on the farther shore Sir Nigel announced to them that they were now within the borders of the land of France. For some miles they still followed the same lonely track, which led them through a dense wood, and then widening out, curved down to an open rolling country, such as they had traversed between Aiguillon and Cahors.

If it were grim and desolate upon the English border, however, what can describe the hideous barrenness of this ten times harried tract of France ? The whole face of the country was scarred and disfigured, mottled over with the black blotches of burned farm-steadings, and the grey gaunt gable-ends of what had been châteaux. Broken fences, crumbling walls, vineyards littered with stones, the shattered arches of bridges—look where you might, the signs of ruin and rapine met the eye. Here and there only, on the farthest sky-line, the gnarled turrets of a castle, or the graceful pinnacles of church or of monastery, showed where the forces of the sword or of the spirit had preserved some small islet of security in this universal flood of misery. Moodily and in silence the little party rode along the narrow and irregular track, their hearts weighed down by this far-stretching land of despair. It was indeed a stricken and a blighted country, and a man might have ridden from Auvergne in the north to the marches of Foix, nor ever seen a smiling village or a thriving homestead.

From time to time as they advanced they saw strange lean figures scraping and scratching amid the weeds and thistles, who, on sight of the band of horsemen, threw up their arms and dived in among the brushwood, as shy and as swift as wild animals. More than once, however, they came on families crouching by the wayside, who were too weak from hunger and disease to fly, so that they could but sit like hares on a tussock, with panting chests and terror in their eyes. So gaunt were these poor folk, so worn and spent—with bent and knotted frames, and sullen, hopeless, mutinous faces—that it made the young Englishmen heart-sick to look upon them. Indeed, it seemed as though all hope and light had gone so far from them that it was not to be brought back ; for when Sir Nigel threw down a handful of silver among them there came no softening of their lined faces, but they clutched greedily at the coins, peering questioningly at him, and champing with their animal jaws. Here and there amid the brushwood the travellers saw the rude bundle of sticks which served them as a home—more like a fowl's nest than the dwelling-place of man. Yet why should they build and strive, when the first adventurer who passed would set torch to their thatch, and when their own feudal lord would wring from them with blows and curses the last fruits of their toil ? They sat at the lowest depth of human misery, and hugged a bitter comfort to their souls as they realised that they could go no lower. Yet they still had the human gift of speech, and would take counsel among themselves in their brushwood hovels, glaring with bleared eyes and pointing with thin fingers at the great widespread châteaux which ate like a cancer into the life of the country-side. When such men who are beyond hope and fear begin in their dim minds to see the source of their woes, it may be an evil time for those who have wronged them. The weak man becomes strong when he has nothing, for then only can he feel the wild, mad thrill of despair. High and strong the châteaux, lowly and weak the brushwood hut ; but God help the seigneur and his lady when the men of the brushwood set their hands to the work of revenge !

Through such country did the party ride for eight or it might be nine miles, until the sun began to slope down in the west and their shadows to stream down the road in front of them. Wary and careful they must be, with watchful eyes to the right and the left, for this was no man's land, and their only passports were those which hung from their belts. Frenchmen and Englishmen, Gascon and Provençal, Brabanter, Tardvenu, Scorcher, Flayer, and Free Companion, wandered and struggled over the whole of this accursed district. So bare and cheerless was the outlook, and so few and poor the dwellings, that Sir Nigel began to have fears as to whether he might find food and quarters for his little troop. It was a relief to him, therefore, when their narrow track opened out upon a larger road, and they saw some little way down it a square white house with a great bunch of holly hung out at the end of a stick from one of the upper windows.

" By Saint Paul ! " said he, " I am right glad ; for I had feared that we might have neither provant nor herbergage. Ride on, Alleyne, and tell this innkeeper that an English knight with his party will lodge with him this night."

Alleyne set spurs to his horse and reached the inn door a long bow-shot before his companions. Neither varlet nor ostler could be seen, so he pushed open the door and called loudly for the landlord. Three times he shouted, but, receiving no reply, he opened an inner door and advanced into the chief guest-room of the hostel.

A very cheerful wood-fire was sputtering and cracking

in an open grate at the farther end of the apartment. At one side of this fire, in a high-backed oak chair, sat a lady, her face turned towards the door. The firelight played over her features, and Alleyne thought that he had never seen such queenly power, such dignity and strength, upon a woman's face. She might have been five-and-thirty years of age, with aquiline nose, firm and yet sensitive mouth, dark curving brows, and deep-set eyes which shone and sparkled with a shifting brilliancy. Beautiful as she was, it was not her beauty which impressed itself upon the beholder ; it was her strength, her power, the sense of wisdom which hung over the broad white brow, the decision which lay in the square jaw and delicately moulded chin. A chaplet of pearls sparkled amid her black hair, with a gauze of silver network flowing back from it over her shoulders ; a black mantle was swathed round her, and she leaned back in her chair as one who is fresh from a journey.

In the opposite corner there sat a very burly and broad-shouldered man, clad in a black jerkin trimmed with sable, with a black velvet cap with curling white feather cocked upon the side of his head. A flask of red wine stood at his elbow, and he seemed to be very much at his ease, for his feet were stuck up on a stool, and between his thighs he held a dish full of nuts. These he cracked between his strong white teeth and chewed in a leisurely way, casting the shells into the blaze. As Alleyne gazed in at him he turned his face half round and cocked an eye at him over his shoulder. It seemed to the young Englishman that he had never seen so hideous a face, for the eyes were of the lightest green, the nose was broken and driven inwards, while the whole countenance was seared and puckered with wounds. The voice, too, when he spoke, was as deep and as fierce as the growl of a beast of prey.

" Young man," said he, " I know not who you may be, and I am not much inclined to bestir myself, but if it were not that I am bent upon taking my ease, I swear, by the sword of Joshua ! that I would lay my dog-whip across your shoulders for daring to fill the air with these discordant bellowings."

Taken aback at this ungentle speech, and scarce knowing how to answer it fitly in the presence of the lady, Alleyne stood with his hand upon the handle of the door while Sir Nigel and his companions dismounted. At the sound of these fresh voices, and of the tongue in which they spoke, the stranger crashed his dish of nuts down upon the floor, and began himself to call for the landlord until the whole house re-echoed with his roarings. With an ashen face the white-aproned host came running at his call, his hands shaking and his very hair bristling with apprehension, " For the sake of God, sirs," he whispered as he passed, " speak him fair and do not rouse him ! For the love of the Virgin, be mild with him ! "

" Who is this, then ? " asked Sir Nigel.

Alleyne was about to explain, when a fresh roar from the stranger interrupted him.

" Thou villain innkeeper," he shouted, " did I not ask you when I brought my lady here whether your inn was clean ? "

" You did, sire."

" Did I not very particularly ask you whether there were any vermin in it ? "

" You did, sire."

" And you answered me ? "

" That there were not, sire."

" And yet ere I have been here an hour I find Englishmen crawling about within it. Where are we to be free from this pestilent race ? Can a Frenchman upon French land not sit down in a French auberge without having his ears pained by the clack of their hideous talk ? Send them packing, innkeeper, or it may be the worse for them and for you."

" I will, sire, I will ! " cried the frightened host, and bustled from the room, while the soft, soothing voice of the woman was heard remonstrating with her furious companion.

" Indeed, gentlemen, you had best go," said mine host. " It is but six miles to Villefranche, where there are very good quarters at the sign of the ' Lion Rouge.' "

" Nay," answered Sir Nigel, " I cannot go until I have seen more of this person, for he appears to be a man from whom much is to be hoped. What is his name and title ? "

" It is not for my lips to name it unless by his desire. But I beg and pray you, gentlemen, that you will go from my house, for I know not what may come of it if his rage should gain the mastery of him."

" By Saint Paul ! " lisped Sir Nigel, " this is certainly a man whom it is worth journeying far to know. Go tell him that a humble knight of England would make his further honourable acquaintance, not from any presumption, pride, or ill-will, but for the advancement of chivalry and the glory of our ladies. Give him greeting from Sir Nigel Loring, and say that the glove which I bear in my cap belongs to the most peerless and lovely of her sex, whom I am now ready to uphold against any lady whose claim he might be desirous of advancing."

The landlord was hesitating whether to carry this message or no, when the door of the inner room was flung open, and the stranger bounded out like a panther from his den, his hair bristling and his deformed face convulsed with anger.

" Still here ! " he snarled. " Dogs of England, must ye be lashed hence ? Tiphaine, my sword ! " He turned to seize his weapon, but as he did so his gaze fell upon the blazonry of Sir Nigel's shield, and he stood staring while the fire in his strange green eyes softened into a sly and humorous twinkle.

" Mort Dieu ! " cried he, " it is my little swordsman of Bordeaux. I should remember that coat-armour, seeing that it is but three days since I looked upon it in the lists by Garonne. Ah ! Sir Nigel, Sir Nigel ! you owe me a return for this," and he touched his right arm, which was girt round just under the shoulder with a silken kerchief.

But the surprise of the stranger at the sight of Sir Nigel

was as nothing compared with the astonishment and the delight which shone upon the face of the knight of Hampshire as he looked upon the strange face of the Frenchman. Twice he opened his mouth and twice he peered again, as though to assure himself that his eyes had not played him a trick.

" Bertrand ! " he gasped at last. " Bertrand du Guesclin ! "

" By Saint Ives ! " shouted the French soldier, with a hoarse roar of laughter, " it is well that I should ride with my visor down, for he that has once seen my face does not need to be told my name. It is indeed I, Sir Nigel, and here is my hand ! I give you my word that there are but three Englishmen in this world whom I would touch save with the sharp edge of the sword : the prince is one, Chandos the second, and you the third ; for I have heard much that is good of you."

" I am growing aged and am somewhat spent in the wars," quoth Sir Nigel ; " but I can lay by my sword now with an easy mind, for I can say that I have crossed swords with him who hath the bravest heart and the strongest arm of all this great kingdom of France. I have longed for it, I have dreamed of it, and now I can scarce bring my mind to understand that this great honour hath indeed been mine."

" By the Virgin of Tennes ! you have given me cause to be very certain of it," said Du Guesclin, with a gleam of his broad white teeth.

" And perhaps, most honoured sir, it would please you to continue the debate. Perhaps you would condescend to go farther into the matter. God He knows that I am unworthy of such honour, yet I can show my four-and-sixty quarterings, and I have been present at some bickerings and scufflings during these twenty years."

" Your fame is very well known to me, and I shall ask my lady to enter your name upon my tablets," said Sir Bertrand. " There are many who wish to advance themselves, and who bide their turn, for I refuse no man who comes on such an errand. At present it may not be, for mine arm is stiff from this small touch, and I would fain do you full honour when we cross swords again. Come in with me, and let your squires come also, that my sweet spouse, the Lady Tiphaine, may say that she hath seen so famed and gentle a knight."

Into the chamber they went in all peace and concord, where the Lady Tiphaine sat like queen on throne for each in turn to be presented to her. Sooth to say, the stout heart of Sir Nigel, which cared little for the wrath of her lion-like spouse, was somewhat shaken by the calm, cold face of this stately dame, for twenty years of camp-life had left him more at ease in the lists than in a lady's boudoir. He bethought him, too, as he looked at her set lips and deep-set questioning eyes, that he had heard strange tales of this same Lady Tiphaine du Guesclin. Was it not she who was said to lay hands upon the sick and raise them from their couches when the leeches had spent their last nostrums ? Had she not forecast the future, and were there not times when in the loneliness of her chamber she was heard to hold converse with some being upon whom mortal eye never rested—some dark familiar who passed where doors were barred and windows high ? Sir Nigel sunk his eye and marked a cross on the side of his leg as he greeted this dangerous dame, and yet ere five minutes had passed he was hers, and not he only but his two young squires as well. The mind had gone out of them, and they could but look at this woman and listen to the words which fell from her lips—words which thrilled through their nerves and stirred their souls like the battle-call of a bugle.

Often in peaceful after-days was Alleyne to think of that scene of the wayside inn of Auvergne. The shadows of evening had fallen, and the corners of the long, low, wood-panelled room were draped in darkness. The spluttering wood-fire threw out a circle of red flickering light which played over the little group of wayfarers, and showed up every line and shadow upon their faces. Sir Nigel sat with elbows upon knees, and chin upon hands, his patch still covering one eye, but his other shining like a star, while the ruddy light gleamed upon his smooth white head. Ford was seated at his left, his lips parted, his eyes staring, and a fleck of deep colour on either cheek, his limbs all rigid as one who fears to move. On the other side the famous French captain leaned back in his chair, a litter of nut-shells upon his lap, his huge head half buried in a cushion, while his eyes wandered with an amused gleam from his dame to the staring, enraptured Englishmen. Then, last of all, that pale clear-cut face, that sweet clear voice, with its high thrilling talk of the deathlessness of glory, of the worthlessness of life, of the pain of ignoble joys, and of the joy which lies in all pains which lead to a noble end. Still, as the shadows deepened, she spoke of valour and virtue, of loyalty, honour and fame, and still they sat drinking in her words while the fire burned down and the red ash turned to grey.

" By the sainted Ives ! " cried Du Guesclin at last, " it is time that we spoke of what we are to do this night, for I cannot think that in this wayside auberge there are fit quarters for an honourable company."

Sir Nigel gave a long sigh as he came back from the dreams of chivalry and hardihood into which this strange woman's words had wafted him. " I care not where I sleep," said he ; " but these are indeed somewhat rude lodgings for this fair lady."

" What contents my lord contents me," quoth she. " I perceive, Sir Nigel, that you are under vow," she added, glancing at his covered eye.

" It is my purpose to attempt some small deed," he answered.

" And the glove—is it your lady's ? "

" It is indeed my sweet wife's."

" Who is doubtless proud of you."

" Say rather I of her," quoth he quickly. " God He knows that I am not worthy to be her humble servant. It is easy, lady, for a man to ride forth in the light of day, and do his devoir when all men have eyes for him. But in a woman's heart there is a strength and truth which asks no praise, and can but be known to him whose treasure it is."

The Lady Tiphaine smiled across at her husband. " You have often told me, Bertrand, that there were very gentle knights among the English," quoth she.

" Aye, aye," said he moodily. " But to horse, Sir Nigel, you and yours, and we shall seek the château of Sir Tristram de Rochefort, which is two miles on this side of Villefranche. He is Seneschal of Auvergne, and mine old war-companion."

" Certes, he would have a welcome for you," quoth Sir Nigel ; " but indeed he might look askance at one who comes without permit over the marches."

" By the Virgin ! when he learns that you have come to draw away these rascals he will be very blithe to look upon your face. Innkeeper, here are ten gold pieces. What is over and above your reckoning you may take off from your charges to the next needy knight who comes this way. Come then, for it grows late, and the horses are stamping in the roadway."

The Lady Tiphaine and her spouse sprang upon their steeds without setting feet to stirrup, and away they jingled down the white moonlit highway, with Sir Nigel at the lady's bridle-arm, and Ford a spear's length behind them. Alleyne had lingered for an instant in the passage, and as he did so there came a wild outcry from a chamber upon the left, and out there ran Aylward and John, laughing together like two schoolboys who are bent upon a prank. At sight of Alleyne they slunk past him with something of a shamefaced air, and springing upon their horses galloped after their party. The hubbub within the chamber did not cease, however, but rather increased with yells of : " À moi, mes amis ! À moi, camar-ades ! À moi, l'honorable champion de l'Évêque de Montaubon ! À la recousse de l'église sainte ! " So shrill was the outcry that both the innkeeper and Alleyne, with every varlet within hearing, rushed wildly to the scene of the uproar.

It was indeed a singular scene which met their eyes. The room was a long and lofty one, stone floored and bare, with a fire at the farther end upon which a great pot was boiling. A deal table ran down the centre, with a wooden wine-pitcher upon it and two horn cups. Some way from it was a smaller table with a single beaker and a broken wine-bottle. From the heavy wooden rafters which formed the roof there hung rows of hooks which held up sides of bacon, joints of smoked beef, and strings of onions for winter use. In the very centre of all these upon the largest hook of all, there hung a fat little red-faced man with enormous whiskers, kicking madly in the air and clawing at rafters, hams, and all else that was within hand-grasp. The huge steel hook had been passed through the collar of his leather jerkin, and there he hung like a fish on a line, writhing, twisting, and screaming, but utterly unable to free himself from his extraordinary position. It was not until Alleyne and the landlord had mounted on the table that they were able to lift him down, when he sank gasping with rage into a seat, and rolled his eyes round in every direction.

" Has he gone ? " quoth he.

" Gone ? Who ? "

" He, the man with the red head, the giant man."

" Yes," said Alleyne, " he hath gone."

" And comes not back ? "

" No."

" The better for him ! " cried the little man, with a long sigh of relief. " Mon Dieu ! What ! am I not the champion of the Bishop of Montaubon ? Ah, could I have descended, could I have come down, ere he fled ! Then you would have seen. You would have beheld a spectacle then. There would have been one rascal the less upon earth. Ma foi, yes ! "

" Good master Pelligny," said the landlord, " these gentlemen have not gone very fast, and I have a horse in the stable at your disposal, for I would rather have such bloody doings as you threaten outside the four walls of mine auberge."

" I hurt my leg and cannot ride," quoth the bishop's champion. " I strained a sinew on the day that I slew the three men at Castelnau."

" God save you, master Pelligny ! " cried the landlord. " It must be an awesome thing to have so much blood upon one's soul. And yet I do not wish to see so valiant a man mishandled, and so I will, for friendship's sake, ride after this Englishman and bring him back to you."

" You shall not stir," cried the champion, seizing the innkeeper in a convulsive grasp. " I have a love for you, Gaston, and I would not bring your house into ill-repute, nor do such scath to these walls and chattels as must befall if two such men as this Englishman and I fall to work here."

" Nay, think not of me ! " cried the innkeeper. " What are my walls when set against the honour of François Poursuivant d'Amour Pelligny, champion of the Bishop of Montaubon ? My horse, André ! "

" By the saints, no ! Gaston, I will not have it ! You have said truly that it is an awesome thing to have such rough work upon one's soul. I am but a rude soldier, yet I have a mind. Mon Dieu ! I reflect, I weigh, I balance. Shall I not meet this man again ? Shall I not bear him in mind ? Shall I not know him by his great paws and his red head ? Ma foi, yes ! "

" And may I ask, sir," said Alleyne, " why it is that you call yourself champion of the Bishop of Montaubon ? "

" You may ask aught which it is becoming to me to answer. The bishop hath need of a champion, because, if any cause be set to test of combat, it would scarce become his office to go down into the lists with leathern shield and cudgel to exchange blows with any varlet. He looks round him then for some tried fighting man, some honest smiter who can give a blow or take one. It is not for me to say how far he hath succeeded, but it is sooth that he who thinks that he hath but to do with the Bishop of Montaubon finds himself face to face with François Poursuivant d'Amour Pelligny."

At this moment there was a clatter of hoofs upon the road, and a varlet by the door cried out that one of the Englishmen was coming back. The champion looked wildly about for some corner of safety, and was clambering up towards the window, when Ford's voice sounded from without, calling upon Alleyne to hasten, or he might scarce find his way. Bidding adieu to landlord and to champion, therefore, he set off at a gallop, and soon overtook the two archers.

" A pretty thing this, John," said he. " Thou wilt have holy Church upon you if you hang her champions upon iron hooks in an inn kitchen."

" It was done without thinking," he answered apologetically, while Aylward burst into a shout of laughter.

" By my hilt ! mon petit," said he, " you would have laughed also could you have seen it. For this man was so swollen with pride that he would neither drink with us, nor sit at the same table with us, nor as much as answer a question, but must needs talk to the varlet all the time that it was well there was peace, and that he had slain more Englishmen than there were tags to his doublet. Our good old John could scarce lay his tongue to French enough to answer him, so he must needs reach out his great hand to him and place him very gently where you saw him. But we must on, for I can scarce hear their hoofs upon the road."

" I think that I can see them yet," said Ford, peering down the moonlit road.

" Pardieu ! yes. Now they ride forth from the shadow. And yonder dark clump is the Castle of Villefranche. En avant, camarades ! or Sir Nigel may reach the gates before us. But hark, mes amis, what sound is that ? "

As he spoke the hoarse blast of a horn was heard from some woods upon the right. An answering call rung

315

forth upon their left, and hard upon it two others from behind them.

" They are the horns of swineherds," quoth Aylward. " Though why they blow them so late I cannot tell."

" Let us on, then," said Ford, and the whole party, setting their spurs to their horses, soon found themselves at the Castle of Villefranche, where the drawbridge had already been lowered and the portcullis raised in response to the summons of Du Guesclin.

29. *How the Blessed Hour of Sight came to the Lady Tiphaine*

SIR TRISTRAM DE ROCHEFORT, Seneschal of Auvergne and Lord of Villefranche, was a fierce and renowned soldier who had grown grey in the English wars. As lord of the marches and guardian of an exposed country-side there was little rest for him even in times of so-called peace, and his whole life was spent in raids and outfalls upon the Brabanters, late-comers, flayers, free companions, and roving archers who wandered over his province. At times he would come back in triumph, and a dozen corpses swinging from the summit of his keep would warn evil-doers that there was still a law in the land. At others his ventures were not so happy, and he and his troop would spur it over the drawbridge with clatter of hoofs hard at their heels and whistle of arrows about their ears. Hard he was of hand and harder of heart, hated by his foes, and yet not loved by those whom he protected, for twice he had been taken prisoner, and twice his ransom had been wrung by dint of blows and tortures out of the starving peasants and ruined farmers. Wolves or watch-dogs, it was hard to say from which the sheep had most to fear.

The Castle of Villefranche was harsh and stern as its master. A broad moat, a high outer wall turreted at the corners, with a great black keep towering above all—so it lay before them in the moonlight. By the light of two flambeaux, protruded through the narrow slit-shaped openings at either side of the ponderous gate, they caught a glimpse of the glitter of fierce eyes and of the gleam of the weapons of the guard. The sight of the two-headed eagle of Du Guesclin, however, was a passport into any fortalice in France, and ere they had passed the gate the old border knight came running forward with hands out-thrown to greet his famous countryman. Nor was he less glad to see Sir Nigel, when the Englishman's errand was explained to him, for these archers had been a sore thorn in his side, and had routed two expeditions which he had sent against them. A happy day it should be for the Seneschal of Auvergne when he should learn that the last yew bow was over the marches.

The material for a feast was ever at hand in days when, if there was grim want in the cottage, there was at least rude plenty in the castle. Within an hour the guests were seated around a board which creaked under the great pasties and joints of meat, varied by those more dainty dishes in which the French excelled, the spiced ortolan and the truffled beccaficoes. The Lady Rochefort, a bright and laughter-loving dame, sat upon the left of her warlike spouse, with the Lady Tiphaine upon the right. Beneath sat Du Guesclin and Sir Nigel, with Sir Amory Monticourt, of the order of the Hospitallers, and Sir Otto Harnit, a wandering knight from the kingdom of Bohemia. These, with Alleyne and Ford, four French squires, and the castle chaplain, made the company who sat together that night and made good cheer in the Castle of Ville-franche. The great fire crackled in the grate, the hooded hawks slept upon their perches, the rough deer hounds with expectant eyes crouched upon the tiled floor ; close at the elbows of the guests stood the dapper little lilac-coated pages ; the laugh and jest circled round and all was harmony and comfort. Little they recked of the brushwood men who crouched in their rags along the fringe of the forest and looked up with wild and haggard eyes at the rich warm glow which shot a golden bar of light from the high arched windows of the castle.

Supper over, the tables dormant were cleared away as by magic, and trestles and bancals arranged round the blazing fire, for there was a bitter nip in the air. The Lady Tiphaine had sunk back in her cushioned chair, and her long dark lashes drooped low over her sparkling eyes. Alleyne, glancing at her, noted that her breath came quick and short, and that her cheeks had blanched to a lily white. Du Guesclin eyed her keenly from time to time, and passed his broad brown fingers through his crisp, curly hair black with the air of a man who is perplexed in his mind.

" These folk here," said the knight of Bohemia, " they do not seem too well fed."

" Ah, canaille ! " cried the Lord of Villefranche. " You would scarce credit it, and yet it is sooth that when I was taken at Poictiers it was all that my wife and my foster-brother could do to raise the money from them for my ransom. The sulky dogs would rather have three twists of a rack, or the thumbikins for an hour, than pay out a denier for their own feudal father and liege lord. Yet there is not one of them but hath an old stocking full of gold pieces hid away in a snug corner."

" Why do they not buy food then ? " asked Sir Nigel. " By Saint Paul ! it seemed to me that their bones were breaking through their skin."

" It is their grutching and grumbling which makes them thin. We have a saying here, Sir Nigel, that if you pummel Jacques Bonhomme he will pat you, but if you pat him he will pummel you. Doubtless you find it so in England."

" Ma foi, no ! " said Sir Nigel. " I have two Englishmen of this class in my train, who are at this instant, I make little doubt, as full of your wine as any cask in your cellar. He who pummelled them might come by such a pat as he would be likely to remember."

" I cannot understand it," quoth the seneschal, " for

the English knights and nobles whom I have met were not men to brook the insolence of the baseborn."

"Perchance, my fair lord, the poor folk are sweeter and of a better countenance in England," laughed the Lady Rochefort. "Mon Dieu! you cannot conceive to yourself how ugly they are! Without hair, without teeth, all twisted and bent; for me, I cannot think how the good God ever came to make such people. I cannot bear it, I, and so my trusty Raoul goes ever before me with a cudgel to drive them from my path."

"Yet they have souls, fair lady, they have souls!" murmured the chaplain, a white-haired man, with a weary, patient face.

"So I have heard you tell them," said the lord of the castle; "and for myself, father, though I am a true son of holy Church, yet I think that you were better employed in saying your mass, and in teaching the children of my men-at-arms, than in going over the country-side to put ideas in these folks' heads which would never have been there but for you. I have heard that you have said to them that their souls are as good as ours, and that it is likely that in another life they may stand as high as the oldest blood of Auvergne. For my part, I believe that there are so many worthy knights and gallant gentlemen in heaven, who know how such things should be arranged, that there is little fear that we shall find ourselves mixed up with base roturiers and swineherds. Tell your beads, father, and con your psalter, but do not come between me and those whom the king has given to me."

"God help them!" cried the old priest. "A higher King that yours has given them to me, and I tell you here in your own castle hall, Sir Tristram de Rochefort, that you have sinned deeply in your dealings with these poor folk, and that the hour will come, and may even now be at hand, when God's hand will be heavy upon you for what you have done." He rose as he spoke, and walked slowly from the room.

"Pest take him!" cried the French knight. "Now

what is a man to do with a priest, Sir Bertrand ?—for one can neither fight him like a man nor coax him like a woman."

" Ah, Sir Bertrand knows, the naughty one ! " cried the Lady Rochefort. " Have we not all heard how he went to Avignon and squeezed fifty thousand crowns out of the Pope ! "

" Ma foi ! " said Sir Nigel, looking with a mixture of horror and admiration at Du Guesclin. " Did not your heart sink within you ? Were you not smitten with fears ? Have you not felt a curse hang over you ? "

" I have not observed it," said the Frenchman carelessly. " But, by Saint Ives ! Tristram, this chaplain of yours seems to me to be a worthy man, and you should give heed to his words, for though I care nothing for the curse of a bad Pope, it would be a grief to me to have aught but a blessing from a good priest."

" Hark to that, my fair lord," cried the Lady Rochefort. " Take heed, I pray thee, for I do not wish to have a blight cast over me, nor a palsy of the limbs. I remember that once before you angered Father Stephen, and my tirewoman said that I lost more hair in seven days than ever before in a month."

" If that be sign of sin, then, by Saint Paul ! I have much upon my soul," said Sir Nigel, amid a general laugh. " But in very truth, Sir Tristram, if I may venture a word of counsel, I should advise that you make your peace with this good man."

" He shall have four silver candlesticks," said the seneschal moodily. " And yet I would that he would leave the folk alone. You cannot conceive in your mind how stubborn and brainless they are. Mules and pigs are full of reason beside them. God He knows that I have had great patience with them. It was but last week that, having to raise some money, I called up to the castle Jean Goubert, who, as all men know, has a casketful of gold pieces hidden away in some hollow tree. I give you my word that I did not so much as lay a stripe upon his fool's back, but after speaking with him, and telling him how needful the money was to me, I left him for the night to think over the matter in my dungeon. What think you that the dog did ? Why, in the morning we found that he had made a rope from strips of his leather jerkin, and had hung himself to the bar of the window."

" For me, I cannot conceive such wickedness ! " cried the lady.

" And there was Gertrude Le Bœuf, as fair a maiden as eye could see, but as bad and bitter as the rest of them. When young Amory de Valance was here last Lammas-tide he looked kindly upon the girl, and even spoke of taking her into his service. What does she do, with her dog of a father ? Why, they tie themselves together and leap into the Linden Pool, where the water is five spears'-length deep. I give you my word that it was a great grief to young Amory, and it was days ere he could cast it from his mind. But how can one serve people who are so foolish and so ungrateful ? "

Whilst the Seneschal of Villefranche had been detailing the evil doings of his tenants, Alleyne had been unable to take his eyes from the face of the Lady Tiphaine. She had lain back in her chair, with drooping eye-lids and a blood-less face, so that he had feared at first that her journey had weighed heavily upon her, and that the strength was ebb-ing out of her. Of a sudden, however, there came a change, for a dash of bright colour flickered up on to either cheek, and her lids were slowly raised again upon eyes which sparkled with such a lustre as Alleyne had never seen in human eyes before, while their gaze was fixed intently, not upon the company, but on the dark tapestry which draped the wall. So transformed and so ethereal was her expression, that Alleyne, in his loftiest dream of archangel or of seraph, had never pictured so sweet, so womanly, and yet so wise a face. Glancing at Du Guesclin, Alleyne saw that he also was watching his wife closely, and from the twitching of his features, and the beads upon his brick-coloured brow, it was easy to see that he was deeply agitated by the change which he marked in her.

"How is it with you, lady?" he asked at last, in a tremulous voice.

Her eyes remained fixed intently upon the wall, and there was a long pause ere she answered him. Her voice, too, which had been so clear and ringing, was now low and muffled as that of one who speaks from a distance.

"All is very well with me, Bertrand," said she. "The blessed hour of sight has come round to me again."

"I could see it come! I could see it come!" he exclaimed, passing his fingers through his hair with the same perplexed expression as before.

"This is untoward, Sir Tristram," he said at last. "And I scarce know in what words to make it clear to you, and to your fair wife, and to Sir Nigel Loring, and to these other stranger knights. My tongue is a blunt one, and fitter to shout word of command than to clear up such a matter as this, of which I can myself understand little. This, however, I know, that my wife is come of a very sainted race, whom God hath in His wisdom endowed with wondrous powers, so that Tiphaine Raquenel was known throughout Brittany ere ever I first saw her at Dinan. Yet these powers are ever used for good, and they are the gift of God and not of the devil, which is the difference betwixt white magic and black."

"Perchance it would be as well that we should send for Father Stephen," said Sir Tristram.

"It would be best that he should come," cried the Hospitaller.

"And bring with him a flask of holy water," added the knight of Bohemia.

"Not so, gentlemen," answered Sir Bertrand. "It is not needful that this priest should be called, and it is in my mind that in asking for this ye cast some slight shadow or slur upon the good name of my wife, as though it were still doubtful whether her power came to her from above or below. If ye have indeed such a doubt I pray that you will say so, that we may discuss the matter in a fitting way."

"For myself," said Sir Nigel, "I have heard such words fall from the lips of this lady that I am of opinion that there is no woman, save only one, who can be in any way compared to her in beauty and in goodness. Should any gentleman think otherwise, I should deem it great honour to run a small course with him, or debate the matter in whatever way might be most pleasing to him."

"Nay, it would ill become me to cast a slur upon a lady who is both my guest and the wife of my comrade-in-arms," said the Seneschal of Villefranche. "I have perceived also that on her mantle there is marked a silver cross, which is surely sign enough that there is nought of evil in these strange powers which you say that she possesses."

This argument of the seneschal's appealed so powerfully to the Bohemian and to the Hospitaller that they at once intimated that their objections had been entirely overcome, while even the Lady Rochefort, who had sat shivering and crossing herself, ceased to cast glances at the door, and allowed her fears to turn to curiosity.

"Among the gifts which have been vouchsafed to my wife," said Du Guesclin, "there is the wondrous one of seeing into the future; but it comes very seldom upon her, and goes as quickly, for none can command it. The blessed hour of sight, as she hath named it, has come but thrice since I have known her, and I can vouch for it that all that she hath told me was true, for on the evening of the Battle of Auray she said that the morrow would be an ill day for me and for Charles of Blois. Ere the sun had sunk again he was dead, and I the prisoner of Sir John Chandos. Yet it is not every question that she can answer, but only those——"

"Bertrand, Bertrand!" cried the lady in the same muttering far-away voice, "the blessed hour passes. Use it, Bertrand, while you may."

"I will, my sweet. Tell me, then, what fortune comes upon me?"

" Danger, Bertrand—deadly, pressing danger—which creeps upon you and you know it not."

The French soldier burst into a thunderous laugh, and his green eyes twinkled with amusement. " At what time during these twenty years would not that have been a true word ? " he cried. " Danger is the air that I breathe. But is this so very close, Tiphaine ? "

" Here—now—close upon you ! " The words came out in broken strenuous speech, while the lady's fair face was writhed and drawn like that of one who looks upon a horror which strikes the words from her lips. Du Guesclin gazed round the tapestried room, at the screens, the tables, the abace, the credence, the buffet with its silver salver, and the half-circle of friendly wondering faces. There was an utter stillness, save for the sharp breathing of the Lady Tiphaine and for the gentle soughing of the wind outside, which wafted to their ears the distant call upon a swineherd's horn.

" The danger may bide," said he, shrugging his broad shoulders. " And now, Tiphaine, tell us what will come of this war in Spain."

" I can see little," she answered, straining her eyes and puckering her brow, as one who would fain clear her sight. " There are mountains, and dry plains, and flash of arms, and shouting of battle-cries. Yet it is whispered to me that by failure you will succeed."

" Ha ! Sir Nigel, how like you that ? " quoth Bertrand, shaking his head. " It is like mead and vinegar, half sweet, half sour. And there is no question which you would ask my lady ? "

" Certes there is. I would fain know, fair lady, how all things are at Twynham Castle, and above all how my sweet lady employs herself."

" To answer this I would fain lay hand upon one whose thoughts turn strongly to this castle which you have named. Nay, my Lord Loring, it is whispered to me that there is another here who hath thought more deeply of it than you."

" Thought more of mine own home ? " cried Sir Nigel. " Lady, I fear that in this matter at least you are mistaken."

" Not so, Sir Nigel. Come hither, young man, young English squire with the grey eyes ! Now give me your hand, and place it here across my brow, that I may see that which you have seen. What is this that rises before me ? Mist, mist, rolling mist with a square black tower above it. See it shreds out, it thins, it rises, and there lies a castle in a green plain, with the sea beneath it, and a great church within a bow-shot. There are two rivers which run through the meadows, and between them lie the tents of the besiegers."

" The besiegers ! " cried Alleyne, Ford, and Sir Nigel all three in a breath.

" Yes, truly, and they press hard upon the castle, for they are an exceeding multitude and full of courage. See how they storm and rage against the gate, while some rear ladders, and others, line after line, sweep the walls with their arrows. There are many leaders who shout and beckon, and one, a tall man with a goldenbeard, who stands before the gate stamping his foot and hallooing them on, as a pricker doth the hounds. But those in the castle fight bravely. There is a woman, two women, who stand upon the walls, and give heart to the men-at-arms. They shower down arrows, darts, and great stones. Ah ! they have struck down the tall leader, and the others give back. The mist thickens and I can see no more."

" By Saint Paul ! " said Sir Nigel, " I do not think that there can be any such doings at Christchurch, and I am very easy of the fortalice so long as my sweet wife hangs the key of the outer bailey at the head of her bed. Yet I will not deny that you have pictured the castle as well as I could have done myself, and I am full of wonderment at all that I have heard and seen."

" I would, Lady Tiphaine," cried the Lady Rochefort, " that you would use your power to tell me what hath befallen my golden bracelet which I wore when hawking upon the second Sunday of Advent, and have never set eyes upon since."

" Nay, lady," said Du Guesclin, " it does not befit so great and wondrous a power to pry and search and play the varlet even to the beautiful châtelaine of Villefranche. Ask a worthy question, and, with the blessing of God, you shall have a worthy answer."

" Then I would fain ask," cried one of the French squires, " as to which may hope to conquer in these wars betwixt the English and ourselves."

" Both will conquer, and each will hold its own," answered the Lady Tiphaine.

" Then we shall still hold Gascony and Guienne ? " cried Sir Nigel.

The lady shook her head. " French land, French blood, French speech," she answered. " They are French, and France shall have them."

" But not Bordeaux ? " cried Sir Nigel excitedly.

" Bordeaux also is for France."

" But Calais ? "

" Calais too."

" Woe worth me then, and ill hail to these evil words ! If Bordeaux and Calais be gone, then what is left for England ? "

" It seems indeed that there are evil times coming upon your country," said Du Guesclin. " In our fondest hopes we never thought to hold Bordeaux. By Saint Ives ! this news hath warmed the heart within me. Our dear country will then be very great in the future, Tiphaine ! "

" Great, and rich, and beautiful," she cried. " Far down the course of time I can see her still leading the nations, a wayward queen among the peoples, great in war, but greater in peace, quick in thought, deft in action, with her people's will for her sole monarch, from the sands of Calais to the blue seas of the south."

" Ha ! " cried Du Guesclin, with his eyes flashing in triumph, " you hear her, Sir Nigel ?—and she never yet said word which was not sooth."

The English knight shook his head moodily. " What of my own poor country ? " said he. " I fear, lady, that what you have said bodes but small good for her."

The lady sat with parted lips, and her breath came quick and fast. " My God ! " she cried, " what is this that is shown me ? Whence come they, these peoples, these lordly nations, these mighty countries which rise up before me ? I look beyond, and others rise, and yet others, far and farther to the shores of the uttermost waters. They crowd ! They swarm ! the world is given to them, and it resounds with the clang of their hammers and the ringing of their church bells. They call them many names, and they rule them this way or that, but they are all English, for I can hear the voices of the people. On I go, and onwards over seas where man hath never yet sailed, and I see a great land under new stars and a stranger sky, and still the land is England. Where have her children not gone ? What have they not done ? Her banner is planted on ice. Her banner is scorched in the sun. She lies athwart the lands, and her shadow is over the seas. Bertrand, Bertrand ! we are undone, for the buds of her bud are even as our choicest flower ! " Her voice rose into a wild cry, and throwing up her arms she sank back white and nerveless into the deep oaken chair.

" It is over," said Du Guesclin moodily, as he raised her drooping head with his strong brown hand. " Wine for the lady, squire ! The blessed hour of sight hath passed."

30. *How the Brushwood Men came to the Château of Villefranche*

IT was late ere Alleyne Edricson, having carried Sir Nigel the goblet of spiced wine which it was his custom to drink after the curling of his hair, was able at last to seek his chamber. It was a stone-flagged room upon the second floor, with a bed in a recess for him, and two smaller pallets on the other side, on which Aylward and Hordle John were already snoring. Alleyne had knelt down to his evening orisons, when there came a tap at his door, and Ford entered with a small lamp in his hand. His face was deadly pale, and his hand shook until the shadows flickered up and down the wall.

" What is it, Ford ? " cried Alleyne, springing to his feet.

" I can scarce tell you," said he, sitting down on the side of the couch, and resting his chin upon his hand. " I know not what to say or what to think."

" Has aught befallen you, then ? "

" Yes, or I have been slave to my own fancy. I tell you, lad, that I am all undone, like a fretted bow-string. Hark hither, Alleyne ! it cannot be that you have forgotten little Tita, the daughter of the old glass-stainer at Bordeaux ? "

" I remember her well."

" She and I, Alleyne, broke the luck groat together ere we parted, and she wears my ring upon her finger. ' Caro mio,' quoth she when last we parted, ' I shall be near thee in the wars, and thy danger will be my danger.' Alleyne, as God is my help, as I came up the stairs this night I saw her stand before me, her face in tears, her hands out as though in warning—I saw it, Alleyne, even as I see those two archers upon their couches. Our very finger-tips seemed to meet, ere she thinned away like a mist in the sunshine."

" I would not give overmuch thought to it," answered Alleyne. " Our minds will play us strange pranks, and bethink you that these words of the Lady Tiphaine du Guesclin have wrought upon us and shaken us."

Ford shook his head. " I saw little Tita as clearly as though I were back at the Rue de Apôtres at Bordeaux," said he. " But the hour is late, and I must go."

" Where do you sleep, then ? "

" In the chamber above you. May the saints be with us all ! " He rose from the couch and left the chamber,

while Alleyne could hear his feet sounding upon the
winding stair. The young squire walked across to the
window and gazed out at the moonlit landscape, his mind
absorbed by the thought of the Lady Tiphaine, and of the
strange words that she had spoken as to what was going
forward at Castle Twynham. Leaning his elbows upon
the stonework, he was deeply plunged in reverie, when in
a moment his thoughts were brought back to Villefranche
and to the scene before him.

The window at which he stood was in the second floor
of that portion of the castle which was nearest to the keep.
In front lay the broad moat with the moon lying upon its
surface, now clear and round, now drawn lengthwise as
the breeze stirred the waters. Beyond, the plain sloped
down to a thick wood, while farther to the left a second
wood shut out the view. Between the two an open glade
stretched, silvered in the moonshine, with the river curving across the lower end of it.

As he gazed, he saw of a sudden a man steal forth from
the wood into the open clearing. He walked with his
head sunk, his shoulders curved, and his knees bent, as
one who strives hard to remain unseen. Ten paces from
the fringe of trees he glanced around, and waving his
hand he crouched down, and was lost to sight among a
belt of furze-bushes. After him there came a second man,
and after him a third, a fourth, and a fifth, stealing across
the narrow open space and darting into the shelter of the
brushwood. Nine-and-seventy Alleyne counted of these
dark figures flitting across the line of the moonlight.
Many bore huge burdens upon their backs, though what
it was that they carried he could not tell at the distance.
Out of the one wood and into the other they passed, all
with the same crouching, furtive gait, until the black
bristle of trees had swallowed up the last of them.

For a moment Alleyne stood in the window, still staring
down at the silent forest, uncertain as to what he should
think of these midnight walkers. Then he bethought
him that there was one beside him who was fitter to

judge on such a matter. His fingers had scarce rested upon Aylward's shoulder ere the bowman was on his feet, with his hand outstretched to his sword.

"Qui va ?" he cried. "Holà ! mon petit. By my hilt ! I thought there had been a camisade. What then, mon gar ?"

"Come hither by the window, Aylward," said Alleyne. "I have seen four-score men pass from yonder shaw across the glade, and nigh every man of them had a great burden on his back. What think you of it ?"

"I think nothing of it, mon camarade ! There are as many masterless folk in this country as there are rabbits on Cowdray Down, and there are many who show their faces by night, but would dance in a hempen collar if they stirred forth in the day. On all the French marches are droves of outcasts, rievers, spoilers, and draw-latches, of whom I judge that these are some, though I marvel that they should dare to come so nigh to the castle of the seneschal. All seems very quiet now," he added, peering out of the window.

"They are in the further wood," said Alleyne.

"And there they may bide. Back to rest, mon petit ; for, by my hilt ! each day now will bring its own work. Yet it would be well to shoot the bolt in yonder door when one is in strange quarters. So !" He threw himself down upon his pallet and in an instant was fast asleep.

It might have been about three o'clock in the morning when Alleyne was aroused from a troubled sleep by a low cry or exclamation. He listened, but, as he heard no more, he set it down as the challenge of the guard upon the walls, and dropped off to sleep once more. A few minutes later he was disturbed by a gentle creaking of his own door, as though someone were pushing cautiously against it, and immediately afterwards he heard the soft thud of cautious footsteps upon the stair which led to the room above, followed by a confused noise and a muffled groan. Alleyne sat up on his couch with all his nerves in a tingle, uncertain whether these sounds might come from a simple cause—some sick archer and visiting leech perhaps—or whether they might have a more sinister meaning. But what danger could threaten them here in this strong castle, under the care of famous warriors, with high walls and a broad moat around them? Who was there that could injure them? He had well-nigh persuaded himself that his fears were a foolish fancy, when his eyes fell upon that which sent the blood cold to his heart and left him gasping, with hands clutching at the counterpane.

Right in front of him was the broad window of the chamber, with the moon shining brightly through it. For an instant something had obscured the light, and now a head was bobbing up and down outside, the face looking in at him, and swinging slowly from one side of the window to the other. Even in that dim light there could be no mistaking those features. Drawn, distorted and blood-stained, they were still those of the young fellow-squire who had sat so recently upon his own couch. With a cry of horror Alleyne sprang from his bed and rushed to the casement, while the two archers, aroused by the sound, seized their weapons and stared about them in bewilderment. One glance was enough to show Edricson that his fears were but too true. Foully murdered, with a score of wounds upon him and a rope round his neck, his poor friend had been cast from the upper window and swung slowly in the night wind, his body rasping against the wall and his disfigured face upon a level with the casement.

" My God! " cried Alleyne, shaking in every limb. " What has come upon us? What devil's deed is this? "

" Here is flint and steel," said John stolidly. " The lamp, Aylward! This moonshine softens a man's heart. Now we may use the eyes which God hath given us."

" By my hilt! " cried Aylward, as the yellow flame flickered up, " it is indeed young master Ford, and I think that this seneschal is a black villain, who dare not face us in the day, but would murther us in our sleep. By the twang of string! if I do not soak a goose's feather with his heart's blood, it will be no fault of Samkin Aylward of the White Company."

" But, Aylward, think of the men whom I saw yester-night," said Alleyne. " It may not be the seneschal. It may be that others have come to the castle. I must to Sir Nigel ere it be too late. Let me go, Aylward, for my place is by his side."

" One moment, mon gar. Put that steel head-piece on the end of my yew-stave. So ! I will put it first through the door ; for it is ill to come out when you can neither see nor guard yourself. Now, camarades, out swords and stand ready ! Holà, by my hilt ! it is time that we were stirring ! "

As he spoke, a sudden shouting broke forth in the castle, with the scream of a woman and the rush of many feet. Then came the sharp clink of clashing steel, and a roar like that of an angry lion—" Notre Dame Du Guesclin ! Saint Ives ! Saint Ives ! " The bowman pulled back the bolt of the door, and thrust out the head-piece at the end of the bow. A crash, the clatter of the steel-cap upon the ground, and, ere the man who struck could heave up for another blow, the archer had passed his sword through his body. " On, camarades, on ! " he cried ; and, break-ing fiercely past two men who threw themselves in his way, he sped down the broad corridor in the direction of the shouting.

A sharp turning, and then a second one, brought them to the head of a short stair, from which they looked straight down upon the scene of the uproar. A square oak-floored hall lay beneath them, from which opened the doors of the principal guest-chambers. This hall was as light as day, for torches burned in numerous sconces upon the walls, throwing strange shadows from the tusked or antlered heads which ornamented them. At the very foot of the stair, close to the open door of their chamber, lay the seneschal and his wife ; she with her head shorn from her shoulders, he thrust through with a sharpened stake, which still protruded from either side of his body. Three servants of the castle lay dead beside them, all torn and draggled, as though a pack of wolves had been upon them. In front of the central guest-chamber stood Du Guesclin and Sir Nigel, half-clad and unarmoured, with the mad joy of battle gleaming in their eyes. Their heads were thrown back, their lips compressed, their blood-stained swords poised over their right shoulders, and their left feet thrown out. Three dead men lay huddled together in front of them ; while a fourth, with the blood squirting from a severed vessel, lay back with updrawn knees, breathing in wheezy gasps. Farther back—all panting together like the wind in a tree—there stood a group of fierce wild creatures, bare-armed and bare-legged, gaunt, unshaven, with deep-set murderous eyes and wild-beast faces. With their flashing teeth, their bristling hair, their mad leapings and screamings, they seemed to Alleyne more like fiends from the pit than men of flesh and blood. Even as he looked, they broke into a hoarse yell and dashed once more upon the two knights, hurling themselves madly upon their sword-points ; clutching, scrambling, biting, tearing, careless of wounds if they could but drag the two soldiers to earth. Sir Nigel was thrown down by the sheer weight of them, and Sir Bertrand with his thunderous war-cry was swinging round his heavy sword to clear a space for him to rise, when the whistle of two long English arrows, and the rush of the squire and the two English archers down the stairs, turned the tide of the combat. The assailants gave back, the knights rushed forward, and in a very few moments the hall was cleared, and Hordle John had hurled the last of the wild men down the steep steps which led from the end of it.

" Do not follow them," cried Du Guesclin. " We are lost if we scatter. For myself I care not a denier, though it is a poor thing to meet one's end at the hands of such scum ; but I have my dear lady here, who must by no means be risked. We have breathing-space now, and I would ask you, Sir Nigel, what it is that you would counsel ? "

" By Saint Paul ! " answered Sir Nigel, " I can by no means understand what hath befallen us, save that I have been woken up by your battle-cry, and, rushing forth, found myself in the midst of this small bickering. Harrow and alas for the lady and the seneschal ! What dogs are they who have done this bloody deed ? "

" They are the Jacks, the men of the brushwood. They have the castle, though I know not how it hath come to pass. Look from this window into the bailey."

" By heaven ! " cried Sir Nigel, " it is as bright as day with the torches. The gates stand open, and there are three thousand of them within the walls. See how they rush and scream and wave ! What is it that they thrust out through the postern door ? My God ! it is a man-at-arms, and they pluck him limb from limb, like hounds on a wolf. Now another, and yet another. They hold the whole castle, for I see their faces at the windows. See, there are some with great bundles on their backs."

" It is dried wood from the forest. They pile them against the walls and set them in a blaze. Who is this who tries to check them ? By Saint Ives ! it is the good priest who spake for them in the hall. He kneels, he prays, he implores ! What ! villains, would ye raise hands against those who have befriended you ? Ah, the butcher has struck him ! He is down ! They stamp him under their feet ! They tear off his gown and wave it in the air ! See now, how the flames lick up the walls ! Are there none left to rally round us ? With a hundred men we might hold our own."

" Oh, for my Company ! " cried Sir Nigel. " But where is Ford, Alleyne ? "

" He is foully murdered, my fair lord."

" The saints receive him ! May he rest in peace ! But here come some at last who may give us counsel, for amid these passages it is ill to stir without a guide."

As he spoke, a French squire, and the Bohemian knight came rushing down the steps, the latter bleeding from a slash across his forehead.

" All is lost ! " he cried. " The castle is taken and on fire, the seneschal is slain and there is nought left for us."

" On the contrary," quoth Sir Nigel, " there is much left to us, for there is a very honourable contention before us, and a fair lady for whom to give our lives. There are many ways in which a man might die, but none better than this."

" You can tell us, Godfrey," said Du Guesclin to the French squire : " how came these men into the castle, and what succours can we count upon ? By Saint Ives ! if we come not quickly to some counsel we shall be burned like young rooks in a nest."

The squire, a dark slender stripling, spoke firmly and quickly, as one who was trained to swift action. " There is a passage under the earth into the castle," said he, " and through it some of the Jacks made their way, casting open the gates for the others. They have had help from within the walls and the men-at-arms were heavy with wine : they must have been slain in their beds, for these devils crept from room to room with soft step and ready knife. Sir Amory the Hospitaller was struck down with an axe as he rushed before us from his sleeping chamber. Save only ourselves, I do not think there are any left alive."

" What, then, would you counsel ? "

" That we make for the keep. It is unused, save in time of war, and the key hangs from my poor lord and master's belt."

" There are two keys there."

" It is the larger. Once there, we might hold the narrow stair ; and at least, as the walls are of a greater thickness, it would be longer ere they could burn them. Could we but carry the lady across the bailey, all might be well with us."

" Nay ; the lady hath seen something of the work of war," said Tiphaine, coming forth, as white, as grave, and as unmoved as ever. " I would not be a hamper to you, my dear spouse and gallant friends. Rest assured of this, that if all else fail I have always a safeguard here "—

drawing a small silver-hilted poniard from her bosom—
" which sets me beyond the fear of these vile and blood-
stained wretches."

" Tiphaine," cried Du Guesclin, " I have always loved
you, and now, by Our Lady of Rennes ! I love you more
than ever. Did I not know that your hand will be as
ready as your words, I would myself turn my last blow
upon you, ere you should fall into their hands. Lead on,
Godfrey ! A new golden pyx shall shine in the Minster
of Dinan if we come through with it."

The attention of the insurgents had been drawn away
from murder to plunder, and all over the castle might be
heard their cries and whoops of delight as they dragged
forth the rich tapestries, the silver flagons, and the carved
furniture. Down in the courtyard half-clad wretches,
their bare limbs all mottled with bloodstains, strutted
about with plumed helmets upon their heads, or with the
Lady Rochefort's silken gowns girt round their loins and
trailing on the ground behind them. Casks of choice
wine had been rolled out from the cellars, and starving
peasants squatted, goblet in hand, draining off vintages
which De Rochefort had set aside for noble and royal
guests. Others, with slabs of bacon and joints of dried
meat upon the ends of their pikes, held them up to the
blaze or tore at them ravenously with their teeth. Yet all
order had not been lost amongst them, for some hundreds
of the better armed stood together in a silent group, leaning upon their rude weapons and looking up at the fire,
which had spread so rapidly as to involve one whole side
of the castle. Already Alleyne could hear the crackling
and roaring of the flames, while the air was heavy with
heat and full of the pungent whiff of burning wood.

31. *How Five Men held the Keep of Ville-franche*

UNDER the guidance of the French squire the party passed down two narrow corridors. The first was empty, but at the head of the second stood a peasant sentry, who started off at the sight of them, yelling loudly to his comrades. " Stop him or we are undone ! " cried Du Guesclin, and had started to run, when Aylward's great war-bow twanged like a harp-string, and the man fell forward upon his face, with twitching limbs and clutching fingers. Within five paces of where he lay a narrow and little-used door led out into the bailey. From beyond it came such a babel of hooting and screaming, horrible oaths and yet more horrible laughter, that the stoutest heart might have shrunk from casting down the frail barrier which faced them.

" Make straight for the keep ! " said Du Guesclin, in a sharp stern whisper. " The two archers in front, the lady in the centre, a squire on either side, while we three knights shall bide behind and beat back those who press upon us. So ! Now open the door, and God have us in His holy keeping ! "

For a few moments it seemed that their object would be attained without danger, so swift and so silent had been their movements. They were half-way across the bailey ere the frantic howling peasants made a movement to stop them. The few who threw themselves in their way were overpowered or brushed aside, while the pursuers were beaten back by the ready weapons of the three cavaliers. Unscathed they fought their way to the door of the keep, and faced round upon the swarming mob, while the squire thrust the great key into the lock.

" My God ! " he cried, " it is the wrong key ! "

" The wrong key ! "

" Dolt, fool that I am ! This is the key of the castle gate ; the other opens the keep. I must back for it ! "

He turned, with some wild intention of retracing his steps, but at the instant a great jagged rock, hurled by a brawny peasant, struck him full upon the ear, and he dropped senseless to the ground.

" This is key enough for me ! " quoth Hordle John, picking up the huge stone, and hurling it against the door with all the strength of his enormous body. The lock shivered, the wood smashed, the stone flew into five pieces, but the iron clamps still held the door in its position. Bending down, he thrust his great fingers under it, and with a heave raised the whole mass of wood and iron from its hinges. For a moment it tottered and swayed, and then, falling outward, buried him in its ruin, while his comrades rushed into the dark archway which led to safety.

" Up the steps, Tiphaine ! " cried Du Guesclin. " Now round, friends, and beat them back." The mob of peasants had surged in upon their heels, but the two trustiest blades in Europe gleamed upon that narrow stair, and four of their number dropped upon the threshold. The others gave back and gathered in a half-circle round the open door, gnashing their teeth and shaking their clenched hands at the defenders. The body of the French squire had been dragged out by them and hacked to pieces. Three or four others had pulled John from under the door, when he suddenly bounded to his feet, and clutching one in either hand dashed them together with such force that they fell senseless across each other upon the ground. With a kick and a blow he freed himself from two others who clung to him, and in a moment he was within the portal with his comrades.

Yet their position was a desperate one. The peasants from far and near had been assembled for this deed of vengeance, and not less than six thousand were within or around the walls of the Château of Villefranche. Ill armed and half starved, they were still desperate men, to whom danger had lost all fears : for what was death that they should shun it to cling to such a life as theirs ? The castle was theirs, and the roaring flames were spurting through the windows and flickering high above the turrets on two sides of the quadrangle. From either side they were sweeping down from room to room and from bastion to bastion in the direction of the keep. Faced by an army, and girt in by fire, were six men and one woman ; but some of them were men so trained to danger and so wise in war that even now the combat was less unequal than it seemed. Courage and resource were penned in by desperation and numbers, while the great yellow sheets of flame threw their lurid glare over the scene of death.

" There is but space for two upon a step to give free play to our sword-arms," said Du Guesclin. " Do you stand with me, Nigel, upon the lowest. France and England will fight together this night. Sir Otto, I pray you to stand behind us with this young squire. The archers may go higher yet and shoot over our heads. I would that we had our harness, Nigel ! "

" Often have I heard my dear Sir John Chandos say that a knight should never, even when a guest, be parted from it. Yet it will be more honour to us if we come well out of it. We have a vantage, since we see them against the light and they can scarce see us. It seems to me that they muster for an onslaught."

" If we can but keep them in play," said the Bohemian, " it is likely that these flames may bring us succour if there be any true men in the country."

" Bethink you, my fair lord," said Alleyne to Sir Nigel, " that we have never injured these men, nor have we cause of quarrel against them. Would it not be well, if but for the lady's sake, to speak them fair, and see if we may not come to honourable terms with them ? "

" Not so, by Saint Paul ! " cried Sir Nigel. " It does not accord with mine honour, nor shall it ever be said that I, a knight of England, was ready to hold parley with men who have a slain a fair lady and a holy priest."

" As well hold parley with a pack of ravening wolves," said the French captain. " Ha ! Notre Dame Du Guesclin ! Saint Ives ! Saint Ives ! "

As he thundered forth his war-cry, the Jacks who had been gathering before the black arch of the gateway rushed in madly in a desperate effort to carry the staircase. Their leaders were a small man, dark in the face, with his beard done up in two plaits, and another larger man, very bowed in the shoulders, with a huge club studded with nails in his hand. The first had not taken three steps ere an arrow from Aylward's bow struck him full in the chest, and he fell coughing and spluttering across the threshold. The other rushed onwards, and breaking between Du Guesclin and Sir Nigel, he dashed out the brains of the Bohemian with a single blow of his clumsy weapon. With three swords through him he still struggled on, and had almost won his way through them ere he fell dead upon the stair. Close at his heels came a hundred furious peasants, who flung themselves again and again against the five swords which confronted them. It was cut and parry and stab as quick as eye could see or hand act. The door was piled with bodies, and the stone floor was slippery with blood. The deep shout of Du Guesclin, the hard hissing breath of the pressing multitude, the clatter of steel, the thud of falling bodies, and the screams of the stricken, made up such a medley as came often in after years to break upon Alleyne's sleep. Slowly and suddenly at last the throng drew off, with many a fierce backward glance, while eleven of their number lay huddled in front of the stair which they had failed to win.

" The dogs have had enough," said Du Guesclin.

" By Saint Paul ! there appear to be some very worthy and valiant persons among them," observed Sir Nigel. " They are men from whom, had they been of better birth, much honour and advancement might be gained. Even as it is, it is a great pleasure to have seen them. But what is this that they are bringing forward ? "

" It is as I feared," growled Du Guesclin. " They will burn us out, since they cannot win their way past us. Shoot straight and hard, archers ; for, by Saint Ives ! our good swords are of little use to us."

As he spoke, a dozen men rushed forward, each screening himself behind a huge fardel of brushwood. Hurling their burdens in one vast heap within the portal, they threw burning torches upon the top of it. The wood had been soaked in oil, for in an instant it was ablaze, and a long hissing yellow flame licked over the heads of the defenders, and drove them farther up to the first floor of the keep. They had scarce reached it, however, ere they found that the wooden joists and planks of the flooring were already on fire. Dry and worm-eaten, a spark upon them became a smoulder, and a smoulder a blaze. A choking smoke filled the air, and the five could scarce grope their way to the staircase which led up to the very summit of the square tower.

Strange was the scene which met their eyes from this eminence. Beneath them on every side stretched the long sweep of peaceful country, rolling plain, and tangled wood, all softened and mellowed in the silver moonshine. No light nor movement, nor any sign of human aid could be seen, but far away the hoarse clangour of a heavy bell rose and fell upon the wintry air. Beneath and around them blazed the huge fire, roaring and crackling on every side of the bailey, and even as they looked the two corner turrets fell in with a deafening crash, and the whole castle was but a shapeless mass, spouting flames and smoke from every window and embrasure. The great black tower upon which they stood rose like a last island of refuge amid this sea of fire ; but the ominous crackling and roaring below showed that it would not be long ere it was engulfed also in the common ruin. At their very feet was the square courtyard, crowded with the howling and dancing peasants, their fierce faces upturned, their clenched hands waving, all drunk with bloodshed and with vengeance. A yell of execrations and a scream of hideous laughter burst from the vast throng, as they saw the faces of the last survivors of their enemies peering down at them from the height of the keep. They still piled the brushwood round the base of the tower, and gambolled hand in hand around the

341

blaze, screaming out the doggerel lines which had long been the watchword of the Jacquerie :

Cessez, cessez, gens d'armes et piétons,
De piller et manger le bonhomme,
Qui de longtemps Jacques Bonhomme
Se nomme.

Their thin shrill voices rose high above the roar of the flames and the crash of the masonry, like the yelping of a pack of wolves who see their quarry before them and know that they have well-nigh run him down.

" By my hilt ! " said Aylward to John, " it is in my mind that we shall not see Spain this journey. It is a great joy to me that I have placed my feather-bed and other things of price with that worthy woman at Lyndhurst, who will now have the use of them. I have thirteen arrows yet, and if one of them fly unfleshed, then, by the twang of string ! I shall deserve my doom. First at him who flaunts with my lady's silken frock. Clap in the clout, by God ! though a hand's-breath lower than I had meant. Now for the rogue with the head upon his pike. Ha ! to the inch, John. When my eye is true, I am better at rovers than at long-butts or hoyles. A good shoot for you also, John ! The villain hath fallen forward into the fire. But I pray you, John, to loose gently, and not to pluck with the drawing-hand, for it is a trick that hath marred many a fine bowman."

Whilst the two archers were keeping up a brisk fire upon the mob beneath them, Du Guesclin and his lady were consulting with Sir Nigel upon their desperate situation.

" 'Tis a strange end for one who has seen so many stricken fields," said the French chieftain. " For me one death is as another, but it is the thought of my sweet lady which goes to my heart."

" Nay, Bertrand, I fear it as little as you," said she. " Had I my dearest wish, it would be that we should go together."

" Well answered, fair lady ! " cried Sir Nigel. " And very sure I am that my own sweet wife would have said the same. If the end be now come, I have had great good fortune in having lived in times when so much glory was to be won, and in knowing so many valiant gentlemen and knights. But why do you pluck my sleeve, Alleyne ? "

" If it please you, my fair lord, there are in this corner two great tubes of iron, with many heavy balls, which may perchance be those bombards and shot of which I have heard."

" By Saint Ives ! it is true," cried Sir Bertrand, striding across to the recess where the ungainly, funnel-shaped, thick-ribbed engines were standing. " Bombards they are, and of good size. We may shoot down upon them."

" Shoot with them, quotha ? " cried Aylward in high disdain, for pressing danger is the great leveller of classes. " How is a man to take aim with these fool's toys, and how can he hope to do scath with them ? "

" I will show you," answered Sir Nigel ; " for here is the great box of powder, and if you will raise it for me, John, I will show you how it may be used. Come hither, where the folk are thickest round the fire. Now, Aylward, crane thy neck and see what would have been deemed an old wife's tale when we first turned our faces to the wars. Throw back the lid, John, and drop the box into the fire."

A deafening roar, a fluff of bluish light, and the great square tower rocked and trembled from its very foundations, swaying this way and that like a reed in the wind. Amazed and dizzy, the defenders, clutching at the cracking parapets for support, saw great stones, burning beams of wood and mangled bodies hurtling past them through the air. When they staggered to their feet once more, the whole keep had settled down upon one side, so that they could scarce keep their footing upon the sloping platform. Gazing over the edge, they looked down upon the horrible destruction which had been caused by the explosion. For forty yards round the portal the ground was black with writhing, screaming figures, who struggled up and hurled themselves down again, tossing this way and that, sightless, scorched, with fire bursting from their tattered clothing. Beyond this circle of death, their comrades, bewildered and amazed, cowered away from this black tower and from these invincible men, who were most to be dreaded when hope was furthest from their hearts.

" A sally, Du Guesclin, a sally ! " cried Sir Nigel. " By Saint Paul ! they are in two minds, and a bold rush may turn them." He drew his sword as he spoke and darted down the winding stairs, closely followed by his four comrades. Ere he was at the first floor, however, he threw up his arms and stopped. " Mon Dieu ! " he said, " we are lost men ! "

" What then ? " cried those behind him.

" The wall hath fallen in, the stair is blocked, and the fire still rages below. By Saint Paul ! friends, we have fought a very honourable fight, and may say in all humbleness that we have done our devoir, but I think that we may now go back to the Lady Tiphaine and say our orisons, for we have played our parts in this world, and it is time that we made ready for another."

The narrow pass was blocked by huge stones littered in wild confusion over each other, with the blue choking smoke reeking up through the crevices. The explosion had blown in the wall and cut off the only path by which they could descend. Pent in, a hundred feet from earth, with a furnace raging under them and a ravening multitude all round who thirsted for their blood, it seemed indeed as though no men had ever come through such peril with their lives. Slowly they made their way back to the summit, but as they came out upon it, the Lady Tiphaine darted forward and caught her husband by the wrist.

" Bertrand," said she, " hush and listen ! I have heard the voices of men all singing together in a strange tongue."

Breathless, they stood and silent, but no sound came up to them, save the roar of the flames and the clamour of their enemies.

" It cannot be, lady," said Du Guesclin. " This night hath overwrought you, and your senses play you false.

What men are there in this country who would sing in a strange tongue ? "

" Holà ! " yelled Aylward, leaping suddenly into the air with waving hands and joyous face. " I thought I heard it ere we went down and now I hear it again. We are saved, comrades ! By these ten finger-bones, we are saved ! It is the marching song of the White Company. Hush ! "

With upraised forefinger and slanting head, he stood listening. Suddenly there came swelling up a deep-voiced rollicking chorus from somewhere out of the dark-ness. Never did choice or dainty ditty of Provence or Languedoc sound more sweetly in the ears than did the rough-tongued Saxon to the six who strained their ears from the blazing keep :

> We'll drink all together
> To the grey goose feather
> And the land where the grey goose flew.

" Ha, by my hilt ! " shouted Aylward, " it is the dear old bow song of the Company. Here come two hundred as tight lads as ever twirled a shaft over their thumb-nails. Hark to the dogs, how lustily they sing ! "

Nearer and clearer, swelling up out of the night, came the gay marching lilt :

> What of the bow ?
> The bow was made in England,
> Of true wood, of yew wood,
>   The wood of English bows ;
> For men who are free
> Love the old yew-tree
>   And the land where the yew-tree grows.
>
> What of the men ?
> The men were bred in England,
> The bowmen, the yeomen,
>   The lads of dale and fell.
> Here's to you and to you,
> To the hearts that are true,
>   And the land where the true hearts dwell.

" They sing very joyfully," said Du Guesclin, " as though they were going to a festival."

" It is their wont when there is work to be done."

" By Saint Paul ! " quoth Sir Nigel, " it is in my mind that they come too late, for I cannot see how we are to come down from this tower."

" There they come, the hearts of gold ! " cried Aylward. " See, they move out from the shadow. Now they cross the meadow. They are on the further side of the moat. Holà, camarades, holà ! Johnston, Eccles, Cooke, Harward, Bligh ! Would ye see a fair lady and two gallant knights done foully to death ? "

" Who is there ? " shouted a deep voice from below. " Who is this who speaks with an English tongue ? "

" It is I, old lad. It is Sam Aylward of the Company ; and here is your captain, Sir Nigel Loring, and four others, all laid out to be grilled like an Easterling's herrings."

" Curse me if I did not think that it was the style of speech from old Samkin Aylward," said the voice, amid a buzz from the ranks. " Wherever there are knocks going there is Sammy in the heart of it. But who are these ill-faced rogues who block the path ? To your kennels, canaille ! What ! you dare look us in the eyes ? Out swords, lads, and give them the flat of them ! Waste not your shafts upon such runagate knaves."

There was little fight left in the peasants, however, still dazed by the explosion, amazed at their own losses, and disheartened by the arrival of the disciplined archers. In a very few minutes they were in full flight for their brush-wood homes, leaving the morning sun to rise upon a blackened and blood-stained ruin, where it had left the night before the magnificent castle of the Seneschal of Auvergne. Already the white lines in the east were deepening into pink as the archers gathered round the keep and took counsel how to rescue the survivors.

" Had we a rope," said Alleyne, " there is one side which is not yet on fire, down which we might slip."

" But how to get a rope ? "

" It is an old trick," quoth Aylward. " Holà ! Johnston, cast me up a rope, even as you did at Maupertius in the war time."

The grizzled archer thus addressed took several lengths of rope from his comrades, and knotting them firmly together, he stretched them out in the long shadow which the rising sun threw from the frowning keep. Then he fixed the yew-stave of his bow upon end and measured the long thin black line which it threw upon the turf.

"A six-foot stave throws a twelve-foot shadow," he muttered. "The keep throws a shadow of sixty paces. Thirty paces of rope will be enow and to spare. Another strand, Watkin! Now pull at the end that all may be safe. So! It is ready for them."

"But how are they to reach it?" asked the young archer beside him.

"Watch and see, young fool's-head," growled the old bowman. He took a long string from his pouch and fastened one end to an arrow.

"All ready, Samkin?"

"Ready, camarade."

"Close to your hand then." With an easy pull he sent the shaft flickering gently up, falling upon the stonework within a foot of where Aylward was standing. The other end was secured to the rope, so that in a minute a good strong cord was dangling from the only sound side of the blazing and shattered tower. The Lady Tiphaine was lowered with a noose drawn fast under the arms, and the other five slid swiftly down amid the cheers and joyous outcry of their rescuers.

32. *How the Company took Counsel Round the Fallen Tree*

"WHERE is Sir Claude Latour?" asked Sir Nigel, as his feet touched the ground.

"He is in camp, near Montpezat, two hours' march from here, my fair lord," said Johnston, the grizzled bowman who commanded the archers.

"Then we shall march thither, for I would fain have

you all back at Dax in time to be in the prince's vanguard."

" My lord," cried Alleyne, joyfully, " here are our chargers in the field, and I see your harness amid the plunder which these rogues have left behind them."

" By Saint Ives ! you speak sooth, young squire," said Du Guesclin. " There is my horse and my lady's jennet. The knaves led them from the stables, but fled without them. Now, Nigel, it is great joy to me to have seen one of whom I have often heard. Yet we must leave you now, for I must be with the King of Spain ere your army crosses the mountains."

" I had thought that you were in Spain with the valiant Henry of Trastamare."

" I have been there, but I came to France to raise succour for him. I shall ride back, Nigel, with four thousand of the best lances of France at my back, so that your prince may find he hath a task which is worthy of him. God be with you, friend, and may we meet again in better times."

" I do not think," said Sir Nigel, as he stood by Alleyne's side, looking after the French knight and his lady, " that in all Christendom you will meet with a more stout-hearted man or a fairer and sweeter dame. But your face is pale and sad, Alleyne. Have you perchance met with some hurt during the ruffle ? "

" Nay, my fair lord, I was but thinking of my friend, Ford, and how he sat upon my couch no later than yesternight."

Sir Nigel shook his head sadly. " Two brave squires have I lost," said he. " I know not why the young shoots should be plucked and an old weed left standing, yet certes there must be some good reason, since God hath so planned it. Did you not note, Alleyne, that the Lady Tiphaine did give us warning last night that danger was coming upon us ? "

" She did, my lord."

" By Saint Paul ! my mind misgives me as to what she

saw at Twynham Castle. And yet I cannot think that any Scottish or French rovers could land in such force as to beleaguer the fortalice. Call the Company together, Aylward ; and let us on, for it will be shame to us if we are not at Dax upon the trysting day."

The archers had spread themselves over the ruins, but a blast upon a bugle brought them all back to the muster with such booty as they could bear with them stuffed into their pouches or slung over their shoulders. As they formed into ranks, each man dropping silently into his place, Sir Nigel ran a questioning eye over them, and a smile of pleasure played over his face. Tall and sinewy, and brown, clear-eyed, hard-featured, with the stern and prompt bearing of experienced soldiers, it would be hard indeed for a leader to seek for a choicer following. Here and there in the ranks were old soldiers of the French wars, grizzled and lean, with fierce puckered features and shaggy bristling brows. The most, however, were young and dandy archers, with fresh English faces, their beards combed out, their hair curling from under their close steel hufkens, with gold or jewelled ear-rings gleaming in their ears, while their gold-spangled baldrics, their silken belts, and the chains which many of them wore round their thick brown necks, all spoke of the brave times which they had had as free companions. Each had a yew or hazel stave slung over his shoulder, plain and serviceable with the older men, but gaudily painted and carved at either end with the others. Steel caps, mail brigandines, white surcoats with the red lion of St. George, and sword or battle-axe swinging from their belts, completed this equipment, while in some cases the murderous maule or five-foot mallet was hung across the bow-stave, being fastened to their leathern shoulder-belt by a hook in the centre of the handle. Sir Nigel's heart beat high as he looked upon their free bearing and fearless faces.

For two hours they marched through forest and marsh-land, along the left bank of the river Aveyron ; Sir Nigel riding behind his Company, with Alleyne at his right hand,

and Johnston, the old master bowman, walking by his left stirrup. Ere they had reached their journey's end the knight had learned all that he would know of his men, their doings and their intentions. Once as they marched they saw upon the farther bank of the river a body of French men-at-arms, riding very swiftly in the direction of Villefranche.

" It is the Seneschal of Toulouse, with his following," said Johnston, shading his eyes with his hand. " Had he been on this side of the water he might have attempted something upon us."

" I think that it would be well that we should cross," said Sir Nigel. " It were pity to balk this worthy seneschal, should he desire to try some small feat of arms."

" Nay, there is no ford nearer than Tourville," answered the old archer. " He is on his way to Villefranche, and short will be the shrift of any Jacks who come into his hands, for he is a man of short speech. It was he and the Seneschal of Beaucaire who hung Peter Wilkins, of the Company, last Lammastide ; for which by the black rood of Waltham ! they shall hang themselves if ever they come into our power. But here are our comrades, Sir Nigel, and here is our camp."

As he spoke, the forest pathway along which they marched opened out into a green glade, which sloped down towards the river. High leafless trees girt it in on three sides, with a thick undergrowth of holly between their trunks. At the farther end of this forest clearing there stood forty or fifty huts, built very nearly from wood and clay, with the blue smoke curling out from the roofs. A dozen tethered horses and mules grazed around the encampment, while a number of archers lounged about : some shooting at marks, while others built up great wooden fires in the open, and hung their cooking kettles above them. At the sight of their returning comrades there was a shout of welcome, and a horseman, who had been exercising his charger behind the camp, came cantering down to them. He was a dapper, brisk man, very richly clad, with a round clean-shaven face, and very bright black eyes, which danced and sparkled with excitement.

"Sir Nigel!" he cried. "Sir Nigel Loring, at last! By my soul! we have awaited you this month past. Right welcome, Sir Nigel! You have had my letter?"

"It was that which brought me here," said Sir Nigel. "But indeed, Sir Claude Latour, it is a great wonder to me that you did not yourself lead these bowmen, for surely they could have found no better leader."

"None, none, by the Virgin of L'Esparre!" he cried, speaking in the strange thick Gascon speech which turns every *v* into a *b*. "But you know what these islanders of yours are, Sir Nigel. They will not be led by any save their own blood and race. There is no persuading them. Not even I, Claude Latour, Seigneur of Montchâteau, master of the high justice, the middle and the low, could gain their favour. They must needs hold a council and put their two hundred thick heads together, and then there comes this fellow Aylward and another, as their spokesmen, to say that they will disband unless an Englishman of good name be set over them. There are many of them, as I understand, who come from some great forest which lies in Hampi, or Hampti—I cannot lay my tongue to the name. Your dwelling is in those parts, and so their thoughts turned to you as their leader. But we had hoped that you would bring a hundred men with you."

"They are already at Dax, where we shall join them," said Sir Nigel. "But let the men break their fast, and we shall then take counsel what to do."

"Come into my hut," said Sir Claude. "It is but poor fare that I can lay before you—milk, cheese, wine and bacon—yet your squire and yourself will doubtless excuse it. This is my house where the pennon flies before the door—a small residence to contain the Lord of Montchâteau."

Sir Nigel sat silent and distrait at his meal, while Alleyne hearkened to the chattering tongue of the Gascon, and to his talk of the glories of his own estate, his successes in love, and his triumphs in war.

" And now that you are here, Sir Nigel," he said at last, " I have many fine ventures all ready for us. I have heard that Montpezat is of no great strength, and that there are two hundred thousand crowns in the castle. At Castlenau there also is a cobbler who is in my pay, and who will throw us a rope any dark night from his house by the town wall. I promise you that you shall thrust your arms elbow deep among good silver pieces ere the nights are moonless again ; for on every hand of us are fair women, rich wine and good plunder, as much as heart could wish."

" I have other plans," answered Sir Nigel curtly ; " for I have come hither to lead these bowmen to the help of the prince, our master, who may have sore need of them ere he set Pedro upon the throne of Spain. It is my purpose to start this very day for Dax upon the Adour, where he hath now pitched his camp."

The face of the Gascon darkened, and his eyes flashed with resentment. " For me," he said, " I care little for this war, and I find the life which I lead a very joyous and pleasant one. I will not go to Dax."

" Nay, think again, Sir Claude," said Sir Nigel gently ; " for you have ever had the name of a true and loyal knight. Surely you will not hold back now when your master hath need of you."

" I will not go to Dax," the other shouted.

" But your devoir—your oath of fealty ? "

" I say that I will not go."

" Then, Sir Claude, I must lead the Company without you."

" If they will follow," cried the Gascon, with a sneer. " These are not hired slaves, but free companions, who will do nothing save by their own good wills. In very sooth, my Lord Loring, they are ill men to trifle with, and it were easier to pluck a bone from a hungry bear than to lead a bowman out of a land of plenty and of pleasure."

" Then I pray you to gather them together," said Sir Nigel, " and I will tell them what is in my mind ; for if I am their leader they must go to Dax, and if I am not, then I know not what I am doing in Auvergne. Have my horse ready, Alleyne ; for, by Saint Paul ! come what may, I must be upon the homeward road ere midday."

A blast upon the bugle summoned the bowmen to counsel, and they gathered in little knots and groups around a great fallen tree, which lay athwart the glade. Sir Nigel sprang lightly upon the trunk, and stood with blinking eye and firm lips looking down at the ring of upturned warlike faces.

" They tell me, bowmen," said he, " that ye have grown so fond of ease and plunder and high living that ye are not to be moved from this pleasant country. But, by Saint Paul ! I will believe no such thing of you, for I can readily see that you are all very valiant men, who would scorn to live here in peace when your prince hath so great a venture before him. Ye have chosen me as a leader, and a leader I will be if ye come with me to Spain ; and I vow to you that my pennon of the five roses shall, if God give me strength and life, be ever where there is most honour to be gained. But if it be your wish to loll and loiter in these glades, bartering glory and renown for vile gold and ill-gotten riches, then ye must find another leader ; for I have lived in honour, and in honour I trust that I shall die. If there be forest men or Hampshire men amongst ye, I call upon them to say whether they will follow the banner of Loring."

" Here's a Romsey man for you ! " cried a young bowman with a sprig of evergreen set in his helmet.

" And a lad from Alresford ! " shouted another.

" And from Milton ! "

" And from Burley ! "

" And from Lymington ! "

" And a little one from Brockenhurst ! " shouted a huge-limbed fellow who sprawled beneath a tree.

" By my hilt ! lads," cried Aylward, jumping upon the

fallen trunk, " I think that we could not look the girls in the eyes if we let the prince cross the mountains and did not pull string to clear a path for him. It is very well in time of peace to lead such a life as we have had together, but now the war-banner is in the wind once more, and, by these ten finger-bones ! if he go alone, old Samkin Aylward will walk beside it."

These words from a man so popular as Aylward decided many of the waverers, and a shout of approval burst from his audience.

" Far be it from me," said Sir Claude Latour suavely, " to persuade you against this worthy archer, or against Sir Nigel Loring ; yet we have been together in many ventures, and perchance it may not be amiss if I say to you what I think upon the matter."

" Peace for the little Gascon ! " cried the archers. " Let every man have his word. Shoot straight for the mark, lad, and fair play for all."

" Bethink you, then," said Sir Claude, " that you go under a hard rule, with neither freedom nor pleasure— and for what ? For sixpence a day, at the most ; while now you may walk across the country and stretch out either hand to gather in whatever you have a mind for. What do we not hear of our comrades who have gone with Sir John Hawkwood to Italy ? In one night they have held to ransom six hundred of the richest noblemen of Mantua. They camp before a great city, and the base burghers come forth with the keys, and then they make great spoil ; or, if it please them better, they take so many horse-loads of silver as a composition ; and so they journey on from state to state, rich and free and feared by all. Now, is not that the proper life for a soldier ? "

" The proper life for a robber ! " roared Hordle John, in his thundering voice.

" And yet there is much in what the Gascon says," said a swarthy fellow in a weather-stained doublet ; " and I for one would rather prosper in Italy than starve in Spain."

" You were always a cur and a traitor, Mark Shaw,"

cried Aylward. " By my hilt ! if you will stand forth and draw your sword I will warrant you that you will see neither one nor the other."

" Nay, Aylward," said Sir Nigel, " we cannot mend the matter by broiling. Sir Claude, I think that what you have said does you little honour, and if my words aggrieve you, I am ever ready to go deeper into the matter with you. But you shall have such men as will follow you, and you may go where you will, so that you come not with us. Let all who love their prince and country stand fast, while those who think more of a well-lined purse step forth upon the farther side."

Thirteen bowmen, with hung heads and sheepish faces, stepped forward with Mark Shaw and ranged themselves behind Sir Claude. Amid the hootings and hissings of their comrades, they marched off together to the Gascon's hut, while the main body broke up their meeting and set cheerily to work packing their possessions, furbishing their weapons, and preparing for the march which lay before them. Over the Tarn and the Garonne, through the vast quagmires of Armagnac, past the swift-flowing Losse, and so down the long valley of the Adour, there was many a long league to be crossed ere they could join themselves to that dark war-cloud which was drifting slowly southwards to the line of snowy peaks, beyond which the banner of England had never yet been seen.

33. *How the Army made the Passage of Roncesvalles*

THE whole vast plain of Gascony and of Languedoc is an arid and profitless expanse in winter, save where the swift-flowing Adour and her snow-fed tributaries, the Louts, the Oloron, and the Pau, run down to the sea of Biscay. South of the Adour the jagged line of mountains which fringe the sky-line send out long granite claws, running down into the lowlands and divid-

ing them into " gaves " or stretches of valley. Hillocks
grow into hills, and hills into mountains, each range over-
lying its neighbour, until they soar up in the giant chain
which raises its spotless and untrodden peaks, white and
dazzling, against the pale blue wintry sky.

A quiet land is this—a land where the slow-moving
Basque, with his flat biretta-cap, his red sash and his
hempen sandals, tills his scanty farm or drives his lean
flock to their hill-side pastures. It is the country of the
wolf and the isard, of the brown bear and the mountain-
goat, a land of bare rock and of rushing water. Yet here
it was that the will of a great prince had now assembled
a gallant army ; so that from the Ardour to the passes of
Navarre the barren valleys and wind-swept wastes were
populous with soldiers and loud with the shouting of
orders and the neighing of horses. For the banners of
war had been flung to the wind once more, and over those
glistening peaks was the highway along which Honour
pointed in an age when men had chosen her as their guide.

And now all was ready for the enterprise. From Dax to
St. Jean Pied-du-Port the country was mottled with the
white tents of Gascons, Aquitanians, and English, all eager
for the advance. From all sides the free companions had
trooped in, until not less than twelve thousand of these
veteran troops were cantoned along the frontiers of
Navarre. From England had arrived the prince's brother,
the Duke of Lancaster, with four hundred knights in his
train and a strong company of archers. Above all, an
heir to the throne had been born in Bordeaux, and the
prince might leave his spouse with an easy mind, for all
was well with mother and with child.

The keys of the mountain passes still lay in the hands
of the shifty and ignoble Charles of Navarre, who had
chaffered and bargained both with the English and with
the Spanish, taking money from the one side to hold them
open and from the other to keep them sealed. The mallet
hand of Edward, however, had shattered all the schemes
and wiles of the plotter. Neither entreaty nor courtly

remonstrance came from the English prince ; but Sir Hugh Calverley passed silently over the border with his company, and the blazing walls of the two cities of Miranda and Puenta de la Reyna warned the unfaithful monarch that there were other metals besides gold, and that he was dealing with a man to whom it was unsafe to lie.   His price was paid, his objections silenced, and the mountain gorges lay open to the invaders.   From the Feast of the Epiphany there was mustering and massing, until, in the first weeks of February—three days after the White Company joined the army—the word was given for a general advance through the defile of Roncesvalles.   At five in the cold winter's morning the bugles were blowing in the hamlet of St. Jean Pied-du-Port, and by six Sir Nigel's Company, three hundred strong, were on their way for the defile, pushing swiftly in the dim light up the steep curving road ; for it was the prince's order that they should be the first to pass through, and that they should remain on guard at the farther end until the whole army had emerged from the mountains.   Day was already breaking in the east, and the summits of the great peaks had turned rosy red, while the valleys still lay in the shadow, when they found themselves with the cliff on either hand and the long rugged pass stretching away before them.

Sir Nigel rode his great black war-horse at the head of his archers, dressed in full armour, with Black Simon bearing his banner behind him, while Alleyne at his bridle-arm carried his blazoned shield and his well-steeled ashen spear.   A proud and happy man was the knight, and many a time he turned in his saddle to look at the long column of bowmen who swung swiftly along behind him.

" By Saint Paul ! Alleyne," said he, " this pass is a very perilous place, and I would that the King of Navarre had held it against us, for it would have been a very honourable venture had it fallen to us to win a passage.   I have heard the minstrels sing of one Sir Roland who was slain by the infidels in these very parts."

" If it please you, my fair lord," said Black Simon, " I know something of these parts, for I have twice served a term with the King of Navarre. There is a hospice of monks yonder, where you may see the roof among the trees, and there it was that Sir Roland was slain. The village upon the left is Orbaiceta, and I know a house therein where the right wine of Jurançon is to be bought, if it would please you to quaff a morning cup."

" There is smoke yonder upon the right."

" That is a village named Les Aldudes, and I know a hostel there also where the wine is of the best. It is said that the innkeeper hath a buried treasure, and I doubt not, my fair lord, that if you grant me leave I could prevail upon him to tell us where he hath hid it."

" Nay, nay, Simon," said Sir Nigel curtly, " I pray you to forget these free-companion tricks. Ha ! Edricson, I see that you stare about you, and in good sooth these mountains must seem wondrous indeed to one who hath but seen Butser or the Portsdown Hill."

The broken and rugged road had wound along the crests of low hills, with wooded ridges on either side of it, over which peeped the loftier mountains, the distant Peak of the South and the vast Altabisca, which towered high above them and cast its black shadow from left to right across the valley. From where they now stood they could look forward down a long vista of beech woods and jagged rock-strewn wilderness, all white with snow, to where the pass opened out upon the uplands beyond. Behind them they could still catch a glimpse of the grey plains of Gascony, and could see her rivers gleaming like coils of silver in the sunshine. As far as eye could see from among the rocky gorges and the bristles of the pine woods there came the quick twinkle and glitter of steel, while the wind brought with it sudden distant bursts of martial music from the great host which rolled by every road and by-path towards the narrow pass of Roncesvalles. On the cliffs on either side might also be seen the flash of arms and the waving of pennons where the force of Navarre looked down upon the army of strangers who passed through their territories.

" By Saint Paul ! " said Sir Nigel, blinking up at them, " I think that we have much to hope for from these cavaliers, for they cluster very thickly upon our flanks. Pass word to the men, Aylward, that they unsling their bows, for I have no doubt that there are some very worthy gentlemen yonder who may give us some opportunity for honourable advancement."

" I hear that the prince hath the King of Navarre as hostage," said Alleyne, " and it is said that he hath sworn to put him to death if there be any attack upon us."

" It was not so that war was made when good King Edward first turned his hand to it," said Sir Nigel sadly. " Ah ! Alleyne, I fear that you will never live to see such things, for the minds of men are more set upon money and gain than of old. By Saint Paul ! it was a noble sight when two great armies would draw together upon a certain day, and all who had a vow would ride forth to discharge themselves of it. What noble spear-runnings have I not seen, and even in a humble way had a part in, when cavaliers would run a course for the easing of their souls and for the love of their ladies ! Never a bad word have I for the French, for, though I have ridden twenty times up to their array, I have never yet failed to find some very gentle and worthy knight or squire who was willing to do what he might to enable me to attempt some small feat of arms. Then, when all cavaliers had been satisfied, the two armies would come to hand-strokes, and fight right merrily until one or other had the vantage. By Saint Paul ! it was not our wont in those days to pay gold for the opening of passes, nor would we hold a king as hostage lest his people come to thrusts with us. In good sooth, if the war is to be carried out in such a fashion, then it is grief to me that I ever came away from Castle Twynham, for I would not have left my sweet lady had I not thought that there were deeds of arms to be done."

" But surely, my fair lord," said Alleyne, " you have

done some great feats of arms since we left the Lady Loring."

" I cannot call any to mind," answered Sir Nigel.

" There was the taking of the sea-rovers and the holding of the keep against the Jacks."

" Nay, nay," said the knight, " these were not feats of arms, but mere wayside ventures and the chances of travel. By Saint Paul ! if it were not that these hills are over steep for Pommers, I would ride to these cavaliers of Navarre and see if there were not some among them who would help me to take this patch from mine eye. It is a sad sight to me to see this very fine pass, which my own Company here could hold against an army, and yet to ride through it with as little profit as though it were the lane from my kennels to the Avon."

All morning Sir Nigel rode in a very ill-humour, with his Company tramping behind him. It was a toilsome march over broken ground and through snow, which came often as high as the knee, yet ere the sun had begun to sink they had reached the spot where the gorge opens out on to the uplands of Navarre, and could see the towers of Pampeluna jutting up against the Southern sky-line. Here the Company were quartered in a scattered mountain hamlet, and Alleyne spent the day looking down upon the swarming army which poured with gleam of spears and flaunt of standards through the narrow pass.

" Holà ! mon gar," said Aylward, seating himself upon a boulder by his side. " This is indeed a sight upon which it is good to look, and a man might go far ere he would see so many brave men and fine horses. By my hilt ! our little lord is wroth because we have come peacefully through the passes, but I will warrant him that we have fighting enow ere we turn our faces northward again. It is said that there are fourscore thousand men behind the King of Spain, with Du Guesclin and all the best lances of France, who have sworn to shed their heart's blood ere this Pedro come again to the throne."

" Yet our own army is a great one," said Alleyne.

" Nay, there are but seven-and-twenty thousand men. Chandos hath persuaded the prince to leave many behind, and indeed I think that he is right, for there is little food and less water in these parts for which we are bound. A man without his meat or a horse without his fodder is like a wet bow-string, fit for little. But voilà, mon petit, here come Chandos and his company, and there is many a pensil and banderole among yonder squadrons which show that the best blood of England is riding under his banners."

Whilst Aylward had been speaking, a strong column of archers had defiled through the pass beneath them. They were followed by a banner-bearer who held high the scarlet wedge upon a silver field which proclaimed the presence of the famous warrior. He rode himself within a spear's-length of his standard, clad from neck to foot in steel, but draped in the long linen gown or parement which was destined to be the cause of his death. His plumed hat was carried behind him by his body-squire and his head was covered by a small purple cap, from under which his snow-white hair curled downwards to his shoulders. With his long beak-like nose and his single gleaming eye, which shone brightly from under a thick tuft of grizzled brow, he seemed to Alleyne to have something of the look of some fierce old bird of prey. For a moment he smiled, as his eye lit upon the banner of the five roses waving from the hamlet ; but his course lay for Pampeluna and he rode after the archers.

Close at his heels came sixteen squires, all chosen from the highest families, and behind them rode twelve hundred English knights, with gleam of steel and tossing of plumes, their harness jingling, their long straight swords clanking against their stirrup-irons, and the beat of their chargers' hoofs like the low deep roar of the sea upon the shore. Behind them marched six hundred Cheshire and Lancashire archers, bearing the badge of the Audleys, followed by the famous Lord Audley himself, with the four valiant squires, Dutton of Dutton, Delves of Doddington, Fowlehurst of Crewe, and Hawkestone of

Wainehill, who had all won such glory at Poictiers. Two hundred heavily armed cavalry rode behind the Audley standard, while close at their heels came the Duke of Lancaster with a glittering train, heralds tabarded with the royal arms riding three deep upon cream-coloured chargers in front of him. On either side of the young prince rode the two Seneschals of Aquitaine, Sir Guiscard d'Angle and Sir Stephen Cossington, the one bearing the banner of the province and the other that of Saint George. Away behind him as far as eye could reach rolled the far-stretching, unbroken river of steel—rank after rank and column after column, with waving of plumes, glitter of arms, tossing of guidons, and flash and flutter of countless armorial devices. All day Alleyne looked down upon the changing scene, and all day the old bowman stood by his elbow, pointing out the crests of famous warriors and the arms of noble houses. Here were the gold mullets of the Pakingtons, the sable and ermine of the Mackworths, the scarlet bars of the Wakes, the gold and blue of the Grosvenors, the cinque-foils of the Cliftons, the annulets of the Musgraves, the silver pinions of the Beauchamps, the crosses of the Molineaux, the bloody chevron of the Woodhouses, the red and silver of the Worsleys, the swords of the Clarks, the boars'-heads of the Lucies, the crescents of the Boyntons, and the wolf and dagger of the Lipscombs. So through the sunny winter day the chivalry of England poured down through the dark pass of Roncesvalles to the plains of Spain.

It was on a Monday that the Duke of Lancaster's division passed safely through the Pyrenees. On the Tuesday there was a bitter frost, and the ground rung like iron beneath the feet of the horses ; yet ere evening the prince himself, with the main battle of his army, had passed the gorge and united with his vanguard at Pampeluna. With him rode the King of Majorca, the hostage King of Navarre, and the fierce Don Pedro of Spain, whose pale blue eyes gleamed with a sinister light as they rested once more upon the distant peaks of the land which had disowned him. Under the royal banners rode many a bold Gascon baron and many a hot-blooded islander. Here were the high stewards of Aquitaine, of Saintonge, of La Rochelle, of Quercy, of Limousin, of Agenois, of Poitou, and of Bigorre, with the banners and musters of their provinces. Here also were the valiant Earl of Angus, Sir Thomas Banaster with his garter over his greave, Sir Nele Loring, second cousin to Sir Nigel, and a long column of Welsh footmen who marched under the red banner of Merlin. From dawn to sundown the long train wound through the pass, their breath reeking up upon the frosty air like the steam from a caldron.

The weather was less keen upon the Wednesday, and the rearguard made good their passage, with the bombards and the waggon-train. Free companions and Gascons made up this portion of the army to the number of ten thousand men. The fierce Sir Hugh Calverley with his yellow mane, and the rugged Sir Robert Knolles, with their war-hardened and veteran companies of English bowmen, headed the long column, while behind them came the turbulent band of the Bastard of Breteuil, Nandon de Bagerant, one-eyed Camus, Black Ortingo, La Nuit, and others whose very names seem to smack of hard hands and ruthless deeds. With them also were the pick of the Gascon chivalry—the old Duc d'Armagnac, his nephew Lord d'Albret, brooding and scowling over his wrongs, the giant Oliver de Clisson, the Captal de Buch, pink of knighthood, the sprightly Sir Perducas d'Albret, the red-bearded Lord d'Esparre, and a long train of needy and grasping border nobles, with long pedigrees and short purses, who had come down from their hill-side strongholds, all hungering for the spoils and the ransoms of Spain. By the Thursday morning the whole army was encamped in the Vale of Pampeluna, and the prince had called his council to meet him in the old palace of the ancient city of Navarre.

34. *How the Company made Sport in the Vale of Pampeluna*

WHILST the council was sitting in Pampeluna the White Company, having encamped in a neighbouring valley, close to the companies of La Nuit and Black Ortingo, were amusing themselves at sword-play, wrestling, and shooting at the shields, which they had placed upon the hill-side to serve them as butts. The younger archers, with their coats of mail thrown aside, their brown or flaxen hair tossing in the wind, and their jerkins turned back to give free play to their brawny chests and arms, stood in lines, each loosing his shaft in turn, while Johnston, Aylward, Black Simon, and half a score of the elders lounged up and down with critical eyes, and a word of rough praise or of curt censure for the marksmen. Behind stood knots of Gascon and Brabant crossbowmen from the companies of Ortingo and of La Nuit, leaning upon their unsightly weapons and watching the practice of the Englishmen.

" A good shot, Hewett, a good shot ! " said old Johnston to a young bowman who stood with his bow in his left hand, gazing with parted lips after his flying shaft. " You see, she finds the ring, as I knew she would from the moment that your string twanged."

" Loose it easy, steady, and yet sharp," said Aylward. " By my hilt ! mon gar, it is very well when you do but shoot at a shield, but when there is a man behind the shield and he rides at you with wave of sword and glint of eyes from behind his vizor, you may find him a less easy mark."

" It is a mark that I have found before now," answered the young bowman.

" And shall again, camarade, I doubt not. But holà ! Johnston, who is this who holds his bow like a crow-keeper ? "

" It is Silas Peterson, of Horsham. Do not wink with

one eye and look with the other, Silas, and do not hop and dance after you shoot, with your tongue out, for that will not speed it upon its way. Stand straight and firm, as God made you. Move not the bow-arm, and steady with the drawing hand."

" I' faith," said Black Simon, " I am a spearman myself and am more fitted for hand-strokes than for such work as this. Yet I have spent my days among bowmen, and I have seen many a brave shaft sped. I will not say but that we have some good marksmen here, and that this Company would be accounted a fine body of archers at any time or place. Yet I do not see any men who bend so strong a bow or shoot as true a shaft as those whom I have known."

" You say sooth," said Johnston, turning his seamed and grizzled face upon the man-at-arms. " See yonder," he added, pointing to a bombard which lay within the camp : " there is what hath done scath to good bowmanship, with its filthy soot and foolish roaring mouth. I wonder that a true knight, like our prince, should carry such a scurvy thing in his train. Robin, thou red-headed lurden, how oft must I tell thee not to shoot straight with a quarter wind blowing across the mark ? "

" By these ten finger-bones ! there were some fine bowmen at the intaking of Calais," said Aylward. " I well remember that, on occasion of an outfall, a Genoan raised his arm over his mantlet and shook it at us, a hundred paces from our line. There were twenty who loosed shafts at him, and when the man was afterwards slain, it was found that he had taken eighteen through his forearm."

" And I can call to mind," remarked Johnston, " that when the great cog ' Christopher,' which the French had taken from us, was moored two hundred paces from the shore, two archers, little Robin Withstaff and Elias Baddlesmere, in four shots each cut every strand of her hempen anchor-cord, so that she well-nigh came upon the rocks."

" Good shooting, i' faith, rare shooting," said Black

Simon. "But I have seen you, Johnston, and you, Samkin Aylward, and one or two others who are still with us, shoot as well as the best. Was it not you, Johnston, who took the fat ox at Finsbury butts against the pick of London town ? "

A sunburnt and black-eyed Brabanter had stood near the old archers, leaning upon a large crossbow and listening to their talk, which had been carried on in that hybrid camp dialect which both nations could understand. He was a squat, bull-necked man, clad in the iron helmet, mail tunic, and woollen gambesson of his class. A jacket with hanging sleeves, slashed with velvet at the neck and wrists, showed that he was a man of some consideration, an under-officer, or file-leader of his company.

" I cannot think," said he, " why you English should be so fond of your six-foot stick. If it amuse you to bend it, well and good ; but why should I strain and pull, when my little moulinet will do all for me, and better than I can do it for myself ? "

" I have seen good shooting with the prod and with the latch," said Aylward, " but, by my hilt ! camarade, with all respect to you and to your bow, I think that is but a woman's weapon, which a woman can point and loose as easily as a man."

" I know not about that," answered the Brabanter, " but this I know, that though I have served for fourteen years, I have never yet seen an Englishman do aught with the long-bow which I could not do better with my arbalest. By the three kings ! I would even go further, and say that I have done things with my arbalest which no Englishman could do with his long-bow."

" Well said, mon gar," cried Aylward. " A good cock has ever a brave call. Now, I have shot little of late, but there is Johnston here who will try a round with you for the honour of the Company."

" And I will lay a gallon of Jurançon wine upon the long-bow," said Black Simon, " though I had rather, for my own drinking, that it were a quart of Twynham ale."

" I take both your challenge and your wager," said the man of Brabant, throwing off his jacket, and glancing keenly about him with his black twinkling eyes. " I cannot see any fitting mark, for I care not to waste a bolt on these shields, which a drunken boor could not miss at a village kermesse."

" This is a perilous man," whispered an English man-at-arms, plucking at Aylward's sleeve. " He is the best marksman of all the crossbow companies, and it was he who brought down the Constable de Bourbon at Brignais. I fear that your man will come by little honour with him."

" Yet I have seen Johnston shoot this twenty years, and I will not flinch from it. How say you, old war-hound, will you not have a flight shot or two with this springald ? "

" Tut, tut, Aylward," said the old bowman. " My day is past, and it is for the younger ones to hold what we have gained. I take it unkindly of thee, Samkin, that thou shouldst call all eyes thus upon a broken bowman who could once shoot a fair shaft. Let me feel that bow, Wilkins ! It is a Scotch bow, I see, for the upper neck is without and the lower within. By the black rood ! it is a good piece of yew, well nocked, well strung, well waxed, and very joyful to the feel. I think even now that I might hit any large and goodly mark with a bow like this. Turn thy quiver to me, Aylward. I love an ash arrow pierced with cornel-wood for a roving shaft."

" By my hilt ! and so do I," cried Aylward. " These three gander-winged shafts are such."

" So I see, comrade. It has been my wont to choose a saddle-backed feather for a dead shaft, and a swine-backed for a smooth flier. I will take the two of them. Ah ! Samkin, lad, the eye grows dim and the hand less firm as the years pass."

" Come then, are you not ready ? " said the Brabanter, who had watched with ill-concealed impatience the slow and methodic movements of his antagonist.

" I will venture a rover with you, or try long-butts or hoyles," said old Johnston. " To my mind the long-bow is a better weapon than the arbalest, but it may be ill for me to prove it."

" So I think," quoth the other with a sneer. He drew his moulinet from his girdle, and, fixing it to the windlass, he drew back the powerful double cord until it had clicked into the catch. Then from his quiver he drew a short thick quarrel, which he placed with the utmost care upon the groove. Word had spread of what was going forward, and the rivals were already surrounded, not only by the English archers of the Company, but by hundreds of arbalestiers and men-at-arms from the bands of Ortingo and La Nuit, to the latter of which the Brabanter belonged.

" There is a mark yonder on the hill," said he ; " mayhap you can discern it."

" I see something," answered Johnston, shading his eyes with his hand ; " but it is a very long shoot."

" A fair shoot—a fair shoot ! Stand aside, Arnaud, lest you find a bolt through your gizzard. Now, comrade, I take no flight shot, and I give you the vantage of watching my shaft."

As he spoke he raised his arbalest to his shoulder and was about to pull the trigger, when a large grey stork flapped heavily into view, skimming over the brow of the hill, and then soaring up into the air to pass the valley. Its shrill and piercing cries drew all eyes upon it, and, as it came nearer, a dark spot which circled above it resolved itself into a peregrine falcon, which hovered over its head, poising itself from time to time, and watching its chance of closing with its clumsy quarry. Nearer and nearer came the two birds, all absorbed in their own contest, the stork wheeling upwards, the hawk still fluttering above it, until they were not a hundred paces from the camp. The Brabanter raised his weapon to the sky, and there came the short deep twang of his powerful string. His bolt struck the stork just where its wing meets the body, and the bird whirled aloft in a last convulsive flutter before falling wounded and flapping to the earth. A roar of applause burst from the cross-bowmen ; but at the instant that the bolt struck its mark old Johnston, who had stood listlessly with arrow on string, bent his bow and sped a shaft through the body of the falcon. Whipping the other from his belt, he set it skimming some few feet from the earth with so true an aim that it struck and transfixed the stork for the second time ere it could reach the ground. A deep-chested shout of delight burst from the archers at the sight of this double feat, and Aylward, dancing with joy, threw his arms round the old marksman and embraced him with such vigour that their mail tunics clanged again.

" Ah ! camarade," he cried, " you shall have a stoup with me for this ! What then, old dog, would not the hawk please thee, but thou must have the stork as well ? Oh, to my heart again ! "

" It is a pretty piece of yew, and well strung," said Johnston with a twinkle in his deep-set grey eyes. " Even an old broken bowman might find the clout with a bow like this."

" You have done very well," remarked the Brabanter in a surly voice. " But it seems to me that you have not yet shown yourself to be a better marksman than I, for I have struck that at which I aimed, and, by the three kings ! no man can do more."

" It would ill beseem me to claim to be a better marksman," answered Johnston, " for I have heard great things of your skill. I did but wish to show that the long-bow could do that which an arbalest could not do, for you could not with your moulinet have your string ready to speed another shaft ere the bird drop to the earth."

" In that you have vantage," said the crossbowman. " By Saint James ! it is now my turn to show you where my weapon has the better of you. I pray you to draw a flight shaft with all your strength down the valley, that we may see the length of your shoot."

" That is a very strong prod of yours," said Johnston, shaking his grizzled head as he glanced at the thick arch and powerful strings of his rival's arbalest. " I have little doubt that you can overshoot me, and yet I have seen bowmen who could send a cloth-yard arrow further than you could speed a quarrel."

" So I have heard," remarked the Brabanter ; " and yet it is a strange thing that these wondrous bowmen are never where I chance to be. Pace out the distances with a wand, at every five-score, and do you, Arnaud, stand at the fifth wand to carry back my bolts to me."

A line was measured down the valley, and Johnston, drawing an arrow to the very head, sent it whistling over the row of wands.

" Bravely drawn ! A rare shoot ! " shouted the by-standers. " It is well up to the fourth mark."

" By my hilt ! it is over it," cried Aylward. " I can see where they have stooped to gather up the shaft."

" We shall hear anon," said Johnston quietly, and presently a young archer came running to say that the arrow had fallen twenty paces beyond the fourth wand.

" Four hundred paces and a score," cried Black Simon. " I' faith it is a very long flight. Yet wood and steel may do more than flesh and blood."

The Brabanter stepped forward with a smile of conscious triumph, and loosed the cord of his weapon. A shout burst from his comrades as they watched the swift and lofty flight of the heavy bolt.

" Over the fourth ! " groaned Aylward. " By my hilt ! I think that it is well up to the fifth."

" It is over the fifth ! " cried a Gascon loudly, and a comrade came running with waving arms to say that the bolt had pitched eight paces beyond the mark of the five hundred.

" Which weapon hath the vantage now ? " cried the Brabanter, strutting proudly about with shouldered arbalest, amid the applause of his companions.

" You can overshoot me," said Johnston, gently.

" Or any other man who ever bent a long-bow," cried his victorious adversary.

" Nay, not so fast," said a huge archer, whose mighty shoulders and red head towered high above the throng of his comrades. " I must have a word with you ere you crow so loudly. Where is my little popper ? By sainted Dick of Hampole ! it will be a strange thing if I cannot outshoot that thing of thine, which to my eyes is more like a rat-trap than a bow. Will you try another flight, or do you stand by your last ? "

" Five hundred and eight paces will serve my turn," answered the Brabanter, looking askance at this new opponent.

" Tut, John," whispered Aylward, " you never were a marksman. Why must you thrust your spoon into this dish ? "

" Easy and slow, Aylward. There are very many things which I cannot do, but there are also one or two which I have the trick of. It is in my mind that I can beat this shoot, if my bow will but hold together."

" Go on, old babe of the woods ! Have at it, Hampshire ! " cried the archers, laughing.

" By my soul ! you may grin," cried John. " But I learned how to make the long shoot from old Hob Miller of Milford."

He took up a great black bow as he spoke, and sitting down upon the ground he placed his two feet on either end of the stave. With an arrow fitted, he then pulled the string towards him with both hands until the head of the shaft was level with the wood. The great bow creaked and groaned and the cord vibrated with the tension.

" Who is this fool's-head who stands in the way of my shoot ? " said he, craning up his neck from the ground.

" He stands on the further side of my mark," answered the Brabanter, " so he has little to fear from you."

" Well, the saints assoil him ! " cried John. " Though I think he is over near to be scathed." As he spoke he raised his two feet, with the bow-stave upon their soles, and his cord twanged with a deep rich hum which might be heard across the valley. The measurer in the distance fell flat upon his face, and then, jumping up again, began to run in the opposite direction.

" Well shot, old lad ! It is indeed over his head," cried the bowmen.

" Mon Dieu ! " exclaimed the Brabanter, " who ever saw such a shoot ! "

" It is but a trick," quoth John. " Many a time have I won a gallon of ale by covering a mile in three flights down Wilverley Chase."

" It fell a hundred and thirty paces beyond the fifth mark," shouted an archer in the distance.

" Six hundred and thirty paces ! Mon Dieu ! but that is a shoot ! And yet it says nothing for your weapon, mon gros camarade, for it was by turning yourself into a cross-bow that you did it."

" By my hilt ! there is truth in that," cried Aylward. " And now, friend, I will myself show you a vantage of the longbow. I pray you to speed a bolt against yonder shield with all your force. It is an inch of elm with bull's hide over it."

" I scarce shot as many shafts at Brignais," growled the man of Brabant ; " though I found a better mark there than a cantle of bull's hide. But what is this, English-man ? The shield hangs not one hundred paces from me, and a blind man could strike it." He screwed up his string to the farthest pitch, and shot his quarrel at the dangling shield. Aylward, who had drawn an arrow from his quiver, carefully greased the head of it, and sped it at the same mark.

" Run, Wilkins," quoth he, " and fetch me the shield."

Long were the faces of the Englishmen and broad the laugh of the crossbowmen as the heavy mantlet was carried towards them, for there in the centre was the thick Brabant bolt driven deeply into the wood, while there was neither sign nor trace of the cloth-yard shaft.

" By the three kings ! " cried the Brabanter, " this time at least there is no gainsaying which is the better weapon, or which the truer hand that held it. You have missed the shield, Englishman."

" Tarry a bit ! Tarry a bit, mon gar ! " quoth Aylward, and turning round the shield he showed a round clear hole in the wood at the back of it. " My shaft has passed through it, camarade, and I trow the one which goes through is more to be feared than that which bides on the way."

The Brabanter stamped his foot with mortification, and was about to make some angry reply, when Alleyne Edricson came riding up to the crowds of archers.

" Sir Nigel will be here anon," said he, " and it is his wish to speak with the Company."

In an instant order and method took the place of general confusion. Bows, steel caps, and jacks were caught up from the grass. A long cordon cleared the camp of all strangers, while the main body fell into four lines with under-officers and file-leaders in front and on either flank. So they stood, silent and motionless, when their leader came riding towards them, his face shining and his whole small figure swelling with the news which he bore.

" Great honour has been done to us, men," cried he : " for of all the army, the prince has chosen us out that we should ride onwards into the lands of Spain to spy upon our enemies. Yet, as there are many of us, and as the service may not be to the liking of all, I pray that those will step forward from the ranks who have the will to follow me."

There was a rustle among the bowmen, but when Sir Nigel looked up at them no man stood forward from his fellows, but the four lines of men stretched unbroken as before. Sir Nigel blinked at them in amazement, and a look of the deepest sorrow shadowed his face.

" That I should have lived to see the day ! " he cried. " What ! not one——"

" My fair lord," whispered Alleyne, " they have all stepped forward."

" Ah, by Saint Paul ! I see how it is with them. I

could not think that they would desert me. We start at dawn to-morrow, and ye are to have the horses of Sir Robert Cheney's company. Be ready, I pray ye, at early cock-crow."

A buzz of delight burst from the archers, as they broke their ranks and ran hither and thither, whooping and cheering like boys who have news of a holiday. Sir Nigel gazed after them with a smiling face, when a heavy hand fell upon his shoulder.

"What ho! my knight-errant of Twynham!" said a voice. "You are off to Ebro, I hear; and, by the holy fish of Tobias! you must take me under your banner."

"What! Sir Oliver Buttesthorn!" cried Sir Nigel. "I had heard that you were come into camp, and had hoped to see you. Glad and proud shall I be to have you with me."

"I have a most particular and weighty reason for wishing to go," said the sturdy knight.

"I can well believe it," returned Sir Nigel; "I have met no man who is quicker to follow where honour leads."

"Nay, it is not for honour that I go, Nigel."

"For what then?"

"For pullets."

"Pullets?"

"Yes, for the rascal vanguard have cleared every hen from the country-side. It was this very morning that Norbury, my squire, lamed his horse in riding round in quest of one, for we have a bag of truffles, and nought to eat with them. Never have I seen such locusts as this vanguard of ours. Not a pullet shall we see until we are in front of them; so I shall leave my Winchester runa-gates to the care of the provost-marshal, and I shall hie south with you, Nigel, with my truffles at my saddle-bow."

"Oliver, Oliver, I know you over well," said Sir Nigel, shaking his head, and the two old soldiers rode off to-gether to their pavilion.

35. *How Sir Nigel Hawked at an Eagle*

TO the south of Pampeluna in the kingdom of Navarre there stretched a high table-land, rising into bare, sterile hills, brown or grey in colour, and strewn with huge boulders of granite. On the Gascon side of the great mountains there had been running streams, meadows, forests, and little nestling villages. Here, on the contrary, were nothing but naked rocks, poor pasture, and savage stone-strewn wastes. Gloomy defiles or barrancas intersected this wild country with mountain torrents dashing and foaming between their rugged sides. The clatter of waters, the scream of the eagle, and the howling of wolves, were the only sounds which broke upon the silence in that dreary and inhospitable region.

Through this wild country it was that Sir Nigel and his Company pushed their way, riding at times through vast defiles where the brown gnarled cliffs shot up on either side of them, and the sky was but a long winding blue slit between the clustering lines of box which fringed the lips of the precipices ; or again leading their horses along the narrow and rocky paths worn by the muleteers upon the edges of the chasm, where under their very elbows they could see the white streak which marked the *gave* which foamed a thousand feet below them. So for two days they pushed their way through the wild places of Navarre, past Fuente, over the rapid Ega, through Estella, until upon a winter's evening the mountains fell away from in front of them, and they saw the broad blue Ebro curving betwixt its double line of homesteads and of villages. The fishers of Viana were aroused that night by rough voices speaking in a strange tongue, and ere morning Sir Nigel and his men had ferried the river and were safe upon the land of Spain.

All the next day they lay in a pine wood near to the town of Logrono, resting their horses and taking counsel as to what they should do. Sir Nigel had with him Sir William Felton, Sir Oliver Buttesthorn, stout old Sir Simon Burley, the Scotch knight-errant, the Earl of Angus, and Sir Richard Causton, all accounted among the bravest knights in the army, together with sixty veteran men-at-arms, and three hundred and twenty archers. Spies had been sent out in the morning, and returned after nightfall to say that the King of Spain was encamped some fourteen miles off in the direction of Burgos, having with him twenty thousand horse and forty-five thousand foot.

A dry-wood fire had been lit, and round this the leaders crouched, the glare beating upon their rugged faces, while the hardy archers lounged and chattered amid the tethered horses, while they munched their scanty provisions.

" For my part," said Sir Simon Burley, " I am of opinion that we have already done that which we have come for. For do we not now know where the king is, and how great a following he hath, which was the end of our journey ? "

" True," answered Sir William Felton, " but I have come on this venture because it is a long time since I have broken a spear in war, and, certes, I shall not go back until I have run a course with some cavalier of Spain. Let those go back who will, but I must see more of these Spaniards ere I turn."

" I will not leave you, Sir William," returned Sir Simon Burley ; " and yet, as an old soldier and one who hath seen much of war, I cannot but think that it is an ill thing for four hundred men to find themselves between an army of sixty thousand on the one side and a broad river on the other."

" Yet," said Sir Richard Causton, " we cannot for the honour of England go back without a blow struck."

" Nor for the honour of Scotland either," cried the Earl of Angus. " By Saint Andrew ! I wish that I may never set eyes upon the water of Leith again, if I pluck my horse's bridle ere I have seen this camp of theirs."

" By Saint Paul ! you have spoken very well," said Sir

Nigel, " and I have always heard that there were very worthy gentlemen among the Scots, and fine skirmishing to be had upon their border. Bethink you, Sir Simon, that we have this news from the lips of common spies, who can scarce tell us as much of the enemy and of his forces as the prince would wish to hear."

" You are the leader in this venture, Sir Nigel," the other answered, " and I do but ride under your banner."

" Yet I would fain have your rede and counsel, Sir Simon. But, touching what you say of the river, we can take heed that we shall not have it at the back of us, for the prince hath now advanced to Salvatierra, and thence to Vittoria, so that if we come upon their camp from the further side we can make good our retreat."

" What then would you propose ? " asked Sir Simon, shaking his grizzled head as one who is but half convinced.

" That we ride forward ere the news reach them that we have crossed the river. In this way we may have sight of their army, and perchance even find occasion for some small deed against them."

" So be it, then," said Sir Simon Burley ; and the rest of the council having approved, a scanty meal was hurriedly snatched, and the advance resumed under the cover of the darkness. All night they led their horses, stumbling and groping through wild defiles and rugged valleys, following the guidance of a frightened peasant who was strapped by the wrist to Black Simon's stirrup-leather. With the early dawn they found themselves in a black ravine, with others sloping away from it on either side, and the bare brown crags rising in long bleak terraces all round them.

" If it please you, fair lord," said Black Simon, " this man hath misled us, and since there is no tree upon which we may hang him, it might be well to hurl him over yonder cliff."

The peasant, reading the soldier's meaning in his fierce eyes and harsh accents, dropped upon his knees, screaming loudly for mercy.

" How comes it, dog ? " asked Sir William Felton in
Spanish. " Where is this camp to which you swore that
you would lead us ? "

" By the sweet Virgin ! By the blessed Mother of
God ! " cried the trembling peasant, " I swear to you that
in the darkness I have myself lost the path."

" Over the cliff with him ! " shouted half a dozen
voices ; but ere the archers could drag him from the rocks
to which he clung Sir Nigel had ridden up and called upon
them to stop.

" How is this, sirs ? " said he. " As long as the prince
doth me the honour to entrust this venture to me, it is for
me only to give orders ; and, by Saint Paul ! I shall be
right blithe to go very deeply into the matter with anyone
to whom my words may give offence. How say you, Sir
William ? Or you, my Lord of Angus ? Or you, Sir
Richard ? "

" Nay, nay, Nigel ! " cried Sir William. " This base
peasant is too small a matter for old comrades to quarrel
over. But he hath betrayed us, and certes he hath merited
a dog's death."

" Hark ye, fellow," said Sir Nigel. " We give you one
more chance to find the path. We are about to gain much
honour, Sir William, in this enterprise, and it would be a
sorry thing if the first blood shed were that of an unworthy boor. Let us say our morning orisons, and it may
chance that ere we finish he may strike upon the track."

With bowed heads and steel caps in hand the archers
stood at their horses' heads, while Sir Simon Burley repeated the Pater, the Ave, and the Credo. Long did
Alleyne bear the scene in mind—the knot of knights in
their dull leaden-hued armour, the ruddy visage of Sir
Oliver, the craggy features of the Scottish earl, the shining
scalp of Sir Nigel, with the dense ring of hard bearded
faces and the long brown heads of the horses, all topped
and circled by the beetling cliffs. Scarce had the last
deep " Amen " broken from the Company, when, in an
instant, there rose the scream of a hundred bugles, with

378

the deep rolling of drums and the clashing of cymbals, all sounding together in one deafening uproar. Knights and archers sprang to arms, convinced that some great host was upon them ; but the guide dropped upon his knees and thanked heaven for its mercies.

" We have found them, caballeros ! " he cried. " This is their morning call. If ye will but deign to follow me, I will set them before you ere a man might tell his beads."

As he spoke he scrambled down one of the narrow ravines, and, climbing over a low ridge at the farther end, he led them into a short valley with a stream purling down the centre of it and a very thick growth of elder and of box upon either side. Pushing their way through the dense brushwood, they looked out upon a scene which made their hears beat harder and their breath come faster.

In front of them there lay a broad plain watered by two winding streams and covered with grass, stretching away to where, in the farthest distance, the towers of Burgos bristled up against the light blue morning sky. Over all this vast meadow there lay a great city of tents— thousands upon thousands of them laid out in streets and in squares like a well-ordered town. High silken pavilions or coloured marquees, shooting up from among the crowd of meaner dwellings, marked where the great lords and barons of Leon and Castile displayed their standards, while over the white roofs, as far as eye could reach, the waving of ancients, pavons, pensils, and banderoles, with flash of gold and glow of colours, proclaimed that all the chivalry of Iberia were mustered in the plain beneath them. Far off, in the centre of the camp, a huge palace of red and white silk with the royal arms of Castile waving from the summit, announced that the gallant Henry lay there in the midst of his warriors.

As the English adventurers, peeping out from behind their brushwood screen, looked down upon this wondrous sight, they could see that the vast army in front of them was already afoot. The first pink light of the rising sun glittered upon the steel caps and breastplates of dense masses of slingers and of crossbowmen, who drilled and marched in the spaces which had been left for their exercise. A thousand columns of smoke reeked up into the pure morning air where the faggots were piled and the camp-kettles already simmering. In the open plain clouds of light horse galloped and swooped with swaying bodies and waving javelins, after the fashion which the Spanish had adopted from their Moorish enemies. All along by the sedgy banks of the rivers long lines of pages led their masters' chargers down to water, while the knights themselves lounged in gaily dressed groups about the doors of their pavilions, or rode out, with their falcons upon their wrists and their greyhounds behind them, in quest of quail or of leveret.

" By my hilt ! mon gar ! " whispered Aylward to Alleyne, as the young squire stood with parted lips and wondering eyes gazing down at the novel scene before him, " we have been seeking them all night, but now that we have found them I know not what we are to do with them."

" You say sooth, Samkin," quoth old Johnston. " I would that we were upon the far side of Ebro again, for there is neither honour nor profit to be gained here. What say you, Simon ? "

" By the rood ! " cried the fierce man-at-arms, " I will see the colour of their blood ere I turn my mare's head for the mountains. Am I a child that I should ride for three days and nought but words at the end of it ? "

" Well said, my sweet honeysuckle ! " cried Hordle John. " I am with you, like hilt to blade. Could I but lay hands upon one of those gay prancers yonder, I doubt not that I should have ransom enough from him to buy my mother a new cow."

" A cow ! " said Aylward. " Say rather ten acres and a homestead on the banks of Avon."

" Say you so ? Then, by Our Lady ! here is for yonder one in the red jerkin."

He was about to push recklessly forward into the open, when Sir Nigel himself darted in front of him, with his hand upon his breast.

" Back ! " said he. " Our time is not yet come, and we must lie here until evening. Throw off your jacks and headpieces, lest their eyes catch the shine, and tether the horses among the rocks."

The order was swiftly obeyed, and in ten minutes the archers were stretched along by the side of the brook, munching the bread and the bacon which they had brought in their bags, and craning their necks to watch the ever-changing scene beneath them. Very quiet and still they lay, save for a muttered jest or whispered order, for twice during the long morning they heard bugle-calls from amid the hills on either side of them, which showed that they had thrust themselves in beween the outposts of the enemy. The leaders sat amongst the box-wood, and took counsel together as to what they should do ; while from below there surged up the buzz of voices, the shouting, the neighing of horses and all the uproar of a great camp.

" What boots it to wait ? " said Sir William Felton. " Let us ride down upon their camp ere they discover us."

" And so say I," cried the Scottish earl ; " for they do not know that there is any enemy within thirty long leagues of them."

" For my part," said Sir Simon Burley, " I think that it is madness, for you cannot hope to rout this great army ; and where are you to go and what are you to do when they have turned upon you ? How say you, Sir Oliver Buttesthorn ? "

" By the apple of Eve ! " cried the fat knight, " it appears to me that this wind brings a very savoury smell of garlic and of onions from their cooking-kettles. I am in favour of riding down upon them at once, if my old friend and comrade here is of the same mind."

" Nay," said Sir Nigel, " I have a plan by which we may attempt some small deed upon them, and yet, by the help of God, may be able to draw off again ; which, as Sir Simon Burley hath said, would be scarce possible in any other way."

" How then, Sir Nigel ? " asked several voices.

" We shall lie here all day ; for amid this brushwood it is ill for them to see us. Then, when evening comes, we shall sally out upon them and see if we may not gain some honourable advancement from them."

" But why then rather than now ? "

" Because we shall have nightfall to cover us when we draw off, so that we may make our way back through the mountains. I would station a score of archers here in the pass, with all our pennons jutting forth from the rocks, and as many nakirs and drums and bugles as we have with us, so that those who follow us in the fading light may think that the whole army of the prince is upon them, and fear to go further. What think you of my plan, Sir Simon ? "

" By my troth ! I think very well of it," cried the prudent old commander. " If four hundred men must needs run a tilt against sixty thousand, I cannot see how they can do it better or more safely."

" And so say I," cried Felton, heartily. " But I wish the day were over, for it will be an ill thing for us if they chance to light upon us."

The words were scarce out of his mouth when there came a clatter of loose stones, the sharp clink of trotting hoofs, and a dark-faced cavalier, mounted upon a white horse, burst through the bushes and rode swiftly down the valley from the end which was farthest from the Spanish camp. Lightly armed, with his vizor open and a hawk perched upon his left wrist, he looked about him with the careless air of a man who is bent wholly upon pleasure, and unconscious of the possibility of danger. Suddenly, however, his eyes lit upon the fierce faces which glared out at him from the brushwood. With a cry of terror, he thrust his spurs into his horse's sides and dashed for the narrow opening of the gorge. For a moment it seemed as though he would have reached it, for he had trampled over or dashed aside the archers who threw themselves in his way ; but Hordle John seized him by the foot in his grasp of iron and dragged him from the saddle, while two others caught the frightened horse.

"Ho, ho ! " roared the great archer. "How many cows wilt buy my mother, if I set thee free ? "

"Hush that bull's bellowing ! " cried Sir Nigel impatiently. "Bring the man here. By Saint Paul ! it is not the first time that we have met ; for, if I mistake not, it is Don Diego Alvarez, who was once at the prince's court."

"It is indeed I," said the Spanish knight, speaking in the French tongue, "and I pray you to pass your sword through my heart ; for how can I live—I, a caballero of Castile—after being dragged from my horse by the base hands of a common archer ? "

"Fret not for that," answered Sir Nigel. "For, in sooth, had he not pulled you down, a dozen cloth-yard shafts had crossed each other in your body."

"By Saint James ! it were better so than to be polluted by his touch," answered the Spaniard, with his black eyes sparkling with rage and hatred. "I trust that I am now the prisoner of some honourable knight or gentleman."

"You are the prisoner of the man who took you, Sir Diego," answered Sir Nigel. "And I may tell you that better men than either you or I have found themselves before now prisoners in the hands of archers of England."

"What ransom, then, does he demand ? " asked the Spaniard.

Big John scratched his red head and grinned in high delight when the question was propounded to him. "Tell him," said he, "that I shall have ten cows and a bull too, if it be but a little one. Also a dress of blue sendall for mother and a red one for Joan ; with five acres of pasture-land, two scythes, and a fine new grindstone. Likewise a small house, with stalls for the cows, and thirty-six gallons of beer for the thirsty weather."

"Tut, tut ! " cried Sir Nigel, laughing. "All these

things may be had for money ; and I think, Don Diego, that five thousand crowns is not too much for so renowned a knight."

" It shall be duly paid him."

" For some days we must keep you with us ; and I must crave leave also to use your shield, your armour and your horse."

" My harness is yours by the law of arms," said the Spaniard, gloomily.

" I do but ask the loan of it. I have need of it this day, but it shall be duly returned to you. Set guards, Aylward, with arrow on string, at either end of the pass ; for it may happen that some other cavaliers may visit us ere the time be come." All day the little band of Englishmen lay in the sheltered gorge, looking down upon the vast host of their unconscious enemies. Shortly after midday, a great uproar of shouting and cheering broke out in the camp, with mustering of men and calling of bugles. Clambering up among the rocks, the companions saw a long rolling cloud of dust along the whole eastern sky-line, with the glint of spears and the flutter of pennons, which announced the approach of a large body of cavalry. For a moment a wild hope came upon them that perhaps the prince had moved more swiftly than had been planned, that he had crossed the Ebro, and that this was his vanguard sweeping to the attack.

" Surely I see the red pile of Chandos at the head of yonder squadron ! " cried Sir Richard Causton, shading his eyes with his hand.

" Not so," answered Sir Simon Burley, who had watched the approaching host with a darkening face. " It is even as I feared. That is the double eagle of Du Guesclin."

" You say very truly," cried the Earl of Angus. " These are the levies of France, for I can see the ensign of the Marshal d'Andreghen, with that of the Lord of Antoing and of Briseuil, and of many another from Brittany and Anjou."

" By Saint Paul ! I am very glad of it," said Sir Nigel. " Of these Spaniards I know nothing ; but the French are very worthy gentlemen, and will do what they can for our advancement."

" There are at the least four thousand of them, and all men-at-arms," cried Sir William Felton. " See, there is Bertrand himself, beside his banner, and there is King Henry, who rides to welcome him. Now they all turn and come into the camp together."

As he spoke, the vast throng of Spaniards and of Frenchmen trooped across the plain, with brandished arms and tossing banners. All day long the sound of revelry and of rejoicing from the crowded camp swelled up to the ears of the Englishmen, and they could see the soldiers of the two nations throwing themselves into each other's arms and dancing hand-in-hand round the blazing fires. The sun had sunk behind a cloud-bank in the west before Sir Nigel at last gave word that the men should resume their arms and have their horses ready. He had himself thrown off his armour, and had dressed himself from head to foot in the harness of the captured Spaniard.

" Sir William," said he, " it is my intention to attempt a small deed, and I ask you therefore that you will lead this outfall upon the camp. For me, I will ride into their camp with my squire and two archers. I pray you to watch me, and to ride forth when I am come among the tents. You will leave twenty men behind here, as we planned this morning, and you will ride back here after you have ventured as far as seems good to you."

" I will do as you order, Nigel ; but what is it that you propose to do ? "

" You will see anon, and indeed it is but a trifling matter. Alleyne, you will come with me, and lead a spare horse by the bridle. I will have the two archers who rode with us through France, for they are trusty men and of stout heart. Let them ride behind us, and let them leave their bows here among the bushes, for it is not my wish that they should know that we are Englishmen. Say no word to any whom we may meet, and, if any speak to you, pass on as though you heard them not. Are you ready ? "

" I am ready, my fair lord," said Alleyne.

" And I," " And I," cried Aylward and John.

" Then the rest I leave to your wisdom, Sir William ; and if God sends us fortune we shall meet you again in this gorge ere it be dark."

So saying, Sir Nigel mounted the white horse of the Spanish cavalier, and rode quietly forth from his concealment with his three companions behind him, Alleyne leading his master's own steed by the bridle. So many small parties of French and Spanish horse were sweeping hither and thither that the small band attracted little notice, and making its way at a gentle trot across the plain they came as far as the camp without challenge or hindrance. On and on they pushed past the endless lines of tents, amid the dense swarms of horsemen and of footmen, until the huge royal pavilion stretched in front of them. They were close upon it when of a sudden there broke out a wild hubbub from a distant portion of the camp, with screams and war-cries and all the wild tumult of battle. At the sound the soldiers came rushing from their tents, knights shouted loudly for their squires, and there was mad turmoil on every hand of bewildered men and plunging horses. At the royal tent a crowd of gorgeously dressed servants ran hither and thither in helpless panic, for the guard of soldiers who were stationed there had already ridden off in the direction of the alarm. A man-at-arms on either side of the doorway were the sole protectors of the royal dwelling.

" I have come for the king," whispered Sir Nigel ; " and, by Saint Paul ! he must back with us or I must bide here."

Alleyne and Aylward sprang from their horses and flew at the two sentries, who were disarmed and beaten down in an instant by so furious and unexpected an attack. Sir Nigel dashed into the royal tent, and was followed by

Hordle John as soon as the horses had been secured. From within came wild screamings and the clash of steel, and then the two emerged once more, their swords and forearms reddened with blood, while John bore over his shoulder the senseless body of a man whose gay surcoat, adorned with the lions and towers of Castile, proclaimed him to belong to the royal house. A crowd of white-faced sewers and pages swarmed at their heels, those behind pushing forwards, while the foremost shrank back from the fierce faces and reeking weapons of the adventurers. The senseless body was thrown across the spare horse, the four sprang to their saddles, and away they thundered with loose reins and busy spurs through the swarming camp.

But confusion and disorder still reigned among the Spaniards, for Sir William Felton and his men had swept through half their camp, leaving a long litter of the dead and the dying to mark their course. Uncertain who were their attackers, and unable to tell their English enemies from their newly arrived Breton allies, the Spanish knights rode wildly hither and thither in aimless fury. The mad turmoil, the mixture of races, and the fading light, were all in favour of the four who alone knew their own purpose among the vast uncertain multitude. Twice ere they reached open ground they had to break their way through small bodies of horse, and once there came a whistle of arrows and singing of stones about their ears ; but, still dashing onwards, they shot out from among the tents and found their own comrades retreating for the mountains at no very great distance from them. Another five minutes of wild galloping over the plain, and they were all back in their gorge, while their pursuers fell back before the rolling of drums and blare of trumpets, which seemed to proclaim that the whole army of the prince was about to emerge from the mountain passes.

" By my soul ! Nigel," cried Sir Oliver, waving a great boiled ham over his head, " I have come by something which I may eat with my truffles ! I had a hard fight for it, for there were three of them with their mouths open and the knives in their hands, all sitting agape round the table when I rushed in upon them. How say you, Sir William, will you not try the smack of the famed Spanish swine though we have but the brook water to wash it down ? "

" Later, Sir Oliver," answered the old soldier, wiping his grimed face. " We must further into the mountains ere we be in safety. But what have we here, Nigel ? "

" It is a prisoner whom I have taken, and in sooth, as he came from the royal tent and wears the royal arms upon his jupon, I trust that he is the King of Spain."

" The King of Spain ! " cried the companions, crowding round in amazement.

" Nay, Sir Nigel," said Felton, peering at the prisoner through the uncertain light. " I have twice seen Henry of Trastamare, and certes this man in no way resembles him."

" Then, by the light of heaven ! I will ride back for him," said Sir Nigel.

" Nay, nay, the camp is in arms, and it would be rank madness. Who are you, fellow ? " he added in Spanish, " and how is it that you dare to wear the arms of Castile ? "

The prisoner was but recovering the consciousness which had been squeezed from him by the grip of Hordle John. " If it please you," he answered, " I and nine others are the body-squires of the King, and must ever wear his arms, so as to shield him from even such perils as have threatened him this night. The king is at the tent of the brave Du Guesclin, where he will sup to-night. But I am a caballero of Aragon, Don Sancho Penelosa, and, though I be no king, I am yet ready to pay a fitting price for my ransom."

" By Saint Paul ! I will not touch your gold," cried Sir Nigel. " Go back to your master and give him greeting from Sir Nigel Loring of Twynham Castle, telling him that I had hoped to make his better acquaintance this night, and that, if I have disordered his tent, it was but in my eagerness to know so famed and courteous a knight.

Spur on, comrades ! for we must cover many a league ere we can venture to light fire or to loosen girth. I had hoped to ride without this patch to-night, but it seems that I must carry it yet a little longer."

36. *How Sir Nigel took the Patch from his Eye*

IT was a cold bleak morning in the beginning of March, and the mist was drifting in dense rolling clouds through the passes of the Cantabrian mountains. The Company, who had passed the night in a sheltered gully, were already astir, some crowding round the blazing fires and others romping or leaping over each other's backs, for their limbs were chilled and the air biting. Here and there, through the dense haze which surrounded them, there loomed out huge pinnacles and jutting boulders of rock ; while high above the sea of vapour there towered up one gigantic peak, with the pink glow of the early sunshine upon its snow-capped head. The ground was wet, the rocks dripping, the grass and evergreens sparkling with beads of moisture ; yet the camp was loud with laughter and merriment, for a messenger had ridden in from the prince with words of heart-stirring praise for what they had done, and with orders that they should still bide in the forefront of the army.

Round one of the fires were clustered four or five of the leading men of the archers, cleaning the rust from their weapons and glancing impatiently from time to time at a great pot which smoked over the blaze. There was Aylward squatting cross-legged in his shirt, while he scrubbed away at his chain-mail brigandine, whistling loudly the while. On one side of him sat old Johnston, who was busy in trimming the feathers of some arrows to his liking ; and on the other Hordle John, who lay with his great limbs all asprawl, and his headpiece balanced upon his uplifted foot. Black Simon of Norwich crouched amid the rocks, crooning an Eastland ballad to himself, while he whetted his sword upon a flat stone which lay across his knees ; while beside him sat Alleyne Edricson, and Norbury, the silent squire of Sir Oliver, holding out their chilled hands towards the crackling faggots.

" Cast on another culpon, John, and stir the broth with thy sword-sheath," growled Johnston, looking anxiously for the twentieth time at the reeking pot.

" By my hilt ! " cried Aylward, " now that John hath come by this great ransom, he will scarce abide the fare of poor archer lads. How say you, camarade ? When you see Hordle once more, there will be no penny ale and fat bacon, but Gascon wines and baked meats every day of the seven."

" I know not about that," said John, kicking his helmet up into the air and catching it in his hand. " I do but know that whether the broth be ready or no, I am about to dip this into it."

" It simmers and it boils," cried Johnston, pushing his hard-lined face through the smoke. In an instant the pot had been plucked from the blaze, and its contents had been scooped up in half a dozen steel headpieces which were balanced betwixt their owners' knees, while, with spoon and with gobbet of bread, they devoured their morning meal.

" It is ill weather for bows," remarked John at last, when, with a long sigh, he had drained the last drop from his helmet. " My strings are as limp as a cow's tail this morning."

" You should rub them with water glue," quoth Johnston. " You remember, Samkin, that it was wetter than this on the morning of Crécy, and yet I cannot call to mind that there was aught amiss with our strings."

" It is in my thoughts," said Black Simon, still pensively grinding his sword, " that we may have need of your strings ere sundown. I dreamed of the red cow last night."

" And what is this red cow, Simon ? " asked Alleyne.

" I know not, young sir ; but I can only say that on the eve of Cadsand, and on the eve of Crécy, and on the eve of Nogent, I dreamed of a red cow ; and now the dream has come upon me again, so I am now setting a very keen edge to my blade."

" Well said, old war-dog ! " cried Aylward. " By my hilt ! I pray that your dream may come true, for the prince hath not set us out here to drink broth or to gather whortleberries. One more fight, and I am ready to hang up my bow, marry a wife, and take to the fire corner. But how now, Robin ? Whom is it that you seek ? "

" The Lord Loring craves your attendance in his tent," said a young archer to Alleyne.

The squire rose and proceeded to the pavilion, where he found the knight seated upon a cushion, with his legs crossed in front of him and a broad ribbon of parchment laid across his knees, over which he was poring with frowning brows and pursed lips.

" It came this morning by the prince's messenger," said he, " and was brought from England by Sir John Fallislee, who is new come from Sussex. What make you of this upon the outer side ? "

" It is fairly and clearly written," Alleyne answered, " and it signifies ' To Sir Nigel Loring, Knight, Constable of Twynham Castle, by the hand of Christopher, the servant of God at the priory of Christchurch.' "

" So I read it," said Sir Nigel. " Now I pray you to read what is set forth within."

Alleyne turned to the letter, and, as his eyes rested upon it, his face turned pale, and a cry of surprise and grief burst from his lips.

" What then ? " asked the knight, peering at him anxiously. " There is nought amiss with the Lady Mary or with the Lady Maude ? "

" It is my brother—my poor unhappy brother ! " cried Alleyne, with his hand to his brow. " He is dead."

" By Saint Paul ! I have never heard that he had shown so much love for you that you should mourn him so."

" Yet he was my brother—the only kith or kin that I had upon earth. Mayhap he had cause to be bitter against me, for his land was given to the Abbey for my upbringing. Alas ! alas ! and I raised my staff against him when last we met ! he has been slain—and slain, I fear, amidst crime and violence."

" Ha ! " said Sir Nigel. " Read on, I pray you."

" ' God be with thee, my honoured lord, and have thee in His holy keeping. The Lady Loring hath asked me to set down in writing what hath befallen at Twynham, and all that concerns the death of thy ill neighbour, the Socman of Minstead. For when ye had left us, this evil man gathered around him all outlaws, villeins and master-less men, until they were come to such a force that they slew and scattered the king's men who went against them. Then, coming forth from the woods, they laid siege to thy castle, and for two days they girt us in and shot hard against us, with such numbers as were a marvel to see. Yet the Lady Loring held the place stoutly, and on the second day the Socman was slain—by his own men, as some think—so that we were delivered from their hands ; for which praise be to all the saints, and more especially to the holy Anselm, upon whose feast it came to pass. The Lady Loring, and the Lady Maude, thy fair daugh-ter, are in good health ; and so also am I, save for an imposthume of the toe-joint, which hath been sent me for my sins. May all the saints preserve thee ! ' "

" It was the vision of the Lady Tiphaine," said Sir Nigel after a pause. " Marked you not how she said that the leader was one with a yellow beard, and how he fell before the gate ? But how came it, Alleyne, that this woman, to whom all things are as crystal, and who hath not said one word which has not come to pass, was yet so led astray as to say that your thoughts turned to Twynham Castle even more than mine own ? "

" My fair lord," said Alleyne, with a flush on his

weather-stained cheeks, " the Lady Tiphaine may have spoken sooth when she said it ; for Twynham Castle is in my heart by day and in my dreams by night."

" Ha ! " cried Sir Nigel, with a sidelong glance.

" Yes, my fair lord ; for, indeed, I love your daughter, the Lady Maude ; and, unworthy as I am, I would yet give my heart's blood to serve her."

" By Saint Paul ! Edricson," said the knight coldly, arching his eyebrows, " you aim high in this matter. Our blood is very old."

" And mine also is very old," answered the squire.

" And the Lady Maude is our single child. All our name and lands centre upon her."

" Alas ! that I should say it, but I also am now the only Edricson."

" And why have I not heard this from you before, Alleyne ? In sooth, I think that you have used me ill."

" Nay, my fair lord, say not so ; for I know not whether your daughter loves me, and there is no pledge between us."

Sir Nigel pondered for a few moments, and then burst out a-laughing. " By Saint Paul ! " said he, " I know not why I should mix in the matter, for I have ever found that the Lady Maude was very well able to look to her own affairs. Since first she could stamp her little foot, she hath ever been able to get that for which she craved ; and if she set her heart on thee, Alleyne, and thou on her, I do not think that this Spanish king, with his threescore thousand men, could hold you apart. Yet this I will say, that I would see you a full knight ere you go to my daughter with words of love. I have ever said that a brave lance should wed her ; and, by my soul ! Edricson, if God spare you, I think that you will acquit yourself well. But enough of such trifles, for we have our work before us, and it will be time to speak of this matter when we see the white cliffs of England once more. Go to Sir William Felton, I pray you, and ask him to come hither, for it is time that we were marching. There is no pass at the further end of the valley, and it is a perilous place should the enemy come upon us."

Alleyne delivered his message, and then wandered forth from the camp, for his mind was all in a whirl with this unexpected news, and with his talk with Sir Nigel. Sitting upon a rock, with his burning brow resting upon his hands, he thought of his brother, of their quarrel, of the Lady Maude in her bedraggled riding-dress, of the grey old castle, of the proud pale face in the armoury, and of the last fiery words with which she had sped him on his way. Then he was but a penniless monk-bred lad, unknown and unfriended. Now he was himself Socman of Minstead, the head of an old stock, and the lord of an estate which, if reduced from its former size, was still ample to preserve the dignity of his family. Further, he had become a man of experience, was counted brave among brave men, had won the esteem and confidence of her father, and above all, had been listened to by him when he told him the secret of his love. As to the gaining of knighthood, in such stirring times it was no great matter for a brave squire of gentle birth to aspire to that honour. He would leave his bones among these Spanish ravines, or he would do some deed which would call the eyes of men upon him.

Alleyne was still seated on the rock, his griefs and his joys drifting swiftly over his mind like the shadow of clouds upon a sunlit meadow, when of a sudden he became conscious of a low, deep sound which came booming up to him through the fog. Close behind him he could hear the murmur of the bowmen, the occasional bursts of hoarse laughter, and the champing and stamping of their horses. Behind it all, however, came that low-pitched, deep-toned hum, which seemed to come from every quarter and to fill the whole air. In the old monastic days he remembered to have heard such a sound when he had walked out one windy night at Bucklershard, and had listened to the long waves breaking upon the shingly shore. Here, however, was neither wind nor sea, and yet the dull murmur arose ever louder and stronger out of the heart of the rolling sea of vapour. He turned and ran to the camp, shouting an alarm at the top of his voice.

It was but a hundred paces, and yet ere he had crossed it every bowman was ready at his horse's head, and the group of knights were out and listening intently to the ominous sound.

" It is a great body of horse," said Sir William Felton, " and they are riding very swiftly hitherwards."

" Yet they must be from the prince's army," remarked Sir Richard Causton, " for they come from the north."

" Nay," said the Earl of Angus, " it is not so certain ; for the peasant with whom we spoke last night said that it was rumoured that Don Tello, the Spanish king's brother, had ridden with six thousand chosen men to beat up the prince's camp. It may be that on their backward road they have come this way."

" By Saint Paul ! " cried Sir Nigel, " I think that it is even as you say, for that same peasant had a sour face and a shifting eye, as one who bore us little goodwill. I doubt not that he has brought these cavaliers upon us."

" But the mist covers us," said Sir Simon Burley. " We have yet time to ride through the further end of the pass."

" Were we a troop of mountain goats we might do so," answered Sir William Felton, " but it is not to be passed by a company of horsemen. If these be indeed Don Tello and his men, then we must bide where we are, and do what we may to make them rue the day that they found us in their path."

" Well spoken, William ! " cried Sir Nigel, in high delight. " If there be so many as has been said, then there will be much honour to be gained from them and every hope of advancement. But the sound has ceased, and I fear that they have gone some other way."

" Or mayhap they have come to the mouth of the gorge, and are marshalling their ranks. Hush and hearken ! for they are no great way from us."

The Company stood peering into the dense fog-wreath amidst a silence so profound that the dripping of the water from the rocks and the breathing of the horses grew loud upon the ear. Suddenly from out the sea of mist came the shrill sound of a neigh, followed by a long blast upon a bugle.

" It is a Spanish call, my fair lord," said Black Simon. " It is used by their prickers and huntsmen when the beast hath not fled, but is still in its lair."

" By my faith," said Sir Nigel, smiling, " if they are in a humour for venerie we may promise them some sport ere they sound the mort over us. But there is a hill in the centre of the gorge on which we might make our stand."

" I marked it yester-night," said Felton, " and no better spot could be found for our purpose, for it is very steep at the back. It is but a bow shot to the left, and, indeed, I can see the shadow of it."

The whole Company, leading their horses, passed across to the small hill which loomed in front of them out of the mist. It was, indeed, admirably designed for defence, for it sloped down in front, all jagged and boulder-strewn, while it fell away behind in a sheer cliff of a hundred feet or more. On the summit was a small, uneven plateau, with a stretch across of a hundred paces, and a depth of half as much again.

" Unloose the horses ! " said Sir Nigel. " We have no space for them, and if we hold our own we shall have horses and to spare when this day's work is done. Nay, keep yours, my fair sirs, for we may have work for them. Aylward, Johnston, let your men form a harrow on either side of the ridge. Sir Oliver and you, my Lord Angus, I give you the right wing, and the left to you, Sir Simon, and to you, Sir Richard Causton. I and Sir William Felton will hold the centre with our men-at-arms. Now order the ranks, and fling wide the banners, for our souls are God's and our bodies the king's, and our swords for Saint George and for England ! "

Sir Nigel had scarcely spoken when the mist seemed to

thin in the valley, and to shred away into long ragged clouds which trailed from the edges of the cliffs. The gorge in which they had camped was a mere wedge-shaped cleft among the hills, three-quarters of a mile deep, with a small rugged rising upon which they stood at the farther end, and the brown crags walling it in on three sides. As the mist parted and the sun broke through it gleamed and shimmered with dazzling brightness upon the armour and head-pieces of a vast body of horsemen who stretched across the barranca from one cliff to the other, and extended backwards until their rearguard were far out upon the plain beyond. Line after line, and rank after rank, they choked the neck of the valley with a long vista of tossing pennons, twinkling lances, waving plumes and streaming banderoles, while the curvets and gambades of the chargers lent a constant motion and shimmer to the glittering many-coloured mass. A yell of exultation, and a forest of waving steel through the length and breadth of their column announced that they could at last see their entrapped enemies, while the swelling notes of a hundred bugles and drums, mixed with the clash of Moorish cymbals, broke forth into a proud peal of martial triumph. Strange it was to these gallant and sparkling cavaliers of Spain to look upon this handful of men upon the hill, the thin lines of bowmen, the knot of knights and men-at-arms with armour rusted and discoloured from long service, and to learn that these were indeed the soldiers whose fame and prowess had been the camp-fire talk of every army in Christendom. Very still and silent they stood, leaning upon their bows, while their leaders took counsel together in front of them. No clang of bugle rose from their stern ranks, but in the centre waved the leopards of England, on the right the ensign of the Company with the roses of Loring, and on the left, over threescore of Welsh bowmen, there floated the red banner of Merlin with the boars' heads of the Buttesthorns. Gravely and sedately they stood beneath the morning sun waiting for the onslaught of their foemen.

" By Saint Paul ! " said Sir Nigel, gazing with puckered eye down the valley, " there appear to be some very worthy people among them. What is this golden banner which waves upon the left ? "

" It is the ensign of the Knights of Calatrava," answered Felton.

" And the other upon the right ? "

" It marks the Knights of Santiago, and I see by his flag that their grand-master rides at their head. There, too, is the banner of Castile amid yonder sparkling squadron which heads the main battle. There are six thousand men-at-arms with ten squadrons of slingers, as far as I may judge their numbers."

" There are Frenchmen among them, my fair lord," remarked Black Simon. " I can see the pennons of De Couvette, De Brieux, Saint Pol and many others who struck in against us for Charles of Blois."

" You are right," said Sir William, " for I can also see them. There is much Spanish blazonry also, if I could but read it. Don Diego, you know the arms of your own land. Who are they who have done us this honour ? "

The Spanish prisoner looked with exultant eyes upon the deep and serried ranks of his countrymen.

" By Saint James ! " said he, " if ye fall this day ye fall by no mean hands, for the flower of the knighthood of Castile ride under the banner of Don Tello, with the chivalry of Asturias, Toledo, Leon, Cordova, Galicia and Seville. I see the guidons of Albornez, Caçorla, Rodriguez, Tavora, with the two great orders, and the knights of France and of Aragon. If you will take my rede you will come to a composition with them, for they will give you such terms as you have given me."

" Nay, by Saint Paul ! it were pity if so many brave men were drawn together, and no little deed of arms to come of it. Ha ! William, they advance upon us ; and, by my soul ! it is a sight that is worth coming over the seas to see."

As he spoke, the two wings of the Spanish host, consisting of the Knights of Calatrava on the one side and of Santiago upon the other, came swooping swiftly down the valley, while the main body followed more slowly behind. Five hundred paces from the English the two great bodies of horse crossed each other, and sweeping round in a curve, retired in feigned confusion towards their centre. Often in bygone days had the Moors tempted the hot-blooded Spaniards from their places of strength by such pretended flights, but there were men upon the hill to whom every ruse and trick of war were as their daily trade and practice. Again and ever nearer came the rallying Spaniards, and again with cry of fear and stooping bodies they swerved off to right and left, but the English still stood stolid and observant among their rocks. The vanguard halted a long bow-shot from the hill, and with waving spears and vaunting shouts challenged their enemies to come forth, while two cavaliers, pricking forward from the glittering ranks, walked their horses slowly between the two arrays with targets braced and lances in rest like the challengers in a tourney.

" By Saint Paul ! " cried Sir Nigel, with his one eye glowing like an ember, " these appear to be two very worthy and debonair gentlemen. I do not call to mind when I have seen any people who seemed of so great a heart and so high of enterprise. We have our horses, Sir William : shall we not relieve them of any vow which they may have upon their souls ? "

Felton's reply was to bound upon his charger, and to urge it down the slope, while Sir Nigel followed not three spears' lengths behind him. It was a rugged course, rocky and uneven; yet the two knights, choosing their men, dashed onwards at the top of their speed, while the gallant Spaniards flew as swiftly to meet them. The one to whom Felton found himself opposed was a tall stripling with a stag's head upon his shield, while Sir Nigel's man was broad and squat, with plain steel harness, and a pink and white torse bound round his helmet. The first struck Felton on the target with such force as to split it from side to side, but Sir William's lance crashed through the camail which shielded the Spaniard's throat, and he fell, screaming hoarsely, to the ground. Carried away by the heat and madness of fight, the English knight never drew rein, but charged straight on into the array of the Knights of Calatrava. Long time the silent ranks upon the hill could see a swirl and eddy deep down in the heart of the Spanish column, with a circle of rearing chargers and flashing blades. Here and there tossed the white plume of the English helmet, rising and falling like the foam upon a wave, with the fierce gleam and sparkle ever circling round it, until at last it had sunk from view, and another brave man had turned from war to peace.

Sir Nigel, meanwhile, had found a foeman worthy of his steel, for his opponent was none other than Sebastian Gomez, the picked lance of the monkish Knights of Santiago, who had won fame in a hundred bloody combats with the Moors of Andalusia. So fierce was their meeting that their spears shivered up to the very grasp, and the horses reared backwards until it seemed that they must crash down upon their riders. Yet with consummate horsemanship they both swung round in a long curvet, and then, plucking out their swords, they lashed at each other like two lusty smiths hammering upon an anvil. The chargers spun round each other, biting and striking, while the two blades wheeled and whizzled and circled in gleams of dazzling light. Cut, parry and thrust followed so swiftly upon each other that the eye could not follow them, until at last, coming thigh to thigh, they cast their arms round each other and rolled off their saddles to the ground. The heavier Spaniard threw himself upon his enemy, and pinning him down beneath him raised his sword to slay him, while a shout of triumph rose from the ranks of his countrymen. But the fatal blow never fell, for even as his arm quivered, before descending, the Spaniard gave a shudder, and, stiffening himself, rolled heavily over upon his side, with the blood gushing from his armpit and from the slit of his vizor. Sir Nigel sprang to his feet with his bloody dagger in his left hand and gazed down upon his adversary, but that fatal and sudden stab in the vital spot, which the Spaniard had exposed by raising his arm, had proved instantly mortal. The Englishman leaped upon his horse and made for the hill, at the very instant that a yell of rage from a thousand voices and the clang of a score of bugles announced the Spanish onset.

But the islanders were ready and eager for the encounter. With feet firmly planted, their sleeves rolled back to give free play to their muscles, their long yellow bow-staves in their left hands, and their quivers slung to the front, they had waited in the four-deep harrow formation which gave strength to their array, and yet permitted every man to draw his arrow freely without harm to those in front. Aylward and Johnston had been engaged in throwing light tufts of grass into the air to gauge the wind force, and a hoarse whisper passed down the ranks from the file-leaders to the men, with scraps of advice and admonition.

" Do not shoot outside the fifteen-score paces," cried Johnston. " We may need all our shafts ere we have done with them."

" Better to overshoot than to undershoot," added Aylward. " Better to strike the rearguard than to feather a shaft in the earth."

" Loose quick and sharp when they come," added another. " Let it be the eye to the string, the string to the shaft, and the shaft to the mark. By Our Lady ! their banners advance, and we must hold our ground now if ever we are to see Southampton Water again."

Alleyne, standing with his sword drawn amidst the archers, saw a long toss and heave of the glittering squadrons. Then the front ranks began to surge slowly forward, to trot, to canter, to gallop, and in an instant the whole vast array was hurtling onward, line after line, the air full of the thunder of their cries, the ground shaking with the beat of their hoofs, the valley choked with the rushing torrent of steel, topped by the waving plumes, the slanting spears and the fluttering banderoles. On they swept over the level and up to the slope, ere they met the blinding storm of the English arrows. Down went whole ranks in a whirl of mad confusion, horses plunging and kicking, bewildered men falling, rising, staggering on or back, while ever new lines of horsemen came spurring through the gaps and urged their chargers up the fatal slope. All around him Alleyne could hear the stern short orders of the master-bowmen, while the air was filled with the keen twanging of the strings and the swish and patter of the shafts. Right across the foot of the hill there had sprung up a long wall of struggling horses and stricken men, which ever grew and heightened as fresh squadrons poured on the attack. One young knight on a grey jennet leaped over his fallen comrades and galloped swiftly up the hill shrieking loudly upon Saint James, ere he fell within a spear-length of the English line, with the feathers of arrows thrusting out from every crevice and joint of his armour. So for five long minutes the gallant horsemen of Spain and France strove ever and again to force a passage until the wailing note of a bugle called them back, and they rode slowly out of bow-shot, leaving their best and their bravest in the ghastly blood-mottled heap behind them.

But there was little rest for the victors. Whilst the knights had charged them in front the slingers had crept round upon either flank and had gained a footing upon the cliffs and behind the outlying rocks. A storm of stones broke suddenly upon the defenders, who, drawn up in lines upon the exposed summit, offered a fair mark to their hidden foes. Johnston, the old archer, was struck upon the temple and fell dead without a groan, while fifteen of his bowmen and six of the men-at-arms were struck down at the same moment. The others lay on their faces to avoid the deadly hail, while at each side of the plateau a fringe of bowmen exchanged shots with the slingers and cross-bowmen among the rocks, aiming mainly at those who had swarmed up the cliffs, and bursting into laughter and cheers when a well-aimed shaft brought one of their opponents toppling down from his lofty perch.

" I think, Nigel," said Sir Oliver, striding across to the little knight, " that we should all acquit ourselves better had we our none-meat, for the sun is high in the heaven."

" By Saint Paul ! " quoth Sir Nigel, plucking the patch from his eye, " I think that I am now clear of my vow, for this Spanish knight was a person from whom much honour might be won. Indeed, he was a very worthy gentleman, of good courage, and great hardiness, and it grieves me that he should have come by such a hurt. As to what you say of food, Oliver, it is not to be thought of, for we have nothing with us upon the hill."

" Nigel ! " cried Sir Simon Burley, hurrying up with consternation upon his face, " Aylward tells me that there are not ten-score arrows left in all their sheaves. See ! they are springing from their horses, and cutting their sollerets that they may rush upon us. Might we not even now make a retreat ? "

" My soul will retreat from my body first ! " cried the little knight. " Here I am, and here I abide, while God gives me strength to lift a sword."

" And so say I ! " shouted Sir Oliver, throwing his mace high into the air and catching it again by the handle.

" To your arms, men ! " roared Sir Nigel. " Shoot while you may, and then out sword, and let us live or die together ! "

37. *How the White Company came to be Disbanded*

THEN up rose from the hill in the rugged Cantabrian valley a sound such as had not been heard in those parts before, nor was again, until the streams which rippled amid the rocks had been frozen by over four hundred

winters and thawed by as many returning springs. Deep
and full and strong it thundered down the ravine, the
fierce battle-call of a warrior race, the last stern welcome
to whoso should join with them in that world-old game
where the stake is death. Thrice it swelled forth and
thrice it sank away, echoing and reverberating amidst the
crags. Then, with set faces, the Company rose up
among the storm of stones, and looked down upon the
thousands who sped swiftly up the slope against them.
Horse and spear had been set aside, but on foot, with
sword and battle-axe, their broad shields slung in front
of them, the chivalry of Spain rushed to the attack.

And now arose a struggle so fell, so long, so evenly
sustained, that even now the memory of it is handed down
amonst the Cantabrian mountaineers, and the ill-omened
knoll is still pointed out by fathers to their children as the
" Altura de los Ingleses," where the men from across the
sea fought the great fight with the knights of the south.
The last arrow was quickly shot, nor could the slingers
hurl their stones, so close were friend and foe. From side
to side stretched the thin line of the English, lightly armed
and quick-footed, while against it stormed and raged the
pressing throng of fiery Spaniards and of gallant Bretons.
The clink of crossing sword-blades, the dull thudding of
heavy blows, the panting and gasping of weary and
wounded men, all rose together in a wild long-drawn
note, which swelled upwards to the ears of the wondering
peasants who looked down from the edges of the cliffs
upon the swaying turmoil of the battle beneath them.
Back and forward reeled the leopard banner, now borne
up the slope by the rush and weight of the onslaught,
now pushing downwards again as Sir Nigel, Burley and
Black Simon, with their veteran men-at-arms, flung themselves madly into the fray. Alleyne, at his lord's right
hand, found himself swept hither and thither in the desperate struggle, exchanging savage thrusts one instant
with a Spanish cavalier, and the next torn away by the
whirl of men and dashed up against some new antagonist.

To the right Sir Oliver, Aylward, Hordle John and the bowmen of the Company fought furiously against the monkish Knights of Santiago, who were led up the hill by their prior—a great deep-chested man, who wore a brown monastic habit over his suit of mail. Three archers he slew in three giant strokes, but Sir Oliver flung his arms round him, and the two, staggering and straining, reeled backwards and fell, locked in each other's grasp, over the edge of the steep cliff which flanked the hill. In vain his knights stormed and raved against the thin line which barred their path; the sword of Aylward and the great axe of John gleamed in the forefront of the battle, and the huge jagged pieces of rock, hurled by the strong arms of the bowmen, crashed and hurtled amid their ranks. Slowly they gave back down the hill, the archers still hanging upon their skirts, with a long litter of writhing and twisted figures to mark the course which they had taken. At the same instant the Welshmen upon the left, led on by the Scotch earl, had charged out from among the rocks which sheltered them, and by the fury of their outfall had driven the Spaniards in front of them in headlong flight down the hill. In the centre only things seemed to be going ill with the defenders. Black Simon was down—dying, as he would wish to have died, like a grim old wolf in its lair—with a ring of his slain around him. Twice Sir Nigel had been overborne, and twice Alleyne had fought over him until he had staggered to his feet once more. Burley lay senseless, stunned by a blow from a mace, and half of the men-at-arms lay littered upon the ground around him. Sir Nigel's shield was broken, his crest shorn, his armour cut and smashed, and the vizor torn from his helmet; yet he sprang hither and thither with light foot and ready hand, engaging two Bretons and a Spaniard at the same instant—thrusting, stooping, dashing in, springing out—while Alleyne still fought by his side, stemming with a handful of men the fierce tide which surged up against them. Yet it would have fared ill with them had not the archers from either side closed in upon the flanks of the attackers, and pressed them very slowly and foot by foot down the long slope, until they were on the plain once more, where their fellows were already rallying for a fresh assault.

But terrible indeed was the cost at which the last had been repelled. Of the three hundred and seventy men who had held the crest, one hundred and seventy-two were left standing, many of whom were sorely wounded and weak from loss of blood. Sir Oliver Buttesthorn, Sir Richard Causton, Sir Simon Burley, Black Simon, Johnston, a hundred and fifty archers and forty-seven men-at-arms had fallen, while the pitiless hail of stones was already whizzing and piping once more about their ears, threatening every instant to further reduce their numbers.

Sir Nigel looked about him at his shattered ranks, and his face flushed with a soldier's pride.

" By Saint Paul ! " he cried, " I have fought in many a little bickering, but never one that I would be more loth to have missed than this. But you are wounded, Alleyne ? "

" It is nought," answered his squire, staunching the blood which dripped from a sword-cut across his forehead.

" These gentlemen of Spain seem to be most courteous and worthy people. I see that they are already forming to continue this debate with us. Form up the bowmen two deep instead of four. By my faith ! some very brave men have gone from among us. Aylward, you are a trusty soldier, for all that your shoulder has never felt accolade, nor your heels worn the gold spurs. Do you take charge of the right ; I will hold the centre, and you, my Lord of Angus, the left."

" Ho ! for Sir Samkin Aylward ! " cried a rough voice among the archers, and a roar of laughter greeted their new leader.

" By my hilt ! " cried the old bowman, " I never thought to lead a wing in a stricken field. Stand close, camarades, for, by these finger-bones ! we must play the man this day."

" Come hither, Alleyne," said Sir Nigel, walking back
to the edge of the cliff which formed the rear of their
position. " And you, Norbury," he continued, beckoning to the squire of Sir Oliver, " do you also come here."

The two squires hurried across to him, and the three
stood looking down into the rocky ravine which lay a
hundred and fifty feet beneath them.

" The prince must hear of how things are with us,"
said the knight. " Another onfall we may withstand, but
they are many and we are few, so that the time must come
when we can no longer form line across the hill. Yet if
help were brought us we might hold the crest until it
comes. See yonder horses which stray among the rocks
beneath us ? "

" I see them, fair lord."

" And see yonder path which winds along the hill upon
the further end of the valley ? "

" I see it."

" Were you on those horses, and riding up yonder
track, steep and rough as it is, I think that ye might gain
the valley beyond. Then on to the prince, and tell him
how we fare."

" But, my fair lord, how can we hope to reach the
horses ? " asked Norbury.

" Ye cannot go round to them, for they would be upon
ye ere ye could come to them. Think ye that ye have
heart enough to clamber down this cliff ? "

" Had we but a rope."

" There is one here. It is but one hundred feet long,
and for the rest ye must trust God and to your fingers.
Can you try it, Alleyne ? "

" With all my heart, my dear lord, but how can I leave
you in such a strait ? "

" Nay, it is to serve me that ye go. And you, Norbury ? "

The silent squire said nothing, but he took up the rope,
and, having examined it, he tied one end firmly round a
projecting rock. Then he cast off his breastplate, thigh-

pieces and greaves, while Alleyne followed his example.

" Tell Chandos, or Calverley, or Knolles, should the prince have gone forward," cried Sir Nigel. " Now may God speed ye, for ye are brave and worthy men."

It was, indeed, a task which might make the heart of the bravest sink within him. The thin cord, dangling down the face of the brown cliff, seemed from above to reach little more than halfway down it. Beyond stretched the rugged rock, wet and shiny, with a green tuft here and there thrusting out from it, but little sign of ridge or foothold. Far below the jagged points of the boulders bristled up, dark and menacing. Norbury tugged thrice with all his strength upon the cord, and then lowered himself over the edge, while a hundred anxious faces peered over at him as he slowly clambered downwards to the end of the rope. Twice he stretched out his foot, and twice he failed to reach the point at which he aimed, but even as he swung himself for a third effort a stone from a sling buzzed like a wasp from amid the rocks and struck him full upon the side of his head. His grasp relaxed, his feet slipped, and in an instant he was a crushed and mangled corpse upon the sharp ridges beneath him.

" If I have no better fortune," said Alleyne, leading Sir Nigel aside, " I pray you, my dear lord, that you will give my humble service to the Lady Maude, and say to her that I was ever her true servant and most unworthy cavalier."

The old knight said no word, but he put a hand on either shoulder, and kissed his squire, with the tears shining in his eyes. Alleyne sprang to the rope, and sliding down swiftly, soon found himself at its extremity. From above it seemed as though rope and cliff were well-nigh touching, but now, when swinging a hundred feet down, the squire found that he could scarce reach the face of the rock with his foot, and that it was as smooth as glass, with no resting-place where a mouse could stand. Some three feet lower, however, his eye lit on a long jagged crack which slanted downwards, and this he must reach if he would save not only his own poor life but that of the eight score men above him. Yet it were madness to spring for that narrow slit with nought but the wet smooth rock to cling to. He swung for a moment, full of thought, and even as he hung there another of the hellish stones sang though his curls, and struck a chip from the face of the cliff. Up he clambered a few feet, drew up the loose end after him, unslung his belt, held on with knee and with elbow while he spliced the long tough leathern belt to the end of the cord ; then lowering himself as far as he could go, he swung backwards and forwards until his hand reached the crack, when he left the rope and clung to the face of the cliff. Another stone struck him on the side, and he heard a sound like a breaking stick, with a keen stabbing pain which shot through his chest. Yet it was no time now to think of pain or ache. There was his lord and his eight score comrades, and they must be plucked from the jaws of death. On he clambered, with his hands shuffling down the long sloping crack, sometimes bearing all his weight upon his arms, at others finding some small shelf or tuft on which to rest his foot. Would he never pass over that fifty feet ? He dared not look down, and could but grope slowly onwards, his face to the cliff, his fingers clutching, his feet scraping and feeling for a support. Every vein and crack and mottling of that face of rock remained for ever stamped upon his memory. At last, however, his foot came upon a broad resting-place, and he ventured to cast a glance downwards. Thank God ! he had reached the highest of those fatal pinnacles upon which his comrade had fallen. Quickly now he sprang from rock to rock until his feet were on the ground, and he had his hand stretched out for the horse's rein, when a sling-stone struck him on the head, and he dropped senseless upon the ground.

An evil blow it was for Alleyne, but a worse one still for him who struck it. The Spanish slinger, seeing the youth lie slain, and judging from his dress that he was no common man, rushed forward to plunder him, knowing well that the bowmen above him had expended their last shaft. He was still three paces, however, from his victim's side when John upon the cliff above plucked up a huge boulder and, poising it for an instant, dropped it with fatal aim upon the slinger beneath him. It struck upon his shoulder and hurled him, crushed and screaming, to the ground, while Alleyne, recalled to his senses by these shrill cries in his very ear, staggered on to his feet, and gazed wildly about him. His eyes fell upon the horses grazing upon the scanty pasture, and in an instant all had come back to him—his mission, his comrades, the need for haste. He was dizzy, sick, faint, but he must not die, and he must not tarry, for his life meant many lives that day. In an instant he was in his saddle and spurring down the valley.

Loud rang the swift charger's hoofs over rock and reef, while the fire flew from the stroke of iron, and the loose stones showered up behind him. But his head was whirling round, the blood was gushing from his brow, his temple, his mouth. Ever keener and sharper was the deadly pain which shot like a red-hot arrow through his side. He felt that his eye was glazing, his senses slipping from him, his grasp upon the reins relaxing. Then, with one mighty effort, he called up all his strength for a single minute. Stooping down he loosened the stirrup-straps, bound his knees tightly to his saddle flaps, twisted his hands in the bridle, and then, putting the gallant horse's head for the mountain path, he dashed the spurs in and fell forward fainting, with his face buried in the coarse black mane.

Little could he ever remember of that wild ride. Half conscious, but ever with one thought beating in his mind, he goaded the horse onwards, rushing swiftly down steep ravines, over huge boulders, along the edges of black abysses. Dim memories he had of beetling cliffs, of a group of huts with wondering faces at the doors, of foaming, clattering water, and of a bristle of mountain beeches. Once, ere he had ridden far, he heard behind him three deep sullen shouts, which told him that his comrades had set their faces to the foe once more. Then all was blank, until he woke to find kindly blue English eyes peering down upon him and to hear the blessed sound of his country's speech.

They were but a foraging party—a hundred archers and as many men-at-arms—but their leader was Sir Hugh Calverley, and he was not a man to bide idle when good blows were to be had not three leagues from him. A scout was sent flying with a message to the camp, and Sir Hugh, with his two hundred men, thundered off to the rescue. With them went Alleyne, still bound to his saddle, still dripping with blood, and swooning and recovering, and swooning once again. On they rode, and on, until at last, topping a ridge, they looked down upon the fateful valley. Alas! and alas! for the sight that met their eyes.

There, beneath them, was the blood-bathed hill, and from the highest pinnacle there flaunted the yellow and white banner with the lions and the towers of the royal house of Castile. Up the long slop rushed ranks and ranks of men—exultant, shouting, with waving pennons and brandished arms. Over the whole summit were dense throngs of knights, with no enemy that could be seen to face them save only that at one corner of the plateau an eddy and swirl amid the crowded mass seemed to show that all resistance was not yet at an end. At the sight a deep groan of rage and of despair went up from the baffled rescuers, and, spurring on their horses, they clattered down the long and winding path which led to the valley beneath.

But they were too late to avenge, as they had been too late to save. Long ere they could gain the level ground, the Spaniards, seeing them riding swiftly amid the rocks, and being ignorant of their numbers, drew off from the captured hill, and, having secured their few prisoners, rode slowly in a long column, with drum-beating and cymbal-clashing, out of the valley. Their rear ranks were already passing out of sight ere the new comers were urging their panting, foaming horses up the slope which had been the scene of that long-drawn and bloody fight.

And a fearsome sight it was that met their eyes ! Across the lower end lay the dense heap of men and horses where the first arrowstorm had burst. Above, the bodies of the dead and the dying—French, Spanish and Aragonese—lay thick and thicker, until they covered the whole ground two and three deep in one dreadful tangle of slaughter. Above them lay the Englishmen in their lines, even as they had stood, and higher yet upon the plateau, a wild medley of the dead of all nations, where the last deadly grapple had left them. In the farther corner, under the shadow of a great rock, there crouched seven bowmen, with great John in the centre of them—all wounded, weary and in sorry case, but still unconquered, with their blood-stained weapons waving and their voices ringing a welcome to their countrymen. Alleyne rode across to John, while Sir Hugh Calverley followed close behind him.

" By Saint George ! " cried Sir Hugh, " I have never seen signs of so stern a fight, and I am right glad that we have been in time to save you."

" You have saved more than us," said John, pointing to the banner which leaned against the rock behind him.

" You have done nobly," cried the old Free Companion, gazing with a soldier's admiration at the huge frame and bold face of the archer. " But why is it, my good fellow, that you sit upon this man ? "

" By the rood ! I had forgot him," John answered, rising and dragging from under him no less a person than the Spanish caballero, Don Diego Alvarez. " This man, my fair lord, means to me a new house, ten cows, one bull —if it be but a little one—a grindstone, and I know not what beside ; so that I thought it well to sit upon him, lest he should take a fancy to leave me."

" Tell me, John," cried Alleyne, faintly, " where is my dear lord, Sir Nigel Loring ? "

" He is dead, I fear. I saw them throw his body across

a horse and ride away with it, but I fear the life had gone from him."

" Now woe worth me ! And where is Aylward ? "

" He sprang upon a riderless horse and rode after Sir Nigel to save him. I saw them throng around him, and he is either taken or slain."

" Blow the bugles ! " cried Sir Hugh, with a scowling brow. " We must back to camp, and ere three days I trust that we may see these Spaniards again. I would fain have ye all in my company."

" We are of the White Company, my fair lord," said John.

" Nay, the White Company is here disbanded," answered Sir Hugh solemnly, looking round him at the lines of silent figures. " Look to the brave squire, for I fear that he will never see the sun rise again."

38. *Of the Home-coming to Hampshire*

IT was a bright July morning four months after that fatal fight in the Spanish barranca. A blue heaven stretched above, a green rolling plain undulated below, intersected with hedgerows and flecked with grazing sheep. The sun was yet low in the heaven, and the red cows stood in the long shadow of the elms, chewing the cud and gazing with great vacant eyes at two horsemen who were spurring it down the long white road which dipped and curved away back to where the towers and pinnacles beneath the flat-topped hill marked the old town of Winchester.

Of the riders, one was young, graceful and fair, clad in plain doublet and hosen of blue Brussels cloth, which served to show his active and well-knit figure. A flat velvet cap was drawn forward to keep the glare from his eyes, and he rode with lips compressed and anxious face, as one who has much care upon his mind. Young as he was, and peaceful as was his dress, the dainty golden spurs

which twinkled upon his heels proclaimed his knighthood, while a long seam upon his brow and a scar upon
his temple gave a manly grace to his refined and delicate
countenance. His comrade was a large red-headed man
upon a great black horse, with a huge canvas bag slung
from his saddle-bow, which jingled and clinked with
every movement of his steed. His broad brown face
was lighted up by a continual smile, and he looked slowly
from side to side with eyes which twinkled and shone with
delight. Well might John rejoice, for was he not back
in his native Hampshire, had he not Don Diego's five
thousand crowns rasping against his knee, and above all
was he not himself squire now to Sir Alleyne Edricson, the
young Socman of Minstead, lately knighted by the sword
of the Black Prince himself, and esteemed by the whole
army as one of the most rising of the soldiers of England ?

For the last stand of the Company had been told
throughout Christendom wherever a brave deed of arms
was loved, and honours had flowed in upon the few who
had survived it. For two months Alleyne had wavered
betwixt death and life, with a broken rib and a shattered
head, yet youth and strength and a cleanly life were all
upon his side, and he awoke from his long delirium to
find that the war was over, that the Spaniards and their
allies had been crushed at Navaretta, and that the prince
himself had heard the tale of his ride for succour, and had
come in person to his bedside to touch his shoulder with
his sword, and to ensure that so brave and true a man
should die, if he could not live, within the order of
chivalry. The instant that he could set foot to ground,
Alleyne had started in search of his lord, but no word
could he hear of him, dead or alive, and he had come
home now sad-hearted in the hope of raising money upon
his estates and so starting upon his quest once more.
Landing at London he had hurried on with a mind full of
care, for he had heard no word from Hampshire since the
short note which had announced his brother's death.

" By the rood ! " cried John, looking around him exultantly, " where have we seen since we left such noble cows, such fleecy sheep, grass so green, or a man so drunk as yonder rogue who lies in the gap of the hedge ? "

" Ah, John," Alleyne answered wearily, " it is well for you, but I never thought that my home-coming would be so sad a one. My heart is heavy for my dear lord and for Aylward, and I know not how I may break the news to the Lady Mary and to the Lady Maude, if they have not yet had tidings of it."

John gave a groan which made the horses shy. " It is indeed a black business," said he. " But be not sad, for I shall give half these crowns to my old mother, and half will I add to the money which you may have, and so we shall buy that yellow cog wherein we sail to Bordeaux, and in it we shall go forth and seek Sir Nigel."

Alleyne smiled, but shook his head. " Were he alive we should have had word of him ere now," said he. " But what is this town before us ? "

" Why, it is Romsey ! " cried John. " See the tower of the old grey church, and the long stretch of the nun-nery. But here sits a very holy man, and I shall give him a crown for his prayers."

Three large stones formed a rough cot by the roadside, and beside it, basking in the sun, sat the hermit, with clay-coloured face, dull eyes and long withered hands. With crossed ankles and sunken head, he sat as though all his life had passed out of him, with the beads slipping slowly through his thin yellow fingers. Behind him lay the narrow cell, clay floored and damp, comfortless, profitless and sordid. Beyond it there lay amid the trees the wattle-and-daub hut of a labourer, the door open, and the single room exposed to the view. The man, ruddy and yellow-haired, stood leaning upon the spade where-with he had been at work upon the garden patch. From behind him came the ripple of a happy woman's laughter, and two young urchins darted forth from the hut, bare-legged and towsy, while the mother, stepping out, laid her hand upon her husband's arm and watched the gambols of the children. The hermit frowned at the untoward noise which broke upon his prayers, but his brow relaxed as he looked upon the broad silver piece which John held out to him.

" There lies the image of our past and of our future," cried Alleyne, as they rode on upon their way. " Now, which is better, to till God's earth, to have happy faces round one's knee, and to love and be loved, or to sit for ever moaning over one's soul, like a mother over a sick babe ? "

" I know not about that," said John, " for it casts a great cloud over me when I think of such matters. But I know that my crown was well spent, for the man had the look of a very holy person. As to the other, there was nought holy about him that I could see, and it would be cheaper for me to pray for myself than to give a crown to one who spent his days in digging for lettuces."

Ere Alleyne could answer there swung round the curve of the road a lady's carriage drawn by three horses abreast with a postilion upon the outer one. Very fine and rich it was, with beams painted and gilt, wheels and spokes carved in strange figures, and over all an arched cover of red and white tapestry. Beneath its shade there sat a stout and elderly lady in a pink *côte-hardie*, leaning back among a pile of cushions, and plucking out her eyebrows with a small pair of silver tweezers. None could seem more safe and secure and at her ease than this lady, yet here also was a symbol of human life, for in an instant, even as Alleyne reined aside to let the carriage pass, a wheel flew out from among its fellows, and over it all toppled—carving, tapestry and gilt—in one wild heap, with the horses plunging, the postilion shouting and the lady screaming from within. In an instant Alleyne and John were on foot, and had lifted her forth all in a shake with fear, but little the worse for her mischance.

" Now woe worth me ! " she cried, " and ill fall on Michael Easover of Romsey ! for I told him that the pin was loose, and yet he must needs gainsay me, like the foolish daffe that he is."

" I trust that you have taken no hurt, my fair lady," said Alleyne, conducting her to the bank, upon which John had already placed a cushion.

" Nay, I have had no scath, though I have lost my silver tweezers. Now, lack-a-day! did God ever put breath into such a fool as Michael Easover of Romsey? But I am much beholden to you, gentle sirs. Soldiers ye are, as one may readily see. I am myself a soldier's daughter," she added, casting a somewhat languishing glance at John, " and my heart ever goes out to a brave man."

" We are indeed fresh from Spain," quoth Alleyne.

" From Spain, say you? Ah! it was an ill and sorry thing that so many should throw away the lives that Heaven gave them. In sooth, it is bad for those who fall, but worse for those who bide behind. I have but now bid farewell to one who hath lost all in this cruel war."

" And how that, lady? "

" She is a young damsel of these parts, and she goes now into a nunnery. Alack! it is not a year since she was the fairest maid from Avon to Itchen, and now it was more than I could abide to wait at Romsey Nunnery to see her put the white veil upon her face, for she was made for a wife and not for the cloister. Did you ever, gentle sir, hear of a body of men called ' The White Company' over yonder? "

" Surely so," cried both the comrades.

" Her father was the leader of it, and her lover served under him as squire. News hath come that not one of the Company was left alive, and so, poor lamb, she hath——"

" Lady! " cried Alleyne, with catching breath, " is it the Lady Maude Loring of whom you speak? "

" It is, in sooth."

" Maude! And in a nunnery! Did, then, the thought of her father's death so move her? "

" Her father! " cried the lady, smiling. " Nay; Maude is a good daughter, but I think it was this young golden-haired squire of whom I have heard who has made her turn her back upon the world."

" And I stand talking here ! " cried Alleyne wildly. " Come, John, come ! "

Rushing to his horse, he swung himself into the saddle, and was off down the road in a rolling cloud of dust as fast as his good steed could bear him.

Great had been the rejoicing amid the Romsey nuns when the Lady Maude Loring had craved admission into their order—for was she not sole child and heiress of the old knight, with farms and fiefs which she could bring to the great nunnery ?   Long and earnest had been the talks of the gaunt lady abbess, in which she had conjured the young novice to turn for ever from the world, and to rest her bruised heart under the broad and peaceful shelter of the Church.   And now, when all was settled, and when abbess and lady superior had had their will, it was but fitting that some pomp and show should mark the glad occasion.   Hence it was that the good burghers of Romsey were all in the streets, that gay flags and flowers brightened the path from the nunnery to the church, and that a long procession wound up to the old arch door, leading up the bride to these spiritual nuptials.   There was lay-sister Agatha with the high gold crucifix, and the three incense-bearers, and the two-and-twenty garbed in white, who cast flowers upon either side of them and sang sweetly the while.   Then, with four attendants, came the novice, her drooping head wreathed with white blossoms, and, behind, the abbess and her council of older nuns, who were already counting in their minds whether their own bailiff could manage the farms of Twynham, or whether a reeve would be needed beneath him to draw the utmost from these new possessions which this young novice was about to bring them.

But alas ! for plots and plans when love and youth and nature, and, above all, fortune are arrayed against them. Who is this travel-stained youth who dares to ride so madly through the lines of staring burghers ?   Why does he fling himself from his horse and stare so strangely about him ?   See how he has rushed through the incense-bearers, thrust aside lay-sister Agatha, scattered the two-and-twenty damosels who sang so sweetly—and he stands before the novice with his hands outstretched, and his face shining, and the light of love in his grey eyes. Her foot is on the very threshold of the church, and yet he bars the way—and she, she thinks no more of the wise words and holy rede of the lady abbess, but she hath given a sobbing cry and hath fallen forward with his arms around her drooping body and her wet cheek upon his breast. A sorry sight this for the gaunt abbess, an ill lesson, too, for the stainless two-and-twenty who have ever been taught that the way of nature is the way of sin. But Maude and Alleyne care little for this. A dank cold air comes out from the black arch before them. Without, the sun shines bright and the birds are singing amid the ivy on the drooping beeches. Their choice is made, and they turn away hand-in-hand, with their backs to the darkness and their faces to the light.

Very quiet was the wedding in the old priory church at Christchurch, where Father Christopher read the service, and there were few to see save the Lady Loring and John, and a dozen bowmen from the castle. The Lady of Twynham had drooped and pined for weary months, so that her face was harsher and less comely than before, yet she still hoped on, for her lord had come through so many dangers that she could scarce believe that he might be stricken down at last. It had been her wish to start for Spain and to search for him, but Alleyne had persuaded her to let him go in her place. There was much to look after, now that the lands of Minstead were joined to those of Twynham, and Alleyne had promised her that if she would but bide with his wife he would never come back to Hampshire again until he had gained some news, good or ill, of her lord and lover.

The yellow cog had been engaged, with Goodwin Hawtayne in command, and a month after the wedding Alleyne rode down to Bucklershard to see if she had come round yet from Southampton. On the way he passed the fishing village of Pitt's Deep, and marked that a little creyer or brig was tacking off the land, as though about to anchor there. On his way back, as he rode towards the village, he saw that she had indeed anchored and that many boats were round her, bearing cargo to the shore.

A bow-shot from Pitt's Deep there was an inn a little back from the road, very large and widespread, with a great green bush hung upon a pole from one of the upper windows. At this window he marked, as he rode up, that a man was seated who appeared to be craning his neck in his direction. Alleyne was still looking up at him, when a woman came rushing from the open door of the inn, and made as though she would climb a tree, looking back the while with a laughing face. Wondering what these doings might mean, Alleyne tied his horse to a tree, and was walking amid the trunks towards the inn, when there shot from the entrance a second woman who made also for the trees. Close at her heels came a burly, brown-faced man, who leaned against the door-post and laughed loudly with his hand to his side.

" Ah, mes belles ! " he cried, " and is it thus you treat me ? Ah, mes petites ! I swear by these finger-bones that I would not hurt a hair of your pretty heads ; but I have been among the black paynim, and, by my hilt ! it does me good to look at your English cheeks. Come, drink a stoup of muscadine with me, mes anges, for my heart is warm to be among ye again."

At the sight of the man Alleyne had stood staring, but at the sound of his voice such a thrill of joy bubbled up in his heart that he had to bite his lip to keep himself from shouting outright. But a deeper pleasure yet was in store. Even as he looked, the window above was pushed outwards, and the voice of the man whom he had seen there came out from it.

" Aylward," cried the voice, " I have seen just now a very worthy person come down the road, though my eyes could scarce discern whether he carried coat-armour. I pray you to wait upon him and tell him that a very humble knight of England abides here, so that if he be in need of advancement, or have any small vow upon his soul, or desire to exalt his lady, I may help him to accomplish it."

Aylward at this order came shuffling forward amid the trees, and in an instant the two men were clinging in each other's arms, laughing and shouting and patting each other in their delight ; while old Sir Nigel came running with his sword, under the impression that some small bickering had broken out, only to embrace and be embraced himself, until all three were hoarse with their questions and outcries and congratulations.

On their journey home through the woods Alleyne learnt their wondrous story, how when Sir Nigel came to his senses, he with his fellow-captive had been hurried to the coast, and conveyed by sea to their captor's castle ; how upon the way they had been taken by a Barbary rover, and how they exchanged their light captivity for a seat on a galley bench and hard labour at the pirate's oars ; how, in the port of Barbary, Sir Nigel had slain the Moorish captain, and had swum, with Aylward, to a small coaster which they had taken and so made their way to England with a rich cargo to reward them for their toils. All this Alleyne listened to, until the dark keep of Twynham towered above them in the gloaming, and they saw the red sun lying athwart the rippling Avon. No need to speak of the glad hearts at Twynham Castle that night, nor of the rich offerings from out of that Moorish cargo which found their way to the chapel of Father Christopher.

Sir Nigel Loring lived for many years, full of honour and laden with every blessing. He rode no more to the wars, but he found his way to every jousting within thirty miles ; and the Hampshire youth treasured it as the highest honour when a word of praise fell from him as to their management of their horses, or their breaking of their lances. So he lived and so he died, the most revered and the happiest man in all his native shire.

For Sir Alleyne Edricson and for his beautiful bride the future had also nought but what was good. Twice he fought in France, and came back each time laden with honours. A high place at court was given to him, and he spent many years at Windsor under the second Richard and the fourth Henry—where he received the honour of the Garter, and won the name of being a brave soldier, a true-hearted gentleman and a great lover and patron of every art and science which refines or ennobles life.

As to John, he took unto himself a village maid, and settled in Lyndhurst, where his five thousand crowns made him the richest franklin for many miles around. For many years he drank his ale every night at the " Pied Merlin," which was now kept by his friend Aylward, who had wedded the good widow to whom he had committed his plunder. The strong men and the bowmen of the country round used to drop in there of an evening to wrestle a fall with John or to shoot a round with Aylward ; but though a silver shilling was to be the prize of the victor, it has never been reported that any man earned much money in that fashion. So they lived, these men, in their own lusty, cheery fashion—rude and rough, but honest, kindly and true. Let us thank God if we have outgrown their vices. Let us pray to God that we may ever hold their virtues. The sky may darken, and the clouds may gather, and again the day may come when Britain may have sore need of her children, on whatever shore of the sea they be found. Shall they not muster at her call ?

SIR NIGEL

1. *The House of Loring*

IN the month of July of the year 1348, between the feasts of St. Benedict and of St. Swithin, a strange thing came upon England, for out of the east there drifted a monstrous cloud, purple and piled, heavy with evil, climbing slowly up the hushed heaven. In the shadow of that strange cloud the leaves drooped in the trees, the birds ceased their calling, and the cattle and the sheep gathered cowering under the hedges. A gloom fell upon all the land, and men stood with their eyes upon the strange cloud and a heaviness upon their hearts. They crept into the churches, where the trembling people were blessed and shriven by the trembling priests. Outside no bird flew, and there came no rustling from the woods, nor any of the homely sounds of Nature. All was still, and nothing moved, save only the great cloud which rolled up and onward, with fold on fold from the black horizon. To the west was the light summer sky, to the east this brooding cloud-bank, creeping ever slowly across, until the last thin blue gleam faded away and the whole vast sweep of the heavens was one great leaden arch.

Then the rain began to fall. All day it rained, and all the night and all the week and all the month, until folk had forgotten the blue heavens and the gleam of the sunshine. It was not heavy, but it was steady and cold and unceasing, so that the people were weary of its hissing and its splashing, with the slow drip from the eaves. Always the same thick evil cloud flowed from east to west with the rain beneath it. None could see for more than a bow-shot from their dwellings for the drifting veil of the rain-storms. Every morning the folk looked upward for a break, but their eyes rested always upon the same endless cloud, until at last they ceased to look up, and their hearts despaired of ever seeing the change. It was raining at Lammas-tide and raining at the Feast of the Assumption and still raining at Michaelmas. The crops and the hay, sodden and black, had rotted in the fields, for they were not worth the garnering. The sheep had died, and the calves also, so there was little to kill when Martinmas came and it was time to salt the meat for winter. They feared a famine, but it was worse than famine which was in store for them.

For the rain had ceased at last, and a sickly autumn sun shone upon a land which was soaked and sodden with water. Wet and rotten leaves reeked and festered under the foul haze which rose from the woods. The fields were spotted with monstrous fungi of a size and colour never matched before—scarlet and mauve and liver and black. It was as though the sick earth had burst into foul pustules ; mildew and lichen mottled the walls, and with that filthy crop Death sprang also from the water-soaked earth. Men died, and women and children, the baron of the castle, the franklin on the farm, the monk in the abbey, and the villein in his wattle-and-daub cottage. All breathed the same polluted reek and all died the same death of corruption. Of those who were stricken none recovered, and the illness was ever the same—gross boils, raving, and the black blotches which gave its name to the disease. All through the winter the dead rotted by the wayside for want of someone to bury them. In many a village no single man was left alive. Then at last the spring came, with sunshine and health and lightness and laughter—the greenest, sweetest, tenderest spring that England had ever known. But only half of England could know it—the other half had passed away with the great purple cloud.

Yet it was there, in that steam of death, in that reek of corruption, that the brighter and freer England was born. There in that dark hour the first streak of the new dawn was seen. For in no way save by a great upheaval and change could the nation break away from that iron feudal system which held her limbs. But now it was a new country which came out from that year of death. The barons were dead in swaths. No high turret nor cunning moat could keep out that black commoner who struck them down. Oppressive laws slackened for want of those who could enforce them, and once slackened could never be enforced again. The labourer would be a slave no longer. The bondsman snapped his shackles. There was much to do and few left to do it. Therefore the few should be free men, name their own price, and work where and for whom they would. It was the black death which cleared the way for the great rising thirty years later which left the English peasant the freest of his class in Europe.

But there were few so far-sighted that they could see that here as ever good was coming out of evil. At the moment misery and ruin were brought into every family. The dead cattle, the ungarnered crops, the untilled lands —every spring of wealth had dried up at the same moment. Those who were rich became poor ; but those who were poor already, and especially those who were poor with the burden of gentility upon their shoulders, found themselves in a perilous state. All through England the smaller gentry were ruined, for they had no trade save war, and they drew their living from the work of others. On many a manor-house there came evil times, and on none more than on the Manor of Tilford, where for many generations the noble family of the Lorings had held their home.

There was a time when the Lorings had held the country from the North Downs to the Lakes of Frensham, and when their grim castle-keep rising above the green meadows which border the River Wey had been the strongest fortalice betwixt Guildford Castle in the east and Winchester in the west. But there came that Barons' War, in which the King used his Saxon subjects as a whip with which to scourge his Norman barons, and Castle

Loring, like so many other great strongholds, was swept
from the face of the land. From that time the Lorings,
with estates sadly curtailed, lived in what had been the
dower-house, with enough for their needs, but shorn of all
their splendour.

And then came their lawsuit with Waverley Abbey,
when the Cistercians laid claim to their richest land, with
peccary, turbary, and feudal rights over the remainder. It
straggled on for years, this great lawsuit, and when it was
finished the men of the Church and the men of the Law
had divided all that was richest of the estate between
them. There was still left the old manor-house, from
which with each generation there came a soldier to uphold
the credit of the name, and to show the five scarlet roses
on the silver shield where it had always been shown—in
the van. There were twelve bronzes in the little chapel,
where Mathew the priest said mass every morning, all of
men of the House of Loring. Two lay with their legs
crossed, as being from the Crusades. Six others rested
their feet upon lions, as having died in war. Four only
lay with the effigy of their hounds to show that they had
passed in peace.

Of this famous but impoverished family, doubly impoverished by law and by pestilence, two members were
living in the year of grace 1349—Lady Ermyntrude Loring
and her grandson Nigel. Lady Ermyntrude's husband
had fallen before the Scottish spearmen at Stirling, and
her son Eustace, Nigel's father, had found a glorious death,
nine years before this chronicle opens, upon the poop of a
Norman galley at the sea-fight of Sluys. The lonely old
woman, fierce and brooding like the falcon mewed in her
chamber, was soft only toward the lad whom she had
brought up. All the tenderness and love of her nature,
so hidden from others that they could not imagine their
existence, were lavished upon him. She could not bear
him away from her, and he, with that respect for authority
which the age demanded, would not go without her
blessing and consent.

So it came about that Nigel, with his lion heart and with the blood of a hundred soldiers thrilling in his veins, still at the age of two-and-twenty, wasted the weary days reclaiming his hawks with leash and lure or training the alans and spaniels who shared with the family the big earthen-floored hall of the manor-house.

Day by day the aged Lady Ermyntrude had seen him wax in strength and in manhood, small of stature, it is true, but with muscles of steel and a soul of fire. From all parts, from the warden of Guildford Castle, from the tilt-yard of Farnham, tales of his prowess were brought back to her, of his daring as a rider, of his debonair courage, of his skill with all weapons ; but still she, who had both husband and son torn from her by a bloody death, could not bear that this, the last of the Lorings, the final bud of so famous an old tree, should share the same fate. With a weary heart, but with a smiling face, he bore with his uneventful days, while she would ever put off the evil time, until the harvest was better, until the monks of Waverley should give up what they had taken, until his uncle should die and leave money for his outfit, or any other excuse with which she could hold him to her side.

And, indeed, there was need for a man at Tilford, for the strife betwixt the Abbey and the manor-house had never been appeased, and still on one pretext or another the monks would clip off yet one more slice of their neighbour's land. Over the winding river, across the green meadows, rose the short square tower and the high grey walls of the grim Abbey, with its bell tolling by day and night, a voice of menace and of dread to the little household.

It is in the heart of the great Cistercian monastery that this chronicle of old days must take its start, as we trace the feud betwixt the monks and the House of Loring with those events to which it gave birth, ending with the coming of Chandos, the strange spear-running of Tilford Bridge, and the deeds with which Nigel won fame in the wars. Elsewhere, in the chronicle of the White Company, it has been set forth what manner of man was Nigel Loring. Those who love him may read herein the things which went to his making. Let us go back together and gaze upon this green stage of England, the scenery, hill, plain and river even as now, the actors in much our very selves, in much also so changed in thought and act that they might be dwellers in another world to ours.

2. *How the Devil came to Waverley*

THE day was the first of May, which was the Festival of the Blessed Apostles Philip and James. The year was the 1349th from man's salvation.

From tierce to sext, and then again from sext to nones, Abbot John of the House of Waverley had been seated in his study while he conducted the many high duties of his office. All round for many a mile on every side stretched the fertile and flourishing estate of which he was the master. In the centre lay the broad Abbey buildings, with church and cloisters, hospitium, chapter-house and frater-house, all buzzing with a busy life. Through the open window came the low hum of the voices of the brethren as they walked in pious converse in the ambulatory below. From across the cloister there rolled the distant rise and fall of a Gregorian chant, where the precentor was hard at work upon the choir, while down in the chapter-house sounded the strident voice of Brother Peter, expounding the rule of Saint Bernard to the novices.

Abbot John rose to stretch his cramped limbs. He looked out at the greensward of the cloister, and at the graceful line of open Gothic arches which skirted a covered walk for the brethren within. Two and two in their black-and-white garb, with slow step and heads inclined, they paced round and round. Several of the more studious had brought their illuminating work from the scriptorium, and sat in the warm sunshine, with their little platters of pigments and packets of gold-leaf before them, their shoulders rounded and their faces sunk low over the white sheets of vellum. There, too, was the copper-worker with his burin and graver. Learning and art were not traditions with the Cistercians as with the parent Order of the Benedictines, and yet the library of Waverley was well filled both with precious books and with pious students.

But the true glory of the Cistercian lay in his outdoor work, and so ever and anon there passed through the cloister some sun-burned monk, soiled mattock or shovel in hand, with his gown looped to his knee, fresh from the fields or the garden. The lush green water-meadows speckled with the heavy-fleeced sheep, the acres of corn-land reclaimed from heather and bracken, the vineyards on the southern slope of Crooksbury Hill, the rows of Hankley fish-ponds, the Frensham marshes drained and sown with vegetables, the spacious pigeon-cotes, all circled the great Abbey round with the visible labours of the Order.

The Abbot's full and florid face shone with a quiet content as he looked out at his huge but well-ordered household. Like every head of a prosperous Abbey, Abbot John, the fourth of the name, was a man of varied accomplishment. Through his own chosen instruments he had to minister a great estate, and to keep order and decorum among a large body of men living a celibate life. He was a rigid disciplinarian toward all beneath him, a supple diplomatist to all above. He held high debate with neighbouring abbots and lords, with bishops, with papal legates, and even on occasion with the King's majesty himself. Many were the subjects with which he must be conversant. Questions of doctrine, questions of building, points of forestry, of agriculture, of drainage, of feudal law, all came to the Abbot for settlement. He held the scales of Justice in all the Abbey banlieue which stretched over many a mile of Hampshire and of Surrey. To the monks his displeasure might mean fasting, exile to some sterner community, or even imprisonment in chains. Over the laymen also he could hold any punishment save only corporeal death, instead of which he had in hand the far more dreadful weapon of spiritual excommunication.

Such were the powers of the Abbot, and it is no wonder that there were masterful lines in the ruddy features of Abbot John, or that the brethren, glancing up, should put on an even meeker carriage and more demure expression as they saw the watchful face in the window above them.

A knock at the door of his study recalled the Abbot to his immediate duties, and he returned to his desk. Already he had spoken with his cellarer and prior, almoner, chaplain, and lector, but now in the tall and gaunt monk who obeyed his summons to enter he recognised the most important and also the most importunate of his agents, Brother Samuel the sacrist, whose office, corresponding to that of the layman's bailiff, placed the material interests of the monastery and its dealings with the outer world entirely under his control, subject only to the check of the Abbot. Brother Samuel was a gnarled and stringy old monk, whose stern and sharp-featured face reflected no light from above, but only that sordid workaday world toward which it was for ever turned. A huge book of accounts was tucked under one of his arms, while a great bunch of keys hung from the other hand, a badge of his office, and also, on occasion of impatience, a weapon of offence, as many a scarred head among rustics and lay brothers could testify.

The Abbot sighed wearily, for he suffered much at the hands of his strenuous agent.

" Well, Brother Samuel, what is your will ? " he asked.

" Holy father, I have to report that I have sold the wool to Master Baldwin of Winchester at two shillings a bale more than it fetched last year, for the murrain among the sheep has raised the price."

" You have done well, brother."

" I have also to tell you that I have distrained Wat the warrener from his cottage ; for his Christmas rent is still unpaid, nor the hen-rents of last year."

" He has a wife and four children, brother." He was a good, easy man, the Abbot, though liable to be overborne by his sterner subordinate.

" It is true, holy father ; but if I should pass him, then how am I to ask the rent of the foresters of Puttenham, or the hinds in the village ? Such a thing spreads from house to house, and where then is the wealth of Waverley? "

" What else, Brother Samuel ? "

" There is the matter of the fish-ponds."

The Abbot's face brightened. It was a subject upon which he was an authority. If the rule of his Order had robbed him of the softer joys of life, he had the keener zest for those which remained.

" How have the char prospered, brother ? "

" They have done well, holy father ; but the carp have died in the Abbot's pond."

" Carp prosper only upon a gravel bottom. They must be put in also in their due proportion, three milters to one spawner, brother sacrist, and the spot must be free from wind, stony and sandy, an ell deep, with willows and grass upon the banks. Mud for tench, brother, gravel for carp."

The sacrist leaned forward with the face of one who bears tidings of woe.

" There are pike in the Abbot's pond," said he.

" Pike ! " cried the Abbot, in horror. " As well shut up a wolf in our sheepfold. How came a pike in the pond ? There were no pike last year, and a pike does not fall with the rain nor rise in the springs. The pond must be drained, or we shall spend next Lent upon stock-fish, and have the brethren down with the great sickness ere Easter Sunday has come to absolve us from our abstinence."

" The pond shall be drained, holy father ; I have already ordered it. Then we shall plant pot-herbs on the mud bottom, and after we have gathered them in, return the fish and water once more from the lower pond, so that they may fatten among the rich stubble."

" Good ! " cried the Abbot. " I would have three fish-stews in every well-ordered house—one dry for herbs, one shallow for the fry and the yearlings, and one deep for the breeders and the table-fish. But still, I have not heard you say how the pike came in the Abbot's pond ? "

A spasm of anger passed over the fierce face of the sacrist, and his keys rattled as his bony hand clasped them more tightly.

" Young Nigel Loring ! " said he. " He swore that he would do us scath, and in this way he has done it."

" How know you this ? "

" Six weeks ago he was seen day by day fishing for pike at the great Lake of Frensham. Twice at night he has been met with a bundle of straw under his arm on the Hankley Down. Well I wot that the straw was wet and that a live pike lay within it."

The Abbot shook his head. " I have heard much of this youth's wild ways ; but now, indeed, he has passed all bounds, if what you say be truth. It was bad enough when it was said that he slew the king's deer in Woolmer Chase, or broke the head of Hobbs the chapman, so that he lay for seven days betwixt life and death in our infirmary, saved only by Brother Peter's skill in the pharmacies of herbs ; but to put pike in the Abbot's pond— why should he play such a devil's prank ? "

" Because he hates the House of Waverley, holy father ; because he swears that we hold his father's land."

" In which there is surely some truth."

" But, holy father, we hold no more than the law has allowed."

" True, brother, and yet, between ourselves, we may admit that the heavier purse may weigh down the scales of Justice. When I have passed the old house and have seen that aged woman with her ruddled cheeks and her baleful eyes look the curses she dare not speak, I have many a time wished that we had other neighbours."

" That we can soon bring about, holy father. Indeed, it is of it that I wished to speak to you. Surely it is not hard for us to drive them from the country-side. There are thirty years' claims of escuage unsettled, and there is

Sergeant Wilkins, the lawyer of Guildford, whom I will warrant to draw up such arrears of dues and rents and issues of hidage and fodder-corn that these folk, who are as beggarly as they are proud, will have to sell the roof-tree over them ere they can meet them. Within three days I will have them at our mercy."

"They are an ancient family and of good repute. I would not treat them too harshly, brother."

"Bethink you of the pike in the carp pond!"

The Abbot hardened his heart at the thought. "It was indeed a devil's deed—when we had but newly stocked it with char and with carp. Well, well, the law is the law, and if you can use it to their hurt it is still lawful to do so. Have these claims been advanced?"

"Deacon, the bailiff, with his two varlets went down to the Hall yesternight on the matter of the escuage, and came screaming back with this young hot-head raging at their heels. He is small and slight, yet he has the strength of many men in the hour of his wrath. The bailiff swears that he will go no more, save with half a score of archers to uphold him."

The Abbot was red with anger at this new offence. "I will teach him that the servants of Holy Church, even though we of the rule of Saint Bernard be the lowliest and humblest of her children, can still defend their own against the froward and the violent! Go, cite this man before the Abbey court. Let him appear in the chapter-house after tierce to-morrow."

But the wary sacrist shook his head. "Nay, holy father, the times are not yet ripe. Give me three days, I pray you, that my case against him may be complete. Bear in mind that the father and the grandfather of this unruly squire were both famous men of their day and the foremost knights in the king's own service, living in high honour and dying in their knightly duty. The Lady Ermyntrude Loring was first lady to the king's mother. Roger FitzAlan of Farnham and Sir Hugh Walcott of Guildford Castle were each old comrades-in-arms of

Nigel's father, and sib to him on the distaff side. Already there has been talk that we have dealt harshly with them. Therefore, my rede is that we be wise and wary and wait until his cup be indeed full."

The Abbot had opened his mouth to reply, when the consultation was interrupted by a most unwonted buzz of excitement from among the monks in the cloister below. Questions and answers in excited voices sounded from one side of the ambulatory to the other. Sacrist and Abbot were gazing at each other in amazement at such a breach of the discipline and decorum of their well-trained flock, when there came a swift step upon the stair, and a white-faced brother flung open the door and rushed into the room.

" Father Abbot ! " he cried. " Alas, alas ! Brother John is dead, and the holy sub-prior is dead, and the Devil is loose in the five-virgate field ! "

3. *The Yellow Horse of Crooksbury*

IN those simple times there was a great wonder and mystery in life. Man walked in fear and solemnity, with Heaven very close above his head, and Hell below his very feet. God's visible hand was everywhere, in the rainbow and the comet, in the thunder and the wind. The Devil, too, raged openly upon the earth ; he skulked behind the hedgerows in the gloaming ; he laughed loudly in the night-time ; he clawed the dying sinner, pounced on the unbaptized babe, and twisted the limbs of the epileptic. A foul fiend slunk ever by a man's side and whispered villainies in his ear, while above him there hovered an angel of grace who pointed to the steep and narrow track. How could one doubt these things, when Pope and priest and scholar and king were all united in believing them, with no single voice of question in the whole wide world ?

Every book read, every picture seen, every tale heard from nurse or mother, all taught the same lesson. And as a man travelled through the world his faith would grow the firmer, for go where he would there were the endless shrines of the saints, each with its holy relic in the centre, and around it the tradition of incessant miracles, with stacks of deserted crutches and silver votive hearts to prove them. At every turn he was made to feel how thin was the veil, and how easily rent, which screened him from the awful denizens of the unseen world.

Hence the wild announcement of the frightened monk seemed terrible rather than incredible to those whom he addressed. The Abbot's ruddy face paled for a moment, it is true, but he plucked the crucifix from his desk and rose valiantly to his feet.

" Lead me to him ! " said he. " Show me the foul fiend who dares to lay his grip upon brethren of the holy house of Saint Bernard ! Run down to my chaplain, brother ! Bid him bring the exorcist with him, and also the blessed box of relics, and the bones of Saint James from under the altar ! With these and a contrite and humble heart we may show front to all the powers of darkness."

But the sacrist was of a more critical turn of mind. He clutched the monk's arm with a grip which left its five purple spots for many a day to come.

" Is this the way to enter the Abbot's own chamber without knock or reverence, or so much as a ' Pax vobiscum ' ? " said he, sternly. " You were wont to be our gentlest novice, of lowly carriage in chapter, devout in psalmody, and strict in the cloister. Pull your wits together and answer me straightly. In what form has the foul fiend appeared, and how has he done this grievous scathe to our brethren ? Have you seen him with your own eyes, or do you repeat from hearsay ? Speak, man, or you stand on the penance-stool in the chapter-house this very hour ! "

Thus adjured, the frightened monk grew calmer in his bearing, though his white lips and his startled eyes, with the gasping of his breath, told of his inward tremors.

" If it please you, holy father, and you, reverend sacrist, it came about in this way. James the sub-prior, and Brother John and I had spent our day from sext onward on Hankley cutting bracken for the cow-houses. We were coming back over the five-virgate field, and the holy sub-prior was telling us a saintly tale from the life of Saint Gregory, when there came a sudden sound like a rushing torrent, and the foul fiend sprang over the high wall which skirts the water-meadow and rushed upon us with the speed of the wind. The lay brother he struck to the ground and trampled into the mire. Then, seizing the good sub-prior in his teeth, he rushed round the field, swinging him as though he were a fardel of old clothes.

"Amazed at such a sight, I stood without movement, and had said a credo and three aves, when the Devil dropped the sub-prior and sprang upon me. With the help of St. Bernard I clambered over the wall, but not before his teeth had found my leg, and he had torn away the whole back skirt of my gown."

As he spoke he turned and gave corroboration to his story by the hanging ruins of his long trailing garment.

"In what shape, then, did Satan appear?" the Abbot demanded.

"As a great yellow horse, holy father—a monster horse, with eyes of fire and the teeth of a griffin."

"A yellow horse!" The sacrist glared at the scared monk. "You foolish brother! how will you behave when you have indeed to face the King of Terrors himself if you can be so frightened by the sight of a yellow horse? It is the horse of Franklin Aylward, my father, which has been distrained by us because he owes the Abbey fifty good shillings, and can never hope to pay it. Such a horse, they say, is not to be found betwixt this and the king's stables at Windsor, for his sire was a Spanish destrier, and his dam an Arab mare of the very breed which Saladin kept for his own use, and even, it has been said, under the shelter of his own tent. I took him in discharge of the debt, and I ordered the varlets who had haltered him to leave him alone in the water-meadow, for I have heard that the beast has indeed a most evil spirit, and has killed more men than one."

" It was an ill day for Waverley that you brought such a monster within its bounds," said the Abbot. " If the sub-prior and brother John be indeed dead, then it would seem that if the horse be not the devil, he is at least the devil's instrument."

" Horse or devil, holy father, I heard him shout with joy as he trampled upon brother John, and had you seen him tossing the sub-prior as a dog shakes a rat, you would perchance have felt even as I did."

" Come, then," cried the Abbot, " let us see with our own eyes what evil has been done."

And the three monks hurried down the stair which led to the cloisters.

They had no sooner descended than their more pressing fears were set at rest, for at that very moment, limping, dishevelled and mud-stained, the two sufferers were being led in amid a crowd of sympathising brethren. Shouts and cries from outside showed, however, that some further drama was in progress, and both Abbot and sacrist hastened onward as fast as the dignity of their office would permit, until they had passed the gates and gained the wall of the meadow. Looking over it, a remarkable sight presented itself to their eyes.

Fetlock deep in the lush grass there stood a magnificent horse, such a horse as a sculptor or a soldier might thrill to see. His colour was a light chestnut, with mane and tail of a more tawny tint. Seventeen hands high, with a barrel and haunches which bespoke tremendous strength, he fined down to the most delicate lines of dainty breed in neck and crest and shoulder. He was indeed a glorious sight as he stood there, his beautiful body leaning back from his widespread and propped forelegs, his head craned high, his ears erect, his mane bristling, his red nostrils opening and shutting with wrath, and his flashing eyes turning from side to side in haughty menace and defiance.

Scattered round in a respectful circle, six of the Abbey lay servants and foresters, each holding a halter, were creeping toward him. Every now and then, with a beautiful toss and swerve and plunge, the great creature would turn upon one of his would-be captors, and with outstretched head, flying mane and flashing teeth, would chase him screaming to the safety of the wall, while the others would close swiftly in behind, and cast their ropes in the hope of catching neck or leg, but only in their turn to be chased to the nearest refuge.

Had two of these ropes settled upon the horse, and had their throwers found some purchase of stump or boulder by which they could hold them, then the man's brain might have won its wonted victory over swiftness and strength. But the brains were themselves at fault which imagined that one such rope would serve any purpose save to endanger the thrower.

Yet so it was, and what might have been foreseen occurred at the very moment of the arrival of the monks. The horse, having chased one of his enemies to the wall, remained so long snorting his contempt over the coping that the others were able to creep upon him from behind. Several ropes were flung, and one noose settled over the proud crest and lost itself in the waving mane. In an instant the creature had turned, and the men were flying for their lives ; but he who had cast the rope lingered, uncertain what use to make of his own success. That moment of doubt was fatal. With a yell of dismay, the man saw the great creature rear above him. Then with a crash the fore-feet fell upon him and dashed him to the ground. He rose screaming, was hurled over once more, and lay a quivering, bleeding heap, while the savage horse, the most cruel and terrible in its anger of all creatures on earth, bit and shook and trampled the writhing body.

A loud wail of horror rose from the lines of tonsured heads which skirted the high wall—a wail which suddenly died away into a long, hushed silence, broken at last by a rapturous cry of thanksgiving and of joy.

On the road which led to the old dark manor-house upon the side of the hill a youth had been riding. His mount was a sorry one, a weedy, shambling, long-haired colt, and his patched tunic of faded purple with stained leather belt presented no very smart appearance ; yet in the bearing of the man, in the poise of his head, in his easy, graceful carriage, and in the bold glance of his large blue eyes, there was that stamp of distinction and of breed which would have given him a place of his own in any assembly. He was of small stature, but his frame was singularly elegant and graceful. His face, though tanned with the weather, was delicate in features, and most eager and alert in expression. A thick fringe of crisp yellow curls broke from under the dark flat cap which he was wearing, and a short golden beard hid the outline of his strong, square chin. One white osprey feather thrust through a gold brooch in the front of his cap gave a touch of grace to his sombre garb. This and other points of his attire, the short hanging mantle, the leather-sheathed hunting-knife, the cross-belt which sustained a brazen horn, the soft doe-skin boots and the prick spurs, would all disclose themselves to an observer ; but at the first glance the brown face set in gold, and the dancing light of the quick, reckless, laughing eyes, were the one strong memory left behind.

Such was the youth who, cracking his whip joyously, and followed by half a score of dogs, cantered on his rude pony down the Tilford Lane, and thence it was that, with a smile of amused contempt upon his face, he observed the comedy in the field and the impotent efforts of the servants of Waverley.

Suddenly, however, as the comedy turned swiftly to black tragedy, this passive spectator leaped into quick strenuous life. With a spring he was off his pony, and with another he was over the stone wall and flying swiftly across the field. Looking up from his victim, the great yellow horse saw this other enemy approach, and spurning the prostrate but still writhing body with his heels, dashed at the newcomer.

But this time there was no hasty flight, no rapturous pursuit to the wall. The little man braced himself straight, flung up his metal-headed whip, and met the horse with a crashing blow upon the head, repeated again and again with every attack. In vain the horse reared and tried to overthrow its enemy with swooping shoulders and pawing hoofs. Cool, swift, and alert, the man sprang swiftly aside from under the very shadow of death, and then again came the swish and thud of the unerring blow from the heavy handle.

The horse drew off, glared with wonder and fury at this masterful man, and then trotted round in a circle, with mane bristling, tail streaming, and ears on end, snorting in its rage and pain. The man, hardly deigning to glance at his fell neighbour, passed on to the wounded forester, raised him in his arms, with a strength which could not have been expected in so slight a body and carried him, groaning, to the wall, where a dozen hands were outstretched to help him over. Then, at his leisure, the young man also climbed the wall, smiling back with cool contempt at the yellow horse, which had come raging after him once more.

As he sprang down, a dozen monks surrounded him to thank him or to praise him ; but he would have turned sullenly away without a word had he not been stopped by Abbot John in person.

" Nay, Squire Loring," said he, " if you be a bad friend to our Abbey, yet we must needs own that you have played the part of a good Christian this day, for if there be breath left in our servant's body it is to you next to our blessed patron Saint Bernard that we owe it."

" By Saint Paul ! I owe you no good-will, Abbot John," said the young man. " The shadow of your Abbey has ever fallen across the house of Loring. As to any small deed that I may have done this day, I ask no thanks for it. It is not for you nor for your house that I have done it, but only because it was my pleasure so to do."

The Abbot flushed at the bold words, and bit his lip with vexation.

It was the sacrist, however, who answered : " It would be more fitting and more gracious," said he, " if you were to speak to the holy Father Abbot in a manner suited to his high rank and to the respect which is due to a Prince of the Church."

The youth turned his bold blue eyes upon the monk, and his sunburned face darkened with anger.

" Were it not for the gown upon your back, and for your silvering hair, I would answer you in another fashion," said he. " You are the lean wolf which growls ever at our door, greedy for the little which hath been left to us. Say and do what you will with me, but by Saint Paul ! if I find that Dame Ermyntrude is bated by your ravenous pack I will beat them off with this whip from the little patch which still remains of all the acres of my fathers."

" Have a care, Nigel Loring, have a care ! " cried the Abbot, with finger upraised. " Have you no fears of the law of England ? "

" A just law I fear and obey."

" Have you no respect for Holy Church ? "

" I respect all that is holy in her. I do not respect those who grind the poor or steal their neighbour's land."

" Rash man, many a one has been blighted by her ban for less than you have now said ! And yet it is not for us to judge you harshly this day. You are young, and hot words come easily to your lips. How fares the forester ? "

" His hurt is grievous, Father Abbot, but he will live," said a brother, looking up from the prostrate form. " With a blood-letting and an electuary, I will warrant him sound within a month."

" Then bear him to the hospital. And now, brother, about this terrible beast who still gazes and snorts at us over the top of the wall as though his thoughts of Holy

Church were as uncouth as those of Squire Nigel himself, what are we to do with him ? "

" Here is Franklin Aylward," said one of the brethren. " The horse was his, and doubtless he will take it back to his farm."

But the stout red-faced farmer shook his head at the proposal. " Not I, in faith ! " said he. " The beast hath chased me twice round the paddock ; it has nigh slain my boy Samkin. He would never be happy till he had ridden it, nor has he ever been happy since. There is not a hind in my employ who will enter his stall. Ill fare the day that ever I took the beast from the Castle stud at Guildford, where they could do nothing with it and no rider could be found bold enough to mount it ! When the sacrist here took it for a fifty-shilling debt he made his own bargain and must abide by it. He comes no more to the Crooksbury farm."

" And he stays no more here," said the Abbot. " Brother sacrist, you have raised the Devil, and it is for you to lay it again."

" That I will most readily," cried the sacrist. " The pittance-master can stop the fifty shillings from my very own weekly dole, and so the Abbey be none the poorer. In the meantime here is Wat with his arbalist and a bolt in his girdle. Let him drive it to the head through this cursed creature, for his hide and his hoofs are of more value than his wicked self."

A hard brown old woodman who had been shooting vermin in the Abbey groves stepped forward with a grin of pleasure. After a lifetime of stoats and foxes, this was indeed a noble quarry which was to fall before him. Fitting a bolt on the nut of his taut crossbow, he had raised it to his shoulder and levelled it at the fierce, proud, dishevelled head which tossed in savage freedom at the other side of the wall. His finger was crooked on the spring, when a blow from a whip struck the bow upward and the bolt flew harmless over the Abbey orchard, while the woodman shrank abashed from Nigel Loring's angry eyes.

" Keep your bolts for your weasels," said he. " Would you take life from a creature whose only fault is that its spirit is so high that it has met none yet who dare control it ? You would slay such a horse as a king might be proud to mount, and all because a country franklin, or a monk, or a monk's varlet, has not the wit nor the hands to master him ? "

The sacrist turned swiftly on the Squire. " The Abbey owes you an offering for this day's work, however rude your words may be," said he. " If you think so much of the horse, you may desire to own it. If I am to pay for it, then with the holy Abbot's permission it is in my gift, and I bestow it freely upon you."

The Abbot plucked at his subordinate's sleeve. " Bethink you, brother sacrist," he whispered, " shall we not have this man's blood upon our heads ? "

" His pride is as stubborn as the horse's, holy father," the sacrist answered, his gaunt face breaking into a malicious smile. " Man or beast, one will break the other, and the world will be the better for it. If you forbid me——"

" Nay, brother, you have bought the horse, and you may have the bestowal of it."

" Then I give it—hide and hoofs, tail and temper—to Nigel Loring, and may it be as sweet and as gentle to him as he hath been to the Abbot of Waverley ! "

The sacrist spoke aloud amid the tittering of the monks, for the man concerned was out of earshot. At the first words which had shown him the turn which affairs had taken he had run swiftly to the spot where he had left his pony. From its mouth he removed the bit and the stout bridle which held it. Then leaving the creature to nibble the grass by the wayside, he sped back whence he came.

" I take your gift, monk," said he, " though I know well why it is that you give it. Yet I thank you, for there are two things upon earth for which I have ever yearned, and which my thin purse could never buy. The one is a noble horse, such a horse as my father's son should have betwixt his thighs, and here is the one of all others which I would have chosen, since some small deed is to be done in the winning of him, and some honourable advancement to be gained. How is the horse called ? "

" Its name," said the franklin, " is Pommers. I warn you, young sir, that none may ride him, for many have tried, and the luckiest is he who has only a staved rib to show for it."

" I thank you for your rede," said Nigel, " and now I see that this is indeed a horse which I would journey far to meet. I am your man, Pommers, and you are my horse, and this night you shall own it, or I will never need horse again. My spirit against thine, and God hold thy spirit high, Pommers, so that the greater be the adventure, and the more hope of honour gained ! "

While he spoke the young Squire had climbed on to the top of the wall and stood there balanced, the very image of grace and spirit and gallantry, his bridle hanging from one hand and his whip grasped in the other. With a fierce snort, the horse made for him instantly, and his white teeth flashed as he snapped ; but again a heavy blow from the loaded whip caused him to swerve, and even at the instant of the swerve, measuring the distance with steady eyes, and bending his supple body for the spring, Nigel bounded into the air and fell with his legs astride the broad back of the yellow horse. For a minute, with neither saddle nor stirrups to help him, and the beast ramping and rearing like a mad thing beneath him, he was hard pressed to hold his own. His legs were like two bands of steel welded on to the swelling arches of the great horse's ribs, and his left hand was buried deep in the tawny mane.

Never had the dull round of the lives of the gentle brethren of Waverley been broken by so fiery a scene. Springing to right and swooping to left, now with its tangled wicked head betwixt its fore-feet, and now pawing eight feet high in the air, with scarlet, furious nostrils and maddened eyes, the yellow horse was a thing of terror and of beauty. But the lithe figure on his back, bending like a reed in the wind to every movement, firm below, pliant above, with calm inexorable face, and eyes which danced and gleamed with the joy of contest, still held its masterful place for all that the fiery heart and the iron muscles of the great beast could do.

Once a long drone of dismay rose from the monks, as, rearing higher and higher yet, a last mad effort sent the creature toppling over backward upon its rider. But, swift and cool, he had writhed from under it ere it fell, spurned it with his foot as it rolled upon the earth, and then seizing its mane as it rose, swung himself lightly on to its back once more. Even the grim sacrist could not but join the cheer, as Pommers, amazed to find the rider still upon his back, plunged and curveted down the field.

But the wild horse only swelled into a greater fury. In the sullen gloom of its untamed heart there rose the furious resolve to dash the life from this clinging rider, even if it meant destruction to beast and man. With red, blazing eyes it looked round for death. On three sides the five-virgate field was bounded by a high wall, broken only at one spot by a heavy four-foot wooden gate. But on the fourth side was a low grey building, one of the granges of the Abbey, presenting a long flank unbroken by door or window. The horse stretched itself into a gallop, and headed straight for that craggy thirty-foot wall. He would break in red ruin at the base of it if he could but dash for ever the life of this man, who claimed mastery over that which had never found its master yet.

The great haunches gathered under it, the eager hoofs drummed the grass, as faster and still more fast the frantic horse bore himself and his rider toward the wall. Would Nigel spring off ? To do so would be to bend his will to that of the beast beneath him. There was a better way than that. Cool, quick and decided, the man swiftly passed both whip and bridle into the left hand which still held the mane. Then with the right he slipped his short mantle from his shoulders, and lying forward along the creature's strenuous, rippling back, he cast the flapping cloth over the horse's eyes.

The result was but too successful, for it nearly brought about the downfall of the rider. When those red eyes, straining for death, were suddenly shrouded in unexpected darkness, the amazed horse propped on its fore-feet and came to so dead a stop that Nigel was shot forward on to its neck, and hardly held himself by his hair-entwined hand. Ere he had slid back into position the moment of danger had passed, for the horse, its purpose all blurred in its mind by this strange thing which had befallen, wheeled round once more, trembling in every fibre, and tossing its petulant head until at last the mantle had been slipped from its eyes and the chilling darkness had melted into the homely circle of sunlit grass once more.

But what was this new outrage which had been inflicted upon it ? What was this defiling bar of iron which was locked hard against its mouth ? What were these straps which galled the tossing neck, this band which spanned its brow ? In those instants of stillness ere the mantle had been plucked away Nigel had lain forward, had slipped the snaffle between the champing teeth, and had deftly secured it.

Blind, frantic fury surged in the yellow horse's heart once more at this new degradation, this badge of serfdom and infamy. His spirit rose high and menacing at the touch. He loathed this place, these people, all and everything which threatened his freedom. He would have done with them for ever ; he would see them no more ! Let him away to the uttermost parts of the earth, to the great plains where freedom is ! Anywhere over the far horizon where he could get away from the defiling bit and the insufferable mastery of man !

He turned with a rush, and one magnificent deer-like bound carried him over the four-foot gate. Nigel's hat had flown off, and his yellow curls streamed behind him as he rose and fell in the leap. They were in the water-meadow now, and the rippling stream twenty feet wide gleamed in front of them, running down to the main current of the Wey. The yellow horse gathered his haunches under him and flew over like an arrow. He took off from behind a boulder and cleared a furze-bush on the farther side. Two stones still mark the leap from hoof-mark to hoof-mark, and they are eleven good paces apart. Under the hanging branch of the great oak tree on the farther side (that *Quercus Tilfordiensis* still shown as the bound of the Abbey's immediate precincts) the great horse passed. He had hoped to sweep off his rider, but Nigel sank low on the heaving back, with his face buried in the flying mane. The rough bough rasped him rudely, but never shook his spirit nor his grip. Rearing, plunging, and struggling, Pommers broke through the sapling grove and was out on the broad stretch of Hankley Down.

And now came such a ride as still lingers in the gossip of the lowly country folk, and forms the rude jingle of that old Surrey ballad, now nearly forgotten, save for the refrain—

> The Doe that sped on Hinde Head,
> The Kestril on the winde,
> And Nigel on the Yellow Horse
> Can leave the world behinde.

Before them lay a rolling ocean of dark heather, knee-deep, swelling in billow on billow up to the clear-cut hill before them. Above stretched one unbroken arch of peaceful blue, with a sun which was sinking down towards the Hampshire hills. Through the deep heather, down the gullies, over the watercourses, up the broken slopes, Pommers flew, his great heart bursting with rage, and every fibre quivering at the indignities which he had endured.

And still, do what he would, the man clung fast to his heaving sides and to his flying mane, silent, motionless, inexorable, letting him do what he would, but fixed as Fate upon his purpose. Over Hankley Down, through Thursley March, with the reeds up to his mud-splashed withers, onward up the long slope of the Headland of the Hinds, down by the Nutcombe Gorge, slipping, blundering, bounding, but never slackening his fearful speed, on went the great yellow horse. The villagers of Shottermill heard the wild clatter of hoofs, but ere they could swing the oxhide curtains of their cottage doors, horse and rider were lost amid the high bracken of the Haslemere Valley. On he went, and on, tossing the miles behind his flying hoofs. No marsh-land could clog him, no hill could hold him back. Up the slope of Linchmere and the long ascent of Fernhurst he thundered as on the level, and it was not until he had flown down the incline of Henley Hill, and the grey castle tower of Midhurst rose over the coppice in front, that at last the eager outstretched neck sank a little on the breast, and the breath came quick and fast. Look where he would in woodland and on Down, his straining eyes could catch no sign of those plains of freedom which he sought.

And yet another outrage ! It was bad that this creature should still cling so tight upon his back, but now he would even go to the intolerable length of checking him and guiding him on the way that he would have him go. There was a sharp pluck at his mouth and his head was turned north once more. As well go that way as another ; but the man was mad indeed if he thought that such a horse as Pommers was at the end of his spirit or his strength. He would soon show him that he was unconquered, if it strained his sinews or broke his heart to do so. Back, then, he flew up the long, long ascent. Would he ever get to the end of it ? Yet he would not own that he could go no farther while the man still kept his grip. He was white with foam and caked with mud. His eyes were gorged with blood, his mouth open and gasping, his nostrils expanded, his coat stark and reeking. On he flew down the long Sunday Hill, until he reached the deep Kingsley Marsh at the bottom. No, it was too much ! Flesh and blood could go no farther. As he struggled out from the reedy slime, with the heavy black mud still clinging to his fetlocks, he at last eased down with sobbing breath, and slowed the tumultuous gallop to a canter.

Oh, crowning infamy! Was there no limit to these degradations? He was no longer even to choose his own pace. Since he had chosen to gallop so far at his own will he must now gallop farther still at the will of another. A spur struck home on either flank. A stinging whip-lash fell across his shoulder. He bounded his own height in the air at the pain and the shame of it. Then, forgetting his weary limbs, forgetting his panting, reeking sides, forgetting everything save this intolerable insult and the burning spirit within, he plunged off once more upon his furious gallop. He was out on the heather slopes again, and heading for Weydown Common. On he flew and on. But again his brain failed him, and again his limbs trembled beneath him, and yet again he strove to ease his pace, only to be driven onward by the cruel spur and the falling lash. He was blind and giddy with fatigue.

He saw no longer where he placed his feet, he cared no longer whither he went, but his one mad longing was to get away from this dreadful thing, this torture which clung to him and would not let him go. Through Thursley village he passed, his eyes straining in his agony, his heart bursting within him, and he had won his way to the crest of Thursley Down, still stung forward by stab and blow, when his spirit weakened, his giant strength ebbed out of him, and with one deep sob of agony the yellow horse sank among the heather. So sudden was the fall that Nigel flew forward over his shoulder, and beast and man lay prostrate and gasping, while the last red rim of the sun sank behind Butser and the first stars gleamed in a violet sky.

The young Squire was the first to recover, and kneeling by the panting, overwrought horse, he passed his hand gently over the tangled mane and down the foam-flecked face. The red eye rolled up at him; but it was wonder, not hatred, a prayer and not a threat, which he could read in it. As he stroked the reeking muzzle, the horse whinnied gently and thrust his nose into the hollow of his hand. It was enough. It was the end of the contest, the acceptance of new conditions by a chivalrous foe from a chivalrous victor.

" You are my horse, Pommers," Nigel whispered, and he laid his cheek against the craning head. " I know you, Pommers, and you know me, and with the help of Saint Paul we shall teach some other folk to know us both. Now let us walk together as far as this moorland pond, for indeed I wot not whether it is you or I who need the water most."

And so it was that some belated monks of Waverley, passing homeward from the outer farms, saw a strange sight, which they carried on with them so that it reached that very night the ears both of sacrist and of Abbot. For, as they passed through Tilford, they had seen horse and man walking side by side and head by head up the manor-house lane. And when they had raised their lanterns on the pair, it was none other than the young Squire himself who was leading home, as a shepherd leads a lamb, the fearsome yellow horse of Crooksbury.

4. *How the Summoner came to the Manor-house of Tilford*

BY the date of this chronicle, the ascetic sternness of the old Norman castles had been humanised and refined, so that the new dwellings of the nobility, if less imposing in appearance, were much more comfortable as places of residence. A gentle race had built their houses rather for peace than for war. He who compares the savage bareness of Pevensey or Guildford with the piled grandeur of Bodmin or Windsor cannot fail to understand the change in manners which they represent.

The earlier castles had a set purpose, for they were built that the invaders might hold down the country ; but when the Conquest was once firmly established, a castle had lost its meaning, save as a refuge from justice or as a centre for civil strife. On the marches of Wales and of Scotland the castle might continue to be a bulwark to the kingdom, and there still grew and flourished ; but in all other places they were rather a menace to the King's majesty, and as such were discouraged and destroyed. By the reign of the third Edward the greater part of the old fighting castles had been converted into dwelling-houses or had been ruined in the civil wars, and left where their grim grey bones are still littered upon the brows of our hills. The new buildings were either great country-houses, capable of defence, but mainly residential, or they were manor-houses with no military significance at all.

Such was the Tilford Manor-house, where the last survivors of the old and magnificent house of Loring still struggled hard to keep a footing and to hold off the monks and the lawyers from the few acres which were left to them. The mansion was a two-storied one, framed in heavy beams of wood, the interstices filled with rude blocks of stone. An outside staircase led up to several sleeping-rooms above. Below, there were only two apartments, the smaller of which was the bower of the aged Lady Ermyntrude. The other was the hall, a very large room, which served as the living-room of the family and as the common dining-room of themselves and of their little group of servants and retainers. The dwellings of these servants, the kitchens, the offices, and the stables were all represented by a row of penthouses and sheds behind the main building. Here lived Charles, the page ; Peter, the old falconer ; Red Swire, who had followed Nigel's grandfather to the Scottish wars ; Weathercote, the broken minstrel ; John, the cook, and other survivors of more prosperous days, who still clung to the old house as the barnacles to some wrecked and stranded vessel.

One evening, about a week after the breaking of the yellow horse, Nigel and his grandmother sat on either side of the large empty fireplace in this spacious apartment.

The supper had been removed, and so had the trestle tables upon which it had been served, so that the room seemed bare and empty. The stone floor was strewed with a thick layer of green rushes, which was swept out every Saturday, and carried with it all the dirt and *débris* of the week. Several dogs were now crouched among these rushes, gnawing and cracking the bones which had been thrown from the table. A long wooden buffet loaded with plates and dishes filled one end of the room, but there was little other furniture, save some benches against the walls, two dorseret chairs, one small table littered with chessmen, and a great iron coffer. In one corner was a high wickerwork stand, and on it two stately falcons were perched, silent and motionless, save for an occasional twinkle of their fierce yellow eyes.

But if the actual fittings of the room would have appeared scanty to one who had lived in a more luxurious age, he would have been surprised on looking up to see the multitude of objects which were suspended above his head. Over the fireplace were the coats-of-arms of a number of houses allied by blood or by marriage to the Lorings. The two cresset-lights which flared upon each side gleamed upon the blue lion of the Percies, the red birds of de Valence, the black engrailed cross of de Mohun, the silver star of de Vere, and the ruddy bars of FitzAlan, all grouped round the famous red roses on the silver shield which the Lorings had borne to glory upon many a bloody field. Then from side to side the room was spanned by heavy oaken beams, from which a great number of objects were hanging. There were mail-shirts of obsolete pattern, several shields, one or two rusted and battered helmets, bow-staves, lances, otter-spears, harness, fishing-rods, and other implements of war or of the chase, while higher still amid the black shadows could be seen rows of hams, flitches of bacon, salted geese, and those other forms of preserved meat which played so great a part in the house-keeping of the Middle Ages.

Dame Ermyntrude Loring, daughter, wife, and mother

of warriors, was herself a formidable figure. Tall and gaunt, with hard craggy features and intolerant dark eyes, even her snow-white hair and stooping back could not entirely remove the sense of fear which she inspired in those around her. Her thoughts and memories went back to harsher times, and she looked upon the England around her as a degenerate and effeminate land which had fallen away from the old standard of knightly courtesy and valour.

The rising power of the people, the growing wealth of the Church, the increasing luxury in life and manners, and the gentler tone of the age were all equally abhorrent to her, so that the dread of her fierce face, and even of the heavy oak staff with which she supported her failing limbs, was widespread through all the country round.

Yet if she was feared she was also respected, for in days when books were few and readers scarce, a long memory and a ready tongue were of the more value ; and where, save from Dame Ermyntrude, could the young un-lettered Squires of Surrey and Hampshire hear of their grandfathers and their battles, or learn that lore of heraldry and chivalry which she handed down from a ruder but a more martial age ? Poor as she was, there was no one in Surrey whose guidance would be more readily sought upon a question of precedence or of conduct than the Dame Ermyntrude Loring.

She sat now with bowed back by the empty fireplace, and looked across at Nigel with all the harsh lines of her old ruddled face softening into love and pride. The young Squire was busy cutting bird-bolts for his crossbow, and whistling softly as he worked. Suddenly he looked up and caught the dark eyes which were fixed upon him. He leaned forward and patted the bony hand.

" What hath pleased you, dear dame ? I read pleasure in your eyes."

" I have heard to-day, Nigel, how you came to win that great war-horse which stamps in our stable."

" Nay, dame ; I had told you that the monks had given it to me."

" You said so, fair son, but never a word more. Yet the horse which you brought home was a very different horse, I wot, to that which was given you. Why did you not tell me ? "

" I should think it shame to talk of such a thing."

" So would your father before you, and his father no less. They would sit silent among the knights when the wine went round and listen to every man's deeds ; but if perchance there was anyone who spoke louder than the rest and seemed to be eager for honour, then afterwards your father would pluck him softly by the sleeve and whisper in his ear to learn if there was any small vow of which he could relieve him, or if he would deign to perform some noble deed of arms upon his person. And if the man were a braggart and would go no further, your father would be silent and none would know it. But if he bore himself well, your father would spread his fame far and wide, but never make mention of himself."

Nigel looked at the old woman with shining eyes. " I love to hear you speak of him," said he. " I pray you to tell me once more of the manner of his death."

" He died as he had lived, a very courtly gentleman. It was at the great sea-battle upon the Norman coast, and your father was in command of the after-guard in the King's own ship. Now the French had taken a great English ship the year before, when they came over and held the narrow seas and burned the town of Southampton. This ship was the *Christopher*, and they placed it in the front of their battle ; but the English closed upon it and stormed over its side, and slew all who were upon it.

" But your father and Sir Lorredan of Genoa, who commanded the *Christopher*, fought upon the high poop, so that all the fleet stopped to watch it, and the King himself cried aloud at the sight, for Sir Lorredan was a famous man-at-arms and bore himself very stoutly that day, and many a knight envied your father that he should have chanced upon so excellent a person. But your father bore him back and struck him such a blow with a mace that he turned the helmet half round on his head, so that he could no longer see through the eyeholes, and Sir Lorredan threw down his sword and gave himself to ransom. But your father took him by the helmet and twisted it until he had it straight upon his head. Then, when he could see once again, he handed him his sword, and prayed him that he would rest himself and then continue, for it was great profit and joy to see any gentleman carry himself so well. So they sat together and rested by the rail of the poop ; but even as they raised their hands again your father was struck by a stone from a mangonel and so died."

" And this Sir Lorredan," cried Nigel, " he died also, as I understand ? "

" I fear that he was slain by the archers, for they loved your father, and they do not see these things with our eyes."

" It was a pity," said Nigel ; " for it is clear that he was a good knight and bore himself very bravely."

" Time was, when I was young, when commoners dared not have laid their grimy hands upon such a man. Men of gentle blood and coat-armour made war upon each other, and the others, spearmen or archers, could scramble amongst themselves. But now all are of a level, and only here and there one like yourself, fair son, who reminds me of the men who are gone."

Nigel leaned forward and took her hands in his. " What I am you have made me," said he.

" It is true, Nigel. I have indeed watched over you as the gardener watches his most precious blossom, for in you alone are all the hopes of our ancient house, and soon —very soon—you will be alone."

" Nay, dear lady, say not that."

" I am very old, Nigel, and I feel the shadow closing in upon me. My heart yearns to go, for all whom I have known and loved have gone before me. And you—it will be a blessed day for you, since I have held you back from that world into which your brave spirit longs to plunge."

" Nay, nay, I have been happy here with you at Tilford."

" We are very poor, Nigel. I do not know where we may find the money to fit you for the wars. Yet we have good friends. There is Sir John Chandos, who has won such credit in the French wars, and who rides ever by the King's bridle-arm. He was your father's friend, and they were squires together. If I sent you to court with a message to him he would do what he could."

Nigel's fair face flushed. " Nay, Dame Ermyntrude, I must find my own gear, even as I have found my own horse, for I had rather ride into battle in this tunic than owe my suit to another."

" I feared that you would say so, Nigel ; but indeed I know not how else we may get the money," said the old woman, sadly. " It was different in the days of my father. I can remember that a suit of mail was but a small matter in those days, for in every English town such things could be made. But year by year, since men have come to take more care of their bodies, there have been added a plate of proof here and a cunning joint there, and all must be from Toledo or Milan, so that a knight must have much metal in his purse ere he puts any on his limbs."

Nigel looked up wistfully at the old armour which was slung on the beams above him. " The ash spear is good," said he, " and so is the oaken shield with facings of steel. Sir Roger FitzAlan handled them and said that he had never seen better. But the armour——"

Lady Ermyntrude shook her old head and laughed. " You have your father's great soul, Nigel, but you have not his mighty breadth of shoulder and length of limb. There was not in all the King's great host a taller or a stronger man. His harness would be little use to you. No, fair son, I rede you that when the time comes you sell this crumbling house and the few acres which are still left, and so go forth to the wars in the hope that with your own right hand you will plant the fortunes of a new House of Loring."

A shadow of anger passed over Nigel's fresh young

face. " I know not if we may hold off these monks and their lawyers much longer. This very day there came a man from Guildford with claims from the Abbey extending back before my father's death."

" Where are they, fair son ? "

" They are flapping on the furze-bushes of Hankley, for I sent his papers and parchments down wind as fast as ever falcon flew."

" Nay ! you were mad to do that, Nigel. And the man, where is he ? "

" Red Swire and old George the Archer threw him into the Thursley bog."

" Alas ! I fear me such things cannot be done in these days, though my father or my husband would have sent the rascal back to Guildford without his ears. But the Church and the Law are too strong now for us who are of gentler blood. Trouble will come of it, Nigel, for the Abbot of Waverley is not one who will hold back the shield of the Church from those who are her servants."

" The Abbot would not hurt us. It is that grey lean wolf of a sacrist who hungers for our land. Let him do his worst. I fear him not."

" He has such an engine at his back, Nigel, that even the bravest must fear him. The ban which blasts a man's soul is in the keeping of his Church, and what have we to place against it ? I pray you to speak him fair, Nigel."

" Nay, dear lady, it is both my duty and my pleasure to do what you bid me ; but I would die ere I ask as a favour that which we can claim as a right. Never can I cast my eyes from yonder window that I do not see the swelling down-lands and the rich meadows, glade and dingle, copse and wood, which have been ours since Norman William gave them to that Loring who bore his shield at Senlac. Now by trick and fraud they have passed away from us, and many a franklin is a richer man than I ; but never shall it be said that I saved the rest by bending my neck to their yoke. Let them do their worst, and let me endure it or fight it as best I may."

The old lady sighed and shook her head. " You speak as a Loring should, and yet I fear that some great trouble will befall us. But let us talk no more of such matters, since we cannot mend them. Where is your citole, Nigel? Will you not play and sing to me ? "

The gentleman of those days could scarce read and write ; but he spoke in two languages, played at least one musical instrument as a matter of course, and possessed a number of other accomplishments, from the imping of hawk's feathers, to the mystery of venery, with knowledge of every beast and bird, its time of grace and when it was seasonable. As far as physical feats went, to vault barebacked upon a horse, to hit a running hare with a crossbow-bolt, or to climb the angle of a castle courtyard, were feats which had come by nature to the young Squire ; but it was very different with music, which had called for many a weary hour of irksome work. Now at last he could master the strings, but both his ear and his voice were not of the best, so that it was well, perhaps, that there was so small and so prejudiced an audience to the Norman-French chanson, which he sang in a high reedy voice with great earnestness of feeling, but with many a slip and quaver, waving his yellow head in cadence to the music—

"A sword ! A sword ! Ah, give me a sword !
   For the world is all to win.
Though the way be hard and the door be barred,
   The strong man enters in.
If Chance and Fate still hold the gate,
   Give me the iron key,
And turret high my plume shall fly,
   Or you may weep for me !

"A horse ! A horse ! Ah, give me a horse !
   To bear me out afar,
Where blackest need and grimmest deed
   And sweetest perils are.
Hold thou my ways from glutted days
   Where poisoned leisure lies,
And point the path of tears and wrath
   Which mounts to high emprise !

> " A heart ! A heart ! Ah, give me a heart
> To rise to circumstance !
> Serene and high and bold to try
> The hazard of the chance,
> With strength to wait, but fixed as fate
> To plan and dare and do,
> The peer of all, and only thrall,
> Sweet lady mine, to you ! "

It may have been that the sentiment went for more than the music, or it may have been the nicety of her own ears had been dulled by age, but old Dame Ermyntrude clapped her lean hands together and cried out in shrill applause.

" Weathercote has indeed had an apt pupil ! " she said. " I pray you that you will sing again."

" Nay, dear dame, it is turn and turn betwixt you and me. I beg that you will recite a romance, you who know them all. For all the years that I have listened I have never yet come to the end of them, and I dare swear that there are more in your head than in all the great books which they showed me at Guildford Castle. I would fain hear ' Doon of Mayence,' or ' The Song of Roland,' or ' Sir Isumbras.' "

So the old dame broke into a long poem, slow and dull in the inception, but quickening as the interest grew, until with darting hands and glowing face she poured forth the verses which told of the emptiness of sordid life, the beauty of heroic death, the high sacredness of love and the bondage of honour. Nigel, with set, still features and brooding eyes, drank in the fiery words, until at last they died upon the old woman's lips and she sank back weary in her chair. Nigel stooped over her and kissed her brow.

" Your words will ever be as a star upon my path," said he. Then carrying over the small table and the chessmen, he proposed that they should play their usual game before they sought their rooms for the night.

But a sudden and rude interruption broke in upon their gentle contest. A dog pricked its ears and barked. The others ran growling to the door. And then there came a

sharp clash of arms, a dull heavy blow as from a club or
sword pommel, and a deep voice from without summoned them to open in the king's name. The old dame
and Nigel had both sprung to their feet, their table over-
turned and their chessmen scattered among the rushes.
Nigel's hand had sought his crossbow, but the Lady
Ermyntrude grasped his arm.

" Nay, fair son ! Have you not heard that it is
in the king's name ? " said she. " Down, Talbot !
Down, Bayard ! Open the door and let his messenger in ! "

Nigel undid the bolt, and the heavy wooden door swung
outward upon its hinges. The light from the flaring cressets beat upon steel caps and fierce bearded faces, with the
glimmer of drawn swords and the yellow gleam of bow-
staves. A dozen armed archers forced their way into the
room. At their head were the gaunt sacrist of Waverley
and a stout elderly man clad in a red-velvet doublet and
breeches, much stained and mottled with mud and clay.
He bore a great sheet of parchment with a fringe of
dangling seals, which he held aloft as he entered.

" I call on Nigel Loring ! " he cried. " I, the officer of
the king's law and the lay summoner of Waverley, call
upon the man named Nigel Loring ! "

" I am he."

" Yes, it is he ! " cried the sacrist. " Archers, do as
you were ordered ! "

In an instant the band threw themselves upon him like
the hounds on a stag. Desperately Nigel strove to gain
his sword, which lay upon the iron coffer. With the convulsive strength which comes from the spirit rather than
from the body, he bore them all in that direction, but the
sacrist snatched the weapon from its place, and the rest
dragged the writhing Squire to the ground and swathed
him in a cord.

" Hold him fast, good archers ! Keep a stout grip on
him ! " cried the summoner. " I pray you, one of you,
prick off these great dogs which snarl at my heels. Stand
off, I say, in the name of the king ! Watkin, come betwixt

me and these creatures, who have as little regard for the law as their master."

One of the archers kicked off the faithful dogs. But there were others of the household who were equally ready to show their teeth in defence of the old house of Loring. From the door which led to their quarters there emerged the pitiful muster of Nigel's threadbare retainers. There was a time when ten knights, forty men-at-arms, and two hundred archers would march behind the scarlet roses. Now at this last rally, when the young head of the house lay bound in his own hall, there mustered at his call the page Charles with a cudgel, John the cook with his longest spit, Red Swire the aged man-at-arms with a formidable axe swung over his snowy head, and Weathercote the minstrel with a boar-spear. Yet this motley array was fired with the spirit of the house, and under the lead of the fierce old soldier they would certainly have flung themselves upon the ready swords of the archers, had the Lady Ermyntrude not swept between them.

" Stand back, Swire ! " she cried. " Back, Weathercote ! Charles, put a leash on Talbot, and hold Bayard back!" Her black eyes blazed upon the invaders until they shrank from that baleful gaze. " Who are you, you rascal robbers, who dare to misuse the king's name and to lay hands upon one whose smallest drop of blood has more worth than all your thrall and caitiff bodies ? "

" Nay, not so fast, dame, not so fast, I pray you ! " cried the stout summoner, whose face had resumed its natural colour, now that he had a woman to deal with. " There is a law of England, mark you, and there are those who serve and uphold it, who are the true men and the king's own lieges. Such a one am I. Then, again, there are those who take such as me and transfer, carry or convey us into a bog or morass. Such a one is this graceless old man with the axe, whom I have seen already this day. There are also those who tear, destroy, or scatter the papers of the law, of which this young man is the chief. Therefore I would rede you, dame, not to rail against us, but to understand that we are the king's men on the king's own service."

" What, then, is your errand in this house at this hour of the night ? "

The summoner cleared his throat pompously, and turning his parchment to the light of the cressets he read out a long document in Norman-French, couched in such a style and such a language that the most involved and foolish of our forms were simplicity itself compared to those by which the men of the long gown made a mystery of that which of all things on earth should be the plainest and the most simple. Despair fell cold upon Nigel's heart and blanched the face of the old dame as they listened to the dread catalogue of claims and suits and issues, questions of peccary and turbary, of house-bote and fire-bote, which ended by a demand for all the lands, hereditaments, tenements, messuages and curtilages, which made up their worldly all.

Nigel, still bound, had been placed with his back against the iron coffer, whence he heard with dry lips and moist brow this doom of his house. Now he broke in on the recital with a vehemence which made the summoner jump :

" You shall rue what you have done this night ! " he cried. " Poor as we are, we have our friends who will not see us wronged, and I will plead my cause before the king's own majesty at Windsor, that he, who saw the father die, may know what things are done in his royal name against the son. But these matters are to be settled in course of law in the king's courts, and how will you excuse yourself for this assault upon my house and person ? "

" Nay, that is another matter," said the sacrist. " The question of debt may indeed be an affair of a civil court. But it is a crime against the law and an act of the Devil which comes within the jurisdiction of the Abbey Court of Waverley when you dare to lay hands upon the summoner or his papers."

" Indeed, he speaks truth," cried the official. " I know no blacker sin."

" Therefore," said the stern monk, " it is the order of the holy father Abbot that you sleep this night in the Abbey cell, and that to-morrow you be brought before him at the court held in the chapter-house so that you receive the fit punishment for this and the many other violent and froward deeds which you have wrought upon the servants of Holy Church. Enough is now said, worthy master summoner. Archers, remove your prisoner ! "

As Nigel was lifted up by four stout archers, the Dame Ermyntrude would have rushed to his aid, but the sacrist thrust her back.

" Stand off, proud woman ! Let the law take its course, and learn to humble your heart before the power of Holy Church. Has your life not taught its lesson, you, whose horn was exalted among the highest and will soon not have a roof above your grey hairs ? Stand back, I say, lest I lay a curse upon you ! "

The old dame flamed suddenly into white wrath as she stood before the angry monk.

" Listen to me while I lay a curse upon you and yours ! " she cried, as she raised her shrivelled arms and blighted him with her flashing eyes : " As you have done to the House of Loring, so may God do to you, until your power is swept from the land of England, and of your great Abbey of Waverley there is nothing left but a pile of grey stones in a green meadow ! I see it ! I see it ! With my old eyes I see it ! From scullion to abbot and from cellar to tower, may Waverley and all within it droop and wither from this night on ! "

The monk, hard as he was, quailed before the frantic figure and the bitter, burning words. Already the summoner and the archers with their prisoner were clear of the house. He turned, and with a clang he shut the heavy door behind him.

5. *How Nigel was Tried by the Abbot of Waverley*

THE law of the Middle Ages, shrouded as it was in old Norman-French dialect, and abounding in uncouth and incomprehensible terms, in deodands and heriots, in infang and outfang, was a fearsome weapon in the hands of those who knew how to use it. It was not for nothing that the first act of the rebel commoners was to hew off the head of the Lord Chancellor. In an age when few knew how to read or to write, these mystic phrases and intricate forms, with the parchments and seals which were their outward expression, struck cold terror into hearts which were steeled against mere physical danger.

Even young Nigel Loring's blithe and elastic spirit was chilled as he lay that night in the penal cell of Waverley, and pondered over the absolute ruin which threatened his house from a source against which all his courage was of no avail. As well take up sword and shield to defend himself against the black death, as against this blight of Holy Church. He was powerless in the grip of the Abbey. Already they had shorn off a field here and a grove there, and now in one sweep they would take in the rest, and where then was the home of the Lorings, and where should Lady Ermyntrude lay her aged head, or his old retainers, broken and spent, eke out the balance of their days ? He shivered as he thought of it.

It was very well for him to threaten to carry the matter before the king, but it was years since Royal Edward had heard the name of Loring, and Nigel knew that the memory of princes was a short one. Besides, the Church was the ruling power in the palace as well as in the cottage, and it was only for very good cause that a king could be expected to cross the purposes of so high a prelate as the Abbot of Waverley, as long as they came within the scope of the law. Where, then, was he to look for help ? With the simple and practical piety of the age, he prayed for the aid of his own particular saints : of Saint Paul, whose adventures by land and sea had always endeared him ; of Saint George, who had gained much honourable advancement from the Dragon ; and of Saint Thomas, who was a gentleman of coat-armour, who would understand and help a person of gentle blood.   Then, much comforted by his naïve orisons, he enjoyed the sleep of youth and health until the entrance of the lay brother with the bread and small beer, which served as breakfast in the morning.

The Abbey court sat in the chapter-house at the canonical hour of tierce, which was nine in the forenoon. At all times the function was a solemn one, even when the culprit might be a villein who was taken poaching on the Abbey estate, or a chapman who had given false measure from his biased scales.   But now, when a man of noble birth was to be tried, the whole legal and ecclesiastical ceremony was carried out with every detail, grotesque or impressive, which the full ritual prescribed.   Mid the distant roll of church music and the slow tolling of the Abbey bell, the white-robed brethren, two and two, walked thrice round the hall singing the *Benedicite* and the *Veni, Creator* before they settled in their places at the desks on either side.   Then in turn each high officer of the Abbey from below upward, the almoner, the lector, the chaplain, the sub-prior and the prior, swept to their wonted places.

Finally there came the grim sacrist, with demure triumph upon his downcast features, and at his heels Abbot John himself, slow and dignified, with pompous walk and solemn, composed face, his iron-beaded rosary swinging from his waist, his breviary in his hand, and his lips muttering as he hurried through his office for the day. He knelt at his high prie-dieu ; the brethren, at a signal from the prior, prostrated themselves upon the floor, and the low deep voices rolled in prayer, echoed back from the arched and vaulted roof like the wash of waves from an ocean cavern.   Finally the monks resumed their seats ;

SIR NIGEL

there entered clerks in seemly black with pens and parchment ; the red-velveted summoner appeared to tell his tale ; Nigel was led in with archers pressing close around him ; and then, with much calling of old French and much legal incantation and mystery, the court of the Abbey was open for business.

It was the sacrist who first advanced to the oaken desk reserved for the witnesses and expounded in hard, dry, mechanical fashion the many claims which the House of Waverley had against the family of Loring. Some generations back, in return for money advanced or for spiritual favour received, the Loring of the day had admitted that his estate had certain feudal duties toward the Abbey. The sacrist held up the crackling yellow parchment with swinging leaden seals on which the claim was based. Amid the obligations was that of escuage, by which the price of a knight's fee should be paid every year. No such price had been paid, nor had any service been done. The accumulated years came now to a greater sum than the fee-simple of the estate. There were other claims also. The sacrist called for his books, and with thin, eager forefinger he tracked them down ; dues for this, and tallage for that, so many shillings this year, and so many nobles that one. Some of it occurred before Nigel was born ; some of it when he was but a child. The accounts had been checked and certified by the sergeant of the law.

Nigel listened to the dread recital, and felt like some young stag who stands at bay with brave pose and heart of fire, but who sees himself compassed round and knows clearly that there is no escape. With his bold young face, his steady blue eyes, and the proud poise of his head, he was a worthy scion of the old house, and the sun, shining through the high oriel window, and showing up the stained and threadbare condition of his once rich doublet, seemed to illuminate the fallen fortunes of his family.

The sacrist had finished his exposition, and the sergeant-at-law was about to conclude a case which Nigel could in

468

no way controvert, when help came to him from an unexpected quarter. It may have been a certain malignity
with which the sacrist urged his suit, it may have been a
diplomatic dislike to driving matters to extremes, or it
may have been some genuine impulse of kindliness, for
Abbot John was choleric but easily appeased. Whatever
the cause, the result was that a white plump hand, raised
in the air with a gesture of authority, showed that the case
was at an end.

" Our brother sacrist hath done his duty in urging this
suit," said he, " for the worldly wealth of this Abbey is
placed in his pious keeping, and it is to him that we
should look if we suffered in such ways, for we are but
the trustees of those who come after us. But to my
keeping has been consigned that which is more precious
still, the inner spirit and high repute of those who follow
the rule of Saint Bernard. Now, it has ever been our
endeavour, since first our saintly founder went down into
the valley of Clairvaux and built himself a cell there, that
we should set an example to all men in gentleness and
humility. For this reason it is that we build our houses
in lowly places, that we have no tower to our Abbey
churches, and that no finery and no metal, save only iron
or lead, come within our walls. A brother shall eat from
a wooden platter, drink from an iron cup, and light
himself from a leaden sconce. Surely it is not for such
an order, who await the exaltation which is promised to
the humble, to judge their own case and so acquire the
lands of their neighbour ! If our cause be just, as indeed
I believe that it is, then it were better that it be judged
at the king's assizes at Guildford, and so I decree that
the case be now dismissed from the Abbey court so that
it can be heard elsewhere."

Nigel breathed a prayer to the three sturdy saints who
had stood by him so manfully and well in the hour of his
need.

" Abbot John," said he, " I never thought that any
man of my name would utter thanks to a Cistercian of

Waverley; but, by Saint Paul! you have spoken like a man this day, for it would indeed be to play with cogged dice if the Abbey's case is to be tried in the Abbey court."

The eighty white-clad brethren looked with half-resentful, half-amused eyes as they listened to this frank address to one who, in their small lives, seemed to be the direct viceregent of Heaven. The archers had stood back from Nigel, as though he were at liberty to go, when the loud voice of the summoner broke in upon the silence.

" If it please you, holy father Abbot," cried the voice, " this decision of yours is indeed *secundum legem* and *intra vires* so far as the civil suit is concerned which lies between this person and the Abbey. That is your affair; but it is I, Joseph the summoner, who have been grievously and criminally mishandled, my writs, papers, and indentures destroyed, my authority flouted, and my person dragged through a bog, quagmire or morass, so that my velvet gabardine and silver badge of office were lost and are, as I verily believe, in the morass, quagmire or bog aforementioned, which is the same bog, morass——"

" Enough!" cried the Abbot, sternly. " Lay aside this foolish fashion of speech, and say straitly what you desire."

" Holy father, I have been the officer of the king's law no less than the servant of Holy Church, and I have been let, hindered, and assaulted in the performance of my lawful and proper duties, whilst my papers, drawn in the king's name, have been shended and rended and cast to the wind. Therefore I demand justice upon this man in the Abbey court, the said assault having been committed within the banlieue of the Abbey's jurisdiction."

" What have you to say to this, brother sacrist?" asked the Abbot in some perplexity.

" I would say, father, that it is within our power to deal gently and charitably with all that concerns ourselves, but that where the king's officer is concerned, we are wanting in our duty if we give him less than the protection that he demands. I would remind you also, holy father, that this is not the first of this man's violence, but that he has before now beaten our servants, defied our authority, and put pike in the Abbot's own fish-pond."

The prelate's heavy cheeks flushed with anger as this old grievance came fresh into his mind. His eyes hardened as he looked at the prisoner. " Tell me, Squire Nigel, did you indeed put pike in the pond ? "

The young man drew himself proudly up. " Ere I answer such a question, father Abbot, do you answer one from me, and tell me what the monks of Waverley have ever done for me that I should hold my hand when I could injure them ? "

A low murmur ran round the room, partly wonder at his frankness, and partly anger at his boldness.

The Abbot settled down in his seat as one who has made up his mind. " Let the case of the summoner be laid before me," said he. " Justice shall be done, and the offender shall be punished, be he noble or simple. Let the plaint be brought before the court."

The tale of the summoner, though rambling and filled with endless legal reiteration, was only too clear in its essence. Red Swire, with his angry face framed in white bristles, was led in, and confessed to his ill-treatment of the official. A second culprit, a little wiry, nut-brown archer from Churt, had aided and abetted in the deed. Both of them were ready to declare that young Squire Nigel Loring knew nothing of the matter. But then there was the awkward incident of the tearing of the writs. Nigel, to whom a lie was an impossibility, had to admit that with his own hands he had shredded those august documents. As to an excuse or an explanation, he was too proud to advance any. A cloud gathered over the brow of the Abbot, and the sacrist gazed with an ironical smile at the prisoner, while a solemn hush fell over the chapter-house as the case ended and only judgment remained.

" Squire Nigel," said the Abbot, " it was for you, who are, as all men know, of ancient lineage in this land, to give a fair example by which others should set their conduct. Instead of this, your manor-house has ever been a centre for the stirring up of strife, and now not content with your harsh showing toward us, the Cistercian monks of Waverley, you have even marked your contempt for the king's law, and through your servants have mishandled the person of his messenger. For such offences it is in my power to call the spiritual terrors of the Church upon your head, and yet I would not be harsh with you, seeing that you are young, and that even last week you saved the life of a servant of the Abbey when in peril. Therefore it is by temporal and carnal means that I will use my power to tame your overbold spirit, and to chasten that head-strong and violent humour which has caused such scandal in your dealings with our Abbey. Bread and water for six weeks from now to the Feast of Saint Benedict, with a daily exhortation from our chaplain, the pious Father Ambrose, may still avail to bend the stiff neck and to soften the hard heart."

At this ignominious sentence, by which the proud heir of the House of Loring would share the fate of the meanest village poacher, the hot blood of Nigel rushed to his face, and his eye glanced round him with a gleam which said more plainly than words that there could be no tame acceptance of such a doom. Twice he tried to speak, and twice his anger and his shame held the words in his throat.

" I am no subject of yours, proud Abbot ! " he cried at last. " My house has ever been vavasor to the king. I deny the power of you and your court to lay sentence upon me. Punish these your own monks, who whimper at your frown, but do not dare to lay your hand upon him who fears you not, for he is a free man, and the peer of any save only the king himself."

The Abbot seemed for an instant taken aback by these bold words, and by the high and strenuous voice in which they were uttered. But the sterner sacrist came as ever to stiffen his will. He held up the old parchment in his hand.

" The Lorings were indeed vavasors to the king," said
he ; " but here is the very seal of Eustace Loring, which
shows that he made himself vassal to the Abbey, and held
his land from it."

" Because he was gentle," cried Nigel, " because he had
no thought of trick or guile."

" Nay ! " said the summoner. " If my voice may be
heard, father Abbot, upon a point of the law, it is of no
weight what the causes may have been why a deed is
subscribed, signed or confirmed, but a court is concerned
only with the terms, articles, covenants, and contracts of
the said deed."

" Besides," said the sacrist, " sentence is passed by the
Abbey court, and there is an end of its honour and good
name if it be not upheld."

" Brother sacrist," said the Abbot, angrily, " methinks
you show overmuch zeal in this case, and certes, we are
well able to uphold the dignity and honour of the Abbey
court without any rede of thine. As to you, worthy
summoner, you will give your opinion when we crave for
it, and not before, or you may yourself get some touch of
the power of our tribunal. But your case hath been tried,
Squire Loring, and judgment given. I have no more to
say."

He motioned with his hand, and an archer laid his
grip upon the shoulder of the prisoner. But that rough
plebeian touch woke every passion of revolt in Nigel's
spirit. Of all his high line of ancestors, was there one
who had been subjected to such ignominy as this ? Would
they not have preferred death ? And should he be the
first to lower their spirit or their traditions ? With a
quick, lithe movement, he slipped under the arm of the
archer, and plucked the short, straight sword from the
soldier's side as he did so. The next instant he had
wedged himself into the recess of one of the narrow
windows, and there were his pale, set face, his burning
eyes, and his ready blade turned upon the assembly.

" By Saint Paul ! " said he, " I never thought to find

honourable advancement under the roof of an abbey, but, perchance, there may be some room for it ere you hale me to your prison."

The chapter-house was in an uproar. Never in the long and decorous history of the Abbey had such a scene been witnessed within its walls. The monks themselves seemed for an instant to be affected by this spirit of daring revolt. Their own lifelong fetters hung more loosely as they viewed this unheard-of defiance of authority. They broke from their seats on either side, and huddled half-scared, half-fascinated, in a large half-circle round the defiant captive, chattering, pointing, grimacing, a scandal for all time. Scourges should fall and penance be done for many a long week before the shadow of that day should pass from Waverley. But meanwhile there was no effort to bring them back to their rule. Everything was chaos and disorder. The Abbot had left his seat of justice and hurried angrily forward, to be engulfed and hustled in the crowd of his own monks like a sheep-dog who finds himself entangled amid a flock.

Only the sacrist stood clear. He had taken shelter behind the half-dozen archers, who looked with some approval and a good deal of indecision at this bold fugitive from justice.

" On him ! " cried the sacrist. " Shall he defy the authority of the court, or shall one man hold six of you at bay ? Close in upon him and seize him. You, Baddlesmere, why do you hold back ? "

The man in question, a tall, bushy-bearded fellow, clad like the others in green jerkin and breeches, with high brown boots, advanced slowly, sword in hand, against Nigel. His heart was not in the business, for these clerical courts were not popular, and everyone had a tender heart for the fallen fortunes of the House of Loring and wished well to its young heir.

" Come, young sir, you have caused scathe enough," said he. " Stand forth and give yourself up ! "

" Come and fetch me, good fellow," said Nigel, with a dangerous smile.

The archer ran in. There was a rasp of steel, a blade flickered like a swift dart of flame, and the man staggered back, with blood running down his forearm and dripping from his fingers. He wrung them and growled a Saxon oath.

" By the black rood of Bromeholm ! " he cried, " I had as soon put my hand down a fox's earth to drag up a vixen from her cubs."

" Stand off ! " said Nigel, curtly. " I would not hurt you ; but, by Saint Paul ! I will not be handled, or someone will be hurt in the handling."

So fierce was his eye and so menacing his blade as he crouched in the narrow bay of the window that the little knot of archers were at a loss what to do. The Abbot had forced his way through the crowd, and stood, purple with outraged dignity, at their side.

" He is outside the law," said he. " He hath shed blood in a court of justice, and for such a sin there is no forgiveness. I will not have my court so flouted and set at nought. He who draws the sword, by the sword also let him perish. Forester Hugh, lay a shaft to your bow ! "

The man, who was one of the Abbey's lay servants, put his weight upon his long bow and slipped the loose end of the string into the upper notch. Then, drawing one of the terrible three-foot arrows, steel-tipped and gaudily winged, from his waist, he laid it to the string.

" Now draw your bow and hold it ready ! " cried the furious Abbot. " Squire Nigel, it is not for Holy Church to shed blood, but there is nought but violence which will prevail against the violent, and on your head be the sin. Cast down the sword which you hold in your hand ! "

" Will you give me freedom to leave your Abbey ? "

" When you have abided your sentence and purged your sin."

" Then I had rather die where I stand than give up my sword."

A dangerous flame lit in the Abbot's eyes. He came of a fighting Norman stock, like so many of those fierce

prelates who, bearing a mace lest they should be guilty of
effusion of blood, led their troops into battle, ever remembering that it was one of their own cloth and dignity who,
crosier in hand, had turned the long-drawn bloody day of
Hastings. The soft accent of the churchman was gone,
and it was the hard voice of the soldier which said—

" One minute I give you, and no more. Then when I
cry ' Loose ! ' drive me an arrow through his body."

The shaft was fitted, the bow was bent, and the stern
eyes of the woodman were fixed on his mark. Slowly the
minute passed, while Nigel breathed a prayer to his three
soldier saints, not that they should save his body in this
life, but that they should have a kindly care for his soul
in the next. Some thought of a fierce wildcat sally crossed
his mind, but once out of his corner he was lost indeed.
Yet at the last he would have rushed among his enemies,
and his body was bent for the spring, when with a deep
sonorous hum, like a breaking harp-string, the cord of the
bow was cloven in twain, and the arrow tinkled upon the
tiled floor. At the same moment a young curly-headed
bowman, whose broad shoulders and deep chest told of
immense strength, as clearly as his frank, laughing face
and honest hazel eyes did of good humour and courage,
sprang forward, sword in hand, and took his place by
Nigel's side.

" Nay, comrades ! " said he. " Samkin Aylward cannot stand by and see a gallant man shot down like a bull at
the end of a baiting. Five against one is long odds, but
two against four is better ; and, by my finger-bones !
Squire Nigel and I leave this room together, be it on our
feet or no."

The formidable appearance of this ally and his high
reputation among his fellows gave a further chill to the
lukewarm ardour of the attack. Aylward's left arm was
passed through his strung bow, and he was known from
Woolmer Forest to the Weald as the quickest, surest
archer that ever dropped a running deer at ten-score paces.

" Nay, Baddlesmere, hold your fingers from your string-case, or I may chance to give your drawing hand a two months' rest," said Aylward. " Swords, if you will, comrades, but no man strings his bow till I have loosed mine."

Yet the angry hearts of both Abbot and sacrist rose higher with a fresh obstacle.

" This is an ill day for your father, Franklin Aylward, who holds the tenancy of Crooksbury," said the sacrist. " He will rue it that ever he begot a son who will lose him his acres and his steading."

" My father is a bold yeoman, and would rue it even more that ever his son should stand by while foul work was afoot," said Aylward, stoutly. " Fall on, comrades ! We are waiting."

Encouraged by promises of reward if they should fall in the service of the Abbey, and by threats of penalties if they should hold back, the four archers were about to close, when a singular interruption gave an entirely new turn to the proceedings.

At the door of the chapter-house, while these fiery doings had been afoot, there had assembled a mixed crowd of lay brothers, servants, and varlets who had watched the development of the drama with the interest and delight with which men hail a sudden break in a dull routine. Suddenly there was an agitation at the back of this group, then a swirl in the centre, and finally the front rank was violently thrust aside, and through the gap there emerged a strange and whimsical figure, who from the instant of his appearance dominated both chapter-house and Abbey, monks, prelates, and archers, as if he were their owner and their master.

He was a man somewhat above middle age, with thin, lemon-coloured hair, a curling moustache, a tufted chin of the same hue, and a high craggy face, all running to a great hook of the nose, like the beak of an eagle. His skin was tanned a brown-red by much exposure to the wind and sun. In height he was tall, and his figure was thin and loose-jointed, but stringy and hard-bitten. One eye was entirely covered by its lid, which lay flat over an empty socket, but the other danced and sparkled with a most roguish light, darting here and there with a twinkle of humour and criticism and intelligence, the whole fire of his soul bursting through that one narrow cranny.

His dress was as noteworthy as his person. A rich purple doublet and cloak was marked on the lapels with a strange scarlet device shaped like a wedge. Costly lace hung round his shoulders, and amid its soft folds there smouldered the dull red of a heavy golden chain. A knight's belt at his waist and a knight's golden spurs twinkling from his doeskin riding-boots proclaimed his rank, and on the wrist of his left gauntlet there sat a demure little hooded falcon of a breed which in itself was a mark of the dignity of the owner. Of weapons he had none, but a mandoline was slung by a black silken band over his back, and the high brown end projected above his shoulder. Such was the man, quaint, critical, masterful, with a touch of what is formidable behind it, who now surveyed the opposing groups of armed men and angry monks with an eye which commanded their attention.

"*Excusez* !" said he, in a lisping French. "*Excusez, mes amis* ! I had thought to arouse you from prayer or meditation, but never have I seen such a holy exercise as this under an abbey's roof, with swords for breviaries and archers for acolytes. I fear that I have come amiss, and yet I ride on an errand from one who permits no delay."

The Abbot, and possibly the sacrist also, had begun to realise that events had gone a great deal farther than they had intended, and that without an extreme scandal it was no easy matter for them to save their dignity and the good name of Waverley. Therefore, in spite of the debonair, not to say disrespectful, bearing of the newcomer, they rejoiced at his appearance and intervention.

"I am the Abbot of Waverley, fair son," said the prelate. "If your message deal with a public matter it may be fitly repeated in the chapter-house ; if not I will give you audience in my own chamber ; for it is clear to me that you are a gentleman of blood and coat-armour who would not lightly break in upon the business of our court—a business which, as you have remarked, is little welcome to men of peace like myself and the brethren of the rule of Saint Bernard."

" *Pardieu* ! Father Abbot," said the stranger. " One had but to glance at you and your men to see that the business was indeed little to your taste, and it may be even less so when I say that rather than see this young person in the window, who hath a noble bearing, further molested by these archers, I will adventure my person on his behalf."

The Abbot's smile turned to a frown at these frank words. " It would become you better, sir, to deliver the message of which you say that you are the bearer, than to uphold a prisoner against the rightful judgment of a court."

The stranger swept the court with his questioning eye. " The message is not for you, good father Abbot. It is for one I know not. I have been to his house, and they have sent me hither. The name is Nigel Loring."

" It is for me, fair sir."

" I had thought as much. I knew your father, Eustace Loring, and though he would have made two of you, yet he has left his stamp plain enough upon your face."

" You know not the truth of this matter," said the Abbot. " If you are a loyal man, you will stand aside, for this young man hath grievously offended against the law, and it is for the king's lieges to give us their support."

" And you have haled him up for judgment," cried the stranger, with much amusement. " It is as though a rookery sat in judgment upon a falcon. I warrant that you have found it easier to judge than to punish. Let me tell you, father Abbot, that this standeth not aright. When powers such as these were given to the like of you, they were given that you might check a brawling underling or correct a drunken woodman, and not that you might drag the best blood in England to your bar and set your archers on him if he questioned your findings."

The Abbot was little used to hear such words of reproof uttered in so stern a voice under his own abbey roof and before his listening monks.

" You may perchance find that an Abbey court has more powers than you wot of, Sir Knight," said he, " if knight indeed you be who are so uncourteous and short in your speech. Ere we go further, I would ask your name and style ? "

The stranger laughed. " It is easy to see that you are indeed men of peace," said he proudly. " Had I shown this sign," and he touched the token upon his lapels, " whether on shield or pennon, in the marches of France or Scotland, there is not a cavalier but would have known the red pile of Chandos."

Chandos, John Chandos, the flower of English chivalry, the pink of knight-errantry, the hero already of fifty desperate enterprises, a man known and honoured from end to end of Europe ! Nigel gazed at him as one who sees a vision. The archers stood back abashed, while the monks crowded closer to stare at the famous soldier of the French wars. The Abbot abated his tone, and a smile came to his angry face.

" We are indeed men of peace, Sir John, and little skilled in warlike blazonry," said he ; " yet stout as are our Abbey walls, they are not so thick that the fame of your exploits has not passed through them and reached our ears. If it be your pleasure to take an interest in this young and misguided squire, it is not for us to thwart your kind intention or to withhold such grace as you request. I am glad indeed that he hath one who can set him so fair an example for a friend."

" I thank you for your courtesy, good father Abbot," said Chandos, carelessly. " This young squire has, however, a better friend than myself, one who is kinder to those he loves and more terrible to those he hates. It is from him I bear a message."

" I pray you, fair and honoured sir," said Nigel, " that you will tell me what is the message that you bear."

" The message, *mon ami*, is that your friend comes into these parts and would have a night's lodging at the Manor-house of Tilford for the love and respect that he bears your family."

" Nay, he is most welcome," said Nigel, " and yet I hope that he is one who can relish a soldier's fare and sleep under a humble roof, for indeed we can but give our best, poor as it is."

" He is indeed a soldier and a good one," Chandos answered, laughing, " and I warrant he has slept in rougher quarters than Tilford Manor-house."

" I have few friends, fair sir," said Nigel, with a puzzled face. " I pray you give me this gentleman's name."

" His name is Edward."

" Sir Edward Mortimer of Kent, perchance, or is it Sir Edward Brocas of whom the Lady Ermyntrude talks?"

" Nay, he is known as Edward only, and if you ask a second name it is Plantagenet, for he who comes to seek the shelter of your roof is your liege lord and mine, the King's high majesty, Edward of England."

6. *In which Lady Ermyntrude Opens the Iron Coffer*

AS in a dream Nigel heard these stupendous and incredible words. As in a dream also he had a vision of a smiling and conciliatory Abbot, of an obsequious sacrist, and of a band of archers who cleared a path for him and for the king's messenger through the motley crowd who had choked the entrance of the Abbey court. A minute later he was walking by the side of Chandos through the peaceful cloister, and in front, in the open archway of the great gate, was the broad yellow road between its borders of green meadow-land. The spring air was the sweeter and the more fragrant for that chill dread of dishonour and captivity which had so recently frozen his ardent heart. He had already passed the portal when a hand plucked at his sleeve, and he turned to find himself confronted by the brown honest face and hazel eyes of the archer who had interfered in his behalf.

" Well," said Aylward, " what have you to say to me, young sir ? "

" What can I say, my good fellow, save that I thank you with all my heart ? By Saint Paul ! if you had been my blood brother you could not have stood by me more stoutly."

" Nay ! but this is not enough."

Nigel coloured with vexation, and the more so as Chandos was listening with his critical smile to their conversation.

" If you had heard what was said in the court," said he, " you will understand that I am not blessed at this moment with much of this world's gear. The black death and the monks have between them been heavy upon our estate. Willingly would I give you a handful of gold for your assistance, since that is what you seem to crave ; but indeed I have it not, and so once more I say that you must be satisfied with my thanks."

" Your gold is nothing to me," said Aylward shortly, " nor would you buy my loyalty if you filled my wallet with rose nobles so long as you were not a man after my own heart. But I have seen you back the yellow horse, and I have seen you face the Abbot of Waverley and you are such a master as I would very gladly serve if you have by chance a place for such a man. I have seen your following, and I doubt not that they were stout fellows in your grandfather's time ; but which of them now would draw a bow-string to his ear ? Through you I have left the service of the Abbey of Waverley, and where can I look now for a post ? If I stay here I am all undone like a fretted bow-string."

" Nay, there can be no difficulty there," said Chandos. " *Pardieu !* a roistering, swaggering dare-devil archer is worth his price on the French border. There are two hundred such who march behind my own person, and I would ask nothing better than to see you among them."

" I thank you, noble sir, for your offer," said Aylward, " and I had rather follow your banner than many another one, for it is well known that it goes ever forward, and I have heard enough of the wars to know that there are small pickings for the man who lags behind. Yet, if the squire will have me, I would choose to fight under the five roses of Loring, for though I was born in the hundred of Ease-bourne and the rape of Chichester, yet I have grown up and learned to use the longbow in these parts, and as the free son of a free franklin I had rather serve my own neighbour than a stranger."

" My good fellow," said Nigel, " I have told you that I could in no wise reward you for such service."

" If you will but take me to the wars I will see to my own reward," said Aylward. " Till then I ask for none, save a corner of your table and six feet of your floor, for it is certain that the only reward I would get from the Abbey for this day's work would be the scourge for my back and the stocks for my ankles. Samkin Aylward is your man, Squire Nigel, from this hour on, and by these ten finger-bones he trusts the Devil will fly away with him if ever he gives you cause to regret it ! " So saying he raised his hand to his steel cap in salute, slung his great yellow bow over his back, and followed on some paces in the rear of his new master.

" *Pardieu !* I have arrived *à la bonne heure*," said Chandos. " I rode from Windsor and came to your manor-house, to find it empty save for a fine old dame, who told me of your troubles. From her I walked across to the Abbey, and none too soon, for what with cloth-yard shafts for your body, and bell, book, and candle for your soul, it was no very cheerful outlook. But here is the very dame herself, I if mistake not."

It was indeed the formidable figure of the Lady Ermyn-trude, gaunt, bowed, and leaning on her staff, which had emerged from the door of the manor-house and advanced to greet them. She croaked with laughter, and shook her stick at the great building as she heard of the discomfiture of the Abbey court. Then she led the way into the hall, where the best which she could provide had been laid out for their illustrious guest. There was Chandos blood in her own veins, traceable back through the de Greys, de Multons, de Valences, de Montagues, and other high and noble strains, so that the meal had been eaten and cleared before she had done tracing the network of intermarriages and connections, with quarterings, impalements, lozenges and augmentations by which the blazonry of the two families might be made to show a common origin. Back to the Conquest and before it there was not a noble family-tree every twig and bud of which was not familiar to the Dame Ermyntrude.

And now, when the trestles were cleared and the three were left alone in the hall, Chandos broke his message to the lady. " King Edward hath ever borne in mind that noble knight, your son, Sir Eustace," said he. " He will journey to Southampton next week, and I am his harbinger. He bade me say, noble and honoured lady, that he would come from Guildford in an easy stage so that he might spend one night under your roof."

The old dame flushed with pleasure, and then turned white with vexation at the words.

" It is in truth great honour to the House of Loring," said she, " yet our roof is now humble and, as you have seen, our fare is plain. The king knows not that we are so poor. I fear lest we seem churlish and niggard in his eyes."

But Chandos reasoned away her fears. The king's retinue would journey on to Farnham Castle. There were no ladies in his party. Though he was king, still he was a hardy soldier, and cared little for his ease. In any case, since he had declared his coming, they must make the best of it. Finally, with all delicacy, Chandos offered his own purse if it would help in the matter. But already the Lady Ermyntrude had recovered her composure.

" Nay, fair kinsman, that may not be," said she. " I will make such preparations as I may for the king. He will bear in mind that if the House of Loring can give nothing else, they have always held their blood and their lives at his disposal."

Chandos was to ride on to Farnham Castle and beyond, but he expressed his desire to have a warm bath ere he left Tilford, for, like most of his fellow-knights, he was much addicted to simmering in the hottest water that he could possibly endure. The bath therefore, a high hooped arrangement like a broader but shorter churn, was carried into the privacy of the guest-chamber, and thither it was that Nigel was summoned to hold him company while he stewed and sweltered in his tub.

Nigel perched himself upon the side of the high bed, swinging his legs over the edge and gazing with wonder and amusement at the quaint face, the ruffled yellow hair, and the sinewy shoulders of the famous warrior, dimly seen amid a pillar of steam. He was in a mood for talk ; so Nigel, with eager lips, plied him with a thousand questions about the wars, hanging upon every word which came back to him, like those of the ancient oracles, out of the mist and the cloud. To Chandos himself, the old soldier for whom war had lost its freshness, it was a renewal of his own ardent youth to listen to Nigel's rapid questions and to mark the rapt attention with which he listened.

"Tell me of the Welsh, honoured sir ? " asked the squire. "What manner of soldiers are the Welsh ? "

" They are very valiant men of war," said Chandos, splashing about in his tub. " There is good skirmishing to be had in their valleys if you ride with a small following. They flare up like a furze-bush in the flames, but if for a short space you may abide the heat of it, then there is a chance that it may be cooler."

" And the Scotch ? " asked Nigel. " You have made war upon them also, as I understand."

" The Scotch knights have no masters in the world, and

he who can hold his own with the best of them, be it a
Douglas, a Murray, or a Seaton, has nothing more to learn.
Though you be a hard man, you will always meet as hard
a one if you ride northward. If the Welsh be like the
furze-fire, then, *pardieu !* the Scotch are the peat, for they
will smoulder and you will never come to the end of them.
I have had many happy hours on the marches of Scotland,
for even if there be no war the Percies of Alnwick or the
Governor of Carlisle can still raise a little bickering with
the border clans."

" I bear in mind that my father was wont to say that
they were very stout spearmen."

" No better in the world, for their spears are twelve foot
long and they hold them in very thick array ; but their
archers are weak, save only the men of Ettrick and Selkirk,
who come from the forest. I pray you to open the lattice,
Nigel, for the steam is overthick. Now, in Wales it is
the spearmen who are weak, and there are no archers in
these islands like the men of Gwent with their bows of
elm, which shoot with such power that I have known a
cavalier to have his horse killed when the shaft had passed
through his mail breeches, his thigh, and his saddle. And
yet, what is the most strongly shot arrow to these new balls
of iron driven by the fire-powder which will crush a man's
armour as an egg is crushed by a stone ? Our fathers
knew them not."

" Then the better for us," cried Nigel, " since there is
at least one honourable venture which is all our own."

Chandos chuckled and turned upon the flushed youth
a twinkling and sympathetic eye. " You have a fashion
of speech which carries me back to the old men whom I
met in my boyhood," said he. " There were some of the
real old knight-errants left in those days and they spoke
as you do. Young as you are, you belong to another age.
Where got you that trick of thought and word ? "

" I have had only one to teach me, the Lady Ermyntrude."

" *Pardieu !* she has trained a proper young hawk ready

to stoop at a lordly quarry," said Chandos. " I would that I had the first unhooding of you. Will you not ride with me to the wars ? "

The tears brimmed over from Nigel's eyes, and he wrung the gaunt hand extended from the bath. " By Saint Paul ! what could I ask better in the world ? I fear to leave her, for she has none other to care for her. But if it can in any way be arranged——"

" The king's hand may smooth it out. Say no more until he is here. But if you wish to ride with me——"

" What could man wish for more ? Is there a squire in England who would not serve under the banner of Chandos ! Whither do you go, fair sir ? And when do you go ? Is it to Scotland ? Is it to Ireland ? Is it to France ? But alas, alas ! "

The eager face had clouded. For the instant he had forgotten that a suit of armour was as much beyond his means as a service of gold plate. Down in a twinkling came all his high hopes to the ground. Oh, these sordid material things, which come between our dreams and their fulfilment ! The squire of such a knight must dress with the best. Yet all the fee-simple of Tilford would scarce suffice for one suit of plate.

Chandos with his quick wit and knowledge of the world had guessed the cause of this sudden change.

" If you fight under my banner it is for me to find the weapons," said he. " Nay, I will not be denied."

But Nigel shook his head sadly. " It may not be. The Lady Ermyntrude would sell this old house and every acre round it, ere she would permit me to accept this gracious bounty which you offer. Yet do I not despair, for only last week I won for myself a noble war-horse for which I paid not a penny, so perchance a suit of armour may also come my way."

" And how won you the horse ? "

" It was given me by the monks of Waverley."

" This is wonderful. *Pardieu !* I should have expected, from what I have seen, that they would have given you little save their malediction."

"They had no use for the horse, and they gave it to me."

"Then we have only to find someone who has no use for a suit of armour and will give it to you. Yet I trust that you will think better of it and let me, since that good lady proves that I am your kinsman, fit you for the wars."

"I thank you, noble sir, and if I should turn to anyone it would indeed be to you ; but there are other ways which I would try first. But I pray you, good Sir John, to tell me of some of your noble spear-runnings against the French, for the whole land rings with the tale of your deeds, and I have heard that in one morning three champions have fallen before your lance. Was it not so ? "

"That it was indeed so these scars upon my body will prove ; but these were the follies of my youth."

"How can you call them follies ? Are they not the means by which honourable advancement may be gained and one's lady exalted ? "

"It is right that you should think so, Nigel. At your age a man should have a hot head and a high heart. I also had both, and fought for my lady's glove or for my vow or for the love of fighting. But as one grows older and commands men one has other things to think of. One thinks less of one's own honour and more of the safety of the army. It is not your own spear, your own sword, your own arm, which will turn the tide of fight ; but a cool head may save a stricken field. He who knows when his horsemen should charge and when they should fight on foot, he who can mix his archers with his men-at-arms in such a fashion that each can support the other, he who can hold up his reserve and pour it into the battle when it may turn the tide, he who has a quick eye for boggy land and broken ground—that is the man who is of more worth to an army than Roland, Oliver, and all the paladins."

" Yet if his knights fail him, honoured sir, all his head-work will not prevail."

" True enough, Nigel ; so may every squire ride to the wars with his soul on fire, as yours is now. But I must linger no longer, for the king's service must be done. I will dress, and when I have bid farewell to the noble Dame Ermyntrude I will on to Farnham ; but you will see me here again on the day that the king comes."

So Chandos went his way that evening, walking his horse through the peaceful lanes and twanging his citole as he went, for he loved music and was famous for his merry songs. The cottagers came from their huts and laughed and clapped as the rich full voice swelled and sank to the cheery tinkling of the strings. There were few who saw him pass that would have guessed that the quaint one-eyed man with the yellow hair was the toughest fighter and craftiest man of war in Europe. Once only, as he entered Farnham, an old broken man-at-arms ran out in his rags and clutched at his horse as a dog gambols round his master. Chandos threw him a kind word and a gold coin as he passed on to the castle.

In the meanwhile young Nigel and the Lady Ermyntrude, left alone with their difficulties, looked blankly in each other's faces.

" The cellar is well-nigh empty," said Nigel. " There are two firkins of small beer and a tun of canary. How can we set such drink before the king and his court ? "

" We must have some wine of Bordeaux. With that and the mottled cow's calf and the fowls and a goose, we can set forth a sufficient repast if he stays only for the one night. How many will be with him ? "

" A dozen, at the least."

The old dame wrung her hands in despair.

" Nay, take it not to heart, dear lady ! " said Nigel. " We have but to say the word and the king would stop at Waverley, where he and his court would find all that they could wish."

" Never ! " cried the Lady Ermyntrude. " It would be

489

shame and disgrace to us for ever if the king were to pass our door when he has graciously said that he was fain to enter in. Nay, I will do it. Never did I think hat I would be forced to this, but I know that he would wish it, and I will do it."

She went to the old iron coffer, and taking a small key from her girdle she unlocked it. The rusty hinges, screaming shrilly as she threw back the lid, proclaimed how seldom it was that she had penetrated into the sacred recesses of her treasure-chest. At the top were some relics of old finery : a silken cloak spangled with gold stars, a coif of silver filigree, a roll of Venetian lace. Beneath were little packets tied in silk which the old lady handled with tender care ; a man's hunting-glove, a child's shoe, a love-knot done in faded green ribbon, some letters in rude rough script, and a vernicle of Saint Thomas. Then from the very bottom of the box she drew three objects, swathed in silken cloth, which she uncovered and laid upon the table. The one was a bracelet of rough gold studded with uncut rubies, the second was a gold salver, and the third was a high goblet of the same metal.

" You have heard me speak of these, Nigel, but never before have you seen them, for indeed I have not opened the hutch for fear that we might be tempted in our great need to turn them into money. I have kept them out of my sight and even out of my thoughts. But now it is the honour of the house which calls, and even these must go. This goblet was that which my husband, Sir Nele Loring, won after the intaking of Belgrade, when he and his comrades held the lists from matins to vespers against the flower of the French chivalry. The salver was given him by the Earl of Pembroke in memory of his valour upon the field of Falkirk."

" And the bracelet, dear lady ? "

" You will not laugh, Nigel ? "

" Nay, why should I laugh ? "

" The bracelet was the prize for the Queen of Beauty which was given to me before all the high-born ladies of

England by Sir Nele Loring a month before our marriage.
The Queen of Beauty, Nigel—I, old and twisted, as you
see me. Five strong men went down before his lance
ere he won that trinket for me. And now in my last
years—— "

"Nay, dear and honoured lady, we will not part
with it."

"Yes, Nigel, he would have it so. I can hear his
whisper in my ear. Honour to him was everything—the
rest nothing. Take it from me, Nigel, ere my heart
weakens. To-morrow you will ride with it to Guildford ;
you will see Thorold the goldsmith ; and you will raise
enough money to pay for all that we shall need for the
king's coming."

She turned her face away to hide the quivering of her
wrinkled features, and the crash of the iron lid covered
the sob which burst from her overwrought soul.

7. *How Nigel went Marketing to Guildford*

IT was on a bright June morning that young Nigel, with
youth and springtime to make his heart light, rode upon
his errand from Tilford to Guildford town. Beneath him
was his great yellow war-horse, caracoling and curveting
as he went, as blithe and free of spirit as his master. In
all England one would scarce have found upon that
morning so high-mettled and so debonair a pair. The
sandy road wound through groves of fir, where the breeze
came soft and fragrant with resinous gums, or over heath-
ery downs, which rolled away to north and to south, vast
and untenanted, for on the uplands the soil was poor and
water scarce. Over Crooksbury Common he passed, and
then across the great Heath of Puttenham, following a
sandy path which wound amid the bracken and the heather,
for he meant to strike the Pilgrim's Way where it turned
eastward from Farnham and from Seale. As he rode he
continually felt his saddle-bag with his hand, for in it,
securely strapped, he had placed the precious treasures of

the Lady Ermyntrude. As he saw the grand tawny neck tossing before him, and felt the easy heave of the great horse and heard the muffled drumming of his hoo˙s, he could have sung and shouted with the joy of living.

Behind him upon the little brown pony which had been Nigel's former mount, rode Samkin Aylward, the bowman, who had taken upon himself the duties of personal attendant and body-guard. His great shoulders and breadth of frame seemed dangerously top-heavy upon the tiny steed, but he ambled along, whistling a merry lilt, and as lighthearted as his master. There was no countryman who had not a nod and no woman who had not a smile for the jovial bowman, who rode for the most part with his face over his shoulder, staring at the last petticoat which had passed him. Once only he met with a harsher greeting. It was from a tall, white-headed, red-faced man whom they met upon the moor.

" Good morrow, dear father ! " cried Aylward. " How is it with you at Crooksbury ? And how are the new black cow and the ewes from Alton, and Mary the dairy-maid, and all your gear ? "

" It ill becomes you to ask, you ne'er-do-weel," said the old man. " You have angered the monks of Waverley, whose tenant I am, and they would drive me out of my farm. Yet there are three more years to run, and do what they may I will bide till then. But little did I think that I should lose my homestead through you, Samkin, and big as you are I would knock the dust out of that green jerkin with a good hazel switch if I had you at Crooksbury."

" Then you shall do it to-morrow morning, good father, for I will come and see you then. But indeed I did not do more at Waverley than you would have done yourself. Look me in the eye, old hot-head, and tell me if you would have stood by while the last Loring—look at him as he rides with his head in the air and his soul in the clouds— was shot down before your very eyes at the bidding of that fat monk ! If you would, then I disown you as my father."

"Nay, Samkin, if it was like that, then perhaps what you did was not so far amiss. But it is hard to lose the old farm when my heart is buried deep in the good brown soil."

"Tut, man! there are three years to run, and what may not happen in three years? Before that time I shall have gone to the wars, and when I have opened a French strong box or two you can buy the good brown soil and snap your fingers at Abbot John and his bailiffs. Am I not as proper a man as Tom Withstaff of Churt? And yet he came back after six months with his pockets full of rose nobles and a French wench on either arm."

"God preserve us from the wenches, Samkin! But indeed I think that if there is money to be gathered you are as likely to get your fist full as any man who goes to the war. But hasten, lad, hasten! Already your young master is over the brow."

Thus admonished, the archer waved his gauntleted hand to his father, and digging his heels into the sides of his little pony soon drew up with the squire. Nigel glanced over his shoulder and slackened speed until the pony's head was up to his saddle.

"Have I not heard, archer," said he, "that an outlaw has been loose in these parts?"

"It is true, fair sir. He was villein to Sir Peter Mandeville, but he broke his bonds and fled into the forests. Men call him the 'Wild Man of Puttenham.'"

"How comes it that he has not been hunted down? If the man be a draw-latch and a robber it would be an honourable deed to clear the country of such an evil."

"Twice the sergeants-at-arms from Guildford have come out against him, but the fox has many earths, and it would puzzle you to get him out of them."

"By Saint Paul! were my errand not a pressing one I would be tempted to turn aside and seek him. Where lives he, then?"

"There is a great morass beyond Puttenham, and across it there are caves in which he and his people lurk."

"His people? He hath a band?"

" There are several with him."

" It sounds a most honourable enterprise," said Nigel. " When the king hath come and gone we will spare a day for the outlaws of Puttenham. I fear there is little chance for us to see them on this journey."

" They prey upon the pilgrims who pass along the Winchester Road, and they are well loved by the folk in these parts, for they rob none of them and have an open hand for all who will help them."

" It is right easy to have an open hand with the money that you have stolen," said Nigel ; " but I fear that they will not try to rob two men with swords at their girdles like you and me, so we shall have no profit from them."

They had passed over the wild moors and had come down now into the main road by which the pilgrims from the west of England made their way to the national shrine of Canterbury. It passed from Winchester, and up the beautiful valley of the Itchen until it reached Farnham, where it forked into two branches, one of which ran along the Hog's Back, while the second wound to the south and came out at St. Catherine's Hill, where stands the Pilgrim's shrine, a grey old ruin now, but once so august, so crowded, and so affluent. It was this second branch upon which Nigel and Aylward found themselves as they rode to Guildford.

No one, as it chanced, was going the same way as themselves, but they met one large drove of pilgrims returning from their journey, with pictures of Saint Thomas and snails' shells or little leaden ampullæ in their hats and bundles of purchases over their shoulders. They were a grimy, ragged, travel-stained crew, the men walking, the women borne on asses. Man and beast, they limped along as if it would be a glad day when they saw their homes once more. These and a few beggars or minstrels, who crouched among the heather on either side of the track in the hope of receiving an occasional farthing from the passer-by, were the only folk they met until they had reached the village of Puttenham. Already there was a hot sun and just breeze enough to send the dust flying down the road, so they were glad to clear their throats with a glass of beer at the ale-stake in the village, where the fair alewife gave Nigel a cold farewell because he had no attentions for her, and Aylward a box on the ears because he had too many.

On the farther side of Puttenham the road runs through thick woods of oak and beech, with a tangled undergrowth of fern and bramble. Here they met a patrol of sergeants-at-arms, tall fellows, well mounted, clad in studded-leather caps and tunics, with lances and swords. They walked their horses slowly on the shady side of the road, and stopped as the travellers came up, to ask if they had been molested on the way.

" Have a care," they added, " for the ' Wild Man ' and his wife are out. Only yesterday they slew a merchant from the west and took a hundred crowns."

" His wife, you say ? "

" Yes, she is ever at his side, and has saved him many a time, for if he has the strength it is she who has the wit. I hope to see their heads together upon the green grass one of these mornings."

The patrol passed downward toward Farnham, and so, as it proved, away from the robbers, who had doubtless watched them closely from the dense brushwood which skirted the road. Coming round a curve, Nigel and Aylward were aware of a tall and graceful woman who sat, wringing her hands and weeping bitterly upon the bank by the side of the track. At such a sight of beauty in distress Nigel pricked Pommers with the spur and in three bounds was at the side of the unhappy lady.

" What ails you, fair dame ? " he asked. " Is there any small matter in which I may stand your friend, or is it possible that anyone hath so hard a heart as to do you an injury ? "

She rose and turned upon him a face full of hope and entreaty.

" Oh, save my poor, poor father ! " she cried. " Have

you perchance seen the way-wardens ? They passed us, and I fear they are beyond call."

" Yes, they have ridden onward, but we may serve as well."

" Then, hasten, hasten, I pray you ! Even now they may be doing him to death. They have dragged him into yonder grove and I have heard his voice growing ever weaker in the distance. Hasten, I implore you ! "

Nigel sprang from his horse and tossed the rein to Aylward.

" Nay, let us go together. How many robbers were there, lady ? "

" Two stout fellows."

" Then I come also."

" Nay, it is not possible," said Nigel. " The wood is too thick for horses, and we cannot leave them in the road."

" I will guard them," cried the lady.

" Pommers is not so easily held. Do you bide here, Aylward, until you hear from me. Stir not, I command you ! "

So saying, Nigel, with the light of adventure gleaming in his joyous eyes, drew his sword and plunged swiftly into the forest.

Far and fast he ran, from glade to glade, breaking through the bushes, springing over the brambles, light as a young deer, peering this way and that, straining his ears for a sound, and catching only the cry of the wood-pigeons. Still on he went, with the constant thought of the weeping woman behind and of the captured man in front. It was not until he was footsore and out of breath that he stopped with his hand to his side, and considered that his own business had still to be done, and that it was time once more that he should seek the road to Guildford.

Meantime Aylward had found his own rough means of consoling the woman in the road, who stood sobbing with her face against the side of Pommers' saddle.

" Nay, weep not, my pretty one," said he. " It brings the tears to my own eyes to see them stream from thine."

" Alas ! good archer, he was the best of fathers, so gentle and so kind ! Had you but known him, you must have loved him."

" Tut, tut ! he will suffer no scathe. Squire Nigel will bring him back to you anon."

" No, no, I shall never see him more. Hold me, archer, or I fall ! "

Aylward pressed his ready arm round the supple waist. The fainting woman leaned with her hand upon his shoulder. Her pale face looked past him, and it was some new light in her eyes, a flash of expectancy, of triumph, of wicked joy, which gave him sudden warning of his danger.

He shook her off and sprang to one side, but only just in time to avoid a crashing blow from a great club in the hands of a man even taller and stronger than himself. He had one quick vision of great white teeth clinched in grim ferocity, a wild flying beard and blazing wild-beast eyes. The next instant he had closed, ducking his head beneath another swing of that murderous cudgel.

With his arms round the robber's burly body and his face buried in his bushy beard, Aylward gasped and strained and heaved. Back and forward in the dusty road the two men stamped and staggered, a grim wrestling match, with life for the prize. Twice the great strength of the outlaw had Aylward nearly down, and twice with his greater youth and skill the archer restored his grip and his balance. Then at last his turn came. He slipped his leg behind the other's knee, and giving a mighty wrench, tore him across it. With a hoarse shout the outlaw toppled backward, and had hardly reached the ground before Aylward had his knee upon his chest and his short sword deep in his beard and pointed to his throat.

" By these ten finger-bones ! " he gasped, " one more struggle and it is your last ! "

The man lay still enough, for he was half-stunned by the crashing fall. Aylward looked round him, but the woman had disappeared. At the first blow struck she

497

had vanished into the forest. He began to have fears for his master, thinking that he perhaps had been lured into some death-trap ; but his forebodings were soon at rest, for Nigel himself came hastening down the road, which he had struck some distance from the spot where he left it.

" By Saint Paul ! " he cried, " who is this man on whom you are perched, and where is the lady who has honoured us so far as to crave our help ! Alas, that I have been unable to find her father ! "

" As well for you, fair sir," said Aylward, " for I am of opinion that her father was the Devil. This woman is, as I believe, the wife of the ' Wild Man of Puttenham,' and this is the ' Wild Man ' himself who set upon me and tried to brain me with his club."

The outlaw, who had opened his eyes, looked with a scowl from his captor to the newcomer.

" You are in luck, archer," said he, " for I have come to grips with many a man, but I cannot call to mind any who have had the better of me."

" You have indeed the grip of a bear," said Aylward ; " but it was a coward deed that your wife should hold me while you dashed out my brains with a stick. It is also a most villainous thing to lay a snare for wayfarers by asking for their pity and assistance, so that it was our own soft hearts which brought us into such danger. The next who hath real need of our help may suffer for your sins."

" When the hand of the whole world is against you," said the outlaw, in a surly voice, " you must fight as best you can."

" You well deserve to be hanged, if only because you have brought this woman, who is fair and gentle-spoken, to such a life," said Nigel. " Let us tie him by the wrist to my stirrup leather, Aylward, and we will lead him into Guildford."

The archer drew a spare bowstring from his case and had bound the prisoner as directed, when Nigel gave a sudden start and cry of alarm.

" Holy Mary ! " he cried. " Where is the saddle-bag ! "

It had been cut away by a sharp knife. Only the two ends of a strap remained. Aylward and Nigel stared at each other in blank dismay. Then the young squire shook his clenched hands and pulled at his yellow curls in his despair.

" The Lady Ermyntrude's bracelet ! My grandfather's cup ! " he cried. " I would have died ere I lost them ! What can I say to her ? I dare not return until I have found them. Oh, Aylward, Aylward ! how came you to let them be taken ? "

The honest archer had pushed back his steel cap and was scratching his tangled head.

" Nay, I know nothing of it. You never said that there was aught of price in the bag, else had I kept a better eye upon it. Certes ! it was not this fellow who took it, since I have never had my hands from him. It can only be the woman who fled with it while we fought."

Nigel stamped about the road in his perplexity. " I would follow her to the world's end if I knew where I could find her, but to search these woods for her is to look for a mouse in a wheat-field. Good Saint George, thou who didst overcome the Dragon, I pray you by that most honourable and knightly achievement that you will be with me now ! And you also, great Saint Julian, patron of all wayfarers in distress ! Two candles shall burn before your shrine at Godalming, if you will but bring me back my saddle-bag. What would I not give to have it back ? "

" Will you give me my life ? " asked the outlaw. " Promise that I go free, and you shall have it back, if it be indeed true that my wife has taken it."

" Nay, I cannot do that," said Nigel. " My honour would surely be concerned, since my loss is a private one ; but it would be to the public scathe that you should go free. By Saint Paul ! it would be an ungentle deed if in order to save my own I let you loose upon the gear of a hundred others."

" I will not ask you to let me loose," said the " Wild Man." " If you will promise that my life be spared I will restore your bag."

" I cannot give such a promise, for it will lie with the sheriff and reeves of Guildford."

" Shall I have your word in my favour ? "

" That I could promise you, if you will give back the bag, though I know not how far my word may avail. But your words are vain, for you cannot think that we will be so fond as to let you go in the hope that you return ? "

" I would not ask it," said the " Wild Man," " for I can get your bag and yet never stir from the spot where I stand. Have I your promise upon your honour and all that you hold dear that you will ask for grace ? "

" You have."

" And that my wife shall be unharmed ? "

" I promise it."

The outlaw laid back his head and uttered a long shrill cry like the howl of a wolf. There was a silent pause, and then, clear and shrill, there rose the same cry no great distance away in the forest. Again the " Wild Man " called, and again his mate replied. A third time he summoned, as the deer bells to the doe in the greenwood. Then with a rustle of brushwood and snapping of twigs the woman was before them once more, tall, pale, graceful, wonderful. She glanced neither at Aylward nor Nigel, but ran to the side of her husband.

" Dear and sweet lord," she cried, " I trust they have done you no hurt. I waited by the old ash, and my heart sank when you came not."

" I have been taken at last, wife."

" Oh, cursed, cursed day ! Let him go, kind, gentle sirs, do not take him from me ! "

" They will speak for me at Guildford," said the " Wild Man." " They have sworn it. But hand them first the bag that you have taken."

She drew it out from under her loose cloak. " Here it is, gentle sir. Indeed it went to my heart to take it, for you had mercy upon me in my trouble. But now I am, as you see, in real and very sore distress. Will you not have mercy now ? Take ruth on us, fair sir ! On my knees I beg it of you, most gentle and kindly squire ! "

Nigel had clutched his bag, and right glad he was to feel that the treasures were all safe within it.

" My promise is given," said he. " I will say what I can ; but the issue rests with others. I pray you to stand up, for indeed I cannot promise more."

" Then I must be content," said she, rising, with a composed face. " I have prayed you to take ruth, and indeed I can do no more ; but ere I go back to the forest I would rede you to be on your guard lest you lose your bag once more. Wot you how I took it, archer ? Nay, it was simple enough, and may happen again, so I make it clear to you. I had this knife in my sleeve, and though it is small it is very sharp. I slipped it down like this. Then, when I seemed to weep with my face against the saddle, I cut down like this—— "

In an instant she had shorn through the stirrup leather which bound her man, and he, diving under the belly of the horse, had slipped like a snake into the brushwood. In passing he had struck Pommers from beneath, and the great horse, enraged and insulted, was rearing high, with two men hanging on his bridle. When at last he had calmed there was no sign left of the " Wild Man " or of his wife. In vain did Aylward, an arrow on his string, run here and there among the great trees and peer down the shadowy glades. When he returned he and his master cast a shame-faced glance at each other.

" I trust that we are better soldiers than jailers," said Aylward, as he climbed on his pony.

But Nigel's frown relaxed into a smile. " At least we have gained back what we lost," said he. " Here I place it on the pommel of my saddle, and I shall not take my eyes from it until we are safe in Guildford town."

So they jogged on together until passing Saint Catharine's shrine they crossed the winding Wey once more, and so found themselves in the steep high street with its heavy-eaved gabled houses, its monkish hospitium upon the left, where good ale may still be quaffed, and its great square-keeped castle upon the right, no grey and grim skeleton of ruin, but very quick and alert, with blazoned banner flying free, and steel caps twinkling from the battlement. A row of booths extended from the castle gate to the high street, and two doors from the Church of the Trinity was that of Thorold the goldsmith, a rich burgess and Mayor of the town.

He looked long and lovingly at the rich rubies and at the fine work upon the goblet. Then he stroked his flowing grey beard as he pondered whether he should offer fifty nobles or sixty, for he knew well that he could sell them again for two hundred. If he offered too much his profit would be reduced. If he offered too little the youth might go as far as London with them, for they were rare and of great worth. The young man was ill-clad, and his eyes were anxious. Perchance he was hard pressed and was ignorant of the value of what he bore. He would sound him.

" These things are old and out of fashion, fair sir," said he. " Of the stones I can scarce say if they are of good quality or not, but they are dull and rough. Yet, if your price be low I may add them to my stock, though indeed this booth was made to sell and not to buy. What do you ask ? "

Nigel bent his brows in perplexity. Here was a game in which neither his bold heart nor his active limbs could help him. It was the new force mastering the old : the man of commerce conquering the man of war—wearing him down and weakening him through the centuries until he had him as his bond-servant and his thrall.

" I know not what to ask, good sir," said Nigel. " It is not for me, nor for any man who bears my name, to chaffer and to haggle. You know the worth of these

things, for it is your trade to do so. The Lady Ermyntrude lacks money, and we must have it against the king's
coming, so give me that which is right and just, and we
will say no more."

The goldsmith smiled. The business was growing
more simple and more profitable. He had intended to
offer fifty, but surely it would be sinful waste to give
more than twenty-five.

" I shall scarce know what to do with them when I
have them," said he. " Yet I should not grudge twenty
nobles if it is a matter in which the king is concerned."

Nigel's heart turned to lead. This sum would not buy
one-half what was needful. It was clear that the Lady
Ermyntrude had overvalued her treasures. Yet he could
not return empty-handed, so if twenty nobles was the real
worth, as this good old man assured him, then he must be
thankful and take it.

" I am concerned by what you say," said he. " You
know more of these things than I can do. However, I
will take——"

" A hundred and fifty," whispered Aylward's voice in
his ear.

" A hundred and fifty," said Nigel, only too relieved to
have found the humblest guide upon these unwonted paths.

The goldsmith started. This youth was not the simple
soldier that he had seemed. That frank face, those blue
eyes, were traps for the unwary. Never had he been
more taken aback in a bargain.

" This is fond talk and can lead to nothing, fair sir,"
said he, turning away and fiddling with the keys of his
strong boxes. " Yet I have no wish to be hard on you.
Take my outside price, which is fifty nobles."

" And a hundred," whispered Aylward.

" And a hundred," said Nigel, blushing at his own
greed.

" Well, well, take a hundred ! " cried the merchant.
" Fleece me, skin me, leave me a loser, and take for your
wares the full hundred ! "

" I should be shamed for ever if I were to treat you so badly," said Nigel. " You have spoken me fair, and I would not grind you down. Therefore, I will gladly take one hundred——"

" And fifty," whispered Aylward.

" And fifty," said Nigel.

" By Saint John of Beverley ! " cried the merchant. " I came hither from the North Country, and they are said to be shrewd at a deal in those parts ; but I had rather bargain with a synagogue full of Jews than with you, for all your gentle ways. Will you indeed take no less than a hundred and fifty ? Alas ! you pluck from me my profits of a month. It is a fell morning's work for me. I would I had never seen you ! " With groans and lamentations he paid the gold pieces across the counter, and Nigel, hardly able to credit his own good fortune, gathered them into the leather saddle-bag.

A moment later with flushed face he was in the street and pouring out his thanks to Aylward.

" Alas, my fair lord ! the man has robbed us now," said the archer. " We could have had another twenty had we stood fast."

" How know you that, good Aylward ? "

" By his eyes, Squire Loring. I wot I have little store of reading where the parchment of a book or the pricking of a blazon is concerned, but I can read men's eyes, and I never doubted that he would give what he has given."

The two travellers had dinner at the monks' hospitium, Nigel at the high table and Aylward among the commonalty. Then again they roamed the high street on business intent. Nigel bought taffeta for hangings, wine, preserves, fruit, damask table-linen, and many other articles of need. At last he halted before the armourer's shop at the castleyard, staring at the fine suits of plate, the engraved pectorals, the plumed helmets, the cunningly jointed gorgets, as a child at a sweet-shop.

" Well, Squire Loring," said Wat the armourer, looking

sidewise from the furnace where he was tempering a sword-blade, " what can I sell you this morning? I swear to you by Tubal Cain, the father of all workers in metal, that you might go from end to end of Cheapside and never see a better suit than that which hangs from yonder hook ! "

" And the price, armourer ? "

" To anyone else, two hundred and fifty rose nobles, To you two hundred."

" And why cheaper to me, good fellow ? "

" Because I fitted your father also for the wars, and a finer suit never went out of my shop. I warrant that it turned many an edge before he laid it aside. We worked in mail in those days, and I had as soon have a well-made thick-meshed mail as any plates ; but a young knight will be in the fashion like any dame of the court, and so it must be plate now, even though the price be trebled."

" Your rede is that the mail is as good ? "

" I am well sure of it."

" Hearken then, armourer ! I cannot at this moment buy a suit of plate, and yet I sorely need steel harness on account of a small deed which it is in my mind to do. Now I have at my home at Tilford that very suit of mail of which you speak, with which my father first rode to the wars. Could you not so alter it that it should guard my limbs also ! "

The armourer looked at Nigel's small upright figure and burst out laughing.

" You jest, Squire Loring ! The suit was made for one who was far above the common stature of man."

" Nay, I jest not. If it will but carry me through one spear-running it will have served its purpose."

The armourer leaned back on his anvil and pondered, while Nigel stared anxiously at his sooty face.

" Right gladly would I lend you a suit of plate for this one venture, Squire Loring, but I know well that if you should be overthrown your harness becomes prize to the victor. I am a poor man with many children, and I dare not risk the loss of it. But as to what you say of the old suit of mail, is it indeed in good condition ? "

" Most excellent, save only at the neck, which is much frayed."

" To shorten the limbs is easy. It is but to cut out a length of the mail and then loop up the links. But to shorten the body—nay, that is beyond the armourer's art."

" It was my last hope. Nay, good armourer, if you have indeed served and loved my gallant father, then I beg you by his memory that you will help me now."

The armourer threw down his heavy hammer with a crash upon the floor.

" It is not only that I loved your father, Squire Loring, but it is that I have seen you, half armed as you were, ride against the best of them at the Castle tilt-yard. Last Martinmas my heart bled for you when I saw how sorry was your harness, and yet you held your own against the stout Sir Oliver with his Milan suit. When go you to Tilford ? "

" Even now."

" Heh, Jenkin, fetch out the cob ! " cried the worthy Wat. " May my right hand lose its cunning if I do not send you into battle in your father's suit ! To-morrow I must be back in my booth, but to-day I give to you without fee and for the sake of the good-will which I bear to your house. I will ride with you to Tilford, and before night you shall see what Wat can do."

So it came about that there was a busy evening at the old Tilford Manor-house, where the Lady Ermyntrude planned and cut and hung the curtains for the hall, and stocked her cupboards with the good things which Nigel had brought from Guildford.

Meanwhile the squire and the armourer sat with their heads touching and the old suit of mail with its gorget of overlapping plates laid out across their knees. Again and again old Wat shrugged his shoulders, as one who has been asked to do more than can be demanded from mortal man. At last, at a suggestion from the squire, he leaned back in his chair and laughed long and loudly in his bushy beard, while the Lady Ermyntrude glared her black displeasure at such plebeian merriment. Then taking his fine chisel and his hammer from his pouch of tools, the armourer, still chuckling at his own thoughts, began to drive a hole through the centre of the steel tunic.

8. How the King Hawked on Crooksbury Heath

THE king and his attendants had shaken off the crowd who had followed them from Guildford along the Pilgrim's Way, and now, the mounted archers having beaten off the more persistent of the spectators, they rode at their ease in a long, straggling, glittering train over the dark undulating plain of heather.

In the van was the king himself, for his hawks were with him and he had some hope of sport. Edward at that time was a well-grown, vigorous man in the very prime of his years, a keen sportsman, an ardent gallant and a chivalrous soldier. He was a scholar too, speaking Latin, French, German, Spanish, and even a little English.

So much had long been patent to the world, but only of recent years had he shown other and more formidable characteristics : a restless ambition which coveted his neighbour's throne, and a wise foresight in matters of commerce, which engaged him now in transplanting Flemish weavers and sowing the seeds of what for many years was the staple trade of England. Each of these varied qualities might have been read upon his face. The brow, shaded by a crimson cap of maintenance, was broad and lofty. The large brown eyes were ardent and bold. His chin was clean-shaven, and the close-cropped dark moustache did not conceal the strong mouth, firm, proud, and kindly, but capable of setting tight in merciless ferocity. His complexion was tanned to copper by a life spent in field sports or in war, and he rode his magnificent black horse carelessly and easily, as one who has grown up in the saddle. His own colour was black also, for his active, sinewy figure was set off by close-fitting velvet of that hue, broken only by a belt of gold, and by a golden border of open pods of the broom-plant.

With his high and noble bearing, his simple yet rich attire and his splendid mount, he looked every inch a king. The picture of gallant man on gallant horse was completed by the noble Falcon of the Isles which fluttered along some twelve feet above his head, " waiting on," as it was termed, for any quarry which might arise. The second bird of the cast was borne upon the gauntleted wrist of Raoul, the chief falconer, in the rear.

At the right side of the monarch and a little behind him rode a youth some twenty years of age, tall, slim, and dark, with noble aquiline features and keen penetrating eyes which sparkled with vivacity and affection as he answered the remarks of the king. He was clad in deep crimson diapered with gold, and the trappings of his white palfrey were of a magnificence which proclaimed the rank of its rider. On his face, still free from moustache or beard, there sat a certain gravity and majesty of expression which showed that, young as he was, great affairs had been in his keeping, and that his thoughts and interests were those of the statesman and the warrior. That great day when, little more than a schoolboy, he had led the van of the victorious army which had crushed the power of France at Crécy had left its stamp upon his features ; but stern as they were they had not assumed that tinge of fierceness which in after-years was to make " The Black Prince " a name of terror on the marches of France. Not yet had the first shadow of fell disease come to poison his nature ere it struck at his life, as he rode that spring day, light and debonair, upon the heath of Crooksbury.

On the left of the king, and so near to him that great intimacy was implied, rode a man about his own age, with the broad face, the projecting jaw, and the flattish nose which are often the outward indications of a pugnacious nature. His complexion was crimson, his large blue eyes somewhat prominent, and his whole appearance full-blooded and choleric. He was short, but massively built, and evidently possessed of immense strength. His voice, however, when he spoke was gentle and lisping, while his manner was quiet and courteous. Unlike the king or the prince, he was clad in light armour and carried a sword by his side and a mace at his saddle-bow, for he was acting as captain of the king's guard, and a dozen other knights in steel followed in the escort. No hardier soldier could Edward have at his side, if, as was always possible in those lawless times, sudden danger were to threaten, for this was the famous knight of Hainault, now naturalised as an Englishman, Sir Walter Manny, who bore as high a reputation for chivalrous valour and for gallant temerity as Chandos himself.

Behind the knights, who were forbidden to scatter and must always follow the king's person, there was a body of twenty or thirty hobelers or mounted bowmen, together with several squires, unarmed themselves but leading spare horses upon which the heavier part of their knights' equipment was carried. A straggling tail of falconers, harbingers, varlets, body-servants and huntsmen holding hounds in leash completed the long and many-coloured train which rose and dipped on the low undulations of the moor.

Many weighty things were on the mind of Edward the king. There was truce for the moment with France, but it was a truce broken by many small deeds of arms, raids, surprises, and ambushes upon either side, and it was certain that it would soon dissolve again into open war. Money must be raised, and it was no light matter to raise it, now that the Commons had once already voted the tenth lamb and the tenth sheaf. Besides, the Black Death had ruined the country, the arable land was all turned to pasture, the labourer, laughing at statutes, would not work under fourpence a day, and all society was chaos. In addition, the Scotch were growling over the border, there was the perennial trouble in half-conquered Ireland, and his allies abroad in Flanders and in Brabant were clamouring for the arrears of their subsidies.

All this was enough to make even a victorious monarch full of care ; but now Edward had thrown it all to the winds and was as light-hearted as a boy upon a holiday. No thought had he for the dunning of Florentine bankers or the vexatious conditions of those busybodies at Westminster. He was out with his hawks, and his thoughts and his talk should be of nothing else. The varlets beat the heather and bushes as they passed, and whooped loudly as the birds flew out.

" A magpie ! A magpie ! " cried the falconer.

" Nay, nay, it is not worthy of your talons, my brown-eyed queen," said the king, looking up at the great bird which flapped from side to side above his head, waiting for the whistle which should give her the signal. " The tercels, falconer—a cast of tercels ! Quick, man, quick ! Ha ! the rascal makes for wood ! He puts in ! Well flown, brave peregrine ! He makes his point. Drive him out to thy comrade. Serve him, varlets ! Beat the bushes ! He breaks ! He breaks ! Nay, come away then ! You will see master magpie no more."

The bird had indeed, with the cunning of its race, flapped its way through brushwood and bushes to the thicker woods beyond, so that neither the hawk amid the cover nor its partner above nor the clamorous beaters could harm it. The king laughed at the mischance and rode on. Continually birds of various sorts were flushed, and each was pursued by the appropriate hawk, the snipe by the tercel, the partridge by the goshawk, even the lark by the little merlin. But the king soon tired of this petty sport and went slowly on his way, still with the magnificent silent attendant flapping above his head.

" Is she not a noble bird, fair son ? " he asked, glancing up as her shadow fell upon him.

" She is indeed, sire. Surely no finer ever came from the isles of the north."

" Perhaps not, and yet I have had a hawk from Barbary as good a footer and a swifter flyer. An Eastern bird in yarak has no peer."

" I had one once from the Holy Land," said de Manny. " It was fierce and keen and swift as the Saracens themselves. They say of old Saladin that in his day his breed of birds, of hounds, and of horses had no equal on earth."

" I trust, dear father, that the day may come when we shall lay our hands on all three," said the prince, looking with shining eyes upon the king. " Is the Holy Land to lie for ever in the grasp of these unbelieving savages, or the Holy Temple to be defiled by their foul presence ? Ah ! my dear and most sweet lord, give to me a thousand lances with ten thousand bowmen like those I led at Crécy, and I swear to you by God's soul that within a year I will have done homage to you for the Kingdom of Jerusalem ! "

The king laughed as he turned to Walter Manny. " Boys will still be boys," said he.

" The French do not count me such ! " cried the young prince, flushing with anger.

" Nay, fair son, there is no one sets you at a higher rate than your father. But you have the nimble mind and quick fancy of youth, turning over from the thing that is half done to a further task beyond. How would we fare in Brittany and Normandy while my young paladin, with his lances and his bowmen, was besieging Ascalon or battering at Jerusalem ? "

" Heaven would help in Heaven's work."

" From what I have heard of the past," said the king, dryly, " I cannot see that Heaven has counted for much as an ally in these wars of the East. I speak with reverence, and yet it is but sooth to say that Richard of the Lion Heart, or Louis of France, might have found the smallest earthly principality of greater service to him than all the celestial hosts. How say you to that, my lord bishop ? "

A stout churchman, who had ridden behind the king

on a solid, bay cob, well suited to his weight and dignity, jogged up to the monarch's elbow.

"How say you, sire? I was watching the goshawk on the partridge, and heard you not."

"Had I said that I would add two manors to the see of Chichester, I warrant that you would have heard me, my lord bishop."

"Nay, fair lord, test the matter by saying so," cried the jovial bishop.

The king laughed aloud. "A fair counter, your reverence. By the rood! you broke your lance that passage. But the question I debated was this : How is it that since the Crusades have manifestly been fought in God's quarrel, we Christians have had so little comfort or support in fighting them? After all our efforts and the loss of more men than could be counted, we are at last driven from the country, and even the military orders, which were formed only for that one purpose, can scarce hold a footing in the islands of the Greek sea. There is not one seaport nor one fortress in Palestine over which the flag of the Cross still waves. Where, then, was our ally?"

"Nay, sire, you open a great debate which extends far beyond this question of the Holy Land, though that may, indeed, be chosen as a fair example. It is the question of all sin, of all suffering, of all injustice—why it should pass without the rain of fire and the lightnings of Sinai. The wisdom of God is beyond our understanding."

The king shrugged his shoulders. "This is an easy answer, my lord bishop. You are a prince of the Church. It would fare ill with an earthly prince who could give no better answer to the affairs which concerned his realm."

"There are other considerations which might be urged, most gracious sire. It is true that the Crusades were a holy enterprise which might well expect the immediate blessing of God ; but the Crusaders—is it certain that they deserved such a blessing? Have I not heard that their camp was the most dissolute ever seen?"

"Camps are camps all the world over, and you cannot

in a moment change a bowman into a saint. But the holy Louis was a crusader after your own heart. Yet his men perished at Mansurah, and he himself at Tunis."

" Bethink you also that this world is but the ante-chamber of the next," said the prelate. " By suffering and tribulation the soul is cleansed, and the true victor may be he who, by the patient endurance of misfortune, merits the happiness to come."

" If that be the true meaning of the Church's blessing, then I hope that it will be long before it rests upon our banners in France," said the king. " But methinks that when one is out with a brave horse and a good hawk, one might find some other subject that theology. Back to the birds, bishop, or Raoul, the falconer, will come to interrupt thee in thy cathedral."

Straightway the conversation came back to the mystery of the woods and the mystery of the rivers, to the dark-eyed hawks and the yellow-eyed, to hawks of the lure and hawks of the fist. The bishop was as steeped in the lore of falconry as the king, and the others smiled as the two wrangled hard over disputed and technical questions : if an eyas trained in the mews can ever emulate the passage hawk taken wild, or how long the young hawks should be placed at hack, and how long weathered before they are fully reclaimed.

Monarch and prelate were still deep in this learned discussion, the bishop speaking with a freedom and assurance which he would never have dared to use in affairs of Church and State, for in all ages there is no such leveller as sport. Suddenly, however, the prince, whose keen eyes had swept from time to time over the great blue heaven, uttered a peculiar call and reined up his palfrey, pointing at the same time into the air.

" A heron ! " he cried. " A heron on passage ! "

To gain the full sport of hawking, a heron must not be put up from its feeding-ground, where it is heavy with its meal, and has no time to get its pace on before it is pounced upon by the more active hawk, but it must be aloft, travelling from point to point, probably from the fish-stream to the heronry. Thus, to catch the bird on passage was the prelude of all good sport. The object to which the prince had pointed was but a black dot in the southern sky, but his strained eyes had not deceived him, and both bishop and king agreed that it was indeed a heron, which grew larger every instant as it flew in their direction.

"Whistle him off, sire ! Whistle off the gerfalcon ! " cried the bishop.

"Nay, nay, he is overfar. She would fly at check."

"Now, sire, now ! " cried the prince, as the great bird, with the breeze behind him, came sweeping down the sky.

The king gave the shrill whistle, and the well-trained hawk raked out to the right and to the left to make sure which quarry she was to follow. Then, spying the heron, she shot up in a swift, ascending curve to meet him.

"Well flown, Margot ! Good bird ! " cried the king, clapping his hands to encourage the hawk, while the falconers broke into the shrill whoop peculiar to the sport.

Going on her curve, the hawk would soon have crossed the path of the heron ; but the latter, seeing the danger in his front, and confident in his own great strength of wing and lightness of body, proceeded to mount higher in the air, flying in such small rings that, to the spectators, it almost seemed as if the bird was going perpendicularly upward.

"He takes the air ! " cried the king. "But strong as he flies, he cannot outfly Margot. Bishop, I lay you ten gold pieces to one that the heron is mine."

"I cover your wager, sire," said the bishop. "I may not take gold so won, and yet I warrant that there is an altar-cloth somewhere in need of repairs."

"You have good store of altar-cloths, bishop, if all the gold I have seen you win at tables goes to the mending of them," said the king. "Ah ! by the rood, rascal, rascal ! See how she flies at check ! "

The quick eyes of the bishop had perceived a drift of rooks which on their evening flight to the rookery were

passing along the very line which divided the hawk from
the heron. A rook is a hard temptation for a hawk to
resist. In an instant the inconstant bird had forgotten all
about the great heron above her, and was circling over the
rooks, flying westward with them as she singled out the
plumpest for her stoop.

" There is yet time, sire ! Shall I cast off her mate ? "
cried the falconer.

" Or shall I show you, sire, how a peregrine may win
where a gerfalcon fails ? " said the bishop. " Ten golden
pieces to one upon my bird."

" Done with you, bishop ! " cried the king, his brow
dark with vexation. " By the rood ! if you were as learned
in the fathers as you are in hawks, you would win to the
throne of Saint Peter ! Cast off your peregrine, and make
your boasting good."

Smaller than the royal gerfalcon, the bishop's bird was
none the less a swift and beautiful creature. From her
perch upon his wrist she had watched with fierce, keen
eyes the birds in the heaven, mantling herself from time
to time in her eagerness. Now, when the button was
undone, and the leash uncast, the peregrine dashed off
with a whir of her sharp-pointed wings, whizzing round
in a great ascending circle which mounted swiftly upward,
growing ever smaller as she approached that lofty point
where, a mere speck in the sky, the heron sought escape
from its enemies. Still higher and higher the two birds
mounted, while the horsemen, their faces upturned,
strained their eyes in their efforts to follow them.

" She rings ! She still rings ! " cried the bishop.
" She is above him ! She has gained her pitch."

" Nay, nay, she is far below," said the king.

" By my soul, my lord bishop is right ! " cried the
prince. " I believe she is above. See ! See ! She swoops ! "

" She binds ! She binds ! " cried a dozen voices as the
two dots blended suddenly into one.

There could be no doubt that they were falling rapidly.
Already they grew larger to the eye. Presently the heron

SIR NIGEL

disengaged himself and flapped heavily away, the worse
for that deadly embrace, while the peregrine, shaking her
plumage, ringed once more so as to get high above the
quarry and deal it a second and more fatal blow. The
bishop smiled, for nothing, as it seemed, could hinder his
victory.

" Thy gold pieces shall be well spent, sire," said he.
" What is lost to the Church is gained by the loser."

But a most unlooked-for chance deprived the bishop's
altar-cloth of its costly mending. The king's gerfalcon,
having struck down a rook, and finding the sport but tame,
bethought herself suddenly of that noble heron, which she
still perceived fluttering over Crooksbury Heath. How
could she have been so weak as to allow these silly,
chattering rooks to entice her away from that lordly bird ?
Even now it was not too late to atone for her mistake. In
a great spiral she shot upwards until she was over the
heron. But what was this ? Every fibre of her, from her
crest to her deck feathers, quivered with jealousy and rage
at the sight of this creature, a mere peregrine, who had
dared to come between a royal gerfalcon and her quarry.
With one sweep of her great wings she shot up until she
was above her rival. The next instant——

" They crab ! They crab ! " cried the king, with a roar
of laughter, following them with his eyes as they hurtled
down through the air.

" Mend thy own altar-cloths, bishop. Not a groat shall
you have from me this journey. Pull them apart, falconer,
lest they do each other an injury. And now, masters, let
us on, for the sun sinks towards the west."

The two hawks, which had come to the ground inter-
locked with clutching talons and ruffled plumes, were torn
apart and brought back bleeding and panting to their
perches, while the heron, after its perilous adventure,
flapped its way heavily onward to settle safely in the
heronry of Waverley. The *cortège*, who had scattered in
the excitement of the chase, came together again, and the
journey was once more resumed.

A horseman who had been riding toward them across the moor now quickened his pace and closed swiftly upon them. As he came nearer, the king and the prince cried out joyously and waved their hands in greeting.

" It is good John Chandos ! " cried the king. " By the rood, John, I have missed your merry songs this week or more ! Glad I am to see that you have your citole slung to your back. Whence come you, then ? "

" I come from Tilford, sire, in the hope that I should meet your majesty."

" It was well thought of. Come, ride here between the prince and me, and we will believe that we are back in France with our war harness on our backs once more. What is your news, Master John ? "

Chandos's quaint face, quivered with suppressed amusement and his one eye twinkled like a star.

" Have you had sport, my liege ? "

" Poor sport, John. We flew two hawks on the same heron. They crabbed, and the bird got free. But why do you smile so ? "

" Because I hope to show you better sport ere you come to Tilford."

" For the hawk ? For the hound ? "

" A nobler sport than either."

" Is this a riddle, John ? What mean you ? "

" Nay, to tell all would be to spoil all. I say again that there is rare sport betwixt here and Tilford, and I beg you, dear lord, to mend your pace that we make the most of the daylight."

Thus adjured, the king set spurs to his horse, and the whole cavalcade cantered over the heath in the direction which Chandos showed. Presently as they came over a slope they saw beneath them a winding river with an old high-backed bridge across it. On the farther side was a village-green with a fringe of cottages and one dark manor-house upon the side of the hill.

" This is Tilford," said Chandos. " Yonder is the house of the Lorings."

The king's expectations had been aroused and his face showed his disappointment.

" Is this the sport that you have promised us, Sir John ?   How can you make good your words ? "

" I will make them good, my liege."

" Where, then, is the sport ? "

On the high crown of the bridge a rider in armour was seated, lance in hand, upon a great yellow steed.   Chandos touched the king's arm and pointed.

" That is the sport," said he.

9. *How Nigel Held the Bridge at Tilford*

THE king looked at the motionless figure, at the little crowd of hushed expectant rustics beyond the bridge, and finally at the face of Chandos, which shone with amusement.

" What is this, John ? " he asked.

" You remember Sir Eustace Loring, sire ? "

" Indeed I could never forget him nor the manner of his death."

" He was a knight-errant in his day."

" That indeed he was—none better have I known."

" So is his son Nigel, as fierce a young war-hawk as ever yearned to use beak and claw ; but held fast in the mews up to now.   This is his trial flight.   There he stands at the bridge-head, as was the wont in our fathers' time, ready to measure himself against all comers."

Of all Englishmen there was no greater knight-errant than the king himself, and none so steeped in every quaint usage of chivalry ; so that the situation was after his own heart.

" He is not yet a knight ? "

" No, sire, only a squire."

" Then he must bear himself bravely this day if he is to make good what he has done.   Is it fitting that a young untried squire should venture to couch his lance against the best in England ? "

" He hath given me his cartel and challenge," said Chandos, drawing a paper from his tunic. " Have I your permission, sire, to issue it ? "

" Surely, John, we have no cavalier more versed in the laws of chivalry than yourself. You know this young man, and you are aware how far he is worthy of the high honour which he asks. Let us hear his defiance."

The knights and squires of the escort, most of whom were veterans of the French war, had been gazing with interest and some surprise at the steel-clad figure in front of them. Now at a call from Sir Walter Manny they assembled round the spot where the king and Chandos had halted. Chandos cleared his throat and read from his paper—

" ' *A tous seigneurs, chevaliers et escuyers,*' so it is headed, gentlemen. It is a message from the good Squire Nigel Loring of Tilford, son of Sir Eustace Loring, of honourable memory. Squire Loring awaits you in arms, gentlemen, yonder upon the crown of the old bridge. Thus says he : ' For the great desire that I, a most humble and unworthy squire, entertain, that I may come to the knowledge of the noble gentlemen who ride with my royal master, I now wait on the Bridge of the Way in the hope that some of them may condescend to do some small deed of arms upon me, or that I may deliver them from any vow which they may have taken. This I say out of no esteem for myself, but solely that I may witness the noble bearing of these famous cavaliers and admire their skill in the handling of arms. Therefore, with the help of Saint George, I will hold the bridge with sharpened lances against any or all who may deign to present themselves while daylight lasts.' "

" What say you to this, gentlemen ? " asked the king, looking round with laughing eyes.

" Truly it is issued in very good form," said the prince. " Neither Claricieux nor Red Dragon nor any herald that ever wore tabard could better it. Did he draw it of his own hand ? "

"He hath a grim old grandmother who is one of the ancient breed," said Chandos. "I doubt not that the Dame Ermyntrude hath drawn a challenge or two before now. But hark ye, sire, I would have a word in your ear—and yours too, most noble prince."

Leading them aside, Chandos whispered some explanations, which ended by them all three bursting into a shout of laughter.

"By the rood! no honourable gentleman should be reduced to such straits," said the king. "It behoves me to look to it. But how now, gentlemen? This worthy cavalier still waits his answer."

The soldiers had all been buzzing together; but now Walter Manny turned to the king with the result of their counsel.

"If it please your majesty," said he, "we are of opinion that this squire hath exceeded all bounds in desiring to break a spear with a belted knight ere he has given his proofs. We do him sufficient honour if a squire ride against him, and with your consent I have chosen my own body-squire, John Widdicombe, to clear the path for us across the bridge."

"What you say, Walter, is right and fair," said the king. "Master Chandos, you will tell our champion yonder what hath been arranged. You will advise him also that it is our royal will that this contest be not fought upon the bridge, since it is very clear that it must end in one or both going over into the river, but that he advance to the end of the bridge and fight upon the plain. You will tell him also that a blunted lance is sufficient for such an encounter, but that a hand-stroke or two with sword or mace may well be exchanged, if both riders should keep their saddles. A blast upon Raoul's horn shall be the signal to close."

Such ventures as these where an aspirant for fame would wait for days at a cross-road, a ford, or a bridge, until some worthy antagonist should ride that way, were very common in the old days of adventurous knight-errantry, and were still familiar to the minds of all men, because the stories of the romancers and the songs of the trouvères were full of such incidents. Their actual occurrence, however, had become rare. There was the more curiosity, not unmixed with amusement, in the thoughts of the courtiers as they watched Chandos ride down to the bridge and commented upon the somewhat singular figure of the challenger. His build was strange, and so also was his figure, for the limbs were short for so tall a man. His head also was sunk forward as if he were lost in thought or overcome with deep dejection.

" This is surely the Cavalier of the Heavy Heart," said Manny. " What trouble has he, that he should hang his head ? "

" Perchance he hath a weak neck," said the king.

" At least he hath no weak voice," the prince remarked, as Nigel's answer to Chandos came to their ears. " By our lady, he booms like a bittern."

As Chandos rode back again to the king, Nigel exchanged the old ash spear which had been his father's for one of the blunted tournament lances which he took from the hands of a stout archer in attendance. He then rode down to the end of the bridge where a hundred-yard stretch of greensward lay in front of him. At the same moment the squire of Sir Walter Manny, who had been hastily armed by his comrades, spurred forward and took up his position.

The king raised his hand ; there was a clang from the falconer's horn, and the two riders, with a thrust of their heels and a shake of their bridles, dashed furiously at each other. In the centre the green strip of marshy meadow land, with the water squirting from the galloping hoofs, and the two crouching men, gleaming bright in the evening sun ; on one side the half circle of motionless horsemen, some in steel, some in velvet, silent and attentive, dogs, hawks, and horses, all turned to stone ; on the other the old peaked bridge, the blue lazy river, the group of open-mouthed rustics, and the dark old manor-house

with one grim face which peered from the upper
window.

A good man was John Widdicombe, but he had met a
better that day. Before that yellow whirlwind of a horse
and that rider who was welded and riveted to his saddle
his knees could not hold their grip. Nigel and Pommers
were one flying missile, with all their weight and strength
and energy centred on the steady end of the lance. Had
Widdicombe been struck by a thunderbolt he could not
have flown faster or farther from his saddle. Two full
somersaults did he make, his plates clanging like cymbals,
ere he lay flat upon his back.

For a moment the king looked grave at that prodigious
fall. Then smiling once more as Widdicombe staggered
to his feet, he clapped his hands loudly in applause.
" A fair course and fairly run ! " he cried. " The five
scarlet roses bear themselves in peace even as I have
seen them in war. How now, my good Walter ? Have
you another squire, or will you clear a path for us yourself ? "

Manny's choleric face had turned darker as he observed
the mischance of his representative. He beckoned now to
a tall knight, whose gaunt and savage face looked out from
his open bassinet as an eagle might from a cage of steel.

" Sir Hubert," said he, " I bear in mind the day when
you overbore the Frenchman at Caen. Will you not be
our champion now ? "

" When I fought the Frenchman, Walter, it was with
naked weapons," said the knight, sternly. " I am a soldier
and I love a soldier's work, but I care not for these tilt-
yard tricks which were invented for nothing but to tickle
the fancies of foolish women."

" Oh, most ungallant speech ! " cried the king. " Had
my good consort heard you she would have arraigned you
to appear at a Court of Love with a jury of virgins to
answer for your sins. But I pray you to take a tilting
spear, good Sir Hubert ! "

" I had as soon take a peacock's feather, my fair lord ;

but I will do it, if you ask me. Here, page, hand me one of those sticks, and let me see what I can do."

But Sir Hubert de Burgh was not destined to test either his skill or his luck. The great bay horse which he rode was as unused to this warlike play as was its master, and had none of its master's stoutness of heart; so that when it saw the levelled lance, the gleaming figure and the frenzied yellow horse rushing down upon it, it swerved, turned and galloped furiously down the river-bank. Amid roars of laughter from the rustics on the one side and from the courtiers on the other, Sir Hubert was seen tugging vainly at his bridle, and bounding onward, clearing gorse-bushes and heather clumps, until he was but a shimmering, quivering gleam upon the dark hillside. Nigel, who had pulled Pommers on to his very haunches at the instant that his opponent turned, saluted with his lance and trotted back to the bridge-head, where he awaited his next assailant.

"The ladies would say that a judgment hath fallen upon our good Sir Hubert for his impious words," said the king.

"Let us hope that his charger may be broken in ere he venture to ride out between two armies," remarked the prince. "They might mistake the hardness of his horse's mouth for a softness of the rider's heart. See where he rides, still clearing every bush upon his path."

"By the rood!" said the king, "if the bold Hubert has not increased his repute as a jouster he has gained great honour as a horseman. But the bridge is still closed, Walter. How say you now? Is this young squire never to be unhorsed, or is your king himself to lay lance in rest ere the way can be cleared? By the head of Saint Thomas! I am in the very mood to run a course with this gentle youth."

"Nay, nay, sire, too much honour hath already been done him!" said Manny, looking angrily at the motion-less horseman. "That this untried boy should be able to say that in one evening he has unhorsed my squire, and seen the back of one of the bravest knights in England, is surely enough to turn his foolish head. Fetch me a spear, Robert ! I will see what I can make of him."

The famous knight took the spear when it was brought to him as a master-workman takes a tool. He balanced it, shook it once or twice in the air, ran his eyes down it for a flaw in the wood, and then finally, having made sure of its poise and weight, laid it carefully in rest under his arm. Then gathering up his bridle so as to have his horse under perfect command, and covering himself with the shield, which was slung round his neck, he rode out to do battle.

Now, Nigel, young and inexperienced, all Nature's aid will not help you against the mixed craft and strength of such a warrior. The day will come when neither Manny nor even Chandos could sweep you from your saddle ; but now, even had you some less cumbrous armour, your chance were small. Your downfall is near ; but as you see the famous black chevrons on a golden ground, your gallant heart, which never knew fear, is only filled with joy and amazement at the honour done you. Your downfall is near, and yet in your wildest dreams you would never guess how strange your downfall is to be.

Again, with a dull thunder of hoofs, the horses gallop over the soft water-meadow. Again, with a clash of metal, the two riders meet. It is Nigel now, taken clean in the face of his helmet with the blunted spear, who flies backward off his horse and falls clanging on the grass.

But, good heavens ! what is this ? Manny has thrown up his hands in horror, and the lance has dropped from his nerveless fingers. From all sides, with cries of dismay, with oaths and shouts and ejaculations to the saints, the horsemen ride wildly in. Was ever so dreadful, so sudden, so complete, an end to a gentle passage-at-arms ? Surely their eyes must be at fault ? Some wizard's trick has been played upon them to deceive their senses. But no, it was only too clear. There on the greensward lay the trunk of the stricken cavalier, and there, a good dozen yards beyond, lay his helmeted head.

" By the Virgin ! " cried Manny, wildly, as he jumped from his horse, " I would give my last gold piece that the work of this evening should be undone ! How came it ? What does it mean ? Hither, my lord bishop, for surely it smacks of witchcraft and the Devil."

With a white face the bishop had sprung down beside the prostrate body, pushing through the knot of horrified knights and squires.

" I fear that the last offices of the Holy Church come too late," said he, in a quivering voice. " Most unfortunate young man ! How sudden an end ! *In medio vitæ*, as the Holy Book has it—one moment in the pride of his youth, the next his head torn from his body. Now God and his saints have mercy upon me and guard me from evil."

The last prayer was shot out of the bishop with an energy and earnestness unusual in his orisons. It was caused by the sudden outcry of one of the squires, who, having lifted the helmet from the ground, cast it down again with a scream of horror.

" It is empty ! " he cried. " It weighs as light as a feather."

" 'Fore God, it is true ! " cried Manny, laying his hand on it. " There is no one in it. With what have I fought, father bishop ? Is it of this world or of the next ? "

The bishop had clambered on his horse the better to consider the point.

" If the foul fiend is abroad," said he, " my place is over yonder by the king's side. Certes, that sulphur-coloured horse hath a very devilish look. I could have sworn that I saw both smoke and flame from its nostrils. The beast is fit to bear a suit of armour which rides and fights, and yet hath no man within it."

" Nay, not too fast, father bishop," said one of the knights. " It may be all that you say and yet come from a human workshop. When I made a campaign in South Germany I have seen at Nuremberg a cunning figure, devised by an armourer, which could both ride and wield a sword. If this be such a one——"

" I thank you all for your very gentle courtesy," said a booming voice from the figure upon the ground.

At the words even the valiant Manny sprang into his saddle. Some rode madly away from the horrid trunk. A few of the boldest lingered.

" Most of all," said the voice, " would I thank the most noble knight, Sir Walter Manny, that he should deign to lay aside his greatness and condescend to do a deed of arms upon so humble a squire."

" 'Fore God ! " said Manny, " if this be the Devil, then the Devil hath a very courtly tongue. I will have him out of his armour, if he blast me ! "

So saying, he sprang once more from his horse and plunging his hand down the slit in the collapsed gorget, he closed it tightly upon a fistful of Nigel's yellow curls. The groan that came forth was enough to convince him that it was indeed a man who lurked within. At the same time his eyes fell upon the hole in the mail corselet which had served the squire as a visor, and he burst into deep-chested mirth. The king, the prince, and Chandos, who had watched the scene from a distance, too much amused by it to explain or interfere, rode up weary with laughter, now that all was discovered.

" Let him out ! " said the king, with his hand to his side. " I pray you to unlace him and let him out ! I have shared in many a spear-running, but never have I been nearer falling from my horse than as I watched this one. I feared the fall had struck him senseless, since he lay so still."

Nigel had indeed lain with all the breath shaken from his body, and as he was unaware that his helmet had been carried off, he had not understood either the alarm or the amusement that he had caused. Now, freed from the great hauberk in which he had been shut like a pea in a pod, he stood blinking in the light, blushing deeply with shame that the shifts to which his poverty had reduced him should be exposed to all these laughing courtiers. It was the king who brought him comfort.

" You have shown that you can use your father's weapons," said he, " and you have proved also that you are the worthy bearer of his name and his arms, for you have within you that spirit for which he was famous. But I wot that neither he nor you would suffer a train of hungry men to starve before your door ; so lead on, I pray you, and if the meat be as good as this grace before it, then it will be a feast indeed."

10. *How the King Greeted His Seneschal of Calais*

IT would have fared ill with the good name of Tilford Manor-house and with the housekeeping of the aged Dame Ermyntrude had the king's whole retinue, with his outer and inner marshal, his justiciar, his chamberlain, and his guard, all gathered under the one roof. But by the foresight and the gentle management of Chandos this calamity was avoided, so that some were quartered at the great Abbey and others passed on to enjoy the hospitality of Sir Roger FitzAlan at Farnham Castle. Only the king himself, the prince, Manny, Chandos, Sir Hubert de Burgh, the bishop, and two or three more remained behind as the guests of the Lorings.

But small as was the party, and humble the surroundings, the king in no way relaxed that love of ceremony, of elaborate form and of brilliant colouring which was one of his characteristics. The sumpter-mules were unpacked, squires ran hither and thither, baths smoked in the bedchambers, silks and satins were unfolded, gold chains gleamed and clinked, so that when, at last, to the long blast of two court trumpeters, the company took their seats at the board, it was the brightest, fairest scene which those old black rafters had ever spanned.

The great influx of foreign knights who had come in their splendour from all parts of Christendom to take part in the opening of the Round Tower of Windsor six years

before, and to try their luck and their skill at the tournament connected with it, had deeply modified the English
fashions of dress. The old tunic, over-tunic, and cyclas
were too sad and simple for the new fashions, so now
strange and brilliant cote-hardies, pourpoints, courtepies,
paltocks, hanselines, and many other wondrous garments,
parti-coloured, or diapered, with looped, embroidered or
escalloped edges, flamed and glittered round the king. He
himself, in black velvet and gold, formed a dark right
centre to the finery around him. On his right sat the
prince, on his left the bishop, while Dame Ermyntrude
marshalled the forces of the household outside, alert and
watchful, pouring in her dishes and her flagons at the right
moment, rallying her tired servants, encouraging the van,
hurrying the rear, hastening up her reserves, the tapping
of her oak stick heard wherever the pressure was the
greatest.

Behind the king, clad in his best, but looking drab and
sorry amid the brilliant costumes round him, Nigel himself, regardless of an aching body and a twisted knee,
waited upon his royal guests, who threw many a merry
jest at him over their shoulders as they still chuckled at·
the adventure of the bridge.

" By the rood ! " said King Edward, leaning back, with
a chicken-bone held daintily between the courtesy fingers
of his left hand, " the play is too good for this country
stage. You must to Windsor with me, Nigel, and bring
with you this great suit of harness in which you lurk.
There you shall hold the lists with your eyes in your
midriff, and unless someone cleave you to the waist I see
not how any harm can befall you. Never have I seen so
small a nut in so great a shell."

The prince, looking back with laughing eyes, saw by
Nigel's flushed and embarrassed face that his poverty
hung heavily upon him.

" Nay," said he kindly, " such a workman is surely
worthy of better tools."

" And it is for his master to see that he has them,"

added the king. " The court armourer will look to it that the next time your helmet is carried away, Nigel, your head shall be inside it."

Nigel, red to the roots of his flaxen hair, stammered out some words of thanks.

John Chandos, however, had a fresh suggestion, and he cocked a roguish eye as he made it—

" Surely, my liege, your bounty is little needed in this case. It is the ancient law of arms that if two cavaliers start to joust, and one either by maladdress or misadventure fail to meet the shock, then his arms become the property of him who still holds the lists. This being so, methinks, Sir Hubert de Burgh, that the fine hauberk of Milan and the helmet of Bordeaux steel in which you rode to Tilford should remain with our young host as some small remembrance of your visit."

The suggestion raised a general chorus of approval and laughter, in which all joined, save only Sir Hubert himself, who, flushed with anger, fixed his baleful eyes upon Chandos's mischievous and smiling face.

" I said that I did not play that foolish game, and I know nothing of its laws," said he ; " but you know well, John, that if you would have a bout with sharpened spear or sword, where two ride to the ground, and only one away from it, you have not far to go to find it."

" Nay, nay, would you ride to the ground ? Surely you had best walk, Hubert," said Chandos. " On your feet I know well that I should not see your back as we have seen it to-day. Say what you will, your horse has played you false, and I claim your suit of harness for Nigel Loring."

" Your tongue is overlong, John, and I am weary of its endless clack ! " said Sir Hubert, his yellow moustache bristling from a scarlet face. " If you claim my harness, do you yourself come and take it. If there is a moon in the sky you may try this very night when the board is cleared."

" Nay, fair sirs," cried the king, smiling from one to the other, " this matter must be followed no further. Do you fill a bumper of Gascony, John, and you also, Hubert. Now pledge each other, I pray you, as good and loyal comrades who would scorn to fight save in your king's quarrel. We can spare neither of you while there is so much work for brave hearts over the sea. As to this matter of the harness, John Chandos speaks truly where it concerns a joust in the lists, but we hold that such a law is scarce binding in this, which was but a wayside passage and a gentle trial of arms. On the other hand, in the case of your squire, Master Manny, there can be no doubt that his suit is forfeit."

"It is a grievous hearing for him, my liege," said Walter Manny ; "for he is a poor man, and hath been at sore pains to fit himself for the wars. Yet what you say shall be done, fair sire. So, if you will come to me in the morning, Squire Loring, John Widdicombe's suit will be handed over to you."

"Then, with the king's leave, I will hand it back to him," said Nigel, troubled and stammering ; "for indeed I had rather never ride to the wars than take from a brave man his only suit of plate."

"There spoke your father's spirit ! " cried the king. "By the rood ! Nigel, I like you full well. Let the matter bide in my hands. But I marvel much that Sir Aymery the Lombard hath not come to us yet from Windsor."

From the moment of his arrival at Tilford, again and again King Edward had asked most eagerly whether Sir Aymery had come, and whether there was any news of him, so that the courtiers glanced at each other in wonder. For Aymery was known to all of them as a famous mercenary of Italy, lately appointed Governor of Calais, and this sudden and urgent summons from the king might well mean some renewal of the war with France, which was the dearest wish of every soldier. Twice the king had stopped his meal and sat with sidelong head, his wine-cup in his hand, listening attentively when some sound like the clatter of hoofs was heard from outside ; but the third time there could be no mistake. The tramp and jingle of the horses broke loud upon the ear, and ended in hoarse voices calling out of the darkness, which were answered by the archers posted as sentries without the door.

"Some traveller has indeed arrived, my liege," said Nigel. "What is your royal will?"

"It can be but Aymery," the king answered, "for it was only to him that I left the message that he should follow me hither. Bid him come in, I pray you, and make him very welcome at your board."

Nigel cast open the door, plucking a torch from its bracket as he did so. Half a dozen men-at-arms sat on their horses outside, but one had dismounted, a short, squat, swarthy man with a rat face and quick, restless brown eyes, which peered eagerly past Nigel into the red glare of the well-lit hall.

"I am Sir Aymery of Pavia," he whispered. "For God's sake, tell me! is the king within?"

"He is at table, fair sir, and he bids you to enter."

"One moment, young man, one moment, and a secret word in your ear. Wot you why it is that the king has sent for me?"

Nigel read terror in the dark cunning eyes which glanced in sidelong fashion into his.

"Nay, I know not."

"I would I knew—I would I was sure ere I sought his presence."

"You have but to cross the threshold, fair sir, and doubtless you will learn from the king's own lips."

Sir Aymery seemed to gather himself as one who braces for a spring into ice-cold water. Then he crossed with a quick stride from the darkness into the light. The king stood up and held out his hand, with a smile upon his long handsome face, and yet it seemed to the Italian that it was the lips which smiled but not the eyes.

"Welcome!" cried Edward. "Welcome to our worthy and faithful Seneschal of Calais! Come, sit here before

531

me at the board, for I have sent for you that I may hear your news from over the sea, and thank you for the care that you have taken of that which is as dear to me as wife or child. Set a place for Sir Aymery there, and give him food and drink, for he has ridden fast and far in our service to-day."

Throughout the long feast which the skill of the Lady Ermyntrude had arranged, Edward chatted lightly with the Italian as well as with the barons near him. Finally, when the last dish was removed and the gravy-soaked rounds of coarse bread which served as plates had been cast to the dogs, the wine-flagons were passed round, and old Weathercote the minstrel entered timidly with his harp in the hope that he might be allowed to play before the king's majesty. But Edward had other sport afoot.

" I pray you, Nigel, to send out the servants so that we may be alone. I would have two men-at-arms at every door lest we be disturbed in our debate, for it is a matter of privacy. And now, Sir Aymery, these noble lords as well as I, your master, would fain hear from your own lips how all goes forward in France."

The Italian's face was calm, but he looked restlessly from one to another along the line of his listeners.

" So far as I know, my liege, all is quiet on the French marches," said he.

" You have not heard, then, that they have mustered or gathered to a head with the intention of breaking the truce and making some attempt upon our dominions ? "

" Nay, sire, I have heard nothing of it."

" You set my mind much at ease, Aymery," said the king ; " for if nothing has come to your ears, then surely it cannot be. It was said that the wild Knight de Chargny had come down to St. Omer with his eyes upon my precious jewel and his mailed hands ready to grasp it."

" Nay, sire, let him come. He will find the jewel safe in its strong box, with a goodly guard over it."

" You are the guard over my jewel, Aymery."

" Yes, sire, I am the guard."

" And you are a faithful guard and one whom I can trust, are you not ? You would not barter away that which is so dear to me when I have chosen you out of all my army to hold it for me ? "

" Nay, sire, what reasons can there be for such questions ? They touch my honour very nearly. You know that I would part with Calais only when I parted with my soul."

" Then you know nothing of de Chargny's attempt ? "

" Nothing, sire."

" Liar and villain ! " yelled the king, springing to his feet and dashing his fist upon the table until the glasses rattled again. " Seize him, archers ! Seize him this instant ! Stand close by either elbow, lest he do himself a mischief ! Now do you dare to tell me to my face, you perjured Lombard, that you know nothing of de Chargny and his plans ? "

" As God is my witness, I know nothing of him ! "

The man's lips were white, and he spoke in a thin, sighing, reedy voice, his eyes wincing away from the fell gaze of the angry king.

Edward laughed bitterly, and drew a paper from his breast.

" You are the judges in this case, you, my fair son, and you, Chandos, and you, Manny, and you, Sir Hubert, and you also, my lord bishop. By my sovereign power I make you a court that you may deal justice upon this man, for by God's eyes I will not stir from this room until I have sifted the matter to the bottom. And first I would read you this letter. It is superscribed to Sir Aymery of Pavia, *nommé* Le Lombard, Château de Calais. Is not that your name and style, you rogue ? "

" It is my name, sire ; but no such letter has come to me."

" Else had your villainy never been disclosed. It is signed ' Isadore de Chargny.' What says my enemy de Chargny to my trusted servant ? Listen ! ' We could not come with the last moon, for we have not gathered sufficient strength, nor have we been able to collect the twenty thousand crowns which are your price. But with the next turn of the moon in the darkest hour, we will come, and you will be paid your money at the small postern gate with the rowan bush beside it.' Well, rogue, what say you now ? "

" It is a forgery ! " gasped the Italian.

" I pray you that you will let me see it, sire," said Chandos. " De Chargny was my prisoner, and so many letters passed ere his ransom was paid that his script is well known to me. Yes, yes, I will swear that this is indeed his. If my salvation were at stake I could swear it."

" If it were indeed written by de Chargny it was to dishonour me," cried Sir Aymery.

" Nay, nay ! " said the young prince. " We all know de Chargny and have fought against him. Many faults he has, a boaster and a brawler, but a braver man and one of greater heart and higher of enterprise does not ride beneath the lilies of France. Such a man would never stoop to write a letter for the sake of putting dishonour upon one of knightly rank. I for one, will never believe it."

A gruff murmur from the others showed that they were of one mind with the prince. The light of the torches from the walls beat upon the line of stern faces at the high table. They had sat like flint, and the Italian shrank from their inexorable eyes. He looked swiftly round, but armed men choked every entrance. The shadow of death had fallen athwart his soul.

" This letter," said the king, " was given by de Chargny to one Dom Beauvais, a priest of St. Omer, to carry into Calais. The said priest, smelling a reward, brought it to one who is my faithful servant, and so it came to me. Straightway I sent for this man that he should come to me. Meanwhile the priest has returned so that de Chargny may think that his message is indeed delivered."

" I know nothing of it," said the Italian, doggedly, licking his dry lips.

A dark flush mounted to the king's forehead, and his eyes were gorged with his wrath.

" No more of this, for God's dignity ! " he cried. " Had we this fellow at the Tower, a few turns of the rack would tear a confession from his craven soul. But why should we need his word for his own guilt ? You have seen, my lords, you have heard ? How say you, fair son ? Is the man guilty ? "

" Sire, he is guilty."

" And you, John ? And you, Walter ? And you, Hubert ? And you, my lord bishop ? You are all of one mind, then. He is guilty of the betrayal of his trust. And the punishment ? "

" It can only be death," said the prince, and each in turn the others nodded their agreement.

" Aymery of Pavia, you have heard your doom," said Edward, leaning his chin upon his hand and glooming at the cowering Italian. " Step forward, you archer at the door—you with the black beard. Draw your sword ! Nay, you white-faced rogue, I would not dishonour this roof-tree by your blood. It is your heels, not your head, that we want. Hack off these golden spurs of knighthood with your sword, archer ! 'Twas I who gave them, and I who take them back. Ha ! they fly across the hall, and with them every bond betwixt you and the worshipful order whose sign and badge they are ! Now lead him out on the heath afar from the house where his carrion can best lie, and hew his scheming head from his body as a warning to all such traitors ! "

The Italian, who had slipped from his chair to his knees, uttered a cry of despair, as an archer seized him by either shoulder. Writhing out of their grip, he threw himself upon the floor and clutched at the king's feet.

" Spare me, my most dread lord, spare me, I beseech you ! In the name of Christ's passion, I implore your grace and pardon ! Bethink you, my good and dear lord, how many years I have served under your banners and how many services I have rendered. Was it not I who found the ford upon the Seine two days before the great battle ? Was it not I also who marshalled the attack at the intaking of Calais ? I have a wife and four children in Italy, great king, and it was the thought of them which led me to fall from my duty, for this money would have allowed me to leave the wars and to see them once again. Mercy, my liege, mercy, I implore ! "

The English are a rough race, but not a cruel one. The king sat with a face of doom ; but the others looked askance and fidgeted in their seats.

" Indeed, my fair liege," said Chandos, " I pray you that you will abate somewhat of your anger."

Edward shook his head curtly. " Be silent, John. It shall be as I have said."

" I pray you, my dear and honoured liege, not to act with overmuch haste in the matter," said Manny. " Bind him and hold him until the morning, for other counsels may prevail."

" Nay, I have spoken. Lead him out ! "

But the trembling man clung to the king's knees in such a fashion that the archers could not disengage his convulsive grip.

" Listen to me a moment, I implore you ! Give me but one minute to plead with you, and then do what you will."

The king leaned back in his chair. " Speak and have done," said he.

" You must spare me, my noble liege. For your own sake I say that you must spare me, for I can set you in the way of such a knightly adventure as will gladden your heart. Bethink you, sire, that this de Chargny and his comrades know nothing of their plans having gone awry. If I do but send them a message they will surely come to the postern gate. Then, if we have placed our bushment with skill, we shall have such a capture and such a ransom as will fill your coffers. He and his comrades should be worth a good hundred thousand crowns."

Edward spurned the Italian away from him with his foot until he sprawled among the rushes, but even as he lay there like a wounded snake his dark eyes never left the king's face.

" You double traitor ! You would sell Calais to de Chargny, and then in turn you would sell de Chargny to me. How dare you suppose that I or any noble knight had such a huckster's soul as to think only of ransoms where honour is to be won ? Could I or any true man be so caitiff and so thrall ? You have sealed your own doom. Lead him out ! "

" One instant, I pray you, my fair and most sweet lord," cried the prince. " Assuage your wrath yet a little while, for this man's rede deserves, perhaps, more thought than we have given it. He has turned your noble soul sick with his talk of ransoms ; but look at it, I pray you, from the side of honour, and where could we find such hope of wor-shipfully winning worship ? I pray you to let me put my body in this adventure, for it is one from which, if rightly handled, much advancement is to be gained."

Edward looked with sparkling eyes at the noble youth at his side.

" Never was hound more keen on the track of a stricken hart than you on the hope of honour, fair son," said he. " How do you conceive the matter in your mind ? "

" De Chargny and his men will be such as are worth going far to meet, for he will have the pick of France under his banner that night. If we did as this man says and awaited him with the same number of lances, then I cannot think that there is any spot in Christendom where one would rather be than in Calais that night."

" By the rood, fair son, you are right ! " cried the king, his face shining with the thought. " Now, which of you, John Chandos or Walter Manny, will take the thing in charge ? " He looked mischievously from one to the other, like a master who dangles a bone between two fierce old hounds. All they had to say was in their burning, longing eyes. " Nay, John, you must not take it amiss ; but it is Walter's turn and he shall have it."

" Shall we not all go under your banner, sire, or that of the prince ? "

" Nay, it is not fitting that the royal banners of England

should be advanced in so small an adventure. And yet, if you have space in your ranks for two more cavaliers, both the prince and I would ride with you that night."

The young man stooped and kissed his father's hand.

" Take this man in your charge, Walter, and do with him as you will. Guard well, lest he betray us once again. Take him from my sight, for his breath poisons the room. And now, Nigel, if that worthy greybeard of thine would fain twang his harp or sing to us—but what in God's name would you have ? "

He had turned, to find his young host upon his knee and his flaxen head bent in entreaty.

" What is it, man ? What do you crave ? "

" A boon, fair liege ! "

" Well, well, am I to have no peace to-night, with a traitor kneeling to me in front, and a true man on his knees behind ? Out with it, Nigel. What would you have ? "

" To come with you to Calais."

" By the rood ! your request is fair enough, seeing that our plot is hatched beneath your very roof. How say you, Walter ? Will you take him, armour and all ? " asked King Edward.

" Say rather will you take me ? " said Chandos. " We are two rivals in honour, Walter, but I am very sure that you would not hold me back."

" Nay, John, I will be proud to have the best lance in Christendom beneath my banner."

" And I to follow so knightly a leader. But Nigel Loring is my squire, and so he comes with us also."

" Then that is settled," said the king, " and now there is no need for hurry, since there can be no move until the moon has changed. So I pray you to pass the flagon once again, and to drink with me to the good knights of France. May they be of great heart and high of enterprise when we all meet once more within the castle wall of Calais ! "

11. *In the Hall of the Knight of Dupplin*

THE king had come and had gone. Tilford Manor-house stood once more dark and silent, but joy and contentment reigned within its walls. In one night every trouble had fallen away like some dark curtain which had shut out the sun. A princely sum of money had come from the king's treasurer, given in such fashion that there could be no refusal. With a bag of gold pieces at his saddle-bow, Nigel rode once more into Guildford, and not a beggar on the way who had not cause to bless his name.

There he had gone first to the goldsmith and had bought back cup and salver and bracelet, mourning with the merchant over the evil chance that gold and gold-work had for certain reasons which only those in the trade could fully understand gone up in value during the last week, so that already fifty gold pieces had to be paid more than the price which Nigel had received. In vain the faithful Aylward fretted and fumed and muttered a prayer that the day would come when he might feather a shaft in the merchant's portly paunch. The money had to be paid.

Thence Nigel hurried to Wat the armourer's, and there he bought that very suit for which he had yearned so short a time before. Then and there he tried it on in the booth, Wat and his boy walking round him with spanner and wrench, fixing bolts and twisting rivets.

" How is that, my fair sir ? " cried the armourer, as he drew the bassinet over the head and fastened it to the camail which extended to the shoulders. " I swear by Tubal Cain that it fits you as the shell fits the crab ! A finer suit never came from Italy or Spain."

Nigel stood in front of a burnished shield which served as a mirror, and he turned this way and that, preening himself like a little shining bird. His smooth breastplate, his wondrous joints with their deft protection by the disks at knee and elbow and shoulder, the beautifully flexible gauntlets and sollerets, the shirt of mail and the close-

fitting greave-plates were all things of joy and of beauty
in his eyes. He sprang about the shop to show his lightness, and then, running out, he placed his hand on the
pommel and vaulted into Pommers' saddle, while Wat and
his boy applauded in the doorway.

Then, springing off and running into the shop again, he
clashed down upon his knees before the image of the Virgin upon the smithy wall. There from his heart he prayed
that no shadow or stain should come upon his soul or his
honour while these arms encased his body, and that he
might be strengthened to use them for noble and godly
ends. A strange turn this to a religion of peace, and yet
for many a century the sword and the faith had upheld
each other, and in a darkened world the best ideal of the
soldier had turned in some dim groping fashion towards
the light. " *Benedictus dominus deus meus qui docet manus
meas ad Prælium et digitos meos ad bellum!* " There
spoke the soul of the knightly soldier.

So the armour was trussed upon the armourer's mule
and went back with them to Tilford, where Nigel put it
on once more for the pleasure of the Lady Ermyntrude,
who clapped her skinny hands and shed tears of mingled
pain and joy—pain that she should lose him, joy that he
should go so bravely to the wars. As to her own future,
it had been made easy for her, since it was arranged that
a steward should look to the Tilford estate while she had
at her disposal a suite of rooms in royal Windsor, where,
with other venerable dames of her own age and standing,
she could spend the twilight of her days discussing long-
forgotten scandals and whispering sad things about the
grandfathers and grandmothers of the young courtiers all
around them. There Nigel might leave her with an easy
mind when he turned his face to France.

But there was one more visit to be paid, and one more
farewell to be spoken ere Nigel could leave the moorlands
where he had dwelt so long. That evening he donned his
brightest tunic, dark purple velvet of Genoa, with trimming of miniver, his hat with the snow-white feather

curling round the front, and his belt of embossed silver round his loins. Mounted on lordly Pommers, with his hawk upon wrist and his sword by his side, never did fairer young gallant or one more modest in mind set forth upon such an errand. It was but the old Knight of Dupplin to whom he would say farewell ; but the Knight of Dupplin had two daughters, Edith and Mary, and Edith was the fairest maid in all the heather-country.

Sir John Buttesthorn, the Knight of Dupplin, was so called because he had been present at that strange battle, some eighteen years before, when the full power of Scotland had been for a moment beaten to the ground by a handful of adventurers and mercenaries, marching under the banner of no nation, but fighting in their own private quarrel. Their exploit fills no pages of history, for it is to the interest of no nation to record it, and yet the rumour and fame of the great fight bulked large in those times, for it was on that day when the flower of Scotland was left dead upon the field, that the world first understood that a new force had arisen in war, and that the English archer, with his robust courage and his skill with the weapon which he had wielded from his boyhood, was a power with which even the mailed chivalry of Europe had seriously to reckon.

Sir John after his return from Scotland had become the king's own head huntsman, famous through all England for his knowledge of venery, until at last, getting overheavy for his horses, he had settled in modest comfort into the old house of Cosford upon the eastern slope of the Hindhead hill. Here, as his face grew redder, and his beard more white, he spent the evening of his days amid hawks and hounds, a flagon of spiced wine ever at his elbow, and his swollen foot perched upon a stool before him. There it was that many an old comrade broke his journey as he passed down the rude road which led from London to Portsmouth, and thither also came the young gallants of the country to hear the stout knight's tales of old wars, or to learn from him that lore of the forest and the chase which none could teach so well as he.

But sooth to say, whatever the old knight might think, it was not merely his old tales and older wine which drew the young men to Cosford, but rather the fair face of his younger daughter, or the strong soul and wise counsel of the elder. Never had two more different branches sprung from the same trunk. Both were tall and of a queenly graceful figure. But there all resemblance began and ended.

Edith was yellow as the ripe corn, blue-eyed, winning, mischievous, with a chattering tongue, a merry laugh, and a smile which a dozen of young gallants, Nigel of Tilford at their head, could share equally among them. Like a young kitten she played with all the things that she found in life, and some there were who thought that already the claws could be felt amid the patting of her velvet touch.

Mary was dark as night, grave-featured, plain-visaged, with steady brown eyes looking bravely at the world from under a strong black arch of brows. None could call her beautiful, and when her fair sister cast her arm around her and placed her cheek against hers, as was her wont when company was there, the fairness of the one and the plainness of the other leaped visibly to the eyes of all, each the clearer for that hard contrast. And yet, here and there, there was one who, looking at her strange strong face, and at the passing gleams far down in her dark eyes, felt that this silent woman, with her proud bearing and her queenly grace, had in her something of strength, of reserve, and of mystery which was more to them than all the dainty glitter of her sister.

Such were the ladies of Cosford towards whom Nigel Loring rode that night with doublet of Genoan velvet and the new white feather in his cap.

He had ridden over Thursley Ridge past that old stone where in days gone by at the place of Thor the wild Saxons worshipped their war-god. Nigel looked at it with a wary eye and spurred Pommers onward as he passed it, for still it was said that wild fires danced round it on the moonless nights, and they who had ears for such things could hear the scream and sob of those whose lives had been ripped from them that the fiend might be honoured. Thor's Stone, Thor's Jumps, Thor's Punch-bowl—the whole countryside was one grim monument to the God of Battles, though the pious monks had changed his uncouth name for that of the Devil his father, so that it was the Devil's Jumps and the Devil's Punch-bowl of which they spoke. Nigel glanced back at the old grey boulder, and he felt for an instant a shudder pass through his stout heart. Was it the chill of the evening air, or was it that some inner voice had whispered to him of the day when he also might lie bound on such a rock and have such a bloodstained pagan crew howling around him ?

An instant later the rock and his vague fear and all things else had passed from his mind, for there, down the yellow sandy path, the setting sun gleaming on her golden hair, her lithe figure bending and swaying with every heave of the cantering horse, was none other than the same fair Edith, whose face had come so often between him and his sleep. His blood rushed hot to his face at the sight, for fearless of all else, his spirit was attracted and yet daunted by the delicate mystery of woman. To his pure and knightly soul not Edith alone, but every woman, sat high and aloof, enthroned and exalted, with a thousand mystic excellencies and virtues which raised her far above the rude world of man. There was joy in contact with them ; and yet there was fear, fear lest his own unworthiness, his untrained tongue or rougher ways should in some way break rudely upon this delicate and tender thing. Such was his thought as the white horse cantered towards him ; but a moment later his vague doubts were set at rest by the frank voice of the young girl, who waved her whip in merry greeting.

" Hail and well met, Nigel ! " she cried. " Whither away this evening ? Sure I am that it is not to see your friends of Cosford, for when did you ever don so brave a doublet for us ? Come, Nigel, her name, that I may hate her for ever ! "

" Nay, Edith," said the young squire, laughing back at the laughing girl. " I was indeed coming to Cosford."

" Then we shall ride back together, for I will go no farther. How think you that I am looking ? "

Nigel's answer was in his eyes as he glanced at the fair flushed face, the golden hair, the sparkling eyes, and the daintily graceful figure set off in a scarlet-and-black riding-dress.

" You are as fair as ever, Edith."

" Oh, cold of speech ! Surely you were bred for the cloisters and not for a lady's bower, Nigel. Had I asked such a question from young Sir George Brocas or the Squire of Fernhurst, he would have raved from here to Cosford. They are both more to my taste than you are, Nigel."

" It is the worse for me, Edith," said Nigel ruefully.

" Nay, but you must not lose heart."

" Have I not already lost it ? " said he.

" That is better," she cried, laughing. " You can be quick enough when you choose, Master Malapert. But you are more fit to speak of high and weary matters with my sister Mary. She will have none of the prattle and courtesy of Sir George, and yet I love them well. But tell me, Nigel, why do you come to Cosford to-night ? "

" To bid you farewell."

" Me alone ? "

" Nay, Edith, you and your sister Mary and the good knight, your father."

" Sir George would have said that he had come for me alone. Indeed you are but a poor courtier beside him. But is it true, Nigel, that you go to France ? "

" Yes, Edith."

" It was so rumoured after the king had been to Tilford. The story goes that the king goes to France and you in his train. Is that true ? "

" Yes, Edith, it is true."

" Tell me, then, to what part you go, and when ? "

" That, alas ! I may not say."

" Oh, in sooth ! " She tossed her fair head and rode onward in silence, with compressed lips and angry eyes.

Nigel glanced at her in surprise and dismay. " Surely, Edith," said he, at last, " you have overmuch regard for my honour that you should wish me to break the word that I have given ? "

" Your honour belongs to you, and my likings belong to me," said she. " You hold fast to the one, and I will do the same by the other."

They rode in silence through Thursley village. Then a thought came to her mind, and in an instant her anger was forgotten and she was hot on a new scent.

" What would you do if I were injured, Nigel ? I have heard my father say that, small as you are, there is no man in these parts could stand against you. Would you be my champion if I suffered wrong ? "

" Surely I or any man of gentle blood would be the champion of any woman who had suffered wrong."

" You or any and I or any—what sort of speech is that ? Is it a compliment, think you, to be mixed with a drove in that fashion ? My question was of you and me. If I were wronged would you be my man ? "

" Try me and see, Edith ! "

" Then I will do so, Nigel. Either Sir George Brocas or the Squire of Fernhurst would gladly do what I ask, and yet I am of a mind, Nigel, to turn to you."

" I pray you to tell me what it is."

" You know Paul de la Fosse of Shalford ? "

" You mean the small man with the twisted back ? "

" He is no smaller than yourself, Nigel, and as to his back there are many folk that I know who would be glad to have his face."

" Nay, I am no judge of that, and I spoke out of no discourtesy. What of the man ? "

" He has flouted me, Nigel, and I would have revenge."

" What—on that poor twisted creature ? "

" I tell you that he has flouted me ! "

" But how ? "

" I should have thought that a true cavalier would have flown to my aid, withouten all these questions. But I will tell you, since I needs must. Know then that he was one of those who came around me and professed to be my own. Then, merely because he thought that there were others who were as dear to me as himself he left me, and now he pays court to Maude Twynham, the little freckle-faced hussy in his village."

" But how has this hurt you, since he was no man of thine ? "

" He was one of my men, was he not ? And he has made game of me to his wench. He has told her things about me. He has made me foolish in her eyes. Yes, yes, I can read it in her saffron face and in her watery gaze when we meet at the church door on Sundays. She smiles—yes, smiles at me ! Nigel, go to him ! Do not slay him, or even wound him, but lay his face open with thy riding-whip, and then come back to me and tell me how I can serve you."

Nigel's face was haggard with the strife within, for desire ran hot in every vein, and yet reason shrank with horror.

" By Saint Paul ! Edith," he cried, " I see no honour nor advancement of any sort in this thing which you have asked me to do. Is it for me to strike one who is no better than a cripple ? For my manhood I could not do such a deed, and I pray you, dear lady, that you will set me some other task."

Her eyes flashed at him in contempt. " And you are a man-at-arms ! " she cried, laughing in bitter scorn. " You are afraid of a little man who can scarce walk. Yes, yes, say what you will, I shall ever believe that you have heard of his skill at fence, and of his great spirit, and that your heart has failed you ! You are right, Nigel. He is indeed a perilous man. Had you done what I asked he would have slain you, and so you have shown your wisdom."

Nigel flushed and winced under the words, but he said no more, for his mind was fighting hard within him, striving to keep that high image of woman which seemed for a moment to totter on the edge of a fall. Together in silence, side by side, the little man and the stately woman, the yellow charger and the white jennet, passed up the sandy winding track with the gorse and the bracken head-high on either side. Soon a path branched off through a gateway marked with the boar-heads of the Buttesthorns, and there was the low widespread house heavily timbered, loud with the barking of dogs. The ruddy knight limped forth with outstretched hand and roaring voice—

" What how, Nigel ! Good welcome and all hail ! I had thought that you had given over poor friends like us, now that the king had made so much of you. The horses, varlets, or my crutch will be across you ! Hush, Lydiard ! Down, Pelamon ! I can scarce hear my voice for your yelping. Mary, a cup of wine for young Squire Loring ! "

She stood framed in the doorway, tall, mystic, silent, with strange, wistful face and deep soul shining in her dark questioning eyes. Nigel kissed the hand that she held out, and all his faith in woman and his reverence came back to him as he looked at her. Her sister had slipped behind her, and her fair elfish face smiled her forgiveness of Nigel over Mary's shoulder.

The Knight of Dupplin leaned his weight upon the young man's arm and limped his way across the great high-roofed hall to his capacious oaken chair.

" Come, come, the stool, Edith ! " he cried. " As God is my help, that girl's mind swarms with gallants as a granary with rats. Well, Nigel, I hear strange tales of your spear-running at Tilford and of the visit of the king. How seemed he ? And my old friend Chandos—many happy hours in the woodlands have we had together—and Manny too, he was ever a bold and a hard rider —what news of them all ? "

Nigel told the old knight all that had occurred, saying little of his own success and much of his own failure, yet the eyes of the dark woman burned the brighter as she sat at her tapestry and listened.

Sir John followed the story with a running fire of oaths, prayers, thumps with his great fist, and flourishes of his crutch.

" Well, well, lad, you could scarce expect to hold your saddle against Manny, and you have carried yourself well. We are proud of you, Nigel, for you are our own man, reared in the heather-country. But indeed I take shame that you are not more skilled in the mystery of the woods, seeing that I have had the teaching of you, and that no one in broad England is my master at the craft. I pray you to fill your cup again whilst I make use of the little time that is left to us."

And straightway the old knight began a long and weary lecture upon the times of grace and when each beast and bird was seasonable, with many anecdotes, illustrations, warnings and exceptions, drawn from his own great experience. He spoke also of the several ranks and grades of the chase : how the hare, hart, and boar must ever take precedence over the buck, the doe, the fox, the marten and the roe, even as a knight banneret does over a knight, while these in turn are of a higher class to the badger, the wildcat, or the otter, who are but the common populace of the world of beasts. Of bloodstains also he spoke—how the skilled hunter may see at a glance if blood be dark and frothy, which means a mortal hurt, or thin and clear, which means that the arrow has struck a bone.

" By such signs," said he, " you will surely know whether to lay on the hounds and cast down the blinks which hinder the stricken deer in its flight. But above all I pray you, Nigel, to have a care in the use of the terms of the craft, lest you should make some blunder at table, so that those who are wiser may have the laugh of you, and we who love you may be shamed."

" Nay, Sir John," said Nigel. " I think that after your teaching I can hold my place with the others."

The old knight shook his white head doubtfully. " There is so much to be learned that there is no one who

can be said to know it all," said he. "For example,
Nigel, it is sooth that for every collection of beasts of the
forest, and for every gathering of birds of the air, there
is their own private name so that none may be confused
with another."

" I know it, fair sir."

" You know it, Nigel, but you do not know each
separate name, else you are a wiser man than I had thought
you. In truth none can say that they know all, though I
have myself pricked off eighty and six for a wager at court,
and it is said that the chief huntsman of the Duke of
Burgundy has counted over a hundred—but it is in my
mind that he may have found them as he went, for there
was none to say him nay. Answer me now, lad, how
would you say if you saw ten badgers together in the
forest ? "

" A cete of badgers, fair sir."

" Good, Nigel—good, by my faith ! And if you walk
in Woolmer Forest and see a swarm of foxes, how would
you call it ? "

" A skulk of foxes."

" And if they be lions ? "

" Nay, fair sir, I am not like to meet several lions in
Woolmer Forest."

" Aye, lad, but there are other forests besides Woolmer,
and other lands besides England, and who can tell how far
afield such a knight-errant as Nigel of Tilford may go,
when he sees worship to be won ? We will say that you
were in the deserts of Nubia, and that afterwards at the
court of the great Sultan you wished to say that you had
seen several lions, which is the first beast of the chase,
being the king of all animals. How then would you
say it ? "

Nigel scratched his head. " Surely, fair sir, I would
be content to say that I had seen a number of lions,
if indeed I could say aught after so wondrous an
adventure."

" Nay, Nigel, a huntsman would have said that he had

seen a pride of lions, and so proved that he knew the language of the chase. Now, had it been boars instead of lions ? "

" One says a singular of boars."

" And if they be swine ? "

" Surely it is a herd of swine."

" Nay, nay, lad, it is indeed sad to see how little you know. Your hands, Nigel, were always better than your head. No man of gentle birth would speak of a herd of swine ; that is the peasant speech. If you drive them it is a herd. If you hunt them it is other. What call you them, then, Edith ? "

" Nay, I know not," said the girl, listlessly. A crumpled note brought in by a varlet was clinched in her right hand and her blue eyes looked afar into the deep shadows of the roof.

" But you can tell us, Mary ? "

" Surely, sweet sir, one talks of a sounder of swine."

The old knight laughed exultantly. " Here is a pupil who never brings me shame ! " he cried. " Be it lore of chivalry or heraldry or woodcraft or what you will, I can always turn to Mary. Many a man can she put to the blush."

" Myself among them," said Nigel.

" Ah, lad, you are a Solomon to some of them. Hark ye ! only last week that jack-fool, the young Lord of Brocas, was here talking of having seen a covey of pheasants in the wood. One such speech would have been the ruin of a young squire at the court. How would you have said it, Nigel ? "

" Surely, fair sir, it should be a nye of pheasants."

" Good, Nigel—a nye of pheasants, even as it is a gaggle of geese or a badling of ducks, a fall of woodcock or a wisp of snipe. But a covey of pheasants ! What sort of talk is that ? I made him sit even where you are sitting, Nigel, and I saw the bottom of two pots of Rhenish ere I let him up. Even then I fear that he had no great profit from his lesson, for he was casting his foolish eyes at Edith when he should have been turning his ears to her father. But where is the wench ? '

" She hath gone forth, father."

" She ever doth go forth when there is a chance of learning aught that is useful indoors. But supper will soon be ready, and there is a boar's ham fresh from the forest with which I would ask your help, Nigel, and a side of venison from the king's own chase. The tineman and verderers have not forgotten me yet, and my larder is ever full. Blow three moots on the horn, Mary, that the varlets may set the table, for the growing shadow and my loosening belt warn me that it is time."

12. *How Nigel fought the Twisted Man of Shalford*

IN the days of which you read all classes, save perhaps the very poor, fared better in meat and in drink than they have ever done since. The country was covered with woodlands—there were seventy separate forests in England alone, some of them covering half a shire. Within these forests the great beasts of the chase were strictly preserved, but the smaller game, the hares, the rabbits, the birds, which swarmed round the coverts, found their way readily into the poor man's pot. Ale was very cheap, and cheaper still was the mead which every peasant could make for himself out of the wild honey in the tree trunks. There were many tea-like drinks also, which were brewed by the poor at no expense : mallow tea, tansy tea, and others the secret of which has passed.

Amid the richer classes there was rude profusion, great joints ever on the sideboard, huge pies, beasts of the field and beasts of the chase, with ale and rough French or Rhenish wines to wash them down. But the very rich had attained to a high pitch of luxury in their food, and cookery was a science in which the ornamentation of the dish was almost as important as the dressing of the food.

It was gilded, it was silvered, it was painted, it was surrounded with flame. From the boar and the peacock
down to such strange food as the porpoise and the hedge-
hog, every dish had its own setting and its own sauce,
very strange and very complex, with flavourings of dates,
currants, cloves, vinegar, sugar and honey, of cinnamon,
ground ginger, sandalwood, saffron, brawn and pines. It
was the Norman tradition to eat in moderation, but to
have a great profusion of the best and of the most delicate
from which to choose. From them came this complex
cookery, so unlike the rude and often guttonous simplicity
of the old Teutonic stock.

Sir John Butteshorn was of that middle class who
fared in the old fashion, and his great oak supper-table
groaned beneath the generous pasties, the mighty joints
and the great flagons. Below were the household, above
on a raised dais the family table, with places ever ready
for those frequent guests who dropped in from the high
road outside. Such a one had just come, an old priest,
journeying from the Abbey of Chertsey to the Priory of
Saint John at Midhurst. He passed often that way, and
never without breaking his journey at the hospitable board
of Cosford.

" Welcome again, good Father Athanasius ! " cried the
burly knight. " Come sit here on my right and give me
the news of the countryside, for there is never a scandal
but the priests are the first to know it."

The priest, a kindly, quiet man, glanced at an empty
place upon the farther side of his host.

" Mistress Edith ? " said he.

" Aye, aye, where is the hussy ? " cried her father, impatiently. " Mary, I beg you to have the horn blown
again, that she may know that the supper is on the table.
What can the little owlet do abroad at this hour of the
night ? "

There was trouble in the priest's gentle eyes as he
touched the knight upon the sleeve. " I have seen
Mistress Edith within this hour," said he. " I fear that

she will hear no horn that you may blow, for she must be at Milford ere now."

" At Milford ? What does she there ? "

" I pray you, good Sir John, to abate your voice somewhat, for indeed this matter is for our private discourse, since it touches the honour of a lady."

" Her honour ? " Sir John's ruddy face had turned redder still, as he stared at the troubled features of the priest. " Her honour, say you—the honour of my daughter ? Make good those words, or never set your foot over the threshold of Cosford again ! "

" I trust that I have done no wrong, Sir John, but indeed I must say what I have seen, else would I be a false friend and an unworthy priest."

" Haste, man, haste ! What in the Devil's name have you seen ? "

" Know you a little man, partly misshapen, named Paul de la Fosse ? "

" I know him well. He is a man of noble family and coat-armour, being the younger brother of Sir Eustace de la Fosse of Shalford. Time was when I had thought that I might call him son, for there was never a day that he did not pass with my girls, but I fear that his crooked back sped him ill in his wooing."

" Alas, Sir John ! It is his mind that is more crooked than his back. He is a perilous man with women, for the Devil hath given him such a tongue and such an eye that he charms them even as the basilisk. Marriage may be in their mind, but never in his, so that I could count a dozen and more whom he has led to their undoing. It is his pride and his boast over the whole countryside."

" Well, well, and what is this to me or mine ? "

" Even now, Sir John, as I rode my mule up the road I met this man speeding towards his home. A woman rode by his side, and though her face was hooded I heard her laugh as she passed me. That laugh I have heard before, and it was under this very roof, from the lips of Mistress Edith."

The knight's knife dropped from his hand. But the debate had been such that neither Mary nor Nigel could fail to have heard it. Mid the rough laughter and clatter of voices from below the little group at the high table had a privacy of their own.

"Fear not, father," said the girl—"indeed, the good Father Athanasius hath fallen into error, and Edith will be with us anon. I have heard her speak of this man many times of late, and always with bitter words."

"It is true, sir," cried Nigel, eagerly. "It was only this very evening as we rode over Thursley Moor that Mistress Edith told me that she counted him not a fly, and that she would be glad if he were beaten for his evil deeds."

But the wise priest shook his silvery locks. "Nay, there is ever danger when a woman speaks like that. Hot hate is twin brother to hot love. Why should she speak so if there were not some bond between them?"

"And yet," said Nigel, "what can have changed her thoughts in three short hours? She was here in the hall with us since I came. By Saint Paul, I will not believe it!"

Mary's face darkened. "I call to mind," said she, "that a note was brought her by Hannekin the stable varlet when you were talking to us, fair sir, of the terms of the chase. She read it and went forth."

Sir John sprang to his feet, but sank into his chair again with a groan.

"Would that I were dead," he cried, "ere I saw dishonour come upon my house, and am so tied with this accursed foot, that I can neither examine if it be true, nor yet avenge it! If my son Oliver were here, then all would be well. Send me this stable varlet that I may question him."

"I pray you, fair and honoured sir," said Nigel, "that you will take me for your son this night, that I may handle this matter in the way which seems best. On jeopardy of my honour I will do all that a man may."

"Nigel, I thank you. There is no man in Christendom to whom I would sooner turn."

" But I would learn your mind in one matter, fair sir. This man, Paul de la Fosse, owns broad acres, as I understand, and comes of noble blood. There is no reason, if things be as we fear, that he should not marry your daughter ? "

" Nay, she could not wish for better."

" It is well. And first I would question this Hannekin ; but it shall be done in such a fashion that none shall know, for indeed it is not a matter for the gossip of servants. But if you will show me the man, Mistress Mary, I will take him out to tend my own horse, and so I shall learn all that he has to tell."

Nigel was absent for some time, and when he returned the shadow upon his face brought little hope to the anxious hearts at the high table.

" I have locked him in the stable-loft, lest he talk too much," said he, " for my questions must have shown him whence the wind blew. It was indeed from this man that the note came, and he had brought with him a spare horse for the lady."

The old knight groaned, and his face sank upon his hands.

" Nay, father, they watch you ! " whispered Mary. " For the honour of our house let us keep a bold face to all." Then, raising her young clear voice, so that it sounded through the room : " If you ride eastward, Nigel, I would fain go with you, that my sister may not come back alone."

" We will ride together, Mary," said Nigel, rising ; then, in a lower voice : " But we cannot go alone, and if we take a servant all is known. I pray you to stay at home and leave the matter with me."

" Nay, Nigel, she may sorely need a woman's aid, and what woman should it be save her own sister ? I can take my tire-woman with us."

" Nay, I shall ride with you myself if your impatience can keep within the powers of my mule," said the old priest.

" But it is not your road, father ? "

" The only road of a true priest is that which leads to the good of others. Come, my children, and we will go together."

And so it was that stout Sir John Buttesthorn, the aged Knight of Dupplin, was left alone at his own high table, pretending to eat, pretending to drink, fidgeting in his seat, trying hard to seem unconcerned with his mind and body in a fever, while below him his varlets and handmaids laughed and jested, clattering their cups and clearing their trenchers, all unconscious of the dark shadow which threw its gloom over the lonely man upon the dais above.

Meantime the Lady Mary upon the white jennet which her sister had ridden on the same evening, Nigel on his war-horse, and the priest on the mule, clattered down the rude winding road which led to London. The country on either side was a wilderness of heather moors and of morasses from which came the strange crying of night-fowl. A half-moon shone in the sky between the rifts of hurrying clouds. The lady rode in silence, absorbed in the thought of the task before them, the danger and the shame.

Nigel chatted in a low tone with the priest. From him he learned more of the evil name of this man whom they followed. His house at Shalford was a den of profligacy and vice. No woman could cross that threshold and depart unstained. In some strange fashion, inexplicable and yet common, the man, with all his evil soul and his twisted body, had yet some strange fascination for women, some mastery over them which compelled them to his will. Again and again he had brought ruin to a household, again and again his adroit tongue and his cunning wit had in some fashion saved him from the punishment of his deeds. His family was great in the county, and his kinsmen held favour with the king, so that his neighbours feared to push things too far against him. Such was the man, malignant and ravenous, who had stooped like some foul night-hawk and borne away to his evil nest the golden beauty of Cosford. Nigel said little as he listened, but he raised his hunting-dagger to his tightened lips, and thrice he kissed the cross of its handle.

They had passed over the moors, and through the village of Milford and the little township of Godalming, until their path turned southward over the Pease marsh, and crossed the meadows of Shalford. There on the dark hillside glowed the red points of light which marked the windows of the house which they sought. A sombre, arched avenue of oak trees led up to it, and then they were in the moon-silvered clearing in front.

From the shadow of the arched door there sprang two rough serving-men, bearded and gruff, great cudgels in their hands, to ask them who they were and what their errand. The Lady Mary had slipped from her horse, and was advancing to the door, but they rudely barred her way.

" Nay, nay, our master needs no more ! " cried one with a hoarse laugh. " Stand back, mistress, whoever you be ! The house is shut, and our lord sees no guests to-night."

" Fellow," said Nigel, speaking low and clear, " stand back from us ! Our errand is with your master."

" Bethink you, my children," cried the old priest, " would it not be best, perchance, that I go in to him, and see whether the voice of the Church may not soften this hard heart ? I fear bloodshed if you enter."

" Nay, father, I pray you to stay here for the nonce," said Nigel. " And you, Mary, do you bide with the good priest, for we know not what may be within."

Again he turned to the door, and again the two men barred his passage.

" Stand back, I say, back for your lives ! " said Nigel. " By Saint Paul ! I should think it shame to soil my sword with such as you, but my soul is set, and no man shall bar my path this night."

The men shrank from the deadly menace of that gentle voice.

" Hold ! " said one of them, peering through the darkness, " is it not Squire Loring of Tilford ? "

" That is indeed my name."

" Had you spoken it, I for one would not have stopped your way. Put down your staff, Wat, for this is no stranger, but the Squire of Tilford."

" As well for him," grumbled the other, lowering his cudgel with an inward prayer of thanksgiving. " Had it been otherwise I should have had blood upon my soul to-night. But our master said nothing of neighbours when he ordered us to hold the door. I will enter and ask him what is his will."

But already Nigel was past them, and had pushed open the outer door. Swift as he was, the Lady Mary was at his very heels, and the two passed together into the hall beyond.

It was a great room, draped and curtained with black shadows, with one vivid circle of light in the centre, where two oil lamps shone upon a small table. A meal was laid upon the table, but only two were seated at it, and there were no servants in the room. At the near end was Edith, her golden hair loose and streaming down over the scarlet and black of her riding-dress.

At the farther end the light beat strongly upon the harsh face and the high-drawn misshapen shoulders of the lord of the house. A tangle of black hair surmounted a high, rounded forehead, the forehead of a thinker, with two deep-set, cold grey eyes twinkling sharply from under tufted brows. His nose was curved and sharp, like the beak of some cruel bird, but below the whole of his clean-shaven, powerful face was marred by the loose, slabbing mouth and the round folds of the heavy chin. His knife in one hand and a half-gnawed bone in the other, he looked fiercely up, like some beast disturbed in his den, as the two intruders broke in upon his hall.

Nigel stopped midway between the door and the table. His eyes and those of Paul de la Fosse were riveted upon each other. But Mary, with her woman's soul flooded over with love and pity, had rushed forward and cast her arms round her younger sister. Edith had sprung up from her chair, and with averted face tried to push the other away from her.

"Edith, Edith ! By the Virgin, I implore you to come back with us, and to leave this wicked man ! " cried Mary. "Dear sister, you would not break our father's heart, nor bring his grey head in dishonour to the grave ! Come back ! Edith, come back and all is well."

But Edith pushed her away, and her fair cheeks were flushed with her anger.

"What right have you over me, Mary, you who are but two years older, that you should follow me over the countryside as though I were a runagate villein and you my mistress ? Do you yourself go back, and leave me to do that which seems best in my own eyes."

But Mary still held her in her arms, and still strove to soften the hard and angry heart.

"Our mother is dead, Edith. I thank God that she died ere she saw you under this roof ! But I stand for her, as I have done all my life, since I am indeed your elder. It is with her voice that I beg and pray you that you will not trust this man further, and that you will come back ere it be too late ! "

Edith writhed from her grasp, and stood flushed and defiant, with gleaming, angry eyes fixed upon her sister.

"You may speak evil of him now," said she, " but there was a time when Paul de la Fosse came to Cosford, and who so gentle and soft-spoken to him then as wise, grave sister Mary ? But he has learned to love another ; so now he is the wicked man, and it is shame to be seen under his roof ! From what I see of my good, pious sister and her cavalier, it is sin for another to ride at night with a man at your side, but it comes easy enough to you. Look at your own eye, good sister, ere you would take the speck from that of another."

Mary stood irresolute and greatly troubled, holding down her pride and her anger, but uncertain how best to deal with this strong, wayward spirit.

" It is not a time for bitter words, dear sister," said she, and again she laid her hand upon her sister's sleeve. " All that you say may be true. There was, indeed, a time when this man was friend to us both, and I know even as you do the power which he may have to win a woman's heart. But I know him now, and you do not. I know the evil that he has wrought, the dishonour that he has brought, the perjury that lies upon his soul, the confidence betrayed, the promise unfulfilled—all this I know. Am I to see my own sister caught in the same well-used trap ? Has it shut upon you, child ? Am I, indeed, already too late ? For God's sake, tell me, Edith, that it is not so ! "

Edith plucked her sleeve from her sister, and made two swift steps to the head of the table. Paul de la Fosse still sat silent with his eyes upon Nigel. Edith laid her hand upon his shoulder.

" This is the man I love, and the only man that I have ever loved. This is my husband," said she.

At the word Mary gave a cry of joy.

" And is it so ? " she cried. " Nay, then all is in honour, and God will see to the rest. If you are man and wife before the altar, then, indeed, why should I, or any other, stand between you ? Tell me that it is indeed so, and I return this moment to make your father a happy man."

Edith pouted like a naughty child. " We are man and wife in the eyes of God. Soon also we shall be wedded before all the world. We do but wait until next Monday, when Paul's brother, who is a priest at Saint Albans, will come to wed us. Already a messenger has sped for him, and he will come, will he not, dear love ? "

" He will come," said the master of Shalford, still with his eyes fixed upon the silent Nigel.

" It is a lie ; he will not come," said a voice from the door.

It was the old priest, who had followed the others as far as the threshold.

" He will not come," he repeated, as he advanced into the room. " Daughter, my daughter, hearken to the words of one who is indeed old enough to be your earthly father. This lie has served before. He has ruined others before you with it. The man has no brother at Saint Albans. I know his brothers well, and there is no priest among them. Before Monday, when it is all too late, you will have found the truth as others have done before you. Trust him not, but come with us ! "

Paul de la Fosse looked up at her with a quick smile and patted the hand upon his shoulder.

" Do you speak to them, Edith," said he.

Her eyes flashed with scorn as she surveyed them each in turn, the woman, the youth, and the priest.

" I have but one word to say to them," said she. " It is that they go hence and trouble us no more. Am I not a free woman ? Have I not said that this is the only man I ever loved ? I have loved him long. He did not know it, and in despair he turned to another. Now he knows all, and never again can doubt come between us. Therefore I will stay here at Shalford and come to Cosford no more save upon the arm of my husband. Am I so weak that I would believe the tales you tell against him ? Is it hard for a jealous woman and a wandering priest to agree upon a lie ? No, no, Mary, you can go hence and take your cavalier and your priest with you, for here I stay, true to my love and safe in my trust upon his honour ! "

" Well spoken, on my faith, my golden bird ! " said the little master of Shalford. " Let me add my own word to that which has been said. You would not grant me any virtue in your unkindly speech, good Lady Mary, and yet you must needs confess that at least I have good store of patience, since I have not set my dogs upon your friends who have come between me and my ease. But even to the most virtuous there comes at last a time when poor human frailty may prevail, and so I pray you to remove both yourself, your priest, and your valiant knight-errant, lest perhaps there be more haste and less dignity when at last you do take your leave. Sit down, my fair love and let us turn once more to our supper." He motioned her to her chair, and he filled her wine-cup as well as his own.

Nigel had said no word since he had entered the room, but his look had never lost its set purpose, nor had his brooding eyes ever wandered from the sneering face of the deformed master of Shalford. Now he turned with swift decision to Mary and to the priest.

" That is over," said he, in a low voice. " You have done all that you could, and now it is for me to play my part as well as I am able. I pray you, Mary, and you, good father, that you will await me outside."

" Nay, Nigel, if there is danger——"

" It is easier for me, Mary, if you are not there. I pray you to go. I can speak to this man more at my ease."

She looked at him with questioning eyes and then obeyed.

Nigel plucked at the priest's gown. " I pray you, father, have you your book of offices with you ? "

" Surely, Nigel, it is ever in my breast."

" Have it ready, father ! "

" For what, my son ? "

" There are two places you may mark : there is the service of marriage, and there is the prayer for the dying. Go with her, father, and be ready at my call."

He closed the door behind them and was alone with this ill-matched couple. They both turned in their chairs to look at him, Edith with a defiant face, the man with a bitter smile upon his lips and malignant hatred in his eyes.

" What," said he, " the knight-errant still lingers ? Have we not heard of his thirst for glory ? What new venture does he see that he should tarry here ? "

Nigel walked to the table. " There is no glory and little venture," said he ; " but I have come for a purpose and I must do it. I learn from your own lips, Edith, that you will not leave this man."

" If you have ears you have heard it."

" You are, as you have said, a free woman, and who can gainsay you ?   But I have known you, Edith, since we played as boy and girl on the heather-hills together. I will save you from this man's cunning and from your own foolish weakness."

" What would you do ? "

" There is a priest without.   He will marry you now. I will see you married ere I leave this hall."

" Or else ? " sneered the man.

" Or else you never leave this hall alive.   Nay, call not for your servants or your dogs !   By Saint Paul !   I swear to you that this matter lies between us three, and that if any fourth comes at your call, you, at least, shall never live to see what comes of it !   Speak then, Paul of Shalford !   Will you wed this woman now, or will you not ? "

Edith was on her feet with outstretched arms between them.

" Stand back, Nigel !   He is small and weak.   You would not do him a hurt !   Did you not say so this very day ?   For God's sake, Nigel, do not look at him so ! There is death in your eyes."

" A snake may be small and weak, Edith, yet every honest man would place his heel upon it.   Do you stand back yourself, for my purpose is set."

" Paul ! "   She turned her eyes to the pale, sneering face.   " Bethink you, Paul !   Why should you not do what he asks ?   What matter to you whether it be now or on Monday ?   I pray you, dear Paul, for my sake let him have his way !   Your brother can read the service again if it so please him.   Let us wed now, Paul, and then all is well."

He had risen from his chair, and he dashed aside her appealing hands.

" You foolish woman," he snarled, " and you, my saviour of fair damsels, who are so bold against a cripple, you have both to learn that if my body be weak, there is the soul of my breed within it !   To marry because a boasting, ranting, country squire would have me do so—no, by the soul of God, I will die first ! On Monday I will marry, and no day sooner, so let that be your answer."

" It is the answer that I wished," said Nigel, " for indeed I see no happiness in this marriage, and the other may well be the better way. Stand aside, Edith ! " He gently forced her to one side and drew his sword.

De la Fosse cried aloud at the sight. " I have no sword. You would not murder me ? " said he, leaning back with haggard face and burning eyes aginst his chair. The bright steel shone in the lamplight. Edith shrank back, her hand over her face.

" Take this sword ! " said Nigel, and he turned the hilt to the cripple. " Now ! " he added, as he drew his hunting-knife. " Kill me if you can, Paul de la Fosse, for as God is my help I will do as much for you ! "

The woman, half swooning and yet spellbound and fascinated, looked on at that strange combat. For a moment the cripple stood with an air of doubt, the sword grasped in his nerveless fingers. Then, as he saw the tiny blade in Nigel's hand, the greatness of the advantage came home to him, and a cruel smile tightened his loose lips. Slowly, step by step he advanced, his chin sunk upon his chest, his eyes glaring from under the thick tangle of his brows like fires through the brushwood. Nigel waited for him, his left hand forward, his knife down by his hip, his face grave, still, and watchful.

Nearer and nearer yet, with stealthy step, and then with a bound and a cry of hatred and rage, Paul de la Fosse had sped his blow. It was well judged and well swung, but point would have been wiser than edge against that supple body and those active feet. Quick as a flash, Nigel had sprung inside the sweep of the blade, taking a flesh wound on his left forearm, as he pressed it under the hilt. The next instant the cripple was on the ground and Nigel's dagger was at his throat.

" You dog ! " he whispered. " I have you at my mercy ! Quick ere I strike, and for the last time ! Will you marry or no ? "

The crash of the fall and the sharp point upon his throat had cowed the man's spirit. He looked up with a white face, and the sweat gleamed upon his forehead. There was terror in his eyes.

" Nay, take your knife from me ! " he cried. " I cannot die like a calf in the shambles."

" Will you marry ? "

" Yes, yes ; I will wed her ! After all, she is a good wench, and I might do worse. Let me up ! I tell you I will marry her ! What more would you have ? "

Nigel stood above him with his foot upon the misshapen body. He had picked up his sword, and the point rested upon the cripple's breast.

" Nay, you will bide where you are ! If you are to live—and my conscience cries loud against it—at least your wedding will be such as your sins have deserved. Lie there, like the crushed worm that you are ! " Then he raised his voice. " Father Athanasius ! " he cried. " What ho ! Father Athanasius ! "

The old priest ran to the cry, and so did the Lady Mary. A strange sight it was that met them now in the circle of light, the frightened girl, half-unconscious against the table, the prostrate cripple, and Nigel with foot and sword upon his body.

" Your book, father ! " cried Nigel. " I know not if what we do is good or ill ; but we must wed them, for there is no way out."

But the girl by the table had given a great cry, and she was clinging and sobbing with her arms round her sister's neck.

" Oh, Mary, I thank the Virgin that you have come ! I thank the Virgin that it is not too late ! What did he say ? He said that he was a de la Fosse, and that he would not be married at the sword-point. My heart went out to him when he said it. But I, am I not a Buttesthorn, and shall it be said that I would marry a man who could be led to the altar with a knife at his throat ? No, no ; I see him as he is ! I know him now, the mean spirit, the

565

lying tongue ! Can I not read in his eyes that he has indeed deceived me, that he would have left me as you say that he has left others ? Take me home, Mary, my sister, for you have plucked me back this night from the very mouth of Hell ! "

And so it was that the master of Shalford, livid and brooding, was left with his wine at his lonely table, while the golden beauty of Cosford, hot with shame and anger, her fair face wet with tears, passed out safe from the house of infamy into the great calm and peace of the starry night.

13. *How the Comrades journeyed down the Old, Old Road*

AND now the season of the moonless nights was drawing nigh and the king's design was ripe. Very secretly his preparations were made. Already the garrison of Calais, which consisted of five hundred archers and two hundred men-at-arms, could, if forewarned, resist any attack made upon it. But it was the king's design not merely to resist the attack, but to capture the attackers. Above all it was his wish to find the occasion for one of those adventurous passages of arms which had made his name famous throughout Christendom as the very pattern and leader of knight-errant chivalry.

But the affair wanted careful handling. The arrival of any reinforcements, or even the crossing of any famous soldier, would have alarmed the French, and warned them that their plot had been discovered. Therefore it was in twos and threes in the creyers and provision ships which were continually passing from shore to shore that the chosen warriors and their squires were brought to Calais. There they were passed at night through the water-gate into the castle where they could lie hidden, unknown to the townsfolk, until the hour for action had come.

Nigel had received word from Chandos to join him at " The Sign of the Broom-Pod " in Winchelsea. Three days beforehand he and Aylward rode from Tilford all armed and ready for the wars. Nigel was in hunting-costume, blithe and gay, with his precious armour and his small baggage trussed upon the back of a spare horse which Aylward led by the bridle. The archer had himself a good black mare, heavy and slow, but strong enough to be fit to carry his powerful frame. In his brigandine of chain mail and his steel cap, with straight strong sword by his side, his yellow long-bow jutting over his shoulder, and his quiver of arrows supported by a scarlet baldric, he was such a warrior as any knight might well be proud to have in his train. All Tilford trailed behind them, as they rode slowly over the long slope of heath land which skirts the flank of Crooksbury Hill.

At the summit of the rise Nigel reined in Pommers and looked back at the little village behind him. There was the old dark manor-house, with one bent figure leaning upon a stick and gazing dimly after him from beside the door. He looked at the high-pitched roof, the old timbered walls, the long trail of swirling blue smoke which rose from the single chimney, and the group of downcast old servants who lingered at the gate—John the cook, Weathercote the minstrel, and Red Swire the broken soldier. Over the river amid the trees he could see the grim, grey tower of Waverley, and even as he looked, the iron bell, which had so often seemed to be the hoarse threatening cry of an enemy, clanged out its call to prayer. Nigel doffed his velvet cap and prayed also—prayed that peace might remain at home, and good warfare, in which honour and fame should await him, might still be found abroad. Then, waving his hand to the people, he turned his horse's head and rode slowly eastward. A moment later Aylward broke from the group of archers and laughing girls who clung to his bridle and his stirrup straps, and rode on, blowing kisses over his shoulder. So at last the two comrades, gentle and simple, were fairly started on their venture.

There are two seasons of colour in those parts : the

yellow, when the countryside is flaming with the gorse-blossoms, and the crimson, when all the long slopes are smouldering with the heather. So it was now. Nigel looked back from time to time, as he rode along the narrow track where the ferns and the ling brushed his feet on either side, and as he looked it seemed to him that, wander where he might, he would never see a fairer scene than that of his own home. Far to the westward, glowing in the morning light, rolled billow after billow of ruddy heather land, until they merged into the dark shadows of Woolmer Forest and the pale clear green of the Butser chalk downs. Never in his life had Nigel wandered far beyond these limits, and the woodlands, the down, and the heather were dear to his soul. It gave him a pang in his heart now as he turned his face away from them ; but if home lay to the westward, out there to the east and south was the great world of adventure, the noble stage where each of his kinsmen in turn had played his manly part and left a proud name behind.

How often he had longed for this day ! And now it had come with no shadow cast behind it. Dame Ermyntrude was under the king's protection. The old servants had their future assured. The strife with the monks of Waverley had been assuaged. He had a noble horse under him, the best of weapons, and a stout follower at his back. Above all he was bound on a gallant errand with the bravest knight in England as his leader. All these thoughts surged together in his mind, and he whistled and sang, as he rode, out of the joy of his heart, while Pommers sidled and curveted in sympathy with the mood of his master. Presently, glancing back, he saw from Aylward's downcast eyes and puckered brow that the archer was clouded with trouble. He reined his horse to let him come abreast of him.

" How now, Aylward ? " said he. " Surely of all men in England you and I should be the most blithe this morning, since we ride forward with all hopes of honourable advancement. By Saint Paul ! ere we see these heather hills once more we shall either worshipfully win worship, or we shall venture our persons in the attempt. These be glad thoughts, and why should you be downcast ? "

Aylward shrugged his broad shoulders, and a wry smile dawned upon his rugged face.

" I am indeed as limp as a wetted bowstring," said he. " It is the nature of a man that he should be sad when he leaves the woman he loves."

" In truth, yes ! " cried Nigel, and in a flash the dark eyes of Mary Buttesthorn rose before him, and he heard her low, sweet, earnest voice as he had heard it that night when they brought her frailer sister back from Shalford Manor, a voice which made all that was best and noblest in a man thrill within his soul. " Yet, bethink you, archer, that what a woman loves in man is not his gross body, but rather his soul, his honour, his fame, the deeds with which he has made his life beautiful. Therefore you are winning love as well as glory when you turn to the wars."

" It may be so," said Aylward ; " but indeed it goes to my heart to see the pretty dears weep, and I would fain weep as well to keep them company. When Mary—or was it Dolly ?—nay, it was Martha, the red-headed girl from the Mill—when she held tight to my baldric it was like snapping my heart-string to pluck myself loose."

" You speak of one name and then of another," said Nigel. " How is she called, then, this maid whom you love ? "

Aylward pushed back his steel cap and scratched his bristling head with some embarrassment.

" Her name," said he, " is Mary Dolly Martha Susan Jane Cicely Theodosia Agnes Johanna Kate."

Nigel laughed as Aylward rolled out this prodigious title.

" I had no right to take you to the wars," said he ; " for by Saint Paul ! it is very clear that I have widowed half the parish. But I saw your aged father the franklin. Bethink you of the joy that will fill his heart when he hears that you have done some small deed in France, and so won honour in the eyes of all."

" I fear that honour will not help him to pay his arrears of rent to the sacrist of Waverley," said Aylward. "Out he will go on the roadside, honour and all, if he does not find ten nobles by next Epiphany. But if I could win a ransom or be at the storming of a rich city, then indeed the old man would be proud of me. ' Thy sword must help my spade, Samkin,' said he as he kissed me good-bye. Ah ! it would indeed be a happy day for him and for all if I could ride back with a saddle-bag full of gold pieces, and please God, I shall dip my hand in some-body's pocket before I see Crooksbury Hill once more ! "

Nigel shook his head, for indeed it seemed hopeless to try to bridge the gulf between them. Already they had made such good progress along the bridle-path through the heather that the little hill of Saint Catharine and the ancient shrine upon its summit loomed up before them. Here they crossed the road from the south to London, and at the crossing two wayfarers were waiting who waved their hands in greeting, the one a tall, slender, dark woman upon a white jennet, the other a very thick and red-faced old man, whose weight seemed to curve the back of the stout grey cob which he bestrode.

" What how, Nigel ! " he cried. " Mary has told me that you make a start this morning, and we have waited here this hour and more on the chance of seeing you pass. Come, lad, and have a last stoup of English ale, for many a time amid the sour French wines you will long for the white foam under your nose, and the good homely twang of it."

Nigel had to decline the draught, for it meant riding into Guildford town, a mile out of his course, but very gladly he agreed with Mary that they should climb the path to the old shrine and offer a last orison together. The knight and Aylward waited below with the horses ; and so it came about that Nigel and Mary found them-selves alone under the solemn old Gothic arches, in front of the dark shadowed recess in which gleamed the golden reliquary of the saint. In silence they knelt side by side in prayer, and then came forth once more out of the gloom and the shadow into the fresh sunlit summer morning. They stopped ere they descended the path, and looked to right and left at the fair meadows and the blue Wey curling down the valley.

" What have you prayed for, Nigel ? " said she.

" I have prayed that God and His saints will hold my spirit high and will send me back from France in such a fashion that I may dare to come to you and to claim you for my own."

" Bethink you well what it is that you say, Nigel," said she. " What you are to me only my own heart can tell ; but I would never set eyes upon your face again rather than abate by one inch that height of honour and worshipful achievement to which you may attain."

" Nay, my dear and most sweet lady, how should you abate it, since it is the thought of you which will serve my arm and uphold my heart ? "

" Think once more, my fair lord, and hold yourself bound by no word which you have said. Let it be as the breeze which blows past our faces and is heard of no more. Your soul yearns for honour. To that has it ever turned. Is there room in it for love also ? or is it possible that both shall live at their highest in one mind ? Do you not call to mind that Galahad and other great knights of old have put women out of their lives that they might ever give their whole soul and strength to the winning of honour ? May it not be that I shall be a drag upon you, that your heart may shrink from some honourable task, lest it should bring risk and pain to me ? Think well before you answer, my fair lord, for indeed my very heart would break if it should ever happen that through love of me your high hopes and great promise should miss fulfilment."

Nigel looked at her with sparkling eyes. The soul which shone through her dark face had transformed it for the moment into a beauty, more lofty and more rare than that of her shallow sister. He bowed before the majesty of the woman, and pressed his lips to her hand.

" You are like a star upon my path which guides me on the upward way," said he. " Our souls are set together upon the finding of honour, and how shall we hold each other back when our purpose is the same ? "

She shook her proud head. " So it seems to you now, fair lord, but it may be otherwise as the years pass. How shall you prove that I am indeed a help and not a hindrance ? "

" I will prove it by my deeds, fair and dear lady," said Nigel. " Here at the shrine of the holy Catharine, on this, the Feast of Saint Margaret, I take my oath that I will do three deeds in your honour as a proof of my high love before I set eyes upon your face again, and these three deeds shall stand as a proof to you that if I love you dearly, still I will not let the thought of you stand betwixt me and honourable achievement ! "

Her face shone with her love and her pride. " I also make my oath," said she, " and I do it in the name of the holy Catharine whose shrine is hard by. I swear that I will hold myself for you until these three deeds be done and we meet once more ; also that if—which may dear Christ forfend !—you fall in doing them then I shall take the veil in Shalford nunnery and look upon no man's face again ! Give me your hand, Nigel."

She had taken a little bangle of gold filigree work from her arm and fastened it upon his sunburnt wirst, reading aloud to him the engraved motto in old French : " *Fais ce que dois, adviegne que pourra—c'est commandé au chevalier.*" Then for one moment they fell into each other's arms and with kiss upon kiss, a loving man and a tender woman, they swore their troth to each other   But the old knight was calling impatiently from below, and together they hurried down the winding path to where the horses waited under the sandy bluff.

As far as the Shalford crossing Sir John rode by

Nigel's arm, and many were the last injunctions which he gave him concerning woodcraft, and great his anxiety lest he confuse a spay with a brocket, or either with a hind. At last, when they came to the reedy edge of the Wey, the old knight and his daughter reined up their horses. Nigel looked back at them ere he entered the dark Chantry woods, and saw them still gazing after him and waving their hands. Then the path wound among the trees and they were lost to sight ; but long afterwards when a clearing exposed once more the Shalford meadows Nigel saw that the old man upon the grey cob was riding slowly toward Saint Catharine's Hill, but that the girl was still where he had seen her last, leaning forward in her saddle and straining her eyes to pierce the dark forest which screened her lover from her view. It was but a fleeting glance through a break in the foliage, and yet in after days of stress and toil in far distant lands it was that one little picture—the green meadow, the reeds, the slow blue winding river, and the eager bending graceful figure upon the white horse—which was the clearest and the dearest image of that England which he had left behind him.

But if Nigel's friends had learned that this was the morning of his leaving, his enemies too were on the alert. The two comrades had just emerged from the Chantry woods and were beginning the ascent of that curving path which leads upward to the old Chapel of the Martyr when, with a hiss like an angry snake, a long white arrow streaked under Pommers and struck quivering in the grassy turf. A second whizzed past Nigel's ear, as he tried to turn, but Aylward struck the great war-horse a sharp blow over the haunches, and it had galloped some hundreds of yards before its rider could pull it up. Aylward followed as hard as he could ride, bending low over his horse's neck, while arrows whizzed all around him.

" By Saint Paul ! " said Nigel, tugging at his bridle and white with anger, " they shall not chase me across the country as though I were a frighted doe. Archer, how dare you to lash my horse when I would have turned and ridden in upon them ? "

" It is well that I did so," said Aylward, " or by these ten finger-bones ! our journey would have begun and ended on the same day. As I glanced round I saw a dozen of them at the least amongst the brushwood. See now how the light glimmers upon their steel caps yonder in the bracken under the great beech-tree. Nay, I pray you, my fair lord, do not ride forward. What chance has a man in the open against all these who lie at their ease in the underwood ? If you will not think of yourself, then consider your horse, which would have a cloth-yard shaft feathered in its hide ere it could reach the wood."

Nigel chafed in impotent anger. " Am I to be shot at like a popinjay at a fair, by any reaver or outlaw that seeks a mark for his bow ? " he cried. " By Saint Paul ! Aylward, I will put on my harness and go further into the matter. Help me to untruss, I pray you ! "

" Nay, my fair lord, I will not help you to your own downfall. It is a match with cogged dice betwixt a horse-man on the moor and archers amid the forest. But these men are no outlaws, or they would not dare to draw their bows within a league of the sheriff of Guildford."

" Indeed, Aylward, I think that you speak truth," said Nigel. " It may be that these are the men of Paul de la Fosse of Shalford, whom I have given little cause to love me. Ah ! there is indeed the very man himself."

They sat their horses with their backs to the long slope which leads up to the old chapel on the hill. In front of them was the dark ragged edge of the wood, with a sharp twinkle of steel here and there in its shadows which spoke of these lurking foes. But now there was a long moot upon a horn, and at once a score of russet-clad bowmen ran forward from amid the trees, spreading out into a scattered line and closing swiftly in upon the travellers. In the midst of them, upon a great grey horse, sat a small misshapen man waving and cheering as one sets hounds on a badger, turning his head this way and that as he whooped and pointed, urging his bowmen onward up the slope.

"Draw them on, my fair lord! Draw them on until we have them out on the down!" cried Aylward, his eyes shining with joy. "Five hundred paces more, and then we may be on terms with them. Nay, linger not, but keep them always just clear of arrow-shot until our turn has come."

Nigel shook and trembled with eagerness, as with his hand on his sword-hilt he looked at the line of eager hurrying men. But it flashed through his mind what Chandos had said of the cool head which is better for the warrior than the hot heart. Aylward's words were true and wise. He turned Pommers' head therefore, and amid a cry of derision from behind them the comrades trotted over the down. The bowmen broke into a run, while their leader screamed and waved more madly than before. Aylward cast many a glance at them over his shoulder.

"Yet a little farther! Yet a little farther still!" he muttered. "The wind is toward them and the fools have forgot that I can overshoot them by fifty paces. Now, my good lord, I pray you for one instant to hold the horses, for my weapon is of more avail this day than thine can be. They may make sorry cheer ere they gain the shelter of the wood once more."

He had sprung from his horse, and with a downward wrench of his arm and a push with his knee he slipped the string into the upper nock of his mighty war-bow. Then in a flash he notched his shaft and drew it to the pile, his keen blue eyes glowing fiercely behind it from under his knotted brows. With thick legs planted sturdily apart, his body laid to the bow, his left arm motionless as wood, his right bunched into a double curve of swelling muscles as he stretched the white well-waxed string, he looked so keen and fierce a fighter that the advancing line stopped for an instant at the sight of him. Two or three loosed off their arrows, but the shafts flew heavily against the head wind, and snaked along the hard turf some score of paces short of the mark. One only, a short bandy-legged man, whose squat figure spoke of enormous muscular strength, ran swiftly in and then drew so strong a bow that the arrow quivered in the ground at Aylward's very feet.

" It is Black Will of Lynchmere," said the bowman. " Many a match have I shot with him, and I know well that no other man on the Surrey marches could have sped such a shaft. I trust that you are houseled and shriven, Will, for I have known you so long that I would not have your damnation upon my soul."

He raised his bow as he spoke, and the string twanged with a rich, deep musical note. Aylward leaned upon his bow-stave as he keenly watched the long swift flight of his shaft, skinning smoothly down the wind.

" On him, on him ! No, over him, by my hilt ! " he cried. " There is more wind than I had thought. Nay, nay, friend, now that I have the length of you, you can scarce hope to loose again."

Black Will had notched an arrow and was raising his bow when Aylward's second shaft passed through the shoulder of his drawing arm. With a shout of anger and pain he dropped his weapon, and dancing in his fury he shook his fist and roared curses at his rival.

" I could slay him ; but I will not, for good bowmen are not so common," said Aylward. " And now, fair sir, we must on, for they are spreading round on either side, and if once they get behind us, then indeed our journey has come to a sudden end. But ere we go I would send a shaft through yonder horseman who leads them on."

" Nay, Aylward, I pray you to leave him," said Nigel. " Villain as he is, he is none the less a gentleman of coat-armour, and should die by some other weapon than thine."

" As you will," said Aylward, with a clouded brow. " I have been told that in the late wars many a French prince and baron has not been too proud to take his death-wound from an English yeoman's shaft, and that nobles of

England have been glad enough to stand by and see it done."

Nigel shook his head sadly. " It is sooth you say, archer, and indeed it is no new thing, for that good knight Richard of the Lion Heart met his end in such a lowly fashion, and so also did Harold the Saxon. But this is a private matter, and I would not have you draw your bow against him. Neither can I ride at him myself, for he is weak in body, though dangerous in spirit. Therefore, we will go upon our way, since there is neither profit nor honour to be gained, nor any hope of advancement."

Aylward, having unstrung his bow, had remounted his horse during this conversation, and the two rode swiftly past the little squat Chapel of the Martyr and over the brow of the hill. From the summit they looked back. The injured archer lay upon the ground, with several of his comrades gathered in a knot around him. Others ran aimlessly up the hill, but were already far behind. The leader sat motionless upon his horse, and as he saw them look back he raised his hand and shrieked his curses at them. An instant later the curve of the ground had hid them from view. So, amid love and hate, Nigel bade adieu to the home of his youth.

And now the comrades were journeying upon that old, old road which runs across the south of England and yet never turns towards London, for the good reason that the place was a poor hamlet when first the road was laid. From Winchester, the Saxon capital, to Canterbury, the holy city of Kent, ran that ancient highway, and on from Canterbury to the narrow straits where, on a clear day, the farther shore can be seen. Along this track as far back as history can trace the metals of the west have been carried, and passed the pack-horses bearing the goods which Gaul sent in exchange. Older than the Christian faith, and older than the Romans, is the old road. North and south are the woods and the marshes, so that only on the high dry turf of the chalk land could a clear track be found. The Pilgrim's Way, it still is called ; but the pilgrims

were the last who ever trod it, for it was already of imme-
morial age before the death of Thomas à Becket gave a new
reason why folk should journey to the scene of his murder.

From the hill of Western Wood the travellers could see
the long white band which dipped and curved and rose
over the green downland, its course marked even in the
hollows by the line of the old yew-trees which flanked it.
Neither Nigel nor Aylward had wandered far from their
own country, and now they rode with light hearts and
eager eyes taking note of all the varied pictures of nature
and of man which passed before them. To their left was
a hilly country, a land of rolling heaths and woods, broken
here and there into open spaces round the occasional farmhouse of a franklin. Hackhurst Down, Dunley Hill, and
Ranmore Common swelled and sank, each merging into
the other. But on the right, after passing the village of
Shere and the old church of Gomshall, the whole south
country lay like a map at their feet. There was the huge
wood of the Weald, one unbroken forest of oak-trees
stretching away to the South Downs, which rose olive-
green against the deep blue sky. Under this great canopy
of trees strange folk lived and evil deeds were done. In
its recesses were wild tribes, little changed from their
heathen ancestors, who danced round the altar of Thor,
and well was it for the peaceful traveller that he could
tread the high open road of the chalk land with no need to
wander into so dangerous a tract, where soft clay, tangled
forest, and wild men all barred his progress.

But apart from the rolling country upon the left and
the great forest-hidden plain upon the right, there was
much upon the road itself to engage the attention of the
wayfarers. It was crowded with people. As far as their
eyes could carry they could see the black dots scattered
thickly upon the thin white band, sometimes single, sometimes several abreast, sometimes in moving crowds, where
a drove of pilgrims held together for mutual protection, or
a nobleman showed his greatness by the number of retainers who trailed at his heels. At that time the main

roads were very crowded, for there were many wandering people in the land. Of all sorts and kinds, they passed in an unbroken stream before the eyes of Nigel and of Aylward, alike only in the fact that one and all were powdered from their hair to their shoes with the grey dust of the chalk.

There were monks journeying from one cell to another, Benedictines with their black gowns looped up to show their white skirts. Carthusians in white, and pied Cistercians. Friars also of the three wandering orders— Dominicans in black, Carmelites in white, and Franciscans in grey. There was no love lost between the cloistered monks and the free friars, each looking on the other as a rival who took from him the oblations of the faithful ; so they passed on the high road as cat passes dog, with eyes askance and angry faces.

Then, besides the men of the Church, there were the men of trade, the merchant in dusty broadcloth and Flanders hat, riding at the head of his line of pack-horses. He carried Cornish tin, West-country wool, or Sussex iron if he traded eastward, or if his head should be turned westward then he bore with him the velvets of Genoa, the ware of Venice, the wine of France, or the armour of Italy and Spain. Pilgrims were everywhere, poor people for the most part, plodding wearily along with trailing feet and bowed heads, thick staves in their hands and bundles over their shoulders. Here and there on a gaily caparisoned palfrey, or in the greater luxury of a horse-litter, some West-country lady might be seen making her easy way to the shrine of Saint Thomas.

Besides all these a constant stream of strange vagabonds drifted along the road ; minstrels who wandered from fair to fair, a foul and pestilent crew ; jugglers and acrobats, quack doctors and tooth-drawers, students and beggars, free workmen in search of better wages, and escaped bondsmen who would welcome any wages at all. Such was the throng which set the old road smoking in a haze of white dust from Winchester to the narrow sea.

But all of the wayfarers those which interested Nigel most were the soldiers. Several times they passed little knots of archers or men-at-arms, veterans from France, who had received their discharge and were now making their way to their southland homes. They were half drunk all of them, for the wayfarers treated them to beer at the frequent inns and ale-stakes which lined the road, so that they cheered and sang lustily as they passed. They roared rude pleasantries at Aylward, who turned in his saddle and shouted his opinion of them until they were out of hearing.

Once, late in the afternoon, they overtook a body of a hundred archers all marching together with two knights riding at their head. They were passing from Guildford Castle to Reigate Castle, where they were in garrison. Nigel rode with the knights for some distance, and hinted that if either was in search of honourable advancement, or wished to do some small deed, or to relieve himself of any vow, it might be possible to find some means of achieving it. They were both, however, grave and elderly men, intent upon their business and with no mind for fond wayside adventures, so Nigel quickened his pace and left them behind.

They had left Boxhill and Headley Heath upon the left, and the towers of Reigate were rising amid the trees in front of them when they overtook a large, cheery, red-faced man, with a forked beard, riding upon a good horse and exchanging a nod or a merry word with all who passed him. With him they rode nearly as far as Bletchingley, and Nigel laughed much to hear him talk ; but always under the raillery there was much earnestness and much wisdom in all his words. He rode at his ease about the country, he said, having sufficient money to keep him from want and to furnish him for the road. He could speak all the three languages of England, the north, the middle, and the south, so that he was at home with the people of every shire and could hear their troubles and their joys. In all parts in town and in country, there was unrest, he said ; for the poor folk were weary of their masters both of the Church and State, and soon there would be such doings in England as had never been seen before.

But above all this man was earnest against the Church : its enormous wealth, its possession of nearly one-third of the whole land of the country, its insatiable greed for more at the very time when it claimed to be poor and lowly. The monks and friars, too, he lashed with his tongue : their roguish ways, their laziness, and their cunning. He showed how their wealth and that of the haughty lord must always be founded upon the toil of poor humble Peter the Plowman, who worked and strove in rain and cold out in the fields, the butt and laughing-stock of everyone, and still bearing up the whole world upon his weary shoulders. He had set it all out in a fair parable ; so now as he rode he repeated some of the verses, chanting them and marking time with his forefinger, while Nigel and Aylward on either side of him with their heads inclined inward listened with the same attention but with very different feelings—Nigel shocked at such an attack upon authority, and Aylward chuckling as he heard the sentiments of his class so shrewdly expressed. At last the stranger halted his horse outside the " Five Angels " at Gatton.

" It is a good inn, and I know the ale of old," said he. " When I had finished that ' Dream of Piers the Plowman,' which I have recited to you, the last verses were thus :

" ' Now have I brought my little booke to an ende
God's blessing be on him who a drinke will me sende '—

I pray you come in with me and share it."

" Nay," said Nigel, " we must on our way, for we have far to go. But give me your name, my friend, for indeed we have passed a merry hour listening to your words."

" Have a care ! " the stranger answered, shaking his head. " You and your class will not spend a merry hour when these words are turned into deeds, and Peter the Plowman grows weary of swinking in the fields and takes up his bow and his staff in order to set this land in order."

"By Saint Paul! I expect that we shall bring Peter to reason, and also those who have put such evil thoughts into his head," said Nigel. "So once more I ask your name, that I may know it if ever I chance to hear that you have been hanged?"

The stranger laughed good-humouredly. "You can call me Thomas Lackland," said he. "I should be Thomas Lack-brain if I were indeed to give my true name, since a good many robbers, some in black gowns and some in steel, would be glad to help me upward in the way you speak of. So good-day to you, squire, and to you also, archer; and may you find your way back with whole bones from the wars!"

That night the comrades slept in Godstone Priory, and early next morning they were well upon their road down the Pilgrim's Way. At Titsey it was said that a band of villains were out in Westerham Wood and had murdered three men the day before; so that Nigel had high hopes of an encounter; but the brigands showed no sign, though the travellers went out of their way to ride their horses along the edges of the forest. Farther on they found traces of their work, for the path ran along the hillside at the base of a chalk quarry, and there in the cutting a man was lying dead. From his twisted limbs and shattered frame it was easy to see that he had been thrown over from above, while his pockets turned outward showed the reason for his murder. The comrades rode past without too close a survey, for dead men were no very uncommon objects on the king's highway, and if sheriff or bailiff should chance upon you near the body you might find yourself caught in the meshes of the law.

Near Sevenoaks their road turned out of the old Canterbury way and pointed south towards the coast, leaving the chalk lands and coming down into the clay of the Weald. It was a wretched, rutted mule-track running through thick forests with occasional clearings in which lay the small Kentish villages, where rude shock-headed peasants with smocks and galligaskins stared with bold, greedy eyes at the travellers. Once on the right they caught a distant view of the Towers of Penshurst, and once they heard the deep tolling of the bells of Bayham Abbey, but for the rest of their day's journey savage peasants and squalid cottages were all that met their eyes, with endless droves of pigs who fed upon the litter of acorns. The throng of travellers who crowded the old road were all gone, and only here and there did they meet or overtake some occasional merchant or messenger bound for Battle Abbey, Pevensey Castle or the towns of the south.

That night they slept in a sordid inn, overrun with rats and with fleas, one mile south of the hamlet of Mayfield. Aylward scratched vigorously and cursed with fervour. Nigel lay without movement or sound. To the man who had learned the old rule of chivalry there were no small ills in life. It was beneath the dignity of his soul to stoop to observe them. Cold and heat, hunger and thirst, such things did not exist for the gentleman. The armour of his soul was so complete that it was proof not only against the great ills of life but even against the small ones ; so the flea-bitten Nigel lay grimly still while Aylward writhed upon his couch.

They were now but a short distance from their destination ; but they had hardly started on their journey through the forest next morning, when an adventure befell them which filled Nigel with the wildest hopes.

Along the narrow winding path between the great oak-trees there rode a dark, sallow man in a scarlet tabard who blew so loudly upon a silver trumpet that they heard the clanging call long before they set eyes on him. Slowly he advanced, pulling up every fifty paces to make the forest ring with another warlike blast. The comrades rode forward to meet him.

" I pray you," said Nigel, " to tell me who you are and why you blow upon this trumpet."

The fellow shook his head, so Nigel repeated the question in French, the common language of chivalry, spoken at that age by every gentleman in Western Europe.

The man put his lips to the trumpet and blew another long note before he answered.

" I am Gaston de Castrier," said he, " the humble squire of the most worthy and valiant knight Raoul de Tubiers, de Pestels, de Grimsard, de Mersac, de Leoy, de Bastanac, who also writes himself Lord of Pons. It is his order that I ride always a mile in front of him to prepare all to receive him, and he desires me to blow upon a trumpet not out of vainglory, but out of greatness of spirit, so that none may be ignorant of his coming should they desire to encounter him."

Nigel sprang from his horse with a cry of joy, and began to unbutton his doublet.

" Quick, Aylward, quick ! " he said. " He comes, a knight-errant comes ! Was there ever such a chance of worshipfully winning worship ? Untruss the harness whilst I loose my clothes ! Good sir, I beg you to warn your noble and valiant master that a poor squire of England would implore him to take notice of him and to do some small deed upon him as he passes."

But already the Lord of Pons had come in sight. He was a huge man upon an enormous horse, so that together they seemed to fill up the whole long dark archway under the oaks. He was clad in full armour of a brazen hue, with only his face exposed, and of this face there was little visible save a pair of arrogant eyes and a great black beard, which flowed through the open visor and down over his breastplate. To the crest of his helmet was tied a small brown glove, nodding and swinging above him. He bore a long lance with a red square banner at the end, charged with a black boar's head, and the same symbol was engraved upon his shield. Slowly he rode through the forest, ponderous, menacing, with dull thudding of his charger's hoofs and constant clank of metal, while always in front of him came the distant peal of the silver trumpet calling all men to admit his majesty and to clear his path ere they be cleared from it.

Never in his dreams had so perfect a vision come to cheer Nigel's heart, and as he struggled with his clothes, glancing up continually at this wondrous traveller, he pattered forth prayers of thanksgiving to the good Saint Paul who had shown such loving-kindness to his unworthy servant and thrown him in the path of so excellent and debonair a gentleman.

But alas! how often at the last instant the cup is dashed from the lips! This joyful chance was destined to change suddenly to unexpected and grotesque disaster— disaster so strange and so complete that through all his life Nigel flushed crimson when he thought of it. He was busily stripping his hunting-costume, and with feverish haste he had doffed boots, hat, hose, doublet and cloak, so that nothing remained save a pink jupon and pair of silken drawers. At the same time Aylward was hastily un-buckling the load with the intention of handing his master his armour piece by piece, when the squire gave one last challenging peal from his silver trumpet into the very ear of the spare horse.

In an instant it had taken to its heels, the precious armour upon its back, and thundered away down the road which they had traversed. Aylward jumped upon his mare, drove his prick spurs into her sides, and galloped after the runaway as hard as he could ride. Thus it came about that in an instant Nigel was shorn of all his little dignity, had lost his two horses, his attendant, and his outfit, and found himself a lonely and unarmed man standing in his shirt and drawers upon the pathway down which the burly figure of the Lord of Pons was slowly advancing.

The knight-errant, whose mind had been filled by the thought of the maiden whom he had left behind at St. Jean—the same whose glove dangled from his helmet— had observed nothing that had occurred. Hence, all that met his eyes was a noble yellow horse, which was tethered by the track, and a small young man, who appeared to be a lunatic, since he had undressed hastily in the heart of the forest, and stood now with an eager anxious face clad in his underlinen amid the scattered *débris* of his garments. Of such a person the high Lord of Pons could take no notice, and so he pursued his inexorable way, his arrogant eyes looking out into the distance and his thoughts set intently upon the maiden of St. Jean. He was dimly aware that the little crazy man in the undershirt ran a long way beside him in his stockings, begging, imploring, and arguing.

" Just one hour, most fair sir, just one hour at the longest, and a poor squire of England shall ever hold himself your debtor ! Do but condescend to rein your horse until my harness comes back to me ! Will you not stoop to show me some small deed of arms ? I implore you, fair sir, to spare me a little of your time and a handstroke or two ere you go upon your way ! "

Lord de Pons motioned impatiently with his gauntleted hand, as one might brush away an importunate fly, but when at last Nigel became desperate in his clamour he thrust his spurs into his great war-horse, and, clashing like a pair of cymbals, he thundered off through the forest. So he rode upon his majestic way, until two days later he was slain by Lord Reginald Cobham in a field near Weybridge.

When after a long chase Aylward secured the spare horse and brought it back, he found his master seated upon a fallen tree, his face buried in his hands and his mind clouded with humiliation and grief. Nothing was said, for the matter was beyond words, and so in moody silence they rode upon their way.

But soon they came upon a scene which drew Nigel's thoughts away from his bitter trouble, for in front of them there rose the towers of a great building with a small grey sloping village around it, and they learned from a passing hind that this was the hamlet and Abbey of Battle. Together they drew rein upon the low ridge and looked down into that valley of death from which even now the reek of blood seems to rise. Down beside that sinister lake and amid those scattered bushes sprinkled over the naked flank of the long ridge was fought that long-drawn struggle between two most noble foes with broad England as the prize of victory. Here, up and down the low hill, hour by hour the grim struggle had waxed and waned, until the Saxon army had died where it stood, king, court, house-carl, and fyrdsman, each in their ranks even as they had fought. And now, after all the stress and toil, the tyranny, the savage revolt, the fierce suppression, God had made His purpose complete, for here were Nigel the Norman and Aylward the Saxon with good-fellowship in their hearts and a common respect in their minds, with the same banner and the same cause, riding forth to do battle for their old mother England.

And now the long ride drew to an end. In front of them was the blue sea, flecked with the white sails of ships. Once more the road passed upwards from the heavy-wooded plain to the springy turf of the chalk downs. Far to the right rose the grim fortalice of Pevensey, squat and powerful, like one great block of rugged stone, the parapet twinkling with steel caps and crowned by the royal banner of England. A flat expanse of reeded marshland lay before them, out of which rose a single wooded hill, crowned with towers, with a bristle of masts rising out of the green plain some distance to the south of it. Nigel looked at it with his hand shading his eyes, and then urged Pommers to a trot. The town was Winchelsea, and there amid that cluster of houses on the hill the gallant Chandos must be awaiting him.

14. *How Nigel chased the Red Ferret*

THEY passed a ferry, wound upward by a curving path, and then, having satisfied a guard of men-at-arms, were admitted through the frowning arch of the Pipewell Gate. There waiting for them, in the middle of the main street, the sun gleaming upon his lemon-coloured beard, and puckering his single eye, stood Chandos himself, his legs apart, his hands behind his back, and a welcoming smile upon his quaint high-nosed face. Behind him a crowd of little boys were gazing with reverent eyes at the famous soldier.

"Welcome, Nigel!" said he, "and you also, good archer! I chanced to be walking on the city wall, and I thought from the colour of your horse that it was indeed you upon the Udimore Road. How have you fared, young squire-errant? Have you held bridges or rescued damsels or slain oppressors on your way from Tilford?"

"Nay, my fair lord, I have accomplished nothing; but I once had hopes——" Nigel flushed at the remembrance.

"I will give you more than hopes, Nigel. I will put you where you can dip both arms to the elbows into danger and honour, where peril will sleep with you at night and rise with you in the morning, and the very air you breathe be laden with it. Are you ready for that, young sir?"

"I can but pray, fair lord, that my spirit will rise to it."

Chandos smiled his approval and laid his thin brown hand on the youth's shoulder.

"Good!" said he. "It is the mute hound which bites the hardest. The babbler is ever the hang-back. Bide with me here, Nigel, and walk upon the ramparts. Archer, do you lead the horses to the Sign of the Broom Pod in the high street, and tell my varlets to see them aboard the cog *Thomas* before nightfall. We sail at the second hour after curfew. Come hither, Nigel, to the crest of the corner turret, for from it I will show you what you have never seen."

It was but a dim and distant white cloud upon the blue water seen far off over the Dungeness Point, and yet the sight of it flushed the young squire's cheeks and sent the blood hot through his veins. It was the fringe of France, that land of chivalry and glory, the stage where name and fame were to be won. With burning eyes he gazed across at it, his heart rejoicing to think that the hour was at hand when he might tread that sacred soil. Then his gaze crossed the immense stretch of the blue sea, dotted over with the sails of fishing-boats, until it rested upon the double harbour beneath packed with vessels of every size and shape, from the pessoners and creyers which plied up and down the coast to the great cogs and galleys which were used either as war-ships or merchantmen as the occasion served. One of them was at that instant passing out to sea, a huge galleass, with trumpets blowing and nakers banging, the flag of Saint George flaunting over the broad purple sail, and the decks sparkling from end to end with steel. Nigel gave a cry of pleasure at the splendour of the sight.

" Aye, lad," said Chandos, " it is the *Trinity of Rye*, the very ship on which I fought at Sluys. Her deck ran blood from stem to stern that day. But turn your eyes this way, I beg you, and tell me if you see aught strange about this town."

Nigel looked down at the noble straight street, at the Roundel Tower, at the fine church of Saint Thomas, and the other fair buildings of Winchelsea.

" It is all new," said he—" church, castle, houses, all are new."

" You are right, fair son. My grandfather can call to mind the time when only the conies lived upon this rock. The town was down yonder by the sea, until one night the waves rose upon it and not a house was left. See, yonder is Rye, huddling also on a hill, the two towns like poor sheep when the waters are out. But down there under the blue water and below the Camber Sand lies the true Winchelsea—tower, cathedral, walls and all, even as my grandfather knew it, when the first Edward was young upon the throne."

For an hour or more Chandos paced upon the ramparts with his young squire at his elbow, and talked to him of his duties and of the secrets and craft of warfare, Nigel drinking in and storing in his memory every word from so revered a teacher. Many a time in after-life, in stress and in danger, he strengthened himself by the memory of that slow walk with the blue sea on one side and the fair town on the other, when the wise soldier and noble-hearted knight poured forth his precept and advice as the master-workman to the apprentice.

" Perhaps, fair son," said he, " you are like so many other lads who ride to the wars, and know so much already that it is waste of breath to advise them ? "

" Nay, my fair lord, I know nothing save that I would fain do my duty and either win honourable advancement or die worshipful on the field."

" You are wise to be humble," said Chandos ; " for indeed he who knows most of war knows best that there is much to learn. As there is a mystery of the rivers and a mystery of woodcraft, even so there is a mystery of war-fare by which battles may be lost and gained ; for all nations are brave, and where the brave meets the brave, it is he who is crafty and war-wise who will win the day. The best hound will run at fault if he be ill laid on, and the best hawk will fly at check if he be badly loosed, and even so the bravest army may go awry if it be ill handled. There are not in Christendom better knights and squires than those of the French, and yet we have had the better of them, for in our Scottish wars and elsewhere we have learned more of this same mystery of which I speak."

" And wherein lies our wisdom, honoured sir ? " asked Nigel. " I also would fain be war-wise, and learn to fight with my wits as well as with my sword."

Chandos shook his head and smiled. " It is in the forest and on the down that you learn to fly the hawk and loose the hound," said he. " So also it is in camp and on the field that the mystery of war can be learned. There only has every great captain come to be its master. To start he must have a cool head, quick to think, soft as wax before his purpose is formed, hard as steel when once he sees it before him. Ever alert he must be, and cautious also, but with judgment to turn his caution into rashness where a large gain may be put against a small stake. An eye for country also, for the trend of the rivers, the slope of the hills, the cover of the woods, and the light green of the bog-land."

Poor Nigel, who had trusted to his lance and to Pommers to break his path to glory, stood aghast at this list of needs.

"Alas!" he cried. "How am I to gain all this?—I, who could scarce learn to read or write, though the good Father Matthew broke a hazel stick a day across my shoulders?"

"You will gain it, fair son, where others have gained it before you. You have that which is the first thing of all, a heart of fire from which other colder hearts may catch a spark. But you must have knowledge also of that which warfare has taught us in olden times. We know, par exemple, that horsemen alone cannot hope to win against good foot-soldiers. Has it not been tried at Courtrai, at Stirling, and again under my own eyes at Crécy, where the chivalry of France went down before our bowmen?"

Nigel stared at him with a perplexed brow. "Fair sir, my heart grows heavy as I hear you. Do you then say that our chivalry can make no head against archers, billmen, and the like?"

"Nay, Nigel, for it has also been very clearly shown that the best foot-soldiers unsupported cannot hold their own against the mailed horsemen."

"To whom, then, is the victory?" asked Nigel.

"To him who can mix his horse and foot, using each to strengthen the other. Apart they are weak. Together they are strong. The archer who can weaken the enemy's line, the horseman who can break it when it is weakened, as was done at Falkirk and Dupplin, there is the secret of our strength. Now, touching this same battle of Falkirk, I pray you for one instant to give it your attention."

With his whip he began to trace a plan of the Scottish battle upon the dust, and Nigel, with knitted brows, was trying hard to muster his small stock of brains, and to profit by the lecture, when their conversation was interrupted by a strange, new arrival.

It was a very stout little man, wheezy and purple with

haste, who scudded down the rampart as if he were blown by the wind, his grizzled hair flying, and his long black gown floating behind him. He was clad in the dress of a respectable citizen, a black jerkin trimmed with sable, a black velvet beaver hat and a white feather. At the sight of Chandos he gave a cry of joy, and quickened his pace, so that when he did at last reach him he could only stand gasping and waving his hands.

" Give yourself time, good Master Wintersole, give yourself time ! " said Chandos, in a soothing voice.

" The papers ! " gasped the little man. " Oh, my Lord Chandos, the papers ! "

" What of the papers, my worthy sir ? "

" I swear by our good patron Saint Leonard, it is no fault of mine ! I had locked them in my coffer. But the lock was forced and the coffer rifled."

A shadow of anger passed over the soldier's keen face.

" How now, Master Mayor ? Pull your wits together, and do not stand there babbling like a three-year child. Do you say that someone hath taken the papers ? "

" It is sooth, fair sir ! Thrice I have been mayor of the town, and fifteen years burgess and jurat, but never once has any public matter gone awry through me. Only last month there came an order from Windsor on a Tuesday for a Friday banquet, a thousand soles, four thousand plaice, two thousand mackerel, five hundred crabs, a thousand lobsters, five thousand whiting——"

" I doubt not, Master Mayor, that you are an excellent fishmonger ; but the matter concerns the papers I gave into your keeping. Where are they ? "

" Taken, fair sir—gone ! "

" And who hath dared to take them ? "

" Alas ! I know not. It was but for as long as you would say an angelus that I left the chamber, and when I came back there was the coffer, broken and empty, upon my table."

" Do you suspect no one ? "

" There was a varlet who hath come with the last few days into my employ. He is not to be found, and I have sent horsemen along both the Udimore Road and that to Rye, that they may seize him. By the help of Saint Leonard they can scarce miss him, for one can tell him a bow-shot off by his hair."

" Is it red ? " asked Chandos, eagerly. " Is it fox-red, and the man a small man pocked with sun spots, and very quick in his movements ? "

" It is the man himself."

Chandos shook his clinched hand with annoyance, and then set off swiftly down the street.

" It is Peter the Red Ferret once more ! " said he. " I knew him of old in France, where he has done us more harm than a company of men-at-arms. He speaks English as he speaks French, and he is of such daring and cunning that nothing is secret from him. In all France there is no more dangerous man, for though he is a gentleman of blood and coat armour, he takes the part of a spy, because it hath the more danger and therefore the more honour."

" But, my fair lord," cried the mayor, as he hurried along, keeping pace with the long strides of the soldier, " I knew that you warned me to take all care of the papers ; but surely there was no matter of great import in it ? It was but to say what stores were to be sent after you to Calais ? "

" Is that not everything ? " cried Chandos, impatiently. " Can you not see, oh foolish Master Wintersole, that the French suspect we are about to make some attempt, and that they have sent Peter the Ferret, as they have sent him many times before, to get tidings of whither we are bound? Now that he knows that the stores are for Calais, then the French near Calais will take his warning, and so the king's whole plan came to nothing."

" Then he will fly by water. We can stop him yet. He has not an hour's start."

" It may be that a boat awaits him at Rye or Hythe ; but it is more like that he has all ready to depart from here. Ah, see yonder! I'll warrant that the Red Ferret is on board!"

Chandos had halted in front of his inn, and now he pointed down to the outer harbour, which lay two miles off across the green plain. It was connected by a long winding canal with the inner dock at the base of the hill, upon which the town was built. Between the two horns formed by the short curving piers a small schooner was running out to sea, dipping and rising before a sharp southerly breeze.

"It is no Winchelsea boat," said the mayor. "She is longer and broader in the beam than ours."

"Horses! bring horses!" cried Chandos. "Come, Nigel, let us go farther into the matter."

A busy crowd of varlets, archers, and men-at-arms swarmed round the gateway of the Sign of the Broom Pod, singing, shouting, and jostling in rough good-fellowship. The sight of the tall thin figure of Chandos brought order among them, and a few minutes later the horses were ready and saddled. A breakneck ride down a steep declivity, and then a gallop of two miles over the sedgy plain carried them to the outer harbour. A dozen vessels were lying there, ready to start for Bordeaux or Rochelle, and the quay was thick with sailors, labourers, and townsmen, and heaped with wine-barrels and wool-packs.

"Who is warden here?" asked Chandos, springing from his horse.

"Badding! Where is Cock Badding? Badding is warden!" shouted the crowd.

A moment later a short swarthy man, bull-necked and deep-chested, pushed through the people. He was clad in rough russet wool with a scarlet cloth tied round his black curly head. His sleeves were rolled up to his shoulders, and his brown arms, all stained with grease and tar, were like two thick gnarled branches from an oaken stump. His savage brown face was fierce and frowning, and was split from chin to temple with the long white wale of an ill-healed wound.

" How now, gentles, will you never wait your turn ? "
he rumbled, in a deep angry voice. " Can you not see
that we are warping the *Rose of Guienne* into midstream
for the ebb-tide ? Is this a time to break in upon us ?
Your goods will go aboard in due season, I promise you ;
so ride back into the town and find such pleasure as you
may, while I and my mates do our work without let or
hindrance."

" It is the gentle Chandos ! " cried someone in the
crowd. " It is the good Sir John."

The rough harbour-master changed his gruffness to
smiles in an instant.

" Nay, Sir John, what would you ? I pray you to
hold me excused if I was short of speech, but we port-
wardens are sore plagued with foolish young lordlings, who
get betwixt us and our work and blame us because we do
not turn an ebb-tide into a flood, or a south wind into a
north. I pray you to tell me how I can serve you."

" That boat ! " said Chandos, pointing to the already
distant sail rising and falling on the waves. "What is it ? "

Cock Badding shaded his keen eyes with his strong
brown hand.

" She has but just gone out," said he. " She is *La
Pucelle*, a small wine-sloop from Gascony, home-bound
and laden with barrel-staves."

" I pray you did any man join at her the last ? "

" Nay, I know not. I saw none."

" But I know," cried a seaman in the crowd. " I was
standing at the wharf-side and was nigh knocked into the
water by a little red-headed fellow, who breathed as though
he had run from the town. Ere I had time to give him a
cuff he had jumped aboard, the ropes were cast off, and
her nose was seaward."

In a few words Chandos made all clear to Badding,
the crowd pressing eagerly round.

" Aye, aye ! " cried a seaman, " the good Sir John is right.
See how she points. It is Picardy and not Gascony that
she will fetch this journey in spite of her wine-staves."

" Then we must lay her aboard ! " cried Cock Badding.
" Come, lads, here is my own *Marie Rose* ready to cast off.
Who's for a trip with a fight at the end of it ? "

There was a rush for the boat ; but the stout little
seaman picked his men. " Go back, Jerry ! Your heart
is good, but you are overfat for the work. You, Luke,
and you, Thomas, and the two Deedes, and William of
Sandgate. You will work the boat. And now we need a
few men of their hands. Do you come, little sir ? "

" I pray you, my dear lord, to let me go ! " cried Nigel.

" Yes, Nigel, you can go, and I will bring your gear
over to Calais this night."

" I will join you there, fair sir, and with the help of
Saint Paul I will bring this Red Ferret with me."

" Aboard, aboard ! Time passes ! " cried Badding, impatiently, while already his seamen were hauling on the
line and raising the mainsail. " Now then, sirrah ! who
are you ? "

It was Aylward who had followed Nigel and was
pushing his way aboard.

" Where my master goes I go also," cried Aylward,
" so stand clear, master-shipman, or you may come by a
hurt."

" By Saint Leonard ! archer," said Cock Badding,
" had I more time I would give you a lesson ere I leave
land. Stand back and give place to others ! "

" Nay, stand back and give place to me ! " cried
Aylward, and seizing Badding round the waist he slung
him into the dock.

There was a cry of anger from the crowd, for Badding
was the hero of all the Cinque Ports and had never yet
met his match in manhood. The epitaph still lingers in
which it was said that he " could never rest until he had
foughten his fill." When, therefore, swimming like a
duck, he reached a rope and pulled himself hand over
hand up to the quay, all stood aghast to see what fell fate
would befall this bold stranger. But Badding laughed
loudly, dashing the salt water from his eyes and hair.

" You have fairly won your place, archer," said he.
" You are the very man for our work. Where is Black
Simon of Norwich ? "

A tall dark young man with a long, stern, lean face
came forward. " I am with you, Cock," said he, " and
I thank you for my place."

" You can come, Hugh Baddlesmere, and you, Hal
Masters, and you, Dicon of Rye. That is enough. Now
off, in God's name, or it will be night ere we can come up
with them ! "

Already the head-sails and the mainsail had been raised,
while a hundred willing hands poled her off from the
wharf. Now the wind caught her ; heeling over, and
quivering with eagerness like an unleashed hound, she
flew through the opening and out into the channel. She
was a famous little schooner, the *Marie Rose* of Winchelsea,
and under her daring owner Cock Badding, half trader
and half pirate, had brought back into port many a rich
cargo taken in mid-channel, and paid for in blood rather
than money. Small as she was, her great speed and the
fierce character of her master had made her a name of
terror along the French coast, and many a bulky East-
lander or Fleming as he passed the narrow seas had
scanned the distant Kentish shore, fearing lest that ill-
omened purple sail with a gold Christopher upon it
should shoot out suddenly from the dim grey cliffs. Now
she was clear of the land, with the wind on her larboard
quarter, every inch of canvas set, and her high sharp bows
smothered in foam, as she dug through the waves.

Cock Badding trod the deck with head erect and jaunty
bearing, glancing up at the swelling sails and then ahead
at the little tilted white triangle, which stood out clear
and hard against the bright blue sky. Behind was the
lowland of the Camber marshes, with the bluffs of Rye
and Winchelsea, and the line of cliffs behind them. On
the larboard rose the great white walls of Folkestone and
of Dover, and far on the distant sky-line the grey shimmer
of those French cliffs for which the fugitives were making.

" By Saint Paul ! " cried Nigel, looking with eager eyes over the tossing waters, " it seems to me, Master Badding, that already we draw in upon them."

The master measured the distance with his keen steady gaze, and then looked up at the sinking sun. " We have still four hours of daylight," said he ; " but if we do not lay her aboard ere darkness falls she will save herself, for the nights are as black as a wolf's mouth, and if she alter her course I know not how we may follow her."

" Unless, indeed, you might guess to which port she was bound and reach it before her."

" Well thought of, little master ! " cried Badding. " If the news be for the French outside Calais, then Amble-teuse would be nearest to Saint Omer. But, my sweeting sails three paces to that lubber's two, and if the wind holds we shall have time and to spare. How now, archer? You do not seem so eager as when you made your way aboard this boat by slinging me into the sea."

Aylward sat on the upturned keel of a skiff which lay upon the deck. He groaned sadly and held his green face between his two hands.

" I would gladly sling you into the sea once more, master-shipman," said he, " if by so doing I could get off this most accursed vessel of thine. Or if you would wish to have your turn, then I would thank you if you would lend me a hand over the side, for indeed, I am but a useless weight upon your deck. Little did I think that Samkin Aylward could be turned into a weakling by an hour of salt water. Alas the day that ever my foot wandered from the good red heather of Crooksbury ! "

Cock Badding laughed loud and long. " Nay, take it not to heart, archer," he cried ; " for better men than you or I have groaned upon this deck. The prince himself with ten of his chosen knights crossed with me once, and eleven sadder faces I never saw. Yet within a month they had shown at Crécy that they were no weaklings, as you will do also, I dare swear, when the time comes. Keep that thick head of thine down upon the planks, and all will be well anon. But we raise her, we raise her with every blast of the wind ! "

It was indeed evident, even to the inexperienced eyes of Nigel, that the *Marie Rose* was closing in swiftly upon the stranger. She was a heavy, bluff-bowed, broad-sterned vessel which laboured clumsily through the seas. The swift, fierce little Winchelsea boat swooping and hissing through the waters behind her was like some keen hawk whizzing down wind at the back of a flapping heavy-bodied duck. Half an hour before *La Pucelle* had been a distant patch of canvas. Now they could see the black hull, and soon the cut of her sails and the lines of her bulwarks. There were at least a dozen men upon her deck, and the twinkle of weapons from among them showed that they were preparing to resist. Cock Badding began to muster his own forces.

He had a crew of seven rough, hardy mariners, who had been at his back in many a skirmish. They were armed with short swords, but Cock Badding carried a weapon peculiar to himself, a twenty-pound blacksmith's hammer, the memory of which, as " Badding's cracker," still lingers in the Cinque Ports. Then there were the eager Nigel, the melancholy Aylward, Black Simon, who was a tried swordsman, and three archers, Baddlesmere, Masters, and Dicon of Rye, all veterans of the French War. The numbers in the two vessels might be about equal ; but Badding as he glanced at the bold harsh faces which looked to him for orders had little fear for the result.

Glancing round, however, he saw something which was more dangerous to his plans than the resistance of the enemy, The wind, which had become more fitful and feebler, now fell suddenly away, until the sails hung limp and straight above them. A belt of calm lay along the horizon, and the waves around had smoothed down into a long oily swell on which the two little vessels rose and fell. The great boom of the *Marie Rose* rattled and jarred with every lurch, and the high thin prow pointed skyward one instant and seaward the next in a way that drew fresh groans from the unhappy Aylward. In vain Cock Badding pulled on his sheets and tried hard to husband every little wandering gust which ruffled for an instant the sleek rollers. The French master was as adroit a sailor, and his boom swung round also as each breath of wind came up from astern.

At last even these fitful puffs died finally away, and a cloudless sky overhung a glassy sea. The sun was almost upon the horizon behind Dungeness Point, and the whole western heaven was bright with the glory of the sunset, which blended sea and sky in one blaze of ruddy light. Like rollers of molten gold, the long swell heaved up Channel from the great ocean beyond. In the midst of the immense beauty and peace of nature the two little dark specks with the white sail and the purple rose and fell, so small upon the vast shining bosom of the waters, and yet so charged with all the unrest and the passion of life.

The experienced eye of the seaman told him that it was hopeless to expect a breeze before nightfall. He looked across at the Frenchman, which lay less than a quarter of a mile ahead, and shook his gnarled fist at the line of heads which could be seen looking back over her stern. One of them waved a white kerchief in derision, and Cock Badding swore a bitter oath at the sight.

" By Saint Leonard of Winchelsea," he cried, " I will rub my side up against her yet ! Out with the skiff, lads, and two of you to the oars. Make fast the line to the mast, Will. Do you go in the boat, Hugh, and I'll make the second. Now, if we bend our backs to it we may have them ere yet night cover them."

The little skiff was swiftly lowered over the side and the slack end of the cable fastened to the after thwart. Cock Badding and his comrades pulled as if they would snap their oars, and the little vessel began slowly to lurch forward over the rollers. But the next moment a larger skiff had splashed over the side of the Frenchman, and no less than four seamen were hard at work under her bows. If the *Marie Rose* advanced a yard the Frenchman was going two. Again Cock Badding raved and shook his fist. He clambered aboard, his face wet with sweat and dark with anger.

" Curse them ! they have the best of us ! " he cried. " I can do no more. Sir John has lost his papers, for indeed now that night is at hand I can see no way in which we can gain them."

Nigel had leaned against the bulwark during these events, watching with keen attention the doings of the sailors, and praying alternately to Saint Paul, Saint George and Saint Thomas for a slant of wind which would put them alongside their enemy. He was silent ; but his hot heart was simmering within him. His spirit had risen even above the discomfort of the sea, and his mind was too absorbed in his mission to have a thought for that which had laid Aylward flat upon the deck. He had never doubted that Cock Badding in one way or another would accomplish his end, but when he heard this speech of despair he bounded off the bulwark and stood before the seaman with his face flushed and all his soul afire.

" By Saint Paul ! master-shipman," he cried, " we should never hold up our heads in honour if we did not go farther into the matter ! Let us do some small deed this night upon the water, or let us never see land again, for indeed we could not wish fairer prospect of winning honourable advancement."

" With your leave, little master, you speak like a fool," said the gruff seaman. " You and all your kind are as children when once the blue water is beneath you. Can you not see that there is no wind, and that the Frenchman can warp her as swiftly as we ? What then would you do ? "

Nigel pointed to the boat which towed astern. " Let us venture forth in her," said he, " and let us take this ship or die worshipful in the attempt."

His bold and fiery words found their echo in the brave

rough hearts around him. There was a deep-chested shout from both archers and seamen. Even Aylward sat up, with a wan smile upon his green face.

But Cock Badding shook his head. " I have never met the man who could lead where I would not follow," said he ; " but by Saint Leonard ! this is a mad business, and I should be a fool if I were to risk my men and my ship. Bethink you, little master, that the skiff can hold only five, though you load her to the water's edge. If there is a man yonder, there are fourteen, and you have to climb their side from the boat. What chance would you have ? Your boat stove in and you in the water—there is the end of it. No man of mine goes on such a fool's errand, and so I swear ! "

" Then, Master Badding, I must crave the loan of your skiff, for by Saint Paul ! the good Lord Chandos' papers are not to be so lightly lost. If no one else will come, then I will go alone."

The shipman smiled at the words ; but the smile died away from his lips when Nigel, with features set like ivory and eyes as hard as steel, pulled on the rope so as to bring the skiff under the counter. It was very clear that he would do even as he said. At the same time Aylward raised his bulky form from the deck, leaned for a moment against the bulwarks, and then tottered aft to his master's side.

" Here is one that will go with you," said he, " or he would never dare show his face to the girls of Tilford again. Come, archers, let us leave these salt herrings in their pickle tub and try our luck out on the water."

The three archers at once ranged themselves on the same side as their comrade. They were bronzed, bearded men, short in stature, as were most Englishmen of that day, but hardy, strong, and skilled with their weapons. Each drew his string from its waterproof case and bent the huge arc of his war-bow as he fitted it into the nocks.

" Now, master, we are at your back," said they, as they pulled and tightened their sword-belts.

But already Cock Badding had been carried away by the hot lust of battle, and had thrown aside every fear and doubt which had clouded him. To see a fight and not to be in it was more than he could bear.

" Nay, have it your own way ! " he cried, " and may Saint Leonard help us, for a madder venture I have never seen ! And yet it may be worth a trial. But if it be done let me have the handling of it, little master, for you know no more of a boat than I do of a war-horse. The skiff can bear five and not a man more. Now, who will come ? "

They had all caught fire, and there was not one who would be left out.

Badding picked up his hammer. " I will come myself," said he, " and you also, little master, since it is your hot head that has planned it. Then there is Black Simon, the best sword of the Cinque Ports. Two archers can pull on the oars, and it may be that they can pick off two or three of these Frenchmen before we close with them. Hugh Baddlesmere, and you, Dicon of Rye—into the boat with you ! "

" What ? " cried Aylward. " Am I to be left behind ? I, who am the squire's own man ? Ill fare the bowman who comes betwixt me and yonder boat ! "

" Nay, Aylward," said his master, " I order that you stay, for indeed you are a sick man."

" But now that the waves have sunk I am myself again. Nay, fair sir, I pray that you will not leave me behind."

" You must needs take the space of a better man ; for what do you know of the handling of a boat," said Badding, shortly. " No more fool's talk, I pray you, for the night will soon fail. Stand aside ! "

Aylward looked hard at the French boat. " I could swim ten times up and down Frensham pond," said he, " and it will be strange if I cannot go as far as that. By these finger-bones, Samkin Aylward may be there as soon as you ! "

The little boat with its five occupants pushed off from the side of the schooner, and dipping and rising, made its slow way towards the Frenchman. Badding and one archer had single oars, the second archer was in the prow, while Black Simon and Nigel huddled into the stern with the water lapping and hissing at their very elbows. A shout of defiance rose from the Frenchman, and they stood in a line along the side of their vessel shaking their fists and waving their weapons. Already the sun was level with Dungeness, and the grey of evening was blurring sky and water into one dim haze. A great silence hung over the broad expanse of nature, and no sound broke it save the dip and splash of the oars and the slow deep surge of the boat upon the swell. Behind them their comrades of the *Marie Rose* stood motionless and silent, watching their progress with eager eyes.

They were near enough now to have a good look at the Frenchmen. One was a big swarthy man with a long black beard. He had a red cap and an axe over his shoulder. There were ten other hardy-looking fellows, all of them well armed, and there were three who seemed to be boys.

" Shall we try a shaft upon them ? " asked Hugh Baddlesmere. " They are well within our bowshot."

" Only one of you can shoot at a time, for you have no footing," said Badding. " With one foot in the prow and one over the thwart you will get your stance. Do what you may, and then we will close in upon them."

The archer balanced himself in the rolling boat with the deftness of a man who has been trained upon the sea, for he was born and bred in the Cinque Ports. Carefully he nocked his arrow, strongly he drew it, steadily he loosed it, but the boat swooped at the instant, and it buried itself in the waves. The second passed over the little ship, and the third stuck in her black side. Then in quick succession—so quick that two shafts were often in the air at the same instant—he discharged a dozen arrows, most of which just cleared the bulwarks and dropped upon the deck. There was a cry on the Frenchman, and the heads vanished from the side.

"Enough!" cried Badding. "One is down, and it may be two. Close in, close in, in God's name, before they rally!"

He and the other bent to their oars; but at the same instant there was a sharp zip in the air and a hard clear sound like a stone striking a wall. Baddlesmere clapped his hand to his head, groaned and fell forward out of the boat, leaving a swirl of blood upon the surface. A moment later the same fierce hiss ended in a loud wooden crash, and a short, thick crossbow-bolt was buried deep in the boat.

"Close in, close in!" roared Badding, tugging at his oar. "Saint George for England! Saint Leonard for Winchelsea! Close in!"

But again that fatal crossbow twanged. Dicon of Rye fell back with a shaft through his shoulder. "God help me, I can no more!" said he.

Badding seized the oar from his hand; but it was only to sweep the boat's head round and pull her back to the *Marie Rose*. The attack had failed.

"What now, master-shipman?" cried Nigel. "What has befallen to stop us? Surely the matter does not end here?"

"Two down out of five," said Badding, "and twelve at the least against us. The odds are too long, little master. Let us go back at least, fill up once more, and raise a mantelet against the bolts, for they have an arbalest which shoots both straight and hard. But what we do we must do quickly, for the darkness falls apace."

Their repulse had been hailed by wild yells of delight from the Frenchmen, who danced with joy and waved their weapons madly over their heads. But before their rejoicings had finished they saw the little boat creeping out once more from the shadow of the *Marie Rose*, a great wooden screen in her bows to protect her from the arrows. Without a pause she came straight and fast for her enemy.

The wounded archer had been put on board, and Aylward would have had his place had Nigel been able to see him upon the deck. The third archer, Hal Masters, had sprung in, and one of the seamen, Wat Finnis of Hythe. With their hearts hardened to conquer or to die, the five ran alongside the Frenchman and sprang upon her deck. At the same instant a great iron weight crashed through the bottom of their skiff, and their feet had hardly left her before she was gone. There was no hope and no escape save victory.

The crossbowman stood under the mast, his terrible weapon at his shoulder, the steel string stretched taut, the heavy bolt shining upon the nut. One life at least he would claim out of this little band. Just for one instant too long did he dwell upon his aim, shifting from the seaman to Cock Badding, whose formidable appearance showed him to be the better prize. In that second of time Hal Masters' string twanged and his long arrow sped through the arbalester's throat. He dropped on the deck, with blood pouring from his mouth.

A moment later Nigel's sword and Badding's hammer had each claimed a victim and driven back the rush of assailants. The five were safe upon the deck, but it was hard for them to keep a footing there. The French seamen, Bretons and Normans, were stout, powerful fellows, armed with axes and swords, fierce fighters and brave men. They swarmed round the little band, attacking them from all sides. Black Simon felled the black-bearded French captain, and at the same instant was cut over the head and lay with his scalp open upon the deck. The seaman Wat of Hythe was killed by a crushing blow from an axe. Nigel was struck down, but was up again like a flash, and drove his sword through the man who had felled him.

But Badding, Masters the archer, and he had been hustled back to the bulwark and were barely holding their own from minute to minute against the fierce crowd who assailed them, when an arrow coming apparently from the

sea struck the foremost Frenchman to the heart. A
moment later a boat dashed up alongside and four more
men from the *Marie Rose* scrambled on to the blood-
stained deck. With one fierce rush the remaining Frenchmen were struck down or were seized by their assailants.
Nine prostrate men upon the deck showed how fierce had
been the attack, how desperate the resistance.

Badding leaned panting upon his blood-clotted hammer. " By Saint Leonard ! " he cried. " I thought that
this little master had been the death of us all. God wot
you were but just in time, and how you came I know not.
This archer has had a hand in it, by the look of him."

Aylward, still pale from his sea-sickness and dripping
from head to foot with water, had been the first man in
the rescue party.

Nigel looked at him in amazement. " I sought you
aboard the ship, Aylward, but I could not lay eyes on
you," said he.

" It was because I was in the water, fair sir, and by
my hilt ! it suits my stomach better than being on it," he
answered. " When you first set forth I swam behind you,
for I saw that the Frenchman's boat hung by a rope, and
I thought that while you kept him in play I might gain
it. I had reached it when you were driven back, so I hid
behind it in the water and said my prayers as I have not
said them for many a day. Then you came again, and no
one had an eye for me, so I clambered into it, cut the rope,
took the oars which I found there, and brought her back
for more men."

" By Saint Paul ! you have acted very wisely and
well," said Nigel, " and I think that of all of us it is you
who have won most honour this day. But of all these
men dead and alive I see none who resembles that Red
Ferret whom my Lord Chandos has described and who has
worked such despite upon us in the past. It would indeed be an evil chance if he has, in spite of all our pains,
made his way to France in some other boat."

" That we shall soon find out," said Badding. " Come

with me, and we will search the ship from truck to keel ere he escapes us."

There was a scuttle at the base of the mast which led down into the body of the vessel, and the Englishmen were approaching this when a strange sight brought them to a stand. A round brazen head had appeared in the square dark opening. An instant afterward a pair of shining shoulders followed. Then slowly the whole figure of a man in complete plate-armour emerged on the deck. In his gauntleted hand he carried a heavy steel mace. With this uplifted he moved towards his enemies, silent save for the ponderous clank of his footfall. It was an inhuman, machine-like figure, menacing and terrible, devoid of all expression, slow-moving, inexorable, and awesome.

A sudden wave of terror passed over the English seamen. One of them tried to pass and get behind the brazen man, but he was pinned against the side by a quick movement and his brains dashed out by a smashing blow from the heavy mace. Wild panic seized the others, and they rushed back to the boat. Aylward strung an arrow, but his bowstring was damp and the shaft rang loudly upon the shining breastplate and glanced off into the sea. Masters struck the brazen head with a sword, but the blade snapped without injuring the helmet, and an instant later the bowman was stretched senseless on the deck. The seamen shrank from this terrible silent creature and huddled in the stern, all the fight gone out of them.

Again he raised his mace and was advancing on the helpless crowd where the brave were encumbered and hampered by the weaklings, when Nigel shook himself clear and bounded forward into the open, his sword in his hand and a smile of welcome upon his lips.

The sun had set, and one long pink gash across the western Channel was closing swiftly into the dull greys of early night. Above, a few stars began to faintly twinkle ; yet the twilight was still bright enough for an observer to see every detail of the scene ; the *Marie Rose*, dipping and rising on the long rollers astern ; the broad French boat with its white deck blotched with blood and littered with bodies ; the group of men in the stern, some trying to advance and some seeking to escape—all a confused, disorderly, struggling rabble.

Then between them and the mast the two figures : the armed shining man of metal, with hand upraised, watchful, silent, motionless, and Nigel, bareheaded and crouching, with quick foot, eager eyes, and fearless, happy face, moving this way and that, in and out, his sword flashing like a gleam of light as he sought at all points for some opening in the brazen shell before him.

It was clear to the man in armour that if he could but pen his antagonist in a corner he would beat him down without fail. But it was not to be done. The unhampered man had the advantage of speed. With a few quick steps he could always glide to either side and escape the clumsy rush. Aylward and Badding had sprung out to Nigel's assistance ; but he shouted to them to stand back, with such authority and anger in his voice that their weapons dropped to their sides. With staring eyes and set features they stood watching that unequal fight.

Once it seemed that all was over with the squire, for in springing back from his enemy he tripped over one of the bodies which strewed the deck and fell flat upon his back, but with a swift wriggle he escaped the heavy blow which thundered down upon him, and springing to his feet he bit deeply into the Frenchman's helmet with a sweeping cut in return. Again the mace fell, and this time Nigel had not quite cleared himself. His sword was beaten down and the blow fell partly upon his left shoulder. He staggered, and once more the iron club whirled upward to dash him to the ground.

Quick as a flash it passed through his mind that he could not leap beyond its reach. But he might get within it. In an instant he had dropped his sword, and springing in he had seized the brazen man round the waist. The mace was shortened and the handle jobbed down once upon the bare flaxen head. Then, with a sonorous clang, and a yell of delight from the spectators, Nigel, with one mighty wrench, tore his enemy from the deck and hurled him down upon his back. His own head was whirling and he felt that his senses were slipping away, but already his hunting knife was out and pointing through the slit in the brazen helmet.

" Give yourself up, fair sir ! " said he.

" Never to fishermen and to archers. I am a gentleman of coat-armour. Kill me ! "

" I also am a gentleman of coat-armour. I promise you quarter."

" Then, sir, I surrender myself to you."

The dagger tinkled down upon the deck. Seamen and archers ran forward, to find Nigel half senseless upon his face. They drew him off, and a few deft blows struck off the helmet of his enemy. A head, sharp-featured, freckled and foxy-red, disclosed itself beneath it. Nigel raised himself on his elbow for an instant.

" You are the Red Ferret ? " said he.

" So my enemies call me," said the Frenchman, with a smile. " I rejoice, sir, that I have fallen to so valiant and honourable a gentleman."

" I thank you, fair sir," said Nigel, feebly. " I also rejoice that I have encountered so debonair a person, and I shall ever bear in mind the pleasure which I have had from our meeting."

So saying he laid his bleeding head upon his enemy's brazen front and sank into a dead faint.

15. *How the Red Ferret came to Cosford*

THE old chronicler in his *Gestes du Sieur Nigel* has bewailed his broken narrative, which rose from the fact that out of thirty-one years of warfare no less than seven were spent by his hero at one time or another in the recovery from his wounds or from those illnesses which arose from privation and fatigue. Here at the very threshold of his career, on the eve of a great enterprise, this very fate befell him.

Stretched upon a couch in a low-roofed and ill-furnished chamber, which looks down from under the machicolated corner turret upon the inner court of the Castle of Calais, he lay half-unconscious and impotent, while great deeds were doing under his window. Wounded in three places, and with his head splintered by the sharp pommel of the Ferret's mace, he hovered between life and death, his shattered body drawing him downward, his youthful spirit plucking him up.

As in some strange dream he was aware of that deed of arms within the courtyard below. Dimly it came back to his memory afterwards, the sudden startled shout, the crash of metal, the slamming of great gates, the roar of many voices, the clang, clang, clang, as of fifty lusty smiths upon their anvils, and then at last the dwindling of the hubbub, the low groans and sudden shrill cries to the saints, the measured murmur of many voices, the heavy clanking of armoured feet.

Sometime in that fell struggle he must have drawn his weakened body as far as the narrow window, and hanging to the iron bars have looked down on the wild scene beneath him. In the red glare of torches held from windows and from roof he saw the rush and swirl of men below, the ruddy light showing back from glowing brass and gleaming steel. As a wild vision it came to him afterwards, the beauty and the splendour, the flying lambrequins, the jewelled crests, the blazonry and richness of surcoat and of shield, where sable and gules, argent and vair, in every pattern of saltire, bend or chevron, glowed beneath him like a drift of many-coloured blossoms, tossing, sinking, stooping into shadow, springing into light. There glared the blood-red gules of Chandos, and he saw the tall figure of his master, a thunderbolt of war, raging in the van. There too were the three black chevrons on the golden shield which marked the noble Manny.

That strong swordsman must surely be the royal Edward himself, since only he and the black-armoured swift-footed youth at his side were marked by no symbol of heraldry.

" Manny ! Manny ! George for England ! " rose the deep-throated bay, and ever the gallant counter-cry : " A Chargny ! A Chargny ! Saint Denis for France ! " thundered amid the clash and thudding of the battle.

Such was the vague whirling memory still lingering in Nigel's mind when at last the mists cleared away from it and he found himself weak but clear on the low couch in the corner turret. Beside him, crushing lavender between his rough fingers and strewing it over floor and sheets, was Aylward the archer. His longbow leaned at the foot of the bed, and his steel cap was balanced on the top of it, while he himself, sitting in his shirt-sleeves, fanned off the flies and scattered the fragrant herbs over his helpless master.

" By my hilt ! " he cried, with a sudden shout, every tooth in his head gleaming with joy, " I thank the Virgin and all the saints for this blessed sight ! I had not dared to go back to Tilford had I lost you. Three weeks have you lain there and babbled like a babe, but now I see in your eyes that you are your own man again."

" I have indeed had some small hurt," said Nigel, feebly ; " but it is shame and sorrow that I should lie here if there is work for my hands. Whither go you, archer ? "

" To tell the good Sir John that you are mending."

" Nay, bide with me a little longer, Aylward. I can call to mind all that has passed. There was a bickering of small boats, was there not, and I chanced upon a most worthy person and exchanged handstrokes with him ? He was my prisoner, was he not ? "

" He was, fair sir."

" And where is he now ? "

" Below in the castle."

A smile stole over Nigel's pale face. " I know what I will do with him," said he.

" I pray you to rest, fair sir," said Aylward, anxiously.
" The king's own leech saw you this morning, and he said
that if the bandage was torn from your head you would
surely die."

" Nay, good archer, I will not move. But tell me
what befell upon the boat ? "

" There is little to tell, fair sir. Had this Ferret not
been his own squire and taken so long a time to don his
harness it is likely that they would have had the better of
us. He did not reach the battle till his comrades were
on their backs. Him we took to the *Marie Rose*, because
he was your man. The others were of no worth, so we
threw them into the sea."

" The quick and the dead ? "

" Every man of them."

" It was an evil deed."

Aylward shrugged his shoulders. " I tried to save
one boy," said he ; " but Cock Badding would not have
it, and he had Black Simon and the others at his back.
' It is the custom of the Narrow Seas,' said they : ' To-
day for them ; to-morrow for us.' Then they tore him
from his hold and cast him screaming over the side. By
my hilt ! I have no love for the sea and its customs, so
I care not if I never set foot on it again when it has once
borne me back to England."

" Nay, there are great happenings upon the sea, and
many worthy people to be found upon ships," said Nigel.
" In all parts, if one goes far enough upon the water, one
would find those whom it would be joy to meet. If one
crosses over the Narrow Sea, as we have done, we come on
the French who are so needful to us ; for how else would
we win worship ? Or if you go south, then in time one
may hope to come to the land of the unbelievers, where
there is fine skirmishing and much honour for him who
will venture his person. Bethink you, archer, how fair a
life it must be when one can ride forth in search of
advancement with some hope of finding many debonair
cavaliers upon the same quest, and then if one be over-

borne one has died for the faith, and the gates of heaven
are open before you. So also the sea to the north is a
help to him who seeks honour, for it leads to the country
of the Eastlanders and to those parts where the heathen
still dwell who turn their faces from the blessed Gospel.
There also a man might find some small deeds to do, and
by Saint Paul ! Aylward, if the French hold the truce and
the good Sir John permits us, I would fain go down into
those parts. The sea is a good friend to the cavalier, for
it takes him where he may fulfil his vows."

Aylward shook his head, for his memories were too
recent ; but he said nothing, because at this instant the
door opened and Chandos entered. With joy in his face
he stepped forward to the couch and took Nigel's hand in
his. Then he whispered a word in Aylward's ear, who
hurried from the room.

" *Pardieu !* this is a good sight," said the knight. " I
trust that you will soon be on your feet again."

" I crave your pardon, my honoured lord, that I have
been absent from your side," said Nigel.

" In truth my heart was sore for you, Nigel ; for you
have missed such a night as comes seldom in any man's
life. All went even as we had planned. The postern
gate was opened, and a party made their way in ; but we
awaited them, and all were taken or slain. But the
greater part of the French had remained without upon the
plain of Nieullet, so we took horse and went out against
them. When we drew near them they were surprised,
but they made good cheer among themselves, calling out
to each other : ' If we fly we lose all. It is better to fight
on, in the hopes that the day may be ours.' This was
heard by our people in the van, who cried out to them :
' By Saint George ! you speak truth. Evil befall him
who thinks of flying ! ' So they held their ground like
worthy people for the space of an hour, and there were
many there whom it is always good to meet : Sir Geoffrey
himself, and Sir Pepin de Werre, with Sir John de Landas,
old Ballieul of the Yellow Tooth, and his brother Hector

the Leopard. But above all Sir Eustace de Ribeaumont was at great pains to meet us worthily, and he was at handstrokes with the king for a long time. Then, when we had slain or taken them all, the prisoners were brought to a feast which was ready for them, and the knights of England waited upon them at the table and made good cheer with them. And all this, Nigel, we owe to you."

The squire flushed with pleasure at the words. " Nay, most honoured lord, it was but a small thing which I have been able to do. But I thank God and our Lady that I have done some service, since it has pleased you to take me with you to the wars. Should it chance——"

But the words were cut short upon Nigel's lips, and he lay back with amazed eyes staring from his pallid face. The door of his little chamber had opened, and who was this, the tall, stately man with the noble presence, the high forehead, the long, handsome face, the dark, brooding eyes —who but the noble Edward of England ?

" Ha, my little cock of Tilford Bridge, I still bear you in mind," said he. " Right glad I was to hear that you had found your wits again, and I trust that I have not helped to make you take leave of them once more."

Nigel's stare of astonishment had brought a smile to the king's lips. Now the squire stammered forth some halting words of gratitude at the honour done to him.

" Nay, not a word," said the king. " But in sooth it is a joy to my heart to see the son of my old comrade Eustace Loring carrying himself so bravely. Had this boat got before us with news of our coming, then all our labour had been in vain, and no Frenchman ventured to Calais that night. But, above all, I thank you for that you have delivered into my hands one whom I had vowed to punish in that he has caused us more scathe by fouler means than any living man. Twice have I sworn that Peter the Red Ferret shall hang, for all his noble blood and coat-armour, if ever he should fall into my hands. Now at last his time has come ; but I would not put him to death until you, who had taken him, could be there to see it done. Nay, thank me not, for I could do no less, seeing that it is to you that I owe him."

But it was not thanks which Nigel was trying to utter. It was hard to frame his words, and yet they must be said.

" Sire," he murmured, " it ill becomes me to cross your royal will——"

The dark Plantagenet wrath gathered upon the king's high brow and gloomed in his fierce, deep-set eyes.

" By God's dignity ! no man has ever crossed it yet and lived unscathed. How now, young sir, what mean such words, to which we are little wont ? Have a care, for this is no light thing which you venture."

" Sire," said Nigel, " in all matters in which I am a free man I am ever your faithful liege, but some things there are which may not be done."

" How ? " cried the king. " In spite of my will ? "

" In spite of your will, sire," said Nigel, sitting up on his couch, with white face and blazing eyes.

" By the Virgin ! " the angry king thundered, " we are come to a pretty pass ! You have been held too long at home, young man. The overstabled horse will kick. The unweathered hawk will fly at check. See to it, Master Chandos ! He is thine to break, and I hold you to it that you break him. And what is it that Edward of England may not do, Master Loring ? "

Nigel faced the king with a face as grim as his own. " You may not put to death the Red Ferret."

" *Pardieu !* And why ? "

" Because he is not thine to slay, sire. Because he is mine. Because I promised him his life, and it is not for you, king though you be, to constrain a man of gentle blood to break his plighted word and lose his honour."

Chandos laid his soothing hand upon his squire's shoulder.

" Excuse him, sire ; he is weak from his wounds," said he. " Perhaps we have stayed over-long, for the leech has ordered repose."

But the angry king was not easily to be appeased. " I

am not wont to be so browbeat," said he, hotly. "This is your squire, Master John. How comes it that you can stand there and listen to his pert talk, and say no word to chide him? Is this how you guide your household? Have you not taught him that every promise given is subject to the king's consent, and that with him only lie the springs of life and death? If he is sick, you, at least, are hale. Why stand you there in silence?"

"My liege," said Chandos, gravely, "I have served you for over a score of years, and have shed my blood through as many wounds in your cause, so that you should not take my words amiss. But indeed, I should feel myself to be no true man if I did not tell you that my Squire Nigel, though perchance he has spoken more bluntly than becomes him, is none the less right in this matter, and that you are wrong. For bethink you, sire——"

"Enough!" cried the king, more furious than ever. "Like master, like man, and I might have known why it is that this saucy squire dares to bandy words with his sovereign lord. He does but give out what he hath taken in. John, John, you grow overbold. But this I tell you, and you also, young man, that as God is my help, ere the sun has set this night the Red Ferret will hang as a warning to all spies and traitors from the highest tower of Calais, that every ship upon the Narrow Seas, and every man for ten miles round may see him as he swings and know how heavy is the hand of the English king. Do you bear it in mind, lest you also may feel its weight!" With a glare like an angry lion he walked from the room, and the iron-clamped door clanged loudly behind him.

Chandos and Nigel looked ruefully at each other. Then the knight patted his squire upon his bandaged head.

"You have carried yourself right well, Nigel. I could not wish for better. Fear not. All will be well."

"My fair and honoured lord," cried Nigel, "I am heavy at heart, for indeed I could do no other, and yet I have brought trouble upon you."

"Nay, the clouds will soon pass. If he does indeed

slay this Frenchman, you have done all that lay within your power, and your mind may rest easy."

" I pray that it will rest easy in Paradise," said Nigel ; " for at the hour that I hear that I am dishonoured and my prisoner slain, I tear this bandage from my head and so end all things. I will not live when once my word is broken."

" Nay, fair son, you take this thing too heavily," said Chandos, with a grave face. " When a man has done all he may there remains no dishonour ; but the king hath a kind heart for all his hot head, and it may be that if I see him I will prevail upon him. Bethink you how he swore to hang the six burghers of this very town, and yet he pardoned them. So keep a high heart, fair son, and I will come with good news ere evening."

For three hours, as the sinking sun traced the shadow higher and ever higher upon the chamber wall, Nigel tossed feverishly upon his couch, his ears straining for the foot-fall of Aylward or of Chandos, bringing news of the fate of the prisoner. At last the door flew open, and there before him stood the one man whom he least expected, and yet would most gladly have seen. It was the Red Ferret himself, free and joyous.

With swift furtive steps he was across the room and on his knees beside the couch, kissing the pendent hand. " You have saved me, most noble sir ! " he cried. " The gallows was fixed and the rope slung, when the good Lord Chandos told the king that you would die by your own hand if I were slain. ' Curse this mule-headed squire ! ' he cried. ' In God's name let him have his prisoner, and let him do what he will with him so long as he troubles me no more ! ' So here I have come, fair sir, to ask you what I shall do."

" I pray you to sit beside me and be at your ease," said Nigel. " In a few words I will tell you what I would have you do. Your armour I will keep that I may have some remembrance of my good fortune in meeting so valiant a gentleman. We are of a size, and I make little doubt that I can wear it. Of ransom I would ask a thousand crowns."

" Nay, nay ! " cried the Ferret. " It would be a sad thing if a man of my position was worth less than five thousand."

" A thousand will suffice, fair sir, to pay my charges for the war. You will not again play the spy, nor do us harm until the truce is broken."

" That I will swear."

" And lastly there is a journey that you shall make."

The Frenchman's face lengthened. " Where you order I must go," said he ; " but I pray you that it is not to the Holy Land."

" Nay," said Nigel ; " but it is to a land which is holy to me. You will make your way back to Southampton."

" I know it well. I helped to burn it down some years ago."

" I rede you to say nothing of that matter when you get there. You will then journey as though to London until you come to a fair town named Guildford."

" I have heard of it. The king hath a hunt there."

" The same. You will then ask for a house named Cosford, two leagues from the town on the side of a long hill."

" I will bear it in mind."

" At Cosford you will see a good knight named Sir John Buttesthorn, and you will ask to have speech with his daughter, the Lady Mary."

" I will do so ; and what shall I say to the Lady Mary, who lives at Cosford on the slope of a long hill two leagues, from the fair town of Guildford ? "

" Say only that I sent my greeting, and that Saint Catharine has been my friend—only that and nothing more. And now leave me, I pray you, for my head is weary and I would fain have sleep."

Thus it came about that a month later on the eve of the Feast of Saint Matthew, the Lady Mary, as she walked from Cosford gates, met with a strange horseman, richly clad, a serving-man behind him, looking shrewdly about him with quick blue eyes, which twinkled from a red and freckled face. At sight of her he doffed his hat and reined his horse.

" This house should be Cosford," said he. " Are you by chance the Lady Mary who dwells there ? "

The lady bowed her proud dark head.

" Then," said he, " Squire Nigel Loring sends you greeting and tells you that Saint Catharine has been his friend." Then, turning to his servant, he cried : " Heh, Raoul, our task is done ! Your master is a free man once more. Come, lad, come, the nearest port to France ! Holà ! Holà ! Holà ! And so without a word more the two, master and man, set spurs to their horses and galloped like madmen down the long slope of Hindhead, until as she looked after them they were but two dark dots in the distance, waist high in the ling and the bracken.

She turned back to the house, a smile upon her face. Nigel had sent her greeting. A Frenchman had brought it. His bringing it had made him a free man. And Saint Catharine had been Nigel's friend. It was at her shrine that he had sworn that three deeds should be done ere he should set eyes upon her again. In the privacy of her room the Lady Mary sank upon her prie-dieu and poured forth the thanks of her heart to the Virgin that one deed was accomplished ; but even as she did so her joy was overcast by the thought of those two others which lay before him.

16. *How the King's Court feasted in Calais Castle*

IT was a bright sunshiny morning when Nigel found himself at last able to leave his turret chamber and to walk upon the rampart of the castle. There was a brisk northern wind, heavy and wet with the salt of the sea, and he felt, as he turned his face to it, fresh life and strength surging in his blood and bracing his limbs. He took his hand from Aylward's supporting arm and stood with his cap off, leaning on the rampart and breathing in the cool strong air. Far off upon the distant sky-line, half hidden by the heave of the waves, was the low white fringe of cliffs which skirted England. Between him and them lay the broad blue Channel, seamed and flecked with flashing foam, for a sharp sea was running and the few ships in sight were labouring heavily. Nigel's eyes traversed the widespread view, rejoicing in the change from the grey wall of his cramped chamber. Finally they settled upon a strange object at his very feet.

It was a long trumpet-shaped engine of leather and iron bolted into a rude wooden stand and fitted with wheels. Beside it lay a heap of metal slugs and lumps of stone. The end of the machine was raised and pointed over the battlement. Behind it stood an iron box which Nigel opened. It was filled with a black coarse powder, like gritty charcoal.

" By Saint Paul ! " said he, passing his hands over the engine, " I have heard men talk of these things, but never before have I seen one. It is none other than one of those wondrous new-made bombards."

" In sooth it is even as you say," Aylward answered, looking at it with contempt and dislike in his face. " I have seen them here upon the ramparts, and have also exchanged a buffet or two with him who had charge of them. He was jack-fool enough to think that with this leather pipe he could outshoot the best archer in Christendom. I lent him a cuff on the ear that laid him across his foolish engine."

" It is a fearsome thing," said Nigel, who had stooped to examine it. " We live in strange times when such things can be made. It is loosed by fire, is it not, which springs from the black dust ? "

" By my hilt ! fair sir, I know not. And yet I call to mind that ere we fell out this foolish bombardman did say something of the matter. The fire-dust is within and so also is the ball. Then you take more dust from this iron box and place it in the hole at the farther end—so. It is now ready. I have never seen one fired, but I wot that this one could be fired now."

" It makes a strange sound, archer, does it not ? " said Nigel, wistfully.

" So I have heard, fair sir—even as the bow twangs, so it also has a sound when you loose it."

" There is no one to hear, since we are alone upon the rampart, nor can it do scathe since it points to sea. I pray you to loose it and I will listen to the sound." He bent over the bombard with an attentive ear, while Aylward, stooping his earnest brown face over the touch-hole, scraped away diligently with a flint and steel. A moment later both he and Nigel were seated some distance off upon the ground, while amid the roar of the discharge and the thick cloud of smoke they had a vision of the long black snake-like engine shooting back upon the recoil. For a minute or more they were struck motionless with astonishment, while the reverberations died away and the smoke-wreaths curled slowly up to the blue heavens.

" Good lack ! " cried Nigel at last, picking himself up and looking round him. " Good lack, and Heaven be my aid ! I thank the Virgin that all stands as it did before. I thought that the castle had fallen."

" Such a bull's bellow I have never heard," cried Aylward, rubbing his injured limbs. " One could hear it from Frensham pond to Guildford Castle. I would not touch one again—not for a hide of the best land in Puttenham ! "

" It may fare ill with your own hide, archer, if you do," said an angry voice behind them. Chandos had stepped from the open door of the corner turret and stood looking at them with a harsh gaze. Presently, as the matter was made clear to him, his face relaxed into a smile.

" Hasten to the warden, archer, and tell him how it befell. You will have the castle and the town in arms. I know not what the king may think of so sudden an alarm. And you, Nigel, how in the name of the saints came you to play the child like this ? "

" I knew not its power, fair lord."

" By my soul, Nigel, I think that none of us know its power. I can see the day when all that we delight in, the splendour and glory of war, may all go down before that which beats through the plate of steel as easily as the leathern jacket. I have bestrode my war-horse in my armour and have looked down at the sooty, smoky bom-bardman beside me, and I have thought that perhaps I was the last of the old and he the first of the new ; that there would come a time when he and his engines would sweep you and me and the rest of us from the field."

" But not yet, I trust, honoured sir ? "

" No, not yet, Nigel. You are still in time to win your spurs even as your fathers did. How is your strength ? "

" I am ready for any task, my good and honoured lord."

" It is well, for work awaits us—good work, pressing work, work of peril and of honour. Your eyes shine and your face flushes, Nigel. I live my own youth over again as I look at you. Know then that though there is truce with the French here, there is not truce in Brittany, where the houses of Blois and of Montfort still struggle for the dukedom. Half Brittany fights for one, and half for the other. The French have taken up the cause of Blois, and we of Montfort, and it is such a war that many a great leader, such as Sir Walter Manny, has first earned his name there. Of late the war has gone against us, and the bloody hands of the Rohans, of Gap-tooth Beaumanoir, of Oliver the Flesher and others have been heavy upon our people. The last tidings have been of disaster, and the king's soul is dark with wrath for that his friend and comrade Gilles de St. Pol has been done to death in the castle of La Brohinière. He will send succours to the country, and we go at their head. How like you that, Nigel ? "

" My honoured lord, what could I ask for better ? "

" Then have your harness ready, for we start within the week. Our path by land is blocked by the French, and we go by sea. This night the king gives a banquet ere he returns to England, and your place is behind my chair. Be in my chamber that you may help me to dress, and so we will go the hall together."

With satin and samite, with velvet and with fur, the noble Chandos was dressed for the king's feast, and Nigel too had donned his best silk jupon, faced with the five scarlet roses, that he might wait upon him. In the great hall of Calais Castle the tables were set, a high table for the lords, a second one for the less distinguished knights, and a third at which the squires might feast when their masters were seated.

Never had Nigel in his simple life at Tilford pictured a scene of such pomp and wondrous luxury. The grim grey walls were covered from ceiling to floor with priceless tapestry of Arras, where hart, hounds and huntsmen circled the great hall with one long living image of the chase. Over the principal table drooped a line of banners, and beneath them rows of emblazoned shields upon the wall carried the arms of the high noblemen who sat beneath. The red light of cressets and of torches burned upon the badges of the great captains of England. The lions and lilies shone over the high dorseret chair in the centre, and the same august device marked with the cadency label indicated the seat of the prince, while glowing to right and to left were the long lines of noble insignia honoured in peace and terrible in war. There shone the gold and sable of Manny, the engrailed cross of Suffolk, the red chevron of Stafford, the scarlet and gold of Audley, the blue lion rampant of the Percies, the silver swallows of Arundel, the red roebuck of the Montacutes, the star of the de Veres, the silver scallops of Russell, the purple lion of de Lacy, and the black crosses of Clinton.

A friendly squire at Nigel's elbow whispered the names of the famous warriors beneath.

"You are young Loring of Tilford, the squire of Chandos, are you not?" said he. "My name is Delves, and I come from Doddington in Cheshire. I am the squire of Sir James Audley, yonder round-backed man

with the dark face and close-cropped beard, who hath the
Saracen head as a crest above him."

" I have heard of him as a man of great valour," said
Nigel, gazing at him with interest.

" Indeed, you may well say so, Master Loring. He is
the bravest knight in England, and in Christendom also,
as I believe. No man hath done such deeds of valour."

Nigel looked at his new acquaintance with hope in his
eyes.

" You speak as it becomes you to speak when you
uphold your own master," said he. " For the same
reason, Master Delves, and in no spirit of ill-will to you, it
behoves me to tell you that he is not to be compared in
name or fame with the noble knight on whom I wait.
Should you hold otherwise, then surely we can debate
the matter in whatever way or time may please you
best."

Delves smiled good-humouredly. " Nay, be not so
hot," said he. " Had you upheld any other knight, save
perhaps Sir Walter Manny, I had taken you at your word,
and your master or mine would have had place for a new
squire. But indeed it is only truth that no knight is
second to Chandos, nor would I draw my sword to lower
his pride of place. Ha, Sir James' cup is low! I must
see to it ! " He darted off, a flagon of Gascony in his
hand. " The king hath had good news to-night," he
continued when he returned. " I have not seen him in so
merry a mind since the night when we took the Frenchmen and he laid his pearl chaplet upon the head of de
Ribeaumont. See how he laughs, and the prince also.
That laugh bodes someone little good, or I am the more
mistaken. Have a care ! Sir John's plate is empty."

It was Nigel's turn to dart away ; but ever in the
intervals he returned to the corner whence he could look
down the hall and listen to the words of the older squire.
Delves was a short, thick-set man past middle age,
weather-beaten and scarred, with a rough manner and
bearing which showed that he was more at his ease in a

tent than a hall. But ten years of service had taught him much, and Nigel listened eagerly to his talk.

" Indeed the king hath some good tidings," he continued. " See now, he has whispered it to Chandos and to Manny. Manny spreads it on to Sir Reginald Cobham, and he to Robert Knolles, each smiling like the devil over a friar."

" Which is Sir Robert Knolles ? " asked Nigel, with interest. " I have heard much of him and his deeds."

" He is the tall hard-faced man in yellow silk, he with the hairless cheeks and the split lip. He is little older than yourself, and his father was a cobbler in Chester, yet he has already won the golden spurs. See how he dabs his great hand in the dish and hands forth the gobbets. He is more used to a camp-kettle than a silver plate. The big man with the black beard is Sir Bartholomew Berghersh, whose brother is the Abbot of Beaulieu. Haste, haste ! for the boar's head is come and the plates to be cleaned."

The table manners of our ancestors at this period would have furnished to the modern eye the strangest mixture of luxury and barbarism. Forks were still unknown, and the courtesy fingers, the index and the middle of the left hand, took their place. To use any others was accounted the worst of manners. A crowd of dogs lay among the rushes growling at each other and quarrelling over the gnawed bones which were thrown to them by the feasters. A slice of coarse bread served usually as a plate, but the king's own high table was provided with silver platters, which were wiped by the squire or page after each course. On the other hand, the table-linen was costly, and the courses, served with a pomp and dignity now unknown, comprised such a variety of dishes and such complex marvels of cookery as no modern banquet could show. Besides all our domestic animals and every kind of game, such strange delicacies as hedgehogs, bustards, porpoises, squirrels, bitterns, and cranes lent variety to the feast.

Each new course, heralded by a flourish of silver

trumpets, was borne in by liveried servants walking two and two, with rubicund marshals strutting in front and behind bearing white wands in their hands, not only as badges of their office, but also as weapons with which to repel any impertinent inroad upon the dishes in the journey from the kitchen to the hall. Boars' heads, enarmed and endored with gilt tusks and flaming mouths, were followed by wondrous pasties moulded to the shape of ships, castles and other devices, with sugar seamen or soldiers who lost their own bodies in their fruitless defence against the hungry attack. Finally came the great nef, a silver vessel upon wheels laden with fruit and sweetmeats which rolled with its luscious cargo down the line of guests. Flagons of Gascony, of Rhine wine, of Canary and of Rochelle were held in readiness by the attendants ; but the age, though luxurious, was not drunken, and the sober habits of the Norman had happily prevailed over the licence of those Saxon banquets where no guest might walk from the table without a slur upon his host. Honour and hardihood go ill with a shaking hand or a blurred eye.

While wine, fruit, and spices were handed round the high tables the squires had been served in turn at the farther end of the hall. Meanwhile round the king there had gathered a group of statesmen and soldiers, talking eagerly among themselves. The Earl of Stafford, the Earl of Warwick, the Earl of Arundel, Lord Beauchamp and Lord Neville were assembled at the back of his chair, with Lord Percy and Lord Mowbray at either side. The little group blazed with golden chains and jewelled chaplets, flame-coloured paltocks and purple tunics.

Of a sudden the king said something over his shoulder to Sir William de Pakyngton the herald, who advanced and stood by the royal chair. He was a tall and noble featured man, with long grizzled beard which rippled down to the gold-linked belt girdling his many-coloured tabard. On his head he had placed the heraldic barret-cap which bespoke his dignity, and he slowly raised his white wand high in the air, while a great hush fell upon the hall.

"My lords of England," said he, "knight bannerets, knights, squires, and all others here present of gentle birth and coat-armour, know that your dread and sovereign lord, Edward, King of England and of France, bids me give you greeting and commands you to come hither that he may have speech with you."

In an instant the tables were deserted and the whole company had clustered in front of the king's chair. Those who had sat on either side of him crowded inward, so that his tall dark figure upreared itself amid the dense circle of his guests.

With a flush upon his olive cheeks and with pride smouldering in his dark eyes, he looked round him at the eager faces of the men who had been his comrades from Sluys and Cadsand to Crécy and Calais. They caught fire from that warlike gleam in his masterful gaze, and a sudden wild, fierce shout pealed up to the vaulted ceiling, a soldierly thanks for what was passed and a promise for what was to come. The king's teeth gleamed in a quick smile, and his large white hand played with the jewelled dagger in his belt.

"By the splendour of God!" said he, in a loud clear voice, "I have little doubt that you will rejoice with me this night, for such tidings have come to my ears as may well bring joy to every one of you. You know well that our ships have suffered great scathe from the Spaniards, who for many years have slain without grace or ruth all of my people who have fallen into their cruel hands. Of late they have sent their ships into Flanders, and thirty great cogs and galleys lie now at Sluys well-filled with archers and men-at-arms and ready in all ways for battle. I have it to-day from a sure hand that, having taken their merchandise aboard, these ships will sail upon the next Sunday, and will make their way through our Narrow Sea. We have for a great time been long-suffering to these people, for which they have done us many contraries and despites, growing ever more arrogant as we grow more patient. It is in my mind therefore that we hie us to-morrow to Winchelsea, where we have twenty ships, and make ready to sally out upon them as they pass. May God and Saint George defend the right!"

A second shout, far louder and fiercer than the first, came like a thunderclap after the king's words. It was the bay of a fierce pack to their trusted huntsman.

Edward laughed again as he looked round at the gleaming eyes, the waving arms, and the flushed joyful faces of his liegemen.

" Who hath fought against these Spaniards ? " he asked. " Is there anyone here who can tell us what manner of men they be ? "

A dozen hands went up into the air; but the king turned to the Earl of Suffolk at his elbow.

" You have fought them, Thomas ? " said he.

" Yes, sire, I was in the great sea-fight eight years ago at the Island of Guernsey, when Lord Lewis of Spain held the sea against the Earl of Pembroke."

" How found you them, Thomas ? "

" Very excellent people, sire, and no man could ask for better. On every ship they have a hundred crossbowmen of Genoa, the best in the world, and their spearmen also are very hardy men. They would throw great cantles of iron from the tops of the masts, and many of our people met their death through it. If we can bar their way in the Narrow Sea, then there will be much hope of honour for all of us."

" Your words are very welcome, Thomas," said the king, " and I make no doubt that they will show themselves to be very worthy of what we prepare for them. To you I give a ship, that you may have the handling of it. You also, my dear son, shall have a ship, that evermore honour may be thine."

" I thank you, my fair and sweet father," said the prince, with joy flushing his handsome boyish face.

" The leading ship shall be mine. But you shall have one, Walter Manny, and you, Stafford, and you, Arundel, and you, Audley, and you, Sir Thomas Holland, and you,

629

Brocas, and you, Berkeley, and you, Reginald. The rest shall be awarded at Winchelsea, whither we sail to-morrow. Nay, John, why do you pluck so at my sleeve ? "

Chandos was leaning forward, with an anxious face. " Surely, my honoured lord, I have not served you so long and so faithfully that you should forget me now. Is there, then, no ship for me ? "

The king smiled, but shook his head. " Nay, John, have I not given you two hundred archers and a hundred men-at-arms to take with you into Brittany ? I trust that your ships will be lying in Saint Malo Bay ere the Spaniards are abreast of Winchelsea. What more would you have, old war-dog ? Wouldst be in two battles at once ? "

" I would be at your side, my liege, when the lion banner is in the wind once more. I have ever been there. Why should you cast me now ? I ask little, dear lord—a galley, a balinger, even a pinnace, so that I may only be there."

" Nay, John, you shall come. I cannot find it in my heart to say you nay. I will find you place in my own ship, that you may indeed be by my side."

Chandos stooped and kissed the king's hand. " My squire ? " he asked.

The king's brows knotted into a frown. " Nay, let him go to Brittany with the others," said he, harshly. " I wonder, John, that you should bring back to my memory this youth whose pertness is too fresh that I should forget it. But someone must go to Brittany in your stead, for the matter presses and our people are hard put to it to hold their own." He cast his eyes over the assembly, and they rested upon the stern features of Sir Robert Knolles.

" Sir Robert," he said, " though you are young in years you are already old in war, and I have heard that you are as prudent in council as you are valiant in the field. To you I commit the charge of this venture to Brittany in place of Sir John Chandos, who will follow thither when our work has been done upon the waters. Three ships lie in Calais port and three hundred men are ready to your hand. Sir John will tell you what our mind is in the matter. And now, my friends and good comrades, you will haste you each to his own quarters, and you will make swiftly such preparations as are needful, for, as God is my aid, I will sail with you to Winchelsea to-morrow ! "

Beckoning to Chandos, Manny and a few of his chosen leaders, the king led them away to an inner chamber, where they might discuss the plans for the future. At the same time the assembly broke up, the knights in silence and dignity, the squires in mirth and noise, but all joyful at heart for the thought of the great days which lay before them.

17. *The Spaniards on the Sea*

MORNING had not yet dawned when Nigel was in the chamber of Chandos preparing him for his departure and listening to the last cheery words of advice and direction from his noble master. That same morning, before the sun was halfway up the heaven, the king's great nef *Philippa*, bearing within it the most of those present at his banquet the night before, set its huge sail, adorned with the lions and the lilies, and turned its brazen beak for England. Behind it went five smaller cogs crammed with squires, archers, and men-at-arms.

Nigel and his companions lined the ramparts of the castle and waved their caps as the bluff, burly vessels, with drums beating and trumpets clanging, a hundred knightly pennons streaming from their decks and the red cross of England over all, rolled slowly out to the open sea. Then, when they had watched them until they were hull down, they turned, with hearts heavy at being left behind, to make ready for their own more distant venture.

It took them four days of hard work ere their preparations were complete, for many were the needs of a small force sailing to a strange country. Three ships had been left to them—the cog *Thomas* of Romney, the *Grace Dieu* of Hythe, and the *Basilisk* of Southampton, into each of which one hundred men were stowed, besides the thirty seamen who formed the crew. In the hold were forty horses, among them Pommers, much wearied by his long idleness, and homesick for the slopes of Surrey, where his great limbs might find the work he craved. Then the food and the water, the bow-staves and the sheaves of arrows, the horseshoes, the nails, the hammers, the knives, the axes, the ropes, the vats of hay, the green fodder, and a score of other things were packed aboard. Always by the side of the ships stood the stern young knight Sir Robert, checking, testing, watching, and controlling, saying little, for he was a man of few words, but with his eyes, his hands, and if need be his heavy dog-whip, wherever they were wanted.

The seamen of the *Basilisk*, being from a free port, had the old feud against the men of the Cinque Ports, who were looked upon by the other mariners of England as being unduly favoured by the king. A ship of the West Country could scarce meet with one from the Narrow Seas without blood flowing. Hence sprang sudden broils on the quay side, when with yell and blow the *Thomases* and *Grace Dieus*, Saint Leonard on their lips and murder in their hearts, would fall upon the *Basilisks*. Then amid the whirl of cudgels and the clash of knives would spring the tiger figure of the young leader, lashing mercilessly to right and left like a tamer among his wolves, until he had beaten them howling back to their work. Upon the morning of the fourth day all was ready, and the ropes being cast off, the three little ships were warped down the harbour by their own pinnaces until they were swallowed up in the swirling folds of a Channel mist.

Though small in numbers it was no mean force which Edward had despatched to succour the hard-pressed English garrisons in Brittany. There was scarce a man among them who was not an old soldier, and their leaders were men of note in council and in war. Knolles flew his flag of the black raven aboard the *Basilisk*. With him were Nigel and his own squire, John Hawthorn. Of his hundred men, forty were Yorkshire dalesmen and forty were men of Lincoln, all noted archers, with old Wat of Carlisle, a grizzled veteran of border warfare, to lead them.

Already Aylward by his skill and strength had won his way to an under-officership among them, and shared with Long Ned Widdington, a huge North Countryman, the reputation of coming next to famous Wat Carlisle in all that makes an archer. The men-at-arms, too, were war-hardened soldiers, with Black Simon of Norwich, the same who had sailed from Winchelsea, to lead them. With his heart filled with hatred for the French who had slain all who were dear to him, he followed like a bloodhound over land and sea to any spot where he might glut his vengeance. Such also were the men who sailed in the other ships— Cheshire men from the Welsh borders in the cog *Thomas*, and Cumberland men, used to Scottish warfare, in the *Grace Dieu*.

Sir James Astley hung his shield of cinquefoil ermine over the quarter of the *Thomas*. Lord Thomas Percy, a cadet of Alnwick, famous already for the high spirit of that house which for ages was the bar upon the landward gate of England, showed his blue lion rampant as leader of the *Grace Dieu*. Such was the goodly company Saint Malo bound, who warped from Calais harbour to plunge into the thick reek of a Channel mist.

A slight breeze blew from the eastward, and the high-ended, round-bodied craft rolled slowly down the Channel. The mist rose a little at times, so that they had sight of each other dipping and rising upon a sleek, oily sea, but again it would sink down, settling over the top, shrouding the great yard, and finally frothing over the deck until even the water alongside had vanished from their view and they were afloat on a little raft in an ocean of vapour. A thin cold rain was falling, and the archers were crowded under the shelter of the overhanging poop and forecastle, where some spent the hours at dice, some in sleep, and many in trimming their arrows or polishing their weapons.

At the farther end, seated on a barrel as a throne of honour, with trays and boxes of feathers around him, was Bartholomew the bowyer and fletcher, a fat, bald-headed man, whose task it was to see that every man's tackle was as it should be, and who had the privilege of selling such extras as they might need. A group of archers with their staves and quivers filed before him with complaints or requests, while half a dozen of the seniors gathered at his back and listened with grinning faces to his comments and rebukes.

" Canst not string it ? " he was saying to a young bowman. " Then surely the string is overshort or the stave overlong. It could not by chance be the fault of thy own baby arms more fit to draw on thy hosen than to dress a warbow. Thou lazy lurdan, thus is it strung ! " He seized the stave by the centre in his right hand, leaned the end on the inside of his right foot, and then, pulling the upper nock down with the left hand, slid the eye of the string easily into place. " Now I pray thee to unstring it again," handing it to the bowman.

The youth, with an effort, did so ; but he was too slow in disengaging his fingers, and the string sliding down with a snap from the upper nock caught and pinched them sorely against the stave. A roar of laughter, like the clap of a wave, swept down the deck as the luckless bowman danced and wrung his hand.

" Serve thee well right, thou redeless fool ! " growled the old bowyer. " So fine a bow is wasted in such hands. How now, Samkin ? I can teach you little of your trade, I trow. Here is a bow dressed as it should be ; but it would, as you say, be the better for a white band to mark the true nocking point in the centre of this red wrapping of silk. Leave it and I will tend to it anon. And you, Wat ? A fresh head on yonder stele ? Lord, that a man should carry four trades under one hat, and be bowyer, fletcher, stringer, and head-maker ! Four men's work for old Bartholomew and one man's pay ! "

" Nay, say no more about that," growled an old wizened bowman, with a brown parchment skin and little beady eyes. " It is better in these days to mend a bow than to bend one. You who never looked a Frenchman in the face are pricked off for ninepence a day, and I who have fought five stricken fields, can earn but fourpence."

" It is in my mind, John of Tuxford, that you have looked in the face more pots of mead than Frenchmen," said the old bowyer. " I am swinking from dawn to night, while you are guzzling in an ale-stake. How now, youngster ? Overbowed ? Put your bow in the tiller. It draws at sixty pounds—not a pennyweight too much for a man of your inches. Lay more body to it, lad, and it will come to you. If your bow be not stiff, how can you hope for a twenty-score flight ? Feathers ? Aye, plenty, and of the best. Here are peacock at a groat each. Surely a dandy archer like you, Tom Beverley, with gold earrings in your ears, would have no feathering but peacocks ? "

" So the shaft fly straight, I care not of the feather," said the bowman, a tall young Yorkshireman, counting out pennies on the palm of his horny hand.

" Grey goose-feathers are but a farthing. These on the left are a halfpenny, for they are of the wild-goose, and the second feather of a fenny goose is worth more than the pinion of a tame one. These in the brass tray are dropped feathers, and a dropped feather is better than a plucked one. Buy a score of these, lad, and cut them saddle-backed or swine-backed, the one for a dead shaft and the other for a smooth flyer, and no man in the company will swing a better-fletched quiver over his shoulder."

It chanced that the opinion of the bowyer on this and other points differed from that of Long Ned of Widding-ton, a surly straw-bearded Yorkshireman, who had listened with a sneering face to his counsel. Now he broke in suddenly upon the bowyer's talk.

" You would do better to sell bows than to try to teach

others how to use them," said he ; " for indeed, Bartholomew, that head of thine has no more sense within it than it has hairs without. If you had drawn string for as many months as I have years you would know that a straight-cut feather flies smoother than a swine-backed, and pity it is that these young bowmen have none to teach them better ! "

This attack upon his professional knowledge touched the old bowyer on the raw. His fat face became suffused with blood and his eyes glared with fury as he turned upon the archer.

" You seven-foot barrel of lies ! " he cried. " All-hallows be my aid, and I will teach you to open your slabbing mouth against me ! Pluck forth your sword and stand out on yonder deck, that we may see who is the man of us twain. May I never twirl a shaft over my thumb-nail if I do not put Bartholomew's mark upon your thick head ! "

A score of rough voices joined at once in the quarrel, some upholding the bowyer and others taking the part of the North Countryman. A red-headed Dalesman snatched up a sword, but was felled by a blow from the fist of his neighbour. Instantly, with a buzz like a swarm of angry hornets, the bowmen were out on the deck ; but ere a blow was struck Knolles was among them with granite face and eyes of fire.

" Stand apart, I say ! I will warrant you enough fighting to cool your blood ere you see England once more Loring, Hawthorn, cut any man down who raises his hand. Have you aught to say, you fox-haired rascal ? " He thrust his face within two inches of that of the red man who had first seized his sword. The fellow shrank back, cowed, from his fierce eyes. " Now stint your noise, all of you, and stretch your long ears. Trumpeter, blow once more ! "

A bugle call had been sounded every quarter of an hour, so as to keep in touch with the other two vessels, who were invisible in the fog. Now the high clear note rang out once more, the call of a fierce sea-creature to its mates, but no answer came back from the thick wall which pent them in. Again and again they called, and again and again with bated breath they waited for an answer.

" Where is the shipman ? " asked Knolles. " What is your name, fellow ? Do you dare call yourself master-mariner ? "

" My name is Nat Dennis, fair sir," said the grey-bearded old seaman. " It is thirty years since first I showed my cartel and blew trumpet for a crew at the water-gate of Southampton. If any man may call himself master-mariner, it is surely I."

" Where are our two ships ? "

" Nay, sir, who can say in this fog ? "

" Fellow, it was your place to hold them together."

" I have but the eyes God gave me, fair sir, and they cannot see through a cloud."

" Had it been fair, I who am a soldier could have kept them in company. Since it was foul, we looked to you, who are called a mariner, to do so. You have not done it. You have lost two of my ships ere the venture is begun."

" Nay, fair sir, I pray you to consider——"

" Enough words ! " said Knolles sternly. " Words will not give me back my two hundred men. Unless I find them before I come to Saint Malo, I swear by Saint Wilfrid of Ripon that it will be an evil day for you ! Enough ! Go forth, and do what you may ! "

For five hours, with a light breeze behind them, they lurched through the heavy fog, the cold rain still matting their beards and shining on their faces. Sometimes they could see a circle of tossing water for a bow-shot or so in each direction, and then the wreaths would crawl in upon them once more and bank them thickly round. They had long ceased to blow the trumpet for their missing com-rades, but had hopes when clear weather came to find them still in sight. By the shipman's reckoning they were now about midway between the two shores.

Nigel was leaning against the bulwarks, his thoughts

away in the dingle at Cosford and out on the heather-clad slopes of Hindhead, when something struck his ear. It was a thin clear clang of metal, pealing out high above the dull murmur of the sea, the creak of the boom, and the flap of the sail. He listened, and again it was borne to his ear.

" Hark, my lord ! " said he to Sir Robert. " Is there not a sound in the fog ? "

They both listened together with sidelong heads. Then it rang clearly forth once more, but this time in another direction. It had been on the bow ; now it was on the quarter. Again it sounded, and again. Now it had moved to the other bow ; now back to the quarter again ; now it was near ; and now so far that it was but a faint tinkle on the ear. By this time every man on board, seamen, archers, and men-at-arms, were crowding the sides of the vessel. All round them there were noises in the darkness, and yet the wall of fog lay wet against their very faces. And the noises were such as were strange to their ears, always the same high musical clashing.

The old shipman shook his head and crossed himself. " In thirty years upon the waters I have never heard the like," said he. " The Devil is ever loose in a fog. Well is he named the Prince of Darkness."

A wave of panic passed over the vessel, and these rough and hardy men, who feared no mortal foe, shook with terror at the shadows of their own minds. They stared into the cloud with blanched faces and fixed eyes, as though each instant some fearsome shape might break in upon them. And as they stared there came a gust of wind. For a moment the fog-bank rose and a circle of ocean lay before them.

It was covered with vessels. On all sides they lay thick upon its surface. They were huge caracks, high-ended and portly, with red sides and bulwarks carved and crusted with gold. Each had one great sail set, and was driving down channel on the same course as the *Basilisk*. Their decks were thick with men, and from their high poops came the weird clashing which filled the air. For one moment they lay there, this wondrous fleet, surging slowly forward, framed in grey vapour. The next the clouds closed in and they had vanished from view. There was a long hush, and then a buzz of excited voices.

" The Spaniards ! " cried a dozen bowmen and sailors.

" I should have known it," said the shipman. " I call to mind on the Biscay coast how they would clash their cymbals after the fashion of the heathen Moor with whom they fight ; but what would you have me do, fair sir ? If the fog rises we are all dead men."

" There were thirty ships at the least," said Knolles with a moody brow. " If we have seen them I trow that they have also seen us. They will lay us aboard."

" Nay, fair sir, it is in my mind that our ship is lighter and faster than theirs. If the fog hold another hour, we should be through them."

" Stand to your arms ! " yelled Knolles. " Stand to your arms ! They are on us ! "

The *Basilisk* had indeed been spied from the Spanish Admiral's ship before the fog closed down. With so light a breeze, and such a fog, he could not hope to find her under sail. But by an evil chance not a bowshot from the great Spanish carack was a low galley, thin and swift, with oars which could speed her against wind or tide. She also had seen the *Basilisk*, and it was to her that the Spanish leader shouted his orders. For a few minutes she hunted through the fog, and then sprang out of it like a lean and stealthy beast upon its prey. It was the sight of the long dark shadow gliding after them which had brought that wild shout of alarm from the lips of the English knight. In another instant the starboard oars of the galley had been shipped, the sides of the two vessels grated together, and a stream of swarthy, red-capped Spaniards were swarming up the sides of the *Basilisk* and dropped with yells of triumph upon her deck.

For a moment it seemed as if the vessel was captured without a blow being struck, for the men of the English ship had run wildly in all directions to look for their arms. Scores of archers might be seen under the shadow of the forecastle and the poop bending their bowstaves to string them with the cords from their leathern cases. Others were scrambling over saddles, barrels, and cases in wild search of their quivers. Each as he came upon his arrows pulled out a few to lend to his less fortunate comrades. In mad haste the men-at-arms also were feeling and grasping in the dark corners, picking up steel caps which would not fit them, hurling them down on the deck, and snatching eagerly at any swords or spears that came their way.

The centre of the ship was held by the Spaniards, and having slain all who stood before them, they were pressing up to either end before they were made to understand that it was no fat sheep but a most fierce old wolf which they had taken by the ears.

If the lesson was late, it was the more thorough. Attacked on both sides and hopelessly outnumbered, the Spaniards, who had never doubted that this little craft was a merchant-ship, were cut off to the last man. It was no fight, but a butchery. In vain the survivors ran screaming prayers to the saints and threw themselves down into the galley alongside. It also had been riddled with arrows from the poop of the *Basilisk*, and both the crew on the deck and the galley-slaves in the outriggers at either side lay dead in rows under the overwhelming shower from above. From stem to rudder every foot of her was furred with arrows. It was but a floating coffin piled with dead and dying men, which wallowed in the waves behind them as the *Basilisk* lurched onward and left her in the fog.

In the first rush on to the *Basilisk*, the Spaniards had seized six of the crew and four unarmed archers. Their throats had been cut and their bodies tossed overboard. Now the Spaniards who littered the deck, wounded and dead, were thrust over the side in the same fashion. One ran down into the hold and had to be hunted and killed squealing under the blows like a rat in the darkness.

Within half an hour no sign was left of this grim meeting in the fog save for the crimson splashes upon bulwarks and deck. The archers, flushed and merry, were unstringing their bows once more, for in spite of the water glue the damp air took the strength from the cords. Some were hunting about for arrows which might have stuck inboard, and some tying up small injuries received in the scuffle. But an anxious shadow still lingered upon the face of Sir Robert, and he peered fixedly about him through the fog.

" Go among the archers, Hawthorn," said he to his squire. " Charge them on their lives to make no sound ! You also, Loring. Go to the afterguard and say the same to them. We are lost if one of these great ships should spy us."

For an hour with bated breath they stole through the fleet, still hearing the cymbals clashing all round them, for in this way the Spaniards held themselves together. Once the wild music came from above their very prow, and so warned them to change their course. Once also a huge vessel loomed for an instant upon their quarter, but they turned two points away from her, and she blurred and vanished. Soon the cymbals were but a distant tinkling, and at last they died gradually away.

" It is none too soon," said the old shipman, pointing to a yellowish tint in the haze above them. " See yonder ! It is the sun which wins through. It will be here anon. Ah ! said I not so ? "

A sickly sun, no larger and far dimmer than the moon, had indeed shown its face, with cloud-wreaths smoking across it. As they looked up it waxed larger and brighter before their eyes—a yellow halo spread around it, one ray broke through, and then a funnel of golden light poured down upon them, widening swiftly at the base. A minute later they were sailing on a clear blue sea with an azure cloud-flecked sky above their heads, and such a scene beneath it as each of them would carry in his memory while memory remained.

They were in mid-channel. The white and green

coasts of Picardy and of Kent lay clear upon either side of them. The wide channel stretched in front, deepening from the light blue beneath their prow to purple on the far skyline. Behind them was that thick bank of cloud from which they had just burst. It lay like a grey wall from east to west, and through it were breaking the high shadowy forms of the ships of Spain. Four of them had already emerged, their red bodies, gilded sides and painted sails shining gloriously in the evening sun. Every instant a fresh golden spot grew out of the fog, which blazed like a star for an instant, and then surged forward to show itself as the brazen beak of the great red vessel which bore it. Looking back, the whole bank of cloud was broken by the widespread line of noble ships which were bursting through it. The *Basilisk* lay a mile or more in front of them and two miles clear of their wing. Five miles farther off, in the direction of the French coast, two other small ships were running down Channel. A cry of joy from Robert Knolles and a hearty prayer for gratitude to the saints from the old shipman hailed them as their missing comrades, the cog *Thomas* and the *Grace Dieu*.

But fair as was the view of their lost friends, and wondrous the appearance of the Spanish ships, it was not on those that the eyes of the men of the *Basilisk* were chiefly bent. A greater sight lay before them—a sight which brought them clustering to the forecastle with eager eyes and pointing fingers. The English fleet was coming forth from the Winchelsea Coast. Already before the fog lifted a fast galleass had brought the news down Channel that the Spanish were on the sea, and the king's fleet was under way. Now their long array of sails, gay with the coats and colours of the towns which had furnished them, lay bright against the Kentish coast from Dungeness Point to Rye. Nine and twenty ships were there from Southampton, Shoreham, Winchelsea, Hastings, Rye, Hythe, Romney, Folkstone, Deal, Dover, and Sandwich. With their great sails slued round to catch the wind they ran out, while the Spanish, like the gallant foes that they have ever been, turned their heads landward to meet them. With flaunting banners and painted sails, blaring trumpets and clashing cymbals, the two glittering fleets, dipping and rising on the long Channel swell, drew slowly together.

King Edward had been lying all day in his great ship the *Philippa*, a mile out from the Camber Sands, waiting for the coming of the Spaniards. Above the huge sail which bore the royal arms flew the red cross of England. Along the bulwarks were shown the shields of forty knights, the flower of English chivalry, and as many pennons floated from the deck. The high ends of the ship glittered with the weapons of the men-at-arms, and the waist was crammed with the archers. From time to time a crash of nakers and blare of trumpets burst from the royal ship, and was answered by her great neighbours, the *Lion* on which the Black Prince flew his flag, the *Christopher* with the Earl of Suffolk, the *Salle du Roi* of Robert of Namur, and the *Grace Marie* of Sir Thomas Holland. Farther off lay the *White Swan*, bearing the arms of Mowbray, the *Palmer of Deal*, flying the black head of Audley, and the *Kentish Man* under the Lord Beauchamp. The rest lay, anchored but ready, at the mouth of Winchelsea Creek.

The king sat upon a keg in the fore part of his ship, with little John of Richmond, who was no more than a schoolboy, perched upon his knee. Edward was clad in the black velvet jacket which was his favourite garb, and wore a small brown beaver hat with a white plume at the side. A rich cloak of fur turned up with miniver drooped from his shoulders. Behind him were a score of his knights, brilliant in silks and sarcenets, some seated on an upturned boat and some swinging their legs from the bulwark.

In front stood John Chandos in a parti-coloured jupon, one foot raised upon the anchor-stock, picking at the strings of his guitar and singing a song which he had learned at Marienburg when last he helped the Teutonic knights against the heathen. The king, his knights, and even the archers in the waist below them, laughed at the merry lilt and joined lustily in the chorus, while the men of the neighbouring ships leaned over the side to hearken to the deep chant rolling over the waters.

But there came a sudden interruption to the song. A sharp, harsh shout came down from the look-out stationed in the circular top at the end of the mast.

" I spy a sail—two sails ! " he cried.

John Bunce, the king's shipman, shaded his eyes and stared at the long fog-bank which shrouded the northern channel. Chandos, with his fingers over the strings of his guitar, the king, the knights, all gazed in the same direction. Two small, dark shapes had burst forth, and then, after some minutes, a third.

" Surely they are the Spaniards ? " said the king.

" Nay, sire," the seaman answered, " the Spaniards are greater ships and are painted red. I know not what these may be."

" But I could hazard a guess ! " cried Chandos. " Surely they are the three ships with my own men on their way to Brittany."

" You have hit it, John," said the king. " But, look, I pray you ! What in the name of the Virgin is that ? "

Four brilliant stars of flashing light had shone out from different points of the cloud-bank. The next instant as many tall ships had swooped forth into the sunshine. A fierce shout rang from the king's ship, and was taken up all down the line, until the whole coast from Dungeness to Winchelsea echoed the warlike greeting. The king sprang up with a joyous face.

" The game is afoot, my friends ! " said he. " Dress, John ! Dress, Walter ! Quick, all of you ! Squires, bring the harness ! Let each tend to himself, for the time is short."

A strange sight it was to see these forty nobles tearing off their clothes, and littering the deck with velvets and satins, while the squire of each, as busy as an ostler before a race, stooped and pulled, and strained and riveted, fastening the bassinets, the leg-pieces, the front and the back plates, until the silken courtier had become the man of steel. When their work was finished, there stood a stern group of warriors where the light dandies had sung and jested round Sir John's guitar. Below in orderly silence the archers were mustering under their officers, and taking their allotted stations. A dozen had swarmed up to their hazardous post in the little tower in the tops.

"Bring wine, Nicholas!" cried the king. "Gentlemen, ere you close your visors I pray you to take a last rouse with me. You will be dry enough, I promise you, before your lips are free once more. To what shall we drink, John?"

"To the men of Spain," said Chandos, his sharp face peering like a gaunt bird through the gap in his helmet. "May their hearts be stout and their spirits high this day!"

"Well said, John!" cried the king; and the knights laughed joyously as they drank. "Now, fair sirs, let each to his post! I am warden here on the forecastle. Do you, John, take charge of the afterguard. Walter, James, William, FitzAlan, Goldesborough, Reginald—you will stay with me! John, you may pick whom you will, and the others will bide with the archers. Now, bear straight at the centre, master shipman. Ere yonder sun sets we will bring a red ship back as a gift to our ladies, or never look upon a lady's face again."

The art of sailing into a wind had not yet been invented, nor was there any fore-and-aft canvas, save for small head sails with which a vessel could be turned. Hence the English fleet had to take a long slant down channel to meet their enemies; but as the Spaniards coming before the wind were equally anxious to engage there was the less delay. With stately pomp and dignity the two great fleets approached.

It chanced that one fine carack had outstripped its consorts and came sweeping along, all red and gold, with a fringe of twinkling steel, a good half-mile before the fleet. Edward looked at her with a kindling eye, for indeed she was a noble sight, with the blue water creaming under her gilded prow.

"This is a most worthy and debonair vessel, Master Bunce," said he to the shipman beside him. "I would fain have a tilt with her. I pray you to hold us straight that we may bear her down."

"If I hold her straight, then one or other must sink, and it may be both," the seaman answered.

"I doubt not that with the help of Our Lady we shall do our part," said the king. "Hold her straight, master-shipman, as I have told you."

Now the two vessels were within arrow flight, and the bolts from the crossbowmen pattered upon the English ship. These short, thick, devil's darts were everywhere humming like great wasps through the air, crashing against the bulwarks, beating upon the deck, ringing loudly on the armour of the knights, or with a soft, muffled thud sinking to the socket in a victim.

The bowmen along either side of the *Philippa* had stood motionless waiting for their orders, but now there was a sharp shout from their leader, and every string twanged together. The air was full of their harping, together with the swish of the arrows, the long-drawn keening of the bowmen, and the short, deep bark of the under-officers. "Steady, steady! Loose steady! Shoot wholly together! Twelve score paces! Ten score! Now eight! Shoot wholly together!" Their gruff shouts broke through the high shrill cry like the deep roar of a wave through the howl of the wind.

As the two great ships hurtled together the Spaniard turned away a few points so that the blow should be a glancing one. None the less it was terrific. A dozen men in the tops of the carack were balancing a huge stone with the intention of dropping it over on the English deck. With a scream of horror they saw the mast cracking beneath them. Over it went, slowly at first, then faster, until with a crash it came down on its side, sending them flying like stones from a sling far out into the sea. A swath of crushed bodies lay across the deck where the mast had fallen. But the English ship had not escaped unscathed. Her mast held, it is true, but the mighty shock not only stretched every man flat upon the deck, but had shaken a score of those who lined her sides into the sea. One bowman was hurled from the top, and his body fell with a dreadful crash at the very side of the prostrate king upon the forecastle. Many were thrown down with broken arms and legs from the high castles at either end into the waist of the ship. Worst of all, the seams had been opened by the crash, and the water was gushing in at a dozen places.

But these were men of experience and discipline, men who had already fought together by sea and by land, so that each knew his place and his duty. Those who could staggered to their feet, and helped up a score or more of knights who were rolling and clashing in the scuppers, unable to rise for the weight of their armour. The bowmen formed up as before. The seamen ran to the gaping seams with oakum and with tar. In ten minutes order had been restored, and the *Philippa*, though shaken and weakened, was ready for battle once more. The king was glaring round him like a wounded boar.

" Grapple my ship with that," he cried, pointing to the crippled Spaniard, " for I would have possession of her ! "

But already the breeze had carried them past it, and a dozen Spanish ships were bearing down full upon them.

" We cannot win back to her, lest we show our flank to these others," said the shipman.

" Let her go her way ! " cried the knights. " You shall have better than her."

" By Saint George ! you speak the truth," said the king, " for she is ours when we have time to take her. These also seem very worthy ships which are drawing up to us, and I pray you, master-shipman, that you will have a tilt with the nearest."

A great carack was within a bowshot of them and crossing their bows. Bunce looked up at his mast, and he saw that already it was shaken and drooping. Another blow and it would be over the side, and his ship a helpless log upon the water. He jammed his helm round, therefore, and ran his ship alongside the Spaniard, throwing out his hooks and iron chains as he did so.

They, no less eager, grappled the *Philippa* both fore and aft, and the two vessels, linked tightly together, surged slowly over the long blue rollers. Over their bulwarks hung a cloud of men locked together in a desperate struggle, sometimes surging forward on to the deck of the Spaniard, sometimes recoiling back on to the king's ship, reeling this way and that, with the swords flickering like silver flames above them, while the long-drawn cry of rage and agony swelled up like a wolf's howl to the calm, blue heaven above them.

But now ship after ship of the English had come up, each throwing its iron over the nearest Spaniard and striving to board her high red sides. Twenty ships were drifting in furious single combat after the manner of the *Philippa*, until the whole surface of the sea was covered with a succession of these desperate duels. The dismasted carack, which the king's ship had left behind it, had been carried by the Earl of Suffolk's *Christopher*, and the water was dotted with the heads of her crew. An English ship had been sunk by a huge stone discharged from an engine, and her men also were struggling in the waves, none having leisure to lend them a hand. A second English ship was caught between two of the Spanish vessels and overwhelmed by a rush of boarders, so that not a man of her was left alive. On the other hand, Mowbray and Audley had each taken the caracks which were opposed to them, and the battle in the centre, after swaying this way and that, was turning now in favour of the Islanders.

The Black Prince, with the *Lion*, the *Grace Marie*, and four other ships, had swept round to turn the Spanish flank ; but the movement was seen, and the Spaniards had ten ships with which to meet it, one of them their great carack, the *St. Iago di Compostella*. To this ship the prince had attached his little cog, and strove desperately to board her ; but her side was so high and the defence so desperate that his men could never get beyond her bulwarks, but were hurled down again and again with a clang and clash to the deck beneath. Her side bristled with crossbowmen, who shot straight down on to the packed waist of the *Lion*, so that the dead lay there in heaps. But the most dangerous of all was a swarthy, black-bearded giant in the tops, who crouched so that none could see him, but rising every now and then with a huge lump of iron between his hands, hurled it down with such force that nothing could stop it. Again and again these ponderous bolts crashed through the deck and hurtled down into the bottom of the ship, starting the planks and shattering all that came in their way.

The prince, clad in the dark armour which gave him his name, was directing the attack from the poop when the shipman rushed wildly up to him with fear on his face.

" Sire ! " he cried. " The ship may not stand against these blows. A few more will sink her ! Already the water floods inboard ! "

The prince looked up, and as he did so the shaggy beard showed once more, and two brawny arms swept downward. A great slug, whizzing down, beat a gaping hole in the deck, and fell rending and riving into the hold below. The master-mariner tore his grizzled hair.

" Another leak ! " he cried. " I pray to Saint Leonard to bear us up this day ! Twenty of my shipmen are bailing with buckets, but the water rises on them fast. The vessel may not float another hour."

The prince had snatched a crossbow from one of his attendants and levelled it at the Spaniard's tops. At the very instant when the seaman stood erect with a fresh bar in his hands, the bolt took him full in the face, and his body fell forward over the parapet, hanging there head downward. A howl of exultation burst from the English at the sight, answered by a wild roar of anger from the Spaniards. A seaman had run from the *Lion's* hold and whispered in the ear of the shipman. He turned an ashen face upon the prince.

" It is even as I say, sire. The ship is sinking beneath our feet ! " he cried.

" The more need that we should gain another," said he. " Sir Henry Stokes, Sir Thomas Stourton, William, John of Clifton, here lies our road ! Advance my banner, Thomas de Mohun ! On, and the day is ours ! "

By a desperate scramble, a dozen men, the prince at their head, gained a footing on the edge of the Spaniard's deck. Some slashed furiously to clear a space, others hung over, clutching the rail with one hand and pulling up their comrades from below. Every instant that they could hold their own their strength increased, till twenty had become thirty, and thirty forty, when of a sudden the newcomers, still reaching forth to their comrades below, saw the deck beneath them reel and vanish in a swirling sheet of foam. The prince's ship had foundered.

A yell went up from the Spaniards as they turned furiously upon the small band who had reached their deck. Already the prince and his men had carried the poop, and from that high station they beat back their swarming enemies. But crossbow darts pelted and thudded among their ranks, till a third of their number were stretched upon the planks. Lined across the deck, they could hardly keep an unbroken front to the leaping, surging crowd who pressed upon them. Another rush, or another after that, must assuredly break them, for these dark men of Spain, hardened by an endless struggle with the Moors, were fierce and stubborn fighters. But hark to this sudden roar upon the farther side of them !

"Saint George ! Saint George ! A Knolles to the rescue ! "

A small craft had run alongside, and sixty men had swarmed on the deck of the *St. Iago.* Caught between two fires, the Spaniards wavered and broke. The fight became a massacre. Down from the poop sprang the prince's men. Up from the waist rushed the newcomers. They were five dreadful minutes of blows and screams and prayers, with struggling figures clinging to the bulwarks and sullen splashes into the water below. Then it was over, and a crowd of weary, overstrained men leaned panting upon their weapons, or lay breathless and exhausted upon the deck of the captured carack.

The prince had pulled up his visor and lowered his beaver. He smiled proudly as he gazed around him and wiped his streaming face.

" Where is the shipman ? " he asked. " Let him lead us against another ship."

" Nay, sire ; the shipman and all his men have sunk in the *Lion*," said Thomas de Mohun, a young knight of the west country, who carried the standard. " We have lost our ship and the half of our following. I fear that we can fight no more."

" It matters the less since the day is already ours," said the prince, looking over the sea. " My noble father's royal banner flies upon yonder Spaniard. Mowbray, Audley, Suffolk, Beauchamp, Namur, Tracey, Stafford, Arundel, each has his flag over a scarlet carack, even as mine floats over this. See, yonder squadron is already far beyond our reach. But surely we owe thanks to you who came at so perilous a moment to our aid. Your face I have seen, and your coat-armour also, young sir, though I cannot lay my tongue to your name. Let me know it, that I may thank you."

He had turned to Nigel, who stood flushed and joyous at the head of the boarders from the *Basilisk*.

" I am but a squire, sire, and can claim no thanks, for there is nothing that I have done. Here is our leader."

The prince's eyes fell upon the shield charged with the Black Raven and the stern young face of him who bore it.

" Sir Robert Knolles," said he. " I had thought you were on your way to Brittany."

" I was so, sire, when I had the fortune to see this battle as I passed."

The prince laughed. " It would indeed be to ask too much, Robert, that you should keep on your course when much honour was to be gathered so close to you. But now I pray you that you will come back with us to Winchelsea, for well I know that my father would fain thank you for what you have done this day."

But Robert Knolles shook his head. " I have your father's command, sire, and without his order I may not go against it. Our people are hard-pressed in Brittany, and it is not for me to linger on the way. I pray you, sire, if you must needs mention me to the king, to crave his pardon that I should have broken my journey thus."

" You are right, Robert. God-speed you on your way ! And I would that I were sailing under your banner, for I see clearly that you will take your people where they may worshipfully win worship. Perchance I also may be in Brittany before the year is past."

The prince turned to the task of gathering his weary people together, and the Basilisks passed over the side once more and dropped down on to their own little ship. They poled her off from the captured Spaniard, and set their sail with their prow for the south. Far ahead of them were their two consorts, beating towards them in the hope of giving help, while down Channel were a score of Spanish ships, with a few of the English vessels hanging upon their skirts. The sun lay low on the water, and its level beams glowed upon the scarlet and gold of fourteen great caracks, each flying the cross of Saint George, and towering high above the cluster of English ships which, with brave waving of flags and blaring of music, were moving slowly towards the Kentish coast.

18. *How Black Simon claimed Forfeit from the King of Sark*

FOR a day and a half the small fleet made good progress, but on the second morning, after sighting Cape de la Hague, there came a brisk land wind which blew them out to sea. It grew into a squall with rain and fog so that they were two more days beating back. Next morning they found themselves in a dangerous rock-studded sea with a small island upon their starboard quarter. It was girdled with high granite cliffs of a reddish hue, and slopes of bright green grassland lay above them. A second smaller island lay beside it. Dennis the shipman shook his head as he looked.

" That is Brechou," said he, " and the larger one is the Island of Sark. If ever I be cast away I pray the saints that I may not be upon yonder coast ! "

Knolles gazed across at it. " You say well, master-shipman," said he. " It does appear to be a rocky and perilous spot."

" Nay, it is the rocky hearts of those who dwell upon it that I had in my mind," the old sailor answered. " We are well safe in three goodly vessels, but had we been here in a small craft I make no doubt that they would have already had their boats out against us."

" Who, then, are these people, and how do they live upon so small and windswept an island ? " asked the soldier.

" They do not live from the island, fair sir, but from what they can gather upon the sea around it. They are broken folk from all countries, justice-fliers, prison-breakers, reavers, escaped bondsmen, murderers and staff-strikers who have made their way to this outland place and hold it against all comers. There is one here who could tell you of them and of their ways, for he was long time prisoner amongst them." The seaman pointed to Black Simon, the dark man from Norwich, who was leaning against the side lost in moody thought and staring with a brooding eye at the distant shore.

" How now, fellow ? " asked Knolles. " What is this I hear ? Is it indeed sooth that you have been a captive upon this island ? "

" It is true, fair sir. For eight months I have been servant to the man whom they call their king. His name is La Muette, and he comes from Jersey, nor is there under God's sky a man whom I have more desire to see."

" Has he, then, mishandled you ? "

Black Simon gave a wry smile and pulled off his jerkin. He lean sinewy back was waled and puckered with white scars.

" He has left his sign of hand upon me," said he. " He swore that he would break me to his will, and thus he tried to do it. But most I desire to see him because he hath lost a wager to me and I would fain be paid."

" This is a strange saying," said Knolles. " What is this wager, and why should he pay you ? "

" It is but a small matter," Simon answered ; " but I am a poor man and the payment would be welcome. Should it have chanced that we stopped at this island I should have craved your leave that I go ashore and ask for that which I have fairly won."

Sir Robert Knolles laughed. " This business tickleth my fancy," said he. " As to stopping at the island, this shipman tells me that we must needs wait a day and a night, for that we have strained our planks. But if you should go ashore, how will you be sure that you will be free to depart, or that you will see this king of whom you speak ? "

Black Simon's dark face was shining with a fierce joy. " Fair sir, I will ever be your debtor if you will let me go. Concerning what you ask, I know this island even as I know the streets of Norwich, as you may well believe, seeing that it is but a small place and I upon it for near a year. Should I land after dark, I could win my way to the king's house, and if he be not dead or distraught with drink I could have speech with him alone, for I know his ways and his hours and how he may be found. I would ask only that Aylward the archer may go with me, that I may have one friend at my side if things should chance to go awry."

Knolles thought awhile. "It is much that you ask," said he, "for by God's truth I reckon that you and this friend of yours are two of my men whom I would be least ready to lose. I have seen you both at grips with the Spaniards and I know you. But I trust you, and if we must indeed stop at this accursed place, then you may do as you will. If you have deceived me, or if this is a trick by which you design to leave me, then God be your friend when next we meet, for man will be of small avail!"

It proved that not only the seams had to be calked but that the cog *Thomas* was out of fresh water. The ships moored therefore near the Isle of Brechou, where springs were to be found. There were no people upon this little patch, but over on the farther island many figures could be seen watching them, and the twinkle of steel from among them showed that they were armed men. One boat had ventured forth and taken a good look at them, but had hurried back with the warning that they were too strong to be touched.

Black Simon found Aylward seated under the poop with his back against Bartholomew the bowyer. He was whistling merrily as he carved a girl's face upon the horn of his bow.

"My friend," said Simon, "will you come ashore to night—for I have need of your help?"

Aylward crowed lustily. "Will I come, Simon? By my hilt, I shall be right glad to put my foot on the good brown earth once more. All my life I have trod it, and yet I would never have learned its worth had I not journeyed in these cursed ships. We will go on shore together, Simon, and we will seek out the women, if there be any there, for it seems a long year since I heard their gentle voices, and my eyes are weary of such faces as Bartholomew's or thine."

Simon's grim features relaxed into a smile. " The only face that you will see ashore, Samkin, will bring you small comfort," said he, " and I warn you that this is no easy errand, but one which may be neither sweet nor fair, for if these people take us our end will be a cruel one."

" By my hilt," said Aylward, " I am with you, gossip, wherever you may go ! Say no more, therefore, for I am weary of living like a cony in a hole, and I shall be right glad to stand by you in your venture."

That night, two hours after dark, a small boat put forth from the *Basilisk*. It contained Simon, Aylward, and two seamen. The soldiers carried their swords, and Black Simon bore a brown biscuit-bag over his shoulder. Under his direction the rowers skirted the dangerous surf which beat against the cliffs until they came to a spot where an outlying reef formed a breakwater. Within was a belt of calm water and a shallow cover with a sloping beach. Here the boat was dragged up and the seamen were ordered to wait, while Simon and Aylward started on their errand.

With the assured air of a man who knows exactly where he is and whither he is going, the man-at-arms began to clamber up a narrow fern-lined cleft among the rocks. It was no easy ascent in the darkness, but Simon climbed on like an old dog hot upon a scent, and the panting Aylward struggled after as best he might. At last they were at the summit and the archer threw himself down upon the grass.

" Nay, Simon, I have not enough breath to blow out a candle," said he. " Stint your haste for a minute, since we have a long night before us. Surely this man is a friend indeed, if you hasten so to see him."

" Such a friend," Simon answered, " that I have often dreamed of our next meeting. Now before that moon has set it will have come."

" Had it been a wench I could have understood it,"
said Aylward. " By these ten finger-bones, if Mary of
the mill or little Kate of Compton had waited me on the
brow of this cliff, I should have come up it and never
known it was there. But surely I see houses and hear
voices over yonder in the shadow ? "

" It is their town," whispered Simon. " There are a
hundred as bloody-minded cut-throats as are to be found
in Christendom beneath those roofs. Hark to that ! "

A fierce burst of laughter came out of the darkness,
followed by a long cry of pain.

" All-hallows be with us ! " cried Aylward. " What is
that ? "

" As like as not some poor devil has fallen into their
clutches, even as I did. Come this way, Samkin, for there
is a peat-cutting where we may hide. Aye, here it is, but
deeper and broader than of old. Now, follow me close, for
if we keep within it we shall find ourselves a stone cast
off the king's house."

Together they crept along the dark cutting. Suddenly
Simon seized Aylward by the shoulder and pushed him
into the shadow of the bank. Crouching in the darkness,
they heard footsteps and voices upon the farther side
of the trench. Two men sauntered along it and stopped
almost at the very spot where the comrades were lying.
Aylward could see their dark figures outlined against the
starry sky.

" Why should you scold, Jacques," said one of them,
speaking a strange half-French, half-English lingo. " *Le
diable t'emporte* for a grumbling rascal. You won a
woman and I got nothing. What more would you have ? "

" You will have your chance off the next ship, *mon
garçon*, but mine is passed. A woman, it is true—an old
peasant out of the fields, with a face as yellow as a kite's
claw. But Gaston, who threw a nine against my eight,
got as fair a little Normandy lass as ever your eyes have
seen. Curse the dice, I say ! And as to my woman, I
will sell her to you for a firkin of Gascony."

" I have no wine to spare, but I will give you a keg of apples," said the other. " I had it out of the *Peter and Paul*, the Falmouth boat that struck in Creux Bay."

" Well, well, your apples may be the worse for keeping, but so is old Marie, and we can cry quits on that. Come round and drink a cup over the bargain."

They shuffled onward in the darkness.

" Heard you ever such villainy ? " cried Aylward, breathing fierce and hard. " Did you hear them, Simon ? A woman for a keg of apples ! And my heart's root is sad for the other one, the girl of Normandy. Surely we can land to-morrow and burn all these water-rats out of their nest."

" Nay, Sir Robert will not waste time or strength ere he reach Brittany."

" Sure I am that if my little master Squire Loring had the handling of it, every woman on this island would be free ere another day had passed."

" I doubt it not," said Simon. " He is one who makes an idol of woman, after the manner of those crazy knight-errants. But Sir Robert is a true soldier and hath only his purpose in view."

" Simon," said Aylward, " the light is not overgood and the place is cramped for sword-play, but if you will step out into the open I will teach you whether my master is a true soldier or not."

" Tut, man ! you are as foolish yourself," said Simon. " Here we are with our work in hand, and yet you must needs fall out with me on our way to it. I say nothing against your master save that he hath the way of his fellows, who follow dreams and fancies. But Knolles looks neither to right nor left, and walks forward to his mark. Now, let us on, for the time passes."

" Simon, your words are neither good nor fair. When we are back on shipboard we will speak further of this matter. Now lead on, I pray you, and let us see some more of this ten-devil island."

For half a mile Simon led the way until they came to

a large house which stood by itself. Peering at it from the edge of the cutting, Aylward could see that it was made from the wreckage of many vessels, for at each corner a prow was thrust out. Lights blazed within, and there came the sound of a strong voice singing a gay song which was taken up by a dozen others in the chorus.

" All is well, lad ! " whispered Simon, in great delight. " That is the voice of the king. It is the very song he used to sing. ' *Les deux filles de Pierre.*' 'Fore God, my back tingles at the very sound of it. Here we will wait until his company take their leave."

Hour after hour they crouched in the peat-cutting, listening to the noisy songs of the revellers within, some French, some English, and all growing fouler and less articular as the night wore on. Once a quarrel broke out and the clamour was like a cageful of wild beasts at feeding-time. Then a health was drunk and there was much stamping and cheering.

Only once was the long vigil broken. A woman came forth from the house and walked up and down, with her face sunk upon her breast. She was tall and slender, but her features could not be seen for a wimple over her head. Weary sadness could be read in her bowed back and dragging steps. Once only they saw her throw her two hands up to Heaven as one who is beyond human aid. Then she passed slowly into the house again. A moment later the door of the hall was flung open, and a shouting, stumbling throng came crowding forth, with whoop and yell, into the silent night. Linking arms and striking up a chorus, they marched past the peat-cutting, their voices dwindling slowly away as they made for their homes.

" Now, Samkin, now ! " cried Simon, and jumping out from the hiding-place, he made for the door. It had not yet been fastened. The two comrades sprang inside. Then Simon drew the bolts so that none might interrupt them.

A long table littered with flagons and beakers lay

before them. It was lit up by a line of torches, which flickered and smoked in their iron sconces. At the farther end a solitary man was seated. His head rested upon his two hands, as if he were befuddled with wine, but at the harsh sound of the snapping bolts he raised his face and looked angrily around him. It was a strange, powerful head, tawny and shaggy like a lion's, with a tangled beard and a large, harsh face, bloated and blotched with vice. He laughed as the newcomers entered, thinking that two of his boon companions had returned to finish a flagon. Then he stared hard, and he passed his hand over his eyes like one who thinks he may be dreaming.

" *Mon Dieu !* " he cried. " Who are you, and whence come you at this hour of the night ? Is this the way to break into our royal presence ? "

Simon approached up one side of the table and Aylward up the other. When they were close to the king, the man-at-arms plucked a torch from its socket and held it to his own face. The king staggered back with a cry, as he gazed at that grim visage.

" *Le diable noir !* " he cried. " Simon, the Englishman ! What make you here ? "

Simon put his hand upon his shoulder. " Sit here ! " said he, and he forced the king into his seat. " Do you sit on the farther side of him, Aylward. We make a merry group, do we not ? Often have I served at this table, but never did I hope to drink at it. Fill your cup, Samkin, and pass the flagon."

The king looked from one to the other with terror in his bloodshot eyes.

" What would you do ? " asked. " Are you mad, that you should come here ? One shout and you are at my mercy."

" Nay, my friend, I have lived too long in your house not to know the ways of it. No man-servant ever slept beneath your roof, for you feared lest your throat would be cut in the night-time. You may shout and shout, if it so please you. It chanced that I was passing on my

660

way from England in those ships which lie off La Brechou, and I thought I would come in and have speech with you."

" Indeed, Simon, I am right glad to see you," said the king, cringing away from the fierce eyes of the soldier. " We were good friends in the past, were we not, and I cannot call to mind that I have ever done you injury. When you made your way to England by swimming to the Levantine there was none more glad in heart than I."

" If I cared to doff my doublet I could show you the marks of what your friendship has done for me in the past," said Simon. " It is printed on my back as clearly as on my memory. Why, you foul dog, there are the very rings upon the wall to which my hands were fastened, and there the stains upon the boards on which my blood has dripped ! Is it not so, you king of butchers ? "

The pirate chief turned whiter still. " It may be that life here was somewhat rough, Simon, but if I have wronged you in any way, I will surely make amends. What do you ask ? "

" I ask only one thing, and I have come hither that I may get it. It is that you pay me forfeit for that you have lost your wager."

" My wager, Simon ! I call to mind no wager."

" But I will call it to your mind, and then I will take my payment. Often have you sworn that you would break my courage. ' By my head ! ' you have cried to me. ' You will crawl at my feet ! ' and again : ' I will wager my head that I will tame you ! ' Yes, yes, a score of times you have said so. In my heart, as I listened, I have taken up your gage. And now, dog, you have lost, and I am here to claim the forfeit."

His long heavy sword flew from its sheath. The king, with a howl of despair, flung his arms round him, and they rolled together under the table. There was a sound like the worrying of dogs ending in a scream. Aylward sat with a ghastly face, and his toes curled with horror at the sight, for he was still new to scenes of strife and his blood was too cold for such a deed. When Simon rose he tossed something into his bag and sheathed his bloody sword.

" Come, Samkin, our work is well done," said he.

" By my hilt, if I had known what it was I would have been less ready to come with you," said the archer. " Could you not have clapped a sword in his fist and let him take his chance in the hall ? "

" Nay, Samkin, if you had such memories as I, you would have wished that he should die like a sheep and not like a man. What chance did he give me when he had the power ? And why should I treat him better ? But, Holy Virgin, what have we here ? "

At the farther end of the table a woman was standing. An open door behind her showed that she had come from the inner room of the house. By her tall figure the comrades knew that she was the same that they had already seen. Her face had once been fair, but now was white and haggard, with wild dark eyes full of a hopeless terror and despair. Slowly she paced up the room, her gaze fixed not upon the comrades, but upon the dreadful thing beneath the table. Then, as she stooped and was sure, she burst into loud laughter and clapped her hands.

" Who shall say there is no God ? " she cried. " Who shall say that prayer is unavailing ? Great sir, brave sir, let me kiss that conquering hand ! "

" Nay, nay, dame, stand back ! Well, if you must needs have one of them, take this which is the clean one."

" It is the other I crave—that which is red with his blood ! Oh ! joyful night when my lips have been wet with it ! Now I can die in peace ! "

" We must go, Aylward," said Simon. " In another hour the dawn will have broken. In daytime a rat could not cross this island and pass unseen. Come, man, and at once ! "

But Aylward was at the woman's side. " Come with us, fair dame," said he. " Surely we can, at least, take you from this island, and no such change can be for the worse."

" Nay," said she, " the saints in Heaven cannot help me now until they take me to my rest. There is no place for me in the world beyond, and all my friends were slain on the day I was taken. Leave me, brave men, and let me care for myself. Already it lightens in the east, and black will be your fate if you are taken. Go, and may the blessing of one who was once a holy nun go with you and guard you from danger ! "

Sir Robert Knolles was pacing the deck in the early morning, when he heard the sound of oars, and there were his two night-birds climbing up the side.

" So, fellow," said he, " have you had speech with the king of Sark ? "

" Fair sir, I have seen him."

" And he has paid his forfeit ? "

" He has paid it, sir ! "

Knolles looked with curiosity at the bag which Simon bore.

" What carry you there ? " he asked.

" The stake that he has lost."

" What was it, then ? A goblet ? A silver plate ? "

For answer Simon opened his bag and shook it out on the deck.

Sir Robert turned away with a whistle. " 'Fore God ! " said he, " it is in my mind that I carry some hard men with me to Brittany."

19. *How a Squire of England met a Squire of France*

SIR ROBERT KNOLLES with his little fleet had sighted the Breton coast near Cancale ; they had rounded the Point du Grouin, and finally had sailed past the port of St. Malo and down the long narrow estuary of the Rance until they were close to the old walled city of Dinan, which was held by that Montfort faction whose cause the English had espoused. Here the horses had been disembarked, the stores were unloaded, and the whole force encamped outside the city, while the leaders waited for news as to the present state of affairs, and where there was most hope of honour and profit.

The whole of France was feeling the effects of that war with England which had already lasted some ten years, but no province was in so dreadful a condition as this unhappy land of Brittany. In Normandy or Picardy the inroads of the English were periodical with intervals of rest between ; but Brittany was torn asunder by constant civil war apart from the grapple of the two great combatants, so that there was no surcease of her sufferings. The struggle had begun in 1341 through the rival claims of Montfort and of Blois to the vacant dukedom. England had taken the part of Montfort, France that of Blois. Neither faction was strong enough to destroy the other, and so after ten years of continual fighting, history recorded a long ineffectual list of surprises and ambushes, of raids and skirmishes, of towns taken and retaken, of alternate victory and defeat, in which neither party could claim a supremacy. It mattered nothing that Montfort and Blois had both disappeared from the scene, the one dead and the other taken by the English. Their wives caught up the red swords which had dropped from the hands of their lords, and the long struggle went on even more savagely than before.

In the south and east the Blois faction held the country, and Nantes the capital was garrisoned and occupied by a strong French army. In the north and west the Montfort party prevailed, for the island kingdom was at their back, and always fresh sails broke the northern sky-line bearing adventurers from over the channel.

Between these two there lay a broad zone comprising all the centre of the country which was a land of blood and violence, where no law prevailed save that of the sword. From end to end it was dotted with castles, some held for one side, some for the other, and many mere robber strongholds, the scenes of gross and monstrous

deeds, whose brute owners, knowing that they could never
be called to account, made war upon all mankind, and
wrung with rack and with flame the last shilling from all
who fell into their savage hands. The fields had long
been untilled. Commerce was dead. From Rennes in
that east to Hennebon in the west, and from Dinan in the
north to Nantes in the south, there was no spot where a
man's life or a woman's honour was safe. Such was the
land, full of darkness and blood, the saddest, blackest
spot in Christendom, into which Knolles and his men
were now advancing.

But there was no sadness in the young heart of Nigel,
as he rode by the side of Knolles at the head of a clump
of spears, nor did it seem to him that Fate had led him
into an unduly arduous path. On the contrary, he blessed
the good fortune which had sent him into so delightful a
country, and it seemed to him as he listened to dreadful
stories of robber barons, and looked round at the black
scars of war which lay branded upon the fair faces of
the hills, that no hero or romancer or trouveur had ever
journeyed through such a land of promise, with so fair a
chance of knightly venture and honourable advancement.

The Red Ferret was one deed toward his vow. Surely
a second, and perhaps a better, was to be found somewhere upon this glorious countryside. He had borne
himself as the others had in the sea-fight, and could not
count it to his credit where he had done no more than
mere duty. Something beyond this was needed for such
a deed as could be laid at the feet of the Lady Mary.
But surely it was to be found here in fermenting war-
distracted Brittany. Then with two done it would be
strange if he could not find occasion for that third one,
which would complete his service and set him free to look
her in the face once more. With the great yellow horse
curveting beneath him, his Guildford armour gleaming in
the sun, his sword clanking against his stirrup-iron, and
his father's tough ash-spear in his hand, he rode with a

light heart and a smiling face, looking eagerly to right and
to left for any chance which his good Fate might send.

The road from Dinan to Caulnes, along which the small
army was moving, rose and dipped over undulating
ground, with a bare marshy plain upon the left where the
river Rance ran down to the sea, while upon the right lay a
wooded country with a few wretched villages, so poor and
sordid that they had nothing with which to tempt the
spoiler. The peasants had left them at the first twinkle
of a steel cap, and lurked at the edges of the woods, ready
in an instant to dive into those secret recesses known only
to themselves. These creatures suffered sorely at the
hands of both parties, but when the chance came they
revenged their wrongs on either in a savage way which
brought fresh brutalities upon their heads.

The newcomers soon had a chance of seeing to what
lengths they would go, for in the roadway near to Caulnes
they came upon an English man-at-arms who had been
waylaid and slain by them. How they had overcome him
could not be told, but how they had slain him within his
armour was horribly apparent, for they had carried such a
rock as eight men could lift, and had dropped it upon him
as he lay, so that he was spread out in his shattered case
like a crab beneath a stone. Many a fist was shaken at
the distant woods and many a curse hurled at those who
haunted them, as the column of scowling soldiers passed
the murdered man whose badge of the Molene cross
showed him to have been a follower of that House of
Bentley, whose head, Sir Walter, was at the time leader of
the British forces in the country.

Sir Robert Knolles had served in Brittany before, and
he marshalled his men on the march with the skill and
caution of the veteran soldier, the man who leaves as little
as possible to chance, having too steadfast a mind to heed
the fool who may think him over-cautious. He had re-
cruited a number of bowmen and men-at-arms at Dinan ;
so that his following was now close upon five hundred
men. In front under his own leadership were fifty

mounted lancers, fully armed and ready for any sudden attack. Behind them on foot came the archers, and a second body of mounted men closed up the rear. Out upon either flank moved small bodies of cavalry, and a dozen scouts, spread fanwise, probed every gorge and dingle in front of the column. So for three days he moved slowly down the Southern Road.

Sir Thomas Percy and Sir James Astley had ridden to the head of the column, and Knolles conferred with them as they marched concerning the plan of their campaign. Percy and Astley were young and hot-headed, with wild visions of dashing deeds and knight-errantry, but Knolles, with cold, clear brain and purpose of iron, held ever his object in view.

" By the holy Dunstan and all the saints of Lindisfarne ! " cried the fiery borderer, " it goes to my heart to ride forward when there are such honourable chances on either side of us. Have I not heard that the French are at Evran beyond the river, and is it not sooth that yonder castle, the towers of which I see above the woods, is in the hands of a traitor, who is false to his liege lord of Montford. There is little profit to be gained upon this road, for the folk seem to have no heart for war. Had we ventured as far over the marches of Scotland as we now are in Brittany, we should not have lacked some honourable venture or chance of winning worship."

" You say truth, Thomas," cried Astley, a red-faced and choleric young man. " It is well certain that the French will not come to us, and surely it is the more needful that we go to them. In sooth, any soldier who sees us would smile that we should creep for three days along this road as though a thousand dangers lay before us, when we have but poor broken peasants to deal with."

But Robert Knolles shook his head. " We know not what are in these woods, or behind these hills," said he, " and when I know nothing it is my wont to prepare for the worst which may befall. It is but prudence so to do."

"Your enemies might find some harsher name for it,"
said Astley, with a sneer. "Nay, you need not think to
scare me by glaring at me, Sir Robert, nor will your ill-
pleasure change my thoughts. I have faced fiercer eyes
than thine, and I have not feared."

"Your speech, Sir James, is neither courteous nor
good," said Knolles, "and if I were a free man I would
cram your words down your throat with the point of my
dagger. But I am here to lead these men in profit and
honour, not to quarrel with every fool who has not the wit
to understand how soldiers should be led. Can you not
see that if I make attempts here and there, as you would
have me do, I shall have weakened my strength before I
come to that part where it can best be spent?"

"And where is that?" asked Percy. "'Fore God,
Astley, it is in my mind that we ride with one who
knows more of war than you or I, and that we would be
wise to be guided by his rede. Tell us then what is in
your mind."

"Thirty miles from here," said Knolles, "there is, as I
am told, a fortalice named Ploermel, and within it is one
Bambro', an Englishman, with a good garrison. No great
distance from him is the Castle of Josselin, where dwells
Robert of Beaumanoir with a great following of Bretons.
It is my intention that we should join Bambro', and so
be in such strength that we may throw ourselves upon
Josselin, and by taking it become the masters of all mid-
Brittany, and able to make head against the Frenchmen
in the south."

"Indeed I think that you can do no better," said Percy,
heartily, "and I swear to you on jeopardy of my soul that
I will stand by you in the matter! I doubt not that
when we come deep into their land they will draw together and do what they may to make head against us;
but up to now I swear by all the saints of Lindisfarne that
I should have seen more war in a summer's day in Liddes-
dale or at the Forest of Jedburgh than any that Brittany
has shown us. But see, yonder horsemen are riding in.

They are our own hobbellers, are they not ? And who are these who are lashed to their stirrups ? "

A small troop of mounted bowmen had ridden out of an oak grove upon the left of the road. They trotted up to where the three knights had halted. Two wretched peasants whose wrists had been tied to their leathers came leaping and straining beside the horses in their effort not to be dragged off their feet. One was a tall, gaunt, yellow-haired man, the other short and swarthy, but both so crusted with dirt, so matted and tangled and ragged, that they were more like beasts of the wood than human beings.

" What is this ? " asked Knolles. " Have I not ordered you to leave the countryfolk at peace ? "

The leader of the archers, old Wat of Carlisle, held up a sword, a girdle and a dagger. " If it please you, fair sir," said he, " I saw the glint of these, and I thought them no fit tools for hands which were made for the spade and the plough. But when we had ridden them down and taken them, there was the Bentley cross upon each, and we knew that they had belonged to yonder dead Englishman upon the road. Surely then, these are two of the villains who have slain him, and it is right that we do justice upon them."

Sure enough, upon sword, girdle and dagger shone the silver Molene cross which had gleamed on the dead man's armour. Knolles looked at them and then at the prisoners with a face of stone. At the sight of those fell eyes they had dropped with inarticulate howls upon their knees, screaming out their protests in a tongue which none could understand.

" We must have the roads safe for wandering Englishmen," said Knolles. " These men must surely die. Hang them to yonder tree."

He pointed to a live oak by the roadside, and rode onward upon his way in converse with his fellow-knights. But the old bowman had ridden after him.

" If it please you, Sir Robert, the bowmen would fain put these men to death in their own fashion," said he.

" So that they die, I care not how," Knolles answered carelessly, and looked back no more.

Human life was cheap in those stern days, when the footmen of a stricken army or the crew of a captured ship were slain without any question or thought of mercy by the victors. War was a rude game, with death for the stake, and the forfeit was always claimed on the one side and paid on the other without doubt or hesitation. Only the knight might be spared, since his ransom made him worth more alive than dead. To men trained in such a school, with death for ever hanging over their own heads, it may well be believed that the slaying of two peasant murderers was a small matter.

And yet there was special reason why upon this occasion the bowmen wished to keep the deed in their own hands. Ever since their dispute aboard the *Basilisk*, there had been ill-feeling between Bartholomew, the old bald-headed bowyer, and long Ned Widdington the dalesman, which had ended in a conflict at Dinan, in which not only they, but a dozen of their friends, had been laid upon the cobble-stones. The dispute raged round their respective knowledge and skill with the bow, and now some quick wit among the soldiers had suggested a grim fashion in which it should be put to the proof, once for all, which could draw the surer shaft.

A thick wood lay two hundred paces from the road upon which the archers stood. A stretch of smooth grassy sward lay between. The two peasants were led out fifty yards from the road, with their faces towards the wood. There they stood, held on a leash, and casting many a wondering, frightened glance over their shoulders at the preparations which were being made behind them.

Old Bartholomew and the big Yorkshireman had stepped out of the ranks and stood side by side, each with his strung bow in his left hand and a single arrow in his right. With care they had drawn on and greased their shooting-gloves and fastened their bracers. They plucked and cast up a few blades of grass to measure the wind, examined every small point of their tackle, turned their sides to the mark, and widened their feet in a firmer stance. From all sides came chaff and counsel from their comrades.

" A three-quarter wind, bowyer ! " cried one. " Aim a body's breadth to the right ! "

" But not thy body's breadth, bowyer," laughed another. " Else may you be overwide."

" Nay, this wind will scarce turn a well-drawn shaft," said a third. " Shoot dead upon him and you will be clap in the clout."

" Steady, Ned, for the good name of the dales," cried a Yorkshireman. " Loose easy and pluck not, or I am five crowns the poorer man."

" A week's pay on Bartholomew ! " shouted another. " Now, old fat-pate, fail me not ! "

" Enough, enough ! Stint your talk ! " cried the old bowman, Wat of Carlisle. " Were your shafts as quick as your tongues there would be no facing you. Do you shoot upon the little one, Bartholomew, and you, Ned, upon the other. Give them law until I cry the word, then loose in your own fashion and at your own time. Are you ready ! Holà, there, Hayward, Beddington, let them run ! "

The leashes were torn away, and the two men, stooping their heads, ran madly for the shelter of the wood amid such a howl from the archers as beaters may give when the hare starts from its form. The two bowmen, each with his arrow drawn to the pile, stood like russet statues, menacing, motionless, their eager eyes fixed upon the fugitives, their bow-staves rising slowly as the distance between them lengthened. The Bretons were halfway to the wood, and still old Wat was silent. It may have been mercy or it may have been mischief, but at least the chase should have a fair chance of life. At six score paces he turned his grizzled head at last.

" Loose ! " he cried.

At the word the Yorkshireman's bowstring twanged. It was not for nothing that he had earned the name of being one of the deadliest archers of the North, and had twice borne away the silver arrow of Selby. Swift and true flew the fatal shaft and buried itself to the feather in the curved back of the long yellow-haired peasant. Without a sound he fell upon his face and lay stone-dead upon the grass, the one short white plume between his dark shoulders to mark where Death had smote him.

The Yorkshireman threw his bowstave into the air and danced in triumph, while his comrades roared their fierce delight in a shout of applause, which changed suddenly into a tempest of hooting and of laughter.

The smaller peasant, more cunning than his comrade, had run more slowly, but with many a backward glance. He had marked his companion's fate and had waited with keen eyes until he saw the bowyer loose his string. At the moment he had thrown himself flat upon the grass and had heard the arrow scream above him, and seen it quiver in the turf beyond. Instantly he had sprung to his feet again, and amid wild whoops and halloos from the bowmen had made for the shelter of the wood. Now he had reached it, and ten score good spaces separated him from the nearest of his persecutors. Surely they could not reach him here. With the tangled brushwood behind him he was as safe as a rabbit at the mouth of his burrow. In the joy of his heart he must needs dance in derision and snap his fingers at the foolish men who had let him slip. He threw back his head, howling at them like a dog, and at the instant an arrow struck him full in the throat and laid him dead among the bracken. There was a hush of surprised silence and then a loud cheer burst from the archers.

" By the rood of Beverley ! " cried old Wat, " I have not seen a finer roving shaft this many a year. In my own best day I could not have bettered it. Which of you loosed it ? "

" It was Aylward of Tilford—Samkin Aylward," cried a score of voices, and the bowman, flushed at his own fame, was pushed to the front.

" Indeed I would that it had been at a nobler mark,"
said he. " He might have gone free for me, but I could
not keep my fingers from the string when he turned to
jeer at us."

" I see well that you are indeed a master-bowman,"
said old Wat, " and it is comfort to my soul to think that
if I fall I leave such a man behind me to hold high the
credit of our craft. Now gather your shafts and on, for
Sir Robert awaits us on the brow of the hill."

All day Knolles and his men marched through the
same wild and deserted country, inhabited only by these
furtive creatures, hares to the strong and wolves to the
weak, who hovered in the shadows of the wood. Ever
and anon upon the tops of the hills they caught a glimpse
of horsemen who watched them from a distance and
vanished when approached. Sometimes bells rang an
alarm from villages among the hills, and twice they passed
castles which drew up their drawbridges at their approach,
and lined their walls with hooting soldiers as they passed.
The Englishmen gathered a few oxen and sheep from the
pastures of each, but Knolles had no mind to break his
strength upon stone walls, and so he went upon his way.

Once at St. Meen they passed a great nunnery, girt
with a high grey lichened wall, an oasis of peace in this
desert of war, the black-robed nuns basking in the sun or
working in the gardens, with the strong gentle hand of
Holy Church shielding them ever from evil. The archers
doffed caps to them as they passed, for the boldest and
roughest dared not cross that line guarded by the dire ban
and blight which was the one only force in the whole
steel-ridden earth which could stand between the weakling
and the spoiler.

The little army halted at St. Meen and cooked its
midday meal. It had gathered into its ranks again and
was about to start, when Knolles drew Nigel to one side.

" Nigel," said he, " it seems to me that I have seldom
set eyes upon a horse which hath more power and promise
of speed than this great beast of thine."

"It is indeed a noble steed, fair sir," said Nigel. Between him and his young leader there had sprung up great affection and respect since the day that they set foot in the *Basilisk*.

"It will be the better if you stretch his limbs, for he grows overheavy," said the knight. "Now, mark me, Nigel! Yonder betwixt the ash-tree and the rock what do you see on the side of the far hill?"

"There is a white dot upon it. Surely it is a horse."

"I have marked it all morning, Nigel. This horseman has kept ever upon our flank, spying upon us or waiting to make some attempt upon us. Now I should be right glad to have a prisoner, for it is my wish to know something of this countryside, and these peasants can speak neither French nor English. I would have you linger here in hiding when we go forward. This man will still follow us. When he does so, yonder wood will lie betwixt you and him. Do you ride round it and come upon him from behind. There is broad plain upon his left, and we will cut him off upon the right. If your horse be indeed the swifter, then you cannot fail to take him."

Nigel had already sprung down and was tightening Pommers' girth.

"Nay, there is no need of haste, for you cannot start until we are two miles upon our way. And above all I pray you, Nigel, none of your knight-errant ways. It is this man that I want, him and the news that he can bring me. Think little of your own advancement and much of the needs of the army. When you get him, ride westwards upon the sun, and you cannot fail to find the road."

Nigel waited with Pommers under the shadow of the nunnery wall, horse and man chafing with impatience, while above them six round-eyed, innocent nun-faces looked down on this strange and disturbing vision from the outer world. At last the long column wound itself out of sight round a curve of the road, and the white dot was gone from the bare green flank of the hill. Nigel bowed his steel head to the nuns, gave his bridle a shake, and bounded off upon his welcome mission. The round-eyed sisters saw yellow horse and twinkling man sweep round the skirt of the wood, caught a last glimmer of him through the tree-trunks, and paced slowly back to their pruning and their planting, their minds filled with the beauty and the terror of that outer world beyond the high grey lichen-mottled wall.

Everything fell out even as Knolles had planned. As Nigel rounded the oak forest, there upon the farther side of it, with only good greensward between, was the rider upon the white horse. Already he was so near that Nigel could see him clearly, a young cavalier, proud in his bearing, clad in purple silk tunic with a red curling feather in his low black cap. He wore no armour, but his sword gleamed at his side. He rode easily and carelessly, as one who cares for no man, and his eyes were for ever fixed upon the English soldiers on the road. So intent was he upon them that he gave no thought to his own safety, and it was only when the low thunder of the great horse's hoofs broke upon his ears that he turned in his saddle, looked very coolly and steadily at Nigel, then gave his own bridle a shake and darted off, swift as a hawk, towards the hills upon the left.

Pommers had met his match that day. The white horse, two parts Arab, bore the lighter weight, since Nigel was clad in full armour. For five miles over the open neither gained a hundred yards upon the other. They had topped the hill and flew down the farther side, the stranger continually turning in his saddle to have a look at his pursuer. There was no panic in his flight, but rather the amused rivalry with which a good horseman who is proud of his mount contends with one who has challenged him. Below the hill was a marshy plain, studded with great Druidic stones, some prostrate, some erect, some bearing others across their tops like the huge doors of some vanished building. A path ran through the marsh, with green rushes as a danger signal on either side of it. Across this path many of the huge stones were lying, but the white horse cleared them in its stride, and Pommers followed close upon his heels. Then came a mile of soft ground where the lighter weight again drew to the front, but it ended in a dry upland, and once again Nigel gained. A sunken road crossed it, but the white cleared it with a mighty spring, and again the yellow followed. Two small hills lay before them with a narrow gorge of deep bushes between. Nigel saw the white horse bounding chest-deep amid the underwood.

Next instant its hind legs were high in the air, and the rider had been shot from its back. A howl of triumph rose from amid the bushes, and a dozen wild figures, armed with club and with spear, rushed upon the prostrate man.

" *A moi, Anglais, moi !* " cried a voice, and Nigel saw the young rider stagger to his feet, strike round him with his sword, and then fall once more before the rush of his assailants.

There was a comradeship among men of gentle blood and bearing which banded them together against all ruffianly or unchivalrous attack. These rude fellows were no soldiers. Their dress and arms, their uncouth cries and wild assault, marked them as banditti—such men as had slain the Englishman upon the road. Waiting in narrow gorges with a hidden rope across the path, they watched for the lonely horseman as a fowler waits by his bird-trap, trusting that they could overthrow the steed and then slay the rider ere he had recovered from his fall.

Such would have been the fate of the stranger, as of so many cavaliers before him, had Nigel not chanced to be close upon his heels. In an instant Pommers had burst through the group who struck at the prostrate man, and in another two of the robbers had fallen before Nigel's sword. A spear rang on his breastplate, but one blow shore off its head, and a second that of the man who held it. In vain they thrust at the steel-girt man. His sword played round them like lightning, and the fierce horse ramped and swooped above them with pawing iron-shod hoofs and eyes of fire. With cries and shrieks they flew off to right and left amid the bushes, springing over boulders and darting under branches where no horseman could follow them. The foul crew had gone as swiftly and suddenly as it had come, and save for four ragged figures littered among the trampled bushes, no sign remained of their passing.

Nigel tethered Pommers to a thorn-bush and then turned his attention to the injured man. The white horse had regained his feet, and stood whinnying gently as he looked down on his prostrate master. A heavy blow, half broken by his sword, had beaten him down and left a great raw bruise upon his forehead. But a stream gurgled through the gorge, and a capful of water dashed over his face brought the senses back to the injured man. He was a mere stripling, with the delicate features of a woman, and a pair of great violet-blue eyes, which looked up presently with a puzzled stare into Nigel's face.

" Who are you ? " he asked. " Ah yes ! I call you to mind. You are the young Englishman who chased me on the great yellow horse. By our Lady of Rocamadour, whose vernicle is round my neck ! I could not have believed that any horse could have kept at the heels of Charlemagne so long. But I will wager you a hundred crowns, Englishman, that I lead you over a five-mile course."

" Nay," said Nigel, " we will wait till you can back a horse ere we talk of racing it. I am Nigel of Tilford, of the family of Loring, a squire by rank, and the son of a knight. How are you called, young sir ? "

" I also am a squire by rank and the son of a knight. I am Raoul de la Roche Pierre de Bras, whose father writes himself Lord of Grosbois, a free vavasor of the noble Count of Toulouse, with the right of fossa and of furca, the high justice, the middle and the low. He sat up and rubbed his eyes. " Englishman, you have saved my life, as I would have saved yours, had I seen such yelping dogs set upon a man of blood and of coat-armour. But now I am yours, and what is your sweet will ? "

"When you are fit to ride, you will come back with me to my people."

"Alas! I feared that you would say so. Had I taken you, Nigel—that is your name, is it not?—had I taken you, I would not have acted thus?"

"How, then, would you have ordered things?" asked Nigel, much taken with the frank and debonair manner of his captive.

"I would not have taken advantage of such a mischance as has befallen me which has put me in your power. I would give you a sword and beat you in fair fight, so that I might send you to give greeting to my dear lady and show her the deeds which I do for her fair sake."

"Indeed, your words are both good and fair," said Nigel. "By Saint Paul! I cannot call to mind that I have ever met a man who bore himself better. But since I am in my armour and you without, I see not how we can debate the matter."

"Surely, gentle Nigel, you could doff your armour."

"Then have I only my underclothes."

"Nay, there shall be no unfairness there, for I also will very gladly strip to my underclothes."

Nigel looked wistfully at the Frenchman; but he shook his head. "Alas! it may not be," said he. "The last words that Sir Robert said to me were that I was to bring you to his side, for he would have speech with you. Would that I could do what you ask, for I also have a fair lady to whom I would fain send you. What use are you to me, Raoul, since I have gained no honour in the taking of you? How is it with you now?"

The young Frenchman had risen to his feet. "Do not take my sword," he said. "I am yours, rescue or no rescue. I think now that I could mount my horse, though indeed my head still rings like a cracked bell."

Nigel had lost all traces of his comrades; but he remembered Sir Robert's words that he should ride upon the sun with the certainty that sooner or later he would strike upon the road. As they jogged slowly along over undulating hills, the Frenchman shook off his hurt, and the two chatted merrily together.

" I had but just come from France," said he, " and I had hoped to win honour in this country, for I have ever heard that the English are very hardy men and excellent people to fight with. My mules and my baggage are at Evran ; but I rode forth to see what I could see, and I chanced upon your army moving down the road, so I coasted it in the hopes of some profit or adventure. Then you came after me, and I would have given all the golden goblets upon my father's table if I had my harness so that I could have turned upon you. I have promised the Countess Beatrice that I will send her an Englishman or two to kiss her hands."

" One might perchance have a worse fate," said Nigel. " Is this fair dame your betrothed ? "

" She is my love," answered the Frenchman. " We are but waiting for the Count to be slain in the wars, and then we mean to marry. And this lady of thine, Nigel ? I would that I could see her."

" Perchance you shall, fair sir," said Nigel, " for all that I have seen of you fills me with desire to go further with you. It is in my mind that we might turn this thing to profit and to honour, for when Sir Robert has spoken with you, I am free to do with you as I will."

" And what will you do, Nigel ? "

" We shall surely try some small deed upon each other, so that either I shall see the Lady Beatrice, or you the Lady Mary. Nay, thank me not, for like yourself, I have come to this country in search of honour, and I know not where I may better find it than at the end of your sword-point. My good lord and master, Sir John Chandos, has told me many times that never yet did he meet French knight nor squire that he did not find great pleasure and profit from their company, and now I very clearly see that he has spoken the truth."

For an hour these two friends rode together, the French-man pouring forth the praises of his lady, whose glove he produced from one pocket, her garter from his vest, and her shoe from his saddle-bag. She was blonde, and when he heard that Mary was dark, he would fain stop then and there to fight the question of colour. He talked too of his great château at Lauta, by the head waters of the pleasant Garonne ; of the hundred horses in the stables, the seventy hounds in the kennels, the fifty hawks in the mews. His English friend should come there when the wars were over, and what golden days would be theirs ! Nigel too, with his English coldness thawing before this young sunbeam of the South, found himself talking of the heather slopes of Surrey, of the forest of Woolmer, even of the sacred chambers of Cosford.

But as they rode onward toward the sinking sun, their thoughts far away in their distant homes, their horses striding together, there came that which brought their minds back in an instant to the perilous hillsides of Brittany.

It was the long blast of a trumpet blown from somewhere on the farther side of a ridge toward which they were riding. A second long-drawn note from a distance answered it.

" It is your camp," said the Frenchman.

" Nay," said Nigel ; " we have pipes with us and a naker or two, but I have heard no trumpet-call from our ranks. It behoves us to take heed, for we know not what may be before us. Ride this way, I pray you, that we may look over and yet be ourselves unseen."

Some scattered boulders crowned the height, and from behind them the two young squires could see the long rocky valley beyond. Upon a knoll was a small square building with a battlement round it. Some distance from it towered a great dark castle, as massive as the rocks on which it stood, with one strong keep at the corner, and four long lines of machicolated walls. Above, a great banner flew proudly in the wind, with some device which glowed red in the setting sun. Nigel shaded his eyes and stared with wrinkled brow.

" It is not the arms of England, nor yet the lilies of France, nor is it the ermine of Brittany," said he. " He who holds this castle fights for his own hand, since his own device flies above it.   Surely it is a head gules on an argent field."

" The bloody head on a silver tray ! " cried the Frenchman.   " Was I not warned against him ?   This is not a man, friend Nigel.   It is a monster who wars upon English, French, and all Christendom.   Have you not heard of the butcher of La Brohinière ? "

" Nay, I have not heard of him."

" His name is accursed in France.   Have I not been told also that he put to death this very year Giles de St. Pol, a friend of the English King ? "

" Yes, in very truth it comes back to my mind now that I heard something of this matter in Calais before we started."

" Then there he dwells, and God guard you if ever you pass under yonder portal, for no prisoner has ever come forth alive !   Since these wars began he hath been a king to himself, and the plunder of eleven years lies in yonder cellars.   How can justice come to him, when no man knows who owns the land ?   But when we have packed you all back to your island, by the Blessed Mother of God, we have a heavy debt to pay to the man who dwells in yonder pile ! "

But even as they watched, the trumpet-call burst forth once more.   It came not from the castle but from the farther end of the valley.   It was answered by a second call from the walls.   Then in a long, straggling line there came a wild troop of marauders streaming homeward from some foray.   In the van, at the head of a body of spearmen, rode a tall and burly man, clad in brazen armour, so that he shone like a golden image in the slanting rays of the sun.   His helmet had been loosened from his gorget and was held before him on his horse's neck.   A great tangled beard flowed over his breastplate, and his hair hung down as far behind.   A squire at his elbow bore high the banner of the bleeding head.   Behind the spearmen were a line of heavily laden mules, and on either side of them a drove of poor country folk, who were being herded into the

681

castle. Lastly came a second strong troop of mounted spearmen, who conducted a score or more of prisoners who marched together in a solid body.

Nigel stared at them, and then springing on his horse, he urged it along the shelter of the ridge so as to reach unseen a spot which was close to the castle gate. He had scarce taken up his new position when the cavalcade reached the drawbridge, and amid yells of welcome from those upon the wall, filed in a thin line across it. Nigel stared hard once more at the prisoners in the rear, and so absorbed was he by the sight that he had passed the rocks and was standing sheer upon the summit.

" By Saint Paul ! " he cried, " it must indeed be so. I see their russet jackets. They are English archers ! "

As he spoke, the hindmost one, a strongly built, broad-shouldered man, looked round and saw the gleaming figure above him upon the hill, with open helmet, and the five roses glowing upon his breast. With a sweep of his hands he had thrust his guardians aside, and for a moment was clear of the throng.

" Squire Loring ! Squire Loring ! " he cried. " It is I, Aylward the archer ! It is I, Samkin Aylward ! " The next minute a dozen hands had seized him, his cries were muffled with a gag, and he was hurled, the last of the band, through the black and threatening archway of the gate. Then with a clang the two iron wings came together, the portcullis swung upward, and captives and captors, robbers and booty, were all swallowed up within the grim and silent fortress.

20. *How the English attempted the Castle of La Brohinière*

FOR some minutes Nigel remained motionless upon the crest of the hill, his heart like lead within him, and his eyes fixed upon the huge grey walls which contained his unhappy henchman. He was roused by a sympathetic hand upon his shoulder, and the voice of his young prisoner in his ear.

" *Peste !* " said he. " They have some of your birds in their cage, have they not ? What, then, my friend ? Keep your heart high ! Is it not the chance of war, to-day to them, to-morrow to thee, and death at last for us all ? And yet I had rather they were in any hands than those of Oliver the Butcher."

" By Saint Paul, we cannot suffer it ! " cried Nigel, distractedly. " This man has come with me from my own home. He has stood between me and death before now. It goes to my very heart that he should call upon me in vain. I pray you, Raoul, to use your wits, for mine are all curdled in my head. Tell me what I should do, and how I may bring him help."

The Frenchman shrugged his shoulders. "As easy to get a lamb unscathed out of a wolves' lair as a prisoner safe from La Brohinière. Nay, Nigel, whither do you go ? Have you, indeed, taken leave of your wits ? "

The squire had spurred his horse down the hillside, and never halted until he was within a bowshot of the gate. The French prisoner followed hard behind him with a buzz of reproaches and expostulations.

" You are mad, Nigel ! " he cried. " What do you hope to do, then ? Would you carry the castle with your own hands ? Halt, man, halt, in the name of the Virgin ! "

But Nigel had no plan in his head, and only obeyed the fevered impulse to do something to ease his thoughts. He paced his horse up and down, waving his spear, and shouting insults and challenges to the garrison. Over the high wall a hundred jeering faces looked down upon him. So rash and wild was his action that it seemed to those within to mean some trap, so the drawbridge was still held high, and none ventured forth to seize him. A few long-range arrows pattered on the rocks, and then, with a deep, booming sound, a huge stone, hurled from a mangonel, sang over the heads of the two squires, and crashed into splinters among the boulders behind them. The Frenchman seized Nigel's bridle, and forced him farther from the gateway.

" By the dear Virgin ! " he cried, " I care not to have those pebbles about my ears, yet I cannot go back alone, so it is very clear, my crazy comrade, that you must come also. Now we are beyond their reach ! But see, my friend Nigel, who are those who crown the height ? "

The sun had sunk behind the western ridge, but the glowing sky was fringed at its lower edge by a score of ruddy, twinkling points. A body of horsemen showed hard and black upon the bare hill. Then they dipped down the slope into the valley, while a band of footmen followed behind.

" They are my people," cried Nigel, joyously. " Come, my friend, hasten, that we may take counsel what we shall do."

Sir Robert Knolles rode a bowshot in front of his men, and his brow was as black as night. Beside him, with crestfallen face, his horse bleeding, his armour dinted and soiled, was the hot-headed knight, Sir James Astley. A fierce discussion raged between them.

" I have done my devoir as best I might," said Astley. " Alone I had ten of them at my sword point. I know not how I have lived to tell it."

" What is your devoir to me ? Where are my thirty bowmen ? " cried Knolles, in bitter wrath. " Ten lie dead upon the ground, and twenty are worse than dead in yonder castle. And all because you must needs show all men how bold you are, and ride into a bushment such as a child could see. Alas for my own folly that ever I should have trusted such a one as you with the handling of men ! "

" By God, Sir Robert, you shall answer to me for those words ! " cried Astley, with a choking voice. " Never has a man dared to speak to me as you have done this day."

" As long as I hold the king's order I shall be master, and by the Lord I will hang you, James, on a near tree if I have further cause of offence ! How now, Nigel ? I see by yonder white horse that you, at least, have not failed me. I will speak with you anon. Percy, bring up your men, and let us gather round this castle, for, as I hope for my soul's salvation, I will not leave it until I have my archers, or the head of him who holds them."

That night the English lay thick round the fortress of La Brohinière, so that none might come forth from it. But if none could come forth it was hard to see how any could win their way in, for it was full of men, the walls were high and strong, and a deep, dry ditch girt it round. But the hatred and fear which its master had raised over the whole countryside could now be plainly seen, for during the night the brushwood men and the villagers came in from all parts with offers of such help as they could give for the intaking of the castle. Knolles set them cutting bushes and tying them into faggots. When morning came he rode out before the wall, and he held counsel with his knights and squires as to how he should enter in.

" By noon," said he, " we shall have so many faggots that we may make our way over the ditch. Then we will beat in the gates and so win a footing."

The young Frenchman had come with Nigel to the conference, and now, amid the silence which followed the leader's proposal, he asked if he might be heard. He was clad in the brazen armour which Nigel had taken from the Red Ferret.

" It may be that it is not for me to join in your counsel," said he, " seeing that I am a prisoner and a Frenchman. But this man is the enemy of all, and we of France owe him a debt even as you do, since many a good Frenchman has died in his cellars. For this reason I crave to be heard."

" We will hear you," said Knolles.

" I have come from Evran yesterday," said he. " Sir Henry Spinnefort, Sir Peter La Roye, and many other brave knights and squires lie there, with a good company of men, all of whom would very gladly join with you to destroy this butcher and his castle, for it is well known amongst us that his deeds are neither good nor fair. There are also bombards which we could drag over the hills, and so beat down this iron gate. If you so order it, I will ride to Evran and bring my companions back with me."

"Indeed, Robert," said Percy, "it is in my mind that this Frenchman speaks very wisely and well."

"And when we have taken the castle—what then ? " asked Knolles.

"Then you could go upon your way, fair sir, and we upon ours. Or if it please you better you could draw together on yonder hill, and we on this one, so that the valley lies between us. Then, if any cavalier wished to advance himself, or to shed a vow and exalt his lady, an opening might be found for him. Surely it would be shame if so many brave men drew together, and no small deed were to come of it."

Nigel clasped his captive's hand to show his admiration and esteem, but Knolles shook his head.

"Things are not ordered thus, save in the tales of the minstrels," said he. "I have no wish that your people at Evran should know our numbers or our plans. I am not in this land for knight-errantry, but I am here to make head against the king's enemies. Has no one aught else to say ? "

Percy pointed to the small outlying fortalice upon the knoll, on which also flew the flag of the bloody head.

"This smaller castle, Robert, is of no great strength, and cannot hold more than fifty men. It is built, as I conceive it, that no one should seize the high ground, and shoot down into the other. Why should we not turn all our strength upon it, since it is the weaker of the twain ? "

But again the young leader shook his head. "If I should take it," said he, "I am still no nearer to my desire, nor will it avail me in getting my bowmen. It may cost a score of men, and what profit shall I have from it ?   Had I bombards, I might place them on yonder hill, but having none it is of little use to me."

" It may be," said Nigel, " that they have scant food or water, and so must come forth to fight us."

" I have made inquiry of the peasants," Knolles answered, " and they are of one mind that there is a well within the castle, and good store of food. Nay, gentlemen, there is no way before us save to take it by arms, and no spot where we can attempt it save through the great gate. Soon we will have so many faggots that we can cast them down into the ditch, and so win our way across. I have ordered them to cut a pine-tree on the hill and shear the branches, so that we may beat down the gate with it. But what is now amiss, and why do they run forward to the castle ? "

A buzz had risen from the soldiers in the camp, and they all crowded in one direction, rushing towards the castle wall. The knights and squires rode after them, and when in view of the main gate, the cause of the disturbance lay before them. On the tower above the portal three men were standing in the garb of English archers, ropes round their necks and their hands bound behind them. Their comrades surged below them with cries of recognition and of pity.

" It is Ambrose ! " cried one. " Surely it is Ambrose of Ingleton."

" Yes, in truth, I see his yellow hair. And the other, him with the beard, it is Lockwood of Skipton. Alas for his wife who keeps the booth by the bridge-head of Ribble ! I wot not who the third may be."

" It is little Johnny Alspaye, the youngest man in the company," cried old Wat, with the tears running down his cheeks. " 'Twas I who brought him from his home. Alas ! alas ! Foul fare the day that ever I coaxed him from his mother's side that he might perish in a far land."

There was a sudden flourish of a trumpet, and the drawbridge fell. Across it strode a portly man with a faded herald's coat. He halted warily upon the farther side, and his voice boomed like a drum.

" I would speak with your leader," he cried.

Knolles rode forward.

"Have I your knightly word that I may advance unscathed with all courteous entreaty as befits a herald ? "

Knolles nodded his head.

The man came slowly and pompously forward. " I am the messenger and liege servant," said he, " of the high baron, Oliver de St. Yvon, Lord of La Brohinière. He bids me to say that if you continue your journey and molest him no further, he will engage upon his part to make no further attack upon you. As to the men whom he holds, he will enrol them in his own honourable service, for he has need of longbowmen, and has heard much of their skill. But if you constrain him or cause him further displeasure by remaining before his castle, he hereby gives you warning that he will hang these three men over his gateway, and every morning another three, until all have been slain. This he has sworn upon the rood of Calvary, and as he has said so he will do upon jeopardy of his soul."

Robert Knolles looked grimly at the messenger. " You may thank the saints that you have had my promise," said he, " else would I have stripped that lying tabard from thy back and the skin beneath it from thy bones, that thy master might have a fitting answer to his message. Tell him that I hold him and all that are within his castle as hostage for the lives of my men, and that should he dare to do them scathe, he and every man that is with him shall hang upon his battlements. Go, and go quickly, lest my patience fail."

There was that in Knolles' cold grey eyes and in his manner of speaking those last words which sent the portly envoy back at a quicker gait than he had come. As he vanished into the gloomy arch of the gateway, the drawbridge swung up with creak and rattle behind him.

A few minutes later a rough-bearded fellow stepped

out over the portal where the condemned archers stood, and seizing the first by the shoulders he thrust him over the wall. A cry burst from the man's lips, and a deep groan from those of his comrades below, as he fell with a jerk which sent him halfway up to the parapet again, and then, after dancing like a child's toy, swung slowly, backward and forward, with limp limbs and twisted neck.

The hangman turned and bowed in mock reverence to the spectators beneath him. He had not yet learned in a land of puny archers how sure and how strong is the English bow. Half a dozen men, old Wat among them, had run forward toward the wall. They were too late to save their comrades, but at least their deaths were speedily avenged. The man was in the act of pushing off the second prisoner when an arrow crashed through his head, and he fell stone dead upon the parapet. But even in falling he had given the fatal thrust, and a second russet figure swung beside the first against the dark background of the castle wall.

There only remained the young lad, Johnny Alspaye, who stood shaking with fear, an abyss below him, and the voices of those who would hurl him over it behind. There was a long pause before anyone would come forth to dare those deadly arrows. Then a fellow, crouching double, ran forward from the shelter, keeping the young archer's body as a shield between him and danger.

"Aside, John! Aside!" cried his comrades from below.

The youth sprang as far as the rope would allow him, and slipped it half over his face in the effort. Three arrows flashed past his side, and two of them buried themselves in the body of the man behind. A howl of delight burst from the spectators as he dropped first upon his knees and then upon his face. A life for a life was no bad bargain.

But it was only a short respite which the skill of his comrades had given to the young archer. Over the parapet there appeared a ball of brass, then a pair of great brazen shoulders, and lastly the full figure of an armoured man. He walked to the edge, and they heard his hoarse guffaw of laughter as the arrows clanged and clattered against his impenetrable mail. He slapped his breastplate as he jeered at them. Well he knew that at the distance no dart ever sped by mortal hands could cleave through his plates of metal. So he stood, the great burly Butcher of La Brohinière, with head uptossed, laughing insolently at his foes. Then, with slow and ponderous tread, he walked toward his boy victim, seized him by the ear, and dragged him across so that the rope might be straight. Seeing that the noose had slipped across the face, he tried to push it down, but the mail glove hampering him, he pulled it off, and grasped the rope above the lad's head with his naked hand.

Quick as a flash old Wat's arrow had sped, and the Butcher sprang back with a howl of pain, his hand skewered by a cloth-yard shaft. As he shook it furiously at his enemies a second grazed his knuckles. With a brutal kick of his metal-shod feet he hurled young Alspaye over the edge, looked down for a few moments at his death agonies, and then walked slowly from the parapet, nursing his dripping hand, the arrows still ringing loudly upon his backpiece as he went.

The archers below, enraged at the death of their comrades, leaped and howled like a pack of ravening wolves.

" By Saint Dunstan," said Percy, looking round at their flushed faces, " if ever we are to carry it, now is the moment, for these men will not be stopped if hate can take them forward."

" You are right, Thomas ! " cried Knolles. " Gather together twenty man-at-arms, each with his shield to cover him. Astley, do you place the bowmen so that no head may show at window or parapet. Nigel, I pray you to order the countryfolk forward with their fardels of faggots. Let the others bring up the lopped pine-tree, which lies yonder behind the horse-lines. Ten men-at-arms can bear it on the right, and ten on the left, having shields over their heads. The gate once down, let every man rush in. And God help the better cause ! "

Swiftly, and yet quietly, the dispositions were made, for these were old soldiers whose daily trade was war. In little groups the archers formed in front of each slit or crevice in the walls, while others scanned the battlements with wary eyes, and sped an arrow at every face which gleamed for an instant above them. The garrison shot forth a shower of crossbow bolts and an occasional stone from their engine, but so deadly was the hail which rained upon them that they had no time to dwell upon their aim, and their discharges were wild and harmless. Under cover of the shafts of the bowmen, a line of peasants ran unscathed to the edge of the ditch, each hurling in the bundle which he bore in his arms, and then hurrying back for another one. In twenty minutes a broad pathway of faggots lay level with the ground upon one side and the gate upon the other. With the loss of two peasants slain by bolts and one archer crushed by a stone, the ditch had been filled up. All was ready for the battering-ram.

With a shout, twenty picked men rushed forward with the pine-tree under their arms, the heavy end turned toward the gate. The arbalesters on the tower leaned over and shot into the midst of them, but could not stop their advance. Two dropped, but the others raising their shields ran onward still shouting, crossed the bridge of faggots, and came with a thundering crash against the door. It splintered from base to arch, but kept its place.

Swinging their mighty weapon, the storming party thudded and crashed upon the gate, every blow loosening and widening the cracks which rent it from end to end. The three knights, with Nigel, the Frenchman Raoul, and the other squires, stood beside the ram, cheering on the men, and chanting to the rhythm of the swing with a loud " Ha ! " at every blow. A great stone loosened from the parapet roared through the air and struck Sir James Astley and another of the attackers, but Nigel and the Frenchman had taken their places in an instant, and the

691

ram thudded and smashed with greater energy than ever. Another blow and another ! the lower part was staving inward, but the great central bar still held firm. Surely another minute would beat it from its sockets.

But suddenly from above there came a great deluge of liquid. A hogshead of it had been tilted from the battlement until soldiers, bridge, and ram were equally drenched in yellow slime. Knolles rubbed his gauntlet in it, held it to his visor, and smelled it.

" Back, back ! " he cried. " Back before it is too late ! "

There was a small barred window above their heads at the side of the gate. A ruddy glare shone through it, and then a blazing torch was tossed down upon them. In a moment the oil had caught and the whole place was a sheet of flame. The fir-tree that they carried, the faggots beneath them, their very weapons, were all in a blaze.

To right and left the men sprang down into the dry ditch, rolling with screams upon the ground in their endeavour to extinguish the flames. The knights and squires protected by their armour strove hard, stamping and slapping, to help those who had but leather jacks to shield their bodies. From above a ceaseless shower of darts and of stones were poured down upon them, while on the other hand the archers, seeing the greatness of the danger, ran up to the edge of the ditch, and shot fast and true at every face which showed above the wall.

Scorched, wearied and bedraggled, the remains of the storming party clambered out of the ditch as best they could, clutching at the friendly hands held down to them, and so limped their way back amid the taunts and howls of their enemies. A long pile of smouldering cinders was all that remainded of their bridge, and on it lay Astley and six other red-hot men glowing in their armour.

Knolles clinched his hands as he looked back at the ruin that was wrought, and then surveyed the group of men who stood or lay around him nursing their burned limbs and scowling up at the exultant figures who waved on the castle wall. Badly scorched himself, the young leader had no thought for his own injuries in the rage and grief which racked his soul.

" We will build another bridge," he cried. " Set the peasants binding faggots once more."

But a thought had flashed through Nigel's mind. " See, fair sir," said he. " The nails of yonder door are red-hot and the wood as white as ashes. Surely we can break our way through it."

" By the Virgin, you speak truly ! " cried the French squire. " If we can cross the ditch the gate will not stop us. Come, Nigel, for our fair ladies' sakes, I will race you who will reach it first, England or France."

Alas for all the wise words of the good Chandos ! Alas for all the lessons in order and discipline learned from the wary Knolles. In an instant, forgetful of all things but this noble challenge, Nigel was running at the top of his speed for the burning gate. Close at his heels was the Frenchman, blowing and gasping, as he rushed along in his brazen armour. Behind came a stream of howling archers and men-at-arms, like a flood which has broken its dam. Down they slipped into the ditch, rushed across it, and clambered on each other's backs up the opposite side. Nigel, Raoul, and two archers gained a foothold in front of the burning gate at the same moment. With blows and kicks they burst it to pieces, and dashed with a yell of triumph through the dark archway beyond. For a moment they thought with mad rapture that the castle was carried. A dark tunnel lay before them, down which they rushed. But alas ! at the farther end it was blocked by a second gateway as strong as that which had been burned. In vain they beat upon it with their swords and axes. On each side the tunnel was pierced with slits, and the crossbow bolts discharged at only a few yards' distance crashed through armour as if it were cloth, and laid man after man upon the stones. They raged and leaped before the great iron-clamped barrier, but the wall itself was as easy to tear down.

It was bitter to draw back ; but it was madness to

remain. Nigel looked round and saw that half his men were down. At the same moment Raoul sank with a gasp at his feet, a bolt driven to its socket through the links of the camail which guarded his neck. Some of the archers, seeing that certain death awaited them, were already running back to escape from the fatal passage.

" By Saint Paul ! " cried Nigel, hotly. " Would you leave our wounded where this butcher may lay his hands upon them ? Let the archers shoot inwards and hold them back from the slits. Now let each man raise one of our comrades, lest we leave our honour in the gate of this castle."

With a mighty effort he had raised Raoul upon his shoulders and staggered with him to the edge of the ditch. Several men were waiting below where the steep bank shielded them from the arrows, and to them Nigel handed down his wounded friend, and each archer in turn did the same. Again and again Nigel went back, until no one lay in the tunnel save seven who had died there. Thirteen wounded were laid in the shelter of the ditch, and there they must remain until night came to cover them. Meanwhile the bowmen on the farther side protected them from attack, and also prevented the enemy from all attempts to build up the outer gate. The gaping smoke-blackened arch was all that they could show for a loss of thirty men, but that at least Knolles was determined to keep.

Burned and bruised, but unconscious of either pain or fatigue for the turmoil of his spirit within him, Nigel knelt by the Frenchman and loosened his helmet. The girlish face of the young squire was white as chalk, and the haze of death was gathering over his violet eyes, but a faint smile played round his lips as he looked up at his English comrade.

" I shall never see Beatrice again," he whispered. " I pray you, Nigel, that when there is a truce you will journey as far as my father's château and tell him how his son died. Young Gaston will rejoice, for to him come the land and the coat, the war-cry and the profit. See them, Nigel, and tell them that I was as forward as the others."

" Indeed, Raoul, no man could have carried himself with more honour or won more worship than you have done this day. I will do your behest when the time comes."

" Surely you are happy, Nigel," the dying squire murmured, " for this day has given you one more deed which you may lay at the feet of your lady-love."

" It might have been so had we carried the gate," Nigel answered sadly ; " but, by Saint Paul ! I cannot count it a deed where I have come back with my purpose unfulfilled. But this is no time, Raoul, to talk of my small affairs. If we take the castle, and I bear a good part in it, then perchance all this may indeed avail."

The Frenchman sat up with that strange energy which comes often as the harbinger of death.

" You will win your Lady Mary, Nigel, and your great deeds will be not three but a score, so that in all Christendom there shall be no man of blood and coat-armour who has not heard your name and your fame. This I tell you—I, Raoul de la Roche Pierre de Bras, dying upon the field of honour. And now kiss me, sweet friend, and lay me back, for the mists close round me and I am gone ! "

With tender hands the squire lowered his comrade's head, but even as he did so there came a choking rush of blood, and the soul had passed. So died a gallant cavalier of France, and Nigel, as he knelt in the ditch beside him, prayed that his own end might be as noble and as debonair.

21. *How the Second Messenger went to Cosford*

UNDER cover of night the wounded men were lifted from the ditch and carried back, while pickets of archers were advanced to the very gate so that none should rebuild it. Nigel, sick at heart over his own failure, the death of his prisoner, and his fears for Aylward, crept back into the camp, but his cup was not yet full, for Knolles was waiting for him with a tongue which cut like a whip-lash. Who was he, a raw squire, that he should lead an attack without orders ? See what his crazy knight-errantry had brought about. Twenty men had been destroyed by it and nothing gained. Their blood was on his head. Chandos should hear of his conduct. He should be sent back to England when the castle had fallen.

Such were the bitter words of Knolles, the more bitter because Nigel felt in his heart that he had indeed done wrong, and that Chandos would have said the same, though, perchance, in kinder words. He listened in silent respect, as his duty was, and then, having saluted his leader, he withdrew apart, threw himself down among the bushes, and wept the hottest tears of his life, sobbing bitterly, with his face between his hands. He had striven hard, and yet everything had gone wrong with him. He was bruised, burned, and aching from head to foot. Yet so high is the spirit above the body that all was nothing compared to the sorrow and shame which racked his soul.

But a little thing changed the current of his thoughts and brought some peace to his mind. He had slipped off his mail gauntlets, and as he did so his fingers lighted upon the tiny bangle which Mary had fastened there when they stood together upon St. Catharine's Hill on the Guildford Road. He remembered the motto curiously worked in filigree of gold. It ran : " *Fais ce que dois, adviegne que pourra—c'est commandé au chevalier.*"

The words rang in his weary brain. He had done what seemed right, come what might. It had gone awry, it is true ; but all things human may do that. If he had carried the castle, he felt that Knolles would have forgiven and forgotten all else. If he had not carried it, it was no fault of his. No man could have done more. If Mary could see she would surely have approved. Dropping into sleep, he saw her dark face, shining with pride and with pity, stooping over him as he lay. She stretched out her hand in his dream and touched him on the shoulder. He sprang up and rubbed his eyes, for fact had woven itself into dream in the strange way that it does, and someone was indeed leaning over him in the gloom, and shaking him from his slumbers. But the gentle voice and soft touch of the Lady Mary had changed suddenly to the harsh accents and rough grip of Black Simon, the fierce Norfolk man-at-arms.

"Surely you are the Squire Loring," he said, peering close to his face in the darkness.

"I am he. What then?"

"I have searched through the camp for you, but when I saw the great horse tethered near these bushes, I thought you would be found hard by. I would have a word with you."

"Speak on."

"This man Aylward the bowman was my friend, and it is the nature that God has given me to love my friends even as I hate my foes. He is also thy servant, and it has seemed to me that you love him also."

"I have good cause so to do."

"Then you and I, Squire Loring, have more reason to strive on his behalf than any of these others, who think more of taking the castle than of saving those who are captives within. Do you not see that such a man as this robber lord would, when all else had failed him, most surely cut the throats of his prisoners at the last instant before the castle fell, knowing well that, come what might, he would have short shrift himself? Is that not certain?"

"By Saint Paul! I had not thought of it."

"I was with you, hammering at the inner gate," said Simon, "and yet once when I thought that it was giving way, I said in my heart, 'Good-bye, Samkin! I shall never see you more.' This Baron has gall in his soul, even as I have myself, and do you think that I would give up my prisoners alive, if I were constrained so to do? No, no ; had we won our way this day, it would have been the death-stroke for them all."

" It may be that you are right, Simon," said Nigel, " and the thought of it should assuage our grief. But if we cannot save them by taking the castle, then surely they are lost indeed."

" It may be so, or it may not," Simon answered slowly. " It is in my mind that if the castle were taken very suddenly, and in such a fashion that they could not foresee it, then perchance we might get the prisoners before they could do them scathe."

Nigel bent forward eagerly, his hand on the soldier's arm.

" You have some plan in your mind, Simon. Tell me what it is."

" I had wished to tell Sir Robert, but he is preparing the assault for to-morrow, and will not be turned from his purpose. I have indeed a plan, but whether it be good or not I cannot say until I have tried it. But first I will tell you what put it into my thoughts. Know, then, that this morning when I was in yonder ditch I marked one of their men upon the wall. He was a big man with a white face, red hair, and a touch of Saint Anthony's fire upon the cheek."

" But what has this to do with Aylward ? "

" I will show you. This evening, after the assault, I chanced to walk with some of my fellows round yonder small fort upon the knoll to see if we could spy a weak spot in it. Some of them came to the wall to curse us, and among them whom should I see but a big man with a white face, red hair, and a touch of Anthony's fire upon his cheek ! What make you of that, Squire Nigel ? "

" That this man had crossed from the castle to the fort."

" In good sooth, it must indeed be so. There are not two such ken-speckled men in the world. But if he crossed from the castle to the fort, it was not above the ground, for our own people were between."

" By Saint Paul ! I see your meaning ! " cried Nigel.

" It is in your mind that there is a passage under the earth from one to the other."

" I am well sure of it."

" Then if we should take the small fort we may pass down this tunnel, and so carry the great castle also."

" Such a thing might happen," said Simon, " and yet it is dangerous also, for surely those in the castle would hear our assault upon the fort and so be warned to bar the passage against us, and to slay the prisoners before we could come."

" What, then, is your rede ? "

" Could we find where the tunnel lay, Squire Nigel, I know not what is to prevent us from digging down upon it and breaking into it so that both fort and castle are at our mercy before either knows that we are there."

Nigel clapped his hands with joy. " 'Fore God ! " he cried. " It is a most noble plan ! But alas ! Simon, I see not how we can tell the course of this passage or where we should dig."

" I have peasants yonder with spades," said Simon. " There are two of my friends, Harding of Barnstable and West-country John, who are waiting for us with their gear. If you will come to lead us, Squire Nigel, we are ready to venture our bodies in the attempt."

What would Knolles say in case they failed ? The thought flashed through Nigel's mind, but another came swiftly behind it. He would not venture farther unless he found hopes of success. And if he did venture farther he would put his life upon it. Giving that, he made amends for all errors. And if, on the other hand, success crowned their efforts, then Knolles would forgive his failure at the gateway. A minute later, every doubt banished from his mind, he was making his way through the darkness under the guidance of Black Simon.

Outside the camp the two other men-at-arms were waiting for them, and the four advanced together. Presently a little group of figures loomed up in the darkness. It was a cloudy night, and a thin rain was falling, which obscured both the castle and the fort ; but a stone had been placed by Simon in the daytime which assured that they were between the two.

" Is blind Andreas there ? " asked Simon.

" Yes, kind sir, I am here," said a voice.

" This man," said Simon, " was once rich and of good repute, but he was beggared by this robber lord, who afterwards put out his eyes so that he has lived for many years in darkness at the charity of others."

" How can he help us in our enterprise if he be indeed blind ? " asked Nigel.

" It is for that very reason, fair lord, that he can be of greater service than any other man," Simon answered ; " for it often happens that when a man has lost a sense the good God will strengthen those that remain. Hence it is that Andreas has such ears that he can hear the sap in the trees or the cheep of the mouse in its burrow. He has come to help us to find the tunnel."

" And I have found it," said the blind man, proudly. " Here I have placed my staff upon the line of it. Twice as I lay there with my ear to the ground I have heard footsteps pass beneath me."

" I trust you make no mistake, old man," said Nigel.

For answer the blind man raised his staff and smote twice upon the ground, once to the right and once to the left. The one gave a dull thud, the other a hollow boom.

" Can you not hear that ? " he asked. " Will you ask me now if I make a mistake ? "

" Indeed, we are much beholden to you ! " cried Nigel. " Let the peasants dig, then, and as silently as they may. Do you keep your ear upon the ground, Andreas, so that if anyone pass beneath us we shall be warned."

So, amid the driving rain, the little group toiled in the darkness. The blind man lay silent, flat upon his face, and twice they heard his warning hiss and stopped their work, while someone passed beneath. In an hour they had dug down to a stone arch which was clearly the outer side of the tunnel roof. Here was a sad obstacle, for it might take long to loosen a stone, and if their work was not done by the break of day then their enterprise was indeed hopeless. They loosened the mortar with a dagger, and at last dislodged one small stone which enabled them to get at the others. Presently a dark hole blacker than the night around them yawned at their feet, and their swords could touch no bottom to it. They had opened the tunnel.

" I would fain enter it first," said Nigel. " I pray you to lower me down." They held him to the full length of their arms, and then letting him drop they heard him land safely beneath them. An instant later the blind man started up with a low cry of alarm.

" I hear steps coming," said he. " They are far off, but they draw nearer."

Simon thrust his head and neck down the hole. " Squire Nigel," he whispered, " can you hear me ? "

" I can hear you, Simon."

" Andreas says that someone comes."

" Then cover over the hole," came the answer. " Quick, I pray you, cover it over ! "

A mantle was stretched across it, so that no glimmer of light should warn the newcomer. The fear was that he might have heard the sound of Nigel's descent. But soon it was clear that he had not done so, for Andreas announced that he was still advancing. Presently Nigel could hear the distant thud of his feet. If he bore a lantern all was lost. But no gleam of light appeared in the black tunnel, and still the footsteps drew nearer.

Nigel breathed a prayer of thanks to all his guardian saints as he crouched close to the slimy wall and waited breathless, his dagger in his hand. Nearer yet and nearer came the steps. He could hear the stranger's coarse breathing in the darkness. Then as he brushed past Nigel bounded upon him with a tiger spring. There was one gasp of astonishment, and not a sound more, for the squire's grip was on the man's throat and his body was pinned motionless against the wall.

" Simon ! Simon ! " cried Nigel, loudly.

The mantle was moved from the hole.

" Have you a cord ? Or your belts linked together may serve."

One of the peasants had a rope, and Nigel soon felt it dangling against his hand. He listened and there was no sound in the passage. For an instant he released his captive's throat. A torrent of prayers and entreaties came forth. The man was shaking like a leaf in the wind. Nigel pressed the point of his dagger against his face and dared him to open his lips. Then he slipped the rope beneath his arms and tied it.

" Pull him up ! " he whispered, and for an instant the grey glimmer above him was obscured.

" We have him, fair sir," said Simon.

" Then drop me the rope and hold it fast."

A moment later Nigel stood among the group of men who had gathered round their captive. It was too dark to see him, and they dare not strike flint and steel.

Simon passed his hand roughly over him and felt a fat clean-shaven face, and a cloth gabardine which hung to the ankles. " Who are you ? " he whispered. " Speak the truth and speak it low, if you would ever speak again."

The man's teeth chattered in his head with cold and fright.

" I speak no English," he murmured.

" French, then," said Nigel.

" I am a holy priest of God. You court the ban of holy Church when you lay hands upon me. I pray you let me go upon my way, for there are those whom I would shrive and housel. If they should die in sin, their damnation is upon you."

" How are you called, then ? "

" I am Dom Peter de Cervolles."

" De Cervolles, the arch-priest, he who heated the brazier when they burned out my eyes," cried old Andreas. " Of all the devils in hell there is none fouler than this one. Friends, friends, if I have done aught for you this night, I ask but one reward, that ye let me have my will of this man."

But Nigel pushed the old man back. "There is no time for this," he said. "Now, hark you, priest—if priest indeed you be—your gown and tonsure will not save you if you play us false, for we are here of a set purpose, and we will go forward with it, come what may. Answer me and answer me truly or it will be an ill night for you. In what part of the castle does this tunnel enter?"

"In the lower cellar."

"What is at the end?"

"An oaken door."

"Is it barred?"

"Yes, it is barred."

"How would you have entered?"

"I would have given the password."

"Who then would have opened?"

"There is a guard within."

"And beyond him?"

"Beyond him are the prison cells and the jailers."

"Who else would be afoot?"

"No one save a guard at the gate and another on the battlement."

"What, then, is the password?"

The man was silent.

"The password, fellow!"

The cold points of two daggers pricked his throat, but still he would not speak.

"Where is the blind man?" asked Nigel. "Here, Andreas, you can have him and do what you will with him."

"Nay, nay," the priest whimpered. "Keep him off me. Save me from blind Andreas! I will tell you everything."

"The password, then, this instant?"

"It is ' *Benedicite* ! ' "

"We have the password, Simon," cried Nigel. "Come, then, let us on to the farther end. These peasants will guard the priest, and they will remain here lest we wish to send a message."

" Nay, fair sir, it is in my mind that we can do better," said Simon. " Let us take the priest with us, so that he who is within may know his voice."

" It is well thought of," said Nigel, " and first let us pray together, for indeed this night may well be our last."

He and the three men-at-arms knelt in the rain and sent up their simple orisons, Simon still clutching tight to his prisoner's wrist.

The priest fumbled in his breast, and drew something forth.

" It is the heart of the blessed confessor Saint Enogat," said he. " It may be that it will ease and assoil your souls if you would wish to handle it."

The four Englishmen passed the flat silver case from hand to hand, each pressing his lips devoutly upon it. Then they rose to their feet. Nigel was the first to lower himself down the hole ; then Simon ; then the priest, who was instantly seized by the other two. The men-at-arms followed them. They had scarcely moved away from the hole when Nigel stopped.

" Surely someone else came after us," said he.

They listened, but no whisper or rustle came from behind them. For a minute they paused and then resumed their journey through the dark. It seemed a long, long way, though in truth it was but a few hundred yards before they came to a door with a glimmer of yellow light around it, which barred their passage. Nigel struck upon it with his hand.

There was the rasping of a bolt and then a loud voice : " Is that you, priest ? "

" Yes, it is I," said the prisoner, in a quavering voice. " Open, Arnold."

The voice was enough. There was no question of pass-words. The door swung inward, and in an instant the janitor was cut down by Nigel and Simon. So sudden and so fierce was the attack that save for the thud of his body no sound was heard. A flood of light burst outward in the passage, and the Englishmen stood with blinking eyes in its glare.

In front of them lay a stone-flagged corridor, across which lay the dead body of the janitor. It had doors on either side of it, and another grated door at the farther end. A strange hubbub, a kind of low droning and whining, filled the air. The four men were standing listening, full of wonder as to what this might mean, when a sharp cry came from behind them. The priest lay in a shapeless heap upon the ground, and the blood was rushing from his gaping throat. Down the passage, a black shadow in the yellow light, there fled a crouching man, who clattered with a stick as he went.

" It is Andreas," cried West-country Will. " He has slain him."

" Then it was he that I heard behind us," said Nigel. " Doubtless he was at our very heels in the darkness. I fear that the priest's cry has been heard."

" Nay," said Simon, " there are so many cries that one more may well pass. Let us take this lamp from the wall and see what sort of devil's den we have around us."

They opened the door upon the right, and so horrible a smell issued from it that they were driven back from it. The lamp which Simon held forward showed a monkey-like creature mowing and grimacing in a corner, man or woman none could tell, but driven crazy by loneliness and horror. In the other cell was a grey-bearded man fettered to the wall, looking blankly before him, a body without a soul, yet with life still in him, for his dull eyes turned slowly in their direction. But it was from behind the central door at the end of the passage that the chorus of sad cries came which filled the air.

" Simon," said Nigel, " before we go farther we will take this outer door from its hinges. With it we will block this passage so that at the worst we may hold our ground here until help comes. Do you back to the camp as fast as your feet can bear you. The peasants will draw you upward through the hole. Give my greetings to Sir Robert and tell him that the castle is taken without fail if he comes this way with fifty men. Say that we have made a lodgment within the walls. And tell him also, Simon, that I would counsel him to make a stir before the gateway so that the guard may be held there whilst we make good our footing behind them. Go, good Simon, and lose not a moment ! "

But the man-at-arms shook his head. " It is I who have brought you here, fair sir, and here I bide through fair and foul. But you speak wisely and well, for Sir Robert should indeed be told what is going forward now that we have gone so far. Harding, do you go with all speed and bear the gentle Nigel's message."

Reluctantly the man-at-arms sped upon his errand. They could hear the racing of his feet and the low jingle of his harness until they died away in the tunnel. Then the three companions approached the door at the end. It was their intention to wait where they were until help should come, but suddenly amid the babel of cries within there broke forth an English voice, shouting in torment.

" My God ! " it cried, " I pray you, comrades, for a cup of water, as you hope for Christ's mercy ! "

A shout of laughter and the thud of a heavy blow followed the appeal.

All the hot blood rushed to Nigel's head at the sound, buzzing in his ears and throbbing in his temples. There are times when the fiery heart of a man must overbear the cold brain of a soldier. With one bound he was at the door, with another he was through it, the men-at-arms at his heels. So strange was the scene before them that for an instant all three stood motionless with horror and surprise.

It was a great vaulted chamber, brightly lit by many torches. At the farther end roared a great fire. In front of it three naked men were chained to posts in such a way that, flinch as they might, they could never get beyond the range of its scorching heat. Yet they were so far from it that no actual burn would be inflicted if they could but keep turning and shifting so as continually to present some fresh portion of their flesh to the flames. Hence they danced and whirled in front of the fire, tossing ceaselessly this way and that within the compass of their chains, wearied to death, their protruding tongues cracked and blackened with thirst, but unable for one instant to rest from their writhings and contortions.

Even stranger was the sight at each side of the room, whence came that chorus of groans which had first struck upon the ears of Nigel and his companions. A line of great hogsheads were placed alongside the walls, and within each sat a man, his head protruding from the top. As they moved within there was a constant splashing and washing of water. The white wan faces all turned together as the door flew open, and a cry of amazement and of hope took the place of those long-drawn moans of despair.

At the same instant two fellows clad in black, who had been seated with a flagon of wine between them at a table near the fire, sprang wildly to their feet, staring with blank amazement at this sudden inrush. That instant of delay deprived them of their last chance of safety. Midway down the room was a flight of stone steps which led to the main door.

Swift as a wild cat Nigel bounded toward it and gained the steps a stride or two before the jailers. They turned and made for the other which led to the passage, but Simon and his comrades were nearer to it than they. Two sweeping blows, two dagger thrusts into writhing figures, and the ruffians who worked the will of the Butcher lay dead upon the floor of their slaughter-house.

Oh, the buzz of joy and of prayer from all those white lips ! Oh, the light of returning hope in all those sunken weary eyes ! One wild shout would have gone up had not Nigel's outstretched hands and warning voice hushed them to silence.

He opened the door behind him. A curving newel

staircase wound upward into the darkness. He listened, but no sound came down. There was a key in the outer lock of the iron door. He whipped it out and turned it on the inner side. The ground that they had gained was safe. Now they could turn to the relief of these poor fellows beside them. A few strong blows struck off the irons and freed the three dancers before the fire. With a husky croak of joy, they rushed across to their comrades' water-barrels, plunged their heads in like horses, and drank and drank and drank. Then in turn the poor shivering wretches were taken out of the barrels, their skins bleached and wrinkled with long soaking. Their bonds were torn from them; but, cramped and fixed, their limbs refused to act, and they tumbled and twisted upon the floor in their efforts to reach Nigel and to kiss his hand.

In a corner lay Aylward, dripping from his barrel and exhausted with cold and hunger. Nigel ran to his side and raised his head. The jug of wine from which the two jailers had drunk still stood upon their table. The squire placed it to the archer's lips, and he took a hearty pull at it.

" How is it with you now, Aylward ? "

" Better, squire, better, but may I never touch water again as long as I live ! Alas ! poor Dicon has gone, and Stephen also—the life chilled out of them. The cold is in the very marrow of my bones. I pray you, let me lean upon your arm as far as the fire, that I may warm the frozen blood and set it running in my veins once more."

A strange sight it was to see these twenty naked men crouching in a half-circle round the fire with their trembling hands extended to the blaze. Soon their tongues at least were thawed, and they poured out the story of their troubles, with many a prayer and ejaculation to the saints for their safe delivery. No food had crossed their lips since they had been taken. The Butcher had commanded them to join his garrison and to shoot upon their comrades from the wall. When they refused he had set aside three of them for execution.

The others had been dragged to the cellar, whither the leering tyrant had followed them. Only one question he had asked them, whether they were of a hot-blooded nature or of a cold. Blows were showered upon them until they answered. Three had said cold, and had been condemned to the torment of the fire. The rest who had said hot were delivered up to the torture of the water-cask. Every few hours this man or fiend had come down to exult over their sufferings and to ask them whether they were ready yet to enter his service. Three had consented and were gone. But the others had all of them stood firm, two of them even to their death.

Such was the tale to which Nigel and his comrades listened while they waited impatiently for the coming of Knolles and his men. Many an anxious look did they cast down the black tunnel, but no glimmer of light and no clash of steel came from its depths. Suddenly, however, a loud and measured sound broke upon their ears. It was a dull metallic clang, ponderous and slow, growing louder and ever louder—the tread of an armoured man. The poor wretches round the fire, all unnerved by hunger and suffering, huddled together with wan, scared faces, their eyes fixed in terror on the door.

" It is he ! " they whispered. " It is the Butcher himself ! "

Nigel had darted to the door and listened intently. There were no footfalls save those of one man. Once sure of that, he softly turned the key in the lock. At the same instant there came a bull's bellow from without.

" Ives ! Bertrand ! " cried the voice. " Can you not hear me coming, you drunken varlets ? You shall cool your own heads in the water-casks, you lazy rascals ! What, not even now ! Open, you dogs. Open, I say ! "

He had thrust down the latch, and with a kick he flung the door wide and rushed inward. For an instant he stood motionless, a statue of dull yellow metal, his eyes fixed upon the empty casks and the huddle of naked men. Then, with the roar of a trapped lion, he turned, but the door had slammed behind him, and Black Simon, with grim figure and sardonic face, stood between.

The Butcher looked round him helplessly, for he was unarmed save for his dagger. Then his eyes fell upon Nigel's roses.

"You are a gentleman of coat-armour," he cried. "I surrender myself to you."

"I will not take your surrender, you black villain," said Nigel. "Draw and defend yourself. Simon, give him your sword."

"Nay, this is madness," said the blunt man-at-arms. "Why should I give the wasp a sting?"

"Give it him, I say. I cannot kill him in cold blood."

"But I can!" yelled Aylward, who had crept up from the fire. "Come, comrades! By these ten finger-bones! has he not taught us how cold blood should be warmed?"

Like a pack of wolves they were on him, and he clanged upon the floor with a dozen frenzied naked figures clutching and clinging above him. In vain Nigel tried to pull them off. They were mad with rage, these tortured starving men, their eyes fixed and glaring, their hair on end, their teeth gnashing with fury, while they tore at the howling, writhing man. Then, with a rattle and clatter, they pulled him across the room by his two ankles and dragged him into the fire.

Nigel shuddered and turned away his eyes as he saw the brazen figure roll out and stagger to his knees, only to be hurled once more into the heart of the blaze. His prisoners screamed with joy and clapped their hands as they pushed him back with their feet until the armour was too hot for them to touch. Then at last he lay still and glowed darkly red, while the naked men danced in a wild half-circle round the fire.

But now at last the supports had come. Lights flashed and armour gleamed down the tunnel. The cellar filled with armed men, while from above came the cries and turmoil of the feigned assault upon the gate. Led by Knolles and Nigel, the storming party rushed upwards and seized the court-yard. The guard of the gate taken in the rear threw down their weapons and cried for mercy. The gate was thrown open and the assailants rushed in, with hundreds of furious peasants at their heels. Some of the robbers died in hot blood, many in cold ; but all died, for Knolles had vowed to give no quarter. Day was just breaking when the last fugitive had been hunted out and slain. From all sides came the yells and whoops of the soldiers, with the rending and riving of doors as they burst into the store-rooms and treasure-chambers. There was a joyous scramble among them for the plunder of eleven years ; gold and jewels, satins and velvets, rich plate and noble hangings were all to be had for the taking.

The rescued prisoners, their hunger appeased and their clothes restored, led the search for booty. Nigel, leaning on his sword by the gateway, saw Aylward totter past, a huge bundle under each arm, another slung over his back, and a smaller packet hanging from his mouth. He dropped it for a moment as he passed his young master.

" By these ten finger-bones ! I am right glad that I came to the war, and no man could ask for a more goodly life," said he. " I have a present here for every girl in Tilford, and my father need never fear the frown of the sacrist of Waverley again. But how of you, Squire Loring ? It standeth not aright that we should gather the harvest whilst you, who sowed it, go forth empty-handed. Come, gentle sir, take these things that I have gathered, and I will go back and find more."

But Nigel smiled and shook his head. " You have gained what your heart desired, and perchance I have done so also," said he.

An instant later Knolles strode up to him with out-stretched hand.

" I ask your pardon, Nigel," said he. " I have spoken too hotly in my wrath."

" Nay, fair sir, I was at fault."

" If we stand here now within this castle, it is to you that I owe it. The king shall know of it, and Chandos also. Can I do aught else, Nigel, to prove to you the high esteem in which I hold you ? "

The squire flushed with pleasure. " Do you send a messenger home to England, fair sir, with news of these doings ? "

" Surely, I must do so. But do not tell me, Nigel, that you would be that messenger. Ask me some other favour, for indeed I cannot let you go."

" Now, God forbid ! " cried Nigel. " By Saint Paul ! I would not be so caitiff and so thrall as to leave you when some small deed might still be done. But I would fain send a message by your messenger."

" To whom ? "

" It is to the Lady Mary, daughter of old Sir John Buttesthorn, who dwells near Guildford."

" But you will write the message, Nigel. Such greetings as a cavalier sends to his lady-love should be under seal."

" Nay, he can carry my message by word of mouth."

" Then I shall tell him, for he goes this morning. What message, then, shall he say to the lady ? "

" He will give her my very humble greeting, and he will say to her that for the second time Saint Catharine has been our friend."

22. *How Robert of Beaumanoir came to Ploermel*

SIR ROBERT KNOLLES and his men passed onward that day, looking back many a time to see the two dark columns of smoke, one thicker and one more slender, which arose from the castle and from the fort of La Brohinière. There was not an archer nor a man-at-arms who did not bear a great bundle of spoil upon his back, and Knolles frowned darkly as he looked upon them. Gladly would he have thrown it all down by the roadside, but he had tried such matters before, and he knew that it was as safe to tear a half-gnawed bone from a bear as their blood-won plunder from such men as these. In any case it was but two days' march to Ploermel, where he hoped to bring his journey to an end.

That night they camped at Mauron, where a small English and Breton garrison held the castle. Right glad were the bowmen to see some of their own countrymen once more, and they spent the night over wine and dice, a crowd of Breton girls assisting, so that next morning their bundles were much lighter, and most of the plunder of La Brohinière was left with the men and women of Mauron. Next day their march lay with a fair sluggish river upon their right, and a great rolling forest upon their left, which covered the whole country. At last, towards evening, the towers of Ploermel rose before them, and they saw against a darkening sky the Red Cross of England waving in the wind. So blue was the river Duc which skirted the road, and so green its banks, that they might indeed have been back beside their own homely streams, the Oxford Thames or the Midland Trent, but ever as the darkness deepened there came in wild gusts the howling of wolves from the forest to remind them that they were in a land of war. So busy had men been for many years in hunting one another that the beasts of the chase had grown to a monstrous degree, until the streets of the towns were no longer safe from the wild inroads of the fierce creatures, the wolves and the bears, who swarmed around them.

It was nightfall when the little army entered the outer gate of the Castle of Ploermel and encamped in the broad bailey-yard. Ploermel was at that time the centre of British power in Mid-Brittany, as Hennebon was in the West, and it was held by a garrison of five hundred men under an old soldier, Richard of Bambro', a rugged Northumbrian, trained in that great school of warriors, the border wars. He who had ridden the marches of the most troubled frontier in Europe, and served his time against the Liddlesdale and Nithsdale raiders, was hardened for a life in the field.

Of late, however, Bambro' had been unable to undertake any enterprise, for his reinforcements had failed him, and amid his following he had but three English knights and seventy men. The rest were a mixed crew of Bretons, Hainaulters, and a few German mercenary soldiers, brave men individually, as those of that stock have ever been, but lacking interest in the cause, and bound together by no common tie of blood or tradition.

On the other hand, the surrounding castles, and especially that of Josselin, were held by strong forces of enthusiastic Bretons, inflamed by a common patriotism, and full of warlike ardour. Robert of Beaumanoir, the fierce seneschal of the house of Rohan, pushed constant forays and excursions against Ploermel, so that town and castle were both in daily dread of being surrounded and besieged. Several small parties of the English faction had been cut off and slain to a man, and so straitened were the others that it was difficult for them to gather provisions from the country round.

Such was the state of Bambro's garrison when on that March evening Knolles and his men streamed into the bailey-yard of his castle.

In the glare of the torches at the inner gate Bambro' was waiting to receive them, a dry, hard, wizened man, small and fierce, with beady black eyes and quick, furtive ways. Beside him, a strange contrast, stood his squire, Croquart, a German, whose name and fame as a man-at-arms were widespread, though, like Robert Knolles himself, he had begun as a humble page. He was a very tall man, with an enormous spread of shoulders, and a pair of huge hands with which he could crack a horseshoe. He was slow and lethargic, save in moments of excitement, and his calm blond face, his dreamy blue eyes, and his long fair hair gave him so gentle an appearance that none save those who had seen him in his berserk mood, raging, an iron giant, in the forefront of the battle, could ever guess how terrible a warrior he might be. Little knight and huge squire stood together under the arch of the donjon and gave welcome to the newcomers, while a swarm of soldiers crowded round to embrace their comrades and to lead them off where they might feed and make merry together.

Supper had been set in the hall of Ploermel, wherein the knights and squires assembled. Bambro' and Croquart were there with Sir Hugh Calverly, an old friend of Knolles and a fellow-townsman, for both were men of Chester. Sir Hugh was a middle-sized flaxen man, with hard grey eyes and fierce, large-nosed face, sliced across with the scar of a sword-cut. There, too, were Geoffrey D'Ardaine, a young Breton seigneur; Sir Thomas Belford, a burly thick-set Midland Englishman; Sir Thomas Walton, whose surcoat of scarlet martlets showed that he was of the Surrey Waltons; James Marshall and John Russell, young English squires; and the two brothers, Richard and Hugh Le Galliard, who were of Gascon blood. Besides these were several squires unknown to fame, and of the newcomers, Sir Robert Knolles, Sir Thomas Percy, Nigel Loring, and two other squires, Allington and Parsons. These were the company who gathered in the torchlight round the table of the Seneschal of Ploermel, and kept high revel with joyous hearts because they thought that much honour and noble deeds lay before them.

But one sad face there was at the board, and that belonged to him at the head of it. Sir Richard Bambro' sat with his chin leaning upon his hand and his eyes downcast upon the cloth, while all around him rose the merry clatter of voices, everyone planning some fresh enterprise which might now be attempted. Sir Robert Knolles was for an immediate advance upon Josselin. Calverly thought that a raid might be made into the South, where the main French power lay. Others spoke of an attack upon Vannes.

To all these eager opinions Bambro' listened in a moody silence, which he broke at last by a fierce execration which drew a hushed attention from the company.

"Say no more, fair sirs," he cried, "for indeed your words are like so many stabs in my heart. All this and more we might have done. But of a truth you are too late."

"Too late?" cried Knolles. "What mean you, Richard?"

"Alas that I should have to say it, but you and all these fair soldiers might be back in England once more for all the profit that I am like to have from your coming. Saw you a rider on a white horse ere you reached the Castle?"

"Nay, I saw him not."

"He came by the western road from Hennebon. Would that he had broken his neck ere he came here. Not an hour ago he left his message, and now hath ridden on to warn the garrison of Malestroit. A truce has been proclaimed for a year betwixt the French king and the English, and he who breaks it forfeits life and estate."

"A truce!" Here was an end to all their fine dreams. They looked blankly at each other all round the table, while Croquart brought his great fist down upon the board until the glasses rattled again. Knolles sat with clinched hands as if he were a figure of stone, while Nigel's heart turned cold and heavy within him. A truce! Where, then, was his third deed, and how might he return without it?

Even as they sat in moody silence there was the call of a bugle from somewhere out in the darkness.

Sir Richard looked up with surprise. "We are not wont to be summoned after once the portcullis is down," said he. "Truce or no truce, we must let no man within our walls until we have proved him. Croquart, see to it!"

The huge German left the room. The company were still seated in despondent silence when he returned.

"Sir Richard," said he, "the brave knight Robert of Beaumanoir and his Squire William de Montaubon are without the gate, and would fain have speech with you."

Bambro' started in his chair. What could the fierce

leader of the Bretons, a man who was red to the elbow with English blood, have to say to them ? On what errand had he left his castle of Josselin to pay this visit to his deadly enemies ? "

" Are they armed ? " he asked.

" They are unarmed."

" Then admit them and bring them hither, but double the guards, and take all heed against surprise."

Places were set at the farther end of the table for these most unexpected guests. Presently the door was swung open, and Croquart, with all form and courtesy, announced the two Bretons, who entered with the proud and lofty air of gallant warriors and high-bred gentlemen.

Beaumanoir was a tall, dark man, with raven hair and long, swarthy beard. He was strong and straight as a young oak, with fiery black eyes, and no flaw in his comely features, save that his front teeth had been dashed from their sockets. His squire, William of Montaubon, was also tall, with a thin, hatchet face, and two small grey eyes set very close upon either side of a long, fierce nose. In Beaumanoir's expression one read only gallantry and frankness ; in Montaubon's there was gallantry also, but it was mixed with the cruelty and cunning of the wolf. They bowed as they entered, and the little English seneschal advanced with outstretched hand to meet them.

" Welcome, Robert, so long as you are beneath this roof," said he. " Perhaps the time may come in another place when we may speak to each other in another fashion."

" So I hope, Richard," said Beaumanoir ; " but, indeed, we of Josselin bear you in high esteem, and are much beholden to you and to your men for all that you have done for us. We could not wish better neighbours, nor any from whom more honour is to be gained. I learn that Sir Robert Knolles and others have joined you, and we are heavy-hearted to think that the orders of our kings should debar us from attempting a venture."

He and his squire sat down at the places set for them, and, filling their glasses, drank to the company.

" What you say is true, Robert," said Bambro', " and
before you came we were discussing the matter among
ourselves, and grieving that it should be so. When heard
you of the truce ? "

" Yester evening a messenger rode from Nantes."

" Our news came to-night from Hennebon. The king's
own seal was on the order. So I fear that for a year, at
least, you will bide at Josselin and we at Ploermel, and
kill time as we may. Perchance we may hunt the wolf
together in the great forest, or fly our hawks on the banks
of the Duc."

" Doubtless we shall do all this, Richard," said Beaumanoir ; " but by Saint Cadoc it is in my mind that, with
good-will upon both sides, we may please ourselves, and
yet stand excused before our kings."

Knights and squires leaned forward in their chairs,
their eager eyes fixed upon him. He broke into a gap-
toothed smile as he looked round at the circle, the wizened
seneschal, the blond giant, Nigel's fresh young face, the
grim features of Knolles, and the yellow, hawk-like
Calverly, all burning with the same desire.

" I see that I need not doubt the good-will," said he,
" and of that I was very certain before I came upon this
errand. Bethink you, then, that this order applies to war
but not to challenges, spear-runnings, knightly exchanges,
or the like. King Edward is too good a knight, and so is
King John, that either of them should stand in the way of
a gentleman who desires to advance himself, or to venture
his body for the exaltation of his lady. Is this not so ? "

A murmur of eager assent rose from the table.

" If you, as the garrison of Ploermel, march upon the
garrison of Josselin, then it is very plain that we have
broken the truce, and upon our heads be it. But if there
be a private bickering betwixt me, for example, and this
young squire whose eyes show that he is very eager for
honour, and if, thereafter, others on each side join in and
fight upon the quarrel, it is in no sense war, but rather
our own private business which no king can alter."

"Indeed, Robert," said Bambro', "all that you say is very good and fair."

Beaumanoir leaned forward towards Nigel, his brimming glass in his hand.

"Your name, squire?" said he.

"My name is Nigel Loring."

"I see that you are young and eager, so I choose you, as I would fain have been chosen when I was of your age."

"I thank you, fair sir," said Nigel. "It is great honour that one so famous as yourself should condescend to do some small deed upon me."

"But we must have cause for quarrel, Nigel. Now, here I drink to the ladies of Brittany, who, of all ladies upon this earth, are the most fair and the most virtuous, so that the least worthy amongst them is far above the best of England. What say you to that, young sir?"

Nigel dipped his finger in his glass, and, leaning over, he placed its wet impress on the Breton's hand.

"This in your face!" said he.

Beaumanoir swept off the red drop of moisture and smiled his approval.

"It could not have been better done," said he. "Why spoil my velvet paltock, as many a hot-headed fool would have done? It is in my mind, young sir, that you will go far. And now, who follows up this quarrel?"

A growl ran round the table.

Beaumanoir ran his eye round and shook his head.

"Alas!" said he, "there are but twenty of you here, and I have thirty at Josselin who are so eager to advance themselves that, if I return without hope for all of them, there will be sore hearts amongst them. I pray you, Richard, since we have been at these pains to arrange matters, that you in turn will do what you may. Can you not find ten more men?"

"But not of gentle blood."

"Nay, it matters not, if they will only fight."

"Of that there can be no doubt, for the castle is full

of archers and men-at-arms who would gladly play a part in the matter."

" Then choose ten," said Beaumanoir.

But for the first time the wolf-like squire opened his thin lips.

" Surely, my lord, you will not allow archers," said he.

" I fear not any man."

" Nay, fair sir, consider that this is a trial of weapons betwixt us, where man faces man. You have seen these English archers, and you know how fast and how strong are their shafts. Bethink you that if ten of them were against us, it is likely that half of us would be down before ever we came to handstrokes."

" By Saint Cadoc, William, I think that you are right," cried the Breton. " If we are to have such a fight as will remain in the memories of men, you will bring no archers and we no crossbows. Let it be steel upon steel. How say you, then ? "

" Surely we can bring ten men-at-arms to make up the thirty that you desire, Robert. It is agreed, then, that we fight on no quarrel of England and France, but over this matter of the ladies in which you and Squire Loring have fallen out. And now the time ? "

" At once."

" Surely at once, or perchance a second messenger may come and this also be forbidden. We will be ready with to-morrow's sunrise."

" Nay, a day later," cried the Breton squire. " Bethink you, my lord, that the three lances of Radenac would take time to come over."

" They are not of our garrison, and they shall not have a place."

" But, fair sir, of all the lances of Brittany——"

" Nay, William, I will not have it an hour later. To-morrow it shall be, Richard."

" And where ? "

" I marked a fitting place even as I rode here this evening. If you cross the river and take the bridle-path

720

through the fields which leads to Josselin you come midway upon a mighty oak standing at the corner of a fair and level meadow. There let us meet at midday to-morrow."

" Agreed ! " cried Bambro'. " But I pray you not to rise, Robert ! The night is still young, and the spices and hippocras will soon be served. Bide with us, I pray you, for if you would fain hear the latest songs from England, these gentlemen have doubtless brought them. To some of us perchance it is the last night, so we would make it a full one."

But the gallant Breton shook his head. " It may indeed be the last night for many," said he, " and it is but right that my comrades should know it. I have no need of monk or friar, for I cannot think that harm will ever come beyond the grave to one who has borne himself as a knight should, but others have other thoughts upon these matters, and would fain have time for prayer and penitence. Adieu, fair sirs, and I drink a last glass to a happy meeting at the midway oak."

23. *How Thirty of Josselin encountered Thirty of Ploermel*

ALL night the Castle of Ploermel rang with warlike preparations, for the smiths were hammering and filing and riveting, preparing the armour for the champions. In the stable yard hostlers were testing and grooming the great war-horses, while in the chapel knights and squires were easing their souls at the knees of old Father Benedict.

Down in the courtyard, meanwhile, the men-at-arms had been assembled, and the volunteers weeded out until the best men had been selected. Black Simon had obtained a place, and great was the joy which shone upon his grim visage. With him were chosen young Nicholas Dagsworth, a gentleman adventurer who was nephew to the famous Sir Thomas, Walter the German, Hulbitée—a huge peasant whose massive frame gave promise which his sluggish spirit failed to fulfil—John Alcock, Robin Adey and Raoul Provost. These with three others made up the required thirty. Great was the grumbling and evil the talk among the archers when it was learned that none of them were to be included, but the bow had been forbidden on either side. It is true that many of them were expert fighters both with axe and with sword, but they were unused to carry heavy armour, and a half-armed man would have short shrift in such a hand-to-hand struggle as lay before them.

It was two hours after tierce, or one hour before noon, on the fourth Wednesday of Lent, in the year of Christ 1351, that the men of Ploermel rode forth from their castle-gate and crossed the bridge of the Duc. In front was Bambro', with his squire, Croquart, the latter on a great roan horse bearing the banner of Ploermel, which was a black rampant lion holding a blue flag upon a field of ermine. Behind him came Robert Knolles and Nigel Loring, with an attendant at their side, who carried the pennon of the black raven. Then rode Sir Thomas Percy, with his blue lion flaunting above him, and Sir Hugh Calverly, whose banner bore a silver owl, followed by the massive Belford, who carried a huge iron club, weighing sixty pounds, upon his saddle-bow, and Sir Thomas Walton, the knight of Surrey. Behind them were four brave Anglo-Bretons, Perrot de Commelain, Le Gaillart, d'Aspremont and d'Ardaine, who fought against their own countrymen because they were partisans of the Countess of Montfort. Her engrailed silver cross upon a blue field was carried at their head. In the rear were five German or Hainault mercenaries, the tall Hulbitée, and the men-at-arms. Altogether of these combatants twenty were of English birth, four were Breton, and six were of German blood.

So, with glitter of armour and flaunting of pennons, their war-horses tossing and pawing, the champions rode down to the midway oak. Behind them streamed hundreds of archers and men-at-arms, whose weapons had been wisely taken from them, lest a general battle should ensue. With them also went the townsfolk, men and women, together with wine-sellers, provision merchants, armourers, grooms, and heralds, with surgeons to tend the wounded and priests to shrive the dying. The path was blocked by this throng, but all over the face of the country, horsemen and footmen, gentle and simple, men and women, could be seen speeding their way to the scene of the encounter.

The journey was not a long one, for presently, as they threaded their way through the fields, there appeared before them a great grey oak which spread its gnarled leafless branches over the corner of a green and level meadow. The tree was black with the peasants who had climbed into it, and all round it was a huge throng, chattering and calling like a rookery at sunset. A storm of hooting broke out from them at the approach of the English, for Bambro' was hated in the country, where he raised money for the Montfort cause by putting every parish to ransom, and maltreating those who refused to pay. There was little amenity in the warlike ways which had been learned upon the Scottish border. The champions rode onward without deigning to take notice of the taunts of the rabble, but the archers turned that way and soon beat the mob to silence. Then they resolved themselves into the keepers of the ground, and pressed the people back until they formed a dense line along the edge of the field, leaving the whole space clear for the warriors.

The Breton champions had not yet arrived, so the English tethered their horses at one side of the ground, and then gathered round their leader. Every man had his shield slung round his neck, and had cut his spear to the length of five feet, so that it might be more manageable for fighting on foot. Besides the spear, a sword or a battle-axe hung at the side of each. They were clad from head to foot in armour, with devices upon the crests and surcoats to distinguish them from their antagonists. At present their visors were still up, and they chatted gaily with each other.

" By Saint Dunstan ! " cried Percy, slapping his gaunt-leted hands together and stamping his steel feet, " I shall be right glad to get to work, for my blood is chilled."

" I warrant you will be warm enough ere you get through," said Calverly.

" Or cold for ever. Candle shall burn and bell toll at Alnwick Chapel if I leave this ground alive ; but come what may, fair sirs, it should be a famous joust, and one which will help us forward. Surely each of us will have worshipfully won worship, if we chance to come through."

" You say truth, Thomas," said Knolles, bracing his girdle. " For my own part I have no joy in such en-counters when there is warfare to be carried out, for it standeth not aright that a man should think of his own pleasure and advancement rather than of the king's cause and the weal of the army. But in times of truce I can think of no better way in which a day may be profitably spent. Why so silent, Nigel ? "

" Indeed, fair sir, I was looking towards Josselin, which lies, as I understand, beyond those woods. I see no sign of this debonair gentleman and of his following. It would be indeed grievous pity if any cause came to hold them back."

Hugh Calverly laughed at the words. " You need have no fear, young sir," said he. " Such a spirit lies in Robert de Beaumanoir that if he must come alone he would ride against us none the less. I warrant that if he were on a bed of death he would be borne here and die on the green field."

" You say truly, Hugh," said Bambro'. " I know him and those who ride behind him. Thirty stouter men or more skilled in arms are not to be found in Christendom. It is in my mind that, come what may, there will be much honour for all of us this day. Ever in my head I have a rhyme which the wife of a Welsh archer gave me when I crossed her hand with a golden bracelet after the intaking of Bergerac. She was of the old blood of Merlin with the power of sight. Thus she said—

> " ' 'Twixt the oak-tree and the river
> Knightly fame and brave endeavour
> Make an honoured name for ever.'

Methinks I see the oak-tree, and yonder is the river. Surely this should betide some good to us."

The huge German squire betrayed some impatience during this speech of his leader. Though his rank was subordinate, no man present had more experience of warfare or was more famous as a fighter than he. He now broke brusquely into the talk.

" We should be better employed in ordering our line and making our plans than in talking of the rhymes of Merlin or such old wives' tales," said he. " It is to our own strong arms and good weapons that we must trust this day. And first I would ask you, Sir Richard, what is your will if perchance you should fall in the midst of the fight ? "

Bambro' turned to the others. " If such should be the case, fair sirs, I desire that my squire, Croquart, should command."

There was a pause, while the knights looked with some chagrin at each other. The silence was broken by Knolles.

" I will do what you say, Richard," said he, " though indeed it is bitter that we who are knights should serve beneath a squire. Yet it is not for us to fall out among ourselves now at this last moment, and I have ever heard that Croquart is a very worthy and valiant man. Therefore, I will pledge you on jeopardy of my soul that I will accept him as leader if you fall."

" So will I also, Richard," said Calverly.

" And I too ! " cried Belford. " But surely I hear music, and yonder are their pennons amid the trees."

They all turned, leaning upon their short spears, and watched the advance of the men of Josselin, as their troop wound its way out from the woodlands. In front rode three heralds with tabards of the ermine of Brittany, blowing loudly upon silver trumpets. Behind them a great man upon a white horse bore the banner of Josselin, which carries nine golden bezants upon a scarlet field. Then came the champions riding two and two, fifteen knights and fifteen squires, each with his pennon displayed. Behind them on a litter was borne an aged priest, the Bishop of Rennes, carrying in his hands the viaticum and the holy oils that he might give the last aid and comfort of the Church to those who were dying. The procession was terminated by hundreds of men and women from Josselin, Guegon, and Helleon, and by the entire garrison of the fortress, who came, as the English had done, without their arms. The head of this long column had reached the field before the rear were clear of the wood, but as they arrived the champions picketed their horses on the farther side, behind which their banner was planted, and the people lined up until they had inclosed the whole lists with a dense wall of spectators.

With keen eyes the English party had watched the armorial blazonry of their antagonists, for those fluttering pennons and brilliant surcoats carried a language which all men could read. In front was the banner of Beaumanoir, blue with silver frets. His motto, "*J'ayme qui m'ayme*," was carried on a second flag by a little page.

"Whose is the shield behind him—silver with scarlet drops?" asked Knolles.

"It is his squire, William of Montaubon," Calverly answered. "And there are the golden lion of Rochefort and the silver cross of Du Bois the Strong. I would not wish to meet a better company than are before us this day. See, there are the blue rings of young Tintiniac, who slew my squire, Hubert, last Lammastide. With the aid of Saint George I will avenge him ere nightfall."

"By the three kings of Almain," growled Croquart,

" we will need to fight hard this day, for never have I seen so many good soldiers gathered together. Yonder is Yves Cheruel, whom they call the man of iron; Caro de Bodegat also, with whom I have had more than one bickering—that is he with the three ermine circles on the scarlet shield. There too is left-handed Alain de Karanais ; bear in mind that his stroke comes on the side where there is no shield."

" Who is the small stout man," asked Nigel—" he with the black and silver shield ? By Saint Paul ! he seems a very worthy person and one from whom much might be gained, for he is nigh as broad as he is long."

" It is Sir Robert Raguenel," said Calverly, whose long spell of service in Brittany had made him familiar with the people. " It is said that he can lift a horse upon his back. Beware a full stroke of that steel mace, for the armour is not made that can abide it. But here is the good Beaumanoir, and surely it is time that we came to grips."

The Breton leader had marshalled his men in a line opposite to the English, and now he strode forward and shook Bambro' by the hand.

" By Saint Cadoc ! this is a very joyous meeting, Richard," said he, " and we have certainly hit upon a very excellent way of keeping a truce."

" Indeed, Robert," said Bambro', " we owe you much thanks, for I can see that you have been at great pains to bring a worthy company against us this day. Surely if all should chance to perish there will be few noble houses in Brittany who will not mourn."

" Nay, we have none of the highest of Brittany," Beaumanoir answered. " Neither a Blois, nor a Leon, nor a Rohan, nor a Conan, fights in our ranks this day. And yet we are all men of blood and coat-armour, who are ready to venture our persons for the desire of our ladies and the love of the high order of knighthood. And now, Richard, what is your sweet will concerning this fight ? "

"That we continue until one or other can endure no longer, for since it is seldom that so many brave men draw together it is fitting that we see as much as is possible of each other."

"Richard, your words are fair and good. It shall be even as you say. For the rest, each shall fight as pleases him best from the time that the herald calls the word. If any man from without shall break in upon us he shall be hanged on yonder oak."

With a salute he drew down his visor and returned to his own men, who were kneeling in a twinkling, many-coloured group, while the old bishop gave them his blessing.

The heralds rode round with a warning to the spectators. Then they halted at the side of the two bands of men, who now stood in a long line facing each other with fifty yards of grass between. The visors had been closed, and every man was now cased in metal from head to foot, some few glowing in brass, the greater number shining in steel. Only their fierce eyes could be seen smouldering in the dark shadow of their helmets. So for an instant they stood glaring and crouching.

Then, with a loud cry of "Allez!" the herald dropped his upraised hand, and the two lines of men shuffled as fast as their heavy armour would permit, until they met with a sharp clang of metal in the middle of the field. There was a sound as of sixty smiths working upon their anvils. Then the babel of yells and shouts from the spectators, cheering on this party or that, rose and swelled, until even the uproar of the combat was drowned in that mighty surge.

So eager were the combatants to engage that in a few moments all order had been lost and the two bands were mixed up in one furious scrambling, clattering throng, each man tossed hither and thither, thrown against one adversary and then against another, beaten and hustled and buffeted, with only the one thought in his mind to thrust with his spear or to beat with his axe against anyone who came within the narrow slit of vision left by his visor.

But alas for Nigel and his hopes of some great deed! His was at least the fate of the brave, for he was the first to fall. With a high heart, he had placed himself in the line as nearly opposite to Beaumanoir as he could, and had made straight for the Breton leader, remembering that in the outset the quarrel had been so ordered that it lay between them. But ere he could reach his goal, he was caught in the swirl of his own comrades, and, being the lighter man, was swept aside, and dashed into the arms of Alain de Karanais, the left-handed swordsman, with such a crash that the two rolled upon the ground together. Light-footed as a cat, Nigel had sprung up first, and was stooping over the Breton squire, when the powerful dwarf Taguenel brought his mace thudding down upon the exposed back of his helmet. With a groan, Nigel fell upon his face, blood gushing from his mouth, nose, and ears. There he lay, trampled over by either party, while that great fight for which his fiery soul had panted was swaying back and forward above his unconscious form.

But Nigel was not long unavenged. The huge iron club of Belford struck the dwarf Raguenel to the ground, while Belford in turn was felled by a sweeping blow from Beaumanoir. Sometimes a dozen were on the ground at one time, but so strong was the armour, and so deftly was the force of a blow broken by guard and shield, that the stricken men were often pulled to their feet once more by their comrades, and were able to continue the fight.

Some, however, were beyond all aid. Croquart had cut at a Breton knight named Jean Rousselot, and had shorn away his shoulder-piece, exposing his neck and the upper part of his arm. Vainly he tried to cover this vulnerable surface with his shield. It was his right side, and he could not stretch it far enough across, nor could he get away on account of the press of men around him. For a time he held his foemen at bay, but that bare patch of white shoulder was a mark for every weapon, until at last a hatchet sank up to the socket in the knight's chest. Almost at the same moment a second Breton, a young squire named Geoffrey Mellon, was slain by a thrust from Black Simon, which found the weak spot beneath the armpit. Three other Bretons, Evan Cheruel, Caro de Bodegat, and Tristan de Pestivien, the first two knights and the latter a squire, became separated from their comrades, and were beaten to the ground with English all around them, so that they had to choose between instant death and surrender. They handed their swords to Bambro', and stood apart, each of them sorely wounded, watching with hot and bitter hearts the mêlée which still surged up and down the field.

But now the combat had lasted twenty minutes without stint or rest, until the warriors were so exhausted with the burden of their armour, the loss of blood, the shock of blows, and their own furious exertions, that they could scarce totter or raise their weapons. There must be a pause if the combat was to have any decisive end.

" *Cessez ! Cessez ! Retirez !* " cried the heralds, as they spurred their horses between the exhausted men.

Slowly the gallant Beaumanoir led the twenty-five men who were left to their original station, where they opened their visors and threw themselves down upon the grass, panting like weary dogs, and wiping the sweat from their bloodshot eyes. A pitcher of wine of Anjou was carried round by a page, and each in turn drained a cup, save only Beaumanoir, who kept his Lent with such strictness that neither food nor drink might pass his lips before sunset. He paced slowly among his men, croaking forth encouragement from his parched lips, and pointing out to them that among the English there was scarce a man who was not wounded, and some so sorely that they could hardly stand. If the fight so far had gone against them, there were still five hours of daylight, and much might happen before the last of them was laid upon his back.

Varlets had rushed forth to draw away the two dead Bretons, and a brace of English archers had carried Nigel from the field. With his own hands, Aylward had unlaced the crushed helmet, and had wept to see the bloodless and unconscious face of his young master. He still breathed, however, and stretched upon the grass by the riverside the bowman tended him with rude surgery, until the water upon his brow and the wind upon his face had coaxed back the life into his battered frame. He breathed with heavy gasps, and some tinge of blood crept back into his cheeks, but still he lay unconscious of the roar of the crowd and of that great struggle which his comrades were now waging once again.

The English had lain for a space, bleeding and breathless, in no better case than their rivals, save that they were still twenty-nine in number. But of this muster there were not nine who were hale men, and some were so weak from loss of blood that they could scarce keep standing. Yet, when the signal was at last given to re-engage, there was not a man upon either side who did not totter to his feet and stagger forward toward his enemies.

But the opening of this second phase of the combat brought one great misfortune and discouragement to the English. Bambro', like the others, had undone his visor, but with his mind full of many cares, he had neglected to make it fast again. There was an opening an inch broad between it and the beaver. As the two lines met, the left-handed Breton squire, Alan de Karanais, caught sight of Bambro's face, and in an instant thrust his short spear through the opening. The English leader gave a cry of pain and fell on his knees, but staggered to his feet again, too weak to raise his shield. As he stood exposed, the Breton knight, Geoffrey Dubois the Strong, struck him such a blow with his axe that he beat in the whole breastplate with the breast behind it. Bambro' fell dead upon the ground, and for a few minutes a fierce fight raged round his body.

Then the English drew back, sullen and dogged, bearing Bambro' with them, and the Bretons, breathing hard, gathered again in their own quarter. At the same instant the three prisoners picked up such weapons as were scattered upon the grass and ran over to join their own party.

" Nay, nay ! " cried Knolles, raising his visor and advancing. " This may not be. You have been held to mercy when we might have slain you, and by the Virgin, I will hold you dishonoured, all three, if you stand not back."

" Say not so, Robert Knolles," Evan Cheruel answered. " Never yet has the word dishonour been breathed with my name ; but I should count myself *fainéant* if I did not fight beside my comrades when chance has made it right and proper that I should do so."

" By Saint Cadoc ! he speaks truly," croaked Beaumanoir, advancing in front of his men. " You are well aware, Robert, that it is the law of war and the usage of chivalry that if the knight to whom you have surrendered be himself slain, the prisoners thereby become released."

There was no answer to this, and Knolles, weary and spent, returned to his comrades.

" I would that we had slain them," said he. " We have lost our leader, and they have gained three men by the same stroke."

" If any more lay down their arms, it is my order that you slay them forthwith," said Croquart, whose bent sword and bloody armour showed how manfully he had borne himself in the fray. " And now, comrades, do not be heavy-hearted because we have lost our leader. Indeed, his rhymes of Merlin have availed him little. By the three kings of Almain ! I can teach you what is better than an old woman's prophecies, and that is that you should keep your shoulders together and your shields so close that none can break between them. Then you will know what is on either side of you, and you can fix your eyes upon the front. Also, if any be so weak or wounded that he must sink his hands, his comrades on right and left can bear him up. Now advance all together in God's name, for the battle is still ours if we bear ourselves like men."

In a solid line the English advanced, while the Bretons ran forward as before to meet them. The swiftest of these was a certain squire, Geoffrey Poulart, who bore a helmet which was fashioned as a cock's head, with high comb above, and long pointed beak in front pierced with the breathing-holes. He thrust with his sword at Calverly, but Belford, who was the next in the line, raised his giant club and struck him a crushing blow from the side. He staggered, and then, pushing forth from the crowd, he ran round and round in circles as one whose brain is stricken, the blood dripping from the holes of his brazen beak. So for a long time he ran, the crowd laughing and cock-crowing at the sight, until at last he stumbled and fell stone dead upon his face. But the fighters had seen nothing of his fate, for desperate and unceasing was the rush of the Bretons and the steady advance of the English line.

For a time it seemed as if nothing would break it, but gap-toothed Beaumanoir was a general as well as a warrior. While his weary, bleeding, hard-breathing men still flung themselves upon the front of the line, he himself, with Raguenel, Tintiniac, Alain de Karanais, and Dubois, rushed round the flank and attacked the English with fury from behind. There was a long and desperate *mêlée*, until once more the heralds, seeing the combatants stand gasping and unable to strike a blow, rode in and called yet another interval of truce.

But in those few minutes while they had been assaulted upon both sides the losses of the English party had been heavy. The Anglo-Breton D'Ardaine had fallen before Beaumanoir's sword, but not before he had cut deeply into his enemy's shoulder. Sir Thomas Walton, Richard of Ireland, one of the squires, and Hulbitée the big peasant had all fallen before the mace of the dwarf Raguenel or the swords of his companions. Some twenty men were still left standing upon either side, but all were in the last state of exhaustion, gasping, reeling, hardly capable of striking a blow.

It was strange to see them as they staggered, with many a lurch and stumble, towards each other once again, for they moved like drunken men, and the scales of their neck-armour and joints were as red as fishes' gills when they raised them. They left foul wet footprints behind them on the green grass as they moved forward once more to their endless contest.

Beaumanoir, faint with the drain of his blood and with a tongue of leather, paused as he advanced.

" I am fainting, comrades," he cried. " I must drink."

" Drink your own blood, Beaumanoir ! " cried Dubois, and the weary men all croaked together in dreadful laughter.

But now the English had learned from experience, and under the guidance of Croquart they fought no longer in a straight line, but in one so bent that at last it became a circle. As the Bretons still pushed and staggered against it they thrust it back on every side, until they had turned it into the most dangerous formation of all, a solid block of men, their faces turned outward, their weapons bristling forth to meet every attack. Thus the English stood, and no assault could move them. They could lean against each other back to back while they waited and allowed their foemen to tire themselves out. Again and again the gallant Bretons tried to make a way through. Again and again they were beaten back by a shower of blows.

Beaumanoir, his head giddy with fatigue, opened his helmet and gazed in despair at this terrible, unbreakable circle. Only too clearly he could see the inevitable result. His men were wearing themselves out. Already many of them could scarce stir hand or foot, and might be dead for any aid which they could give him in winning the fight. Soon all would be in the same plight. Then these cursed English would break their circle to swarm over his helpless men and to strike them down. Do what he might, he could see no way by which such an end might be prevented. He cast his eyes round in his agony, and there was one of his Bretons slinking away to the side of the lists. He could scarce credit his senses when he saw by the scarlet and silver that the deserter was his own well-tried squire, William of Montaubon.

" William ! William ! " he cried. " Surely you would not leave me ? "

But the other's helmet was closed and he could hear nothing. Beaumanoir saw that he was staggering away as swiftly as he could. With a cry of bitter despair, he drew into a knot as many of his braves as could still move, and together they made a last rush upon the English spears. This time he was firmly resolved, deep in his gallant soul, that he would come no foot back, but would find his death there among his foemen or carve a path into the heart of their ranks. The fire in his breast spread from man to man of his followers, and amid the crashing of blows they still locked themselves against the English shields and drove hard for an opening in their ranks.

But all was vain ! Beaumanoir's head reeled. His senses were leaving him. In another minute he and his men would have been stretched senseless before this terrible circle of steel, when suddenly the whole array fell in pieces before his eyes ; his enemies, Croquart, Knolles, Calverly, Belford, all were stretched upon the ground together, their weapons dashed from their hands and their bodies too exhausted to rise. The surviving Bretons had but strength to fall upon them dagger in hand, and to wring from them their surrender with the sharp point stabbing through their visors. Then victors and van-quished lay groaning and panting in one helpless and blood-smeared heap.

To Beaumanoir's simple mind it has seemed that at the supreme moment the Saints of Brittany had risen at their country's call. Already, as he lay gasping, his heart was pouring forth its thanks to his patron Saint Cadoc.

But the spectators had seen clearly enough the earthly cause of this sudden victory, and a hurricane of applause from one side, with a storm of hooting from the other, showed how different was the emotion which it raised in minds which sympathised with the victors or the vanquished.

William of Montaubon, the cunning squire, had made his way across to the spot where the steeds were tethered, and had mounted his own great roussin. At first it was thought that he was about to ride from the field, but the howl of execration from the Breton peasants changed suddenly to a yell of applause and delight as he turned the beast's head for the English circle and thrust his long prick spurs into its side. Those who faced him saw this sudden and unexpected appearance. Time was when both horse and rider must have winced away from the shower of their blows. But now they were in no state to meet such a rush. They could scarce raise their arms. Their blows were too feeble to hurt this mighty creature. In a moment it had plunged through the ranks, and seven of them were on the grass. It turned and rushed through them again, leaving five others helpless beneath its hoofs. No need to do more! Already Beaumanoir and his companions were inside the circle, the prostrate men were helpless, and Josselin had won.

That night a train of crestfallen archers, bearing many a prostrate figure, marched sadly into Ploermel Castle. Behind them rode ten men, all weary, all wounded, and all with burning hearts against William of Montaubon for the foul trick that he had served them.

But over at Josselin, yellow gorse-blossoms in their helmets, the victors were borne in on the shoulders of a shouting mob, amid the fanfare of trumpets and the beating of drums. Such was the combat of the Midway Oak, where brave men met brave men, and such honour was gained that from that day he who had fought in the battle of the Thirty was ever given the highest place and the post of honour, nor was it easy for any man to pretend to have been there, for it has been said by that great chronicler who knew them all, that not one on either side failed to carry to his grave the marks of that stern encounter.

24. *How Nigel was called to his Master*

"MY sweet ladye," wrote Nigel, in a script which it would take the eyes of love to read, "there hath been a most noble meeting in the fourth sennight of Lent betwixt some of our own people and sundry most worthy persons of this country, which ended, by the grace of our lady, in so fine a joust that no man living can call to mind so fair an occasion. Much honour was gained by the Sieur de Beaumanoir and also by an Almain named Croquart, with whom I hope to have some speech when I am hale again, for he is a most excellent person and very ready to advance himself or to relieve another from a vow. For myself I had hoped, with Godde's help, to venture that third small deed which might set me free to haste to your sweet side, but things have gone awry with me, and I early met with such scathe and was of so small comfort to my friends that my heart is heavy within me, and in sooth I feel that I have lost honour rather than gained it. Here I have lain since the Feast of the Virgin, and here I am like still to be, for I can move no limb, save only my hand ; but grieve not, sweet lady, for Saint Catharine hath been our friend since in so short a time I had two such ventures as the Red Ferret and the intaking of the Reaver's fortalice. It needs but one more deed, and sickerly when I am hale once more it will not be long ere I seek it out. Till then, if my eyes may not rest upon you, my heart at least is ever at thy feet."

So he wrote from his sick-room in the Castle of Ploermel late in the summer, but yet another summer had come before his crushed head had mended and his wasted limbs had gained their strength once more. With despair he heard of the breaking of the truce, and of the fight at Mauron, in which Sir Robert Knolles and Sir Walter

Bentley crushed the rising power of Brittany—a fight in which many of the thirty champions of Josselin met their end. Then, when with renewed strength and high hopes in his heart he went forth to search for the famous Croquart, who proclaimed himself ever ready night and day to meet any man with any weapon, it was only to find that, in trying the paces of his new horse, the German had been cast into a ditch and had broken his neck. In the same ditch perished Nigel's last chance of soon accomplishing that deed which should free him from his vow.

There was truce once more over all Christendom, and mankind was sated with war, so that only in far-off Prussia, where the Teutonic knights waged ceaseless battle with the Lithuanian heathen, could he hope to find his heart's desire. But money and high knightly fame were needed ere a man could go upon the northern crusade, and ten years were yet to pass ere Nigel should look from the battlements of Marienberg on the waters of the Frische Haff, or should endure the torture of the hot plate when bound to the Holy Woden stone of Memel. Meanwhile, he chafed his burning soul out through the long seasons of garrison life in Brittany, broken only by one visit to the château of the father of Raoul, when he carried to the Lord of Grosbois the news of how his son had fallen like a gallant gentleman under the gateway of La Brohinière.

And then, then at last, when all hope was well-nigh dead in his heart, there came one glorious July morning which brought a horseman bearing a letter to the Castle of Vannes, of which Nigel was now seneschal. It contained but few words, short and clear as the call of a war-trumpet. It was Chandos who wrote. He needed his squire at his side, for his pennon was in the breeze once more. He was at Bordeaux. The prince was starting at once for Bergerac, whence he would make a great raid into France. It would not end without a battle. They had sent word of their coming, and the good French king had promised to be at great pains to receive them. Let Nigel hasten at once. If the army had left, then let him

738

follow after with all speed. Chandos had three other squires, but would very gladly see his fourth once again, for he had heard much of him since he parted, and nothing which he might not have expected to hear of his father's son. Such was the letter which made the summer sun shine brighter and the blue sky seem of a still fairer blue upon that happy morning in Vannes.

It is a weary way from Vannes to Bordeaux. Coastwise ships are hard to find, and winds blow north when all brave hearts would fain be speeding south. A full month has passed from the day when Nigel received his letter before he stood upon the quayside of the Garonne amid the stacked barrels of Gascon wine and helped to lead Pommers down the gang-planks. Not Aylward himself had a worse opinion of the sea than the great yellow horse, and he whinnied with joy as he thrust his muzzle into his master's outstretched hand, and stamped his ringing hoofs upon the good firm cobblestones. Beside him, slapping his tawny shoulder in encouragement, was the lean spare form of Black Simon, who had remained ever under Nigel's pennon.

But Aylward, where he was ? Alas ! two years before he and the whole of Knolles' company of archers had been drafted away on the king's service to Guienne, and since he could not write the squire knew not whether he was alive or dead. Simon, indeed, had thrice heard of him from wandering archers, each time that he was alive and well and newly married, but as the wife in one case was a fair maid, and in another a dark, while in the third she was a French widow, it was hard to know the truth.

Already the army had been gone a month, but news of it came daily to the town, and such news as all men could read, for through the landward gates there rolled one constant stream of waggons, pouring down the Libourne Road, and bearing the booty of southern France. The town was full of foot soldiers, for none but mounted men had been taken by the prince. With sad faces and longing eyes they watched the passing of the train of plunder-laden carts, piled high with rich furniture, silks, velvets, tapestries, carvings, and precious metals, which had been the pride of many a lordly home in fair Auvergne or the wealthy Bourbonnais.

Let no man think that in these wars England alone was face to face with France alone. There is glory and to spare without trifling with the truth. Two provinces in France, both rich and warlike, had become English through a royal marriage, and these, Guienne and Gascony, furnished many of the most valiant soldiers under the island flag. So poor a country as England could not afford to keep a great force overseas, and so must needs have lost the war with France through want of power to uphold the struggle. The feudal system enabled an army to be drawn rapidly together with small expense, but at the end of a few weeks it dispersed again as swiftly, and only by a well-filled money-chest could it be held together. There was no such chest in England, and the king was for ever at his wits' end how to keep his men in the field.

But Guienne and Gascony were full of knights and squires who were always ready to assemble from their isolated castles for a raid into France, and these with the addition of those English cavaliers who fought for honour, and a few thousand of the formidable archers, hired for fourpence a day, made an army with which a short campaign could be carried on. Such were the materials of the prince's force, some eight thousand strong, who were now riding in a great circle through southern France, leaving a broad wale of blackened and ruined country behind them.

But France, even with her south-western corner in English hands, was still a very warlike power, far richer and more populous than her rival. Single provinces were so great that they were stronger than many a kingdom. Normandy in the north, Burgundy in the east, Brittany in the west, and Languedoc in the south were each capable of fitting out a great army of its own. Therefore the brave and spirited John, watching from Paris this insolent raid into his dominions, sent messengers in hot haste to all these great feudatories, as well as to Lorraine, Picardy, Auvergne, Hainault, Vermandois, Champagne, and to the German mercenaries over his eastern border, bidding all of them to ride hard, with bloody spur, day and night, until they should gather to a head at Chartres.

There a great army had assembled early in September, while the prince, all unconscious of its presence, sacked towns and besieged castles from Bourges to Issodun, passing Romorantin, and so onward to Vierzon and to Tours. From week to week there were merry skirmishes at barriers, brisk assaults of fortresses in which much honour was won, knightly meetings with detached parties of Frenchmen and occasional spear-runnings, where noble champions deigned to venture their persons. Houses, too, were to be plundered, while wine and women were in plenty. Never had either knights or archers had so pleasant and profitable an excursion, so that it was with high heart and much hope of pleasant days at Bordeaux with their pockets full of money that the army turned south from the Loire and began to retrace its steps to the seaboard city.

But now its pleasant and martial promenade changed suddenly to very serious work of war. As the prince moved south he found that all supplies had been cleared away from in front of him and that there was neither fodder for the horses nor food for the men. Two hundred waggons laden with spoil rolled at the head of the army, but the starving soldiers would soon have gladly changed it all for as many loads of bread and meat. The light troops of the French had preceded them, and burned or destroyed everything that could be of use. Now also for the first time the prince and his men became aware that a great army was moving upon the eastern side of them, streaming southward in the hope of cutting off their retreat to the sea. The sky glowed with their fires at night, and the autumn sun twinkled and gleamed from one end of the horizon to the other upon the steel caps and flashing weapons of a mighty host.

Anxious to secure his plunder, and conscious that the

levies of France were far superior in number to his own force, the prince redoubled his attempts to escape ; but his horses were exhausted and his starving men were hardly to be kept in order. A few more days would unfit them for battle. Therefore, when he found near the village of Maupertuis a position in which a small force might have a chance to hold its own, he gave up the attempt to out-march his pursuers, and he turned at bay, like a hunted boar, all tusks and eyes of flame.

While these high events had been in progress, Nigel with Black Simon and four other men-at-arms from Bordeaux were hastening northward to join the army. As far as Bergerac they were in a friendly land, but thence onward they rode over a blackened landscape with many a roofless house, its two bare gable-ends sticking upward— a " Knolles' mitre," as it was afterwards called, when Sir Robert worked his stern will upon the country. For three days they rode northward, seeing many small parties of French in all directions, but too eager to reach the army to ease their march in the search of adventures.

Then at last after passing Lusignan they began to come in touch with English foragers, mounted bowmen for the most part, who were endeavouring to collect supplies either for the army or for themselves. From them Nigel learned that the prince, with Chandos ever at his side, was hastening south and might be met within a short day's march. As he still advanced these English stragglers became more and more numerous, until at last he overtook a considerable column of archers moving in the same direction as his own party. These were men whose horses had failed them and who had therefore been left behind on the advance, but were now hastening to be in in time for the impending battle. A crowd of peasant girls accompanied them upon their march, and a whole train of laden mules were led beside them.

Nigel and his little troop of men-at-arms were riding past the archers when Black Simon, with a sudden exclamation, touched his leader upon the arm.

" See yonder, fair sir," he cried, with gleaming eyes, " there where the wastrel walks with the great fardel upon his back ! Who is he who marches behind him ? "

Nigel looked, and was aware of a stunted peasant who bore upon his rounded back an enormous bundle very much larger than himself. Behind him walked a burly broad-shouldered archer, whose stained jerkin and battered headpiece gave token of long and hard service. His bow was slung over his shoulder, and his arms were round the waists of two buxom Frenchwomen, who tripped along beside him with much laughter and many saucy answers flung back over their shoulders to a score of admirers behind them.

" Aylward ! " cried Nigel, spurring forward.

The archer turned his bronzed face, stared for an instant with wild eyes, and then, dropping his two ladies, who were instantly carried off by his comrades, he rushed to seize the hand which his young master held down to him.

" Now, by my hilt, Squire Nigel, this is the fairest sight of my lifetime ! " he cried. " And you, old leather-face ! Nay, Simon, I would put my arms round your dried herring of a body, if I could but reach you. Here is Pommers too, and I read in his eye that he knows me well, and is as ready to put his teeth into me as when he stood in my father's stall."

It was like a whiff of the heather-perfumed breezes of Hankley to see his homely face once more. Nigel laughed with sheer joy as he looked at him.

" It was an ill day when the king's service called you from my side," said he, " and by Saint Paul ! I am right glad to set eyes upon you once more ! I see well that you are in no wise altered, but the same Aylward that I have ever known. But who is this varlet with the great bundle who waits upon your movements ? "

" It is no less than a feather-bed, fair sir, which he bears upon his back, for I would fain bring it to Tilford, and yet it is overlarge for me when I take my place with my fellows in the ranks. But indeed this war has been a

most excellent one, and I have already sent half a waggon-
load of my gear back to Bordeaux to await my home-
coming. Yet I have my fears when I think of all the
rascal foot-archers who are waiting there, for some folk
have no grace or honesty in their souls, and cannot
keep their hands from that which belongs to another.
But if I may throw my leg over yonder spare horse I will
come on with you, fair sir, for indeed it would be joy to
my heart to know that I was riding under your banner
once again."

So Aylward, having given instructions to the bearer of
his feather-bed, rode away in spite of shrill protests from
his French companions, who speedily consoled themselves
with those of his comrades who seemed to have most to
give.

Nigel's party was soon clear of the column of archers
and riding hard in the direction of the prince's army.
They passed by a narrow and winding track, through the
great wood of Nouaille, and found before them a marshy
valley down which ran a sluggish stream. Along its
farther bank hundreds of horses were being watered, and
beyond was a dense block of waggons. Through these
the comrades passed, and then topped a small mound, from
which the whole strange scene lay spread before them.

Down the valley the slow stream meandered, with
marshy meadows on either side. A mile or two lower a
huge drove of horses were to be seen assembled upon the
bank. They were the steeds of the French cavalry, and
the blue haze of a hundred fires showed where King John's
men were camping. In front of the mound upon which
they stood the English line was drawn, but there were few
fires, for indeed, save their horses, there was little for them
to cook. Their right rested upon the river, and their
array stretched across a mile of ground, until the left was
in touch with a tangled forest which guarded it from flank
attack. In front was a long, thick hedge and much broken
ground, with a single deeply rutted country road cutting
through it in the middle. Under the hedge and along

the whole front of the position lay swarms of archers upon the grass, the greater number slumbering peacefully with sprawling limbs in the warm rays of the September sun. Behind were the quarters of the various knights, and from end to end flew the banners and pennons marked with the devices of the chivalry of England and Guienne.

With a glow in his heart Nigel saw those badges of famous captains and leaders, and knew that now at last he also might show his coat-armour in such noble company. There was the flag of Jean Grailly, the Captal de Buch, five silver shells on a black cross, which marked the presence of the most famous soldier of Gascony, while beside it waved the red lion of the noble Knight of Hainault, Sir Eustace d'Ambreticourt. These two coats Nigel knew, as did every warrior in Europe, but a dense grove of pennoned lances surrounded them, bearing charges which were strange to him, from which he understood that these belonged to the Guienne division of the army. Farther down the line the famous English ensigns floated on the wind, the scarlet and gold of Warwick, the silver star of Oxford, the golden cross of Suffolk, the blue and gold of Willoughby, and the gold-fretted scarlet of Audley. In the very centre of them all was one which caused all others to pass from his mind, for close to the royal banner of England, crossed with the label of the prince, there waved the war-worn flag with the red wedge upon the golden field which marked the quarters of the noble Chandos.

At the sight Nigel set spurs to his horse, and a few minutes later had reached the spot. Chandos, gaunt from hunger and want of sleep, but with the old fire lurking in his eye, was standing by the prince's tent, gazing down at what could be seen of the French array, and heavy with thought. Nigel sprang from his horse and was within touch of his master when the silken hanging of the royal tent was torn violently aside and Edward rushed out.

He was without his armour and clad in a sober suit

745

of black, but the high dignity of his bearing and the imperious anger which flushed his face proclaimed the leader and the prince. At his heels was a little white-haired ecclesiastic in a flowing gown of scarlet sendal, expostulating and arguing in a torrent of words.

" Not another word, my Lord Cardinal," cried the angry prince. " I have listened to you overlong, and by God's dignity ! that which you say is neither good nor fair in my ears. Hark you, John, I would have your counsel. What think you is the message which my Lord Cardinal of Perigord has carried from the king of France ? He says that of his clemency he will let my army pass back to Bordeaux if we will restore to him all that we have taken, remit all ransoms, and surrender my own person with that of a hundred nobles of England and Guienne to be held as prisoners. What think you, John ? "

Chandos smiled. " Things are not done in that fashion," said he.

" But, my lord Chandos," cried the Cardinal, " I have made it clear to the prince that indeed it is a scandal to all Christendom and a cause of mocking to the heathen, that two great sons of the Church should turn their swords thus upon each other."

" Then bid the king of France keep clear of us," said the prince.

" Fair son, you are aware that you are in the heart of his country, and that it standeth not aright that he should suffer you to go forth as you came. You have but a small army, three thousand bowmen and five thousand men-at-arms at the most, who seem in evil case for want of food and rest. The king has thirty thousand men at his back, of which twenty thousand are expert men-at-arms. It is fitting therefore that you make such terms as you may, lest worse befall."

" Give my greetings to the king of France and tell him that England will never pay ransom for me. But it seems to me, my Lord Cardinal, that you have our numbers and condition very ready upon your tongue, and I would fain know how the eye of a Churchman can read a line of battle so easily. I have seen that these knights of your household have walked freely to and fro within our camp, and I much fear that when I welcomed you as envoys I have in truth given my protection to spies. How say you, my Lord Cardinal ? "

" Fair prince, I know not how you can find it in your heart or conscience to say such evil words."

" There is this red-bearded nephew of thine, Robert de Duras. See where he stands yonder, counting and prying. Hark hither, young sir ! I have been saying to your uncle the Cardinal that it is in my mind that you and your comrades have carried news of our disposition to the French king. How say you ? "

The knight turned pale and sank his eyes. " My lord," he murmured, " it may be that I have answered some questions."

" And how will such answers accord with your honour, seeing that we have trusted you since you came in the train of the cardinal ? "

" My lord, it is true that I am in the train of the cardinal, and yet I am liege man of King John and a knight of France, so I pray you to assuage your wrath against me."

The prince ground his teeth and his piercing eyes blazed upon the youth.

" By my father's soul ! I can scarce forbear to strike you to the earth ! But this I promise you, that if you show that sign of the Red Griffin in the field and if you be taken alive in to-morrow's battle, your head shall most assuredly be shorn from your shoulders ! "

" Fair son, indeed you speak wildly," cried the Cardinal. " I pledge you my word that neither my nephew Robert nor any of my train will take part in the battle. And now I leave you, sire, and may God assoil your soul, for indeed in all this world no men stand in greater peril than you and those who are around you, and I rede you that you spend the night in such ghostly exercises as may best prepare you for that which may befall." So saying the cardinal bowed, and with his household walking behind him set off for the spot where they had left their horses, whence they rode to the neighbouring abbey.

The angry prince turned upon his heel and entered his tent once more, while Chandos, glancing round, held out a warm welcoming hand to Nigel.

" I have heard much of your noble deeds," said he. " Already your name rises as a squire-errant. I stood no higher, nor so high, at your age."

Nigel flushed with pride and pleasure. " Indeed, my dear lord, it is very little that I have done. But now that I am back at your side I hope that in truth I shall learn to bear myself in worthy fashion, for where else should I win honour if it be not under your banner ? "

" Truly, Nigel, you have come at a very good time for advancement. I cannot see how we can leave this spot without a great battle which will live in men's minds for ever. In all our fights in France I cannot call to mind any in which they have been so strong or we so weak as now, so that there will be the more honour to be gained. I would that we had two thousand more archers. But I doubt not that we shall give them much trouble ere they drive us out from amidst these hedges. Have you seen the French ? "

" Nay, fair sir, I have but this moment arrived."

" I was about to ride forth myself to coast their army and observe their countenance, so come with me ere the night fall, and we shall see what we can of their order and dispositions."

There was a truce between the two forces for the day, on account of the ill-advised and useless interposition of the Cardinal of Perigord. Hence when Chandos and Nigel had pushed their horses through the long hedge which fronted the position they found that many small parties of the knights of either army were riding up and down on the plain outside. The greater number of these groups were French, since it was very necessary for them to know as much as possible of the English defences ; and many of their scouts had ridden up to within a hundred yards of the hedge, where they were sternly ordered back by the pickets of archers on guard.

Through these scattered knots of horsemen Chandos rode, and as many of them were old antagonists it was " Ha, John ! " on the one side, and " Ha, Raoul ! " " Ha, Nicholas ! " " Ha, Guichard ! " upon the other, as they brushed past them. Only one cavalier greeted them amiss, a large, red-faced man, the Lord Clermont, who by some strange chance bore upon his surcoat a blue virgin standing amid golden sunbeams, which was the very device which Chandos had donned for the day. The fiery Frenchman dashed across their path and drew his steed back on its haunches.

" How long is it, my lord Chandos," said he, hotly, " since you have taken it upon yourself to wear my arms ? "

Chandos smiled. " It is surely you who have mine," said he, " since this surcoat was worked for me by the good nuns of Windsor a long year ago."

" If it were not for the truce," said Clermont, " I would soon show you that you have no right to wear it."

" Look for it then in the battle to-morrow, and I also will look for yours." Chandos answered. " There we can very honourably settle the matter."

But the Frenchman was choleric and hard to appease. " You English can invent nothing," said he, " and you take for your own whatever you see handsome belonging to others." So, grumbling and fuming, he rode upon his way, while Chandos, laughing gaily, spurred onward across the plain.

The immediate front of the English lines was shrouded with scattered trees and bushes which hid the enemy ; but when they had cleared these a fair view of the great French army lay before them. In the centre of the huge camp was a long and high pavilion of red silk, with the silver lilies of the king at one end of it, and the golden oriflamme of the battle-flag of old France at the other.

Like the reeds of a pool from side to side of the broad array, and dwindling away as far as their eyes could see, were the banners and pennons of high barons and famous knights, but above them all flew the ducal standards which showed that the feudal muster of all the warlike provinces of France was in the field before them.

With a kindling eye Chandos looked across at the proud ensigns of Normandy, of Burgundy, of Auvergne, of Champagne, of Vermandois, and of Berry, flaunting and gleaming in the rays of the sinking sun. Riding slowly down the line he marked with attentive gaze the camp of the crossbowmen, the muster of the German mercenaries, the numbers of the foot-soldiers, the arms of every proud vassal or vavasor which might give some guide as to the power of each division. From wing to wing and round the flanks he went, keeping ever within crossbow-shot of the army, and then at last having noted all things in his mind he turned his horse's head and rode slowly back, heavy with thought, to the English lines.

25. *How the King of France held Counsel at Maupertuis*

THE morning of Sunday, the nineteenth of September, in the year of our Lord 1356, was cold and fine. A haze which rose from the marshy valley of Muisson covered both camps and set the starving Englishmen shivering, but it cleared slowly away as the sun rose. In the red silken pavilion of the French king—the same which had been viewed by Nigel and Chandos the evening before—a solemn mass was held by the Bishop of Chalons, who prayed for those who were about to die, with little thought in his mind that his own last hour was so near at hand. Then, when communion had been taken by the king and his four young sons the altar was cleared away, and a great red-covered table placed lengthwise down the tent, round which John might assemble his council and determine how best he should proceed. With the silken roof, rich tapestries of Arras round the walls and eastern rugs beneath the feet, his palace could furnish no fairer chamber.

King John, who sat upon the canopied dais at the upper end, was now in the sixth year of his reign and the thirty-sixth of his life. He was a short burly man, ruddy-faced and deep-chested, with dark kindly eyes and a most noble bearing. It did not need the blue cloak sewed with silver lilies to mark him as the king. Though his reign had been short, his fame was already widespread over all Europe as a kindly gentleman and a fearless soldier—a fit leader for a chivalrous nation. His elder son, the Duke of Normandy, still hardly more than a boy, stood beside him, his hand upon the king's shoulder, and John half turned from time to time to fondle him. On the right, at the same high dais, was the king's younger brother, the Duke of Orleans, a pale heavy-featured man, with a languid manner and intolerant eyes. On the left was the Duke of Bourbon, sad-faced and absorbed, with that gentle melancholy in his eyes and bearing which comes often with the premonition of death. All these were in their armour, save only for their helmets, which lay upon the board before them.

Below, grouped around the long red table, was an assembly of the most famous warriors in Europe. At the end nearest the king was the veteran soldier the Duke of Athens, son of a banished father, and now high constable of France. On one side of him sat the red-faced and choleric Lord Clermont, with the same blue virgin in golden rays upon his surcoat which had caused his quarrel with Chandos the night before. On the other was a noble-featured grizzly-haired soldier, Arnold d'Andreghen, who shared with Clermont the honour of being Marshal of France. Next to them sat Lord James of Bourbon, a brave warrior who was afterwards slain by the White Company at Brignais, and beside him a little group of German noblemen, including the Earl of Salzburg and the Earl of Nassau, who had ridden over the frontier with their formidable mercenaries at the bidding of the French king. The ridged armour and the hanging nasals of their bassinets were enough in themselves to tell every soldier that they were from beyond the Rhine. At the other side of the table was a line of proud and war-like lords, Fiennes, Chatillon, Nesle, de Landas, de Beaujeu, with the fierce knight-errant de Chargny, he who had planned the surprise of Calais, and Eustace de Ribeaumont, who had upon the same occasion won the prize of valour from the hands of Edward of England. Such were the chiefs to whom the king now turned for assistance and advice.

" You have already heard, my friends," said he, " that the Prince of Wales has made no answer to the proposal which we sent by the Lord Cardinal of Perigord. Certes this is as it should be, and though I have obeyed the call of Holy Church I had no fears that so excellent a prince as Edward of England would refuse to meet us in battle. I am now of opinion that we should fall upon them at once, lest perchance the Cardinal's cross should again come betwixt our swords and our enemies."

A buzz of joyful assent arose from the meeting, and even from the attendant men-at-arms who guarded the door. When it had died away the Duke of Orleans rose in his place beside the king.

" Sire," said he, " you speak as we would have you do, and I for one am of opinion that the Cardinal of Perigord has been an ill friend of France, for why should we bargain for a part when we have but to hold out our hands in order to grasp the whole ? What need is there for words ? Let us spring to horse forthwith and ride over this handful of marauders who have dared to lay waste your fair dominions. If one them of go hence save as our prisoner we are the more to blame."

" By Saint Denis, brother ! " said the king, smiling, " if words could slay you would have had them all upon their backs ere ever we left Chartres. You are new to war, but when you have had experience of a stricken field or two you know that things must be done with forethought and in order or they may go awry. In our father's time we sprang to horse and spurred upon these English at Crécy and elsewhere as you advise, but we had little profit from it, and now we are grown wiser. How say you, Sieur de Ribeaumont ? You have coasted their lines and observed their countenance. Would you ride down upon them, as my brother has advised, or how would you order the matter ? "

De Ribeaumont, a tall dark-eyed, handsome man, paused ere he answered.

" Sire," he said at last, " I have indeed ridden along their front and down their flanks in company with Lord Landas and Lord de Beaujeu, who are here at your council to witness to what I say. Indeed, sire, it is in my mind that though the English are few in number yet they are in such a position amongst these hedges and vines that you would be well-advised if you were to leave them alone, for they have no food and must retreat, so that you will be able to follow them and to fight them to better advantage."

A murmur of disapproval rose from the company and the Lord Clermont, marshal of the army, sprang to his feet, his face red with anger.

" Eustace, Eustace," said he, " I bear in mind the days when you were of great heart and high enterprise, but since King Edward gave you yonder chaplet of pearls you have ever been backward against the English ! "

" My Lord Clermont," said de Ribeaumont, sternly, " it is not for me to brawl at the king's council and in the face of the enemy, but we will go further into this matter at some other time. Meanwhile, the king has asked me for my advice and I have given it as best I might."

" It had been better for your honour, Sir Eustace, had you held your peace," said the Duke of Orleans. " Shall we let them slip from our fingers when we have them here and are fourfold their number ? I know not where we should dwell afterwards, for I am very sure that we should be ashamed to ride back to Paris, or to look our ladies in the eyes again."

" Indeed, Eustace, you have done well to say what is in your mind," said the king ; " but I have already said that we shall join battle this morning, so that there is no room here for further talk. But I would fain have heard from you how it would be wisest and best that we attack them?"

" I will advise you, sire, to the best of my power. Upon their right is a river with marshes around it, and upon their left a great wood, so that we can advance only upon the centre. Along their front is a thick hedge, and behind it I saw the green jerkins of their archers, as thick as the sedges by the river. It is broken by one road where only four horsemen could ride abreast, which leads through the position. It is clear then, that if we are to drive them back we must cross the great hedge, and I am very sure that the horses will not face it with such a storm of arrows beating from behind it. Therefore, it is my counsel that we fight upon foot, as the English did at Crécy, for indeed we may find that our horses will be more hindrance than help to us this day."

" The same thought was in my own mind, sire," said Arnold d'Andreghen, the veteran marshal. " At Crécy the bravest had to turn their backs, for what can a man do with a horse which is mad with pain and fear ? If we advance upon foot we are our own masters, and if we stop the shame is ours."

" The counsel is good," said the Duke of Athens, turning his shrewd wizened face to the king ; " but one thing only I would add to it. The strength of these people lies in their archers, and if we could throw them into disorder, were it only for a short time, we should win the hedge ; else they will shoot so strongly that we must lose many men before we reach it, for indeed we have learned that no armour will keep out their shafts when they are close."

" Your words, fair sir, are both good and wise," said the king, " but I pray you to tell us how you would throw these archers into disorder ? "

" I would choose three hundred horsemen, sire, the

best and most forward in the army. With these I would ride up the narrow road, and so turn to right and left, falling upon the archers behind the hedge. It may be that the three hundred would suffer sorely, but what are they among so great a host, if a road may be cleared for their companions ? "

" I would say a word to that, sire," cried the German Count of Nassau. " I have come here with my comrades to venture our persons in your quarrel ; but we claim the right to fight in our own fashion, and we would count it dishonour to dismount from our steeds out of fear of the arrows of the English. Therefore, with your permission, we will ride to the front, as the Duke of Athens has advised, and so clear a path for the rest of you."

" This may not be ! " cried the Lord Clermont, angrily. " It would be strange indeed if Frenchmen could not be found to clear a path for the army of the King of France. One would think to hear you talk, my Lord Count, that your hardihood was greater than our own, but by our Lady of Rocamadour you will learn before nightfall that it is not so. It is for me, who am a marshal of France, to lead these three hundred, since it is an honourable venture."

" And I claim the same right for the same reason," said Arnold of Andreghen.

The German count struck the table with his mailed fist.

" Do what you like ! " said he. " But this only I can promise you, that neither I nor any of the German riders will descend from our horses so long as they are able to carry us, for in our country it is only people of no consequence who fight upon their feet."

The Lord Clermont was leaning angrily forward with some hot reply when King John intervened.

" Enough, enough ! " he said. " It is for you to give your opinions, and for me to tell you what you will do. Lord Clermont, and you, Arnold, you will choose three hundred of the bravest cavaliers in the army and you will endeavour to break these archers. As to you and your Germans, my Lord Nassau, you will remain upon horseback, since you desire it, and you will follow the marshals and support them as best you may. The rest of the army will advance upon foot, in three other divisions as arranged : yours, Charles," and he patted his son, the Duke of Normandy, affectionately upon the hand ; " yours Philip," he glanced at the Duke of Orleans ; " and the main battle which is my own. To you, Geoffrey de Chargny, I intrust the oriflamme this day. But who is this knight and what does he desire ? "

A young knight, ruddy bearded and tall, a red griffin upon his surcoat, had appeared in the opening of the tent. His flushed face and dishevelled dress showed that he had come in haste.

" Sire," said he, " I am Robert de Duras, of the household of the Cardinal de Perigord. I have told you yesterday all that I have learned of the English camp. This morning I was again admitted to it, and I have seen their waggons moving to the rear. Sire, they are in flight for Bordeaux."

" 'Fore God, I knew it ! " cried the Duke of Orleans, in a voice of fury. " Whilst we have been talking they have slipped through our fingers. Did I not warn you ? "

" Be silent, Philip ! " said the king angrily. " But you, sir, have you seen this with your own eyes ? "

" With my own eyes, sire, and I have ridden straight from their camp."

King John looked at him with a stern gaze. " I know not how it accords with your honour to carry such tidings in such a fashion," said he ; " but we cannot choose but take advantage of it. Fear not, brother Philip, it is in my mind that you will see all that you would wish of the Englishmen before nightfall. Should we fall upon them whilst they cross the ford it will be to our advantage. Now, fair sirs, I pray you to hasten to your posts and to carry out all that we have agreed. Advance the oriflamme, Geoffrey, and do you marshal the divisions, Arnold. So may God and Saint Denis have us in their holy keeping this day ! "

The Prince of Wales stood upon that little knoll where Nigel had halted the day before. Beside him were Chandos, and a tall sun-burned warrior of middle age, the Gascon Captal de Buch. The three men were all attentively watching the distant French lines, while behind them a column of waggons wound down to the ford of the Muisson.

Close in the rear four knights in full armour with open visors sat their horses and conversed in undertones with each other. A glance at their shields would have given their names to any soldier, for they were all men of fame who had seen much warfare. At present they were awaiting their orders, for each of them commanded the whole or part of a division of the army. The youth upon the left, dark, slim, and earnest, was William Montacute, Earl of Salisbury, only twenty-eight years of age, and yet a veteran of Crécy. How high he stood in reputation is shown by the fact that the command of the rear, the post of honour in a retreating army, had been given to him by the prince. He was talking to a grizzled harsh-faced man, somewhat over middle age, with lion features and fierce light-blue eyes which gleamed as they watched the distant enemy. It was the famous Robert de Ufford, Earl of Suffolk, who had fought without a break from Cadsand onward through the whole Continental War. The other tall silent soldier, with the silver star gleaming upon his surcoat, was John de Vere, Earl of Oxford, and he listened to the talk of Thomas Beauchamp, a burly, jovial, ruddy nobleman and a tried soldier, who leaned forward and tapped his mailed hand upon the other's steel-clad thigh. They were old battle-companions, of the same age and in the very prime of life, with equal fame and equal experience of the wars. Such was the group of famous English soldiers who sat their horses behind the prince and waited for their orders.

" I would that you had laid hands upon him," said the prince angrily, continuing his conversation with Chandos, " and yet, perchance, it was wiser to play this trick and make them think that we were retreating."

" He has certainly carried the tidings," said Chandos, with a smile. " No sooner had the waggons started than I saw him gallop down the edge of the wood."

" It was well thought of, John," the prince remarked, " for it would indeed be great comfort if we could turn their own spy against them. Unless they advance upon us, I know not how we can hold out another day, for there is not a loaf left in the army ; and yet if we leave this position, where shall we hope to find such another ? "

" They will stoop, fair sir, they will stoop to our lure. Even now Robert de Duras will be telling them that the waggons are on the move, and they will hasten to overtake us lest we pass the ford. But who is this, who rides so fast ? Here perchance may be tidings."

A horseman had spurred up to the knoll. He sprang from the saddle, and sank on one knee before the prince.

" How now, my Lord Audley," said Edward. " What would you have ? "

" Sir," said the knight, still kneeling with bowed head before his leader, " I have a boon to ask of you."

" Nay, James, rise ! Let me hear what I can do."

The famous knight-errant, pattern of chivalry for all time, rose and turned his swarthy face and dark earnest eyes upon his master.

" Sir," said he, " I have ever served most loyally my lord your father and yourself, and shall continue so to do so long as I have life. Dear sir, I must now acquaint you that formerly I made a vow if ever I should be in any battle under your command that I would be fore-most or die in the attempt. I beg therefore that you will graciously permit me to honourably quit my place among the others, that I may post myself in such wise as to accomplish my vow."

The prince smiled, for it was very sure that vow or no vow, permission or no permission, Lord James Audley would still be in the van.

" Go, James," said he, shaking his hand, " and God

grant that this day you may shine in valour above all knights. But hark, John, what is that ? "

Chandos cast up his fierce nose like the eagle which smells slaughter afar.

" Surely, sir, all is forming even as we had planned it."

From far away there came a thunderous shout. Then another and yet another.

" See, they are moving ! " cried the Captal de Buch.

All morning they had watched the gleam of the armed squadrons who were drawn up in front of the French camp. Now, while a great blare of trumpets was borne to their ears, the distant masses flickered and twinkled in the sunlight.

" Yes, yes, they are moving ! " cried the prince.

" They are moving ! They are moving ! " Down the line the murmur ran. And then, with a sudden impulse, the archers at the hedge sprang to their feet and the knights behind them waved their weapons in the air, while one tremendous shout of warlike joy carried their defiance to the approaching enemy. Then there fell such a silence that the pawing of the horses or the jingle of their harness struck loud upon the ear, until amid the hush there rose a low deep roar like the sound of the tide upon the beach, ever growing and deepening as the host of France drew near.

26. *How Nigel found his Third Deed*

FOUR archers lay behind a clump of bushes ten yards in front of the thick hedge which shielded their companions. Amid the long line of bowmen those behind them were their own company, and in the main the same who were with Knolles in Brittany. The four in front were their leaders : old Wat of Carlisle, Ned Widdington the red-headed dalesman, the bald bowyer Bartholomew, and Samkin Aylward, newly rejoined after a week's absence. All four were munching bread and apples, for Aylward had brought in a full haversack, and divided them freely among his starving comrades. The old borderer and the Yorkshireman were gaunt and hollow-eyed with privation, while the bowyer's round face had fallen in so that the skin hung in loose pouches under his eyes and beneath his jaws.

Behind them lines of haggard, wolfish men glared through the underwood, silent and watchful save that they burst into a fierce yelp of welcome when Chandos and Nigel galloped up, sprang from their horses and took their station beneath them. All along the green fringe of bowmen might be seen the steel-clad figures of knights and squires who had pushed their way into the front line to share the fortune of the archers.

" I call to mind that I once shot six ends with a Kentish woldsman at Ashford——" began the bowyer.

" Nay, nay, we have heard that story ! " said old Wat, impatiently. " Shut thy clap, Bartholomew, for it is no time for redeless gossip ! Walk down the line, I pray you, and see if there be no frayed string nor broken nock nor loosened whipping to be mended."

The stout bowyer passed down the fringe of bowmen, amid a running fire of rough wit. Here and there a bow was thrust out at him through the hedge for his professional advice.

" Wax your heads ! " he kept crying. " Pass down the wax-pot and wax your heads. A waxed arrow will pass where a dry will be held. Tom Beverley, you jack-fool ! where is your bracer-guard ? Your string will flay your arm ere you reach your up-shot this day. And you, Watkin, draw not to your mouth, as is your wont, but to your shoulder. You are so used to the wine-pot that the string must needs follow it. Nay, stand loose, and give space for your drawing arms, for they will be on us anon."

He ran back and joined his comrades in the front, who had now risen to their feet. Behind them a half-mile of archers stood behind the hedge, each with his great war-bow strung, half a dozen shafts loose behind him, and eighteen more in the quiver slung across his front. With arrow on string, their feet firm-planted, their fierce eager faces peering through the branches, they awaited the coming storm.

The broad flood of steel, after oozing slowly forward, had stopped about a mile from the English front. The greater part of the army had then descended from their horses, while a crowd of varlets and ostlers led them to the rear. The French formed themselves now into three great divisions, which shimmered in the sun like silver pools, reed-capped with many a thousand of banners and pennons. A space of several hundred yards divided each, At the same time two bodies of horsemen formed themselves in front. The first consisted of three hundred men in one thick column, the second of a thousand, riding in a more extended line.

The prince had ridden up to the line of archers. He was in dark armour, his visor open, and his handsome aquiline face all glowing with spirit and martial fire. The bowmen yelled at him, and he waved his hands to them as a huntsman cheers his hounds.

" Well, John, what think you now ? " he asked. " What would my noble father not give to be by our side this day ? Have you seen that they have left their horses ? "

" Yes, my fair lord, they have learned their lesson," said Chandos. " Because we have had good fortune upon our feet at Crécy and elsewhere, they think that they have found the trick of it. But it is in my mind that it is very different to stand when you are assailed, as we have done, and to assail others when you must drag your harness for a mile and come weary to the fray."

" You speak wisely, John. But these horsemen who form in front and ride slowly toward us, what make you of them ? "

" Doubtless they hope to cut the strings of our bowmen and so clear a way for the others. But they are indeed a chosen band, for mark you, fair sir, are not those the colours of Clermont upon the left, and of d'Andreghen upon the right, so that both marshals ride with the vanguard ? "

" By God's soul, John ! " cried the prince, " it is very sure that you can see more with one eye than any man in this army with two. But it is even as you say. And this larger band behind ? '

" They should be Germans, fair sir, by the fashion of their harness."

The two bodies of horsemen had moved slowly over the plain, with a space of nearly a quarter of a mile between them. Now, having come two bowshots from the hostile line, they halted. All that they could see of the English was the long hedge, with an occasional twinkle of steel through its leafy branches, and behind that the spearheads of the men-at-arms rising from amid the brushwood and the vines. A lovely autumn countryside with changing many-tinted foliage lay stretched before them, all bathed in peaceful sunshine, and nothing save those flickering fitful gleams to tell of the silent and lurking enemy who barred their way. But the bold spirit of the French cavaliers rose the higher to the danger. The clamour of their war-cries filled the air, and they tossed their pennoned spears over their heads in menace and defiance. From the English line it was a noble sight, the gallant, pawing, curveting horses, the many-coloured twinkling riders, the swoop and wave and toss of plume and banner.

Then a bugle rang forth. With a sudden yell every spur struck deep, every lance was laid in rest, and the whole gallant squadron flew like a glittering thunderbolt for the centre of the English line.

A hundred yards they had crossed, and yet another hundred, but there was no movement in front of them, and no sound save their own hoarse battle-cries and the thunder of their horses. Ever swifter and swifter they flew. From behind the hedge it was a vision of horses, white, bay, and black, their necks stretched, their nostrils distended, their bellies to the ground, while of the rider one could but see a shield with a plume-tufted visor above it, and a spear-head twinkling in front.

Then of a sudden the prince raised his hand and gave a cry. Chandos echoed it, it swelled down the line, and with one mighty chorus of twanging strings and hissing shafts the long-pent storm broke at last.

Alas for the noble steeds ! Alas for the gallant men ! When the lust of battle is over who would not grieve to see that noble squadron break into red ruin before the rain of arrows beating upon the faces and breasts of the horses ? The front rank crashed down, and the others piled themselves upon the top of them, unable to check their speed, or to swerve aside from the terrible wall of their shattered comrades which had so suddenly sprung up before them. Fifteen feet high was that blood-spurting mound of screaming, kicking horses and writhing, struggling men. Here and there on the flanks a horseman cleared himself and dashed for the hedge, only to have his steed slain under him and to be hurled from his saddle. Of all the three hundred gallant riders, not one ever reached that fatal hedge.

But now in a long rolling wave of steel the German battalion roared swiftly onward. They opened in the centre to pass that terrible mound of death, and then spurred swiftly in upon the archers. They were brave men, well led, and in their open lines they could avoid the clubbing together which had been the ruin of the vanguard ; yet they perished singly even as the others had perished together. A few were slain by the arrows. The greater number had their horses killed under them, and were so shaken and shattered by the fall that they could not raise their limbs, overweighted with iron, from the spot where they lay.

Three men riding together broke through the bushes which sheltered the leaders of the archers, cut down Widdington the Dalesman, spurred onward through the hedge, dashed over the bowmen behind it, and made for the prince. One fell with an arrow through his head, a second was beaten from his saddle by Chandos, and the third was slain by the prince's own hand. A second band broke through near the river, but were cut off by Lord Audley and his squires, so that all were slain. A single horseman whose steed was mad with pain, an arrow in its eye and a second in its nostril, sprang over the hedge and clattered through the whole army, disappearing amid whoops and laughter into the woods behind. But none others won as far as the hedge. The whole front of the position was fringed with a litter of German wounded or dead, while one great heap in the centre marked the downfall of the gallant French three hundred.

While these two waves of the attack had broken in front of the English position, leaving this blood-stained wreckage behind them, the main divisions had halted and made their last preparations for their own assault. They had not yet begun their advance, and the nearest was still half a mile distant, when the few survivors from the forlorn hope, their maddened horses bristling with arrows, flew past them on either flank.

At the same moment the English archers and men-at-arms dashed through the hedge, and dragged all who were living out of that tangled heap of shattered horses and men. It was a mad wild rush, for in a few minutes the fight must be renewed, and yet there was a rich harvest of wealth for the lucky man who could pick a wealthy prisoner from amid the crowd. The nobler spirits disdained to think of ransoms while the fight was still unsettled ; but a swarm of needy soldiers, Gascons and English, dragged the wounded out by the leg or the arm, and with daggers at their throats demanded their names title, and means. He who had made a good prize hurried him to the rear where his own servants could guard him, while he who was disappointed too often drove the dagger home and then rushed once more into the tangle in the hope of better luck. Clermont, with an arrow through the sky-blue virgin on his surcoat, lay dead within ten paces of the hedge ; d'Andreghen was dragged by a penniless squire from under a horse and became his prisoner. The Earls of Salzburg and of Nassau were both found helpless on the ground and taken to the rear. Aylward cast his thick arms round Count Otto von Langenbeck, and laid him, helpless from a broken leg, behind his bush. Black Simon had made prize of Bernard, Count of Ventadour, and hurried him through the hedge. Everywhere there was rushing and shouting, brawling and buffeting, while amid it all a swarm of archers were seeking their shafts, plucking them from the dead, and sometimes even from the wounded. Then there was a sudden cry of warning. In a moment every man was back in his place once more, and the line of the hedge was clear.

It was high time ; for already the first division of the French was close upon them. If the charge of the horse-men had been terrible from its rush and its fire, this steady advance of a huge phalanx of armoured footmen was even more fearsome to the spectator. They moved very slowly, on account of the weight of their armour, but their progress was the more regular and inexorable. With elbows touching—their shields slung in front, their short five-foot spears carried in their right hands, and their maces or swords ready at their belts, the deep column of men-at-arms moved onward. Again the storm of arrows beat upon them, clinking and thudding on the armour. They crouched double behind their shields as they met it. Many fell, but still the slow tide lapped onward. Yelling they surged up to the hedge, and lined it for half a mile, struggling hard to pierce it.

For five minutes the long straining ranks faced each other with fierce stab of spear on one side and heavy beat of axe or mace upon the other. In many parts the hedge was pierced or levelled to the ground, and the French men-at-arms were raging among the archers, hacking and hewing among the lightly armed men. For a moment it seemed as if the battle was on the turn.

But John de Vere, Earl of Oxford, cool, wise, and crafty in war, saw and seized his chance. On the right flank a marshy meadow skirted the river. So soft was it that a heavy-armed man would sink to his knees. At his order a spray of light bowmen was thrown out from the battle-line and forming upon the flank of the French poured their arrows into them. At the same moment Chandos, with Audley, Nigel, Bartholomew Burghersh, the Captal de Buch, and a score of other knights sprang upon their horses, and charging down the narrow lane rode over the French line in front of them. Once through it they spurred to left and right, trampling down the dismounted men-at-arms.

A fearsome sight was Pommers that day, his red eyes rolling, his nostrils gaping, his tawny mane tossing, and his savage teeth gnashing in fury, as he tore and smashed and ground beneath his ramping hoofs all that came before him. Fearsome too was the rider, ice-cool, alert, concentrated of purpose, with heart of fire and muscles of steel. A very angel of battle he seemed as he drove his maddened horse through the thickest of the press ; but, strive as he would, the tall figure of his master upon his coal-black steed was ever half a length before him.

Already the moment of danger was passed. The French line had given back. Those who had pierced the hedge had fallen like brave men amid the ranks of their foemen. The division of Warwick had hurried up from the vineyards to fill the gaps of Salisbury's battle line. Back rolled the shining tide, slowly at first, even as it had advanced, but quicker now as the bolder fell and the weaker shredded out and shuffled with ungainly speed for a place of safety. Again there was a rush from behind the hedge. Again there was a reaping of that strange crop of bearded arrows which grew so thick upon the ground, and again the wounded prisoners were seized and dragged in brutal haste to the rear. Then the line was restored, and the English, weary, panting and shaken, awaited the next attack.

But a great good fortune had come to them—so great that as they looked down the valley they could scarce credit their own senses. Behind the division of the dauphin, which had pressed them so hard, stood a second division hardly less numerous, led by the Duke of Orleans. The fugitives from in front, blood-smeared and be-draggled, blinded with sweat and with fear, rushed amid its ranks in their flight, and in a moment, without a blow being struck, had carried them off in their wild rout. This vast array, so solid and so martial, thawed suddenly away like a snow-wreath in the sun. It was gone, and in its place thousands of shining dots scattered over the whole plain as each man made his own way to the spot where he could find his horse and bear himself from the field. For a moment it seemed that the battle was won, and a thunder-shout of joy pealed up from the English line.

But as the curtain of the duke's division was drawn away it was only to disclose stretching far behind it, and spanning the valley from side to side, the magnificent array of the French king, solid, unshaken, and preparing its ranks for the attack. Its numbers were as great as those of the English army ; it was unscathed by all that was past, and it had a valiant monarch to lead it to the charge. With the slow deliberation of the man who means to do or to die, its leader marshalled its ranks for the supreme effort of the day.

Meanwhile during that brief moment of exultation when the battle appeared to be won, a crowd of hot-headed young knights and squires swarmed and clamoured round the prince, beseeching that he would allow them to ride forth.

" See this insolent fellow who bears three martlets upon a field gules ! " cried Sir Maurice Berkeley. " He stands betwixt the two armies as though he had no dread of us."

" I pray you, sir, that I may ride out to him since he seems ready to attempt some small deed," pleaded Nigel.

" Nay, fair sirs, it is an evil thing that we should break our line, seeing that we still have much to do," said the prince. " See ! he rides away, and so the matter is settled."

" Nay, fair prince," said the young knight who had

spoken first. " My grey horse, Lebryte, could run him down ere he could reach shelter. Never since I left Severn side have I seen steed as fleet as mine. Shall I not show you ? " In an instant he had spurred the charger and was speeding across the plain.

The Frenchman, John de Helennes, a squire of Picardy, had waited with a burning heart, his soul sick at the flight of the division in which he had ridden. In the hope of doing some redeeming exploit, or of meeting his own death, he had loitered between the armies, but no movement had come from the English lines. Now he had turned his horse's head to join the king's array, when the low drumming of hoofs sounded behind him, and he turned to find a horseman hard upon his heels. Each had drawn his sword, and the two armies paused to view the fight. In the first bout Sir Maurice Berkeley's lance was struck from his hand, and as he sprang down to recover it the Frenchman ran him through the thigh, dismounted from his horse, and received his surrender. As the unfortunate Englishman hobbled away at the side of his captor a roar of laughter burst from both armies at the spectacle.

" By my ten finger-bones ! " cried Aylward, chuckling behind the remains of his bush, " he found more on his distaff that time than he knew how to spin. Who was the knight ? '

" By his arms," said old Wat, " he should either be a Berkeley of the West, or a Popham of Kent."

" I call to mind that I shot a match of six ends once with a Kentish woldsman——" began the fat bowyer.

" Nay, nay, stint thy talk, Bartholomew ! " cried old Wat. " Here is poor Ned with his head cloven, and it would be more fitting if you were saying aves for his soul, instead of all this bobance and boasting. How now, Tom of Beverley ? "

" We have suffered sorely in this last bout, Wat. There are forty of our men upon their backs, and the Dean foresters on the right are in worse case still."

" Talking will not mend it, Tom, and if all but one were on their backs he must still hold his ground."

While the archers were chatting, the leaders of the army were in solemn conclave just behind them. Two divisions of the French had been repulsed, and yet there was many an anxious face as the older knights looked across the plain at the unbroken array of the French king moving slowly toward them. The line of the archers was much thinned and shredded. Many knights and squires had been disabled in the long and fierce combat at the hedge. Others, exhausted by want of food, had no strength left and were stretched panting upon the ground. Some were engaged in carrying the wounded to the rear and laying them under the shelter of the trees, while others were replacing their broken swords or lances from the weapons of the slain. The Captal de Buch, brave and experienced as he was, frowned darkly and whispered his misgivings to Chandos.

But the prince's courage flamed the higher as the shadow fell, while his dark eyes gleamed with a soldier's pride as he glanced round him at his weary comrades, and then at the dense masses of the king's battle which now, with a hundred trumpets blaring and a thousand pennons waving, rolled slowly over the plain.

" Come what may, John, this has been a most noble meeting," said he. " They will not be ashamed of us in England. Take heart, my friends, for if we conquer we shall carry the glory ever with us ; but if we be slain then we die most worshipfully and in high honour, as we have ever prayed that we might die, and we leave behind us our brothers and kinsmen who will assuredly avenge us. It is but one more effort and all will be well. Warwick, Oxford, Salisbury, Suffolk, every man to the front ! My banner to the front also ! Your horses, fair sirs ! The archers are spent, and our own good lances must win the field this day. Advance, Walter, and may God and Saint George be with England ! "

Sir Walter Woodland, riding a high black horse, took

station by the prince, with the royal banner resting in a socket by his saddle. From all sides the knights and squires crowded in upon it, until they formed a great squadron containing the survivors of the battalions of Warwick and Salisbury, as well as those of the prince. Four hundred men-at-arms who had been held in reserve were brought up and thickened the array, but even so Chandos's face was grave as he scanned it, and then turned his eyes upon the masses of the Frenchmen.

" I like it not, fair sir. The weight is overgreat," he whispered to the prince.

" How would you order it, John ? Speak what is in your mind."

" We should attempt something upon their flank whilst we hold them in front. How say you, Jean ? "

He turned to the Captal de Buch, whose dark, resolute face reflected the same misgivings.

" Indeed, John, I think as you do," said he. " The French king is a very valiant man, and so are those who are about him, and I know not how we may drive them back unless we can do as you advise. If you will give me only a hundred men I will attempt it."

" Surely the task is mine, fair sir, since the thought has come from me," said Chandos.

" Nay, John, I would keep you at my side. But you speak well, Jean, and you shall do even as you have said. Go, ask the Earl of Oxford for a hundred men-at-arms and as many hobbelers, that you may ride round the mound yonder, and so fall upon them unseen. Let all that are left of the archers gather on each side, shoot away their arrows, and then fight as best they may. Wait till they are past yonder thorn-bush and then, Walter, bear my banner straight against that of the King of France. Fair sirs, may God and the thought of your ladies hold high your hearts ! "

The French monarch, seeing that his footmen had made no impression upon the English, and also that the hedge had been well-nigh levelled to the ground in the course of the combat, so that it no longer presented an obstacle, had ordered his followers to remount their horses, and it was as a solid mass of cavalry that the chivalry of France advanced to their last supreme effort. The king was in the centre of the front line, Geoffrey de Chargny with the golden oriflamme upon his right, and Eustace de Ribeaumont with the royal lilies upon his left. At his elbow was the Duke of Athens, High Constable of France, and round him were the nobles of the court, fiery and furious, yelling their war-cries, as they waved their weapons over their heads. Six thousand gallant men of the bravest race in Europe, men whose very names are like blasts of a battle-trumpet—Beaujeus and Chatillons, Tancarvilles and Ventadours—pressed hard behind the silver lilies.

Slowly they moved at first, walking their horses that they might be the fresher for the shock. Then they broke into a trot which was quickening into a gallop when the remains of the hedge in front of them was beaten in an instant to the ground and the broad line of the steel-clad chivalry of England swept grandly forth to the final shock. With loose rein and busy spur the two lines of horsemen galloped at the top of their speed straight and hard for each other. An instant later they met with a thunder-crash which was heard by the burghers on the wall of Poictiers, seven good miles away.

Under that frightful impact horses fell dead with broken necks, and many a rider, held in his saddle by the high pommel, fractured his thighs with the shock. Here and there a pair met breast to breast, the horses rearing straight upward and falling back upon their masters. But for the most part the line had opened in the gallop, and the cavaliers, flying through the gaps, buried themselves in the enemy's ranks. Then the flanks shredded out, and the thick press in the centre loosened until there was space to swing a sword and to guide a steed. For ten acres there was one wild tumultuous swirl of tossing heads, of gleaming weapons which rose and fell, of upthrown hands, of tossing plumes and of lifted shields, while the din of a thousand war-cries and the clash-clash of metal upon metal rose and swelled like the roar and beat of an ocean surge upon a rock-bound coast. Backward and forward swayed the mighty throng, now down the valley and now up, as each side in turn put forth its strength for a fresh rally. Locked in one long deadly grapple, great England and gallant France with iron hearts and souls of fire strove and strove for mastery.

Sir Walter Woodland, riding hard upon his high black horse, had plunged into the swelter and headed for the blue and silver banner of King John. Close at his heels in a solid wedge rode the prince, Chandos, Nigel, Lord Reginald Cobham, Audley, with his four famous squires, and a score of the flower of the English and Gascon knighthood. Holding together and bearing down opposition by a shower of blows and by the weight of their powerful horses, their progress was still very slow, for ever fresh waves of French cavaliers surged up against them and broke in front only to close in again upon their rear. Sometimes they were swept backwards by the rush, sometimes they gained a few paces, sometimes they could but keep their foothold, and yet from minute to minute that blue and silver flag which waved above the press grew ever a little closer. A dozen furious hard-breathing French knights had broken into their ranks, and clutched at Sir Walter Woodland's banner, but Chandos and Nigel guarded it on one side, Audley with his squires on the other, so that no man laid his hand upon it and lived.

But now there was a distant crash and a roar of " Saint George for Guienne ! " from behind. The Captal de Buch had charged home. " Saint George for England ! " yelled the main attack, and ever the counter-cry came back to them from afar. The ranks opened in front of them. The French were giving way. A small knight with golden scroll-work upon his armour threw himself upon the prince and was struck dead by his mace. It was the Duke of Athens, Constable of France, but none had time to note it, and the fight rolled on over his body. Looser still were the French ranks. Many were turning their horses, for that ominous roar had shaken their resolution. The little English wedge poured onward, the prince, Chandos, Audley, and Nigel ever in the van.

A huge warrior in black, bearing a golden banner, appeared suddenly in a gap of the shredding ranks. He tossed his precious burden to a squire, who bore it away. Like a pack of hounds on the very haunch of a deer the English rushed yelling for the oriflamme. But the black warrior flung himself across their path. " Chargny ! Chargny *à la recousse* ! " he roared with a voice of thunder. Sir Reginald Cobham dropped before his battle-axe, so did the Gascon de Clisson. Nigel was beaten down on to the crupper of his horse by a sweeping blow ; but at the same instant Chandos's quick blade passed through the Frenchman's camail and pierced his throat. So died Geoffrey de Chargny ; but the oriflamme was saved.

Dazed with the shock, Nigel still kept his saddle, and Pommers, his yellow hide mottled with blood, bore him onward with the others. The French horsemen were now in full flight ; but one stern group of knights stood firm, like a rock in a rushing torrent, beating off all, whether friend or foe, who tried to break the ranks. The oriflamme had gone, and so had the blue and silver banner, but here were desperate men ready to fight to the death. In their ranks honour was to be reaped. The prince and his following hurled themselves upon them, while the rest of the English horsemen swept onward to secure the fugitives and to win their ransoms. But the nobler spirits —Audley, Chandos, and the others—would have thought it shame to gain money while there was work to be done or honour to be won. Furious was the wild attack, desperate the prolonged defence. Men fell from their saddles for very exhaustion.

Nigel, still at his place near Chandos's elbow, was hotly attacked by a short broad-shouldered warrior upon a stout white cob, but Pommers reared with pawing forefeet and dashed the smaller horse to the ground. The falling rider clutched Nigel's arm and tore him from the saddle, so that the two rolled upon the grass under the stamping hoofs, the English squire on the top and his shortened sword glimmered before the visor of the gasping, breathless Frenchman.

" *Je me rends ! je me rends !* " he panted.

For a moment a vision of rich ransoms passed through Nigel's brain. That noble palfrey, that gold-flecked armour, meant fortune to the captor. Let others have it ! There was work still to be done. How could he desert the prince and his noble master for the sake of a private gain ? Could he lead a prisoner to the rear when honour beckoned him to the van ? He staggered to his feet, seized Pommers by the mane, and swung himself into the saddle.

An instant later he was by Chandos's side once more and they were bursting together through the last ranks of the gallant group who had fought so bravely to the end. Behind them was one long swath of the dead and the wounded. In front the whole wide plain was covered with the flying French and their pursuers.

The prince reined up his steed and opened his visor, while his followers crowded round him with waving weapons and frenzied shouts of victory.

" What now, John ! " cried the smiling prince, wiping his streaming face with his ungauntleted hand. " How fares it then ? "

" I am little hurt, fair lord, save for a crushed hand and a spear-prick in the shoulder. But you, sir ? I trust you have no scathe ? "

" In truth, John, with you at one elbow and Lord Audley at the other, I know not how I could come to harm. But alas ! I fear that Sir James is sorely stricken."

The gallant Lord Audley had dropped upon the ground and the blood oozed from every crevice of his battered armour. His four brave squires—Dutton of Dutton, Delves of Doddington, Fowlhurst of Crewe, and Hawkstone of Wainhill—wounded and weary themselves, but with no thought save for their master, unlaced his helmet and bathed his pallid blood-stained face.

He looked up at the prince with burning eyes. " I thank you, sir, for deigning to consider so poor a knight as myself," said he, in a feeble voice.

The prince dismounted and bent over him. " I am bound to honour you very much, James," said he, " for by your valour this day you have won glory and renown above us all, and your prowess has proved you to be the bravest knight."

" My lord," murmured the wounded man, " you have a right to say what you please ; but I wish it were as you say."

" James," said the prince, " from this time onward I make you a knight of my own household, and I settle upon you five hundred marks of yearly income from my own estates in England."

" Sir," the knight answered, " God make me worthy of the good fortune you bestow upon me. Your knight I will ever be, and the money I will divide with your leave amongst these four squires who have brought me whatever glory I have won this day." So saying his head fell back, and he lay white and silent upon the grass.

" Bring water ! " said the prince. " Let the royal leech see to him ; for I had rather lose many men than the good Sir James. Ha, Chandos, what have we here ? "

A knight lay across the path with his helmet beaten down upon his shoulders. On his surcoat and shield were the arms of a red griffin.

" It is Robert de Duras, the spy," said Chandos.

" Well for him that he has met his end," said the angry prince. " Put him on his shield, Hubert, and let four archers bear him to the monastery. Lay him at the feet of the cardinal and say that by this sign I greet him. Place my flag on yonder high bush, Walter, and let my tent be raised there, that my friends may know where to seek me."

The flight and pursuit had thundered far away, and

the field was deserted save for the numerous groups of weary horsemen who were making their way back, driving their prisoners before them. The archers were scattered over the whole plain, rifling the saddle-bags and gathering the armour of those who had fallen, or searching for their own scattered arrows.

Suddenly, however, as the prince was turning toward the bush which he had chosen for his headquarters, there broke out from behind him an extraordinary uproar and a group of knights and squires came pouring toward him, all arguing, swearing and abusing each other in French and English at the tops of their voices. In the midst of them limped a stout little man in gold-spangled armour, who appeared to be the object of the contention, for one would drag him one way and one another, as though they would pull him limb from limb.

"Nay, fair sirs, gently, gently, I pray you!" he pleaded. "There is enough for all, and no need to treat me so rudely."

But ever the hubbub broke out again, and swords gleamed as the angry disputants glared furiously at each other. The prince's eyes fell upon the small prisoner, and he staggered back with a gasp of astonishment.

"King John!" he cried.

A shout of joy rose from the warriors around him. "The king of France! The king of France a prisoner!" they cried in an ecstasy.

"Nay, nay, fair sirs, let him not hear that we rejoice! Let no word bring pain to his soul!" Running forward the prince clasped the French king by the two hands.

"Most welcome, sire!" he cried. "Indeed it is good for us that so gallant a knight should stay with us for some short time, since the chance of war has so ordered it. Wine there! Bring wine for the king!"

But John was flushed and angry. His helmet had been roughly torn off, and blood was smeared upon his cheek. His noisy captors stood around him in a circle, eyeing him hungrily like dogs who have been beaten from their quarry. There were Gascons and English, knights, squires, and archers, all pushing and straining.

" I pray you, fair prince, to get rid of these rude fellows," said King John, " for indeed they have plagued me sorely. By Saint Denis ! my arm has been well-nigh pulled from its socket."

" What wish you then ? " asked the prince, turning angrily upon the noisy swarm of his followers.

" We took him, fair lord. He is ours ! " cried a score of voices. They closed in, all yelping together like a pack of wolves. " It was I, fair lord ! "—" Nay, it was I ! "—" You lie, you rascal, it was I ! " Again their fierce eyes glared and their blood-stained hands sought the hilts of their weapons.

" Nay, this must be settled here and now ! " said the prince. " I crave your patience, fair and honoured sir, for a few brief minutes, since indeed much ill-will may spring from this if it be not set at rest. Who is this tall knight who can scarce keep his hands from the king's shoulder ? "

" It is Denis de Morbecque, my lord, a knight of Saint Omer, who is in our service, being an outlaw from France."

" I call him to mind. How, then, Sir Denis ? What say you in this matter ? "

" He gave himself to me, fair lord. He had fallen in the press, and I came upon him and seized him. I told him that I was a knight from Artois, and he gave me his glove. See here, I bear it in my hand."

" It is true, fair lord ! It is true ! " cried a dozen French voices.

" Nay, sir, judge not too soon ! " shouted an English squire, pushing his way to the front. " It was I who had him at my mercy, and he is my prisoner, for he spoke to this man only because he could tell by his tongue that he was his own countryman. I took him, and here are a score to prove it."

" It is true, fair lord ! We saw it, and it was even so ! " cried a chorus of Englishmen.

At all times there are growling and snapping between

the English and their allies of France. The prince saw
how easily this might set a light to such a flame as could
not readily be quenched. It must be stamped out now
ere it had time to mount

" Fair and honoured lord," he said to the king, " again
I pray you for a moment of patience. It is your word
and only yours which can tell us what is just and right.
To whom were you graciously pleased to commit your
royal person ? "

King John looked up from the flagon which had been
brought to him and wiped his lips with the dawnings of a
smile upon his ruddy face.

" It was not this Englishman," he said, and a cheer
burst from the Gascons, " nor was it this bastard Frenchman," he added. " To neither of them did I surrender."

There was a hush of surprise.

" To whom then, sire ? " asked the prince.

The king looked slowly round. " There was a devil of
a yellow horse," said he. " My poor palfrey went over
like a skittle-pin before a ball. Of the rider I know
nothing save that he bore red roses on a silver shield.
Ah ! by Saint Denis, there is the man himself, and there
his thrice-accursed horse ! "

His head swimming, and moving as if in a dream,
Nigel found himself the centre of the circle of armed and
angry men.

The prince laid his hand upon his shoulder. " It is
the little cock of Tilford Bridge," said he. " On my
father's soul, I have ever said that you would win your
way. Did you receive the king's surrender ? "

" Nay, fair lord, I did not receive it."

" Did you hear him give it ? "

" I heard, sir, but I did not know that it was the king.
My master Lord Chandos had gone on, and I followed
after."

" And left him lying. Then the surrender was not
complete, and by the laws of war the ransom goes to
Denis de Morbecque, if his story be true."

" It is true," said the king. " He was the second."

" Then the ransom is yours, Denis. But for my part I swear by my father's soul that I had rather have the honour this squire has gathered than all the richest ransoms of France."

At these words spoken before that circle of noble warriors Nigel's heart gave one great throb, and he dropped upon his knee before the prince.

" Fair lord, how can I thank you ? " he murmured. " These words at least are more than any ransom."

" Rise up ! " said the smiling prince, and he smote with his sword upon his shoulder. " England has lost a brave squire, and has gained a gallant knight. Nay, linger not, I pray ! Rise up, Sir Nigel."

27. *How the Third Messenger came to Cosford*

TWO months have passed, and the long slopes of Hindhead are russet with the faded ferns—the fuzzy brown pelt which wraps the chilling earth. With whoop and scream the wild November wind sweeps over the great rolling downs, tossing the branches of the Cosford beeches, and rattling at the rude latticed windows. The stout old knight of Dupplin, grown even a little stouter, with whiter beard to fringe an ever redder face, sits as of yore at the head of his own board. A well-heaped platter, flanked by a foaming tankard stands before him. At his right sits the Lady Mary, her dark, plain, queenly face marked deep with those years of weary waiting, but bearing the gentle grace and dignity which only sorrow and restraint can give. On his left is Mathew, the old priest. Long ago the golden-haired beauty had passed from Cosford to Fernhurst, where the young and beautiful Lady Edith Brocas is the belle of all Sussex, a sunbeam of smiles and merriment, save perhaps when her thoughts for an instant fly back to that dread night when she was plucked from under the very talons of the foul hawk of Shalford.

The old knight looked up as a fresh gust of wind with a dash of rain beat against the window behind him.

" By Saint Hubert, it is a wild night," said he. " I had hoped to-morrow to have a flight at a heron of the pool or a mallard at the brook. How fares it with little Katherine the peregrine, Mary ? "

" I have joined the wing, father, and I have imped the feathers ; but I fear it will be Christmas ere she can fly again."

" This is a hard saying," said Sir John ; " for indeed I have seen no bolder better bird. Her wing was broken by a heron's beak last Sabbath sennight, holy father, and Mary has the mending of it."

" I trust, my son, that you had heard mass ere you turned to worldly pleasure upon God's holy day," Father Mathew answered.

" Tut, tut ! " said the old knight, laughing. " Shall I make confession at the head of my own table ? I can worship the good God amongst His own works, the woods and the fields, better than in yon pile of stone and wood. But I call to mind a charm for a wounded hawk which was taught me by the fowler of Gaston de Foix. How did it run ? ' The lion of the tribe of Judah, the root of David, has conquered.' Yes, those were the words to be said three times as you walk round the perch where the bird is mewed."

The old priest shook his head. " Nay, these charms are tricks of the devil," said he. " Holy Church lends them no countenance, for they are neither good nor fair. But how is it now with your tapestry, Lady Mary ? When last I was beneath this roof you had half done in five fair colours the story of Theseus and Ariadne."

" It is half done still, holy father."

" How is this, my daughter ? Have you, then, so many calls ? "

" Nay, holy father, her thoughts are otherwhere," Sir

John answered. " She will sit an hour at a time, the needle in her hand and her soul a hundred leagues from Cosford House. Ever since the prince's battle——"

" Good father, I beg you——"

" Nay, Mary, none can hear me, save your own confessor, Father Mathew. Ever since the prince's battle, I say, when we heard that young Nigel had won such honour, she is brain-wode, and sits ever—well, even as you see her now."

An intent look had come into Mary's eyes ; her gaze was fixed upon the dark rain-splashed window. It was a face carved from ivory, white-lipped and rigid, on which the old priest looked.

" What is it, my daughter ? What do you see ? "

" I see nothing, father."

" What is it, then, that disturbs you ? "

" I hear, father."

" What do you hear ? "

" There are horsemen on the road."

The old knight laughed. " So it goes on, father. What day is there that a hundred horsemen do not pass our gate, and yet every clink of hoofs sets her poor heart a-trembling. So strong and steadfast she has ever been, my Mary, and now no sound too slight to shake her to the soul ! Nay, daughter, nay, I pray you ! "

She had half-risen from her chair, her hands clinched and her dark, startled eyes still fixed upon the window.

" I hear them, father ! I hear them amid the wind and the rain ! Yes, yes, they are turning—they have turned ! My God, they are at our very door ! "

" By Saint Hubert, the girl is right ! " cried old Sir John, beating his fist upon the board. " Ho, varlets, out with you to the yard ! Set the mulled wine on the blaze once more ! There are travellers at the gate, and it is no night to keep a dog waiting at our door. Hurry, Hannekin ! Hurry, I say, or I will haste you with my cudgel ! "

Plainly to the ears of all men could be heard the stamping of the horses. Mary had stood up, quivering in every

limb. An eager step at the threshold, the door was flung
wide, and there in the opening stood Nigel, the rain
gleaming upon his smiling face, his cheeks flushed with
the beating of the wind, his blue eyes shining with tenderness and love. Something held her by the throat, the
light of the torches danced up and down ; but her strong
spirit rose at the thought that others should see that inner
holy of holies of her soul. There is a heroism of women
to which no valour of man can attain. Her eyes only
carried him her message as she held out her hand.

"Welcome, Nigel ! " said she.

He stooped and kissed it.

"Saint Catharine has brought me home," said he.

A merry supper it was at Cosford Manor that night,
with Nigel at the head between the jovial old knight and
the Lady Mary, while at the farther end Samkin Aylward
wedged between two servant maids kept his neighbours
in alternate laughter and terror as he told his tales of the
French Wars. Nigel had to turn his doeskin heels and show
his little golden spurs. As he spoke of what was passed
Sir John clapped him on the shoulder, while Mary took his
strong right hand in hers, and the good old priest, smiling,
blessed them both. Nigel had drawn a little golden
ring from his pocket, and it twinkled in the torchlight.

"Did you say that you must go on your way to-morrow, father ? " he asked the priest.

"Indeed, fair son, the matter presses."

"But you may bide the morning ? "

"It will suffice if I start at noon."

"Much may be done in a morning." He looked at
Mary, who blushed and smiled. "By Saint Paul ! I
have waited long enough."

"Good, good ! " chuckled the old knight, with wheezy
laughter. "Even so I wooed your mother, Mary.
Wooers were brisk in the olden time. To-morrow is
Tuesday, and Tuesday is ever a lucky day. Alas ! that
the good Dame Ermyntrude is no longer with us to see
it done ! The old hound must run us down, Nigel, and

I hear its bay upon my own heels ; but my heart will rejoice that before the end I may call you son. Give me your hand, Mary, and yours, Nigel. Now, take an old man's blessing, and may God keep and guard you both, and give you your desert, for I believe on my soul that in all this broad land there dwells no nobler man nor any woman more fitted to be his mate."

There let us leave them, their hearts full of gentle joy, the golden future of hope and promise stretching out before their youthful eyes. Alas for those green spring dreamings ! How often do they fade and wither until they fall and rot, a dreary sight, by the wayside of life ! But here, by God's blessing, it was not so, for they burgeoned and they grew, ever fairer and more noble, until the whole wide world might marvel at the beauty of it.

It has been told elsewhere how as the years passed Nigel's name rose higher in honour ; but still Mary's would keep pace with it, each helping and sustaining the other upon an ever higher path. In many lands did Nigel carve his fame, and ever as he returned spent and weary from his work he drank fresh strength and fire and craving for honour from her who glorified his home. At Twynham Castle they dwelled for many years, beloved and honoured by all. Then in the fullness of time they came back to the Tilford Manor-house and spent their happy, healthy age amid those heather downs where Nigel had passed his first lusty youth, ere ever he turned his face to the wars. Thither also came Aylward when he had left the Pied Merlin where for many a year he sold ale to the men of the forest.

But the years pass ; the old wheel turns and ever the thread runs out. The wise and the good, the noble and the brave, they come from the darkness, and into the darkness they go, whence, whither, and why, who may say ? Here is the slope of Hindhead. The fern still glows russet in November, the heather still burns red in July ; but where now is the Manor of Cosford ? Where is the old house of Tilford ? Where, but for a few scattered grey stones, is the mighty pile of Waverley ? And yet even gnawing Time has not eaten all things away. Walk with me towards Guildford, reader, upon the busy highway. Here, where the high green mound rises before us, mark yonder roofless shrine which still stands foursquare to the winds. It is St. Catharine's, where Nigel and Mary plighted their faith. Below lies the winding river, and over yonder you still see the dark Chantry woods which mount up to the bare summit, on which, roofed and whole, stands that Chapel of the Martyr where the comrades beat off the archers of the crooked Lord of Shalford. Down yonder on the flanks of the long chalk hills one traces the road by which they made their journey to the wars. And now turn hither to the north, down this sunken winding path ! It is all unchanged since Nigel's day. Here is the Church of Compton. Pass under the aged and crumbling arch. Before the steps of that ancient altar, unrecorded and unbrassed, lies the dust of Nigel and of Mary. Near them is that of Maude their daughter, and of Alleyne Edricson, whose spouse she was ; their children and children's children are lying by their side. Here too, near the old yew in the churchyard, is the little mound which marks where Samkin Aylward went back to that good soil from which he sprang.

So lie the dead leaves ; but they and such as they nourish for ever that great old trunk of England, which still sheds forth another crop and another, each as strong and as fair as the last. The body may lie in mouldering chancel, or in crumbling vault, but the rumour of noble lives, the record of valour and truth, can never die, but lives on in the soul of the people. Our own work lies ready to our hands ; and yet our strength may be the greater and our faith the firmer if we spare an hour from present toils to look back upon the women who were gentle and strong, or the men who loved honour more than life on this green stage of England where for a few short years we play our little part.

THE EXPLOITS OF BRIGADIER GERARD

1. *How the Brigadier came to the Castle of Gloom* [1]

YOU do very well, my friends, to treat me with some little reverence, for in honouring me you are honouring both France and yourselves. It is not merely an old, grey-moustached officer whom you see eating his omelette or draining his glass, but it is a fragment of history. In me you see one of the last of those wonderful men, the men who were veterans when they were yet boys, who learned to use a sword earlier than a razor, and who during a hundred battles had never once let the enemy see the colour of their knapsacks. For twenty years we were teaching Europe how to fight, and even when they had learned their lesson it was only the thermometer, and never the bayonet, which could break the Grand Army down. Berlin, Naples, Vienna, Madrid, Lisbon, Moscow—we stabled our horses in them all. Yes, my friends, I say again that you do well to send your children to me with flowers, for these ears have heard the trumpet calls of France, and these eyes have seen her standards in lands where they may never be seen again.

Even now, when I doze in my arm-chair, I can see those great warriors stream before me—the green-jacketed chasseurs, the giant cuirassiers, Poniatowsky's lancers, the white-mantled dragoons, the nodding bear-skins of the horse grenadiers. And then there comes the thick, low rattle of the drums, and through wreaths of dust and smoke I see the line of high bonnets, the row of brown faces, the swing and toss of the long, red plumes

---

[1] The term Brigadier is used throughout in its English and not in its French sense.

amid the sloping lines of steel. And there rides Ney with his red head, and Lefebvre with his bulldog jaw, and Lannes with his Gascon swagger ; and then amidst the gleam of brass and the flaunting feathers I catch a glimpse of *him*, the man with the pale smile, the rounded shoulders, and the far-off eyes. There is an end of my sleep, my friends, for up I spring from my chair, with a cracked voice calling and a silly hand outstretched, so that Madame Titaux has one more laugh at the old fellow who lives among the shadows.

Although I was a full Chief of Brigade when the wars came to an end, and had every hope of soon being made a General of Division, it is still rather to my earlier days that I turn when I wish to talk of the glories and the trials of a soldier's life. For you will understand that when an officer has so many men and horses under him, he has his mind full of recruits and remounts, fodder and farriers, and quarters, so that even when he is not in the face of the enemy, life is a very serious matter for him. But when he is only a lieutenant or a captain, he has nothing heavier than his epaulettes upon his shoulders, so that he can clink his spurs and swing his dolman, drain his glass and kiss his girl, thinking of nothing save of enjoying a gallant life. That is the time when he is likely to have adventures, and it is often to that time that I shall turn in the stories which I may have for you. So it will be to-night when I tell you of my visit to the Castle of Gloom ; of the strange mission of Sub-Lieutenant Duroc, and of the horrible affair of the man who was once known as Jean Carabin, and afterwards as the Baron Straubenthal.

You must know, then, that in the February of 1807, immediately after the taking of Danzig, Major Legendre and I were commissioned to bring four hundred remounts from Prussia into Eastern Poland.

The hard weather, and especially the great battle at Eylau, had killed so many of the horses that there was some danger of our beautiful Tenth of Hussars becoming a battalion of light infantry. We knew, therefore, both the Major and I, that we should be very welcome at the front. We did not advance very rapidly, however, for the snow was deep, the roads detestable, and we had but twenty returning invalids to assist us. Besides, it is impossible, when you have a daily change of forage, and sometimes none at all, to move horses faster than a walk. I am aware that in the story-books the cavalry whirls past at the maddest of gallops ; but for my own part, after twelve campaigns, I should be very satisfied to know that my brigade could always walk upon the march and trot in the presence of the enemy. This I say of the hussars and chasseurs, mark you, so that it is far more the case with cuirassiers or dragoons.

For myself I am fond of horses, and to have four hundred of them, of every age and shade and character, all under my own hands, was a very great pleasure to me. They were from Pomerania for the most part, though some were from Normandy and some from Alsace, and it amused us to notice that they differed in character as much as the people of those provinces. We observed also, what I have often proved since, that the nature of a horse can be told by his colour, from the coquettish light bay, full of fancies and nerves, to the hardy chestnut, and from the docile roan to the pig-headed rusty-black. All this has nothing in the world to do with my story, but how is an officer of cavalry to get on with his tale when he finds four hundred horses waiting for him at the outset ? It is my habit, you see, to talk of that which interests myself and so I hope that I may interest you.

We crossed the Vistula opposite Marienwerder, and had got as far as Riesenberg, when Major Legendre came into my room in the post-house with an open paper in his hand.

" You are to leave me," said he, with despair upon his face.

It was no very great grief to me to do that, for he was,

if I may say so, hardly worthy to have such a subaltern. I saluted, however, in silence.

" It is an order from General Lasalle," he continued ; " you are to proceed to Rossel instantly, and to report yourself at the headquarters of the regiment."

No message could have pleased me better. I was already very well thought of by my superior officers. It was evident to me, therefore, that this sudden order meant that the regiment was about to see service once more, and that Lasalle understood how incomplete my squadron would be without me. It is true that it came at an inconvenient moment, for the keeper of the posthouse had a daughter—one of those ivory-skinned, black-haired Polish girls—with whom I had hoped to have some further talk. Still, it is not for the pawn to argue when the fingers of the player move him from the square ; so down I went, saddled my big black charger, Rataplan, and set off instantly upon my lonely journey.

My word, it was a treat for those poor Poles and Jews, who have so little to brighten their dull lives, to see such a picture as that before their doors ! The frosty morning air made Rataplan's great black limbs and the beautiful curves of his back and sides gleam and shimmer with every gambade. As for me, the rattle of hoofs upon a road, and the jingle of bridle chains which comes with every toss of a saucy head, would even now set my blood dancing through my veins. You may think, then, how I carried myself in my five-and-twentieth year—I, Étienne Gerard, the picked horseman and surest blade in the ten regiments of hussars. Blue was our colour in the Tenth—a sky-blue dolman and pelisse with a scarlet front—and it was said of us in the army that we could set a whole population running, the women towards us, and the men away. There were bright eyes in the Riesenberg windows that morning which seemed to beg me to tarry ; but what can a soldier do, save to kiss his hand and shake his bridle as he rides upon his way ?

HOW HE CAME TO THE CASTLE OF GLOOM

It was a bleak season to ride through the poorest and ugliest country in Europe, but there was a cloudless sky above, and a bright, cold sun, which shimmered on the huge snow-fields. My breath reeked into the frosty air, and Rataplan sent up two feathers of steam from his nostrils, while the icicles drooped from the side-irons of his bit. I let him trot to warm his limbs, while for my own part I had too much to think of to give much heed to the cold. To north and south stretched the great plains, mottled over with dark clumps of fir and lighter patches of larch. A few cottages peeped out here and there, but it was only three months since the Grand Army had passed that way, and you know what that meant to a country. The Poles were our friends, it was true, but out of a hundred thousand men, only the Guard had waggons, and the rest had to live as best they might. It did not surprise me, therefore, to see no signs of cattle and no smoke from the silent houses. A weal had been left across the country where the great host had passed, and it was said that even the rats were starved wherever the Emperor had led his men.

By midday I had got as far as the village of Saalfeldt, but as I was on the direct road for Osterode, where the Emperor was wintering, and also for the main camp of the seven divisions of infantry, the highway was choked with carriages and carts. What with artillery caissons and waggons and couriers, and the ever-thickening stream of recruits and stragglers, it seemed to me that it would be a very long time before I should join my comrades. The plains, however, were five feet deep in snow, so there was nothing for it but to plod upon our way. It was with joy, therefore, that I found a second road which branched away from the other, trending through a fir-wood towards the north. There was a small auberge at the cross-roads, and a patrol of the Third Hussars of Conflans —the very regiment of which I was afterwards colonel— were mounting their horses at the door. On the steps stood their officer, a slight, pale young man, who looked more like a young priest from a seminary than a leader of the devil-may-care rascals before him.

"Good-day, sir," said he, seeing that I pulled up my horse.

"Good-day," I answered. "I am Lieutenant Étienne Gerard, of the Tenth."

I could see by his face that he had heard of me. Everybody had heard of me since my duel with the six fencing masters. My manner, however, served to put him at his ease with me.

"I am Sub-Lieutenant Duroc, of the Third," said he.

"Newly joined?" I asked.

"Last week."

I had thought as much, from his white face and from the way in which he let his men lounge upon their horses. It was not so long, however, since I had learned myself what it was like when a schoolboy has to give orders to veteran troopers. It made me blush, I remember, to shout abrupt commands to men who had seen more battles than I had years, and it would have come more natural for me to say, "With your permission, we shall now wheel into line," or, "If you think it best, we shall trot." I did not think the less of the lad, therefore, when I observed that his men were somewhat out of hand, but I gave them a glance which stiffened them in their saddles.

"May I ask, monsieur, whether you are going by this northern road?" I asked.

"My orders are to patrol it as far as Arensdorf," said he.

"Then I will, with your permission, ride so far with you," said I. "It is very clear that the longer way will be the faster."

So it proved, for this road led away from the army into a country which was given over to Cossacks and marauders, and it was as bare as the other was crowded. Duroc and I rode in front, with our six troopers clattering in the rear. He was a good boy, this Duroc, with his head full of the nonsense that they teach at St. Cyr, knowing more about Alexander and Pompey than how to mix a horse's fodder or care for a horse's feet. Still, he was, as I have said, a good boy, unspoiled as yet by the camp. It pleased me to hear him prattle away about his sister Marie and about his mother in Amiens. Presently we found ourselves at the village of Hayenau. Duroc rode up to the post-house and asked to see the master.

" Can you tell me," said he, " whether the man who calls himself the Baron Straubenthal lives in these parts? "

The postmaster shook his head, and we rode upon our way. I took no notice of this, but when, at the next village, my comrade repeated the same question, with the same result, I could not help asking him who this Baron Straubenthal might be.

" He is a man," said Duroc, with a sudden flush upon his boyish face, " to whom I have a very important message to convey."

Well, this was not satisfactory, but there was something in my companion's manner which told me that any further questioning would be distasteful to him. I said nothing more, therefore, but Duroc would still ask every peasant whom we met whether he could give him any news of the Baron Straubenthal.

For my own part I was endeavouring, as an officer of light cavalry should, to form an idea of the lay of the country, to note the course of the streams, and to mark the places where there should be fords. Every step was taking us farther from the camp round the flanks of which we were travelling. Far to the south a few plumes of grey smoke in the frosty air marked the position of some of our outposts. To the north, however, there was nothing between ourselves and the Russian winter quarters. Twice on the extreme horizon I caught a glimpse of the glitter of steel, and pointed it out to my companion. It was too distant for us to tell whence it came, but we had little doubt that it was from the lance-heads of marauding Cossacks.

The sun was just setting when we rode over a low hill

and saw a small village upon our right, and on our left a high black castle, which jutted out from amongst the pine-woods. A farmer with his cart was approaching us—a matted-haired, downcast fellow, in a sheepskin jacket.

"What village is this?" asked Duroc.

"It is Arensdorf," he answered, in his barbarous German dialect.

"Then here I am to stay the night," said my young companion. Then, turning to the farmer, he asked his eternal question, "Can you tell me where the Baron Straubenthal lives?"

"Why, it is he who owns the Castle of Gloom," said the farmer, pointing to the dark turrets over the distant fir forest.

Duroc gave a shout like the sportsman who sees his game rising in front of him. The lad seemed to have gone off his head—his eyes shining, his face deathly white, and such a grim set about his mouth as made the farmer shrink away from him. I can see him now, leaning forward on his brown horse, with his eager gaze fixed upon the great black tower.

"Why do you call it the Castle of Gloom?" I asked.

"Well, it's the name it bears upon the country-side," said the farmer. "By all accounts there have been some black doings up yonder. It's not for nothing that the wickedest man in Poland has been living there these fourteen years past."

"A Polish nobleman?" I asked.

"Nay, we breed no such men in Poland," he answered.

"A Frenchman, then?" cried Duroc.

"They say that he came from France."

"And with red hair?"

"As red as a fox."

"Yes, yes, it is my man," cried my companion, quivering all over in his excitement. "It is the hand of Providence which has led me here. Who can say that there is not justice in this world? Come, Monsieur

Gerard, for I must see the men safely quartered before I can attend to this private matter."

He spurred on his horse, and ten minutes later we were at the door of the inn of Arensdorf, where his men were to find their quarters for the night.

Well, all this was no affair of mine, and I could not imagine what the meaning of it might be. Rossel was still far off, but I determined to ride on for a few hours and take my chance of some wayside barn in which I could find shelter for Rataplan and myself. I had mounted my horse, therefore, after tossing off a cup of wine, when young Duroc came running out of the door and laid his hand upon my knee.

"Monsieur Gerard," he panted, "I beg of you not to abandon me like this!"

"My good sir," said I, "if you would tell me what is the matter and what you would wish me to do, I should be better able to tell you if I could be of any assistance to you."

"You can be of the very greatest," he cried. "Indeed, from all that I have heard of you, Monsieur Gerard, you are the one man whom I should wish to have by my side to-night."

"You forget that I am riding to join my regiment."

"You cannot, in any case, reach it to-night. To-morrow will bring you to Rossel. By staying with me you will confer the very greatest kindness upon me, and you will aid me in a matter which concerns my own honour and the honour of my family. I am compelled, however, to confess to you that some personal danger may possibly be involved."

It was a crafty thing for him to say. Of course, I sprang from Rataplan's back and ordered the groom to lead him back into the stables.

"Come into the inn," said I, "and let me know exactly what it is that you wish me to do."

He led the way into a sitting-room, and fastened the door lest we should be interrupted. He was a well-grown lad, and as he stood in the glare of the lamp, with the light beating upon his earnest face and upon his uniform of silver grey, which suited him to a marvel, I felt my heart warm towards him. Without going so far as to say that he carried himself as I had done at his age, there was at least similarity enough to make me feel in sympathy with him.

" I can explain it all in a few words," said he. " If I have not already satisfied your very natural curiosity, it is because the subject is so painful a one to me that I can hardly bring myself to allude to it. I cannot, however, ask for your assistance without explaining to you exactly how the matter lies.

" You must know, then, that my father was the well-known banker, Christophe Duroc, who was murdered by the people during the September massacres. As you are aware, the mob took possession of the prisons, chose three so-called judges to pass sentence upon the unhappy aristocrats, and then tore them to pieces when they were passed out into the street. My father had been a bene-factor of the poor all his life. There were many to plead for him. He had the fever, too, and was carried in, half-dead, upon a blanket. Two of the judges were in favour of acquitting him ; the third, a young Jacobin, whose huge body and brutal mind had made him a leader among these wretches, dragged him, with his own hands, from the litter, kicked him again and again with his heavy boots, and hurled him out of the door, where in an instant he was torn limb from limb under circum-stances which are too horrible for me to describe. This, as you perceive, was murder, even under their own unlawful laws, for two of their own judges had pronounced in my father's favour.

" Well, when the days of order came back again, my elder brother began to make inquiries about this man. I was only a child then, but it was a family matter, and it was discussed in my presence. The fellow's name was Carabin. He was one of Sansterre's Guard, and a noted duellist. A foreign lady named the Baroness Straubenthal having been dragged before the Jacobins, he had gained her liberty for her on the promise that she with her money and estates should be his. He had married her, taken her name and title, and escaped out of France at the time of the fall of Robespierre. What had become of him we had no means of learning.

" You will think, doubtless, that it would be easy for us to find him, since we had both his name and his title. You must remember, however, that the Revolution left us without money, and that without money such a search is very difficult. Then came the Empire, and it became more difficult still, for, as you are aware, the Emperor considered that the 18th Brumaire brought all accounts to a settlement, and that on that day a veil had been drawn across the past. None the less, we kept our own family story and our own family plans.

" My brother joined the army, and passed with it through all Southern Europe, asking everywhere for the Baron Straubenthal. Last October he was killed at Jena, with his mission still unfulfilled. Then it became my turn, and I have the good fortune to hear of the very man of whom I am in search at one of the first Polish villages which I have to visit, and within a fortnight of joining my regiment. And then, to make the matter even better, I find myself in the company of one whose name is never mentioned throughout the army save in connection with some daring and generous deed."

This was all very well, and I listened to it with the greatest interest, but I was none the clearer as to what young Duroc wished me to do.

" How can I be of service to you ? " I asked.

" By coming up with me."

" To the Castle ? "

" Precisely."

" When ? "

" At once."

" But what do you intend to do ? "

" I shall know what to do. But I wish you to be with me, all the same."

Well, it was never in my nature to refuse an adventure, and, besides, I had every sympathy with the lad's feelings. It is very well to forgive one's enemies, but one wishes to give them something to forgive also. I held out my hand to him, therefore.

" I must be on my way for Rossel to-morrow morning, but to-night I am yours," said I.

We left our troopers in snug quarters, and, as it was but a mile to the Castle, we did not disturb our horses. To tell the truth, I hate to see a cavalry man walk, and I hold that just as he is the most gallant thing upon earth when he has his saddle-flaps between his knees, so he is the most clumsy when he has to loop up his sabre and his sabre-tasche in one hand and turn in his toes for fear of catching the rowels of his spurs. Still, Duroc and I were of the age when one can carry things off, and I dare swear that no woman at least would have quarrelled with the appearance of the two young hussars, one in blue and one in grey, who set out that night from the Arensdorf post-house. We both carried our swords, and for my own part I slipped a pistol from my holster into the inside of my pelisse, for it seemed to me that there might be some wild work before us.

The track which led to the castle wound through a pitch-black fir-wood, where we could see nothing save the ragged patch of stars above our heads. Presently, however, it opened up, and there was the Castle right in front of us, about as far as a carbine would carry. It was a huge, uncouth place, and bore every mark of being exceedingly old, with turrets at every corner, and a square keep on the side which was nearest to us. In all its great shadow there was no sign of light save from a single window, and no sound came from it. To me there was something awful in its size and its silence, which corresponded so well with its sinister name. My companion

pressed on eagerly, and I followed him along the ill-kept
path which led to the gate.

There was no bell or knocker upon the great iron-
studded door, and it was only by pounding with the hilts
of our sabres that we could attract attention. A thin,
hawk-faced man, with a beard up to his temples, opened it
at last. He carried a lantern in one hand, and in the other
a chain which held an enormous black hound. His
manner at the first moment was threatening, but the sight
of our uniforms and of our faces turned it into one
of sulky reserve.

" The Baron Straubenthal does not receive visitors
at so late an hour," said he, speaking in very excellent
French.

" You can inform Baron Straubenthal that I have come
eight hundred leagues to see him, and that I'll not leave
until I have done so," said my companion. I could not
myself have said it with a better voice and manner.

The fellow took a sidelong look at us, and tugged at his
black beard in his perplexity.

" To tell the truth, gentlemen," said he, " the Baron
has a cup or two of wine in him at this hour, and you would
certainly find him a more entertaining companion if you
were to come again in the morning."

He had opened the door a little wider as he spoke, and
I saw by the light of the lamp in the hall behind him that
three other rough fellows were standing there, one of
whom held another of these monstrous hounds. Duroc
must have seen it also, but it made no difference to his
resolution.

" Enough talk," said he, pushing the man to one side.
" It is with your master that I have to deal."

The fellows in the hall made way for him as he strode
in among them, so great is the power of one man who
knows what he wants over several who are not sure of
themselves. My companion tapped one of them upon
the shoulder with as much assurance as though he owned
him.

" Show me to the Baron," said he.

The man shrugged his shoulders, and answered something in Polish. The fellow with the beard, who had shut and barred the front door, appeared to be the only one among them who could speak French.

" Well, you shall have your way," said he, with a sinister smile. " You shall see the Baron. And perhaps, before you have finished, you will wish that you had taken my advice."

We followed him down the hall, which was stone-flagged and very spacious, with skins scattered upon the floor, and the heads of wild beasts upon the walls. At the father end he threw open a door, and we entered.

It was a small room, scantily furnished, with the same marks of neglect and decay which met us at every turn. The walls were hung with discoloured tapestry, which had come loose at one corner, so as to expose the rough stonework behind. A second door, hung with a curtain, faced us upon the other side. Between lay a square table, strewn with dirty dishes and the sordid remains of a meal. Several bottles were scattered over it. At the head of it, and facing us, there sat a huge man with a lion-like head and a great shock of orange-coloured hair. His beard was of the same glaring hue ; matted and tangled and coarse as a horse's mane. I have seen some strange faces in my time, but never one more brutal than that, with its small, vicious, blue eyes, its white, crumpled cheeks, and the thick, hanging lip which protruded over his monstrous beard. His head swayed about on his shoulders, and he looked at us with the vague, dim gaze of a drunken man. Yet he was not so drunk but that our uniforms carried their message to him.

" Well, my brave boys," he hiccoughed. " What is the latest news from Paris, eh ? You're going to free Poland, I hear, and have meantime all become slaves yourselves—slaves to a little aristocrat with his grey coat and his three-cornered hat. No more citizens either, I am told, and nothing but monsieur and madame. My faith, some more heads will have to roll into the sawdust basket some of these mornings."

Duroc advanced in silence, and stood by the ruffian's side.

" Jean Carabin," said he.

The Baron started, and the film of drunkenness seemed to be clearing from his eyes.

" Jean Carabin," said Duroc, once more.

He sat up and grasped the arms of his chair.

" What do you mean by repeating that name, young man ? " he asked.

" Jean Carabin, you are a man whom I have long wished to meet."

" Supposing that I once had such a name, how can it concern you, since you must have been a child when I bore it ? "

" My name is Duroc."

" Not the son of—— ? "

" The son of the man you murdered.

The Baron tried to laugh, but there was terror in his eyes.

" We must let bygones be bygones, young man," he cried. " It was our life or theirs in those days : the aristocrats or the people. Your father was of the Gironde. He fell. I was of the mountain. Most of my comrades fell. It was all the fortune of war. We must forget all this and learn to know each other better, you and I." He held out a red, twitching hand as he spoke.

" Enough," said young Duroc. " If I were to pass my sabre through you as you sit in that chair, I should do what is just and right. I dishonour my blade by crossing it with yours. And yet you are a Frenchman, and have even held a commission under the same flag as myself. Rise, then, and defend yourself ! "

" Tut, tut ! " cried the Baron. " It is all very well for you young bloods——"

Duroc's patience could stand no more. He swung his open hand into the centre of the great orange beard.

I saw a lip fringed with blood, and two glaring blue eyes above it.

" You shall die for that blow."

" That is better," said Duroc.

" My sabre ! " cried the other. " I will not keep you waiting, I promise you ! " and he hurried from the room.

I have said that there was a second door covered with a curtain. Hardly had the Baron vanished when there ran from behind it a woman, young and beautiful. So swiftly and noiselessly did she move that she was between us in an instant, and it was only the shaking curtains which told us whence she had come.

" I have seen it all," she cried. " Oh, sir, you have carried yourself splendidly." She stooped to my companion's hand, and kissed it again and again ere he could disengage it from her grasp.

" Nay, madame, why should you kiss my hand ? " he cried.

" Because it is the hand which struck him on his vile, lying mouth. Because it may be the hand which will avenge my mother. I am his step-daughter. The woman whose heart he broke was my mother. I loathe him, I fear him. Ah, there is his step ! " In an instant she had vanished as suddenly as she had come. A moment later, the Baron entered with a drawn sword in his hand, and the fellow who had admitted us at his heels.

" This is my secretary," said he. " He will be my friend in this affair. But we shall need more elbow-room than we can find here. Perhaps you will kindly come with me to a more spacious apartment."

It was evidently impossible to fight in a chamber which was blocked by a great table. We followed him out, therefore, into the dimly-lit hall. At the farther end a light was shining through an open door.

" We shall find what we want in here," said the man with the dark beard. It was a large, empty room, with rows of barrels and cases round the walls. A strong lamp stood upon a shelf in the corner. The floor was level and true, so that no swordsman could ask for more. Duroc drew his sabre and sprang into it. The Baron stood back with a bow and motioned me to follow my companion. Hardly were my heels over the threshold when the heavy door crashed behind us and the key screamed in the lock. We were taken in a trap.

For a moment we could not realise it. Such incredible baseness was outside all our experiences. Then, as we understood how foolish we had been to trust for an instant a man with such a history, a flush of rage came over us, rage against his villainy and against our own stupidity. We rushed at the door together, beating it with our fists and kicking with our heavy boots. The sound of our blows and of our execrations must have resounded through the Castle. We called to this villain, hurling at him every name which might pierce even into his hardened soul. But the door was enormous—such a door as one finds in mediæval castles—made of huge beams clamped together with iron. It was as easy to break as a square of the Old Guard. And our cries appeared to be of as little avail as our blows, for they only brought for answer the clattering echoes from the high roof above is. When you have done some soldiering, you soon learn to put up with what cannot be altered. It was I, then, who first recovered my calmness, and prevailed upon Duroc to join with me in examining the apartment which had become our dungeon.

There was only one window, which had no glass in it, and was so narrow that one could not so much as get one's head through. It was high up, and Duroc had to stand upon a barrel in order to see from it.

" What can you see ? " I asked.

" Fir-woods and an avenue of snow between them," said he. " Ah ! " he gave a cry of surprise.

I sprang upon the barrel beside him. There was, as he said, a long, clear strip of snow in front. A man was riding down it, flogging his horse and galloping like a madman. As we watched, he grew smaller and smaller, until he was swallowed up by the black shadows of the forest.

" What does that mean ? " asked Duroc.

" No good for us," said I. " He may have gone for some brigands to cut our throats. Let us see if we cannot find a way out of this mouse-trap before the cat can arrive."

The one piece of good fortune in our favour was that beautiful lamp. It was nearly full of oil, and would last us until morning. In the dark our situation would have been far more difficult. By its light we proceeded to examine the packages and cases which lined the walls. In some places there was only a single line of them, while in one corner they were piled nearly to the ceiling. It seemed that we were in the storehouse of the Castle, for there were a great number of cheeses, vegetables of various kinds, bins full of dried fruits, and a line of wine barrels. One of these had a spigot in it, and as I had eaten little during the day, I was glad of a cup of claret, and some food. As to Duroc, he would take nothing, but paced up and down the room in a fever of anger and impatience. " I'll have him yet ! " he cried, every now and then. " The rascal shall not escape me ! "

This was all very well, but it seemed to me, as I sat on a great round cheese eating my supper, that this youngster was thinking rather too much of his own family affairs and too little of the fine scrape into which he had got me. After all, his father had been dead fourteen years, and nothing could set that right ; but here was Étienne Gerard, the most dashing lieutenant in the whole Grand Army, in imminent danger of being cut off at the very outset of his brilliant career. Who was ever to know the heights to which I might have risen if I were knocked on the head in this hole-and-corner business, which had nothing whatever to do with France or the Emperor ? I could not help thinking what a fool I had been, when I had a fine war before me and everything which a man could desire, to go off on a hare-brained expedition of this sort, as if it were not enough to have a quarter of a million Russians to fight against, without plunging into all sorts of private quarrels as well.

" That is all very well," I said at last, as I heard Duroc muttering his threats. " You may do what you like to him when you get the upper hand. At present the question rather is, what is *he* going to do to us ? "

" Let him do his worst ! " cried the boy. " I owe a duty to my father."

" That is mere foolishness," said I. " If you owe a duty to your father, I owe one to my mother, which is to get out of this business safe and sound."

My remark brought him to his senses.

" I have thought too much of myself ! " he cried. " Forgive me, Monsieur Gerard. Give me your advice as to what I should do."

" Well," said I, " it is not for our health that they have shut us up here among the cheeses. They mean to make an end of us if they can. That is certain. They hope that no one knows that we have come here, and that none will trace us if we remain. Do your hussars know where you have gone to ? "

" I said nothing."

" Hum ! It is clear that we cannot be starved here. They must come to us if they are to kill us. Behind a barricade of barrels we could hold our own against the five rascals whom we have seen. That is, probably, why they have sent that messenger for assistance."

" We must get out before he returns."

" Precisely, if we are to get out at all."

" Could we not burn down this door ? " he cried.

" Nothing could be easier," said I. " There are several casks of oil in the corner. My only objection is that we should ourselves be nicely toasted, like two little oyster pâtés."

" Can you not suggest something ? " he cried, in despair. " Ah, what is that ? "

There had been a low sound at our little window, and

a shadow came between the stars and ourselves. A small, white hand was stretched into the lamplight. Something glittered between the fingers.

" Quick ! quick ! " cried a woman's voice.

We were on the barrel in an instant.

" They have sent for the Cossacks. Your lives are at stake. Ah, I am lost ! I am lost ! "

There was the sound of rushing steps, a hoarse oath, a blow, and the stars were once more twinkling through the window. We stood helpless upon the barrel with our blood cold with horror. Half a minute afterwards we heard a smothered scream, ending in a choke. A great door slammed somewhere in the silent night.

" Those ruffians have seized her. They will kill her," I cried.

Duroc sprang down with the inarticulate shouts of one whose reason has left him. He struck the door so frantically with his naked hands that he left a blotch of blood with every blow.

" Here is the key ! " I shouted, picking one from the floor. " She must have thrown it in at the instant that she was torn away."

My companion snatched it from me with a shriek of joy. A moment later he dashed it down upon the boards. It was so small that it was lost in the enormous lock. Duroc sank upon one of the boxes with his head between his hands. He sobbed in his despair. I could have sobbed, too, when I thought of the woman and how helpless we were to save her.

But I am not easily baffled. After all, this key must have been sent to us for a purpose. The lady could not bring us that of the door, because this murderous step-father of hers would most certainly have it in his pocket. Yet this other must have a meaning, or why should she risk her life to place it in our hands ? It would say little for our wits if we could not find out what that meaning might be.

I set to work moving all the cases out from the wall,

and Duroc, gaining new hope from my courage, helped me with all his strength. It was no light task, for many of them were large and heavy. On we went, working like maniacs, slinging barrels, cheeses and boxes pell-mell into the middle of the room. At last there only remained one huge barrel of vodki, which stood in the corner. With our united strength we rolled it out, and there was a little low wooden door in the wainscot behind it. The key fitted, and with a cry of delight we saw it swing open before us. With the lamp in my hand, I squeezed my way in, followed by my companion.

We were in the powder-magazine of the Castle—a rough, walled cellar, with barrels all round it, and one with the top staved in in the centre. The powder from it lay in a black heap upon the floor. Beyond there was another door, but it was locked.

" We are no better off than before," cried Duroc. " We have no key."

" We have a dozen ! " I cried.

" Where ? "

I pointed to the line of powder barrels.

" You would blow this door open ? "

" Precisely."

" But you would explode the magazine."

It was true, but I was not at the end of my resources.

" We will blow open the store-room door," I cried.

I ran back and seized a tin box which had been filled with candles. It was about the size of my busby—large enough to hold several pounds of powder. Duroc filled it while I cut off the end of a candle. When we had finished, it would have puzzled a colonel of engineers to make a better petard. I put three cheeses on the top of each other and placed it above them, so as to lean against the lock. Then we lit our candle-end and ran for shelter, shutting the door of the magazine behind us.

It is no joke, my friends, to be among all those tons of powder, with the knowledge that if the flame of the explosion should penetrate through one thin door our blackened limbs would be shot higher than the Castle keep. Who could have believed that a half-inch of candle could take so long to burn ? My ears were straining all the time for the thudding of the hoofs of the Cossacks who were coming to destroy us. I had almost made up my mind that the candle must have gone when there was a smack like a bursting bomb, our door flew to bits, and pieces of cheese, with a shower of turnips, apples, and splinters of cases, were shot in among us. As we rushed out we had to stagger through an impenetrable smoke, with all sorts of débris beneath our feet, but there was a glimmering square where the dark door had been. The petard had done its work.

In fact, it had done more for us than we had even ventured to hope. It had shattered gaolers as well as gaol. The first thing that I saw as I came out into the hall was a man with a butcher's axe in his hand, lying flat upon his back, with a gaping wound across his forehead. The second was a huge dog, with two of its legs broken, twisting in agony upon the floor. As it raised itself up I saw the two broken ends flapping like flails. At the same instant I heard a cry, and there was Duroc, thrown against the wall, with the other hound's teeth in his throat. He pushed it off with his left hand, while again and again he passed his sabre through its body, but it was not until I blew out its brains with my pistol that the iron jaws relaxed, and the fierce, bloodshot eyes were glazed in death.

There was no time for us to pause. A woman's scream from in front—a scream of mortal terror—told us that even now we might be too late. There were two other men in the hall, but they cowered away from our drawn swords and furious faces. The blood was streaming from Duroc's neck and dyeing the grey fur of his pelisse. Such was the lad's fire, however, that he shot in front of me, and it was only over his shoulder that I caught a glimpse of the scene as we rushed into the chamber in which we had first seen the master of the Castle of Gloom.

The Baron was standing in the middle of the room, with his tangled mane bristling like an angry lion. He was, as I have said, a huge man with enormous shoulders ; and as he stood there, with his face flushed with rage and his sword advanced, I could not but think that, in spite of all his villainies, he had a proper figure for a grenadier. The lady lay cowering in a chair behind him. A weal across one of her white arms and a dog-whip upon the floor were enough to show that our escape had hardly been in time to save her from his brutality. He gave a howl like a wolf as we broke in, and was upon us in an instant, hacking and driving, with a curse at every blow.

I have already said that the room gave no space for swordsmanship. My young companion was in front of me in the narrow passage between the table and the wall, so that I could only look on without being able to aid him. The lad knew something of his weapon, and was as fierce and active as a wild cat, but in so narrow a space the weight and strength of the giant gave him the advantage. Besides, he was an admirable swordsman. His parade and riposte were as quick as lightning. Twice he touched Duroc upon the shoulder, and then, as the lad slipped on a lunge, he whirled up his sword to finish him before he could recover his feet. I was quicker than he, however, and took the cut upon the pommel of my sabre.

" Excuse me," said I, " but you have still to deal with Étienne Gerard."

He drew back and leaned against the tapestry-covered wall, breathing in little, hoarse gasps, for his foul living was against him.

" Take your breath," said I. " I will await your convenience."

" You have no cause of quarrel against me," he panted.

" I owe you some little attention," said I, " for having shut me up in your store-room. Besides, if all other were wanting, I see cause enough upon that lady's arm."

"Have your way, then!" he snarled, and leaped at me like a madman. For a minute I saw only the blazing blue eyes, and the red glazed point which stabbed and stabbed, rasping off to right or to left, and yet ever back at my throat and my breast. I had never thought that such good sword-play was to be found at Paris in the days of the Revolution. I do not suppose that in all my little affairs I have met six men who had a better know-ledge of their weapon. But he knew that I was his master. He read death in my eyes, and I could see that he read it. The flush died from his face. His breath came in shorter and in thicker gasps. Yet he fought on, even after the final thrust had come, and died still hacking and cursing, with foul cries upon his lips, and his blood clotting upon his orange beard. I who speak to you have seen so many battles, that my old memory can scarce contain their names, and yet of all the terrible sights which these eyes have rested upon, there is none which I care to think of less than of that orange beard with the crimson stain in the centre, from which I had drawn my sword-point.

It was only afterwards that I had time to think of all this. His monstrous body had hardly crashed down upon the floor, before the woman in the corner sprang to her feet, clapping her hands together and screaming out in her delight. For my part I was disgusted to see a woman take such delight in a deed of blood, and I gave no thought as to the terrible wrongs which must have befallen her before she could so far forget the gentleness of her sex. It was on my tongue to tell her sharply to be silent, when a strange, choking smell took the breath from my nostrils, and a sudden, yellow glare brought out the figures upon the faded hangings.

"Duroc, Duroc!" I shouted, tugging at his shoulder. "The Castle is on fire!"

The boy lay senseless upon the ground exhausted by his wounds. I rushed out into the hall to see whence the danger came. It was our explosion which had set alight to the dry framework of the door. Inside the store-room some of the boxes were already blazing. I glanced in, and as I did so my blood was turned to water by the sight of the powder barrels beyond, and of the loose heap upon the floor. It might be seconds, it could not be more than minutes, before the flames would be at the edge of it. These eyes will be closed in death, my friends, before they cease to see those crawling lines of fire and the black heap beyond.

How little I can remember what followed. Vaguely I can recall how I rushed into the chamber of death, how I seized Duroc by one limp hand and dragged him down the hall, the woman keeping pace with me and pulling at the other arm. Out of the gateway we rushed, and on down the snow-covered path until we were on the fringe of the fir forest. It was at that moment that I heard a crash behind me, and, glancing round, saw a great spout of fire shoot up into the wintry sky. An instant later there seemed to come a second crash, far louder than the first. I saw the fir trees and the stars whirling round me and I fell unconscious across the body of my comrade.

It was some weeks before I came to myself in the post-house of Arensdorf, and longer still before I could be told all that had befallen me. It was Duroc, already able to go soldiering, who came to my bedside and gave me an account of it. He it was who told me how a piece of timber had struck me on the head and laid me almost dead upon the ground. From him, too, I learned how the Polish girl had run to Arensdorf, how she had roused our hussars, and how she had only just brought them back in time to save us from the spears of the Cossacks who had been summoned from their bivouac by that same black-bearded secretary whom we had seen galloping so swiftly over the snow. As to the brave lady who had twice saved our lives, I could not learn very much about her at that moment from Duroc, but when I chanced to meet him in Paris two years later, after the campaign of Wagram, I was not very much surprised to find that I needed no introduction to his bride, and that by the queer turns of fortune he had himself, had he chosen to use it, that very name and title of the Baron Straubenthal, which showed him to be the owner of the blackened ruins of the Castle of Gloom.

2. *How the Brigadier slew the Brothers of Ajaccio*

WHEN the Emperor needed an agent he was always very ready to do me the honour of recalling the name of Étienne Gerard, though it occasionally escaped him when rewards were to be distributed. Still, I was a colonel at twenty-eight, and the chief of a brigade at thirty-one, so that I have no reason to be dissatisfied with my career. Had the wars lasted another two or three years I might have grasped my bâton, and the man who had his hand upon that was only one stride from a throne. Murat had changed his hussar's cap for a crown, and another light cavalry man might have done as much. However, all those dreams were driven away by Waterloo, and, although I was not able to write my name upon history, it is sufficiently well known by all who served with me in the great wars of the Empire.

What I want to tell you to-night is about the very singular affair which first started me upon my rapid upward course, and which had the effect of establishing a secret bond between the Emperor and myself.

There is just one little word of warning which I must give you before I begin. When you hear me speak, you must always bear in mind that you are listening to one who has seen history from the inside. I am talking about what my ears have heard and my eyes have seen, so you must not try to confute me by quoting the opinions of some student or man of the pen, who has written a book of history or memoirs. There is much which is unknown by such people, and much which never will be known by the world. For my own part, I could tell you some very surprising things were it discreet to do so. The facts which I am about to relate to you to-night were kept secret by me during the Emperor's life-time, because I gave him my promise that it should be so, but I do not think that there can be any harm now in my telling the remarkable part which I played.

You must know, then, that at the time of the Treaty of Tilsit I was a simple lieutenant in the 10th Hussars, without money or interest. It is true that my appearance and my gallantry were in my favour, and that I had already won a reputation as being one of the best swordsmen in the army ; but among the host of brave men who surrounded the Emperor it needed more than this to ensure a rapid career. I was confident, however, that my chance would come, though I never dreamed that it would take so remarkable a form.

When the Emperor returned to Paris, after the declaration of peace in the year 1807, he spent much of his time with the Empress and the Court at Fontainebleau. It was the time when he was at the pinnacle of his career. He had in three successive campaigns humbled Austria, crushed Prussia, and made the Russians very glad to get upon the right side of the Niemen. The old Bulldog over the Channel was still growling, but he could not get very far from his kennel. If we could have made a perpetual peace at that moment, France would have taken a higher place than any nation since the days of the Romans. So I have heard the wise folk say, though for my part I had other things to think of. All the girls were glad to see the army back after its long absence, and you may be sure that I had my share of any favours that were going. You may judge how far I was a favourite in those days when I say that even now, in my sixtieth year——

But why should I dwell upon that which is already sufficiently well known ?

Our regiment of hussars was quartered with the horse
chasseurs of the guard at Fontainebleau. It is, as you
know, but a little place, buried in the heart of the forest,
and it was wonderful at this time to see it crowded with
Grand Dukes and Electors and Princes, who thronged
round Napoleon like puppies round their master, each
hoping that some bone might be thrown to him. There
was more German than French to be heard in the street,
for those who had helped us in the late war had come to
beg for a reward, and those who had opposed us had come
to try and escape their punishment.

And all the time our little man, with his pale face and
his cold, grey eyes, was riding to the hunt every morning,
silent and brooding, all of them following in his train, in
the hope that some word would escape him. And then,
when the humour seized him, he would throw a hundred
square miles to that man, or tear as much off the other,
round off one kingdom by a river, or cut off another by
a chain of mountains. That was how he used to do
business, this little artilleryman, whom we had raised so
high with our sabres and our bayonets. He was very
civil to us always, for he knew where his power came from.
We knew also, and showed it by the way in which we
carried ourselves. We were agreed, you understand,
that he was the finest leader in the world, but we did not
forget that he had the finest men to lead.

Well, one day I was seated in my quarters playing cards
with young Morat, of the horse chasseurs, when the door
opened and in walked Lasalle, who was our Colonel.
You know what a fine, swaggering fellow he was, and
the sky-blue uniform of the Tenth suited him to a marvel.
My faith, we youngsters were so taken by him that we all
swore and diced and drank and played the deuce whether
we liked it or no, just that we might resemble our Colonel !
We forgot that it was not because he drank or gambled
that the Emperor was going to make him the head of the

light cavalry, but because he had the surest eye for the nature of a position or for the strength of a column, and the best judgment as to when infantry could be broken, or whether guns were exposed, of any man in the army. We were too young to understand all that, however, so we waxed our moustaches and clinked our spurs and let the ferrules of our scabbards wear out by trailing them along the pavement in the hope that we should all become Lasalles. When he came clanking into my quarters, both Morat and I sprang to our feet.

" My boy," said he, clapping me on the shoulder, " the Emperor wants to see you at four o'clock."

The room whirled round me at the words, and I had to lean my hands upon the edge of the card-table.

" What ? " I cried. " The Emperor ! "

" Precisely," said he, smiling at my astonishment.

" But the Emperor does not know of my existence, Colonel," I protested. " Why should he send for me ? "

" Well, that's just what puzzles me," cried Lasalle, twirling his moustache. " If he wanted the help of a good sabre, why should he descend to one of my lieu-tenants when he might have found all that he needed at the head of the regiment ? However," he added, clapping me on the shoulder again in his hearty fashion, " every man has his chance. I have had mine, otherwise I should not be Colonel of the Tenth. I must not grudge you yours. Forwards, my boy, and may it be the first step towards changing your busby for a cocked hat."

It was but two o'clock, so he left me, promising to come back and to accompany me to the palace. My faith, what a time I passed, and how many conjectures did I make as to what it was that the Emperor could want of me ! I paced up and down my little room in a fever of anticipation. Sometimes I thought that perhaps he had heard of the guns which we had taken at Austerlitz ; but then, there were so many who had taken guns at Auster-litz, and two years had passed since the battle. Or it might be that he wished to reward me for my affair with the aide-de-camp of the Russian Emperor. But then again a cold fit would seize me, and I would fancy that he had sent for me to reprimand me. There were a few duels which he might have taken in ill part, and there were one or two little jokes in Paris since the peace.

But, no! I considered the words of Lasalle. "If he had need of a brave man," said Lasalle.

It was obvious that my Colonel had some idea of what was in the wind. If he had not known that it was to my advantage, he would not have been so cruel as to con-gratulate me. My heart glowed with joy as this convic-tion grew upon me, and I sat down to write to my mother and to tell her that the Emperor was waiting, at that very moment, to have my opinion upon a matter of importance. It made me smile as I wrote it to think that, wonderful as it appeared to me, it would probably only confirm my mother in her opinion of the Emperor's good sense.

At half-past three I heard a sabre come clanking against every step of my wooden stair. It was Lasalle, and with him was a lame gentleman, very neatly dressed in black with dapper ruffles and cuffs. We did not know many civilians, we of the army, but, my word, this was one whom we could not afford to ignore! I had only to glance at those twinkling eyes, the comical, upturned nose, and the straight, precise mouth, to know that I was in the presence of the one man in France whom even the Emperor had to consider.

"This is Monsieur Étienne Gerard, Monsieur de Talleyrand," said Lasalle.

I saluted, and the statesman took me in from the top of my panache to the rowel of my spur, with a glance that played over me like a rapier point.

"Have you explained to the lieutenant the circum-stances under which he is summoned to the Emperor's presence?" he asked, in his dry, creaking voice.

They were such a contrast, these two men, that I could not help glancing from one to the other of them : the black, sly politician, and the big, sky-blue hussar with one fist on his hip and the other on the hilt of his sabre. They both took their seats as I looked, Talleyrand without a sound, and Lasalle with a clash and a jingle like a prancing charger.

" It's this way, youngster," said he, in his brusque fashion ; " I was with the Emperor in his private cabinet this morning when a note was brought in to him. He opened it, and as he did so he gave such a start that it fluttered down on to the floor. I handed it up to him again, but he was staring at the wall in front of him as if he had seen a ghost. ' Fratelli dell' Ajaccio,' he muttered ; and then again, ' Fratelli dell' Ajaccio.' I don't pretend to know more Italian than a man can pick up in two campaigns, and I could make nothing of this. It seemed to me that he had gone out of his mind ; and you would have said so also, Monsieur de Talleyrand, if you had seen the look in his eyes. He read the note, and then he sat for half an hour or more without moving."

" And you ? " asked Talleyrand.

" Why, I stood there not knowing what I ought to do. Presently he seemed to come back to his senses.

" ' I suppose, Lasalle,' said he, ' that you have some gallant young officers in the Tenth ? '

" ' They are all that, sire,' I answered.

" ' If you had to pick one who was to be depended upon for action, but who would not think too much— you understand me, Lasalle—which would you select ? ' he asked.

" I saw that he needed an agent who would not penetrate too deeply into his plans.

" ' I have one,' said I, ' who is all spurs and moustaches, with never a thought beyond women and horses.'

" ' That is the man I want,' said Napoleon. ' Bring him to my private cabinet at four o'clock.'

" So, youngster, I came straight away to you at once, and mind that you do credit to the 10th Hussars."

I was by no means flattered by the reasons which had led to my Colonel's choice, and I must have shown as

much in my face, for he roared with laughter and Talleyrand gave a dry chuckle also.

" Just one word of advice before you go, Monsieur
Gerard," said he : " you are now coming into troubled
waters, and you might find a worse pilot than myself.
We have none of us any idea as to what this little affair
means, and, between ourselves, it is very important for
us, who have the destinies of France upon our shoulders,
to keep ourselves in touch with all that goes on. You
understand me, Monsieur Gerard ? "

I had not the least idea what he was driving at, but I
bowed and tried to look as if it was clear to me.

" Act very guardedly, then, and say nothing to any-
body," said Talleyrand. " Colonel de Lasalle and I will
not show ourselves in public with you, but we will await
you here, and we will give you our advice when you have
told us what has passed between the Emperor and yourself. It is time that you started now, for the Emperor
never forgives unpunctuality."

Off I went on foot to the palace, which was only a
hundred paces off. I made my way to the ante-chamber,
where Duroc, with his grand new scarlet and gold coat,
was fussing about among the crowd of people who were
waiting. I heard him whisper to Monsieur de Caulain-
court that half of them were German Dukes who
expected to be made Kings, and the other half German
Dukes who expected to be made paupers. Duroc, when
he heard my name, showed me straight in, and I found
myself in the Emperor's presence.

I had, of course, seen him in camp a hundred times,
but I had never been face to face with him before. I
have no doubt that if you had met him without knowing
in the least who he was, you would simply have said that
he was a sallow little fellow with a good forehead and
fairly well-turned calves. His tight white cashmere
breeches and white stockings showed off his legs to
advantage. But even a stranger must have been struck
by the singular look of his eyes, which could harden into

an expression which would frighten a grenadier. It is said that even Auguereau, who was a man who had never known what fear was, quailed before Napoleon's gaze, at a time, too, when the Emperor was but an unknown soldier. He looked mildly enough at me, however, and motioned me to remain by the door. De Meneval was writing to his dictation, looking up at him between each sentence with his spaniel eyes.

"That will do. You can go," said the Emperor, abruptly. Then, when the secretary had left the room, he strode across with his hands behind his back, and he looked me up and down without a word. Though he was a small man himself, he was very fond of having fine-looking fellows about him, and so I think that my appearance gave him pleasure. For my own part, I raised one hand to the salute and held the other upon the hilt of my sabre, looking straight ahead of me, as a soldier should.

"Well, Monsieur Gerard," said he, at last, tapping his forefinger upon one of the brandebourgs of gold braid upon the front of my pelisse, " I am informed that you are a very deserving young officer. Your Colonel gives me an excellent account of you."

I wished to make a brilliant reply, but I could think of nothing save Lasalle's phrase that I was all spurs and moustaches, so it ended in my saying nothing at all. The Emperor watched the struggle which must have shown itself upon my features, and when, finally, no answer came he did not appear to be displeased.

" I believe that you are the very man that I want," said he. "Brave and clever men surround me upon every side. But a brave man who——" He did not finish his sentence, and for my own part I could not understand what he was driving at. I contented myself with assuring him that he could count upon me to the death.

" You are, as I understand, a good swordsman?" said he.

" Tolerable, sire," I answered.

"You were chosen by your regiment to fight the champion of the Hussars of Chambarant?" said he.

I was not sorry to find that he knew so much of my exploits.

"My comrades, sire, did me that honour," said I.

"And for the sake of practice you insulted six fencing masters in the week before your duel?"

"I had the privilege of being out seven times in as many days, sire," said I.

"And escaped without a scratch?"

"The fencing master of the 23rd Light Infantry touched me on the left elbow, sire."

"Let us have no more child's play of the sort, monsieur," he cried, turning suddenly to that cold rage of his which was so appalling. "Do you imagine that I place veteran soldiers in these positions that you may practise quarte and tierce upon them? How am I to face Europe if my soldiers turn their points upon each other? Another word of your duelling, and I break you between these fingers."

I saw his plump white hands flash before my eyes as he spoke, and his voice had turned to the most discordant hissing and growling. My word, my skin pringled all over as I listened to him, and I would gladly have changed my position for that of the first man in the steepest and narrowest breach that ever swallowed up a storming party. He turned to the table, drank off a cup of coffee, and then when he faced me again every trace of this storm had vanished, and he wore that singular smile which came from his lips but never from his eyes.

"I have need of your services, Monsieur Gerard," said he. "I may be safer with a good sword at my side, and there are reasons why yours should be the one which I select. But first of all I must bind you to secrecy. Whilst I live what passes between us to-day must be known to none but ourselves."

I thought of Talleyrand and of Lasalle, but I promised.

"In the next place, I do not want your opinions or

conjectures, and I wish you to do exactly what you are told."

I bowed.

"It is your sword that I need, and not your brains. I will do the thinking. Is that clear to you?"

"Yes, sire."

"You know the Chancellor's Grove, in the forest?"

I bowed.

"You know also the large double fir-tree where the hounds assembled on Tuesday?"

Had he known that I met a girl under it three times a week, he would not have asked me. I bowed once more without remark.

"Very good. You will meet me there at ten o'clock to-night."

I had got past being surprised at anything which might happen. If he had asked me to take his place upon the Imperial throne I could only have nodded my busby.

"We shall then proceed into the wood together," said the Emperor. "You will be armed with a sword, but not with pistols. You must address no remark to me, and I shall say nothing to you. We will advance in silence. You understand?"

"I understand, sire."

"After a time we shall see a man, or more probably two men, under a certain tree. We shall approach them together. If I signal to you to defend me, you will have your sword ready. If, on the other hand, I speak to these men, you will wait and see what happens. If you are called upon to draw, you must see that neither of them, in the event of there being two, escapes from us. I shall myself assist you."

"Sire," I cried, "I have no doubt that two would not be too many for my sword; but would it not be better that I should bring a comrade than that you should be forced to join in such a struggle?"

"Ta, ta, ta," said he. "I was a soldier before I

was an Emperor. Do you think, then, that artillerymen have not swords as well as the hussars ? But I ordered you not to argue with me. You will do exactly what I tell you. If swords are once out, neither of these men is to get away alive."

" They shall not, sire," said I.

" Very good. I have no more instructions for you. You can go."

I turned to the door, and then an idea occurring to me I turned.

" I have been thinking, sire——" said I.

He sprang at me with the ferocity of a wild beast. I really thought he would have struck me.

" Thinking ! " he cried. " You, *you !* Do you imagine I chose you out because you could think ? Let me hear of your doing such a thing again ! You, the one man—but, there ! You meet me at the fir-tree at ten o'clock."

My faith, I was right glad to get out of the room. If I have a good horse under me, and a sword clanking against my stirrup-iron, I know where I am. And in all that relates to green fodder or dry, barley and oats and rye, and the handling of squadrons upon the march, there is no one who can teach me very much. But when I meet a Chamberlain and a Marshal of the Palace, and have to pick my words with an Emperor, and find that every-body hints instead of talking straight out, I feel like a troop-horse who has been put in a lady's calèche. It is not my trade, all this mincing and pretending. I have learned the manners of a gentleman, but never those of a courtier. I was right glad then to get into the fresh air again, and I ran away up to my quarters like a school-boy who has just escaped from the seminary master.

But as I opened the door, the very first thing that my eye rested upon was a long pair of sky-blue legs with hussar boots, and a short pair of black ones with knee-breeches and buckles. They both sprang up together to greet me.

"Well, what news?" they cried, the two of them.

"None," I answered.

"The Emperor refused to see you?"

"No, I have seen him."

"And what did he say?"

"Monsieur de Talleyrand," I answered, "I regret to say that it is quite impossible for me to tell you anything about it. I have promised the Emperor."

"Pooh, pooh, my dear young man," said he, sidling up to me, as a cat does when it is about to rub itself against you. "This is all among friends, you understand, and goes no farther than these four walls. Besides, the Emperor never meant to include me in this promise."

"It is but a minute's walk to the palace, Monsieur de Talleyrand," I answered; "if it would not be troubling you too much to ask you to step up to it and bring back the Emperor's written statement that he did not mean to include you in this promise, I shall be happy to tell you every word that passed."

He showed his teeth at me then like the old fox that he was.

"Monsieur Gerard appears to be a little puffed up," said he. "He is too young to see things in their just proportion. As he grows older he may understand that it is not always very discreet for a subaltern of cavalry to give such very abrupt refusals."

I did not know what to say to this, but Lasalle came to my aid in his downright fashion.

"The lad is quite right," said he. "If I had known that there was a promise I should not have questioned him. You know very well, Monsieur de Talleyrand, that if he had answered you, you would have laughed in your sleeve and thought as much about him as I think of the bottle when the burgundy is gone. As for me, I promise you that the Tenth would have had no room for him, and that we should have lost our best swordsman if I had heard him give up the Emperor's secret."

But the statesman became only the more bitter when he saw that I had the support of my Colonel.

" I have heard, Colonel de Lasalle," said he, with an icy dignity, " that your opinion is of great weight upon the subject of light cavalry. Should I have occasion to seek information about that branch of the army, I shall be very happy to apply to you. At present, however, the matter concerns diplomacy, and you will permit me to form my own views upon that question. As long as the welfare of France and the safety of the Emperor's person are largely committed to my care, I will use every means in my power to secure them, even if it should be against the Emperor's own temporary wishes. I have the honour, Colonel de Lasalle, to wish you a very good day ! "

He shot a most unamiable glance in my direction, and, turning upon his heel, he walked with little, quick, noiseless steps out of the room.

I could see from Lasalle's face that he did not at all relish finding himself at enmity with the powerful Minister. He rapped out an oath or two, and then, catching up his sabre and his cap, he clattered away down the stairs. As I looked out of the window I saw the two of them, the big blue man and the limping black one, going up the street together. Talleyrand was walking very rigidly, and Lasalle was waving his hands and talking, so I suppose he was trying to make his peace.

The Emperor had told me not to think, and I endeavoured to obey him. I took up the cards from the table where Morat had left them, and I tried to work out a few combinations at écarté. But I could not remember which were trumps, and I threw them under the table in despair. Then I drew my sabre and practised giving point until I was weary, but it was all of no use at all. My mind *would* work, in spite of myself. At ten o'clock I was to meet the Emperor in the forest. Of all extraordinary combinations of events in the whole world, surely this was the last which would have occurred to me when I rose from my couch that morning. But the responsibility—the dreadful responsibility! It was all upon my shoulders. There was no one to halve it with me. It made me cold all over. Often as I have faced death upon the battle-field, I have never known what real fear was until that moment. But then I considered that after all I could but do my best like a brave and honourable gentleman, and above all obey the orders which I had received, to the very letter. And, if all went well, this would surely be the foundation of my fortunes. Thus, swaying between my fears and my hopes, I spent the long, long evening until it was time to keep my appointment.

I put on my military overcoat, as I did not know how much of the night I might have to spend in the woods, and I fastened my sword outside it. I pulled off my hussar boots also, and wore a pair of shoes and gaiters, that I might be lighter upon my feet. Then I stole out of my quarters and made for the forest, feeling very much easier in my mind, for I am always at my best when the time of thought has passed and the moment for action arrived.

I passed the barracks of the Chasseurs of the Guards, and the line of cafés all filled with uniforms. I caught a glimpse as I went by of the blue and gold of some of my comrades, amid the swarm of dark infantry coats and the light green of the Guides. There they sat, sipping their wine and smoking their cigars, little dreaming what their comrade had on hand. One of them, the chief of my squadron, caught sight of me in the lamplight, and came shouting after me into the street. I hurried on, however, pretending not to hear him, so he, with a curse at my deafness, went back at last to his wine bottle.

It is not very hard to get into the forest at Fontainebleau. The scattered trees steal their way into the very streets, like the tirailleurs in front of a column. I turned into a path, which led to the edge of the woods, and then I pushed rapidly forward towards the old fir-tree. It was a place which, as I have hinted, I had my own reasons for knowing well, and I could only thank the Fates that it was not one of the nights upon which Léonie would be waiting for me. The poor child would have died of terror at sight of the Emperor. He might have been too harsh with her—and worse still, he might have been too kind.

There was a half moon shining, and, as I came up to our trysting-place, I saw that I was not the first to arrive. The Emperor was pacing up and down, his hands behind him and his face sunk somewhat forward upon his breast. He wore a grey great-coat with a capote over his head. I had seen him in such a dress in our winter campaign in Poland, and it was said that he used it because the hood was such an excellent disguise. He was always fond, whether in the camp or in Paris, of walking round at night, and overhearing the talk in the cabarets or round the fires. His figure, however, and his way of carrying his head and his hands were so well known that he was always recognised, and then the talkers would say whatever they thought would please him best.

My first thought was that he would be angry with me for having kept him waiting, but as I approached him, we heard the big church clock of Fontainebleau clang out the hour of ten. It was evident, therefore, that it was he who was too soon, and not I too late. I remembered his order that I should make no remark, so contented myself with halting within four paces of him, clicking my spurs together, grounding my sabre and saluting. He glanced at me, and then without a word he turned and walked slowly through the forest, I keeping always about the same distance behind him. Once or twice he seemed to me to look apprehensively to right and to left, as if he feared that someone was observing us. I looked also, but although I have the keenest sight, it was quite impossible to see anything except the ragged patches of moonshine between the great black shadows of the trees. My ears are as quick as my eyes, and once or twice I thought that I heard a twig crack ; but you know how many sounds there are in a forest at night, and how difficult it is even to say what direction they come from.

We walked for rather more than a mile, and I knew exactly what our destination was, long before we got there. In the centre of one of the glades, there is the shattered stump of what must at some time have been a most gigantic tree. It is called the Abbot's Beech, and there are so many ghostly stories about it, that I know many a brave soldier who would not care about mounting sentinel over it. However, I cared as little for such folly as the Emperor did, so we crossed the glade and made straight for the old broken trunk. As we approached, I saw that two men were waiting for us beneath it.

When I first caught sight of them they were standing rather behind it, as if they were not anxious to be seen, but as we came nearer they emerged from its shadow and walked forward to meet us. The Emperor glanced back at me, and slackened his pace a little so that I came within arm's length of him. You may think that I had my hilt well to the front, and that I had a very good look at these two people who were approaching us.

The one was tall, remarkably so, and of very spare frame, while the other was rather below the usual height, and had a brisk, determined way of walking. They each wore black cloaks, which were slung right across their figures, and hung down upon one side, like the mantles of Murat's dragoons. They had flat black caps, like those I have since seen in Spain, which threw their faces into darkness, though I could see the gleam of their eyes from beneath them. With the moon behind them and their long black shadows walking in front, they were such figures as one might expect to meet at night near the Abbot's Beech. I can remember that they had a stealthy way of moving, and that as they approached, the moon-shine formed two white diamonds between their legs and the legs of their shadows.

The Emperor had paused, and these two strangers came to a stand also within a few paces of us. I had drawn up close to my companion's elbow, so that the four of us were facing each other without a word spoken. My eyes were particularly fixed upon the taller one, because he was slightly the nearer to me, and I became certain as I watched him that he was in the last state of nervousness. His lean figure was quivering all over, and I heard a quick, thin panting like that of a tired dog. Suddenly one of them gave a short, hissing signal. The tall man bent his back and his knees like a diver about to spring, but before he could move, I had jumped with drawn sabre in front of him. At the same instant the smaller man bounded past me, and buried a long poniard in the Emperor's heart.

My God! the horror of that moment! It is a marvel that I did not drop dead myself. As in a dream, I saw the grey coat whirl convulsively round, and caught a glimpse in the moonlight of three inches of red point which jutted out from between the shoulders. Then down he fell with a dead man's gasp upon the grass, and the assassin, leaving his weapon buried in his victim, threw up both his hands and shrieked with joy. But I— I drove my sword through his midriff with such frantic force, that the mere blow of the hilt against the end of his breast-bone sent him six paces before he fell, and left my reeking blade ready for the other. I sprang round upon him with such a lust for blood upon me as I had never felt, and never have felt, in all my days. As I turned, a dagger flashed before my eyes, and I felt the cold wind of it pass my neck and the villain's wrist jar upon my shoulder. I shortened my sword, but he winced away from me, and an instant afterwards was in full flight, bounding like a deer across the glade in the moonlight.

But he was not to escape me thus. I knew that the murderer's poniard had done its work. Young as I was, I had seen enough of war to know a mortal blow. I paused but for an instant to touch the cold hand.

" Sire! Sire! " I cried, in an agony; and then as

no sound came back, and nothing moved, save an ever-widening dark circle in the moonlight, I knew that all was indeed over. I sprang madly to my feet, threw off my great-coat, and ran at the top of my speed after the remaining assassin.

Ah, how I blessed the wisdom which had caused me to come in shoes and gaiters! And the happy thought which had thrown off my coat. He could not get rid of his mantle, this wretch, or else he was too frightened to think of it. So it was that I gained upon him from the beginning. He must have been out of his wits, for he never tried to bury himself in the darker parts of the woods, but he flew on from glade to glade, until he came to the heath-land which leads up to the great Fontainebleau quarry. There I had him in full sight, and knew that he could not escape me. He ran well, it is true—ran as a coward runs when his life is the stake. But I ran as Destiny runs when it gets behind a man's heels. Yard by yard I drew in upon him. He was rolling and staggering. I could hear the rasping and crackling of his breath. The great gulf of the quarry suddenly yawned in front of his path, and glancing at me over his shoulder, he gave a shriek of despair. The next instant he had vanished from my sight.

Vanished utterly, you understand. I rushed to the spot, and gazed down into the black abyss. Had he hurled himself over? I had almost made up my mind that he had done so, when a gentle sound rising and falling came out of the darkness beneath me. It was his breathing once more, and it showed me where he must be. He was hiding in the tool-house.

At the edge of the quarry and beneath the summit there is a small platform upon which stands a wooden hut for the use of the labourers. It was into this, then, that he had darted. Perhaps he had thought, the fool, that, in the darkness, I would not venture to follow him. He little knew Étienne Gerard. With a spring I was on the platform, with another I was through the doorway, and then, hearing him in the corner, I hurled myself down upon the top of him.

He fought like a wild cat, but he never had a chance with his shorter weapon. I think that I must have transfixed him with that first mad lunge, for, though he struck and struck, his blows had no power in them, and presently his dagger tinkled down upon the floor. When I was sure that he was dead, I rose up and passed out into the moonlight. I climbed on to the heath again, and wandered across it as nearly out of my mind as a man could be.

With the blood singing in my ears, and my naked sword still clutched in my hand, I walked aimlessly on until, looking round me, I found that I had come as far as the glade of the Abbot's Beech and saw in the distance that gnarled stump which must ever be associated with the most terrible moment of my life. I sat down upon a fallen trunk with my sword across my knees and my head between my hands, and I tried to think about what had happened and what would happen in the future.

The Emperor had committed himself to my care. The Emperor was dead. Those were the two thoughts which clanged in my head, until I had no room for any other ones. He had come with me and he was dead. I had done what he had ordered when living. I had revenged him when dead. But what of all that? The world would look upon me as responsible. They might even look upon me as the assassin. What could I prove? What witnesses had I? Might I not have been the accomplice of these wretches? Yes, yes, I was eternally dishonoured—the lowest, most despicable creature in all France. This, then, was the end of my fine military ambitions—of the hopes of my mother. I laughed bitterly at the thought. And what was I to do now? Was I to go into Fontainebleau, to wake up the palace, and to inform them that the great Emperor had been murdered within a pace of me? I could not do it—no, I could not do it! There was but one course for an honourable gentleman whom Fate had placed in so cruel a position. I would fall upon my dishonoured sword, and so share, since I could not avert, the Emperor's fate. I rose with my nerves strung to this last piteous deed, and as I did so, my eyes fell upon something which struck the breath from my lips. The Emperor was standing before me !

He was not more than ten yards off, with the moon shining straight upon his cold, pale face. He wore his grey overcoat, but the hood was turned back, and the front open, so that I could see the green coat of the Guides, and the white breeches. His hands were clasped behind his back, and his chin sunk forward upon his breast, in the way that was usual with him.

" Well," said he, in his hardest and most abrupt voice, " what account do you give of yourself ? "

I believe that, if he had stood in silence for another minute, my brain would have given way. But those sharp military accents were exactly what I needed to bring me to myself. Living or dead, here was the Emperor standing before me and asking me questions. I sprang to the salute.

" You have killed one, I see," said he, jerking his head towards the beech.

" Yes, sire."

" And the other escaped ? "

" No, sire, I killed him also."

" What ! " he cried. " Do I understand that you have killed them both ? " He approached me as he spoke with a smile which set his teeth gleaming in the moonlight.

" One body lies there, sire," I answered. " The other is in the tool-house at the quarry."

" Then the Brothers of Ajaccio are no more," he cried, and after a pause, as if speaking to himself : " The shadow has passed me for ever." Then he bent forward and laid his hand upon my shoulder.

" You have done very well, my young friend," said he. " You have lived up to your reputation."

He was flesh and blood, then, this Emperor. I could feel the little, plump palm that rested upon me. And yet I could not get over what I had seen with my own eyes, and so I stared at him in such bewilderment that he broke once more into one of his smiles.

" No, no, Monsieur Gerard," said he, " I am not a ghost, and you have not seen me killed. You will come here, and all will be clear to you."

He turned as he spoke, and led the way towards the great beech stump.

The bodies were still lying upon the ground, and two men were standing beside them. As we approached I saw from the turbans that they were Roustem and Mustafa, the two Mameluke servants. The Emperor paused when he came to the grey figure upon the ground, and turning back the hood which shrouded the features, he showed a face which was very different from his own.

" Here lies a faithful servant who has given up his life for his master," said he. " Monsieur de Goudin resembles me in figure and in manner, as you must admit."

What a delirium of joy came upon me when these few words made everything clear to me. He smiled again as he saw the delight which urged me to throw my arms round him and to embrace him, but he moved a step away, as if he had divined my impulse.

" You are unhurt ? " he asked.

" I am unhurt, sire. But in another minute I should in my despair——"

" Tut, tut ! " he interrupted. " You did very well. He should himself have been more on his guard. I saw everything which passed."

" You saw it, sire ! "

" You did not hear me follow you through the wood, then ? I hardly lost sight of you from the moment that you left your quarters until poor De Goudin fell. The counterfeit Emperor was in front of you and the real one behind. You will now escort me back to the palace."

He whispered an order to his Mamelukes, who saluted

in silence and remained where they were standing. For my part, I followed the Emperor with my pelisse bursting with pride. My word, I have always carried myself as a hussar should, but Lasalle himself never strutted and swung his dolman as I did that night. Who should clink his spurs and clatter his sabre if it were not I—I, Étienne Gerard—the confidant of the Emperor, the chosen swordsman of the light cavalry, the man who slew the would-be assassins of Napoleon? But he noticed my bearing and turned upon me like a blight.

" Is that the way you carry yourself on a secret mission ? " he hissed, with that cold glare in his eyes. " Is it thus that you will make your comrades believe that nothing remarkable has occurred ? Have done with this nonsense, monsieur, or you will find yourself transferred to the sappers, where you would have harder work and duller plumage."

That was the way with the Emperor. If ever he thought that anyone might have a claim upon him, he took the first opportunity to show him the gulf that lay between. I saluted and was silent, but I must confess to you that it hurt me after all that had passed between us. He led on to the palace, where we passed through the side door and up into his own cabinet. There were a couple of grenadiers at the staircase, and their eyes started out from under their fur caps, I promise you, when they saw a young lieutenant of hussars going up to the Emperor's room at midnight. I stood by the door, as I had done in the afternoon, while he flung himself down in an arm-chair, and remained silent so long that it seemed to me that he had forgotten all about me. I ventured at last upon a slight cough to remind him.

" Ah, Monsieur Gerard," said he, " you are very curious, no doubt, as to the meaning of all this ? "

" I am quite content, sire, if it is your pleasure not to tell me," I answered.

" Ta, ta, ta," said he, impatiently. " These are only words. The moment that you were outside that door you would begin making inquiries about what it means. In two days your brother officers would know about it, in three days it would be all over Fontainebleau, and it would be in Paris on the fourth. Now, if I tell you enough to appease your curiosity, there is some reasonable hope that you may be able to keep the matter to yourself."

He did not understand me, this Emperor, and yet I could only bow and be silent.

" A few words will make it clear to you," said he, speaking very swiftly and pacing up and down the room. " They were Corsicans, these two men. I had known them in my youth. We had belonged to the same society —Brothers of Ajaccio, as we called ourselves. It was founded in the old Paoli days, you understand, and we had some strict rules of our own which were not infringed with impunity."

A very grim look came over his face as he spoke, and it seemed to me that all that was French had gone out of him, and that it was the pure Corsican, the man of strong passions and of strange revenges, who stood before me. His memory had gone back to those early days of his, and for five minutes, wrapped in thought, he paced up and down the room with his quick little tiger steps. Then with an impatient wave of his hands he came back to his palace and to me.

" The rules of such a society," he continued, " are all very well for a private citizen. In the old days there was no more loyal brother than I. But circumstances change, and it would be neither for my welfare nor for that of France that I should now submit myself to them. They wanted to hold me to it, and so brought their fate upon their own heads. These were the two chiefs of the order, and they had come from Corsica to summon me to meet them at the spot which they named. I knew what such a summons meant. No man had ever returned from obeying one. On the other hand, if I did not go, I was sure that disaster would follow. I am a brother myself, you remember, and I know their ways."

Again there came that hardening of his mouth and cold glitter of his eyes.

" You perceive my dilemma, Monsieur Gerard," said he. " How would you have acted yourself, under such circumstances ?"

" Given the word to the 10th Hussars, sire," I cried. " Patrols could have swept the woods from end to end, and brought these two rascals to your feet."

He smiled, but he shook his head.

" I had very excellent reasons why I did not wish them taken alive," said he. " You can understand that an assassin's tongue might be as dangerous a weapon as an assassin's dagger. I will not disguise from you that I wished to avoid scandal at all cost. That was why I ordered you to take no pistols with you. That also is why my Mamelukes will remove all traces of the affair, and nothing more will be heard about it. I thought of all possible plans, and I am convinced that I selected the best one. Had I sent more than one guard with De Goudin into the woods, then the brothers would not have appeared. They would not change their plans nor miss their chance for the sake of a single man. It was Colonel Lasalle's accidental presence at the moment when I received the summons which led to my choosing one of his hussars for the mission. I selected you, Monsieur Gerard, because I wanted a man who could handle a sword, and who would not pry more deeply into the affair than I desired. I trust that, in this respect, you will justify my choice as well as you have done in your bravery and skill."

" Sire," I answered, " you may rely upon it."

" As long as I live," said he, " you never open your lips upon this subject."

" I dismiss it entirely from my mind, sire. I will efface it from my recollections as if it had never been. I will promise you to go out of your cabinet at this moment exactly as I was when I entered it at four o'clock."

" You cannot do that," said the Emperor, smiling.

"You were a lieutenant at that time. You will permit me, Captain, to wish you a very good-night."

3. *How the Brigadier held the King*

HERE, upon the lapel of my coat, you may see the ribbon of my decoration, but the medal itself I keep in a leathern pouch at home, and I never venture to take it out unless one of the modern peace generals, or some foreigner of distinction who finds himself in our little town, takes advantage of the opportunity to pay his respects to the well-known Brigadier Gerard. Then I place it upon my breast, and I give my moustache the old Marengo twist which brings a grey point into either eye. Yet with it all I fear that neither they, nor you either, my friends, will ever realise the man that I was. You know me only as a civilian—with an air and a manner, it is true—but still merely as a civilian. Had you seen me as I stood in the doorway of the inn at Alamo, on the 1st of July, in the year 1810, you would then have known what the hussar may attain to.

For a month I had lingered in that accursed village, and all on account of a lance-thrust in my ankle, which made it impossible for me to put my foot to the ground. There were three besides myself at first : old Bouvet, of the Hussars of Berchény, Jacques Regnier, of the Cuirassiers, and a funny little voltigeur captain whose name I forget ; but they all got well and hurried on to the front, while I sat gnawing my fingers and tearing my hair, and even, I must confess, weeping from time to time as I thought of my Hussars of Conflans, and the deplorable condition in which they must find themselves when deprived of their colonel. I was not a chief of brigade yet, you understand, although I already carried myself like one, but I was the youngest colonel in the whole service, and my regiment was wife and children to me. It went to my heart that they should be so bereaved. It is true that Villaret, the senior major, was an excellent soldier ; but still, even among the best there are degrees of merit.

Ah, that happy July day of which I speak, when first I limped to the door and stood in the golden Spanish sunshine ! It was but the evening before that I had heard from the regiment. They were at Pastores, on the other side of the mountains, face to face with the English—not forty miles from me by road. But how was I to get to them ? The same thrust which had pierced my ankle had slain my charger. I took advice both from Gomez, the landlord, and from an old priest who had slept that night in the inn, but neither of them could do more than assure me that there was not so much as a colt left upon the whole country-side.

The landlord would not hear of my crossing the mountains without an escort, for he assured me that El Cuchillo, the Spanish guerrilla chief, was out that way with his band, and that it meant a death by torture to fall into his hands. The old priest observed, however, that he did not think a French hussar would be deterred by that, and if I had had any doubts, they would of course have been decided by his remark.

But a horse ! How was I to get one ? I was standing in the doorway, plotting and planning, when I heard the clink of shoes, and, looking up, I saw a great bearded man, with a blue cloak frogged across in military fashion, coming towards me. He was riding a big black horse with one white stocking on his near fore-leg.

" Halloa, comrade ! " said I, as he came up to me.

" Halloa ! " said he.

" I am Colonel Gerard, of the Hussars," said I. " I have lain here wounded for a month, and I am now ready to rejoin my regiment at Pastores."

" I am Monsieur Vidal, of the commissariat," he answered, " and I am myself upon my way to Pastores. I should be glad to have your company, Colonel, for I hear that the mountains are far from safe."

" Alas," said I, " I have no horse. But if you will sell

me yours, I will promise that an escort of hussars shall be sent back for you."

He would not hear of it, and it was in vain that the landlord told him dreadful stories of the doings of El Cuchillo, and that I pointed out the duty which he owed to the army and to the country. He would not even argue, but called loudly for a cup of wine. I craftily asked him to dismount and to drink with me, but he must have seen something in my face, for he shook his head ; and then, as I approached him with some thought of seizing him by the leg, he jerked his heels into his horse's flanks, and was off in a cloud of dust.

My faith ! it was enough to make a man mad to see this fellow riding away so gaily to join his beef-barrels, and his brandy-casks, and then to think of my five hundred beautiful hussars without their leader. I was gazing after him with bitter thoughts in my mind, when who should touch me on the elbow but the little priest whom I have mentioned.

" It is I who can help you," he said. " I am myself travelling south."

I put my arms about him and, as my ankle gave way at the same moment, we nearly rolled upon the ground together.

" Get me to Pastores," I cried, " and you shall have a rosary of golden beads." I had taken one from the Convent of Spiritu Santo. It shows how necessary it is to take what you can when you are upon a campaign, and how the most unlikely things may become useful.

" I will take you," he said, in very excellent French, " not because I hope for any reward, but because it is my way always to do what I can do serve my fellow-man, and that is why I am so beloved wherever I go."

With that he led me down the village to an old cow-house, in which we found a tumble-down sort of diligence, such as they used to run early in this century, between some of our remote villages. There were three old mules, too, none of which were strong enough to carry a man, but together they might draw the coach. The sight of their gaunt ribs and spavined legs gave me more delight than the whole two hundred and twenty hunters of the Emperor which I have seen in their stalls at Fontainebleau. In ten minutes the owner was harnessing them into the coach, with no very good will, however, for he was in mortal dread of this terrible Cuchillo. It was only by promising him riches in this world, while the priest threatened him with perdition in the next, that we at last got him safely upon the box with the reins between his fingers. Then he was in such a hurry to get off, out of fear lest we should find ourselves in the dark in the passes, that he hardly gave me time to renew my vows to the innkeeper's daughter. I cannot at this moment recall her name, but we wept together as we parted, and I can remember that she was a very beautiful woman. You will understand, my friends, that when a man like me, who has fought the men and kissed the women in fourteen separate kingdoms, gives a word of praise to the one or the other, it has a little meaning of its own.

The little priest had seemed a trifle grave when we kissed good-bye, but he soon proved himself the best of companions in the diligence. All the way he amused me with tales of his little parish up in the mountains, and I in my turn told him stories about the camp ; but, my faith, I had to pick my steps, for when I said a word too much he would fidget in his seat and his face would show the pain that I had given him. And of course it is not the act of a gentleman to talk in anything but a proper manner to a religious man, though, with all the care in the world, one's words may get out of hand sometimes.

He had come from the north of Spain, as he told me, and was going to see his mother in a village of Estremadura, and as he spoke about her little peasant home, and her joy in seeing him, it brought my own mother so vividly to my thoughts that the tears started to my eyes. In his simplicity he showed me the little gifts which he was taking to her, and so kindly was his manner that I could readily believe him when he said he was loved wherever he went. He examined my own uniform with as much curiosity as a child, admiring the plume of my busby, and passing his fingers through the sable with which my dolman was trimmed. He drew my sword, too, and then when I told him how many men I had cut down with it, and set my finger on the notch made by the shoulder-bone of the Russian Emperor's aide-de-camp, he shuddered and placed the weapon under the leathern cushion, declaring that it made him sick to look at it.

Well, we had been rolling and creaking on our way whilst this talk had been going forward, and as we reached the base of the mountains we could hear the rumbling of cannon far away upon the right. This came from Massena, who was, as I knew, besieging Ciudad Rodrigo. There was nothing I should have wished better than to have gone straight to him, for if, as some said, he had Jewish blood in his veins, he was the best Jew that I have heard of since Joshua's time. If you were in sight of his beaky nose and bold, black eyes, you were not likely to miss much of what was going on. Still, a siege is always a poor sort of a pick-and-shovel business, and there were better prospects with my hussars in front of the English. Every mile that passed, my heart grew lighter and lighter, until I found myself shouting and singing like a young ensign fresh from St. Cyr, just to think of seeing all my fine horses and my gallant fellows once more.

As we penetrated the mountains the road grew rougher and the pass more savage. At first we had met a few muleteers, but now the whole country seemed deserted, which is not to be wondered at when you think that the French, the English, and the guerrillas had each in turn had command over it. So bleak and wild was it, one great brown wrinkled cliff succeeding another, and the pass growing narrower and narrower, that I ceased to look out, but sat in silence, thinking of this and that, of women whom I had loved and of horses which I had handled. I was suddenly brought back from my dreams, however, by observing the difficulties of my companion, who was trying with a sort of brad-awl, which he had drawn out, to bore a hole through the leathern strap which held up his water-flask. As he worked with twitching fingers the strap escaped his grasp, and the wooden bottle fell at my feet. I stooped to pick it up, and I as did so the priest silently leaped upon my shoulders and drove his brad-awl into my eye!

My friends, I am, as you know, a man steeled to face every danger. When one has served from the affair of Zurich to that last fatal day of Waterloo, and has had the special medal, which I keep at home in a leathern pouch, one can afford to confess when one is frightened. It may console some of you, when your own nerves play you tricks, to remember that you have heard even me, Brigadier Gerard, say that I have been scared. And besides my terror at this horrible attack, and the maddening pain of my wound, there was a sudden feeling of loathing such as you might feel were some filthy tarantula to strike its fangs into you.

I clutched the creature in both hands, and, hurling him on to the floor of the coach, I stamped on him with my heavy boots. He had drawn a pistol from the front of his soutane, but I kicked it out of his hand, and again I fell with my knees upon his chest. Then, for the first time, he screamed horribly, while I, half blinded, felt about for the sword which he had so cunningly concealed. My hand had just lighted upon it, and I was dashing the blood from my face to see where he lay that I might transfix him, when the whole coach turned partly over upon its side, and my weapon was jerked out of my grasp by the shock.

Before I could recover myself the door was burst open, and I was dragged by the heels on to the road. But even as I was torn out on to the flint stones, and realised that thirty ruffians were standing around me, I was filled with joy, for my pelisse had been pulled over my head in the struggle and was covering one of my eyes, and it was with my wounded eye that I was seeing this gang of brigands. You see for yourself by this pucker and scar how the thin blade passed between socket and ball, but it was only at that moment, when I was dragged from the coach, that I understood that my sight was not gone for ever. The creature's intention, doubtless, was to drive it through into my brain, and indeed he loosened some portion of the inner bone of my head, so that I afterwards had more trouble from that wound than from any one of the seventeen which I have received.

They dragged me out, these sons of dogs, with curses and execrations, beating me with their fists and kicking me as I lay upon the ground. I had frequently observed that the mountaineers wore cloth swathed round their feet, but never did I imagine that I should have so much cause to be thankful for it. Presently, seeing the blood upon my head, and that I lay quiet, they thought that I was unconscious, whereas I was storing every ugly face among them into my memory, so that I might see them all safely hanged if ever my chance came round. Brawny rascals they were, with yellow handkerchiefs round their heads, and great red sashes stuffed with weapons. They had rolled two rocks across the path, where it took a sharp turn, and it was these which had torn off one of the wheels of the coach and upset us. As to this reptile, who had acted the priest so cleverly and had told me so much of his parish and his mother, he, of course, had known where the ambuscade was laid and had attempted to put me beyond all resistance at the moment when we reached it.

I cannot tell you how frantic their rage was when they drew him out of the coach and saw the state to which I had reduced him. If he had not got all his deserts, he had, at least, something as a souvenir of his meeting with Étienne Gerard, for his legs dangled aimlessly about, and though the upper part of his body was convulsed with rage and pain, he sat straight down upon his feet when they tried to set him upright. But all the time his two little black eyes, which had seemed so kindly and so innocent in the coach, were glaring at me like a wounded cat, and he spat, and spat, and spat in my direction. My faith! when the wretches jerked me on to my feet again, and when I was dragged off up one of the mountain paths, I understood that a time was coming when I was to need all my courage and resource. My enemy was carried upon the shoulders of two men behind me, and I could hear his hissing and his reviling, first in one ear and then in the other, as I was hurried up the winding track.

I suppose that it must have been for an hour that we ascended, and what with my wounded ankle and the pain from my eye, and the fear lest this wound should have spoiled my appearance, I have made no journey to which I look back with less pleasure. I have never been a good climber at any time, but it is astonishing what you can do, even with a stiff ankle, when you have a copper-coloured brigand at each elbow and a nine-inch blade within touch of your whiskers.

We came at last to a place where the path wound over a ridge, and descended upon the other side through thick pine-trees into a valley which opened to the south. In time of peace I had little doubt that the villains were all smugglers, and that these were the secret paths by which they crossed the Portuguese frontier. There were many mule-tracks, and once I was surprised to see the marks of a large horse where a stream had softened the track. These were explained when, on reaching a place where there was a clearing in the fir wood, I saw the animal itself haltered to a fallen tree. My eyes had hardly rested upon it, when I recognised the great black limbs and the white near fore-leg. It was the very horse which I had begged for in the morning.

What, then, had become of Commissariat Vidal? Was it possible that there was another Frenchman in as perilous a plight as myself? The thought had hardly entered my head when our party stopped and one of them uttered a peculiar cry. It was answered from among the brambles which lined the base of a cliff at one side of a clearing, and an instant later ten or a dozen more brigands came out from amongst them, and the two parties greeted each other. The new-comers surrounded my friend of the brad-awl with cries of grief and sympathy, and then, turning upon me, they brandished their knives and howled at me like the gang of assassins that they were. So frantic were their gestures that I was convinced that my end had come, and was just bracing myself to meet it in a manner which should be worthy of my past reputation, when one of them gave an order and I was dragged roughly across the little glade to the brambles from which this new band had emerged.

A narrow pathway led through them to a deep grotto in the side of the cliff. The sun was already setting outside, and in the cave itself it would have been quite dark but for a pair of torches which blazed from a socket on either side. Between them there was sitting at a rude table a very singular-looking person, whom I saw instantly, from the respect with which the others addressed him, could be none other than the brigand chief who had received, on account of his dreadful character, the sinister name of El Cuchillo.

The man whom I had injured had been carried in and placed upon the top of a barrel, his helpless legs dangling about in front of him, and his cat's eyes still darting glances of hatred at me. I understood, from the snatches of talk which I could follow between the chief and him, that he was the lieutenant of the band, and that part of his duties was to lie in wait with his smooth tongue and his peaceful garb for travellers like myself. When I thought of how many gallant officers may have been lured to their death by this monster of hypocrisy, it gave me a glow of pleasure to think that I had brought his villainies to an end—though I feared it would be at the price of a life which neither the Emperor nor the army could well spare.

As the injured man, still supported upon the barrel by two comrades, was explaining in Spanish all that had befallen him, I was held by several of the villains in front of the table at which the chief was seated, and had an excellent opportunity of observing him. I have seldom seen any man who was less like my idea of a brigand, and especially of a brigand with such a reputation that in a land of cruelty he had earned so dark a nickname. His face was bluff and broad and bland, with ruddy cheeks and comfortable little tufts of side-whiskers, which gave him the appearance of a well-to-do grocer of the Rue St. Antoine. He had not any of those flaring sashes or gleaming weapons which distinguished his followers, but on the contrary he wore a good broadcloth coat like a respectable father of a family, and save for his brown leggings there was nothing to indicate a life among the mountains. His surroundings, too, corresponded with himself, and beside his snuff-box upon the table there stood a great brown book, which looked like a commercial ledger. Many other books were ranged along a plank between two powder-casks, and there was a great litter of papers, some of which had verses scribbled upon them. All this I took in while he, leaning indolently back in his chair, was listening to the report of his lieutenant. Having heard everything, he ordered the cripple to be carried out again, and I was left with my three guards, waiting to hear my fate. He took up his pen, and tapping his forehead with the handle of it, he pursed up his lips and looked out of the corner of his eyes at the roof of the grotto.

" I suppose," said he at last, speaking very excellent French, " that you are not able to suggest a rhyme for the word Covilha."

I answered him that my acquaintance with the Spanish language was so limited that I was unable to oblige him.

" It is a rich language," said he, " but less prolific in

rhymes than either the German or the English. That is why our best work has been done in blank verse, a form of composition which is capable of reaching great heights. But I fear that such subjects are somewhat outside the range of a hussar."

I was about to answer that if they were good enough for a guerrilla, they could not be too much for the light cavalry, but he was already stooping over his half-finished verse. Presently he threw down the pen with an exclamation of satisfaction, and declaimed a few lines which drew a cry of approval from the three ruffians who held me. His broad face blushed like a young girl who receives her first compliment.

" The critics are in my favour, it appears," said he ; " we amuse ourselves in our long evenings by singing our own ballads, you understand. I have some little facility in that direction, and I do not at all despair of seeing some of my poor efforts in print before long, and with ' Madrid ' upon the title-page, too. But we must get back to business. May I ask what your name is ? "

" Étienne Gerard."

" Rank ? "

" Colonel."

" Corps ? "

" The Third Hussars of Conflans."

" You are young for a colonel."

" My career has been an eventful one."

" Tut, that makes it the sadder," said he, with his bland smile.

I made no answer to that, but I tried to show him by my bearing that I was ready for the worst which could befall me.

" By the way, I rather fancy that we have had some of your corps here," said he, turning over the pages of his big brown register. " We endeavour to keep a record of our operations. Here is a heading under June 24th. Have you not a young officer named Soubiron, a tall, slight youth with light hair ? "

" Certainly."

" I see that we buried him upon that date."

" Poor lad !" I cried. " And how did he die ? "

" We buried him."

" But before you buried him ? "

" You misunderstand me, Colonel. He was not dead before we buried him."

" You buried him alive ! "

For a moment I was too stunned to act. Then I hurled myself upon the man, as he sat with that placid smile of his upon his lips, and I would have torn his throat out had the three wretches not dragged me away from him. Again and again I made for him, panting and cursing, shaking off this man and that, straining and wrenching, but never quite free. At last, with my jacket torn nearly off my back and blood dripping from my wrists, I was hauled backwards in the bight of a rope and cords passed round my ankles and my arms.

" You sleek hound ! " I cried. " If ever I have you at my sword's point, I will teach you to maltreat one of my lads. You will find, you blood-thirsty beast, that my Emperor has long arms, and though you lie here like a rat in its hole, the time will come when he will tear you out of it, and you and your vermin will perish together."

My faith, I have a rough side to my tongue, and there was not a hard word that I had learned in fourteen campaigns which I did not let fly at him ; but he sat with the handle of his pen tapping against his forehead and his eyes squinting up at the roof as if he had conceived the idea of some new stanza. It was this occupation of his which showed me how I might get my point into him.

" You spawn ! " said I ; " you think that you are safe here, but your life may be as short as that of your absurd verses, and God knows that it could not be shorter than that."

Ah, you should have seen him bound from his chair when I said the words. This vile monster, who dispensed death and torture as a grocer serves out his figs, had one raw nerve, then, which I could prod at pleasure. His face grew livid, and those little bourgeois side-whiskers quivered and thrilled with passion.

" Very good, Colonel. You have said enough," he cried, in a choking voice. " You say that you have had a very distinguished career. I promise you also a very distinguished ending. Colonel Étienne Gerard of the Third Hussars shall have a death of his own."

" And I only beg," said I, " that you will not com-memorate it in verse." I had one or two little ironies to utter, but he cut me short by a furious gesture which caused my three guards to drag me from the cave.

Our interview, which I have told you as nearly as I can remember it, must have lasted some time, for it was quite dark when we came out, and the moon was shining very clearly in the heavens. The brigands had lighted a great fire of the dried branches of the fir-trees ; not, of course, for warmth, since the night was already very sultry, but to cook their evening meal. A huge copper pot hung over the blaze, and the rascals were lying all round in the yellow glare, so that the scene looked like one of those pictures which Junot stole out of Madrid. There are some soldiers who profess to care nothing for art and the like, but I have always been drawn towards it myself, in which respect I show my good taste and my breeding. I remember, for example, that when Lefebvre was selling the plunder after the fall of Danzig, I bought a very fine picture, called " Nymphs Surprised in a Wood," and I carried it with me through two campaigns, until my charger had the misfortune to put his hoof through it.

I only tell you this, however, to show you that I was never a mere rough soldier like Rapp or Ney. As I lay in that brigands' camp, I had little time or inclination to think about such matters. They had thrown me down under a tree, the three villains squatting round and smoking their cigarettes within hands' touch of me. What to do I could not imagine. In my whole career I do not suppose that I have ten times been in as hopeless a situation. "But courage," thought I. "Courage, my brave boy! You were not made a Colonel of Hussars at twenty-eight because you could dance a cotillon. You are a picked man, Étienne; a man who has come through more than two hundred affairs, and this little one is surely not going to be the last." I began eagerly to glance about for some chance of escape, and as I did so I saw something which filled me with great astonishment.

I have already told you that a large fire was burning in the centre of the glade. What with its glare, and what with the moonlight, everything was as clear as possible. On the other side of the glade there was a single tall fir-tree which attracted my attention because its trunk and lower branches were discoloured, as if a large fire had recently been lit underneath it. A clump of bushes grew in front of it which concealed the base. Well, as I looked towards it, I was surprised to see projecting above the bush, and fastened apparently to the tree, a pair of fine riding boots with the toes upwards. At first I thought that they were tied there, but as I looked harder I saw that they were secured by a great nail which was hammered through the foot of each. And then, suddenly, with a thrill of horror, I understood that these were not empty boots; and moving my head a little to the right, I was able to see who it was that had been fastened there, and why a fire had been lit beneath the tree. It is not pleasant to speak or to think of horrors, my friends, and I do not wish to give any of you bad dreams to-night—but I cannot take you among the Spanish guerrillas without showing you what kind of men they were, and the sort of warfare that they waged. I will only say that I understood why Monsieur Vidal's horse was waiting masterless in the grove, and that I hoped he had met this terrible fate with sprightliness and courage, as a good Frenchman ought.

It was not a very cheering sight for me, as you can imagine. When I had been with their chief in the grotto I had been so carried away by my rage at the cruel death of young Soubiron, who was one of the brightest lads who ever threw his thigh over a charger, that I had never given a thought to my own position. Perhaps it would have been more politic had I spoken the ruffian fair, but it was too late now. The cork was drawn and I must drain the wine. Besides, if the harmless commissariat man were put to such a death, what hope was there for me, who had snapped the spine of their lieutenant? No, I was doomed in any case, and it was as well perhaps that I should have put the best face on the matter. This beast could bear witness that Étienne Gerard had died as he had lived, and that one prisoner at least had not quailed before him. I lay there thinking of the various girls who would mourn for me, and of my dear old mother, and of the deplorable loss which I should be, both to my regiment and to the Emperor, and I am not ashamed to confess to you that I shed tears as I thought of the general consternation which my premature end would give rise to.

But all the time I was taking the very keenest notice of everything which might possibly help me. I am not a man who would lie like a sick horse waiting for the farrier sergeant and the pole-axe. First I would give a little tug at my ankle cords, and then another at those which were round my wrists, and all the time that I was trying to loosen them I was peering round to see if I could find something which was in my favour. There was one thing which was very evident. A hussar is but half formed without a horse, and there was my other half quietly grazing within thirty yards of me. Then I observed yet another thing. The path by which we had come over the mountains was so steep that a horse could only be led across it slowly and with difficulty, but in the other direction the ground appeared to be more open, and to lead straight down into a gently-sloping valley. Had I but my feet in yonder stirrups and my sabre in my hand, a single bold dash might take me out of the power of these vermin of the rocks.

I was still thinking it over and straining with my wrists
and my ankles, when their chief came out from his grotto,
and after some talk with his lieutenant, who lay groaning
near the fire, they both nodded their heads and looked
across at me. He then said some few words to the band,
who clapped their hands and laughed uproariously.
Things looked ominous, and I was delighted to feel that
my hands were so far free that I could easily slip them
through the cords if I wished. But with my ankles I
feared that I could do nothing, for when I strained it
brought such pain into my lance-wound that I had to
gnaw my moustache to keep from crying out. I could
only lie still, half-free and half-bound, and see what turn
things were likely to take.

For a little I could not make out what they were after.
One of the rascals climbed up a well-grown fir-tree upon
one side of the glade, and tied a rope round the top of the
trunk. He then fastened another rope in the same
fashion to a similar tree upon the other side. The two
loose ends were now dangling down, and I waited with
some curiosity, and just a little trepidation also, to see
what they would do next. The whole band pulled upon
one of the ropes until they had bent the strong young
tree down into a semicircle, and they then fastened it to
a stump, so as to hold it so. When they had bent the
other tree down in a similar fashion, the two summits
were within a few feet of each other, though, as you understand, they would each spring back into their original
position the instant that they were released. I already saw
the diabolical plan which these miscreants had formed.

" I presume that you are a strong man, Colonel," said
the chief, coming towards me with his hateful smile.

" If you will have the kindness to loosen these cords,"
I answered, " I will show you how strong I am."

" We were all interested to see whether you were as
strong as these two young saplings," said he. " It is
our intention, you see, to tie one end of each rope round
your ankles and then let the trees go. If you are stronger

than the trees, then, of course, no harm would be done ; if, on the other hand, the trees are stronger than you, why, in that case, Colonel, we may have a souvenir of you upon each side of our little glade."

He laughed as he spoke, and at the sight of it the whole forty of them laughed also. Even now if I am in my darker humour, or if I have a touch of my old Lithuanian ague, I see in my sleep that ring of dark, savage faces, with their cruel eyes, and the firelight flashing upon their strong white teeth.

It is astonishing—and I have heard many make the same remark—how acute one's senses become at such a crisis as this. I am convinced that at no moment is one living so vividly, so acutely, as at the instant when a violent and foreseen death overtakes one. I could smell the resinous fagots, I could see every twig upon the ground, I could hear every rustle of the branches, as I have never smelled or seen or heard save at such times of danger. And so it was that long before anyone else, before even the time when the chief had addressed me, I had heard a low, monotonous sound, far away indeed, and yet coming nearer at every instant. At first it was but a murmur, a rumble, but by the time he had finished speaking, while the assassins were untying my ankles in order to lead me to the scene of my murder, I heard, as plainly as ever I heard anything in my life, the clinking of horseshoes and the jingling of bridle-chains, with the clank of sabres against stirrup-irons. Is it likely that I, who had lived with the light cavalry since the first hair shaded my lip, would mistake the sound of troopers on the march ?

" Help, comrades, help ! " I shrieked, and though they struck me across the mouth and tried to drag me up to the trees, I kept on yelling, " Help me, my brave boys ! Help me, my children ! They are murdering your colonel ! "

For the moment my wounds and my troubles had brought on a delirium, and I looked for nothing less than my five hundred hussars, kettle-drums and all, to appear at the opening of the glade.

But that which really appeared was very different to anything which I had conceived. Into the clear space there came galloping a fine young man upon a most beautiful roan horse. He was fresh-faced and pleasant-looking, with the most debonair bearing in the world and the most gallant way of carrying himself—a way which reminded me somewhat of my own. He wore a singular coat which had once been red all over, but which was now stained to the colour of a withered oak-leaf wherever the weather could reach it. His shoulder straps, however, were of golden lace, and he had a bright metal helmet upon his head, with a coquettish white plume upon one side of its crest. He trotted his horse up the glade, while behind him rode four cavaliers in the same dress—all clean-shaven, with round, comely faces, looking to me more like monks than dragoons. At a short, gruff order they halted with a rattle of arms, while their leader cantered forward, the fire beating upon his eager face and the beautiful head of his charger. I knew, of course, by the strange coats that they were English. It was the first sight that I had ever had of them, but from their stout bearing and their masterful way I could see at a glance that what I had always been told was true, and that they were excellent people to fight against.

"Well, well, well!" cried the young officer, in sufficiently bad French, "what game are you up to here? Who was that who was yelling for help, and what are you trying to do to him?"

It was at that moment that I learned to bless those months which Obriant, the descendant of the Irish kings, had spent in teaching me the tongue of the English. My ankles had just been freed, so that I had only to slip my hands out of the cords, and with a single rush I had flown across, picked up my sabre where it lay by the fire, and hurled myself on to the saddle of poor Vidal's horse. Yes, for all my wounded ankle, I never put foot to stirrup, but was in the seat in a single bound. I tore the halter from the tree, and before these villains could so much as snap a pistol at me I was beside the English officer.

" I surrender to you, sir," I cried ; though I daresay my English was not very much better than his French. " If you will look at that tree to the left you will see what these villains do to the honourable gentlemen who fall into their hands."

The fire had flared up at that moment, and there was poor Vidal exposed before them, as horrible an object as one could see in a nightmare. " Godam ! " cried the officer, and " Godam ! " cried each of the four troopers, which is the same as with us when we cry " Mon Dieu ! " Out rasped the five swords, and the four men closed up. One, who wore a sergeant's chevrons, laughed and clapped me on the shoulder.

" Fight for your skin, froggy," said he.

Ah, it was so fine to have a horse between my thighs and a weapon in my grip. I waved it above my head and shouted in my exultation. The chief had come forward with that odious smiling face of his.

" Your excellency will observe that this Frenchman is our prisoner," said he.

" You are a rascally robber," said the Englishman, shaking his sword at him. " It is a disgrace to us to have such allies. By my faith, if Lord Wellington were of my mind we would swing you up on the nearest tree."

" But my prisoner ? " said the brigand, in his suave voice.

" He shall come with us to the British camp."

" Just a word in your ear before you take him."

He approached the young officer, and then turning as quick as a flash, he fired his pistol in my face. The bullet scored its way through my hair and burst a hole on each side of my busby. Seeing that he had missed me, he raised the pistol and was about to hurl it at me when the English sergeant, with a single back-handed cut, nearly severed his head from his body. His blood had not reached the ground, nor the last curse died on his lips, before the whole horde was upon us, but with a dozen bounds and as many slashes we were all safely out of the glade, and galloping down the winding track which led to the valley.

It was not until we had left the ravine far behind us and were right out in the open fields that we ventured to halt, and to see what injuries we had sustained. For me, wounded and weary as I was, my heart was beating proudly, and my chest was nearly bursting my tunic to think that I, Étienne Gerard, had left this gang of murderers so much by which to remember me. My faith, they would think twice before they ventured again to lay hands upon one of the Third Hussars. So carried away was I that I made a small oration to these brave Englishmen, and told them who it was that they had helped to rescue. I would have spoken of glory also, and of the sympathies of brave men, but the officer cut me short.

" That's all right," said he. " Any injuries, Sergeant ? "

" Trooper Jones's horse hit with a pistol bullet on the fetlock."

" Trooper Jones to go with us. Sergeant Halliday, with troopers Harvey and Smith, to keep to the right until they touch the vedettes of the German Hussars."

So these three jingled away together, while the officer and I, followed at some distance by the trooper whose horse had been wounded, rode straight down in the direction of the English camp. Very soon we had opened our hearts, for we each liked the other from the beginning. He was of the nobility, this brave lad, and he had been sent out scouting by Lord Wellington to see if there were any signs of our advancing through the mountains. It is one advantage of a wandering life like mine, that you learn to pick up those bits of knowledge which distinguish the man of the world. I have, for example, hardly ever met a Frenchman who could repeat an English title correctly. If I had not travelled I should not be able to say with confidence that this young man's real name was Milor the Hon. Sir Russell, Bart., this last being an honourable distinction, so that it was as the Bart that I usually addressed him, just as in Spanish one might say " the Don."

As we rode beneath the moonlight in the lovely Spanish night, we spoke our minds to each other, as if we were brothers. We were both of an age, you see, both of the light cavalry also (the Sixteenth Light Dragoons was his regiment), and both with the same hopes and ambitions. Never have I learned to know a man so quickly as I did the Bart. He gave me the name of a girl whom he had loved at a garden called Vauxhall, and, for my own part, I spoke to him of little Coralie, of the Opera. He took a lock of hair from his bosom, and I a garter. Then we nearly quarrelled over hussar and dragoon, for he was absurdly proud of his regiment, and you should have seen him curl his lip and clap his hand to his hilt when I said that I hoped it might never be its misfortune to come in the way of the Third. Finally, he began to speak about what the English call sport, and he told such stories of the money which he had lost over which of two cocks could kill the other, or which of two men could strike the other the most in a fight for a prize, that I was filled with astonishment. He was ready to bet upon anything in the most wonderful manner, and when I chanced to see a shooting star he was anxious to bet that he would see more than me, twenty-five francs a star, and it was only when I explained that my purse was in the hands of the brigands that he would give over the idea.

Well, we chatted away in this very amiable fashion until the day began to break, when suddenly we heard a great volley of musketry from somewhere in front of us. It was very rocky and broken ground, and I thought, although I could see nothing, that a general engagement had broken out. The Bart laughed at my idea, however, and explained that the sound came from the English camp, where every man emptied his piece each morning so as to make sure of having a dry priming.

" In another mile we shall be up with the outposts," said he.

I glanced round at this, and I perceived that we had trotted along at so good a pace during the time that we were keeping up our pleasant chat, that the dragoon with the lame horse was altogether out of sight. I looked on every side, but in the whole of that vast rocky valley there was no one save only the Bart and I—both of us armed, you understand, and both of us well mounted. I began to ask myself whether after all it was quite necessary that I should ride that mile which would bring me to the British outposts.

Now, I wish to be very clear with you on this point, my friends, for I would not have you think that I was acting dishonourably or ungratefully to the man who had helped me away from the brigands. You must remember that of all duties the strongest is that which a commanding officer owes to his men. You must also bear in mind that war is a game which is played under fixed rules, and when these rules are broken one must at once claim the forfeit. If, for example, I had given a parole, then I should have been an infamous wretch had I dreamed of escaping. But no parole had been asked of me. Out of over-confidence, and the chance of the lame horse dropping behind, the Bart had permitted me to get upon equal terms with him. Had it been I who had taken him, I should have used him as courteously as he had me, but, at the same time, I should have respected his enterprise so far as to have deprived him of his sword, and seen that I had at least one guard beside myself. I reined up my horse and explained this to him, asking him at the same time whether he saw any breach of honour in my leaving him.

He thought about it, and several times repeated that which the English say when they mean " Mon Dieu."

" You would give me the slip, would you ? " said he.

" If you can give no reason against it."

" The only reason that I can think of," said the Bart, " is that I should instantly cut your head off if you were to attempt it."

" Two can play at that game, my dear Bart," said I.

" Then we'll see who can play at it best," he cried, pulling out his sword.

I had drawn mine also, but I was quite determined not to hurt this admirable young man who had been my benefactor.

" Consider," said I, " you say that I am your prisoner. I might with equal reason say that you are mine. We are alone here, and though I have no doubt that you are an excellent swordsman, you can hardly hope to hold your own against the best blade in the six light cavalry brigades."

His answer was a cut at my head. I parried and shore off half of his white plume. He thrust at my breast. I turned his point and cut away the other half of his cockade.

" Curse your monkey-tricks ! " he cried, as I wheeled my horse away from him.

" Why should you strike at me ? " said I. " You see that I will not strike back."

" That's all very well," said he ; " but you've got to come along with me to the camp."

" I shall never see the camp," said I.

" I'll lay you nine to four you do," he cried, as he made at me, sword in hand.

But those words of his put something new into my head. Could we not decide the matter in some better way than fighting ? The Bart was placing me in such a position that I should have to hurt him, or he would certainly hurt me. I avoided his rush, though his sword-point was within an inch of my neck.

" I have a proposal," I cried. " We shall throw dice as to which is the prisoner of the other."

He smiled at this. It appealed to his love of sport.

" Where are your dice ? " he cried.

" I have none."

" Nor I. But I have cards."

" Cards let it be," said I.

" And the game ? "

" I leave it to you."

" Écarté, then—the best of three."

I could not help smiling as I agreed, for I do not suppose that there were three men in France who were my masters at the game. I told the Bart as much as we dismounted. He smiled also as he listened.

" I was counted the best player at Watier's," said he. " With even luck you deserve to get off if you beat me."

So we tethered our two horses and sat down one on either side of a great flat rock. The Bart took a pack of cards out of his tunic, and I had only to see him shuffle to convince me that I had no novice to deal with. We cut and the deal fell to him.

My faith, it was a stake worth playing for. He wished to add a hundred gold pieces a game, but what was money when the fate of Colonel Étienne Gerard hung upon the cards ? I felt as though all those who had reason to be interested in the game—my mother, my hussars, the Sixth Corps d'Armée, Ney, Massena, even the Emperor himself—were forming a ring round us in that desolate valley. Heavens, what a blow to one and all of them should the cards go against me ! But I was confident, for my écarté play was as famous as my swordsmanship, and save old Bouvet of the Hussars of Berchény, who won seventy-six out of one hundred and fifty games off me, I have always had the best of a series.

The first game I won right off, though I must confess that the cards were with me, and that my adversary could have done no more. In the second, I never played better and saved a trick by a finesse, but the Bart voled me once, marked the king, and ran out in the second hand. My faith, we were so excited that he laid his helmet down beside him and I my busby.

" I'll lay my roan mare against your black horse," said he.

" Done ! " said I.

" Sword against sword."

" Done ! " said I.

" Saddle, bridle and stirrups ! " he cried.

" Done ! " I shouted.

I had caught this spirit of sport from him. I would have laid my hussars against his dragoons had they been ours to pledge.

And then began the game of games. Oh, he played, this Englishman—he played in a way that was worthy of such a stake. But I, my friends, I was superb ! Of the five which I had to make to win, I gained three on the first hand. The Bart bit his moustache and drummed his hands, while I already felt myself at the head of my dear little rascals. On the second, I turned the king, but lost two tricks—and my score was four to his two. When I saw my next hand I could not but give a cry of delight. " If I cannot gain my freedom on this," thought I, " I deserve to remain for ever in chains."

Give me the cards, landlord, and I will lay them out on the table for you.

Here was my hand : knave and ace of clubs, queen and knave of diamonds, and king of hearts. Clubs were trumps, mark you, and I had but one point between me and freedom. He knew it was the crisis, and he undid his tunic. I threw my dolman on the ground. He led the ten of spades. I took it with my ace of trumps. One point in my favour. The correct play was to clear the trumps, and I led the knave. Down came the queen upon it, and the game was equal. He led the eight of spades, and I could only discard my queen of diamonds. Then came the seven of spades, and the hair stood straight up on my head. We each threw down a king at the final. He had won two points, and my beautiful hand had been mastered by his inferior one. I could have rolled on the ground as I thought of it. They used to play very good écarté at Watier's in the year '10. I say it—I, Brigadier Gerard.

The last game was now four all. This next hand must settle it one way or the other. He undid his sash, and I put away my sword-belt. He was cool, this Englishman, and I tried to be so also, but the perspiration would trickle into my eyes. The deal lay with him, and I may confess to you, my friends, that my hands shook so that I could hardly pick my cards from the rock. But when I raised them, what was the first thing that my eyes rested upon ? It was the king, the king, the glorious king of trumps ! My mouth was open to declare it when the words were frozen upon my lips by the appearance of my comrade.

He held his cards in his hand, but his jaw had fallen, and his eyes were staring over my shoulder with the most dreadful expression of consternation and surprise. I whisked round, and I was myself amazed at what I saw.

Three men were standing quite close to us—fifteen metres at the farthest. The middle one was of a good height, and yet not too tall—about the same height, in fact, that I am myself. He was clad in a dark uniform with a small cocked hat, and some sort of white plume upon the side. But I had little thought of his dress. It was his face, his gaunt cheeks, his beak-like nose, his masterful blue eyes, his thin, firm slit of a mouth which made one feel that this was a wonderful man, a man of a million. His brows were tied into a knot, and he cast such a glance at my poor Bart from under them that one by one the cards came fluttering down from his nerveless fingers. Of the two other men, one, who had a face as brown and hard as though it had been carved out of old oak, wore a bright red coat, while the other, a fine portly man with bushy side-whiskers, was in a blue jacket with gold facings. Some little distance behind, three order-lies were holding as many horses, and an escort of dragoons was waiting in the rear.

" Heh, Crauford, what the deuce is this ? " asked the thin man.

" D'you hear, sir ? " cried the man with the red coat. " Lord Wellington wants to know what this means."

My poor Bart broke into an account of all that had occurred, but that rock-face never softened for an instant.

" Pretty fine, 'pon my word, General Crauford," he broke in. " The discipline of this force must be maintained, sir. Report yourself at headquarters as a prisoner."

It was dreadful to me to see the Bart mount his horse and ride off with hanging head. I could not endure it. I threw myself before this English General. I pleaded with him for my friend, I told him how I, Colonel Gerard, would witness what a dashing young officer he was. Ah, my eloquence might have melted the hardest heart ; I brought tears to my own eyes, but none to his. My voice broke, and I could say no more.

" What weight do you put on your mules, sir, in the French service ? " he asked. Yes, that was all this phlegmatic Englishman had to answer to these burning words of mine. That was his reply to what would have made a Frenchman weep upon my shoulder.

" What weight on a mule ? " asked the man with the red coat.

" Two hundred and ten pounds," said I.

" Then you load them deucedly badly," said Lord Wellington. " Remove the prisoner to the rear."

His dragoons closed in upon me, and I—I was driven mad, as I thought that the game had been in my hands, and that I ought at that moment to be a free man. I held the cards up in front of the General.

" See, my lord ! " I cried ; " I played for my freedom and I won, for, as you perceive, I hold the king."

For the first time a slight smile softened his gaunt face.

" On the contrary," said he, as he mounted his horse, " it is I who won, for, as you perceive, my King holds you."

4. *How the King held the Brigadier*

MURAT was undoubtedly an excellent cavalry officer, but he had too much swagger, which spoils many a good soldier. Lasalle, too, was a very dashing leader, but he ruined himself with wine and folly. Now I, Étienne Gerard, was always totally devoid of swagger, and at the same time I was very abstemious, except, maybe, at the end of a campaign, or when I met an old comrade-in-arms. For these reasons I might, perhaps, had it not been for a certain diffidence, have claimed to be the most valuable officer in my own branch of the Service. It is true that I never rose to be more than a chief of brigade, but then, as everyone knows, no one had a chance of rising to the top unless he had the good fortune to be with the Emperor in his early campaigns. Except Lasalle, and Labau, and Drouet, I can hardly remember any one of the generals who had not already made his name before the Egyptian business. Even I, with all my brilliant qualities, could only attain the head of my brigade, and also the special medal of honour, which I received from the Emperor himself, and which I keep at home in a leathern pouch.

But though I never rose higher than this, my qualities were very well known to those who had served with me, and also to the English. After they had captured me in the way which I described to you the other night, they kept a very good guard over me at Oporto, and I promise you that they did not give such a formidable opponent a chance of slipping through their fingers. It was on the 10th of August that I was escorted on board the transport which was to take us to England, and behold me before the end of the month in the great prison which had been built for us at Dartmoor ! " L'hôtel Français, et Pension," we used to call it, for you understand that we were all brave men there, and that we did not lose our spirits because we were in adversity.

It was only those officers who refused to give their parole who were confined at Dartmoor, and most of the prisoners were seamen, or from the ranks. You ask me, perhaps, why it was that I did not give this parole, and so enjoy the same good treatment as most of my brother officers. Well, I had two reasons, and both of them were sufficiently strong.

In the first place, I had so much confidence in myself, that I was quite convinced that I could escape. In the second, my family, though of good repute, has never been wealthy, and I could not bring myself to take anything from the small income of my mother. On the other hand, it would never do for a man like me to be outshone by the bourgeois society of an English country town, or to be without the means of showing courtesies and attentions to those ladies whom I should attract. It was for these reasons that I preferred to be buried in the dreadful prison of Dartmoor. I wish now to tell you of my adventures in England, and how far Milor Wellington's words were true when he said that his King would hold me.

And first of all I may say that if it were not that I have set off to tell you about what befell myself, I could keep you here until morning with my stories about Dartmoor itself, and about the singular things which occurred there. It was one of the very strangest places in the whole world, for there, in the middle of that great desolate waste, were herded together seven or eight thousand men—warriors, you understand, men of experience and courage. Around there were a double wall and a ditch, and warders and soldiers ; but, my faith ! you could not coop men like that up like rabbits in a hutch ! They would escape by twos and tens and twenties, and then the cannon would boom, and the search parties run, and we, who were left behind, would laugh and dance and shout " Vive l'Empereur " until the warders would turn their muskets upon us in their passion. And then we would have our little mutinies, too, and up would come the infantry and

the guns from Plymouth, and that would set us yelling
" Vive l'Empereur " once more, as though we wished
them to hear us in Paris. We had lively moments at
Dartmoor, and we contrived that those who were about
us should be lively also.

You must know that the prisoners there had their own
Courts of Justice, in which they tried their own cases,
and inflicted their own punishments. Stealing and
quarrelling were punished—but most of all treachery.
When I came there first there was a man, Meunier, from
Rheims, who had given information of some plot to
escape. Well, that night, owing to some form or other
which had to be gone through, they did not take him out
from among the other prisoners, and though he wept and
screamed, and grovelled upon the ground, they left him
there amongst the comrades whom he had betrayed.
That night there was a trial with a whispered accusation
and a whispered defence, a gagged prisoner, and a judge
whom none could see. In the morning, when they came
for their man with papers for his release, there was not
as much of him left as you could put upon your thumb-
nail. They were ingenious people, these prisoners, and
they had their own way of managing.

We officers, however, lived in a separate wing, and a
very singular group of people we were. They had left
us our uniforms, so that there was hardly a corps which
had served under Victor, or Massena, or Ney, which was
not represented there, and some had been there from the
time when Junot was beaten at Vimiera. We had
chasseurs in their green tunics, and hussars, like myself,
and blue-coated dragoons, and white-fronted lancers, and
voltigeurs, and grenadiers, and men of the artillery
and engineers. But the greater part were naval officers,
for the English had had the better of us upon the seas.
I could never understand this until I journeyed myself
from Oporto to Plymouth, when I lay for seven days
upon my back, and could not have stirred had I seen the
eagle of the regiment carried off before my eyes. It was

in perfidious weather like this that Nelson took advantage of us.

I had no sooner got into Dartmoor than I began to plan to get out again, and you can readily believe that, with wits sharpened by twelve years of warfare, it was not very long before I saw my way.

You must know, in the first place, that I had a very great advantage in having some knowledge of the English language. I learned it during the months that I spent before Danzig, from Adjutant Obriant, of the Regiment Irlandais, who was sprung from the ancient kings of the country. I was quickly able to speak it with some facility, for I do not take long to master anything to which I set my mind. In three months I could not only express my meaning, but I could use the idioms of the people. It was Obriant who taught me to say " Be jabers," just as we might say " Ma foi " ; and also " The curse of Crummle ! " which means " Ventre bleu ! " Many a time I have seen the English smile with pleasure when they have heard me speak so much like one of themselves.

We officers were put two in a cell, which was very little to my taste, for my room-mate was a tall, silent man named Beaumont, of the Flying Artillery, who had been taken by the English cavalry at Astorga.

It is seldom I meet a man of whom I cannot make a friend, for my disposition and manners are—as you know them. But this fellow had never a smile for my jests, nor an ear for my sorrows, but would sit looking at me with his sullen eyes, until sometimes I thought that his two years of captivity had driven him crazy. Ah, how I longed that old Bouvet, or any of my comrades of the hussars, was there, instead of this mummy of a man. But such as he was I had to make the best of him, and it was very evident that no escape could be made unless he were my partner in it, for what could I possibly do without him observing me ? I hinted at it, therefore, and then by degrees I spoke more plainly, until it seemed to me that I had prevailed upon him to share my lot.

I tried the walls, and I tried the floor, and I tried the ceiling, but though I tapped and probed, they all appeared to be very thick and solid. The door was of iron, shutting with a spring lock, and provided with a small grating, through which a warder looked twice in every night. Within there were two beds, two stools, two washstands —nothing more. It was enough for my wants, for when had I had as much during those twelve years spent in camps ? But how was I to get out ? Night after night I thought of my five hundred hussars, and had dreadful nightmares, in which I fancied that the whole regiment needed shoeing, or that my horses were all bloated with green fodder, or that they were foundered from bogland, or that six squadrons were clubbed in the presence of the Emperor. Then I would awake in a cold sweat, and set to work picking and tapping at the walls once more ; for I knew very well that there is no difficulty which cannot be overcome by a ready brain and a pair of cunning hands.

There was a single window in our cell, which was too small to admit a child. It was further defended by a thick iron bar in the centre. It was not a very promising point of escape, as you will allow, but I became more and more convinced that our efforts must be directed towards it. To make matters worse, it only led out into the exercise yard, which was surrounded by two high walls. Still, as I said to my sullen comrade, it is time to talk of the Vistula when you are over the Rhine. I got a small piece of iron, therefore, from the fittings of my bed, and I set to work to loosen the plaster at the top and the bottom of the bar. Three hours I would work, and then leap into my bed upon the sound of the warder's step. Then another three hours, and then very often another yet, for I found that Beaumont was so slow and clumsy at it that it was on myself only that I could rely.

I pictured to myself my Third of Hussars waiting just outside that window, with kettledrums and standards and leopard-skin shabracks all complete. Then I would work like a madman, until my iron was crusted with blood, as if with rust. And so, night by night, I loosened that stony plaster, and hid it away in the stuffing of my pillow, until the hour came when the iron shook ; and then with one good wrench it came off in my hand, and my first step had been made towards freedom.

You will ask me what better off I was, since, as I have said, a child could not have fitted through the opening. I will tell you. I had gained two things—a tool and a weapon. With the one I might loosen the stone which flanked the window. With the other I might defend myself when I had scrambled through. So now I turned my attention to that stone, and I picked and picked with the sharpened end of my bar until I had worked out the mortar all round. You understand, of course, that during the day I replaced everything in its position, and that the warder was never permitted to see a speck upon the floor. At the end of three weeks I had separated the stone, and had the rapture of drawing it through, and seeing a hole left with ten stars shining through it, where there had been but four before. All was ready for us now, and I replaced the stone, smearing the edges of it round with a little fat and soot, so as to hide the cracks where the mortar should have been. In three nights the moon would be gone, and that seemed the best time for our attempt.

I had now no doubt at all about getting into the yard, but I had very considerable misgivings as to how I was to get out again. It would be too humiliating, after trying here, and trying there, to have to go back to my hole again in despair, or to be arrested by the guards outside, and thrown into those damp underground cells which are reserved for prisoners who are caught in escaping. I set to work, therefore, to plan what I should do. I have never, as you know, had the chance of showing what I could do as a general. Sometimes, after a glass or two of wine, I have found myself capable of thinking out surprising combinations, and have felt that if Napoleon had entrusted me with an army corps, things might have gone differently with him. But however that may be, there is no doubt that in the small stratagems of war, and in that quickness of invention which is so necessary for an officer of light cavalry, I could hold my own against anyone. It was now that I had need of it, and I felt sure that it would not fail me.

The inner wall which I had to scale was built of bricks, twelve feet high, with a row of iron spikes, three inches apart, upon the top. The outer I had only caught a glimpse of once or twice, when the gate of the exercise yard was open. It appeared to be about the same height, and was also spiked at the top. The space between the walls was over twenty feet, and I had reason to believe that there were no sentries there, except at the gates. On the other hand, I knew that there was a line of soldiers outside. Behold the little nut, my friends, which I had to open with no crackers, save these two hands.

One thing upon which I relied was the height of my comrade Beaumont. I have already said that he was a very tall man, six feet at least, and it seemed to me that if I could mount upon his shoulders, and get my hands upon the spikes, I could easily scale the wall. Could I pull my big companion up after me ? That was the question, for when I set forth with a comrade, even though it be one for whom I bear no affection, nothing on earth would make me abandon him. If I climbed the wall and he could not follow me, I should be compelled to return to him. He did not seem to concern himself much about it, however, so I hoped that he had confidence in his own activity.

Then another very important matter was the choice of the sentry who should be on duty in front of my window at the time of our attempt. They were changed every two hours to ensure their vigilance, but I, who watched them closely each night out of my window, knew that there was a great difference between them. There were some who were so keen that a rat could not cross the yard unseen, while others thought only of their own ease, and could sleep as soundly leaning upon a musket as if they were at home upon a feather bed. There was one especially, a fat, heavy man, who would retire into the shadow of the wall and doze so comfortably during his two hours, that I have dropped pieces of plaster from my window at his very feet, without his observing it. By good luck, this fellow's watch was due from twelve to two upon the night which we had fixed upon for our enterprise.

As the last day passed, I was so filled with nervous agitation that I could not control myself, but ran ceaselessly about my cell, like a mouse in a cage. Every moment I thought that the warder would detect the looseness of the bar, or that the sentry would observe the unmortared stone, which I could not conceal outside, as I did within. As for my companion, he sat brooding upon the end of his bed, looking at me in a sidelong fashion from time to time, and biting his nails like one who is deep in thought.

" Courage, my friend ! " I cried, slapping him upon the shoulder. " You will see your guns before another month be past."

" That is very well," said he. " But whither will you fly when you get free ? "

" To the coast," I answered. " All comes right for a brave man, and I shall make straight for my regiment."

" You are more likely to make straight for the underground cells, or for the Portsmouth hulks," said he.

" A soldier takes his chances," I remarked. " It is only the poltroon who reckons always upon the worst."

I raised a flush in each of his sallow cheeks at that, and I was glad of it, for it was the first sign of spirit which I had ever observed in him. For a moment he put his hand out towards his water-jug, as though he would have hurled it at me, but then he shrugged his shoulders and sat in silence once more, biting his nails, and scowling down at the floor. I could not but think, as I looked at him, that perhaps I was doing the Flying Artillery a very bad service by bringing him back to them.

I never in my life have known an evening pass as slowly as that one. Towards nightfall a wind sprang up, and as the darkness deepened it blew harder and harder, until a terrible gale was whistling over the moor. As I looked out of my window I could not catch a glimpse of a star, and the black clouds were flying low across the heavens. The rain was pouring down, and what with its hissing and splashing, and the howling and screaming of the wind, it was impossible for me to hear the steps of the sentinels. " If I cannot hear them," thought I, " then it is unlikely that they can hear me "; and I waited with the utmost impatience until the time when the inspector should have come round for his nightly peep through our grating. Then, having peered through the darkness, and seen nothing of the sentry, who was doubtless crouching in some corner out of the rain, I felt that the moment was come. I removed the bar, pulled out the stone, and motioned to my companion to pass through.

" After you, Colonel," said he.

" Will you not go first ? " I asked.

" I had rather you showed me the way."

" Come after me, then, but come silently, as you value your life."

In the darkness I could hear the fellow's teeth chattering, and I wondered whether a man ever had such a partner in a desperate enterprise. I seized the bar, however, and mounting upon my stool, I thrust my head and shoulders into the hole. I had wriggled through as far as my waist, when my companion seized me suddenly by the knees, and yelled at the top of his voice : " Help ! Help ! A prisoner is escaping ! "

Ah, my friends, what did I not feel at that moment ! Of course, I saw in an instant the game of this vile creature. Why should he risk his skin in climbing walls when he might be sure of a free pardon from the English for having prevented the escape of one so much more distinguished than himself ? I had recognised him as a poltroon and a sneak, but I had not understood the depth of baseness to which he could descend. One who has spent his life among gentlemen and men of honour does not think of such things until they happen.

The blockhead did not seem to understand that he was lost more certainly than I. I writhed back in the darkness, and seizing him by the throat, I struck him twice with my iron bar. At the first blow he yelped as a little cur does when you tread upon its paw. At the second, down he fell with a groan upon the floor. Then I seated myself upon my bed, and waited resignedly for whatever punishment my gaolers might inflict upon me.

But a minute passed and yet another, with no sound save the heavy, snoring breathing of the senseless wretch upon the floor. Was it possible, then, that amid the fury of the storm his warning cries had passed unheeded ? At first it was but a tiny hope, another minute and it was probable, another and it was certain. There was no sound in the corridor, none in the courtyard. I wiped the cold sweat from my brow, and asked myself what I should do next.

One thing seemed certain. The man on the floor must die. If I left him I could not tell how short a time it might be before he gave the alarm. I dare not strike a light, so I felt about in the darkness until my hand came upon something wet, which I knew to be his head. I raised my iron bar, but there was something, my friends, which prevented me from bringing it down. In the heat of fight I have slain many men—men of honour, too, who had done me no injury. Yet here was this wretch, a creature too foul to live, who had tried to work me so great a mischief, and yet I could not bring myself to crush his skull in. Such deeds are very well for a Spanish partida—or for that matter a sansculotte of the Faubourg St. Antoine—but not for a soldier and a gentleman like me.

However, the heavy breathing of the fellow made me hope that it might be a very long time before he recovered his senses. I gagged him, therefore, and bound him with strips of blankets to the bed, so that in his weakened condition there was good reason to think that, in any case, he might not get free before the next visit of the warder. But now again I was faced with new difficulties, for you will remember that I had relied upon his height to help me over the walls. I could have sat down and shed tears of despair had not the thought of my mother and of the Emperor come to sustain me. " Courage ! " said I. " If it were anyone but Étienne Gerard he would be in a bad fix now ; that is a young man who is not so easily caught."

I set to work therefore upon Beaumont's sheet as well as my own, and by tearing them into strips and then plaiting them together, I made a very excellent rope. This I tied securely to the centre of my iron bar, which was a little over a foot in length. Then I slipped out into the yard, where the rain was pouring and the wind screaming louder than ever. I kept in the shadow of the prison wall, but it was as black as the ace of spades, and I could not see my own hand in front of me. Unless I walked into the sentinel I felt that I had nothing to fear from him. When I had come under the wall I threw up my bar, and to my joy it stuck the very first time between the spikes at the top. I climbed up my rope, pulled it after me, and dropped down on the other side. Then I scaled the second wall, and was sitting astride among the spikes upon the top, when I saw something twinkle in the darkness beneath me. It was the bayonet of the sentinel below, and so close was it (the second wall being rather lower than the first) that I could easily, by leaning over, have unscrewed it from its socket. There he was, humming a tune to himself, and cuddling up against the wall to keep himself warm, little thinking that a desperate man within a few feet of him was within an ace of stabbing him to the heart with his own weapon. I was already bracing myself for the spring when the fellow, with an oath, shouldered his musket, and I heard his steps squelching through the mud as he resumed his beat. I slipped down my rope, and, leaving it hanging, I ran at the top of my speed across the moor.

Heavens, how I ran! The wind buffeted my face and buzzed in my nostrils. The rain pringled upon my skin and hissed past my ears. I stumbled into holes. I tripped over bushes. I fell among brambles. I was torn and breathless and bleeding. My tongue was like leather, my feet like lead, and my heart beating like a kettle-drum. Still I ran, and I ran, and I ran.

But I had not lost my head, my friends. Everything was done with a purpose. Our fugitives always made for the coast. I was determined to go inland, and the more so as I had told Beaumont the opposite. I would fly to the north, and they would seek me in the south. Perhaps you will ask me how I could tell which was which on such a night. I answer that it was by the wind. I had observed in the prison that it came from the north, and so, as long as I kept my face to it, I was going in the right direction.

Well, I was rushing along in this fashion when, suddenly, I saw two yellow lights shining out of the darkness in front of me. I paused for a moment, uncertain what I should do. I was still in my hussar uniform, you understand, and it seemed to me that the very first thing that I should aim at was to get some dress which should not betray me. If these lights came from a cottage, it was probable enough that I might find what I wanted there. I approached, therefore, feeling very sorry that I had left my iron bar behind ; for I was determined to fight to the death before I should be retaken.

But very soon I found that there was no cottage there. The lights were two lamps hung upon each side of a carriage, and by their glare I saw that a broad road lay in front of me. Crouching among the bushes, I observed that there were two horses to the equipage, that a small post-boy was standing at their heads, and that one of the wheels was lying in the road beside him. I can see them now, my friends : the steaming creatures, the stunted lad with his hands to their bits, and the big, black coach, all shining with the rain, and balanced upon its three wheels. As I looked, the window was lowered, and a pretty little face under a bonnet peeped out from it.

" What shall I do ? " the lady cried to the post-boy, in a voice of despair. " Sir Charles is certainly lost, and I shall have to spend the night upon the moor."

" Perhaps I can be of some assistance to madame," said I, scrambling out from among the bushes into the glare of the lamps. A woman in distress is a sacred thing to me, and this one was beautiful. You must not forget that, although I was a colonel, I was only eight-and-twenty years of age.

My word, how she screamed, and how the post-boy stared ! You will understand that after that long race in the darkness, with my shako broken in, my face smeared with dirt, and my uniform all stained and torn with brambles, I was not entirely the sort of gentleman whom one would choose to meet in the middle of a lonely moor. Still, after the first surprise, she soon understood that I was her very humble servant, and I could even read in her pretty eyes that my manner and bearing had not failed to produce an impression upon her.

" I am sorry to have startled you, madame," said I. " I chanced to overhear your remark, and I could not refrain from offering you my assistance." I bowed as I spoke. You know my bow, and can realise what its effect was upon the lady.

" I am much indebted to you, sir," said she. " We have had a terrible journey since we left Tavistock. Finally, one of our wheels came off, and here we are helpless in the middle of the moor. My husband, Sir Charles, has gone on to get help, and I much fear that he must have lost his way."

I was about to attempt some consolation, when I saw

beside the lady a black travelling coat, faced with astrakhan, which her companion must have left behind him. It was exactly what I needed to conceal my uniform. It is true that I felt very much like a highway robber, but then, what would you have ? Necessity has no law, and I was in an enemy's country.

" I presume, madame, that this is your husband's coat," I remarked. " You will, I am sure, forgive me, if I am compelled to——" I pulled it through the window as I spoke.

I could not bear to see the look of surprise and fear and disgust which came over her face.

" Oh, I have been mistaken in you ! " she cried. " You came to rob me, then, and not to help me. You have the bearing of a gentleman, and yet you steal my husband's coat."

" Madame," said I, " I beg that you will not condemn me until you know everything. It is quite necessary that I should take this coat, but if you will have the goodness to tell me who it is who is fortunate enough to be your husband, I shall see that the coat is sent back to him."

Her face softened a little, though she still tried to look severe. " My husband," she answered, " is Sir Charles Meredith, and he is travelling to Dartmoor Prison, upon important Government business. I only ask you, sir, to go upon your way, and to take nothing which belongs to him."

" There is only one thing which belongs to him that I covet," said I.

" And you have taken it from the carriage," she cried.

" No," I answered. " It still remains there."

She laughed in her frank English way.

" If, instead of paying me compliments, you were to return my husband's coat——" she began.

" Madame," I answered, " what you ask is quite impossible. If you will allow me to come into the carriage, I will explain to you how necessary this coat is to me."

Heavens knows into what foolishness I might have plunged myself had we not, at this instant, heard a faint halloa in the distance, which was answered by a shout from the little post-boy. In the rain and the darkness, I saw a lantern some distance from us, but approaching rapidly.

" I am sorry, madame, that I am forced to leave you," said I. " You can assure your husband that I shall take every care of his coat." Hurried as I was, I ventured to pause a moment to salute the lady's hand, which she snatched through the window with an admirable pretence of being offended at my presumption. Then, as the lantern was quite close to me, and the post-boy seemed inclined to interfere with my flight, I tucked my precious overcoat under my arm, and dashed off into the darkness.

And now I set myself to the task of putting as broad a stretch of moor between the prison and myself as the remaining hours of darkness would allow. Setting my face to the wind once more, I ran until I fell from exhaustion. Then, after five minutes of panting among the heather, I made another start, until again my knees gave way beneath me. I was young and hard, with muscles of steel, and a frame which had been toughened by twelve years of camp and field. Thus I was able to keep up this wild flight for another three hours, during which I still guided myself, you understand, by keeping the wind in my face. At the end of that time I calculated that I had put nearly twenty miles between the prison and myself. Day was about to break, so I crouched down among the heather upon the top of one of those small hills which abound in that country, with the intention of hiding myself until nightfall. It was no new thing for me to sleep in the wind and the rain, so, wrapping myself up in my thick warm cloak, I soon sank into a doze.

But it was not a refreshing slumber. I tossed and

tumbled amid a series of vile dreams, in which everything seemed to go wrong with me. At last, I remember, I was charging an unshaken square of Hungarian Grenadiers, with a single squadron upon spent horses, just as I did at Elchingen. I stood in my stirrups to shout "Vive l'Empereur!" and as I did so, there came the answering roar from my hussars, "Vive l'Empereur!" I sprang from my rough bed, with the words still ringing in my ears, and then, as I rubbed my eyes, and wondered if I were mad, the same cry came again, five thousand voices in one long-drawn yell. I looked out from my screen of brambles, and saw in the clear light of morning the very last thing that I should either have expected or chosen.

It was Dartmoor Prison! There it stretched, grim and hideous, within a furlong of me. Had I run on for a few more minutes in the dark, I should have butted my shako against the wall. I was so taken aback at the sight, that I could scarcely realise what had happened. Then it all became clear to me, and I struck my head with my hands in my despair. The wind had veered from north to south during the night, and I, keeping my face always towards it, had run ten miles out and ten miles in, winding up where I had started. When I thought of my hurry, my falls, my mad rushing and jumping, all ending in this, it seemed so absurd, that my grief changed suddenly to amusement, and I fell among the brambles, and laughed, and laughed, until my sides were sore. Then I rolled myself up in my cloak and considered seriously what I should do.

One lesson which I have learned in my roaming life, my friends, is never to call anything a misfortune until you have seen the end of it. Is not every hour a fresh point of view? In this case I soon perceived that accident had done for me as much as the most profound cunning. My guards naturally commenced their search from the place where I had taken Sir Charles Meredith's coat, and from my hiding-place I could see them hurrying along the road to that point. Not one of them ever dreamed that I could have doubled back from there, and I lay quite undisturbed in the little bush-covered cup at the summit of my knoll. The prisoners had, of course, learned of my escape, and all day exultant yells, like that which had aroused me in the morning, resounded over the moor, bearing a welcome message of sympathy and companionship to my ears. How little did they dream that on the top of that very mound, which they could see from their windows, was lying the comrade whose escape they were celebrating? As for me—I could look down upon this poor herd of idle warriors, as they paced about the great exercise yard, or gathered in little groups, gesticulating joyfully over my success. Once I heard a howl of execration, and I saw Beaumont, his head all covered with bandages, being led across the yard by two of the warders. I cannot tell you the pleasure which this sight gave me, for it proved that I had not killed him, and also that the others knew the true story of what had passed. They had all known me too well to think that I could have abandoned him.

All that long day I lay behind my screen of bushes, listening to the bells which struck the hours below. My pockets were filled with bread which I had saved out of my allowance, and on searching my borrowed overcoat I came upon a silver flask, full of excellent brandy and water, so that I was able to get through the day without hardship. The only other things in the pockets were a red silk handkerchief, a tortoise-shell snuff-box, and a blue envelope, with a red seal, addressed to the Governor of Dartmoor Prison. As to the first two, I determined to send them back when I should return the coat itself.

The letter caused me more perplexity, for the Governor had always shown me every courtesy, and it offended my sense of honour that I should interfere with his correspondence. I had almost made up my mind to leave it under a stone upon the roadway within musket-shot of the gate. This would guide them in their search for me, however, and so, on the whole, I saw no better way than just to carry the letter with me in the hope that I might find some means of sending it back to him. Meanwhile I packed it safely away in my innermost pocket.

There was a warm sun to dry my clothes, and when night fell I was ready for my journey. I promise you that there were no mistakes this time. I took the stars for my guides, as every hussar should be taught to do, and I put eight good leagues between myself and the prison. My plan now was to obtain a complete suit of clothes from the first person whom I could waylay, and I should then find my way to the north coast, where there were many smugglers and fishermen who would be ready to earn the reward which was paid by the Emperor to those who brought escaping prisoners across the Channel. I had taken the panache from my shako so that it might escape notice, but even with my fine overcoat I feared that sooner or later my uniform would betray me. My first care must be to provide myself with a complete disguise.

When day broke, I saw a river upon my right and a small town upon my left—the blue smoke reeking up above the moor. I should have liked well to have entered it, because it would have interested me to see something of the customs of the English, which differ very much from those of other nations. Much as I should have wished, however, to have seen them eat their raw meat and sell their wives, it would have been dangerous until I had got rid of my uniform. My cap, my moustache and my speech would all help to betray me. I continued to travel towards the north therefore, looking about me continually, but never catching a glimpse of my pursuers.

About mid-day I came to where, in a secluded valley, there stood a single small cottage without any other building in sight. It was a neat little house, with a rustic porch and a small garden in front of it, with a swarm of cocks and hens. I lay down among the ferns and watched it, for it seemed to be exactly the kind of place where I might obtain what I wanted. My bread was finished, and I was exceedingly hungry after my long journey ; I determined, therefore, to make a short recon-naissance, and then to march up to this cottage, summon it to surrender, and help myself to all that I needed. It could at least provide me with a chicken and with an omelette. My mouth watered at the thought.

As I lay there, wondering who could live in this lonely place, a brisk little fellow came out through the porch, accompanied by another older man, who carried two large clubs in his hands. These he handed to his young companion, who swung them up and down, and round and round, with extraordinary swiftness. The other, standing beside him, appeared to watch him with great attention, and occasionally to advise him. Finally he took a rope, and began skipping like a girl, the other still gravely observing him. As you may think, I was utterly puzzled as to what these people could be, and could only surmise that the one was a doctor, and the other a patient who had submitted himself to some singular method of treatment.

Well, as I lay watching and wondering, the older man brought out a great-coat, and held it while the other put it on and buttoned it to his chin. The day was a warmish one, so that this proceeding amazed me even more than the other. " At least," thought I, " it is evident that his exercise is over " ; but, far from this being so, the man began to run, in spite of his heavy coat, and as it chanced, he came right over the moor in my direction. His companion had re-entered the house, so that this arrangement suited me admirably. I would take the small man's clothing, and hurry on to some village where I could buy provisions. The chickens were certainly tempting, but still there were at least two men in the house, so perhaps it would be wiser for me, since I had no arms, to keep away from it.

I lay quietly then among the ferns. Presently I heard

the steps of the runner, and there he was quite close to me, with his huge coat, and the perspiration running down his face. He seemed to be a very solid man—but small—so small that I feared that his clothes might be of little use to me. When I jumped out upon him he stopped running, and looked at me in the greatest astonishment."

" Blow my dickey," said he, " give it a name, guv'nor ! Is it a circus, or what ? "

That was how he talked, though I cannot pretend to tell you what he meant by it.

" You will excuse me, sir," said I, " but I am under the necessity of asking you to give me your clothes."

" Give you what ? " he cried.

" Your clothes."

" Well, if this don't lick cock-fighting ! " said he. " What am I to give you my clothes for ? "

" Because I need them."

" And suppose I won't ? "

" Be jabers," said I, " I shall have no choice but to take them."

He stood with his hands in the pockets of his great-coat, and a most amused smile upon his square-jawed, clean-shaven face.

" You'll take them, will you ? " said he. " You're a very leery cove, by the look of you, but I can tell you that you've got the wrong sow by the ear this time. I know who you are. You're a runaway Frenchy, from the prison yonder, as anyone could tell with half an eye. But you don't know who I am, else you wouldn't try such a plant as that. Why, man, I'm the Bristol Bustler, nine stone champion, and them's my training quarters down yonder."

He stared at me as if this announcement of his would have crushed me to the earth, but I smiled at him in my turn, and looked him up and down, with a twirl of my moustache.

" You may be a very brave man, sir," said I, " but when I tell you that you are opposed to Colonel Étienne Gerard, of the Hussars of Conflans, you will see the necessity of giving up your clothes without further parley."

" Look here, mounseer, drop it ! " he cried ; " this'll end by your getting pepper."

" Your clothes, sir, this instant ! " I shouted, advancing fiercely upon him.

For answer he threw off his heavy great-coat, and stood in a singular attitude, with one arm out, and the other across his chest, looking at me with a curious smile. For myself, I knew nothing of the methods of fighting which these people have, but on horse or on foot, with arms or without them, I am always ready to take my own part. You understand that a soldier cannot always choose his own methods, and that it is time to howl when you are living among wolves. I rushed at him, therefore, with a warlike shout, and kicked him with both my feet. At the same moment my heels flew into the air, I saw as many flashes as at Austerlitz, and the back of my head came down with a crash upon a stone. After that I can remember nothing more.

When I came to myself I was lying upon a truckle-bed, in a bare, half-furnished room. My head was ringing like a bell, and when I put up my hand, there was a lump like a walnut over one of my eyes. My nose was full of a pungent smell, and I soon found that a strip of paper soaked in vinegar was fastened across my brow. At the other end of the room this terrible little man was sitting with his knee bare, and his elderly companion was rubbing it with some liniment. The latter seemed to be in the worst of tempers, and he kept up a continual scolding, which the other listened to with a gloomy face.

" Never heard tell of such a thing in my life," he was saying. " In training for a month with all the weight of it on my shoulders, and then when I get you as fit as a trout, and within two days of fighting the likeliest man on the list, you let yourself into a bye-battle with a foreigner."

" There, there ! Stow your gab ! " said the other, sulkily. " You're a very good trainer, Jim, but you'd be better with less jaw."

" I should think it was time to jaw," the elderly man answered. " If this knee don't get well before next Wednesday, they'll have it that you fought a cross, and a pretty job you'll have next time you look for a backer."

" Fought a cross ! " growled the other. " I've won nineteen battles, and no man ever so much as dared to say the word ' cross ' in my hearin'. How the deuce was I to get out of it when the cove wanted the very clothes off my back ? "

" Tut, man ; you knew that the beak and the guards were within a mile of you. You could have set them on to him as well then as now. You'd have got your clothes back again all right."

" Well, strike me ! " said the Bustler. " I don't often break my trainin', but when it comes to givin' up my clothes to a Frenchy who couldn't hit a dint in a pat o' butter, why, it's more than I can swaller."

" Pooh, man, what are the clothes worth ? D'you know that Lord Rufton alone has five thousand pounds on you ? When you jump the ropes on Wednesday, you'll carry every penny of fifty thousand into the ring. A pretty thing to turn up with a swollen knee and a story about a Frenchman ! "

" I never thought he'd ha' kicked," said the Bustler.

" I suppose you expected he'd fight Broughton's rules, and strict P.R. ? Why, you silly, they don't know what fighting is in France."

" My friends," said I, sitting up on my bed, " I do not understand very much of what you say, but when you speak like that it is foolishness. We know so much about fighting in France, that we have paid our little visit to nearly every capital in Europe, and very soon we are coming to London. But we fight like soldiers, you understand, and not like gamins in the gutter. You strike me on the head. I kick you on the knee. It is child's play. But if you will give me a sword, and take another one, I will show you how we fight over the water."

They both stared at me in their solid, English way.

" Well, I'm glad you're not dead, mounseer," said the elder one at last. " There wasn't much sign of life in you when the Bustler and me carried you down. That head of yours ain't thick enough to stop the crook of the hardest hitter in Bristol."

" He's a game cove, too, and he came for me like a bantam," said the other, still rubbing his knee. " I got my old left-right in, and he went over as if he had been pole-axed. It wasn't my fault, mounseer. I told you you'd get pepper if you went on."

" Well, it's something to say all your life, that you've been handled by the finest light-weight in England," said the older man, looking at me with an expression of congratulation upon his face. " You've had him at his best, too—in the pink of condition, and trained by Jim Hunter."

" I am used to hard knocks," said I, unbuttoning my tunic, and showing my two musket wounds. Then I bared my ankle also, and showed the place in my eye where the guerrilla had stabbed me.

" He can take his gruel," said the Bustler.

" What a glutton he'd have made for the middle-weights," remarked the trainer ; "with six months' coaching he'd astonish the Fancy. It's a pity he's got to go back to prison."

I did not like that last remark at all. I buttoned up my coat and rose from the bed.

" I must ask you to let me continue my journey," said I.

" There's no help for it, mounseer," the trainer answered. " It's a hard thing to send such a man as you back to such a place, but business is business, and there's a twenty-pound reward. They were here this morning, looking for you, and I expect they'll be round again."

His words turned my heart to lead.

"Surely, you would not betray me!" I cried. "I will send you twice twenty pounds on the day that I set foot upon France. I swear it upon the honour of a French gentleman."

But I only got head-shakes for a reply. I pleaded, I argued, I spoke of the English hospitality and the fellowship of brave men, but I might as well have been addressing the two great wooden clubs which stood balanced upon the floor in front of me. There was no sign of sympathy upon their bull-faces.

"Business is business, mounseer," the old trainer repeated. "Besides, how am I to put the Bustler into the ring on Wednesday if he's jugged by the beak for aidin' and abettin' a prisoner of war? I've got to look after the Bustler, and I take no risks."

This, then, was the end of all my struggles and strivings. I was to be led back again like a poor silly sheep who has broken through the hurdles. They little knew me who could fancy that I should submit to such a fate. I had heard enough to tell me where the weak point of these two men was, and I showed, as I have often showed before, that Étienne Gerard is never so terrible as when all hope seems to have deserted him. With a single spring I seized one of the clubs and swung it over the head of the Bustler.

"Come what may," I cried, "*you* shall be spoiled for Wednesday."

The fellow growled out an oath, and would have sprung at me, but the other flung his arms round him and pinned him to the chair.

"Not if I know it, Bustler," he screamed. "None of your games while I am by. Get away out of this, Frenchy. We only want to see your back. Run away, run away, or he'll get loose!"

It was good advice, I thought, and I ran to the door, but

as I came out into the open air my head swam round and I had to lean against the porch to save myself from falling. Consider all that I had been through, the anxiety of my escape, the long, useless flight in the storm, the day spent amid wet ferns, with only bread for food, the second journey by night, and now the injuries which I had received in attempting to deprive the little man of his clothes. Was it wonderful that even I should reach the limits of my endurance ?

I stood there in my heavy coat and my poor battered shako, my chin upon my chest, and my eyelids over my eyes. I had done my best, and I could do no more. It was the sound of horses' hoofs which made me at last raise my head, and there was the grey-moustached Governor of Dartmoor prison not ten paces in front of me, with six mounted warders behind him !

" So, Colonel," said he, with a bitter smile, " we have found you once more."

When a brave man has done his utmost, and has failed, he shows his breeding by the manner in which he accepts his defeat. For me, I took the letter which I had in my pocket, and stepping forward, I handed it, with such grace of manner as I could summon, to the Governor.

" It has been my misfortune, sir, to detain one of your letters," said I.

He looked at me in amazement, and beckoned to the warders to arrest me. Then he broke the seal of the letter. I saw a curious expression come over his face as he read it.

" This must be the letter which Sir Charles Meredith lost," said he.

" It was in the pocket of his coat."

" You have carried it for two days ? "

" Since the night before last."

" And never looked at the contents ? "

I showed him by my manner that he had committed an indiscretion in asking a question which one gentleman should not have put to another.

To my surprise he burst out into a roar of laughter.

" Colonel," he said, wiping the tears from his eyes, " you have really given both yourself and us a great deal of unnecessary trouble. Allow me to read the letter which you carried with you in your flight."

And this was what I heard :

" On receipt of this you are directed to release Colonel Étienne Gerard, of the 3rd Hussars, who has been exchanged against Colonel Mason, of the Horse Artillery, now in Verdun."

And as he read it, he laughed again, and the warders laughed, and the two men from the cottage laughed, and then, as I heard this universal merriment, and thought of all my hopes and fears, and my struggles and dangers, what could a debonair soldier do but lean against the porch once more, and laugh as heartily as any of them ? And of them all was it not I who had the best reason to laugh, since in front of me I could see my dear France, and my mother, and the Emperor, and my horsemen ; while behind lay the gloomy prison, and the heavy hand of the English King ?

5. *How the Brigadier took the Field against the Marshal Millefleurs*

MASSENA was a thin, sour little fellow, and after his hunting accident he had only one eye, but when it looked out from under his cocked hat there was not much upon a field of battle which escaped it. He could stand in front of a battalion, and with a single sweep tell you if a buckle or a gaiter button were out of place. Neither the officers nor the men were very fond of him, for he was, as you know, a miser, and soldiers love that their leaders should be free-handed. At the same time, when it came to work they had a very high respect for him, and they would rather fight under him than under anyone except the Emperor himself, and

Lannes, when he was alive. After all, if he had a tight grasp upon his money-bags, there was a day also, you must remember, when that same grip was upon Zurich and Genoa. He clutched on to his positions as he did to his strong box, and it took a very clever man to loosen him from either.

When I received his summons I went gladly to his head-quarters, for I was always a great favourite of his, and there was no officer of whom he thought more highly. That was the best of serving with those good old generals, that they knew enough to be able to pick out a fine soldier when they saw one. He was seated alone in his tent, with his chin upon his hand, and his brow as wrinkled as if he had been asked for a subscription. He smiled, however, when he saw me before him.

"Good day, Colonel Gerard."

"Good day, Marshal."

"How is the Third of Hussars ? "

"Seven hundred incomparable men upon seven hundred excellent horses."

"And your wounds—are they healed ? "

"My wounds never heal, Marshal," I answered.

"And why ? "

"Because I have always new ones."

"General Rapp must look to his laurels," said he, his face all breaking into wrinkles as he laughed. "He has had twenty-one from the enemy's bullets, and as many from Larrey's knives and probes. Knowing that you were hurt, Colonel, I have spared you of late."

"Which hurt me most of all."

"Tut, tut ! Since the English got behind these accursed lines of Torres Vedras, there has been little for us to do. You did not miss much during your imprisonment at Dartmoor. But now we are on the eve of action."

"We advance ? "

"No, retire."

My face must have shown my dismay. What, retire before this sacred dog of a Wellington—he who had listened unmoved to my words, and had sent me to his land of fogs ? I could have sobbed as I thought of it.

" What would you have ? " cried Massena, impatiently. " When one is in check, it is necessary to move the king."

" Forwards," I suggested.

He shook his grizzled head.

" The lines are not to be forced," said he. " I have already lost General St. Croix and more men than I can replace. On the other hand, we have been here at Santarem for nearly six months. There is not a pound of flour nor a jug of wine on the country-side. We must retire."

" There are flour and wine in Lisbon," I persisted.

" Tut, you speak as if an army could charge in and charge out again like your regiment of hussars. If Soult were here with thirty thousand men—but he will not come. I sent for you, however, Colonel Gerard, to say that I have a very singular and important expedition which I intend to place under your direction."

I pricked up my ears, as you can imagine. The Marshal unrolled a great map of the country and spread it upon the table. He flattened it out with his little, hairy hands.

" This is Santarem," he said, pointing.

I nodded.

" And here, twenty-five miles to the east, is Almeixal, celebrated for its vintages and for its enormous Abbey."

Again I nodded ; I could not think what was coming.

" Have you heard of the Marshal Millefleurs ? " asked Massena.

" I have served with all the Marshals," said I, " but there is none of that name."

" It is but the nickname which the soldiers have given him," said Massena. " If you had not been away from us for some months, it would not be necessary for me to tell you about him. He is an Englishman, and a man of good breeding. It is on account of his manners that they have given him his title. I wish you to go to this polite Englishman at Almeixal."

"Yes, Marshal."

"And to hang him to the nearest tree."

"Certainly, Marshal."

I turned briskly upon my heels, but Massena recalled me before I could reach the opening of his tent.

"One moment, Colonel," said he ; "you had best learn how matters stand before you start. You must know, then, that this Marshal Millefleurs, whose real name is Alexis Morgan, is a man of very great ingenuity and bravery. He was an officer in the English Guards, but having been broken for cheating at cards, he left the army. In some manner he gathered a number of English deserters round him and took to the mountains. French stragglers and Portuguese brigands joined him, and he found himself at the head of five hundred men. With these he took possession of the Abbey of Almeixal, sent the monks about their business, fortified the place, and gathered in the plunder of all the country round."

"For which it is high time he was hanged," said I, making once more for the door.

"One instant !" cried the Marshal, smiling at my impatience. "The worst remains behind. Only last week the Dowager Countess of La Ronda, the richest woman in Spain, was taken by these ruffians in the passes as she was journeying from King Joseph's Court to visit her grandson. She is now a prisoner in the Abbey, and is only protected by her——"

"Grandmotherhood," I suggested.

"Her power of paying a ransom," said Massena. "You have three missions, then : To rescue this unfortunate lady ; to punish this villain ; and, if possible, to break up this nest of brigands. It will be a proof of the confidence which I have in you when I say that I can only spare you half a squadron with which to accomplish all this."

My word, I could hardly believe my ears ! I thought that I should have had my regiment at the least.

" I would give you more," said he, " but I commence my retreat to-day, and Wellington is so strong in horse that every trooper becomes of importance. I cannot spare you another man. You will see what you can do, and you will report yourself to me at Abrantes not later than to-morrow night."

It was very complimentary that he should rate my powers so high, but it was also a little embarrassing. I was to rescue an old lady, to hang an Englishman, and to break up a band of five hundred assassins—all with fifty men. But after all, the fifty men were Hussars of Conflans, and they had an Étienne Gerard to lead them. As I came out into the warm Portuguese sunshine my confidence had returned to me, and I had already begun to wonder whether the medal which I had so often deserved might not be waiting for me at Almeixal.

You may be sure that I did not take my fifty men at haphazard. They were all old soldiers of the German wars, some of them with three stripes, and most of them with two. Oudet and Papilette, two of the best sub-officers in the regiment, were at their head. When I had them formed up in fours, all in silver grey and upon chestnut horses, with their leopard skin shabracks and their little red panaches, my heart beat high at the sight. I could not look at their weather-stained faces, with the great moustaches which bristled over their chin-straps, without feeling a glow of confidence, and, between ourselves, I have no doubt that that was exactly how they felt when they saw their young Colonel on his great black war-horse riding at their head.

Well, when we got free of the camp and over the Tagus, I threw out my advance and my flankers, keeping my own place at the head of the main body. Looking back from the hills above Santarem, we could see the dark lines of Massena's army, with the flash and twinkle of the sabres and bayonets as he moved his regiments into position for their retreat. To the south lay the scattered red patches of the English outposts, and behind the grey smoke-cloud which rose from Wellington's camp—thick, oily smoke, which seemed to our poor starving fellows to bear with it the rich smell of seething camp-kettles. Away to the west lay a curve of blue sea flecked with the white sails of the English ships.

You will understand that as we were riding to the east, our road lay away from both armies. Our own marauders, however, and the scouting parties of the English, covered the country, and it was necessary with my small troop that I should take every precaution. During the whole day we rode over desolate hill-sides, the lower portions covered by the budding vines, but the upper turning from green to grey, and jagged along the skyline like the back of a starved horse. Mountain streams crossed our path running west to the Tagus, and once we came to a deep, strong river, which might have checked us had I not found the ford by observing where houses had been built opposite each other upon either bank. Between them, as every scout should know, you will find your ford. There was none to give us information, for neither man nor beast, nor any living thing except great clouds of crows, was to be seen during our journey.

The sun was beginning to sink when we came to a valley clear in the centre, but shrouded by huge oak trees upon either side. We could not be more than a few miles from Almeixal, so it seemed to me to be best to keep among the groves, for the spring had been an early one and the leaves were already thick enough to conceal us. We were riding then in open order among the great trunks, when one of my flankers came galloping up.

"There are English across the valley, Colonel," he cried, as he saluted.

"Cavalry or infantry?"

"Dragoons, Colonel," said he; "I saw the gleam of their helmets, and heard the neigh of a horse."

Halting my men I hastened to the edge of the wood.

There could be no doubt about it. A party of English cavalry was travelling in a line with us, and in the same direction. I caught a glimpse of their red coats and of their flashing arms glowing and twinkling among the tree-trunks. Once, as they passed through a small clearing, I could see their whole force, and I judged that they were of about the same strength as my own—a half squadron at the most.

You who have heard some of my little adventures will give me credit for being quick in my decisions, and prompt in carrying them out. But here I must confess that I was in two minds. On the one hand there was the chance of a fine cavalry skirmish with the English. On the other hand, there was my mission at the Abbey of Almeixal, which seemed already to be so much above my power. If I were to lose any of my men, it was certain that I should be unable to carry out my orders. I was sitting my horse, with my chin in my gauntlet, looking across at the rippling gleams of light from the further wood, when suddenly one of these red-coated Englishmen rode out from the cover, pointing at me and breaking into a shrill whoop and halloa as if I had been a fox. Three others joined him, and one who was a bugler sounded a call, which brought the whole of them into the open. They were, as I had thought, a half squadron, and they formed a double line with a front of twenty-five, their officer—the one who had whooped at me—at their head.

For my own part, I had instantly brought my own troopers into the same formation, so that there we were, hussars and dragoons, with only two hundred yards of grassy sward between us. They carried themselves well, those red-coated troopers, with their silver helmets, their high white plumes, and their long, gleaming swords ; while, on the other hand, I am sure that they would acknowledge that they had never looked upon finer light horsemen than the fifty hussars of Conflans who were facing them. They were heavier, it is true, and they may have seemed the smarter, for Wellington used to make them burnish their metal work, which was not usual among us. On the other hand, it is well known that the English tunics were too tight for the sword-arm, which gave our men an advantage. As to bravery, foolish, inexperienced people of every nation always think that their own soldiers are braver than any others. There is no nation in the world which does not entertain this idea. But when one has seen as much as I have done, one understands that there is no very marked difference, and that although nations differ very much in discipline, they are all equally brave—except that the French have rather more courage than the rest.

Well, the cork was drawn and the glasses ready, when suddenly the English officer raised his sword to me as if in a challenge, and cantered his horse across the grassland. My word, there is no finer sight upon earth than that of a gallant man upon a gallant steed ! I could have halted there just to watch him as he came with such careless grace, his sabre down by his horse's shoulder, his head thrown back, his white plume tossing—youth and strength and courage, with the violet evening sky above and the oak trees behind. But it was not for me to stand and stare. Étienne Gerard may have his faults, but, my faith, he was never accused of being backward in taking his own part. The old horse, Rataplan, knew me so well that he had started off before ever I gave the first shake to the bridle.

There are two things in this world that I am very slow to forget ; the face of a pretty woman, and the legs of a fine horse. Well, as we drew together, I kept on saying, " Where have I seen those great roan shoulders ? Where have I seen that dainty fetlock ? " Then suddenly I remembered, and as I looked up at the reckless eyes and the challenging smile, whom should I recognise but the man who had saved me from the brigands and played me for my freedom—he whose correct title was Milor the Hon. Sir Russell, Bart !

" Bart ! " I shouted.

He had his arm raised for a cut, and three parts of his body open to my point, for he did not know very much about the use of the sword. As I brought my hilt to the salute he dropped his hand and stared at me.

" Halloa ! " said he. " It's Gerard ! " You would have thought by his manner that I had met him by appointment. For my own part, I would have embraced him had he but come an inch of the way to meet me.

" I thought we were in for some sport," said he. " I never dreamed that it was you."

I found this tone of disappointment somewhat irritating. Instead of being glad at having met a friend, he was sorry at having missed an enemy.

" I should have been happy to join in your sport, my dear Bart," said I. " But I really cannot turn my sword upon a man who saved my life."

" Tut, never mind about that."

" No, it is impossible. I should never forgive myself."

" You make too much of a trifle."

" My mother's one desire is to embrace you. If ever you should be in Gascony——"

" Lord Wellington is coming there with 60,000 men."

" Then one of them will have a chance of surviving," said I, laughing. " In the meantime, put your sword in your sheath ! "

Our horses were standing head to tail, and the Bart put out his hand and patted me on the thigh.

" You're a good chap, Gerard," said he. " I only wish you had been born on the right side of the Channel."

" I was," said I.

" Poor devil ! " he cried, with such an earnestness of pity that he set me laughing again. " But look here, Gerard," he continued ; " this is all very well, but it is not business, you know. I don't know what Massena would say to it, but our Chief would jump out of his riding-boots if he saw us. We weren't sent out here for a picnic—either of us."

" What would you have ? "

" Well, we had a little argument about our hussars and dragoons, if you remember. I've got fifty of the Sixteenth all chewing their carbine bullets behind me. You've got as many fine-looking boys over yonder, who seem to be fidgeting in their saddles. If you and I took the right flanks we should not spoil each other's beauty—though a little blood-letting is a friendly thing in this climate."

There seemed to me to be a good deal of sense in what he said. For the moment Mr. Alexis Morgan and the Countess of La Ronda and the Abbey of Almeixal went right out of my head, and I could only think of the fine level turf and of the beautiful skirmish which we might have.

" Very good, Bart," said I. " We have seen the front of your dragoons. We shall now have a look at their backs."

" Any betting ? " he asked.

" The stake," said I, " is nothing less than the honour of the Hussars of Conflans."

" Well, come on ! " he answered. " If we break you, well and good—if you break us, it will be all the better for Marshal Millefleurs."

When he said that I could only stare at him in astonishment.

" Why for Marshal Millefleurs ? " I asked.

" It is the name of a rascal who lives out this way. My dragoons have been sent by Lord Wellington to see him safely hanged."

" Name of a name ! " I cried. " Why, my hussars have been sent by Massena for that very object."

We burst out laughing at that, and sheathed our swords. There was a whirr of steel from behind us as our troopers followed our example.

" We are allies ! " he cried.

" For a day."

" We must join forces."

" There is no doubt of it."

And so, instead of fighting, we wheeled our half squadrons round and moved in two little columns down the valley, the shakos and the helmets turned inwards, and the men looking their neighbours up and down, like old fighting dogs with tattered ears who have learned to respect each other's teeth. The most were on the broad grin, but there were some on either side who looked black and challenging, especially the English sergeant and my own sub-officer Papilette. They were men of habit, you see, who could not change all their ways of thinking in a moment. Besides, Papilette had lost his only brother at Busaco. As for the Bart and me, we rode together at the head and chatted about all that had occurred to us since that famous game of écarté of which I have told you.

For my own part, I spoke to him of my adventures in England. They are a very singular people, these English. Although he knew that I had been engaged in twelve campaigns, yet I am sure that the Bart thought more highly of me because I had had an affair with the Bristol Bustler. He told me, too, that the Colonel who presided over his court-martial for playing cards with a prisoner acquitted him of neglect of duty, but nearly broke him because he thought that he had not cleared his trumps before leading his suit. Yes, indeed, they are a singular people.

At the end of the valley the road curved over some rising ground before winding down into another wider valley beyond. We called a halt when we came to the top ; for there, right in front of us, at the distance of about three miles, was a scattered, grey town, with a single enormous building upon the flank of the mountain which overlooked it. We could not doubt that we were at last in sight of the Abbey that held the gang of rascals whom we had come to disperse. It was only now, I think, that we fully understood what a task lay in front of us, for the place was a veritable fortress, and it was evident that cavalry should never have been sent out upon such an errand.

"That's got nothing to do with us," said the Bart; "Wellington and Massena can settle that between them."

"Courage!" I answered. "Piré took Leipzig with fifty hussars."

"Had they been dragoons," said the Bart, laughing, "he would have had Berlin. But you are senior officer; give us a lead, and we'll see who will be the first to flinch."

"Well," said I, "whatever we do must be done at once, for my orders are to be on my way to Abrantes by to-morrow night. But we must have some information first, and here is someone who should be able to give it to us."

There was a square, whitewashed house standing by the roadside, which appeared, from the bush hanging over the door, to be one of those wayside tabernas which are provided for the muleteers. A lantern was hung in the porch, and by its light we saw two men, the one in the brown habit of a Capuchin monk, and the other girt with an apron, which showed him to be the landlord. They were conversing together so earnestly that we were upon them before they were aware of us. The innkeeper turned to fly, but one of the Englishmen seized him by the hair, and held him tight.

"For mercy's sake, spare me," he yelled. "My house has been gutted by the French, and harried by the English, and my feet have been burned by the brigands. I swear by the Virgin that I have neither money nor food in my inn, and the good Father Abbot, who is starving upon my doorstep, will be witness to it."

"Indeed, sir," said the Capuchin, in excellent French, "what this worthy man says is very true. He is one of the many victims to these cruel wars, although his loss is but a feather-weight compared to mine. Let him go," he added, in English, to the trooper, "he is too weak to fly, even if he desired to."

In the light of the lantern I saw that this monk was a magnificent man, dark and bearded, with the eyes of a hawk, and so tall that his cowl came up to Rataplan's ears. He wore the look of one who had been through much suffering, but he carried himself like a king, and we could form some opinion of his learning when we each heard him talk our own language as fluently as if he were born to it.

" You have nothing to fear," said I, to the trembling innkeeper. " As to you, father, you are, if I am not mistaken, the very man who can give us the information which we require."

" All that I have is at your service, my son. But," he added, with a wan smile, " my Lenten fare is always somewhat meagre, and this year it has been such that I must ask you for a crust of bread if I am to have the strength to answer your questions."

We bore two days' rations in our haversacks, so that he soon had the little he asked for. It was dreadful to see the wolfish way in which he seized the piece of dried goat's flesh which I was able to offer him.

" Time presses, and we must come to the point," said I. " We want your advice as to the weak points of yonder Abbey, and concerning the habits of the rascals who infest it."

He cried out something which I took to be Latin, with his hands clasped and his eyes upturned. " The prayer of the just availeth much," said he, " and yet I had not dared to hope that mine would have been so speedily answered. In me you see the unfortunate Abbot of Almeixal, who has been cast out by this rabble of three armies with their heretical leader. Oh ! to think of what I have lost ! " his voice broke, and the tears hung upon his lashes.

" Cheer up, sir," said the Bart. " I'll lay nine to four that we have you back again by to-morrow night."

" It is not of my own welfare that I think," said he, " nor even of that of my poor, scattered flock. But it is of the holy relics which are left in the sacrilegious hands of these robbers."

" It's even betting whether they would ever bother their heads about them," said the Bart. " But show us the way inside the gates, and we'll soon clear the place out for you."

In a few short words the good Abbot gave us the very points that we wished to know. But all that he said only made our task more formidable. The walls of the Abbey were forty feet high. The lower windows were barricaded, and the whole building loopholed for musketry fire. The gang preserved military discipline, and their sentries were too numerous for us to hope to take them by surprise. It was more than ever evident that a battalion of grenadiers and a couple of breaching pieces were what was needed. I raised my eyebrows, and the Bart began to whistle.

" We must have a shot at it, come what may," said he.

The men had already dismounted, and, having watered their horses, were eating their suppers. For my own part I went into the sitting-room of the inn with the Abbot and the Bart, that we might talk about our plans.

I had a little cognac in my *sauve vie*, and I divided it among us—just enough to wet our moustaches.

" It is unlikely," said I, " that those rascals know anything about our coming. I have seen no signs of scouts along the road. My own plan is that we should conceal ourselves in some neighbouring wood, and then, when they open their gates, charge down upon them and take them by surprise."

The Bart was of opinion that this was the best that we could do, but, when we came to talk it over, the Abbot made us see that there were difficulties in the way.

" Save on the side of the town, there is no place within a mile of the Abbey where you could shelter man or horse," said he. " As to the townsfolk, they are not to be trusted. I fear, my son, that your excellent plan would have little chance of success in the face of the vigilant guard which these men keep."

"I see no other way," answered I. "Hussars of Conflans are not so plentiful that I can afford to run half a squadron of them against a forty-foot wall with five hundred infantry behind it."

"I am a man of peace," said the Abbot, "and yet I may, perhaps, give a word of counsel. I know these villains and their ways. Who should do so better, seeing that I have stayed for a month in this lonely spot, looking down in weariness of heart at the Abbey which was my own? I will tell you now what I should myself do if I were in your place."

"Pray tell us, father," we cried, both together.

"You must know that bodies of deserters, both French and English, are continually coming in to them, carrying their weapons with them. Now, what is there to prevent you and your men from pretending to be such a body, and so making your way into the Abbey?"

I was amazed at the simplicity of the thing, and I embraced the good Abbot. The Bart, however, had some objections to offer.

"That is all very well," said he, "but if these fellows are as sharp as you say, it is not very likely that they are going to let a hundred armed strangers into their crib. From all I have heard of Mr. Morgan, or Marshal Millefleurs, or whatever the rascal's name is, I give him credit for more sense than that."

"Well, then," I cried, "let us send fifty in, and let them at daybreak throw open the gates to the other fifty, who will be waiting outside."

We discussed the question at great length and with much foresight and discretion. If it had been Massena and Wellington instead of two young officers of light cavalry, we could not have weighed it all with more judgment. At last we agreed, the Bart and I, that one of us should indeed go with fifty men, under pretence of being deserters, and that in the early morning he should gain command of the gate and admit the others. The Abbot, it is true, was still of opinion that it was dangerous to divide our force, but finding that we were both of the same mind, he shrugged his shoulders and gave in.

"There is only one thing that I would ask," said he. "If you lay hands upon this Marshal Millefleurs—this dog of a brigand—what will you do with him?"

"Hang him," I answered.

"It is too easy a death," cried the Capuchin, with a vindictive glow in his dark eyes. "Had I my way with him—but, oh, what thoughts are these for a servant of God to harbour!" He clapped his hands to his forehead like one who is half demented by his troubles, and rushed out of the room.

There was an important point which we had still to settle, and that was whether the French or the English party should have the honour of entering the Abbey first. My faith, it was asking a great deal of Étienne Gerard that he should give place to any man at such a time! But the poor Bart pleaded so hard, urging the few skirmishes which he had seen against my four-and-seventy engagements, that at last I consented that he should go. We had just clasped hands over the matter when there broke out such a shouting and cursing and yelling from the front of the inn, that out we rushed with our drawn sabres in our hands, convinced that the brigands were upon us.

You may imagine our feelings when, by the light of the lantern which hung from the porch, we saw a score of our hussars and dragoons all mixed in one wild heap, red coats and blue, helmets and busbies, pommelling each other to their hearts' content. We flung ourselves upon them, imploring, threatening, tugging at a lace collar, or at a spurred heel, until, at last, we had dragged them all apart. There they stood, flushed and bleeding, glaring at each other, and all panting together like a line of troop horses after a ten-mile chase. It was only with our drawn swords that we could keep them from each other's throats. The poor Capuchin stood in the porch in his long brown habit, wringing his hands and calling upon all the saints for mercy.

He was, indeed, as I found upon inquiry, the innocent cause of all the turmoil, for, not understanding how soldiers look upon such things, he had made some remark to the English sergeant that it was a pity that his squadron was not as good as the French. The words were not out of his mouth before a dragoon knocked down the nearest hussar, and then, in a moment, they all flew at each other like tigers. We would trust them no more after that, but the Bart moved his men to the front of the inn, and I mine to the back, the English all scowling and silent, and our fellows shaking their fists and chattering, each after the fashion of their own people.

Well, as our plans were made, we thought it best to carry them out at once, lest some fresh cause of quarrel should break out between our followers. The Bart and his men rode off, therefore, he having first torn the lace from his sleeves, and the gorget and sash from his uniform, so that he might pass as a simple trooper. He explained to his men what it was that was expected of them, and though they did not raise a cry or wave their weapons as mine might have done, there was an expression upon their stolid and clean-shaven faces which filled me with confidence. Their tunics were left unbuttoned, their scabbards and helmets stained with dirt, and their harness badly fastened, so that they might look the part of deserters, without order or discipline. At six o'clock next morning they were to gain command of the main gate of the Abbey, while at that same hour my hussars were to gallop up to it from outside. The Bart and I pledged our words to it before he trotted off with his detachment. My sergeant, Papilette, with two troopers, followed the English at a distance, and returned in half an hour to say that, after some parley, and the flashing of lanterns upon them from the grille, they had been admitted into the Abbey.

So far, then, all had gone well. It was a cloudy night

with a sprinkling of rain, which was in our favour, as there was the less chance of our presence being discovered. My vedettes I placed two hundred yards in every direction, to guard against a surprise, and also to prevent any peasant who might stumble upon us from carrying the news to the Abbey. Oudin and Papilette were to take turns of duty, while the others with their horses had snug quarters in a great wooden granary. Having walked round and seen that all was as it should be, I flung myself upon the bed which the innkeeper had set apart for me, and fell into a dreamless sleep.

No doubt you have heard my name mentioned as being the beau-ideal of a soldier, and that not only by friends and admirers like our fellow-townsfolk, but also by old officers of the great wars who have shared the fortunes of those famous campaigns with me. Truth and modesty compel me to say, however, that this is not so. There are some gifts which I lack—very few, no doubt—but still, amid the vast armies of the Emperor there may have been some who were free from those blemishes which stood between me and perfection. Of bravery I say nothing. Those who have seen me in the field are best fitted to speak about that. I have often heard the soldiers discussing round the camp-fires as to who was the bravest man in the Grand Army. Some said Murat and some said Lasalle, and some Ney ; but for my own part, when they asked me, I merely shrugged my shoulders and smiled. It would have seemed mere conceit if I had answered that there was no man braver than Brigadier Gerard. At the same time, facts are facts, and a man knows best what his own feelings are. But there are other gifts besides bravery which are necessary for a soldier, and one of them is that he should be a light sleeper. Now, from my boyhood onwards, I have been hard to wake, and it was this which brought me to ruin upon that night.

It may have been about two o'clock in the morning that I was suddenly conscious of a feeling of suffocation.

I tried to call out, but there was something which prevented me from uttering a sound. I struggled to rise, but I could only flounder like a hamstrung horse. I was strapped at the ankles, strapped at the knees, and strapped again at the wrists. Only my eyes were free to move, and there at the foot of my couch, by the light of a Portuguese lamp, whom should I see but the Abbot and the innkeeper !

The latter's heavy, white face had appeared to me when I looked upon it the evening before to express nothing but stupidity and terror. Now, on the contrary, every feature bespoke brutality and ferocity. Never have I seen a more dreadful-looking villain. In his hand he held a long, dull-coloured knife. The Abbot, on the other hand, was as polished and as dignified as ever. His Capuchin gown had been thrown open, however, and I saw beneath it a black, frogged coat, such as I have seen among the English officers. As our eyes met he leaned over the wooden end of the bed and laughed silently until it creaked again.

" You will, I am sure, excuse my mirth, my dear Colonel Gerard," said he. " The fact is, that the expression upon your face when you grasped the situation was just a little funny. I have no doubt that you are an excellent soldier, but I hardly think that you are fit to measure wits with the Marshal Millefleurs, as your fellows have been good enough to call me. You appear to have given me credit for singularly little intelligence, which argues, if I may be allowed to say so, a want of acuteness upon your own part. Indeed, with the single exception of my thick-headed compatriot, the British dragoon, I have never met anyone who was less competent to carry out such a mission."

You can imagine how I felt and how I looked, as I listened to this insolent harangue, which was all delivered in that flowery and condescending manner which had gained this rascal his nickname. I could say nothing, but they must have read my threat in my eyes, for the fellow who had played the part of the innkeeper whispered something to his companion.

" No, no, my dear Chenier, he will be infinitely more valuable alive," said he. " By the way, Colonel, it is just as well that you are a sound sleeper, for my friend here, who is a little rough in his ways, would certainly have cut your throat if you had raised any alarm. I should recommend you to keep in his good graces, for Sergeant Chenier, late of the 7th Imperial Light Infantry, is a much more dangerous person than Captain Alexis Morgan, of His Majesty's foot-guards."

Chenier grinned and shook his knife at me, while I tried to look the loathing which I felt at the thought that a soldier of the Emperor could fall so low.

" It may amuse you to know," said the Marshal, in that soft, suave voice of his, " that both your expeditions were watched from the time that you left your respective camps. I think that you will allow that Chenier and I played our parts with some subtlety. We had made every arrangement for your reception at the Abbey, though we had hoped to receive the whole squadron instead of half. When the gates are secured behind them, our visitors find themselves in a very charming little mediæval quadrangle, with no possible exit, commanded by musketry fire from a hundred windows. They may choose to be shot down ; or they may choose to surrender. Between ourselves, I have not the slightest doubt that they have been wise enough to do the latter. But since you are naturally interested in the matter, we thought that you would care to come with us and see for yourself. I think I can promise you that you will find your titled friend waiting for you at the Abbey with a face as long as your own."

The two villains began whispering together, debating, as far as I could hear, which was the best way of avoiding my vedettes.

" I will make sure that it is all clear upon the other side of the barn," said the Marshal at last. " You will stay here, my good Chenier, and if the prisoner gives any trouble you will know what to do."

So we were left together, this murderous renegade and I—he sitting at the end of the bed, sharpening his knife upon his boot in the light of the single smoky little oil-lamp. As to me, I only wonder now, as I look back upon it, that I did not go mad with vexation and self-reproach as I lay helplessly upon the couch, unable to utter a word or move a finger, with the knowledge that my fifty gallant lads were so close to me, and yet with no means of letting them know the straits to which I was reduced. It was no new thing for me to be a prisoner ; but to be taken by these renegades, and to be led into their Abbey in the midst of their jeers, befooled and outwitted by their insolent leaders—that was indeed more than I could endure. The knife of the butcher beside me would cut less deeply than that.

I twitched softly at my wrists, and then at my ankles, but whichever of the two had secured me was no bungler at his work. I could not move either of them an inch. Then I tried to work the handkerchief down over my mouth, but the ruffian beside me raised his knife with such a threatening snarl that I had to desist. I was lying still looking at his bull neck, and wondering whether it would ever be my good fortune to fit it for a cravat, when I heard returning steps coming down the inn passage and up the stairs. What word would the villain bring back ? If he found it impossible to kidnap me, he would probably murder me where I lay. For my own part, I was indifferent which it might be, and I looked at the doorway with the contempt and defiance which I longed to put into words. But you can imagine my feelings, my dear friends, when, instead of the tall figure and dark, sneering face of the Capuchin, my eyes fell upon the grey pelisse and huge moustaches of my good little sub-officer, Papilette !

The French soldier of those days had seen too much to be ever taken by surprise. His eyes had hardly rested upon my bound figure and the sinister face beside me before he had seen how the matter lay.

" Sacred name of a dog ! " he growled, and out flashed his great sabre. Chenier sprang forward at him with his knife, and then, thinking better of it, he darted back and stabbed frantically at my heart. For my own part, I had hurled myself off the bed on the side opposite to him, and the blade grazed my side before ripping its way through blanket and sheet. An instant later I heard the thud of a heavy fall, and then almost simultaneously a second object struck the floor—something lighter but harder, which rolled under the bed. I will not horrify you with details, my friends. Suffice it that Papilette was one of the strongest swordsmen in the regiment, and that his sabre was heavy and sharp. It left a red blotch upon my wrists and my ankles, as it cut the thongs which bound me.

When I had thrown off my gag, the first use which I made of my lips was to kiss the sergeant's scarred cheeks. The next was to ask him if all was well with the command. Yes, they had had no alarms. Oudin had just relieved him, and he had come to report. Had he seen the Abbot ? No, he had seen nothing of him. Then we must form a cordon and prevent his escape. I was hurrying out to give the orders, when I heard a slow and measured step enter the door below, and come creaking up the stairs.

Papilette understood it all in an instant. " You are not to kill him," I whispered, and thrust him into the shadow on one side of the door ; I crouched on the other. Up he came, up and up, and every footfall seemed to be upon my heart. The brown skirt of his gown was not over the threshold before we were both on him, like two wolves on a buck. Down we crashed, the three of us, he fighting like a tiger, and with such amazing strength that he might have broken away from the two of us. Thrice he got to his feet, and thrice we had him over again, until Papilette made him feel that there was a point to his sabre. He had sense enough then to know that the game was up, and to lie still while I lashed him with the very cords which had been round my own limbs.

" There has been a fresh deal, my fine fellow," said I, " and you will find that I have some of the trumps in *my* hand this time."

" Luck always comes to the aid of a fool," he answered. " Perhaps it is as well, otherwise the world would fall too completely into the power of the astute. So, you have killed Chenier, I see. He was an insubordinate dog, and always smelt abominably of garlic. Might I trouble you to lay me upon the bed ? The floor of these Portuguese tabernas is hardly a fitting couch for anyone who has prejudices in favour of cleanliness."

I could not but admire the coolness of the man, and the way in which he preserved the same insolent air of condescension in spite of this sudden turning of the tables. I dispatched Papilette to summon a guard, whilst I stood over our prisoner with my drawn sword, never taking my eyes off him for an instant, for I must confess that I had conceived a great respect for his audacity and resource.

" I trust," said he, " that your men will treat me in a becoming manner."

" You will get your deserts—you may depend upon that."

" I ask nothing more. You may not be aware of my exalted birth, but I am so placed that I cannot name my father without treason, nor my mother without a scandal. I cannot *claim* Royal honours, but these things are so much more graceful when they are conceded without a claim. The thongs are cutting my skin. Might I beg you to loosen them ? "

" You do not give me credit for much intelligence," I remarked, repeating his own words.

" *Touché*," he cried, liked a pinked fencer. " But here come your men, so it matters little whether you loosen them or not."

I ordered the gown to be stripped from him and placed

him under a strong guard. Then, as morning was already breaking, I had to consider what my next step was to be. The poor Bart and his Englishmen had fallen victims to the deep scheme which might, had we adopted all the crafty suggestions of our adviser, have ended in the capture of the whole instead of the half of our force. I must extricate them if it were still possible. Then there was the old lady, the Countess of La Ronda, to be thought of. As to the Abbey, since its garrison was on the alert it was hopeless to think of capturing that. All turned now upon the value which they placed upon their leader. The game depended upon my playing that one card. I will tell you how boldly and how skilfully I played it.

It was hardly light before my bugler blew the assembly, and out we trotted on to the plain. My prisoner was placed on horseback in the very centre of the troops. It chanced that there was a large tree just out of musket-shot from the main gate of the Abbey, and under this we halted. Had they opened the great doors in order to attack us, I should have charged home upon them; but, as I had expected, they stood upon the defensive, lining the long wall and pouring down a torrent of hootings and taunts and derisive laughter upon us. A few fired their muskets, but finding that we were out of reach they soon ceased to waste their powder. It was the strangest sight to see that mixture of uniforms, French, English and Portuguese cavalry, infantry and artillery, all wagging their heads and shaking their fists at us.

My word, their hubbub soon died away when we opened our ranks, and showed whom we had got in the midst of us! There was silence for a few seconds, and then such a howl of rage and grief! I could see some of them dancing like madmen upon the wall. He must have been a singular person, this prisoner of ours, to have gained the affection of such a gang.

I had brought a rope from the inn, and we slung it over the lower bough of the tree.

" You will permit me, monsieur, to undo your collar," said Papilette, with mock politeness.

" If your hands are perfectly clean," answered our prisoner, and set the whole half-squadron laughing.

There was another yell from the wall, followed by a profound hush as the noose was tightened round Marshal Millefleurs' neck. Then came a shriek from a bugle, the Abbey gates flew open, and three men rushed out waving white cloths in their hands. Ah, how my heart bounded with joy at the sight of them. And yet I would not advance an inch to meet them, so that all the eagerness might seem to be upon their side. I allowed my trumpeter, however, to wave a handkerchief in reply, upon which the three envoys came running towards us. The Marshal, still pinioned, and with the rope round his neck, sat his horse with a half smile, as one who is slightly bored and yet strives out of courtesy not to show it. If I were in such a situation I could not wish to carry myself better, and surely I can say no more than that.

They were a singular trio, these ambassadors. The one was a Portuguese caçadore in his dark uniform, the second a French chasseur in the lightest green, and the third a big English artilleryman in blue and gold. They saluted, all three, and the Frenchman did the talking.

" We have thirty-seven English dragoons in our hands," said he. " We give you our most solemn oath that they shall all hang from the Abbey wall within five minutes of the death of our Marshal."

" Thirty-seven ! " I cried. " You have fifty-one."

" Fourteen were cut down before they could be secured."

" And the officer ? "

" He would not surrender his sword save with his life. It was not our fault. We would have saved him if we could."

Alas for my poor Bart ! I had met him but twice, and yet he was a man very much after my heart. I have always had a regard for the English for the sake of that one friend. A braver man and a worse swordsman I have never met.

I did not, as you may think, take these rascals' word for anything. Papilette was dispatched with one of them, and returned to say that it was too true. I had now to think of the living.

" You will release the thirty-seven dragoons if I free your leader ? "

" We will give you ten of them."

" Up with him ? " I cried.

" Twenty," shouted the chasseur.

" No more words," said I. " Pull on the rope ! "

" All of them," cried the envoy, as the cord tightened round the Marshal's neck.

" With horses and arms ? "

They could see that I was not a man to jest with.

" All complete," said the chasseur, sulkily.

" And the Countess of La Ronda as well ? " said I.

But here I met with firmer opposition. No threats of mine could induce them to give up the Countess. We tightened the cord. We moved the horse. We did all but leave the Marshal suspended. If once I broke his neck the dragoons were dead men. It was as precious to me as to them.

" Allow me to remark," said the Marshal, blandly, " that you are exposing me to a risk of a quinsy. Do you not think, since there is a difference of opinion upon this point, that it would be an excellent idea to consult the lady herself ? We would neither of us, I am sure, wish to override her own inclinations."

Nothing could be more satisfactory. You can imagine how quickly I grasped at so simple a solution. In ten minutes she was before us, a most stately dame, with her grey curls peeping out from under her mantilla. Her face was as yellow as though it reflected the countless doubloons of her treasury.

" This gentleman," said the Marshal, " is exceedingly anxious to convey you to a place where you will never see us more. It is for you to decide whether you would wish to go with him, or whether you prefer to remain with me."

She was at his horse's side in an instant. " My own Alexis," she cried, " nothing can ever part us."

He looked at me with a sneer upon his handsome face.

" By the way, you made a small slip of the tongue, my dear Colonel," said he. " Except by courtesy, no such person exists as the Dowager Countess of La Ronda. The lady whom I have the honour to present to you is my very dear wife, Mrs. Alexis Morgan—or shall I say Madame la Maréchale Millefleurs ? "

It was at this moment that I came to the conclusion that I was dealing with the cleverest, and also the most unscrupulous, man whom I had ever met. As I looked upon this unfortunate old woman my soul was filled with wonder and disgust. As for her, her eyes were raised to his face with such a look as a young recruit might give to the Emperor.

" So be it," said I at last ; " give me the dragoons and let me go."

They were brought out with their horses and weapons, and the rope was taken from the Marshal's neck.

" Good-bye, my dear Colonel," said he. " I am afraid that you will have rather a lame account to give of your mission, when you find your way back to Massena, though, from all I hear, he will probably be too busy to think of you. I am free to confess that you have extricated yourself from your difficulties with greater ability than I had given you credit for. I presume that there is nothing which I can do for you before you go ? "

" There is one thing."

" And that is ? "

" To give fitting burial to this young officer and his men."

" I pledge my word to it."

" And there is one other."

" Name it."

" To give me five minutes in the open with a sword in your hand and a horse between your legs."

" Tut, tut ! " said he. " I should either have to cut short your promising career, or else to bid adieu to my own bonny bride. It is unreasonable to ask such a request of a man in the first joys of matrimony."

I gathered my horsemen together and wheeled them into column.

" Au revoir," I cried, shaking my sword at him. " The next time you may not escape so easily."

" Au revoir," he answered. " When you are weary of the Emperor, you will always find a commission waiting for you in the service of the Marshal Millefleurs."

6. *How the Brigadier played for a Kingdom*

IT has sometimes struck me that some of you, when you have heard me tell these little adventures of mine, may have gone away with the impression that I was conceited. There could not be a greater mistake than this, for I have always observed that really fine soldiers are free from this failing. It is true that I have had to depict myself sometimes as brave, sometimes as full of resource, always as interesting ; but, then, it really was so, and I had to take the facts as I found them. It would be an unworthy affectation if I were to pretend that my career has been anything but a fine one. The incident which I will tell you to-night, however, is one which you will understand that only a modest man would describe. After all, when one has attained such a position as mine, one can afford to speak of what an ordinary man might be tempted to conceal.

You must know, then, that after the Russian campaign the remains of our poor army were quartered along the western bank of the Elbe, where they might thaw their frozen blood and try, with the help of the good German beer, to put a little between their skin and their bones. There were some things which we could not hope to regain, for I dare say that three large commissariat fourgons would not have sufficed to carry the fingers and the toes which the army had shed during that retreat. Still, lean and crippled as we were, we had much to be thankful for when we thought of our poor comrades whom we had left behind, and of the snowfields—the horrible, horrible snowfields. To this day, my friends, I do not care to see red and white together. Even my red cap thrown down upon my white counterpane has given me dreams in which I have seen those monstrous plains, the reeling, tortured army, and the crimson smears which glared upon the snow behind them. You will coax no story out of me about that business, for the thought of it is enough to turn my wine to vinegar and my tobacco to straw.

Of the half-million who crossed the Elbe in the autumn of the year '12, about forty thousand infantry were left in the spring of '13. But they were terrible men, these forty thousand : men of iron, eaters of horses, and sleepers in the snow ; filled, too, with rage and bitterness against the Russians. They would hold the Elbe until the great army of conscripts, which the Emperor was raising in France, should be ready to help them to cross it once more.

But the cavalry was in a deplorable condition. My own hussars were at Borna, and when I paraded them first, I burst into tears at the sight of them. My fine men and my beautiful horses—it broke my heart to see the state to which they were reduced. " But, courage," I thought, " they have lost much, but their Colonel is still left to them." I set to work, therefore, to repair their disasters, and had already constructed two good squadrons, when an order came that all colonels of cavalry should repair instantly to the depôts of the regiments in France to organise the recruits and the remounts for the coming campaign.

You will think, doubtless, that I was overjoyed at

this chance of visiting home once more. I will not deny that it was a pleasure to me to know that I should see my mother again, and there were a few girls who would be very glad at the news ; but there were others in the army who had a stronger claim. I would have given my place to any who had wives and children whom they might not see again. However, there is no arguing when the blue paper with the little red seal arrives, so within an hour I was off upon my great ride from the Elbe to the Vosges. At last I was to have a period of quiet. War lay behind my mare's tail and peace in front of her nostrils. So I thought, as the sound of the bugles died in the distance, and the long, white road curled away in front of me through plain and forest and mountain, with France somewhere beyond the blue haze which lay upon the horizon.

It is interesting, but it is also fatiguing, to ride in the rear of an army. In the harvest time our soldiers could do without supplies, for they had been trained to pluck the grain in the fields as they passed, and to grind it for themselves in their bivouacs. It was at that time of year, therefore, that those swift marches were performed which were the wonder and the despair of Europe. But now the starving men had to be made robust once more, and I was forced to draw into the ditch continually as the Coburg sheep and the Bavarian bullocks came streaming past with waggon loads of Berlin beer and good French cognac. Sometimes, too, I would hear the dry rattle of the drums and the shrill whistle of the fifes, and long columns of our good little infantry men would swing past me with the white dust lying thick upon their blue tunics. These were old soldiers drawn from the garrisons of our German fortresses, for it was not until May that the new conscripts began to arrive from France.

Well, I was rather tired of this eternal stopping and dodging, so that I was not sorry when I came to Altenburg to find that the road divided, and that I could take the southern and quieter branch. There were few wayfarers between there and Greiz, and the road wound through groves of oaks and beeches, which shot their branches across the path. You will think it strange that a Colonel of hussars should again and again pull up his horse in order to admire the beauty of the feathery branches and the little, green, new-budded leaves, but if you had spent six months among the fir trees of Russia you would be able to understand me.

There was something, however, which pleased me very much less than the beauty of the forests, and that was the words and looks of the folk who lived in the woodland villages. We had always been excellent friends with the Germans, and during the last six years they had never seemed to bear us any malice for having made a little free with their country. We had shown kindnesses to the men and received them from the women, so that good, comfortable Germany was a second home to all of us. But now there was something which I could not understand in the behaviour of the people. The travellers made no answer to my salute ; the foresters turned their heads away to avoid seeing me ; and in the villages the folk would gather into knots in the roadway and would scowl at me as I passed. Even women would do this, and it was something new for me in those days to see anything but a smile in a woman's eyes when they were turned upon me.

It was in the hamlet of Schmolin, just ten miles out of Altenburg, that the thing became most marked. I had stopped at the little inn there just to damp my moustache and to wash the dust out of poor Violette's throat. It was my way to give some little compliment, or possibly a kiss, to the maid who served me ; but this one would have neither the one nor the other, but darted a glance at me like a bayonet-thrust. Then when I raised my glass to the folk who drank their beer by the door they turned their backs on me, save only one fellow, who cried, " Here's a toast for you, boys ! Here's to the letter T ! " At that they all emptied their beer mugs

918

and laughed ; but it was not a laugh that had good-fellowship in it.

I was turning this over in my head and wondering what their boorish conduct could mean, when I saw, as I rode from the village, a great T new carved upon a tree. I had already seen more than one in my morning's ride, but I had given no thought to them until the words of the beer-drinker gave them an importance. It chanced that a respectable-looking person was riding past me at the moment, so I turned to him for information.

" Can you tell me, sir," said I, " what this letter T is ? "

He looked at it and then at me in the most singular fashion. " Young man," said he, " it is not the letter N." Then before I could ask further he clapped his spurs into his horse's ribs and rode, stomach to earth, upon his way.

At first his words had no particular significance in my mind, but as I trotted onwards Violette chanced to half turn her dainty head, and my eyes were caught by the gleam of the brazen N's at the end of the bridle-chain. It was the Emperor's mark.   And those T's meant something which was opposite to it. Things had been happening in Germany, then, during our absence, and the giant sleeper had begun to stir.   I thought of the mutinous faces that I had seen, and I felt that if I could only have looked into the hearts of these people I might have had some strange news to bring into France with me.   It made me the more eager to get my remounts, and to see ten strong squadrons behind my kettle-drums once more.

While these thoughts were passing through my head I had been alternately walking and trotting, as a man should who has a long journey before, and a willing horse beneath, him. The woods were very open at this point, and beside the road there lay a great heap of fagots. As I passed there came a sharp sound from among them, and, glancing round, I saw a face looking out at me—a hot, red face, like that of a man who is beside himself with excitement and anxiety. A second glance told me that it was the very person with whom I had talked an hour before in the village.

" Come nearer ! " he hissed. " Nearer still ! Now dismount and pretend to be mending the stirrup leather. Spies may be watching us, and it means death to me if I am seen helping you."

" Death ! " I whispered. " From whom ? "

" From the Tugendbund. From Lutzow's night-riders. You Frenchmen are living on a powder magazine, and the match has been struck that will fire it."

" But this is all strange to me," said I, still fumbling at the leathers of my horse. " What is this Tugend-bund ? "

" It is the secret society which has planned the great rising which is to drive you out of Germany, just as you have been driven out of Russia."

" And these T's stand for it ? "

" They are the signal. I should have told you all this in the village, but I dared not be seen speaking with you. I galloped through the woods to cut you off, and concealed both my horse and myself."

" I am very much indebted to you," said I, " and the more so as you are the only German that I have met to-day from whom I have had common civility."

" All that I possess I have gained through contracting for the French armies," said he. " Your Emperor has been a good friend to me. But I beg that you will ride on now, for we have talked long enough. Beware only of Lutzow's night-riders ! "

" Banditti ? " I asked.

" All that is best in Germany," said he. " But for God's sake ride forwards, for I have risked my life and exposed my good name in order to carry you this warning."

Well, if I had been heavy with thought before, you can think how I felt after my strange talk with the man among the fagots. What came home to me even more than his words was his shivering, broken voice, his twitching face, and his eyes glancing swiftly to right and left, and opening in horror whenever a branch cracked upon a tree. It was clear that he was in the last extremity of terror, and it is possible that he had cause, for shortly after I had left him I heard a distant gunshot and a shouting from somewhere behind me. It may have been some sportsman halloaing to his dogs, but I never again heard of or saw the man who had given me my warning.

I kept a good look-out after this, riding swiftly where the country was open, and slowly where there might be an ambuscade. It was serious for me, since 500 good miles of German soil lay in front of me ; but somehow I did not take it very much to heart, for the Germans had always seemed to me to be a kindly, gentle people, whose hands closed more readily round a pipe-stem than a sword-hilt—not out of want of valour, you understand, but because they are genial, open souls, who would rather be on good terms with all men. I did not know then that beneath that homely surface there lurks a devilry as fierce as, and far more persistent than, that of the Castilian or the Italian.

And it was not long before I had shown to me that there was something more serious abroad than rough words and hard looks. I had come to a spot where the road runs upwards through a wild tract of heathland and vanishes into an oak wood. I may have been half-way up the hill when, looking forward, I saw something gleaming under the shadow of the tree-trunks, and a man came out with a coat which was so slashed and spangled with gold that he blazed like a fire in the sunlight. He appeared to be very drunk, for he reeled and staggered as he came towards me. One of his hands was held up to his ear and clutched a great red handkerchief, which was fixed to his neck.

I had reined up the mare and was looking at him with some disgust, for it seemed strange to me that one who wore so gorgeous a uniform should show himself in such a state in broad daylight. For his part, he looked hard in my direction and came slowly onwards, stopping from time to time and swaying about as he gazed at me. Suddenly, as I again advanced, he screamed out his thanks to Christ, and, lurching forwards, he fell with a crash upon the dusty road. His hands flew forward with the fall, and I saw that what I had taken for a red cloth was a monstrous wound, which had left a great gap in his neck, from which a dark blood-clot hung, like an epaulette upon his shoulder.

" My God ! " I cried, as I sprang to his aid. " And I thought that you were drunk ! "

" Not drunk, but dying," said he. " But thank Heaven that I have seen a French officer while I have still strength to speak."

I laid him among the heather and poured some brandy down his throat. All round us was the vast country-side, green and peaceful, with nothing living in sight save only the mutilated man beside me.

" Who has done this ? " I asked, " and what are you ? You are French, and yet the uniform is strange to me."

" It is that of the Emperor's new guard of honour. I am the Marquis of Château St. Arnaud, and I am the ninth of my blood who has died in the service of France. I have been pursued and wounded by the night-riders of Lutzow, but I hid among the brushwood yonder, and waited in the hope that a Frenchman might pass. I could not be sure at first if you were friend or foe, but I felt that death was very near, and that I must take the chance."

" Keep your heart up, comrade," said I ; " I have seen a man with a worse wound who has lived to boast of it."

" No, no," he whispered ; " I am going fast." He laid his hand upon mine as he spoke, and I saw that his finger-nails were already blue. " But I have papers here in my tunic which you must carry at once to the

Prince of Saxe-Felstein, at his Castle of Hof. He is still true to us, but the Princess is our deadly enemy. She is striving to make him declare against us. If he does so, it will determine all those who are wavering, for the King of Prussia is his uncle and the King of Bavaria his cousin. These papers will hold him to us if they can only reach him before he takes the last step. Place them in his hands to-night, and, perhaps, you will have saved all Germany for the Emperor. Had my horse not been shot, I might, wounded as I am——" he choked, and the cold hand tightened into a grip, which left mine as bloodless as itself. Then, with a groan, his head jerked back, and it was all over with him.

Here was a fine start for my journey home. I was left with a commission of which I knew little, which would lead me to delay the pressing needs of my hussars, and which at the same time was of such importance that it was impossible for me to avoid it. I opened the Marquis's tunic, the brilliance of which had been devised by the Emperor in order to attract those young aristocrats from whom he hoped to raise these new regiments of his Guard. It was a small packet of papers which I drew out, tied up with silk, and addressed to the Prince of Saxe-Felstein. In the corner, in a sprawling, untidy hand, which I knew to be the Emperor's own, was written : " Pressing and most important." It was an order to me, those four words—an order as clear as if it had come straight from the firm lips with the cold grey eyes looking into mine. My troopers might wait for their horses, the dead Marquis might lie where I had laid him amongst the heather, but if the mare and her rider had a breath left in them the papers should reach the Prince that night.

I should not have feared to ride by the road through the wood, for I have learned in Spain that the safest time to pass through a guerrilla country is after an outrage, and that the moment of danger is when all is peaceful. When I came to look upon my map, however, I saw that

Hof lay further to the south of me, and that I might reach it more directly by keeping to the moors. Off I set, therefore, and had not gone fifty yards before two carbine shots rang out of the brushwood and a bullet hummed past me like a bee. It was clear that the night-riders were bolder in their ways than the brigands of Spain, and that my mission would have ended where it had begun if I had kept to the road.

It was a mad ride, that—a ride with a loose rein, girth-deep in heather and in gorse, plunging through bushes, flying down hill-sides, with my neck at the mercy of my dear little Violette. But she—she never slipped, she never faltered, as swift and as surefooted as if she knew that her rider carried the fate of all Germany beneath the buttons of his pelisse. And I—I had long borne the name of being the best horseman in the six brigades of light cavalry, but I never rode as I rode then. My friend the Bart has told me of how they hunt the fox in England, but the swiftest fox would have been captured by me that day. The wild pigeons which flew overhead did not take a straighter course than Violette and I below. As an officer, I have always been ready to sacrifice myself for my men, though the Emperor would not have thanked me for it, for he had many men, but only one—well, cavalry leaders of the first class are rare.

But here I had an object which was indeed worth a sacrifice, and I thought no more of my life than of the clods of earth that flew from my darling's heels.

We struck the road once more as the light was failing, and galloped into the little village of Lobenstein. But we had hardly got upon the cobble-stones when off came one of the mare's shoes, and I had to lead her to the village smithy. His fire was low, and his day's work done, so that it would be an hour at the least before I could hope to push on to Hof. Cursing at the delay, I strode into the village inn and ordered a cold chicken and some wine to be served for my dinner. It was but a few miles to Hof, and I had every hope that I might deliver my papers to the Prince on that very night, and be on my way for France next morning with dispatches for the Emperor in my bosom. I will tell you now what befell me in the inn of Lobenstein.

The chicken had been served and the wine drawn, and I had turned upon both as a man may who has ridden such a ride, when I was aware of a murmur and a scuffling in the hall outside my door. At first I thought that it was some brawl between peasants in their cups, and I left them to settle their own affairs. But of a sudden there broke from among the low, sullen growl of the voices such a sound as would send Étienne Gerard leaping from his death-bed. It was the whimpering cry of a woman in pain. Down clattered my knife and my fork, and in an instant I was in the thick of the crowd which had gathered outside my door.

The heavy-cheeked landlord was there and his flaxen-haired wife, the two men from the stables, a chamber-maid and two or three villagers. All of them, women and men, were flushed and angry, while there in the centre of them, with pale cheeks and terror in her eyes, stood the loveliest woman that ever a soldier would wish to look upon. With her queenly head thrown back, and a touch of defiance mingled with her fear, she looked as she gazed round her like a creature of a different race from the vile, coarse-featured crew who surrounded her. I had not taken two steps from my door before she sprang to meet me, her hand resting upon my arm and her blue eyes sparkling with joy and triumph.

"A French soldier and gentleman!" she cried. "Now at last I am safe."

"Yes, madam, you are safe," said I, and I could not resist taking her hand in mine in order that I might re-assure her. "You have only to command me," I added, kissing the hand as a sign that I meant what I was saying.

"I am Polish," she cried; "the Countess Palotta is my name. They abuse me because I love the French.

I do not know what they might have done to me had Heaven not sent you to my help."

I kissed her hand again lest she should doubt my intentions. Then I turned upon the crew with such an expression as I know how to assume. In an instant the hall was empty.

" Countess," said I, " you are now under my protection. You are faint, and a glass of wine is necessary to restore you." I offered her my arm and escorted her into my room, where she sat by my side at the table and took the refreshment which I offered her.

How she blossomed out in my presence, this woman, like a flower before the sun ! She lit up the room with her beauty. She must have read my admiration in my eyes, and it seemed to me that I also could see something of the sort in her own. Ah ! my friends, I was no ordinary-looking man when I was in my thirtieth year. In the whole light cavalry it would have been hard to find a finer pair of whiskers. Murat's may have been a shade longer, but the best judges are agreed that Murat's were a shade too long. And then I had a manner. Some women are to be approached in one way and some in another, just as a siege is an affair of fascines and gabions in hard weather and of trenches in soft. But the man who can mix daring with timidity, who can be outrageous with an air of humility, and presumptuous with a tone of deference, that is the man whom mothers have to fear. For myself, I felt that I was the guardian of this lonely lady, and knowing what a dangerous man I had to deal with, I kept strict watch upon myself. Still, even a guardian has his privileges, and I did not neglect them.

But her talk was as charming as her face. In a few words she explained that she was travelling to Poland, and that her brother who had been her escort had fallen ill upon the way. She had more than once met with ill-treatment from the country folk because she could not conceal her good-will towards the French. Then turning from her own affairs she questioned me about the army, and so came round to myself and my own exploits. They were familiar to her, she said, for she knew several of Ponia-towski's officers, and they had spoken of my doings. Yet she would be glad to hear them from my own lips. Never have I had so delightful a conversation. Most women make the mistake of talking rather too much about their own affairs, but this one listened to my tales just as you are listening now, ever asking for more and more and more. The hours slipped rapidly by, and it was with horror that I heard the village clock strike eleven, and so learned that for four hours I had forgotten the Emperor's business.

"Pardon me, my dear lady," I cried, springing to my feet, "but I must on instantly to Hof."

She rose also, and looked at me with a pale, reproachful face. "And me?" she said. "What is to become of me?"

"It is the Emperor's affair. I have already stayed far too long. My duty calls me, and I must go."

"You must go? And I must be abandoned alone to these savages? Oh, why did I ever meet you? Why did you ever teach me to rely upon your strength?" Her eyes glazed over, and in an instant she was sobbing upon my bosom.

Here was a trying moment for a guardian! Here was a time when he had to keep a watch upon a forward young officer. But I was equal to it. I smoothed her rich brown hair and whispered such consolations as I could think of in her ear, with one arm round her, it is true, but that was to hold her lest she should faint. She turned her tear-stained face to mine. "Water," she whispered. "For God's sake, water!"

I saw that in another moment she would be senseless. I laid the drooping head upon the sofa, and then rushed furiously from the room, hunting from chamber to chamber for a carafe. It was some minutes before I could get one and hurry back with it. You can imagine my feelings to find the room empty and the lady gone.

Not only was she gone, but her cap and silver-mounted riding switch which had lain upon the table were gone also. I rushed out and roared for the landlord. He knew nothing of the matter, had never seen the woman before, and did not care if he never saw her again. Had the peasants at the door seen anyone ride away ? No, they had seen nobody. I searched here and searched there, until at last I chanced to find myself in front of a mirror, where I stood with my eyes staring and my jaw as far dropped as the chin-strap of my shako would allow.

Four buttons of my pelisse were open, and it did not need me to put my hand up to know that my precious papers were gone. Oh ! the depth of cunning that lurks in a woman's heart. She had robbed me, this creature, robbed me as she clung to my breast. Even while I smoothed her hair, and whispered kind words into her ear, her hands had been at work beneath my dolman. And here I was, at the very last step of my journey, without the power of carrying out this mission which had already deprived one good man of his life, and was likely to rob another one of his credit. What would the Emperor say when he heard that I had lost his dispatches ? Would the army believe it of Étienne Gerard ? And when they heard that a woman's hand had coaxed them from me, what laughter there would be at mess-table and at camp-fire ! I could have rolled upon the ground in my despair.

But one thing was certain—all this affair of the fracas in the hall and the persecution of the so-called Countess was a piece of acting from the beginning. This villainous innkeeper must be in the plot. From him I might learn who she was and where my papers had gone. I snatched my sabre from the table and rushed out in search of him. But the scoundrel had guessed what I would do, and had made his preparations for me. It was in the corner of the yard that I found him, a blunderbuss in his hands and a mastiff held upon a leash by his son. The two stable-hands, with pitchforks, stood upon either side, and the wife held a great lantern behind him, so as to guide his aim.

" Ride away, sir, ride away ! " he cried, with a crackling voice. " Your horse is at the door, and no one will meddle with you if you go your way ; but if you come against us, you are alone against three brave men."

I had only the dog to fear, for the two forks and the blunderbuss were shaking about like branches in a wind. Still, I considered that, though I might force an answer with my sword-point at the throat of this fat rascal, still I should have no means of knowing whether that answer was the truth. It would be a struggle, then, with much to lose and nothing certain to gain. I looked them up and down, therefore, in a way that set their foolish weapons shaking worse than ever, and then, throwing myself upon my mare, I galloped away with the shrill laughter of the landlady jarring upon my ears.

I had already formed my resolution. Although I had lost my papers, I could make a very good guess as to what their contents would be, and this I would say from my own lips to the Prince of Saxe-Felstein, as though the Emperor had commissioned me to convey it in that way. It was a bold stroke and a dangerous one, but if I went too far I could afterwards be disavowed. It was that or nothing, and when all Germany hung on the balance the game should not be lost if the nerve of one man could save it.

It was midnight when I rode into Hof, but every window was blazing, which was enough in itself, in that sleepy country, to tell the ferment of excitement in which the people were. There was hooting and jeering as I rode through the crowded streets, and once a stone sang past my head, but I kept upon my way, neither slowing nor quickening my pace, until I came to the palace. It was lit from base to battlement, and the dark shadows, coming and going against the yellow glare, spoke of the turmoil within. For my part, I handed my mare to a groom at the gate, and striding in I demanded, in such a voice as an ambassador should have, to see the Prince instantly, upon business which would brook no delay.

The hall was dark, but I was conscious as I entered of a buzz of innumerable voices, which hushed into silence as I loudly proclaimed my mission. Some great meeting was being held then—a meeting which, as my instincts told me, was to decide this very question of war and peace. It was possible that I might still be in time to turn the scale for the Emperor and for France. As to the major-domo, he looked blackly at me, and showing me into a small ante-chamber he left me. A minute later he returned to say that the Prince could not be disturbed at present, but that the Princess would take my message.

The Princess! What use was there in giving it to her? Had I not been warned that she was German in heart and soul, and that it was she who was turning her husband and her State against us?

" It is the Prince that I must see," said I.

" Nay, it is the Princess," said a voice at the door, and a woman swept into the chamber. " Von Rosen, you had best stay with us. Now, sir, what is it that you have to say to either Prince or Princess of Saxe-Felstein ? "

At the first sound of the voice I had sprung to my feet. At the first glance I had thrilled with anger. Not twice in a lifetime does one meet that noble figure, that queenly head, and those eyes as blue as the Garonne, and as chilling as her winter waters.

" Time presses, sir ! " she cried, with an impatient tap of her foot. " What have you to say to me ? "

" What have I to say to you ? " I cried. " What can I say, save that you have taught me never to trust a woman more ? You have ruined and dishonoured me for ever."

She looked with arched brows at her attendant.

" Is this the raving of fever, or does it come from some less innocent cause ? " said she. " Perhaps a little blood-letting——"

" Ah, you can act ! " I cried. " You have shown me that already."

" Do you mean that we have met before ? "

" I mean that you have robbed me within the last two hours."

" This is past all bearing," she cried, with an admirable affectation of anger. " You claim, as I understand, to be an ambassador, but there are limits to the privileges which such an office brings with it."

" You brazen it admirably," said I. " Your Highness will not make a fool of me twice in one night." I sprang forward and, stooping down, caught up the hem of her dress. " You would have done well to change it after you had ridden so far and so fast," said I.

It was like the dawn upon a snow-peak to see her ivory cheeks flush suddenly to crimson.

" Insolent ! " she cried, " Call the foresters and have him thrust from the palace ! "

" I will see the Prince first."

" You will never see the Prince. Ah ! Hold him, Von Rosen, hold him ! "

She had forgotten the man with whom she had to deal —was it likely that I would wait until they could bring their rascals ? She had shown me her cards too soon. Her game was to stand between me and her husband. Mine was to speak face to face with him at any cost. One spring took me out of the chamber. In another I had crossed the hall. An instant later I had burst into the great room from which the murmur of the meeting had come. At the far end I saw a figure upon a high chair under a daïs. Beneath him was a line of high dignitaries, and then on every side I saw vaguely the heads of a vast assembly. Into the centre of the room I strode, my sabre clanking, my shako under my arm.

" I am the messenger of the Emperor," I shouted. " I bear his message to His Highness the Prince of Saxe-Felstein."

The man beneath the daïs raised his head, and I saw

that his face was thin and wan, and that his back was bowed as though some huge burden was balanced between his shoulders.

" Your name, sir ? " he asked.

" Colonel Étienne Gerard, of the Third Hussars."

Every face in the gathering was turned upon me, and I heard the rustle of the innumerable necks and saw countless eyes without meeting one friendly one amongst them. The woman had swept past me, and was whispering, with many shakes of her head and dartings of her hands, into the Prince's ear. For my own part I threw out my chest and curled my moustache, glancing round in my own debonair fashion at the assembly. They were men, all of them, professors from the college, a sprinkling of their students, soldiers, gentlemen, artisans, all very silent and serious. In one corner there sat a group of men in black, with riding-coats drawn over their shoulders. They leaned their heads to each other, whispering under their breath, and with every movement I caught the clank of their sabres or the clink of their spurs.

" The Emperor's private letter to me informs me that it is the Marquis Château St. Arnaud who is bearing his dispatches," said the Prince.

" The Marquis has been foully murdered," I answered, and a buzz rose up from the people as I spoke. Many heads were turned, I noticed, towards the dark men in the cloaks.

" Where are your papers ? " asked the Prince.

" I have none."

A fierce clamour rose instantly around me. " He is a spy ! He plays a part ! " they cried. " Hang him ! " roared a deep voice from the corner, and a dozen others took up the shout. For my part, I drew out my handkerchief and flicked the dust from the fur of my pelisse. The Prince held out his thin hands, and the tumult died away.

" Where, then, are your credentials, and what is your message ? "

" My uniform is my credential, and my message is for your private ear."

He passed his hand over his forehead with the gesture of a weak man who is at his wits' end what to do. The Princess stood beside him with her hand upon his throne, and again whispered in his ear.

" We are here in council together, some of my trusty subjects and myself," said he. " I have no secrets from them, and whatever message the Emperor may send to me at such a time concerns their interests no less than mine."

There was a hum of applause at this, and every eye was turned once more upon me. My faith, it was an awkward position in which I found myself, for it is one thing to address eight hundred hussars, and another to speak to such an audience on such a subject. But I fixed my eyes upon the Prince, and tried to say just what I should have said if we had been alone, shouting it out, too, as though I had my regiment on parade.

" You have often expressed friendship for the Emperor," I cried. " It is now at last that this friendship is about to be tried. If you will stand firm, he will reward you as only he can reward. It is an easy thing for him to turn a Prince into a King and a province into a power. His eyes are fixed upon you, and though you can do little to harm him, you can ruin yourself. At this moment he is crossing the Rhine with two hundred thousand men. Every fortress in the country is in his hands. He will be upon you in a week, and if you have played him false, God help both you and your people. You think that he is weakened because a few of us got the chilblains last winter. Look there ! " I cried, pointing to a great star which blazed through the window above the Prince's head. " That is the Emperor's star. When it wanes, he will wane—but not before."

You would have been proud of me, my friends, if you could have seen and heard me, for I clashed my sabre as I spoke, and swung my dolman as though my regiment

933

was picketed outside in the courtyard. They listened to me in silence, but the back of the Prince bowed more and more as though the burden which weighed upon it was greater than his strength. He looked round with haggard eyes.

"We have heard a Frenchman speak for France," said he. "Let us have a German speak for Germany."

The folk glanced at each other, and whispered to their neighbours. My speech, as I think, had its effect, and no man wished to be the first to commit himself in the eyes of the Emperor. The Princess looked round her with blazing eyes, and her clear voice broke the silence.

"Is a woman to give this Frenchman his answer?" she cried. "Is it possible, then, that among the night-riders of Lutzow, there is none who can use his tongue as well as his sabre?"

Over went a table with a crash, and a young man had bounded upon one of the chairs. He had the face of one inspired—pale, eager, with wild hawk eyes, and tangled hair. His sword hung straight from his side, and his riding-boots were brown with mire.

"It is Korner!" the people cried. "It is young Korner, the poet! Ah, he will sing, he will sing."

And he sang! It was soft, at first, and dreamy, telling of old Germany, the mother of nations, of the rich, warm plains, and the grey cities, and the fame of dead heroes. But then verse after verse rang like a trumpet-call. It was of the Germany of now, the Germany which had been taken unawares and overthrown, but which was up again, and snapping the bonds upon her giant limbs. What was life that one should covet it? What was glorious death that one should shun it? The mother, the great mother, was calling. Her sigh was in the night wind. She was crying to her own children for help. Would they come? Would they come? Would they come?

Ah, that terrible song, the spirit face and the ringing voice! Where were I, and France, and the Emperor?

They did not shout, these people—they howled. They were up on the chairs and the tables. They were raving, sobbing, the tears running down their faces. Korner had sprung from the chair, and his comrades were round him with their sabres in the air. A flush had come into the pale face of the Prince, and he rose from his throne.

"Colonel Gerard," said he, "you have heard the answer which you are to carry to your Emperor. The die is cast, my children. Your Prince and you must stand or fall together."

He bowed to show that all was over, and the people with a shout made for the door to carry the tidings into the town. For my own part, I had done all that a brave man might, and so I was not sorry to be carried out amid the stream. Why should I linger in the palace? I had had my answer and must carry it, such as it was. I wished neither to see Hof nor its people again until I entered it at the head of a vanguard. I turned from the throng, then, and walked silently and sadly in the direction in which they had led the mare.

It was dark down there by the stables, and I was peering round for the ostler, when suddenly my two arms were seized from behind. There were hands at my wrists and at my throat, and I felt the cold muzzle of a pistol under my ear.

"Keep your lips closed, you French dog," whispered a fierce voice. "We have him, captain."

"Have you the bridle?"

"Here it is."

"Sling it over his head."

I felt the cold coil of leather tighten round my neck. An ostler with a stable lantern had come out and was gazing upon the scene. In its dim light I saw stern faces breaking everywhere through the gloom, with the black caps and dark cloaks of the night-riders.

"What would you do with him, captain?" cried a voice.

"Hang him at the palace gate."

" An ambassador ? "

" An ambassador without papers."

" But the Prince ? "

" Tut, man, do you not see that the Prince will then be committed to our side ? He will be beyond all hope of forgiveness. At present he may swing round to-morrow as he has done before. He may eat his words, but a dead hussar is more than he can explain."

" No, no, Von Strelitz, we cannot do it," said another voice.

" Can we not ? I shall show you that ! " and there came a jerk on the bridle which nearly pulled me to the ground. At the same instant a sword flashed and the leather was cut through within two inches of my neck.

" By Heaven, Korner, this is rank mutiny," cried the captain. " You may hang yourself before you are through with it."

" I have drawn my sword as a soldier and not as a brigand," said the young poet. " Blood may dim its blade, but never dishonour. Comrades, will you stand by and see this gentleman mishandled ? "

A dozen sabres flew from their sheaths, and it was evident that my friends and my foes were about equally balanced. But the angry voices and the gleam of steel had brought the folk running from all parts.

" The Princess ! " they cried. " The Princess is coming ! "

And even as they spoke I saw her in front of us, her sweet face framed in the darkness. I had cause to hate her, for she had cheated and befooled me, and yet it thrilled me then and thrills me now to think that my arms have embraced her, and that I have felt the scent of her hair in my nostrils. I know not whether she lies under her German earth, or whether she still lingers, a grey-haired woman in her Castle of Hof, but she lives ever, young and lovely, in the heart and memory of Étienne Gerard.

" For shame ! " she cried, sweeping up to me, and

tearing with her own hands the noose from my neck.
" You are fighting in God's own quarrel, and yet you
would begin with such a devil's deed as this. This man
is mine, and he who touches a hair of his head will answer
for it to me."

They were glad enough to slink off into the darkness
before those scornful eyes. Then she turned once more
to me.

" You can follow me, Colonel Gerard," she said. " I
have a word that I would speak to you."

I walked behind her to the chamber into which I had
originally been shown. She closed the door, and then
looked at me with the archest twinkle in her eyes.

" Is it not confiding of me to trust myself with you ? "
said she. " You will remember that it is the Princess of
Saxe-Felstein and not the poor Countess Palotta of
Poland."

" Be the name what it might," I answered, " I helped
a lady whom I believed to be in distress, and I have been
robbed of my papers and almost of my honour as a
reward."

" Colonel Gerard," said she, " we have been playing
a game, you and I, and the stake was a heavy one. You
have shown by delivering a message which was never
given to you that you would stand at nothing in the cause
of your country. My heart is German and yours is
French, and I also would go all lengths, even to deceit
and to theft, if at this crisis I could help my suffering
fatherland. You see how frank I am."

" You tell me nothing that I have not seen."

" But now that the game is played and won, why
should we bear malice ? I will say this, that if ever I
were in such a plight as that which I pretended in the inn
of Lobenstein, I should never wish to meet a more gallant
protector or a truer-hearted gentleman than Colonel
Étienne Gerard. I had never thought that I could feel
for a Frenchmen as I felt for you when I slipped the
papers from your breast."

" But you took them, none the less."

" They were necessary to me and to Germany. I knew the arguments which they contained and the effect which they would have upon the Prince. If they had reached him all would have been lost."

" Why should your Highness descend to such expedients when a score of these brigands, who wished to hang me at your castle gate, would have done the work as well ? "

" They are not brigands, but the best blood of Germany," she cried, hotly. " If you have been roughly used, you will remember the indignities to which every German has been subjected, from the Queen of Prussia downwards. As to why I did not have you waylaid upon the road, I may say that I had parties out on all sides, and that I was waiting at Lobenstein to hear of their success. When instead of their news you yourself arrived I was in despair, for there was only the one weak woman betwixt you and my husband. You see the straits to which I was driven before I used the weapon of my sex."

" I confess that you have conquered me, your Highness, and it only remains for me to leave you in possession of the field."

" But you will take your papers with you." She held them out to me as she spoke. " The Prince has crossed the Rubicon now, and nothing can bring him back. You can return these to the Emperor, and tell him that we refused to receive them. No one can accuse you then of having lost your dispatches. Good-bye, Colonel Gerard, and the best I can wish you is that when you reach France you may remain there. In a year's time there will be no place for a Frenchman upon this side of the Rhine."

And thus it was that I played the Princess of Saxe-Felstein with all Germany for a stake, and lost my game to her. I had much to think of as I walked my poor, tired Violette along the highway which leads westward from Hof. But amid all the thoughts there came back to me always the proud, beautiful face of the German woman, and the voice of the soldier-poet as he sang from the chair. And I understood then that there was something terrible in this strong, patient Germany—this mother root of nations—and I saw that such a land, so old and so beloved, never could be conquered. And as I rode I saw that the dawn was breaking, and that the great star at which I had pointed through the palace window was dim and pale in the western sky.

7. *How the Brigadier won his Medal*

THE Duke of Tarentum, or Macdonald, as his old comrades prefer to call him, was, as I could perceive, in the vilest of tempers. His grim, Scotch face was like one of those grotesque door-knockers which one sees in the Faubourg St. Germain. We heard afterwards that the Emperor had said in jest that he would have sent him against Wellington in the South, but that he was afraid to trust him within the sound of the pipes. Major Charpentier and I could plainly see that he was smouldering with anger.

" Brigadier Gerard of the Hussars," said he, with the air of the corporal with the recruit.

I saluted.

" Major Charpentier of the Horse Grenadiers."

My companion answered to his name.

" The Emperor has a mission for you."

Without more ado he flung open the door and announced us.

I have seen Napoleon ten times on horseback to once on foot, and I think that he does wisely to show himself to the troops in this fashion, for he cuts a very good figure in the saddle. As we saw him now he was the shortest man out of six by a good hand's breadth, and yet I am no very big man myself, though I ride quite heavy enough for a hussar. It is evident, too, that his body is too long for his legs. With his big, round head, his curved shoulders, and his clean-shaven face, he is more like a Professor at the Sorbonne than the first soldier in France. Every man to his taste, but it seems to me that, if I could clap a pair of fine light cavalry whiskers, like my own, on to him, it would do him no harm. He has a firm mouth, however, and his eyes are remarkable. I have seen them once turned on me in anger, and I had rather ride at a square on a spent horse than face them again. I am not a man who is easily daunted, either.

He was standing at the side of the room, away from the window, looking up at a great map of the country which was hung upon the wall. Berthier stood beside him, trying to look wise, and just as we entered, Napoleon snatched his sword impatiently from him and pointed with it on the map. He was talking fast and low, but I heard him say, " The valley of the Meuse," and twice he repeated " Berlin." As we entered, his aide-de-camp advanced to us, but the Emperor stopped him and beckoned us to his side.

" You have not yet received the cross of honour, Brigadier Gerard ? " he asked.

I replied that I had not, and was about to add that it was not for want of having deserved it, when he cut me short in his decided fashion.

" And you, Major ? " he asked.

" No, sire."

" Then you shall both have your opportunity now."

He led us to the great map upon the wall and placed the tip of Berthier's sword on Rheims.

" I will be frank with you, gentlemen, as with two comrades. You have both been with me since Marengo, I believe ? " He had a strangely pleasant smile, which used to light up his pale face with a kind of cold sunshine. " Here at Rheims are our present headquarters on this the 14th of March. Very good. Here is Paris, distant by road a good twenty-five leagues. Blucher lies to the north, Schwarzenberg to the south." He prodded at the map with the sword as he spoke.

" Now," said he, " the further into the country these people march, the more completely I shall crush them. They are about to advance upon Paris. Very good. Let them do so. My brother, the King of Spain, will be there with a hundred thousand men. It is to him that I send you. You will hand him this letter, a copy of which I confide to each of you. It is to tell him that I am coming at once, in two days' time, with every man and horse and gun to his relief. I must give them forty-eight hours to recover. Then straight to Paris! You understand me, gentlemen ? "

Ah, if I could tell you the glow of pride which it gave me to be taken into the great man's confidence in this way. As he handed our letters to us I clicked my spurs and threw out my chest, smiling and nodding to let him know that I saw what he would be after. He smiled also, and rested his hand for a moment upon the cape of my dolman. I would have given half my arrears of pay if my mother could have seen me at that instant.

" I will show you your route," said he, turning back to the map. " Your orders are to ride together as far as Bazoches. You will then separate, the one making for Paris by Oulchy and Neuilly, and the other to the north by Braine, Soissons and Senlis. Have you anything to say, Brigadier Gerard ? "

I am a rough soldier, but I have words and ideas. I had begun to speak about glory and the peril of France when he cut me short.

" And you, Major Charpentier ? "

" If we find our route unsafe, are we at liberty to choose another ? " said he.

" Soldiers do not choose, they obey." He inclined his head to show that we were dismissed, and turned round to Berthier. I do not know what he said, but I heard them both laughing.

Well, as you may think, we lost little time in getting

upon our way. In half an hour we were riding down the High Street of Rheims, and it struck twelve o'clock as we passed the Cathedral. I had my little grey mare, Violette, the one which Sebastiani had wished to buy after Dresden. It is the fastest horse in the six brigades of light cavalry, and was only beaten by the Duke of Rovigo's racer from England. As to Charpentier, he had the kind of horse which a horse grenadier or a cuirassier would be likely to ride : a back like a bedstead, you understand, and legs like the posts. He is a hulking fellow himself, so that they looked a singular pair. And yet in his insane conceit he ogled the girls as they waved their handkerchiefs to me from the windows, and he twirled his ugly red moustache up into his eyes, just as if it were to him that their attention was addressed.

When we came out of the town we passed through the French camp, and then across the battle-field of yesterday, which was still covered both by our own poor fellows and by the Russians. But of the two the camp was the sadder sight. Our army was thawing away. The Guards were all right, though the young guard was full of conscripts. The artillery and the heavy cavalry were also good if there were more of them, but the infantry privates with their under-officers looked like schoolboys with their masters. And we had no reserves. When one considered that there were 80,000 Prussians to the north and 150,000 Russians and Austrians to the south, it might make even the bravest man grave.

For my own part, I confess that I shed a tear until the thought came that the Emperor was still with us, and that on that very morning he had placed his hand upon my dolman and had promised me a medal of honour. This set me singing, and I spurred Violette on, until Charpentier had to beg me to have mercy on his great, snorting, panting camel. The road was beaten into paste and rutted two feet deep by the artillery, so that he was right in saying that it was not the place for a gallop.

I have never been very friendly with this Charpentier ;

and now for twenty miles of the way I could not draw a word from him. He rode with his brows puckered and his chin upon his breast, like a man who is heavy with thought. More than once I asked him what was on his mind, thinking that, perhaps, with my quicker intelligence I might set the matter straight. His answer always was that it was his mission of which he was thinking, which surprised me, because, although I had never thought much of his intelligence, still it seemed to me to be impossible that anyone could be puzzled by so simple and soldierly a task.

Well, we came at last to Bazoches, where he was to take the southern road and I the northern. He half turned in his saddle before he left me, and he looked at me with a singular expression of inquiry in his face.

" What do you make of it, Brigadier ? " he asked.

" Of what ? "

" Of our mission."

" Surely it is plain enough."

" You think so ? Why should the Emperor tell us his plans ? "

" Because he recognised our intelligence."

My companion laughed in a manner which I found annoying.

" May I ask what you intend to do if you find these villages full of Prussians ? " he asked.

" I shall obey my orders."

" But you will be killed."

" Very possibly."

He laughed again, and so offensively that I clapped my hand to my sword. But before I could tell him what I thought of his stupidity and rudeness he had wheeled his horse, and was lumbering away down the other road. I saw his big fur cap vanish over the brow of the hill, and then I rode upon my way, wondering at his conduct. From time to time I put my hand to the breast of my tunic and felt the paper crackle beneath my fingers. Ah, my precious paper, which should be turned into the little silver medal for which I had yearned so long. All the way from Braine to Sermoise I was thinking of what my mother would say when she saw it.

I stopped to give Violette a meal at a wayside auberge on the side of a hill not far from Soissons—a place surrounded by old oaks, and with so many crows that one could scarce hear one's own voice. It was from the innkeeper that I learned that Marmont had fallen back two days before, and that the Prussians were over the Aisne. An hour later, in the fading light, I saw two of their vedettes upon the hill to the right, and then, as darkness gathered, the heavens to the north were all glimmering from the lights of a bivouac.

When I heard that Blucher had been there for two days, I was much surprised that the Emperor should not have known that the country through which he had ordered me to carry my precious letter was already occupied by the enemy. Still, I thought of the tone of his voice when he said to Charpentier that a soldier must not choose, but must obey. I should follow the route he had laid down for me as long as Violette could move a hoof or I a finger upon her bridle. All the way from Sermoise to Soissons, where the road dips up and down, curving among fir woods, I kept my pistol ready and my sword-belt braced, pushing on swiftly where the path was straight, and then coming slowly round the corners in the way we learned in Spain.

When I came to the farmhouse which lies to the right of the road, just after you cross the wooden bridge over the Crise, near where the great statue of the Virgin stands, a woman cried to me from the field, saying that the Prussians were in Soissons. A small party of their lancers, she said, had come in that very afternoon, and a whole division was expected before midnight. I did not wait to hear the end of her tale, but clapped spurs into Violette, and in five minutes was galloping her into the town.

Three Uhlans were at the mouth of the main street,

their horses tethered, and they gossiping together, each with a pipe as long as my sabre. I saw them well in the light of an open door, but of me they could have seen only the flash of Violette's grey side and the black flutter of my cloak. A moment later I flew through a stream of them rushing from an open gateway. Violette's shoulder sent one of them reeling, and I stabbed at another but missed him. Pang, pang, went two carbines, but I had flown round the curve of the street, and never so much as heard the hiss of the balls. Ah, we were great, both Violette and I. She lay down to it like a coursed hare, the fire flying from her hoofs. I stood in my stirrups and brandished my sword. Someone sprang for my bridle. I sliced him through the arm, and I heard him howling behind me. Two horsemen closed upon me. I cut one down and outpaced the other. A minute later I was clear of the town, and flying down a broad white road with the black poplars on either side. For a time I heard the rattle of hoofs behind me, but they died and died until I could not tell them from the throbbing of my own heart. Soon I pulled up and listened, but all was silent. They had given up the chase.

Well, the first thing that I did was to dismount and to lead my mare into a small wood through which a stream ran. There I watered her and rubbed her down, giving her two pieces of sugar soaked in cognac from my flask. She was spent from the sharp chase, but it was wonderful to see how she came round with a half-hour's rest. When my thighs closed upon her again, I could tell by the spring and the swing of her that it would not be her fault if I did not win my way safe to Paris.

I must have been well within the enemy's lines now, for I heard a number of them shouting one of their rough drinking songs out of a house by the roadside, and I went round by the fields to avoid it. At another time two men came out into the moonlight (for by this time it was a cloudless night) and shouted something in German, but I galloped on without heeding them, and they were afraid to fire, for their own hussars are dressed exactly as I was. It is best to take no notice at these times, and then they put you down as a deaf man.

It was a lovely moon, and every tree threw a black bar across the road. I could see the country-side just as if it were daytime, and very peaceful it looked, save that there was a great fire raging somewhere in the north. In the silence of the night-time, and with the knowledge that danger was in front and behind me, the sight of that great distant fire was very striking and awesome. But I am not easily clouded, for I have seen too many singular things, so I hummed a tune between my teeth, and thought of little Lisette, whom I might see in Paris. My mind was full of her when, trotting round a corner, I came straight upon half-a-dozen German dragoons, who were sitting round a brushwood fire by the roadside.

I am an excellent soldier. I do not say this because I am prejudiced in my own favour, but because I really am so. I can weigh every chance in a moment, and decide with as much certainty as though I had brooded for a week. Now I saw like a flash that, come what might, I should be chased, and on a horse which had already done a long twelve leagues. But it was better to be chased onwards than to be chased back. On this moonlit night, with fresh horses behind me, I must take my risk in either case ; but if I were to shake them off, I preferred that it should be near Senlis than near Soissons.

All this flashed on me as if by instinct, you understand. My eyes had hardly rested on the bearded faces under the brass helmets before my rowels had touched Violette, and she off with a rattle like a pas-de-charge. Oh, the shouting and rushing and stamping from behind us ! Three of them fired and three swung themselves on to their horses. A bullet rapped on the crupper of my saddle with a noise like a stick on a door. Violette sprang madly forward, and I thought she had been wounded, but it was only a graze above the near fore-fetlock. Ah, the dear little mare, how I loved her when I felt her settle down into that long, easy gallop of hers, her hoofs going like a Spanish girl's castanets. I could not hold myself, I turned on my saddle and shouted and raved, " Vive l'Empereur ! " I screamed and laughed at the gust of oaths that came back to me.

But it was not over yet. If she had been fresh she might have gained a mile in five. Now she could only hold her own with a very little over. There was one of them, a young boy of an officer, who was better mounted than the others. He drew ahead with every stride. Two hundred yards behind him were two troopers, but I saw every time that I glanced round that the distance between them was increasing. The other three who had waited to shoot were a long way in the rear.

The officer's mount was a bay—a fine horse, though not to be spoken of with Violette ; yet it was a powerful brute, and it seemed to me that in a few miles its freshness might tell. I waited until the lad was a long way in front of his comrades, and then I eased my mare down a little —a very, very little, so that he might think he was really catching me. When he came within pistol-shot of me I drew and cocked my own pistol, and laid my chin upon my shoulder to see what he would do. He did not offer to fire, and I soon discerned the cause. The silly boy had taken his pistols from his holsters when he had camped for the night. He wagged his sword at me now and roared some threat or other. He did not seem to understand that he was at my mercy. I eased Violette down until there was not the length of a long lance between the grey tail and the bay muzzle.

" Rendez-vous ! " he yelled.

" I must compliment monsieur upon his French," said I, resting the barrel of my pistol upon my bridle-arm, which I have always found best when shooting from the saddle. I aimed at his face, and could see, even in the moonlight, how white he grew when he understood that it was all up with him. But even as my finger pressed the trigger I thought of his mother, and I put my ball through his horse's shoulder. I fear he hurt himself in the fall, for it was a fearful crash, but I had my letter to think of, so I stretched the mare into a gallop once more.

But they were not so easily shaken off, these brigands. The two troopers thought no more of their young officer than if he had been a recruit thrown in the riding-school. They left him to the others and thundered on after me. I had pulled up on the brow of a hill, thinking that I had heard the last of them ; but, my faith, I soon saw there was no time for loitering, so away we went, the mare tossing her head and I my shako, to show what we thought of two dragoons who tried to catch a hussar. But at this moment, even while I laughed at the thought, my heart stood still within me, for there at the end of the long white road was a black patch of cavalry waiting to receive me. To a young soldier it might have seemed the shadow of the trees, but to me it was a troop of hussars and, turn where I could, death seemed to be waiting for me.

Well, I had the dragoons behind me and the hussars in front. Never since Moscow have I seemed to be in such peril. But for the honour of the brigade I had rather be cut down by a light cavalryman than by a heavy. I never drew bridle, therefore, or hesitated for an instant, but I let Violette have her head. I remember that I tried to pray as I rode, but I am a little out of practice at such things, and the only words I could remember were the prayer for fine weather which we used at the school on the evening before holidays. Even this seemed better than nothing, and I was pattering it out, when suddenly I heard French voices in front of me. Ah, mon Dieu, but the joy went through my heart like a musket-ball. They were ours—our own dear little rascals from the corps of Marmont. Round whisked my two dragoons and galloped for their lives, with the moon gleaming on their brass helmets, while I trotted up to my friends with no undue haste, for I would have them understand that though a hussar may fly, it is not in his nature to fly very fast. Yet I fear that Violette's heaving flanks and foam-spattered muzzle gave the lie to my careless bearing.

Who should be at the head of the troop but old Bouvet, whom I saved at Leipzig! When he saw me his little pink eyes filled with tears, and, indeed, I could not but shed a few myself at the sight of his joy. I told him of my mission, but he laughed when I said that I must pass through Senlis.

" The enemy is there," said he. " You cannot go."

" I prefer to go where the enemy is," I answered.

" But why not go straight to Paris with your dispatch ? Why should you choose to pass through the one place where you are almost sure to be taken or killed ? "

" A soldier does not choose—he obeys," said I, just as I had heard Napoleon say it.

Old Bouvet laughed in his wheezy way, until I had to give my moustachios a twirl and look him up and down in a manner which brought him to reason.

" Well," said he, " you had best come along with us, for we are all bound for Senlis. Our orders are to reconnoitre the place. A squadron of Poniatowski's Polish Lancers are in front of us. If you must ride through it, it is possible that we may be able to go with you."

So away we went, jingling and clanking through the quiet night until we came up with the Poles—fine old soldiers all of them, though a trifle heavy for their horses. It was a treat to see them, for they could not have carried themselves better if they had belonged to my own brigade. We rode together, until in the early morning we saw the lights of Senlis. A peasant was coming along with a cart, and from him we learned how things were going there.

His information was certain, for his brother was the Mayor's coachman, and he had spoken with him late the night before. There was a single squadron of Cossacks —or a polk, as they call it in their frightful language— quartered upon the Mayor's house, which stands at the corner of the market-place, and is the largest building in the town. A whole division of Prussian infantry was encamped in the woods to the north, but only the Cossacks were in Senlis. Ah, what a chance to avenge ourselves upon these barbarians, whose cruelty to our poor countryfolk was the talk at every camp fire.

We were into the town like a torrent, hacked down the vedettes, rode over the guard, and were smashing in the doors of the Mayor's house before they understood that there was a Frenchman within twenty miles of them. We saw horrid heads at the windows—heads bearded to the temples, with tangled hair and sheepskin caps, and silly, gaping mouths. " Hourra ! Hourra ! " they shrieked, and fired with their carbines, but our fellows were into the house and at their throats before they had wiped the sleep out of their eyes. It was dreadful to see how the Poles flung themselves upon them, like starving wolves upon a herd of fat bucks—for, as you know, the Poles have a blood feud against the Cossacks. The most were killed in the upper rooms, whither they had fled for shelter, and the blood was pouring down into the hall like rain from a roof. They are terrible soldiers, these Poles, though I think they are a trifle heavy for their horses. Man for man, they are as big as Kellermann's cuirassiers. Their equipment is, of course, much lighter, since they are without the cuirass, back-plate and helmet.

Well, it was at this point that I made an error—a very serious error it must be admitted. Up to this moment I had carried out my mission in a manner which only my modesty prevents me from describing as remarkable. But now I did that which an official would condemn and a soldier excuse.

There is no doubt that the mare was spent, but still it is true that I might have galloped on through Senlis and reached the country, where I should have had no enemy between me and Paris. But what hussar can ride past a fight and never draw rein ? It is to ask too much of him. Besides, I thought that if Violette had an hour of rest I might have three hours the better at the other end. Then on the top of it came those heads at the windows, with their sheepskin hats and their barbarous cries. I sprang from my saddle, threw Violette's bridle over a rail-post, and ran into the house with the rest. It is true that I was too late to be of service, and that I was nearly wounded by a lance-thrust from one of these dying savages. Still, it is a pity to miss even the smallest affair, for one never knows what opportunity for advancement may present itself. I have seen more soldierly work in outpost skirmishes and little gallop-and-hack affairs of the kind than in any of the Emperor's big battles.

When the house was cleared I took a bucket of water out for Violette, and our peasant guide showed me where the good Mayor kept his fodder. My faith, but the little sweetheart was ready for it. Then I sponged down her legs, and leaving her still tethered I went back into the house to find a mouthful for myself, so that I should not need to halt again until I was in Paris.

And now I come to the part of my story which may seem singular to you, although I could tell you at least ten things every bit as queer which have happened to me in my lifetime. You can understand that, to a man who spends his life in scouting and vedette duties on the bloody ground which lies between two great armies, there are many chances of strange experiences. I'll tell you, however, exactly what occurred.

Old Bouvet was waiting in the passage when I entered, and he asked me whether we might not crack a bottle of wine together. " My faith, we must not be long," said he. " There are ten thousand of Theilmann's Prussians in the woods up yonder."

" Where is the wine ? " I asked.

" Ah, you may trust two hussars to find where the wine is," said he, and taking a candle in his hand, he led the way down the stone stairs into the kitchen.

When we got there we found another door, which

opened on to a winding stair with the cellar at the bottom. The Cossacks had been there before us, as was easily seen by the broken bottles littered all over it. However, the Mayor was a *bon-vivant*, and I do not wish to have a better set of bins to pick from. Chambertin, Graves, Alicant, white wine and red, sparkling and still, they lay in pyramids peeping coyly out of sawdust. Old Bouvet stood with his candle looking here and peeping there, purring in his throat like a cat before a milk-pail. He had picked upon a Burgundy at last, and had his hand outstretched to the bottle when there came a roar of musketry from above us, a rush of feet, and such a yelping and screaming as I have never listened to. The Prussians were upon us !

Bouvet is a brave man : I will say that for him. He flashed out his sword and away he clattered up the stone steps, his spurs clinking as he ran. I followed him, but just as we came out into the kitchen passage a tremendous shout told us that the house had been recaptured.

" It is all over," I cried, grasping at Bouvet's sleeve.

" There is one more to die," he shouted, and away he went like a madman up the second stair. In effect, I should have gone to my death also had I been in his place, for he had done very wrong in not throwing out his scouts to warn him if the Germans advanced upon him. For an instant I was about to rush up with him, and then I bethought myself that, after all, I had my own mission to think of, and that if I were taken the important letter of the Emperor would be sacrificed. I let Bouvet die alone, therefore, and I went down into the cellar again, closing the door behind me.

Well, it was not a very rosy prospect down there either. Bouvet had dropped the candle when the alarm came, and I, pawing about in the darkness, could find nothing but broken bottles. At last I came upon the candle, which had rolled under the curve of a cask, but, try as I would with my tinder-box, I could not light it. The reason was that the wick had been wet in a puddle of wine, so suspecting that this might be the case, I cut the end off with my sword. Then I found that it lighted easily enough. But what to do I could not imagine. The scoundrels upstairs were shouting themselves hoarse, several hundred of them from the sound, and it was clear that some of them would soon want to moisten their throats. There would be an end to a dashing soldier and of the mission and of the medal. I thought of my mother and I thought of the Emperor. It made me weep to think that the one would lose so excellent a son and the other the best light cavalry officer he ever had since Lasalle's time. But presently I dashed the tears from my eyes. " Courage ! " I cried, striking myself upon the chest. " Courage, my brave boy ! Is it possible that one who has come safely from Moscow without so much as a frost-bite will die in a French wine-cellar ? " At the thought I was up on my feet and clutching at the letter in my tunic, for the crackle of it gave me courage.

My first plan was to set fire to the house in the hope of escaping in the confusion. My second to get into an empty wine-cask. I was looking round to see if I could find one, when suddenly, in the corner, I espied a little low door, painted of the same grey colour as the wall, so that it was only a man with quick sight who would have noticed it. I pushed against it, and at first I imagined that it was locked. Presently, however, it gave a little, and then I understood that it was held by the pressure of something on the other side. I put my feet against a hogshead of wine, and I gave such a push that the door flew open and I came down with a crash upon my back, the candle flying out of my hands, so that I found myself in darkness once more. I picked myself up and stared through the black archway into the gloom beyond.

There was a slight ray of light coming from some slit or grating. The dawn had broken outside, and I could dimly see the long, curving sides of several huge casks, which made me think that perhaps this was where the Mayor kept his reserves of wine while they were maturing.

At any rate, it seemed to be a safer hiding-place than the outer cellar, so gathering up my candle, I was just closing the door behind me, when I suddenly saw something which filled me with amazement, and even, I confess, with the smallest little touch of fear.

I have said that at the farther end of the cellar there was a dim grey fan of light striking downwards from somewhere near the roof. Well, as I peered through the darkness, I suddenly saw a great, tall man skip into this belt of daylight, and then out again into the darkness at the further end. My word, I gave such a start that my shako nearly broke its chin-strap! It was only a glance, but, none the less, I had time to see that the fellow had a hairy Cossack cap on his head, and that he was a great, long-legged, broad-shouldered brigand, with a sabre at his waist. My faith, even Étienne Gerard was a little staggered at being left alone with such a creature in the dark.

But only for a moment. " Courage ! " I thought. " Am I not a hussar, a brigadier, too, at the age of thirty-one, and the chosen messenger of the Emperor ? " After all, this skulker had more cause to be afraid of me than I of him. And then suddenly I understood that he was afraid—horribly afraid. I could read it from his quick step and his bent shoulders as he ran among the barrels, like a rat making for its hole. And, of course, it must have been he who had held the door against me, and not some packing-case or wine-cask as I had imagined. He was the pursued, then, and I the pursuer. Aha, I felt my whiskers bristle as I advanced upon him through the darkness ! He would find that he had no chicken to deal with, this robber from the North. For the moment I was magnificent.

At first I had feared to light my candle lest I should make a mark of myself, but now, after cracking my shin over a box, and catching my spurs in some canvas, I thought the bolder course the wiser. I lit it, therefore, and then I advanced with long strides, my sword in my hand. " Come out, you rascal ! " I cried. " Nothing can save you. You will at last meet with your deserts."

I held my candle high, and presently I caught a glimpse of the man's head staring at me over a barrel. He had a gold chevron on his black cap, and the expression of his face told me in an instant that he was an officer and a man of refinement.

" Monsieur," he cried, in excellent French, " I surrender myself on a promise of quarter. But if I do not have your promise, I will then sell my life as dearly as I can."

" Sir," said I, " a Frenchman knows how to treat an unfortunate enemy. Your life is safe." With that he handed his sword over the top of the barrel, and I bowed with the candle on my heart. " Whom have I the honour of capturing ? " I asked.

" I am the Count Boutkine, of the Emperor's own Don Cossacks," said he. " I came out with my troop to reconnoitre Senlis, and as we found no sign of your people we determind to spend the night here."

" And would it be an indiscretion," I asked, " if I were to inquire how you came into the back cellar ? "

" Nothing more simple," said he. " It was our intention to start at early dawn. Feeling chilled after dressing, I thought that a cup of wine would do me no harm, so I came down to see what I could find. As I was rummaging about, the house was suddenly carried by assault so rapidly that by the time I had climbed the stairs it was all over. It only remained for me to save myself, so I came down here and hid myself in the back cellar, where you have found me."

I thought of how old Bouvet had behaved under the same conditions, and the tears sprang to my eyes as I contemplated the glory of France. Then I had to consider what I should do next. It was clear that this Russian Count, being in the back cellar while we were in the front one, had not heard the sounds which would have told him that the house was once again in the hands of his own allies. If he should once understand this the tables would be turned, and I should be his prisoner instead of he being mine. What was I to do ? I was at my wits' end, when suddenly there came to me an idea so brilliant that I could not but be amazed at my own invention.

" Count Boutkine," said I, " I find myself in a most difficult position."

" And why ? " he asked.

" Because I have promised you your life."

His jaw dropped a little.

" You would not withdraw your promise ? " he cried.

" If the worst comes to the worst I can die in your defence," said I ; " but the difficulties are great."

" What is it, then ? " he asked.

" I will be frank with you," said I. " You must know that our fellows, and especially the Poles, are so incensed against the Cossacks that the mere sight of the uniform drives them mad. They precipitate themselves instantly upon the wearer and tear him limb from limb. Even their officers cannot restrain them."

The Russian grew pale at my words and the way in which I said them.

" But this is terrible," said he.

" Horrible ! " said I. " If we were to go up together at this moment I cannot promise how far I could protect you."

" I am in your hands," he cried. " What would you suggest that we should do ? Would it not be best that I should remain here ? "

" That worst of all."

" And why ? "

" Because our fellows will ransack the house presently, and then you would be cut to pieces. No, no, I must go and break it to them. But even then, when once they see that accursed uniform, I do not know what may happen."

" Should I, then, take the uniform off ? "

" Excellent ! " I cried. " Hold, we have it ! You will take your uniform off and put on mine. That will make you sacred to every French soldier."

" It is not the French I fear so much as the Poles."

" But my uniform will be a safeguard against either."

" How can I thank you ? " he cried. " But you— what are you to wear ? "

" I will wear yours."

" And perhaps fall a victim to your generosity ? "

" It is my duty to take the risk," I answered ; " but I have no fears. I will ascend in your uniform. A hundred swords will be turned upon me. ' Hold ! ' I will shout, ' I am the Brigadier Gerard ! ' Then they will see my face. They will know me. And I will tell them about you. Under the shield of these clothes you will be sacred."

His fingers trembled with eagerness as he tore off his tunic. His boots and breeches were much like my own, so there was no need to change them, but I gave him my hussar jacket, my dolman, my shako, my sword-belt and my sabre-tasche, while I took in exchange his high sheep-skin cap with the gold chevron, his fur-trimmed coat and his crooked sword. Be it well understood that in changing the tunics I did not forget to change my thrice-precious letter also from my old one to my new.

" With your leave," said I, " I shall now bind you to a barrel."

He made a great fuss over this, but I have learned in my soldiering never to throw away chances, and how could I tell that he might not, when my back was turned, see how the matter really stood, and break in upon my plans ? He was leaning against a barrel at the time, so I ran six times round it with a rope, and then tied it with a big knot behind. If he wished to come upstairs he would, at least, have to carry a thousand litres of good French wine for a knapsack. I then shut the door of the back cellar behind me, so that he might not hear what was going forward, and tossing the candle away I ascended the kitchen stair.

There were only about twenty steps, and yet, while I came up them, I seemed to have time to think of everything that I had ever hoped to do. It was the same feeling that I had at Eylau when I lay with my broken leg and saw the horse artillery galloping down upon me. Of course, I knew that if I were taken I should be shot instantly as being disguised within the enemy's lines. Still, it was a glorious death—in the direct service of the Emperor—and I reflected that there could not be less than five lines, and perhaps seven, in the *Moniteur* about me. Palaret had eight lines, and I am sure that he had not so fine a career.

When I made my way out into the hall, with all the nonchalance in my face and manner that I could assume, the very first thing that I saw was Bouvet's dead body, with his legs drawn up and a broken sword in his hand. I could see by the black smudge that he had been shot at close quarters. I should have wished to salute as I went by, for he was a gallant man, but I feared lest I should be seen, and so I passed on.

The front of the hall was full of Prussian infantry, who were knocking loopholes in the wall, as though they expected that there might be yet another attack. Their officer, a little man, was running about giving directions. They were all too busy to take much notice of me, but another officer, who was standing by the door with a long pipe in his mouth, strode across and clapped me on the shoulder, pointing to the dead bodies of our poor hussars, and saying something which was meant for a jest, for his long beard opened and showed every fang in his head. I laughed heartily also, and said the only Russian words that I knew. I learned them from little Sophie, at Wilna, and they meant : " If the night is fine we shall meet under the oak tree, but if it rains we shall meet in the byre." It was all the same to this German, however, and I have no doubt that he gave me credit for saying something very witty indeed, for he roared laughing, and slapped me on my shoulder again. I nodded to him and marched out of the hall-door as coolly as if I were the commandant of the garrison.

There were a hundred horses tethered about outside, most of them belonging to the Poles and hussars. Good little Violette was waiting with the others, and she whinnied when she saw me coming towards her. But I would not mount her. No. I was much too cunning for that. On the contrary, I chose the most shaggy little Cossack horse that I could see, and I sprang upon it with as much assurance as though it had belonged to my father before me. It had a great bag of plunder slung over its neck, and this I laid upon Violette's back, and led her along beside me. Never have you seen such a picture of the Cossack returning from the foray. It was superb.

Well, the town was full of Prussians by this time. They lined the side-walks and pointed me out to each other, saying, as I could judge from their gestures, " There goes one of those devils of Cossacks. They are the boys for foraging and plunder."

One or two officers spoke to me with an air of authority, but I shook my head and smiled, and said, " If the night is fine we shall meet under the oak tree, but if it rains we shall meet in the byre," at which they shrugged their shoulders and gave the matter up. In this way I worked along until I was beyond the northern outskirt of the town. I could see in the roadway two lancer vedettes with their black and white pennons, and I knew that when I was once past these I should be a free man once more. I made my pony trot, therefore, Violette rubbing her nose against my knee all the time, and looking up at me to ask how she had deserved that this hairy doormat of a creature should be preferred to her. I was not more than a hundred yards from the Uhlans when, suddenly, you can imagine my feelings when I saw a real Cossack coming galloping along the road towards me.

Ah, my friend, you who read this, if you have any heart, you will feel for a man like me, who had gone through so many dangers and trials, only at this very last moment to be confronted with one which appeared to put an end to everything. I will confess that for a moment I lost heart, and was inclined to throw myself down in my despair, and to cry out that I had been betrayed. But, no ; I was not beaten even now. I opened two buttons of my tunic so that I might get easily at the Emperor's message, for it was my fixed determination when all hope was gone to swallow the letter and then die sword in hand. Then I felt that my little, crooked sword was loose in its sheath, and I trotted on to where the vedettes were waiting. They seemed inclined to stop me, but I pointed to the other Cossack, who was still a couple of hundred yards off, and they, understanding that I merely wished to meet him, let me pass with a salute.

I dug my spurs into my pony then, for if I were only far enough from the lancers I thought I might manage the Cossack without much difficulty. He was an officer, a large, bearded man, with a gold chevron in his cap, just the same as mine. As I advanced he unconsciously aided me by pulling up his horse, so that I had a fine start of the vedettes. On I came for him, and I could see wonder changing to suspicion in his brown eyes as he looked at me and at my pony, and at my equipment. I do not know what it was that was wrong, but he saw something which was as it should not be. He shouted out a question, and then when I gave no answer he pulled out his sword. I was glad in my heart to see him do so, for I had always rather fight than cut down an unsuspecting enemy. Now I made at him full tilt, and, parrying his cut, I got my point in just under the fourth button of his tunic. Down he went, and the weight of him nearly took me off my horse before I could disengage. I never glanced at him to see if he were living or dead, for I sprang off my pony and on to Violette, with a shake of my bridle and a kiss of my hand to the two Uhlans behind me. They galloped after me, shouting, but Violette had had her rest, and was just as fresh as when she started. I took the first side road to the west and then the first to the south, which would take me away from the enemy's country. On we went and on, every stride taking me farther from my foes and nearer to my friends. At last, when I reached the end of a long stretch of road, and looking back from it could see no sign of any pursuers, I understood that my troubles were over.

And it gave me a glow of happiness, as I rode, to think that I had done to the letter what the Emperor had ordered. What would he say when he saw me ? What could he say which would do justice to the incredible way in which I had risen above every danger ? He had ordered me to go through Sermoise, Soissons and Senlis, little dreaming that they were all three occupied by the enemy. And yet I had done it. I had borne his letter in safety through each of these towns. Hussars, dragoons, lancers, Cossacks and infantry—I had run the gauntlet of all of them, and had come out unharmed.

When I had got as far as Dammartin I caught a first glimpse of our own outposts. There was a troop of dragoons in a field, and of course I could see from the horsehair crests that they were French, I galloped towards them in order to ask them if all was safe between there and Paris, and as I rode I felt such a pride at having won my way back to my friends again, that I could not refrain from waving my sword in the air.

At this a young officer galloped out from among the dragoons, also brandishing his sword, and it warmed my heart to think that he should come riding with such ardour and enthusiasm to greet me. I made Violette caracole, and as we came together I brandished my sword more gallantly than ever, but you can imagine my feelings when he suddenly made a cut at me which would certainly have taken my head off if I had not fallen forward with my nose in Violette's mane. My faith, it whistled just over my cap like an east wind. Of course, it came from this accursed Cossack uniform which, in my excitement, I had forgotten all about, and this young dragoon had imagined that I was some Russian champion who was challenging the French cavalry. My word, he was a frightened man when he understood how near he had been to killing the celebrated Brigadier Gerard.

Well, the road was clear, and about three o'clock in the afternoon I was at St. Denis, though it took me a long two hours to get from there to Paris, for the road was blocked with commissariat waggons and guns of the artillery reserve, which was going north to Marmont and Mortier. You cannot conceive the excitement which my appearance in such a costume made in Paris, and when I came to the Rue de Rivoli I should think I had a quarter of a mile of folk riding or running behind me. Word had got about from the dragoons (two of whom had come with me), and everybody knew about my adventures and how I had come by my uniform. It was a triumph—men shouting and women waving their handkerchiefs and blowing kisses from the windows.

Although I am a man singularly free from conceit, still I must confess that, on this one occasion, I could not restrain myself from showing that this reception gratified me. The Russian's coat had hung very loose upon me, but now I threw out my chest until it was as tight as a sausage-skin. And my little sweetheart of a mare tossed her mane and pawed with her front hoofs, frisking her tail about as though she said, " We've done it together this time. It is to us that commissions should be entrusted." When I kissed her between the nostrils as I dismounted at the gate of the Tuileries, there was as much shouting as if a bulletin had been read from the Grand Army.

I was hardly in costume to visit a King ; but, after all, if one has a soldierly figure one can do without all that. I was shown up straight away to Joseph, whom I had often seen in Spain. He seemed as stout, as quiet and as amiable as ever. Talleyrand was in the room with him, or I suppose I should call him the Duke of Benevento, but I confess that I like old names best. He read my letter when Joseph Buonaparte handed it to him, and then he looked at me with the strangest expression in those funny little, twinkling eyes of his.

" Were you the only messenger ? " he asked.

" There was one other, sir," said I. " Major Charpentier, of the Horse Grenadiers.'

" He has not yet arrived," said the King of Spain.

" If you had seen the legs of his horse, sire, you would not wonder at it," I remarked.

" There may be other reasons," said Talleyrand, and he gave that singular smile of his.

Well, they paid me a compliment or two, though they might have said a good deal more and yet have said too little. I bowed myself out, and very glad I was to get away, for I hate a Court as much as I love a camp. Away I went to my old friend Chaubert, in the Rue Miromesnil, and there I got his hussar uniform, which fitted me very well. He and Lisette and I supped together in his rooms, and all my dangers were forgotten. In the morning I found Violette ready for another twenty-league stretch. It was my intention to return instantly to the Emperor's headquarters, for I was, as you may well imagine, impatient to hear his words of praise, and to receive my reward.

I need not say that I rode back by a safe route, for I had seen quite enough of Uhlans and Cossacks. I passed through Meaux and Château Thierry, and so in the evening I arrived at Rheims, where Napoleon was still lying. The bodies of our fellows and of St. Prest's Russians had all been buried, and I could see changes in the camp also. The soldiers looked better cared for ; some of the cavalry had received remounts, and everything was in excellent order. It was wonderful what a good general can effect in a couple of days.

When I came to the headquarters I was shown

straight into the Emperor's room. He was drinking coffee at a writing-table, with a big plan drawn out on paper in front of him. Berthier and Macdonald were leaning one over each shoulder, and he was talking so quickly that I don't believe that either of them could catch a half of what he was saying. But when his eyes fell upon me he dropped the pen on to the chart, and he sprang up with a look in his pale face which struck me cold.

" What the deuce are you doing here ? " he shouted. When he was angry he had a voice like a peacock.

" I have the honour to report to you, sire," said I, " that I have delivered your dispatch safely to the King of Spain."

" What ! " he yelled, and his two eyes transfixed me like bayonets. Oh, those dreadful eyes, shifting from grey to blue, like steel in the sunshine. I can see them now when I have a bad dream.

" What has become of Charpentier ? " he asked.

" He is captured," said Macdonald.

" By whom ? "

" The Russians."

" The Cossacks ? "

" No, a single Cossack."

" He gave himself up ? "

" Without resistance."

" He is an intelligent officer. You will see that the medal of honour is awarded to him."

When I heard those words I had to rub my eyes to make sure that I was awake.

" As to you," cried the Emperor, taking a step forward as if he would have struck me, " you brain of a hare, what do you think that you were sent upon this mission for ? Do you conceive that I would send a really important message by such a hand as yours, and through every village which the enemy holds ? How you came through them passes my comprehension ; but if your fellow-messenger had had but as little sense as you, my whole plan of campaign would have been ruined. Can you not see, coglione, that this message contained false news, and that it was intended to deceive the enemy whilst I put a very different scheme into execution?"

When I heard those cruel words and saw the angry, white face which glared at me, I had to hold the back of a chair, for my mind was failing me and my knees would hardly bear me up. But then I took courage as I reflected that I was an honourable gentleman, and that my whole life had been spent in toiling for this man and for my beloved country.

"Sire," said I, and the tears would trickle down my cheeks whilst I spoke, "when you are dealing with a man like me you would find it wiser to deal openly. Had I known that you had wished the dispatch to fall into the hands of the enemy, I would have seen that it came there. As I believed that I was to guard it, I was prepared to sacrifice my life for it. I do not believe, sire, that any man in the world ever met with more toils and perils than I have done in trying to carry out what I thought was your will."

I dashed the tears from my eyes as I spoke, and with such fire and spirit as I could command I gave him an account of it all, of my dash through Soissons, my brush with the dragoons, my adventure in Senlis, my rencontre with Count Boutkine in the cellar, my disguise, my meeting with the Cossack officer, my flight, and how at the last moment I was nearly cut down by a French dragoon. The Emperor, Berthier and Macdonald listened with astonishment on their faces. When I had finished Napoleon stepped forward and he pinched me by the ear.

"There, there!" said he. "Forget anything which I may have said. I would have done better to trust you. You may go."

I turned to the door, and my hand was upon the handle, when the Emperor called upon me to stop.

"You will see," said he, turning to the Duke of

Tarentum, " that Brigadier Gerard has the special medal of honour, for I believe that if he has the thickest head he has also the stoutest heart in my army."

8. *How the Brigadier was tempted by the Devil*

THE spring is at hand, my friends. I can see the little green spear-heads breaking out once more upon the chestnut trees, and the café tables have all been moved into the sunshine. It is more pleasant to sit there, and yet I do not wish to tell my little stories to the whole town. You have heard my doings as a lieu-tenant, as a squadron officer, as a colonel, as the chief of a brigade. But now I suddenly become something higher and more important. I become history.

If you have read of those closing years of the life of the Emperor which were spent in the Island of St. Helena, you will remember that, again and again, he implored permission to send out one single letter which should be unopened by those who held him. Many times he made this request, and even went so far as to promise that he would provide for his own wants and cease to be an expense to the British Government if it were granted to him. But his guardians knew that he was a terrible man, this pale, fat gentleman in the straw hat, and they dared not grant him what he asked. Many have wondered who it was to whom he could have had anything so secret to say. Some have supposed that it was to his wife, and some that it was to his father-in-law ; some that it was to the Emperor Alexander, and some to Marshal Soult. What will you think of me, my friends, when I tell you it was to me—to me, the Brigadier Gerard—that the Emperor wished to write ? Yes, humble as you see me, with only my 100 francs a month of half-pay between me and hunger, it is none the less true that I was always in the Emperor's mind, and that he would have given his left hand for five minutes' talk with me. I will tell you to-night how this came about.

It was after the Battle of Fére-Champenoise, where the conscripts in their blouses and their sabots made such a fine stand, that we, the more long-headed of us, began to understand that it was all over with us. Our reserve ammunition had been taken in the battle, and we were left with silent guns and empty caissons. Our cavalry, too, was in a deplorable condition, and my own brigade had been destroyed in the charge at Craonne. Then came the news that the enemy had taken Paris, that the citizens had mounted the white cockade ; and finally, most terrible of all, that Marmont and his corps had gone over to the Bourbons. We looked at each other, and asked how many more of our generals were going to turn against us. Already there were Jourdan, Marmont, Murat, Bernadotte and Jomini—though nobody minded much about Jomini, for his pen was always sharper than his sword. We had been ready to fight Europe, but it looked now as though we were to fight Europe and half France as well.

We had come to Fontainebleau by a long, forced march, and there we were assembled, the poor remnants of us, the corps of Ney, the corps of my cousin Gerard, and the corps of Macdonald : twenty-five thousand in all, with seven thousand of the guard. But we had our prestige, which was worth fifty thousand, and our Emperor, who was worth fifty thousand more. He was always among us, serene, smiling, confident, taking his snuff and playing with his little riding-whip. Never in the days of his greatest victories have I admired him as much as I did during the Campaign of France.

One evening I was with a few of my officers, drinking a glass of wine of Suresnes. I mention that it was wine of Suresnes just to show you that times were not very good with us. Suddenly I was disturbed by a message from Berthier that he wished to see me. When I speak of my old comrades-in-arms, I will, with your permission, leave out all the fine foreign titles which they had picked up during the wars. They are excellent for a Court, but you never heard them in the camp, for we could not afford to do away with our Ney, our Rapp, or our Soult—names which were as stirring to our ears as the blare of our trumpets blowing the reveille. It was Berthier, then, who sent to say that he wished to see me.

He had a suite of rooms at the end of the gallery of Francis the First, not very far from those of the Emperor. In the ante-chamber were waiting two men whom I knew well : Colonel Despienne, of the 57th of the line, and Captain Tremeau, of the Voltigeurs. They were both old soldiers—Tremeau had carried a musket in Egypt —and they were also both famous in the army for their courage and their skill with weapons. Tremeau had become a little stiff in the wrist, but Despienne was capable at his best of making me exert myself. He was a tiny fellow, about three inches short of the proper height for a man—he was exactly three inches shorter than myself—but both with the sabre and with the small-sword he had several times almost held his own against me when we used to exhibit at Verron's Hall of Arms in the Palais Royal. You may think that it made us sniff something in the wind when we found three such men called together into one room. You cannot see the lettuce and dressing without suspecting a salad.

" Name of a pipe ! " said Tremeau, in his barrack-room fashion. " Are we then expecting three champions of the Bourbons ? "

To all of us the idea appeared not improbable. Certainly in the whole army we were the very three who might have been chosen to meet them.

" The Prince of Neufchâtel desires to speak with the Brigadier Gerard," said a footman, appearing at the door.

In I went, leaving my two companions consumed with impatience behind me. It was a small room, but very gorgeously furnished. Berthier was seated opposite to me at a little table, with a pen in his hand and a note-book open before him. He was looking weary and slovenly—very different from that Berthier who used to give the fashion to the army, and who had so often set us poorer officers tearing our hair by trimming his pelisse with fur one campaign, and with grey astrakhan the next. On his clean-shaven, comely face there was an expression of trouble, and he looked at me as I entered his chamber in a way which had in it something furtive and displeasing.

" Chief of Brigade Gerard ! " said he.

" At your service, your Highness ! " I answered.

" I must ask you, before I go farther, to promise me, upon your honour as a gentleman and a soldier, that what is about to pass between us shall never be mentioned to any third person."

My word, this was a fine beginning ! I had no choice but to give the promise required.

" You must know, then, that it is all over with the Emperor," said he, looking down at the table and speaking very slowly, as if he had a hard task in getting out the words. " Jourdan at Rouen and Marmont at Paris have both mounted the white cockade, and it is rumoured that Talleyrand has talked Ney into doing the same. It is evident that further resistance is useless, and that it can only bring misery upon our country. I wish to ask you, therefore, whether you are prepared to join me in laying hands upon the Emperor's person, and bringing the war to a conclusion by delivering him over to the allies ? "

I assure you that when I heard this infamous proposition put forward by the man who had been the earliest friend of the Emperor, and who had received greater favours from him than any of his followers, I could only stand and stare at him in amazement. For his part he tapped his pen-handle against his teeth, and looked at me with a slanting head.

" Well ? " he asked.

" I am a little deaf on one side," said I, coldly. " There

are some things which I cannot hear. I beg that you will permit me to return to my duties."

" Nay, but you must not be headstrong," rising up and laying his hand upon my shoulder. " You are aware that the Senate has declared against Napoleon, and that the Emperor Alexander refuses to treat with him."

" Sir," I cried, with passion, " I would have you know that I do not care the dregs of a wine-glass for the Senate or for the Emperor Alexander either."

" Then for what do you care ? "

" For my own honour and for the service of my glorious master, the Emperor Napoleon."

" That is all very well," said Berthier, peevishly, shrugging his shoulders. " Facts are facts, and as men of the world, we must look them in the face. Are we to stand against the will of the nation ? Are we to have civil war on the top of all our misfortunes ? And, besides, we are thinning away. Every hour comes the news of fresh desertions. We have still time to make our peace, and, indeed, to earn the highest reward, by giving up the Emperor."

I shook so with passion that my sabre clattered against my thigh.

" Sir," I cried, " I never thought to have seen the day when a Marshal of France would have so far degraded himself as to put forward such a proposal. I leave you to your own conscience ; but as for me, until I have the Emperor's own order, there shall always be the sword of Étienne Gerard between his enemies and himself."

I was so moved by my own words and by the fine position which I had taken up, that my voice broke, and I could hardly refrain from tears. I should have liked the whole army to have seen me as I stood with my head so proudly erect and my hand upon my heart proclaiming my devotion to the Emperor in his adversity. It was one of the supreme moments of my life.

" Very good," said Berthier, ringing a bell for the

lackey. " You will show the Chief of Brigade Gerard into the salon."

The footman led me into an inner room, where he desired me to be seated. For my own part, my only desire was to get away, and I could not understand why they should wish to detain me. When one has had no change of uniform during a whole winter's campaign, one does not feel at home in a palace.

I had been there about a quarter of an hour when the footman opened the door again, and in came Colonel Despienne. Good heavens, what a sight he was ! His face was as white as a guardsman's gaiters, his eyes projecting, the veins swollen upon his forehead, and every hair of his moustache bristling like those of an angry cat. He was too angry to speak, and could only shake his hands at the ceiling and make a gurgling in his throat. " Parricide ! Viper ! " those were the words that I could catch as he stamped up and down the room.

Of course it was evident to me that he had been subjected to the same infamous proposals as I had, and that he had received them in the same spirit. His lips were sealed to me, as mine were to him, by the promise which we had taken, but I contented myself with muttering " Atrocious ! Unspeakable ! "—so that he might know that I was in agreement with him.

Well, we were still there, he striding furiously up and down, and I seated in the corner, when suddenly a most extraordinary uproar broke out in the room which we had just quitted. There was a snarling, worrying growl, like that of a fierce dog which has got his grip. Then came a crash and a voice calling for help. In we rushed, the two of us, and, my faith, we were none too soon.

Old Tremeau and Berthier were rolling together upon the floor, with the table upon the top of them. The Captain had one of his great, skinny yellow hands upon the Marshal's throat, and already his face was lead-coloured, and his eyes were starting from their sockets. As to Tremeau, he was beside himself, with foam upon the corners of his lips, and such a frantic expression upon him that I am convinced, had we not loosened his iron grip, finger by finger, that it would never have relaxed while the Marshal lived. His nails were white with the power of his grasp.

" I have been tempted by the devil ! " he cried, as he staggered to his feet. " Yes, I have been tempted by the devil ! "

As to Berthier, he could only lean against the wall, and pant for a couple of minutes, putting his hands up to his throat and rolling his head about. Then, with an angry gesture, he turned to the heavy blue curtain which hung behind his chair.

The curtain was torn to one side and the Emperor stepped out into the room. We sprang to the salute, we three old soldiers, but it was all like a scene in a dream to us, and our eyes were as far out as Berthier's had been. Napoleon was dressed in his green-coated chasseur uniform, and he held his little, silver-headed switch in his hand. He looked at us each in turn, with a smile upon his face—that frightful smile in which neither eyes nor brow joined—and each in turn had, I believe, a pringling on his skin, for that was the effect which the Emperor's gaze had upon most of us. Then he walked across to Berthier and put his hand upon his shoulder.

" You must not quarrel with blows, my dear Prince," said he ; " they are your title to nobility." He spoke in that soft, caressing manner which he could assume. There was no one who could make the French tongue sound so pretty as the Emperor, and no one who could make it more harsh and terrible.

" I believe he would have killed me," cried Berthier, still rolling his head about.

" Tut, tut ! I should have come to your help had these officers not heard your cries. But I trust that you are not really hurt ! " He spoke with earnestness, for he was in truth very fond of Berthier—more so than of any man, unless it were of poor Duroc.

Berthier laughed, though not with a very good grace. " It is new for me to receive my injuries from French hands," said he.

" And yet it was in the cause of France," returned the Emperor. Then, turning to us, he took old Tremeau by the ear. " Ah, old grumbler," said he, " you were one of my Egyptian grenadiers, were you not, and had your musket of honour at Marengo. I remember you very well, my good friend. So the old fires are not yet extinguished ! They still burn up when you think that your Emperor is wronged. And you, Colonel Despienne, you would not even listen to the tempter. And you, Gerard, your faithful sword is ever to be between me and my enemies. Well, well, I have had some traitors about me, but now at last we are beginning to see who are the true men."

You can fancy, my friends, the thrill of joy which it gave us when the greatest man in the whole world spoke to us in this fashion. Tremeau shook until I thought he would have fallen, and the tears ran down his gigantic moustache. If you had not seen it, you could never believe the influence which the Emperor had upon those coarse-grained, savage old veterans.

" Well, my faithful friends," said he, " if you will follow me into this room, I will explain to you the meaning of this little farce which we have been acting. I beg, Berthier, that you will remain in this chamber, and so make sure that no one interrupts us."

It was new for us to be doing business with a Marshal of France as sentry at the door. However, we followed the Emperor as we were ordered, and he led us into the recess of the window, gathering us around him and sinking his voice as he addressed us.

" I have picked you out of the whole army," said he, " as being not only the most formidable but also the most faithful of my soldiers. I was convinced that you were all three men who would never waver in your fidelity to me. If I have ventured to put that fidelity to the proof, and to watch you while attempts were at my orders made upon your honour, it was only because, in the days when I have found the blackest treason amongst my own flesh and blood, it is necessary that I should be doubly circumspect. Suffice it that I am well convinced now that I can rely upon your valour."

" To the death, sire ! " cried Tremeau, and we both repeated it after him.

Napoleon drew us all yet a little closer to him, and sank his voice still lower.

" What I say to you now I have said to no one—not to my wife or my brothers ; only to you. It is all up with us, my friends. We have come to our last rally. The game is finished, and we must make provision accordingly."

My heart seemed to have changed to a nine-pounder ball as I listened to him. We had hoped against hope, but now when he, the man who was always serene and who always had reserves—when he, in that quiet, impassive voice of his, said that everything was over, we realised that the clouds had shut for ever, and the last gleam gone. Tremeau snarled and gripped at his sabre, Despienne ground his teeth, and for my own part I threw out my chest and clicked my heels to show the Emperor that there were some spirits which could rise to adversity.

" My papers and my fortune must be secured," whispered the Emperor. " The whole course of the future may depend upon my having them safe. They are our base for the next attempt—for I am very sure that these poor Bourbons would find that my footstool is too large to make a throne for them. Where am I to keep these precious things ? My belongings will be searched—so will the houses of my supporters. They must be secured and concealed by men whom I can trust with that which is more precious to me than my life. Out of the whole of France, you are those whom I have chosen for this sacred trust.

" In the first place, I will tell you what these papers

are. You shall not say that I have made you blind agents in the matter. They are the official proof of my divorce from Josephine, of my legal marriage to Marie Louise, and of the birth of my son and heir, the King of Rome. If we cannot prove each of these, the future claim of my family to the throne of France falls to the ground. Then there are securities to the value of forty millions of francs —an immense sum, my friends, but of no more value than this riding-switch when compared to the other papers of which I have spoken. I tell you these things that you may realise the enormous importance of the task which I am committing to your care. Listen, now, while I inform you where you are to get these papers, and what you are to do with them.

" They were handed over to my trusty friend, the Countess Walewski, at Paris, this morning. At five o'clock she starts for Fontainebleau in her blue berline. She should reach here between half-past nine and ten. The papers will be concealed in the berline, in a hiding-place which none know but herself. She has been warned that her carriage will be stopped outside the town by three mounted officers, and she will hand the packet over to your care. You are the younger man, Gerard, but you are of the senior grade. I confide to your care this amethyst ring, which you will show the lady as a token of your mission, and which you will leave with her as a receipt for her papers.

" Having received the packet, you will ride with it into the forest as far as the ruined dove-house—the Colombier. It is possible that I may meet you there—but if it seems to me to be dangerous, I will send my body-servant, Mustapha, whose directions you may take as being mine. There is no roof to the Colombier, and to-night will be a full moon. At the right of the entrance you will find three spades leaning against the wall. With these you will dig a hole three feet deep in the north-eastern corner —that is, in the corner to the left of the door, and nearest Fontainebleau. Having buried the papers, you will replace the soil with great care, and you will then report to me at the palace."

These were the Emperor's directions, but given with an accuracy and minuteness of detail such as no one but himself could put into an order. When he had finished, he made us swear to keep his secret as long as he lived, and as long as the papers should remain buried. Again and again he made us swear it before he dismissed us from his presence.

Colonel Despienne had quarters at the " Sign of the Pheasant," and it was there that we supped together. We were all three men who had been trained to take the strangest turns of fortune as part of our daily life and business, yet we were all flushed and moved by the extraordinary interview which we had had, and by the thought of the great adventure which lay before us. For my own part, it had been my fate three several times to take my orders from the lips of the Emperor himself, but neither the incident of the Ajaccio murderers nor the famous ride which I made to Paris appeared to offer such opportunities as this new and most intimate commission.

" If things go right with the Emperor," said Despienne, " we shall all live to be marshals yet."

We drank with him to our future cocked hats and our bâtons.

It was agreed between us that we should make our way separately to our rendezvous, which was to be the first milestone upon the Paris road. In this way we should avoid the gossip which might get about if three men who were so well known were to be seen riding out together. My little Violette had cast a shoe that morning, and the farrier was at work upon her when I returned, so that my comrades were already there when I arrived at the trysting-place. I had taken with me not only my sabre, but also my new pair of English rifled pistols, with a mallet for knocking in the charges. They had cost me a hundred and fifty francs at Trouvel's, in the Rue de Rivoli, but they would carry far further and straighter than the others. It was with one of them that I had saved old Bouvet's life at Leipzig.

The night was cloudless, and there was a brilliant moon behind us, so that we always had three black horsemen riding down the white road in front of us. The country is so thickly wooded, however, that we could not see very far. The great palace clock had already struck ten, but there was no sign of the Countess. We began to fear that something might have prevented her from starting.

And then suddenly we heard her in the distance. Very faint at first were the birr of wheels and the tat-tat-tat of the horses' feet. Then they grew louder and clearer and louder yet, until a pair of yellow lanterns swung round the curve, and in their light we saw the two big brown horses tearing along with the high, blue carriage at the back of them. The postilion pulled them up panting and foaming within a few yards of us. In a moment we were at the window and had raised our hands in a salute to the beautiful pale face which looked out at us.

" We are the three officers of the Emperor, madame," said I, in a low voice, leaning my face down to the open window. " You have already been warned that we should wait upon you."

The Countess had a very beautiful, cream-tinted complexion of a sort which I particularly admire, but she grew whiter and whiter as she looked up at me. Harsh lines deepened upon her face until she seemed, even as I looked at her, to turn from youth into age.

" It is evident to me," she said, " that you are three impostors."

If she had struck me across the face with her delicate hand she could not have startled me more. It was not her words only, but the bitterness with which she hissed them out.

" Indeed, madame," said I. " You do us less than justice. These are the Colonel Despienne and Captain

Tremeau. For myself, my name is Brigadier Gerard, and I have only to mention it to assure anyone who has heard of me that——"

"Oh, you villains!" she interrupted. "You think that because I am only a woman I am very easily to be hoodwinked! You miserable impostors!"

I looked at Despienne, who had turned white with anger, and at Tremeau, who was tugging at his moustache.

"Madame," said I, coldly, "when the Emperor did us the honour to entrust us with this mission, he gave me this amethyst ring as a token. I had not thought that three honourable gentlemen would have needed such corroboration, but I can only confute your unworthy suspicions by placing it in your hands."

She held it up in the light of the carriage lamp, and the most dreadful expression of grief and of horror contorted her face.

"It is his!" she screamed, and then, "Oh, my God, what have I done? What have I done?"

I felt that something terrible had befallen. "Quick, madame, quick!" I cried. "Give us the papers!"

"I have already given them."

"Given them! To whom?"

"To three officers."

"When?"

"Within the half-hour."

"Where are they?"

"God help me, I do not know. They stopped the berline, and I handed them over to them without hesitation, thinking that they had come from the Emperor."

It was a thunder-clap. But those are the moments when I am at my finest.

"You remain here," said I, to my comrades. "If three horsemen pass you, stop them at any hazard. The lady will describe them to you. I will be with you presently." One shake of the bridle, and I was flying into Fontainebleau as only Violette could have carried me. At the palace I flung myself off, rushed up the stairs, brushed aside the lackeys who would have stopped me, and pushed my way into the Emperor's own cabinet. He and Macdonald were busy with pencil and compasses over a chart. He looked up with an angry frown at my sudden entry, but his face changed colour when he saw that it was I.

"You can leave us, Marshal," said he, and then, the instant the door was closed: "What news about the papers?"

"They are gone!" said I, and in a few curt words I told him what had happened. His face was calm, but I saw the compasses quiver in his hand.

"You must recover them, Gerard!" he cried. "The destinies of my dynasty are at stake. Not a moment is to be lost! To horse, sir, to horse!"

"Who are they, sire?"

"I cannot tell. I am surrounded with treason. But they will take them to Paris. To whom should they carry them but to the villain Talleyrand? Yes, yes, they are on the Paris road, and may yet be overtaken. With the three best mounts in my stables and——"

I did not wait to hear the end of the sentence. I was already clattering down the stair. I am sure that five minutes had not passed before I was galloping Violette out of the town with the bridle of one of the Emperor's own Arab chargers in either hand. They wished me to take three, but I should have never dared to look my Violette in the face again. I feel that the spectacle must have been superb when I dashed up to my comrades and pulled the horses on to their haunches in the moonlight.

"No one has passed?"

"No one."

"Then they are on the Paris road. Quick! Up and after them!"

They did not take long, those good soldiers. In a flash they were upon the Emperor's horses, and their own left masterless by the roadside. Then away we went upon our long chase, I in the centre, Despienne upon my right, and Tremeau a little behind, for he was the heavier man. Heavens, how we galloped! The twelve flying hoofs roared and roared along the hard, smooth road. Poplars and moon, black bars and silver streaks, for mile after mile our course lay along the same chequered track, with our shadows in front and our dust behind. We could hear the rasping of bolts and the creaking of shutters from the cottages as we thundered past them, but we were only three dark blurs upon the road by the time that the folk could look after us. It was just striking midnight as we raced into Corbail; but an ostler with a bucket in either hand was throwing his black shadow across the golden fan which was cast from the open door of the inn.

" Three riders ! " I gasped. " Have they passed ? "

" I have just been watering their horses," said he. " I should think they——"

" On, on, my friends ! " and away we flew, striking fire from the cobblestones of the little town. A gendarme tried to stop us, but his voice was drowned by our rattle and clatter. The houses slid past, and we were out on the country road again, with a clear twenty miles between ourselves and Paris. How could they escape us, with the finest horses in France behind them ? Not one of the three had turned a hair, but Violette was always a head and shoulders to the front. She was going within herself too, and I knew by the spring of her that I had only to let her stretch herself, and the Emperor's horses would see the colour of her tail.

" There they are ! " cried Despienne.

" We have them ! " growled Tremeau.

" On, comrades, on ! " I shouted, once more.

A long stretch of white road lay before us in the moonlight. Far away down it we could see three cavaliers, lying low upon their horses' necks. Every instant they grew larger and clearer as we gained upon them. I could see quite plainly that the two upon either side were wrapped in mantles and rode upon chestnut horses, whilst the man between them was dressed in a chasseur uniform and mounted upon a grey. They were keeping abreast, but it was easy enough to see from the way in which he gathered his legs for each spring that the centre horse was far the fresher of the three. And the rider appeared to be the leader of the party, for we continually saw the glint of his face in the moonshine as he looked back to measure the distance between us. At first it was only a glimmer, then it was cut across with a moustache, and at last when we began to feel their dust in our throats I could give a name to my man.

" Halt, Colonel de Montluc ! " I shouted. " Halt in the Emperor's name ! "

I had known him for years as a daring officer and an unprincipled rascal. Indeed, there was a score between us, for he had shot my friend, Treville, at Warsaw, pulling his trigger, as some said, a good second before the drop of the handkerchief.

Well, the words were hardly out of my mouth when his two comrades wheeled round and fired their pistols at us. I heard Despienne give a terrible cry, and at the same instant both Tremeau and I let drive at the same man. He fell forward with his hands swinging on each side of his horse's neck. His comrade spurred on to Tremeau, sabre in hand, and I heard the crash which comes when a strong cut is met by a stronger parry. For my own part I never turned my head, but I touched Violette with the spur for the first time and flew after the leader. That he should leave his comrades and fly was proof enough that I should leave mine and follow.

He had gained a couple of hundred paces, but the good little mare set that right before we could have passed two milestones. It was in vain that he spurred and thrashed like a gunner driver on a soft road. His hat flew off with his exertions, and his bald head gleamed in the moonshine. But do what he might, he still heard the rattle of the hoofs growing louder and louder behind him. I could not have been twenty yards from him, and the shadow head was touching the shadow haunch, when he turned with a curse in his saddle and emptied both his pistols, one after the other, into Violette.

I have been wounded myself so often that I have to stop and think before I can tell you the exact number of times. I have been hit by musket balls, by pistol bullets and by bursting shells, besides being pierced by bayonet, lance, sabre and finally by a brad-awl, which was the most painful of any. Yet out of all these injuries I have never known the same deadly sickness as came over me when I felt the poor, silent, patient creature, which I had come to love more than anything in the world except my mother and the Emperor, reel and stagger beneath me. I pulled my second pistol from my holster and fired point-blank between the fellow's broad shoulders. He slashed his horse across the flank with his whip, and for a moment I thought that I had missed him. But then on the green of his chasseur jacket I saw an ever-widening black smudge, and he began to sway in his saddle, very slightly at first, but more and more with every bound, until at last over he went, with his foot caught in the stirrup and his shoulders thud-thud-thudding along the road, until the drag was too much for the tired horse, and I closed my hand upon the foam-spattered bridle-chain. As I pulled him up it eased the stirrup leather, and the spurred heel clinked loudly as it fell.

" Your papers ! " I cried, springing from my saddle. " This instant ! "

But even as I said it, the huddle of the green body and the fantastic sprawl of the limbs in the moonlight told me clearly enough that it was all over with him. My bullet had passed through his heart, and it was only his own iron will which had held him so long in the saddle. He had lived hard, this Montluc, and I will do him justice to say that he died hard also.

But it was the papers—always the papers—of which I

thought. I opened his tunic and I felt in his shirt. Then I searched his holsters and his sabre-tasche. Finally I dragged off his boots, and undid his horse's girth so as to hunt under the saddle. There was not a nook or crevice which I did not ransack. It was useless. They were not upon him.

When this stunning blow came upon me I could have sat down by the roadside and wept. Fate seemed to be fighting against me, and that is an enemy from whom even a gallant hussar might not be ashamed to flinch. I stood with my arm over the neck of my poor wounded Violette, and I tried to think it all out, that I might act in the wisest way. I was aware that the Emperor had no great respect for my wits, and I longed to show him that he had done me an injustice. Montluc had not the papers. And yet Montluc had sacrificed his companions in order to make his escape. I could make nothing of that. On the other hand, it was clear that, if he had not got them, one or other of his comrades had. One of them was certainly dead. The other I had left fighting with Tremeau, and if he escaped from the old swordsman he had still to pass me. Clearly, my work lay behind me.

I hammered fresh charges into my pistols after I had turned this over in my head. Then I put them back in the holsters, and I examined my little mare, she jerking her head and cocking her ears the while, as if to tell me that an old soldier like herself did not make a fuss about a scratch or two. The first shot had merely grazed her off-shoulder, leaving a skin-mark, as if she had brushed a wall. The second was more serious. It had passed through the muscle of her neck, but already it had ceased to bleed. I reflected that if she weakened I could mount Montluc's grey, and meanwhile I led him along beside us, for he was a fine horse, worth fifteen hundred francs at the least, and it seemed to me that no one had a better right to him than I.

Well, I was all impatience now to get back to the others, and I had just given Violette her head, when suddenly I saw something glimmering in a field by the roadside. It was the brass-work upon the chasseur hat which had flown from Montluc's head ; and at the sight of it a thought made me jump in the saddle. How could the hat have flown off ? With its weight, would it not have simply dropped ? And here it lay, fifteen paces from the roadway ! Of course, he must have thrown it off when he had made sure that I would overtake him. And if he threw it off—I did not stop to reason any more, but sprang from the mare with my heart beating the *pas-de-charge*. Yes, it was all right this time. There, in the crown of the hat was stuffed a roll of papers in a parchment wrapper bound with yellow ribbon. I pulled it out with the one hand, and, holding the hat in the other, I danced for joy in the moonlight. The Emperor would see that he had not made a mistake when he put his affairs into the charge of Étienne Gerard.

I had a safe pocket on the inside of my tunic just over my heart, where I kept a few little things which were dear to me, and into this I thrust my precious roll. Then I sprang upon Violette, and was pushing forward to see what had become of Tremeau, when I saw a horseman riding across the field in the distance. At the same instant I heard the sound of hoofs approaching me, and there in the moonlight was the Emperor upon his white charger, dressed in his grey overcoat and his three-cornered hat, just as I had seen him so often upon the field of battle.

" Well ! " he cried, in the sharp, sergeant-major way of his. " Where are my papers ? "

I spurred forward and presented them without a word. He broke the ribbon and ran his eyes rapidly over them. Then, as we sat our horses head to tail, he threw his left arm across me with his hand upon my shoulder. Yes, my friends, simple as you see me, I have been embraced by my great master.

" Gerard," he cried, " you are a marvel ! "

I did not wish to contradict him, and it brought a

flush of joy upon my cheeks to know that he had done me justice at last.

" Where is the thief, Gerard ? " he asked.

" Dead, sire."

" You killed him ? "

" He wounded my horse, sire, and would have escaped had I not shot him."

" Did you recognise him ? "

" De Montluc is his name, sire—a Colonel of Chasseurs."

" Tut," said the Emperor. " We have got the poor pawn, but the hand which plays the game is still out of our reach." He sat in silent thought for a little, with his chin sunk upon his chest. " Ah, Talleyrand, Talleyrand," I heard him mutter, " if I had been in your place and you in mine, you would have crushed a viper when you held it under your heel. For five years I have known you for what you are, and yet I have let you live to sting me. Never mind, my brave," he continued, turning to me, " there will come a day of reckoning for everybody, and when it arrives, I promise you that my friends will be remembered as well as my enemies."

" Sire," said I, for I had had time for thought as well as he, " if your plans about these papers have been carried to the ears of your enemies I trust you do not think that it was owing to any indiscretion upon the part of myself or of my comrades."

" It would be hardly reasonable for me to do so," he answered, " seeing that this plot was hatched in Paris, and that you only had your orders a few hours ago."

" Then how—— ? "

" Enough," he cried, sternly. " You take an undue advantage of your position."

That was always the way with the Emperor. He would chat with you as with a friend and a brother, and then when he had wiled you into forgetting the gulf which lay between you, he would suddenly, with a word or with a look, remind you that it was as impassable as ever. When I have fondled my old hound until he has been encouraged to paw my knees, and I have then thrust him down again, it has made me think of the Emperor and his ways.

He reined his horse round, and I followed him in silence and with a heavy heart. But when he spoke again his words were enough to drive all thought of myself out of my mind.

" I could not sleep until I knew how you had fared," said he. " I have paid a price for my papers. There are not so many of my old soldiers left that I can afford to lose two in one night."

When he said " two " it turned me cold.

" Colonel Despienne was shot, sire," I stammered.

" And Captain Tremeau cut down. Had I been a few minutes earlier, I might have saved him. The other escaped across the fields."

I remembered that I had seen a horseman a moment before I had met the Emperor. He had taken to the fields to avoid me, but if I had known, and Violette been unwounded, the old soldier would not have gone unavenged. I was thinking sadly of his sword-play, and wondering whether it was his stiffening wrist which had been fatal to him, when Napoleon spoke again.

" Yes, Brigadier," said he, " you are now the only man who will know where these papers are concealed."

It must have been imagination, my friends, but for an instant I may confess that it seemed to me that there was a tone in the Emperor's voice which was not altogether one of sorrow. But the dark thought had hardly time to form itself in my mind before he let me see that I was doing him an injustice.

" Yes, I have paid a price for my papers," he said, and I heard them crackle as he put his hand up to his bosom. " No man has ever had more faithful servants—no man since the beginning of the world."

As he spoke we came upon the scene of the struggle. Colonel Despienne and the man whom we had shot lay together some distance down the road, while their horses grazed contentedly beneath the poplars. Captain Tremeau lay in front of us upon his back, with his arms and legs stretched out, and his sabre broken short off in his hand. His tunic was open, and a huge blood-clot hung like a dark handkerchief out of a slit in his white shirt. I could see the gleam of his clenched teeth from under his immense moustache.

The Emperor sprang from his horse and bent down over the dead man.

" He was with me since Rivoli," said he, sadly. " He was one of my old grumblers in Egypt."

And the voice brought the man back from the dead. I saw his eyelids shiver. He twitched his arm, and moved the sword-hilt a few inches. He was trying to raise it in salute. Then the mouth opened, and the hilt tinkled down on to the ground.

" May we all die as gallantly," said the Emperor, as he rose, and from my heart I added " Amen."

There was a farm within fifty yards of where we were standing, and the farmer, roused from his sleep by the clatter of hoofs and the cracking of pistols, had rushed out to the roadside. We saw him now, dumb with fear and astonishment, staring open-eyed at the Emperor. It was to him that we committed the care of the four dead men and of the horses also. For my own part, I thought it best to leave Violette with him and to take De Montluc's grey with me, for he could not refuse to give me back my own mare, whilst there might be difficulties about the other. Besides, my little friend's wound had to be considered, and we had a long return ride before us.

The Emperor did not at first talk much upon the way. Perhaps the deaths of Despienne and Tremeau still weighed heavily upon his spirits. He was always a reserved man, and in those times, when every hour brought him the news of some success of his enemies or defection of his friends, one could not expect him to be a merry companion. Nevertheless, when I reflected that he was carrying in his bosom those papers which he valued so highly, and which only a few hours ago appeared to be for ever lost, and when I further thought that it was I, Étienne Gerard, who had placed them there, I felt that I had deserved some little consideration. The same idea may have occurred to him, for when we had at last left the Paris high road, and had entered the forest, he began of his own accord to tell me that which I should have most liked to have asked him.

"As to the papers," said he, "I have already told you that there is no one now, except you and me, who knows where they are to be concealed. My Mameluke carried the spades to the pigeon-house, but I have told him nothing. Our plans, however, for bringing the packet from Paris have been formed since Monday. There were three in the secret, a woman and two men. The woman I would trust with my life; which of the two men has betrayed us I do not know, but I think that I may promise to find out."

We were riding in the shadow of the trees at the time, and I could hear him slapping his riding-whip against his boot, and taking pinch after pinch of snuff, as was his way when he was excited.

"You wonder, no doubt," said he, after a pause, "why these rascals did not stop the carriage at Paris instead of at the entrance to Fontainebleau."

In truth, the objection had not occurred to me, but I did not wish to appear to have less wits than he gave me credit for, so I answered that it was indeed surprising.

"Had they done so they would have made a public scandal, and run a chance of missing their end. Short of taking the berline to pieces, they could not have discovered the hiding-place. He planned it well—he could always plan well—and he chose his agents well also. But mine were the better."

It is not for me to repeat to you, my friends, all that was said to me by the Emperor as we walked our horses amid the black shadows and through the moon-silvered glades of the great forest. Every word of it is impressed upon my memory, and before I pass away it is likely that I will place it all upon paper, so that others may read it in the days to come. He spoke freely of his past, and something also of his future; of the devotion of Macdonald, of the treason of Marmont, of the little King of Rome, concerning whom he talked with as much tenderness as any bourgeois father of a single child; and, finally, of his father-in-law, the Emperor of Austria, who would, he thought, stand between his enemies and himself. For myself, I dared not say a word, remembering how I had already brought a rebuke upon myself; but I rode by his side, hardly able to believe that this was indeed the great Emperor, the man whose glance sent a thrill through me, who was now pouring out his thoughts to me in short, eager sentences, the words rattling and racing like the hoofs of a galloping squadron. It is possible that, after the word-splittings and diplomacy of a Court, it was a relief to him to speak his mind to a plain soldier like myself.

In this way the Emperor and I—even after years it sends a flush of pride into my cheeks to be able to put those words together—the Emperor and I walked our horses through the Forest of Fontainebleau, until we came at last to the Colombier. The three spades were propped against the wall upon the right-hand side of the ruined door, and at the sight of them the tears sprang to my eyes as I thought of the hands for which they were intended. The Emperor seized one and I another.

"Quick!" said he. "The dawn will be upon us before we get back to the palace."

We dug the hole, and placing the papers in one of my pistol holsters to screen them from the damp, we laid them at the bottom and covered them up. We then carefully removed all marks of the ground having been disturbed, and we placed a large stone upon the top. I dare say that since the Emperor was a young gunner, and helped to train his pieces against Toulon, he had not worked so hard with his hands. He was mopping his forehead with his silk handkerchief long before we had come to the end of our task.

The first grey cold light of morning was stealing through the tree trunks when we came out together from the old pigeon-house. The Emperor laid his hand upon my shoulder as I stood ready to help him to mount.

" We have left the papers there," said he, solemnly, " and I desire that you shall leave all thought of them there also. Let the recollection of them pass entirely from your mind, to be revived only when you receive a direct order under my own hand and seal. From this time onwards you forget all that has passed."

" I forget it, sire," said I.

We rode together to the edge of the town, where he desired that I should separate from him. I had saluted, and was turning my horse, when he called me back.

" It is easy to mistake the points of the compass in the forest," said he. " Would you not say that it was in the north-eastern corner that we buried them ? "

" Buried what, sire ? "

" The papers, of course," he cried, impatiently.

" What papers, sire ? "

" Name of a name ! Why, the papers that you have recovered for me."

" I am really at a loss to know what your Majesty is talking about."

He flushed with anger for a moment, and then he burst out laughing.

" Very good, Brigadier ! " he cried. " I begin to believe that you are as good a diplomatist as you are a soldier, and I cannot say more than that."

So that was my strange adventure in which I found myself the friend and confident agent of the Emperor. When he returned from Elba he refrained from digging up the papers until his position should be secure, and they still remained in the corner of the old pigeon-house after his exile to St. Helena. It was at this time that he was desirous of getting them into the hands of his own supporters, and for that purpose he wrote me, as I afterwards learned, three letters, all of which were intercepted by his guardians. Finally, he offered to support himself and his own establishment—which he might very easily have done out of the gigantic sum which belonged to him —if they would only pass one of his letters unopened. This request was refused, and so, up to his death in '21, the papers still remained where I have told you. How they came to be dug up by Count Bertrand and myself, and who eventually obtained them, is a story which I would tell you, were it not that the end has not yet come.

Some day you will hear of those papers, and you will see how, after he has been so long in his grave, that great man can still set Europe shaking. When that day comes, you will think of Étienne Gerard, and you will tell your children that you have heard the story from the lips of the man who was the only one living of all who took part in that strange history—the man who was tempted by Marshal Berthier, who led that wild pursuit upon the Paris road, who was honoured by the embrace of the Emperor, and who rode with him by moonlight in the Forest of Fontainebleau. The buds are bursting and the birds are calling, my friends. You may find better things to do in the sunlight than listening to the stories of an old, broken soldier. And yet you may well treasure what I say, for the buds will have burst and the birds sung in many seasons before France will see such another ruler as he whose servants we were proud to be.

ADVENTURES OF GERARD

1. *How the Brigadier lost his Ear*

IT was the old Brigadier who was talking in the café.

I have seen a great many cities, my friends. I would not dare to tell you how many I have entered as a conqueror with eight hundred of my little fighting devils clanking and jingling behind me. The cavalry were in front of the Grande Armée, and the Hussars of Conflans were in front of the cavalry, and I was in front of the Hussars. But of all the cities which we visited Venice is the most ill-built and ridiculous. I cannot imagine how the people who laid it out thought that the cavalry could manœuvre. It would puzzle Murat or Lasalle to bring a squadron into that square of theirs. For this reason we left Kellermann's heavy brigade and also my own Hussars at Padua on the mainland. But Suchet with the infantry held the town, and he had chosen me as his aide-de-camp for that winter, because he was pleased about the affair of the Italian fencing-master at Milan. The fellow was a good swordsman, and it was fortunate for the credit of French arms that it was I who was opposed to him. Besides, he deserved a lesson, for if one does not like a *prima donna's* singing one can always be silent, but it is intolerable that a public affront should be put upon a pretty woman. So the sympathy was all with me, and after the affair had blown over and the man's widow had been pensioned, Suchet chose me as his own galloper, and I followed him to Venice, where I had the strange adventure which I am about to tell you.

You have not been to Venice ? No, for it is seldom

that the French travel. We were great travellers in those days. From Moscow to Cairo we had travelled everywhere, but we went in larger parties than were convenient to those whom we visited, and we carried our passports in our limbers. It will be a bad day for Europe when the French start travelling again, for they are slow to leave their homes ; but when they have done so no one can say how far they will go if they have a guide like our little man to point out the way. But the great days are gone and the great men are dead, and here am I, the last of them, drinking wine of Suresnes and telling old tales in a café.

But it is of Venice that I would speak. The folks there live like water-rats upon a mud-bank ; but the houses are very fine, and the churches, especially that of St. Mark, are as great as any I have seen. But, above all, they are all proud of their statues and their pictures, which are the most famous in Europe. There are many soldiers who think that because one's trade is to make war one should never have a thought above fighting and plunder. There was old Bouvet, for example—the one who was killed by the Prussians on the day that I won the Emperor's medal ; if you took him away from the camp and the canteen, and spoke to him of books, or of art, he would sit and stare at you. But the highest soldier is a man like myself who can understand the things of the mind and the soul. It is true that I was very young when I joined the army, and that the quarter-master was my only teacher ; but if you go about the world with your eyes open you cannot help learning a great deal.

Thus I was able to admire the pictures in Venice, and to know the names of the great men, Michael Titiens, and Angelus, and the others, who had painted them. No one can say that Napoleon did not admire them also, for the very first thing which he did when he captured the town was to send the best of them to Paris. We all took what we could get, and I had two pictures for my share. One of them, called " Nymphs Surprised," I kept for myself, and the other, " Saint Barbara," I sent as a present to my mother.

It must be confessed, however, that some of our men behaved very badly in this matter of the statues and the pictures. The people at Venice were very much attached to them, and as to the four bronze horses which stood over the gate of their great church, they loved them as dearly as if they had been their children. I have always been a judge of a horse, and I had a good look at these ones, but I could not see that there was much to be said for them. They were too coarse-limbed for light cavalry chargers, and they had not the weight for the gun-teams. However, they were the only four horses, alive or dead, in the whole town, so it was not to be expected that the people would know any better. They wept bitterly when they were sent away, and ten French soldiers were found floating in the canals that night. As a punishment for these murders a great many more of their pictures were sent away, and the soldiers took to breaking the statues and firing their muskets at the stained-glass windows. This made the people furious, and there was very bad feeling in the town. Many officers and men disappeared during that winter, and even their bodies were never found.

For myself I had plenty to do, and I never found the time heavy on my hands. In every country it has been my custom to try to learn the language. For this reason I always look round for some lady who will be kind enough to teach it to me, and then we practise it together. This is the most interesting way of picking it up, and before I was thirty I could speak nearly every tongue in Europe ; but it must be confessed that what you learn is not of much use for the ordinary purposes of life. My business, for example, has usually been with soldiers and peasants, and what advantage is it to be able to say to them that I love only them, and that I will come back when the wars are over ?

Never have I had so sweet a teacher as in Venice.

Lucia was her first name, and her second—but a gentleman forgets second names. I can say this with all discretion, that she was of one of the senatorial families of Venice, and that her grandfather had been Doge of the town. She was of an exquisite beauty—and when I, Étienne Gerard, use such a word as " exquisite," my friends, it has a meaning. I have judgment, I have memories, I have the means of comparison. Of all the women who have loved me there are not twenty to whom I could apply such a term as that. But I say again that Lucia was exquisite. Of the dark type I do not recall her equal unless it were Dolores of Toledo. There was a little brunette whom I loved at Santarem when I was soldiering under Massena in Portugal—her name has escaped me. She was of a perfect beauty, but she had not the figure nor the grace of Lucia. There was Agnes, also. I could not put one before the other, but I do none an injustice when I say that Lucia was the equal of the best.

It was over this matter of pictures that I had first met her, for her father owned a palace on the farther side of the Rialto Bridge upon the Grand Canal, and it was so packed with wall-paintings that Suchet sent a party of sappers to cut some of them out and send them to Paris. I had gone down with them, and after I had seen Lucia in tears it appeared to me that the plaster would crack if it were taken from the support of the wall. I said so, and the sappers were withdrawn. After that I was the friend of the family, and many a flask of Chianti have I cracked with the father and many a sweet lesson have I had from the daughter. Some of our French officers married in Venice that winter, and I might have done the same, for I loved her with all my heart; but Étienne Gerard had his sword, his horse, his regiment, his mother, his Emperor and his career. A debonair Hussar has room in his heart for love, but none for a wife. So I thought then, my friends, but I did not see the lonely days when I should long to clasp those vanished hands, and turn my head away when I saw old comrades with their tall children standing round their chairs. This love which I had thought was a joke and a plaything—it is only now that I understand that it is the moulder of one's life, the most solemn and sacred of all things. . . . Thank you, my friend, thank you ! It is a good wine, and a second bottle cannot hurt.

And now I will tell you how my love for Lucia was the cause of one of the most terrible of all the wonderful adventures which have ever befallen me, and how it was that I came to lose the top of my right ear. You have often asked me why it was missing. To-night for the first time I will tell you.

Suchet's headquarters at that time was the old palace of the Doge Dandolo, which stands on the lagoon not far from the place of San Marco. It was near the end of the winter, and I had returned one night from the Theatre Goldini, when I found a note from Lucia and a gondola waiting. She prayed me to come to her at once as she was in trouble. To a Frenchman and a soldier there was but one answer to such a note. In an instant I was in the boat and the gondolier was pushing out into the dark lagoon. I remember that as I took my seat in the boat I was struck by the man's great size. He was not tall, but he was one of the broadest men that I have ever seen in my life. But the gondoliers of Venice are a strong breed, and powerful men are common enough among them. The fellow took his place behind me and began to row.

A good soldier in an enemy's country should everywhere and at all times be on the alert. It has been one of the rules of my life, and if I have lived to wear grey hairs it is because I have observed it. And yet upon that night I was as careless as a foolish young recruit who fears lest he should be thought to be afraid. My pistols I had left behind in my hurry. My sword was at my belt, but it is not always the most convenient of weapons. I lay back in my seat in the gondola, lulled by the gentle swish of the water and the steady creaking of the oar. Our way lay through a network of narrow canals with high houses towering on either side and a thin slit of star-spangled sky above us. Here and there, on the bridges which spanned the canal, there was the dim glimmer of an oil lamp, and sometimes there came a gleam from some niche, where a candle burned before the image of a saint. But save for this it was all black, and one could only see the water by the white fringe which curled round the long black nose of our boat. It was a place and a time for dreaming. I thought of my own past life, of all the great deeds in which I had been concerned, of the horses that I had handled, and of the women that I had loved. Then I thought also of my dear mother, and I fancied her joy when she heard the folk in the village talking about the fame of her son. Of the Emperor also I thought, and of France, the dear fatherland, the sunny France, mother of beautiful daughters and of gallant sons. My heart glowed within me as I thought of how we had brought her colours so many hundred leagues beyond her borders. To her greatness I would dedicate my life. I placed my hand upon my heart as I swore it, and at that instant the gondolier fell upon me from behind.

When I say that he fell upon me I do not mean merely that he attacked me, but that he really did tumble upon me with all his weight. The fellow stands behind you and above you as he rows, so that you can neither see him nor can you in any way guard against such an assault. One moment I had sat with my mind filled with sublime resolutions, the next I was flattened out upon the bottom of the boat, the breath dashed out of my body, and this monster pinning me down. I felt the fierce pants of his hot breath upon the back of my neck. In an instant he had torn away my sword, and slipped a sack over my head, and had tied a rope firmly round the outside of it. There was I at the bottom of the gondola as helpless as a trussed fowl. I could not shout, I could not move ; I was a mere bundle. An instant later I heard once more the swishing of the water and the creaking of the oar. This fellow had done his work and had resumed his journey as quietly and unconcernedly as if he were accustomed to clap a sack over a colonel of Hussars every day of the week.

I cannot tell you the humiliation and also the fury which filled my mind as I lay there like a helpless sheep being carried to the butcher's. I, Étienne Gerard, the champion of the six brigades of light cavalry and the first swordsman of the Grand Army, to be overpowered by a single, unarmed man in such a fashion! Yet I lay quiet, for there is a time to resist and there is a time to save one's strength. I had felt the fellow's grip upon my arms, and I knew that I would be a child in his hands. I waited quietly, therefore, with a heart which burned with rage, until my opportunity should come.

How long I lay there at the bottom of the boat I cannot tell; but it seemed to me to be a long time, and always there were the hiss of the waters and the steady creaking of the oars. Several times we turned corners, for I heard the long, sad cry which these gondoliers give when they wish to warn their fellows that they are coming. At last, after a considerable journey, I felt the side of the boat scrape up against a landing-place. The fellow knocked three times with his oar upon wood, and in answer to his summons I heard the rasping of bars and the turning of keys. A great door creaked back upon its hinges.

"Have you got him?" asked a voice, in Italian.

My monster gave a laugh and kicked the sack in which I lay.

"Here he is," said he.

"They are waiting." He added something which I could not understand.

"Take him, then," said my captor. He raised me in his arms, ascended some steps, and I was thrown down upon a hard floor. A moment later the bars creaked and the key whined once more. I was a prisoner inside a house.

From the voices and the steps there seemed now to be several people round me. I understand Italian a great deal better than I speak it, and I could make out very well what they were saying.

" You have not killed him, Matteo ? "

" What matter if I have ? "

" My faith, you will have to answer for it to the tribunal."

" They will kill him, will they not ? "

" Yes, but it is not for you or me to take it out of their hands."

" Tut ! I have not killed him. Dead men do not bite, and his cursed teeth met in my thumb as I pulled the sack over his head."

" He lies very quiet."

"Tumble him out and you will find he is lively enough."

The cord which bound me was undone and the sack drawn from over my head. With my eyes closed I lay motionless upon the floor.

" By the saints, Matteo, I tell you that you have broken his neck."

" Not I. He has only fainted. The better for him if he never came out of it again."

I felt a hand within my tunic.

" Matteo is right," said a voice. " His heart beats like a hammer. Let him lie and he will soon find his senses."

I waited for a minute or so and then I ventured to take a stealthy peep from between my lashes. At first I could see nothing, for I had been so long in darkness and it was but a dim light in which I found myself. Soon, however, I made out that a high and vaulted ceiling covered with painted gods and goddesses was arching over my head. This was no mean den of cut-throats into which I had been carried, but it must be the hall of some Venetian palace. Then, without movement, very slowly and stealthily I had a peep at the men who surrounded me. There was the gondolier, a swart, hard-faced, murderous ruffian, and beside him were three other men, one of them a little, twisted fellow with an air of authority and several keys in his hand, the other two tall young servants in a smart livery. As I listened to their talk I saw that the small man was the steward of the house, and that the others were under his orders.

There were four of them, then, but the little steward might be left out of the reckoning. Had I a weapon I should have smiled at such odds as those. But, hand to hand, I was no match for the one even without three others to aid him. Cunning, then, not force, must be my aid. I wished to look round for some mode of escape, and in doing so I gave an almost imperceptible movement of my head. Slight as it was it did not escape my guardians.

" Come, wake up, wake up ! " cried the steward.

" Get on your feet, little Frenchman," growled the gondolier. " Get up, I say ! " and for the second time he spurned me with his foot.

Never in the world was a command obeyed so promptly as that one. In an instant I had bounded to my feet and rushed as hard as I could run to the back of the hall. They were after me as I have seen the English hounds follow a fox, but there was a long passage down which I tore. It turned to the left and again to the left, and then I found myself back in the hall once more. They were almost within touch of me and there was no time for thought. I turned towards the staircase, but two men were coming down it. I dodged back and tried the door through which I had been brought, but it was fastened with great bars and I could not loosen them. The gondolier was on me with his knife, but I met him with a kick on the body which stretched him on his back. His dagger flew with a clatter across the marble floor. I had no time to seize it, for there were half a dozen of them now clutching at me. As I rushed through them the little steward thrust his leg before me and I fell with a crash, but I was up in an instant, and breaking from their grasp I burst through the very middle of them and made for a door at the other end of the hall. I reached it well in front of them, and I gave a shout of triumph as the handle turned freely in my hand, for I could see that it led to the outside and that all was clear for my escape. But I had forgotten this strange city in which I was. Every house is an island. As I flung open the door, ready to bound out into the street, the light of the hall shone upon the deep, still, black water which lay flush with the topmost step. I shrank back, and in an instant my pursuers were on me. But I am not taken so easily.

Again I kicked and fought my way through them, though one of them tore a handful of hair from my head in his effort to hold me. The little steward struck me with a key and I was battered and bruised, but once more I cleared a way in front of me. Up the grand staircase I rushed, burst open the pair of huge folding doors which faced me, and learned at last that my efforts were in vain.

The room into which I had broken was brilliantly lighted. With its gold cornices, its massive pillars, and its painted walls and ceilings it was evidently the grand hall of some famous Venetian palace. There are many hundred such in this strange city, any one of which has rooms which would grace the Louvre or Versailles. In the centre of this great hall there was a raised dais, and upon it in a half circle there sat twelve men all clad in black gowns, like those of a Franciscan monk, and each with a mask over the upper part of his face.

A group of armed men—rough-looking rascals—were standing round the door, and amid them facing the dais was a young fellow in the uniform of the light infantry. As he turned his head I recognised him. It was Captain Auret, of the 7th, a young Basque with whom I had drunk many a glass during the winter. He was deadly white, poor wretch, but he held himself manfully amid the assassins who surrounded him. Never shall I forget the sudden flash of hope which shone in his dark eyes when he saw a comrade burst into the room, or the look of despair which followed as he understood that I had come not to change his fate but to share it.

You can think how amazed these people were when I hurled myself into their presence. My pursuers had crowded in behind me and choked the doorway, so that all further flight was out of the question. It is at such instants that my nature asserts itself. With dignity I advanced towards the tribunal. My jacket was torn, my hair was dishevelled, my head was bleeding, but there was that in my eyes and in my carriage which made them realise that no common man was before them. Not a hand was raised to arrest me until I halted in front of a formidable old man whose long grey beard and masterful manner told me that both by years and by character he was the man in authority.

" Sir," said I, " you will perhaps tell me why I have been forcibly arrested and brought to this place. I am an honourable soldier, as is this other gentleman here, and I demand that you will instantly set us both at liberty."

There was an appalling silence to my appeal. It is not pleasant to have twelve masked faces turned upon you and to see twelve pairs of vindictive Italian eyes fixed with fierce intentness upon your face. But I stood as a debonair soldier should, and I could not but reflect how much credit I was bringing upon the Hussars of Conflans by the dignity of my bearing. I do not think that anyone could have carried himself better under such difficult circumstances. I looked with a fearless face from one assassin to another, and I waited for some reply.

It was the greybeard who at last broke the silence.

" Who is this man ? " he asked.

" His name is Gerard," said the little steward at the door.

" Colonel Gerard," said I. " I will not deceive you. I am Étienne Gerard, *the* Colonel Gerard, five times mentioned in dispatches and recommended for the sword of honour. I am aide-de-camp to General Suchet, and I demand my instant release, together with that of my comrade in arms."

The same terrible silence fell upon the assembly, and the same twelve pairs of merciless eyes were bent upon my face. Again it was the greybeard who spoke.

" He is out of his order. There are two names upon our list before him."

" He escaped from our hands and burst into the room."

" Let him await his turn. Take him down to the wooden cell."

" If he resist us, your excellency ? "

" Bury your knives in his body. The tribunal will uphold you. Remove him until we have dealt with the others."

They advanced upon me and for an instant I thought of resistance. It would have been a heroic death, but who was there to see it or to chronicle it ? I might be only postponing my fate, and yet I had been in so many bad places and come out unhurt that I had learned always to hope and to trust my star. I allowed these rascals to seize me, and I was led from the room, the gondolier walking at my side with a long naked knife in his hand. I could see in his brutal eyes the satisfaction which it would give him if he could find some excuse for plunging it into my body.

They are wonderful places, these great Venetian houses, palaces and fortresses and prisons all in one. I was led along a passage and down a bare stone stair until we came to a short corridor from which three doors opened. Through one of these I was thrust and the spring lock closed behind me. The only light came dimly through a small grating which opened on the passage. Peering and feeling, I carefully examined the chamber in which I had been placed. I understood from what I had heard that I should soon have to leave it again in order to appear before this tribunal, but still it is not my nature to throw away any possible chances.

The stone floor of the cell was so damp and the walls for

some feet high were so slimy and foul that it was evident they were beneath the level of the water. A single slanting hole high up near the ceiling was the only aperture for light or air. Through it I saw one bright star shining down upon me, and the sight filled me with comfort and with hope. I have never been a man of religion, though I have always had a respect for those who were, but I remember that night that the star shining down the shaft seemed to be an all-seeing eye which was upon me, and I felt as a young and frightened recruit might feel in battle when he saw the calm gaze of his colonel turned upon him.

Three of the sides of my prison were formed of stone, but the fourth was of wood, and I could see that it had only recently been erected. Evidently a partition had been thrown up to divide a single large cell into two smaller ones. There was no hope for me in the old walls, in the tiny window, or in the massive door. It was only in this one direction of the wooden screen that there was any possibility of exploring. My reason told me that if I should pierce it—which did not seem very difficult—it would only be to find myself in another cell as strong as that in which I then was. Yet I had always rather be doing something than doing nothing, so I bent all my attention and all my energies upon the wooden wall. Two planks were badly joined and so loose that I was certain I could easily detach them. I searched about for some tool, and I found one in the leg of a small bed which stood in the corner. I forced the end of this into the chink of the planks, and I was about to twist them outwards when the sound of rapid footsteps caused me to pause and to listen.

I wish I could forget what I heard. Many a hundred men have I seen die in battle, and I have slain more myself than I care to think of, but all that was fair fight and the duty of a soldier. It was a very different matter to listen to a murder in this den of assassins. They were pushing someone along the passage, someone who resisted and who clung to my door as he passed. They must have taken him into the third cell, the one which was farthest from me. "Help! help!" cried a voice, and then I heard a blow and a scream. "Help! help!" cried the voice again, and then "Gerard! Colonel Gerard!" It was my poor captain of infantry whom they were slaughtering. "Murderers! murderers!" I yelled, and I kicked at my door, but again I heard him shout, and then everything was silent. A minute later there was a heavy splash, and I knew that no human eye would ever see Auret again. He had gone as a hundred others had gone whose names were missing from the roll-calls of their regiments during that winter in Venice.

The steps returned along the passage, and I thought that they were coming for me. Instead of that they opened the door of the cell next to mine, and they took someone out of it. I heard the steps die away up the stair. At once I renewed my work upon the planks, and within a very few minutes I had loosened them in such a way that I could remove and replace them at pleasure. Passing through the aperture I found myself in the farther cell, which, as I expected, was the other half of the one in which I had been confined. I was not any nearer to escape than I had been before, for there was no other wooden wall which I could penetrate, and the spring lock of the door had been closed. There were no traces to show who was my companion in misfortune. Closing the two loose planks behind me, I returned to my own cell, and waited there with all the courage which I could command for the summons which would probably be my death-knell.

It was a long time in coming, but at last I heard the sound of feet once more in the passage, and I nerved myself to listen to some other odious deed and to hear the cries of the poor victim. Nothing of the kind occurred, however, and the prisoner was placed in the cell without violence. I had no time to peep through my hole of communication, for next moment my own door was flung open and my rascally gondolier, with the other assassins, came into the cell.

"Come, Frenchman," said he. He held his blood-stained knife in his great hairy hand, and I read in his fierce eyes that he only looked for some excuse in order to plunge it into my heart. Resistance was useless. I followed without a word. I was led up the stone stair and back into that gorgeous chamber in which I had left the secret tribunal. I was ushered in, but to my surprise it was not on me that their attention was fixed. One of their own number, a tall, dark young man, was standing before them and was pleading with them in low, earnest tones. His voice quivered with anxiety and his hands darted in and out or writhed together in an agony of entreaty. "You cannot do it! You cannot do it!" he cried. "I implore the tribunal to reconsider this decision."

"Stand aside, brother," said the old man who presided. "The case is decided and another is up for judgment."

"For Heaven's sake be merciful!" cried the young man.

"We have already been merciful," the other answered. "Death would have been a small penalty for such an offence. Be silent and let judgment take its course."

I saw the young man throw himself in an agony of grief into his chair. I had no time, however, to speculate as to what it was which was troubling him, for his eleven colleagues had already fixed their stern eyes upon me. The moment of fate had arrived.

"You are Colonel Gerard?" said the terrible old man.

"I am."

"Aide-de-camp to the robber who calls himself General Suchet, who in turn represents that arch-robber Buonaparte?"

It was on my lips to tell him that he was a liar, but there is a time to argue and a time to be silent.

"I am an honourable soldier," said I. "I have obeyed my orders and done my duty."

The blood flushed into the old man's face and his eyes blazed through his mask.

"You are thieves and murderers, every man of you," he cried. "What are you doing here? You are Frenchmen. Why are you not in France? Did we invite you to Venice? By what right are you here? Where are our pictures? Where are the horses of St. Mark? Who are you that you should pilfer those treasures which our fathers through so many centuries have collected? We were a great city when France was a desert. Your drunken, brawling, ignorant soldiers have undone the work of saints and heroes. What have you to say to it?"

He was, indeed, a formidable old man, for his white beard bristled with fury and he barked out the little sentences like a savage hound. For my part I could have told him that his pictures would be safe in Paris, that his horses were really not worth making a fuss about, and that he could see heroes—I say nothing of saints—without going back to his ancestors or even moving out of his chair. All this I could have pointed out, but one might as well argue with a Mameluke about religion. I shrugged my shoulders and said nothing.

"The prisoner has no defence," said one of my masked judges.

"Has anyone any observation to make before judgment is passed?" The old man glared round him at the others.

"There is one matter, your excellency," said another. "It can scarce be referred to without reopening a brother's wounds, but I would remind you that there is a very particular reason why an exemplary punishment should be inflicted in the case of this officer."

"I had not forgotten it," the old man answered. "Brother, if the tribunal has injured you in one direction, it will give you ample satisfaction in another."

The young man who had been pleading when I entered the room staggered to his feet.

"I cannot endure it," he cried. "Your excellency must forgive me. The tribunal can act without me. I am ill! I am mad!" He flung his hands up with a furious gesture and rushed from the room.

"Let him go! Let him go!" said the president. "It is, indeed, more than can be asked of flesh and blood that he should remain under this roof. But he is a true Venetian, and when the first agony is over he will understand that it could not be otherwise."

I had been forgotten during this episode, and though I am not a man who is accustomed to being overlooked I should have been all the happier had they continued to neglect me. But now the old president glared at me again like a tiger who comes back to his victim.

"You shall pay for it all, and it is but justice that you should," said he. "You, an upstart adventurer and foreigner, have dared to raise your eyes in love to the grand-daughter of a Doge of Venice who was already betrothed to the heir of the Loredans. He who enjoys such privileges must pay a price for them."

"It cannot be higher than they are worth," said I.

"You will tell us that when you have made a part payment," he said. "Perhaps your spirit may not be so proud by that time. Matteo, you will lead this prisoner to the wooden cell. To-night is Monday. Let him have no food or water, and let him be led before the tribunal again on Wednesday night. We shall then decide upon the death which he is to die."

It was not a pleasant prospect, and yet it was a reprieve. One is thankful for small mercies when a hairy savage with a bloodstained knife is standing at one's elbow. He dragged me from the room and I was thrust down the stairs and back into my cell. The door was locked and I was left to my reflections.

My first thought was to establish connection with my neighbour in misfortune. I waited until the steps had died away, and then I cautiously drew aside the two boards and peeped through. The light was very dim, so dim that I could only just discern a figure huddled in the corner, and I could hear the low whisper of a voice which prayed as one prays who is in deadly fear. The boards must have made a creaking. There was a sharp exclamation of surprise.

" Courage, friend, courage ! " I cried. " All is not lost. Keep a stout heart, for Étienne Gerard is by your side."

" Étienne ! " It was a woman's voice which spoke— a voice which was always music to my ears. I sprang through the gap and I flung my arms round her. " Lucia ! Lucia ! " I cried.

It was " Étienne ! " and " Lucia ! " for some minutes, for one does not make speeches at moments like that. It was she who came to her senses first.

" Oh, Étienne, they will kill you. How came you into their hands ? "

" In answer to your letter."

" I wrote no letter."

" The cunning demons ! But you ? "

" I came also in answer to your letter."

" Lucia, I wrote no letter."

" They have trapped us both with the same bait."

" I care nothing about myself, Lucia. Besides, there is no pressing danger with me. They have simply returned me to my cell."

" Oh, Étienne, Étienne, they will kill you. Lorenzo is there."

" The old greybeard ? "

" No, no, a young dark man. He loved me, and I thought I loved him until—until I learned what love is, Étienne. He will never forgive you. He has a heart of stone."

" Let them do what they like. They cannot rob me of the past, Lucia. But you—what about you ? "

" It will be nothing, Étienne. Only a pang for an

instant and then all over. They mean it as a badge of infamy, dear, but I will carry it like a crown of honour since it was through you that I gained it."

Her words froze my blood with horror. All my adventures were insignificant compared to this terrible shadow which was creeping over my soul.

"Lucia! Lucia!" I cried. "For pity's sake tell me what these butchers are about to do. Tell me, Lucia! Tell me!"

"I will not tell you, Étienne, for it would hurt you far more than it would me. Well, well, I will tell you lest you should fear it was something worse. The president has ordered that my ear be cut off, that I may be marked for ever as having loved a Frenchman."

Her ear! The dear little ear which I had kissed so often. I put my hand to each little velvet shell to make certain that this sacrilege had not yet been committed. Only over my dead body should they reach them. I swore it to her between my clenched teeth.

"You must not care, Étienne. And yet I love that you should care all the same."

"They shall not hurt you—the fiends!"

"I have hopes, Étienne. Lorenzo is there. He was silent while I was judged, but he may have pleaded for me after I was gone."

"He did. I heard him."

"Then he may have softened their hearts."

I knew that it was not so, but how could I bring myself to tell her? I might as well have done so, for with the quick instinct of woman my silence was speech to her.

"They would not listen to him! You need not fear to tell me, dear, for you will find that I am worthy to be loved by such a soldier. Where is Lorenzo now?"

"He left the hall."

"Then he may have left the house as well."

"I believe that he did."

"He has abandoned me to my fate. Étienne, Étienne, they are coming!"

Afar off I heard those fateful steps and the jingle of distant keys. What were they coming for now, since there were no other prisoners to drag to judgment. It could only be to carry out the sentence upon my darling. I stood between her and the door, with the strength of a lion in my limbs. I would tear the house down before they should touch her.

"Go back! Go back!" she cried. "They will murder you, Étienne. My life, at least, is safe. For the love you bear me, Étienne, go back. It is nothing. I will make no sound. You will not hear that it is done."

She wrestled with me, this delicate creature, and by main force she dragged me to the opening between the cells. But a sudden thought had crossed my mind.

"We may yet be saved," I whispered. "Do what I tell you at once and without argument. Go into my cell. Quick!"

I pushed her through the gap and helped her to replace the planks. I had retained her cloak in my hands, and with this wrapped round me I crept into the darkest corner of her cell. There I lay when the door was opened and several men came in. I had reckoned that they would bring no lantern, for they had none with them before. To their eyes I was only a black blur in the corner.

"Bring a light," said one of them.

"No, no; curse it!" cried a rough voice, which I knew to be that of the ruffian Matteo. "It is not a job that I like, and the more I saw it the less I should like it. I am sorry, signora, but the order of the tribunal has to be obeyed."

My impulse was to spring to my feet and to rush through them all and out by the open door. But how would that help Lucia? Suppose that I got clear away, she would be in their hands until I could come back with help, for single-handed I could not hope to clear a way for her. All this flashed through my mind in an instant, and I saw that the only course for me was to lie still, take what came, and wait my chance. The fellow's coarse hand felt among my curls—those curls in which only a woman's fingers had ever wandered. The next instant he gripped my ear, and a pain shot through me as if I had been touched with a hot iron. I bit my lip to stifle a cry, and I felt the blood run warm down my neck and back.

" There, thank Heaven that's over," said the fellow, giving me a friendly pat on the head. " You're a brave girl, signora, I'll say that for you, and I only wish you'd have better taste than to love a Frenchman. You can blame him and not me for what I have done."

What could I do save to lie still and grind my teeth at my own helplessness ? At the same time my pain and my rage were always soothed by the reflection that I had suffered for the woman whom I loved. It is the custom of men to say to ladies that they would willingly endure any pain for their sake, but it was my privilege to show that I had said no more than I meant. I thought also how nobly I would seem to have acted if ever the story came to be told, and how proud the regiment of Conflans might well be of their colonel. These thoughts helped me to suffer in silence while the blood still trickled over my neck and dripped upon the stone floor. It was that sound which nearly led to my destruction.

" She's bleeding fast," said one of the valets. " You had best fetch a surgeon or you will find her dead in the morning."

" She lies very still and she has never opened her mouth," said another. " The shock has killed her."

" Nonsense ; a young woman does not die so easily." It was Matteo who spoke. " Besides, I did but snip off enough to leave the tribunal's mark upon her. Rouse up, signora, rouse up ! "

He shook me by the shoulder, and my heart stood still for fear he should feel the epaulette under the mantle.

" How is it with you now ? " he asked.

I made no answer.

"Curse it! I wish I had to do with a man instead of a woman, and the fairest woman in Venice," said the gondolier. "Here, Nicholas, lend me your handkerchief and bring a light."

It was all over. The worst had happened. Nothing could save me. I still crouched in the corner, but I was tense in every muscle, like a wild cat about to spring. If I had to die I was determined that my end should be worthy of my life.

One of them had gone for a lamp, and Matteo was stooping over me with a handkerchief. In another instant my secret would be discovered. But he suddenly drew himself straight and stood motionless. At the same instant there came a confused murmuring sound through the little window far above my head. It was the rattle of oars and the buzz of many voices. Then there was a crash upon the door upstairs, and a terrible voice roared: "Open! Open in the name of the Emperor!"

The Emperor! It was like the mention of some saint which, by its very sound, can frighten the demons. Away they ran with cries of terror—Matteo, the valets, the steward, all of the murderous gang. Another shout and then the crash of a hatchet and the splintering of planks. There were the rattle of arms and the cries of French soldiers in the hall. Next instant feet came flying down the stair and a man burst frantically into my cell.

"Lucia!" he cried, "Lucia!" He stood in the dim light, panting and unable to find his words. Then he broke out again. "Have I not shown you how I love you, Lucia? What more could I do to prove it? I have betrayed my country, I have broken my vow, I have ruined my friends, and I have given my life in order to save you."

It was young Lorenzo Loredan, the lover whom I had superseded. My heart was heavy for him at the time, but after all it is every man for himself in love, and if one fails in the game it is some consolation to lose to one who can be a graceful and considerate winner. I was about to point this out to him, but at the first word I uttered he gave a shout of astonishment, and, rushing out, he seized the lamp which hung in the corridor and flashed it in my face.

" It is you, you villain ! " he cried. " You French coxcomb. You shall pay me for the wrong which you have done me."

But the next instant he saw the pallor of my face and the blood which was still pouring from my head.

" What is this ? " he asked. " How come you to have lost your ear ? "

I shook off my weakness and, pressing my handkerchief to my wound, I rose from my couch, the debonair colonel of Hussars.

" My injury, sir, is nothing. With your permission we will not allude to a matter so trifling and so personal."

But Lucia had burst through from her cell and was pouring out the whole story while she clasped Lorenzo's arm.

" This noble gentleman—he has taken my place, Lorenzo ! He has borne it for me. He has suffered that I might be saved."

I could sympathise with the struggle which I could see in the Italian's face. At last he held out his hand to me.

" Colonel Gerard," he said, " you are worthy of a great love. I forgive you, for if you have wronged me you have made a noble atonement. But I wonder to see you alive. I left the tribunal before you were judged, but I understood that no mercy would be shown to any Frenchman since the destruction of the ornaments of Venice."

" He did not destroy them," cried Lucia. " He has helped to preserve those in our palace."

" One of them, at any rate," said I, as I stooped and kissed her hand.

This was the way, my friends, in which I lost my ear.

Lorenzo was found stabbed to the heart in the Piazza of St. Mark within two days of the night of my adventure. Of the tribunal and its ruffians, Matteo and three others were shot, the rest banished from the town. Lucia, my lovely Lucia, retired into a convent at Murano after the French had left the city, and there she still may be, some gentle lady abbess who has perhaps long forgotten the days when our hearts throbbed together, and when the whole great world seemed so small a thing beside the love which burned in our veins. Or perhaps it may not be so. Perhaps she has not forgotten. There may still be times when the peace of the cloister is broken by the memory of the old soldier who loved her in those distant days. Youth is past and passion is gone, but the soul of the gentleman can never change, and still Étienne Gerard would bow his grey head before her and would very gladly lose this other ear if he might do her a service.

2. *How the Brigadier captured Saragossa*

HAVE I ever told you, my friends, the circumstances connected with my joining the Hussars of Conflans at the time of the siege of Saragossa, and the very remarkable exploit which I performed in connection with the taking of that city ? No ? Then you have indeed something still to learn. I will tell it to you exactly as it occurred. Save for two or three men and a score or two of women, you are the first who have ever heard the story.

You must know, then, that it was in the 2nd Hussars—called the Hussars of Chamberan—that I had served as a lieutenant and as a junior captain. At the time I speak of I was only twenty-five years of age, as reckless and desperate a man as any in that great army. It chanced that the war had come to a halt in Germany, while it was still raging in Spain ; so the Emperor, wishing to reinforce the Spanish army, transferred me as senior captain to the

Hussars of Conflans, which were at that time in the 5th Army Corps under Marshal Lannes.

It was a long journey from Berlin to the Pyrenees. My new regiment formed part of the force which, under Marshal Lannes, was then besieging the Spanish town of Saragossa. I turned my horse's head in that direction, therefore, and behold me a week or so later at the French headquarters, whence I was directed to the camp of the Hussars of Conflans.

You have read, no doubt, of this famous siege of Saragossa, and I will only say that no general could have had a harder task than that with which Marshal Lannes was confronted. The immense city was crowded with a horde of Spaniards—soldiers, peasants, priests—all filled with the most furious hatred of the French, and the most savage determination to perish before they would surrender. There were eighty thousand men in the town and only thirty thousand to besiege them. Yet we had a powerful artillery, and our Engineers were of the best. There was never such a siege, for it is usual that when the fortifications are taken the city falls ; but here it was not until the fortifications were taken that the real fighting began. Every house was a fort and every street a battlefield, so that slowly, day by day, we had to work our way inwards, blowing up the houses with their garrisons until more than half the city had disappeared. Yet the other half was as determined as ever, and in a better position for defence, since it consisted of enormous convents and monasteries with walls like the Bastille, which could not be so easily brushed out of our way. This was the state of things at the time that I joined the army.

I will confess to you that cavalry are not of much use in a siege, although there was a time when I would not have permitted anyone to have made such an observation. The Hussars of Conflans were encamped to the south of the town, and it was their duty to throw out patrols and to make sure that no Spanish force was advancing from that quarter. The colonel of the regiment was not a good soldier, and the regiment was at that time very far from being in the high condition which it afterwards attained. Even in that one evening I saw several things which shocked me ; for I had a high standard, and it went to my heart to see an ill-arranged camp, an ill-groomed horse, or a slovenly trooper. That night I supped with twenty-six of my new brother-officers, and I fear that in my zeal I showed them only too plainly that I found things very different to what I was accustomed to in the army of Germany. There was silence in the mess after my remarks, and I felt that I had been indiscreet when I saw the glances that were cast at me. The colonel especially was furious, and a great major named Olivier, who was the fire-eater of the regiment, sat opposite to me curling his huge black moustaches, and staring at me as if he would eat me. However, I did not resent his attitude, for I felt that I had indeed been indiscreet, and that it would give a bad impression if upon this my first evening I quarrelled with my superior officer.

So far I admit that I was wrong, but now I come to the sequel. Supper over, the colonel and some other officers left the room, for it was in a farmhouse that the mess was held. There remained a dozen or so, and a goat-skin of Spanish wine having been brought in, we all made merry. Presently this Major Olivier asked me some questions concerning the army of Germany and as to the part which I had myself played in the campaign. Flushed with the wine, I was drawn on from story to story. It was not unnatural, my friends. You will sympathise with me. Up there I had been the model for every officer of my years in the army. I was the first swordsman, the most dashing rider, the hero of a hundred adventures. Here I found myself not only unknown, but even disliked. Was it not natural that I should wish to tell these brave comrades what sort of man it was that had come among them ? Was it not natural that I should wish to say, " Rejoice, my friends, rejoice ! It is no ordinary man who has joined you to-night, but it is

I, *the* Gerard, the hero of Ratisbon, the victor of Jena, the man who broke the square at Austerlitz ? " I could not say all this. But I could at least tell them some incidents which would enable them to say it for themselves. I did so. They listened unmoved. I told them more. At last, after my tale of how I had guided the army across the Danube, one universal shout of laughter broke from them all. I sprang to my feet, flushed with shame and anger. They had drawn me on. They were making game of me. They were convinced that they had to do with a braggart and a liar. Was this my reception in the Hussars of Conflans ? I dashed the tears of mortification from my eyes, and they laughed the more at the sight.

" Do you know, Captain Pelletan, whether Marshal Lannes is still with the army ? " asked the major.

" I believe that he is, sir," said the other.

" Really, I should have thought that his presence was hardly necessary now that Captain Gerard has arrived."

Again there was a roar of laughter. I can see the ring of faces, the mocking eyes, the open mouths—Olivier with his great black bristles, Pelletan thin and sneering, even the young sub-lieutenants convulsed with merriment. Heavens, the indignity of it ! But my rage had dried my tears. I was myself again, cold, quiet, self-contained, ice without and fire within.

" May I ask, sir," said I to the major, " at what hour the regiment is paraded ? "

" I trust, Captain Gerard, that you do not mean to alter our hours," said he, and again there was a burst of laughter, which died away as I looked slowly round the circle.

" What hour is the assembly ? " I asked, sharply, of Captain Pelletan.

Some mocking answer was on his tongue, but my glance kept it there. " The assembly is at six," he answered.

" I thank you," said I. I then counted the company,

and found that I had to do with fourteen officers, two of whom appeared to be boys fresh from St. Cyr. I could not condescend to take any notice of their indiscretion. There remained the major, four captains and seven lieutenants.

" Gentlemen," I continued, looking from one to the other of them, " I should feel myself unworthy of this famous regiment if I did not ask you for satisfaction for the rudeness with which you have greeted me, and I should hold you to be unworthy of it if on any pretext you refused to grant it."

" You will have no difficulty upon that score," said the major. " I am prepared to waive my rank and to give you every satisfaction in the name of the Hussars of Conflans."

" I thank you," I answered. " I feel, however, that I have some claim upon these other gentlemen who laughed at my expense."

" Whom would you fight, then ? " asked Captain Pelletan.

" All of you," I answered.

They looked in surprise from one to the other. Then they drew off to the other end of the room, and I heard the buzz of their whispers. They were laughing. Evidently they still thought that they had to do with some empty braggart. Then they returned.

" Your request is unusual," said Major Olivier, " but it will be granted. How do you propose to conduct such a duel ? The terms lie with you."

" Sabres," said I. " And I will take you in order of seniority, beginning with you, Major Olivier, at five o'clock. I will thus be able to devote five minutes to each before the assembly is blown. I must, however, beg you to have the courtesy to name the place of meeting, since I am still ignorant of the locality."

They were impressed by my cold and practical manner. Already the smile had died away from their lips. Olivier's face was no longer mocking, but it was dark and stern.

" There is a small open space behind the horse lines,"
said he. " We have held a few affairs of honour there,
and it has done very well. We shall be there, Captain
Gerard, at the hour you name."

I was in the act of bowing to thank them for their
acceptance when the door of the mess-room was flung
open and the colonel hurried into the room, with an
agitated face.

" Gentlemen," said he, " I have been asked to call for
a volunteer from among you for a service which involves
the greatest possible danger. I will not disguise from
you that the matter is serious in the last degree, and that
Marshal Lannes has chosen a cavalry officer because he
can be better spared than an officer of infantry or of
Engineers. Married men are not eligible. Of the
others, who will volunteer ! "

I need not say that all the unmarried officers stepped
to the front. The colonel looked round in some
embarrassment. I could see his dilemma. It was
the best man who should go, and yet it was the best
man whom he could least spare.

" Sir," said I, " may I be permitted to make a suggestion ? "

He looked at me with a hard eye. He had not forgotten my observations at supper. " Speak ! " said he.

" I would point out, sir," said I, " that this mission
is mine both by right and by convenience."

" Why so, Captain Gerard ? "

" By right, because I am the senior captain. By convenience, because I shall not be missed in the regiment,
since the men have not yet learned to know me."

The colonel's features relaxed.

" There is certainly truth in what you say, Captain
Gerard," said he. " I think that you are indeed best
fitted to go upon this mission. If you will come with
me I will give you your instructions."

I wished my new comrades good-night as I left the
room, and I repeated that I should hold myself at their

disposal at five o'clock next morning. They bowed in silence, and I thought that I could see, from the expression of their faces, that they had already begun to take a more just view of my character.

I had expected that the colonel would at once inform me what it was that I had been chosen to do, but instead of that he walked on in silence, I following behind him. We passed through the camp and made our way across the trenches and over the ruined heaps of stones which marked the old wall of the town. Within there was a labyrinth of passages, formed among the debris of the houses which had been destroyed by the mines of the Engineers. Acres and acres were covered with splintered walls and piles of brick which had once been a populous suburb. Lanes had been driven through it and lanterns placed at the corners with inscriptions to direct the way-farer. The colonel hurried onwards until at last, after a long walk, we found our way barred by a high grey wall which stretched right across our path. Here behind a barricade lay our advanced guard. The colonel led me into a roofless house, and there I found two general officers, a map stretched over a drum in front of them, they kneeling beside it and examining it carefully by the light of a lantern. The one with the clean-shaven face and the twisted neck was Marshal Lannes, the other was General Razout, the head of the Engineers.

" Captain Gerard has volunteered to go," said the colonel.

Marshal Lannes rose from his knees and shook me by the hand.

" You are a brave man, sir," said he. " I have a present to make to you," he added, handing me a very tiny glass tube. " It has been specially prepared by Dr. Fardet. At the supreme moment you have but to put it to your lips and you will be dead in an instant."

This was a cheerful beginning. I will confess to you, my friends, that a cold chill passed up my back and my hair rose upon my head.

" Excuse me, sir," said I, as I saluted, " I am aware that I have volunteered for a service of great danger, but the exact details have not yet been given to me."

" Colonel Perrin," said Lannes, severely, " it is unfair to allow this brave officer to volunteer before he has learned what the perils are to which he will be exposed."

But already I was myself once more.

" Sir," said I, " permit me to remark that the greater the danger the greater the glory, and that I could only repent of volunteering if I found that there were no risks to be run."

It was a noble speech, and my appearance gave force to my words. For the moment I was an heroic figure. As I saw Lannes's eyes fixed in admiration upon my face it thrilled me to think how splendid was the début which I was making in the army of Spain. If I died that night my name would not be forgotten. My new comrades and my old, divided in all else, would still have a point of union in their love and admiration of Étienne Gerard.

" General Razout, explain the situation ! " said Lannes, briefly.

The Engineer officer rose, his compasses in his hand. He led me to the door and pointed to the high grey wall which towered up amongst the debris of the shattered houses.

" That is the enemy's present line of defence," said he. " It is the wall of the great Convent of the Madonna. If we can carry it the city must fall, but they have run countermines all round it, and the walls are so enormously thick that it would be an immense labour to breach it with artillery. We happen to know, however, that the enemy have a considerable store of powder in one of the lower chambers. If that could be exploded the way would be clear for us."

" How can it be reached ? " I asked.

" I will explain. We have a French agent within the town named Hubert. This brave man has been in constant communication with us, and he had promised to explode the magazine. It was to be done in the early morning, and for two days running we have had a storming party of a thousand Grenadiers waiting for the breach to be formed. But there has been no explosion, and for these two days we have had no communication from Hubert. The question is, what has become of him ? "

" You wish me to go and see ? "

" Precisely. Is he ill, or wounded, or dead ? Shall we still wait for him, or shall we attempt the attack elsewhere ? We cannot determine this until we have heard from him. This is a map of the town, Captain Gerard. You perceive that within this ring of convents and monasteries are a number of streets which branch off from a central square. If you come so far as this square you will find the cathedral at one corner. In that corner is the street of Toledo. Hubert lives in a small house between a cobbler's and a wine-shop, on the right-hand side as you go from the cathedral. Do you follow me ? "

" Clearly."

" You are to reach that house, to see him, and to find out if his plan is still feasible or if we must abandon it." He produced what appeared to be a roll of dirty brown flannel. " This is the dress of a Franciscan friar," said he. " You will find it the most useful disguise."

I shrank away from it.

" It turns me into a spy," I cried. " Surely I can go in my uniform ? "

" Impossible ! How could you hope to pass through the streets of the city ? Remember, also, that the Spaniards take no prisoners, and that your fate will be the same in whatever dress you are taken."

It was true, and I had been long enough in Spain to know that that fate was likely to be something more serious than mere death. All the way from the frontier I had heard grim tales of torture and mutilation. I enveloped myself in the Franciscan gown.

" Now I am ready."

" Are you armed ? "

" My sabre."

" They will hear it clank. Take this knife and leave your sword. Tell Hubert that at four o'clock before dawn the storming party will again be ready. There is a sergeant outside who will show you how to get into the city. Good-night, and good luck ! "

Before I had left the room the two generals had their cocked hats touching each other over the map. At the door an under-officer of Engineers was waiting for me. I tied the girdle of my gown, and taking off my busby I drew the cowl over my head. My spurs I removed. Then in silence I followed my guide.

It was necessary to move with caution, for the walls above were lined by the Spanish sentries, who fired down continually at our advanced posts. Slinking along under the very shadow of the great convent, we picked our way slowly and carefully among the piles of ruins until we came to a large chestnut tree. Here the sergeant stopped.

" It is an easy tree to climb," said he. " A scaling ladder would not be simpler. Go up it, and you will find that the top branch will enable you to step upon the roof of that house. After that it is your guardian angel who must be your guide, for I can help you no more."

Girding up the heavy brown gown, I ascended the tree as directed. A half-moon was shining brightly, and the line of roof stood out dark and hard against the purple, starry sky. The tree was in the shadow of the house. Slowly I crept from branch to branch until I was near the top. I had but to climb along a stout limb in order to reach the wall. But suddenly my ears caught the patter of feet, and I cowered against the trunk and tried to blend myself with its shadow. A man was coming towards me on the roof. I saw his dark figure creeping along, his body crouching, his head advanced, the barrel of his gun protruding. His whole bearing was full of caution and suspicion. Once or twice he paused, and then came on again until he had reached the edge of the parapet within a few yards of me. Then he knelt down, levelled his musket, and fired.

I was so astonished at this sudden crash at my very elbow that I nearly fell out of the tree. For an instant I could not be sure that he had not hit me. But when I heard a deep groan from below, and the Spaniard leaned over the parapet and laughed aloud, I understood what had occurred. It was my poor, faithful sergeant who had waited to see the last of me. The Spaniard had seen him standing under the tree and had shot him. You will think that it was good shooting in the dark, but these people use trebucos, or blunderbusses, which are filled up with all sorts of stones and scraps of metal, so that they will hit you as certainly as I have hit a pheasant on a branch. The Spaniard stood peering down through the darkness, while an occasional groan from below showed that the sergeant was still living. The sentry looked round and everything was still and safe. Perhaps he thought that he would like to finish off this accursed Frenchman, or perhaps he had a desire to see what was in his pockets ; but whatever his motive he laid down his gun, leaned forward, and swung himself into the tree. The same instant I buried my knife in his body, and he fell with a loud crashing through the branches and came with a thud to the ground. I heard a short struggle below and an oath or two in French. The wounded sergeant had not waited long for his vengeance.

For some minutes I did not dare to move, for it seemed certain that someone would be attracted by the noise. However, all was silent save for the chimes striking midnight in the city. I crept along the branch and lifted myself on to the roof. The Spaniard's gun was lying there, but it was of no service to me, since he had the powder-horn at his belt. At the same time, if it were found it would warn the enemy that something had happened, so I thought it best to drop it over the wall. Then I looked round for the means of getting off the roof and down into the city.

It was very evident that the simplest way by which I could get down was that by which the sentinel had got up, and what this was soon became evident. A voice along the roof called " Manuelo ! Manuelo ! " several times, and, crouching in the shadow, I saw in the moonlight a bearded head, which protruded from a trap-door. Receiving no answer to his summons the man climbed through, followed by three other fellows all armed to the teeth. You will see here how important it is not to neglect small precautions, for had I left the man's gun where I found it a search must have followed, and I should certainly have been discovered. As it was, the patrol saw no sign of their sentry and thought, no doubt, that he had moved along the line of the roofs. They hurried on, therefore, in that direction, and I, the instant that their backs were turned, rushed to the open trap-door and descended the flight of steps which led from it. The house appeared to be an empty one, for I passed through the heart of it and out, by an open door, into the street beyond.

It was a narrow and deserted lane, but it opened into a broader road, which was dotted with fires, round which a great number of soldiers and peasants were sleeping. The smell within the city was so horrible that one wondered how people could live in it, for during the months that the siege had lasted there had been no attempt to cleanse the streets or to bury the dead. Many people were moving up and down from fire to fire, and among them I observed several monks. Seeing that they came and went unquestioned, I took heart and hurried on my way in the direction of the great square. Once a man rose from beside one of the fires and stopped me by seizing my sleeve. He pointed to a woman who lay motionless upon the road, and I took him to mean that she was dying, and that he desired me to administer the last offices of the Church. I sought refuge, however, in the very little Latin that was left to me. " Ora pro nobis," said I, from the depths of my cowl. " Te deum laudamus. Ora pro nobis." I raised my hand as I spoke and pointed forwards. The fellow released my sleeve and shrank back in silence, while I, with a solemn gesture, hurried upon my way.

As I had imagined, this broad boulevard led out into the central square, which was full of troops and blazing with fires. I walked swiftly onwards, disregarding one or two people who addressed remarks to me. I passed the cathedral and followed the street which had been described to me. Being upon the side of the city which was farthest from our attack, there were no troops encamped in it, and it lay in darkness, save for an occasional glimmer in a window. It was not difficult to find the house to which I had been directed, between the wine-shop and the cobbler's. There was no light within, and the door was shut. Cautiously I pressed the latch, and I felt that it had yielded. Who was within I could not tell, and yet I must take the risk. I pushed the door open and entered.

It was pitch-dark within—the more so as I had closed the door behind me. I felt round and came upon the edge of a table. Then I stood still and wondered what I should do next, and how I could gain some news of this Hubert, in whose house I found myself. Any mistake would cost me not only my life, but the failure of my mission. Perhaps he did not live alone. Perhaps he was only a lodger in a Spanish family, and my visit might bring ruin to him as well as to myself. Seldom in my life have I been more perplexed. And then, suddenly, something turned my blood cold in my veins. It was a voice, a whispering voice, in my very ear. " Mon Dieu !" cried the voice in a tone of agony. " Oh, mon Dieu ! mon Dieu ! " Then there was a dry sob in the darkness, and all was still once more.

It thrilled me with horror, that terrible voice ; but it thrilled me also with hope, for it was the voice of a Frenchman.

" Who is there ? " I asked.

There was a groaning, but no reply.

" Is that you, Monsieur Hubert ? "

" Yes, yes," sighed the voice, so low that I could hardly hear it. " Water, water, for Heaven's sake, water ! "

I advanced in the direction of the sound, but only to come in contact with the wall. Again I heard a groan, but this time there could be no doubt that it was above my head. I put up my hands, but they felt only empty air.

" Where are you ? " I cried.

" Here ! Here ! " whispered the strange, tremulous voice. I stretched my hand along the wall, and I came upon a man's naked foot. It was as high as my face, and yet, so far as I could feel, it had nothing to support it. I staggered back in amazement. Then I took a tinder-box from my pocket and struck a light. At the first flash a man seemed to be floating in the air in front of me, and I dropped the box in my amazement. Again, with tremulous fingers, I struck the flint against the steel, and this time I lit not only the tinder, but the wax taper. I held it up, and if my amazement was lessened, my horror was increased by that which it revealed.

The man had been nailed to the wall as a weasel is nailed to the door of a barn. Huge spikes had been driven through his hands and his feet. The poor wretch was in his last agony, his head sunk upon his shoulder and his blackened tongue protruded from his lips. He was dying as much from thirst as from his wounds, and these inhuman wretches had placed a beaker of wine upon the table in front of him to add a fresh pang to his tortures. I raised it to his lips. He had still strength enough to swallow, and the light came back a little to his dim eyes.

" Are you a Frenchman ? " he whispered.

" Yes. They have sent me to learn what had befallen you."

" They discovered me. They have killed me for it.

But before I die let me tell you what I know. A little more of that wine, please ! Quick ! Quick ! I am very near the end. My strength is going. Listen to me ! The powder is stored in the Mother Superior's room. The wall is pierced, and the end of the train is in Sister Angela's cell, next the chapel. All was ready two days ago. But they discovered a letter, and they tortured me."

" Good Heavens ! have you been hanging here for two days ? "

" It seems like two years. Comrade, I have served France, have I not ? Then do one little service for me. Stab me to the heart, dear friend ! I implore you, I entreat you, to put an end to my sufferings."

The man was indeed in a hopeless plight, and the kindest action would have been that for which he begged. And yet I could not in cold blood drive my knife into his body, although I knew how I should have prayed for such a mercy had I been in his place. But a sudden thought crossed my mind. In my pocket I held that which would give an instant and painless death. It was my own safeguard against torture, and yet this poor soul was in very pressing need of it, and he had deserved well of France.

I took out my phial and emptied it into the cup of wine. I was in the act of handing it to him when I heard a sudden clash of arms outside the door. In an instant I put out my light and slipped behind the window-curtains. Next moment the door was flung open, and two Spaniards strode into the room—fierce, swarthy men in the dress of citizens, but with muskets slung over their shoulders. I looked through the chink in the curtains in an agony of fear lest they had come upon my traces, but it was evident that their visit was simply in order to feast their eyes upon my unfortunate compatriot. One of them held the lantern which he carried up in front of the dying man, and both of them burst into a shout of mocking laughter. Then the eyes of the man with the lantern fell upon the flagon of wine upon the table. He picked it up, held it, with a devilish grin, to the lips of Hubert, and then, as the poor wretch involuntarily inclined his head forward to reach it, snatched it back and took a long gulp himself. At the same instant he uttered a loud cry, clutched wildly at his own throat, and fell stone-dead upon the floor. His comrade stared at him in horror and amazement. Then, overcome by his own superstitious fears, he gave a yell of terror and rushed madly from the room. I heard his feet clattering wildly on the cobble-stones until the sound died away in the distance.

The lantern had been left burning upon the table, and by its light I saw, as I came out from behind my curtain, that the unfortunate Hubert's head had fallen forward upon his chest and that he also was dead. That motion to reach the wine with his lips had been his last. A clock ticked loudly in the house, but otherwise all was absolutely still. On the wall hung the twisted form of the French-man, on the floor lay the motionless body of the Spaniard, all dimly lit by the horn lantern. For the first time in my life a frantic spasm of terror came over me. I had seen ten thousand men in every conceivable degree of mutilation stretched upon the ground, but the sight had never affected me like those two silent figures who were my companions in that shadowy room. I rushed into the street as the Spaniard had done, eager only to leave that house of gloom behind me, and I had run as far as the cathedral before my wits came back to me. There I stopped panting in the shadow, and, my hand pressed to my side, I tried to collect my scattered senses and to plan out what I should do. As I stood there, breathless, the great brass bells roared twice above my head. It was two o'clock. Four was the hour when the storming party would be in its place. I had still two hours in which to act.

The cathedral was brilliantly lit within, and a number of people were passing in and out ; so I entered, thinking that I was less likely to be accosted there and that I might have quiet to form my plans. It was certainly a singular sight, for the place had been turned into a hospital, a refuge and a storehouse. One aisle was crammed with provisions, another was littered with sick and wounded, while in the centre a great number of helpless people had taken up their abode and had even lit their cooking fires upon the mosaic floors. There were many at prayer, so I knelt in the shadow of a pillar and I prayed with all my heart that I might have the good luck to get out of this scrape alive, and that I might do such a deed that night as would make my name as famous in Spain as it had already become in Germany. I waited until the clock struck three and then I left the cathedral and made my way towards the Convent of the Madonna, where the assault was to be delivered. You will understand, you who know me so well, that I was not the man to return tamely to the French camp with the report that our agent was dead and that other means must be found of entering the city. Either I should find some means to finish his uncompleted task or there would be a vacancy for a senior captain in the Hussars of Conflans.

I passed unquestioned down the broad boulevard, which I have already described, until I came to the great stone convent which formed the outwork of the defence. It was built in a square with a garden in the centre. In this garden some hundreds of men were assembled, all armed and ready, for it was known, of course, within the town that this was the point against which the French attack was likely to be made. Up to this time our fighting all over Europe had always been done between one army and another. It was only here in Spain that we learned how terrible a thing it is to fight against a people. On the one hand there is no glory, for what glory could be gained by defeating this rabble of elderly shopkeepers, ignorant peasants, fanatical priests, excited women and all the other creatures who made up the garrison ? On the other hand there were extreme discomfort and danger, for these people would give you no rest, would observe no rules of war, and were desperately earnest in their desire by hook or by crook to do you an injury. I began to realise how odious was our task as I looked upon the motley but ferocious groups who were gathered round the watch fires in the garden of the Convent of the Madonna. It was not for us soldiers to think about politics, but from the beginning there always seemed to be a curse upon this war in Spain.

However, at the moment I had no time to brood over such matters as these. There was, as I have said, no difficulty in getting as far as the convent garden, but to pass inside the convent unquestioned was not so easy. The first thing which I did was to walk round the garden, and I was soon able to pick out one large stained-glass window which must belong to the chapel. I had understood from Hubert that the Mother Superior's room in which the powder was stored was near to this, and that the train had been laid through a hole in the wall from some neighbouring cell. I must at all costs get into the convent. There was a guard at the door, and how could I get in without explanations ? But a sudden inspiration showed me how the thing might be done. In the garden was a well, and beside the well were a number of empty buckets. I filled two of these and approached the door. The errand of a man who carries a bucket of water in each hand does not need to be explained. The guard opened to let me through. I found myself in a long stone-flagged corridor lit with lanterns, with the cells of the nuns leading out from one side of it. Now at last I was on the high road to success. I walked on without hesitation, for I knew by my observations in the garden which way to go for the chapel.

A number of Spanish soldiers were lounging and smoking in the corridor, several of whom addressed me as I passed. I fancy it was for my blessing that they asked, and my " Ora pro nobis " seemed to entirely satisfy them. Soon I had got as far as the chapel, and it was easy to see that the cell next door was used as a magazine, for the floor was all black with powder in front of it. The door was shut, and two fierce-looking fellows stood on guard outside it, one of them with a key stuck in his belt. Had we been alone it would not have been long before it would have been in my hand, but with his comrade there it was impossible for me to hope to take it by force. The cell next door to the magazine on the far side from the chapel must be the one which belonged to Sister Angela. It was half open. I took my courage in both hands, and leaving my buckets in the corridor, I walked unchallenged into the room.

I was prepared to find half a dozen fierce Spanish desperadoes within, but what actually met my eyes was even more embarrassing. The room had apparently been set aside for the use of some of the nuns, who for some reason had refused to quit their home. Three of them were within, one an elderly, stern-faced dame who was evidently the Mother Superior, the others young ladies of charming appearance. They were seated together at the far side of the room, but they all rose at my entrance, and I saw with some amazement, by their manner and expressions, that my coming was both welcome and expected. In a moment my presence of mind had returned, and I saw exactly how the matter lay. Naturally, since an attack was about to be made upon the convent, these sisters had been expecting to be directed to some place of safety. Probably they were under vow not to quit the walls, and they had been told to remain in this cell until they had received further orders. In any case I adapted my conduct to this supposition, since it was clear that I must get them out of the room, and this would give me a ready excuse to do so. I first cast a glance at the door and observed that the key was within. I then made a gesture to the nuns to follow me. The Mother Superior asked me some question, but I shook my head impatiently and beckoned to her again. She hesitated, but I stamped my foot and called them forth in so imperious a manner that they came at once. They would be safer in the chapel, and thither I led them, placing them at the end which was farthest from the magazine. As the three nuns took their places before the altar my heart bounded with joy and pride within me, for I felt that the last obstacle had been lifted from my path.

And yet how often have I not found that this is the very moment of danger ? I took a last glance at the Mother Superior and to my dismay I saw that her piercing dark eyes were fixed, with an expression in which surprise was deepening into suspicion, upon my right hand. There were two points which might well have attracted her attention. One was that it was red with the blood of the sentinel whom I had stabbed in the tree. That alone might count for little, as the knife is as familiar as the breviary to the monks of Saragossa. But on my forefinger I wore a heavy gold ring—the gift of a German baroness whose name I may not mention. It shone brightly in the light of the altar lamp. Now, a ring upon a friar's hand is an impossibility, since they are vowed to absolute poverty. I turned quickly and made for the door of the chapel, but the mischief was done. As I glanced back I saw that the Mother Superior was already hurrying after me. I ran through the chapel door and along the corridor, but she called out some shrill warning to the two guards in front. Fortunately I had the presence of mind to call out also, and to point down the passage as if we were both pursuing the same object, Next instant I had dashed past them, sprang into the cell. slammed the heavy door, and fastened it upon the inside. With a bolt above and below and a huge lock in the centre it was a piece of timber that would take some forcing.

Even now if they had had the wit to put a barrel of powder against the door I should have been ruined. It was their only chance, for I had come to the final stage of my adventure. Here at last, after such a string of dangers as few men have ever lived to talk of I was at one end of the powder train, with the Saragossa magazine at the other. They were howling like wolves out in the passage, and muskets were crashing against the door. I paid no heed to their clamour, but I looked eagerly round for that train of which Hubert had spoken. Of course, it must be at the side of the room next to the magazine. I crawled along it on my hands and knees, looking into every crevice, but no sign could I see. Two bullets flew through the door and flattened themselves against the wall. The thudding and smashing grew ever louder. I saw a grey pile in a corner, flew to it with a cry of joy, and found that it was only dust. Then I got back to the side of the door where no bullets could ever reach me—they were streaming freely into the room—and I tried to forget this fiendish howling in my ear and to think out where this train could be. It must have been carefully laid by Hubert lest these nuns should see it. I tried to imagine how I should myself have arranged it had I been in his place. My eye was attracted by a statue of St. Joseph which stood in the corner. There was a wreath of leaves along the edge of the pedestal, with a lamp burning amidst them. I rushed across to it and tore the leaves aside. Yes, yes, there was a thin black line, which disappeared through a small hole in the wall. I tilted over the lamp, and threw myself on the ground. Next instant came a roar like thunder, the walls wavered and tottered around me, the ceiling clattered down from above and over the yell of the terrified Spaniards was heard the terrific shout of the storming column of the Grenadiers. As in a dream—a happy dream—I heard it, and then I heard no more.

When I came to my senses two French soldiers were propping me up, and my head was singing like a kettle. I staggered to my feet and looked around me. The plaster had fallen, the furniture was scattered, and there were rents in the bricks, but no signs of a breach. In fact, the walls of the convent had been so solid that the explosion of the magazine had been insufficient to throw them down. On the other hand, it had caused such a panic among the defenders that our stormers had been able to carry the windows and throw open the doors almost without resistance. As I ran out into the corridor I found it full of troops, and I met Marshal Lannes himself, who was entering with his staff. He stopped and listened eagerly to my story.

" Splendid, Captain Gerard, splendid ! " he cried. " These facts will certainly be reported to the Emperor."

" I would suggest to your excellency," said I, " that I have only finished the work that was planned and carried out by Monsieur Hubert, who gave his life for the cause."

" His services will not be forgotten," said the Marshal. " Meanwhile, Captain Gerard, it is half-past four, and you must be starving after such a night of exertion. My staff and I will breakfast inside the city. I assure you that you will be an honoured guest."

" I will follow your excellency," said I. " There is a small engagement which detains me."

He opened his eyes.

" At this hour ? "

" Yes, sir," I answered. " My fellow-officers, whom I never saw until last night, will not be content unless they catch another glimpse of me the first thing this morning."

" Au revoir, then," said Marshal Lannes, as he passed upon his way.

I hurried through the shattered door of the convent. When I reached the roofless house in which we had held the consultation the night before, I threw off my gown, and I put on the busby and sabre which I had left there. Then, a hussar once more, I hurried onwards to the grove which was our rendezvous. My brain was still reeling from the concussion of the powder, and I was exhausted by the many emotions which had shaken me during that terrible night. It is like a dream, all that walk in the first dim grey light of dawn, with the smouldering camp-fires around me and the buzz of the waking army. Bugles and drums in every direction were mustering the infantry, for the explosion and the shouting had told their own tale. I strode onwards until, as I entered the little clump of cork oaks behind the horse lines, I saw my twelve comrades waiting in a group, their sabres at their sides. They looked at me curiously as I approached. Perhaps with my powder-blackened face and my blood-stained hands I seemed a different Gerard to the young captain whom they had made game of the night before.

" Good morning, gentlemen," said I. " I regret exceedingly if I have kept you waiting, but I have not been master of my own time."

They said nothing, but they still scanned me with curious eyes. I can see them now, standing in a line before me, tall men and short men, stout men and thin men ; Olivier, with his warlike moustache ; the thin, eager face of Pelletan ; young Oudin, flushed by his first duel ; Mortier, with the sword-cut across his wrinkled brow. I laid aside my busby and drew my sword.

" I have one favour to ask you, gentlemen," said I. " Marshal Lannes has invited me to breakfast, and I cannot keep him waiting."

" What do you suggest ? " asked Major Olivier.

" That you release me from my promise to give you five minutes each, and that you will permit me to attack you all together." I stood upon my guard as I spoke.

But their answer was truly beautiful and truly French. With one impulse the twelve swords flew from their scabbards and were raised in salute. There they stood, the twelve of them, motionless, their heels together, each with his sword upright before his face.

I staggered back from them. I looked from one to the other. For an instant I could not believe my own eyes. They were paying me homage, these, the men who had jeered me ! Then I understood it all. I saw the effect that I had made upon them and their desire to make reparation. When a man is weak he can steel himself against danger, but not against emotion. " Comrades," I cried, " comrades——! " but I could say no more. Something seemed to take me by the throat and choke me. And then in an instant Olivier's arms were round me, Pelletan had seized me by the right hand, Mortier by the left, some were patting me on the shoulder, some were clapping me on the back, on every side smiling faces were looking into mine ; and so it was that I knew that I had won my footing in the Hussars of Conflans.

3. *How the Brigadier slew the Fox*

IN all the great hosts of France there was only one officer towards whom the English of Wellington's army retained a deep, steady and unchangeable hatred. There were plunderers among the French, and men of violence, gamblers, duellists and *roués*. All these could be forgiven, for others of their kidney were to be found among the ranks of the English. But one officer of Massena's force had committed a crime which was unspeakable, unheard of, abominable ; only to be alluded to with curses late in the evening, when a second bottle had loosened the tongues of men. The news of it was carried back to England, and country gentlemen who knew little of the details of the war grew crimson with passion when they heard of it, and yeomen of the shires raised freckled fists to Heaven and swore. And yet who should be the doer of this dreadful deed but our friend the brigadier, Étienne Gerard, of the Hussars of Conflans, gay-riding, plume-tossing, debonair, the darling of the ladies and of the six brigades of light cavalry.

But the strange part of it is that this gallant gentleman did this hateful thing, and made himself the most un-popular man in the Peninsula, without ever knowing that he had done a crime for which there is hardly a name amid all the resources of our language. He died of old age, and never once in that imperturbable self-confidence which adorned or disfigured his character knew that so many thousand Englishmen would gladly have hanged him with their own hands. On the contrary, he numbered this adventure among those other exploits which he has given to the world, and many a time he chuckled and hugged himself as he narrated it to the eager circle who gathered round him in that humble café where, between his dinner and his dominoes, he would tell, amid tears and laughter, of that inconceivable Napoleonic past when France, like an angel of wrath, rose up, splendid and terrible, before a cowering continent. Let us listen to him as he tells the story in his own way and from his own point of view.

You must know, my friends (said he), that it was towards the end of the year eighteen hundred and ten that I and Massena and the others pushed Wellington backwards until we had hoped to drive him and his army into the Tagus. But when we were still twenty-five miles from Lisbon we found that we were betrayed, for what had this Englishman done but build an enormous line of works and forts at a place called Torres Vedras, so that even we were unable to get through them ! They lay across the whole peninsula, and our army was so far from home that we did not dare to risk a reverse, and we had already learned at Busaco that it was no child's play to fight against these people. What could we do, then, but sit down in front of these lines and blockade them to the best of our power ? There we remained for six months, amid such anxieties that Massena said afterwards that he had not one hair which was not white upon his body. For my own part, I did not worry much about our situation, but I looked after our horses, who were in great need of rest and green fodder. For the rest, we drank the wine of the country and passed the time as best we might. There was a lady at Santarem—but my lips are sealed.

It is the part of a gallant man to say nothing, though he may indicate that he could say a great deal.

One day Massena sent for me, and I found him in his tent with a great plan pinned upon the table. He looked at me in silence with that single piercing eye of his, and I felt by his expression that the matter was serious. He was nervous and ill at ease, but my bearing seemed to reassure him. It is good to be in contact with brave men.

" Colonel Étienne Gerard," said he, " I have always heard that you are a very gallant and enterprising officer."

It was not for me to confirm such a report, and yet it would be folly to deny it, so I clinked my spurs together and saluted.

" You are also an excellent rider."

I admitted it.

" And the best swordsman in the six brigades of light cavalry."

Massena was famous for the accuracy of his information.

" Now," said he, " if you will look at this plan you will have no difficulty in understanding what it is that I wish you to do. These are the lines of Torres Vedras. You will perceive that they cover a vast space, and you will realise that the English can only hold a position here and there. Once through the lines, you have twenty-five miles of open country which lie between them and Lisbon. It is very important to me to learn how Wellington's troops are distributed throughout that space, and it is my wish that you should go and ascertain."

His words turned me cold.

" Sir," said I, " it is impossible that a colonel of light cavalry should condescend to act as a spy."

He laughed and clapped me on the shoulder. " You would not be a Hussar if you were not a hot-head," said he. " If you will listen you will understand that I have not asked you to act as a spy. What do you think of that horse ? "

He had conducted me to the opening of his tent, and there was a chasseur who led up and down a most admirable creature. He was a dapple grey, not very tall— a little over fifteen hands perhaps—but with the short head and splendid arch of the neck which comes with the Arab blood. His shoulders and haunches were so muscular, and yet his legs so fine, that it thrilled me with joy just to gaze upon him. A fine horse or a beautiful woman, I cannot look at them unmoved, even now when seventy winters have chilled my blood. You can think how it was in the year '10.

" This," said Massena, " is Voltigeur, the swiftest horse in our army. What I desire is that you should start to-night, ride round the lines upon the flank, make your way across the enemy's rear, and return upon the other flank, bringing me news of his dispositions. You will wear a uniform, and will, therefore, if captured, be safe from the death of a spy. It is probable that you will get through the lines unchallenged, for the posts are very scattered. Once through, in daylight you can outride anything which you meet, and if you keep off the roads you may escape entirely unnoticed. If you have not reported yourself by to-morrow night I will understand that you are taken, and I will offer them Colonel Petrie in exchange."

Ah, how my heart swelled with pride and joy as I sprang into the saddle and galloped this grand horse up and down to show the marshal the mastery which I had of him ! He was magnificent—we were both magnificent, for Massena clapped his hands and cried out in his delight. It was not I, but he, who said that a gallant beast deserves a gallant rider. Then, when for the third time, with my panache flying and my dolman streaming behind me, I thundered past him, I saw upon his hard old face that he had no longer any doubt that he had chosen the man for his purpose. I drew my sabre, raised the hilt to

my lips in salute, and galloped on to my own quarters.
Already the news had spread that I had been chosen for a
mission, and my little rascals came swarming out of their
tents to cheer me. Ah! it brings the tears to my old
eyes when I think how proud they were of their colonel.
And I was proud of them also. They deserved a dashing
leader.

The night promised to be a stormy one, which was
very much to my liking. It was my desire to keep my
departure most secret, for it was evident that if the English
heard that I had been detached from the army they
would naturally conclude that something important was
about to happen. My horse was taken, therefore,
beyond the picket line, as if for watering, and I followed
and mounted him there. I had a map, a compass and a
paper of instructions from the marshal, and with these in
the bosom of my tunic, and a sabre at my side, I set out
upon my adventure. A thin rain was falling, and there
was no moon, so you may imagine that it was not very
cheerful. But my heart was light at the thought of the
honour which had been done me, and the glory which
awaited me. This exploit should be one more in that
brilliant series which was to change my sabre into a
bâton. Ah, how we dreamed, we foolish fellows, young,
and drunk with success! Could I have foreseen that night
as I rode, the chosen man of 60,000, that I should spend
my life planting cabbages on a hundred francs a month!
Oh, my youth, my hopes, my comrades! But the wheel
turns and never stops. Forgive me, my friends, for an
old man has his weakness.

My route, then, lay across the face of the high ground
of Torres Vedras, then over a streamlet, past a farmhouse
which had been burned down and was now only a land-
mark, then through a forest of young cork oaks, and so to
the monastery of San Antonio, which marked the left of
the English position. Here I turned south and rode
quietly over the downs, for it was at this point that
Massena thought that it would be most easy for me to

find my way unobserved through the position. I went very slowly, for it was so dark that I could not see my hand in front of me. In such cases I leave my bridle loose, and let my horse pick its own way. Voltigeur went confidently forward, and I was very content to sit upon his back, and to peer about me, avoiding every light. For three hours we advanced in this cautious way, until it seemed to me that I must have left all danger behind me. I then pushed on more briskly, for I wished to be in the rear of the whole army by daybreak. There are many vineyards in these parts which in winter become open plains, and a horseman finds few difficulties in his way.

But Massena had underrated the cunning of these English, for it appears that there was not one line of defence, but three, and it was the third which was the most formidable, through which I was at that instant passing. As I rode, elated at my own success, a lantern flashed suddenly before me, and I saw the glint of polished gun-barrels and the gleam of a red coat.

" Who goes there ? " cried a voice—such a voice ! I swerved to the right and rode like a madman, but a dozen quirts of fire came out of the darkness, and the bullets whizzed all round my ears. That was no new sound to me, my friends, though I will not talk like a foolish conscript and say that I have ever liked it. But at least it had never kept me from thinking clearly, and so I knew that there was nothing for it but to gallop hard and try my luck elsewhere. I rode round the English picket, and then, as I heard nothing more of them, I concluded rightly that I had at last come through their defences. For five miles I rode south, striking a tinder from time to time to look at my pocket compass. And then in an instant—I feel the pang once more as my memory brings back the moment—my horse, without a sob or stagger, fell stone dead beneath me !

I had not known it, but one of the bullets from that infernal picket had passed through his body. The gallant creature had never winced nor weakened, but had gone while life was in him. One instant I was secure on the swiftest, most graceful horse in Massena's army. The next he lay upon his side, worth only the price of his hide, and I stood there that most helpless, most ungainly of creatures, a dismounted hussar. What could I do with my boots, my spurs, my trailing sabre ? I was far inside the enemy's lines. How could I hope to get back again ? I am not ashamed to say that I, Étienne Gerard, sat upon my dead horse and sank my face in my hands in my despair. Already the first streaks were whitening in the east. In half an hour it would be light. That I should have won my way past every obstacle, and then at this last instant be left at the mercy of my enemies, my mission ruined, and myself a prisoner—was it not enough to break a soldier's heart ?

But courage, my friends ! We have these moments of weakness, the bravest of us ; but I have a spirit like a slip of steel, for the more you bend it the higher it springs. One spasm of despair, and then a brain of ice and a heart of fire. All was not yet lost. I, who had come through so many hazards, would come through this one also. I rose from my horse and considered what had best be done.

And first of all it was certain that I could not get back. Long before I could pass the lines it would be broad daylight. I must hide myself for the day, and devote the next night to my escape. I took the saddle, holsters and bridle from my poor Voltigeur, and I concealed them among some bushes, so that no one finding him could know that he was a French horse. Then, leaving him lying there, I wandered on in search of some place where I might be safe for the day. In every direction I could see camp fires upon the sides of the hills, and already figures had begun to move around them. I must hide quickly or I was lost. But where was I to hide ? It was a vineyard in which I found myself, the poles of the vines still standing, but the plants gone. There was no cover there. Besides, I should want some food and water before another night had come. I hurried wildly onwards through the waning darkness, trusting that chance would be my friend. And I was not disappointed. Chance is a woman, my friend, and she has her eye always upon a gallant hussar.

Well, then, I stumbled through the vineyard, something loomed in front of me, and I came upon a great square house with another long, low building upon one side of it. Three roads met there, and it was easy to see that this was the *posada*, or wine-shop. There was no light in the windows, and everything was dark and silent, but, of course, I knew that such comfortable quarters were certainly occupied, and probably by someone of importance. I have learned, however, that the nearer the danger may really be the safer the place, and so I was by no means inclined to trust myself away from this shelter. The low building was evidently the stable, and into this I crept, for the door was unlatched. The place was full of bullocks and sheep, gathered there, no doubt, to be out of the clutches of marauders. A ladder led to a loft, and up this I climbed, and concealed myself very snugly among some bales of hay upon the top. This loft had a small open window, and I was able to look down upon the front of the inn and also upon the road Then I crouched and waited to see what would happen.

It was soon evident that I had not been mistaken when I had thought that this might be the quarters of some person of importance. Shortly after daybreak an English light dragoon arrived with a despatch, and from then onwards the place was in a turmoil, officers continually riding up and away. Always the same name was upon their lips: " Sir Stapleton—Sir Stapleton." It was hard for me to lie there with a dry moustache and watch the great flagons which were brought out by the landlord to these English officers. But it amused me to look at their fresh-coloured, clean-shaven, careless faces, and to wonder what they would think if they knew that so celebrated a person was lying so near to them. And then, as I lay and watched, I saw a sight which filled me with surprise.

It is incredible, the insolence of these English ! What do you suppose Milord Wellington had done when he found that Massena had blockaded him and that he could not move his army ? I might give you many guesses. You might say that he had raged, that he had despaired, that he had brought his troops together and spoken to them about glory and the fatherland before leading them to one last battle. No, Milord did none of these things. But he sent a fleet ship to England to bring him a number of fox-dogs, and he with his officers settled themself down to chase the fox. It is true what I tell you. Behind the lines of Torres Vedras these mad Englishmen made the fox-chase three days in the week. We had heard of it in the camp, and now I myself was to see that it was true.

For, along the road which I have described, there came these very dogs, thirty or forty of them, white and brown, each with its tail at the same angle, like the bayonets of the Old Guard. My faith, but it was a pretty sight ! And behind and amidst them there rode three men with peaked caps and red coats, whom I understood to be the hunters. After them came many horsemen with uniforms of various kinds, stringing along the road in twos and threes, talking together and laughing. They did not seem to be going above a trot, and it appeared to me that it must indeed be a slow fox which they hoped to catch. However, it was their affair, not mine, and soon they had all passed my window and were out of sight. I waited and I watched, ready for any chance which might offer.

Presently an officer, in a blue uniform not unlike that of our flying artillery, came cantering down the road—an elderly, stout man he was, with grey side-whiskers. He stopped and began to talk with an orderly officer of dragoons, who waited outside the inn, and it was then that I learned the advantage of the English which had been taught me. I could hear and understand all that was said.

" Where is the meet ? " said the officer, and I thought that he was hungering for his bifstek. But the other answered him that it was near Altara, so I saw that it was a place of which he spoke.

" You are late, Sir George," said the orderly.

" Yes, I had a court-martial. Has Sir Stapleton Cotton gone ? "

At this moment a window opened, and a handsome young man in a very splendid uniform looked out of it.

" Halloa, Murray ! " said he. " These cursed papers keep me, but I will be at your heels."

" Very good, Cotton. I am late already, so I will ride on."

" You might order my groom to bring round my horse," said the young general at the window to the orderly below, while the other went on down the road.

The orderly rode away to some outlying stable, and then in a few minutes there came a smart English groom with a cockade in his hat, leading by the bridle a horse— and, oh, my friends, you have never known the perfection to which a horse can attain until you have seen a first-class English hunter. He was superb : tall, broad, strong, and yet as graceful and agile as a deer. Coal black he was in colour, and his neck, and his shoulder, and his quarters, and his fetlocks—how can I describe him all to you ? The sun shone upon him as on polished ebony, and he raised his hoofs in a little playful dance so lightly and prettily, while he tossed his mane and whinnied with impatience. Never have I seen such a mixture of strength and beauty and grace. I had often wondered how the English Hussars had managed to ride over the Chasseurs of the Guards in the affair at Astorga, but I wondered no longer when I saw the English horses.

There was a ring for fastening bridles at the door of the inn, and the groom tied the horse there while he entered the house. In an instant I had seen the chance which

Fate had brought to me. Were I in that saddle I should be better off than when I started. Even Voltigeur could not compare with this magnificent creature. To think is to act with me. In one instant I was down the ladder and at the door of the stable. The next I was out and the bridle was in my hand. I bounded into the saddle. Somebody, the master or the man, shouted wildly behind me. What cared I for his shouts! I touched the horse with my spurs, and he bounded forward with such a spring that only a rider like myself could have sat him. I gave him his head and let him go—it did not matter to me where, so long as we left this inn far behind us. He thundered away across the vineyards, and in a very few minutes I had placed miles between myself and my pursuers. They could no longer tell, in that wild country, in which direction I had gone. I knew that I was safe, and, so riding to the top of a small hill, I drew my pencil and note-book from my pocket, and proceeded to make plans of those camps which I could see, and to draw the outline of the country.

He was a dear creature upon whom I sat, but it was not easy to draw upon his back, for every now and then his two ears would cock, and he would start and quiver with impatience. At first I could not understand this trick of his, but soon I observed that he only did it when a peculiar noise—" Yoy, yoy, yoy "—came from somewhere among the oak woods beneath us. And then suddenly this strange cry changed into a most terrible screaming, with the frantic blowing of a horn. Instantly he went mad—this horse. His eyes blazed. His mane bristled. He bounded from the earth and bounded again, twisting and turning in a frenzy. My pencil flew one way and my note-book another. And then, as I looked down into the valley, an extraordinary sight met my eyes. The hunt was streaming down it. The fox I could not see, but the dogs were in full cry, their noses down, their tails up, so close together that they might have been one great yellow and white moving carpet.

And behind them rode the horsemen—my faith, what a sight ! Consider every type which a great army could show ; some in hunting dress, but the most in uniforms ; blue dragoons, red dragoons, red-trousered hussars, green riflemen, artillerymen, gold-slashed lancers, and most of all red, red, red, for the infantry officers ride as hard as the cavalry. Such a crowd, some well mounted, some ill, but all flying along as best they might, the subaltern as good as the general, jostling and pushing, spurring and driving, with every thought thrown to the winds save that they should have the blood of this absurd fox ! Truly, they are an extraordinary people, the English ! But I had little time to watch the hunt or to marvel at these islanders, for of all these mad creatures the very horse upon which I sat was the maddest. You understand that he was himself a hunter, and that the crying of these dogs was to him what the call of a cavalry trumpet in the street yonder would be to me. It thrilled him. It drove him wild. Again and again he bounded into the air, and then, seizing the bit between his teeth, he plunged down the slope, and galloped after the dogs. I swore, and tugged, and pulled, but I was powerless. This English general rode his horse with a snaffle only, and the beast had a mouth of iron. It was useless to pull him back. One might as well try to keep a grenadier from a wine bottle. I gave it up in despair, and, settling down in the saddle, I prepared for the worst which could befall.

What a creature he was ! Never have I felt such a horse between my knees. His great haunches gathered under him with every stride, and he shot forward ever faster and faster, stretched like a greyhound, while the wind beat in my face and whistled past my ears. I was wearing our undress jacket, a uniform simple and dark in itself—though some figures give distinction to any uniform—and I had taken the precaution to remove the long panache from my busby. The result was that, amidst the mixture of costumes in the hunt, there was no reason why mine should attract attention, or why these men, whose thoughts were all with the chase, should give any heed to me. The idea that a French officer might be riding with them was too absurd to enter their minds. I laughed as I rode, for, indeed, amid all the danger, there was something of comic in the situation.

I have said that the hunters were very unequally mounted, and so, at the end of a few miles, instead of being one body of men, like a charging regiment, they were scattered over a considerable space, the better riders well up to the dogs, and the others trailing away behind. Now, I was as good a rider as any, and my horse was the best of them all, and so you can imagine that it was not long before he carried me to the front. And when I saw the dogs streaming over the open, and the red-coated huntsman behind them, and only seven or eight horsemen between us, then it was that the strangest thing of all happened, for I, too, went mad—I, Étienne Gerard! In a moment it came upon me, this spirit of sport, this desire to excel, this hatred of the fox. Accursed animal, should he then defy us? Vile robber, his hour was come! Ah, it is a great feeling, this feeling of sport, my friends, this desire to trample the fox under the hoofs of your horse. I have made the fox-chase with the English. I have also, as I may tell you some day, fought the box-fight with the Bustler, of Bristol. And I say to you that this sport is a wonderful thing—full of interest as well as madness.

The farther we went the faster galloped my horse, and soon there were but three men as near the dogs as I was. All thought of fear of discovery had vanished. My brain throbbed, my blood ran hot—only one thing upon earth seemed worth living for, and that was to overtake this infernal fox. I passed one of the horsemen—a hussar like myself. There were only two in front of me now—the one in a black coat, the other the blue artilleryman whom I had seen at the inn. His grey whiskers streamed in the wind, but he rode magnificently. For a mile or more we kept in this order, and then, as we galloped up a steep slope, my lighter weight brought me to the front. I passed them both, and when I reached the crown I was riding level with the little, hard-faced English huntsman. In front of us were the dogs, and then, a hundred paces beyond them, was a brown wisp of a thing, the fox itself, stretched to the uttermost. The sight of him fired my blood. " Aha, we have you then, assassin ! " I cried, and shouted my encouragement to the huntsman. I waved my hand to show him that there was one upon whom he could rely.

And now there were only the dogs between me and my prey. These dogs, whose duty it is to point out the game, were now rather a hindrance than a help to us, for it was hard to know how to pass them. The huntsman felt the difficulty as much as I, for he rode behind them and could make no progress towards the fox. He was a swift rider, but wanting in enterprise. For my part, I felt that it would be unworthy of the Hussars of Conflans if I could not overcome such a difficulty as this. Was Étienne Gerard to be stopped by a herd of fox-dogs ? It was absurd. I gave a shout and spurred my horse.

" Hold hard, sir ! Hold hard ! " cried the huntsman. He was uneasy for me, this good old man, but I re-assured him by a wave and smile. The dogs opened in front of me. One or two may have been hurt, but what would you have ? The egg must be broken for the omelette. I could hear the huntsman shouting his con-gratulations behind me. One more effort, and the dogs were all behind me. Only the fox was in front.

Ah, the joy and pride of that moment ! To know that I had beaten the English at their own sport. Here were three hundred all thirsting for the life of this animal, and yet it was I who was about to take it. I thought of my comrades of the light cavalry brigade, of my mother, of the Emperor, of France. I had brought honour to each and all. Every instant brought me nearer to the fox. The moment for action had arrived, so I unsheathed my sabre.

I waved it in the air, and the brave English all shouted behind me.

Only then did I understand how difficult is this fox-chase, for one may cut again and again at the creature and never strike him once. He is small, and turns quickly from a blow. At every cut I heard those shouts of encouragement behind me, and they spurred me to yet another effort. And then at last the supreme moment of my triumph arrived. In the very act of turning I caught him fair with such another back-handed cut as that with which I killed the aide-de-camp of the Emperor of Russia. He flew into two pieces, his head one way and his tail another. I looked back and waved the blood-stained sabre in the air. For the moment I was exalted —superb!

Ah! how I should have loved to have waited to have received the congratulations of these generous enemies. There were fifty of them in sight, and not one of them who was not waving his hand and shouting. They are not really such a phlegmatic race, the English. A gallant deed in war or in sport will always warm their hearts. As to the old huntsman, he was the nearest to me, and I could see with my own eyes how overcome he was by what he had seen. He was like a man paralysed—his mouth open, his hand, with outspread fingers, raised in the air. For a moment my inclination was to return and embrace him. But already the call of duty was sounding in my ears, and these English, in spite of all the fraternity which exists among sportsmen, would certainly have made me prisoner. There was no hope for my mission now, and I had done all that I could do. I could see the lines of Massena's camp no very great distance off, for, by a lucky chance, the chase had taken us in that direction. I turned from the dead fox, saluted with my sabre, and galloped away.

But they would not leave me so easily, these gallant huntsmen. I was the fox now, and the chase swept bravely over the plain. It was only at the moment when

I started for the camp that they could have known that I was a Frenchman, and now the whole swarm of them were at my heels. We were within gunshot of our pickets before they would halt, and then they stood in knots and would not go away, but shouted and waved their hands at me. No, I will not think that it was in enmity. Rather would I fancy that a glow of admiration filled their breasts, and that their one desire was to embrace the stranger who had carried himself so gallantly and well.

4. *How the Brigadier saved an Army*

I HAVE told you, my friends, how we held the English shut up for six months, from October, 1810, to March, 1811, within their lines of Torres Vedras. It was during this time that I hunted the fox in their company, and showed them that amidst all their sportsmen there was not one who could outride a Hussar of Conflans. When I galloped back into the French lines with the blood of the creature still moist upon my blade, the outposts who had seen what I had done raised a frenzied cry in my honour, whilst these English hunters still yelled behind me, so that I had the applause of both armies. It made the tears rise to my eyes to feel that I had won the admiration of so many brave men. These English are generous foes. That very evening there came a packet under a white flag addressed " To the hussar officer who cut down the fox." Within I found the fox itself in two pieces, as I had left it. There was a note also, short but hearty as the English fashion is, to say that as I had slaughtered the fox it only remained for me to eat it. They could not know that it was not our French custom to eat foxes, and it showed their desire that he who had won the honours of the chase should also partake of the game. It is not for a Frenchman to be outdone in politeness, and so I returned it to these brave hunters, and begged them to accept it as a side-dish for their next *déjeuner de la chasse*. It is thus that chivalrous opponents make war.

I had brought back with me from my ride a clear plan of the English lines, and this I laid before Massena that very evening.

I had hoped that it would lead him to attack, but all the marshals were at each other's throats, snapping and growling like so many hungry hounds. Ney hated Massena, and Massena hated Junot, and Soult hated them all. For this reason nothing was done. In the meantime food grew more and more scarce, and our beautiful cavalry was ruined for want of fodder. With the end of the winter we had swept the whole country bare, and nothing remained for us to eat, although we sent our forage parties far and wide. It was clear even to the bravest of us that the time had come to retreat. I was myself forced to admit it.

But retreat was not so easy. Not only were the troops weak and exhausted from want of supplies, but the enemy had been much encouraged by our long inaction. Of Wellington we had no great fear. We had found him to be brave and cautious, but with little enterprise. Besides, in that barren country his pursuit could not be rapid. But on our flanks and in our rear there had gathered great numbers of Portuguese militia, of armed peasants, and of guerillas. These people had kept a safe distance all the winter, but now that our horses were foundered they were as thick as flies all round our outposts, and no man's life was worth a sou when once he fell into their hands. I could name a dozen officers of my own acquaintance who were cut off during that time, and the luckiest was he who received a ball from behind a rock through his head or his heart. There were some whose deaths were so terrible that no report of them was ever allowed to reach their relatives. So frequent were these tragedies, and so much did they impress the imagination of the men, that it became very difficult to induce them to leave the camp. There was one especial scoundrel, a guerilla chief named Manuelo, "The Smiler," whose exploits filled our men with horror. He was a large, fat man of jovial aspect, and he lurked with a fierce gang among the mountains which lay upon our left flank. A volume might be written of this fellow's cruelties and brutalities, but he was certainly a man of power, for he organised his brigands in a manner which made it almost impossible for us to get through his country. This he did by imposing a severe discipline upon them and enforcing it by cruel penalties, a policy by which he made them formidable, but which had some unexpected results, as I will show you in my story. Had he not flogged his own lieutenant—— But you will hear of that when the time comes.

There were many difficulties in connection with a retreat, but it was very evident that there was no other possible course, and so Massena began to quickly pass his baggage and his sick from Torres Novas, which was his headquarters, to Coimbra, the first strong post on his line of communications. He could not do this unperceived, however, and at once the guerillas came swarming closer and closer upon our flanks. One of our divisions, that of Clausel, with a brigade of Montbrun's cavalry, was far to the south of the Tagus, and it became very necessary to let them know that we were about to retreat, for otherwise they would be left unsupported in the very heart of the enemy's country. I remember wondering how Massena would accomplish this, for simple couriers could not get through, and small parties would be certainly destroyed. In some way an order to fall back must be conveyed to these men, or France would be the weaker by fourteen thousand men. Little did I think that it was I, Colonel Gerard, who was to have the honour of a deed which might have formed the crowning glory of any other man's life, and which stands high among those exploits which have made my own so famous.

At that time I was serving on Massena's staff, and he

had two other aides-de-camp, who were also very brave and intelligent officers. The name of one was Cortex and of the other Duplessis. They were senior to me in age, but junior in every other respect. Cortex was a small, dark man, very quick and eager. He was a fine soldier, but he was ruined by his conceit. To take him at his own valuation, he was the first man in the army. Duplessis was a Gascon, like myself, and he was a very fine fellow, as all Gascon gentlemen are. We took it in turn, day about, to do duty, and it was Cortex who was in attendance upon the morning of which I speak. I saw him at breakfast, but afterwards neither he nor his horse was to be seen. All day Massena was in his usual gloom, and he spent much of his time staring with his telescope at the English lines and at the shipping in the Tagus. He said nothing of the mission upon which he had sent our comrade, and it was not for us to ask him any questions.

That night, about twelve o'clock, I was standing outside the Marshal's headquarters when he came out and stood motionless for half an hour, his arms folded upon his breast, staring through the darkness towards the east. So rigid and intent was he that you might have believed the muffled figure and the cocked hat to have been the statue of the man. What he was looking for I could not imagine ; but at last he gave a bitter curse, and, turning on his heel, he went back into the house, banging the door behind him.

Next day the second aide-de-camp, Duplessis, had an interview with Massena in the morning, after which neither he nor his horse was seen again. That night, as I sat in the ante-room, the Marshal passed me, and I observed him through the window standing and staring to the east exactly as he had done before. For fully half an hour he remained there, a black shadow in the gloom. Then he strode in, the door banged, and I heard his spurs and his scabbard jingling and clanking through the passage. At the best he was a savage old man, but when he was crossed I had almost as soon face the Emperor himself. I heard him that night cursing and stamping above my head, but he did not send for me, and I knew him too well to go unsought.

Next morning it was my turn, for I was the only aide-de-camp left. I was his favourite aide-de-camp. His heart went out always to a smart soldier. I declare that I think there were tears in his black eyes when he sent for me that morning.

" Gerard ! " said he. " Come here ! "

With a friendly gesture he took me by the sleeve and he led me to the open window which faced the east. Beneath us was the infantry camp, and beyond that the lines of the cavalry with the long rows of picketed horses. We could see the French outposts, and then a stretch of open country, intersected by vineyards. A range of hills lay beyond, with one well-marked peak towering above them. Round the base of these hills was a broad belt of forest. A single road ran white and clear, dipping and rising until it passed through a gap in the hills.

" This," said Massena, pointing to the mountain, " is the Sierra de Merodal. Do you perceive anything upon the top ? "

I answered that I did not.

" Now ? " he asked, and he handed me his field-glass.

With its aid I perceived a small mound or cairn upon the crest.

" What you see," said the Marshal, " is a pile of logs which was placed there as a beacon. We laid it when the country was in our hands, and now, although we no longer hold it, the beacon remains undisturbed. Gerard, that beacon must be lit to-night. France needs it, the Emperor needs it, the army needs it. Two of your comrades have gone to light it, but neither has made his way to the summit. To-day it is your turn, and I pray that you may have better luck."

It is not for a soldier to ask the reason for his orders,

and so I was about to hurry from the room, but the Marshal laid his hand upon my shoulder and held me.

" You shall know all, and so learn how high is the cause for which you risk your life," said he. " Fifty miles to the south of us, on the other side of the Tagus, is the army of General Clausel. His camp is situated near a peak named the Sierra d'Ossa. On the summit of this peak is a beacon, and by this beacon he has a picket. It is agreed between us that when at midnight he shall see our signal fire he shall light his own as an answer, and shall then at once fall back upon the main army. If he does not start at once I must go without him. For two days I have endeavoured to send him his message. It must reach him to-day, or his army will be left behind and destroyed."

Ah, my friends, how my heart swelled when I heard how high was the task which Fortune had assigned to me ! If my life were spared, here was one more splendid new leaf for my laurel crown. If, on the other hand, I died, then it would be a death worthy of such a career. I said nothing, but I cannot doubt that all the noble thoughts that were in me shone in my face, for Massena took my hand and wrung it.

" There is the hill and there the beacon," said he. " There is only this guerilla and his men between you and it. I cannot detach a large party for the enterprise, and a small one would be seen and destroyed. Therefore to you alone I commit it. Carry it out in your own way, but at twelve o'clock this night let me see the fire upon the hill."

" If it is not there," said I, " then I pray you, Marshal Massena, to see that my effects are sold and the money sent to my mother." So I raised my hand to my busby and turned upon my heel, my heart glowing at the thought of the great exploit which lay before me.

I sat in my own chamber for some little time consider-ing how I had best take the matter in hand. The fact that neither Cortex nor Duplessis, who were very zealous and active officers, had succeeded in reaching the summit of the Sierra de Merodal showed that the country was very closely watched by the guerillas. I reckoned out the distance upon a map. There were ten miles of open country to be crossed before reaching the hills. Then came a belt of forest on the lower slopes of the mountain, which may have been three or four miles wide. And then there was the actual peak itself, of no very great height, but without any cover to conceal me. Those were the three stages of my journey.

It seemed to me that once I had reached the shelter of the wood all would be easy, for I could lie concealed within its shadows and climb upwards under the cover of night. From eight till twelve would give me four hours of darkness in which to make the ascent. It was only the first stage, then, which I had seriously to consider.

Over that flat country there lay the inviting white road, and I remembered that my comrades had both taken their horses. That was clearly their ruin, for nothing could be easier than for the brigands to keep watch upon the road, and to lay an ambush for all who passed along it. It would not be difficult for me to ride across country, and I was well horsed at that time, for I had not only Violette and Rataplan, who were two of the finest mounts in the army, but I had the splendid black English hunter which I had taken from Sir Cotton. However, after much thought, I determined to go upon foot, since I should then be in a better state to take advantage of any chance which might offer. As to my dress, I covered my hussar uniform with a long cloak, and I put a grey forage cap upon my head. You may ask me why I did not dress as a peasant, but I answer that a man of honour has no desire to die the death of a spy. It is one thing to be murdered, and it is another to be justly executed by the laws of war. I would not run the risk of such an end.

In the late afternoon I stole out of the camp and passed through the line of our pickets. Beneath my cloak I had a field-glass and a pocket pistol, as well as my sword. In my pocket were tinder, flint and steel.

For two or three miles I kept under cover of the vineyards, and made such good progress that my heart was high within me, and I thought to myself that it only needed a man of some brains to take the matter in hand to bring it easily to success. Of course, Cortex and Duplessis galloping down the high road would be easily seen, but the intelligent Gerard lurking among the vines was quite another person. I dare say I had got as far as five miles before I met any check. At that point there is a small winehouse, round which I perceived some carts and a number of people, the first that I had seen. Now that I was well outside the lines I knew that every person was my enemy, so I crouched lower while I stole along to a point from which I could get a better view of what was going on. I then perceived that these people were peasants, who were loading two waggons with empty wine-casks. I failed to see how they could either help or hinder me, so I continued upon my way.

But soon I understood that my task was not so simple as had appeared. As the ground rose the vineyards ceased, and I came upon a stretch of open country studded with low hills. Crouching in a ditch I examined them with a glass, and I very soon perceived that there was a watcher upon every one of them, and that these people had a line of pickets and outposts thrown forward exactly like our own. I had heard of the discipline which was practised by this scoundrel whom they called " The Smiler," and this, no doubt, was an example of it. Between the hills there was a cordon of sentries, and, though I worked some distance round to the flank, I still found myself faced by the enemy. It was a puzzle what to do. There was so little cover that a rat could hardly cross without being seen. Of course, it would be easy enough to slip through at night, as I had done with the English at Torres Vedras ; but I was still far from the mountain, and I could not in that case reach it in time to light the midnight beacon. I lay in my ditch and I made a thousand plans, each more dangerous than the last. And then suddenly I had that flash of light which comes to the brave man who refuses to despair.

You remember I have mentioned that two waggons were loading up with empty casks at the inn. The heads of the oxen were turned to the east, and it was evident that those waggons were going in the direction which I desired. Could I only conceal myself upon one of them, what better and easier way could I find of passing through the lines of the guerillas ? So simple and so good was the plan that I could not restrain a cry of delight as it crossed my mind, and I hurried away instantly in the direction of the inn. There, from behind some bushes, I had a good look at what was going on upon the road.

There were three peasants with red montero caps loading the barrels, and they had completed one waggon and the lower tier of the other. A number of empty barrels still lay outside the winehouse waiting to be put on. Fortune was my friend—I have always said that she is a woman and cannot resist a dashing young hussar. As I watched, the three fellows went into the inn, for the day was hot, and they were thirsty after their labour. Quick as a flash I darted out from my hiding-place, climbed on to the waggon, and crept into one of the empty casks. It had a bottom but no top, and it lay upon its side with the open end inwards. There I crouched like a dog in its kennel, my knees drawn up to my chin ; for the barrels were not very large and I am a well-grown man. As I lay there out came the three peasants again, and presently I heard a crash upon the top of me, which told that I had another barrel above me. They piled them upon the cart until I could not imagine how I was ever to get out again. However, it is time to think of crossing the Vistula when you are over the Rhine, and I had no doubt that if chance and my own wits had carried me so far they would carry me farther.

Soon, when the waggon was full, they set forth upon

their way, and I within my barrel chuckled at every step, for it was carrying me whither I wished to go. We travelled slowly, and the peasants walked beside the waggons. This I knew, because I heard their voices close to me. They seemed to me to be very merry fellows, for they laughed heartily as they went. What the joke was I could not understand. Though I speak their language fairly well I could not hear anything comic in the scraps of their conversation which met my ear.

I reckoned that at the rate of walking of a team of oxen we covered about two miles an hour. Therefore, when I was sure that two and a half hours had passed—such hours, my friends, cramped, suffocated and nearly poisoned with the fumes of the lees—when they had passed, I was sure that the dangerous open country was behind us, and that we were upon the edge of the forest and the mountain. So now I had to turn my mind upon how I was to get out of my barrel. I had thought of several ways, and was balancing one against the other, when the question was decided for me in a very simple but unexpected manner.

The waggon stopped suddenly with a jerk, and I heard a number of gruff voices in excited talk. " Where, where ? " cried one. " On our cart," said another. " Who is he ? " said a third. " A French officer ; I saw his cap and his boots." They all roared with laughter. " I was looking out of the window of the *posada* and I saw him spring into the cask like a toreador with a Seville bull at his heels." " Which cask, then ? " " It was this one," said the fellow, and, sure enough, his fist struck the wood beside my head.

What a situation, my friends, for a man of my standing ! I blush now, after forty years, when I think of it. To be trussed like a fowl and to listen helplessly to the rude laughter of these boors—to know, too, that my mission had come to an ignominious and even ridiculous end. I would have blessed the man who would have sent a bullet through the cask and freed me from my misery.

I heard the crashing of the barrels as they hurled them off the waggon, and then a couple of bearded faces and the muzzles of two guns looked in at me. They seized me by the sleeves of my coat, and they dragged me out into the daylight. A strange figure I must have looked as I stood blinking and gaping in the blinding sunlight. My body was bent like a cripple's, for I could not straighten my stiff joints, and half my coat was as red as an English soldier's from the lees in which I had lain. They laughed and laughed, these dogs, and as I tried to express by my bearing and gestures the contempt in which I held them, their laughter grew all the louder. But even in these hard circumstances I bore myself like the man I am, and as I cast my eye slowly round I did not find that any of the laughers were very ready to face it.

That one glance round was enough to tell me exactly how I was situated. I had been betrayed by these peasants into the hands of an outpost of guerillas. There were eight of them, savage-looking, hairy creatures, with cotton handkerchiefs under their sombreros, and many-buttoned jackets with coloured sashes round the waist. Each had a gun and one or two pistols stuck in his girdle. The leader, a great bearded ruffian, held his gun against my ear while the others searched my pockets, taking from me my overcoat, my pistol, my glass, my sword, and, worst of all, my flint and steel and tinder. Come what might I was ruined, for I had no longer the means of lighting the beacon even if I should reach it.

Eight of them, my friends, with three peasants, and I unarmed ! Was Étienne Gerard in despair ? Did he lose his wits ? Ah, you know me too well ; but they did not know me yet, these dogs of brigands. Never have I made so supreme and astounding an effort as at this very instant when all seemed lost. Yet you might guess many times before you would hit upon the device by which I escaped them. Listen and I will tell you.

They had dragged me from the waggon when they searched me, and I stood, still twisted and warped, in the midst of them. But the stiffness was wearing off, and already my mind was very actively looking out for some method of breaking away. It was a narrow pass in which the brigands had their outposts. It was bounded on the one hand by a steep mountain side. On the other the ground fell away in a very long slope, which ended in a bushy valley many hundreds of feet below. These fellows, you understand, were hardy mountaineers, who could travel either up hill or down very much quicker than I. They wore abarcas, or shoes of skin, tied on like sandals, which gave them a foothold everywhere. A less resolute man would have despaired. But in an instant I saw and used the strange chance which Fortune had placed in my way. On the very edge of the slope was one of the wine-barrels. I moved slowly towards it, and then with a tiger spring I dived into it feet foremost, and with a roll of my body I tipped it over the side of the hill.

Shall I ever forget that dreadful journey—how I bounded and crashed and whizzed down that terrible slope? I had dug in my knees and elbows, bunching my body into a compact bundle so as to steady it; but my head projected from the end, and it was a marvel that I did not dash out my brains. There were long, smooth slopes and then came steeper scarps where the barrel ceased to roll, and sprang into the air like a goat, coming down with a rattle and crash which jarred every bone in my body. How the wind whistled in my ears, and my head turned and turned until I was sick and giddy and nearly senseless! Then, with a swish and a great rasping and crackling of branches, I reached the bushes which I had seen so far below me. Through them I broke my way, down a slope beyond, and deep into another patch of underwood, where striking a sapling my barrel flew to pieces. From amid a heap of staves and hoops I crawled out, my body aching in every inch of it, but my heart singing loudly with joy and my spirit high within me, for I knew how great was the feat which I had accomplished, and I already seemed to see the beacon blazing on the hill.

A horrible nausea had seized me from the tossing which I had undergone, and I felt as I did upon the ocean when first I experienced those movements of which the English have taken so perfidious an advantage. I had to sit for a few moments with my head upon my hands beside the ruins of my barrel. But there was no time for rest. Already I heard shouts above me which told that my pursuers were descending the hill. I dashed into the thickest part of the underwood, and I ran and ran until I was utterly exhausted. Then I lay panting and listened with all my ears, but no sound came to them. I had shaken off my enemies.

When I had recovered my breath I travelled swiftly on, and waded knee-deep through several brooks, for it came into my head that they might follow me with dogs. On gaining a clear place and looking round me, I found to my delight that in spite of my adventures I had not been much out of my way. Above me towered the peak of Merodal, with its bare and bold summit shooting out of the groves of dwarf oaks which shrouded its flanks. These groves were the continuation of the cover under which I found myself, and it seemed to me that I had nothing to fear now until I reached the other side of the forest. At the same time I knew that every man's hand was against me, that I was unarmed, and that there were many people about me. I saw no one, but several times I heard shrill whistles, and once the sound of a gun in the distance.

It was hard work pushing one's way through the bushes, and so I was glad when I came to the larger trees and found a path which led between them. Of course, I was too wise to walk upon it, but I kept near it and followed its course. I had gone some distance, and had, as I imagined, nearly reached the limit of the wood, when a strange, moaning sound fell upon my ears. At first I thought it was the cry of some animal, but then there came words, of which I only caught the French exclamation, " Mon Dieu ! " With great caution I advanced in the direction from which the sound proceeded, and this is what I saw.

On a couch of dried leaves there was stretched a man dressed in the same grey uniform which I wore myself. He was evidently horribly wounded, for he held a cloth to his breast which was crimson with his blood. A pool had formed all round his couch, and he lay in a haze of flies, whose buzzing and droning would certainly have called my attention if his groans had not come to my ear. I lay for a moment, fearing some trap, and then, my pity and loyalty rising above all other feelings, I ran forward and knelt by his side. He turned a haggard face upon me, and it was Duplessis, the man who had gone before me. It needed but one glance at his sunken cheeks and glazing eyes to tell me that he was dying.

" Gerard ! " said he ; " Gerard ! "

I could but look my sympathy, but he, though the life was ebbing swiftly out of him, still kept his duty before him, like the gallant gentleman he was.

" The beacon, Gerard ! You will light it ? "

" Have you flint and steel ? "

" It is here."

" Then I will light it to-night."

" I die happy to hear you say so. They shot me, Gerard. But you will tell the Marshal that I did my best."

" And Cortex ? "

" He was less fortunate. He fell into their hands and died horribly. If you see that you cannot get away, Gerard, put a bullet into your own heart. Don't die as Cortex did."

I could see that his breath was failing, and I bent low to catch his words.

" Can you tell me anything which can help me in my task ? " I asked.

" Yes, yes ; De Pombal He will help you. Trust

De Pombal." With the words his head fell back and he was dead.

"Trust De Pombal. It is good advice." To my amazement a man was standing at the very side of me. So absorbed had I been in my comrade's words and intent on his advice that he had crept up without my observing him. Now I sprang to my feet, and faced him. He was a tall, dark fellow, black-haired, black-eyed, black-bearded, with a long, sad face. In his hand he had a wine bottle and over his shoulder was slung one of the trebucos, or blunderbusses, which these fellows bear. He made no effort to unsling it, and I understood that this was the man to whom my dead friend had commended me.

"Alas, he is gone!" said he, bending over Duplessis. "He fled into the wood after he was shot, but I was fortunate enough to find where he had fallen and to make his last hours more easy. This couch was my making and I had brought this wine to slake his thirst."

"Sir," said I, "in the name of France I thank you. I am but a colonel of light cavalry, but I am Étienne Gerard, and the name stands for something in the French army. May I ask——"

"Yes, sir, I am Aloysius de Pombal, younger brother of the famous nobleman of that name. At present I am the first lieutenant in the band of the guerilla chief who is usually known as Manuelo, 'The Smiler.'"

My word, I clapped my hand to the place where my pistol should have been, but the man only smiled at the gesture.

"I am his first lieutenant, but I am also his deadly enemy," said he. He slipped off his jacket and pulled up his shirt as he spoke. "Look at this!" he cried, and he turned upon me a back which was all scored and lacerated with red and purple weals. "This is what 'The Smiler' has done to me, a man with the noblest blood of Portugal in my veins. What I will do to 'The Smiler' you have still to see."

There was such fury in his eyes and in the grin of his white teeth that I could no longer doubt his truth, with that clotted and oozing back to corroborate his words.

" I have ten men sworn to stand by me," said he. " In a few days I hope to join your army, when I have done my work here. In the meanwhile——" A strange change came over his face, and he suddenly slung his musket to the front : " Hold up your hands, you French hound ! " he yelled. " Up with them, or I blow your head off ! "

You start, my friends ! You stare ! Think, then, how I stared and started at this sudden ending of our talk. There was the black muzzle, and there the dark, angry eyes behind it. What could I do ? I was helpless. I raised my hands in the air. At the same moment voices sounded from all parts of the wood, there were crying and calling and rushing of many feet. A swarm of dreadful figures broke through the green bushes, a dozen hands seized me, and I, poor, luckless, frenzied I, was a prisoner once more. Thank God, there was no pistol which I could have plucked from my belt and snapped at my own head. Had I been armed at that moment I should not be sitting here in this café and telling you these old-world tales.

With grimy, hairy hands clutching me on every side I was led along the pathway through the wood, the villain De Pombal giving directions to my captors. Four of the brigands carried up the dead body of Duplessis. The shadows of evening were already falling when we cleared the forest and came out upon the mountain-side. Up this I was driven until we reached the headquarters of the guerillas, which lay in a cleft close to the summit of the mountain. There was the beacon which had cost me so much, a square stack of wood, immediately above our heads. Below were two or three huts, which had belonged, no doubt, to goatherds, and which were now used to shelter these rascals. Into one of these I was cast, bound and helpless, and the dead body of my poor comrade was laid beside me.

I was lying there with the one thought still consuming me, how to wait a few hours and to get at that pile of faggots above my head, when the door of my prison opened and a man entered. Had my hands been free I should have flown at his throat, for it was none other than De Pombal. A couple of brigands were at his heels, but he ordered them back and closed the door behind him.

" You villain ! " said I.

" Hush ! " he cried. " Speak low, for I do not know who may be listening, and my life is at stake. I have some words to say to you, Colonel Gerard ; I wish well to you, as I did to your dead companion. As I spoke to you beside his body I saw that we were surrounded, and that your capture was unavoidable. I should have shared your fate had I hesitated. I instantly captured you myself, so as to preserve the confidence of the band. Your own sense will tell you that there was nothing else for me to do. I do not know now whether I can save you, but at least I will try."

This was a new light upon the situation. I told him that I could not tell how far he spoke the truth, but that I would judge him by his actions.

" I ask nothing better," said he. " A word of advice to you ! The chief will see you now. Speak him fair, or he will have you sawn between two planks. Contradict nothing he says. Give him such information he wants. It is your only chance. If you can gain time something may come in our favour. Now, I have no more time. Come at once, or suspicion may be awakened." He helped me to rise and then, opening the door, he dragged me out very roughly, and with the aid of the fellows outside he brutally pushed and thrust me to the place where the guerilla chief was seated, with his rude followers gathered round him.

A remarkable man was Manuelo, " The Smiler." He was fat and florid and comfortable, with a big, clean-shaven face and a bald head, the very model of a kindly father of a family. As I looked at his honest smile I could scarcely believe that this was, indeed, the infamous ruffian whose name was a horror through the English Army as well as our own. It is well known that Trent, who was a British officer, afterwards had the fellow hanged for his brutalities. He sat upon a boulder and he beamed upon me like one who meets an old acquaintance. I observed, however, that one of his men leaned upon a long saw, and the sight was enough to cure me of all delusions.

" Good evening, Colonel Gerard," said he. " We have been highly honoured by General Massena's staff : Major Cortex one day, Colonel Duplessis the next, and now Colonel Gerard. Possible the Marshal himself may be induced to honour us with a visit. You have seen Duplessis, I understand. Cortex you will find nailed to a tree down yonder. It only remains to be decided how we can best dispose of yourself."

It was not a cheering speech ; but all the time his fat face was wreathed in smiles, and he lisped out his words in the most mincing and amiable fashion. Now, however, he suddenly leaned forward, and I read a very real intensity in his eyes.

" Colonel Gerard," said he, " I cannot promise you your life, for it is not our custom, but I can give you an easy death or I can give you a terrible one. Which shall it be ? "

" What do you wish me to do in exchange ? "

" If you would die easy I ask you to give me truthful answers to the questions which I ask."

A sudden thought flashed through my mind.

" You wish to kill me," said I ; " it cannot matter to you how I die. If I answer your questions, will you let me choose the manner of my own death ? "

" Yes, I will," said he, " so long as it is before midnight to-night."

" Swear it ! " I cried.

" The word of a Portuguese gentleman is sufficient," said he.

" Not a word will I say until you have sworn it."

He flushed with anger and his eyes swept round towards the saw. But he understood from my tone that I meant what I said, and that I was not a man to be bullied into submission. He pulled a cross from under his zammara or jacket of black sheepskin.

" I swear it," said he.

Oh, my joy as I heard the words ! What an end—what an end for the first swordsman of France ! I could have laughed with delight at the thought.

" Now, your questions ! " said I.

" You swear in turn to answer them truly ? "

" I do, upon the honour of a gentleman and a soldier." It was, as you perceive, a terrible thing that I promised, but what was it compared to what I might gain by compliance ?

" This is a very fair and a very interesting bargain," said he, taking a note-book from his pocket. " Would you kindly turn your gaze towards the French camp ? "

Following the direction of his gesture, I turned and looked down upon the camp in the plain beneath us. In spite of the fifteen miles one could in that clear atmosphere see every detail with the utmost distinctness. There were the long squares of our tents and our huts, with the cavalry lines and the dark patches which marked the ten batteries of artillery. How sad to think of my magnificent regiment waiting down yonder, and to know that they would never see their colonel again! With one squadron of them I could have swept all these cut-throats off the face of the earth. My eager eyes filled with tears as I looked at the corner of the camp where I knew that there were eight hundred men, any one of whom would have died for his colonel. But my sadness vanished when I saw behind the tents the plumes of smoke which marked the headquarters at Torres Novas.

There was Massena, and, please God, at the cost of my life his mission would that night be done. A spasm of pride and exultation filled my breast. I should have liked to have had a voice of thunder that I might call to them, " Behold, it is I, Étienne Gerard, who will die in order to save the army of Clausel ! " It was, indeed, sad to think that so noble a deed should be done, and that no one should be there to tell the tale.

" Now," said the brigand chief, " you see the camp and you see also the road which leads to Coimbra. It is crowded with your fourgons and your ambulances. Does this mean that Massena is about to retreat ? "

One could see the dark moving lines of waggons with an occasional flash of steel from the escort. There could, apart from my promise, be no indiscretion in admitting that which was already obvious.

" He will retreat," said I.

" By Coimbra ? "

" I believe so."

" But the army of Clausel ? "

I shrugged my shoulders.

" Every path to the south is blocked. No message can reach them. If Massena falls back the army of Clausel is doomed."

" It must take its chance," said I.

" How many men has he ? "

" I should say about fourteen thousand."

" How much cavalry ? "

" One brigade of Montbrun's Division."

" What regiments ? "

" The 4th Chasseurs, the 9th Hussars and a regiment of Cuirassiers."

" Quite right," said he, looking at his note-book. " I can tell you speak the truth, and Heaven help you if you don't." Then, division by division, he went over the whole army, asking the composition of each brigade. Need I tell you that I would have had my tongue torn out before I would have told him such things had I not a greater end in view ? I would let him know all if I could but save the army of Clausel.

At last he closed his note-book and replaced it in his pocket. " I am obliged to you for this information, which shall reach Lord Wellington to-morrow," said he. " You have done your share of the bargain ; it is for me now to perform mine. How would you wish to die ? As a soldier you would, no doubt, prefer to be shot, but some think that a jump over the Merodal precipice is really an easier death. A good few have taken it, but we were, unfortunately, never able to get an opinion from them afterwards. There is the saw, too, which does not appear to be popular. We could hang you, no doubt, but it would involve the inconvenience of going down to the wood. However, a promise is a promise, and you seem to be an excellent fellow, so we will spare no pains to meet your wishes."

" You said," I answered, " that I must die before midnight. I will choose, therefore, just one minute before that hour."

" Very good," said he. " Such clinging to life is rather childish, but your wishes shall be met."

" As to the method," I added, " I love a death which all the world can see. Put me on yonder pile of faggots and burn me alive, as saints and martyrs have been burned before me. That is no common end, but one which an Emperor might envy."

The idea seemed to amuse him very much.

" Why not ? " said he. " If Massena has sent you to spy upon us, he may guess what the fire upon the mountain means."

" Exactly," said I. " You have hit upon my very reason. He will guess, and all will know, that I have died a soldier's death."

" I see no objection whatever," said the brigand, with his abominable smile. " I will send some goat's flesh and wine into your hut. The sun is sinking, and it is nearly eight o'clock. In four hours be ready for your end."

It was a beautiful world to be leaving. I looked at the golden haze below, where the last rays of the sinking sun shone upon the blue waters of the winding Tagus and gleamed upon the white sails of the English transports. Very beautiful it was, and very sad to leave ; but there are things more beautiful than that. The death that is died for the sake of others, honour, and duty, and loyalty, and love—these are the beauties far brighter than any which the eye can see. My breast was filled with admiration for my own most noble conduct, and with wonder whether any soul would ever come to know how I had placed myself in the heart of the beacon which saved the army of Clausel. I hoped so and I prayed so, for what a consolation it would be to my mother, what an example to the army, what a pride to my hussars ! When De Pombal came at last into my hut with the food and the wine, the first request I made him was that he would write an account of my death and send it to the French camp. He answered not a word, but I ate my supper with a better appetite from the thought that my glorious fate would not be altogether unknown.

I had been there about two hours when the door opened again, and the chief stood looking in. I was in darkness, but a brigand with a torch stood beside him, and I saw his eyes and his teeth gleaming as he peered at me.

" Ready ? " he asked.

" It is not yet time."

" You stand out for the last minute ? "

" A promise is a promise."

" Very good. Be it so. We have a little justice to do among ourselves, for one of my fellows has been mis-behaving. We have a strict rule of our own which is no respecter of persons, as De Pombal here could tell you. Do you truss him and lay him on the faggots, De Pombal, and I will return to see him die."

De Pombal and the man with the torch entered, while

I heard the steps of the chief passing away. De Pombal closed the door.

" Colonel Gerard," said he, " you must trust this man, for he is one of my party. It is neck or nothing. We may save you yet. But I take a great risk, and I want a definite promise. If we save you, will you guarantee that we have a friendly reception in the French camp and that all the past will be forgotten ? "

" I do guarantee it."

" And I trust your honour. Now, quick, quick, there is not an instant to lose ! If this monster returns we shall die horribly, all three."

I stared in amazement at what he did. Catching up a long rope he wound it round the body of my dead comrade, and he tied a cloth round his mouth so as to almost cover his face.

" Do you lie there ! " he cried, and he laid me in the place of the dead body. " I have four of my men waiting, and they will place this upon the beacon." He opened the door and gave an order. Several of the brigands entered and bore out Duplessis. For myself I remained upon the floor, with my mind in a turmoil of hope and wonder.

Five minutes later De Pombal and his men were back.

" You are laid upon the beacon," said he ; " I defy anyone in the world to say it is not you, and you are so gagged and bound that no one can expect you to speak or move. Now, it only remains to carry forth the body of Duplessis and to toss it over the Merodal precipice."

Two of them seized me by the head and two by the heels and carried me, stiff and inert, from the hut. As I came into the open air I could have cried out in my amazement. The moon had risen above the beacon, and there, clear outlined against its silver light, was the figure of the man stretched upon the top. The brigands were either in their camp or standing round the beacon, for none of them stopped or questioned our little party. De Pombal led them in the direction of the precipice.

At the brow we were out of sight, and there I was allowed to use my feet once more. De Pombal pointed to a narrow, winding track.

" This is the way down," said he, and then, suddenly, " Dios mio, what is that ? "

A terrible cry had risen out of the woods beneath us. I saw that De Pombal was shivering like a frightened horse.

" It is that devil," he whispered. " He is treating another as he treated me. But on, on, for Heaven help us if he lays his hands upon us ! "

One by one we crawled down the narrow goat track. At the bottom of the cliff we were back in the woods once more. Suddenly a yellow glare shone above us, and the black shadows of the tree-trunks started out in front. They had fired the beacon behind us. Even from where we stood we could see that impassive body amid the flames, and the black figures of the guerillas as they danced, howling like cannibals, round the pile. Ha ! how I shook my fist at them, the dogs, and how I vowed that one day my hussars and I would make the reckoning level !

De Pombal knew how the outposts were placed and all the paths which led through the forest. But to avoid these villains we had to plunge among the hills and walk for many a weary mile. And yet how gladly would I have walked those extra leagues if only for one sight which they brought to my eyes ! It may have been two o'clock in the morning when we halted upon the bare shoulder of a hill over which our path curled. Looking back we saw the red glow of the embers of the beacon as if volcanic fires were bursting from the tall peak of Merodal. And then, as I gazed, I saw something else—something which caused me to shriek with joy and to fall upon the ground, rolling in my delight. For, far away upon the southern horizon, there winked and twinkled one great yellow light, throbbing and flaming, the light of no house, the light of no star, but the answering beacon of

Mount d'Ossa, which told that the army of Clausel knew what Étienne Gerard had been sent to tell them.

5. *How the Brigadier triumphed in England*

I HAVE told you, my friends, how I triumphed over the English at the fox-hunt when I pursued the animal so fiercely that even the herd of trained dogs was unable to keep up, and alone with my own hand I put him to the sword. Perhaps I have said too much of the matter, but there is a thrill in the triumphs of sport which even warfare cannot give, for in warfare you share your successes with your regiment and your army, but in sport it is you yourself unaided who have won the laurels. It is an advantage which the English have over us that in all classes they take great interest in every form of sport. It may be that they are richer than we, or it may be that they are more idle ; but I was surprised when I was a prisoner in that country to observe how widespread was this feeling, and how much it filled the minds and the lives of the people. A horse that will run, a cock that will fight, a dog that will kill rats, a man that will box—they would turn away from the Emperor in all his glory in order to look upon any of these.

I could tell you many stories of English sport, for I saw much of it during the time that I was the guest of Lord Rufton, after the order for my exchange had come to England. There were months before I could be sent back to France, and during that time I stayed with this good Lord Rufton at his beautiful house at High Combe, which is at the northern end of Dartmoor. He had ridden with the police when they had pursued me from Princetown, and he had felt towards me when I was over-taken as I would myself have felt had I, in my own country, seen a brave and debonair soldier without a friend to help him. In a word, he took me to his house, clad me, fed me and treated me as if he had been my brother. I will say this of the English, that they were always generous enemies, and very good people with whom to fight. In the Peninsula the Spanish outposts would present their muskets at ours, but the British their brandy flasks. And of all these generous men there was none who was the equal of this admirable milord, who held out so warm a hand to an enemy in distress.

Ah! what thoughts of sport it brings back to me, the very name of High Combe! I can see it now, the long, low, brick house, warm and ruddy, with white plaster pillars before the door. He was a great sportsman this Lord Rufton, and all who were about him were of the same sort. But you will be pleased to hear that there were few things in which I could not hold my own, and in some I excelled. Behind the house was a wood in which pheasants were reared, and it was Lord Rufton's joy to kill these birds, which was done by sending in men to drive them out while he and his friends stood outside and shot them as they passed. For my part I was more crafty, for I studied the habits of the birds, and stealing out in the evening I was able to kill a number of them as they roosted in the trees. Hardly a single shot was wasted, but the keeper was attracted by the sound of the firing, and he implored me in his rough English fashion to spare those that were left. That night I was able to place twelve birds as a surprise upon Lord Rufton's supper table, and he laughed until he cried, so overjoyed was he to see them. " Gad, Gerard, you'll be the death of me yet! " he cried. Often he said the same thing, for at every turn I amazed him by the way in which I entered into the sports of the English.

There is a game called cricket which they play in the summer, and this also I learned. Rudd, the head gardener, was a famous player of cricket, and so was Lord Rufton himself. Before the house was a lawn, and here it was that Rudd taught me the game. It is a brave pastime, a game for soldiers, for each tries to strike the other with the ball, and it is but a small stick with which you may ward it off. Three sticks behind show the spot beyond which you may not retreat. I can tell you that it is no game for children, and I will confess that, in spite of my nine campaigns, I felt myself turn pale when first the ball flashed past me. So swift was it that I had not time to raise my stick to ward it off, but by good fortune it missed me and knocked down the wooden pins which marked the boundary. It was for Rudd then to defend himself and for me to attack. When I was a boy in Gascony I learned to throw both far and straight, so that I made sure that I could hit this gallant Englishman. With a shout I rushed forward and hurled the ball at him. It flew as swift as a bullet towards his ribs, but without a word he swung his staff and the ball rose a surprising distance in the air. Lord Rufton clapped his hands and cheered. Again the ball was brought to me, and again it was for me to throw. This time it flew past his head, and it seemed to me that it was his turn to look pale. But he was a brave man, this gardener, and again he faced me. Ah, my friends, the hour of my triumph had come ! It was a red waistcoat that he wore, and at this I hurled the ball. You would have said that I was a gunner, not a hussar, for never was so straight an aim. With a despairing cry—the cry of the brave man who is beaten—he fell upon the wooden pegs behind him, and they all rolled upon the ground together. He was cruel, this English milord, and he laughed so that he could not come to the aid of his servant. It was for me, the victor, to rush forwards to embrace this intrepid player, and to raise him to his feet with words of praise, and encouragement, and hope. He was in pain and could not stand erect, yet the honest fellow confessed that there was no accident in my victory. " He did it a-purpose ! He did it a-purpose ! " Again and again he said it. Yes, it is a great game this cricket, and I would gladly have ventured upon it again, but Lord Rufton and Rudd said that it was late in the season, and so they would play no more.

How foolish of me, the old broken man, to dwell upon these successes, and yet I will confess that my age has been very much soothed and comforted by the memory of the women who have loved me and the men whom I have overcome. It is pleasant to think that five years afterwards, when Lord Rufton came to Paris after the peace, he was able to assure me that my name was still a famous one in the north of Devonshire for the fine exploits that I had performed. Especially, he said, that they still talked over my boxing match with the Honourable Baldock. It came about in this way. Of an evening many sportsmen would assemble at the house of Lord Rufton, where they would drink much wine, make wild bets, and talk of their horses and their foxes. How well I remember those strange creatures. Sir Barrington, Jack Lupton of Barnstaple, Colonel Addison, Johnny Miller, Lord Sadler, and my enemy, the Honourable Baldock. They were of the same stamp all of them, drinkers, madcaps, fighters, gamblers, full of strange caprices and extraordinary whims. Yet they were kindly fellows in their rough fashion, save only this Baldock, a fat man who prided himself on his skill at the box-fight. It was he who, by his laughter against the French because they were ignorant of sport, caused me to challenge him in the very sport at which he excelled. You will say that it was foolish, my friends, but the decanter had passed many times, and the blood of youth ran hot in my veins. I would fight him, this boaster; I would show him that if we had not skill, at least we had courage. Lord Rufton would not allow it. I insisted. The others cheered me on and slapped me on the back. "No, dash it, Baldock, he's our guest," said Rufton. "It's his own doing," the other answered. "Look here, Rufton, they can't hurt each other if they wear the mawleys," cried Lord Sadler. And so it was agreed.

What the mawleys were I did not know; but presently they brought out four great puddings of leather, not unlike a fencing-glove, but larger. With these our hands were covered after we had stripped ourselves of our coats and our waistcoats. Then the table, with the glasses, and decanters, was pushed into the corner of the room, and behold us, face to face ! Lord Sadler in the armchair with a watch in his open hand. " Time ! " said he.

I will confess to you, my friends, that I felt at that moment a tremor such as none of my many duels have ever given me. With sword or pistol I am at home ; but here I only understood that I must struggle with this fat Englishman and do what I could, in spite of these great puddings upon my hands, to overcome him. And at the very outset I was disarmed of the best weapon that was left to me. " Mind, Gerard, no kicking ! " said Lord Rufton in my ear. I had only a pair of thin dancing slippers, and yet the man was fat, and a few well-directed kicks might have left me the victor. But there is an etiquette just as there is in fencing, and I refrained. I looked at this Englishman and I wondered how I should attack him. His ears were large and prominent. Could I seize them I might drag him to the ground. I rushed in, but I was betrayed by this flabby glove, and twice I lost my hold. He struck me, but I cared little for his blows, and again I seized him by the ear. He fell, and I rolled upon him and thumped his head upon the ground. How they cheered and laughed, these gallant Englishmen, and how they clapped me on the back !

" Even money on the Frenchman," cried Lord Sadler.

" He fights foul," cried the enemy, rubbing his crimson ears. " He savaged me on the ground."

" You must take your chance of that," said Lord Rufton coldly.

" Time," cried Lord Sadler, and once again we advanced to the assault.

He was flushed, and his small eyes were as vicious as those of a bulldog. There was hatred on his face. For my part I carried myself lightly and gaily. A French gentleman fights, but he does not hate. I drew myself up before him, and I bowed as I have done in the duello. There can be grace and courtesy as well as defiance in a bow ; I put all three into this one, with a touch of ridicule in the shrug which accompanied it. It was at this moment that he struck me. The room spun round with me. I fell upon my back. But in an instant I was on my feet again and had rushed to a close combat. His ear, his hair, his nose, I seized them each in turn. Once again the mad joy of the battle was in my veins. The old cry of triumph rose to my lips. " Vive l'Empereur ! " I yelled as I drove my head into his stomach. He threw his arm round my neck, and holding me with one hand he struck me with the other. I buried my teeth in his arm, and he shouted with pain. " Call him off, Rufton ! " he screamed. " Call him off, man ! He's worrying me ! " They dragged me away from him. Can I ever forget it ?—the laughter, the cheering, the congratulations ! Even my enemy bore me no ill will, for he shook me by the hand. For my part I embraced him on each cheek. Five years afterwards I learned from Lord Rufton that my noble bearing upon that evening was still fresh in the memory of my English friends.

It is not, however, of my own exploits in sport that I wish to speak to you to-night, but it is of the Lady Jane Dacre and the strange adventure of which she was the cause. Lady Jane Dacre was Lord Rufton's sister and the lady of his household. I fear that until I came it was lonely for her, since she was a beautiful and refined woman with nothing in common with those who were about her. Indeed, this might be said of many women in the England of those days, for the men were rude and rough and coarse, with boorish habits and few accomplishments, while the women were the most lovely and tender that I have ever known. We became great friends, the Lady Jane and I, for it was not possible for me to drink three bottles of port after dinner like those Devonshire gentlemen and so I would seek refuge in her drawing-room, where evening after evening she would play the harpsicord and I would sing the songs of my own land. In those peaceful moments I would find a refuge from the misery which filled me, when I reflected that my regiment was left in the front of the enemy without the chief whom they had learned to love and to follow. Indeed, I could have torn my hair when I read in the English papers of the fine fighting which was going on in Portugal and on the frontiers of Spain, all of which I had missed through my misfortune in falling into the hands of Milord Wellington.

From what I have told you of the Lady Jane you will have guessed what occurred, my friends. Étienne Gerard is thrown into the company of a young and beautiful woman. What must it mean for him? What must it mean for her? It was not for me, the guest, the captive, to make love to the sister of my host. But I was reserved. I was discreet. I tried to curb my own emotions and to discourage hers. For my own part I fear that I betrayed myself, for the eye becomes more eloquent when the tongue is silent. Every quiver of my fingers as I turned over her music-sheets told her my secret. But she—she was admirable. It is in these matters that women have a genius for deception. If I had not penetrated her secret I should often have thought that she forgot even that I was in the house. For hours she would sit lost in a sweet melancholy, while I admired her pale face and her curls in the lamp-light, and thrilled within me to think that I had moved her so deeply. Then at last I would speak, and she would start in her chair and stare at me with the most admirable pretence of being surprised to find me in the room. Ah! how I longed to hurl myself suddenly at her feet, to kiss her white hand, to assure her that I had surprised her secret and that I would not abuse her confidence. But, no, I was not her equal, and I was under her roof as a castaway enemy. My lips were sealed. I endeavoured to imitate her own wonderful affectation of indifference, but, as you may think, I was eagerly alert for any opportunity of serving her.

One morning Lady Jane had driven in her phaeton to Okehampton, and I strolled along the road which led to that place in the hope that I might meet her on her return. It was the early winter, and banks of fading fern sloped down to the winding road. It is a bleak place this Dartmoor, wild and rocky—a country of wind and mist. I felt as I walked that it is no wonder Englishmen should suffer from the spleen. My own heart was heavy within me, and I sat upon a rock by the wayside looking out on the dreary view with my thoughts full of trouble and foreboding. Suddenly, however, as I glanced down the road I saw a sight which drove everything else from my mind, and caused me to leap to my feet with a cry of astonishment and anger.

Down the curve of the road a phaeton was coming, the pony tearing along at full gallop. Within was the very lady whom I had come to meet. She lashed at the pony like one who endeavours to escape from some pressing danger, glancing ever backwards over her shoulder. The bend of the road concealed from me what it was that had alarmed her, and I ran forward not knowing what to expect. The next instant I saw the pursuer, and my amazement was increased at the sight. It was a gentleman in the red coat of an English fox-hunter, mounted on a great grey horse. He was galloping as if in a race, and the long stride of the splendid creature beneath him soon brought him up to the lady's flying carriage. I saw him stoop and seize the reins of the pony, so as to bring it to a halt. The next instant he was deep in talk with the lady, he bending forward in his saddle and speaking eagerly, she shrinking away from him as if she feared and loathed him.

You may think, my dear friends, that this was not a sight at which I could calmly gaze. How my heart thrilled within me to think that a chance should have been given to me to serve the Lady Jane ! I ran—oh, good Lord, how I ran ! At last breathless, speechless, I reached the phaeton. The man glanced up at me with his blue English eyes, but so deep was he in his talk that he paid no heed to me, nor did the lady say a word. She still leaned back, her beautiful pale face gazing up at him. He was a good-looking fellow—tall, and strong, and brown ; a pang of jealousy seized me as I looked at him. He was talking low and fast, as the English do when they are in earnest.

" I tell you, Jinny, it's you and only you that I love," said he. " Don't bear malice, Jinny. Let bygones by bygones. Come now, say it's all over."

" No, never, George, never ! " she cried.

A dusky red suffused his handsome face. The man was furious.

" Why can't you forgive me, Jinny ? "

" I can't forget the past."

" By George, you must ! I've asked enough. It's time to order now. I'll have my rights. D'ye hear ? " His hand closed upon her wrist.

At last my breath had returned to me.

" Madame," I said, as I raised my hat, " do I intrude, or is there any possible way in which I can be of service to you ? "

But neither of them minded me any more than if I had been a fly who buzzed between them. Their eyes were locked together.

" I'll have my rights, I tell you. I've waited long enough."

" There's no use bullying, George."

" Do you give in ? "

" No, never ! "

" Is that your final answer ? "

" Yes, it is."

He gave a bitter curse and threw down her hand.

" All right, my lady, we'll see about this."

" Excuse me, sir," said I, with dignity.

" Oh, go to blazes ! " he cried, turning on me with his furious face. The next instant he had spurred his horse and was galloping down the road once more.

Lady Jane gazed after him until he was out of sight, and I was surprised to see that her face wore a smile and not a frown. Then she turned to me and held out her hand.

" You are very kind, Colonel Gerard. You meant well, I am sure."

" Madame," said I, " if you can oblige me with the gentleman's name and address I will arrange that he shall never trouble you again."

" No scandal, I beg of you," she cried.

" Madame, I could not so far forget myself. Rest assured that no lady's name would ever be mentioned by me in the course of such an incident. In bidding me to go to blazes this gentleman has relieved me from the embarrassment of having to invent a cause of quarrel."

" Colonel Gerard," said the lady, earnestly, " you must give me your word as a soldier and a gentleman that this matter goes no farther, and also that you will say nothing to my brother about what you have seen. Promise me ! "

" If I must."

" I hold you to your word. Now drive with me to High Combe, and I will explain as we go."

The first words of her explanation went into me like a sabre-point.

" That gentleman," said she, " is my husband."

" Your husband ! "

" You must have known that I was married." She seemed surprised at my agitation.

" I did not know."

" He is Lord George Dacre. We have been married two years. There is no need to tell you how he wronged me. I left him and sought a refuge under my brother's roof. Up till to-day he has left me there unmolested. What I must above all things avoid is the chance of a duel betwixt my husband and my brother. It is horrible to think of. For this reason Lord Rufton must know nothing of this chance meeting of to-day."

" If my pistol could free you from this annoyance——"

" No, no, it is not to be thought of. Remember your promise, Colonel Gerard. And not a word at High Combe of what you have seen ! "

Her husband ! I had pictured in my mind that she was a young widow. This brown-faced brute with his " go to blazes " was the husband of this tender dove of a woman. Oh, if she would but allow me to free her from so odious an encumbrance ! There is no divorce so quick and certain as that which I could give her. But a promise is a promise, and I kept it to the letter. My mouth was sealed. In a week I was to be sent back from Plymouth to St. Malo, and it seemed to me that I might never hear the sequel of the story. And yet it was destined that it should have a sequel, and that I should play a very pleasing and honourable part in it.

It was only three days after the event which I have described when Lord Rufton burst hurriedly into my room. His face was pale, and his manner that of a man in extreme agitation.

" Gerard," he cried, " have you seen Lady Jane Dacre ? "

I had seen her after breakfast, and it was now midday.

" By Heaven, there's villainy here ! " cried my poor friend, rushing about like a madman. " The bailiff has been up to say that a chaise and pair were seen driving full split down the Tavistock Road. The blacksmith heard a woman scream as it passed his forge. Jane has disappeared. By the Lord, I believe that she has been kidnapped by this villain Dacre." He rang the bell furiously. " Two horses this instant ! " he cried. " Colonel Gerard, your pistols ! Jane comes back with me this night from Gravel Hanger, or there will be a new master in High Combe Hall."

Behold us then within half an hour, like two knight-errants of old, riding forth to the rescue of this lady in distress. It was near Tavistock that Lord Dacre lived, and at every house and toll-gate along the road we heard the news of the flying post-chaise in front of us, so there could be no doubt whither they were bound. As we rode Lord Rufton told me of the man whom we were pursuing. His name, it seems, was a household word throughout all England for every sort of mischief. Wine, women, dice, cards, racing—in all forms of debauchery he had earned for himself a terrible name. He was of an old and noble family, and it had been hoped that he had sowed his wild oats when he married the beautiful Lady Jane Rufton. For some months he had indeed behaved well, and then he had wounded her feelings in their most tender part by some unworthy *liaison*. She had fled from his house and taken refuge with her brother, from whose care she had now been dragged once more, against her will. I ask you if two men could have had a fairer errand than that upon which Lord Rufton and myself were riding?

" That's Gravel Hanger," he cried at last, pointing with his crop ; and there on the green side of a hill was an old brick and timber building as beautiful as only an English country house can be. " There's an inn by the park-gate, and there we shall leave our horses," he added.

For my own part it seemed to me that with so just a cause we should have done best to ride boldly up to his door and summon him to surrender the lady. But there I was wrong. For the one thing which every Englishman fears is the law. He makes it himself, and when he has once made it it becomes a terrible tyrant before whom the bravest quails. He will smile at breaking his neck, but he will turn pale at breaking the law. It seems, then, from what Lord Rufton told me as we walked through the park, that we were on the wrong side of the law in this matter. Lord Dacre was in the right in carrying off his wife, since she did indeed belong to him, and our own position now was nothing better than that of burglars and trespassers. It was not for burglars to openly approach the front door. We could take the lady by force or by craft, but we could not take her by right, for the law was against us. This was what my friend explained to me as we crept up towards the shelter of a shrubbery which was close to the windows of the house. Thence we could examine this fortress, see whether we could effect a lodgment in it, and, above all, try to establish some communication with the beautiful prisoner inside.

There we were, then, in the shrubbery, Lord Rufton and I, each with a pistol in the pockets of our riding-coats, and with the most resolute determination in our hearts that we should not return without the lady. Eagerly we scanned every window of the wide-spread house. Not a sign could we see of the prisoner or of anyone else; but on the gravel drive outside the door were the deep-sunk marks of the wheels of the chaise. There was no doubt that they had arrived. Crouching among the laurel bushes we held a whispered council of war, but a singular interruption brought it to an end.

Out of the door of the house there stepped a tall, flaxen-haired man, such a figure as one would choose for the flank of a grenadier company. As he turned his brown face and his blue eyes towards us I recognised Lord Dacre. With long strides he came down the gravel path straight for the spot where we lay.

" Come out, Ned !" he shouted ; " you'll have the gamekeeper putting a charge of shot into you. Come out, man, and don't skulk behind the bushes."

It was not a very heroic situation for us. My poor friend rose with a crimson face. I sprang to my feet also and bowed with such dignity as I could muster.

" Halloa ! it's the Frenchman, is it ? " said he, without returning my bow. " I've got a crow to pluck with him already. As to you, Ned, I knew you would be hot on our scent, and so I was looking out for you. I saw you cross the park and go to ground in the shrubbery. Come in, man, and let us have all the cards on the table."

He seemed master of the situation, this handsome giant of a man, standing at his ease on his own ground while we slunk out of our hiding-place. Lord Rufton had said not a word, but I saw by his darkened brow and his sombre eyes that the storm was gathering. Lord Dacre led the way into the house, and we followed close at his heels. He ushered us himself into an oak-panelled sitting-room, closing the door behind us. Then he looked me up and down with insolent eyes.

" Look here, Ned," said he, " time was when an English family could settle their own affairs in their own way. What has this foreign fellow got to do with your sister and my wife ? "

" Sir," said I, " permit me to point out to you that this is not a case merely of a sister or a wife, but that I am the friend of the lady in question, and that I have the privilege which every gentleman possesses of protecting a woman against brutality. It is only by a gesture that I can show you what I think of you." I had my riding glove in my hand, and I flicked him across the face with it. He drew back with a bitter smile and his eyes were as hard as flint.

" So you've brought your bully with you, Ned ? " said he. " You might at least have done your fighting yourself, if it must come to a fight."

" So I will," cried Lord Rufton. " Here and now."

" When I've killed this swaggering Frenchman," said Lord Dacre. He stepped to a side table and opened a brass-bound case. " By Gad," said he, " either that man or I go out of this room feet foremost. I meant well by you, Ned ; I did, by George, but I'll shoot this led-captain of yours as sure as my name's George Dacre. Take your choice of pistols, sir, and shoot across this table. The barkers are loaded. Aim straight and kill me if you can, for, by the Lord, if you don't, you're done."

In vain Lord Rufton tried to take the quarrel upon himself. Two things were clear in my mind—one that the Lady Jane had feared above all things that her husband and brother should fight, the other that if I could but kill this big milord, then the whole question would be settled for ever in the best way. Lord Rufton did not want him. Lady Jane did not want him. There-fore, I, Étienne Gerard, their friend, would pay the debt of gratitude which I owed them by freeing them of this encumbrance. But, indeed, there was no choice in the matter, for Lord Dacre was as eager to put a bullet into me as I could be to do the same service to him In vain Lord Rufton argued and scolded. The affair must continue.

" Well, if you must fight my guest instead of myself, let it be to-morrow morning with two witnesses," he cried at last ; " this is sheer murder across the table."

" But it suits my humour, Ned," said Lord Dacre.

" And mine, sir," said I.

" Then I'll have nothing to do with it," cried Lord Rufton. " I tell you, George, if you shoot Colonel Gerard under these circumstances you'll find yourself in the dock instead of on the bench. I won't act as second, and that's flat."

" Sir," said I, " I am perfectly prepared to proceed without a second."

" That won't do. It's against the law," cried Lord Dacre. " Come, Ned, don't be a fool. You see we mean to fight. Hang it, man, all I want you to do is to drop a handkerchief."

" I'll take no part in it."

" Then I must find someone who will," said Lord Dacre. He threw a cloth over the pistols, which lay upon the table, and he rang the bell. A footman entered. " Ask Colonel Berkeley if he will step this way. You will find him in the billiard-room."

A moment later there entered a tall thin Englishman with a great moustache, which was a rare thing amid that clean-shaven race. I have heard since that they were worn only by the Guards and the Hussars. This Colonel Berkeley was a guardsman. He seemed a strange, tired, languid, drawling creature with a long black cigar thrusting out, like a pole from a bush, amidst that immense moustache. He looked from one to the other of us with true English phlegm, and he betrayed not the slightest surprise when he was told our intention.

" Quite so," said he ; " quite so."

" I refuse to act, Colonel Berkeley," cried Lord Rufton. " Remember, this duel cannot proceed without you, and I hold you personally responsible for anything that happens."

This Colonel Berkeley appeared to be an authority upon the question, for he removed the cigar from his mouth and he laid down the law in his strange, drawling voice.

" The circumstances are unusual, but not irregular, Lord Rufton," said he. " This gentleman has given a blow, and this other gentleman has received it. That is a clear issue. Time and conditions depend upon the person who demands satisfaction. Very good. He claims it here and now, across the table. He is acting within his rights. I am prepared to accept the responsibility."

There was nothing more to be said. Lord Rufton sat moodily in the corner, with his brows drawn down and his hands thrust deep into the pockets of his riding-breeches. Colonel Berkeley examined the two pistols and laid them both in the centre of the table. Lord Dacre was at one end and I at the other, with eight feet of shining mahogany between us. On the hearthrug, with his back to the fire, stood the tall colonel, his handkerchief in his left hand, his cigar between two fingers of his right.

" When I drop the handkerchief," said he, " you will pick up your pistols and you will fire at your own convenience. Are you ready ? "

" Yes," we cried.

His hand opened, and the handkerchief fell. I bent swiftly forward and seized a pistol, but the table, as I have said, was eight feet across, and it was easier for this long-armed milord to reach the pistols than it was for me. I had not yet drawn myself straight before he fired, and to this it was that I owe my life. His bullet would have blown out my brains had I been erect. As it was it whistled through my curls. At the same instant, just as I threw up my own pistol to fire, the door flew open, and a pair of arms were thrown round me. It was the beautiful, flushed, frantic face of Lady Jane which looked up into mine.

" You shan't fire ! Colonel Gerard, for my sake, don't fire," she cried. " It is a mistake, I tell you—a mistake, a mistake ! He is the best and dearest of husbands. Never again shall I leave his side." Her hands slid down my arm and closed upon my pistol.

" Jane, Jane," cried Lord Rufton ; " come with me. You should not be here. Come away."

" It is all confoundedly irregular," said Colonel Berkeley.

" Colonel Gerard, you won't fire, will you ? My heart would break if he were hurt."

" Hang it all, Jinny, give the fellow fair play," cried Lord Dacre. " He stood my fire like a man, and I won't see him interfered with. Whatever happens, I can't get worse than I deserve."

But already there had passed between me and the lady a quick glance of the eyes which told her everything. Her hands slipped from my arm. " I leave my husband's life and my own happiness to Colonel Gerard," said she.

How well she knew me, this admirable woman ! I stood for an instant irresolute, with the pistol cocked in my hand. My antagonist faced me bravely, with no blenching of his sunburnt face and no flinching of his bold, blue eyes.

" Come, come, sir, take your shot ! " cried the colonel from the mat.

" Let us have it, then," said Lord Dacre.

I would, at least, show them how completely his life was at the mercy of my skill. So much I owed to my own self-respect. I glanced round for a mark. The colonel was looking towards my antagonist, expecting to see him drop. His face was sideways to me, his long cigar projecting from his lips with an inch of ash at the end of it. Quick as a flash I raised my pistol and fired.

"Permit me to trim your ash, sir," said I, and I bowed with a grace which is unknown among these islanders.

I am convinced that the fault lay with the pistol and not with my aim. I could hardly believe my own eyes when I saw that I had snapped off the cigar within half an inch of his lips. He stood staring at me with the ragged stub of the cigar-end sticking out from his singed moustache. I can see him now with his foolish, angry eyes and his long, thin, puzzled face. Then he began to talk. I have always said that the English are not really a phlegmatic or a taciturn nation if you stir them out of their groove. No one could have talked in a more animated way than this colonel. Lady Jane put her hands over her ears.

"Come, come, Colonel Berkeley," said Lord Dacre, sternly, "you forget yourself. There is a lady in the room."

The colonel gave a stiff bow.

"If Lady Dacre will kindly leave the room," said he, "I will be able to tell this infernal little Frenchman what I think of him and his monkey tricks."

I was splendid at that moment, for I ignored the words that he had said and remembered only the extreme provocation.

"Sir," said I, "I freely offer you my apologies for this unhappy incident. I felt that if I did not discharge my pistol Lord Dacre's honour might feel hurt, and yet it was quite impossible for me, after hearing what this lady had said, to aim it at her husband. I looked round for a mark, therefore, and I had the extreme misfortune to blow your cigar out of your mouth when my intention had merely been to snuff the ash. I was betrayed by my pistol. This is my explanation, sir, and if after listening to my apologies you still feel that I owe you satisfaction,

I need not say that it is a request which I am unable to refuse."

It was certainly a charming attitude which I had assumed, and it won the hearts of all of them. Lord Dacre stepped forward and wrung me by the hand. " By George, sir," said he, " I never thought to feel towards a Frenchman as I do to you. You're a man and a gentleman, and I can't say more." Lord Rufton said nothing, but his hand-grip told me all that he thought. Even Colonel Berkeley paid me a compliment, and declared that he would think no more about the unfortunate cigar. And she—ah, if you could have seen the look she gave me, the flushed cheek, the moist eye, the tremulous lip ! When I think of my beautiful Lady Jane it is at that moment that I recall her. They would have had me stay to dinner, but you will understand, my friends, that this was no time for either Lord Rufton or myself to remain at Gravel Hanger. This reconciled couple desired only to be alone. In the chaise he had persuaded her of his sincere repentance, and once again they were a loving husband and wife. If they were to remain so, it was best perhaps that I should go. Why should I unsettle that domestic peace ? Even against my own will my mere presence and appearance might have their effect upon the lady. No, no, I must tear myself away—even her persuasions were unable to make me stop. Years afterwards I heard that the household of the Dacres was among the happiest in the whole country, and that no cloud had ever come again to darken their lives. Yet I dare say if he could have seen into his wife's mind— but there, I say no more ! A lady's secret is her own, and I fear that she and it are buried long years ago in some Devonshire churchyard. Perhaps all that gay circle are gone and the Lady Jane only lives now in the memory of an old half-pay French brigadier. He at least can never forget.

6. *How the Brigadier rode to Minsk*

I WOULD have a stronger wine to-night, my friends, a wine of Burgundy rather than of Bordeaux. It is that my heart, my old soldier heart, is heavy within me. It is a strange thing, this age which creeps upon one. One does not know, one does not understand ; the spirit is ever the same, and one does not remember how the poor body crumbles. But there comes a moment when it is brought home, when quick as the sparkle of a whirling sabre it is clear to us, and we see the men we were and the men we are. Yes, yes, it was so to-day, and I would have a wine of Burgundy to-night, White Burgundy—Montrachet—— Sir, I am your debtor !

It was this morning in the Champ de Mars. Your pardon, friends, while an old man tells his trouble. You saw the review. Was it not splendid ? I was in the enclosure for veteran officers who have been decorated. This ribbon on my breast was my passport. The cross itself I keep at home in a leathern pouch. They did us honour, for we were placed at the saluting point, with the Emperor and the carriages of the Court upon our right.

It is years since I have been to a review, for I cannot approve of many things which I have seen. I do not approve of the red breeches of the infantry. It was in white breeches that the infantry used to fight. Red is for the cavalry. A little more, and they would ask our busbies and our spurs ! Had I been seen at a review they might well have said that I, Étienne Gerard, had condoned it. So I have stayed at home. But this war of the Crimea is different. The men go to battle. It is not for me to be absent when brave men gather.

My faith, they march well, those little infantrymen ! They are not large, but they are very solid and they carry themselves well. I took off my hat to them as they passed. Then there came the guns. They were good

guns, well horsed, and well manned. I took off my hat
to them. Then came the engineers, and to them also I
took off my hat. There are no braver men than the
engineers. Then came the cavalry : lancers, cuirassiers, chasseurs and spahis. To all of them in turn I
was able to take off my hat, save only to the spahis. The
Emperor had no spahis. But when all of the others had
passed, what think you came at the close ? A brigade of
hussars, and at the charge ! Oh, my friends, the pride
and the glory and the beauty, the flash and the sparkle,
the roar of the hoofs, and the jingle of chains, the tossing
manes, the noble heads, the rolling cloud and the dancing
waves of steel ! My heart drummed to them as they
passed. And the last of all, was it not my own old
regiment ? My eyes fell upon the grey and silver dolmans,
with the leopard-skin shabracks, and at that instant the
years fell away from me and I saw my own beautiful
men and horses, even as they had swept behind their
young colonel, in the pride of our youth and our strength,
just forty years ago. Up flew my cane. " Chargez !
En avant ! Vive l'Empereur ! " It was the past calling
to the present. But, oh, what a thin, piping voice !
Was this the voice that had once thundered from wing
to wing of a strong brigade ? And the arm that could
scarce wave a cane, were these the muscles of fire and
steel which had no match in all Napoleon's mighty host ?
They smiled at me. They cheered me. The Emperor
laughed and bowed. But to me the present was a dim
dream, and what was real were my eight hundred dead
hussars and the Étienne of long ago. Enough—a brave
man can face age and fate as he faced Cossacks and
Uhlans. But there are times when Montrachet is better
than the wine of Bordeaux.

It is to Russia that they go, and so I will tell you a
story of Russia. Ah, what an evil dream of the night it
seems ! Blood and ice. Ice and blood. Fierce faces
with snow upon the whiskers. Blue hands held out for
succour. And across the great white plain the one long

black line of moving figures, trudging, trudging, a hundred miles, another hundred, and still always the same white plain. Sometimes there were fir-woods to limit it, sometimes it stretched away to the cold blue sky, but the black line stumbled on and on. Those weary, ragged, starving men, the spirit frozen out of them, looked neither to right nor left, but with sunken faces and rounded backs trailed onwards and ever onwards, making for France as wounded beasts make for their lair. There was no speaking, and you could scarce hear the shuffle of feet in the snow. Once only I heard them laugh. It was outside Wilna when an aide-de-camp rode up to the head of that dreadful column and asked if that were the Grand Army. All who were within hearing looked round, and when they saw those broken men, those ruined regiments, those fur-capped skeletons who were once the Guard, they laughed, and the laugh crackled down the column like a *feu de joie*. I have heard many a groan and cry and scream in my life, but nothing so terrible as the laugh of the Grand Army.

But why was it that these helpless men were not destroyed by the Russians? Why was it that they were not speared by the Cossacks or herded into droves, and driven as prisoners into the heart of Russia? On every side as you watched the black snake winding over the snow you saw also dark, moving shadows which came and went like cloud drifts on either flank and behind. They were the Cossacks, who hung round us like wolves round the flock. But the reason why they did not ride in upon us was that all the ice of Russia could not cool the hot hearts of some of our soldiers. To the end there were always those who were ready to throw themselves between these savages and their prey. One man above all rose greater as the danger thickened, and won a higher name amid disaster than he had done when he led our van to victory. To him I drink this glass—to Ney, the red-maned Lion, glaring back over his shoulder at the enemy who feared to tread too closely on his heels. I can see him now, his broad white face convulsed with fury, his light blue eyes sparkling like flints, his great voice roaring and crashing amid the roll of the musketry. His glazed and featherless cocked hat was the ensign upon which France rallied during those dreadful days.

It is well known that neither I nor the regiment of Hussars of Conflans were at Moscow. We were left behind on the lines of communication at Borodino. How the Emperor could have advanced without us is incomprehensible to me, and, indeed, it was only then that I understood that his judgment was weakening, and that he was no longer the man that he had been. However, a soldier has to obey orders, and so I remained at this village, which was poisoned by the bodies of thirty thousand men who had lost their lives in the great battle. I spent the late autumn in getting my horses into condition and reclothing my men, so that when the army fell back on Borodino my hussars were the best of the cavalry, and were placed under Ney in the rear-guard. What could he have done without us during those dreadful days ? " Ah, Gerard," said he one evening—but it is not for me to repeat the words. Suffice it that he spoke what the whole army felt. The rear-guard covered the army, and the Hussars of Conflans covered the rear-guard. There was the whole truth in a sentence. Always the Cossacks were on us. Always we held them off. Never a day passed that we had not to wipe our sabres. That was soldiering indeed.

But there came a time between Wilna and Smolensk when the situation became impossible. Cossacks and even cold we could fight, but we could not fight hunger as well. Food must be got at all costs. That night Ney sent for me to the waggon in which he slept. His great head was sunk on his hands. Mind and body, he was wearied to death.

" Colonel Gerard," said he, " things are going very badly with us. The men are starving. We must have food at all costs."

" The horses," I suggested.

" Save your handful of cavalry, there are none left."

" The band," said I.

He laughed, even in his despair.

" Why the band ? " he asked.

" Fighting men are of value."

" Good ! " said he. " You would play the game down to the last card, and so would I. Good, Gerard, good ! " He clasped my hand in his. " But there is one chance for us yet, Gerard." He unhooked a lantern from the roof of the waggon, and he laid it on a map which was stretched before him. " To the south of us," said he, " there lies the town of Minsk. I have word from a Russian deserter that much corn has been stored in the town hall. I wish you to take as many men as you think best, set forth for Minsk, seize the corn, load any carts which you may collect in the town, and bring them to me between here and Smolensk. If you fail, it is but a detachment cut off. If you succeed, it is new life to the army."

He had not expressed himself well, for it was evident that if we failed it was not merely the loss of a detachment. It is quality as well as quantity which counts. And yet how honourable a mission, and how glorious a risk ! If mortal men could bring it, then the corn should come from Minsk. I said so, and spoke a few burning words about a brave man's duty until the Marshal was so moved that he rose and, taking me affectionately by the shoulders, pushed me out of the waggon.

It was clear to me that in order to succeed in my enterprise I should take a small force and depend rather upon surprise than upon numbers. A large body could not conceal itself, would have great difficulty in getting food, and would cause all the Russians around us to concentrate for its certain destruction. On the other hand, if a small body of cavalry could get past the Cossacks unseen it was probable that they would find no troops to oppose them, for we knew that the main Russian army was several days' march behind us. This corn was meant, no doubt, for their consumption. A squadron of hussars and thirty Polish lancers were all whom I chose for the venture. That very night we rode out of the camp, and struck south in the direction of Minsk.

Fortunately there was but half a moon, and we were able to pass without being attacked by the enemy. Twice we saw great fires burning amid the snow, and around them a thick bristle of long poles. These were the lances of Cossacks, which they had stood upright while they slept. It would have been a great joy to us to have charged in amongst them, for we had much to revenge, and the eyes of my comrades looked longingly from me to those red flickering patches in the darkness. My faith, I was sorely tempted to do it, for it would have been a good lesson to teach them that they must keep a few miles between themselves and a French army. It is the essence of good generalship, however, to keep one thing before one at a time, and so we rode silently on through the snow, leaving these Cossack bivouacs to right and left. Behind us the black sky was all mottled with a line of flame, which showed where our own poor wretches were trying to keep themselves alive for another day of misery and starvation.

All night we rode slowly onwards, keeping our horses' tails to the Pole Star. There were many tracks in the snow, and we kept to the line of these, that no one might remark that a body of cavalry had passed that way. These are the little precautions which mark the experienced officer. Besides, by keeping to the tracks we were most likely to find the villages, and only in the villages could we hope to get food. The dawn of day found us in a thick fir-wood, the trees so loaded with snow that the light could hardly reach us. When we had found our way out of it it was full daylight, the rim of the rising sun peeping over the edge of the great snow-plain and turning it crimson from end to end. I halted my hussars and lancers under the shadow of the wood, and I studied the country. Close to us there was a small farmhouse. Beyond, at a distance of several miles, was a village. Far away on the skyline rose a considerable town all bristling with church towers. This must be Minsk. In no direction could I see any signs of troops. It was evident that we had passed through the Cossacks, and that there was nothing between us and our goal. A joyous shout burst from my men when I told them our position, and we advanced rapidly towards the village.

I have said, however, that there was a small farmhouse immediately in front of us. As we rode up to it I observed that a fine grey horse with a military saddle was tethered by the door. Instantly I galloped forward, but before I could reach it a man dashed out of the door, flung himself on to the horse, and rode furiously away, the crisp, dry snow flying up in a cloud behind him. The sunlight gleamed upon his gold epaulettes, and I knew that he was a Russian officer. He would raise the whole country-side if we did not catch him. I put spurs to Violette and flew after him. My troopers followed; but there was no horse among them to compare with Violette, and I knew well that if I could not catch the Russian I need expect no help from them.

But it is a swift horse indeed and a skilful rider who can hope to escape from Violette with Étienne Gerard in the saddle. He rode well, this young Russian, and his mount was a good one, but gradually we wore him down. His face glanced continually over his shoulder—a dark, handsome face, with eyes like an eagle—and I saw as I closed with him that he was measuring the distance between us. Suddenly he half turned; there were a flash and a crack as his pistol bullet hummed past my ear. Before he could draw his sword I was upon him; but he still spurred his horse, and the two galloped together over the plain, I with my leg against the Russian's and my left hand upon his right shoulder. I saw his hand fly up to his mouth. Instantly I dragged him across my pommel and seized him by the throat, so that he could not swallow. His horse shot from under him, but I held him fast, and Violette came to a stand. Sergeant Oudin of the hussars was the first to join us. He was an old soldier, and he saw at a glance what I was after.

" Hold tight, Colonel," said he ; " I'll do the rest."

He slipped out his knife, thrust the blade between the clenched teeth of the Russian, and turned it so as to force his mouth open. There, on his tongue, was the little wad of wet paper which he had been so anxious to swallow. Oudin picked it out, and I let go of the man's throat. From the way in which, half strangled as he was, he glanced at the paper I was sure that it was a message of extreme importance. His hands twitched as if he longed to snatch it from me. He shrugged his shoulders, however, and smiled good-humouredly when I apologised for my roughness.

" And now to business," said I, when he had done coughing and hawking. " What is your name ? "

" Alexis Barakoff."

" Your rank and regiment ? "

" Captain of the Dragoons of Grodno."

" What is this note which you were carrying ? "

" It is a line which I had written to my sweetheart."

" Whose name," said I, examining the address, " is the Hetman Platoff. Come, come, sir, this is an important military document, which you are carrying from one general to another. Tell me this instant what it is."

" Read it, and then you will know." He spoke perfect French, as do most of the educated Russians. But he knew well that there is not one French officer in a thousand who knows a word of Russian. The inside of the note contained one single line which ran like this :—

" Pustj Franzuzy pridutt v Minsk. Min gotovy."

I stared at it, and I had to shake my head. Then I showed it to my hussars, but they could make nothing of it. The Poles were all rough fellows who could not read or write, save only the sergeant, who came from Memel, in East Prussia, and knew no Russian. It was maddening, for I felt that I had possession of some important secret upon which the safety of the army might depend, and yet I could make no sense of it. Again I entreated our prisoner to translate it, and offered him his freedom if he would do so. He only smiled at my request. I could not but admire him, for it was the very smile which I should have myself smiled had I been in his position.

" At least," said I, " tell us the name of this village."

" It is Dobrova."

" And that is Minsk over yonder, I suppose ? "

" Yes, that is Minsk."

" Then we shall go to the village and we shall very soon find someone who will translate this despatch."

So we rode onward together, a trooper with his carbine on either side of our prisoner. The village was but a little place, and I set a guard at the ends of the single street, so that no one could escape from it. It was necessary to call a halt and to find some food for the men and horses, since they had travelled all night and had a long journey still before them.

There was one large stone house in the centre of the village, and to this I rode. It was the house of the priest —a snuffy and ill-favoured old man who had not a civil answer to any of our questions. An uglier fellow I never met, but, my faith, it was very different with his only daughter, who kept house for him. She was a brunette, a rare thing in Russia, with creamy skin, raven hair and a pair of the most glorious dark eyes that ever kindled at the sight of a hussar. From the first glance I saw that she was mine. It was no time for love-making when a soldier's duty had to be done, but still, as I took the simple meal which they laid before me, I chatted lightly with the lady, and we were the best of friends before an hour had passed. Sophie was her first name, her second I never knew. I taught her to call me Étienne, and I tried to cheer her up, for her sweet face was sad and there were tears in her beautiful dark eyes. I pressed her to tell me what it was which was grieving her.

"How can I be otherwise," said she, speaking French with a most adorable lisp, "when one of my poor country-men is a prisoner in your hands? I saw him between two of your hussars as you rode into the village."

"It is the fortune of war," said I. "His turn to-day; mine, perhaps, to-morrow."

"But consider, Monsieur——" said she.

"Étienne," said I.

"Oh, Monsieur——"

"Étienne," said I.

"Well, then," she cried, beautifully flushed and desperate, "consider, Étienne, that this young officer will be taken back to your army and will be starved or frozen, for if, as I hear, your own soldiers have a hard march, what will be the lot of a prisoner?"

I shrugged my shoulders.

"You have a kind face, Étienne," said she; "you would not condemn this poor man to certain death. I entreat you to let him go."

Her delicate hand rested upon my sleeve, her dark eyes looked imploringly into mine.

A sudden thought passed through my mind. I would grant her request, but I would demand a favour in return. At my order the prisoner was brought up into the room.

"Captain Barakoff," said I, "this young lady has begged me to release you, and I am inclined to do so. I would ask you to give your parole that you will remain in this dwelling for twenty-four hours, and take no steps to inform anyone of our movements."

"I will do so," said he.

"Then I trust in your honour. One man more or less can make no difference in a struggle between great armies, and to take you back as a prisoner would be to condemn you to death. Depart, sir, and show your gratitude not to me, but to the first French officer who falls into your hands."

When he was gone I drew my paper from my pocket.

" Now, Sophie," said I, " I have done what you asked me and all that I ask in return is that you will give me a lesson in Russian."

" With all my heart," said she.

" Let us begin on this," said I, spreading out the paper before her. " Let us take it word for word and see what it means."

She looked at the writing with some surprise. " It means," said she, " if the French come to Minsk all is lost." Suddenly a look of consternation passed over her beautiful face. " Great heavens ! " she cried, " what is it that I have done ? I have betrayed my country ! Oh, Étienne, your eyes are the last for whom this message is meant. How could you be so cunning as to make a poor, simple-minded and unsuspecting girl betray the cause of her country ? "

I consoled my poor Sophie as best I might, and I assured her that it was no reproach to her that she should be outwitted by so old a campaigner and so shrewd a man as myself. But it was no time now for talk. This message made it clear that the corn was indeed at Minsk, and that there were no troops there to defend it. I gave a hurried order from the window, the trumpeter blew the assembly, and in ten minutes we had left the village behind us and were riding hard for the city, the gilded domes and minarets of which glimmered above the snow of the horizon. Higher they rose and higher, until at last, as the sun sank towards the west, we were in the broad main street, and galloped up it amid the shouts of the moujiks and the cries of frightened women until we found ourselves in front of the great town-hall. My cavalry I drew up in the square, and I, with my two sergeants, Oudin and Papilette, rushed into the building.

Heavens ! shall I ever forget the sight which greeted us ? Right in front of us was drawn up a triple line of Russian grenadiers. Their muskets rose as we entered and a crashing volley burst into our very faces, Oudin and Papilette dropped upon the floor, riddled with bullets. For myself, my busby was shot away and I had two holes through my dolman. The grenadiers ran at me with their bayonets. " Treason ! " I cried. " We are betrayed ! Stand to your horses ! " I rushed out of the hall, but the whole square was swarming with troops. From every side street dragoons and Cossacks were riding down upon us, and such a rolling fire had burst from the surrounding houses that half my men and horses were on the ground. " Follow me ! " I yelled, and sprang upon Violette, but a giant of a Russian dragoon officer threw his arms round me, and we rolled on the ground together. He shortened his sword to kill me, but, changing his mind, he seized me by the throat and banged my head against the stones until I was unconscious. So it was that I became the prisoner of the Russians.

When I came to myself my only regret was that my captor had not beaten out my brains. There in the grand square of Minsk lay half my troopers dead or wounded, with exultant crowds of Russians gathered round them. The rest, in a melancholy group, were herded into the porch of the town-hall, a sotnia of Cossacks keeping guard over them. Alas ! what could I say, what could I do ? It was evident that I had led my men into a carefully baited trap. They had heard of our mission, and they had prepared for us. And yet there was that despatch which had caused me to neglect all precautions and to ride straight into the town. How was I to account for that ? The tears ran down my cheeks as I surveyed the ruin of my squadron, and as I thought of the plight of my comrades of the Grand Army who awaited the food which I was to have brought them. Ney had trusted me, and I had failed him. How often he would strain his eyes over the snowfields for that convoy of grain which should never gladden his sight ! My own fate was hard enough. An exile in Siberia was the best which the future could bring me. But you will believe me, my friends, that it was not for his own sake, but for that of his starving comrades, that Étienne Gerard's cheeks were lined by his tears, frozen even as they were shed.

" What's this ? " said a gruff voice at my elbow ; and I turned to face the huge, black-bearded dragoon who had dragged me from my saddle. " Look at the Frenchman crying ! I thought that the Corsican was followed by brave men, and not by children."

" If you and I were face to face and alone, I should let you see which is the better man," said I.

For answer the brute struck me across the face with his open hand. I seized him by the throat, but a dozen of his soldiers tore me away from him, and he struck me again while they held my hands.

" You base hound," I cried, " is this the way to treat an officer and a gentleman ? "

" We never asked you to come to Russia," said he. " If you do you must take such treatment as you can get. I would shoot you off-hand if I had my way."

" You will answer for this some day," I cried, as I wiped the blood from my moustache.

" If the Hetman Platoff is of my way of thinking you will not be alive this time to-morrow," he answered, with a ferocious scowl. He added some words in Russian to his troops, and instantly they all sprang to their saddles. Poor Violette, looking as miserable as her master, was led round and I was told to mount her. My left arm was tied with a thong which was fastened to the stirrup-iron of a sergeant of dragoons. So in most sorry plight I and the remnant of my men set forth from Minsk.

Never have I met such a brute as this man Sergine, who commanded the escort. The Russian army contains the best and the worst in the world, but a worse than Major Sergine of the Dragoons of Kieff I have never seen in any force outside of the guerillas of the Peninsula. He was a man of great stature, with a fierce, hard face and a bristling black beard, which fell over his cuirass. I have been told since that he was noted for his strength and his bravery, and I could answer for it that he had the grip of a bear, for I had felt it when he tore me from my saddle. He was a wit, too, in his way, and made continual remarks in Russian at our expense which set all his dragoons and Cossacks laughing. Twice he beat my comrades with his riding-whip, and once he approached me with the lash swung over his shoulder, but there was something in my eyes which prevented it from falling. So in misery and humiliation, cold and starving, we rode in a disconsolate column across the vast snow-plain. The sun had sunk, but still in the long northern twilight we pursued our weary journey. Numbed and frozen, with my head aching from the blows it had received, I was borne onwards by Violette, hardly conscious of where I was or whither I was going. The little mare walked with a sunken head, only raising it to snort her contempt for the mangy Cossack ponies who were round her.

But suddenly the escort stopped, and I found that we had halted in the single street of a small Russian village. There was a church on one side, and on the other was a large stone house, the outline of which seemed to me to be familiar. I looked around me in the twilight, and then I saw that we had been led back to Dobrova, and that this house at the door of which we were waiting was the same house of the priest at which we had stopped in the morning. Here it was that my charming Sophie in her innocence had translated the unlucky message which had in some strange way led us to our ruin. To think that only a few hours before we had left this very spot with such high hopes and all fair prospects for our mission, and now the remnants of us waited as beaten and humiliated men for whatever lot a brutal enemy might ordain ! But such is the fate of the soldier, my friends—kisses to-day, blows to-morrow, Tokay in a palace, ditch-water in a hovel, furs or rags, a full purse or an empty pocket, ever swaying from the best to the worst, with only his courage and his honour unchanging.

The Russian horsemen dismounted, and my poor

fellows were ordered to do the same. It was already late, and it was clearly their intention to spend the night in this village. There were great cheering and joy amongst the peasants when they understood that we had all been taken, and they flocked out of their houses with flaming torches, the women carrying out tea and brandy for the Cossacks. Amongst others, the old priest came forth—the same whom we had seen in the morning. He was all smiles now, and he bore with him some hot punch on a salver, the reek of which I can remember still. Behind her father was Sophie. With horror I saw her clasp Major Sergine's hand as she congratulated him upon the victory he had won and the prisoners he had made. The old priest, her father, looked at me with an insolent face, and made insulting remarks at my expense, pointing at me with his lean and grimy hand. His fair daughter Sophie looked at me also, but she said nothing, and I could read her tender pity in her dark eyes. At last she turned to Major Sergine and said something to him in Russian, on which he frowned and shook his head impatiently. She appeared to plead with him, standing there in the flood of light which shone from the open door of her father's house. My eyes were fixed upon the two faces, that of the beautiful girl and of the dark, fierce man, for my instinct told me that it was my own fate which was under debate. For a long time the soldier shook his head, and then, at last softening before her pleadings, he appeared to give way. He turned to where I stood with my guardian sergeant beside me.

" These good people offer you the shelter of their roof for the night," said he to me, looking me up and down with vindictive eyes. " I find it hard to refuse them, but I tell you straight that for my part I had rather see you on the snow. It would cool your hot blood, you rascal of a Frenchman ! "

I looked at him with the contempt that I felt.

" You were born a savage, and you will die one," said I.

My words stung him, for he broke into an oath, raising his whip as if he would strike me.

" Silence, you crop-eared dog ! " he cried. " Had I my way some of the insolence would be frozen out of you before morning." Mastering his passion, he turned upon Sophie with what he meant to be a gallant manner. " If you have a cellar with a good lock," said he, " the fellow may lie in it for the night, since you have done him the honour to take an interest in his comfort. I must have his parole that he will not attempt to play us any tricks, as I am answerable for him until I hand him over to the Hetman Platoff to-morrow."

His supercilious manner was more than I could endure. He had evidently spoken French to the lady in order that I might understand the humiliating way in which he referred to me.

" I will take no favour from you," said I. " You may do what you like, but I will never give you my parole."

The Russian shrugged his great shoulders, and turned away as if the matter were ended.

" Very well, my fine fellow, so much the worse for your fingers and toes. We shall see how you are in the morning after a night in the snow."

" One moment, Major Sergine," cried Sophie. " You must not be so hard upon this prisoner. There are some special reasons why he has a claim upon our kindness and mercy."

The Russian looked with suspicion upon his face from her to me.

" What are the special reasons ? You certainly seem to take a remarkable interest in this Frenchman," said he.

" The chief reason is that he has this very morning of his own accord released Captain Alexis Barakoff, of the Dragoons of Grodno."

" It is true," said Barakoff, who had come out of the house. " He captured me this morning, and he released me upon parole rather than take me back to the French army, where I should have been starved."

" Since Colonel Gerard has acted so generously you will surely, now that fortune has changed, allow us to offer him the poor shelter of our cellar upon this bitter night," said Sophie. " It is a small return for his generosity."

But the dragoon was still in the sulks.

" Let him give me his parole first that he will not attempt to escape," said he. " Do you hear, sir ? Do you give me your parole ? "

" I give you nothing," said I.

" Colonel Gerard," cried Sophie, turning to me with a coaxing smile, " you will give *me* your parole, will you not ? "

" To you, mademoiselle, I can refuse nothing. I will give you my parole, with pleasure."

" There, Major Sergine," cried Sophie, in triumph, " that is surely sufficient. You have heard him say that he gives me his parole. I will be answerable for his safety."

In an ungracious fashion my Russian bear grunted his consent, and so I was led into the house, followed by the scowling father and by the big, black-bearded dragoon. In the basement there was a large and roomy chamber, where the winter logs were stored. Thither it was that I was led, and I was given to understand that this was to be my lodging for the night. One side of this bleak apartment was heaped up to the ceiling with faggots of firewood. The rest of the room was stone-flagged and bare-walled, with a single, deep-set window upon one side, which was safely guarded with iron bars. For light I had a large stable lantern, which swung from a beam of the low ceiling. Major Sergine smiled as he took this down, and swung it round so as to throw its light into every corner of that dreary chamber.

" How do you like our Russian hotels, monsieur ? " he asked, with his hateful sneer. " They are not very grand, but they are the best that we can give you. Perhaps the next time that you Frenchmen take a fancy to travel you will choose some other country where they will make you more comfortable." He stood laughing at me, his white teeth gleaming through his beard. Then he left me, and I heard the great key creak in the lock.

For an hour of utter misery, chilled in body and soul, I sat upon a pile of faggots, my face sunk upon my hands and my mind full of the saddest thoughts. It was cold enough within those four walls, but I thought of the sufferings of my poor troopers outside, and I sorrowed with their sorrow. Then I paced up and down, and I clapped my hands together and kicked my feet against the walls to keep them from being frozen. The lamp gave out some warmth, but still it was bitterly cold, and I had had no food since morning. It seemed to me that everyone had forgotten me, but at last I heard the key turn in the lock, and who should enter but my prisoner of the morning, Captain Alexis Barakoff. A bottle of wine projected from under his arm, and he carried a great plate of hot stew in front of him.

" Hush ! " said he ; " not a word ! Keep up your heart ! I cannot stop to explain, for Sergine is still with us. Keep awake and ready ! " With these hurried words he laid down the welcome food and ran out of the room.

" Keep awake and ready ! " The words rang in my ears. I ate my food and I drank my wine, but it was neither food nor wine which had warmed the heart within me. What could those words of Barakoff mean ? Why was I to remain awake ? For what was I to be ready ? Was it possible that there was a chance yet of escape ? I have never respected the man who neglects his prayers at all other times and yet prays when he is in peril. It is like a bad soldier who pays no respect to the colonel save when he would demand a favour of him. And yet when I thought of the salt-mines of Siberia on the one side and of my mother in France upon the other, I could not help a prayer rising not from my lips, but from my heart, that the words of Barakoff might mean all that I hoped. But hour after hour struck upon the village clock, and still I heard nothing save the call of the Russian sentries in the street outside.

Then at last my heart leaped within me, for I heard a light step in the passage. An instant later the key turned, the door opened, and Sophie was in the room.

" Monsieur—— " she cried.

" Étienne," said I.

" Nothing will change you," said she. " But is it possible that you do not hate me ? Have you forgiven me the trick which I played you ? "

" What trick ? " I asked.

" Good heavens ! is it possible that even now you have not understood it ? You asked me to translate the despatch. I have told you that it meant, ' If the French come to Minsk all is lost.' "

" What did it mean, then ? "

" It means, ' Let the French come to Minsk. We are awaiting them.' "

I sprang back from her.

" You betrayed me ! " I cried. " You lured me into this trap. It is to you that I owe the death and capture of my men. Fool that I was to trust a woman ! "

" Do not be unjust, Colonel Gerard. I am a Russian woman, and my first duty is to my country. Would you not wish a French girl to have acted as I have done ? Had I translated the message correctly you would not have gone to Minsk and your squadron would have escaped. Tell me that you forgive me ! "

She looked bewitching as she stood pleading her cause in front of me. And yet, as I thought of my dead men, I could not take the hand which she held out to me.

" Very good," said she, as she dropped it by her side. " You feel for your own people and I feel for mine, and so we are equal. But you have said one wise and kindly thing within these walls, Colonel Gerard. You have said, ' One man more or less can make no difference in a struggle between two great armies.' Your lesson of nobility is not wasted. Behind those faggots is an unguarded door. Here is the key to it. Go forth, Colonel Gerard, and I trust that we may never look upon each other's face again."

I stood for an instant with the key in my hand and my head in a whirl. Then I handed it back to her.

" I cannot do it," I said.

" Why not ? "

" I have given my parole."

" To whom ? " she asked.

" Why, to you."

" And I release you from it."

My heart bounded with joy. Of course, it was true what she said. I had refused to give my parole to Sergine. I owed him no duty. If she relieved me from my promise my honour was clear. I took the key from her hand.

" You will find Captain Barakoff at the end of the village street," she said. " We of the North never forget either an injury or a kindness. He has your mare and your sword waiting for you. Do not delay an instant, for in two hours it will be dawn."

So I passed out into the starlit Russian night, and had that last glimpse of Sophie as she peered after me through the open door. She looked wistfully at me as if she expected something more than the cold thanks which I gave her, but even the humblest man has his pride, and I will not deny that mine was hurt by the deception which she had played upon me. I could not have brought myself to kiss her hand, far less her lips. The door led into a narrow alley, and at the end of it stood a muffled figure who held Violette by the bridle.

" You told me to be kind to the next French officer whom I found in distress," said he. " Good luck ! Bon voyage ! " he whispered, as I bounded into the saddle. " Remember, ' Poltava ' is the watchword."

It was well that he had given it to me, for twice I had

to pass Cossack pickets before I was clear of the lines. I had just ridden past the last vedettes and hoped that I was a free man again when there was a soft thudding in the snow behind me, and a heavy man upon a great black horse came swiftly after me. My first impulse was to put spurs to Violette. My second, as I saw a long black beard against a steel cuirass, was to halt and await him.

" I thought that it was you, you dog of a Frenchman," he cried, shaking his drawn sword at me. " So you have broken your parole, you rascal ? "

" I gave no parole."

" You lie, you hound ! "

I looked around and no one was coming. The vedettes were motionless and distant. We were all alone, with the moon above and the snow beneath. Fortune has ever been my friend.

" I gave you no parole."

" You gave it to the lady."

" Then I will answer for it to the lady."

" That would suit you better, no doubt. But, unfortunately, you will have to answer for it to me."

" I am ready."

" Your sword, too ! There is treason in this ! Ah, I see it all ! The woman has helped you. She shall see Siberia for this night's work."

The words were his death-warrant. For Sophie's sake I could not let him go back alive. Our blades crossed, and an instant later mine was through his black beard and deep in his throat. I was on the ground almost as soon as he, but the one thrust was enough. He died, snapping his teeth at my ankles like a savage wolf.

Two days later I had rejoined the army at Smolensk, and was a part once more of that dreary procession which tramped onwards through the snow, leaving a long weal of blood to show the path which it had taken.

Enough, my friends ; I would not reawaken the memory of those days of misery and death. They still come to haunt me in my dreams. When we halted at last in Warsaw, we had left behind us our guns, our transport, three-fourths of our comrades. But we did not leave behind us the honour of Étienne Gerard. They have said that I broke my parole. Let them beware how they say it to my face, for the story is as I tell it, and old as I am my forefinger is not too weak to press a trigger when my honour is in question.

7. *How the Brigadier bore himself at Waterloo*

I—THE STORY OF THE FOREST INN

OF all the great battles in which I had the honour of drawing my sword for the Emperor and for France there was not one which was lost. At Waterloo, although, in a sense, I was present, I was unable to fight, and the enemy was victorious. It is not for me to say that there is a connection between these two things. You know me too well, my friends, to imagine that I would make such a claim. But it gives matter for thought, and some have drawn flattering conclusions from it. After all, it was only a matter of breaking a few English squares and the day would have been our own. If the Hussars of Conflans, with Étienne Gerard to lead them, could not do this, then the best judges are mistaken. But let that pass. The Fates had ordained that I should hold my hand and that the Empire should fall. But they had also ordained that this day of gloom and sorrow should bring such honour to me as had never come when I swept on the wings of victory from Boulogne to Vienna. Never had I burned so brilliantly as at that supreme moment when the darkness fell upon all around me. You are aware that I was faithful to the Emperor in his adversity, and that I refused to sell my sword and my honour to the Bourbons. Never again was I to feel my war horse between my knees, never again to hear the kettledrums and silver trumpets behind me as I rode in front of my little rascals. But it comforts my heart, my friends, and it brings the tears to my eyes, to think how great I was upon that last day of my soldier life, and to remember that of all the remarkable exploits which have won me the love of so many beautiful women, and the respect of so many noble men, there was none which, in splendour, in audacity, and in the great end which was attained, could compare with my famous ride upon the night of June 18th, 1815. I am aware that the story is often told at mess-tables and in barrack-rooms, so that there are few in the army who have not heard it, but modesty has sealed my lips, until now, my friends, in the privacy of these intimate gatherings, I an inclined to lay the true facts before you.

In the first place, there is one thing which I can assure you. In all his career Napoleon never had so splendid an army as that with which he took the field for that campaign. In 1813 France was exhausted. For every veteran there were five children—Marie Louises as we called them, for the Empress had busied herself in raising levies while the Emperor took the field. But it was very different in 1815. The prisoners had all come back— the men from the snows of Russia, the men from the dungeons of Spain, the men from the hulks in England. These were the dangerous men, veterans of twenty battles, longing for their old trade, and with hearts filled with hatred and revenge. The ranks were full of soldiers who wore two and three chevrons, every chevron meaning five years' service. And the spirit of these men was terrible. They were raging, furious, fanatical, adoring the Emperor as a Mameluke does his prophet, ready, to fall upon their own bayonets if their blood could serve him. If you had seen these fierce old veterans going into battle, with their flushed faces, their savage eyes, their furious yells, you would wonder that anything could stand against them. So high was the spirit of France at that time that every other spirit would have quailed before it; but these people, these English, had neither spirit nor soul, but only solid, immovable beef, against which we broke ourselves in vain. That was it, my friends! On the one side, poetry, gallantry, self-sacrifice—all that is beautiful and heroic. On the other side, beef. Our hopes, our ideals, our dreams—all were shattered on that terrible beef of Old England.

You have read how the Emperor gathered his forces, and then how he and I, with a hundred and thirty thousand veterans, hurried to the northern frontier and fell upon the Prussians and the English. On the 16th of June Ney held the English in play at Quatre Bras while we beat the Prussians at Ligny. It is not for me to say how far I contributed to that victory, but it is well known that the Hussars of Conflans covered themselves with glory. They fought well, these Prussians, and eight thousand of them were left upon the field. The Emperor thought that he had done with them, as he sent Marshal Grouchy with thirty-two thousand men to follow them up and to prevent their interfering with his plans. Then, with nearly eighty thousand men, he turned upon these " Goddam " Englishmen. How much we had to avenge upon them, we Frenchmen—the guineas of Pitt, the hulks of Portsmouth, the invasion of Wellington, the perfidious victories of Nelson! At last the day of punishment seemed to have arisen.

Wellington had with him sixty-seven thousand men, but many of them were known to be Dutch and Belgian, who had no great desire to fight against us. Of good troops he had not fifty thousand. Finding himself in the presence of the Emperor in person with eighty thousand men, this Englishman was so paralysed with fear that he could neither move himself nor his army. You have seen the rabbit when the snake approaches. So stood the English upon the ridge of Waterloo. The night before, the Emperor, who had lost an aide-de-camp at Ligny, ordered me to join his staff, and I had left my hussars to the charge of Major Victor. I know not which of us was the most grieved, they or I, that I should be called away upon the eve of battle ; but an order is an order, and a good soldier can but shrug his shoulders and obey. With the Emperor I rode across the front of the enemy's position on the morning of the 18th, he looking at them through his glass and planning which was the shortest way to destroy them. Soult was at his elbow, and Ney and Foy and others who had fought the English in Portugal and Spain. " Have a care, sire," said Soult, " the English infantry is very solid."

" You think them good soldiers because they have beaten you," said the Emperor, and we younger men turned away our faces and smiled. But Ney and Foy were grave and serious. All the time the English line, chequered with red and blue and dotted with batteries, was drawn up silent and watchful within a long musket-shot of us. On the other side of the shallow valley our own people, having finished their soup, were assembling for the battle. It had rained very heavily ; but at this moment the sun shone out and beat upon the French army, turning our brigades of cavalry into so many dazzling rivers of steel, and twinkling and sparkling on the innumerable bayonets of the infantry. At the sight of that splendid army, and the beauty and majesty of its appearance, I could contain myself no longer ; but, rising in my stirrups, I waved my busby and cried, " Vive l'Empereur ! " a shout which growled and roared and clattered from one end of the line to the other, while the horsemen waved their swords and the footmen held up their shakos upon their bayonets. The English remained petrified upon their ridge. They knew that their hour had come.

And so it would have come if at that moment the word had been given and the whole army had been permitted to advance. We had but to fall upon them and to sweep them from the face of the earth. To put aside all ques-tion of courage, we were the more numerous, the older soldiers, and the better led. But the Emperor desired to do all things in order, and he waited until the ground should be drier and harder, so that his artillery could manœuvre. So three hours were wasted, and it was eleven o'clock before we saw Jerome Buonaparte's columns advance upon our left and heard the crash of the guns which told that the battle had begun. The loss of those three hours was our destruction. The attack upon the left was directed upon a farmhouse which was held by the English Guards, and we heard the three loud shouts of apprehension which the defenders were compelled to utter. They were still holding out, and D'Erlon's corps was advancing upon the right to engage another portion of the English line, when our attention was called away from the battle beneath our noses to a distant portion of the field of action.

The Emperor had been looking through his glass to the extreme left of the English line, and now he turned suddenly to the Duke of Dalmatia, or Soult, as we soldiers preferred to call him.

" What is it, Marshal ? " said he.

We all followed the direction of his gaze, some raising our glasses, some shading our eyes. There was a thick wood over yonder, then a long, bare slope, and another wood beyond. Over this bare strip between the two woods there lay something dark, like the shadow of a moving cloud.

" I think that they are cattle, sire," said Soult.

At that instant there came a quick twinkle from amid the dark shadow.

" It is Grouchy," said the Emperor, and he lowered his glass. " They are doubly lost, these English. I hold them in the hollow of my hand. They cannot escape me."

He looked round, and his eyes fell upon me.

" Ah ! here is the prince of messengers," said he. " Are you well mounted, Colonel Gerard ? "

I was riding my little Violette, the pride of the brigade. I said so.

" Then ride hard to Marshal Grouchy, whose troops you see over yonder. Tell him that he is to fall upon the left flank and rear of the English while I attack them in front. Together we shall crush them and not a man escape."

I saluted and rode off without a word, my heart dancing with joy that such a mission should be mine. I looked at that long, solid line of red and blue looming through the smoke of the guns, and I shook my fist at it as I went. " We shall crush them and not a man escape." They were the Emperor's words, and it was I, Étienne Gerard, who was to turn them into deeds. I burned to reach the Marshal, and for an instant I thought of riding through the English left wing, as being the shortest cut. I have done bolder deeds and come out safely, but I reflected that if things went badly with me and I was taken or shot the message would be lost and the plans of the Emperor miscarry. I passed in front of the cavalry therefore, past the chasseurs, the lancers of the guard, the carabineers, the horse grenadiers, and, lastly, my own little rascals, who followed me wistfully with their eyes. Beyond the cavalry the Old Guard was standing, twelve regiments of them, all veterans of many battles, sombre and severe, in long blue overcoats, and high bearskins from which the plumes had been removed. Each bore within the goatskin knapsack upon his back the blue and white parade uniform which they would use for their entry into Brussels next day. As I rode past them I reflected that these men had never been beaten, and, as I looked at their weather-beaten faces and their stern and silent bearing, I said to myself that they never would be beaten. Great heavens, how little could I foresee what a few more hours would bring !

On the right of the Old Guard were the Young Guard and the 6th Corps of Lobau, and then I passed Jacquinot's Lancers and Marbot's Hussars, who held the extreme flank of the line. All these troops knew nothing of the corps which was coming towards them through the wood, and their attention was taken up in watching the battle which raged upon their left. More than a hundred guns were thundering from each side, and the din was so great that of all the battles which I have fought I cannot recall more than half-a-dozen which were as noisy. I looked back over my shoulder, and there were two brigades of cuirassiers, English and French, pouring down the hill together, with the sword-blades playing over them like summer lightning. How I longed to turn Violette, and to lead my hussars into the thick of it ! What a picture ! Étienne Gerard with his back to the battle, and a fine cavalry action raging behind him. But duty is duty, so I rode past Marbot's vedettes and on in the direction of the wood, passing the village of Frishermont upon my left.

In front of me lay the great wood, called the Wood of Paris, consisting mostly of oak trees, with a few narrow paths leading through it. I halted and listened when I reached it ; but out of its gloomy depths there came no blare of trumpet, no murmur of wheels, no tramp of horses to mark the advance of that great column which with my own eyes I had seen streaming towards it. The battle roared behind me, but in front all was as silent as that grave in which so many brave men would shortly sleep. The sunlight was cut off by the arches of leaves above my head, and a heavy damp smell rose from the sodden ground. For several miles I galloped at such a pace as few riders would care to go with roots below and branches above. Then, at last, for the first time I caught a glimpse of Grouchy's advance guard. Scattered parties of hussars passed me on either side, but some distance off, among the trees. I heard the beating of a drum far away, and the low, dull murmur which an army makes upon the march. Any moment I might come upon the staff and deliver my message to Grouchy in person, for I knew well that on such a march a Marshal of France would certainly ride with the van of his army.

Suddenly the trees thinned in front of me, and I understood with delight that I was coming to the end of the wood, whence I could see the army and find the Marshal. Where the track comes out from amid the trees there is a small cabaret, where woodcutters and waggoners drink their wine. Outside the door of this I reined up my horse for an instant while I took in the scene which was before me. Some few miles away I saw a second great forest, that of St. Lambert, out of which the Emperor had seen the troops advancing. It was easy to see, however, why there had been so long a delay in their leaving one wood and reaching the other, because between the two ran the deep defile of the Lasnes, which had to be crossed. Sure enough, a long column of troops—horse, foot and guns—was streaming down one side of it and swarming up the other, while the advance guard was already among the trees on either side of me. A battery of horse artillery was coming along the road, and I was about to gallop up to it and ask the officer in command if he could tell me where I should find the Marshal, when suddenly I observed that, though the gunners were dressed in blue, they had not the dolman trimmed with red brandenburgs as our own horse-gunners wear it. Amazed at the sight, I was looking at these soldiers to left and right when a hand touched my thigh, and there was the landlord, who had rushed from his inn.

" Madman ! " he cried, " why are you here ? What are you doing ? "

" I am seeking Marshal Grouchy."

" You are in the heart of the Prussian army. Turn and fly ! "

" Impossible ; this is Grouchy's corps."

" How do you know ? "

" Because the Emperor has said it."

" Then the Emperor has made a terrible mistake ! I tell you that a patrol of Silesian hussars has this instant left me. Did you not see them in the wood ? "

" I saw hussars."

" They are the enemy."

" Where is Grouchy ? "

" He is behind. They have passed him."

" Then how can I go back ? If I go forward I may see him yet. I must obey my orders and find him wherever he is."

The man reflected for an instant.

" Quick ! quick ! " he cried, seizing my bridle. " Do what I say and you may yet escape. They have not observed you yet. Come with me and I will hide you until they pass."

Behind his house there was a low stable, and into this he thrust Violette. Then he half led and half dragged me into the kitchen of the inn. It was a bare, brick-floored room. A stout, red-faced woman was cooking cutlets at the fire.

" What's the matter now ? " she asked, looking with a frown from me to the innkeeper. " Who is this you have brought in ? "

" It is a French officer, Marie. We cannot let the Prussians take him."

" Why not ? "

" Why not ? Sacred name of a dog, was I not myself a soldier of Napoleon ? Did I not win a musket of honour among the Vélites of the Guard ? Shall I see a comrade taken before my eyes ? Marie, we must save him."

But the lady looked at me with most unfriendly eyes.

" Pierre Charras," she said, " you will not rest until you have your house burned over your head. Do you not understand, you blockhead, that if you fought for Napoleon it was because Napoleon ruled Belgium ? He does so no longer. The Prussians are our allies and this is our enemy. I will have no Frenchman in this house. Give him up ! "

The innkeeper scratched his head and looked at me in despair, but it was very evident to me that it was neither for France nor for Belgium that this woman cared, but that it was the safety of her own house that was nearest her heart.

" Madame," said I, with all the dignity and assurance I could command, " the Emperor is defeating the English and the French army will be here before evening. If you have used me well you will be rewarded, and if you have denounced me you will be punished and your house will certainly be burned by the provost-marshal."

She was shaken by this, and I hastened to complete my victory by other methods.

" Surely," said I, " it is impossible that anyone so beautiful can also be hard-hearted ? You will not refuse me the refuge which I need."

She looked at my whiskers and I saw that she was softened. I took her hand, and in two minutes we were on such terms that her husband swore roundly that he would give me up himself if I pressed the matter farther.

" Besides, the road is full of Prussians," he cried. " Quick ! quick ! into the loft ! "

" Quick ! quick ! into the loft ! " echoed his wife, and together they hurried me towards a ladder which led to a trap-door in the ceiling. There was loud knocking at the door, so you can think that it was not long before my spurs went twinkling through the hole and the board was dropped behind me. An instant later I heard the voices of the Germans in the rooms below me.

The place in which I found myself was a single long attic, the ceiling of which was formed by the roof of the house. It ran over the whole of one side of the inn, and through the cracks in the flooring I could look down either upon the kitchen, the sitting-room or the bar at my pleasure. There were no windows, but the place was in the last stage of disrepair, and several missing slates upon the roof gave me light and the means of observation. The place was heaped with lumber— fodder at one end and a huge pile of empty bottles at the other. There was no door or window save the hole through which I had come up.

I sat upon the heap of hay for a few minutes to steady myself and to think out my plans. It was very serious that the Prussians should arrive upon the field of battle earlier than our reserves, but there appeared to be only one corps of them, and a corps more or less makes little difference to such a man as the Emperor. He could afford to give the English all this and beat them still. The best way in which I could serve him, since Grouchy was behind, was to wait here until they were past, and then to resume my journey, to see the Marshal, and to give him his orders. If he advanced upon the rear of the English instead of following the Prussians all would be well. The fate of France depended upon my judgment and my nerve. It was not the first time, my friends, as you are well aware, and you know the reasons that I had to trust that neither nerve nor judgment would ever fail me. Certainly, the Emperor had chosen the right man for his mission. " The prince of messengers " he had called me. I would earn my title.

It was clear that I could do nothing until the Prussians had passed, so I spent my time in observing them. I have no love for these people, but I am compelled to say that they kept excellent discipline, for not a man of them entered the inn, though their lips were caked with dust and they were ready to drop with fatigue. Those who had knocked at the door were bearing an insensible comrade, and having left him they returned at once to the ranks. Several others were carried in the same fashion and laid in the kitchen, while a young surgeon, little more than a boy, remained behind in charge of them. Having observed them through the cracks in the floor, I next turned my attention to the holes in the roof, from which I had an excellent view of all that was passing outside. The Prussian corps was still streaming past. It was easy to see that they had made a terrible march and had little food, for the faces of the men were ghastly, and they were plastered from head to foot with mud from their falls upon the foul and slippery roads. Yet, spent as they were, their spirit was excellent, and they pushed and hauled at the gun-carriages when the wheels sank up to the axles in the mire and the weary horses were floundering knee-deep unable to draw them through. The officers rode up and down the column encouraging the more active with words of praise, and the laggards with blows from the flat of their swords. All the time from over the wood in front of them there came the tremendous roar of the battle, as if all the rivers on earth had united in one gigantic cataract, booming and crashing in a mighty fall. Like the spray of the cataract was the long veil of smoke which rose high over the trees. The officers pointed to it with their swords, and with hoarse cries from their parched lips the mud-stained men pushed onwards to the battle. For an hour I watched them pass, and I reflected that their vanguard must have come into touch with Marbot's vedettes and that the Emperor knew already of their coming. " You are going very fast up the road, my friends, but you will come down it a great deal faster," said I to myself, and I consoled myself with the thought.

But an adventure came to break the monotony of this long wait. I was seated beside my loophole and congratulating myself that the corps was nearly past, and that the road would soon be clear for my journey, when suddenly I heard a loud altercation break out in French in the kitchen.

" You shall not go ! " cried a woman's voice.

" I tell you that I will ! " said a man's, and there was a sound of scuffling.

In an instant I had my eye to the crack in the floor. There was my stout lady, like a faithful watch-dog, at the bottom of the ladder ; while the young German surgeon, white with anger, was endeavouring to come up it. Several of the German soldiers who had recovered from their prostration were sitting about on the kitchen floor and watching the quarrel with stolid, but attentive, faces. The landlord was nowhere to be seen.

" There is no liquor there," said the woman.

" I do not want liquor ; I want hay or straw for these men to lie upon. Why should they lie on the bricks when there is straw overhead ?

" There is no straw."

" What is up there ? "

" Empty bottles."

" Nothing else ? "

" No."

For a moment it looked as if the surgeon would abandon his intention, but one of the soldiers pointed up to the ceiling. I gathered from what I could understand of his words that he could see the straw sticking out between the planks. In vain the woman protested. Two of the soldiers were able to get upon their feet and to drag her aside, while the young surgeon ran up the ladder, pushed open the trap-door, and climbed into the loft. As he swung the door back I slipped behind it, but as luck would have it he shut it again behind him, and there we were left standing face to face.

Never have I seen a more astonished young man.

" A French officer ! " he gasped.

" Hush ! " said I. " Hush ! Not a word above a whisper." I had drawn my sword.

" I am not a combatant," he said ; " I am a doctor. Why do you threaten me with your sword ? I am not armed."

" I do not wish to hurt you, but I must protect myself. I am in hiding here."

" A spy ! "

" A spy does not wear such a uniform as this, nor do you find spies on the staff of an army. I rode by mistake into the heart of this Prussian corps, and I concealed myself here in the hope of escaping when they are past. I will not hurt you if you do not hurt me, but if you do not swear that you will be silent as to my presence you will never go down alive from this attic."

" You can put up your sword sir," said the surgeon,

1132

and I saw a friendly twinkle in his eyes. " I am a Pole by birth, and I have no ill-feeling to you or your people. I will do my best for my patients, but I will do no more. Capturing hussars is not one of the duties of a surgeon. With your permission I will now descend with this truss of hay to make a couch for these poor fellows below."

I had intended to exact an oath from him, but it is my experience that if a man will not speak the truth he will not swear the truth, so I said no more. The surgeon opened the drap-door, threw out enough hay for his purpose, and then descended the ladder, letting down the door behind him. I watched him anxiously when he rejoined his patients, and so did my good friend the landlady, but he said nothing and busied himself with the needs of the soldiers.

By this time I was sure that the last of the army corps was past, and I went to my loop-hole confident that I should find the coast clear, save, perhaps, for a few stragglers, whom I could disregard. The first corps was indeed past, and I could see the last files of the infantry disappearing into the wood ; but you can imagine my disappointment when out of the Forest of St. Lambert I saw a second corps emerging, as numerous as the first. There could be no doubt that the whole Prussian army, which we thought we had destroyed at Ligny, was about to throw itself upon our right wing while Marshal Grouchy had been coaxed away upon some fool's errand. The roar of guns, much nearer than before, told me that the Prussian batteries which had passed me were already in action. Imagine my terrible position ! Hour after hour was passing ; the sun was sinking towards the west. And yet this cursed inn, in which I lay hid, was like a little island amid a rushing stream of furious Prussians. It was all-important that I should reach Marshal Grouchy, and yet I could not show my nose without being made prisoner. You can think how I cursed and tore my hair. How little do we know what is in store for us ! Even while I raged against my ill-fortune, that same fortune was reserving me for a far higher task than to carry a message to Grouchy—a task which could not have been mine had I not been held tight in that little inn on the edge of the Forest of Paris.

Two Prussian corps had passed and a third was coming up, when I heard a great fuss and the sound of several voices in the sitting-room. By altering my position I was able to look down and see what was going on.

Two Prussian generals were beneath me, their heads bent over a map which lay upon the table. Several aides-de-damp and staff officers stood round in silence. Of the two generals one was a fierce old man, white-haired and wrinkled, with a ragged grizzled moustache and a voice like the bark of a hound. The other was younger, but long-faced and solemn. He measured distances upon the map with the air of a student, while his companion stamped and fumed and cursed like a corporal of hussars. It was strange to see the old man so fiery and the young one so reserved. I could not understand all that they said, but I was very sure about their general meaning.

" I tell you we must push on and ever on ! " cried the old fellow, with a furious German oath. " I promised Wellington that I would be there with the whole army even if I had to be strapped to my horse. Bülow's corps is in action, and Zeithen's shall support it with every man and gun. Forwards, Gneisenau, forwards ! "

The other shook his head.

" You must remember, your excellency, that if the English are beaten they will make for the coast. What will your position be then, with Grouchy between you and the Rhine ? "

" We shall beat them, Gneisenau ; the Duke and I will grind them to powder between us. Push on, I say ! The whole war will be ended in one blow. Bring Pirsch up, and we can throw sixty thousand men into the scale while Thielmann holds Grouchy beyond Wavre."

Gneisenau shrugged his shoulders, but at that instant an orderly appeared at the door.

"An aide-de-camp from the Duke of Wellington," said he

"Ha, ha!" cried the old man; "let us hear what he has to say."

An English officer, with mud and blood all over his scarlet jacket, staggered into the room. A crimson-stained handkerchief was knotted round his arm, and he held the table to keep himself from falling.

"My message is to Marshal Blucher," says he.

"I am Marshal Blucher. Go on! go on!" cried the impatient old man.

"The Duke bade me to tell you, sir, that the British army can hold its own, and that he has no fears for the result. The French cavalry has been destroyed, two of their divisions of infantry have ceased to exist, and only the Guard is in reserve. If you give us a vigorous support the defeat will be changed to absolute rout and——" His knees gave way under him, and he fell in a heap upon the floor.

"Enough! enough!" cried Blucher. "Gneisenau, send an aide-de-camp to Wellington and tell him to rely upon me to the full. Come on, gentlemen, we have our work to do! He bustled eagerly out of the room, with all his staff clanking behind him, while two orderlies carried the English messenger to the care of the surgeon.

Gneisenau, the Chief of the Staff, had lingered behind for an instant, and he laid his hand upon one of the aides-de-camp. The fellow had attracted my attention, for I have always a quick eye for a fine man. He was tall and slender, the very model of a horseman; indeed, there was something in his appearance which made it not unlike my own. His face was dark and as keen as that of a hawk, with fierce black eyes under thick, shaggy brows, and a moustache which would have put him in the crack squadron of my hussars. He wore a green coat with white facings, and a horsehair helmet—a dragoon, as I conjectured, and as dashing a cavalier as one would wish to have at the end of one's sword-point.

" A word with you, Count Stein," said Gneisenau.
" If the enemy are routed, but if the Emperor escapes,
he will rally another army, and all will have to be done
again. But if we can get the Emperor, then the war is
indeed ended. It is worth a great effort and a great risk
for such an object as that."

The young dragoon said nothing, but he listened
attentively.

" Suppose the Duke of Wellington's words should
prove to be correct, and the French army should be driven
in utter rout from the field, the Emperor will certainly
take the road back through Genappe and Charleroi as
being the shortest to the frontier. We can imagine that
his horses will be fleet, and that the fugitives will make
way for him. Our cavalry will follow the rear of the
beaten army, but the Emperor will be far away at the
front of the throng."

The young dragoon inclined his head.

" To you, Count Stein, I commit the Emperor. If
you take him your name will live in history. You have
the reputation of being the hardest rider in our army.
Do you choose such comrades as you may select—ten
or a dozen should be enough. You are not to engage in
the battle, nor are you to follow the general pursuit, but
you are to ride clear of the crowd, reserving your energies
for a nobler end. Do you understand me ? "

Again the dragoon inclined his head. This silence
impressed me. I felt that he was indeed a dangerous
man.

" Then I leave the details in your own hands. Strike
at no one except the highest. You cannot mistake the
Imperial carriage, nor can you fail to recognise the
figure of the Emperor. Now I must follow the Marshal.
Adieu ! If ever I see you again I trust that it will be to
congratulate you upon a deed which will ring through
Europe."

The dragoon saluted, and Gneisenau hurried from the
room. The young officer stood in deep thought for a

few moments. Then he followed the Chief of the Staff. I looked with curiosity from my loophole to see what his next proceeding would be. His horse, a fine, strong chestnut with two white stockings, was fastened to the rail of the inn. He sprang into the saddle, and, riding to intercept a column of cavalry which was passing, he spoke to an officer at the head of the leading regiment. Presently, after some talk, I saw two hussars—it was a hussar regiment—drop out of the ranks and take up their position beside Count Stein. The next regiment was also stopped, and two lancers were added to his escort. The next furnished him with two dragoons, and the next with two cuirassiers. Then he drew his little group of horsemen aside, and he gathered them round him, explaining to them what they had to do. Finally the nine soldiers rode off together and disappeared into the Wood of Paris.

I need not tell you, my friends, what all this portended. Indeed, he had acted exactly as I should have done in his place. From each colonel he had demanded the two best horsemen in the regiment, and so he had assembled a band who might expect to catch whatever they should follow. Heaven help the Emperor if, without an escort, he should find them on his track !

And I, dear friends—imagine the fever, the ferment, the madness, of my mind ! All thought of Grouchy had passed away. No guns were to be heard to the east. He could not be near. If he should come up he would not now be in time to alter the event of the day. The sun was already low in the sky and there could not be more than two or three hours of daylight. My mission might be dismissed as useless. But here was another mission, more pressing, more immediate, a mission which meant the safety, and perhaps the life, of the Emperor. At all costs, through every danger, I must get back to his side. But how was I to do it ? The whole Prussian army was now between me and the French lines. They blocked every road, but they could not block the path of duty when Étienne Gerard sees it lie before him. I could not wait longer. I must be gone.

There was but the one opening to the loft, and so it was only down the ladder that I could descend. I looked into the kitchen, and I found that the young surgeon was still there. In a chair sat the wounded English aide-de-camp, and on the straw lay two Prussian soldiers in the last stage of exhaustion. The others had all recovered and been sent on. These were my enemies, and I must pass through them in order to gain my horse. From the surgeon I had nothing to fear ; the Englishman was wounded, and his sword stood with his cloak in a corner ; the two Germans were half insensible, and their muskets were not beside them. What could be simpler ? I opened the trap-door, slipped down the ladder, and appeared in the midst of them, my sword drawn in my hand.

What a picture of surprise ! The surgeon, of course, knew all, but to the Englishman and the two Germans it must have seemed that the god of war in person had descended from the skies. With my appearance, with my figure, with my silver and grey uniform, and with that gleaming sword in my hand, I must indeed have been a sight worth seeing. The two Germans lay petrified, with staring eyes. The English officer half rose, but sat down again from weakness, his mouth open and his hand on the back of his chair.

" What the deuce ! " he kept on repeating, " what the deuce ! "

" Pray do not move," said I ; " I will hurt no one, but woe to the man who lays hands upon me to stop me. You have nothing to fear if you leave me alone, and nothing to hope if you try to hinder me. I am Colonel Étienne Gerard, of the Hussars of Conflans."

" The deuce ! " said the Englishman. " You are the man that killed the fox." A terrible scowl had darkened his face. The jealousy of sportsmen is a base passion. He hated me, this Englishman, because I had been before him in transfixing the animal. How different are our natures ! Had I seen him do such a deed I would have embraced him with cries of joy. But there was no time for argument.

" I regret it, sir," said I ; " but you have a cloak here and I must take it."

He tried to rise from his chair and reach his sword, but I got between him and the corner where it lay.

" If there is anything in the pockets——"

" A case," said he.

" I would not rob you," said I ; and raising the coat I took from the pockets a silver flask, a square wooden case and a field-glass. All these I handed to him. The wretch opened the case, took out a pistol, and pointed it straight at my head.

" Now, my fine fellow," said he, " put down your sword and give yourself up."

I was so astonished at this infamous action that I stood petrified before him. I tried to speak to him of honour and gratitude, but I saw his eyes fix and harden over the pistol.

" Enough talk ! " said he. " Drop it ! "

Could I endure such a humiliation ? Death were better than to be disarmed in such a fashion. The word " Fire ! " was on my lips when in an instant the Englishman vanished from before my face, and in his place was a great pile of hay, with a red-coated arm and two Hessian boots waving and kicking in the heart of it. Oh, the gallant landlady ! It was my whiskers that had saved me.

" Fly, soldier, fly ! " she cried, and she heaped fresh trusses of hay from the floor on to the struggling Englishman. In an instant I was out in the courtyard, had led Violette from her stable, and was on her back. A pistol bullet whizzed past my shoulder from the window, and I saw a furious face looking out at me. I smiled my contempt and spurred out into the road. The last of the Prussians had passed, and both my road and my duty lay clear before me. If France won, all was well. If France lost, then on me and on my little mare depended that which was more than victory or defeat—the safety and the life of the Emperor. " On, Étienne, on ! " I cried. " Of all your noble exploits, the greatest, even if it be the last, lies now before you ! "

II—The Story of the Nine Prussian Horsemen

I told you when last we met, my friends, of the important mission from the Emperor to Marshal Grouchy, which failed through no fault of my own, and I described to you how during a long afternoon I was shut up in the attic of a country inn, and was prevented from coming out because the Prussians were all around me. You will remember also how I overheard the Chief of the Prussian Staff give his instructions to Count Stein, and so learned the dangerous plan which was on foot to kill or capture the Emperor in the event of a French defeat. At first I could not have believed in such a thing, but since the guns had thundered all day, and since the sound had made no advance in my direction, it was evident that the English had at least held their own and beaten off all our attacks.

I have said that it was a fight that day between the soul of France and the beef of England, but it must be confessed that we found the beef was very tough. It was clear that if the Emperor could not defeat the English when alone, then it might, indeed, go hard with him now that sixty thousand of these cursed Prussians were swarming on his flank. In any case, with this secret in my possession, my place was by his side.

I had made my way out of the inn in the dashing manner which I have described to you when last we met, and I left the English aide-de-camp shaking his foolish fist out of the window. I could not but laugh as I looked back at him, for his angry red face was framed and frilled with hay. Once out on the road I stood erect in my stirrups, and I put on the handsome black riding-coat, lined with red, which had belonged to him. It fell to the top of my high boots, and covered my tell-tale uniform completely. As to my busby, there are many such in the German service, and there was no reason why it should attract attention. So long as no one spoke to me there was no reason why I should not ride through the whole of the Prussian army ; but though I understood German, for I had many friends among the German ladies during the pleasant years that I fought all over that country, still I spoke it with a pretty Parisian accent which could not be confounded with their rough, unmusical speech. I knew that this quality of my accent would attract attention, but I could only hope and pray that I would be permitted to go my way in silence.

The Forest of Paris was so large that it was useless to think of going round it, and so I took my courage in both hands and galloped on down the road in the track of the Prussian army. It was not hard to trace it, for it was rutted two feet deep by the gunwheels and the caissons. Soon I found a fringe of wounded men, Prussians and French, on each side of it, where Bülow's advance had come into touch with Marbot's Hussars. One old man with a long white beard, a surgeon, I suppose, shouted at me, and ran after me still shouting, but I never turned my head and took no notice of him save to spur on faster. I heard his shouts long after I had lost sight of him among the trees.

Presently I came up with the Prussian reserves. The infantry were leaning on their muskets or lying exhausted on the wet ground, and the officers stood in groups listening to the mighty roar of the battle and discussing the reports which came from the front. I hurried past at the top of my speed, but one of them rushed out and stood in my path with his hand up as a signal to me to stop. Five thousand Prussian eyes were turned upon me. There was a moment ! You turn pale, my friends, at the thought of it. Think how every hair upon me stood on end. But never for one instant did my wits or my courage desert me. " General Blucher ! " I cried. Was it not my guardian angel who whispered the words in my ear ! The Prussian sprang from my path, saluted and pointed forwards. They are well disciplined, these Prussians, and who was he that he should dare to stop the officer who bore a message to the general ? It was a talisman that would pass me out of every danger, and my heart sang within me at the thought. So elated was I that I no longer waited to be asked, but as I rode through the army I shouted to right and left, " General Blucher ! General Blucher ! " and every man pointed me onwards and cleared a path to let me pass. There are times when the most supreme impudence is the highest wisdom. But discretion must also be used, and I must admit that I became indiscreet. For as I rode upon my way, ever nearer to the fighting line, a Prussian officer of Uhlans gripped my bridle and pointed to a group of men who stood near a burning farm. " There is Marshal Blucher. Deliver your message ! " said he, and sure enough my terrible old grey-whiskered veteran was there within a pistol shot, his eyes turned in my direction.

But the good guardian angel did not desert me. Quick as a flash there came into my memory the name of the general who commanded the advance of the Prussians. " General Bülow ! " I cried. The Uhlan let go my bridle. " General Bülow ! General Bülow ! " I shouted as every stride of the dear little mare took me nearer my own people. Through the burning village of Plancenoit I galloped, spurred my way between two columns of Prussian infantry, sprang over a hedge, cut down a Silesian hussar who flung himself before me, and an instant afterwards, with my coat flying open to show the uniform below, I passed through the open files of the tenth of the line and was back in the heart of Lobau's corps once more. Outnumbered and outflanked, they were being slowly driven in by the pressure of the

Prussian advance. I galloped onwards, anxious only to find myself by the Emperor's side.

But a sight lay before me which held me fast as though I had been turned into some noble equestrian statue. I could not move, I could scarce breathe, as I gazed upon it. There was a mound over which my path lay, and as I came out on the top of it I looked down the long, shallow valley of Waterloo. I had left it with two great armies on either side and a clear field between them. Now there were but long, ragged fringes of broken and exhausted regiments upon the two ridges, but a real army of dead and wounded lay between. For two miles in length and half a mile across the ground was strewed and heaped with them. But slaughter was no new sight to me, and it was not that which held me spell-bound. It was that up the long slope of the British position was moving a walking forest—black, tossing, waving, unbroken. Did I not know the bearskins of the Guard? And did I not also know, did not my soldier's instinct tell me, that it was the last reserve of France; that the Emperor, like a desperate gamester, was staking all upon his last card? Up they went and up—grand, solid, unbreakable, scourged with musketry, riddled with grape, flowing onwards in a black, heavy tide, which lapped over the British batteries. With my glass I could see the English gunners throw themselves under their pieces or run to the rear. On rolled the crest of the bearskins, and then, with a crash which was swept across to my ears, they met the British infantry. A minute passed, and another, and another. My heart was in my mouth. They swayed back and forwards; they no longer advanced; they were held. Great Heaven! was it possible that they were breaking? One black dot ran down the hill, then two, then four, then ten, then a great, scattered, struggling mass, halting, breaking, halting and at last shredding out and rushing madly downwards. "The Guard is beaten! The Guard is beaten!" From all around me I heard the cry. Along the whole line the infantry turned their faces and the gunners flinched from their guns.

" The Old Guard is beaten ! The Guard retreats ! " An officer with a livid face passed me yelling out these words of woe. " Save yourselves ! Save yourselves ! You are betrayed ! " cried another. " Save yourselves ! Save yourselves ! " Men were rushing madly to the rear, blundering and jumping like frightened sheep. Cries and screams rose from all around me. And at that moment, as I looked at the British position, I saw what I can never forget. A single horseman stood out black and clear upon the ridge against the last red angry glow of the setting sun. So dark, so motionless against that grim light, he might have been the very spirit of Battle brooding over that terrible valley. As I gazed he raised his hat high in the air, and at the signal, with a low, deep roar like a breaking wave, the whole British army flooded over their ridge and came rolling down into the valley. Long steel-fringed lines of red and blue, sweeping waves of cavalry, horse batteries rattling and bounding—down they came on to our crumbling ranks. It was over. A yell of agony, the agony of brave men who see no hope, rose from one flank to the other, and in an instant the whole of that noble army was swept in a wild, terror-stricken crowd from the field. Even now, dear friends, I cannot, as you see, speak of that dreadful moment with a dry eye or with a steady voice.

At first I was carried away in that wild rush, whirled off like a straw in a flooded gutter. But, suddenly, what should I see amongst the mixed regiments in front of me but a group of stern horsemen, in silver and grey, with a broken and tattered standard held aloft in the heart of them. Not all the might of England and of Prussia could break the Hussars of Conflans. But when I joined them it made my heart bleed to see them. The major, seven captains, and five hundred men were left upon the field. Young Captain Sabbatier was in command, and when I asked him where were the five missing squadrons he pointed back and answered : " You will find them round one of those British squares." Men and horses were at their last gasp, caked with sweat and dirt, their black tongues hanging out from their lips ; but it made me thrill with pride to see how that shattered remnant still rode knee to knee, with every man, from the boy trumpeter to the farrier-sergeant, in his own proper place. Would that I could have brought them on with me as an escort for the Emperor ! In the heart of the Hussars of Conflans he would be safe indeed. But the horses were too spent to trot. I left them behind me with orders to rally upon the farmhouse of St. Aunay, where we had camped two nights before. For my own part I forced my horse through the throng in search of the Emperor.

There were things which I saw then, as I pressed through that dreadful crowd, which can never be banished from my mind. In evil dreams there comes back to me the memory of that flowing stream of livid, staring, screaming faces upon which I looked down. It was a nightmare. In victory one does not understand the horror of war. It is only in the cold chill of defeat that it is brought home to you. I remember an old Grenadier of the Guard lying at the side of the road with his broken leg doubled at a right angle. " Comrades, comrades, keep off my leg ! " he cried, but they tripped and stumbled over him all the same. In front of me rode a lancer officer without his coat. His arm had just been taken off in the ambulance. The bandages had fallen. It was horrible. Two gunners tried to drive through with their gun. A chasseur raised his musket and shot one of them through the head. I saw a major of cuirassiers draw his two holster pistols and shoot first his horse and then himself. Beside the road a man in a blue coat was raging and raving like a madman. His face was black with powder, his clothes were torn, one epaulette was gone, the other hung dangling over his breast. Only when I came close to him did I recognise that it was Marshal Ney. He howled at the flying troops and his voice was hardly human. Then he raised the stump of his sword—it was broken three inches from the hilt. "Come and see how a Marshal of France can die!" he cried. Gladly would I have gone with him, but my duty lay elsewhere. He did not, as you know, find the death he sought, but he met it a few weeks later in cold blood at the hands of his enemies.

There is an old proverb that in attack the French are more than men, in defeat they are less than women. I knew that it was true that day. But even in that rout I saw things which I can tell with pride. Through the fields which skirt the road moved Cambronne's three reserve battalions of the Guard, the cream of our army. They walked slowly in square, their colours waving over the sombre lines of the bearskins. All around them raged the English cavalry and the black Lancers of Brunswick, wave after wave thundering up, breaking with a crash, and recoiling in ruin. When last I saw them the English guns, six at a time, were smashing grape-shot through their ranks, and the English infantry were closing in upon three sides and pouring volleys into them; but still, like a noble lion with fierce hounds clinging to its flanks, the glorious remnant of the Guard, marching slowly, halting, closing up, dressing, moved majestically from their last battle. Behind them the Guards' battery of twelve-pounders was drawn up upon the ridge. Every gunner was in his place, but no gun fired. "Why do you not fire?" I asked the colonel as I passed. "Our powder is finished." "Then why not retire?" "Our appearance may hold them back for a little. We must give the Emperor time to escape." Such were the soldiers of France.

Behind this screen of brave men the others took their breath, and then went on in less desperate fashion. They had broken away from the road, and all over the country-side in the twilight I could see the timid, scattered, frightened crowd who ten hours before had formed the finest army that ever went down to battle. I with my splendid mare was soon able to get clear of the throng, and just after I passed Genappe I overtook the Emperor with the remains of his Staff. Soult was with him still, and so were Drouot, Lobau and Bertrand, with five Chasseurs of the Guard, their horses hardly able to move. The night was falling, and the Emperor's haggard face gleamed white through the gloom as he turned it towards me.

" Who is that ? " he asked.

" It is Colonel Gerard," said Soult.

" Have you seen Marshal Grouchy ? "

" No, sire. The Prussians were between."

" It does not matter. Nothing matters now. Soult, I will go back."

He tried to turn his horse, but Bertrand seized his bridle. " Ah, sire," said Soult, " the enemy has had good fortune enough already." They forced him on among them. He rode in silence with his chin upon his breast, the greatest and the saddest of men. Far away behind us those remorseless guns were still roaring. Sometimes out of the darkness would come shrieks and screams and the low thunder of galloping hoofs. At the sound we would spur our horses and hasten onwards through the scattered troops. At last, after riding all night in the clear moonlight, we found that we had left both pursued and pursuers behind. By the time we passed over the bridge at Charleroi the dawn was breaking. What a company of spectres we looked in that cold, clear, searching light, the Emperor with his face of wax, Soult blotched with powder, Lobau dabbled with blood ! But we rode more easily now and had ceased to glance over our shoulders, for Waterloo was more than thirty miles behind us. One of the Emperor's carriages had been picked up at Charleroi, and we halted now on the other side of the Sambre, and dismounted from our horses.

You will ask me why it was that during all this time I had said nothing of that which was nearest my heart, the need for guarding the Emperor. As a fact, I had tried to speak of it both to Soult and to Lobau, but their minds were so overwhelmed with the disaster and so distracted by the pressing needs of the moment that it was impossible to make them understand how urgent was my message. Besides, during this long flight we had always had numbers of French fugitives beside us on the road, and, however demoralised they might be, we had nothing to fear from the attack of nine men. But now, as we stood round the Emperor's carriage in the early morning, I observed with anxiety that not a single French soldier was to be seen upon the long, white road behind us. We had outstripped the army. I looked round to see what means of defence were left to us. The horses of the Chasseurs of the Guard had broken down, and only one of them, a grey-whiskered sergeant, remained. There were Soult, Lobau and Bertrand ; but for all their talents, I had rather, when it came to hard knocks, have a single quarter-master-sergeant of hussars at my side than the three of them put together. There remained the Emperor himself, the coachman and a valet of the household who had joined us at Charleroi—eight all told ; but of the eight only two, the chasseur and I, were fighting soldiers who could be depended upon at a pinch. A chill came over me as I reflected how utterly helpless we were. At that moment I raised my eyes, and there were the nine Prussian horsemen coming over the hill.

On either side of the road at this point are long stretches of rolling plain, part of it yellow with corn and part of it rich grass land watered by the Sambre. To the south of us was a low ridge, over which was the road to France. Along this road the little group of cavalry was riding. So well had Count Stein obeyed his instructions that he had struck far to the south of us in his determination to get ahead of the Emperor. Now he was riding from the direction in which we were going—the last in which we could expect an enemy. When I caught that first glimpse of them they were still half a mile away.

" Sire ! " I cried, " the Prussians ! "

They all started and stared. It was the Emperor who broke the silence.

" Who says they are Prussians ? "

" I do, sire—I, Étienne Gerard ! "

Unpleasant news always made the Emperor furious against the man who broke it. He railed at me now in the rasping, croaking, Corsican voice which only made itself heard when he had lost his self-control.

" You were always a buffoon," he cried. " What do you mean, you numskull, by saying that they are Prussians ? How could Prussians be coming from the direction of France ? You have lost any wits that you ever possessed."

His words cut me like a whip, and yet we all felt towards the Emperor as an old dog does to its master. His kick is soon forgotten and forgiven. I would not argue or justify myself. At the first glance I had seen the two white stockings on the forelegs of the leading horse, and I knew well that Count Stein was on its back. For an instant the nine horsemen had halted and surveyed us. Now they put spurs to their horses, and with a yell of triumph they galloped down the road. They had recognised that their prey was in their power.

At that swift advance all doubt had vanished. " By heavens, sire, it is indeed the Prussians ! " cried Soult. Lobau and Bertrand ran about the road like two frightened hens. The sergeant of chasseurs drew his sabre with a volley of curses. The coachman and the valet cried and wrung their hands. Napoleon stood with a frozen face, one foot on the step of the carriage. And I—ah, my friends, I was magnificent ! What words can I use to do justice to my own bearing at that supreme instant of my life ! So coldly alert, so deadly cool, so clear in brain and ready in hand. He had called me a numskull and a buffoon. How quick and how noble was my revenge ! When his own wits failed him, it was Étienne Gerard who supplied the want.

To fight was absurd ; to fly was ridiculous. The
Emperor was stout, and weary to death. At the best he
was never a good rider. How could he fly from these,
the picked men of an army ? The best horseman in
Prussia was among them. But I was the best horseman
in France. I, and only I, could hold my own with them.
If they were on *my* track instead of the Emperor's, all
might still be well. These were the thoughts which
flashed so swiftly through my mind that in an instant I
had sprung from the first idea to the final conclusion.
Another instant carried me from the final conclusion to
prompt and vigorous action. I rushed to the side of the
Emperor, who stood petrified, with the carriage between
him and our enemies. " Your coat, sire ! your hat ! "
I cried. I dragged them off him. Never had he been so
hustled in his life. In an instant I had them on and had
thrust him into the carriage. The next I had sprung on
to his famous white Arab and had ridden clear of the
group upon the road.

You have already divined my plan ; but you may well
ask how could I hope to pass myself off as the Emperor.
My figure is as you still see it, and his was never beautiful,
for he was both short and stout. But a man's height is
not remarked when he is in the saddle, and for the rest
one had but to sit forward on the horse and round one's
back and carry oneself like a sack of flour. I wore the
little cocked hat and the loose grey coat with the silver
star which was known to every child from one end of
Europe to the other. Beneath me was the Emperor's own
famous white charger. It was complete.

Already as I rode clear the Prussians were within two
hundred yards of us. I made a gesture of terror and
despair with my hands, and I sprang my horse over the
bank which lined the road. It was enough. A yell of
exultation and of furious hatred broke from the Prussians.
It was the howl of starving wolves who scent their prey.
I spurred my horse over the meadow-land and looked back
under my arm as I rode. Oh, the glorious moment when

one after the other I saw eight horsemen come over the bank at my heels ! Only one had stayed behind, and I heard shouting and the sounds of a struggle. I remembered my old sergeant of chasseurs, and I was sure that number nine would trouble us no more. The road was clear, and the Emperor free to continue his journey.

But now I had to think of myself. If I were overtaken the Prussians would certainly make short work of me in their disappointment. If it were so—if I lost my life—I should still have sold it at a glorious price. But I had hopes that I might shake them off. With ordinary horsemen upon ordinary horses I should have had no difficulty in doing so, but here both steeds and riders were of the best. It was a grand creature that I rode, but it was weary with its long night's work, and the Emperor was one of those riders who do not know how to manage a horse. He had little thought for them, and a heavy hand upon their mouths. On the other hand Stein and his men had come both far and fast. The race was a fair one.

So quick had been my impulse, and so rapidly had I acted upon it, that I had not thought enough of my own safety. Had I done so in the first instance I should, of course, have ridden straight back the way we had come, for so I should have met our own people. But I was off the road and had galloped a mile over the plain before this occurred to me. Then when I looked back I saw that the Prussians had spread out into a long line, so as to head me off from the Charleroi road. I could not turn back, but at least I could edge towards the north. I knew that the whole face of the country was covered with our flying troops, and that sooner or later I must come upon some of them.

But one thing I had forgotten—the Sambre. In my excitement I never gave it a thought until I saw it, deep and broad, gleaming in the morning sunlight. It barred my path, and the Prussians howled behind me. I galloped to the brink, but the horse refused the plunge.

I spurred him, but the bank was high and the stream deep. He shrank back trembling and snorting. The yells of triumph were louder every instant. I turned and rode for my life down the river bank. It formed a loop at this part, and I must get across somehow, for my retreat was blocked. Suddenly a thrill of hope ran through me, for I saw a house on my side of the stream and another on the farther bank. Where there are two such houses it usually means that there is a ford between them. A sloping path led to the brink, and I urged my horse down it. On he went, the water up to the saddle, the foam flying right and left. He blundered once and I thought we were lost, but he recovered and an instant later was clattering up the farther slope. As we came out I heard the splash behind me as the first Prussian took the water. There was just the breadth of the Sambre between us.

I rode with my head sunk between my shoulders in Napoleon's fashion, and I did not dare to look back for fear they should see my moustache. I had turned up the collar of the grey coat so as partly to hide it. Even now if they found out their mistake they might turn and overtake the carriage. But when once we were on the road I could tell by the drumming of their hoofs how far distant they were, and it seemed to me that the sound grew perceptibly louder, as if they were slowly gaining upon me. We were riding now up the stony and rutted lane which led from the ford. I peeped back very cautiously from under my arm and I perceived that my danger came from a single rider, who was far ahead of his comrades. He was a hussar, a very tiny fellow, upon a big black horse, and it was his light weight which had brought him into the foremost place. It is a place of honour ; but it is also a place of danger, as he was soon to learn. I felt the holsters, but, to my horror, there were no pistols. There was a field-glass in one and the other was stuffed with papers. My sword had been left behind with Violette. Had I only my own weapons and my own little mare I could have played with these rascals. But I was not entirely unarmed. The Emperor's own sword hung to the saddle. It was curved and short, the hilt all crusted with gold—a thing more fitted to glitter at a review than to serve a soldier in his deadly need. I drew it, such as it was, and I waited my chance. Every instant the clink and clatter of the hoofs grew nearer. I heard the panting of the horse, and the fellow shouted some threat at me. There was a turn in the lane, and as I rounded it I drew up my white Arab on his haunches. As we spun round I met the Prussian hussar face to face. He was going too fast to stop, and his only chance was to ride me down. Had he done so he might have met his own death, but he would have injured me or my horse past all hope of escape. But the fool flinched as he saw me waiting, and flew past me on my right. I lunged over my Arab's neck and buried my toy sword in his side. It must have been the finest steel and as sharp as a razor, for I hardly felt it enter, and yet his blood was within three inches of the hilt. His horse galloped on and he kept his saddle for a hundred yards before he sank down with his face on the mane, and then dived over the side of the neck on to the road. For my own part, I was already at his horse's heels. A few seconds had sufficed for all that I have told.

I heard the cry of rage and vengeance which rose from the Prussians as they passed their dead comrade, and I could not but smile as I wondered what they could think of the Emperor as a horseman and a swordsman. I glanced back cautiously as before, and I saw that none of the seven men stopped. The fate of their comrade was nothing compared to the carrying out of their mission. They were as untiring and as remorseless as bloodhounds. But I had a good lead, and the brave Arab was still going well. I thought that I was safe. And yet it was at that very instant that the most terrible danger befell me. The lane divided, and I took the smaller of the two divisions because it was the more grassy and the easier for the horse's hoofs. Imagine my horror when, riding through a gate, I found myself in a square of stables and farm-buildings, with no way out save that by which I had come ! Ah, my friends, if my hair is snowy white, have I not had enough to make it so ?

To retreat was impossible. I could hear the thunder of the Prussians' hoofs in the lane. I looked round me, and Nature has blessed me with that quick eye which is the first of gifts to any soldier, but most of all to a leader of cavalry. Between a long, low line of stables and the farmhouse there was a pig-sty. Its front was made of bars of wood four feet high ; the back was of stone, higher than the front. What was beyond I could not tell. The space between the front and the back was not more than a few yards. It was a desperate venture, and yet I must take it. Every instant the beating of those hurrying hoofs was louder and louder. I put my Arab at the pig-sty. She cleared the front beautifully, and came down with her forefeet upon the sleeping pig within, slipping forward upon her knees. I was thrown over the wall beyond, and fell upon my hands and face in a soft flower-bed. My horse was upon one side of the wall, I upon the other, and the Prussians were pouring into the yard. But I was up in an instant, and had seized the bridle of the plunging horse over the top of the wall. It was built of loose stones, and I dragged down a few of them to make a gap. As I tugged at the bridle and shouted the gallant creature rose to the leap, and an instant afterwards she was by my side and I with my foot on the stirrup.

An heroic idea had entered my mind as I mounted into the saddle. These Prussians, if they came over the pig-sty, could only come one at once, and their attack would not be formidable when they had not had time to recover from such a leap. Why should I not wait and kill them one by one as they came over ? It was a glorious thought. They would learn that Étienne Gerard was not a safe man to hunt. My hand felt for my sword, but you can imagine my feelings, my friends, when I came upon an empty scabbard. It had been shaken out when the horse had tripped over that infernal pig. On what absurd trifles do our destinies hang—a pig on one side, Étienne Gerard on the other ! Could I spring over the wall and get the sword ? Impossible ! The Prussians were already in the yard. I turned my Arab and resumed my flight.

But for a moment it seemed to me that I was in a far worse trap than before. I found myself in the garden of the farmhouse, an orchard in the centre and flower-beds all round. A high wall surrounded the whole place. I reflected, however, that there must be some point of entrance, since every visitor could not be expected to spring over the pig-sty. I rode round the wall. As I expected, I came upon a door with a key upon the inner side. I dismounted, unlocked it, opened it, and there was a Prussian lancer sitting his horse within six feet of me.

For a moment we each stared at the other. Then I shut the door and locked it again. A crash and a cry came from the other end of the garden. I understood that one of my enemies had come to grief in trying to get over the pig-sty. How could I ever get out of this *cul-de-sac* ? It was evident that some of the party had galloped round, while some had followed straight upon my tracks. Had I my sword I might have beaten off the lancer at the door, but to come out now was to be butchered. And yet if I waited some of them would certainly follow me on foot over the pig-sty, and what could I do then ? I must act at once or I was lost. But it is at such moments that my wits are most active and my actions most prompt. Still leading my horse, I ran for a hundred yards by the side of the wall away from the spot where the lancer was watching. There I stopped, and with an effort I tumbled down several of the loose stones from the top of the wall. The instant I had done so I hurried back to the door. As I had expected, he

thought I was making a gap for my escape at that point,
and I heard the thud of his horse's hoofs as he galloped
to cut me off. As I reached the gate I looked back, and
I saw a green-coated horseman, whom I knew to be
Count Stein, clear the pig-sty and gallop furiously with
a shout of triumph across the garden. " Surrender,
your Majesty, surrender ! " he yelled ; " we will give
you quarter ! " I slipped through the gate, but had no
time to lock it on the other side. Stein was at my very
heels, and the lancer had already turned his horse.
Springing upon my Arab's back, I was off once more with
a clear stretch of grass land before me. Stein had to
dismount to open the gate, to lead his horse through, and
to mount again before he could follow. It was he that I
feared rather than the lancer, whose horse was coarse-
bred and weary. I galloped hard for a mile before I
ventured to look back, and then Stein was a musket-shot
from me, and the lancer as much again, while only
three of the others were in sight. My nine Prussians
were coming down to more manageable numbers, and
yet one was too much for an unarmed man.

It had surprised me that during this long chase I had
seen no fugitives from the army, but I reflected that I was
considerably to the west of their line of flight, and that I
must edge more towards the east if I wished to join them.
Unless I did so it was probable that my pursuers, even if
they could not overtake me themselves, would keep me in
view until I was headed off by some of their comrades
coming from the north. As I looked to the eastward I
saw afar off a line of dust which stretched for miles across
the country. This was certainly the main road along
which our unhappy army was flying. But I soon had
proof that some of our stragglers had wandered into these
side tracks, for I came suddenly upon a horse grazing at
the corner of a field, and beside him, with his back against
the bank, his master, a French cuirassier, terribly
wounded and evidently at the point of death. I sprang
down, seized his long, heavy sword, and rode on with it.

Never shall I forget the poor man's face as he looked at me with his failing sight. He was an old, grey-moustached soldier, one of the real fanatics, and to him this last vision of his Emperor was like a revelation from on high. Astonishment, love, pride—all shone in his pallid face. He said something—I fear they were his last words—but I had no time to listen, and I galloped on my way.

All this time I had been on the meadowland, which was intersected in this part by broad ditches. Some of them could not have been less than from fourteen to fifteen feet, and my heart was in my mouth as I went at each of them, for a slip would have been my ruin. But whoever selected the Emperor's horses had done his work well. The creature, save when it balked on the bank of the Sambre, never failed me for an instant. We cleared everything in one stride. And yet we could not shake off those infernal Prussians. As I left each watercourse behind me I looked back with renewed hope, but it was only to see Stein on his white-legged chestnut flying over it as lightly as I had done myself. He was my enemy, but I honoured him for the way in which he carried himself that day.

Again and again I measured the distance which separated him from the next horseman. I had the idea that I might turn and cut him down, as I had the hussar, before his comrade could come to his help. But the others had closed up and were not far behind. I reflected that this Stein was probably as fine a swordsman as he was a rider, and that it might take me some little time to get the better of him. In that case the others would come to his aid and I should be lost. On the whole, it was wiser to continue my flight.

A road with poplars on either side ran across the plain from east to west. It would lead me towards the long line of dust which marked the French retreat. I wheeled my horse, therefore, and galloped down it. As I rode I saw a single house in front of me upon the right, with a

great bush hung over the door to mark it as an inn.
Outside there were several peasants, but for them I cared
nothing. What frightened me was to see the gleam of a
red coat, which showed that there were British in the
place. However, I could not turn and I could not stop,
so there was nothing for it but to gallop on and to take my
chance. There were no troops in sight, so these men
must be stragglers or marauders, from whom I had little
to fear. As I approached I saw that there were two of
them sitting drinking on a bench outside the inn door.
I saw them stagger to their feet, and it was evident that
they were both very drunk. One stood swaying in the
middle of the road. "It's Boney! So help me, it's
Boney!" he yelled. He ran with his hands out to
catch me, but luckily for himself his drunken feet stumbled
and he fell on his face on the road. The other was more
dangerous. He had rushed into the inn, and just as I
passed I saw him run out with his musket in his hand.
He dropped upon one knee, and I stooped forward
over my horse's neck. A single shot from a Prussian or
an Austrian is a small matter, but the British were at that
time the best shots in Europe, and my drunkard seemed
steady enough when he had a gun at his shoulder. I
heard the crack and my horse gave a convulsive spring
which would have unseated many a rider. For an
instant I thought he was killed, but when I turned in my
saddle I saw a stream of blood running down the off
hind-quarter. I looked back at the Englishman, and the
brute had bitten the end off another cartridge and was
ramming it into his musket, but before he had it primed
we were beyond his range. These men were foot-soldiers
and could not join in the chase, but I heard them whooping and tally-hoing behind me as if I had been a fox.
The peasants also shouted and ran through the fields
flourishing their sticks. From all sides I heard cries, and
everywhere were the rushing, waving figures of my
pursuers. To think of the great Emperor being
chivied over the country-side in this fashion! It made

me long to have these rascals within the sweep of my sword.

But now I felt that I was nearing the end of my course. I had done all that a man could be expected to do—some would say more—but at last I had come to a point from which I could see no escape. The horses of my pursuers were exhausted, but mine was exhausted and wounded also. It was losing blood fast, and we left a red trail upon the white, dusty road. Already his pace was slackening, and sooner or later he must drop under me. I looked back, and there were the five inevitable Prussians—Stein, a hundred yards in front, then a lancer, and then three others riding together. Stein had drawn his sword, and he waved it at me. For my own part I was determined not to give myself up. I would try how many of these Prussians I could take with me into the other world. At this supreme moment all the great deeds of my life rose in a vision before me, and I felt that this, my last exploit, was indeed a worthy close to such a career. My death would be a fatal blow to those who loved me, to my dear mother, to my hussars, to others who shall be nameless. But all of them had my honour and my fame at heart, and I felt that their grief would be tinged with pride when they learned how I had ridden and how I had fought upon this last day. Therefore I hardened my heart and, as my Arab limped more and more upon his wounded leg, I drew the great sword which I had taken from the cuirassier, and I set my teeth for my supreme struggle. My hand was in the very act of tightening the bridle, for I feared that if I delayed longer I might find myself on foot fighting against five mounted men. At that instant my eye fell upon something which brought hope to my heart and a shout of joy to my lips.

From a grove of trees in front of me there projected the steeple of a village church. But there could not be two steeples like that, for the corner of it had crumbled away or been struck by lightning, so that it was of a most fantastic shape. I had seen it only two days before, and it was the church of the village of Gosselies. It was not the hope of reaching the village which set my heart singing with joy, but it was that I knew my ground now, and that farmhouse not half a mile ahead, with its gable end sticking out from amid the trees, must be that very farm of St. Aunay where we had bivouacked, and which I had named to Captain Sabbatier as the rendezvous of the Hussars of Conflans. There they were, my little rascals, if I could but reach them. With every bound my horse grew weaker. Each instant the sound of the pursuit grew louder. I heard a gust of crackling German oaths at my very heels. A pistol bullet sighed in my ears. Spurring frantically and beating my poor Arab with the flat of my sword I kept him at the top of his speed. The open gate of the farmyard lay before me. I saw the twinkle of steel within. Stein's horse's head was within ten yards of me as I thundered through. " To me, comrades ! To me ! " I yelled. I heard a buzz as when the angry bees swarm from their nest. Then my splendid white Arab fell dead under me, and I was hurled on to the cobble-stones of the yard, where I can remember no more.

Such was my last and most famous exploit, my dear friends, a story which rang through Europe and has made the name of Étienne Gerard famous in history. Alas ! that all my efforts could only give the Emperor a few weeks more liberty, since he surrendered upon July 15th to the English. But it was not my fault that he was not able to collect the forces still waiting for him in France, and to fight another Waterloo with a happier ending. Had others been as loyal as I was the history of the world might have been changed, the Emperor would have preserved his throne, and such a soldier as I would not have been left to spend his life in planting cabbages or to while away his old age telling stories in a café. You ask me about the fate of Stein and the Prussian horsemen ! Of the three who dropped upon the way I know nothing. One you will remember that I killed. There remained five, three of whom were cut down by my hussars, who, for the instant, were under the impression that it was indeed the Emperor whom they were defending. Stein was taken, slightly wounded, and so was one of the Uhlans. The truth was not told to them, for we thought it best that no news, or false news, should get about as to where the Emperor was, so that Count Stein still believed that he was within a few yards of making that tremendous capture. " You may well love and honour your Emperor," said he, " for such a horseman and such a swordsman I have never seen." He could not understand why the young colonel of hussars laughed so heartily at his words—but he has learned since.

8. *The Last Adventure of the Brigadier*

I WILL tell you no more stories, my dear friends. It is said that man is like the hare, which runs in a circle and comes back to die at the point from which it started. Gascony has been calling to me of late. I see the blue Garonne winding among the vineyards and the bluer ocean towards which its waters sweep. I see the old town also, and the bristle of masts from the side of the long stone quay. My heart hungers for the breath of my native air and the warm glow of my native sun. Here in Paris are my friends, my occupations, my pleasures. There all who have known me are in their grave. And yet the south-west wind as it rattles on my windows seems always to be the strong voice of the motherland calling her child back to that bosom into which I am ready to sink. I have played my part in my time. The time has passed. I must pass also. Nay, dear friends, do not look sad, for what can be happier than a life completed in honour and made beautiful with friendship and love ? And yet it is solemn also when a man approaches the end of the long road and sees the turning which leads him into the unknown. But the Emperor and all his Marshals have ridden round that dark turning and passed into the beyond. My hussars, too—there are not fifty men who are not waiting yonder. I must go. But on this the last night I will tell you that which is more than a tale—it is a great historical secret. My lips have been sealed, but I see no reason why I should not leave behind me some account of this remarkable adventure, which must otherwise be entirely lost, since I, and only I of all living men, have a knowledge of the facts.

I will ask you to go back with me to the year 1821. In that year our great Emperor had been absent from us for six years, and only now and then from over the seas we heard some whisper which showed that he was still alive. You cannot think what a weight it was upon our hearts for us who loved him to think of him in captivity eating his giant soul out upon that lonely island. From the moment we rose until we closed our eyes in sleep the thought was always with us, and we felt dishonoured that he, our chief and master, should be so humiliated without our being able to move a hand to help him. There were many who would most willingly have laid down the remainder of their lives to bring him a little ease, and yet all that we could do was to sit and grumble in our cafés and stare at the map, counting up the leagues of water which lay between us. It seemed that he might have been in the moon for all that we could do to help him. But that was only because we were all soldiers and knew nothing of the sea.

Of course, we had our own little troubles to make us bitter, as well as the wrongs of our Emperor. There were many of us who had held high rank and would hold it again if he came back to his own. We had not found it possible to take service under the white flag of the Bourbons, or to take an oath which might turn our sabres against the man whom we loved. So we found ourselves with neither work nor money. What could we do save gather together and gossip and grumble, while those who had a little paid the score and those who had nothing shared the bottle ? Now and then, if we were lucky, we managed to pick a quarrel with one of the Garde du Corps, and if we left him on his back in the Bois we felt that we had struck a blow for Napoleon once again. They came to know our haunts in time, and they avoided them as if they had been hornets' nests.

There was one of these—the Sign of the Great Man— in the Rue Varennes, which was frequented by several of the more distinguished and younger Napoleonic officers. Nearly all of us had been colonels or aides-de-camp, and when any man of less distinction came among us we generally made him feel that he had taken a liberty. There were Captain Lepine, who had won the medal of honour at Leipzig ; Colonel Bonnet, aide-de-camp to Macdonald ; Colonel Jourdan, whose fame in the army was hardly second to my own ; Sabbatier of my own hussars, Meunier of the Red Lancers, Le Breton of the Guards, and a dozen others. Every night we met and talked, played dominoes, drank a glass or two and wondered how long it would be before the Emperor would be back and we at the head of our regiments once more. The Bourbons had already lost any hold they ever had upon the country, as was shown a few years afterwards, when Paris rose against them and they were hunted for the third time out of France. Napoleon had but to show himself on the coast, and he would have marched without firing a musket to the capital, exactly as he had done when he came back from Elba.

Well, when affairs were in this state there arrived one night in February, in our café, a most singular little man. He was short but exceedingly broad, with huge shoulders, and a head which was a deformity, so large was it. His heavy brown face was scarred with white streaks in a most extraordinary manner, and he had grizzled whiskers such as seamen wear. Two gold ear-rings in his ears, and plentiful tattooing upon his hands and arms, told us also that he was of the sea before he introduced himself as Captain Fourneau, of the Emperor's navy. He had letters of introduction to two of our number, and there could be no doubt that he was devoted to the cause. He won our respect, too, for he had seen as much fighting as any of us, and the burns upon his face were caused by his standing to his post upon the *Orient*, at the Battle of the Nile, until the vessel blew up underneath him. Yet he would say little about himself, but he sat in the corner of the café watching us all with a wonderfully sharp pair of eyes and listening intently to our talk.

One night I was leaving the café when Captain Four-neau followed me, and touching me on the arm he led me without saying a word for some distance until we reached his lodgings. "I wish to have a chat with you," said he, and so conducted me up the stair to his room. There he lit a lamp and handed me a sheet of paper which he took from an envelope in his bureau. It was dated a few months before from the Palace of Schönbrunn at Vienna. "Captain Fourneau is acting in the highest interests of the Emperor Napoleon. Those who love the Emperor should obey him without question—Marie Louise." That is what I read. I was familiar with the signature of the Empress, and I could not doubt that this was genuine.

"Well," said he, "are you satisfied as to my credentials ? "

"Entirely."

"Are you prepared to take your orders from me ? "

"This document leaves me no choice."

"Good ! In the first place, I understand from something you said in the café that you can speak English ? "

"Yes, I can."

"Let me hear you do so."

I said in English, "Whenever the Emperor needs the help of Étienne Gerard, I am ready night and day to give my life in his service." Captain Fourneau smiled.

"It is funny English," said he, "but still it is better than no English. For my own part I speak English like an Englishman. It is all that I have to show for six years spent in an English prison. Now I will tell you why I have come to Paris. I have come in order to choose an agent who will help me in a matter which affects the interests of the Emperor. I was told that it was at the café of the Great Man that I would find the pick of his old officers, and that I could rely upon every man there being devoted to his interests. I studied you all, therefore, and I have come to the conclusion that you are the one who is most suited for my purpose."

I acknowledged the compliment. "What is it that you wish me to do ? " I asked.

"Merely to keep me company for a few months," said he. "You must know that after my release in England I settled down there, married an English wife, and rose to command a small English merchant ship, in which I have made several voyages from Southampton to the Guinea coast. They look on me there as an Englishman. You can understand, however, that with my feelings about the Emperor I am lonely sometimes, and that it would be an advantage to me to have a companion who would sympathise with my thoughts. One gets very bored on these long voyages, and I would make it worth your while to share my cabin."

He looked hard at me with his shrewd grey eyes all the time that he was uttering this rigmarole, and I gave him a glance in return which showed him that he was not dealing with a fool. He took out a canvas bag full of money.

"There are a hundred pounds in gold in this bag," said he. "You will be able to buy some comforts for your voyage. I should recommend you to get them in Southampton, whence we will start in ten days. The name of the vessel is the *Black Swan*. I return to Southampton to-morrow, and I shall hope to see you in the course of the next week."

"Come now," said I, "tell me frankly what is the destination of our voyage ? "

" Oh, didn't I tell you ? " he answered. " We are bound for the Guinea coast of Africa."

" Then how can that be in the highest interests of the Emperor ? " I asked.

" It is in his highest interests that you ask no indiscreet questions and I give no indiscreet replies," he answered, sharply. So he brought the interview to an end, and I found myself back in my lodgings with nothing save this bag of gold to show that this singular interview had indeed taken place.

There was every reason why I should see the adventure to a conclusion, and so within a week I was on my way to England. I passed from St. Malo to Southampton, and on inquiry at the docks I had no difficulty in finding the *Black Swan*, a neat little vessel of a shape which is called, as I learned afterwards, a brig. There was Captain Fourneau himself upon the deck, and seven or eight rough fellows hard at work grooming her and making her ready for sea. He greeted me and led me down to his cabin.

" You are plain Mr. Gerard now," said he, " and a Channel Islander. I would be obliged to you if you would kindly forget your military ways and drop your cavalry swagger when you walk up and down my deck. A beard, too, would seem more sailor-like than those moustaches."

I was horrified by his words, but, after all, there are no ladies on the high seas, and what did it matter ? He rang for the steward.

" Gustav," said he, " you will pay every attention to my friend, Monsieur Étienne Gerard, who makes this voyage with us. This is Gustav Kerouan, my Breton steward," he explained, " and you are very safe in his hands——"

This steward, with his harsh face and stern eyes, looked a very warlike person for so peaceful an employment. I said nothing, however, though you may guess that I kept my eyes open. A berth had been prepared for me next the cabin, which would have seemed comfortable enough had it not contrasted with the extraordinary splendour of Fourneau's quarters. He was certainly a most luxurious person, for his room was new-fitted with velvet and silver in a way which would have suited the yacht of a noble better than a little West African trader. So thought the mate, Mr. Burns, who could not hide his amusement and contempt whenever he looked at it. This fellow, a big, solid red-headed Englishman, had the other berth connected with the cabin. There was a second mate named Turner, who lodged in the middle of the ship, and there were nine men and one boy in the crew, three of whom, as I was informed by Mr. Burns, were Channel Islanders like myself. This Burns, the first mate, was much interested to know why I was coming with them.

" I come for pleasure," said I.

He stared at me.

" Ever been to the West Coast ? " he asked.

I said that I had not.

" I thought not," said he. " You'll never come again for that reason, anyhow."

Some three days after my arrival we untied the ropes by which the ship was tethered and we set off upon our journey. I was never a good sailor, and I may confess that we were far out of sight of any land before I was able to venture upon deck. At last, however, upon the fifth day I drank the soup which the good Kerouan brought me, and I was able to crawl from my bunk and up the stair. The fresh air revived me, and from that time onwards I accommodated myself to the motion of the vessel. My beard had begun to grow also, and I have no doubt that I should have made as fine a sailor as I have a soldier had I chanced to be born to that branch of the service. I learned to pull the ropes which hoisted the sails, and also to haul round the long sticks to which they are attached. For the most part, however, my duties were to play écarté with Captain Fourneau, and to act as his companion. It was not strange that he should need one, for neither of his mates could read nor write, though each of them was an excellent seaman. If our captain had died suddenly I cannot imagine how we should have found our way in that waste of waters, for it was only he who had the knowledge which enabled him to mark our place upon the chart. He had this fixed upon the cabin wall, and every day he put our course upon it so that we could see at a glance how far we were from our destination. It was wonderful how well he could calculate it, for one morning he said that we should see the Cape Verd light that very night, and there it was, sure enough, upon our left front the moment that darkness came. Next day, however, the land was out of sight, and Burns, the mate, explained to me that we should see no more until we came to our port in the Gulf of Biafra. Every day we flew south with a favouring wind, and always at noon the pin upon the chart was moved nearer and nearer to the African coast. I may explain that palm oil was the cargo which we were in search of, and that our own lading consisted of coloured cloths, old muskets and such other trifles as the English sell to the savages.

At last the wind which had followed us so long died away, and for several days we drifted about on a calm and oily sea under a sun which brought the pitch bubbling out between the planks upon the deck. We turned and turned our sails to catch every wandering puff, until at last we came out of this belt of calm and ran south again with a brisk breeze, the sea all round us being alive with flying fishes. For some days Burns appeared to be uneasy, and I observed him continually shading his eyes with his hand and staring at the horizon as if he were looking for land. Twice I caught him with his red head against the chart in the cabin, gazing at that pin, which was always approaching and yet never reaching the African coast. At last one evening, as Captain Fourneau and I were playing écarté in the cabin, the mate entered with an angry look upon his sunburned face.

"I beg your pardon, Captain Fourneau," said he. "But do you know what course the man at the wheel is steering?"

"Due south," the captain answered, with his eyes fixed upon his cards.

"And he should be steering due east."

"How do you make that out?"

The mate gave an angry growl.

"I may not have much education," said he, "but let me tell you this, Captain Fourneau. I've sailed these waters since I was a little nipper of ten, and I know the line when I'm on it, and I know the doldrums, and I know how to find my way to the oil rivers. We are south of the line now, and we should be steering due east instead of due south if your port is the port that the owners sent you to."

"Excuse me, Mr. Gerard. Just remember that it is my lead," said the captain, laying down his cards. "Come to the map here, Mr. Burns, and I will give you a lesson in practical navigation. Here is the trade wind from the south-west and here is the line, and here is the port that we want to make, and here is a man who will have his own way aboard his own ship." As he spoke he seized the unfortunate mate by the throat and squeezed him until he was nearly senseless. Kerouan, the steward, had rushed in with a rope, and between them they gagged and trussed the man, so that he was utterly helpless.

"There is one of our Frenchmen at the wheel. We had best put the mate overboard," said the steward.

"That is safest," said Captain Fourneau.

But that was more than I could stand. Nothing would persuade me to agree to the death of a helpless man. With a bad grace Captain Fourneau consented to spare him, and we carried him to the after-hold, which lay under the cabin. There he was laid among the bales of Manchester cloth.

"It is not worth while to put down the hatch," said

Captain Fourneau. " Gustav, go to Mr. Turner, and tell him that I would like to have a word with him."

The unsuspecting second mate entered the cabin, and was instantly gagged and secured as Burns had been. He was carried down and laid beside his comrade. The hatch was then replaced.

" Our hands have been forced by that red-headed dolt," said the captain, " and I have had to explode my mine before I wished. However, there is no great harm done, and it will not seriously disarrange my plans. Kerouan, you will take a keg of rum forward to the crew and tell them that the captain gives it to them to drink his health on the occasion of crossing the line. They will know no better. As to our own fellows, bring them down to your pantry so that we may be sure that they are ready for business. Now, Colonel Gerard, with your permission we will resume our game of écarté."

It is one of those occasions which one does not forget. This captain, who was a man of iron, shuffled and cut, dealt and played as if he were in his café. From below we heard the inarticulate murmurings of the two mates, half smothered by the handkerchiefs which gagged them. Outside the timbers creaked and the sails hummed under the brisk breeze which was sweeping us upon our way. Amid the splash of the waves and the whistle of the wind we heard the wild cheers and shoutings of the English sailors as they broached the keg of rum. We played half a dozen games, and then the captain rose. " I think they are ready for us now," said he. He took a brace of pistols from a locker, and he handed one of them to me.

But we had no need to fear resistance, for there was no one to resist. The Englishman of those days, whether soldier or sailor, was an incorrigible drunkard. Without drink he was a brave and good man. But if drink were laid before him it was a perfect madness—nothing could induce him to take it with moderation. In the dim light of the den which they inhabited, five senseless figures and two shouting, swearing, singing madmen represented the crew of the *Black Swan*. Coils of rope were brought forward by the steward, and with the help of two French seamen (the third was at the wheel) we secured the drunkards and tied them up, so that it was impossible for them to speak or move. They were placed under the forehatch, as their officers had been under the after one, and Kerouan was directed twice a day to give them food and drink. So at last we found that the *Black Swan* was entirely our own.

Had there been bad weather I do not know what we should have done, but we still went gaily upon our way with a wind which was strong enough to drive us swiftly south, but not strong enough to cause us alarm. On the evening of the third day I found Captain Fourneau gazing eagerly out from the platform in the front of the vessel. "" Look, Gerard, look ! " he cried and pointed over the pole which struck out in front.

A light blue sky rose from a dark blue sea, and far away, at the point where they met, was a shadowy something like a cloud, but more definite in shape.

" What is it ? " I cried.

" It is land."

" And what land ? "

I strained my ears for the answer, and yet I knew already what the answer would be.

" It is St. Helena."

Here, then, was the island of my dreams ! Here was the cage where our great Eagle of France was confined ! All those thousands of leagues of water had not sufficed to keep Gerard from the master whom he loved. There he was, there on that cloud-bank yonder over the dark blue sea. How my eyes devoured it ! How my soul flew in front of the vessel—flew on and on to tell him that he was not forgotten, that after many days one faithful servant was coming to his side ! Every instant the dark blur upon the water grew harder and clearer. Soon I could see plainly enough that it was indeed a mountainous island. The night fell, but still I knelt upon the deck, with my eyes fixed upon the darkness which covered the spot where I knew that the great Emperor was. An hour passed and another one, and then suddenly a little golden twinkling light shone out exactly ahead of us. It was the light of the window of some house—perhaps of his house. It could not be more than a mile or two away. Oh, how I held out my hands to it !—they were the hands of Étienne Gerard, but it was for all France that they were held out.

Every light had been extinguished aboard our ship, and presently, at the direction of Captain Fourneau, we all pulled upon one of the ropes, which had the effect of swinging round one of the sticks above us, and so stopping the vessel. Then he asked me to step down to the cabin.

" You understand everything now, Colonel Gerard," said he, " and you will forgive me if I did not take you into my complete confidence before. In a matter of such importance I make no man my confidant. I have long planned the rescue of the Emperor, and my remaining in England and joining their merchant service was entirely with that design. All has worked out exactly as I expected. I have made several successful voyages to the West Coast of Africa, so that there was no difficulty in my obtaining the command of this one. One by one I got these old French man-of-war's-men among the hands. As to you, I was anxious to have one tried fighting man in case of resistance, and I also desired to have a fitting companion for the Emperor during his long homeward voyage. My cabin is already fitted up for his use. I trust that before to-morrow morning he will be inside it, and we out of sight of this accursed island."

You can think of my emotion, my friends, as I listened to these words. I embraced the brave Fourneau, and implored him to tell me how I could assist him.

" I must leave it all in your hands," said he. " Would that I could have been the first to pay him homage, but it would not be wise for me to go. The glass is falling, there is a storm brewing, and we have the land under our lee. Besides, there are three English cruisers near the island which may be upon us at any moment. It is for me, therefore, to guard the ship and for you to bring off the Emperor."

I thrilled at the words.

"Give me your instructions!" I cried.

"I can only spare you one man, for already I can hardly pull round the yards," said he. "One of the boats has been lowered, and this man will row you ashore and await your return. The light which you see is indeed the light of Longwood. All who are in the house are your friends, and all may be depended upon to aid the Emperor's escape. There is a cordon of English sentries, but they are not very near to the house. Once you have got as far as that you will convey our plans to the Emperor, guide him down to the boat, and bring him on board."

The Emperor himself could not have given his instructions more shortly and clearly. There was not a moment to be lost. The boat with the seaman was waiting alongside. I stepped into it, and an instant afterwards we had pushed off. Our little boat danced over the dark waters, but always shining before my eyes was the light of Longwood, the light of the Emperor, the star of hope. Presently the bottom of the boat grated upon the pebbles of the beach. It was a deserted cove, and no challenge from a sentry came to disturb us. I left the seaman by the boat and began to climb the hill-side.

There was a goat-track winding in and out among the rocks, so I had no difficulty in finding my way. It stands to reason that all paths in St. Helena would lead to the Emperor. I came to a gate. No sentry—and I passed through. Another gate—still no sentry! I wondered what had become of this cordon of which Fourneau had spoken. I had come now to the top of my climb, for there was the light burning steadily right in front of me. I concealed myself and took a good look round, but still I could see no sign of the enemy. As I approached I saw the house, a long, low building with a veranda. A man was walking up and down upon the path in front. I crept nearer and had a look at him. Perhaps it was this cursed Hudson Lowe. What a triumph if I could not only rescue the Emperor, but also avenge him! But it was more likely that this man was an English sentry. I crept nearer still, and the man stopped in front of the lighted window, so that I could see him. No; it was no soldier, but a priest. I wondered what such a man could be doing there at two in the morning. Was he French or English? If he were one of the household I might take him into my confidence. If he were English he might ruin all my plans. I crept a little nearer still, and at that moment he entered the house, a flood of light pouring out through the open door. All was clear for me now, and I understood that not an instant was to be lost. Bending myself double I ran swiftly forward to the lighted window. Raising my head I peeped through, and there was the Emperor lying dead before me!

My friends, I fell down upon the gravel walk as senseless as if a bullet had passed through my brain. So great was the shock that I wonder that I survived it. And yet in half an hour I had staggered to my feet again, shivering in every limb, my teeth chattering, and there I stood staring with the eyes of a maniac into that room of death.

He lay upon a bier in the centre of the chamber, calm, composed, majestic, his face full of that reserve power which lightened our hearts upon the day of battle. A half-smile was fixed upon his pale lips, and his eyes, half-opened, seemed to be turned on mine. He was stouter than when I had seen him at Waterloo, and there was a gentleness of expression which I had never seen in life. On either side of him burned rows of candles, and this was the beacon which had welcomed us at sea, which had guided me over the water, and which I had hailed as my star of hope. Dimly I became conscious that many people were kneeling in the room; the little Court, men and women, who had shared his fortunes, Bertrand, his wife, the priest, Montholon—all were there. I would have prayed too, but my heart was too heavy and bitter for prayer. And yet I must leave, and I could not leave him without a sign. Regardless of whether I was seen or not, I drew myself erect before my dead leader, brought my heels together, and raised my hand in a last salute. Then I turned and hurried off through the darkness, with the picture of the wan, smiling lips and the steady grey eyes dancing always before me.

It had seemed to me but a little time that I had been away, and yet the boatman told me that it was hours. Only when he spoke of it did I observe that the wind was blowing half a gale from the sea and that the waves were roaring in upon the beach. Twice we tried to push out our little boat, and twice it was thrown back by the sea. The third time a great wave filled it and stove the bottom. Helplessly we waited beside it until the dawn broke, to show a raging sea and a flying scud above it. There was no sign of the *Black Swan*. Climbing the hill we looked down, but on all the great torn expanse of the ocean there was no gleam of a sail. She was gone. Whether she had sunk, or whether she was recaptured by her English crew, or what strange fate may have been in store for her, I do not know. Never again in this life did I see Captain Fourneau to tell him the result of my mission. For my own part I gave myself up to the English, my boatman and I pretending that we were the only survivors of a lost vessel—though, indeed, there was no pretence in the matter. At the hands of their officers I received that generous hospitality which I have always encountered, but it was many a long month before I could get a passage back to the dear land outside of which there can be no happiness for so true a Frenchman as myself.

And so I tell you in one evening how I bade good-bye to my master, and I take my leave also of you, my kind friends, who have listened so patiently to the long-winded stories of an old broken soldier. Russia, Italy, Germany, Spain, Portugal and England, you have gone with me to all these countries, and you have seen through my dim eyes something of the sparkle and splendour of those great days, and I have brought back to you some shadow of those men whose tread shook the earth. Treasure it in your minds and pass it on to your children, for the memory of a great age is the most precious treasure that a nation can possess. As the tree is nurtured by its own cast leaves, so it is these dead men and vanished days which may bring out another blossoming of heroes, of rulers, and of sages. I go to Gascony, but my words stay here in your memory, and long after Étienne Gerard is forgotten a heart may be warmed or a spirit braced by some faint echo of the words that he has spoken. Gentlemen, an old soldier salutes you and bids you farewell.